977-828-1

PRESENTED TO

_____

BY

_____

DATE

_____

The Illustrated
Children's
Old Testament

The Illustrated
Children's
Old Testament

PAINTINGS BY

Bill Farnsworth

HARCOURT BRACE & COMPANY

SAN DIEGO   NEW YORK   LONDON

Editorial Staff

General Editor & Art Director: Christopher Morris

Project Editor: Elinor Williams

Contributing Editor: Gail Rice

Designer: Trina Stahl

Editorial Assistant: Joseph Sheehan

Library of Congress Cataloging-in-Publication Data available upon request.

ISBN 0-15-238220-8

First edition

A B C D E

Printed in the United States of America

A Note on the Text

For the content of *The Illustrated Children's Old Testament,* we have drawn on various traditional texts, especially the Authorized (King James) Version. We have modified traditional wording as necessary to avoid the unnecessary use of old-fashioned or difficult terms. However, we have not supplied any commentary or interpretation beyond what appears in the original text. This is the Bible itself, presented here in a form that is understandable and accessible to children.

Old Testament is the traditional Christian name for this material, which is traditionally known to members of the Jewish religion as the *Hebrew Bible* or *Tanach.* It is known to both groups as the *Scriptures,* which literally means "the writings."

We wish to thank the following consultants who reviewed this Old Testament text for its publication in *The Illustrated Bible for Children*:

Dr. Gleason L. Archer
Professor Emeritus
Old Testament and Semitic Languages
Trinity Evangelical School
Deerfield, Illinois

Dr. Tamara C. Eskenazi
Associate Professor of Bible
Hebrew Union College
Los Angeles, California

Dr. George Mason
Ph.D. in Systematic Theology
Pastor, Wilshire Baptist Church
Dallas, Texas

Sr. Patricia McDonald, S.H.C.J.
Assistant Professor
Department of Theology
Mount St. Mary's College
Emmitsburg, Maryland

We also wish to thank Rabbi A. James Rudin, National Director of Interreligious Affairs for the American Jewish Committee, for his additional comments on the text.

We hope that this book will serve as an intermediate stage between Bible picture books without text and a complete Bible in a standard translation. Our editorial policies have been explicitly devised for the young reader, such as the use of large and readable type, the inclusion of colorful illustrations to accompany the text, and the presentation of the episodes in narrative form.

This is the story of the Children of Israel. We invite you to read it.

The Publishers

A Note on the Paintings

In the paintings that I have created for this book, I have been inspired by the many famous artists throughout history who have depicted scenes from the Bible. I hope my own efforts have been faithful to the great tradition that they established. I wish to dedicate my work on this project to my father, John Farnsworth.

Bill Farnsworth

Table of Contents

Publisher's and Artist's Notes vii

Contents of The Old Testament xi

Paintings of The Old Testament xvi

The Lands of the Bible (Map) .... xviii–xix

The Exodus of the Israelites (Map) xviii

The Old Testament **1–149**

Additional Information on The Old Testament 150–155

    The Geography of the Holy Land 150

    Biblical Plants and Animals 152

    Ancient Egypt 154

Notes on the Text 156–160

Bible Dictionary 161–172

Contents of The Old Testament

THE CREATION   1
"In the beginning God created the heaven and the earth."

THE GARDEN OF EDEN   6
"On the day you eat fruit from this tree, you shall surely die."

THE FORBIDDEN FRUIT   8
"The serpent tempted me, and I did eat."

CAIN AND ABEL   11
"Am I my brother's keeper?"

THE LORD SPEAKS TO NOAH   13
"Behold, I will bring a flood of waters upon the earth."

NOAH AND THE ARK   14
"Bring into the ark two of every sort of every living thing."

NOAH HEARS GOD'S PROMISE   18
"I do set my rainbow in the cloud."

THE TOWER OF BABEL   19
"We will build a tower whose top may reach up to heaven."

ABRAHAM   20
"Say that you are my sister, and I will live because of you."

ABRAHAM AND LOT   21
"Let there be no fighting between us, for we are one family."

ABRAHAM AND SARAH   22
"You will be the father of many nations."

SODOM AND GOMORRAH   23
"Escape for your lives, and do not look behind you."

THE TEST FOR ABRAHAM   24
"But where is the lamb for the burnt offering?"

ISAAC AND REBEKAH   26
"I will draw water for your camels also."

JACOB AND ESAU 28
"What good is this birthright to me?"

JACOB'S LADDER 30
"This land on which you lie, I give to you and your descendants."

RACHEL AND LEAH 32
"I will serve you seven years."

JACOB AND THE ANGEL 35
"I will not let you go unless you bless me."

THE COAT OF MANY COLORS 36
"And all your bundles stood around mine and bowed down to it."

JOSEPH IN EGYPT 39
"My master has not kept anything in this house from me but you."

PHARAOH'S DREAMS 40
"Seven thin, sick cows followed, and ate the seven healthy cows."

JOSEPH AND HIS BROTHERS 42
"And Joseph's brothers came and bowed down before him."

BENJAMIN IN EGYPT 44
"Search, and let whoever took the cup die."

THE BIRTH OF MOSES 46
"I will call his name Moses, because I took him up out of the water."

THE BURNING BUSH 48
"And the angel of the Lord appeared to Moses in a flame of fire."

THE LORD'S MESSAGE TO MOSES 50
"I have come to deliver my people out of the hand of the Egyptians."

PHARAOH AND THE ISRAELITES 52
"All the waters were turned to blood."

THE PLAGUES OF EGYPT 54
"And the frogs came up, and covered the land of Egypt."

PASSOVER 56
"Among the children of Israel, neither man nor beast will be harmed."

THE PARTING OF THE SEA   58
"The waters formed a wall on their right hand, and on their left."

IN THE WILDERNESS   60
"I will rain bread from heaven for you."

THE TEN COMMANDMENTS   62
"All that the Lord has spoken, we will do."

ON THE MOUNTAINTOP   64
"I will give you stone tablets of the laws I have written."

THE TABERNACLE   65
"They shall keep the sabbath throughout the generations."

THE GOLDEN CALF   66
"They sat down to eat and drink, and they rose up to sing and dance."

LAWS AND OBSERVANCES   70
"You shall love your neighbor as yourself."

THE JOURNEY TO CANAAN   71
"The land surely flows with milk and honey."

THE DEATH OF MOSES   73
"I have brought you to see the land with your own eyes."

THE WALLS OF JERICHO   74
"Shout, for the Lord has given you the city."

GIDEON'S TRUMPET   76
"He blew his trumpet to call Israel to battle."

SAMSON   79
"No razor may touch his hair."

SAMSON AND DELILAH   80
"Samson bent with all his might, and the temple fell."

RUTH AND NAOMI   84
"For wherever you go, I will go, and wherever you stay, I will stay."

SAMUEL IS CALLED   87
"Speak, Lord, for your servant is listening."

A KING FOR ISRAEL   89
"Listen to the voice of the people, for they have rejected me."

SAUL AND SAMUEL   90
"It is better to obey the Lord than to make sacrifices to him."

THE SHEPHERD BOY   92
"Send me your son David, who is with the sheep."

DAVID AND GOLIATH   94
"Am I a dog, that you come to me with sticks?"

SAUL'S JEALOUSY   98
"Would you kill an innocent man without reason?"

DAVID AND JONATHAN   100
"The Lord will be between me and you forever."

THE WITCH OF ENDOR   102
"Find me a woman who can raise the spirits."

DAVID BECOMES KING   104
"How the mighty are fallen!"

DAVID AND BATHSHEBA   106
"With this deed, you have scorned the Lord."

DAVID AND ABSALOM   108
"Behold, my own son wants to kill me."

THE DEATH OF DAVID   110
"I swear by the Lord God that Solomon shall sit on my throne."

SOLOMON'S DREAM   111
"Give me, therefore, an understanding heart."

KING SOLOMON'S WISDOM   112
"Bring me a sword! We will divide this living child in two."

SOLOMON BUILDS A TEMPLE   115
"I have built you a house to dwell in forever."

THE QUEEN OF SHEBA   116
"And all the earth came to hear the wisdom of King Solomon."

A DIVIDED KINGDOM   118
    "I will take the kingdom away from your son."

THE PROPHET ELIJAH   120
    "A chariot of fire and horses of fire came."

THE RETURN TO JERUSALEM   122
    "The people mocked the messengers of God."

ESTHER BECOMES QUEEN   124
    "And the king loved her above all women."

MORDECAI AND HAMAN   126
    "What should be done for a man that the king wants to honor?"

GOD'S SERVANT JOB   128
    "And the Lord said to Satan, 'Have you considered my servant Job?'"

PSALMS   132
    "Yea, though I walk through the valley of the shadow of death."

PROVERBS   135
    "Pride goes before destruction, and a haughty spirit before a fall."

ECCLESIASTES   136
    "For every thing there is a season."

THE SONG OF SONGS   137
    "Arise, my love, my fair one, and come away."

ISAIAH   138
    "And the leopard shall lie down with the kid."

KING NEBUCHADNEZZAR   140
    "And Daniel understood visions and dreams."

HANDWRITING ON THE WALL   141
    "The fingers of a man's hand came forth and wrote on the wall."

DANIEL IN THE LION'S DEN   144
    "O Daniel, has your God been able to save you from the lions?"

JONAH AND THE WHALE   146
    "So they took up Jonah, and they threw him into the sea."

Paintings of The Old Testament

The Creation	1	Joseph in the Pit	37
Let There Be Light	2	Jacob Sees Joseph's Coat	38
The Earth Is Formed	3	Potiphar and His Wife	39
God Creates Living Things	5	Pharoah's Dreams	40–41
Adam, the First Man	6	Joseph Meets His Brothers	42
Adam and Eve	7	The Cup Is Stolen	44
The Serpent Tempts Eve	8	Jacob Meets Joseph	45
Adam and Eve Hide From God	9	Moses in the Bulrushes	46–47
The Flaming Sword	10	The Burning Bush	49
Cain and Abel	11	Moses Hears God Speak	50
East of Eden	12	The Serpent Becomes a Rod	51
Noah's Ark	15	The Israelites in Slavery	52
The Great Flood	16	Aaron's Rod	53
The Dove Returns	17	The Plagues of Egypt	54–55
The Tower of Babel	19	The Exodus From Egypt	56–57
The Land of Abraham	21	The Parting of the Red Sea	59
Sarah in the Tent	22	Lost in the Wilderness	60
Lot's Wife	23	Manna from Heaven	61
Abraham and Isaac	25	The Ten Commandments	62–63
Rebekah at the Well	26	Moses on the Mountaintop	64
Rebekah Meets Isaac	27	The Tabernacle	65
Jacob and Esau	28	The Golden Calf	66–67
Isaac Blesses Jacob	29	Moses Brings the Tablets	69
Jacob's Ladder	30–31	Moses Hears the People	71
Jacob Speaks to Laban	32	The Land of Milk and Honey	72
Jacob Meets the Angel	34	The Promised Land	73
Joseph and His Brothers	36	The Battle of Jericho	74–75

Gideon and the Angel 76

Gideon's Trumpet 77

Samson Fights a Lion 78

Samson and Delilah 80–81

The Blind Samson 83

Ruth in the Field 85

Naomi and the Child 86

Samuel in the Temple 87

The Lord Calls to Samuel 88

Samuel Becomes King 89

The Tearing of the Robe 90–91

David and His Flock 92

David Plays His Harp 93

Goliath of Gath 94

David and Goliath 97

Saul Throws His Spear 98–99

David Is Found 101

Samuel Appears to Saul 102–103

A Great Battle in the Valley 104

David Becomes King 105

David Sees Bathsheba 106

Absalom, Absalom! 109

Zadok Anoints Solomon 110

The Lord Comes to Solomon 111

King Solomon's Wisdom 112–113

Building the Temple 114

The Queen of Sheba 116–117

Departing for Israel 118–119

The Prophet Elijah 120

The Chariot of Fire 121

Rebuilding the Temple 123

Queen Vashti 124

The Crowning of Esther 125

Mordecai on Parade 127

The Blessings of Job 128

The Sufferings of Job 129–130

Job's Blessings Are Restored 131

The Prophecy of Isaiah 138

The Peaceable Kingdom 139

King Nebuchadnezzar 140

King Belshazzar Is Warned 141

Handwriting on the Wall 142–143

Daniel in the Lion's Den 144-145

Jonah and the Whale 146–147

Jonah Is Saved 148

The Lord Speaks to Jonah 149

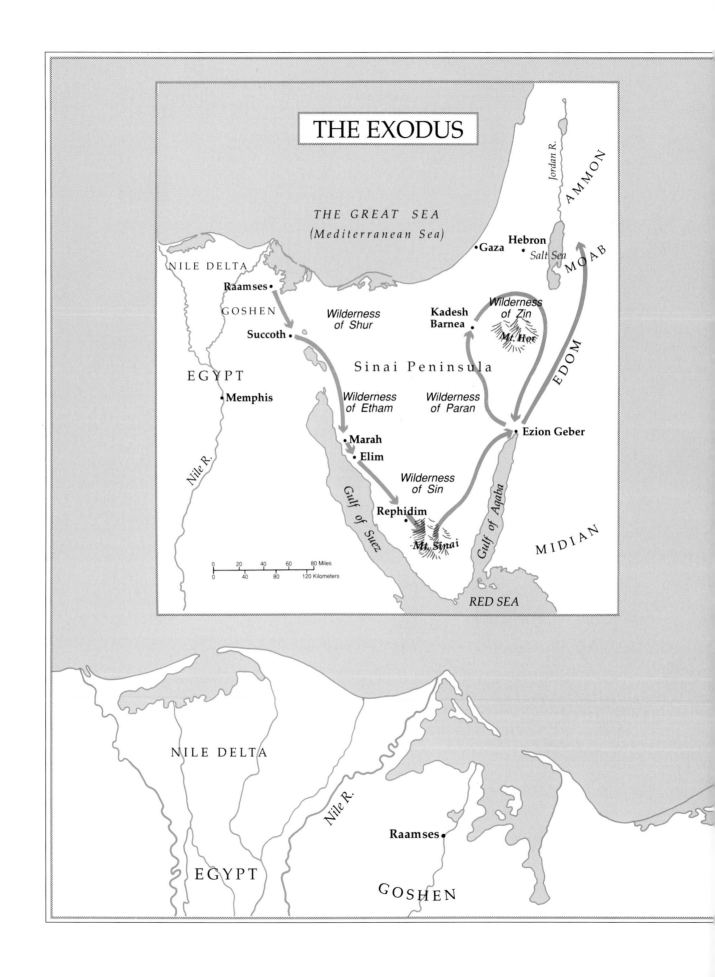

THE EXODUS

THE GREAT SEA
(*Mediterranean Sea*)

Jordan R.

AMMON

NILE DELTA

•Gaza **Hebron**• *Salt Sea*

MOAB

Raamses•

GOSHEN

Wilderness of Shur

Kadesh Barnea• *Wilderness of Zin*

Succoth•

EDOM

Mt. Hor

S i n a i   P e n i n s u l a

EGYPT

Wilderness of Etham

Wilderness of Paran

•**Memphis**

•**Marah**

Ezion Geber•

•**Elim**

Wilderness of Sin

Nile R.

Gulf of Suez

Gulf of Aqaba

Rephidim•

Mt. Sinai

MIDIAN

| 0 | 20 | 40 | 60 | 80 Miles |
| 0 | 40 | 80 | 120 Kilometers |

RED SEA

NILE DELTA

Nile R.

Raamses•

EGYPT

GOSHEN

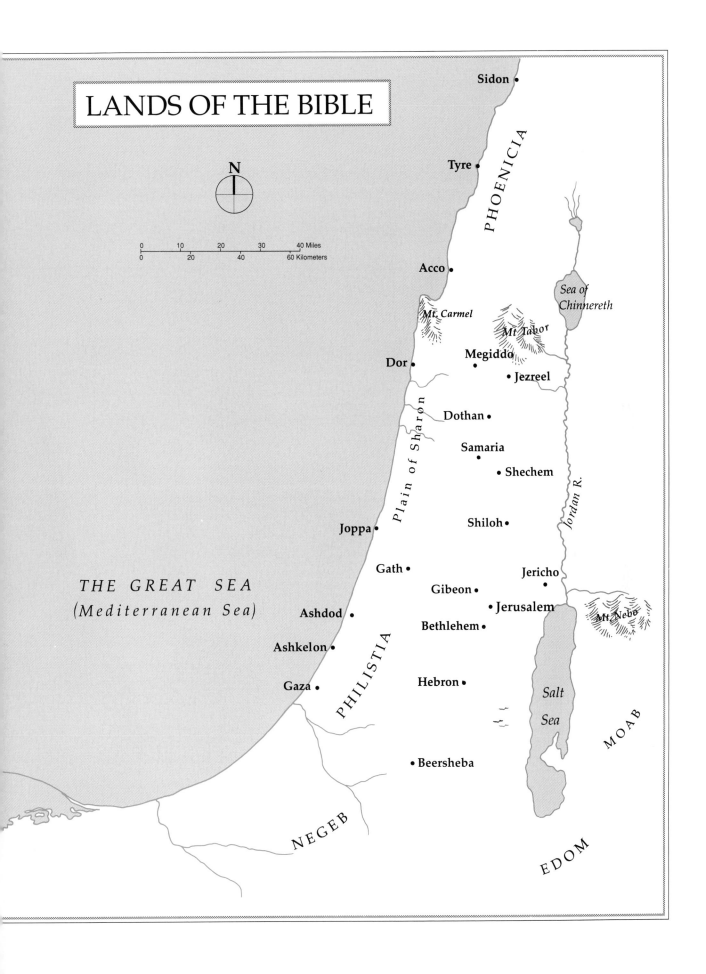

LANDS OF THE BIBLE

N

| 0 | 10 | 20 | 30 | 40 Miles |
| 0 | 20 | 40 | 60 Kilometers |

THE GREAT SEA
(Mediterranean Sea)

Sidon •

PHOENICIA

Tyre •

Acco •

Sea of Chinnereth

Mt. Carmel

Mt Tabor

Megiddo
•

Dor •

• Jezreel

Plain of Sharon

Dothan •

Samaria

• Shechem

Jordan R.

Shiloh •

Joppa •

Gath •

Jericho
•

Gibeon •

• Jerusalem

Ashdod •

Bethlehem •

Mt Nebo

Ashkelon •

Gaza •

Hebron •

Salt Sea

PHILISTIA

MOAB

• Beersheba

NEGEB

EDOM

THE CREATION

In the beginning God created the heavens and the earth.

And the earth was without form, and empty, and darkness was upon the face of the deep. And the spirit of God moved upon the face of the waters.

And God said, "Let there be light." And there was light.

And God saw the light, that it was good, and God divided the light from the darkness.

And God called the light Day, and the darkness God called Night. And the evening and the morning were one day.

And God said, "Let there be an expanse of sky in the midst of the waters. Let this expanse divide the waters above from the waters that are below."

And God made the expanse of sky, and divided the waters that were above from the waters that were below. And it was so.

And God called the expanse heaven. And the evening and the morning were a second day.

And God said, "Let the waters under the heavens be gathered together into one place, and let the dry land appear."

And God called the dry land Earth, and the gathering together of the waters God called the Seas. And God saw that it was good. And God said, "Let the earth bring forth grass, let the plants give seed, and let the trees bear fruit." And it was so.

And that was a third day.

And God said, "Let there be lights in the heavens to divide the day from the night, and let them be for signs, and for seasons, and for days, and years."

And God made two great lights: the greater light to rule the day, and the lesser light to rule the night. God made the stars also. And God set all these lights in the heavens to give light on the earth. And God saw that it was good.

And that was a fourth day.

And then God said, "Let the waters bring forth all the moving creatures that have life, and birds that may fly above the earth in the open sky."

And God created great sea monsters, and every living creature that moves in the sea, which the waters brought forth in great number, all of their kind. And God created every winged bird, all of their kind. And God saw that it was good.

And God blessed them, saying, "Be fruitful, and multiply, and fill the waters in the seas, and let birds multiply over the earth."

And that was a fifth day.

And God said, "Let the earth bring forth all living creatures, each of his own kind: cattle and animals of the field, and creeping things, and wild beasts of the forest." And it was so.

And so God made the animals of the earth, each of their own kind, and God saw that it was good.

And God said, "Let us make humans in our image, after our likeness. Let them rule over the fish of the sea, and the birds of the air, and over the animals of the field, and over all the earth, and over every creeping thing that crawls upon the earth."

And so God created human beings in his own image. He created them male and female. And God blessed them, and he said to them, "Be fruitful, and multiply, and restore the earth, and master it." And God saw everything that he had made, and God saw that it was very good.

And that was the sixth day.

Then the heavens and the earth were finished, and all the things that filled them. And on the seventh day God ended his work. Then God rested from all the work he had done.

And God blessed the seventh day, and made it holy, because on that day God rested.

GENESIS 1; 2:1–3

THE GARDEN OF EDEN

These then are the generations of the heavens and the earth, from the day the Lord God made the world.

No plant of the field was yet in the earth, for the Lord God had not caused it to rain upon the earth, and there was no one to farm the land.

But there went up a mist from the earth, and watered the whole face of the ground.

So the Lord God formed a man out of the dust of the ground, and breathed into his nostrils the breath of life. And he became a living being.

And then the Lord God planted a garden in the east, in Eden. And in the garden, he made trees grow that were beautiful to see and that had fruit that was good to eat. In the middle of the garden, he put the tree of life, and the tree of the knowledge of good and evil.

The Lord God took the man and put him into the garden to work it and keep it. The Lord God commanded the man, saying, "You may eat freely of the fruit from every tree in the garden, except from the tree of the knowledge of good and evil. For on the day that you eat fruit from this tree, you shall surely die."

And then the Lord God said, "It is not good that the man should be alone; I will make him a companion." And then he brought every living creature to the man to see what he would call them. And the man gave names to the birds of the air, and to every beast of the field. But for Adam there was not a companion.

So the Lord God made Adam fall into a deep sleep, and as he slept, the Lord God took one of his ribs, and closed up the flesh. From the rib, which the Lord God took from the man, he made a woman, and brought her to the man.

And Adam said, "This at last is bone of my bones, and flesh of my flesh. She shall be called Woman."

Therefore, a man shall leave his father and his mother, and shall cleave to his wife; and they shall be one flesh. And the man and the woman were both naked, and they were not ashamed.

GENESIS 2:4–25

THE FORBIDDEN FRUIT

The serpent was more clever than any beast of the field that the Lord God had made. He said to the woman, "Has God said that you shall not eat from every tree of the garden?"

The woman said, "We may eat the fruit of the trees of the garden, but not from the one tree that is in the middle of the garden. For God has said: 'You shall not eat from it, nor touch it, or you will die.'"

But the serpent said, "Surely you will not die, for God knows that on the day you eat from the tree, your eyes shall be opened, and you shall be like gods, knowing good and evil."

And when the woman saw that the tree was good for food, and that it was beautiful, and that it was a tree to make one wise, she took its fruit, and she did eat. And she also gave the fruit to her husband, who was with her. And he did eat.

And then their eyes were opened, and they knew that they were naked. They sewed fig leaves together, and made themselves clothing.

Then they heard the voice of the Lord God, while they were walking in the garden in the cool of the day. And Adam and his wife hid themselves from the sight of the Lord among the trees of the garden.

The Lord God called to Adam, and said, "Where are you?"

And Adam said, "I heard your voice in the garden, and I was afraid, because I was naked. So I hid myself."

And the Lord God said, "Who told you that you were naked? Have you eaten of the tree from which I commanded you not to eat?"

Then the man said, "The woman whom you gave to be with me gave me fruit from the tree, and I did eat."

And the Lord God said to the woman, "What is this that you have done?"

And the woman said, "The serpent tricked me, and I did eat."

So the Lord God said to the serpent, "Because you have done this, you are more cursed than any beast of the field. You shall go on your belly, and you shall eat dust all the days of your life."

To the woman the Lord said, "I will greatly increase your sorrow and suffering in childbearing. In sorrow you will bring forth children."

And to Adam he said, "Because you listened to your wife and ate of the tree from which I commanded you not to eat, the ground is cursed for you. In sorrow you shall eat of it for all the days of your life. In the sweat of your brow you shall eat bread until you return to the ground. For out of the ground you were taken: dust you are, and to dust you shall return."

Then the Lord God made coats of skins to clothe Adam and his wife. And he said, "The man has become as one of us, to know good and evil. Now, he might put forth his hand and also take fruit from the tree of life, and eat, and so live forever."

Therefore the Lord God sent Adam and Eve forth from the garden of Eden. East of the garden, he placed angels and a flaming sword that turned every way, to guard the tree of life.

GENESIS 3

CAIN AND ABEL

Adam called his wife Eve, because she was the mother of all living. Adam and Eve had a son, Cain. And Eve said, "I have gotten a man from the Lord."

Then Eve gave birth to Cain's brother, Abel. Abel became a keeper of sheep, and Cain was a farmer who worked the land.

In time it came to pass that Cain brought an offering of the fruit of the ground to the Lord. And Abel also brought the most prized of his flock. The Lord respected Abel and his offering. But the Lord did not respect Cain and his offering.

Cain was very angry, and his face showed his unhappiness. Then the Lord said to him, "Why are you angry, and why do you look so unhappy? If you do well, will you not be accepted? If you do not do well, sin lies in wait at your door. But you must rule over it."

Cain talked with Abel his brother, and it came to pass, when they were in the field, that Cain rose up against Abel, and killed him.

And the Lord said to Cain, "Where is Abel your brother?"

Cain answered, "I do not know. Am I my brother's keeper?"

And the Lord said, "What have you done? The voice of your brother's blood cries out to me from the ground. Now you are cursed from the earth, which has opened its mouth to receive your brother's blood from your hand. When you plant in the ground, it shall no longer give its fruit for you. You shall be a fugitive and a wanderer on the earth."

Cain cried to the Lord, "My punishment is greater than I can bear. You have driven me out this day from the face of the earth. I shall be hidden from your sight; and I shall be a fugitive and a wanderer. It shall come to pass that anyone who finds me shall kill me."

And so the Lord said to him, "Whoever should kill Cain, I shall take revenge on him seven times over." Then the Lord set a mark upon Cain, so that anyone finding him would not kill him.

And Cain went out from the sight of the Lord, and lived in the land of Nod, to the east of Eden.

GENESIS 4:1–16

12

THE LORD SPEAKS TO NOAH

And then it came to pass, that people began to multiply on the face of the earth, and daughters were born to them.

Then the sons of God saw that the daughters of mankind were pleasing to the eye, and they took as wives whichever ones they chose.

And the Lord said, "My spirit shall not always contend in man, because he is flesh. Therefore the days of his life shall be one hundred and twenty years."

There were giants on the earth in those days, and also after that. When the sons of God joined with the daughters of men and had children with them, these same children became mighty men, the famous ones of old.

And God saw that the wickedness of man was great on the earth, and that every imagination of the thoughts of his heart was continually evil. And the Lord regretted that he had made man on the earth, and it brought sadness to the Lord in his heart.

Then the Lord said, "I will destroy man whom I have created from the face of the earth; both man and beast, and also the creeping things, and the birds of the air; for I am sorry that I have made them."

But Noah found grace in the eyes of the Lord. Noah was a just man and was perfect in his time, and he walked with God. Noah was the son of Lamech, and the grandson of Methuselah. And Noah had three sons: Shem, Ham, and Japheth.

The earth was sinful in the eyes of God, and it was filled with violence. And God looked upon the earth, and saw that it was evil, for all flesh had corrupted his way upon the earth.

And God said to Noah, "The end of all living things is now at hand, for the earth is filled with violence, and I will destroy all the creatures that live on it."

GENESIS 6:1–13

NOAH AND THE ARK

God said to Noah, "Make me an ark, a huge boat, of cypress wood. Make many rooms in the ark, and cover the ark with tar both inside and out.

"You shall make it in this way: The ark shall be 300 cubits long, 50 cubits wide, and 30 cubits high. You shall make an opening around the top of the ark. Make it one cubit wide. You shall set a door in the side. And the ark shall have lower, second, and third decks.

"And behold, I will bring a flood of waters upon the earth, to destroy all flesh, all things that contain the breath of life, from under heaven; and everything that is in the earth shall die.

"But I will make a covenant, a solemn promise to you. You and all your family will come into the ark, for I have seen that you are an honorable man in this generation. By this covenant, you shall come into the ark, you, and your sons, and your wife, and your sons' wives with you."

This Noah did, according to all that God commanded him.

Then the Lord said, "Bring with you into the ark two of every sort of every living thing, to keep them alive. And they shall be male and female. Gather also all food that is eaten, and take it into the ark for you and for them.

"Take seven pairs of every clean beast, a male and female of each, and two each of all beasts that are wild, the male and the female. Take seven pairs of all the birds of the air, the male and the female. Do this in order to keep them alive on the face of the earth.

"Seven days from now, I will make it rain upon the earth for forty days and forty nights. And every living thing that I have made I will destroy from the face of the earth."

And Noah did all that the Lord commanded him.

GENESIS 6:14–22; 7:1–5

Then Noah went into the ark, and his sons, and his wife, and his sons' wives went into the ark with him. Clean beasts, and beasts that were not clean, and birds, and everything that creeps upon the earth went, two by two, into the ark, the male and the female, as God had commanded Noah.

And it came to pass after seven days, that the waters of the flood were upon the earth. On the seventeenth day of the second month, all the fountains of the great deep were broken, and the windows of heaven were opened. And the rain was upon the earth for forty days and forty nights.

The flood was forty days on the earth; and the waters increased greatly, and lifted the ark up above the earth. And the ark floated upon the face of the waters. Still the waters increased, and covered the high mountains. Every living thing on the face of the earth was destroyed. Only Noah remained alive, and those that were with him in the ark.

But God remembered Noah and every creature that was with him in the ark; and God made a wind pass over the earth, and the waters grew calm. Then the fountains of the deep and the windows of heaven were stopped, and the rain no longer came down from the sky.

On the seventeenth day of the seventh month, the ark rested upon the mountains of Ararat. And then the waters went down until the tops of the mountains were seen.

And then at the end of forty days, Noah opened the window of the ark and sent out a raven. It flew back and forth, until the waters had dried up from the earth.

Noah also sent out a dove to see if the waters had gone off from the face of the ground. But the dove found no place to rest her foot, and she returned. Noah put out his hand and took her into the ark.

And so Noah waited another seven days, and again he sent out the dove from the ark. The dove came to him in the evening, and in her mouth was an olive leaf. Then Noah knew the waters had gone down from off the earth.

And on the first day of the first month of the next year, Noah removed the covering of the ark, and he looked out. And, behold, the face of the ground was dry.

GENESIS 7:6–24; 8:1–13

17

NOAH HEARS GOD'S PROMISE

On the twenty-seventh day of the second month, God said to Noah, "Go forth from the ark and bring every living thing with you, that they may be fruitful and multiply upon the earth." And Noah with his sons, his wife, and his sons' wives, and every beast, every creeping thing, and every bird, went out from the ark.

Noah built an altar to the Lord. He took one of every clean beast and one of every clean bird, and he made burnt offerings on the altar. And then the Lord smelled a sweet odor, and the Lord said in his heart, "I will not again curse the ground for man's sake; for man may be tempted by evil even from his youth. Neither will I again destroy every thing living, as I have done. While the earth remains, planting time and harvest, cold and heat, summer and winter, and day and night, shall go on without stopping."

And God spoke to Noah, saying to him, "I establish my covenant, a solemn promise, with you, and with your children after you; and with every living creature that is with you; never again shall all flesh be cut off by the waters of a flood; never shall there be a flood to destroy the earth."

Then God said, "This is my token of the covenant that I make between me and you and every living creature that is with you. I do set my rainbow in the cloud, and it shall be as a token of an agreement between me and the earth.

"It will come to pass, when I bring a cloud over the earth, that the rainbow shall be seen in the cloud, and I will remember my covenant and the waters shall no more become a flood to destroy all flesh."

And God said to Noah, "This is the token of the covenant that I have established between me and all living creatures that are upon the earth."

GENESIS 8:20–22; 9:1–17

THE TOWER OF BABEL

The whole earth once had one language and one speech. And as the people journeyed from the east, they found a plain in the land of Shinar, and so they settled there. There they said to one another, "Let us make bricks, and bake them hard. And here we will build us a city and a tower, whose top may reach up to the sky. And then we will make us a name, so that we cannot be scattered abroad on the face of the earth." And then the Lord came down to see the city and the tower, which the people had built. And the Lord said, "Behold, the people now all have one language, and this they begin to do. Now, nothing will stop them from doing whatever it is they can imagine. Let us then confuse their language, so that they cannot understand one another's speech."

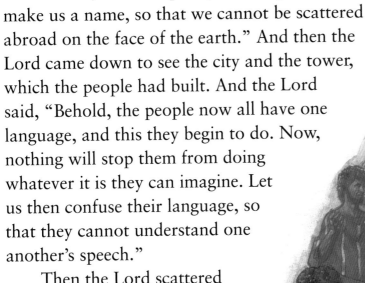

Then the Lord scattered people from there all over the face of the earth. And they stopped building the city.

Therefore the city is called Babel, because it was there that the Lord confused the language of all the earth; and from there he did scatter the people all over the earth.

Genesis 11:1–9

19

ABRAHAM

Abraham was the son of Terah, and he was descended from Shem, the son of Noah. He lived in the land of Haran.

The Lord said to Abraham, "Go out of your country, from your birthplace and from your father's house, to a land that I will show you. And I will make a great nation of you, and I will bless you, and make your name great. And in you all families of the earth shall be blessed."

So Abraham took Sarah and Lot, his brother's son, and they went out into the land of Canaan. There the Lord appeared to Abraham and said, "To your descendants I will give this land." And Abraham built there an altar to the Lord, and he called upon the name of the Lord.

But there was a famine in Canaan, and Abraham went down to Egypt to live there, for the famine was terrible in the land. And Abraham said to Sarah his wife, "I know that you are a beautiful woman, and when the Egyptians see you, they will kill me but keep you alive. So, say that you are my sister, and I will live because of you."

And so it came about that the princes of Egypt saw Sarah and praised her before Pharaoh. And she was taken into Pharaoh's house. Pharaoh treated Abraham well for Sarah's sake, and gave him livestock and servants.

But the Lord sent great plagues upon Pharaoh and his household because of Sarah. And Pharaoh called Abraham to him, and said, "What have you done to me? Why did you say Sarah was your sister, so I would take her as my wife? Take your wife and go your way."

And Pharaoh sent Abraham away with his wife and all that he had. And Abraham, Sarah, and Lot took their possessions and traveled out of Egypt. They settled in a place between Bethel and Ai, where Abraham had built the altar to the Lord.

GENESIS 12; 13:1–4

ABRAHAM AND LOT

Abraham was very rich in cattle, in silver, and in gold. And Lot also had flocks, and herds, and tents. And the land was not able to support them both. There was fighting between the herdsmen of Abraham and the herdsmen of Lot.

Abraham said to Lot, "Let there be no fighting between us, for we are of one family. The whole land is before us. You choose the land to the left hand or to the right, and I will take the other."

Lot lifted up his eyes, and looked out over all the plain of Jordan. And he saw that the land was well watered everywhere. So Lot chose for himself all the plain of Jordan, and journeyed east. Then Abraham and Lot separated from one another, and Abraham stayed in the land of Canaan.

The Lord said to Abraham, "Lift up your eyes, and look from where you are northward, and southward, and eastward, and westward. All the land that you see there, I will give to you and your descendants forever."

GENESIS 13:5–15

ABRAHAM AND SARAH

When Abraham was ninety-nine years old, the Lord came and said to him, "I am the Almighty God, and I will make my covenant with you. You will be the father of many nations. I will give to you, and to your descendants after you, the land of Canaan for an everlasting possession. And I will be their God."

Then the Lord appeared again to Abraham as he sat in the tent door in the heat of the day. And the Lord said, "I will surely return to you at this time next year; and Sarah your wife will have a son."

Sarah heard this from the tent door. Abraham and Sarah were old and far along in years, and Sarah had become too old to have a child.

Therefore Sarah laughed to herself, saying, "As old as I am, how is it that I will have a child?" But the Lord said to Abraham, "Why did Sarah laugh? Is anything too hard for the Lord? At the right time, I will return to you, and Sarah shall have a son."

GENESIS 17:1–8; 18:10–14

SODOM AND GOMORRAH

Sodom and Gomorrah were cities on the plain of Jordan. The Lord said, "Because the sins of these cities are very great, I will go down to judge them."

Abraham asked the Lord, "Will you destroy the righteous with the wicked? If there are fifty who are innocent within the city, will you not forgive the place for them? Shall not the Judge of all the earth be just?"

And the Lord said, "If I find in Sodom fifty righteous men within the city, then I will spare all the place for their sake."

And then two angels came to Sodom, and said to Lot, "Bring your family out of this place, for the Lord has sent us to destroy it." The angels brought Lot out of the city, and one said to him, "Escape for your lives, and do not look behind you."

Then the Lord rained brimstone and fire out of heaven on Sodom and Gomorrah, and he destroyed the cities and all those within them. But Lot's wife looked behind her, and she was turned into a pillar of salt.

GENESIS 18:20–32; 19:20–26

THE TEST FOR ABRAHAM

The Lord did as he had spoken, and Sarah bore Abraham a son in his old age. And Abraham called the son that was born to Sarah by the name of Isaac. And the child grew.

Then it came to pass that God said to Abraham, "Take your only son Isaac, whom you love, into the land of Moriah. Offer him there for a burnt sacrifice on one of the mountains that I shall show you."

And Abraham rose early in the morning, and saddled his donkey, and took two servants and Isaac his son, and he set out for the place that God had told him. And on the third day, Abraham lifted his eyes, and saw the place far off. He gave Isaac his son the wood to carry for the burnt offering, and he took glowing embers and a knife. And they went on together.

Isaac said to his father Abraham, "Here are the fire and the wood, but where is the lamb for the burnt offering?" And Abraham said, "God himself will provide a lamb for the burnt offering."

Then they came to the place that God had told Abraham of, and Abraham built an altar there. He bound Isaac his son and laid him on the wood of the altar. Then Abraham stretched out his hand, and took the knife to kill his son.

But the angel of the Lord called to Abraham from heaven, and said, "Do not lay your hand upon your son; for now I know that you fear God, seeing that you have not kept your only son from me."

Abraham looked up and saw a ram caught in the bushes behind him. And he sacrificed the ram instead of his son.

The angel of the Lord said, "Because you have not withheld your only son, I will bless you and multiply your descendants as the stars of the heaven and as the sand upon the seashore. And through your descendants, all the nations of the earth shall be blessed, because you have obeyed my voice."

GENESIS 21:1–3; 22:1–18

ISAAC AND REBEKAH

When Abraham was very old, he said to the eldest servant of his house, "Swear by the Lord that you will go to my country, to my relatives, and take a wife for my son Isaac." And he did so swear.

And so the servant took ten camels, and went to the city of Nahor in Mesopotamia. In the evening, he waited at a well outside the city as the women came to draw water. As he waited, Rebekah came to fill her pitcher at the well. She was the daughter of Bethuel, the son of Nahor, Abraham's brother. Rebekah was not married and was very beautiful.

The servant said to her, "May I drink a little water from your pitcher?" And Rebekah said, "Drink, my lord." When she had given him a drink, she said, "I will draw water for your camels also."

When the camels had finished drinking, the servant gave Rebekah a golden earring that weighed half a shekel, and two bracelets that weighed ten shekels. And he said to her, "Whose daughter are you? Is there room in your father's house for us to spend the night?"

Rebekah ran to tell her family of these things, and her brother Laban came to the servant and invited him to their home. They gave food and water to his camels, and set meat before him. But the servant said, "I will not eat until I have told you my errand." And he told them that he was Abraham's servant, and that he had come to find a wife for his master's son Isaac.

Then Laban and Bethuel said, "Take Rebekah, and go, and let her become your master's son's wife, as the Lord has said."

And they called Rebekah, and said, "Will you go with this man?" And she said, "I will go."

One evening, Isaac went out to the field, and he saw the camels were coming. When Rebekah saw Isaac, she got down from the camel, and said, "Who is that man who is coming to meet us?" And the servant said, "It is my master." So Rebekah covered her face with her veil.

Isaac brought Rebekah into his mother Sarah's tent; and Rebekah became his wife, and he loved her.

GENESIS 24

JACOB AND ESAU

Isaac prayed to the Lord that Rebekah would have a child. And the Lord answered Isaac's prayer. Then Rebekah felt two children struggling together within her. Rebekah went to ask the Lord about this, and the Lord said to her, "You are carrying two nations: one shall be stronger than the other, and the elder shall serve the younger."

Rebekah's firstborn twin was red and hairy all over, and he was called Esau. His brother was born with his hand holding Esau's heel. He was called Jacob.

The boys grew. Esau became a skillful hunter, a man of the field. And Jacob was a quiet, thoughtful man, dwelling in tents. And Isaac loved Esau, for he liked to eat the venison that Esau brought. But Rebekah loved Jacob.

One day, Esau came from the field, and he was weak from hunger. He asked Jacob for some of the bean soup that he was cooking. Esau said to Jacob, "Feed me, I beg you, for I am faint with hunger." But Jacob said to Esau, "Sell me this day your birthright."

Esau said, "I am about to die of hunger. What good is this birthright to me?" So he sold his birthright to Jacob.

And then Jacob gave Esau bread and bean soup, and Esau did eat, and went on his way.

And that was how Esau gave up his birthright.

When Isaac was old, his eyes were so dim that he could not see. He called Esau to him and said, "Make me the tasty stew that I love, and my soul will bless you before I die."

But Rebekah heard what Isaac said to Esau, and she said to Jacob, "Do as I command you and fetch me two young goats. I will make the stew that your father loves, so you can take it to him, and he will bless you before his death."

Jacob said, "Esau is a hairy man; I am a smooth man. My father may feel me and curse me as a deceiver, not bless me." But he brought her the young goats. Rebekah put Esau's best clothes on Jacob, and she put the skins of the young goats on Jacob's hands and on his neck.

Jacob took the stew to his father and he said, "I am Esau, your firstborn." But Isaac said, "Come near that I may feel if you are Esau." Isaac felt him and said, "The voice is Jacob's voice, but the hands are the hands of Esau." But Isaac did not recognize Jacob, for his hands were hairy like Esau's hands. Isaac blessed Jacob, saying, "Let people serve you, and nations bow down to you. Be lord over your brothers."

When Esau returned, he cried to his father, "Bless me also." But Isaac answered, "Your brother has taken away your blessing. What can I do for you now, my son?" And Esau lifted up his voice and wept.

Genesis 25, 27

JACOB'S LADDER

Then Esau hated Jacob because of the stolen blessing. He said to himself, "The time of my father's death must be near. After the days of mourning for my father are over, then I will kill my brother Jacob."

Rebekah was told of these words of Esau, and she said to Jacob, "Your brother Esau plans to kill you. Go now to my brother Laban in Haran. Stay there for a time until your brother's anger is gone, and he forgets what you have done to him." She said to Isaac, "If Jacob takes a wife from this land of Canaan, what good will my life be to me?"

So Isaac blessed Jacob, and said, "Do not take a wife from Canaan, but go to Haran, and take a wife from the daughters of Laban, your mother's brother."

And so Jacob went toward Haran. Then he came upon a place where he spent the night. He took a stone from this place and he put it down for his pillow, and then lay down to sleep.

Jacob dreamed that a ladder was set upon the earth, with its top reaching to heaven. And the angels of God were going up and down on the ladder.

The Lord stood above it, and he said, "I am the Lord, the God of Abraham and of Isaac. This land on which you lie, I give to you and your descendants. I am with you and I will keep you wherever you go, and I will bring you back to this land."

GENESIS 27:41–46; 28:1–2, 10–15

30

RACHEL AND LEAH

Jacob continued on with his journey, and then he came into Haran. There he stopped by a well where shepherds watered their flocks. As he spoke with the shepherds, Rachel came by with her father's sheep. Rachel was the daughter of Laban, his mother's brother. And when Jacob saw Rachel, he kissed her and wept loudly.

Then Jacob told Rachel that he was Rebekah's son, and she ran and told her father. Laban ran to meet Jacob, and embraced him, and brought him to his house. And so Jacob stayed with Laban for about one month.

Then Laban said to Jacob, "Though you are of my family, you should not work for nothing. What shall your wages be?"

Now Laban had two daughters: Leah the elder had tender eyes, but Rachel was beautiful. And Jacob loved Rachel. So he said, "I will serve you seven years, for Rachel your younger daughter."

And so Jacob worked seven years for Rachel, but they seemed only a few days to him, because of his love for her.

Then Jacob said to Laban, "Give me my wife, for the seven years have passed." And Laban gathered all the men of the place, and made a feast. In the evening, Laban took his daughter Leah and brought her to Jacob in bed.

And then in the morning, Jacob found that it was Leah, and not Rachel. He said to Laban, "What is this you have done to me? Did I not work for you for seven years for Rachel? Why then have you tricked me?"

Laban said to him, "It cannot be done in our land to give the younger daughter in marriage before the firstborn. But we will give you Rachel also, if you shall promise to serve me another seven years." So Jacob promised and was given Rachel. And he loved her more than Leah.

When the Lord saw that Leah was not loved, he blessed her with children. But Rachel had none. Leah had six sons, and then a daughter, Dinah.

But God finally remembered Rachel and heard her prayers. And so Rachel bore a son, and called him Joseph.

Jacob worked for yet another six years, and Laban gave him cattle. And Jacob had many cattle, and he became a man of great wealth. Then Jacob heard Laban's sons say, "Jacob has taken away all our father's wealth." And then Jacob saw in the face of Laban, that Laban was not as friendly to him as before.

And then the Lord said to Jacob, "Return to the land of your fathers, and to your family, and I will be with you."

So Jacob spoke first to Rachel and Leah. Then he set his sons and his wives upon camels, and he carried away all his cattle, and all his goods, to go to the land of Canaan.

And as Jacob went on his way, he sent messengers before him to tell his brother Esau in the land of Seir, that he was returning home and wished for his favor. But the messengers returned to Jacob, saying, "Your brother Esau comes to meet you, with four hundred men."

GENESIS 29–32

JACOB AND THE ANGEL

Jacob was greatly afraid and distressed, and so he asked God to deliver him from the hand of his brother Esau. And Jacob sent ahead a present of goats, and sheep, and camels, and cattle to his brother.

That night, Jacob sent on his wives and his children, and he was left alone. In that place, a stranger wrestled with Jacob until daybreak. And when he saw that he could not defeat Jacob, he touched the hollow of Jacob's thigh. And the thigh was greatly strained. Then he said, "Let me go, for the day is breaking." But Jacob said, "I will not let you go unless you bless me."

And the man said to him, "What is your name?" And he said, "Jacob." Then the man said, "Your name shall no longer be Jacob, but Israel. For you have battled with God and with men, and have won." And he blessed Jacob there.

Then Jacob looked up and saw Esau and his four hundred men coming. And Jacob passed in front of his family, and bowed to the ground seven times, until he came near to his brother.

And Esau ran to meet Jacob, and embraced him, and kissed him. And they wept.

Then Esau said, "Why did you send me this present? I have enough, my brother. Keep what you have for yourself."

And Jacob said, "No, if I have found grace in your eyes, please accept my present, so I will know that you are pleased with me."

And Esau accepted the present. Then he returned that day to Seir, and Jacob journeyed on to the land of Canaan.

And it came to pass that Rachel gave birth to another son, and she died. Jacob called his son Benjamin.

And Jacob went to Isaac in Hebron, where the aged Isaac died; and his sons Esau and Jacob buried him.

GENESIS 32–33, 35

35

THE COAT OF MANY COLORS

Jacob lived in the land of Canaan. And this is the story of the sons of Jacob, Joseph and his brothers.

Joseph, who was seventeen years old, was feeding the flock of sheep with his brothers. Now, Jacob loved Joseph more than all his other children, because he was the son of his old age. He made Joseph a coat of many colors.

When his brothers saw that their father loved Joseph the most, they hated Joseph and could not speak kindly to him.

Joseph dreamed a dream, and he told it to his brothers. He said to them, "I have dreamed that we were tying up bundles of grain in the field, and then my own bundle rose up and stood straight, and all your bundles stood around it and bowed down to mine."

Then his brothers said to him, "Will you then rule over us? Will we have to bow down to you?" And they hated him all the more for his dreams, and for his words.

One day Jacob called Joseph to him and said, "Go, I pray you. See whether all is well with your brothers, and with their flocks, and bring me word of them." So Joseph went into the fields, and he found his brothers in Dothan.

When the brothers saw Joseph coming from far off, they said to one another, "Look, here comes the boy who dreams." And they plotted against him. "Come, let us kill him," they said. "We will throw him into some pit, and say that an evil beast has eaten him. Then we shall see what will become of his dreams."

But Rueben, the oldest of the brothers, heard this. He said, "Let us not kill him. Do not shed his blood, but only throw him into this pit that is here in the wilderness, and do not lay your hand upon him." For Reuben meant to rescue Joseph from his brothers, and return him to his father.

So when Joseph came up to his brothers, they seized him and stripped off his coat of many colors. They took him and threw him into a dry pit. Then they sat down to eat.

Then Joseph's brothers looked up and saw a band of Ishmaelites coming with their camels, bearing goods to carry to Egypt. The brother named Judah said, "Come, let us sell him to the Ishmaelites, and let us bring no more harm to him. After all, he is our brother, and our own flesh and blood." And his brothers agreed.

As they were eating, some Midianite traders came by. They lifted Joseph up out of the pit and sold him to the Ishmaelites for twenty pieces of silver. When Reuben returned to the pit, he saw that Joseph was not there. He tore at his clothes, and he cried out to his brothers, "The boy is gone! And now, where will I go?"

The brothers took Joseph's coat of many colors. Then they killed a young goat, and they dipped the coat in its blood. Then they brought the bloody coat to their father. "We found this," they said. "Tell us if you know whether it is your son's coat or not?"

Jacob knew that it was Joseph's coat, and he said, "It is my son's coat. Some wild beast has eaten him. My son Joseph has been torn to pieces, there is no doubt."

Jacob wept, and put on funeral clothes, and he mourned for his son for many days.

Meanwhile, Joseph had been sold as a slave in Egypt. He was sold to Potiphar, the captain of the Pharaoh's guards.

GENESIS 37

JOSEPH IN EGYPT

And Potiphar saw that the Lord was with Joseph, and he made Joseph the chief servant over his house, and he let Joseph manage all that he had. And it came to pass that the Lord blessed the Egyptian's house for Joseph's sake.

Now Joseph was a handsome man, and Potiphar's wife desired him. But Joseph refused her, saying, "My master has not kept anything in this house from me, but you, his wife. How can I do this great wrong, and commit a sin against God?"

Then Potiphar's wife grew angry. She told Potiphar that Joseph had mocked her, and turned and run away when she had cried out. When Joseph's master heard his wife's words, he became angry. And he had Joseph put into the prison where the king's prisoners were kept.

But the Lord was with Joseph and showed him mercy, and the keeper of the prison put Joseph in charge of the other prisoners.

Genesis 39

PHARAOH'S DREAMS

Once Pharaoh was angry with his chief butler and with his chief baker, and he put them in the place where Joseph was a prisoner.

There in prison, each one dreamed a dream. When Joseph came in to them in the morning, he asked, "Why do you look so sad today?"

And the chief butler said to Joseph, "I dreamed of a vine with three branches that blossomed and brought forth grapes. And I pressed the grapes into Pharaoh's cup, and gave the cup to Pharaoh."

Joseph said, "Within three days, Pharaoh will set you free, and you shall serve him as you did before. When you do, remember me. Show kindness, and speak of me to Pharaoh, that I may be set free."

Then the chief baker said, "I dreamed I had three baskets of bread on my head. In the top basket there were all kinds of baked goods for Pharaoh, but the birds ate them from the basket."

And Joseph said, "Within three days Pharaoh shall hang you on a tree, and the birds shall eat the flesh from you."

And in three days time all these things came to pass, just as Joseph had said they would happen. Yet the chief butler did not remember Joseph, but forgot him.

At the end of two full years, Pharaoh dreamed that he stood by the river, and seven cows, fat and healthy, came from the river and ate the grass. But then seven thin, sickly cows followed, and they ate the seven healthy cows. Then Pharaoh dreamed that seven ears of grain, plump and tasty, came up on one stalk. But seven thin and diseased ears swallowed up the good ears.

Pharaoh was troubled, and he told the wise men his dreams. But no one could tell him what they meant. Then Pharaoh's chief butler remembered Joseph, the Hebrew who could interpret dreams.

So Pharaoh called for Joseph and told him his dreams. And Joseph said, "God has shown Pharaoh what he is about to do. The seven good cows and the seven good ears are seven years of great plenty. The seven sickly cows and the seven diseased ears are seven years of famine that will follow. Let Pharaoh find a wise man and set him over the land of Egypt, to store food against the seven years of famine."

Then Pharaoh said to Joseph, "You shall be over my house, and all my people shall be ruled according to your word. Only I will be greater than you." And during the seven years of plenty, Joseph stored food in the cities. And Joseph had a wife, Asenath, and they had two sons: Manasseh and Ephraim.

GENESIS 40; 41:1–52

JOSEPH AND HIS BROTHERS

After the seven years of plenty in the land of Egypt were ended, then the seven years of famine began. This was just as Joseph had said. The famine was over all the face of the earth, but there was food in Egypt. So all nations came to Joseph in Egypt to buy grain.

Now when Jacob saw that there was grain in Egypt, he said to his sons, "Go down to Egypt, and buy grain there, that we may live and not die."

So Joseph's ten brothers went down to buy grain in Egypt. But Jacob did not send Benjamin, Joseph's brother, with the others, for fear that some harm might come to him.

And Joseph's brothers came and bowed down before him with their faces to the ground. Joseph saw his brothers, and he knew them, but he did not make himself known to them.

Joseph spoke roughly to the brothers, saying to them, "Where do you come from?"

And they said, "We have come from the land of Canaan to buy food."

Then Joseph remembered the dreams that he had dreamed, and said, "You are spies; you come here to see the weaknesses of this land." And he put them in prison for three days.

On the third day, Joseph said, "If you are honest men, let one of you stay in prison while the rest take grain home. But bring your youngest brother to me, so I shall know that your words are true. Then you shall not die."

The brothers said one to another, "We are guilty because we saw the suffering of our brother Joseph's soul, and would not help him. Therefore, this trouble has come upon us."

And when Joseph heard them, he turned away and wept. Then he took Simeon and tied him up before their eyes. And the others loaded their donkeys with grain, and they returned to Jacob.

When Jacob heard their story, he said, "My son Benjamin shall not go with you, for his brother Joseph is dead. If any harm should come to Benjamin, I shall go down to my grave in sorrow."

But the famine was still great in the land of Canaan. And when they had eaten up all the grain that they had brought out of Egypt, Jacob said, "Go again, buy us a little food."

And Judah said, "The man did solemnly say that we shall not see his face again unless our brother is with us. If you will send Benjamin with us, then we will go down to Egypt. And if I do not bring him back to you, then I will bear the blame for this forever."

Then their father said, "If it must be so, do this: take the man a present of the best fruits in the land, a little balm, and a little honey, spices, myrrh, and nuts. Take your brother Benjamin also, and go again to him."

GENESIS 42; 43:1–14

BENJAMIN IN EGYPT

The brothers went to Egypt, and Joseph's servant took them to his house. And when Joseph saw Benjamin, he hurried into his own room to weep, for he was deeply moved to see his brother.

They sat before him, and Joseph sent them food from his plate. To Benjamin, he gave five times as much as to any of the others. And they drank and were merry with him. Then Joseph told his servant to fill his brothers' sacks with grain and to put each man's money in the top of the sack. And in Benjamin's sack, he also put his own silver cup.

As soon as the morning was light, the brothers were sent on their way. When they were not far out of the city, Joseph's servant caught up with them, saying, "Why have you rewarded good with evil, and taken the cup from which my lord drinks?"

And they said, "God forbid that we should steal from your lord. Search, and let whoever took the cup die." When the cup was found in Benjamin's sack, the brothers tore their clothes in anguish, and they returned to the city.

When the brothers returned to the city, Joseph said to them, "Let the one in whose sack the cup was found remain here as my servant."

But Judah said, "Let me stay in my brother's place, for how shall I return to my father if Benjamin is not with me? Surely it will kill him."

Then Joseph wept loudly, and he said, "I am Joseph your brother, whom you sold into Egypt. God has sent me to you to save your lives.

"Hurry, and go to my father, and say to him, 'This is what your son Joseph wishes to tell you: Come to me now and live in the land of Goshen, you, and your children, and your children's children, and all that you have. There I will take care of you, for there are five years of famine yet to come.'"

And they did as Joseph said. And then Joseph went up to Goshen to meet Jacob his father. He presented himself to him, and he fell upon his neck, and he wept on his neck for a good while. And Jacob said, "Now let me die, since I have seen your face, and you are still alive."

But Jacob lived in the land of Egypt for seventeen years, and his family grew and multiplied there. And then when Jacob died, his sons carried his coffin into the land of Canaan and buried him there.

FROM GENESIS 43–45, 47, 50

THE BIRTH OF MOSES

There rose up a new ruler of Egypt, who did not know of Joseph. He said to his people, "The people of Israel are stronger than we are. In time of war they might join with our enemies and fight against us. Come, let us deal cleverly with them, and get them out of our land."

Therefore the Egyptians put masters over the Israelites. They made their lives bitter with slavery, and with all kinds of hard work in the fields. But the more the children of Israel were made to suffer, the more they multiplied and grew. Then Pharaoh ordered all his people, "Every son of Israel that is born you shall throw into the river to drown, and every daughter you shall let live."

Now there was an Israelite of the house of Levi, who took as his wife a daughter of Levi. She had a baby son, and when she saw he was a healthy child, she hid him for three months.

When the mother could no longer hide her baby, she made him a basket of bulrushes. She sealed it with mud and tar, and she put the child in it. Then she laid the basket in the reeds by the river's edge.

The baby's sister stood far off, to watch what would happen to him. Then the daughter of Pharaoh came down to wash herself at the river. She and her servants walked along by the riverside. When she saw the basket among the reeds, she sent her servant to fetch it.

She opened the basket, and she saw that the baby was in it. The baby cried, and she felt sorry for him. She said, "This is one of the Hebrews' children."

Then the baby's sister came forward, and she said to Pharaoh's daughter, "Shall I go and call a nurse from the Hebrew women, one who will care for this child for you?"

Pharaoh's daughter said to her, "Go." And the girl went off and called the child's mother. Pharaoh's daughter said to the mother, "Take this child away, and nurse him for me, and I will pay you for it." Then the woman took the child away, and cared for him.

And when the child grew up, his mother brought him back to Pharaoh's daughter, and Pharaoh's daughter took him to become her son. And she said, "I will call his name 'Moses,' because I took him up out of the water."

EXODUS 1; 2:1–10

THE BURNING BUSH

And it came to pass in those days, when Moses was grown, that he went out among his people, and he watched them at their hard labors. And he saw an Egyptian beating a Hebrew.

Then Moses looked this way and that way. And when he saw that no one was around, he killed the Egyptian, and hid him in the sand.

The next day Moses saw two Hebrews fighting, and he said to one of them, "Why do you hit your brother?"

And the man said, "Who made you a prince and a judge over us? Do you intend to kill me, as you killed that Egyptian?" Then Moses was afraid, and said to himself, "What I did has become known."

Now when Pharaoh heard of this thing, he meant to kill Moses. But Moses fled from Pharaoh, and went to live in the land of Midian.

There in Midian Moses lived with the priest Jethro, who gave him his daughter Zipporah. And she bore him a son, and Moses called his son Gershom.

In the process of time, the king of Egypt died, and the children of Israel groaned because of their slavery.

And then God heard their groaning, and God remembered his covenant with Abraham, with Isaac, and with Jacob.

Moses tended the flock of Jethro, and he led it to the mountain of God, to Horeb. And then the angel of the Lord appeared to Moses in a flame of fire out of the midst of a bush. Moses looked, and, behold, the bush was filled with fire, but the bush was not destroyed by the fire.

And God called to Moses out of the midst of the bush, "Moses, Moses." And Moses said, "Here I am."

And God said, "I am the God of your father, the God of Abraham, the God of Isaac, and the God of Jacob." And Moses hid his face, for he was afraid to look upon God.

EXODUS 2:11–25; 3:1–6

THE LORD'S MESSAGE TO MOSES

Then God said to Moses, "I have surely seen the suffering of my people in the land of Egypt, and have heard their cry, for I know their sorrows.

"And I have come down to deliver them out of the hand of the Egyptians, and to bring them up out of that land, into a land flowing with milk and honey.

"Come now therefore, and I will send you to Pharaoh, so that you may bring forth my people, the children of Israel, out of the land of Egypt."

And Moses answered the Lord and said, "Who am I, that I should go to Pharaoh, and bring forth the children of Israel out of Egypt?" And God said, "Certainly I will be with you."

But Moses said to God, "And when I come to the children of Israel, and say to them, 'The God of your fathers has sent me to you,' they shall say to me, 'What is his name?' What shall I say to them?"

And God said to Moses, "I AM THAT I AM. This you shall say to the children of Israel: 'I AM has sent me to you.'"

But Moses said, "They will not believe me, nor listen to my voice. They will say, 'The Lord has not appeared to you.'"

And God said, "What is that in your hand?" And Moses said, "A rod." Then God said, "Throw it on the ground." And Moses threw the rod on the ground, and it became a serpent. And God said, "Take it by the tail." Moses caught the serpent, and it became a rod in his hand.

God said, "This will be a sign so that the children of Israel may believe that the Lord God of their fathers has appeared to you."

Then Moses said, "O my Lord, I do not speak well, and I am slow of speech." God was angry with Moses, and he said, "Is not Aaron the Levite your brother? I know that he can speak well. You shall put words in his mouth, and he will be your spokesman to the people. And you shall take this rod in your hand to perform the signs for them."

And so Moses took his wife and his sons, and he returned to the land of Egypt. He took the rod of God in his hand.

Aaron met Moses in the wilderness, and Moses told him of the words of the Lord. Moses and Aaron went and gathered together the people of Israel. And Aaron spoke the words the Lord had spoken to Moses, and showed the signs to them. And the people believed, and they bowed their heads and worshipped.

Exodus 3:7–22; 4

PHARAOH AND THE ISRAELITES

Afterward Moses and Aaron went to Pharaoh, and they said, "This the Lord God of Israel says, 'You must let my people go, that they may hold a feast to me in the wilderness.'"

And Pharaoh said, "Who is the Lord that I should obey his voice? I do not know the Lord, and I will not let Israel go."

That same day, Pharaoh commanded the officers of the people, saying, "You shall give the people no more straw to make bricks, but let them gather straw for themselves. Yet they must make as many bricks as they made before." The officers did as Pharaoh commanded.

Then the people said to Moses and Aaron, "The Lord look on you and judge, because you have made us hated in the eyes of Pharaoh."

And Moses returned to the Lord, and said, "Why have you sent me, for since I came to Pharaoh, he has done evil and has not let the people go."

The Lord said, "Say to the children of Israel that I am the Lord, and I will bring you out from under the burdens of the Egyptians."

But the children of Israel would not listen to Moses, for their spirit was crushed by their hard labor.

Then the Lord said to Moses, "I have made you like God to Pharaoh, and Aaron your brother shall be your prophet."

So Moses and Aaron went to Pharaoh. Aaron threw down his rod before Pharaoh and his servants, and it became a serpent.

And so Pharaoh called on the magicians of Egypt, and each one threw down his rod, and all the rods became serpents. And then Aaron's rod swallowed up their rods.

But all this hardened the Pharaoh's heart, and so Pharaoh would not listen to them.

Then God told Moses to say to Pharaoh, "The Lord God of the Hebrews has sent me to you, saying, 'Let my people go, that they may serve me in the wilderness.'"

In the morning, when Pharaoh was standing by the river's edge, Aaron lifted up the rod and struck the waters of the river. All the waters were turned to blood.

And the fish in the river died, and the river stank. The Egyptians could not drink of the water, and there was blood throughout all the land of Egypt.

But the magicians of Egypt did the same with their spells, and Pharaoh's heart was hardened. And still he would not listen to them.

Exodus 5; 7:1–22

53

THE PLAGUES OF EGYPT

Then the Lord spoke to Moses, "Say to Aaron, 'Stretch out your hand with your rod, over the streams, over the rivers, and over the ponds, and cause frogs to come upon the land of Egypt.'"

And Aaron stretched out his hand over the waters of Egypt, and the frogs came up, and covered the land of Egypt.

And then the magicians cast their spells and brought frogs upon the land of Egypt.

Pharaoh said to Moses, "Ask the Lord to take away the frogs, and then I will let your people go."

And the Lord did according to Moses' request, and the frogs died out of the land of Egypt. But when Pharaoh saw that the frogs were gone, he hardened his heart, and would not listen to them.

Then the Lord had Aaron stretch out his rod and strike the dust of the land. It became lice in man and in beast, throughout the land of Egypt. Then the magicians tried to bring forth lice with their spells, but they could not.

And the Lord sent a swarm of flies into all the land of Egypt. But in the land of Goshen, where his people lived, there were no flies.

Pharaoh called for Moses and for Aaron, and said, "Go and sacrifice to your God." And the Lord removed all the swarms of flies. Not one remained.

But Pharaoh hardened his heart at this time also, and he would not let the people go.

Then the Lord sent a plague upon the cattle. All the cattle of Egypt died. But not one of the cattle of the Israelites died. When Pharaoh heard this, it hardened his heart, and he did not let the people go.

Then the Lord told Moses to take ashes of the furnace and sprinkle them up toward heaven. And the ashes became boils, breaking out on man and on beast. And the boils were upon all the Egyptians.

Moses stretched his rod toward heaven, and the Lord sent thunder and hail. Fire ran along the ground upon the land of Egypt. Only in the land of Goshen, where the children of Israel were, there was no hail. Then Pharaoh said to Moses, "Beg the Lord to stop the hail, and I will let you go."

So Moses prayed to the Lord, and the thunder and hail stopped. But when Pharaoh saw the hail had stopped, he hardened his heart and would not let the children of Israel go.

Then the Lord brought locusts to the land. They covered the face of the whole earth, so that the land was darkened. And the locusts ate every green thing throughout Egypt.

And the Lord sent a mighty wind to blow away the locusts. Still Pharaoh would not let the children of Israel go. Then the Lord sent a thick darkness over the land, so the Egyptians could not see one another. But all the Israelites had light where they lived.

Still the Lord hardened Pharaoh's heart, and he would not let the people go. Then Pharoah said to Moses, "Go away, and see my face no more." And Moses said, "You have spoken well. I will see your face no more."

EXODUS 8–10

55

PASSOVER

And the Lord said to Moses, "I will bring one more plague upon Pharaoh and on Egypt. Afterwards, he will let you go."

And Moses said, "This the Lord says, 'About midnight I will go out into the midst of Egypt, and all the firstborn of Egypt will die, from the firstborn of the Pharaoh who sits on the throne, even to the firstborn of the servants, and all the firstborn of the beasts. But among the children of Israel, neither man nor beast will be harmed.'"

And the Lord spoke to Moses and Aaron, saying, "On the tenth day of this month each Israelite family shall take a lamb into their house. On the fourteenth day of the same month, the whole assembly of the congregation of Israel shall kill the lambs in the same evening.

"They shall take the lamb's blood and smear it on the side posts and the upper doorpost of the houses. And they shall eat the flesh quickly that night, for it is the Lord's Passover." And the Lord said, "For I will pass through the land of Egypt this night, and I will kill all the firstborn in the land of Egypt, both man and beast."

And then the children of Israel went away, and they did as the Lord had commanded Moses and Aaron. And so it came to pass, that at midnight the Lord killed all the firstborn in the land of Egypt.

Then Pharaoh and all his servants rose up in the night. And there was a great cry in all of Egypt, for there was not a house without one that was dead. And Pharaoh called for Moses and Aaron by night, and he said, "Rise up, and go away from my people. Go now and serve the Lord. Take your flocks and your herds, and be gone."

And so it came to pass the same day, that the Lord did bring the children of Israel out of the land of Egypt.

EXODUS 11, 12

THE PARTING OF THE SEA

The Lord went before the Israelites by day in a pillar of cloud to lead them. At night, he went in a pillar of fire to give them light. And they camped in the wilderness between Migdol and the sea.

And when Pharaoh was told the Israelites had fled, he said, "Why have we let Israel go from serving us?" Then he took all his chariots and horses, and his army, and he pursued the Israelites. And so the Egyptians overtook the Israelites camped by the sea.

As Pharaoh and the Egyptians drew near, the Israelites were afraid, and they said to Moses, "Why have you brought us out from Egypt to die in the wilderness?"

And Moses said to the people, "Do not be afraid, for the Lord will fight for you. Never again will you see the Egyptians."

And the Lord told Moses to lift up his rod, and stretch out his hand over the sea and divide it, so the children of Israel could cross over on dry ground.

Moses stretched out his hand over the sea, and the Lord made a strong east wind blow all through the night, dividing the waters. Then the children of Israel crossed on the dry ground in the middle of the sea. The waters formed a wall on their right hand, and on their left.

The Egyptians with all Pharaoh's horses, his chariots, and his horsemen followed the Israelites into the sea. Then the Lord told Moses to stretch out his hand over the sea so that the waters would come back upon the Egyptians. Moses stretched forth his hand. The waters returned and covered the army of Pharaoh, and not one of them remained alive.

Thus the Lord saved the children of Israel, and they saw the great work that the Lord had done for them. And Moses and the Israelites gave thanks to the Lord.

EXODUS 13:21; 14

IN THE WILDERNESS

Moses brought Israel from the Red Sea, and the Israelites went out into the wilderness of Shur. They wandered for three days, but they found no water.

Then they came to Marah, but they could not drink the waters, because the waters were bitter. They complained, saying, "What shall we drink?"

Moses cried out to the Lord, and the Lord showed him a tree. When he threw it into the waters, the waters became sweet.

And then they came to Elim, where there were twelve wells of water, and seventy palm trees, and they camped there.

So they continued on their journey and came to the wilderness of Sin. And the children of Israel said to Moses and Aaron, "We would rather have died by the hand of the Lord in Egypt, for you have brought us out to this wilderness to die of hunger."

And then the Lord said to Moses, "Behold, I will rain bread from heaven for you, and each day the people shall go out and gather enough for that day.

"But on the sixth day, they shall gather twice as much as they gather on the other days."

And so it came to pass that in the evening quails came up and covered the camp. In the morning when the dew was gone, there lay a small round thing, as small as frost on the ground.

When the children of Israel saw it, they said, "What is it?"

And Moses said to them, "This is manna, the bread that the Lord has given you to eat. This is what he commands you: Gather enough to eat for one day, and let no one leave any till the morning."

But some did not listen, and left it until morning. And the manna smelled and was full of worms. And Moses was angry with them.

On the sixth day, they gathered twice as much manna, for the seventh day was the rest of the holy Sabbath. But some people went out on the seventh day to gather manna, and they found none.

The Lord said to Moses, "How long will you refuse to keep my commandments? The Lord has given you the Sabbath. This is why on the sixth day, he gives you enough bread for two days. Let no man go out of his place on the seventh day." So the people rested on that day.

And the children of Israel ate manna for forty years, until they came to the borders of the land of Canaan.

FROM EXODUS 15:22–27; 16:1–35

THE TEN COMMANDMENTS

In the third month, the children of Israel came into the wilderness of Sinai, and camped at the foot of the mountain.

Moses went up the mountain, and God said, "Tell the children of Israel, if you will obey my voice, you shall be a treasure to me above all people, and a holy nation."

And Moses told the people God's words. And the people answered together, "All that the Lord has spoken, we will do."

And the Lord said to Moses, "I will come to you in a thick cloud, so that the people will hear when I speak with you, and will believe you forever."

And Moses brought the people to the mountain. And Mount Sinai was covered in smoke, because the Lord had come down upon it in fire. When the horn sounded long and became louder, Moses spoke. And God's voice answered him in thunder. God spoke all these words:

I am the Lord thy God, who has brought thee out of the land of Egypt, out of the house of bondage.

Thou shalt have no other gods before me.

Thou shalt not make unto thee any graven image, or any likeness of anything that is in heaven above, or that is in the earth beneath. Thou shalt not bow down thyself to them, nor serve them: for I the Lord thy God am a jealous God.

Thou shalt not take the name of the Lord thy God in vain.

Remember the Sabbath day, to keep it holy.

Honor thy father and thy mother.

Thou shalt not kill.

Thou shalt not commit adultery.

Thou shalt not steal.

Thou shalt not bear false witness against thy neighbor.

Thou shalt not covet thy neighbor's house, thou shalt not covet thy neighbor's wife, nor his servants, nor his animals, nor anything that is thy neighbor's.

EXODUS 19; 20:1–17

ON THE MOUNTAINTOP

All the people heard the thunder, and they saw the lightning and the smoking mountain, and stood far off.

They said to Moses, "You speak with us and we will hear, but do not let God speak with us, or we may die."

But Moses said, "Do not be afraid. God has come to test you, so you will not sin." So he went near the thick darkness where God was.

The Lord said to Moses, "Say this to the children of Israel: 'You have seen for yourselves that I have talked with you from heaven.'"

And then God gave laws for the children of Israel to obey.

Moses told them the Lord's words. And with one voice, all the people answered, "All the words that the Lord has said, we will do."

Then the Lord said to Moses, "Come up the mountain, and I will give you stone tablets of the laws that I have written, so that you may teach them."

Moses went to the mountain. And the sight of the glory of the Lord was like a blazing fire in the eyes of the children of Israel.

Moses went into the midst of a cloud and went up the mountain. And he was up on the mountain for forty days and forty nights.

FROM EXODUS 20:18–22; 24:3, 12–18

THE TABERNACLE

The Lord spoke to Moses, saying, "Speak to the people of Israel, and let them make me a sanctuary, so that I may dwell among them. They shall build the Tabernacle, according to the pattern I show you.

"You shall make an ark of acacia wood, and overlay it with pure gold, both inside and out. And you shall make upon it a crown of gold.

"And you shall make the altar for burnt offerings of acacia wood, with horns on each corner. The altar shall be overlaid with brass.

"Make a lampstand with six branches, and put on it seven lamps, that they may give light. And you shall command the children of Israel to bring you pure oil to keep the lamp burning always.

"And tell the children of Israel that they shall keep the Sabbath throughout the generations, for it is a sign between me and them forever.

"And I will dwell among the children of Israel, and I will be their God."

FROM EXODUS 25–31

THE GOLDEN CALF

And when the people saw that Moses delayed so long to come down from the mountain, they got together and went to Aaron. They said, "Make us gods to lead us, for we do not know what has become of Moses."

And so Aaron said, "Take off your golden earrings, and bring them to me." So the people took off their earrings, and Aaron melted them down, and had a calf made from the gold. When Aaron saw the calf, he built an altar before it, and he said, "Tomorrow we shall make a feast to the Lord." The people rose early in the morning and made burnt offerings and peace offerings. Then they sat down to eat and drink, and they rose up to sing and dance.

And so the Lord said to Moses, "Go down from the mountain, because your people, that you brought out of Egypt, have become sinful. They have turned aside quickly from my commandments, and they are worshipping a golden calf."

And then the Lord said to Moses, "I have seen this people, and they are a stiff-necked people. Now therefore leave me alone, for my anger burns hot against them. I shall destroy them, and make a great nation of you."

But Moses pleaded with the Lord, saying, "Why are you angry against your people, that you brought out of Egypt? If you should destroy them now, the Egyptians will mock you. They will say you brought the people out only to kill them in the mountains, and remove them from the face of the earth.

"Remember Abraham, Isaac, and Jacob, your servants, whose children you swore you would multiply as the stars of heaven, and give the land to their descendants forever."

And the Lord repented of the evil which he had thought to do to his people.

Then Moses went down from the mountain. The two tablets with the writing of God engraved on both sides were in his hands.

But as soon as he came near the camp, he saw the calf and the dancing. And his anger became great. He threw the tablets from his hands and broke them at the foot of the mountain.

Then Moses took the calf which they had made, and he burned it and ground it to powder. He scattered it upon the water and made the children of Israel drink it.

And Moses said to Aaron, "What did this people do, that you have brought so great a sin upon them?"

And Aaron said, "Do not be angry, for you know that the people are always ready to do wrong."

Then Moses stood at the gate of the camp, and said, "Let whoever is on the Lord's side come to me." And all the sons of Levi gathered around him. And Moses said to them, "Each one take his sword and kill everyone who worshipped the golden calf, even if he is a brother or friend or neighbor."

They did as Moses said, and three thousand people died that day.

On the next day, Moses said to the people, "You have sinned a great sin. Now I will go up to the Lord, and perhaps he shall forgive you for your sin."

So Moses returned to the Lord, and asked him to forgive the great sin of the children of Israel.

The Lord said to Moses, "You and the people that you brought out of Egypt go forth to the land I swore to give to Abraham, to Isaac, and to Jacob. I will send an angel before you to a land flowing with milk and honey."

Then the Lord said to Moses, "Carve two tablets of stone, and I will write on them the words that were on the first tablets, which you broke."

Then Moses carved two tablets of stone, and went up on Mount Sinai. And the Lord descended and stood with him there. And Moses bowed his head and worshipped.

And Moses was with the Lord for forty days and forty nights. And he wrote the commandments on the tablets.

Then Moses came down from the mountain, and the skin on his face shone with the glory of God.

EXODUS 32–34

LAWS AND OBSERVANCES

The Lord said to Moses, "Speak to the children of Israel, and tell them my laws." These are some of the laws the Lord told to Moses.

"These are the beasts that you shall eat of all the beasts on the earth. Whatever has a cloven, or divided, hoof, and chews a cud, you shall eat. But you shall not eat the camel, the badger, the hare, or the swine, for their flesh is unclean to you.

"You shall eat whatever has fins and scales in the waters, in the seas, and in the rivers. But all in the seas and the rivers that do not have fins and scales shall be an abomination to you."

"You shall not live as they do in the land of Egypt, which you have left, nor live as they do in the land of Canaan, where I shall bring you. You shall follow my laws and shall keep my commandments, for I am the Lord your God."

"When you harvest your land, you shall not wholly harvest the corners of the field, nor gather the grain that falls to the ground. And you shall not gather every grape of your vineyard, but shall leave some for the poor and the stranger: I am the Lord your God."

"You shall not curse the deaf, nor put a stumbling block before the blind, but you shall fear your God.

"You shall be just to all people; and neither be partial to the poor nor favor the rich. You shall not seek revenge, nor bear any grudge against the children of your people, but you shall love your neighbor as yourself."

"When a stranger lives among you in your land, do not do him wrong. He shall be like one born among you, and you shall love him as yourself. For you yourselves were strangers once, in the land of Egypt. I am the Lord your God."

LEVITICUS 11:1–12; 18:3–5; 19:9–18,33–34

70

THE JOURNEY TO CANAAN

The people of Israel departed from Mount Sinai, and the ark of the Lord was carried before them. The cloud of the Lord was above them when they set out from their camp. When the people complained, this displeased the Lord. He grew angry.

The children of Israel wept, and they said, "Who will give us food to eat? We remember the fish that we ate in Egypt, and the cucumbers, and the melons, and the leeks, and the onions, and the garlic. But now our soul is dried away, and there is nothing to eat but this manna."

Moses heard the people weep, and he also was displeased. And he said to the Lord, "Why have you given to me this burden of all the people? Where shall I find food to give to them? For they cry out to me, saying, 'Give us meat, that we may eat.' I am not able to bear this burden of the people alone; it is too heavy for me."

So the Lord told Moses to gather seventy elders of Israel, who would bear the burden of the people with him, so that Moses would not have to bear it alone.

Then the Lord told Moses to send a man from each tribe to spy out the land of Canaan.

71

And so Moses sent them out, saying, "See what the land is like, and see if there are many people, and if they are strong or weak."

So the men went, and they came to the valley of Eshcol. And there they cut down one cluster of grapes so heavy that they had to carry it on a pole between two men. And they also brought pomegranates and figs.

They returned to the camp after forty days, and they said, "The land surely flows with milk and honey. But the people there are fierce and are as tall as giants. Their cities are very great, and they are protected by high walls."

And then the children of Israel wept, and they said, "It would have been better to have died in Egypt or in the wilderness, than to be brought here to fall by the sword. Let us stone Moses and Aaron, and choose a new leader to take us back to Egypt."

Then the Lord appeared to them, and said, "All of you who are twenty years and older, except for Caleb and Joshua who believed in me, shall not come into the land. You will wander for forty years and will die in the wilderness. But I will bring your children into the land."

But after hearing these words from God, the people said, "We are here, so we will go up to the land that the Lord has promised us."

Moses said, "Do not go now, or you will be struck down by your enemies, for the Lord is not with you." But they went out of the camp, and went up to the hill country. And their enemies in the hill country came, and they defeated the people of Israel and drove them away.

FROM NUMBERS 11, 13, 14

72

THE DEATH OF MOSES

After the forty years had passed,
the Israelites arrived at the river Jordan.
By that time Moses was a very old man, and the Lord said to him,
"The days approach when you must go and sleep with your fathers."

Moses said to the people, "Hear, O Israel: The Lord our God, the
Lord is one. You shall love the Lord your God with all your heart, and
all your soul, and all your might. These words that I command you this
day shall be upon your heart. You shall teach them to your children,
and shall speak of them when you sit in your house, when you walk by
the way, when you lie down, and when you rise up."

Then Moses went up Mount Nebo, and from the mountaintop the
Lord showed him all the land of Canaan, saying, "This is the land that
I swore to give to Abraham, to Isaac, and to Jacob. I have brought you
to see this land with your own eyes, but you shall not go into it."

So Moses, the servant of the Lord, died in the land of Moab. And
they buried him in the valley, and to this day, no one knows the place
of his grave. And the children of Israel wept for Moses for thirty days.

FROM DEUTERONOMY 6, 31, 34

THE WALLS OF JERICHO

*T*hen the Lord spoke to Joshua, saying, "Moses my servant is dead, now therefore you must rise and cross the river Jordan to the land that I give to the children of Israel. Be strong and brave, and be careful to obey all the law that my servant Moses has given you."

And then Joshua commanded the people, "Prepare food, for in three days you shall cross the Jordan to take the land that the Lord has given to you."

Then Joshua sent two men to spy secretly in the city of Jericho. There they stayed in the house of a woman named Rahab. Then the king of Jericho sent soldiers to Rahab.

The men said, "Give us the men who entered your house, for they have come to spy on our land."

But Rahab told the soldiers that the men had already gone off, and she said, "Go after them quickly." Then Rahab hid the spies on the roof of her house, and she said to them, "I know that the Lord has given you this land. We fear you, for we have heard of how the Lord dried the waters of the Red Sea for you and destroyed the Egyptians. Since I have shown you kindness, I beg that you will save my father, and my mother, and brothers, and my sisters, and all that they have."

And so the men promised this, and Rahab let them down by a rope through the window, for her house was on the town wall. And she said to them, "Now get away to the mountain, before the soldiers can find you."

When the two men returned, they said to Joshua, "Truly the Lord has delivered the land into our hands, for all the people of this country fear us."

On the next day, as the priests who carried the ark stepped into the Jordan, the waters all stopped and rose up in one place upstream. All the Israelites passed over on dry ground. Then the Lord said to Joshua, "I shall give into your hand Jericho, and its king, and all of its mighty men."

And then it came to pass, that for six days, seven priests blowing rams' horns went with the ark of the Lord around the city, with the armed men in front of them. And Joshua commanded the people not to shout or make any sound.

On the seventh day, when the priests blew the trumpets, Joshua said to the people, "Now shout; for the Lord has given you the city."

And as soon as the people heard the sound of the horns, they gave a great shout. And just then the walls of Jericho fell down flat.

Then the people burned the city, and destroyed all that was in it, except for Rahab and her family. And the gold and the silver, they put into the treasury of the house of the Lord.

JOSHUA 1–6

GIDEON'S TRUMPET

The Israelites lived in Canaan for many years, but they disobeyed the Lord. And he made the Midianites rule over them for seven years.

A young Israelite named Gideon was threshing wheat in a wine press, to hide it from the Midianites. An angel of the Lord came and said, "The Lord is with you. You will save Israel from the Midianites."

Gideon said, "How will I save Israel? My family is poor, and I am the youngest of them. If I am favored by the Lord, show me a sign."

And Gideon prepared food and put it on a rock. The angel of the Lord stretched out his rod. Fire burst from the rock and burned up the food. Then the angel of the Lord disappeared. That night the Lord said to Gideon, "Destroy your father's altar of Baal and build an altar to the Lord in its place." And Gideon did as the Lord commanded.

When the men of the city learned what he had done, they said to his father, "Bring out your son, that we may kill him." But his father said, "If Baal is a god, let him defend himself."

Then all the Midianites and Amalekites joined together to destroy the Israelites. But the spirit of the Lord came over Gideon, and he blew his trumpet made of a ram's horn, to call Israel to battle.

And the Lord said to Gideon, "There are too many people with you, and they will say that they have won the battle on their own without the Lord's help. Let anyone who is afraid return home." Then twenty-two thousand left, and only ten thousand remained.

But the Lord said, "There are still too many." So Gideon brought the people to the water to drink. The Lord chose those who put their hand to the water to drink, instead of bowing down. And of these there were three hundred men.

And Gideon divided the three hundred men into three companies, and each man had a trumpet, an empty pitcher, and a torch. They came to the Midianite camp in the middle of the night, and they blew the trumpets, and broke the pitchers, and held high the torches. The Midianites cried out in confusion and fear, and they ran away.

JUDGES 6–7

SAMSON

Once again the children of Israel disobeyed the Lord, and he made the Philistines rule over them for forty years. And the angel of the Lord appeared to the wife of Manoah, who had no children, and said to her, "You shall have a son. No razor may touch his hair, for he will be a Nazirite from birth, and will free Israel from the Philistines."

When the child was born, she called him Samson. He grew strong and mighty, and the Lord blessed him.

Once when Samson went to the vineyards of Timnah, a young lion attacked him. The spirit of the Lord came over him, and he tore the lion apart with his bare hands. After a time he returned to see the dead body of the lion, and there was a swarm of bees and honey in it. Samson took the honey in his hands and ate it, and gave some to his mother and father to eat.

Samson married a Philistine woman, but he grew angry with her and went back to live in his father's house. When Samson returned to visit his wife, her father said, "I thought that you hated her, so I gave her to your friend." Then Samson caught three hundred foxes, and tied them tail to tail, and put a torch between each set of tails. He set the torches afire and sent the foxes into the fields to burn down the crops.

Then the Philistines went into Judah to capture Samson for what he had done. And three thousand men of Judah went to Samson and said, "We have come to bind you and give you to the Philistines." And they bound him with ropes. But when the Philistines saw Samson and began shouting against him, the spirit of the Lord came over Samson. The ropes became like burnt threads, and he tore them off easily.

Then he found the fresh jawbone of an ass, and with it he killed a thousand Philistines. And Samson led the people of Israel for twenty years.

JUDGES 13–15

SAMSON AND DELILAH

Samson loved a woman from the valley of Sorek, whose name was Delilah. The lords of the Philistines came to her and said, "Find out where his great strength comes from and how we can capture him, and we will each give you eleven hundred pieces of silver."

So Delilah said to Samson, "Tell me where your great strength comes from, and how you could be captured." And he said, "If they tie me with seven new bowstrings, I shall become weak and the same as other men." Delilah bound Samson with seven new bowstrings. And there were men hiding in wait in her room. Then she cried out, "The Philistines are upon you." But Samson broke the bowstrings as easily as a thread of flax is broken when it touches fire.

Delilah said, "You have mocked me and told me lies. Now tell me how you might be captured." And he said, "If they tie me up with new ropes that have never been used, I shall become weak and the same as other men."

80

So Delilah took new ropes and tied him, and she cried out, "The Philistines are upon you." The men were hiding in the room, but Samson broke the ropes from off his arms like threads. And Delilah said, "How can you say you love me when you mock me and will not tell me where your strength comes from?" And every day she urged him to tell her.

Then Samson grew annoyed and told her the truth and said, "No razor has ever touched my hair, for I have been a Nazirite since my birth. If I am shaved, I shall become weak, and be like any other man."

When Delilah saw that Samson had told her the truth, she sent for the Philistines, and they came with the money for her. Then she made Samson fall asleep with his head on her lap. Then she called for a man to shave off his hair, and Samson's strength left him. And so Delilah cried out, "The Philistines are upon you."

And Samson awoke from his sleep, and said, "I will go out and shake myself free as I did the other times." But now Samson's strength had gone from him, and he did not know that the Lord was no longer with him.

The Philistines seized Samson, and they put out his eyes. Then they brought him down to Gaza and bound him with chains of brass. And they made him grind grain in the prison house.

But the hair of his head began to grow again after he had been shaved.

The lords of the Philistines gathered the people together to offer a great sacrifice to their god, and to rejoice, for they said, "Our god has delivered Samson our enemy into our hand."

And when the people saw Samson and saw that he was blind, they praised their god, and they said, "Our god has given to us our enemy, and the destroyer of our country who has killed so many of us."

And it came to pass, when their hearts were merry, that they called for Samson to be brought out of the prison house so they could mock him and make fun of him. Then Samson was brought out, and they set him between the pillars of the temple, and they mocked him.

But Samson said to the young boy that led him by the hand, "Take me so that I may feel the pillars that the temple rests on, so that I may lean upon them."

Now the temple was full of men and women, and all the lords of the Philistines were there. And there were more than three thousand men and women upon the roof, who had come to mock Samson and to make fun of him.

And Samson called to the Lord, "O Lord God, remember me, I pray you, and give me strength only this once, O God, that I may have revenge on the Philistines for taking my two eyes." And Samson took hold of the two middle pillars upon which the temple rested. He leaned upon the pillars, one with his right hand, and the other with his left. Then he said, "Let me die with the Philistines." And Samson bent with all his might, and the temple fell upon the lords and all the people that were there.

So the dead that Samson killed at his death were more than all those he had killed in his life.

JUDGES 16: 4–30

RUTH AND NAOMI

In the days when the judges ruled over Israel, there was a famine in the land. Elimelech, a man of Judah, took his wife Naomi and his two sons to live in the country of Moab. And there he finally died.

And his two sons took wives from among the women of Moab. One was named Orpah, the other Ruth. And they lived there about ten years. Then it happened that both of the sons also died, and Naomi was left alone without her sons or her husband.

So Naomi went with her two daughters-in-law so that she might return to Judah, for she had heard that the Lord had visited the land of his people and given them bread.

And Naomi said to her two daughters-in-law, "Go, return each of you to your mother's house. May the Lord be kind to you, as you were kind to your dead, and to me. And may the Lord grant that you find rest in the house of a new husband." Then Naomi kissed them, and they lifted up their voices and wept.

They said to her, "Surely we will return with you to your people." But Naomi said, "Why will you go with me? Can I have yet more sons to be your husbands? Turn back, go your way, for I am too old to have a husband. Even if I should have a husband, and should bear him sons, would you wait until they were grown? No, you must go. It gives me great sorrow for your sake that the Lord has turned against me."

And they lifted up their voices, and wept again. Orpah kissed her mother-in-law, but Ruth clung to her. Then Naomi said to Ruth, "Look, your sister-in-law has gone back to her people and to her gods. Return now after her."

And Ruth said, "Do not ask me to leave you. For wherever you go, I will go. Wherever you stay, I will stay. Your people will be my people, and your God will be my God." So they continued on, and came to Bethlehem at the beginning of the barley harvest.

Now, Boaz was a wealthy relative of Naomi's husband. And Ruth said to Naomi, "I shall go to the field and gather grain." And when she went to the fields to gather stalks of grain left by the workers, she came to a field that belonged to Boaz.

Boaz came to his field from Bethlehem, and asked his servant who was in charge of the workers, "Who is this woman?" And the servant said, "It is the Moabite woman that came back with Naomi. She asked to gather grain after the reapers, and she has worked from morning until now without a rest."

Then Boaz said to Ruth, "Do not go to gather grain in another field, but stay here with the women. And when you are thirsty, drink the water the young men have drawn." Ruth bowed to the ground and said, "Why are you so kind to me, a stranger?"

And Boaz answered, "I have heard all that you have done for your mother-in-law, and how you left your father and mother and your country to come to our land."

Then he said to the young men, "Let her gather grain among the sheaves, and let some fall on purpose, and leave it for her."

So Ruth took the grain she had gathered in the field of Boaz to Naomi. And she continued to gather in his fields until the end of the harvest, and she lived with her mother-in-law. Then Naomi said to Ruth, "Boaz is our relative, and he is threshing the grain. Go there, but do not let him see you until he has finished eating and drinking."

When Boaz had eaten and drunk, he went to lie down at the end of the pile of grain. It came to pass at midnight, that he was startled, and he turned over in his sleep. He saw a woman lying at his feet. And he said to her, "Who are you?" And she answered, "I am Ruth."

Then Boaz said, "May the Lord bless you for the kindness you have shown." And Ruth lay at his feet until the morning.

So Boaz took Ruth for his wife. And she had a son. The women said to Naomi, "Blessed be the Lord, who has not left you without a family. For your daughter-in-law, who loves you, and who is better to you than seven sons, has borne a son. And he shall care for you in your old age."

And so Naomi took the child in her arms and she cared for him. His name was Obed, and he became the father of Jesse. And Jesse was the father of David, who became king of Israel.

RUTH 1–4

SAMUEL IS CALLED

Now Hannah was the wife of a Levite named Elkanah, and Hannah had no children. And she wept, and she did not eat.

Then Hannah went to the temple at Shiloh, where the ark of the Lord was kept, and she made a promise, saying, "O Lord of hosts, if you will remember me and give me a man-child, I will give him to the Lord all the days of his life." And so then in time Hannah had a son, and she called him Samuel.

When the child was still very young, Hannah said to Elkanah, "I prayed for this child, and now the Lord has given him to me. Therefore I have lent him to the Lord for as long as he shall live." And they brought the child to the priest Eli at the temple in Shiloh, and Samuel served the Lord.

Each year Samuel's mother made him a little coat, and she brought it to him when she came to the temple with her husband to offer the yearly sacrifice.

And it came to pass that one night, when Samuel had lain down to sleep, the Lord called him. Samuel ran to Eli, and said, "Here I am, for you called me." And Eli said, "I did not call you; lie down again." And so Samuel went and lay down.

And the Lord called to him yet again, "Samuel." And Samuel got up and went to Eli, and said, "Here I am, for you did call me."

But Eli answered, "I did not call you, my son; lie down yet again."

And the Lord called Samuel a third time. And again he arose and went to Eli, and said, "Here I am, for you did call me."

Then Eli understood that the Lord had called the child, and he said to Samuel, "If he calls you again, say, 'Speak Lord, for your servant is listening.'"

Then the Lord came and called as before, "Samuel, Samuel." And Samuel answered, "Speak, for your servant is listening."

And then the Lord told Samuel that he would punish Eli and his descendants because Eli had not stopped his sons from doing evil.

In the morning, Eli said, "What did the Lord say to you? Do not hide it from me." So Samuel told him.

Then Eli said, "It is the Lord, let him do what seems good."

And Samuel grew, and the Lord was with him, and let none of his words fall to the ground. And all Israel, from Dan to Beersheba, knew that Samuel was a prophet of the Lord.

1 SAMUEL 1–3

A KING FOR ISRAEL

And it came to pass when Samuel was old, that the people of Israel came to him, and said, "Find us a king to judge us like all the other nations." But this displeased Samuel, and so he prayed to the Lord. And the Lord said to Samuel, "Listen to the voice of the people, for they have rejected me. But tell them the ways in which a king would rule over them."

So Samuel said to the people, "A king will take your sons as horsemen for his chariots. He will make them plow his ground and reap his harvest, and make his weapons. And he will take your daughters for cooks and bakers. And he will take a tenth of all you have, and you shall become his servants. And you shall cry out on that day, but the Lord will not hear you."

Nevertheless the people said, "We will have a king over us like all the other nations, to judge us, and to lead us, and to fight our battles."

And so the Lord said to Samuel, "Listen to their voice, and find them a king."

1 SAMUEL 8

SAUL AND SAMUEL

Now there was a man of Benjamin, whose name was Kish, who had a son named Saul. There was not a man among the people of Israel more handsome than Saul, and he stood taller than all others. And the Lord told Samuel to choose Saul to be the first king of Israel.

So Saul took over the kingdom of Israel, and he fought against all his enemies on every side; against Moab, and against Ammon, and against Edom, and against the Philistines. And wherever Saul turned, he delivered Israel out of the hands of its enemies.

Samuel said to Saul, "The Lord remembers what the Amalekites did to Israel when they were coming out of Egypt. Now he wants you to go and completely destroy all that the Amalekites have. And do not spare a single man, woman, or child, or any of the animals."

And so then Saul called his men together, and they completely destroyed the Amalekites with the sword. But Saul and the people spared the king of the Amalekites and the best of all the animals.

The Lord told Samuel, "I am sorry that I made Saul the king, for he has turned his back on me and has not done my commandments."

Then Samuel got up early the next morning to meet Saul. He said to Samuel, "I have done what was commanded by the Lord." But Samuel said, "Then why do I hear the sounds of sheep and of oxen?"

Saul said, "They have brought them from the Amalekites, for the people spared the best of the sheep and oxen to sacrifice to the Lord. The rest we have completely destroyed."

And then Samuel said, "Did the Lord not send you to destroy the Amalekites? Why did you not listen to him, and do evil in his sight? It is better to obey the voice of the Lord than to make sacrifices to him."

Saul said, "I have sinned because I feared the people and listened to them. Now, I pray you, pardon my sin, so that I may worship the Lord." But Samuel said, "You have rejected the Lord, and the Lord has rejected you from being king of Israel."

Then as Samuel turned to leave, Saul took hold of his robe, and it tore. Samuel said to Saul, "The Lord has torn the kingdom of Israel from you on this day." So Samuel went to Ramah, and Saul went to his house. And the Lord repented that he had made Saul the king of Israel.

1 SAMUEL 9:1–2; 15

THE SHEPHERD BOY

The Lord said to Samuel, "How long will you mourn for Saul? Go to Bethlehem, for I will provide a king from among Jesse's sons."

And so Samuel went to Bethlehem and he gathered the people to sacrifice to the Lord, and Jesse came with his sons. When Samuel saw Eliab, Jesse's first son, he said, "Surely the Lord will choose him."

But the Lord said, "Do not judge by his looks or by his height, for the Lord sees not as man sees. Man looks at the outward appearance, but the Lord looks at the heart."

And Jesse made seven of his sons pass before Samuel, and they were all tall and strong. But Samuel said to Jesse, "The Lord has not chosen these. Are all your sons here?"

And Jesse said, "The youngest stayed behind to tend the sheep."

Samuel said, "Send and fetch him." And Jesse sent, and brought David in. Now, David was handsome and had a fine appearance. And the Lord said, "Arise and anoint him, for this is the one."

Then Samuel took the horn of oil and anointed him, and the spirit of the Lord came upon David from that day forward.

Now the spirit of the Lord had left Saul, and an evil spirit from the Lord frightened him. And Saul's servants said to him, "Let us find you a skillful player on the harp, and when the evil spirit is on you, he shall play and you shall feel well."

And then Saul said, "Find a man that can play well, and bring him to me."

Then a young man said, "I have seen a son of Jesse who is skillful in playing, and who is a brave and handsome man." So Saul sent a message to Jesse, saying, "Send me your son David, who is with the sheep."

Then David came to Saul, and stood before him. And Saul loved him greatly, and made him his armor-bearer.

So it came to pass, when the evil spirit was on Saul, that David played the harp for him. And Saul felt well and the evil spirit left him.

1 SAMUEL 16

93

DAVID AND GOLIATH

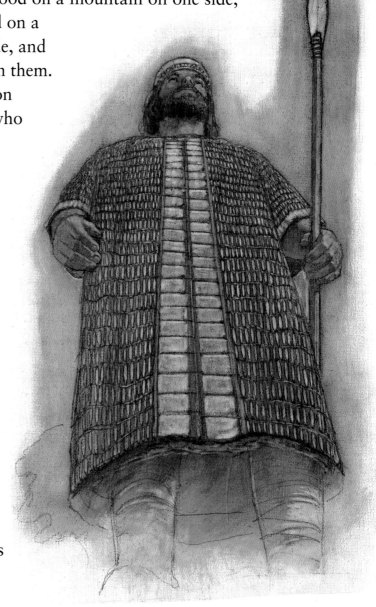

The Philistines gathered together all their armies in battle, and were camped in Judah. Saul and all the men of Israel gathered together, and pitched their camp by the valley of Elah.

And the Philistines stood on a mountain on one side, and all the Israelites stood on a mountain on the other side, and there was a valley between them.

Then a huge champion named Goliath of Gath, who stood nearly ten feet tall, came out from the camp of the Philistines.

He had a helmet of brass upon his head, and he was armed with a coat of bronze. His spear was a huge beam, and its top was made of iron.

Goliath stood and cried out to the armies of Israel, "Why are all of you coming out to battle? Choose a man, and let him come down to me. If he is able to fight and kill me, then we Philistines will be your servants; but if I kill him, then you will be our servants."

And then the Philistine said, "I defy the armies of Israel today. Send a man out to me, so that we may fight each other." When Saul and the Israelites heard the words of the Philistine, they became very upset, and they were greatly afraid.

Now David had returned from Saul to feed his father's sheep at Bethlehem. And Jesse said to David his son, "Take this food to your brothers at the camp with Saul, and see if they are well."

David rose early in the morning and went, as his father had said. And David came to Saul's army and talked with his brothers. Goliath came up, and he spoke the same words. And David heard them.

And when all the men of Israel saw Goliath, they fled from him, and were greatly afraid. They said, "Have you seen this man who comes up to us? Surely he comes to defy Israel. And it shall be that the king will reward the man who kills him with great riches, and will give that man his daughter."

And then David said to the men that stood by him, "Who is this Philistine that he should defy the armies of God?" Then Eliab, David's eldest brother, heard what David said to the men. And Eliab was angry with David, and said, "Why did you come here? With whom have you left the sheep? You have come only to see the battle."

And David said, "What have I done now? May I not even speak?" And David turned away from his brother toward another and spoke in the same way.

David's words were repeated to Saul, and he sent for David. And David said to Saul, "Let no man's heart fail because of Goliath. I will go and fight with this Philistine."

But Saul said, "You cannot fight this Philistine, for you are but a boy and he is a man of war."

David said, "When I guarded my father's sheep, there came a lion and a bear, who took a lamb from the flock. And I went out after him, and hit him, and took the lamb out of his mouth. And when he rose against me, I caught him by his beard, and hit him, and killed him. I killed both the lion and the bear. This Philistine will be as one of them, because he has defied the armies of God."

David then said, "The Lord that saved me from the paw of the lion, and from the paw of the bear, he will also save me from the hand of this Philistine."

And Saul said, "Go, and the Lord be with you." Then he gave David his own armor, and he put a helmet of brass on David's head, and he armed him with a coat of bronze.

But David took off the armor, because he was not used to it. He took his staff in his hand. Then he chose five smooth stones out of the brook, and he put them in his shepherd's bag. His slingshot was in his hand, and he went nearer to the Philistine.

Then the Philistine came on and he came near David, with his shield-bearer in front of him. And when the Philistine saw David, he looked at him with scorn, for he was but a youth. The Philistine said to David, "Am I a dog, that you come to me with sticks?" Then he cursed David, and said, "Come to me, and I will give your flesh to the birds of the air, and to the beasts of the field."

And David said, "You come to me with a sword and a spear, and with a shield, but I come to you in the name of the Lord God of Israel, whom you have defied. Today the Lord will deliver you into my hands, and I will strike you, and take your head from you. I will give your dead body to the birds of the air and to the wild beasts of the earth, so the earth may know that there is a God of Israel. And all who are here will know that the Lord does not save with sword and spear, for the battle is the Lord's and he will give you into our hands."

And when the Philistine drew near to meet David, David ran out quickly to meet him. And David put his hand in his bag, and took out a stone, and threw it with his slingshot. The stone hit the Philistine so that it sunk into his forehead. And he fell on his face to the earth.

So David triumphed over the Philistine with a slingshot and a stone. When the Philistines saw that their champion was dead, they fled. And the men of Israel arose, and shouted, and chased after them as far as Gath and the gates of Ekron.

1 SAMUEL 17:1–52

SAUL'S JEALOUSY

Saul took David that day, and would not let him return again to his father's house. David went wherever Saul sent him, and acted wisely. So Saul set him over the men of war.

When they returned from fighting the Philistines, the women of Israel came singing and dancing joyously to meet Saul. And they sang: "Saul has killed his thousands, and David his ten thousands." Saul was angered by these words, and he eyed David jealously from that day on.

The next day, the evil spirit from God came upon Saul, and David played the harp for him, as at other times.

There was a spear in Saul's hand. Saul threw the spear, thinking he would pin David to the wall. But twice David escaped from the spear.

Then Saul was afraid of David, because the Lord was with him. So he made David captain over a thousand men, and sent him away. And David won all his battles, because the Lord was with him. And all of Israel and Judah loved David.

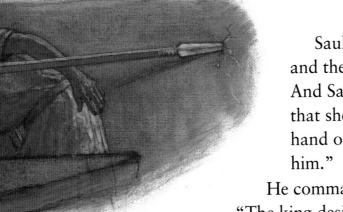

Saul's daughter Michal loved David, and they told Saul, and this pleased him. And Saul said, "I will give her to him, that she may be a trap for him, that the hand of the Philistines will be against him."

He commanded his servants to tell David, "The king desires you to be his son-in-law. As payment for your bride, he wants you to kill one hundred Philistines." Saul thought David would die by the hand of the Philistines.

But David and his men killed two hundred Philistines, and Saul gave him Michal for his wife. And Saul saw that the Lord was with David, and that Michal loved him.

Now Saul spoke to his son Jonathan and to all his servants, saying that they should kill David. But Jonathan liked David very much and he warned him.

Jonathan told David, saying, "My father wants to kill you, so hide yourself in a secret place. I will talk to my father about you. And what I see, I will tell you."

Then Jonathan said to Saul, "Do not sin against your servant David, for he has not sinned against you. Would you kill an innocent man without reason?" And Saul listened to Jonathan, and swore David would not be killed. And then Jonathan told David, and brought him to Saul.

But the evil spirit again came upon Saul as he sat in his house with his spear in his hand. David was playing his harp.

Again Saul tried to pin David to the wall with his spear, but David slipped away, and the spear went into the wall. And David escaped into the night.

So David ran away, and he escaped from Saul. And David came to Samuel in Ramah and told him what Saul had done.

1 SAMUEL 18; 19:1–18

99

DAVID AND JONATHAN

David came back from Ramah secretly to meet Jonathan, and said to him, "What have I done that your father should want to kill me?" And Jonathan said, "You shall not die. My father does nothing without telling me, so why should he hide this from me?"

But David answered, "Your father knows well that we are dearest friends, so he has not told you. But as the Lord lives, there is but one step between me and death." Then Jonathan said, "Whatever you wish, I shall do for you."

And David said, "Tomorrow is the new moon, when I should eat with the king. If he asks for me, tell him I have gone to Bethlehem. If he says it is well, I shall be at peace. But if he is angry, you will know that he means to kill me." And Jonathan agreed to do as David asked. And they swore before God to be friends and to be kind to each other forever, for Jonathan loved David as he loved his own soul.

Then Jonathan said, "On the third day from now, come near the stone Ezel. And I will shoot three arrows as though I were shooting at a mark. I will send a lad to find the arrows. If I say that the arrows are on this side of you, take them and come, for there will be no harm to you. But if I say the arrows are beyond you, go your way, for the Lord will have warned you." So David hid himself in the field.

When the new moon came, Jonathan went to eat with his father. But David's place was empty. Saul said nothing, but on the second day, he said to Jonathan, "Why does the son of Jesse not come to the meal?" And Jonathan answered, "He has gone to Bethlehem to offer a sacrifice with his family."

Then Saul grew angry, and said to him, "You fool. You have chosen David over your own family. For as long as the son of Jesse lives, you shall not have this kingdom. Go now and bring him to me, for he shall surely die."

But Jonathan said, "Why should he be put to death? What has he done?" Then Saul threw his spear at Jonathan. And Jonathan left the table in a rage.

In the morning, Jonathan took a boy with him and went to the field where David was hiding. Jonathan said to the boy, "Run, find the arrows that I shoot." As the boy ran, Jonathan shot an arrow. Then he cried, "The arrow is beyond you. Hurry, go quickly, do not stay." Then the boy brought the arrow to his master, and Jonathan sent him back to the city.

David came out of his hiding place and bowed down three times. Then they kissed one another and wept. And Jonathan said to David, "Go in peace, for we have both sworn in the name of the Lord that the Lord will be between me and you, and between my children and yours forever." And so then David went into hiding, and Jonathan returned to the city.

David's brothers and many other men joined him, and David was their leader. They won many battles, and David's fame continued to grow.

FROM 1 SAMUEL 20; 21:1; 22:1–2

THE WITCH OF ENDOR

Saul gathered together all his men of war to find David and his followers. David knew that Saul wanted to kill him. Twice, Saul came so near to him that David might have killed him. But each time, David chose not to. David said to Saul, "Let the Lord judge between you and me, and deliver me out of your hands."

Saul said, "You are more righteous than I, for you have rewarded me with good, and I have rewarded you with evil."

About that time, Samuel died. And all Israel gathered together and mourned him, and they buried him at Ramah.

Then the Philistines gathered their forces to fight against Israel. When Saul saw the army of the Philistines, he was afraid, and his heart trembled. He asked the Lord for help, but the Lord did not answer.

Then Saul said to his servants, "Find me a woman who can raise the spirits, so that I may go to her." And they said to him, "There is a witch at Endor."

So Saul went to the woman at Endor, and said, "Bring up for me the one I shall name."

Then the woman said, "Whose spirit shall I bring up?" And Saul said to her, "Bring me up Samuel." And so then Samuel rose up from the earth.

Saul saw that it was Samuel, and he bowed to the ground. Samuel said, "Why have you disturbed me?"

Saul answered, "I am greatly distressed, for the Philistines make war against me, and God has turned away and will not answer me."

Samuel said, "Why then do you ask me, since the Lord has now become your enemy? He has torn the kingdom from your hand and given it to David, because you did not obey him at Amalek.

"Tomorrow you and your sons shall be with me, and the Lord will deliver the army of Israel into the hand of the Philistines."

Then Saul was filled with fear, and he fell down full length upon the ground. There was no strength in him, for he had eaten nothing all day and all night. And so the woman brought food before Saul and his servants, and they did eat. Then they rose up, and went away.

FROM 1 SAMUEL 22; 25:1; 28:1–20

DAVID BECOMES KING

Now the Philistines fought against Israel, and the men of Israel fled from before them. Many Israelites fell dead on Mount Gilboa. And the Philistines killed Jonathan, and Abinadab, and Malchishua, Saul's sons. Saul was badly wounded by arrows, and fell on his own sword, so that he would not die by the hand of his enemies.

When the men of Israel on the other side of the valley saw that Saul and his sons were dead, and that the Israelites were fleeing, they abandoned their cities and fled as well. And the Philistines came and lived in the cities.

When David heard that Saul and Jonathan had fallen, he tore his clothes and wept. And all the men that were with him mourned and wept.

And then David said, "The beauty of Israel is slain upon the high places! How are the mighty fallen! Tell it not in Gath; publish it not in Ashkelon; lest the daughters of the Philistines rejoice.

"Saul and Jonathan were lovely and pleasant in their lives, and in their death they are not divided. They were swifter than eagles, they were stronger than lions. How are the mighty fallen in the midst of the battle!"

And so the men of Judah came to Hebron. There they anointed David as king over Judah. Later all the tribes of Israel came to David in Hebron and anointed him king over Israel.

And so David ruled over the country for forty years. And during this reign, the Israelites defeated their enemies and rebuilt their cities.

David captured the city of Jerusalem, and he made it a holy city. And there he brought the ark of the covenant, in which the law of God was kept. And so Jerusalem became known as the City of David.

FROM 1 SAMUEL 31:1–4; 2 SAMUEL 1–3, 5, 6

DAVID AND BATHSHEBA

And it came to pass one evening, that David arose from his bed and walked on the roof of his house. From the roof he saw a woman washing herself, and the woman was very beautiful to look upon.

So David asked about the woman. And someone said, "Is that not Bathsheba, the daughter of Eliam and the wife of Uriah the Hittite?"

David sent messengers to her, and she came to be with him. And then she returned to her house. In time, the woman sent a message to David, saying "I am with child."

So David sent for Uriah her husband. And when Uriah came to him, David asked him for a report on the army and the war. Then David said to Uriah, "Wait here today, and tomorrow I will let you return to the army."

In the morning, David wrote to Joab the captain of the army and sent the letter to him in the hand of Uriah. In the letter, David wrote, "Put Uriah in the very front of the hottest battle, and then retreat from him, so he will be struck down, and die."

And as Joab was attacking the city, he assigned Uriah to the place where he knew there were brave men. And so the brave men of the city came out and they fought with Joab's men, and Uriah the Hittite was killed.

When Bathsheba heard that Uriah her husband was dead, she mourned for him. And when the time of mourning was past, David sent for her and brought her to his house. Bathsheba became his wife, and she bore him a son. But the thing that David had done displeased the Lord.

And the Lord sent Nathan the prophet to David, and he said, "Why have you despised the commandment of the Lord? In secret, you have killed Uriah the Hittite and have taken his wife to be your wife."

And David said to Nathan, "I have sinned against the Lord."

Then Nathan said, "The Lord has put away your sin, so you shall not die for it. But with this deed, you have scorned the Lord, and the child that is born to you shall surely die."

And then the Lord struck the child that Bathsheba had borne to David, and the child was very sick. David prayed to God for the child, and he fasted, and lay all night upon the ground. But on the seventh day, the child died.

David arose from the ground, and washed himself, and went to worship in the house of the Lord. Then he came to his own house, and when the servants set bread before him, he did eat.

Then his servants said to him, "What is this that you do? You did fast and weep for the child while it was alive, but now that the child is dead, you rise and eat bread."

And David said, "While the child was alive, I fasted and wept, for I thought perhaps God would be gracious to me, and the child would live. But now that he is dead, why should I fast? Can I bring him back again?"

And David comforted Bathsheba his wife, and Bathsheba bore him another son, and he called him by the name Solomon. And the Lord loved Solomon.

FROM 2 SAMUEL 11:2–27; 12:9–24

DAVID AND ABSALOM

Absalom, a son of David, had a beautiful sister, whose name was Tamar, and Amnon her half brother disgraced her. When King David heard about this, he was very angry.

After two years had passed, Absalom said to his servants, "Watch for a time when Amnon's heart is merry with wine, and then kill him. Do not be afraid." So Absalom's servants did as he had commanded. And then Absalom fled, and he went to live in Geshur for three years.

Then David sent for Absalom to return to Jerusalem. But he said, "Let him go to his own house, and not see my face." So Absalom lived for two years in Jerusalem, and did not see the king. And then David called for Absalom, and he came and bowed, and David kissed him.

But it came to pass that Absalom sent spies throughout Israel, saying, "As soon as you hear the sound of the trumpet, you will know that Absalom reigns in Hebron."

And a messenger came to David, and said to him, "The hearts of the men of Israel are with Absalom." Then the king and his followers fled to the wilderness between Jerusalem and the river Jordan.

As David made his way through the mountains, a man named Shimei cursed him and threw stones at him. David's servant said, "Why should this man curse the king? Let me go over and take off his head!" But David said, "Behold, even my own son wants to kill me. Let this man alone, and let him curse me."

The armies of David and Absalom met near the forest of Ephraim. David said to his men, "Deal gently with the young man Absalom, for my sake." And there was a great slaughter of twenty thousand men.

Absalom rode upon a mule, and the mule went under a great oak tree. Absalom's head was caught up in its branches, and the mule ran away. Then Joab took three spears in his hand, and he put them through the heart of Absalom, while he was still alive in the tree.

When the battle was over, the men ran to tell David that the Lord had delivered to them those who had lifted up their hand against the king. And David said, "Is Absalom safe?" And then a man said, "The Lord has avenged you today of all who rose up against you."

And again the king asked, "Is Absalom safe?" And the man answered, "May all the enemies of my lord the king be as that young man is."

Then the king went to his chamber, and wept. And he cried, "O my son Absalom, my son, my son Absalom! Would God I had died for you, O Absalom, my son, my son!"

FROM 2 SAMUEL 13–16, 18

109

THE DEATH OF DAVID

When King David was very old, his son Adonijah said, "I will be king," for he was now the oldest, and a handsome man.

But Nathan the prophet spoke to Bathsheba, saying to her, "Have you not heard that Adonijah reigns in the land, and David does not know it? Go to David and ask him if he did not swear that Solomon should sit on his throne."

And as Bathsheba talked with the king, Nathan also came in. And he said, "My lord, have you said that Adonijah shall reign after you, and not told your servant?" Then David said, "I swear by the Lord God that Solomon shall sit on my throne."

And so Zadok the priest anointed Solomon. And the earth shook with the sound of the people rejoicing.

David commanded Solomon, saying to him, "Be strong and show yourself to be a man. Walk in the ways of the Lord your God, and keep his commandments, that you may do well in all that you do."

Then David slept with his fathers and was buried in Jerusalem, the city of David. And David had reigned over Israel for forty years; then Solomon sat upon the throne of David his father. And he established a mighty kingdom.

FROM 1 KINGS 1; 2:1, 10–12

SOLOMON'S DREAM

Solomon took the daughter of Pharaoh king of Egypt as his wife, and he brought her into the city of David. Solomon loved the Lord, and he went to Gibeon to offer a thousand burnt offerings upon the altar there. In Gibeon the Lord appeared to Solomon in a dream, and God said, "Ask what I shall give you."

And Solomon said, "You have made me king in my father's place, and I am only a little child, who does not even know how to go out or come in. And I am in the midst of the people you have chosen, a great people, too many to be counted.

"Give me, therefore, an understanding heart to judge your people, that I may tell the difference between good and bad."

And this speech pleased the Lord, and so he said to Solomon, "Because you have not asked for a long life, or riches for yourself, or death for your enemies, I have done according to your words. I have given you a wise and an understanding heart. There were none like you before, and no other shall arise like you. And I have also given you that for which you did not ask, both riches and honor."

And Solomon awoke; and behold, it was all a dream.

1 KINGS 3:1–15

111

KING SOLOMON'S WISDOM

Once two women came to the court of King Solomon, and stood before him. "Oh, my king," said one woman, "I and this woman live in the same house. A child was born to me in that house. Then, three days later, another child was born to this woman.

"Only the two of us were in the house that night, and her baby died, because she lay on top of it as she slept. But then she got up at midnight, and took my living child from beside me, and put her own dead child in its place.

"When I awoke in the morning to nurse my child, I saw then that it was dead. But as I looked closely at it in the light, I knew that this was not my son, the one born to me." Then the second woman said, "No, no, the living one is my son! The dead one is her son!"

But the first woman answered back, "The dead one is yours! My son is the one who is alive!"

King Solomon said, "This first woman says, 'My son is the one that lives, and yours is the one that is dead.' Then this second woman answers, 'No, your son is the dead one; mine is the living one.'

"Bring me a sword!" the king said. "We will divide this living child in two, and give half to one mother, and half to the other."

Then the first woman spoke, and said, "Oh, no, my king! Do not kill the living child! Give it to her!" For the living child was really hers, and her heart went out to her son as she thought that he might be killed.

But the second woman only said, "Yes, divide the child in two. That way it will be neither mine nor hers alone."

At that King Solomon said, "Put the sword away. We will not kill this child. For we now know that this first woman is its mother. Give the living child to her."

And all of Israel heard of this judgment of King Solomon, and they knew that the wisdom of God was in him.

1 KINGS 3:16–28

SOLOMON BUILDS A TEMPLE

Judah and Israel lived safely, every man under his vine and under his fig tree, for there was peace all around. God gave Solomon wisdom and understanding, and largeness of heart.

Solomon said, "David my father could not build a temple for the Lord because there were wars all about him. But now the Lord has given me peace on every side, so I will build a temple for the Lord my God."

From Lebanon there came cedar and cypress wood, and craftsmen to cut and carve it. Solomon gathered laborers from all Israel to lay the foundation, put up the walls, and make the ceiling. And all the temple and the altar, he overlaid in pure gold. With much beauty, skill, and careful detail, Solomon built the rooms and the furniture of the temple.

Solomon then assembled the congregation of Israel, and the priests brought up the ark of the Lord to the temple, to the most holy place. It came to pass, when the priests had come out of the holy place, that a bright cloud filled it, so that the priests could not perform their service. For the glory of the Lord had filled the house of the Lord.

Then Solomon cried out to the Lord, "I have built you a house to dwell in forever." And he stood before the altar in the presence of all the congregation of Israel. He spread out his hands toward heaven, and said, "Lord God of Israel, there is no God like you, in heaven above, or on earth beneath."

And Solomon blessed the congregation, saying, "The Lord our God be with us, as he was with our fathers; let him not leave us. And may the Lord maintain his people Israel at all times, so that all the people of the earth may know that the Lord is God, and that there is none else. Let your hearts therefore be true to the Lord our God, to keep his commandments, and to walk in his laws, as on this day."

1 KINGS 5–9

THE QUEEN OF SHEBA

When the Queen of Sheba heard of Solomon's fame, she came to test him with hard questions. And she brought to Jerusalem a great train of camels bearing spices, and gold, and precious stones.

When she came to Solomon, she told him all that was on her mind. And Solomon answered all her questions, for there was nothing he could not explain to her.

And when the Queen of Sheba had seen the temple and Solomon's palace, and the food on his table, and all his servants and the richness of their clothing, she was breathless with amazement.

She said to the king, "It was a true report that I heard in my own land about you and your wisdom. But I did not believe those words, until I came and saw with my own eyes.

"And, behold, not even half was told to me; your wisdom and riches are far more than what I heard."

Then she said, "Happy are your men and your servants, who stand before you and hear your wisdom. Blessed be the Lord your God, who delights in you, and who set you on the throne of Israel."

And she gave the king all the spices and gold and precious stones that she had brought. And King Solomon gave the Queen of Sheba whatever she desired, and gifts from his royal treasury as well. Then she and her servants returned to her own country.

And all the earth came to hear the wisdom of King Solomon that God had put in his heart. And every man brought Solomon his present: cups of gold and silver, and clothing, and armor, and spices, horses, and mules.

And so King Solomon was greater than all the kings of the earth for riches and for wisdom.

1 KINGS 10:1–25

A DIVIDED KINGDOM

King Solomon loved many foreign women: the daughter of Pharaoh, and also Moabite, Ammonite, Edomite, Sidonite, and Hittite women. God had warned the Israelites, saying to them, "You shall not marry these women, for they will surely turn you away from your gods." But King Solomon still held to these women that he loved.

When Solomon was old, his wives turned his heart away from God, and he built altars for their gods. The Lord was angry, and said, "Because you have not kept my commandments, I will take the kingdom away from your son. But I will give him one tribe for the sake of your father David and for Jerusalem."

Solomon ruled in Jerusalem over all Israel for forty years. Then he died, and he was buried in the city of David his father. Rehoboam his son ruled in his place. The people protested against the heavy taxes and labor that Solomon had demanded from them, but Rehoboam would not lighten their loads. So the tribes of the north rebelled against the house of David. But the tribe of Judah still followed Rehoboam.

Now Rehoboam was not as wise as his father Solomon nor as brave as his grandfather David, and he could not win back the tribes of the north. They established a kingdom, and called it Israel. And their king was Jeroboam, the son of Solomon's servant. And the Lord was God over both of these kingdoms.

FROM 1 KINGS 11:1–13, 42–43; 12

THE PROPHET ELIJAH

Then the prophet Elijah came from Gilead and said to Ahab, the seventh king of Israel, "As the Lord God of Israel lives, there shall not be dew or rain these years." For King Ahab had done more evil in the eyes of the Lord than any of those before him. He had taken the Sidonian Jezebel as his wife, and built a temple to Baal. And there was no rain in Israel for three years.

Then Elijah went again to Ahab, and told him to gather all the people of Israel and the priests of Baal on Mount Carmel. And Elijah said to them, "If the Lord be God, follow him; but if Baal is god, then follow him." And so the priests of Baal prepared an offering, and called to Baal to turn it to flames. All day they cried out, but there was no answer.

Then Elijah prepared an offering to the Lord, and he said, "Lord God of Israel, let this people know that you are the Lord God." And the fire of the Lord fell, and it burned up the offering, and the wood, and the stones, and the dust.

The people fell on their faces, and cried, "The Lord is God." Then after Elijah had prayed for rain, the heavens became black with clouds and wind, and a great rain fell. The Lord told Elijah to choose Elisha, the son of Shaphat, to be prophet in his place. And Elijah found Elisha plowing in the field, and Elisha got up and went with Elijah.

Now when the Lord was about to take Elijah up to heaven, Elijah said to Elisha, "What shall I do for you, before I am taken from you?"

And Elisha said to him, "I pray you, let me inherit a double share of your spirit."

And Elijah said, "You have asked a hard thing. Nevertheless, if you see me when I am taken from you, it shall be so; but if you do not see me, it shall not be so."

But as they walked on and talked, a chariot of fire and horses of fire suddenly came between the two of them. And Elijah was taken up by a whirlwind into heaven.

And Elisha saw it, and he cried, "My father, my father; the chariot of Israel, and its horsemen!" And he saw Elijah no more.

And when the sons of the prophets saw Elisha, they said, "The spirit of Elijah does rest on Elisha," and they bowed to the ground before him.

FROM 1 KINGS 16, 17; 2 KINGS 2:1–15

121

THE RETURN TO JERUSALEM

During the years after Elisha's death, the priests and the people of Israel sinned against the Lord and worshipped the gods of the heathen, and they polluted the house of the Lord in Jerusalem. And God sent his messengers, because he had mercy on his people. But the people mocked the messengers of God, and despised his words, until the anger of the Lord became so great that it could not be calmed.

Therefore the Lord brought the Chaldeans down upon them. They killed the young men, and had no mercy on the people. And they took to Babylon all the treasure of the house of God, and all the treasures of the king. The Chaldeans burned down the house of God, and they broke down the wall of Jerusalem. The people who had not been killed were taken to Babylon as slaves.

Then Cyrus the king of Persia captured Babylon. He sent an order throughout his kingdom, saying, "The Lord God of heaven has given me all the kingdoms of the earth, and he has commanded me to build him a house in Jerusalem in Judah. Therefore, let any among his people go up to Jerusalem, and the Lord his God be with him." And the tribes of Judah and Benjamin came out of exile, and went again to Jerusalem.

In the second year of the return to Jerusalem, the builders laid the foundation of the temple. And with trumpets and cymbals, they sang together and gave praise to the Lord.

But the enemies of the people of Judah and Benjamin set out to weaken them, and troubled them while they were building. They hired counsellors against the people, to frustrate their purpose. This went on through all the days of Cyrus, even up to the time of King Darius. But when Darius became king of Persia, he ordered that the house of God should be rebuilt, and all the treasures replaced there.

And when the temple was finished, the children of Israel dedicated it to God with joy and with sacrifices.

FROM 2 CHRONICLES 36:14–23; EZRA 1–10

ESTHER BECOMES QUEEN

Now it came to pass that King Ahasuerus of Persia decided to give a banquet in the garden of his palace in Shushan. He invited all the princes and nobles to show them the riches of his glorious kingdom and the honor of his majesty. And the banquet lasted for seven days.

On the seventh day, when the king was merry with wine, he commanded his servants to bring Vashti the queen before him, so the people and the princes could see how beautiful she was. But the queen refused to come at the king's command. The king was very angry and embarrassed, and he ruled that Vashti could never again come before him. He ordered his servants to find another queen better than she.

So the servants gathered all the young maidens of the kingdom in Shushan in the custody of the king's officer. And the maiden who pleased the king would become queen instead of Vashti.

Now in the palace of Shushan there lived a certain Jewish man by the name of Mordecai, whose ancestors had been carried away from Jerusalem. And Mordecai had become like a father to his cousin Esther, after her own parents had died. She was a young and beautiful woman.

It came to pass that Esther was taken to King Ahasuerus, and he loved her more than all other women. He set the royal crown upon her head and made her queen instead of Vashti. But Esther did not tell the king she was a Jew. Mordecai had warned her not to let this be known.

In those days, Mordecai often sat by the palace gates, and one day, he overheard two of the king's officers plotting to kill the king. And so Mordecai told Queen Esther, who warned the king of the plot. Both the men were hanged. And then, in the king's presence, this story was written in the book of the history of the kingdom.

ESTHER 1–2

125

MORDECAI AND HAMAN

It came to pass that King Ahasuerus placed Haman above all the princes of the kingdom. All the king's servants had to bow down to him, but Mordecai did not bow down. Haman was very angry, and he decided to destroy all of Mordecai's people, the Jews, in the kingdom.

So he told King Ahasuerus, "There is a certain people who follow different laws and who do not obey you. If it so pleases you, have an order issued that they should be destroyed." And the king told Haman to do what seemed best. Then letters in the king's name were sent out, saying that all Jews should be killed, and their property taken away.

Mordecai told Queen Esther to beg the king to save her people. But Esther said, "If I go to the king's court without being called, I shall be put to death." And Mordecai said, "Speak now, or you too will be killed with all of your people. For who knows if you have not come to the kingdom for just such a time as this?"

So Esther went to the king's court. When the king saw her, he held out his golden scepter, and said, "What is your request, Queen Esther? For even if you ask for half of the kingdom, it shall be given to you."

Esther answered, "I would like you and Haman to come to a banquet that I have prepared." So the king and Haman dined with Esther, and after they had eaten, the king again asked what he could give her. And she said, "Come again tomorrow to dine with me, and I will tell you my request." And Haman was pleased because no other prince had been invited to the banquet but him. But he said to himself, "All this is as nothing so long as Mordecai the Jew will not bow down to me." So Haman had a gallows built on which to hang Mordecai.

That night the king had the book of the kingdom read to him. When the king heard again how Mordecai had once saved his life, he asked, "What honor has been given to Mordecai?" And the king's servants said, "Nothing has been given to him."

Then the king said to Haman, "What should be done for a man that the king wants to honor?" And Haman thought to himself, "Who else could the king wish to honor other than myself?" So he said, "Let this man wear the king's crown, and let him parade through the city on the king's horse." So the king said, "Hurry then, take my robes and the horse, and do this for Mordecai." And so Haman did as the king had ordered. But then he hurried off to his house, covering his head and weeping with sorrow.

That night the king and Haman again went to the banquet that Queen Esther had prepared. After they had eaten, she said, "Please, let my life and the lives of my people be spared, for we are to be destroyed." And the king asked, "Who dares to do this?" And Esther said, "The enemy is this wicked Haman."

So the king had Haman hanged on the gallows that he had built for Mordecai. And all the Jews were spared. And throughout the land, the Jews celebrated with joy and gladness.

ESTHER 1–9

GOD'S SERVANT JOB

There was a man named Job in the land of Uz. He was a perfect and righteous man; he feared God and did not do evil.

Now, Job had seven sons and three daughters. He also had seven thousand sheep, and three thousand camels, and many oxen and asses, and a rich household. And so this man was the greatest of all the men of the east.

There was a day when the sons of God came to present themselves before the Lord, and Satan also came among them. And the Lord said to Satan, "Where have you come from?" And Satan answered, "From going to and fro on the earth, and from walking up and down on it."

Then the Lord said to Satan, "Have you considered my servant Job, for there is none like him on earth, a perfect and righteous man, one who fears God and does no evil?"

And Satan answered, "Job has every reason to love God. But if you take away all his riches, he will curse you to your face."

So the Lord said to Satan, "All that Job has is in your power. But do not touch Job himself."

Then one day a messenger came to Job and said, "The Sabeans have taken your oxen and asses, and they have killed your servants with the edge of the sword. Only I alone have escaped to tell you."

While he was still speaking, another messenger came to Job and said, "A fire has fallen from heaven, and has burned up all your sheep, and your servants. Only I alone have escaped to tell you."

While he was still speaking, another messenger came to Job and said, "The Chaldeans have carried away your camels, and they have killed your servants with the edge of the sword. Only I alone have escaped to tell you."

And while he was speaking, still another came, and he said, "A great wind came and knocked down the house in which your sons and daughters were eating and drinking. They are all dead. Only I alone have escaped to tell you."

Then Job arose, and tore his clothes, and fell to the ground and worshipped, saying, "Naked I came from my mother's body, and naked I shall return. The Lord gave, and the Lord has taken away. Blessed be the name of the Lord." And Job did not sin, nor did he curse God.

Once again there was a day when the sons of God came before the Lord, and Satan came among them. The Lord said to Satan, "Have you considered my servant Job? Although you moved me against him with no cause, he still holds fast to his honor and integrity."

And Satan answered, "A man will give everything he has for his life. If you put out your hand now, and touch his bone and his flesh, he will curse you to your face." And the Lord said, "He is in your power; only do not take his life."

So Satan caused Job to suffer from terrible sores, from the soles of his feet to the crown of his head. And Job sat down among the ashes and scraped himself with a piece of pottery. Then his wife said to him, "Do you still hold fast to your integrity? Curse God, and die."

But Job answered, "You speak foolishly. Shall we receive good at the hand of God, and not receive evil?" And in all this, Job did not sin with the words that came from his lips.

Three of Job's friends heard of his troubles, and came to comfort him. They sat with him, but did not speak, for they saw his grief was very great. At the end of seven days, Job cursed the day he was born. Then his friends tried to comfort him, and one of them said to him, "Suffering does not come up from the dust, nor does trouble sprout

from the ground. Man is born to trouble, as the sparks fly upward. But if I were in your place, I would seek God, and put my case before him. God does great things that cannot be understood, and miracles that cannot be counted."

And Job said, "Oh, that I knew where I might find God, so that I might put my case before him! I would know the words with which he would answer me, and understand what he would say."

Then the Lord answered Job out of the whirlwind, saying, "I will question you, and you shall answer me. Where were you when I laid the foundation of the earth? When the morning stars sang together, and all the sons of God shouted for joy? And who shut in the sea with doors when it burst forth? Have you commanded the morning, and caused the dawn to know its place? Have you seen the doors of the shadow of death? Have you seen the treasures of the snow, or of the hail? Do you know how the light is parted, that scatters the east wind upon the earth? Will you hunt prey for the lions or provide food for the raven? Have you given the horse strength? Does the hawk fly by your wisdom? He that finds fault with the Lord, let him answer."

Then Job answered the Lord, "I know you can do everything, and that no thought can be hidden from you. I spoke about what I did not understand, things too wonderful to know. I have heard of you by my ears, but now my eyes see you. Therefore I repent in dust and ashes."

And the Lord accepted Job's words, and he blessed the later life of Job even more than the beginning, for he gave Job twice as much as he had given him before. Seven more sons and three more daughters were born to Job. And he lived to be a very old man.

Job 1–42

FROM *THE BOOK OF PSALMS*

O Lord our Lord, how excellent is thy name in all the earth!
who hast set thy glory above the heavens.
Out of the mouth of babes and sucklings hast thou ordained
strength because of thine enemies, that thou mightest still the
enemy and the avenger.
When I consider thy heavens, the work of thy fingers, the moon
and the stars, which thou has ordained;
What is man, that thou are mindful of him? and the son of
man, that thou visiteth him?
For thou has made him a little lower than the angels, and hast
crowned him with glory and honor.
Thou madest him to have dominion over the works of thy
hands: thou hast put all things under his feet:
All sheep and oxen, yea, and the beasts of the field;
The fowl of the air, and the fish of the sea, and whatsoever
passeth through the paths of the seas.
O Lord our Lord, how excellent is thy name in all the earth!

PSALM 8

Make a joyful noise unto the Lord, all ye lands.
Serve the Lord with gladness: come before his presence with
singing.
Know ye that the Lord he is God: it is he that hath made us,
and not we ourselves; we are his people, and the sheep of his
pasture.
Enter into his gates with thanksgiving, and into his courts with
praise: be thankful unto him, and bless his name.
For the Lord is good; his mercy is everlasting: and his truth
endureth to all generations.

PSALM 100

The Lord is my shepherd; I shall not want.

*He maketh me to lie down in green pastures: he leadeth me
    beside the still waters.*

*He restoreth my soul: he leadeth me in the paths of
    righteousness for his name's sake.*

*Yea, though I walk through the valley of the shadow of death, I
    will fear no evil: for thou art with me; thy rod and thy staff
    they comfort me.*

*Thou preparest a table before me in the presence of mine
    enemies: thou anointest my head with oil; my cup runneth
    over.*

*Surely goodness and mercy shall follow me all the days of my
    life: and I will dwell in the house of the Lord forever.*

Psalm 23

*I will lift up mine eyes unto the hills, from whence cometh my
    help.*

My help cometh from the Lord, which made heaven and earth.

*He will not suffer thy foot to be moved; he that keepeth thee
    will not slumber.*

Behold, he that keepeth Israel shall neither slumber nor sleep.

*The Lord is thy keeper: the Lord is thy shade upon thy right
    hand.*

The sun shall not smite thee by day, nor the moon by night.

*The Lord shall preserve thee from all evil: he shall preserve thy
    soul.*

*The Lord shall preserve thy going out and thy coming in from
    this time forth, and even for evermore.*

Psalm 121

By the rivers of Babylon, there we sat down, yea, we wept,
 when we remembered Zion.
We hanged our harps upon the willows in the midst thereof.
For there they that carried us away captive required of us a
 song; and they that wasted us required of us mirth, saying,
 "Sing us one of the songs of Zion."
How shall we sing the Lord's song in a strange land?
If I forget thee, O Jerusalem, let my right hand forget her
 cunning.
If I do not remember thee, let my tongue cleave to the roof of
 my mouth; if I prefer not Jerusalem above my chief joy.
Remember, O Lord, the children of Edom in the day of
 Jerusalem; who said, "Raze it, raze it, even to the foundation
 thereof."
O daughter of Babylon, who art to be destroyed; happy shall
 he be, that rewardeth thee as thou hast served us.
Happy shall he be, that taketh and dasheth thy little ones
 against the stones.

PSALM 137

The Lord reigneth, he is clothed with majesty; the Lord is
 clothed with strength, wherewith he hath girded himself: the
 world also is stabilized, that it cannot be moved.
Thy throne is established of old: thou art from everlasting.
The floods have lifted up, O Lord, the floods have lifted up
 their voice; the floods lift up their waves.
The Lord on high is mightier than the noise of many waters,
 yea, than the mighty waves of the sea.
Thy testimonies are very sure: holiness becometh thine house,
 O Lord, forever.

PSALM 93

134

FROM PROVERBS

*A wise son makes a glad father: but a foolish son is the
  heaviness of his mother.*
*The wicked flee when no man pursues: but the righteous are
  bold as a lion.*
*He that spares his rod hates his son: but he that loves him
  chastens him sometimes.*
He that troubles his own house shall inherit the wind.
A soft answer turns away wrath.
*Better is a dinner of herbs where love is, than a stalled ox and
  hatred therewith.*
Pride goes before destruction, and a haughty spirit before a fall.
Even a fool, when he holds his peace, is counted wise.
A friend loves at all times, and a brother is born for adversity.
Better is a neighbor that is near than a brother far off.
*A merry heart does good like a medicine: but a broken spirit
  dries the bones.*
*Even a child is known by his doings, whether his work be pure,
  and whether it be right.*
A good name is rather to be chosen than great riches.
*Train up a child in the way he should go; and when he is old,
  he will not depart from it.*
The borrower is servant to the lender.
*Riches certainly make themselves wings; they fly away as an
  eagle toward heaven.*
Despise not your mother when she is old.
Let another man praise you, and not your own mouth.
*Wealth makes many friends; but the poor is separated from his
  neighbor.*
*A false witness shall not be unpunished, and he that speaks lies
  shall not escape.*

FROM *ECCLESIASTES*

*Vanity of vanities, says the Preacher, vanity of vanities; all is
vanity.*

*What does a man gain from all the labor he takes under the sun?
One generation passes away, and another generation comes:
but the earth remains forever.*

*The sun also rises, and the sun goes down, and hastens to his
place where he arose.*

*All the rivers run into the sea; yet the sea is not full; unto the
place from whence the rivers come, there they return again.*

*All things are full of labor; man cannot utter it: the eye is not
satisfied with seeing, nor the ear filled with hearing.*

*The thing that has been, it is that which shall be; and that which
is done is that which shall be done: and there is no new thing
under the sun.*

*For every thing there is a season, and a time for every purpose
under heaven:*

*A time to be born, and a time to die; a time to plant, and a time
to pluck up that which is planted;*

*A time to kill, and a time to heal; a time to break down, and a
time to build up;*

*A time to weep, and a time to laugh; a time to mourn, and a time
to dance;*

*A time to cast away stones, and a time to gather stones together;
a time to embrace, and a time to refrain from embracing;*

*A time to get, and a time to lose; a time to keep, and a time to
cast away;*

*A time to rend, and a time to sew; a time to keep silence, and a
time to speak;*

*A time to love, and a time to hate; a time of war, and a time of
peace.*

FROM *THE SONG OF SONGS*

*I have compared you, O my love, to a company of horses in
   Pharaoh's chariots.
Your cheeks are comely with rows of jewels, your neck with
   chains of gold.
We will make you borders of gold with studs of silver.*

*I am the rose of Sharon, and the lily of the valleys.
As the lily among thorns, so is my love among the daughters.
As the apple tree among the trees of the wood, so is my beloved
   among the sons.*

*My beloved spoke, and said unto me, "Rise up, my love, my fair
   one, and come away.
For, lo, the winter is past, the rain is over and gone;
The flowers appear on the earth; the time of the singing of birds
   is come, and the voice of the turtle is heard in our land;
The fig tree puts forth her green figs, and the vines with the
   tender grape give a good smell. Arise, my love, my fair one,
   and come away."*

*Who is this that comes out of the wilderness like pillars of
   smoke, perfumed with myrrh and frankincense, with all
   powders of the merchant?*

*Awake, O north wind; and come, thou south; blow upon my
   garden, that the spices thereof may flow out. Let my beloved
   come into his garden, and eat his pleasant fruits.*

*Until the day break, and the shadows flee away, get me to the
   mountain of myrrh, and to the hill of frankincense.*

FROM *THE BOOK OF ISAIAH*

"Come now, and let us reason together, " said the Lord: "For though your sins be scarlet, they shall be as white as snow; though they be red like crimson, they shall be as white as wool."

The Lord shall judge among the nations, and he shall rebuke many people. They shall beat their swords into plowshares, and their spears into pruning hooks: nation shall not lift up sword against nation, neither shall they learn war any more.

Holy, holy, holy, is the Lord of hosts: the earth is full of his glory.

Therefore the Lord himself shall give you a sign: Behold, a virgin shall be with child, and bear a son, and shall call his name Immanuel.

Butter and honey shall he eat, that he may know to refuse the evil, and choose the good.

For unto us a child is born, unto us a son is given: and the government shall be upon his shoulder: and his name shall be called Wonderful Counselor, Mighty God, Everlasting Father, Prince of Peace.

And there shall come forth a rod out of the stem of Jesse, and a branch shall grow out of his roots.

And the Spirit of the Lord shall rest upon him, the spirit of wisdom and of understanding, the spirit of counsel and of might, the spirit of knowledge and of the fear of the Lord.

The wolf also shall dwell with the lamb, and the leopard shall lie down with the kid, and the calf and the young lion and the fatling together. And a little child shall lead them.

And the cow and the bear shall feed; their young ones shall lie down together: and the lion shall eat straw like the ox.

And the suckling child shall play on the hole of the asp, and the weaned child shall put his hand on the den of the cockatrice.

They shall not hurt nor destroy in all my holy mountain: for the earth shall be full of the knowledge of the Lord, as the waters cover the sea.

A voice cries in the wilderness: "Prepare you the way of the Lord, make straight in the desert a highway for our God.

"Every valley shall be raised up, and every mountain and hill shall be made low; and the crooked shall be made straight, and the rough places made plain.

"And the glory of the Lord shall be revealed, and all who are flesh shall see it together: for the mouth of the Lord has spoken."

ISAIAH 1, 6, 7, 9, 11, 40

KING NEBUCHADNEZZAR

In the third year of the reign of Jehoiakim, king of Judah, King Nebuchadnezzar of Babylon captured Jerusalem. He took some of the vessels of the house of God back to his land, to the house of his god.

King Nebuchadnezzar had certain of the Israelite children brought to his palace. These children were handsome, and skillful and clever, and were quick to understand. The king wanted the children to learn the ways and the language of the Babylonians, so they could serve him.

Now among those chosen from Judah were these four: Daniel, Hananiah, Mishael, and Azariah. They were given Babylonian names: Daniel was called Belteshazzar; and Hananiah was called Shadrach; Mishael was called Meshach; and Azariah was called Abednego.

Daniel and the others did not eat the king's rich food and wine, because it was against God's law. But they were more healthy than those who did, even though they lived on only vegetables and water.

God gave these young men knowledge and skill in all learning, and Daniel understood visions and dreams. The king spoke with them. And in all matters of wisdom and understanding, he found them ten times better than all the magicians and astrologers in his kingdom.

DANIEL 1:1–7, 17–20

HANDWRITING ON THE WALL

King Belshazzar ruled Babylon after the death of his ancestor Nebuchadnezzar. One night King Belshazzar held a great banquet for one thousand of his lords, and he drank wine before the thousand.

While Belshazzar tasted the wine, he had brought to him the golden and silver vessels which Nebuchadnezzar had taken from the temple of the house of God, which was in Jerusalem. And when the vessels were brought in, the king and his guests did drink wine from them. As they drank the wine, they praised their gods of gold and silver, of bronze, iron, wood, and stone.

Then suddenly the fingers of a man's hand came forth and wrote on the wall of the banquet room. The king saw the hand as it wrote.

Then the king's face was changed, and his thoughts were troubled. His knees knocked against each other and his legs were weak. He cried out loud to bring in all his astrologers and soothsayers.

And the king spoke, and he said to these wise men of Babylon,

"Whoever can read this writing, and can show me the meaning of it, shall be dressed in scarlet, and have a chain of gold about his neck. And he shall be the third ruler in the kingdom."

Then all the king's wise men came in, but they could not read the writing, nor could they interpret it for the king.

And so King Belshazzar was very troubled. Now the queen mother spoke and said, "O king, do not let your thoughts trouble you, for there is a man in your kingdom, whose name is Daniel. Wisdom like the wisdom of the holy gods is found in him, and your ancestor King Nebuchadnezzar made him the master of all the magicians. This man can interpret dreams and solve problems."

Then Daniel was brought in, and Belshazzar said to him, "Are you Daniel, who was brought out of Jerusalem as a captive by my father the king? I have heard of you, and I have heard that the spirit of the gods is in you, and that light and understanding and excellent wisdom are found in you. If you can read the writing and can tell me what it means, you shall be clothed in scarlet, and have a chain of gold around your neck, and you shall be the third ruler in the kingdom."

142

And Daniel said, "Let your gifts be given to another, but I will read the writing and interpret it for you. O, Belshazzar, you have not humbled your heart, but have lifted yourself against the Lord. You have brought the vessels from his house, and you and your guests have drunk wine from them. And you have worshipped the gods of silver and gold, of brass, iron, wood, and stone. But you have not glorified the God who holds your life in his hand."

Then Daniel said, "This is the writing that was written: MENE, MENE, TEKEL, UPHARSIN ("Numbered, Weighed, and Divided"). And this is what the writing means: God has numbered the days of your kingdom, and finished it. You are weighed on the balance scales, and are found lacking. Your kingdom is divided and is given to the Medes and Persians." That very night, King Belshazzar was killed; and then Darius the Mede took over the kingdom.

DANIEL 5

143

DANIEL IN THE LION'S DEN

King Darius the Mede appointed one hundred and twenty princes to rule over the whole kingdom. He preferred Daniel above the others, and set him over them all. These men tried to find fault with Daniel, but they could find none. They said, "We shall not find any chance to complain against Daniel, except where it concerns the law of his God."

Then they went to King Darius and said, "We have decided to issue an order that anyone who asks a favor of any god or man for thirty days shall be put in the den of lions." And King Darius signed the order.

Even though Daniel knew that the king had signed the order, he knelt three times a day, and prayed. Then he gave thanks to his God, as he had done before.

The men found him praying, and they went to King Darius, and they said, "Daniel does not pay attention to you, O king, or to your order. He kneels three times a day to pray to his God."

When the king heard this, he was not pleased, and he set his heart on saving Daniel. But the men said, "You know it is our law: no order that the king gives may be changed."

So the king ordered that Daniel be put into the den of lions. But then he said to him, "Your God whom you serve always, he will deliver you." And a stone was put over the mouth of the den.

Then the king went to his palace, but he could not eat or sleep. Early in the morning he arose and hurried to the den of lions. When he came to the den he cried out in a sad voice, "O Daniel, has your God been able to save you from the lions?"

And Daniel said to the king, "My God has sent his angel and has shut the lions' mouths, and they have not hurt me. For I have been found innocent before God, and before you."

The king was very glad for Daniel, and he had him taken from the den of lions. And there was not a mark or a hurt upon Daniel, because he believed in his God.

King Darius put the men who had accused Daniel into the den of lions, and the lions overpowered them.

Then the king wrote to his people, saying, "Let all fear the God of Daniel, the living God whose kingdom will not be destroyed. For God works many signs and wonders in heaven and on earth, and God has saved Daniel from the power of the lions."

DANIEL 6

JONAH AND THE WHALE

The word of the Lord came to Jonah, the son of Amittai, saying, "Arise now, and go up to Nineveh, that great city, and warn the people there that I will destroy them because of their wickedness." But Jonah fled from the presence of the Lord, and he boarded a ship for Tarshish.

But the Lord sent out a great wind, and there was a mighty storm in the sea, so strong that it seemed as if the ship would break apart. The sailors were afraid, and each man cried to his god. And they threw the cargo into the sea to lighten the ship.

The sailors said to one another, "Let us cast lots to see who has brought this evil upon us." So they cast lots, and the lot fell on Jonah.

They said to him, "Of what people are you? And what have you done to bring this evil upon us?" And Jonah answered them, "I am a Hebrew; and I fear the Lord, the God of heaven, who has made the sea and the dry land."

Then Jonah told them that he had fled from the presence of the Lord. They were very frightened, and said, "What shall we do to you, so that the sea will be calm for us?" And Jonah said, "Throw me into the sea, and it will grow calm, for I know it is because of me that this great storm has come upon you." But the men rowed hard to bring the ship to land. But the sea was too rough, and they could not reach it.

So they took up Jonah, and they threw him into the sea. And the sea stopped raging. Then the men greatly feared the Lord, and they offered a sacrifice and made vows to him. Then the Lord prepared a great fish to swallow Jonah. And Jonah was in the belly of the fish for three days and three nights.

Then Jonah prayed to the Lord from out of the fish's belly, and said, "O Lord my God, I am sent out of your sight, yet I will look again toward your holy temple. And I will sacrifice to you with the voice of thanksgiving." And the Lord spoke to the fish, and it spit up Jonah out upon the dry land.

Then the word of the Lord came to Jonah the second time, saying, "Arise, and go up to Nineveh, that great city, and preach as I have told you." So Jonah went to Nineveh, as the Lord commanded.

And as Jonah entered the city, he began crying out, "In forty days, Nineveh shall be destroyed." And the people of Nineveh believed God, and proclaimed a fast. From the greatest of them to the least of them, they repented of their evil. When God saw that they had turned from their evil way, he repented, and he did not destroy them.

But this displeased Jonah, and he was very angry. And he said to the Lord, "Did I not flee from you, because I knew that you are a gracious God, and merciful, and slow to anger, and one who repents of evil? Now, I beg you, take my life, for it is better for me to die than to live." Then the Lord said, "Are you right to be so angry?"

So Jonah went out, and he made himself a shelter on the east side of the city. He sat under it, so that he might see what would become of the city.

And the Lord God made a vine grow over the shelter to shade Jonah's head. And Jonah was very glad of the vine.

But in the morning, God sent a worm to eat away at the vine until it dried up and died. And when the sun rose, God sent a hot east wind. And the sun beat upon Jonah's unshaded head until he grew faint, and wished again to die.

Then God said to Jonah, "Are you right to be angry at the vine?"

Jonah said, "I am right to be angry, angry enough to die."

And then the Lord said, "You have pity for this vine, which you did neither plant nor take care of, and which came up in a night, and then died in a night.

"Should I not then pity Nineveh, that great city, in which there are more than one hundred twenty thousand persons who cannot tell their right hand from their left, and also many cattle?"

JONAH 1–4

149

GEOGRAPHY OF THE HOLY LAND

The Holy Land does not have a single type of geography. The landscape changes from flat coastal plains to high mountains to valleys that lie well below sea level. This differing geography fits into a small area that measures only about 150 miles from north to south, running from Dan to Beersheba.

The Holy Land is surrounded by great natural barriers. The Mediterranean Sea (called the Great Sea in ancient times) lies to the west. There are high mountains to the north and vast, empty desert areas to the south and the east.

Deserts and Farmland

The soil of the land of Israel varied greatly, from desert regions that supported only shepherds and tribes of nomads, to fertile regions in which there were many productive farmlands. Even today, the change in the terrain from farmland to desert is obvious as one moves inland from the seacoast. The prevailing west-to-east winds pick up moisture from the Mediterranean and then lose it in the form of rain as they rise upward to the highlands. As the now-dry winds descend into the Jordan valley, the lack of rainfall there creates the desert areas.

The land of Israel is also on the border of two climate zones, the Mediterranean and the Sahara-Arabian, so that any change in the landscape causes a marked change in the climate. In the winter, the Mediterranean climate brings rain, while the Sahara-Arabian climate remains dry. The winds from the west pass over the Mediterranean, bringing rain, while winds from the south blow over dry land and, thus do not bring rain. Although the average rainfall in Biblical times has been calculated at about ten inches per year, more than twenty inches might fall in the north, with less than two inches in the south.

The Coastal Plain

Around the southern end of the Holy Land near Gaza, the coastal strip of land along the Mediterranean is about twelve and one-half miles wide. Here, near the open sea, the land has many natural springs and is covered with vegetation, including fruit and sycamore trees.

Just north of this area, great sand dunes, reaching heights of 150 feet, cut off a rolling, treeless plain from the sea. Running along the east side of this plain a row of low foothills, called the Shephelah in the Bible, extend to the mountainous region of Judah.

Farther north there is a fertile region that in Biblical times could be easily reached from the chief city of Jerusalem. Above this region is the Plain of Sharon, which was covered with wooded areas and served as grazing land for sheep and goats sent down from the high country when vegetation was scarce.

As it continues north, this strip narrows and is only about two miles wide at the ancient city of Caesarea. Somewhat north of this point, the coastal plains are interrupted by the Carmel range, which extends out to the very edge of the sea. Beyond the mountains, the plains again pick up, forming the Bay of Acre. The Biblical city of Acco was located here, surrounded by the fertile and well-populated plain of Acre. A bit farther north on this same narrow strip lay the ancient city of Tyre, not far below the northern boundary of the Holy Land.

Even with its long shoreline, this area has a lack of natural harbors, and so Israel never developed as a seagoing nation.

The Highlands

The high country of the Holy Land is bordered on the south by the desert region of the Negev, which literally means "parched country." The low hills of the Shephelah extend from the coastal plain to the mountainous ridge, which runs lengthwise through the center of the region.

The settlements in this region were protected from surprise attack by the high elevation and the rough terrain. Securely perched high in the mountains, they overlooked the coastal plain to the west and the great valley

150

to the east. Hebron, one of the southernmost settlements, is 3,000 feet above sea level. Because of its central location and position in the mountains, King David chose Jerusalem as his capital city.

Northward, the land opens to the valleys of Samaria, which are less than 600 feet above sea level. Mount Gerizim, a sacred high place of the Samaritans, rises above the valley at a height of 2,800 feet. Shechem lies in the pass between it and Mount Ebal to the north, which rises to 3,120 feet. This pass forms a sharp division between northern and southern Samaria.

At this point the Carmel ridge turns west into the Mediterranean Sea. Along the northeastern edge of this ridge is the Plain of Esdraelon; its western region is known as the Plain of Megiddo and the eastern section as the Plain of Jezreel. This triangular-shaped plain, 200 feet above sea level, is the most fertile area in all of the Holy Land.

To the north lies the region of Galilee. The lower portion of this area, which slopes up from the Plain of Esdraelon is known as "Lower Galilee," and the land continuing to rise up toward Syria is "Upper Galilee." The mountains in Galilee are high, reaching elevations of about 4,000 feet. The highlands keep rising into Lebanon, where the snow-covered cap of Mount Hermon reaches 9,700 feet above sea level.

At the most northern point in Galilee, the mountains drop abruptly to the Jordan valley on the east. The streams of the region of Lower Galilee lead to the Sea of Galilee, with Mount Tabor on the southeastern corner providing a view over the entire region.

The Great Rift Valley

A great rift, or opening, divides the Holy Land lengthwise into two sections. It is the deepest ditch on the face of the earth. It is part of a huge fault that runs some 350 miles, from the mountains of Lebanon in the north to the Gulf of Aqaba in the south. This rift, called "the Ghor" or "the valley," is 1,268 feet below sea level at its greatest depth, and the highlands drop steeply to it from elevations of 3,000 feet.

The Jordan River, fed by streams from Mount Hermon, runs through the Great Rift, falling about nine feet with each mile that it flows. The Jordan ends in the Dead Sea to the south. The river supplies water for the lakes along its path, including the Sea of Galilee (Lake Galilee). This heart-shaped body of fresh water is thirteen miles long and eight miles wide at its widest point. Its surface lies 680 feet below sea level. The land is marshy where the Jordan River enters the lake. The area around the lake was originally named for Zebulun and Naphtali, the Hebrew tribes that settled there, and the lake itself is called the Lake of Chinneroth in the Old Testament.

It is 65 miles from the Sea of Galilee to the Dead Sea, but the Jordan loops and twists almost 200 miles to travel this distance. The Great Rift widens below the Sea of Galilee from a beginning of about four miles to a width of thirteen to fourteen miles. At the bottom of this broad section is a deep depression of one hundred or more feet that is the actual river bottom. Gray hills still cover the slopes leading to the lower level, and the depression itself was once covered by jungle-like plant growth, providing a home for many wild animals. This area is called "the Zor" or "thicket."

As the Rift continues southward, the river bottom narrows and vegetation decreases, for rainfall is rare in this area and little water seeps down from the parched western slopes of the highlands. There are oases in this region, however, including one with a great spring near which one of the oldest cities on earth, the Biblical Jericho, was settled.

The Jordan River ends in the Dead Sea, its incoming waters taken up by the hot sun and dry air of the region. The water of the Dead Sea is so salty that a person will not sink in it, and its Hebrew name is literally "Sea of Salt." It is 53 miles long and nine to ten feet wide, and it lies 1,286 feet below sea level. The water level is as deep as 1,300 feet, although in Biblical times one could wade across the southern part. From the southern end of the Dead Sea, the Rift continues for another 100 miles to the Gulf of Aqaba.

BIBLICAL PLANTS AND ANIMALS

The Holy Land of Biblical times covered an area that had different amounts of rainfall and different kinds of soil in various places. This meant that many different kinds of plants grew in the different regions.

The Natural Plant Life

Along the coast of the Great Sea (Mediterranean Sea) lay the marshy soil of Sharon and parts of Esdraelon, with some areas covered by forest. The land of the Philistines had few trees, except in the valley bottoms. But up the coast to the north, groves of sycamore trees covered the land.

The hill country of Judah and Samaria was covered with thick oak and pine forests. The plant growth was thicker on the northern and western slopes, where the rainfall was greater and the evaporation less than on the eastern and southern slopes.

A ground cover of scrub woodland and shrubs stretched into the semidesert area, extending into what is now Jordan. The western slopes of the hills of Galilee were rich with trees and vegetation. Along with the pine forests, there were hawthorns, plantains, and wild pear trees. The country to the south and east of the highlands was covered with grass. The hills of the desert areas were often barren, but the wadis (gullies or stream beds) had a thin line of saltbush and tamarisk. In the Great Rift Valley, low-lying areas with enough heat and moisture became marshes that were almost impossible to cross. Tropical plants such as papyrus and doum palms grew there, with tamarisk jungle in the flood plain of the Jordan River.

The Crops

As people cleared away the old wild plant growth, they planted farm crops. In place of forest trees, they grew olives; in place of the scrub woodland, they planted grape vines; and in place of the grasses, they grew grains, such as wheat and barley. In the Bible, these crops are often mentioned together because they provided the basic needs of the people.

The Bible also speaks of the food called pulse (lentils, peas, and beans) that was an important part of the people's diet. Jacob bought his brother Esau's birthright with pottage, a stew made of pulse. And even though they were threatened by King Nebuchadnezzar of Babylon, Daniel and his companions chose to eat pulse instead of the daily provision of the king's meat.

Grain was grown between the olive trees, and pulse between the grape vines. Together these crops provided a well-balanced diet that a farmer could raise with the help of only his family, and he would consider himself fortunate to have this food.

The Promised Land in which the Israelites had settled was rich and fruitful, and it provided the people with more than simply the necessities of their everyday lives. In the summer there were also foods that were considered to be special treats, such as figs, pomegranates, and spices and nuts:

One basket had very good figs, like first-ripe figs. (Jeremiah 24:2)

Your shoots are an orchard of pomegranates with all choicest fruits. (Song of Solomon 4:13)

. . . carry down to the man a present, a little balm and a little honey, gum, myrrh, pistachio nuts, and almonds. (Genesis 43:11)

The Wild Animals

But the Promised Land could also be dangerous. Wild animals such as lions, bears, wolves, jackals, and hyenas were a danger to farm animals, or even to people, who wandered too far from their villages or farms. These wild animals were a constant threat to the flocks of sheep:

David said to Saul, "Your servant used to keep sheep for his father; and when there came a lion, or a bear, and took a lamb from the flock, I went after him and smote him." (1 Samuel 17:34)

Although the people feared the mighty lion, they also respected its courage and strength:

The lion, which is mightiest among beasts and does not turn back before any. (Proverbs 30:30)

There were many snakes and reptiles in the land, such as cobras, asps, adders, green lizards and monitor lizards, and white or gray geckos. Some of the snakes were poisonous.

In the rivers and lakes of the Holy Land, carp, catfish, and other fish lived along with the hippopotamus and the crocodile. It may be that these two animals were the two large beasts mentioned in the Bible, the "behemoth" (hippopotamus) and the "leviathan" (crocodile).

Birds of all kinds were in the land, those that could fly and those that could not. Many were birds of prey, such as the eagle and the hawk.

The forests, the plains, and the desert were full of game animals that the people could hunt. King Solomon's table was provided with "harts, gazelles, roebucks, and fatted fowl." (1 Kings 4:23). In addition to those the people had already tamed, wild goats and asses roamed the hills and plains.

There were also many insects in the land of the Bible, including bees, which were the source of honey. Lice, flies, grasshoppers, wasps, and locusts were there along with hundreds of kinds of butterflies and beetles. Some insects were eaten, but others, such as the centipede and the scorpion, the Israelites were forbidden to eat:

Yet among the winged insects that go on all fours you may eat those which have legs above their feet, with which to leap on the earth;

Of them you may eat: the locust according to its kind, the bald locust according to its kind, the cricket according to its kind, and the grasshopper according to its kind.

But all other winged insects which have four feet are an abomination to you. (Leviticus 11:21–23)

The Domesticated Animals

The people of Israel depended upon their flocks of goats and sheep as well as on their crops for food. The sheep were a fat-tailed variety that provided milk, meat, and wool. They were also the source of sheepskin coats that protected the shepherds against the cold. These sheep were highly valued and were often offered in sacrifice.

Goats were raised together with the sheep, even though they were able to range farther into the desert. They also provided meat and milk, and their coarse hair was used to make the heavy cloth for tents. It may be that sheep dogs were used. But it seems that for the most part the Israelites did not think of dogs as pets or work animals.

By the time the kings ruled in Israel, the camel had become the major means of transport in the desert. Its speed and endurance enabled desert tribes, such as the Midianites, to make sudden raids upon the farms and villages of the Israelites, laying waste the land.

The ass, the mule, and the ox were the main work animals of the shepherds and the farmers. Almost every family had an ass or a donkey. These large animals worked hard and could easily travel 25 miles in a day.

The ox was prized most highly. The farmer used it to plow the heavy soil and as a beast of burden. The nomads used oxen to transport all their goods and to carry women and children.

Horses were not common and were considered by the Israelites primarily as animals of war. The chariots of the Egyptians who pursued the people of Israel were pulled by horses. They were also included on the list of animals the Jews brought with them on their return from exile in Babylon. Always the horse was spoken of with great admiration.

Do you give the horse his might? Do you clothe his neck with strength?

Do you make him leap like the locust? His majestic snorting is terrible.

He paws in the valley, and exults in his strength; he goes out to meet the weapons. (Job 39:19–22)

ANCIENT EGYPT

At the time that Abraham, Isaac, and Jacob lived, Egypt had been a powerful country for well over a thousand years. For a time, Egypt was overrun by foreign invaders and its power declined. But, during what historians call The New Kingdom, which dates from about the year 1500 B.C., Egypt became the world's strongest nation. King Thutmose III brought Palestine and Syria into the Egyptian empire and established control over Nubia and Kush.

The Nile River

Almost from its beginning, this country along the Nile grew in numbers and strength. Extending the length of the land, the river provided a means of transportation and communication for the settlements along its banks. The river also made farming possible.

The Nile River flooded sometime in July each year. In September, the flood waters would recede, leaving a layer of rich, fertile soil (alluvium). This flood area was very hot and dry, with little rainfall.

In spite of the dry climate, crops could be planted with confidence because of the regularity of the Nile's flooding pattern. The people created extensive irrigation systems to water the crops, which made it possible for the land to support a large population.

The fertile land was planted with wheat, barley, and rye. Bread was made from the wheat and a thick beer from the barley. All the grains were important in feeding both the people and their livestock. Grain was stored in granaries in the cities for use in times of famine. Overseers recorded the amount of grain that was put in and taken out:

And that food shall be for store to the land against the seven years of famine, which shall be in the land of Egypt. (Genesis 41:36)

It was so important that provisions be made for times of famine that one-fifth of the produce was given to the Egyptian ruler, the Pharaoh, for distribution in times of need:

And it shall come to pass in the increase, that ye shall give the fifth part unto Pharaoh, and four parts shall be your own, for seed of the field, and for your food, and for them of your households, and for food for your little ones. (Genesis 47:24)

Many kinds of vegetables and fruits, such as dates, figs, and pomegranates, grew in the rich soil. The people were able to catch fish from the Nile, as well as the ducks and geese that lived there. Their cattle furnished them with milk, cheese, and butter. Wealthy Egyptians regularly ate beef or the meat of gazelles and antelopes. They also had fancy baked goods and drank grape, date, or palm wines.

Flax was also raised and was made into linen. In the hot climate, cool linen garments were worn by both men and women, and some of the yarn was used for trading.

The farmer was respected far above the shepherd in Egypt, and few people wanted to tend the flocks. When Joseph's family came to Egypt, he instructed them to tell Pharaoh that they were shepherds, so they would be sent to settle on the grasslands of Goshen:

And it shall come to pass, when Pharaoh shall call you, and shall say, "What is your occupation?"

That ye shall say, "Thy servants' trade hath been about cattle from our youth even until now, both we, and also our fathers: that ye may dwell in the land of Goshen: for every shepherd is an abomination unto the Egyptians." (Genesis 46:33–34)

The Pharaoh

The Egyptians believed that the visible world had been created by divine forces out of a watery waste. These forces also brought into existence the gods who governed every aspect of human life. So, the people of Egypt worshiped many gods. The farmers relied on Re, the sun god, and the goddess Rennutet

for their good harvests. Isis ruled with her husband and brother, Osiris, over plant life and the dead. Their son, Horus, was the sky god.

The people of each city and town of ancient Egypt also worshipped their own god as well as the major gods. The great city of Memphis had a creator god called Ptah. The people of Thebes worshipped the sun god Amon. The gods were often pictured as animals or as humans with animal heads.

The king of Egypt lived in a Great House, which was called a Per-ao (or Pharaoh in Hebrew), which gives us his title. Pharaoh was considered to be a god on earth. He assured the rise of the Nile, which in turn assured the prosperity, peace, and order of the land. The Pharaoh was an absolute ruler, and his will became reality as soon as it was spoken. The Egyptians recognized no power on earth greater than his.

But one person alone could not rule such a great empire, and the Pharaoh needed help in governing as the god-king. To the priests fell the care of the temples, which gave them great power. Viziers and governors were appointed by the Pharaoh to aid him in running the country. Joseph was one:

Thou shalt be over my house, and according unto thy word shall all my people be ruled: only in the throne will I be greater than thou. (Genesis 41:40)

The Pharaoh also had a large army of foot soldiers and charioteers. Although horses were not originally found in Egypt, they were later brought in from other countries to pull the chariots. Later the Egyptians raised horses themselves.

The Afterlife

According to the Egyptians, a person's soul or spirit consisted of three parts: *akh* was the part of a person that became an "excellent spirit" and traveled through the floor of the burial chamber to the underworld; *ka* was the exact double of a person (the "shadow" or "name") to which funerary offerings were made; and *ba* was the manifestation of the soul that could enter or leave the dead body.

The Egyptians loved life so much that they wanted to enjoy it even after death. The inscriptions, paintings, and furniture in the tombs were put there for the enjoyment of the dead in the afterlife. This desire also led to the practice of embalming bodies by a process called mummification:

So Joseph died, being an hundred and ten years old: and they embalmed him and he was put in a coffin in Egypt. (Genesis 50:26)

The huge pyramids of Egypt were built as tombs for the pharaohs. The oldest one still standing is the pyramid of Zoser, which was built around 2700 B.C. The Great Pyramid of King Khufu at Giza is probably the most famous. It originally stood about 480 feet high and covered 275 square yards. The base is almost precisely aligned with the points of the compass, and its elevation does not vary more than one half inch. It was made of over 2,300,000 huge stone blocks, some weighing as much as 33,000 pounds. The stones were not joined with any type of mortar, but dressed to fit together so perfectly that even something so thin as a piece of paper cannot be slipped between them..

Structures such as the pyramids and the great cities of Egypt required many thousands of workers to construct them.

Therefore they did set over them taskmasters to afflict them with their burdens. And they built for Pharaoh treasure cities, Pithom and Raamses. (Exodus 1:11)

During the time the fields were flooded, the farm workers could help in the building. But slaves were needed in addition to the farmers and the skilled craftsmen. These slaves were taken in battle or bought from traders or merchants.

In spite of their mighty position in the ancient world, the people of Egypt seemed to have been cheerful and brooded very little about the place of man before the gods. Life was relatively sure and peaceful for these inhabitants of one of the earliest civilized kingdoms on the earth.

NOTES ON THE TEXT

The Creation, Pages 1–4: Light was God's first creation following the initial creation of the heaven and the earth. "And God said, 'Let there be light.'" Throughout the Bible, light is associated with God and with life.

The term "man," which occurs frequently in the Creation and elsewhere in the text, is a rendering of the Hebrew word *Adam,* which has been translated as *man* in the collective sense of "human being" rather than in the specific sense of "a male person."

The break that occurs in the account of Creation between the end of Genesis 1 and the beginning of Genesis 2 is a reflection of the fact that the early Bible was not divided into chapters. Formal chapter divisions were added later, in the Middle Ages, and they do not always reflect a change in subject matter.

The Garden of Eden, Pages 6–7: The location of the Garden of Eden has never been determined, but both Egypt and Mesopotamia have been considered to be possibilities. The name *Eden* means "delight" or "pleasure" in Hebrew. This has been traced to a Sumerian word that means "plain." Sumer was one of the earliest civilizations in the Mesopotamian plain, watered by the Tigris and Euphrates Rivers. The soil of this area was extremely fertile and has been under cultivation for thousands of years.

The Forbidden Fruit, Pages 8–10: The fruit that Adam and Eve eat in the Garden of Eden has traditionally been pictured as an apple. Actually, the Bible does not mention a specific kind of fruit, saying only that "when the woman saw that the tree was good for food, and that it was beautiful, and that it was a tree to make one wise, she took its fruit, and she did eat."

Cain and Abel, Pages 11–12: This tells of the first crime and the resulting punishment. God banished Cain for the murder of his brother and set a mark upon him. The mark of Cain has come to be associated with a murderer. But the mark is to protect Cain, "so that anyone finding him would not kill him." His punishment comes from God, not from man.

The Lord Speaks to Noah, Page 13: The statements given here and elsewhere divide the animal kingdom into four groups: man, beast, creeping things, and the birds of the air.

Many ancient peoples thought of living things as falling into four categories: those that walk the earth on two legs (humans); those that walk on four legs (animals), those that go along the earth or in the water (snakes, fish, insects); those that fly above the earth (birds).

Noah and the Ark, Pages 14–17: Noah sends forth a dove from the ark to see if the waters had dried up from the earth. The dove eats only plants, so if it finds food, Noah will know the waters have receded. The then dove returns with an olive leaf in her mouth. Knowing that olive trees grow at a low elevation, Noah has the sign that "the waters had gone down from off the earth."

The universal use of a dove holding an olive branch in its mouth as a symbol of peace can be traced to this account.

Noah Hears God's Promise, Page 18: A rainbow appears when the sun emerges after a storm, indicating that the storm is over. After the flood that God sent to punish the wickedness of humanity, he sets a rainbow in a cloud as a sign of his covenant with all living things that "the waters shall no more become a flood to destroy all flesh."

The Tower of Babel, Page 19: The city in which the people try to build a tower to heaven is known as Babel, a word that itself sounds like meaningless talk. The word, which is Assyrian, means "gate of God," but it is very close to the Hebrew word, *balal,* which means "to confuse." The term "Babel" has come to indicate a scene of noise and confusion, such as resulted here when God confused the people's language.

Abraham, Pages 20–21: Abraham is considered to be the founder of the Hebrew people. Two groups that are currently in conflict in the Middle East regard him as a common ancestor: the Jews are descended from him through his son Isaac, and the Arabs are descended from him through Ishmael, his son by Hagar, the servant of Sarah.

Abraham and Sarah, Page 22: Though Abraham had been promised the land of Canaan by the Lord, he is now very old. Up to this point, he has no children to whom he can pass on the promised land.

Sodom and Gomorrah, Page 23: The lost cities of Sodom and Gomorrah were on the Jordanian Plain near the Dead Sea. The term *sodomy* derives from the idea that the people of Sodom were sexually depraved. The Lord destroyed the cities because he could not find even ten innocent men within them.

The Test for Abraham, Page 24: The Bible often refers to sacrifices being offered to God as a form of worship or respect, or to atone for sins. The thing sacrificed had to be valuable, and thus was usually in the form of food, typically cereal grains such as wheat, or an animal, such as a sheep or calf. In the case of animal sacrifice, the term "burnt offering" means that the animal was burned on a fire.

Isaac and Rebekah, Pages 26–27: Although most marriages were negotiated by the parents, the final arrangements required the consent of the prospective bride. Even though Rebekah's father and brother have agreed to give her in marriage to Isaac, Rebekah's consent is also needed.

It was a sign of respect for both men and women to dismount at the approach of a person of importance, and for a woman to appear veiled. When Rebekah sees a man approaching, she gets down from the camel. And when the servant tells her it is his master, Rebekah covers her face with her veil. (It was not necessary for her to be veiled before the servant.)

Jacob and Esau, Pages 28–30: It was the right of the firstborn, at his father's death, to become the head of the family and receive the largest share of the property, which in Deuteronomy is fixed as a "double portion." Jacob's superiority over Esau, which symbolizes the superiority of Israel over Edom, is thought to have been brought about because of Esau's willingness to give up his birthright to Jacob merely in return for some food.

The blessing that Jacob receives by deceiving Isaac is God's blessing, which brings with it good fortune for the person receiving it and all associated with him. In this case, even Laban prospers under Jacob's blessing.

Rachel and Leah, Pages 32–33: Leah is brought to Jacob heavily veiled, probably with a long mantle with which her whole body could be wrapped. In the dark, after the celebration of the wedding feast, it is not unlikely that Jacob could mistake Leah for Rachel. This deception by Laban may be regarded as divine retribution for Jacob's earlier deception of his father.

At this time it was possible for a man to marry one woman and then later to marry the woman's sister, as Jacob does in this case with Leah and Rachel. However, after the giving of the Law at Sinai, the marrying of two sisters was forbidden.

Jacob and the Angel, Page 35: The Jewish dietary custom of not eating the "sinew of the hip" stems from the strained thigh that Jacob receives here as he wrestles with the angel. The angel then gives Jacob the name "Israel," which in this sense means "he who perseveres with God."

The Coat of Many Colors, Pages 36–39: Joseph's special coat was probably a long robe with full, wide sleeves, which differed from the knee-length ordinary sleeveless tunic that most people wore. Often tribal chiefs wore such robes woven in many colors as an insignia of their rulership. In giving Joseph such a coat, Jacob marked him as the leader of the tribes after Jacob's death.

Pharaoh's Dreams, Pages 40–41: Isolated as a prisoner in a foreign land, Joseph is still able to win a special place in the court of the ruler by his ability to interpret dreams. Many years later in another country, Daniel is able to do the same thing in the court of King Nebuchadnezzar and later also in the court of his son King Belshazzar (see pages 140–145).

Joseph and His Brothers, Pages 42–43: During the famine, Joseph's brothers "came and bowed down to him with their faces to the ground." Although they were unaware of it, they were fulfilling the prediction of Joseph's dream of the bundles of grain (page 36).

Benjamin in Egypt, Pages 44–45: Joseph is described here as weeping on three different occasions: first as he sees his brother Benjamin, then when he reveals to his brothers who he really is, and finally when he reunites with his father Jacob.

The Birth of Moses, Pages 46–47: God's striking down of the firstborn of both man and beasts in the land of Egypt (Exodus 11:5) can be seen as a just retribution for the Pharaoh's order to slay all the male babies of the Israelites.

Moses, Pages 48–51: Since Moses went on to speak many times as the leader of his people, it is ironic that here he resists taking on this role and thus is provided with a spokesman, his brother Aaron.

Pharaoh and the Israelites, Pages 52–53: In ancient Egypt, bricks were used for paving as well as for buildings. Chopped straw and refuse were mixed with the clay in order to increase its consistency. Archaeologists have excavated some bricks in Egypt made with good straw, some with roots and bits of straw, and some with no straw at all.

The Plagues of Egypt, Pages 54–55: Pharaoh is impressed with the power of God only when a crisis exists and he needs help. Each time a plague comes upon the Egyptians, he promises to let the Israelites go if the Lord will stop the plague. But after the plague has been lifted, Pharaoh always goes back on his promise.

Passover, Pages 56–57: The lamb was the most common offering in Jewish sacrifices, both to offer thanks and to remove sin. When Abraham is about to sacrifice his son, God provides a ram to replace Isaac.

The Parting of the Sea, Page 58: The Hebrew name for the sea that the Israelites crossed is "the Sea of Reeds" or "Reed Sea." It is in the Greek version of the Old Testament that it is first called "the Red Sea." Its exact location is not known, but it may be the northern part of the present Red Sea.

In the Wilderness, Pages 60–61: Large flocks of quail still migrate across the Sinai Peninsula between Arabia and Europe. Often these birds can be easily captured when, exhausted by their long flight, they roost on the ground or in low bushes.

The Ten Commandments, Pages 62–64: In the Sixth Commandment, the word "kill" is also translated as "murder."

The Tabernacle, Page 65: Pure olive oil was used for all sacred purposes. The olives were gently pounded in a mortar, and the first drops were considered to be of the purest quality. Because no sunlight fell into the sanctuary, the lamp had to be kept burning at all times.

The Golden Calf, Pages 66–68: The Hebrew word actually refers to a "young bull" rather than a calf. The bull was a common religious symbol to the Egyptians and among many Semitic tribes, representing energy and strength. In recent years archaeologists have found such idols in the Middle East. Although traditional depictions of this scene usually show the idol as larger than life size, the actual examples that have been have found are much smaller, a fact that is reflected in our painting on pp. 66–67.

The Journey to Canaan, Pages 71–72: The number forty has special significance in the Bible. Here the Israelites explore the land for forty days, and the Lord then condemns them to wander in the desert for forty years, one year for each of these days. Also, the Great Flood remains on the earth for forty days, and Moses spends forty days on the mountain.

The Death of Moses, Page 73: Moses led the Israelites out of slavery, and God showed him the promised land of Canaan from a mountain. But Moses did not go into the land; he died first.

The Walls of Jericho, Pages 74–75: At the beginning of the Israelites' flight from Egypt, God parted the waters of the sea to allow them to cross safely. In this episode, the waters of the Jordan River dry up and the Israelites cross on dry ground into the Promised Land.

Gideon's Trumpet, Pages 76–77: The trumpet or horn of the Old Testament was not a musical instrument, but was used to make a loud sound. It was usually made of the curved horn of a cow or ram, and was used primarily to give signals in war or to announce important events. The horn, called a *shofar*, is still used by Jews at solemn festivals.

Samson, Pages 79–82: The Nazirites were a group devoted to the Lord by a special vow. According to this vow, it was forbidden for them to drink alcohol, cut their hair, touch or go near a dead body, or eat unclean food. This vow was originally a lifelong obligation, and it was considered a sin against God to tempt a Nazirite to break it.

Ruth and Naomi, Pages 84–86: When Boaz orders his men to leave some grain in the field for Ruth, he is following a law from Leviticus, which states that the corners of the field should not be harvested and grain that falls to the ground should not be gathered but should be left "for the poor and the strangers." Boaz goes even further by telling the men to "let some fall on purpose."

Samuel Is Called, Pages 87–88: It was believed that God is responsible for the ability of a woman to have a successful pregnancy and bear a child. Thus a woman who was barren (unable to have children) would be regarded as one who is without divine approval, and the woman so affected felt disgrace in the eyes of the world. Sarah, Hannah, and Elizabeth were all barren until they were very old, when God granted them sons.

Saul and Samuel, Pages 89–91: The Amalekites roamed the region from the boundary of Judah to the Sinai peninsula and were probably people the Israelites found already in the land. During the Exodus from Egypt, the Amalekites harassed the Israelites and fought to prevent them from entering the region. The Lord then had Moses write that "I will utterly blot out the remembrance of Amalek from under heaven." (Exodus 17:14)

The Shepherd Boy, Pages 92–93: The position of armor-bearer was held by a young man who carried the shield, breastplate, a supply of darts, and other weapons for his chief. He also delivered the death blow to those his chief struck down.

David and Goliath, Pages 94–96: The Philistine warrior Goliath is a giant, descended from the race of giants mentioned in Genesis, who were said to have been on the earth in those early times (see p. 13). Archaeologists have excavated human skeletons of about the same height as Goliath.

Saul's Jealousy, Pages 98–99: Saul's periods of black melancholy and flashes of homicidal violence were attributed to an evil spirit from God; today he might be diagnosed as having a form of mental illness.

David and Jonathan, Pages 100–101: Jonathan goes to eat with his father Saul at the time of the new moon. The moon, along with the sun, was considered a fertilizing power, as well as a source of light. The appearance of the new moon was an occasion for celebration, often including the blowing of trumpets and an offering of sacrifices.

The Witch of Endor, Pages 102–103: A spirit, usually an underground spirit, was thought to be able to dwell in a human being. Such spirits were supposed to have the power of calling up and consulting the dead. Saul goes to consult the witch even though his own policy explicitly forbids this.

David Becomes King, Pages 104–105: The high places that David mentions were his mountain strongholds, not the high places of worship.

David and Bathsheba, Pages 106–107: The Hittites were the earliest known inhabitants of what is now Turkey. They were a leading military and cultural power in the Middle East for several hundred years. The few who still remained in the time of David joined with the Israelites, taking Hebrew names, such as Uriah.

What David did was wrong, even though he was the king. And it is clear that David is aware of this, for when the prophet Nathan rebukes him, David replies, "I have sinned against the Lord."

David and Absalom, Pages 108–109: David's leniency with his sons had a significant impact on the affairs of Israel. Amnon was not punished by David for the rape of his sister, Tamar, though he should have been exiled. Absalom was allowed to return from exile, unpunished for the murder of his brother. The deaths of Amnon and Absalom moved Solomon closer to becoming king, though he was originally far down the line of succession.

The Death of David, Page 110: It was not a strict practice that the oldest son had to become king on the death of his father. Thus there is no objection when Solomon ascends to the throne in place of Adonijah, the eldest of David's remaining sons.

Solomon's Dream, Page 111: This dream has been linked to the practice of sleeping in a sacred place in order to receive a communication from the Lord, since Gibeon was a great high place to which Solomon went to offer sacrifice. There is no indication, however, that he was intentionally seeking this communication. In fact, the Lord is pleased that Solomon does not ask for riches and honor for himself, and so grants him these things.

King Solomon's Wisdom, Pages 112–113: The true mother would rather see her child given to another woman than have the child be killed. The false mother, whose own child was already dead, was willing to let this child die. King Solomon's decision parallels the Lord's action with respect to Solomon: he received riches and honor from the Lord specifically because he did not ask for them; here the woman who would give up the child is the one who receives it.

Solomon Builds a Temple, Page 115: The original Temple of Jerusalem that was built by Solomon was later destroyed by the Babylonians under King Nebuchadnezzar, in about 586 B.C. The Temple was then rebuilt and destroyed several other times, most recently by the Romans in 70 A.D. Today only remnants of the Temple of Herod the Great remain standing, most notably the Western Wall, which is still a major religious site. It is also known as the Wailing Wall because of the prayers said there to mourn the destruction of the Temple.

The Queen of Sheba, Pages 116–117: There were no major military operations in King Solomon's reign, but he put himself in a position of strength by establishing a strong standing army. Estimates as to the size of Solomon's army vary, but he probably had about 1,400 chariots, 4,000 stables for chariot horses, and some 12,000 horses.

A Divided Kingdom, Pages 118–119: The many marriages of King Solomon were probably for political reasons, to strengthen ties with foreign powers. However, even though kings and persons of wealth or authority were permitted to have multiple wives, the Biblical accounts of men who did this, such as Solomon, Jacob, and David, seem to illustrate the troubles inherent in this practice.

The Prophet Elijah, Pages 120–121: There is evidence that the worship of Baal existed in ancinet Palestine as early as 1800 B.C. Although many minor local gods bore the name, Baal was specifically the name of the Amorite god of winter rain and storm. Sculptures show him as a warrior-god, who carried a thunderbolt-spear and a mace. His association with fertility was expressed by the bull, whose horns he wore on his helmet.

The Return to Jerusalem, Page 122: The foreign rulers of Jerusalem were usually very hostile toward the Jewish religion and Jewish holy places. Two notable exceptions to this harsh policy were the Persian kings Cyrus the Great and Darius the Great (Darius I). After the Chaldeans (Babylonians) had destroyed Jerusalem in about 586 B.C., Cyrus in turn conquered Babylonia in 538 B.C. His policy of restoring the Jewish state was later continued by Darius, who ruled from 522 to 486 B.C.

Esther, Pages 124–125: The name Ahasuerus is a Hebrew version of Xerxes, the Persian name by which this ruler is more often known historically.

Mordecai and Haman, Pages 126–127: The saving of the Jews from Haman is still celebrated on the 14th and 15th of the month of Adar (which falls in either February or March). It is called the Feast of Purim, which means "lots," because of the lot that Haman cast to determine the date for the destruction of the Jews.

Job, Pages 128–131: The name *Satan* is a Hebrew word. "The Satan" means "the accuser" or "the adversary." In the early passages of the Old Testament, there is no reference to a distinct being called Satan. It is not until the story of Job that Satan appears as a being whose function is to search out human sin. However, even here he does not have the power to act without the permission of God and thus is not an independent evil force.

Isaiah, Pages 138–139: The word "virgin" (Authorized Version, New International Version) is rendered as "young woman" in the Revised Standard Version. The Hebrew word is *almah,* the feminine form of *elem,* "young man."

The wolf of ancient Palestine was larger and lighter in color than the wolf of northern Europe. It is rarely seen today and seldom travels in packs, although it is often found in pairs. The wolf was one of the greatest terrors of the shepherd, ravaging the flocks at night. Lions have been extinct in Palestine since the Crusades, but they must have been common there at one time. Their terrifying roar has been compared to the voice of God, and the nation of Israel has been likened to the lion.

King Nebuchadnezzar, Page 140: Visions and dreams were believed to reveal the future. People such as Daniel, who could understand and explain these visions and dreams, were highly regarded by kings, who consulted with them before making important decisions about the rule of the kingdom.

Handwriting on the Wall, Pages 141–143: The dye used to provide the color scarlet was derived from the cochineal insect, which attaches itself to leaves and twigs. In Hebrew, it is called "the scarlet worm." Clothing of scarlet was a mark of distinction and prosperity for those wearing it.

Daniel in the Lion's Den, Pages 144–145: During the time of the Babylonian exile, Jerusalem assumed great importance in the religious life of the people. It was the place toward which their prayers were offered. So the offense here is not only that Daniel prays in violation of the king's edict, but also that his prayers are directed toward Jerusalem.

Jonah and the Whale, Pages 146–149: The fish that swallowed Jonah is usually considered to be a whale, in spite of the phrase "a great fish." Scientifically speaking, a whale is a mammal rather than a fish, but in earlier times whales were described as "great fish." The distinction between fish and sea mammals is a modern conception.

BIBLE DICTIONARY

This Bible Dictionary provides a selected list of words from *The Illustrated Children's Old Testament*. It explains all the words in the book that could be difficult for a modern reader to understand.

The Dictionary includes three kinds of words. First, it has words that are no longer in common use, such as *thou*, which is an older word meaning "you." Second, it has words that are still well-known today, but that have a different meaning in the Old Testament, such as *company*, which used to mean a large group of people rather than a business. Third, it has words that are still used today on some occasions, but that are not part of our everyday language, such as *decree, rebuke,* or *righteous.*

abomination something that is very bad, wrong, or hateful.

acacia a type of tree whose hard wood is used for building.

adultery sex between a married man and someone who is not his wife, or between a married woman and someone who is not her husband.

adversity a time of trouble or difficulty; a problem that must be overcome.

almighty having complete or unlimited power. "Almighty God" means "all-powerful God."

altar 1. a raised platform or table where sacrifices or offerings to God or a god are made. **2.** a table or stand used as a sacred place in a religious ceremony.

Amen a word meaning "That is right" or "Let it be so," which is often said at the end of a prayer to agree with what has been said.

angel a messenger of God; a spiritual being who serves God or is with God.

anguish great pain or suffering; deep sorrow.

anoint 1. to rub or sprinkle a special kind of oil on a person's body. **2.** to do this as a sign that the person has taken on some high office or special position.

anointest an older word for *anoints.* "Thou anointest" means "you anoint" (rub with oil).

ark the large ship built by Noah to save his family and pairs of every different kind of animal during the great flood.

ark of the covenant a special box that was built to hold the two stone tablets on which the Ten Commandments were written.

armor a metal coat worn into battle by a soldier to protect his body against enemy weapons.

armor-bearer a person, usually a boy or young man, who went along with a soldier to carry his heavy armor to the battlefield.

art an older word for *are.* "Thou art" means "you are."

asp a small, highly poisonous snake. The kind mentioned in the Bible is usually identified as the Egyptian cobra.

ass a long-eared animal related to the horse, used for riding and for carrying or pulling loads; now more often called a *donkey.*

astrologer a person who claims to be able to tell what will happen by studying the stars.

avenge to have revenge against a person; do something to make up for an earlier wrong or injury. Someone who takes revenge against another person is an **avenger.**

babe another word for *baby.*

balance or **balances** an instrument that is used for weighing things; the thing to be weighed is placed on one side and balanced by a certain amount of weight on the other side.

balm 1. a soft oil or ointment spread on the body as a medicine. **2.** anything that helps to ease pain or suffering.

band a large group of people. A "band of angels" means "a large number of angels."

banquet a large and special meal; a feast.

barley a type of grain plant similar to wheat, widely grown for food.

barren 1. not producing crops or fruit. A *barren* field is one in which no useful plants grow. **2.** a word used to describe a woman who cannot have children.

bear 1. to pick up and take along; carry. "Bearing gifts" means "Bringing gifts." **2.** to give birth or life to. "To bear a child" means "to have a child." **3.** to have or give. "To bear the blame" means "to have the blame."

161

"Bear false witness" means "give witness (testify) in a false way."

bear a type of large, heavy wild animal; the kind mentioned in the Bible is the Syrian bear.

beast another word for an animal, especially a wild animal.

becometh an older word for *becomes*.

behold a command or statement meaning, "See this" or "Look, and you will see."

beloved very much loved; greatly loved.

birthright something that a person has the right to receive because of being born into a certain family; an inheritance. In former times, this often meant that the oldest son in a family would get all or most of the father's land when he died.

bless 1. to make holy or sacred. 2. to be *blessed* means to have the favor of God.

boils a disease in which large, painful sores break out on the skin.

bold not afraid; having courage; brave.

bondage the condition of being held as a slave or prisoner; slavery.

bore a past tense form of the verb *bear*. "She bore a son" means "She gave birth to a son."

borne a past tense form of the verb *bear*. "She has borne a son" means "She has given birth to a son."

borrower a person who borrows something from another.

bramble a type of shrub or vine that has sharp thorns.

bread 1. a common food made by baking flour or meal from grain. 2. food in general; any type of food.

breathless out of breath; breathing hard, as from running fast.

brimstone an older name for sulfur, a chemical element that catches fire very easily.

brother 1. a man or boy who has the same parents as some other person. 2. a person who is very close to another in some way, as by being part of the same group.

bulrush a type of plant having tall, very thin stems and growing in or near water.

burden 1. a heavy load to carry. 2. a serious problem or difficulty to deal with.

burnt offering see OFFERING.

bushel a large basket used to hold fruit, grain, or other food crops.

butler a male servant who has charge of the household of a wealthy or powerful person.

captive someone who is held prisoner, especially a prisoner in war. To be held in **captivity** means to be held as a prisoner.

cast 1. to throw. To *cast* something away is to throw it away. 2. to put out. To *cast* a spell is to put a magic spell on someone.

cast lots to gamble by throwing (casting) some kind of object (lot) and betting on how the throw will come out. Throwing dice is a modern form of casting lots.

cattle 1. the common farm animals that produce milk and beef. 2. farm animals in general; any farm animals.

cedar a type of tree known for its fine wood, often used in ancient times for temples and other important buildings.

chamber a room, especially a bedroom or other private room.

chamberlain an officer or high-ranking servant in the household of a king.

champion 1. in modern use, a person or team that wins an important game or contest, such as a sports event. 2. in older use, a man who was the strongest fighter in an army and who fought at the head of the army.

chariot a small two-wheeled cart pulled by one or more horses, formerly used in warfare.

chasten to punish in order to make better; punish in a firm but not cruel way.

child 1. a young person; a son or daughter. 2. a member of a certain tribe or nation, thought of as a son or daughter of the person who began that group. "The children of Israel" means "all the people of Israel," not just the younger people of Israel.

children see CHILD.

clean 1. free from dirt; not dirty. 2. free from a disease, such as leprosy. 3. acceptable to God. A *clean* beast was an animal that was acceptable to be eaten or to be used for sacrifice

cleave to hold or stick tight; cling.

cloven divided or split into parts. Some animals, such as cattle, deer, and sheep, have a *cloven* hoof, meaning that the front of the foot is divided in two.

cockatrice a poisonous snake. The cockatrice was supposed to be so deadly that it could kill something just by looking at it.

coffin a large box in which a dead body is placed for burial.

comely pleasing to look at; pretty or beautiful.

cometh an older word for *comes*. "My help cometh" means "my help comes."

commandment 1. an order or command that must be obeyed or that should be obeyed. 2. one of the Ten Commandments that were given by God to Moses.

company 1. in modern use, a group of people who do business together. 2. in older use, any large group or collection of people or things acting or moving together.

congregation a large group of people gathered together, especially a group gathered to worship God.

contend to act against some enemy or opposing force; struggle against.

counsel advice or guidance given to a person about what to do.

counselor a person who guides others as to what to do.

covenant a serious and lasting agreement to do or not do a certain thing.

covet to want very much to have something that belongs to another person; want to take for one's own.

craftsman a man who is skilled in doing work with his hands.

creature any living being, especially a living thing other than a human.

crimson a strong, deep shade of the color red, like the color of blood.

cubit an ancient measure of length based on the length of the arm, equal to about 18–22 inches.

cud in grass-eating animals such as cattle, a mass of partly-digested food chewed a second time.

cunning very smart and skillful; able to do or learn things quickly.

curse to wish great harm to a person; call on God or a god to bring evil to someone.

cursed under a curse; having had evil or harm come to oneself.

custody the fact of guarding or keeping safe; care or protection.

cymbal one of a pair of round metal plates that are struck together to make a ringing sound.

cypress a tall tree whose wood is often used for building.

dart a small arrow used as a weapon, thrown by hand rather than shot from a bow.

dasheth an older word meaning "throws down hard."

deceiver a person who deceives or tricks another person.

decree 1. an important order issued by a king or other ruler. 2. to give such an order.

deed an action that a person has done; something that is done.

defy to speak out or go against someone in a bold way. Goliath *defied* the army of Israel to send someone out to fight him.

deliver 1. to send to a certain place. 2. in older use, to take away from some harm or evil; save. Daniel was *delivered* (saved) from the danger he faced in the lions' den.

den a place where wild animals live, such as a cave or a hole in the ground.

deny to answer something that has been said by saying that it is not true. A person can deny that something happened, deny that he knows someone, and so on.

descend 1. to go or come down. 2. to be born later as a relative of a certain person who lived earlier. A grandchild is *descended* from his or her grandparents.

descendant a person who is part of a certain family or group, and who is directly related to those who lived earlier in this family or group.

despise to dislike very much; hate.

destruction the fact of being destroyed; complete ruin or disaster.

dominion the power to rule over or to control something.

draw to pull or take something up from a lower place, as in getting water from a river or a well.

dwell to live in a certain place.

elder 1. older. The *elder* son in a family is the older son. 2. one of the older people in a group or tribe. 3. **elders.** a group of older men who have certain authority in a tribe or nation, either by ruling themselves or by advising the ruler.

eldest oldest. The *eldest* daughter in a family is the oldest daughter.

ember a piece of wood in a fire, almost burned away but still glowing with heat.

embrace to put the arms tightly around; hug or hold tightly.

endureth an older word for *endures.* "It endureth forever" means "It endures (lasts) forever."

enraged in a great rage; very angry.

envy a feeling of wanting what someone else has or of being jealous of that person.

everlasting going on for all time; lasting forever.

evermore for all time; forever.

evil very bad or wrong; not done in a good or right way.

exile the fact of being forced out of one's country to live in another country.

face of the earth the surface of the earth; the ground everywhere on earth.

faint to feel *faint* is to be weak and sick, as from being very hungry or very tired.

fair **1.** doing or deciding things in the right way; doing what is right. **2.** good-looking; pretty or beautiful.

faith **1.** a strong belief or trust that something will happen in a certain way, without the need for facts or evidence to prove this. **2.** especially, belief in the power and goodness of God.

false god a being or object that is worshipped as a god but that is not the true God of the Bible.

false witness see WITNESS.

fame the fact of being famous; being well-known to people.

famine a time when food is very scarce and people have little or nothing to eat.

fast to go for a long time without eating anything, by one's own choice rather than because there is no food to eat.

father **1.** a male parent. **2.** a man who is the ancestor of some family, tribe, or nation, especially the person who began that group.

fatling a young calf, pig, or other such animal that is being fed extra food to make it fatter for eating.

feast **1.** a large or special meal with certain kinds of food. **2.** a holiday or celebration that includes such a special meal. The **Feast of Unleavened Bread,** or Passover, is held each year to celebrate the time when the Israelites were led out of slavery in Egypt.

fig a type of small tree that is widely grown for its sweet fruit.

firstborn the oldest child in a family.

flax a plant whose fibers are used to make thread for clothing.

fled a past tense form of the verb *flee.* "He fled" means "He ran away."

flee to go away from some danger; run away.

flesh **1.** the soft part of the body between the skin and the bones. **2.** the body of an animal eaten as food; meat. **3.** the physical part of a person; the body as opposed to the spirit or soul. **4.** people in general; human beings.

flock a group of sheep or other animals moving or kept together.

follower a person who goes along with another and does what that person says; someone who obeys or believes in another person.

forbid to make a rule or law against something; not allow something to be done. Something that is not allowed in this way is **forbidden.**

forgive to accept that another person has done wrong and agree not to punish or hate the person for it.

forgiveness the act of forgiving; saying that a person who has done wrong will not be punished for it.

forsake to give up something and go away from it; leave behind or abandon.

forth out of or away from. To **go forth** means to go out from some place to another place. To **bring forth** something means to bring it out from inside, such as a child that is born from its mother's body, or plants that come up from the ground.

fountain a large stream or flow of water coming up from the earth.

fowl a bird or birds; any kind of bird.

frankincense a sweet-smelling substance that comes from certain trees, used as a perfume and in religious ceremonies.

fro short for *from.* See TO AND FRO.

fruit **1.** a part of certain plants eaten as a sweet food. Apples, peaches, and pears are fruit. **2.** any plant part that can be eaten as food.

fruitful **1.** having or giving much fruit. **2.** having many children.

fugitive a person who tries to get away from danger or from some punishment.

gallows a stand or platform used to execute people by hanging.

generation **1.** one stage in the life of a family. A mother and father, their children, and their grandchildren are three generations. **2.** the time between the birth of one generation and the next, thought of as a period of about thirty years.

gird **1.** to put a belt or band around the waist; tie up one's clothes with a belt. **2.** to get ready for some effort or struggle, as if getting dressed for a battle.

glorify to bring or give glory to someone.

glory high honor, praise, or standing; the fact of being great.

grace **1.** a feeling of what is good and right to do; being good and pure. **2.** the giving of love and forgiveness by God.

gracious filled with or showing grace; giving love and forgiveness.

grain the seed or small fruit of a plant eaten as food, especially a plant such as wheat, corn, or barley.

graven carved or engraved. A **graven image** is a carved statue or figure. In early times people who did not worship God would sometimes worship a graven image instead, as of an animal or a manlike being.

great **1.** very, very good; excellent or outstanding. **2.** very large in some way.

164

grief great sadness about something bad that has happened; being very sad.

grudge a feeling that a person holds for a long time of wanting to act against someone who has harmed him or her in the past.

hail rain that falls in a frozen form, like small balls of ice.

hail a word that is used to give honor to a person. "Hail" means "I praise you" or "I salute you."

harden to make harder. The expression "His heart was hardened" means "He was cold and stubborn" or "He had no feelings."

hare a small animal that is closely related to a rabbit, but is larger and has longer ears.

harp a musical instrument with long strings stretched tight in a wooden frame.

harvest the time of the year when food plants are cut or picked so that the part that is to be eaten is taken off.

hast an older word for *have*. "Thou hast" means "you have."

haste or **hasten** to move fast; go quickly.

hath an older word for *has*. "The thing that hath been" means "the thing that has been."

haughty too proud of what one has or has done; thinking oneself to be better than others.

heart 1. the body part that sends blood to the rest of the body. 2. this part thought of as the center of a person's feelings.

heathen a person who does not worship God; someone who worships false gods.

heaven 1. the place of God and the angels; the kingdom beyond the universe ruled over by God. 2. **the heavens.** the skies above the earth, where the sun, moon, planets, and stars are.

heavenly coming from or having to do with heaven. Angels are *heavenly* beings.

heavens see HEAVEN.

herdsman a man who takes care of a herd of animals in the field.

high priest the religious leader of the Jewish people in Biblical times.

holy 1. belonging to or coming from God; sacred. 2. very good and pure; without sin.

hoof the foot of certain grass-eating animals, such as a horse or cow.

horn 1. a sharp part sticking out from the head of some animals, such as cattle. 2. this part of an animal, dried and hollowed out and used to make a loud sound by blowing into it.

host 1. a person who entertains or receives other people as guests. 2. a large number of

people or things; a great many. A *host* of angels or a *heavenly host* is a great number of angels.

hosts great numbers. See HOST.

house 1. any building where people live, especially the building a single family lives in. 2. a family, including its relatives who lived in the past. The *house* of David is a name for people who are directly related to King David.

humble 1. not too proud; not having too high an opinion of oneself. 2. to make a person humble; take away pride.

hymn a song to praise or give honor to God; a holy song.

image a picture or figure that is meant to look like something or to represent it in some way.

incense a substance from certain plants that has a sweet smell when it is burned. The burning of incense can be a part of a religious ceremony.

inherit 1. to get land, money, or property owned by another person, especially one's parent, when that person dies. 2. to come to be the owner of something; come to have.

inn a place for travelers to stay while on a journey.

innkeeper a person who owns or is in charge of an inn.

integrity a sense of being honest and doing the right thing; good character and good actions.

interpret 1. to explain the meaning of words from another language. 2. to explain the meaning of something that seems hard to understand, such as a dream or some unusual sign or writing. An **interpreter** is someone who explains things in this way.

issue to come out; be given out.

jealous 1. wanting something that another person has; feeling that someone else is better off than yourself and disliking the person for it. 2. expecting or demanding that someone be true or loyal to you.

judge 1. a person who has charge of a court of law. 2. a leader who decides matters of law and also has other authority; the early Israelites were ruled by judges rather than kings. 3. anyone who considers the actions of others and decides if they are right or wrong. 4. to decide in this way.

judgment the act or fact of judging someone.

just deciding or judging something in the right way; fair and honest.

keep 1. to have something and hold onto it. 2. to go along with; obey. To *keep* a commandment means to obey it and do what it says.

165

keeper 1. a person who keeps or watches over animals, such as a flock of sheep. 2. someone who watches over and takes care of a person.

keepeth an older word for *keeps*. "He keepeth thee safe" means "he keeps you safe."

kid a small goat or baby goat.

kingdom the place ruled over by a king.

labor to do work, especially hard outdoor work.

laborer a person who works; a worker.

lamp in older use, a small container giving off light from the burning of oil.

land 1. the dry part of the earth, the area that is not ocean or sky. 2. a certain area of the earth where a group of people live, and that they think of as their own.

leadeth an older word for *leads*. "He leadeth me" means "He leads me." "Leadeth not" means "does not lead."

leek a type of plant that is somewhat like an onion, often used in soups and as a flavoring.

lend to give money to someone else with the promise that it will be paid back later.

lender a person who lends money to someone else.

lest an older word meaning "so that it will not happen." "Lest he escape" means "so that he will not escape."

let 1. to permit something to happen; allow something. 2. to cause to happen; bring about. "Let your light shine" means "make your light shine."

lice tiny insects that live in the hair or on the skin of animals, eating by sucking blood from the animal.

lighten to make lighter; make less heavy.

likeness 1. a picture or object that looks just like a person or animal. 2. something that is meant to look or be just like another thing.

loaves more than one loaf of bread.

locust a type of insect, a large grasshopper. Since ancient times, they have been known to travel over the earth in swarms of millions and millions of insects, eating all the plants in their way and causing great damage.

lots see CAST LOTS.

madest an older word for *made*. "Thou madest" means "you made."

magician 1. a person who can do tricks that do not seem possible, such as making something suddenly appear or disappear. 2. in older use, a person who claimed to have special powers to make strange things happen or to control the way people acted.

maiden a young woman, especially one who has not been married.

maketh an older word for *makes*. "He maketh me" means "he makes me."

man 1. a male adult person. 2. any person. "No man knows the place of his grave" means "no person knows the place of his grave; no one knows." 3. people in general. "The Lord does not see as man sees" means "as people see; as we see."

manna 1. a food that suddenly came to the Israelites by a miracle when they were starving in the wilderness. 2. any food or other thing that is suddenly supplied at a time when it is badly needed.

master a person who is in charge of a household or farm; someone who gives orders to a servant or slave.

men 1. more than one man; male people. 2. people in general, both male and female. "Let all men fear God" means "Let all people fear God."

mene, mene, tekel, upharsin the four words that appear on the wall in the Book of Daniel as a judgment of King Belshazzar; they are often translated as "numbered, numbered, weighed, divided," with the idea of judging something by counting and weighing it.

merchant a person who owns a business or who buys and sell things.

merciful having or showing the quality of mercy; kind and forgiving toward others.

mercy the treating of other people in a gentle rather than a cruel way; being kind to someone who is under one's power. It is an act of mercy to forgive a person for doing wrong rather than to severely punish that person.

midst the central part or place; the middle. "In the midst of" means "in the middle of."

might great power or strength; force.

might another form of the word "may," referring to something that could happen.

mightest an older word meaning "might." "Thou mightest" means "you might."

mighty having great power or strength; having might.

milk and honey an expression used to stand for a rich land that is filled with food.

mindful knowing about or aware of. To be *mindful* of something is to keep it in mind.

mine belonging to the person who is speaking. In older use, "I will lift up mine eyes" means "I will lift up my eyes."

miracle 1. something very unusual that cannot be explained in an ordinary way; an amazing thing that seems to go against the laws of nature. 2. especially, actions of this kind done or caused by God.

mirth the act of laughing; laughter.

mock to make fun of someone in a cruel way; tease and laugh at someone to hurt the person.

mourn to feel or show sadness because someone has died, especially a close family member.

multiply 1. to become much larger in number. **2.** to have many children or offspring.

multitude a very large number of things or people; very many.

myrrh a sweet-smelling substance that comes from certain trees, used as a perfume and in religious ceremonies.

nard a shorter name for **spikenard,** a very expensive perfume that was brought from Asia.

nation 1. a large area of land having certain definite borders and a single government; a country. **2.** in older use, a large group of people thought of as related to each other or somehow joined together.

neighbor 1. a person who lives next door to or near someone. **2.** in older use, any person who is near to or has dealings with another.

noble a person who is born into a rich or powerful family; a person who has a high rank in society.

nostrils the openings of the nose through which air passes.

notorious well-known for doing something bad.

now 1. at the present time; at this time. **2.** it is so; certainly. "Now Boaz was a rich man" means "It is true that Boaz was a rich man." **3.** at the time spoken about; at that time. "Now Laban had two daughters" means "At that time Laban had two daughters."

nurse 1. a woman who takes care of sick people. **2.** of a mother, to give milk from the breast to her baby. **3.** in older times, a woman who was hired to give milk to another woman's baby.

odor a smell, especially a strong, powerful smell.

offer 1. to present something to be received by another. **2.** to give up something valuable as a sign of worship of God.

offering something that is presented to God or a god; food or other objects of value given as a sign of worship. A burnt offering was something that was specially burned as a gift to God.

oil 1. in modern use, another name for petroleum, a product found underground that is used to produce gasoline and other fuels. **2.** any of various animal, vegetable, or mineral products that do not mix easily with water and that generally are greasy and able to burn easily. In earlier times, lamps gave off light by the burning of certain types of oil rather than by means of electricity. **3.** a special type of oil used to rub on the body for healing purposes or as part of a ceremony.

ointment a substance put on the skin for healing purposes.

olive a tree that is widely grown in warm climates for its fruit, which is eaten and is also used to make oil.

ordain 1. to name a person as a priest or other religious leader by holding a special ceremony. **2.** to order or cause something to happen.

overlay to put over; put one layer on top of another. Something that is **overlaid** with gold has a layer of gold on top of it.

overpower to have more power than another; defeat or take over another by being stronger.

overshadow 1. to come over as a shadow; cast a shadow upon. **2.** to do better or be more important than another; be more noticed than another.

ox one animal of the type known as *oxen*. See OXEN.

oxen 1. another name for cattle, the common farm animals used for milk and food. **2.** especially, large male animals of this type used for food or to pull heavy loads.

pardon to forgive someone for a crime or wrong and end the person's punishment for it.

partial 1. not total or complete; being a part. **2.** favoring one person or side over another, especially in an unfair way.

pass an older word meaning "to happen." "It came to pass that" means "It happened that."

passeth an older word meaning "passes."

Passover or **passover** a Jewish holiday to celebrate the time when God freed the Israelites from slavery in Egypt.

pasture a field in which grass grows for farm animals to eat.

perish to stop being alive; die.

persecute 1. to charge someone unfairly with a crime; try to punish an innocent person. **2.** to punish someone unfairly or too harshly, especially because of who the person is or what he or she believes.

Pharaoh the title of the early kings of Egypt.

Philistines a group of people who often fought wars against the Israelites. The term *Philistine* is used today to describe someone

as being narrow-minded, with no appreciation for art and culture.

pillar a high tower or column, straight and tall like a tree.

pit a large, deep hole.

pity a feeling of being sorry for someone else who is suffering or in trouble.

plague a dangerous disease that can spread very quickly from one person to another. In past times a plague could sweep through an entire country and kill thousands of people.

plain **1.** a large, flat area of land. **2.** of ground, flat and smooth.

plot a secret plan made to hurt someone or to carry out some wrong action.

plow to break up hard ground for farming, so that plants will grow better.

plowshare the blade of a **plow**, a tool used in farming to break up hard ground for planting.

pluck to pull something out with a quick, hard motion.

plump fat in a healthy or attractive way.

pollute **1.** to cause air or water to become dirty with waste matter. **2.** to harm or ruin something by wrongdoing.

pomegranate a type of reddish fruit with many seeds.

pool in older use, any small pond or other such natural collection of water.

pray **1.** to communicate with God; speak to God in some way. **2.** to ask that something be done; make a request.

prayer the act of praying; communicating with God.

preach to speak in public about God and religion; give a speech or talk on God.

preparest an older word meaning "to prepare." "Thou preparest" means "you prepare" (you make ready).

presence the fact of being with someone, especially someone important. To be in the *presence* of the king means to be with the king.

priest a person who is specially chosen or trained to perform certain religious acts; a religious leader.

proclaim to state publicly that something is true; make an official statement. A statement of this kind is a **proclamation**.

profit **1.** money that is made from some kind of business dealing. **2.** any kind of benefit or advantage. **3.** to make a profit; gain money or some other benefit.

prophecy a statement about something that will come true in the future; a statement saying what the future will bring.

prophet **1.** a person who tells about things that will happen in the future. **2.** a person who brings a message from God; someone who speaks for God. **3.** a person chosen or inspired by God to be a leader.

proverb a short and usually simple saying that contains an important truth, and that can be used as a guide for good living.

pruning hook a pole with a long blade at one end, used to cut branches from trees.

psalm a song or poem in praise of God; a song to or about God.

publish **1.** to make a book available for the public to read. **2.** in older use, to make something public; make known to people.

pure **1.** not mixed with any other thing; free from anything that spoils or ruins. **2.** honest and good; not evil in any way.

pursue to run or go after; chase.

quail a type of small game bird that feeds along the ground.

rabbi **1.** in modern use, a Jewish religious leader; a person who has carefully studied Jewish religious law and who is qualified to be the leader of a Jewish congregation. **2.** in older use, a teacher of Jewish religious law.

ram an adult male sheep.

raven a large black bird of the crow family.

raze to tear down or knock down a building; completely destroy a building.

realm the land or country that is ruled by a king; a kingdom.

reap to cut or pick plants for food; harvest a food crop, especially a grain crop such as wheat or barley.

reaper someone who reaps; a person who harvests grain or other food crops.

rebel **1.** to rise up and fight against a leader or government; fight to be free of one's ruler. **2.** a person who fights in this way.

rebellion the act of fighting against one's government or ruler; fighting for freedom from a ruler.

rebellious wanting or trying to rebel; fighting against one's ruler.

rebuke to punish or criticize someone for wrongdoing.

refrain to keep from doing something; not do something.

reign **1.** to rule as a king; rule over a kingdom. **2.** the time during which a king rules.

reigneth an older word for *reigns*. "He reigneth" means "he reigns" (he rules).

reject to turn away from; not accept.

rejoice to be very happy about something that has happened; give great thanks.

rend to tear something apart, especially a piece of clothing; tear into pieces.

repent to feel truly sorry for something one has done wrong and decide not to do it again; change away from a bad way of acting.

restore to bring something back to the way it was before; return to a state of health or a better condition.

restoreth an older word for *restores*. "He restoreth" means "he restores."

retreat to run or move away from the enemy during battle; go back from the enemy.

revenge a wrong or harm done by someone to another person, in return for something that the other person has done earlier to him or her.

rewardeth an older word for *rewards*. "He rewardeth" means "he rewards."

righteous knowing what is right to do and acting in this way; good, honest, and fair.

righteousness the fact of being righteous; being good, honest, and fair.

rod 1. a long, thin piece of wood; a stick. 2. such a stick used to beat someone as a punishment.

royal having to do with a king; done by or belonging to a king.

runneth an older word for *runs*. "Runneth over" means "runs over" (overflows).

sabbath or **Sabbath** the seventh day of the week; a day off from work, set aside to rest and worship God.

sacrifice 1. to give something valuable to God as a sign of respect or worship, or as a way of making up for wrongdoing. The Israelites *sacrificed* farm animals such as young sheep or goats, and also bundles of newly-harvested grain. 2. the thing that is offered up to God in this way.

saith an older word for *says*. "Saith the Lord" means "the Lord says."

sanctuary a building or part of a building that is set aside for worship of God; a holy place.

save 1. to hold on to something and keep it for later use. 2. to rescue someone from danger. 3. to keep someone from sin and the punishments of sin.

scarlet a very bright red color.

scepter a special decorated rod or stick held or carried by a king or other ruler as a sign of royal power.

scorn 1. to act as if someone is not worth respect or attention; ignore or look down on a person. 2. the feeling that someone is unimportant and not worthy of respect.

scribe 1. a person whose job is writing things down. In earlier times before printing machines were invented, scribes made copies of books by hand. 2. in the ancient Jewish religion, a person who studied religious law and made copies of holy writings.

scripture 1. a book of holy writing; a book about God. 2. see SCRIPTURE.

Scripture or **Scriptures** the writings of the Bible.

sea 1. a large body of salt water; an ocean. 2. a large body of fresh water, such as the Sea of Galilee.

serpent a snake, especially a poisonous snake.

servant 1. a person who lives in the house of another and is paid by that person to do housework, such as cooking or washing. 2. any person who serves another.

shall another word for *will*. "You shall make it in this way" means "you will make it this way" or "you should make it this way."

shalt an older word for *shall*. "Thou shalt not steal" means "you shall not steal."

sheaves large pieces of grain or other plants that have been gathered together in a bundle.

shekel 1. a small unit of weight used in ancient times; one pound is about 30 shekels. 2. a gold or silver coin having the weight of one shekel.

shepherd a person who takes care of a flock of sheep.

shield a large, heavy piece of wood or metal. In ancient times warriors held up shields as they fought in battle to protect themselves against enemy arrows, swords, and so on.

shield-bearer a person who carried a warrior's shield to the battlefield.

sickly not in good health; sick or likely to become sick.

sin something that it is very wrong to do; something that is against the laws of God or that does not follow the word of God.

sinful filled with sin; doing wrong against the laws of God.

sinner a person who sins; someone who breaks the laws of God.

slain an older word meaning "killed."

slaughter the killing of a great many; the death of many people or animals at one time.

slave a person who is held prisoner by another and forced to work for that person without any pay. In ancient times, people who lost a war were often forced to become the slaves of the winning side.

slavery the fact of being a slave; being forced to work for another without pay.

slay an older word meaning "to kill."

sling or **slingshot** a simple weapon used to throw a stone through the air at a high speed, made up of a leather strap or string with a pouch at the end to hold the stone. The thrower spins the sling quickly overhead and then lets go of one end to make the stone fly out.

slumber to be in a deep, sound sleep.

smite to hit hard. To *smite* someone means to hit the person with the fist or with a weapon.

soothsayer a person who claims to be able to tell what will happen in the future, by studying such signs as the flight of birds.

sow to plant seeds in the ground or scatter them on the ground, so that plants will grow.

spare **1.** to not use something; be able to do without something. **2.** to not kill or harm a person who is under one's power.

spell a magic power that can cause something strange or amazing to happen.

spice something that is added to food to make it taste better. Pepper, ginger, nutmeg, and cinnamon are spices.

spin to draw out and twist fibers to form thread or yarn for making clothing.

spokesman a person who speaks for someone else, especially someone who speaks for a group or for the leader of the group.

stabilized made stable; made so that it will not move off its position or course.

staff a long, thin stick or pole, somewhat like a modern broomstick.

stank an older word meaning "smelled bad."

stature the way a person stands. A person of great *stature* is very tall.

statute a rule or law.

stiff-necked not willing to give in or obey; stubborn.

strike to hit hard; hit with the fist or a weapon.

stud a small knob or head that stands out on the surface of something.

stumbling block an obstacle or block in a person's path that the person might trip over.

suckling a baby, or a pig or other such animal, that is still so young that it feeds by sucking its mother's milk rather than eating solid food.

swear **1.** to say in a very serious way that one will do something or that something is true. **2.** especially, to make a promise to God to do something. **3.** to use bad or foul language; curse.

swine another name for a pig or hog.

swore a past tense form of SWEAR.

synagogue a place of worship for the Jewish religion.

tabernacle a holy place set aside for the worship of God.

tablet a flat, smooth piece of stone, used in early times for writing as paper is used today.

taketh an older word meaning *takes*. "He taketh away" means "he takes away."

talent **1.** in modern use, the ability or skill to do something well. **2.** in ancient times, a heavy unit of weight, or a large unit of money based on this weight.

temple **1.** a building used for the worship of God. **2. Temple.** a special building of this type in Jerusalem. Several different Temples were built at different times in history.

tempt to try to get someone to do a bad thing; influence or persuade a person to do wrong

temptation the fact of being tempted; being influenced to do wrong.

tend to take care of. To *tend* sheep means to take care of them.

test **1.** a set of questions used to find out how much a student has learned. **2.** a difficult task used to find out what a person knows or believes.

testament a statement that something is true or real.

testimony **1.** a statement made by a witness in court as to what he or she knows to be true about the case on trial. **2.** any such statement about what is true.

thankful glad that something happened; giving thanks.

thee an older form of the word *you*. "I have told thee" means "I have told you."

thereof of or from that. "He went to the river and drank the water thereof" means "He went to the river and drank water from it."

therewith with that. "A heavy rain came, and strong winds therewith" means "A heavy rain came, and strong winds with it."

thine an older form of the word *your*. "In thine house" means "in your house."

thou an older form of the word *you*. "Thou has made him" means "you have made him."

thresh to separate grain from the plant on which it grows, so that it can be used for food.

thy an older form of the word *your*. "Thy father and mother" means "your father and mother."

thyself an older form of the word *yourself*. "Do this thyself" means "do this yourself."

to and fro here and there; from one place to another.

170

token 1. a small metal disk used in place of a coin, as in a machine. 2. an object or sign that stands for something.

tomb a building, room, or other place used to bury the dead.

train in older use, a long line of people traveling together on horses, camels, or other animals.

tremble to move quickly back and forth; shake, especially from fear.

tribe a number of people who form a single group under one leader. The members of a tribe all relate their families to one common ancestor. The Levites were a tribe descended from Levi, the son of Jacob.

triumph to win a battle or contest; be the winner.

turtledove a type of dove, a bird known for its soft, cooing song. The phrase "the voice of the *turtle*" in the Song of Songs refers to the singing of this bird.

unclean 1. not clean; dirty. 2. not acceptable to God; against the rules of God. Jewish law has declared certain foods to be unclean, such as pork or shellfish.

unleavened bread a special kind of bread that does not rise when it is baked and looks like a flat, thin cracker.

unto an older word for *to*. "Do unto others" means "do to others."

upright 1. standing straight up; vertical. 2. having a strong and honest character; being an honorable person.

utter to say something; speak out loud.

vain 1. having no value or purpose; worthless or empty. 2. **in vain**. for no reason or for the wrong reason. "To take the Lord's name in vain" means to use the name of God in the wrong way, as in cursing someone.

vanities things that have no effect or value; useless things.

vanity something that has no value or purpose; an action that does not do anything useful.

venison 1. in modern use, the meat of a deer. 2. in older use, the meat of any wild animal.

vessel 1. a boat or ship. 2. a cup or glass used to drink from.

vineyard a place where grape vines are grown, especially for making wine.

virgin a woman who has never had sex with a man.

vision 1. the power to see, or a thing that a person sees. 2. something a person sees that is not like an ordinary sight, such as the appearance of a dead person or an angel.

visiteth an older word for *visits*. "He visiteth" means "he visits."

void having nothing in it; without anything; empty.

vow 1. a very serious promise to do something. 2. to make such a promise.

wages payment that is made to a person for work done.

want 1. to be interested in getting or doing something. 2. in older use, to be without something one needs or should have.

wanting not having; being without something; lacking.

wayside the side of a road or path.

weaned of a young child or young animal, no longer feeding on its mother's milk, but eating solid food instead.

weep to cry; shed tears. To say that someone *wept* means that the person cried.

wept see WEEP.

whence from what place or from where. "From whence you came" means "from where you came."

wherewith an older word that means "with which."

whirlwind a strong wind that spins around in a circle.

whosoever whoever; whichever person.

wicked very bad; evil.

wickedness the fact of being very bad; being evil.

wilderness a wild place away from where people live; a forest, desert, or wasteland.

wisdom the fact of being wise; knowing a great deal.

wither of a plant, to dry up and die.

witness 1. a person who tells in a court of law what he or she has seen or knows about the case on trial. 2. a person who tells others what he or she has seen or knows. 3. **false witness.** a lie or untrue statement by a person about what he or she knows or has seen.

woe bad luck or evil; a bad thing that happens.

word 1. a sound or group of letters that has a separate meaning. 2. a message or statement from God.

worship to give honor to God; show one's love and respect for God.

wrath great anger; the fact of being very angry about something.

ye an older word for *you*.

yea an older word for *yes*.

yearn to want something very much.

youth 1. the time of being young. 2. a young person, especially a young boy.

Dedication

To Mary Anne and Misha

M. M.

For Grayson, Kieran, Liam, and Erica

J. C.

Manuel C. Molles Jr. is an emeritus Professor of Biology at the University of New Mexico, where he has been a member of the faculty and curator in the Museum of Southwestern Biology since 1975. He teaches ecology and advises graduate students. He received his B.S. from Humboldt State University and his Ph.D. from the Department of Ecology and Evolutionary Biology at the University of Arizona. Seeking to broaden his geographic perspective, he has taught and conducted ecological research in Latin America, the Caribbean, and Europe. He was awarded a Fulbright Research Fellowship to conduct research on river ecology in Portugal, and has held visiting professor appointments in the Department of Zoology at the University of Coimbra, Portugal, in the Laboratory of Hydrology at the Polytechnic University of Madrid, Spain, and at the University of Montana's Flathead Lake Biological Station.

Originally trained as a marine ecologist and fisheries biologist, the author has worked mainly on river and riparian ecology at the University of New Mexico. His research has covered a wide range of ecological levels, including behavioural ecology, population biology, community ecology, ecosystem ecology, biogeography of stream insects, and the influence of a large-scale climate system (El Niño) on the dynamics of southwestern river and riparian ecosystems. His current research concerns the influence of climate change and climatic variability on the dynamics of populations and communities along steep gradients of temperature and moisture in the mountains of the Southwest. Throughout his career, Dr. Molles has attempted to combine research, teaching, and service, involving undergraduate as well as graduate students in his ongoing projects. At the University of New Mexico, he has taught a broad range of lower division, upper division, and graduate courses, including Principles of Biology, Evolution and Ecology, Stream Ecology, Limnology and Oceanography, Marine Biology, and Community and Ecosystem Ecology. He has taught courses in Global Change and River Ecology at the University of Coimbra, Portugal, and General Ecology and Groundwater and Riparian Ecology at the Flathead Lake Biological Station. Dr. Manuel Molles was named Teacher of the Year by the University of New Mexico for 1995–96 and Potter Chair in Plant Ecology in 2000.

James F. Cahill Jr., or "JC" as he is generally known, is a Professor of Biology at the University of Alberta. He received his B.A. in Cultural Ecology and Biology from Trinity College (CT) in 1992 and his Ph.D. in Ecology from the University of Pennsylvania in 1997. After first teaching ecology at several schools in the United States, he joined the faculty at the University of Alberta in 1999.

JC is an experimental plant ecologist, with diverse research interests. At the core of his research programs are studies focused on understanding the mechanisms of plant competition and its role in structuring plant communities. Over time, his research interests have expanded to include plant–animal interactions, soil ecology, evolution of ecological traits, and plant behavioural ecology. JC has led large, multi-investigator projects examining the combined impacts of grazing and climate change on the sustainability of Canada's grasslands, and another project studying the linkages among the mountain pine beetle, pine trees, and soil fungi. His research contributions have been recognized by the scientific community, both by being asked to serve as an Associate Editor at the *Journal of Ecology,* as well as by being awarded a Discovery Accelerator Grant by NSERC, the main funding organization for ecology in Canada. JC maintains an active research lab in Edmonton, which includes postdoctoral researchers, graduate students, and undergraduates. He is always looking for motivated new students, so don't hesitate to send him a note if interested in this type of research!

Being a professor is about more than just conducting research; and teaching and service are important aspects of the job. JC has taught a wide variety of courses for undergraduate and graduate students, including Principles of Ecology, Fundamentals of Plant Biology, Plant Ecology, Methods in Plant Ecology, Plant–Animal Interactions, Ecology of Belowground Communities, Current Topics in Plant Ecology, and Advanced Ecology. It was through his experiences in the classroom that JC realized how much difficulty many students were having relating to the ecological concepts being presented. It was his desire to enhance student learning that led to his participation in this textbook.

BRIEF CONTENTS

1   Introduction to Ecology   1

SECTION 1   Natural History and Evolution   13

2   Life on Land   14
3   Life in Water   51
4   Evolution and Speciation   89

SECTION 2   Individuals   115

5   Temperature Relations   116
6   Water Relations   146
7   Energy and Nutrient Relations   174
8   Behavioural Ecology   202
9   Life Histories and the Niche   231

SECTION 3   Population Ecology   261

10   Distribution and Abundance of Populations and Species   262
11   Population Structure   293
12   Population Dynamics and Growth   310

SECTION 4   Interactions   334

13   Competition   335
14   Herbivory and Predation   361
15   Mutualism, Parasitism, and Disease   391

SECTION 5   Communities and Ecosystems   420

16   Community Structure and Function   421
17   Species Interactions and Community Structure   446
18   Disturbance, Succession, and Stability   468
19   Production and Energy Flow   501
20   Nutrient and Elemental Cycling   524

SECTION 6   Large-Scale Ecology   550

21   Landscape Ecology   551
22   Macroecology   577
23   Global Ecology   607

About the New Edition   xi

Chapter 1 Introduction to Ecology   1

Chapter Concepts   1
1.1   Overview of Ecology   2
1.2   Sampling Ecological Research   4
Ecology In Action: The Scientific Method   10
Summary   12
Review Questions   12

SECTION 1

Natural History and Evolution   13

Chapter 2 Life on Land   14

Chapter Concepts   14
2.1   Large-Scale Patterns of Climatic Variation   16
   Concept 2.1 Review   19
2.2   Soil: Foundation of Terrestrial Biomes   19
   Concept 2.2 Review   22
Ecology In Action: Natural History of Soils   22
2.3   Natural History and Geography of Biome   23
   Concept 2.3 Review   46
Ecological Tools and Approaches: Biomes of Canada and Winter Ecology   46
Summary   49
Review Questions   50

Chapter 3 Life in Water   51

Chapter Concepts   51
3.1   The Hydrologic Cycle   52
   Concept 3.1 Review   54
3.2   Life in Water and the Natural History of Aquatic Environments   54
Ecology In Action: What Lies Below?   62
   Concept 3.2 Review   84
Ecological Tools and Approaches: Reconstructing Lake Communities   84
Summary   87
Review Questions   88

Chapter 4 Evolution and Speciation   89

Chapter Concepts   89
4.1   Variation Within Populations   92
   Concept 4.1 Review   95
4.2   Evolution   96
Ecology In Action: Human-Induced Evolution   98
   Concept 4.2 Review   106
4.3   Speciation   106
   Concept 4.3 Review   110
Ecological Tools and Approaches: Integrating Population Genetics and Ecology   111
Summary   113
Review Questions   114

SECTION 2

Individuals   115

Chapter 5 Temperature Relations   116

Chapter Concepts   116
5.1   Microclimates   117
   Concept 5.1 Review   121
5.2   Evolutionary Trade-Offs   121
   Concept 5.2 Review   122
5.3   Temperature and Performance of Organisms   122
Ecology In Action: Impacts of Stream Temperature on Salmon Recruitment   123
   Concept 5.3 Review   128
5.4   Regulating Body Temperature   128
   Concept 5.4 Review   137
5.5   Surviving Extreme Temperatures   137
   Concept 5.5 Review   142
Ecological Tools and Approaches: Climatic Warming and the Local Extinction of a Land Snail   142
Summary   144
Review Questions   145

Chapter 6 Water Relations   146

Chapter Concepts   146
6.1   Water Availability   147
   Concept 6.1 Review   153

6.2 **Water Regulation on Land** 153

Ecology In Action: Dams, Flows, and Cottonwoods 159
Concept 6.2 Review 165

6.3 **Water and Salt Balance in Aquatic Environments** 165
Concept 6.3 Review 169

Ecological Tools and Approaches: Using Stable Isotopes to Study Water Uptake by Plants 169

Summary 171
Review Questions 172

Chapter 7 Energy and Nutrient Relations 174

Chapter Concepts 174

7.1 **Energy Sources** 175
Concept 7.1 Review 188

7.2 **Energy and Nutrient Limitation** 188
Concept 7.2 Review 191

7.3 **Energy and Nutrient Capture** 191
Concept 7.3 Review 196

Ecology In Action: Using Ecological Knowledge to Predict C$_4$ Plant Distributions in a Changing World 196

Ecological Tools and Approaches: Bioremediation—Using the Trophic Diversity of Bacteria to Solve Environmental Problems 198

Summary 199
Review Questions 200

Chapter 8 Behavioural Ecology 202

Chapter Concepts 202

8.1 **Evolution and Behaviour** 203
Concept 8.1 Review 208

8.2 **Sociality** 208

Ecology In Action: Human–Wildlife Conflict 209
Concept 8.2 Review 215

8.3 **Mating Systems and Mate Choice** 216
Concept 8.3 Review 226

Ecological Tools and Approaches: Using Game Theory to Understand Behaviour 226

Summary 229
Review Questions 230

Chapter 9 Life Histories and the Niche 231

Chapter Concepts 231

9.1 **Trade-Offs** 232

Ecology In Action: How Life Histories Influence Extinction Risk 241
Concept 9.1 Review 244

9.2 **Life-History Classification** 244
Concept 9.2 Review 250

9.3 **Fundamental and Realized Niches** 250
Concept 9.3 Review 253

Ecological Tools and Approaches: Using Life-History Information as Indicators of Biological Effects of Climate Change 254

Summary 258
Review Questions 259

SECTION 3

Population Ecology 261

Chapter 10 Distribution and Abundance of Populations and Species 262

Chapter Concepts 262

10.1 **Distribution Limits** 264
Concept 10.1 Review 267

10.2 **Dispersal** 267
Concept 10.2 Review 272

10.3 **Metapopulations** 272
Concept 10.3 Review 274

10.4 **Distribution Patterns** 274
Concept 10.4 Review 280

Ecology In Action: Using Ecology to Protect Threatened Species 280

10.5 **Organism Size and Population Density** 282
Concept 10.5 Review 284

10.6 **Commonness and Rarity** 284
Concept 10.6 Review 286

Ecological Tools and Approaches: Estimating Abundance 286

Summary 290
Review Questions 291

Chapter 11 Population Structure 293

Chapter Concepts 293

11.1 **Patterns of Survival** 295
Concept 11.1 Review 299

Ecology In Action: Unintended Consequences of Ecological Research 300

11.2 **Age Distribution** 301
Concept 11.2 Review 303

11.3 **Sex Ratios** 303
Concept 11.3 Review 305

Ecological Tools and Approaches: Using Population Structure to Assess the Impact of Human-Mediated Change 305

Summary 308
Review Questions 309

Chapter 12 Population Dynamics
and Growth   310

Chapter Concepts   310
**12.1 BIDE (Birth, Immigration, Death, Emigration)
Dynamics   311**
Concept 12.1 Review   315
12.2 Rates of Population Change   316
Concept 12.2 Review   319
12.3 Geometric and Exponential Population Growth   319
Concept 12.3 Review   322
12.4 Logistic Population Growth   323
Concept 12.4 Review   326

Ecology In Action: Fisheries   326

Ecological Tools and Approaches: The Human Population   328
Summary   332
Review Questions   333

SECTION 4

Interactions   334

Chapter 13 Competition   335

Chapter Concepts   335
13.1 Forms of Competition   337
Concept 13.1 Review   338
13.2 Evidence of Competition in Natural Systems   338
Concept 13.2 Review   343
13.3 Mathematical and Laboratory Models   343
Concept 13.3 Review   349
13.4 Competition and Niches   349

Ecology In Action: The Role of Competition in Forest
Management   354
Concept 13.4 Review   356

Ecological Tools and Approaches: Identifying the Mechanisms
by Which Plants Compete   357
Summary   358
Review Questions   359

Chapter 14 Herbivory and Predation   361

Chapter Concepts   361
14.1 Herbivory and Plant Defence   362

Ecology In Action: Invasive Species and Exploitative
Relationships   368
Concept 14.1 Review   370
14.2 Impacts of Predators on Prey Populations   370
Concept 14.2 Review   375
**14.3 Predator–Prey Dynamics in a Mathematical
Model   375**
Concept 14.3 Review   378
14.4 Predator Avoidance   378
Concept 14.4 Review   385

Ecological Tools and Approaches: Evolution and
Exploitation   385
Summary   389
Review Questions   389

Chapter 15 Mutualism, Parasitism,
and Disease   391

Chapter Concepts   391
15.1 Complex Interactions   393
Concept 15.1 Review   399
15.2 Ecology of Disease   399
Concept 15.2 Review   403
15.3 Mutualist–Exploiter Continuum   404

Ecology In Action: Impacts of Mycorrhizae on Forest
Sustainability   410
Concept 15.3 Review   412
15.4 Evolution of Mutualism   412
Concept 15.4 Review   414

Ecological Tools and Approaches: Mutualism
and Humans   414
Summary   417
Review Questions   418

SECTION 5

Communities and Ecosystems   420

Chapter 16 Community Structure and
Function   421

Chapter Concepts   421
16.1 Species Abundances and Diversity   423
Concept 16.1 Review   428
16.2 Environmental Complexity and Species Diversity   428
Concept 16.2 Review   433
16.3 Functional Consequences of Diversity   433
Concept 16.3 Review   436

Ecology In Action: Indicators of Human Impacts   436
16.4 Genetic Diversity and Ecological Processes   438
Concept 16.4 Review   440

Ecological Tools and Approaches: Sampling
Communities   440
Summary   444
Review Questions   445

Chapter 17 Species Interactions and Community
Structure   446

Chapter Concepts   446
**17.1 Ecological Networks Across Trophic Boundaries: Food
Webs   447**
Concept 17.1 Review   451

17.2 Community Assembly: Competitive Asymmetries   451
Concept 17.2 Review   453
17.3 Community Assembly: Keystone Species   454
Ecology In Action: Keystone Species, Ecosystem Engineers,
and Conservation Biology   459
Concept 17.3 Review   461
17.4 Mutualistic Keystones   461
Concept 17.4 Review   463
Ecological Tools and Approaches: Humans as Keystone
Species   463
Summary   466
Review Questions   466

Chapter 18 Disturbance, Succession,
and Stability   468
Chapter Concepts   468
18.1 Disturbance and Diversity   470
Concept 18.1 Review   474
Ecology In Action: Using Disturbances for Conservation   474
18.2 Community and Ecosystem Stability   475
Concept 18.2 Review   479
18.3 Community Changes During Succession   479
Concept 18.3 Review   485
18.4 Ecosystem Changes During Succession   485
Concept 18.4 Review   489
18.5 Mechanisms of Succession   490
Concept 18.5 Review   496
Ecological Tools and Approaches: Using Repeat Photography to
Detect Long-Term Change   496
Summary   498
Review Questions   499

Chapter 19 Production and Energy Flow   501
Chapter Concepts   501
19.1 Patterns of Terrestrial Primary Production   503
Ecology In Action: Interactions Across Community Boundaries   506
Concept 19.1 Review   508
19.2 Patterns of Aquatic Primary Production   508
Concept 19.2 Review   512
19.3 Trophic Levels   512
Concept 19.3 Review   516
19.4 Biotic Influences   516
Concept 19.4 Review   519
Ecological Tools and Approaches: Using Stable Isotope Analysis
to Trace Energy Flow Through Ecosystems   519
Summary   522
Review Questions   522

Chapter 20 Nutrient and Elemental Cycling   524
Chapter Concepts   524
20.1 Nutrient Cycles   526
Concept 20.1 Review   529

20.2 Rates of Decomposition   529
Ecology In Action: How Decomposition Can Change
the World   532
Concept 20.2 Review   534
20.3 Organisms and Nutrients   535
Concept 20.3 Review   539
20.4 Human Impacts on Elemental Cycles   539
Concept 20.4 Review   546
Ecological Tools and Approaches: Altering Aquatic
and Terrestrial Ecosystems   546
Summary   548
Review Questions   548

SECTION 6

Large-Scale Ecology   550

Chapter 21 Landscape Ecology   551
Chapter Concepts   551
21.1 Origins of Landscapes   553
Concept 21.1 Review   558
21.2 Landscape Structure   558
Concept 21.2 Review   561
21.3 Landscape Processes   561
Concept 21.3 Review   569
Ecology In Action: Linear Disturbances Across the
Landscape   569
Ecological Tools and Approaches: Linking Population,
Behavioural, and Landscape Ecology   571
Summary   575
Review Questions   576

Chapter 22 Macroecology   577
Chapter Concepts   577
22.1 Ecological Niche Modelling   578
Concept 22.1 Review   582
22.2 Area, Isolation, and Species Richness   582
Concept 22.2 Review   586
22.3 The Equilibrium Model of Island Biogeography   586
Concept 22.3 Review   591
22.4 Latitudinal Gradients in Species Richness   591
Concept 22.4 Review   595
22.5 Historical and Regional Influences   595
Ecology In Action: Biodiversity Hotspots   597
Concept 22.5 Review   600
Ecological Tools and Approaches: Global Positioning Systems,
Remote Sensing, and Geographic Information Systems   600
Summary   604
Review Questions   605

Chapter 23 Global Ecology   607

Chapter Concepts   607

23.1 Patterns of Biological Diversity Change Through Time   609

Concept 23.1 Review   *618*

23.2 Human Activity Transforms the World   618

Ecology In Action: Being an Ecologist   624

Concept 23.2 Review   *628*

23.3 Ecologically Informed Decision Making   628

Concept 23.3 Review   *632*

Ecological Tools and Approaches: Cooperative Research Networks & Distributed Ecology   633

Summary   635

Review Questions   636

Appendix A: Building a Statistical Toolbox   AP-1

Glossary   GL-1

References   RE-1

Credits   CR-1

Index   IN-1

Environmental issues are of pressing concern to Canadians. Discussions of environmental sustainability, increased development, resource extraction, species at risk, and global responsibility are common in the news and among the Canadian public. When faced with choices, it is the science of ecology that provides lawmakers, land managers, and the public the information they need to make informed decisions. However, ecology is a young science, and the rapidly increasing pace of discovery and ever-increasing list of environmental concerns makes teaching ecology very challenging. As we attempt to educate students to understand and design solutions to environmental problems, every facet of ecology is important. Ideally, an introductory course in ecology would include the foundations of all the major ecological subdisciplines. Including such breadth, and developing it to sufficient depth, is difficult within the time constraints most of us face in the classroom. The Third Canadian edition of *Ecology: Concepts & Applications* provides careful organization, clear and relevant Canadian and global examples, and a conceptual approach to ease this task. This book is designed with the goal of enhancing student understanding of key ecological principles and concepts, rather than being an encyclopedic source of information.

Introductory Audience

We have written this book for students taking their first undergraduate course in ecology. Ecology is an integrative discipline, and thus a foundation in other sciences is important. We have assumed that students in this course have some knowledge of basic chemistry and mathematics and that they have had a course in general biology that included introductions to physiology, biological diversity, and evolution.

Unique Approach

In an address at the 1991 meeting of the Ecological Society of America in San Antonio, Texas, eminent ecologist Paul Risser challenged ecology instructors to focus their attention on the major concepts of the field. If we subdivide a large and dynamic subject such as ecology too finely, we cannot teach it in one or even two academic terms. Risser proposed that by focusing on major concepts, however, we may provide students with a robust framework of the discipline upon which they can build.

This book attempts to address Risser's challenge. **Each chapter is organized around two to six major concepts, presenting the student with a manageable and meaningful synthesis of the subject.** We have found that while beginning students can often absorb a few central concepts well, they can easily get lost in a sea of details. In this book, each concept is accompanied by case studies and research results that reinforce the central concept being discussed. This approach introduces students to the research methods used in the various areas of ecology, with a strong focus on a scientific approach to understanding ecological principles. Wherever possible, the original research and the scientists who did the research are presented. Allowing the scientists who created this field to emerge from the background and lead students through the discipline breathes life into the subject and helps students retain information. This approach also helps students understand that science is not a list of facts; instead it consists of active debates, hard work, and real people.

Accessible Writing

Science is fun, and there is no reason reading about science should be dull. Instead, we believe textbooks should be engaging to the students, helping them learn the material. The opportunity to discover a bit of knowledge that no one has ever before known is a reason many of us became researchers in the first place. However, this sense of enjoyment and excitement is missing from most textbooks, where writing most resembles the terseness of a scientific article. We believe a textbook that is not read is of little value, no matter how strong the content contained between the covers. Thus we use a writing style that is accessible to students—one your students are most certain to notice. Brief narratives, attempts at humour, and continued emphasis on the organisms being studied and the people who study them draw the student into each chapter and concept. Such an approach eases understanding of ecology, increasing the value of this text for the students.

Organized Around Key Concepts

Natural history and evolution are the foundations of ecology, and concepts from these disciplines run throughout the entire textbook. The textbook begins with a brief introduction to the nature and history of the discipline of ecology, followed by Section I, which includes three chapters on natural history—life on land, life in water, and a chapter on evolution. Sections II through VI build a hierarchical perspective through the traditional subdisciplines of ecology: Section II concerns the ecology of individuals; Section III focuses on population ecology; Section IV presents the ecology of interactions; Section V summarizes community and ecosystem ecology; and finally, Section VI discusses large-scale ecology and includes chapters on landscape, macro- and global ecology. In summary, the book begins with the natural history of the planet, considers portions of the whole in the middle chapters, and ends with another perspective of the entire planet in the concluding chapter.

Within each chapter, key concepts are highlighted both in the first listing of chapter concepts and at the beginning of each section in which the concepts are discussed. The concept numbers are repeated in the concept review questions that conclude each section. Thus, the beginning and end of each concept is clearly signalled for the student.

Unique Benefits of Molles and Cahill

Teach the foundations of ecology using Canadian examples to help students relate to the material. In this text we focus on the major themes of ecology and include the foundational studies that all students should learn. However, ecology is more than a set of graphs and abstract concepts. At its core are a diversity of species, each with its own unique characteristics and interesting stories. Where possible, we highlight species students would be familiar with in Canada and research conducted at Canadian universities. By placing complex ideas into a familiar context, students become more engaged and can focus their learning on the ideas the instructor is teaching. Importantly, we do not sacrifice presentation of foundational studies and examples of ecological principles simply to increase the "Canadian content" of the text.

Link the science of ecology to real-world problems. All chapters include an "Ecology In Action" box in which we highlight how the ecological principles are being used in real-world situations in Canada and around the world. Examples include human-induced evolution in natural populations, fishery management and collapse, using behavioural ecology to reduce human–wildlife conflict, and many others. These boxes emphasize to students that ecology is not an abstract science, but instead is central to solving real issues of societal concern.

Emphasize the linkage between ecology and evolutionary biology. Evolution results in species that we find on the planet and the diversity of ecological processes that occur. Without ecology, there would be no natural selection. These two disciplines are separated more by time-scales than by concepts, and we emphasize the linkage between them throughout the text. Evolution serves as a thread that helps link the chapters together, facilitating understanding for the students of ecology, as well as providing a link to other disciplines of biology.

Enhance quantitative understanding of students. Ecology is a quantitative discipline, and shying away from this would provide a misleading representation of this field of research. However, students often struggle with many aspects of ecology, including interpreting graphs, understanding statistics, and the value of models for addressing ecological questions. We are very aware of both the importance of these skills, as well as their difficulty for many students.

To help students learn how to understand graphical information, we have embedded text boxes into the figures in the text. These boxes guide the students toward understanding the main points of the graphs, while they read the text on their own. We also provide instructors with versions of the figures without the textboxes for use during lectures, allowing them to guide the students themselves during lecture.

Within each chapter we also discuss the general statistical approaches that researchers used, while providing the details of different statistical methods in an appendix. The statistical appendix is written in a friendly tone, outlining the most common statistics used in ecology. For those instructors who incorporate statistics into their lectures, this appendix could be an early assigned reading. For those instructors who reduce the quantitative aspects of ecology, the appendix could serve as a resource for the students. This approach allows for a focus on key concepts in each chapter, while also giving instructors flexibility in how they present statistical information to their students.

Many major concepts in ecology come from the use of models and we include many of these in the text. To help students understand, rather than simply memorize, these models, we spend significant amounts of text explaining the details of each model. For those instructors who choose to teach these models in their courses, our approach allows the text to reinforce lecture concepts.

Changes in the Third Edition

The first edition of Molles and Cahill was the first ecology text specifically for the Canadian market. It was widely adopted throughout Canada at universities and colleges along all three coasts. As a result of real instructors using both the first and second editions of this text with real students, we have received helpful feedback as to what aspects of the text worked well, and what parts needed to be refined. At the same time, we have actively sought comments from instructors using other texts in their courses, providing unique perspectives and ideas about how this text could be enhanced. Through the incorporation of these comments, along with our own ideas that have emerged from our own experiences inside and outside of the classroom, we believe this edition will be even more effective at enhancing student learning and the teaching of ecology.

In this edition, the chapter design has been changed to more effectively emphasize the key concepts, facilitating student learning. In all chapters we have also enhanced the overall flow of information and updated it to ensure the material presented is current and accurate. In total, we have included 30 new images and illustrations to help enhance understanding of chapter concepts. Many other existing illustrations have been modified to offer greater clarity. In addition to these general changes throughout the text, several chapters have been significantly altered, warranting particular notice.

In *Chapter 2* we have added a version of Whittaker's classic schematic showing the relationship between biome type and climate.

In *Chapter 3*, and throughout the text, we have enhanced our clarity regarding peatland habitats, including the addition of more effective images.

In *Chapter 4* we have improved the clarity of the discussion or the causes of phenotypic variation and the importance of phenotypic plasticity. There are also new case studies of stabilizing and disruptive selection to reinforce these important concepts.

In *Chapter 5* we have clarified the foundational concept of the theory of allocation. We have also expanded the discussion of cushion plants, including a new case study along an elevation gradient.

In *Chapter 8* we now provide more introductory background into the general field of behavioural ecology, and have clarified issues related to human–wildlife conflict.

In *Chapter 9* we have updated the presentation of Charnov's planar life-history classification. We have also

expanded our discussion about life history and extinction risk to include marine examples.

In **Chapter 10** we are now more thorough in our overview of the central ecological processes influencing populations, and include sections on both dispersal and metapopulations.

In **Chapter 11** we now emphasize the long-term consistency in ecological processes, by adding an example of *Tyrannosaur* survivorship curves.

In **Chapter 12** we have extensively edited our presentation of population dynamics to enhance student understanding of these challenging concepts. We have also updated information on human population growth, including the changes observed in Canada.

In **Chapter 13** the discussion on self-thinning in plants has been rewritten, allowing for more clarity.

Chapter 16 has been substantially rewritten and renamed *Community Structure and Function*. In this chapter we emphasize the linkage between ecological patterns and processes. We now discuss the concepts of alpha, beta, and gamma diversity, and have clarified the presentation of species abundance patterns. We have added a new section on the functional consequences of both species and genetic diversity, and present current information regarding biodiversity-function relationships. The new Ecology In Action section focuses on using biological indicators as measures of ecosystem health and human impacts.

Chapter 18 has been expanded to include concepts of disturbance, succession, and stability. The ecological concept of stability, divided into resistance and resilience, is given its own section, including new artwork. To help students relate to this material,

we include a discussion about how increased marine diversity is associated with a reduced frequency of fishery collapse.

In **Chapter 19** we have added a discussion on marine dead zones, linking these to land-use patterns and controls of primary productivity. We have also increased the focus of this chapter on production and energy flow though the addition of a conceptual diagram, and moving unrelated material to different chapters.

In **Chapter 20** we adopt a more synthetic approach to the presentation of nutrient and elemental cycling, and now present information regarding human impacts on carbon and nitrogen cycles here. We have added a section on the role of vertebrates in nutrient cycling within aquatic systems, further emphasizing the biotic aspects of these important topics. The presentation of the Hubbard Brook whole watershed experiment has been enhanced. A new Ecological Tools and Applications section focuses on the impacts of cities on nutrient fluxes.

In **Chapter 23** you will find that although it remains titled Global Ecology, the content has been substantially modified. We now begin the chapter emphasizing the dynamic aspects of ecological processes and patterns. These include biodiversity patterns over deep evolutionary time, including presentation of past and present mass-extinction events. We then present information about impacts of human activities on the global ecological system, including the impacts of agriculture and deforestation, as well as the appropriation of global net primary productivity. We conclude with a section discussing ecologically informed decision making, and how ecological knowledge is being used to guide conservation programs. A new Ecology In Action section has been included, describing many of the potential careers available to students of ecology.

The features of this textbook are unique and were carefully planned to enhance the students' comprehension of ecology. All chapters beyond the introductory Chapter 1 are based on a distinctive learning system, featuring the following key components:

Introduction:
The introduction to each chapter presents students with the flavour of the subject and important background information. Some introductions include historical events related to the subject; others present an example of an ecological process. All attempt to engage students and draw them into the discussion that follows.

Concepts:
The goal of this book is to build a foundation of ecological knowledge around key concepts. These key concepts are listed after the chapter introduction to alert students to the major topics to follow, and to provide a place where students can find a list of the important points of each chapter. The sections in which concepts are discussed reinforce concepts with a focus on published studies. This case-study approach supports the concepts with evidence, and introduces students to the methods and people that have created the discipline of ecology. At the end of each concept is a brief concept review that includes several questions specific to the material the students just read. These boxes serve as an immediate indicator to students as to whether they understood this section, or if they need additional help.

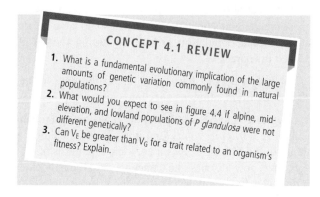

CONCEPT 4.1 REVIEW

1. What is a fundamental evolutionary implication of the large amounts of genetic variation commonly found in natural populations?

2. What would you expect to see in figure 4.4 if alpine, mid-elevation, and lowland populations of *P. glandulosa* were not different genetically?

3. Can V_E be greater than V_G for a trait related to an organism's fitness? Explain.

Illustrations:
A great deal of effort has been put into the development of illustrations, both photographs and line art. The goal has been to create more effective pedagogical tools through skilful design and use of colour, and to rearrange the traditional presentation of information in figures and captions. Much explanatory material is located within the illustrations, providing students with key information where they need it most.

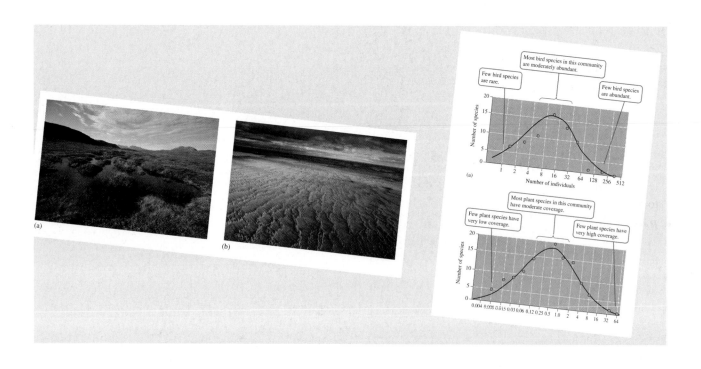

Ecology In Action: Many undergraduate students want to know how abstract ideas and general relationships can be applied to the ecological problems facing us all. They are concerned with the practical side of ecology and want to know more about the tools of science. Including applications in each chapter motivates students to learn more of the underlying principles of ecology. In addition, it seems that environmental problems are now so numerous and so pressing that they have erased a once easy distinction between general and applied ecology.

Ecological Tools and Approaches

Ecological Tools and Approaches: To understand the results of science, an understanding of the methods of science is required. We believe it is important for students to understand that science is a process, not simply a list of facts. Therefore, in each chapter we highlight a method, or a conceptual approach to understanding, that allows researchers to address questions relevant to the concepts presented in that chapter. These examples are varied, including sampling designs, game theory, stable isotopes, and many others.

End-of-Chapter Material

- *Summary* The chapter summary reviews the main points of the content. The concepts around which each chapter is organized are boldfaced and redefined in the summary to re-emphasize the main points of the chapter.

- *Review Questions* The review questions are designed to help students think more deeply about each concept and to reflect on alternative views. These questions supplement the concept review questions located at the end of each concept section. They range from specific to more integrative, and provide feedback to the students about any remaining gaps in the information presented. Our intent is to also use these questions to take students beyond the foundation established in the main body of the chapter, and ask them to use their newly found knowledge in novel ways.

End-of-Book Material

- *Appendix* A student-friendly appendix, "Building a Statistical Toolbox," appears at the end of the textbook to give instructors flexibility in terms of how and when to include statistics in their course. Two additional appendices are available on the Online Learning Centre at www.mcgrawhill.ca/olc/molles: "Statistical Tables" and "Answers to Concept Review Questions."

- *Glossary*

- *References* References are an important part of any scientific work and we give credit to the researchers whose hard work made this book possible.

- *Index*

McGraw-Hill Connect® is a web-based assignment and assessment platform that gives students the means to better connect with their coursework, with their instructors, and with the important concepts that they will need to know for success now and in the future.

With Connect, instructors can deliver assignments, quizzes, and tests online. Instructors can edit existing questions and author entirely new problems; track individual student performance—by question, assignment or in relation to the class overall—with detailed grade reports; and integrate grade reports easily with Learning Management Systems (LMS) such as WebCT and Blackboard.

By choosing Connect, instructors are providing their students with a powerful tool for improving academic performance and truly mastering course material. Connect allows students to practise important skills at their own pace and on their own schedule. Importantly, students' assessment results and instructors' feedback are all saved online—so students can continually review their progress and plot their course to success.

Connect also provides 24/7 online access to an eBook—an online edition of the text—to help them successfully complete their work, wherever and whenever they choose.

Key Features

Simple Assignment Management
With Connect, creating assignments is easier than ever, so you can spend more time teaching and less time managing.

- Create and deliver assignments easily with custom interactive exercises and testbank material to assign online.
- Streamline lesson planning, student progress reporting, and assignment grading to make classroom management more efficient than ever.
- Go paperless with the eBook and online submission and grading of student assignments.

Smart Grading
When it comes to studying, time is precious. Connect helps students learn more efficiently by providing feedback and practice material when they need it, where they need it.

- Automatically score assignments, giving students immediate feedback on their work and side-by-side comparisons with correct answers.
- Access and review each response; manually change grades or leave comments for students to review.
- Reinforce classroom concepts with practice tests and instant quizzes.

Instructor Library
The Connect Instructor Library is your course-creation hub. It provides all the critical resources you'll need to build your course, just how you want to teach it.

- Assign eBook readings and draw from a rich collection of textbook-specific assignments.
- Access instructor resources
  - **Computerized Test Bank**, Anurani Dev, *Trent University*
  - **Connect**, David Locky, *Grant Macewan University*
  - **Microsoft® PowerPoint® Lecture Slides**, Tara Hayes, *Sheridan College*
  - **Class Activities**, David Locky, *Grant Macewan University*
  - **Answers to Review Questions**, David Locky, *Grant Macewan University*
  - **Answers to Concept Reviews**, David Locky, *Grant Macewan University*
- View assignments and resources created for past sections.
- Post your own resources for students to use.

eBook
Connect reinvents the textbook learning experience for the modern student. Every Connect subject area is seamlessly integrated with Connect eBooks, which are designed to keep students focused on the concepts key to their success.

- Provide students with a Connect eBook, allowing for anytime, anywhere access to the textbook.
- Merge media, animation, and assessments with the text's narrative to engage students and improve learning and retention.
- Pinpoint and connect key concepts in a snap using the powerful eBook search engine.
- Manage notes, highlights, and bookmarks in one place for simple, comprehensive review.

Superior Learning Solutions and Support

The McGraw-Hill Ryerson team is ready to help you assess and integrate any of our products, technology, and services into your course for optimal teaching and learning performance. Whether it's helping your students improve their grades, or putting your entire course online, the McGraw-Hill Ryerson team is here to help you do it. Contact your Learning Solutions Consultant today to learn how to maximize all of McGraw-Hill Ryerson's resources!

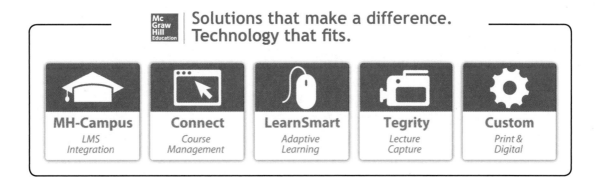

For more information on the latest technology and Learning Solutions offered by McGraw-Hill Ryerson and its partners, please visit us online: www.mcgrawhill.ca/he/solutions.

Acknowledgments

A complete list of the people who have helped with the development of this third edition would be impossibly long, and thus I only mention a few individuals here. First, I thank Manuel Molles for providing me with the opportunity to add my own view of ecology to what was already a very strong textbook.

I wish to acknowledge the broad ecological research community in Canada. I have been overwhelmed by the generosity of spirit and willingness to help me complete this project. Thank you to the many professors who adopted the previous editions of this text and provided substantial feedback, making the development of this third edition possible. Thank you too to the students, though typically without choice, who purchased this book. I hope my efforts have improved your understanding of ecology.

During the development of this third edition I relied quite heavily on several colleagues who freely shared their ideas and expertise, including: Suzanne Bayley, Erin Bayne, David Coltman, Andy Derocher, John Gamon, David Hik, Lindsay Leighton, Jan Murie, Heather Proctor, and Rolf Vinebrooke. Thank you to the many students and postdocs who frequently gave of their time to discuss aspects of the book, and who were able to quickly adapt to my suddenly busier schedule. In particular I thank Tan Bao, Pamela Belter, Jon Bennett, Kurt Illerbrun, Frank Forcino, Stephen Mayor, Samson Nyanumba, Morgan Randall, Gisela Stotz, and Shannon White.

I also acknowledge the help throughout the publishing process given by many individuals associated with McGraw-Hill Ryerson during this project, including: Leanna MacLean, Group Product Manager; Kamilah Reid-Burrell, Product Developer; Indu Arora, Permissions Editor; Kelly Dickson, Group Product Development Manager; Stephanie Gay, Supervising Editor; and Cat Haggert, Copy Editor.

I offer particular thanks to my friends and family who have offered support during this project. These people have been a wonderful group, and I regret not being able to list them all here. Instead, I name just a few, including my children Erica, Liam, Kieran, and Grayson; my parents Teena, Brooks, Jim, and Ellen; and my friends Benoit, Cathy, Cam, Simita, Clive, Melanie, Lee, Naomi, Rich, Faye, Jennifer, Samantha, and Jan. I also offer my thanks to Colleen St. Clair, the love of my life, for support and encouragement throughout this project. I will do my best to not talk about the textbook for another few years.

Finally, thank you to the many reviewers of this edition listed below, and those who reviewed the second edition of this text and draft chapters of this edition. All have given much of their time and expertise to help improve this textbook for use by students in Canada.

James F. Cahill, Jr.

Reviewers of our Third Canadian Edition

Nigel Waltho, Carleton University
David Locky, Grant MacEwan University
Joan Sharp, Simon Fraser University
Anurani Persaud, Trent University
Wayne Goodey, University of British Columbia

Lisa Poirier, University of Northern British Columbia
Kerri Finlay, University of Regina
Ken Oakes, University of Waterloo
Rebecca Rooney, University of Waterloo
Dr. Christopher Lottie, York University

INTRODUCTION TO ECOLOGY

CHAPTER CONCEPTS

1.1 Ecologists study environmental relationships ranging from those of individual organisms to factors influencing global-scale processes.

1.2 Ecologists design their studies based on their research questions, the temporal and spatial scale of their studies, and available research tools.

Ecology in Action: The Scientific Method

Summary

Review Questions

What is ecology? **Ecology** is the branch of science dedicated to the study of relationships between organisms and the environment. Humans have been students of ecology as long as we have existed as a species. The earliest hunters and gatherers had to be familiar with the habits of their prey, where to find food plants, and when fruits would ripen. Farmers and ranchers are aware of how variations in weather and soils affect their crops and livestock, how yields change depending upon what species grow together, as well as how pests and pathogens impact their crops and livelihood. All of this is ecology, and the need of people to understand how the natural world works continues to this day. A modern fisher, hunter, rancher, or farmer who does not understand the patterns of nature will not be successful. A society that ignores ecological changes is at risk of losing the life-sustaining services ecosystems provide. Increasingly, modern society is turning to ecologists to offer solutions to problems generated by anthropogenic activities and a continually increasing population size.

From these roots in natural history and close observation grew the academic discipline of ecology. The academic study of ecology is relatively new, emerging as a separate scientific discipline only in the nineteenth century. The term *ecology* comes from the Greek word for house, *oīkos,* and much of ecology is focused on understanding how organisms interact with each other and their environment.

Most people no longer live in rural areas surrounded by large expanses of natural areas. Instead the human population is increasingly centred in cities and urban areas. Does this mean that the study of ecology, or its need, is disappearing? No. Ecological processes do not end at park boundaries. Rather, they occur in all living systems, be they managed farms or fisheries, urban landscapes, or expanses of wild waters and native species. Cities are not sterile areas devoid of any life other than people. Instead, cities contain a diverse set of flora and fauna, spread in a patchwork of parks, waterways, golf courses, tree-lined boulevards, and gardens. Natural selection is as strong a force in cities as in pristine natural areas, and how individual organisms interact with their local environment influences their success. This too is ecology.

Taking a step back, we see that cities are just one part of a larger landscape made up of a mixture of agriculture areas; protected wilderness, rivers, and lakes; and urban areas. Organisms move in and out of these patches, corridors, waterways, and islands. Plants spread pollen and seed across vast distances, with potential movement of genes and seed across the landscape. No single area on the landscape is in complete isolation, and indeed, activities in one area can influence the interactions among organisms and their environment in another. This too is ecology.

Taking an even broader view, we see changes in temperature, varied patterns of precipitation, and altered air and water circulation are occurring across the planet. We see grasslands disappearing in the face of agricultural expansion, fisheries collapsing through overexploitation, and nitrogen and other chemicals falling from the sky as a consequence of industrial development. These changes to the environment influence organisms of all types. This too is ecology.

Behind the simple definition of ecology lies a broad scientific discipline that almost defies definition. Ecologists may study individual organisms, entire grasslands or lakes, individual countries and coastlines, or even the whole planet. The measurements made by ecologists include counts of individuals, frequency of births and deaths, spatial patterns of distribution, and rates of processes such as photosynthesis and decomposition. Ecology is an interdisciplinary science, and ecologists generally need to know as much about plant biology, animal biology, microbiology, and molecular biology as they do about geography, soil science, chemistry, and physics. While most people tend to think of ecologists as people "out in the field," many ecologists make critical advances through lab experiments and the development of theoretical models and computer simulations. Our simple definition of *ecology* does not effectively describe the great breadth of the discipline or the diversity of its practitioners.

Although ecology is broad as a scientific discipline, it does have limits. Perhaps most importantly, ecology is a science; it is not a political philosophy or a way of life. Being an ecologist does not mean that you necessarily recycle, wear patchouli, enjoy eating granola, wear field cloths to the office, or have some fetish for home composting. This does not mean that ecologists, similar to all others, cannot try to live in a sustainable manner. Being scientists does not preclude ecologists from advocating policy decisions based upon their scientific knowledge. Nor does it mean that ecologists are to be excluded from political debate. Instead, those social and political actions are a form of environmental activism, not the scientific study of ecological processes. Ecologists may (and often should) participate in such debates, but the debates themselves are not part of the science of ecology. The ecologist is the person who applies a scientific approach to understanding the relationships between organisms and the environment. Or put another way, making coffee requires the use of chemistry, but drinking coffee does not make you a chemist.

Similarly, ecology is not simply about knowing the names of the birds, fish, and plants that you find outside. That is natural history. As we will discuss in chapters 2 and 3, natural history serves as a foundation for much ecological research; however, such activities should not be confused with the science of ecology itself. Ecology is about understanding the mechanisms causing the patterns that occur in the natural world. Natural history generally stops at describing the patterns.

Even within these limits, the science of ecology covers substantial intellectual terrain. To get a better idea of what ecology is, we will briefly review the scope of the discipline.

1.1 Overview of Ecology

Ecologists study environmental relationships ranging from those of individual organisms to factors influencing global-scale processes. The discipline of ecology addresses environmental relationships ranging from those of individual organisms to factors influencing the state of the entire

biosphere. This broad range of subjects can be arranged as levels in a hierarchy of ecological organization, such as that imbedded in the brief table of contents of this book. Figure 1.1 attempts to display such a hierarchy graphically.

Historically, the ecology of individuals (the base of figure 1.1), has been the domain of **physiological** and

behavioural ecologists. These subdisciplines have a strong footing in evolutionary theory, and rely on a detailed understanding of organismal biology to help understand ecological patterns and processes. Physiological ecologists study the morphological and physiological mechanisms organisms use to gather energy and cope with biotic and abiotic stressors in the environment. Behavioural ecologists focus principally on the determinants of individual behaviour, and how that can influence interactions among individuals and the environment. However, the distinction among these subdisciplines is often blurred. For instance, researchers in all areas may study how individuals acquire food or cope with cold weather. There is a strong conceptual linkage between studies of individuals and those of populations. **Population ecology** is centred on the factors influencing population structure and dynamics, where a population is a group of individuals of a single species inhabiting a defined area. The processes studied by population ecologists include the distribution and abundance of species, population growth and regulation, and many aspects of conservation biology. Population ecologists are particularly interested in how the environment influences these processes, including biotic and abiotic components of the environment.

Individuals interact with others from a number of species, and these interactions form the basis of the next level of organization within ecology, **community ecology**. Community ecologists study interactions such as predation, parasitism, mutualism, and competition. Some community ecologists emphasize the evolutionary effects of the interaction on the species involved, and others explore the effect the interaction has on the properties of ecological communities, such as species diversity or the provision of ecological services.

Ecosystem ecology has an even broader scope of study, including the biological, chemical, and physical processes and interactions that occur within a location. One goal of ecosystem ecology is to understand the controls on nutrient cycling and energy flow through ecosystems.

To simplify their studies, ecologists often identify and study isolated communities and ecosystems. However, all natural communities and ecosystems are open systems subject to exchanges of materials, energy, and organisms with other communities and ecosystems. The study of these exchanges, especially among ecosystems, is the intellectual territory of **landscape ecology**. However, landscapes themselves are not isolated, but are instead part of regions subject to large-scale and long-term regional processes. These regional processes and patterns are the subjects of **macroecology**. Macroecology in turn leads us to the largest spatial scale and highest level of ecological organization—the biosphere, which falls within the realm of **global ecology**.

In addition to organizing ecology by subdisciplines and spatial extent of study, we can see there is great variation in the temporal scale of ecological research. For example, physiological ecologists might be interested in how a small subcanopy tree can alter its rate of photosynthesis in response to a 0.3 second burst of sunlight. Alternatively, that same researcher may want to explore the lifetime consequences

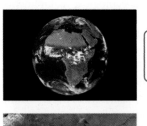

Biosphere

What role does concentration of atmospheric CO_2 play in the regulation of global temperature?

Region

How has geologic history influenced regional patterns of biodiversity?

Landscape

What factors control the movement of mammals in a fragmented landscape?

Ecosystem

How do changes in temperatures alter nutrient cycling and primary productivity?

Community

How can multiple species of grazers coexist within a single grassland?

Populations

What factors control population growth rates?

Individuals

How do animals choose what food to consume?

Figure 1.1 Levels of ecological organization and examples of the kinds of questions asked by ecologists working at each level. These ecological levels correspond broadly to sections II to VI of this book.

of these short "sunflecks" on the plant's reproductive output. These are both questions in physiological ecology, but occur at completely different temporal scales. Ecological studies can occur at even longer time scales. For example, there is currently concern that the southern edge of the boreal forest will move as a function of climate change, atmospheric nitrogen deposition, and altered fire regimes. Such "migration" may take centuries. At even deeper time scales, fossil evidence shows shifts in ecological communities over millennia. As is likely apparent, different temporal scales of ecological processes will require completely different research methods.

1.2 Sampling Ecological Research

Ecologists design their studies based on their research questions, the temporal and spatial scale of their studies, and available research tools. While the overview of ecology presented in the previous section offers a brief preview of the material covered in this book, it is by necessity a rough sketch and highly abstract. To move beyond the abstraction represented by figure 1.1 we need to connect it to the work of the scientists that have created, or continue to create the discipline of ecology. As you will see, the diversity of approaches used by different ecologists is spectacularly varied. Some will focus on construction of theory from first principles, leading to a series of testable hypotheses. Some will take these hypotheses and challenge them with data collected through careful observation. Others will perform experimental manipulations in the lab, and others perform such tests in the field. These studies may last weeks, seasons, decades, or even millennia. Studies may involve a focus on individuals, small or large populations, communities, or even entire regions. In all cases, the methods used differ. Combined, ecologists have built a rich body of knowledge, theory, and general understanding of the functioning of the natural world. Though a young science, ecology has made substantial progress. You will learn of that progress in subsequent chapters; here we briefly review the research approaches of several ecologists who have worked at a broad range of ecological levels and time scales.

The Ecology of Forest Birds: Old Tools and New

Robert MacArthur gazed intently through his binoculars. He was watching a small bird, called a warbler, searching for insects in the top of a spruce tree. To the casual observer it might have seemed that MacArthur was a weekend bird-watcher. Yes, he was intensely interested in the birds he was watching, but his scientific observations lead to the development of fundamental ecological theory.

The year was 1955, and MacArthur was studying the ecology of five species of warblers that live together in the spruce forests of northeastern North America. All five warbler species, Cape May (*Dendroica tigrina*), yellow-rumped (*D. coronata*), black-throated green (*D. virens*), blackburnian (*D. fusca*), and bay-breasted (*D. castanea*), are approximately

the same size and shape and all feed upon insects. Existing ecological theory predicted that two species with identical ecological requirements would compete with each other and that, as a consequence, they could not live in the same environment indefinitely. However, MacArthur could see with his own eyes that this theory was not correct, as the birds were clearly living together. As a scientist, he wanted to understand how species with apparently similar ecological requirements could coexist.

The question of what factors allow for the coexistence of the five warbler species falls within the realm of community ecology. MacArthur was interested in patterns that he could observe during a few years of field research, and thus he was working in a short-to-moderate time scale. MacArthur's work would prove to be a landmark study, serving as a model for future generations of ecologists. At first it may not be clear why a study of five bird species could be of such importance. However, underneath the specifics of his study was a strong research question, "what factors allow, or prevent, species coexistence?," along with well designed and executed research methodologies. The presence of the research question and how MacArthur addressed it demonstrates how MacArthur was able to conduct a scientific study, as opposed to simply documenting natural history.

The warblers fed mainly by gleaning insects from the bark and foliage of trees. MacArthur predicted that these warblers might be able to coexist and not compete with each other if they fed on insects living in different zones within trees. To map where the warblers fed, he subdivided trees into vertical and horizontal zones. He then carefully recorded the amount of time warblers spent feeding in each.

Using the most basic of field equipment—binoculars and a stopwatch—MacArthur's prediction proved to be correct. His quantitative observations demonstrated that the five warbler species in his study area fed in different zones in spruce trees. As figure 1.2 shows, the Cape May warbler fed mainly among new needles and buds at the tops of trees. The feeding zone of the blackburnian warbler overlapped broadly with that of the Cape May warbler but extended farther down the tree. The black-throated green warbler fed toward the trees' interiors. The bay-breasted warbler concentrated its feeding in the interior of trees. Finally, the yellow-rumped warbler fed mostly on the ground and low in the trees. MacArthur's observations showed that though these warblers live in the same forest, they extract food from different parts of that forest. He concluded that feeding in different zones may reduce competition among the warblers of spruce forests. Although to a casual observer it would appear as though these five bird species were feeding on the same food (insects) in the same locations (spruce trees) at the same time, close study by MacArthur showed they subdivided their environment by having slightly different feeding behaviours.

MacArthur's study (1958) of foraging by warblers is a true classic in ecology. However, like most studies it raised as many questions as it answered. Scientific research is important both for what it teaches us directly about nature and for how it stimulates other studies that improve our understanding.

Cape May warbler

Blackburnian warbler

Black-throated green warbler

New needles and buds at top of tree

New needles and buds of upper branches

New needles and buds and some older needles

Bay-breasted warbler

Yellow-rumped warbler

Old needles and bare and lichen-covered middle branches

Bare or lichen-covered lower trunk and middle branches

Figure 1.2   Warbler feeding zones. The warbler species that coexist in the forests of northeastern North America feed in distinctive zones within spruce trees, thereby reducing the potential for competition.

Science is a long, iterative process that involves the hard work of many different labs across the planet. MacArthur's work stimulated numerous studies of competition by many ecologists. Some of these studies produced results that supported MacArthur's initial theories, and others produced different results. All added to our knowledge of competition and of ecology.

Nearly half a century later, ecologists are still interested in understanding the movement of birds. However, new research tools have allowed scientists to study long-distance migration, not only movement within individual trees. Keith Hobson of Environment Canada has been a leader in developing stable isotope analysis for the study of ecological questions (Hobson 1999). Isotopes of a chemical element have different atomic masses as a result of having different numbers of neutrons. Carbon, for instance, has three isotopes: ^{12}C, ^{13}C, and ^{14}C. Of these three, ^{12}C and ^{13}C are stable isotopes because they do not undergo radioactive decay, whereas ^{14}C decays radioactively and is therefore unstable. Stable isotopes have proven useful in the study of ecological processes—for example, identifying food sources—because the proportions of various isotopes differ across the environment. Stable isotopic analysis provides ecologists with a new tool capable of revealing ecological relationships that would otherwise remain invisible, even to an ecologist with a new pair of binoculars.

Ryan Norris of Guelph University (Norris et al. 2005) has worked to refine the research tools needed to understand the feeding habitats of wide-ranging migratory birds. Norris's particular research focus is on migratory patterns, a pattern of nature quite familiar to any who live in the cold winters that cover much of Canada. In this particular study, the focal species was the American redstart (*Setophaga ruticilla*), another colourful member of the warbler family Parulidae (fig. 1.3). American redstarts are long-distance migrants, nesting in temperate North America during the summer and spending the winters in tropical Central America, northern South America, and the Caribbean islands.

Historically, studies of migratory bird species have focused on their temperate breeding grounds. However, there is much evidence that the success of an individual migratory bird during the breeding season depends on the conditions it experienced on its tropical wintering grounds. For example, it has been well established that male migratory birds arriving early on the breeding grounds are generally in better physical condition compared to those arriving later. Early arrivals also

Figure 1.3   A male American redstart, *Setophaga ruticilla*.

generally obtain the best breeding territories and have higher reproductive success.

Variation in arrival times and physical condition led ecologists to ponder the connection between events on the wintering grounds and subsequent reproductive success among birds in their breeding habitats. To answer such a question, we need a great deal of information, including where individual birds live on the wintering grounds, how the winter habitat correlates with physical condition during migration, how winter habitat influences time of arrival on the breeding grounds, and whether winter habitat correlates with reproductive success on the breeding grounds (fig. 1.4). The complexity of ecological questions has often led to the development of more powerful research tools.

Ecologists can bring samples taken in the field into the lab back in Canada and use stable isotope analysis to track habitat use by American redstarts on their wintering grounds. In Jamaica, older male American redstarts, along with some females, spend the winter in higher-productivity mangrove forest habitats, pushing most females and younger males into poorer-quality, dry scrub habitat. The dominant plants in these two habitats and the insects that feed on them contain different proportions of the carbon isotopes ^{12}C and ^{13}C. Therefore, blood samples taken from birds can reveal whether they spent their winters in the productive mangrove habitat (lower ^{13}C) or in the poor scrub habitat (higher ^{13}C). As a consequence, today's ecologist can analyze a very small sample of blood from an American redstart when it arrives on its temperate breeding ground and know much about the habitat where it spent the winter.

The studies of MacArthur and Norris show how field studies can be used to address ecological questions concerning interactions among individuals and species both within individual trees and across a large geographic extent. But what happens when humans cause changes to ecosystems, such as increased temperature, logging, or fertilizer runoff? To answer these whole-system questions, some ecologists have taken the experimental approach and applied it at amazing spatial scales.

Ecosystem Controls: Using Large-Scale Experiments to Understand Ecosystems

In the early 1960s, scientists and politicians around the world were seeing previously clear lakes turn pea-green, a process called **eutrophication**. Observers quickly realized that some nutrient was likely being added to these lakes, causing rapid algal growth. The question that was resisting an answer was which nutrient was to blame. In the mid-1960s, the Fisheries Research Board of Canada established the Freshwater Institute to search for the cause of eutrophication. At the time, lab studies were giving conflicting answers, contributing to a heated debate between scientists and industry representatives. The leaders of the Freshwater Institute realized that resolution would not be found by adding nutrients to beakers in a lab. Instead, they needed to do their experiments on a much grander scale—adding nutrients to whole lakes. In 1968, the Experimental Lakes Area (ELA) was established in Ontario, and David Schindler (fig. 1.5) was hired as "Leader of Experimental Lake Investigations."

ELA is a world-class research facility consisting of 17 watersheds containing 46 individual lakes. Under Schindler's research direction, the research team began to add different nutrients in different combinations to different lakes, measuring the response of each ecosystem. Adding a bit of fertilizer to a beaker in a lab is a relatively trivial exercise. Fertilizing a lake was much more complicated, involving motor boats, 200-litre barrels, and significant amounts of time.

In several landmark papers (e.g., Schindler 1974, 1977), Schindler was able to show that phosphorus (P) was the nutrient responsible for eutrophication. This can be seen clearly in

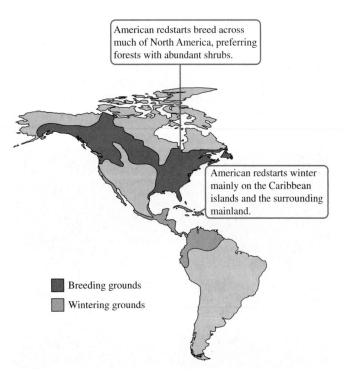

American redstarts breed across much of North America, preferring forests with abundant shrubs.

American redstarts winter mainly on the Caribbean islands and the surrounding mainland.

■ Breeding grounds
■ Wintering grounds

Figure 1.4 The breeding and wintering grounds of the American redstart, *Setophaga ruticilla.*

Figure 1.5 Dave Schindler conducting field work in a lake in Jasper National Park.

Figure 1.6 Lake 226 at the Experimental Lakes Area divided in half. The eutrophied half in the background had phosphorus added, while the clear half in the foreground did not.

a photograph of Lake 226 (fig. 1.6). For this experiment, the scientists split the lake in half, adding nitrogen and carbon to one side and nitrogen, carbon, and phosphorus to the other. The phosphorus addition caused a dramatic shift in this ecosystem: eutrophication. The next question that emerged was where the phosphorus in eutrophied lakes was coming from. It quickly became apparent that the common household detergents people used contained significant amounts of phosphorus, and as waste water this phosphorus entered lakes and streams causing eutrophication. In other words, ecological research lead to the realization that simply doing the dishes and washing clothes was resulting in the detrimental fertilization of aquatic ecosystems. Schindler travelled throughout North America and the world, explaining his research to many levels of government. Because of his work, detergents containing phosphorus have been banned from many places throughout the world, substantially improving the quality of freshwater ecosystems and of people's lives.

When Schindler was conducting this research, many other scientists around the world were trying to answer the same question. Why did Schindler's approach work where others' failed? The answer is similar to what we saw with the work of Ryan Norris. To answer hard and important questions, scientists need to be creative, often developing or enhancing the basic tools of ecological research. In this example, the underlying mechanisms driving eutrophication requires the ability of the microflora and fauna to shift in species composition as nutrient levels increase, and this could not easily be captured in a small-scale study using beakers. Another aspect that small-scale experiments neglected was the exchange of nitrogen and carbon with the atmosphere. In windswept lakes, more CO_2 from the atmosphere mixed into the water, supporting the increased photosynthesis that occurs during algal blooms. In beaker experiments, there was no such CO_2 exchange between the water and the atmosphere, and thus when phosphorus was added, algal growth often became carbon limited. Lab experiments rarely ever include all species

from natural areas, nor do they allow for surface–atmosphere interactions, and thus the conditions needed for eutrophication were better found in the field than the lab.

Research at ELA has continued, and Schindler has since moved to the University of Alberta and continues research in aquatic ecology with significant impacts on governmental policy. As time passed and questions were answered, the research focus shifted. Ongoing studies explore the effect of acidification on lake communities and whether these ecosystems can recover; the impacts of climate change; the consequences of introducing fish to historically fishless lakes; and the impacts of tars and development on the health of local streams and rivers. Using the basic experimental approach refined in the 1960s, Schindler and colleagues continue to address many of the most pressing questions in freshwater ecology (Schindler et al. 1985, 1990). Despite the size of these ecosystem experiments, questions occur over even larger spatial scales, and a group of landscape and geographic ecologists are willing to tackle them.

Change: Using Information About the Organism to Describe and Predict Temporal and Spatial Changes in Species Distributions

The earth and its life are always changing, and this will be the dominant theme of chapter 23, the final chapter in this book. Though the rapid changes associated with eutrophication and pine beetle outbreaks and the impacts of oil development often make the front pages of the newspapers, many ecological and evolutionary changes occur over such long periods of time and such broad spatial extents that they are difficult to study, and even more difficult to distil down to a sound bite for a reporter. As is often the case, a critical step in studying large-scale and long-term ecological questions is combining the right research tool with detailed knowledge of the biology of the organisms being studied.

Margaret Davis (1983, 1989) carefully searched through a sample of lake sediments for pollen. The sediments had come from a lake in the Appalachian Mountains, and the pollen they contained would help her document changes near the lake during the past several thousands of years. Davis is a paleoecologist, and she has spent much of her professional career studying changes in the distributions of plants during the last 20,000 years. During this period the earth underwent rapid climate change, with advancing and retreating glacier fields throughout regions of the Northern Hemisphere. By understanding plant biology, Davis' work is proving invaluable to understanding how modern species are likely to respond to prolonged periods of environmental change.

Some of the pollen produced by plants that live near a lake falls on the lake surface, sinks, and becomes trapped in lake sediments. As sediments build up over the centuries, this pollen is preserved and forms a historical record of the kinds of plants that lived nearby. As the lakeside vegetation changes, the mix of pollen preserved in the lake's sediments also changes. In the example shown in figure 1.7, the earliest appearance of pollen from spruce trees, *Picea* spp., is in the lake sediments from about 12,000 years ago and pollen from

Lake profile

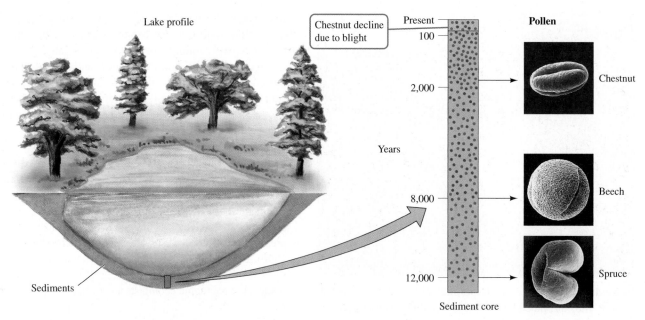

Chestnut decline due to blight

Present
100
2,000

8,000

12,000

Years

Sediment core

Pollen

Chestnut

Beech

Spruce

Sediments

Figure 1.7   The vegetation history of landscapes can be reconstructed using the pollen contained within the sediments of nearby lakes.

beech, *Fagus grandifolia,* first appears in the sediments from about 8,000 years ago. Chestnut pollen does not appear in the sediments until about 2,000 years ago. The pollen from all three tree species continues in the sediment record until about 1920, when chestnut blight killed most of the chestnut trees in the vicinity of the lake. Thus, the pollen preserved in the sediments of individual lakes can be used to construct a paleoecological record. By studying many different lakes, Davis could study changes in vegetation across an entire continent.

The biology of organisms can be used not only as a record of change, but also as a tool to predict and understand future changes. One difficulty in understanding changes that occur over large regions, or even across the planet, is difficulty in collecting data at such spatial scale. Once again, ecologists have developed critical research tools.

Trevor Platt is a research scientist in Canada's Department of Fisheries and Oceans. He has spent the last several decades working to understand large-scale patterns in marine productivity. Platt has been particularly interested in determining the factors that control variation in marine **primary productivity**, and in developing tools to measure it (Platt 1975; Platt and Jassby 1976). Marine ecologists and oceanographers are very interested in understanding the growth of phytoplankton, as these small photosynthetic organisms serve as the base of most marine food webs. Why do people care about changes to the small organisms? Changes in marine productivity can lead to changes in the abundances of other species, including the abundance of fish and crustaceans harvested by people. This in turn can influence the economic well-being of many coastal communities. A great challenge in Platt's work is that marine systems are enormous, at least in comparison to the size of most terrestrial habitats, and physically sampling such a large area is generally not practical. So, Platt used his knowledge of phytoplankton biology to help develop a number of methods by which these organisms could be sampled remotely, such as spectral reflectance patterns

received from satellite imagery. Platt and his colleagues have further enhanced these techniques over time, allowing ecologists to study productivity over large spatial extents (fig. 1.8).

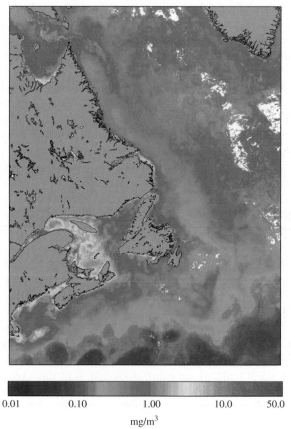

0.01   0.10   1.00   10.0   50.0

mg/m^3

Figure 1.8   By understanding the spectral properties of chlorophyll, ecologists are able to estimate primary productivity across large geographic areas. Shown here are chlorophyll-a abundances (an indicator of productivity) in early July 2009 across a broad area of the Atlantic Zone of Canada.

Figure 1.9 Boundaries within landscapes created by human activity (background) and natural environmental gradients (foreground).

Figure 1.10 Marie-Josée Fortin answers ecological questions by developing and applying statistical methods to empirical data.

This work is proving critical to understanding how marine systems change in response to shifting climates, and how changes in primary production can influence the success or failure of marine fisheries.

The detection of spatial patterns is just as important on land as it is in the ocean. Although terrestrial systems tend to be smaller than marine ones, they also tend to be heavily fragmented by natural barriers (e.g., streams) and a diversity of human activities (fig. 1.9). Some organisms tend to live near edges of disturbances, and others only in interior regions. To understand how much habitat remains (or is destroyed), it is critical to be able to identify the boundaries of one community from another. Marie-Josée Fortin of the University of Toronto and her colleagues (fig. 1.10) have been exploring and expanding the statistical tools available to ecologists (Fortin et al. 2000, 2005).

There exist a variety of types of ecological boundaries. **Ecotones** are transitions from one type of ecosystem to another, for instance the transition from an agricultural field into the surrounding forest (fig. 1.9). Historically, ecologists have often ignored ecotones, focusing research in areas of a "typical" forest, grassland, or other ecosystem. However, as the natural world becomes more and more fragmented through human activities and as large-scale disturbances increase in frequency, the amount of transitional area in a landscape increases exponentially. The plant and animal species that occupy transition zones are often at their physiological limits, and may be particularly sensitive to any additional environmental change. If one is able to accurately measure the location of transition zones, then one can also measure whether these locations change over time. Boundary delimitation is also important for land managers and conservation groups. For example, many municipalities have strict regulations regarding land development, particularly in

wetland areas. For these to be enforced requires someone to literally draw a line separating the two. Placing the line in the wrong place causes either unnecessary loss of income for the landowner or preventable ecological damage to the community. None of this work can be done without clear and accurate methods for identifying boundaries. In ecology, mathematical tools, such as those developed by Fortin, can be just as important as binoculars, lab equipment, and a strong back.

As you will see throughout this text, some ecological methods, particularly quantitative methods, can be applied to questions conducted on a diversity of taxa in a number of different locations. For example, although Fortin and colleagues have generally focused on identifying ecotones in the forests of Quebec, they have recently applied the same tools to exploring the geographic ranges and distribution limits of animals. Superficially these questions appear unrelated. However, they are linked by important conceptual issues: Where is the boundary? How wide is it? Is it straight (i.e., mostly human-made) or is it curvy (i.e., driven by environmental factors and species interactions)? Identifying range expansion and contraction of animal and plant species has important ecological and conservation implications. Fortin and her group are at the forefront of landscape ecology, both developing new statistical methods and applying them to address issues of broad ecological concern.

As we have seen so far in this chapter, different quantitative tools are needed to address different ecological questions. Schindler and his colleagues were able to convincingly show the main impact of added phosphorus on lake eutrophication through strong experiments and clear photographs. Fortin has developed complex statistical methods and models to help ecologists understand how boundaries move through time and space. Most ecologists require a statistical toolbox somewhere between these two examples, and in fact other research by Schindler and Fortin also requires a diversity of statistical approaches. Because so many of the questions in ecology are conceptually complex, it is essential that as you learn ecology you also become familiar with basic statistical approaches. We have provided you with an introduction to

many statistical tests that are commonly used by ecologists, and that will be discussed throughout the text (appendix A). We encourage you to read this appendix before diving into the remaining 22 chapters, as that information will help guide your understanding of how ecologists actually make discoveries. We end this chapter with an overview of the scope of ecology.

The Scope of Ecology

With this brief review of research approaches and topics, we return to the question asked at the beginning of the chapter: What is ecology? Ecology is indeed the study of relationships between organisms and the environment. However, as you can see from the research we have reviewed, ecologists examine those relationships over a large range of temporal and spatial scales using a wide variety of approaches. Ecology includes Fortin's studies of forests in Quebec and Davis' studies of vegetation movement across North America. Ecology also includes the observational studies of MacArthur, as well as the whole-ecosystem manipulations of Schindler. Some ecological studies, such as Norris' measures of stable isotopes, involve long hours at a bench in a lab. Other studies, such as those of Platt, rely on the use of satellites that orbit Earth. Some ecologists study processes that take place over short periods of time over small spatial scales, while others ask questions that involve millennia and cover large regions of earth. All this is ecology.

As fun and enjoyable as it is to spend summers conducting field work in beautiful locations throughout the world, one factor that differentiates an ecologist from eco-tourists and natural historians is a strict reliance on the scientific method. Ecologists are scientists answering complex questions in natural and managed systems; we are not simply observing the landscape. If you want to predict the impacts of climate change on local species diversity, bring in an ecologist. If you want to understand how predators may alter prey densities,

bring in an ecologist. If you want to determine the importance of a given patch of habitat on the migration of an endangered animal, bring in an ecologist. Critical to our ability to find answers to these questions is our ability to objectively identify and evaluate relationships in complex data sets. Though it may come as a surprise to many, ecology is among the more quantitative disciplines of biology. As a result, a strong understanding of quantitative methods and statistics is critical to the success of students of ecology, and we again encourage you read appendix A. As fun and enjoyable as it is to read several pages of statistical methods, we also encourage you to not limit learning to reading and listening to lectures. Natural history is also a foundation of ecology, and understanding ecology is intimately intertwined with observing nature and doing ecology.

However, ecology is a science principally concerned with understanding interactions between organisms and the environment. As such, field studies—both controlled observations and experimental manipulations—are of particular importance and value to the discipline. This will not be the case for many subdisciplines of biology or other branches of science. Thus, the reason the ecologists in your department often "head to the field" is one of scientific necessity—field data are the ultimate test of the accuracy or theory, predictions, and expectations. Though one will be able to learn the core principles of ecology from this text and your instructors, one is less able to "do" ecology without getting dirty in the field.

The brief survey of ecology in this chapter has only hinted at the conceptual and methodological basis for the research described. Throughout this book we emphasize the foundations of ecology. Each chapter focuses on a few ecological concepts, and we explore some of the applications and tools associated with the concepts introduced. We continue our exploration of ecology in section I with the natural history of life on land and in water. Natural history is the foundation upon which ecologists built modern ecology.

ECOLOGY IN ACTION

The Scientific Method

Ecologists explore the relationships between organisms and environment using the methods of science. The series of boxes called "Ecology In Action" that are found in all the chapters of this book provide discussions of various examples showing how ecologists are addressing real-world problems. Taken together, these boxes demonstrate the breadth of research conducted by ecologists. Unifying these boxes is

one central idea: science can be used to answer questions of societal concern. To begin with, we present here not an example from the field, but instead an overview of the scientific method.

Let us begin this discussion with the most basic question. What is science? The word *science* comes from the Latin word, *scientia,* meaning "to know." Broadly speaking, science is a

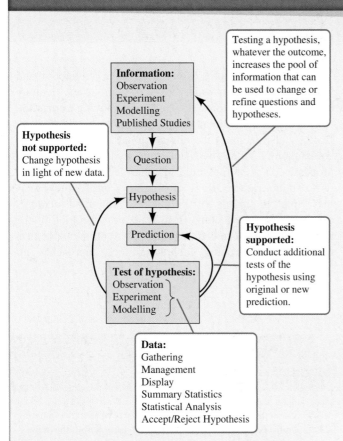

Testing a hypothesis, whatever the outcome, increases the pool of information that can be used to change or refine questions and hypotheses.

Information:
Observation
Experiment
Modelling
Published Studies

Hypothesis not supported:
Change hypothesis in light of new data.

Question

Hypothesis

Prediction

Hypothesis supported:
Conduct additional tests of the hypothesis using original or new prediction.

Test of hypothesis:
Observation
Experiment
Modelling

Data:
Gathering
Management
Display
Summary Statistics
Statistical Analysis
Accept/Reject Hypothesis

Figure 1.11 Graphic summary of the scientific method. The scientific method centres on the use of information to propose and test hypotheses through observation, experiment, and modelling.

way of obtaining knowledge about the natural world using certain formal procedures. There are a number of different philosophies and approaches to conducting science, but they all share the same goal—understanding the natural world. One approach to science is particularly common, and is generally referred to as "the scientific method." We outline it here in figure 1.11. Despite a great diversity of approaches to doing science, sound scientific studies have many methodological characteristics in common. The most universal and critical

aspects of the scientific method are asking interesting questions and forming testable hypotheses.

Questions are the guiding lights of the scientific process. Without them, exploration of nature lacks focus and yields little understanding of the world. Let's consider some questions asked by the ecologists discussed in this chapter. The main question asked by Robert MacArthur in his studies of warblers was: "How can several species of insect-eating warblers live in the same forest without one species eventually excluding the others through competition?" David Schindler asked, "What nutrients cause lake eutrophication?" While this focus on questions may seem obvious, one of the most common questions asked of scientists at seminars and professional meetings is, "What is your question?"

If scientists are in the business of asking questions about nature, where does a hypothesis enter the process? The word *hypothesis* itself can be defined in many ways, and here we use a general definition of a potential answer to a question. For MacArthur, one hypothesis was: "Several warbler species are able to coexist because each species feeds on insects living in different zones within trees." The central hypothesis of the Schindler study was: "Increased phosphorus, not nitrogen or carbon, is responsible for lake eutrophication." A single research question may generate multiple alternative hypotheses, rather than a simple yes/no contrast. For example, an alternative hypothesis for MacArthur's study could have been, "Several warbler species are able to coexist because each species feeds on insects at different times within trees." In science, there can be more than a single factually correct answer, and researchers who ignore alternative explanations to the patterns they observe do so at their own intellectual peril!

Once a scientist proposes a hypothesis (or multiple alternative hypotheses), the next step in the scientific method is to determine its validity by testing predictions that follow from each hypothesis (more accurately scientists typically test *null hypotheses,* an issue that is discussed in appendix A). Three fundamental ways to collect the data needed to test hypotheses are through observation, experiments, and modelling. These approaches, which are all represented in the research presented here in chapter 1 and in figure 1.11, will be discussed in detail throughout the text.

SUMMARY

1.1 Ecologists study environmental relationships ranging from those of individual organisms to factors influencing global-scale processes.

The research focus and questions posed by ecologists differ across the levels of organization studied.

1.2 Ecologists design their studies based on their research questions, the temporal and spatial scale of their studies, and available research tools.

With this brief review of research approaches and topics, we return to the question asked at the beginning of the chapter: What is ecology? Ecology is indeed the study of relationships between organisms and the environment. However, as you can see from the studies we have reviewed, ecologists study those relationships over a large range of temporal and spatial scales using a wide variety of approaches. Ecology includes Davis's studies of vegetation moving across the North American continent over a span of thousands of years. Ecology also includes the observational studies of birds in contemporary forests by MacArthur. Ecologists may study processes on plots measured in square centimetres or, like those studying the ecology of migratory birds, study areas may span thousands of kilometres. Important ecological discoveries have come from Nadkarni's probing of the rain forest canopy and from traces of stable isotopes in a droplet of blood. Ecology includes all these approaches and many more.

REVIEW QUESTIONS

1. Faced with the complexity of nature, ecologists have divided the field of ecology into subdisciplines, each of which focuses on one of the levels of organization pictured in figure 1.1. What is the advantage of developing such subdisciplines within ecology?

2. What are the pitfalls of subdividing nature in the way it is represented in figure 1.1? In what ways does figure 1.1 misrepresent nature?

3. What could you do to verify that the distinct feeding zones used by the warblers studied by MacArthur (see fig. 1.2) are the result of ongoing competition between the different species of warblers? How might you examine the role of competition in keeping some American redstarts out of the most productive feeding areas on their wintering grounds?

4. David Schindler chose to conduct an experiment manipulating an entire ecosystem, rather than small areas within the ecosystem. What are the potential costs and benefits of such large-scale approaches to science?

5. How can an understanding of the biology of individual species help ecologists understand long-term population changes?

6. In ecology, there are experimentalists and theorists; some work in the field, some in the lab. Why is there value in using a diversity of philosophical approaches and tools in addressing research questions?

7. How can scientific information be used to inform political decisions? How much evidence is "sufficient" before a scientist advocates for a particular solution?

For more information on the resources available from McGraw-Hill Ryerson, go to **www.mcgrawhill.ca/he/solutions**.

NATURAL HISTORY AND EVOLUTION

The science of ecology is built upon a foundation of natural history and evolutionary biology. In section I, we describe some of the common terrestrial and aquatic ecosystems that occur around the world and the dominant environmental factors that influence these systems. We conclude with an overview of evolution, a set of biological processes intimately intertwined with ecological interactions.

Chapter 2   Life on Land
Chapter 3   Life in Water
Chapter 4   Evolution and Speciation

LIFE ON LAND

CHAPTER 2

CHAPTER CONCEPTS

2.1 Uneven heating of the earth's spherical surface by the sun and the tilt of the earth on its axis combine to produce predictable latitudinal variation in climate.

Concept 2.1 Review

2.2 Soil structure results from the long-term interaction of climate, organisms, topography, and parent mineral material.

Concept 2.2 Review

Ecology in Action: Natural History of Soils

2.3 The geographic distribution of terrestrial biomes corresponds closely to variation in climate, especially prevailing temperature and precipitation.

Concept 2.3 Review

Ecological Tools and Approaches: Biomes of Canada and Winter Ecology

Summary

Review Questions

atural history is the study of how organisms in a particular area are influenced by factors such as climate, soils, predators, competitors, mutualists, and evolutionary history. A solid understanding of natural history provides the foundation for modern ecology and conservation biology. One of the most dramatic restoration successes that depended upon understanding both natural history and ecology comes from Costa Rica. Daniel Janzen's goal was to restore tropical dry forest to Guanacaste National Park. Janzen is an ecologist, and like Robert MacArthur (chapter 1), he gives us a great example of how a combination of the scientific method and detailed observation can lead to significant discoveries. Perhaps not too surprisingly, Guanacaste National Park contains the guanacaste tree, *Enterolobium cyclocarpum* (fig. 2.1*a*). The guanacaste tree, a member of the pea family, produces disk-shaped fruit about 10 cm in diameter and 4 to 10 mm thick. Each year, a large tree produces up to 5,000 of these fruits, which fall to the ground when ripe. As Janzen studied the guanacaste tree, he asked a simple question, why does the guanacaste tree produce so much fruit? His answer was that the fruit of the tree should promote seed dispersal by animals.

Janzen, however, knew of no native animals of the size and behaviour that would make them dependable dispersers of guanacaste seeds. Dependable dispersers would be necessary to speed restoration of tropical dry forests across Guanacaste National Park. Had the guanacaste tree evolved an elaborate fruit and made thousands of them each year in the absence of native dispersers? On the surface, it appeared so, but this did not seem to make sense. Without some means of dispersing their seeds, the majority of offspring would fall from the tree and remain at the base of the maternal plant. This appears to be a dangerous place for seedlings to grow, as their mother would cast shade over them and draw resources from the soils around them.

Janzen's plans for restoration of tropical dry forests were guided by his knowledge of natural history. As he considered the long-term natural history of Central American dry forest, he found what he was looking for: a whole host of large herbivorous animals, including gomphotheres (elephant-like animals), ground sloths, camels, and horses (fig. 2.1*b*). The dry forest had once supported plenty of potential dispersers of guanacaste seeds, all of which became extinct about 10,000 years ago. For thousands of years following these extinctions, the guanacaste tree continued its annual production of fruits, but there were few large animals to consume them. Then, about 500 years ago, Europeans introduced horses and cattle, which ate the fruits of the guanacaste tree and dispersed its seeds around the landscape. Janzen recognized the practical value of livestock as seed dispersers and included them in his plan for tropical dry forest restoration.

(a)

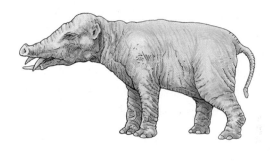

(b)

Figure 2.1   (*a*) A guanacaste tree, *Enterolobium cyclocarpum,* growing in Costa Rica. Guanacaste trees, which produce large amounts of edible fruit, require large herbivores to disperse their seeds. (*b*) An artistic rendering of *Phiomia,* a now-extinct gomphothere, in comparison to a modern day African Elephant. Gomphotheres are putative consumers of the guanacaste fruit.

From this footing in natural history, Janzen then applied a formal scientific method, as we described in chapter 1. He first tested, and confirmed, the hypothesis that contemporary horses could act as effective seed dispersers for the guanacaste tree. After this test, he applied his knowledge by incorporating horses into the management plan for Guanacaste National Park. The guanacaste tree and other trees in a similar predicament would have their dispersers, and restoration of tropical dry forest would be accelerated. However, he alone could not change the practices of the park. Instead, he realized success would require collaboration and cooperation from people of various sectors of society—those that live around the park as well as those that govern the country.

Janzen's pioneering work (1981a, 1981b) shows how natural history, along with science and community engagement, can be used to address a practical problem. Janzen's work also shows the impact that humans have on ecological interactions; both in their influence on species extinctions as well as working with governments to effect positive change through restoration. This theme—that people are not separate from ecological processes—will be common throughout the book.

Because the science of ecology continues to rest upon a solid foundation of natural history, we devote chapters 2 and 3 to the natural history of the biosphere. In chapter 2, we examine the natural history of life on land. Before we begin that discussion, we need to introduce some of the challenges of life on land, and the broad classification of terrestrial biomes. We also discuss the development and ecology of soils, the living system that supports all terrestrial biomes.

Life on Land and Terrestrial Biomes

Life on land can be brutal. Most terrestrial organisms are essentially bags of water surrounded by dry air. As a result, they are at constant threat of dehydration due to evaporation of the water contained within their tissues. Even when an organism can keep their water inside, low temperatures make that water dangerous. When ice crystals form, they puncture and destroy living cells, leading to organ damage and even death. Heat, too, can be a significant challenge for terrestrial organisms. At high temperatures proteins denature, reducing the efficiency of many biological processes. An even more basic problem of life on land is the cruel and persistent force of gravity. Compared to aquatic organisms, there is no natural buoyancy for organisms that live on land. Elaborate structures are required to simply stand, let alone grow and move. Dealing with all of these stressors requires specific traits, such as woody tissues in plants, the ability to sweat or pant for some mammals, or the ability to lower the freezing point of water as is found among some amphibians. The physiological ecology of dealing with abiotic stressors is discussed in section II. Here, we describe how common abiotic conditions, such as temperature and precipitation, result in predictable characteristics in the species that live under such conditions.

Chapter 2 focuses on major divisions of the terrestrial environment called **biomes**. Biomes are distinguished primarily by the commonly observed plant species, and each

is associated with a particular climate. Because each biome will contain different types of plants and animals and occur in regions with very different climates, their natural histories differ a great deal. The main goal of chapter 2 is to take a large-scale perspective of nature before delving, in later chapters, into finer details of structure and process. We pay particular attention to the geographic distributions of the major biomes, the climate associated with each, their soils, the common characteristics of the species able to live under those conditions, and the extent of human influences. Now let's move on to the central concepts of this chapter, which concern patterns of climatic variation, soil structure and ecology, and the global distribution of the major biomes.

2.1 Large-Scale Patterns of Climatic Variation

Uneven heating of the earth's spherical surface by the sun and the tilt of the earth on its axis combine to produce predictable latitudinal variation in climate. In chapter 1, ecology was defined as the study of the relationships between organisms and their environment. Consequently, understanding geographic and seasonal variations in temperature and precipitation is fundamental to studying ecology. Several attributes of climate vary predictably over the earth. For instance, average temperatures are lower and more seasonal (varying predictably over the year) at middle and high latitudes than near the equator. Deserts, which are concentrated in a narrow band of latitudes around the globe, receive little precipitation, which generally falls unpredictably in time and space. However, average climatic conditions over a large geographic extent do not necessarily indicate the typical climate for a given location within that broad area. For example, unique geographic features allow wineries to exist in the Niagara Peninsula in southern Ontario, even though the broader region has a climate unsuitable for commercial grape production. In this section, we will discuss the major mechanisms that produce these and other patterns of climatic variation, leaving these local exceptions to later chapters.

Temperature, Precipitation, and Atmospheric Circulation

Much of the earth's climatic variation is caused by uneven heating of its surface by the sun. This uneven heating results from the spherical shape of the earth and the angle at which the earth rotates on its axis as it orbits the sun. Because the earth is a sphere, the sun's rays are most concentrated where the sun is directly overhead. However, the latitude at which the sun is directly overhead changes with the seasons. This seasonal change occurs because the earth's axis of rotation is not perpendicular to its plane of orbit about the sun, but is tilted approximately 23.5° away from the perpendicular (fig. 2.2).

Because this tilted angle of rotation is maintained throughout Earth's orbit about the sun, the amount of solar energy received by the Northern and Southern Hemispheres

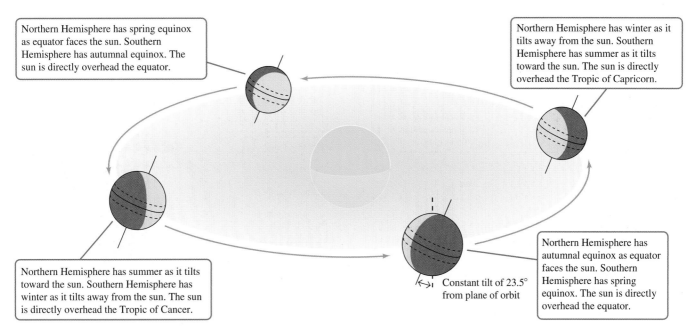

Figure 2.2 The seasons in the Northern and Southern Hemispheres.

changes seasonally. During the northern summer, the Northern Hemisphere is tilted toward the sun and receives more solar energy than the Southern Hemisphere. During the northern summer solstice on approximately June 21, the sun is directly overhead at the tropic of Cancer, at 23.5° N latitude. During the northern winter solstice, on approximately December 21, the sun is directly overhead at the tropic of Capricorn, at 23.5° S latitude. During the northern winter, the Northern Hemisphere is tilted away from the sun and the Southern Hemisphere receives more solar energy. The sun is directly overhead at the equator during the spring and autumnal equinoxes, on approximately March 21 and September 23. On those dates, the Northern and Southern Hemispheres receive approximately equal amounts of solar radiation.

This regular shift in the latitude at which the sun is directly overhead drives the changes we associate with the different seasons of the year. At high latitudes, in both the Northern and Southern Hemispheres, seasonal shifts in input of solar energy produce winters with low average temperatures and shorter day lengths and summers with high average temperatures and longer day lengths. In contrast, between the tropics of Cancer and Capricorn, seasonal variations in temperature and day length are slight, while precipitation may vary greatly. What produces spatial and temporal variation in precipitation?

Heating of the earth's surface and atmosphere drives circulation of the atmosphere and influences patterns of precipitation. As shown in figure 2.3*a*, the sun constantly heats air at the equator, causing the air to expand and rise. This warm, moist air cools as it rises. Since cool air holds less water vapour than warm air, the water vapour carried by this rising air mass condenses and forms clouds, which produce the heavy rainfall associated with tropical environments.

Eventually, this equatorial air mass ceases to rise and spreads to the north and south. This high-altitude air is dry, since the moisture it once held fell as tropical rains. As this air mass moves away from the intensity of solar warming found at the equator, it cools, increasing its density. Eventually, this denser air sinks back to the earth's surface at about 30° latitude, where it again spreads both to the north and south. This dry air draws moisture from the lands over which it flows, creating a band of deserts.

Air moving from 30° latitude back to the equator completes a thermal loop, which forms the Hadley cell. As figure 2.3*b* shows, there are three atmospheric cells on either side of the equator, called the Hadley, Ferrel, and Polar cells. The Polar cell functions in a manner similar to the Hadley cell, driven by air movement associated with warming at 60° latitude and cooling at the poles. The Polar cell is primarily responsible for the weather patterns associated with most northerly and southerly areas, bringing cool weather from the poles. Though displayed as single narrow arrows in figure 2.3, it is important to recognize that each cell surrounds all longitudes around the earth.

The Ferrel cell occurs at mid-latitudes, and is driven in part by the effects of the Hadley and Polar cells. When moist air flowing from the Hadley cell rises as it meets cold air flowing from the Polar cell, moisture picked up from desert regions at lower latitudes condenses to form the clouds that produce the abundant precipitation of temperate regions.

The patterns of atmospheric circulation shown in figure 2.3*b* suggest that air movement is directly north and south. However, this does not reflect what we observe from the earth's surface as the earth rotates from west to east. An observer at tropical latitudes observes winds that blow from the northeast in the Northern Hemisphere and from the southeast in the Southern Hemisphere (fig. 2.4). These are the *northeast* and *southeast trades*. Someone studying winds within the temperate belt between 30° and 60° latitude would observe that winds blow mainly from the west. These are the *westerlies* of temperate latitudes. At high latitudes, our

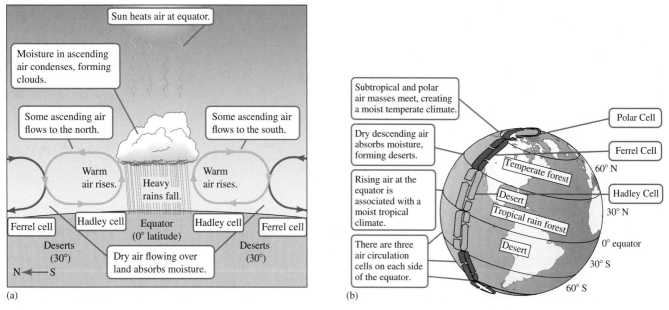

Figure 2.3 (*a*) Solar-driven air circulation. (*b*) Latitude and atmospheric circulation.

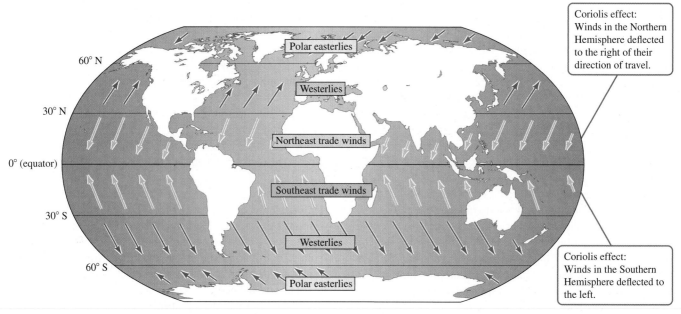

Figure 2.4 The Coriolis effect and wind direction.

observer would find that the predominant wind direction is from the east. These are the *polar easterlies.*

Why don't winds move directly north to south? The prevailing winds do not move in a straight north–south direction because of the **Coriolis effect**. In the Northern Hemisphere, the Coriolis effect causes an apparent deflection of winds to the right of their direction of travel and to the left in the Southern Hemisphere. We say "apparent" deflection because we see this deflection only if we make our observations from the surface of the earth. To an observer in space, it would appear that winds move in approximately a straight line, while the earth rotates beneath them.

Geographic variation in temperature and precipitation is very complex, but also very important to the science of

ecology. The distribution of biomes we discuss in this chapter is substantially influenced by geographic variation in temperature and precipitation. How can we study and represent variation in these climatic variables without being overwhelmed by a mass of numbers? This practical problem is addressed by a visual device called a climate diagram.

Climate Diagrams

Climate diagrams were developed by Heinrich Walter (1985) as a tool to explore the relationship between the distribution of terrestrial vegetation and climate. Climate diagrams summarize a great deal of useful climatic information, including seasonal variation in temperature and precipitation, the length

and intensity of wet and dry seasons, and the portion of the year during which average minimum temperature is above and below 0°C.

As shown in figures 2.5 and 2.6, climate diagrams summarize climatic information using a standardized structure. The months of the year are plotted on the horizontal axis, beginning with January and ending with December for locations in the Northern Hemisphere, and beginning with July and ending with June in the Southern Hemisphere. Temperature is plotted on the left vertical axis and precipitation on the right vertical axis. Temperature and precipitation are plotted on different scales so that 10°C is equivalent to 20 mm of precipitation.

Because the temperature and precipitation scales are constructed so that 10°C equals 20 mm of precipitation, the relative positions of the temperature and precipitation lines reflect water availability. In general, adequate moisture for plant growth exists when the precipitation line lies above the temperature line. These moist periods are indicated in the figure by blue shading. When the temperature line lies above the precipitation line, potential evaporation rate exceeds precipitation. These dry periods are indicated by gold shading in the climate diagram. Notice that gold shading of the climate diagram for Yuma, Arizona (fig. 2.6a), indicates year-round drought, while the blue shading of the climate diagram for Kuala Lumpur (fig. 2.6b) indicates moist conditions year-round. Climate diagrams for wet areas such as tropical rain forest compress the precipitation scale for precipitation above 100 mm so that 10°C is equivalent to 200 mm of precipitation. With this change in scale, rainfall data from very wet climates can fit on a graph of convenient size. This change in scale is represented by darker

shading in the climate diagram for Kuala Lumpur, Malaysia (fig. 2.6b). Notice that the precipitation at Kuala Lumpur exceeds 100 mm during all months of the year.

The climate diagram for Dzamiin Uuded, Mongolia (fig. 2.6c), is much more complex than those of either the rain forest or hot desert. This complexity results from the much greater seasonal change in the cold desert climate. Dzamiin Uuded is moist from October to April. These moist periods are separated by the months of May to September, when the temperature line rises above the precipitation line, indicating drought. During October to April, the mean *minimum* temperature at Dzamiin Uuded is below freezing (0°C). The months when the mean minimum temperature is above freezing are May through September.

Climate diagrams also include the mean annual temperature, which is presented in the upper left corner (e.g., 27.5°C at Kuala Lumpur). The mean annual precipitation (e.g., 86 mm at Yuma, Arizona) is presented in the upper right corner of each climate diagram. The elevation of each site, in metres above sea level (e.g., 962 m at Dzamiin Uuded), is also presented in the upper right corner.

As you can see, climate diagrams efficiently summarize important environmental variables. In the following section, we discuss another central aspect of all terrestrial biomes: soil.

CONCEPT 2.1 REVIEW

1. How would seasonality in temperature and precipitation be affected if the earth's rotation on its axis were perpendicular to its plane or orbit about the sun?
2. Why does the annual rainy season in regions near 23° N begin in June?

2.2 Soil: Foundation of Terrestrial Biomes

Soil structure results from the long-term interaction of climate, organisms, topography, and parent mineral material. What is **soil** and why should an ecologist care? It is fair to say that there are few topics that many biology students find less interesting than soils (though decomposition, a topic discussed in chapter 20, is a close second!). An ecologist studies wolves, elk, caribou, and the beauty of the North, right? Yes, some ecologists study those things, and many important questions have been answered. However, none of those things would exist without soil. Soil is a complex mixture of living and nonliving material upon which most terrestrial life depends. In addition to its importance in sustaining the communities and ecosystems that we can easily see, soils themselves are complex ecological systems. The amount of organic material, living and dead, found in soil is not trivial. In fact, it is estimated that there is more organic carbon stored below ground than above ground (Schimel 1995), leading to

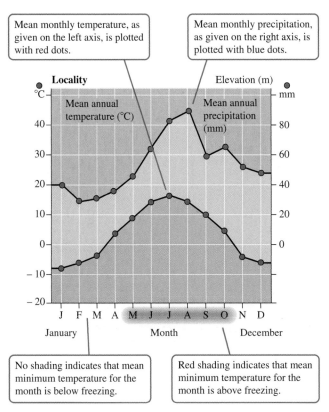

Figure 2.5 The structure of climate diagrams.

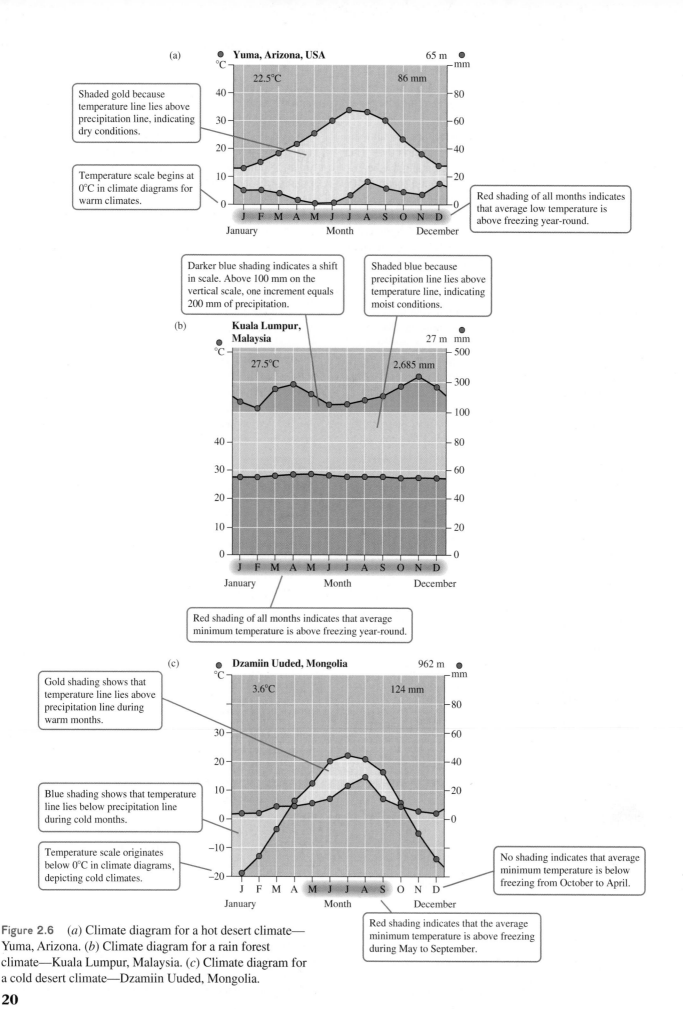

Figure 2.6 (*a*) Climate diagram for a hot desert climate—Yuma, Arizona. (*b*) Climate diagram for a rain forest climate—Kuala Lumpur, Malaysia. (*c*) Climate diagram for a cold desert climate—Dzamiin Uuded, Mongolia.

the logical conclusion that "the terrestrial world is brown and black, not green" (Wall et al. 2005). Although most students may imagine ecology to be primarily about the study of the charismatic megafauna that you see on nature shows and hear about from environmental lobbying groups, the reality is that much of what drives the world's systems occurs below our feet. It may then come as no surprise that a growing number of ecologists are realizing that if we want to understand the ecological interactions in communities, or the movement of energy and nutrients within ecosystems, it is critical that ecologists understand what happens below ground at least as well as what happens on the surface. Here we provide an overview of the natural history of soils, including their structure, development, and biodiversity.

From the surface, many soils look quite similar: a dark base covered with a layer of fallen leaves and branches. However, when the soil is broken and a pit is dug, one will typically find differently coloured layers, or horizons, which merge into one another as you dig deeper into the soil (fig. 2.7). At the surface of the soil lies the majority of the organic matter. In Canada, this organic horizon will be called either the O horizon or the LFH horizon. **O horizons** are found in soils in

which the plant material is primarily aquatic in nature (e.g., peat mosses), and **LFH horizons** are generally found in more upland sites. Regardless of the designation, at the surface of the organic horizon you will find freshly fallen organic matter such as whole leaves, twigs, flowers, and fruits. This organic litter is the food source and home to a wide variety of organisms, and their activity results in the deeper portions of the organic horizon containing highly fragmented and partially decomposed organic matter. Small organic horizons are found in areas with little litter deposition (e.g., deserts and farmland) or high decomposition rates (e.g., tropical rainforests), and deep organic horizons are found in areas with substantial litter inputs and/or low decomposition rates (e.g., bogs and fens).

The **A horizon** contains a mixture of mineral materials, such as clay, silt, and sand, as well as organic material derived from the organic horizon above. The A horizon also supports substantial biological activity, including burrowing animals such as earthworms, which can mix organic matter from the organic horizon into the A horizon. As a result, the A horizon is generally rich in mineral nutrients, including those essential for plant growth. With rainfall, the A horizon is leached of clays, iron, aluminum, silicates, and **humus** (partially

Figure 2.7 Soil profile exposed in a boreal forest site, showing LFH, A, B, and C horizons.

decomposed organic matter), all of which gradually move down through the soil profile into the B horizon.

The **B horizon** contains the materials leached from above, often resulting in a distinctive banding pattern. Below the B horizon is the **C horizon**, consisting of weathered parent material, which has been broken down through the actions of frost, water, microbial activity, and deep penetrating roots. This weathering results in the production of the sand, silt, clay, and rock fragments that we generally associate with soils. Under the C horizon we find unweathered parent material, which is often bedrock.

Although soils appear static, their structure is actually in a constant state of flux due to the interactive actions of climate, organisms, topography, parent material, and time (Jenny 1980). Plants secrete numerous **root exudates**, which, along with the living roots and plant litter, serve as substrates for bacterial, fungal, and animal species. The growth and activity of these organisms provides stability to the mineral components of the soil, allowing the development and maintenance of complex canals of air spaces and cavities within the soil. Climate affects the rates of weathering of parent materials, leaching of organic and inorganic substances, erosion, and decomposition of organic matter through direct weathering effects. Climate can also alter decomposition by directly impacting the activity of soil organisms, as well as indirectly altering soil activity by influencing the type and amount of plant species that can grow in a given area.

Soil is a complex and dynamic entity. It forms the medium in which organisms grow, and the activities of those organisms, in turn, affect soil structure. As with many aspects of ecology, it is often difficult to separate organisms from their environment. The biome discussions that follow provide additional information on soils by including aspects of soil structure and chemistry characteristic of each biome.

CONCEPT 2.2 REVIEW

1. Desert soils and agricultural soils support greatly different amounts of plant growth, but both generally have limited organic layers. Why?
2. Can soils be developed in the absence of plants?

ECOLOGY IN ACTION

Natural History of Soils

In each chapter of the book, we will provide an example of how ecologists use their understanding of the natural world to address questions of societal concern. These "Ecology In Action" boxes demonstrate that the science of ecology can provide great insights into many of the pressing environmental issues that we currently face in Canada and across the globe. Some of the examples will be specific studies, while others, such as this one, will discuss a general topic. In this first chapter on the natural history of terrestrial ecosystems, we address an issue of fundamental importance: how many terrestrial species are there?

It turns out, this simple question is very difficult to answer, and no firm number exists. More specifically, no number exists that has resulted in broad agreement among scientists.

Researchers at Redpath Museum at McGill University are cataloguing the biodiversity of Canada. They have developed a user-friendly Web site (The Canadian Biodiversity Web Site) to help people see the diversity of species found in Canada (Bernhardt 2010). They report that across the world, up to 1.8 million species have been described by scientists (approximately 70,000 in Canada), with nearly half being insects. These counts include both terrestrial and aquatic species, though it is generally accepted that there is more species diversity on land than in aquatic systems. Does this mean there are approximately 2 million species on the planet? Absolutely

not. Estimates of true global biodiversity range from 2 to 100 million, though all of these are simply educated guesses. Scientists are now realizing how little natural history is actually known, even in our own backyards.

A fundamental goal of ecology is to understand the processes that influence the distribution and abundance of organisms. This knowledge can be used to address a variety of environmental issues that people face throughout the world, such as climate change, controlling the spread of invasive species, and trying to integrate agriculture, economic development, human housing, and wilderness within a limited amount of land. However, before we are able to explain patterns of abundance, we must first know the organisms we are studying. In many locations (e.g., North America), and for many groups (e.g., birds and mammals), species are so well studied that researchers are unlikely to ever know someone who has identified a new species, let alone find one themselves. Does this mean the days of natural history are over? If not, then where can more natural history make significant contributions to our ability to understand the science of ecology? The natural history and biodiversity of locations with high species diversity, such as tropical forests, are generally poorly documented, and many (non-vertebrate) species remain to be described by scientists.

For those of us with more modest budgets, and for those who want to find a very large number of new species, the

answer will be much closer to home. In fact, large amounts of undescribed biodiversity are literally underneath your feet. Soils are the "poor man's tropical rainforest," (Usher et al. 1979) home to countless numbers of fungi, bacteria, micro- and mesofauna, algae, bryophytes, and other types of organisms. The diversity of these systems is staggering, with many more species unidentified than there are identified (fig. 2.8). The relatively small size and subterranean habitat of these organisms has greatly impeded efforts at identifying and understanding the ecology of soils. Nonetheless, although many people will go their whole lives without seeing a bear, wolf, or whale in its natural environment, every day we each likely walk upon dozens or hundreds of species new to science in the soils below us. Only recently have ecologists appreciated that our lack of knowledge of the most basic natural history of these groups of organisms may be a serious impediment to understanding how natural systems function.

For example, the activity of these soil organisms strongly influences the rates of carbon and nutrient cycling, soil respiration, and the transfer of nutrients to vascular plants. They also provide food and habitat for larger organisms, and are key to the development of soil structure. Although our understanding of exactly how these processes emerge from the complex web of soil interactions is still limited, it is very clear that changes in composition of communities of soil organisms is likely to alter the efficiency of these processes. Such changes can have significant impacts on a variety of issues of concern to people, including carbon sequestration, primary production, litter buildup, and nutrient leaching. As you will see throughout this book, human activities are changing the composition of species in communities across the planet, with unknown consequences for ecological functioning. Such changes occur in the soil as well. For example, Dennis Parkinson of the University of Calgary has shown the introduction of earthworm, *Dendrobaena octaedra,* to boreal forest soils alters fungal biodiversity and plant growth (Scheu and Parkinson 1994; McLean and Parkinson 2000). Similar changes are likely to be found in response to other human-mediated changes on the landscape and in the climate.

The first step in understanding how the members of the soil community alter ecological processes will be to understand what organisms are there. Although soils do not represent the world that surface dwellers like humans typically inhabit, they are home to large numbers of small organisms that greatly affect our lives. It will be up to the next generation of natural historians and ecologists to determine how.

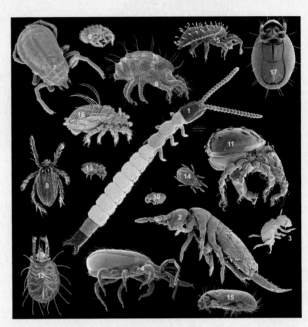

Figure 2.8   A diversity of species live within the soils, the ecology of which remains to be explored. Shown are species of arthropods from the following taxa: 1. Diplura (Japygidae), 2. Collembola (Entomobryidae), 3. Collembola (Neelidae), 4–17 Acari, 4. Mesostigmata (Ologamasidae), 5. Mesostigmata (Zerconidae), 6. Prostigmata (Stigmaeidae), 7. Prostigmata (Labidostomatidae), 8. Prostigmata (Trombiculidae), 9. Endeostigmata (Terpnacaridae), 10. Endeostigmata (Nanorchestidae), 11. Oribatida (Hermanniidae), 12. Oribatida (Phenopelopidae), 13. Oribatida (Brachychthoniidae), 14. Oribatida (Suctobelboideae), 15. Oribatida (Lohmannidae), 16. Oribatida (Cosmochthoniidae), 17. Oribatida (Phthiracaroidea). These species include predators (1, 4, 5, 6, 7), microbivores/detritivores (2, 3, 10, 13–17), parasites (8), and fungivores (9, 11, 12).

2.3 Natural History and Geography of Biome

The geographic distribution of terrestrial biomes corresponds closely to variation in climate, especially prevailing temperature and precipitation. In this section, we discuss the climate, soils, and organisms of the earth's major biomes and how they have been influenced by humans. However, don't be concerned if you know of some places that do not quite fit any of the biomes discussed. Dividing the world into biomes is a very subjective process, and biomes are not truly distinctive entities. Instead they change gradually along environmental gradients, and unique geography can result in disjunct distributions. Even within a large biome, such as the boreal forest, no two locations will be exactly alike. Because of this variability, not all ecologists will agree on whether there are 7, 17, or 27 biomes. Here we present nine biomes that capture the majority of the major regions of the world (fig. 2.9a).

What determines where the different biomes are located? That answer to this is simple, "nearly everything," as you will see in subsequent chapters of the book. However, for now, we follow the lead of ecologists in the early twentieth century who often focused on how climate and soils influence the distribution of vegetation. One of the most influential depictions of climate-biome relationships was provided by Robert Whittaker (Whittaker 1975; fig. 2.9*b*). In viewing both of the

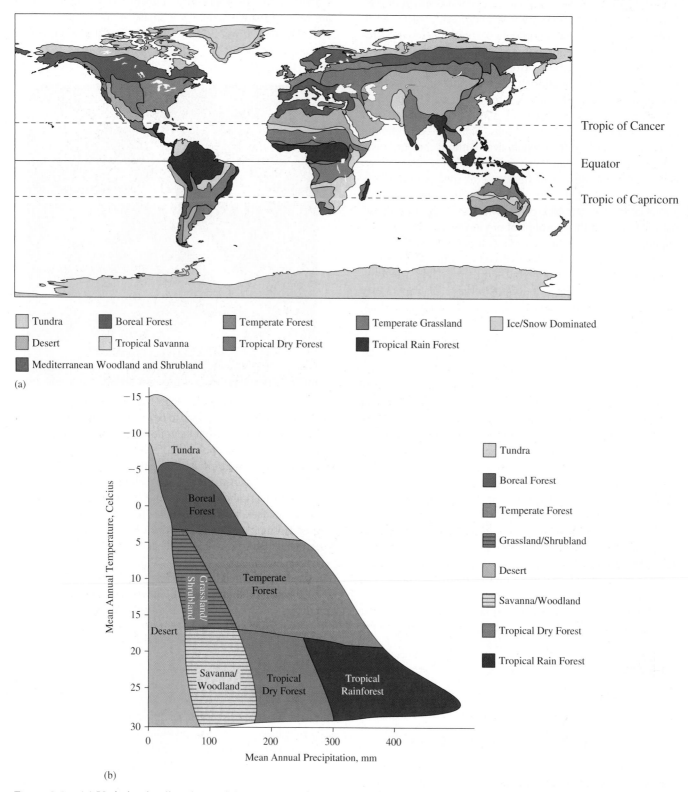

Figure 2.9   (*a*) Variation in climatic conditions results in geographic variation in the distribution of biome types across the planet. Clear areas indicate the locations of major bodies of water. (*b*) The distribution of terrestrial biomes can be largely described by differences in precipitation and temperature (modified from Whittaker 1975). You will note that the specific types of biomes described by Whittaker (and presented in this figure) differ slightly from that found in 2.9*a*.

diagrams in figure 2.9, it is important to recognize the boundaries are fairly subjective, and their value lies in the presentation of general concepts, rather than being precisely drawn maps and figures. A more detailed understanding of the factors that lead to the development and persistence of each of these nine biomes is provided below.

Tundra

Starting at the most northerly areas of vegetation, we find an open landscape of mosses, lichens, and dwarf willows, dotted with small ponds and laced with clear streams (fig. 2.10). This is the **tundra**—home to some and a destination to many. If it is summer and surface soils have thawed, movement through the tundra will be cushioned by a mat of lichens and mosses, punctuated by occasionally sinking into soggy accumulations of peat. The air will be filled with the cries of nesting birds that visit during the brief summer, feeding upon the population explosions of their plant and animal prey. After long and cold winters, the summer air can be quite warm, at least for those of us accustomed to cold Canadian winters.

Geography

The arctic tundra rings the top of the globe, covering most of the lands north of the Arctic Circle (fig. 2.11). Tundra extends from northern-most Scandinavia, across northern European Russia, through northern Siberia, and across northern Alaska

Figure 2.10 The tundra at the base of the Torngat mountains in Labrador consists primarily of low-growing mosses, lichens, perennial herbaceous plants, and shrubs.

and Canada. It reaches far south of the Arctic Circle into the Hudson Bay region of Canada, and is also found in patches on the coast of Greenland and in northern Iceland.

Climate

The tundra climate is typically cold and dry with short summers (fig. 2.11). However, the tundra usually does not get quite

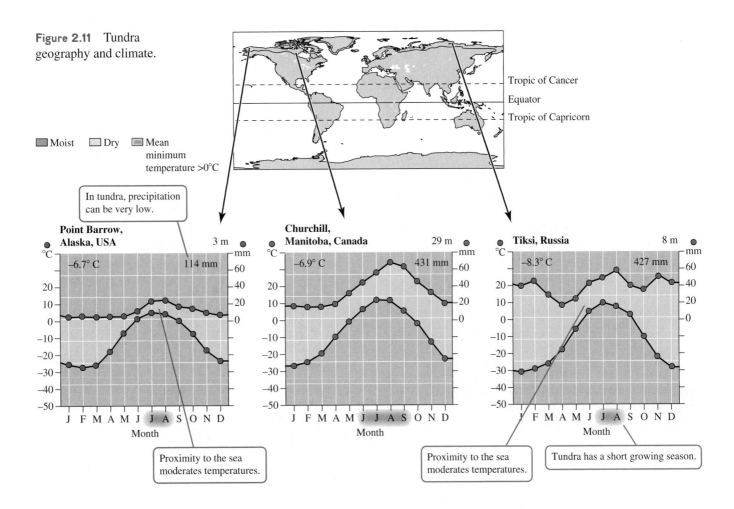

Figure 2.11 Tundra geography and climate.

Tropic of Cancer
Equator
Tropic of Capricorn

◼ Moist   ☐ Dry   ◼ Mean minimum temperature >0°C

In tundra, precipitation can be very low.

Point Barrow, Alaska, USA   3 m
°C   mm
−6.7° C   114 mm

Churchill, Manitoba, Canada   29 m
°C   mm
−6.9° C   431 mm

Tiksi, Russia   8 m
°C   mm
−8.3° C   427 mm

J F M A M J J A S O N D
Month

Proximity to the sea moderates temperatures.

Proximity to the sea moderates temperatures.

Tundra has a short growing season.

as cold in the winter or quite as warm in the summer as does the boreal forest to the south. Precipitation on the tundra varies from less than 200 mm to a little over 600 mm. Still, because average annual temperatures are so low, precipitation exceeds evaporation. As a consequence, the short summers are soggy and the tundra landscape is filled with ponds and streams.

Soils

Soil building is slow in the cold tundra climate. Because rates of decomposition are low, organic matter accumulates in deposits of peat and humus. Surface soils thaw each summer but are often underlain by **permafrost** that may be many metres thick. Permafrost is a layer of soil that remains frozen even during the summer months. The annual freezing and thawing of surface soil overtop permafrost combines with the actions of water and gravity to produce a variety of surface processes that are largely limited to the tundra. One of these processes, **solifluction**, slowly moves soils down slopes. In addition, freezing and thawing can bring stones to the surface of the soil, forming a netlike, or polygonal, pattern on the surface of tundra soils (fig. 2.12).

Biology

The open tundra landscape is dominated by a patchwork of perennial herbaceous plants, especially grasses, sedges, and mosses. Lichens, associations of fungi and algae, are also highly abundant, and can be fed upon by reindeer and caribou. The woody vegetation of the tundra consists of dwarf willows and birches along with a variety of low-growing shrubs, all of which can also be browsed upon by a variety of animals.

Figure 2.12   Ice wedges form netlike polygons on the surface of the tundra. Aerial photo of polygonal peat plateau, Wapusk National Park, Manitoba.

The short periods of warm weather suitable for plant growth present significant challenges to the residents of the tundra. Plants of the tundra are generally very slow growing, with nearly all of the living biomass below ground. Plants tend to be very short with strong stems, able to withstand the often fierce winds of the north. In the most northerly reaches of the tundra, the sun will never set during the summer, and the plants are able to photosynthesize nearly continuously.

The tundra is one of the last biomes on Earth that still supports substantial numbers of large native mammals, including caribou, reindeer, musk ox, bear, and wolves. Small mammals such as arctic fox, weasel, lemming, and ground squirrel are also abundant. Resident birds such as the ptarmigan and snowy owl are joined each summer by a host of migratory bird species. Insects, though not as diverse as in biomes farther south, are very abundant. Each summer, swarms of mosquitoes and other insects emerge from the many tundra ponds and streams.

Human Influences

In the past, human presence in the tundra was largely limited to small populations of hunters and nomadic herders. Recently, however, human development has increased markedly, with intense exploration and extraction of oil, natural gas, and a variety of minerals such as diamonds. An equally pressing concern in the North is the impact of rapidly rising temperatures on the permafrost and rates of decomposition. Because of patterns of global air and ocean circulation, areas of the arctic tundra are rapidly warming. Although this is a general global concern, the deep expanses of permafrost in the arctic raise a unique concern within the tundra biome. As permafrost melts, the rich organic material it contains becomes available to soil microbes and insects for decomposition, potentially releasing enormous amounts of CO_2 into the atmosphere, amplifying the greenhouse effect and global warming. The exact extent to which this will occur is still unclear, in large part because of the difficulties in working in the North, and our general lack of understanding of the ecology of soils. Such concerns make it clear that human activity can have significant impacts on even the most isolated of regions on the planet. The ecological responses that occur as a result of human activities can in turn have dramatic consequences for humans across the planet. Recent discoveries of large tracts of oil and natural gas in the far North, along with technological developments allowing for more economically viable resource extraction, will ensure increased pressure on the natural environment for generations to come.

Boreal Forest

The **boreal forest**, or **taiga**, is a world of wood and water that covers over 11% of the earth's land area. This biome extends around the globe in a repeating pattern: forest-water, forest-water, etc. In places, the trees are so close together you can barely walk through them (fig. 2.13). In other places, the forest is open and you can wander wherever you like on its soft floor of needles and duff. In sunny patches in the forest you will find berry bushes of many varieties where wildlife and humans

Figure 2.13 Boreal forests, such as this one in Kluane National Park, Yukon, are dominated by a few species of conifer trees.

alike pause and snack on an assortment of fruits. A trek through a boreal forest eventually leads to the edge of a lake, river, fen, or bog, where shade and cover give way to light and space. Along the lake margins grow willows and plants that require lots of light for growth and reproduction. The summer forest is coloured green, grey, and brown; the autumn adds brilliant splashes of yellow and red; and the long northern winter turns the boreal forest into a land of white solitude.

Geography

The term, "boreal" comes from the Greek word for north, reflecting the fact that boreal forests are confined to the Northern Hemisphere. Boreal forests extend from Scandinavia, through European Russia, across Siberia, to central Alaska, and across all of central Canada in a band between 50° and 65° N latitude (fig. 2.14). These forests are bounded in the south either by temperate forests or temperate grasslands and in the north by tundra. Fingers of boreal forest extend from the west to east coasts of North America and reappear in western Europe, extending to the eastern coast of Asia. As can be seen in figure 2.9*a*, the Southern Hemisphere does not contain large expanses of land at southern latitudes equivalent to those that contain the boreal forests of the north. As a result, although there are coniferous forests in locations in the Southern Hemisphere, there is no southern equivalent to the large and nearly circumpolar boreal forest.

Climate

The boreal forest is found where winters are usually longer than six months, and the summers too short to support temperate forest (fig. 2.14). The boreal forest zone includes some fairly moderate climates, such as that at Umeå, Sweden, where the climate is moderated by the nearby Baltic Sea. However, boreal forests are also found in some of the most variable climates on Earth. For instance, the temperature at Verkhoyansk,

Figure 2.14 Boreal forest geography and climate.

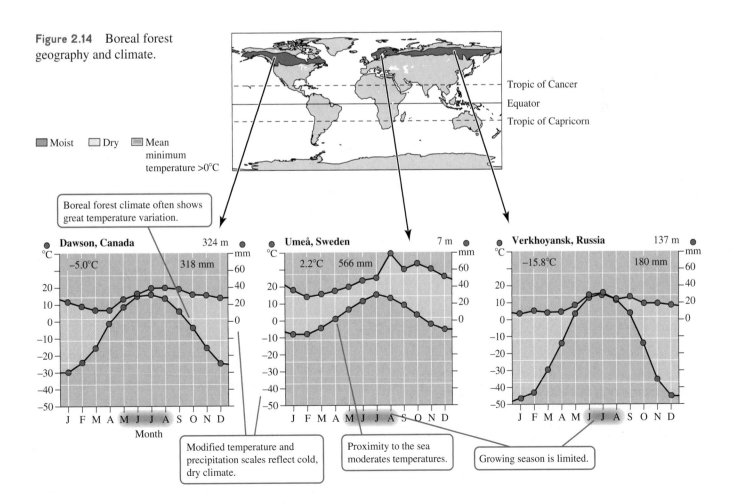

Tropic of Cancer
Equator
Tropic of Capricorn

☐ Moist ☐ Dry ☐ Mean minimum temperature >0°C

Boreal forest climate often shows great temperature variation.

Dawson, Canada 324 m −5.0°C 318 mm

Umeå, Sweden 7 m 2.2°C 566 mm

Verkhoyansk, Russia 137 m −15.8°C 180 mm

Month

Modified temperature and precipitation scales reflect cold, dry climate.

Proximity to the sea moderates temperatures.

Growing season is limited.

Russia, in central Siberia, ranges from about –70°C in winter to over 30°C in summer, an annual temperature range of 100°C! Precipitation in the boreal forest is moderate, ranging from about 200 to 600 mm. Yet, because of low temperatures and long winters, evaporation rates are low, and drought is either infrequent or brief. When droughts do occur, however, forest fires can burn vast areas of boreal forest.

Soils

Boreal forest soils are highly variable. In some areas they will be thin and acidic with low fertility; in other areas they will have thick organic layers of high fertility. Low temperatures and low pH typically slow down decomposition of plant litter and the rate of soil building, and specific soil characteristics are influenced by the type and depth of bedrock. Typically, nutrients are tied up in a thick layer of plant litter that carpets the forest floor. In turn, most trees in boreal forests have a dense network of shallow roots that, along with associated mycorrhizal fungi, tap directly into the nutrients bound up in this litter layer. The topsoil, which underlies the litter layer, is thin. In the more extreme boreal forest climates, the subsoil is permanently frozen in a layer of permafrost that may be several metres thick.

Biology

The boreal forest is generally dominated by evergreen conifers such as spruce, fir, and pines. Larch, a deciduous conifer, dominates in the most extreme Siberian climates. Deciduous aspen and birch trees grow throughout the Canadian boreal forests, and may be dominant during the early stages of recovery following fire. Willows grow along the shores of rivers and lakes. Along the base of most trees and on the forest floor lies a lush carpet of mosses and other non-vascular plants. These plants trap much of the rainfall, and are home to a large diversity of insects and other organisms. Between the moss and canopy layers the forest is fairly open with little herbaceous vegetation under the often thick forest canopy. The plants of the boreal have adapted to cold winters and low nutrient availability.

A characteristic of all forests, including the boreal, is a steep vertical gradient in light as one moves from the top of the canopy to the soil surface. Leaves on the outside of the canopy receive the full intensity of sunlight, reflecting and absorbing much of the visible light. As you move down through the canopy, light levels attenuate, changing in both intensity and colour (less blue and red penetrate the canopy than green). There is also a strong vertical gradient in ambient temperatures as you move down through the canopy to the soil surface. These vertical changes have significant impacts in what types of species are able to be active and grow at different heights in the forest.

Scattered throughout much of the boreal forests of the world are large expanses of bogs and fens dominated by a variety of moss species. These areas have waterlogged "soils," with islands of vascular plants centred around a few trees and shrubs. They are home to countless species, including many plants that feed upon the insects they capture with their leaves. The boreal forest is the winter home of migratory caribou and reindeer and the year-round home of moose and woodland bison. Wolves and bear are major predators of the boreal

Figure 2.15   Well pads, roads, and seismic lines associated with oil and gas extraction in the boreal forest.

forest, and many smaller mammals such as lynx, wolverine, snowshoe hare, porcupines, and red squirrels also live in boreal forests. The boreal forest is the nesting habitat for many birds that migrate from the tropics each spring and the year-round home of other birds such as crossbills and spruce grouse.

Human Influences

Ancient cave paintings in southern France and northern Spain, made during the last ice age when the climate was much colder, reveal that humans have consumed boreal forest animals, such as the migratory reindeer, for tens of thousands of years. In Eurasia, from Lapland in Scandinavia to Siberia, hunting of reindeer eventually gave way to domestication and herding. Northern peoples have also long harvested the berries that grow in abundance in the boreal forest. The many berry dishes of Scandinavia are living testimony to this heritage.

For most of human history, human development in the boreal forest was relatively light, in contrast to grasslands (explored in the next section). Recently, however, the boreal has become the site of extensive development. As demand for wood products increases, even low-value trees within boreal forests are being cut for lumber and pulp. Extensive oil and gas deposits are no longer too remote and expensive to develop, and exploration and extraction (fig. 2.15) are occurring in increasingly large areas. Although the impacts of each of these developments are relatively small, there is increasing awareness that the combined effects of all activities may have large impacts on the boreal forest. However, there continue to be new pressures placed on the forest, ones of tremendous potential economic gain. For example, Alberta currently has allowed oil sand mining in about 3,000 km² of boreal forest. However, deeper deposits occur in over 125,000 km², raising the potential for extensive deforestation and development.

Temperate Forest

Old-growth **temperate forest** (fig. 2.16) contains the largest living organisms on Earth, perhaps the largest that have ever lived: the sequoias of western North America and the giant

Eucalyptus trees of southern Australia. Enter the subdued light of this cool, moist realm, this world of mushrooms and decaying leaves, and feel yourself shrink before the giants of living world. At dusk in the heart of an old-growth forest, it is easy to understand how cultures around the earth came to make the temperate forest the haunt of diverse mythical creatures such as the nymphs and elves of European folk tales.

Geography

Temperate forest can be found between 30° and 55° latitude. However, the majority of this biome lies between 40° and 50° (fig. 2.17). In Asia, temperate forest originally covered much of Japan, eastern China, Korea, and eastern Siberia. In western Europe, temperate forests extended from southern Scandinavia to northwestern Iberia and from the British Isles through eastern Europe. North American temperate forests are found from the Atlantic sea coast to the Great Plains and reappear on the West Coast as temperate coniferous forests that extend from northern California through southeastern Alaska. In the Southern Hemisphere, temperate forests are found in southern Chile, New Zealand, and southern Australia.

Climate

Temperate forests, which may be either coniferous or deciduous, occur where temperatures are not extreme and where annual precipitation averages anywhere from about 650 mm to over 3,000 mm (fig. 2.17). These forests generally receive more winter precipitation than temperate grasslands. Deciduous trees usually dominate temperate forests, where

Figure 2.16   Old-growth redwood forest in western North America. Redwoods are the tallest trees in the world, with some individual trees growing to heights of over 100 m.

Figure 2.17   Temperate forest geography and climate.

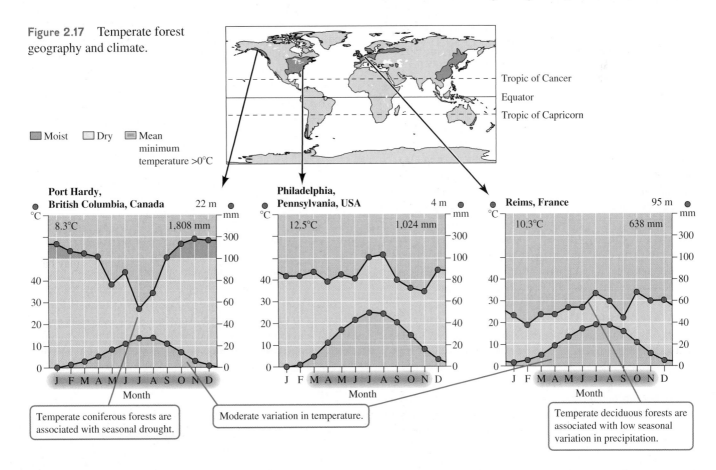

Temperate coniferous forests are associated with seasonal drought.

Moderate variation in temperature.

Temperate deciduous forests are associated with low seasonal variation in precipitation.

the growing season is moist and at least four months long. In deciduous forests, winters last from three to four months. Though snowfall may be heavy, winters in deciduous forests are relatively mild. Where winters are more severe or the summers drier, conifers are more abundant than deciduous trees. The temperate coniferous forests of the Pacific Coast of North America receive most of their precipitation during fall, winter, and spring and are subject to summer drought.

Soils

Temperate forest soils are usually fertile, though as in the boreal forest, there exists variability. The most fertile soils in this biome develop under deciduous forests, where they are generally neutral or slightly acidic in pH and rich in both organic matter and inorganic nutrients. Nutrient movement between soil and vegetation tends to be slower and more conservative in coniferous forests; nutrient movement within deciduous forests is generally more dynamic. For example, each year temperate deciduous forests recycle about twice the amount of nitrogen recycled by temperate coniferous forests of similar age.

Biology

While the diversity of trees found in temperate forests is lower than that of tropical forests, temperate forest biomass can be as great, or greater. Temperate forests are vertically stratified. Starting at ground level, you will find the lowest layer of vegetation, the herb layer. Above the herb layer is a layer of shrubs and saplings, then shade-tolerant understory trees, and finally the canopy, formed by the largest trees. The height of this canopy varies from about 40 m to over 100 m. Young saplings of canopy trees have no immediate hope of reaching the canopy high above. Many species will have a "sapling bank," with individual plants staying under 1 m in height for decades. When an opening appears in the canopy, these saplings grow rapidly to fill the space.

Birds, mammals, and insects make use of all layers of the forest from beneath the forest floor to above the canopy. Small arboreal mammals such as deer mice, tree squirrels, and flying squirrels use the tree canopy. Other mammals such as deer, bear, and fox live on the forest floor. Bats and other animals find homes inside cavities of large trees. Still others burrow into the rich forest soil. But the most important consumers of all are the fungi and bacteria, largely unnoticed members of entirely different kingdoms. They, along with a diversity of microscopic invertebrate animals, consume the large quantities of wood stored on the floor of old-growth temperate forest (fig. 2.18). The activities of these organisms recycle nutrients, a process upon which the function of the entire forest depends. Thus, the temperate forest, realm of the giants of the biosphere, emerges as a partnership of the great and the very small.

Human Influences

What, besides being large cities, do Toronto, Tokyo, Beijing, Moscow, Warsaw, Berlin, Paris, London, New York, Washington, D.C., Boston, Chicago, and Vancouver have in common?

Figure 2.18   Massive amounts of wood are stored on the forest floor of old-growth temperate coniferous forests of the Pacific Northwest, such as this one in southeastern Alaska.

They are all built on lands that once supported temperate forests. The first human settlements in temperate forests were concentrated along forest margins, usually along streams and rivers. Eventually agriculture was practised in these forest clearings, and animals and plant products were harvested from the surrounding forest. This was the circumstance several thousand years ago, in Europe and Asia, and five centuries ago, in North America. Since those times, most of the ancient forests have fallen before axe and saw. For example, the Black Forest of central Europe, where forest still survives, has been largely replaced by tree plantations.

Few tracts of the old-growth deciduous forest that once covered most of the eastern half of the continent remain, and there are fierce conflicts among disparate interests over the fate of the remaining 1%–2% of old-growth forests in western North America. Finding a way to preserve a sense of wilderness in the face of unprecedented human expansion and development will be a challenge for years to come. One encouraging sign is that many temperate deciduous forests are able to recover following years of logging and agriculture. Throughout much of eastern North America, there has been an increase in forest cover over the last several decades as old and unproductive agricultural fields have been abandoned.

Temperate Grassland

In their original state, **temperate grasslands** extended unbroken over vast areas (fig. 2.19). Nothing other than the open sea feels quite like standing in the middle of unobstructed prairie, under a dome of blue sky. It is no accident that early visitors from forested Europe and eastern North America often referred to the prairie in the American Midwest as a "sea of grass" and to the wagons that crossed them as "prairie schooners." Prairies were the home of the bison and pronghorn and of the nomadic cultures of Eurasia and North America.

Geography

Temperate grassland is the largest biome in North America and is even more extensive in Eurasia (fig. 2.20). In North America,

(a)   (b)

Figure 2.19   (*a*) Pronghorn, native grazers of the temperate grasslands of North America. (*b*) Badlands region of southeastern Alberta, Canada.

Figure 2.20   Temperate grassland distribution and climate.

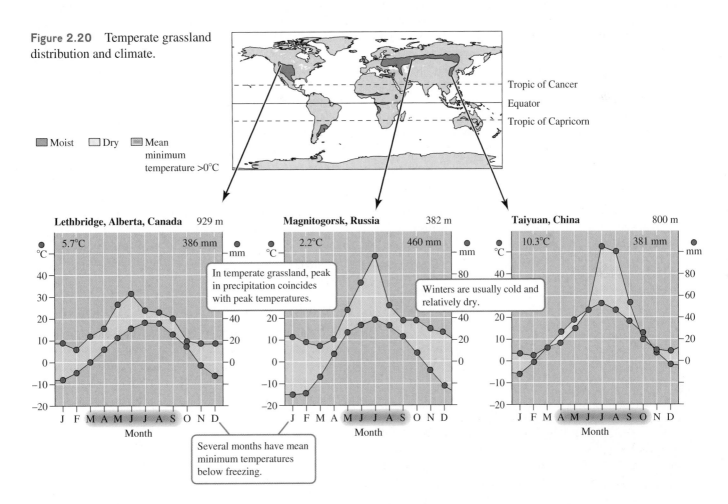

the prairies of the Great Plains extend from southern Canada to the Gulf of Mexico and from the Rocky Mountains to the deciduous forests of the east. Additional grasslands are found on the Palouse prairies of Idaho and Washington and in the central valley and surrounding foothills of California. In Eurasia, the temperate grassland biome forms a virtually unbroken band from eastern Europe all the way to eastern China. In the Southern Hemisphere, temperate grassland occurs in Argentina, Uruguay, southern Brazil, New Zealand, and Australia.

Climate

Temperate grasslands receive between 300 and 1,000 mm of precipitation annually. Though wetter than deserts, temperate grasslands experience droughts that may persist for several

years. The maximum precipitation usually occurs in summer during the height of the growing season. This summer peak in precipitation is clearly shown in the climate diagrams for Lethbridge, Alberta, Canada; Magnitogorsk, Russia; and Taiyuan, China (fig. 2.20).

Soils

Temperate grassland soils are derived from a wide variety of parent materials. The most productive temperate grassland soils are deep, basic or neutral, and fertile, and contain large quantities of organic matter. The black prairie soils of North America and Eurasia, famous for their fertility, contain the greatest amount of organic matter. The brown soils of the more arid grasslands contain less organic matter.

Biology

Temperate grassland is thoroughly dominated by herbaceous vegetation. A combination of fire, drought, and grazing exclude woody vegetation from temperate grasslands, where trees and shrubs are often limited to the margins of streams and rivers. These factors also result in strong pressures on plants to protect themselves from these stresses. It is not surprising to find up to 80% of the living biomass of some grasslands below ground. In addition to grasses, which make up the bulk of vegetative biomass, there can be a striking diversity of other herbaceous vegetation. Spring graces temperate grasslands with showy anemones, sunflowers, prairie smoke, and other wild flowers; up to 70 species can bloom simultaneously on the species-rich North American prairie (fig. 2.21). The height of grassland vegetation varies from about 5 cm in dry, short-grass prairies to over 300 cm in the wetter tall-grass prairies.

Temperate grasslands once supported huge herds of roving herbivores: bison and pronghorns in North America (see fig. 2.19a); and wild horses and Saiga antelope in Eurasia. As do fishes in the open sea, the herbivores of the open grassland banded together in social groups; their attendant predators,

the steppe and prairie wolves, banded together as well. North American prairies were also the historical home of the grizzly bear. However, human pressures have been so great that these animals have been pushed into the mountains. In many of the grasslands of the world, animals built for speed no longer have great predators from which they need to flee. The smaller animals, such as grasshoppers and mice, inconspicuous among the herbaceous vegetation, continue to be even more numerous than the large herbivores. Grassland animals of intermediate size generally have one of two lifestyles: there are the burrowing, like the badger and prairie dog, and the fleet, like the swift fox and prairie falcon.

Human Influences

The extent of agricultural development in North America and throughout the world has left grasslands among the most critically endangered biomes. The first human populations on temperate grasslands were nomadic hunters, soon followed by the nomadic herders. Later, came the farmers with their plows, who broke the sod and tapped into fertile soils built up over thousands of years. Under the plow, temperate grasslands have produced some of the most fertile farmlands on the earth and fed much of the world. However, continuous agriculture has caused the loss of as much as 35% to 40% of the organic matter in the soils in just 35 to 40 years of cultivation. The more arid grasslands, with their frequent droughts, do not appear capable of supporting farming indefinitely without extensive irrigation. The future of agriculture in temperate grasslands hinges on several unanswered questions, including: Can the losses of organic matter and nutrients be reversed? What level of agricultural production can be sustained over the long term? Unfortunately, development in grasslands is often "invisible" to the average citizen, as many of us grew up viewing grasslands as the place for farms and ranches, rather than as a wild and intact natural region.

Mediterranean Woodland and Shrubland

The **Mediterranean woodland and shrubland** climate was the climate of the classical Greeks and the coastal Native American tribes of Old California. The mild temperate climate experienced by these cultures was accompanied by high biological richness (fig. 2.22).

Geography

Mediterranean woodlands and shrublands occur on all continents except Antarctica (fig. 2.23). They are most extensive around the Mediterranean Sea and in North America, where they extend from California into northern Mexico. They are also found in central Chile, southern Australia, and southern Africa. Under present climatic conditions, Mediterranean woodlands and shrublands grow between about 30° and 40° latitude. The far-flung geographic distribution of Mediterranean woodland and shrubland is reflected in the diversity of names for this biome. In western North America, it is called *chaparral*. In Spain, the most common name for Mediterranean woodland and shrubland is *matoral*. Farther east in the Mediterranean basin, the biome is referred to as *garrigue*.

Figure 2.21 Large numbers of plant species can flower at once in this grassland in Kinsella, Alberta.

Figure 2.22 A Mediterranean woodland in California shown during the cool moist season, when the herbaceous vegetation is still green.

Meanwhile in the Southern Hemisphere, South Africans call the biome *fynbos,* while Australians refer to at least one form of it as *mallee.* While the names for this biome vary widely, its climate does not.

Climate

The Mediterranean woodland and shrubland climate is cool and moist during fall, winter, and spring. In most regions the Mediterranean woodland and shrubland summers are hot and dry. The danger of frost varies considerably from one region to another. When they do occur, however, frosts are usually not severe. The combination of dry summers and dense vegetation, rich in essential oils, creates ideal conditions for frequent and intense fires.

Soils

The soils of Mediterranean woodlands and shrublands are generally of low to moderate fertility. Some soils, such as those of the South African *fynbos,* have exceptionally low fertility. Fire in the Mediterranean woodlands and shrublands of southern California can cause 40-fold increases in soil losses through erosion. Fire coupled with overgrazing have stripped the soil from some Mediterranean woodland and shrubland landscapes.

Figure 2.23 Mediterranean woodland and shrubland distribution and climate.

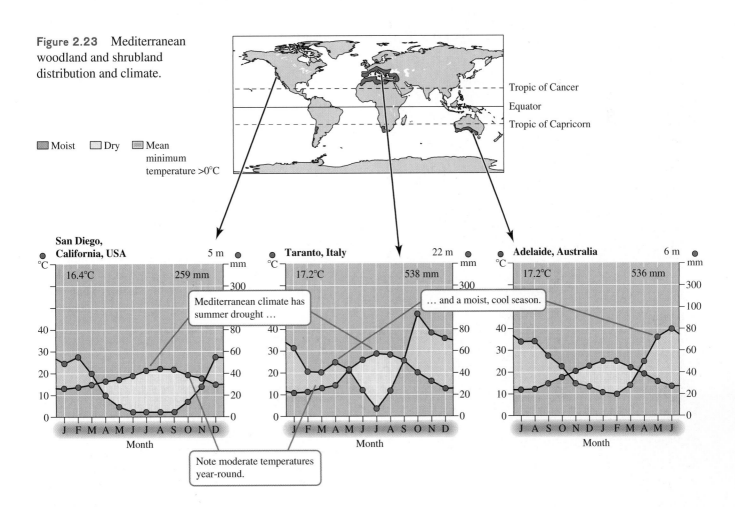

Biology

The plants and animals of Mediterranean woodlands and shrublands, like their desert neighbours, show several adaptations to drought. Trees and shrubs are typically evergreen and have small, tough leaves. This vegetation conserves both water and nutrients; many plants have well-developed mutualistic relationships with microbes that fix atmospheric nitrogen.

The process of decomposition is greatly slowed during the dry summer and then started again with the coming of fall and winter rains. Curiously, this intermittent decomposition may speed the process sufficiently so that average rates of decomposition are comparable to those in temperate forests.

Fire, a common occurrence in Mediterranean woodlands and shrublands, has resulted in the selection for fire-resistant plants. Many Mediterranean woodland trees have thick, tough bark that is resistant to fire (fig. 2.24). In contrast, many shrubs in Mediterranean woodlands are rich in oils and burn readily but re-sprout rapidly. Most herbaceous plants grow during the cool, moist season and then die back in summer, thus avoiding both drought and fire.

The animals of the Mediterranean woodlands and shrublands, both vertebrates and invertebrates, are highly diverse.

Figure 2.24 The thick bark of the cork oak of the Mediterranean region protects the tree from fire.

In addition to resident species, many migratory birds and some migratory insects spend the winter in Mediterranean woodland and shrubland climates, as do some human populations. The plants and animals of this region have been derived from diverse evolutionary lineages. For example, in the Mediterranean woodlands and shrublands of North America, the native browsers, herbivores that feed on the buds, twigs, and bark of woody plants, are deer. Around the Mediterranean Sea, in addition to deer, there are wild sheep and goats. In southern Africa, the native browsers are small antelope, and in Australia, they are kangaroos.

Human Influences

Human activity has had a substantial influence on the structure of landscapes in the Mediterranean woodlands and shrublands. Whether in southern France or southern California, people generally find the climate agreeable in this region. High population densities, coupled with a long history of human occupation, have left an indelible mark on Mediterranean woodlands and shrublands. For example, the open oak woodlands of southern Spain and Portugal are the product of an agricultural management system that is thousands of years old.

Desert

In the sparse **desert** landscape, sculpted by wind and water, the ecologist grows to appreciate geology, hydrology, and climate as much as organisms (fig. 2.25). In the desert, drought and flash floods, and heat and bitter cold, often go hand in hand. For many species, the desert is the centre of their world, not the edge, and thus many desert organisms flourish where others would starve or wither away.

Geography

Deserts occupy about 20% of the land surface of the earth. Two bands of deserts ring the globe, one at about 30° N latitude and one at about 30° S (fig. 2.26). These bands correspond to latitudes where dry subtropical air descends (see fig. 2.3), drying the landscape as it spreads north and south. Other deserts are found either deep in the interior of continents, for example, the Gobi of central Asia, or in the rain shadow of mountains, for example, the Great Basin Desert of North America. Few may realize that the Great Basin Desert extends into Canada (fig. 2.26). Still other deserts are found along the cool western coasts of continents, for example, the Atacama of South America and the Namib of southwestern Africa, where air circulating across a cool ocean delivers a great deal of fog to the coast but little rain.

Climate

Environmental conditions vary considerably from one desert to another. Some, such as the Atacama and central Sahara, receive very little rainfall and fit the stereotype of deserts as extremely dry places. Other deserts, such as some parts of the Sonoran Desert of North America, may receive nearly 300 mm of rainfall annually. Whatever their mean annual rainfall, however, water loss in deserts due to evaporation and

(a)

(b)

Figure 2.25 Deserts differ across the world. (*a*) Acacia trees between a gravel plain and sand dunes in the Namib Desert of southwestern Africa. (*b*) The landscape around the deserts of Osoyoos, British Columbia.

Figure 2.26 Desert distribution and climate.

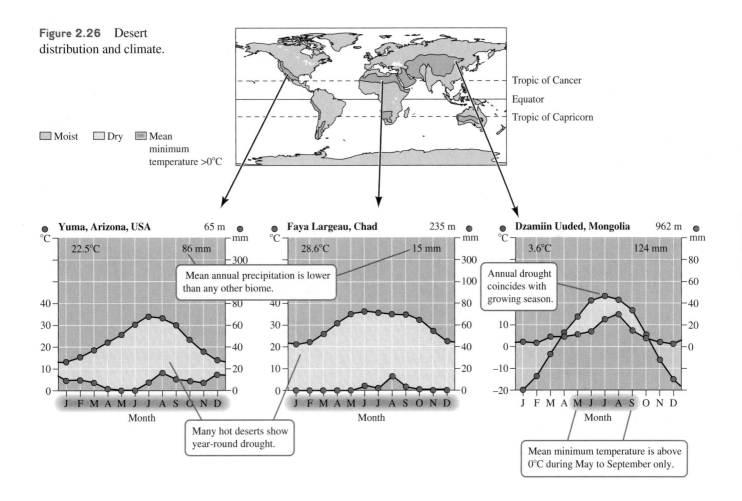

transpiration by plants exceeds precipitation during most of the year. It is a lack of available water, rather than hot temperatures, that makes a desert. Even large expanses of Antarctica and Canada's North are considered deserts.

Figure 2.26 includes the climate diagrams of two hot deserts. Notice that drought conditions prevail during all months, and that during some months average temperatures exceed 30°C at both Yuma, Arizona, and Faya Largeau, Chad.

The maximum shade temperatures in any biome, which were greater than 56°C, were recorded in the deserts of North Africa and western North America. However, some deserts can be bitterly cold. For example, average winter temperatures at Dzamiin Uuded, Mongolia, in the Gobi Desert of central Asia, sometimes fall to –20°C. Notice that the average annual temperature at Dzamiin Uuded is only 3.6°C and the growing season, as indicated by the months shaded red on the

climate diagram, lasts only five months. The relatively moist period at Dzamiin Uuded occurs during the cold season when average temperatures are below 0°C.

Soils

Desert soils are generally low in organic matter, with the soils consisting primarily of sand and rock. However, the soils under desert shrubs often contain large amounts of organic matter and form islands of fertility. Desert animals can affect soil properties. For example, in North America, kangaroo rats change the texture and elevate the nutrient content of surface soils by burrowing and hoarding seeds. In Middle Eastern deserts, porcupines and isopods strongly influence a variety of soil properties.

Desert soils, particularly those in poorly drained valleys and lowlands, often contain high concentrations of salts. Salts accumulate in these soils as water evaporates from the soil surface, thereby increasing the aridity of the desert environment by making it harder for plants to extract water from the soils.

Biology

The desert landscape is sparse. Plant cover is absent from many places, exposing soils and other geological features. Desert vegetation is typically grey-green, rather than the dark greens familiar in forests. By displaying lighter colours, many desert plants protect their photosynthetic surfaces from intense sunlight and reduce evaporative water loss. Other plant adaptations include small leaves, producing leaves only in response to rainfall and then dropping them during dry periods, or having no leaves at all (fig. 2.27). Some desert plants, such as cacti, have taken reduced leaf area to an extreme, with photosynthesis occurring in green stems while the leaves have been modified into spines (fig. 2.27a). Many of the columnar cacti species further minimize the harmful effects of the strong desert sun by growing directly toward the sun. At first this seems counterintuitive, but as you can see in figure 2.27, this action exposes the minimum amount of surface area to direct sunlight, reducing transpiration and heat imbalance. Some desert plants avoid drought almost entirely by remaining dormant in the soil as seeds, which germinate and grow only during infrequent wet periods. Because these wet periods can be so short-lived, the growth rates of many desert annual plant species are among the fastest on the planet.

In deserts, animal abundance tends to be low but diversity can be high. Most desert animals use behaviour to avoid environmental extremes. In summer, many avoid the heat of the day by being active at dusk and dawn or at night. In winter, the same species may be active during the day. Animals also use body orientation to minimize heat gain in the summer.

Human Influences

Many human cultures have arisen independently in the deserts of North America, Australia, Africa, and Asia. Compared to true desert species, however, humans are profligate water users. Consequently, human populations in desert regions are

(a)

(b)

Figure 2.27   Convergence among desert plants: (*a*) cactus in North America, (*b*) *Euphorbia* in Africa.

concentrated around oases and river valleys. Despite natural limitations in water availability, human settlements in deserts frequently display fountains, ancient and modern water diversions, agricultural schemes, and large urban centres complete with artificial lakes and golf courses. Pushed, the desert blooms. Unfortunately, many desert landscapes have been pushed until they now grow little but salt crystals.

The desert is one biome that, because of human activity, is increasing in area. Plowing, overgrazing, and deforestation of arid regions all lead to soil erosion. Once the O horizon blows away, it is difficult for it to be re-established and desert-ification often occurs.

Tropical Savanna

Stand in the middle of a savanna, a tropical grassland dotted with scattered trees, and your eye will be drawn to the horizon for the approach of thunderstorms or wandering herds of wildlife (fig. 2.28). The **tropical savanna** is the kingdom of the farsighted, the stealthy, and the swift, and is the birth-place of humankind. It was from here that humans eventually moved out into every biome on the face of the earth.

Geography

Most tropical savannas occur north and south of tropical dry forests within 10° to 20° of the equator. In Africa south of the Sahara Desert, tropical savannas extend from the west to the east coasts, cut a north–south swath across the east African highlands, and reappear in south-central Africa (fig. 2.29). In South America, tropical savannas occur in south-central Brazil and cover a great deal of Venezuela and Columbia. Tropical savannas are also the natural vegetation of much of northern Australia in the region just south of the tropical dry forest. The savanna is the natural vegetation of an area in southern Asia just east of the Indus River in eastern Pakistan and northwestern India.

Climate

Life on the savanna cycles to the rhythms of alternating dry and wet seasons (fig. 2.29). Here, however, seasonal drought combines with another important physical factor: fire. The rains come in summer and are accompanied by intense light-ning. This lightning often starts fires, particularly at the begin-ning of the wet season when the savanna is tinder dry. These fires kill young trees while the grasses survive and quickly re-sprout. Consequently, fires help maintain the tropical savanna as a landscape of grassland and scattered trees.

The savanna climate is generally drier than that of tropi-cal dry forests. The longer dry season and lower annual precipitation of most savannas are shown by the climate dia-grams for Tahoua, Niger, and Longreach, Australia (fig. 2.29). The mean rainfall for these two areas is within the range (300–500 mm) occurring on most savannas. However, the cli-mate diagram for San Fernando, Venezuela (fig. 2.29) shows that some savannas receive as much rainfall as a tropical dry forest. Other savannas occur in areas that are as dry as deserts. What keeps the wet savannas near San Fernando from being replaced by forest, and how can savannas persist under desert-like conditions? The answer lies deep in the savanna soils.

Figure 2.28 Tropical savanna and grazers in Kenya. The tropical savanna landscape is partially maintained by periodic fires that reduce the density of woody vegetation.

Figure 2.29 Tropical savanna distribution and climate.

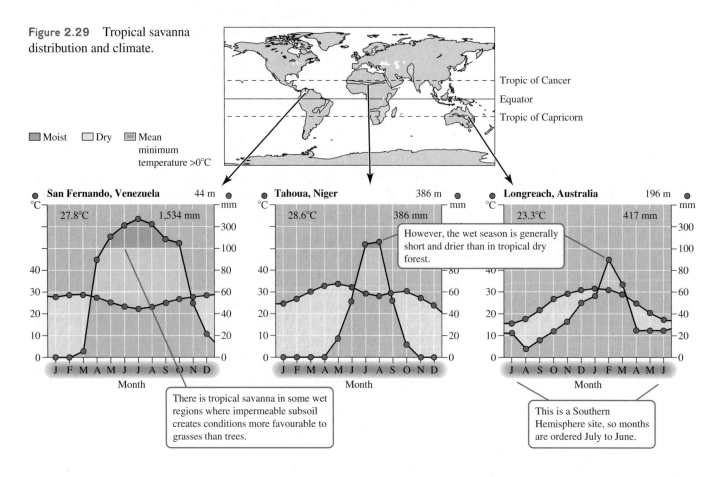

There is tropical savanna in some wet regions where impermeable subsoil creates conditions more favourable to grasses than trees.

However, the wet season is generally short and drier than in tropical dry forest.

This is a Southern Hemisphere site, so months are ordered July to June.

Soils

Soil layers with low permeability to water play a key role in maintaining many tropical savannas. For instance, because a dense, impermeable subsoil retains water near the surface, savannas occur in areas of southwest Africa that would otherwise support only desert. Impermeable soils also help savannas persist in wet areas, particularly in South America. Trees do not move onto savannas where an impermeable subsoil keeps surface soils waterlogged during the wet season. In these landscapes, scattered trees occur only where soils are well drained.

Biology

The tropical savanna is populated by wandering animals that move in response to seasonal and year-to-year variations in rainfall and food availability. The wandering consumers of the Australian savannas include kangaroos, large flocks of birds, and, for at least 40,000 years, humans. The African savanna is home to a host of well-known mobile consumers, such as elephants, wildebeest, giraffes, zebras, lions, and, again, humans (see fig. 2.28).

The parklike landscape of the savanna is maintained by a dynamic interplay of physical and biological forces. The diverse mammalian herbivores of the African savanna harvest all above-ground parts of the vegetation, from low herbs to the tops of trees. As noted, fire plays a key role in maintaining the savanna landscape. Frequent fires have selected for fire resistance in the savanna flora. The few tree species on the savanna resist fire well enough to be unaffected by low-intensity fires, and some even require fire for dispersal and germination of their seed. Although tropical savannas are confined to an area between the tropics of Cancer and Capricorn, there also exist more temperate savannas throughout the world. For example, the aspen parkland is a mosaic of aspen stand and grasslands, extending through much of western Canada. Though parklands are often thought of simply as transition zones from the grasslands to the south and boreal to the north, they are true savannas, home to bison, wolves, raptors, and bear.

Human Influences

Humans are, in some measure, a product of the savanna, and in turn the savanna has been influenced by human activity. One of the factors that forged an indelible link between us and this biome is fire. Long before the appearance of hominids, fire played a role in the ecology of the tropical savanna. Later, the savanna was the classroom where early humans observed and learned to use, control, and make fire. Eventually, humans began to purposely set fire to the savanna, which, in turn, helped to maintain and spread the savanna itself. We had entered the business of large-scale manipulation of nature.

Originally, humans subsisted on the savanna by hunting and gathering. In time, they shifted from hunting to pastoralism, replacing wild game with domestic grazers and browsers. Today, livestock ranching is the main source of livelihood in all the savanna regions.

Tropical Dry Forest

During the dry season, the **tropical dry forest** is all earth tones; in the rainy season, it's an emerald tangle (fig. 2.30). Life in the tropical dry forest responds to the rhythms of the annual solar cycle, which drives the oscillation between wet and dry seasons. During the dry season, most trees in the tropical dry forest are dormant. Then, as the rains approach, trees flower and insects appear to pollinate them. Eventually, as the first storms of the wet season arrive, the trees produce their leaves and transform the landscape into a lush green forest.

Geography

Tropical dry forests occupy a substantial portion of the earth's surface between about 10° and 25° latitude (fig. 2.31). In Africa, tropical dry forests are found both north and south of the central African rain forests. In the Americas, tropical dry forests are the natural vegetation of extensive areas south and north of the Amazon rain forest. Tropical dry forests also extend up the west coast of Central America and into North America along the west coast of Mexico. In Asia, tropical dry forests are the natural vegetation of most of India and the Indochina peninsula. Australian tropical dry forests form a continuous band across the northern and northeastern portions of the continent.

Climate

The climate of tropical dry forests is more seasonal than that of tropical rain forests. The three climate diagrams shown in figure 2.31 each show a dry season lasting for six to seven months, followed by a season of abundant rainfall. This wet season lasts for about five months in Acapulco, Mexico, and Bombay, India, and about six months in Darwin, Australia. Heavy rains occur during the wet season at all three sites, with wet season monthly precipitation similar to that found in tropical rain forests. The climate diagrams also indicate more seasonal variation in temperature than we will see in the climate diagrams for the tropical rain forest. Notice here that the seasonal rains in the tropical dry forest come during the warmer part of the year.

Soils

The soils of many tropical dry forests are of great age, particularly those in the parts of Africa, Australia, India, and Brazil that were once part of the ancient southern continent of Gondwana. The soils of tropical dry forests tend to be less acidic than those of rain forests and are generally richer in nutrients. However, the annual pulses of torrential rain make the soils of tropical dry forest highly vulnerable to erosion, particularly when deforested and converted to agriculture.

Biology

The plants of the tropical dry forest are strongly influenced by physical factors. For example, the height of the dry forest is correlated with average precipitation. Trees are tallest in the wettest areas. In the driest places, where the trees are smallest and the landscape more open, the tropical dry forest can blend into areas of tropical savanna or even desert. In addition, in the driest habitats, all trees drop their leaves during the dry season; in wetter areas over 50% may be evergreen. Many plant species in the tropical dry forest produce fruits that are attractive to animals and, as in the tropical rain forest, have animal-dispersed seeds. However, wind-dispersed seeds are also common in more open tropical dry forests.

The tropical dry forest shares many animal species with the rain forest and savanna, including monkeys, parrots, and large cats such as the tiger in Asia and the jaguar in the Americas. The lives of dry forest animals, like those of its plants, are organized around alternating wet and dry seasons. Many dry

(a)

(b)

Figure 2.30   The same view of a tropical dry forest in Guanacaste, Costa Rica during the wet and dry seasons.

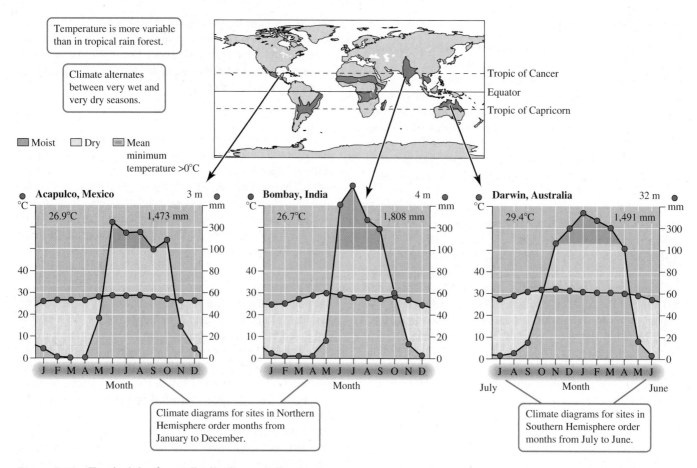

Figure 2.31 Tropical dry forest distribution and climate.

forest birds, mammals, and insects make seasonal migrations to wetter habitats along rivers or to the nearest rain forest.

Human Influences

Peter Murphy and Ariel Lugo (1986) studied the patterns of human settlement in the tropical forests of Central America. They divided the types of forests into rain forest, wet forest, moist forest, dry forest, and very dry forest. Their analysis showed a very uneven pattern of human settlement. Murphy and Lugo calculated that tropical rain forest and tropical wet forest include approximately 7% of the human population of Central America. In contrast, tropical dry forest and moist forest include about 79% of the Central American population. The population density—the number of people per square kilometre—in tropical dry and moist forests is more than 10 times higher than in tropical wet and rain forests.

Heavy human settlement has devastated the tropical dry forest. Extensive clearing for agriculture has reduced tropical dry forest in Central America and Mexico to less than 2% of its former area. People have replaced tropical dry forests with cattle ranches, grain farms, and cotton fields. Tropical dry forests are more vulnerable to human exploitation than tropical rain forests because the dry season makes them more accessible and easier to burn.

Intensive settlement and agricultural development have whittled away at tropical dry forests over a period of centuries.

In contrast, rain forests are disappearing in a recent push involving far fewer people but an enormous application of mechanical energy. This energy is directed at the extraction of lumber and minerals and at large-scale conversion of land from rain forest to agriculture. Though human impacts on tropical dry forests and rain forests have differed in tempo, their ecological consequences appear to be the same—massive loss of biological diversity.

Tropical Rain Forest

The **tropical rain forest** is nature's most extravagant garden (fig. 2.32). Beyond its tangled edge, a rain forest opens into a surprisingly spacious interior, illuminated by dim greenish light shining through a ceiling of leaves. High above towers the forest canopy, home to many rain forest species and the aerial laboratory of a few rain forest ecologists. The architecture of rain forests, with their vaulted ceilings and spires, has invited comparisons to cathedrals and mansions. However, this cathedral is alive from ceiling to sub-basement. In the rain forest, the sounds of evening and morning, the brilliant flashes of colour, and rich scents carried on moist night air speak of abundant life, in seemingly endless variety.

Geography

Tropical rain forests straddle the equator in three major regions: Southeast Asia, West Africa, and South and Central

Figure 2.32 Tropical rain forest in Borneo. Within the three-dimensional framework of tropical rain forests live a higher diversity of organisms than in any other terrestrial biome.

America (fig. 2.33). Most rain forest occurs within 10° of latitude north or south of the equator. Outside this equatorial band are the rain forests of Central America and Mexico, southeastern Brazil, eastern Madagascar, southern India, and northeastern Australia.

Climate

The global distribution of rain forests corresponds to areas where conditions are warm and wet year-round (fig. 2.33). Temperatures in tropical rain forests vary little from month to month and often change as much in a day as they do over the entire year. Though rain forests have a reputation for being extremely hot places, they are not. Average temperatures are about 25° to 27°C, lower than the average maximum summer temperatures in many deserts and temperate regions. Annual rainfall ranges from about 2,000 to 4,000 mm, and some rain forests receive even more precipitation. To support a tropical rain forest, rainfall must be fairly evenly distributed throughout the year. Notice that the climate diagrams for Belem, Kisangani, and Kuala Lumpur indicate moist conditions throughout the year. In summary, the tropical rain forest climate is warm, moist, and one of the least seasonal on the earth.

Soils

Heavy rains gradually leach nutrients from rain forest soils and rapid decomposition in the warm, moist rain forest climate keeps the organic horizon narrow. Consequently, rain forest soils are often nutrient-poor, acidic, thin, and low in

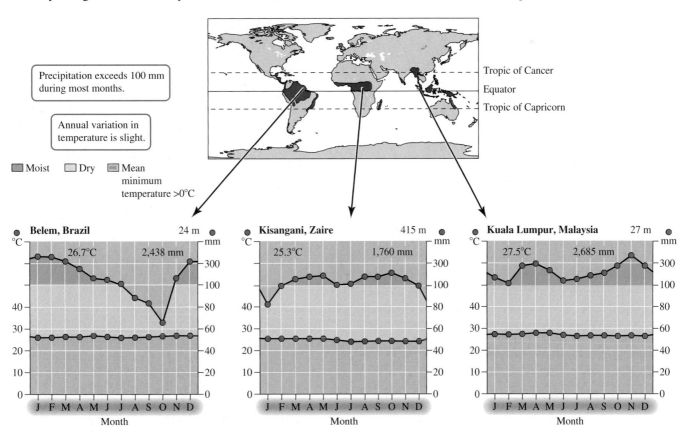

Figure 2.33 Tropical rain forest distribution and climate.

organic matter. In many areas, **lateritic soils** occur. These soils are the result of extensive weathering of the parent rocks, resulting in high concentrations of iron and aluminum, and low concentrations of essential plant nutrients. In many rain forests, more nutrients are tied up in living tissue than in soil. As a result, rain forest plants are adept at conserving and acquiring nutrients. Large numbers of free-living fungi, bacteria, and soil animals rapidly scavenge nutrients from plant litter and animal wastes, further tightening the nutrient economy of the rain forest. It is often only a matter of minutes before insects and other organisms attack the feces left behind by the myriad animals of the rainforest.

Some rain forests, however, occur where soils are very fertile. For instance, rain forests grow on young volcanic soils that have not yet been leached of their nutrients by heavy tropical rains. Fertile rain forest soils also occur along rivers, where a fresh nutrient supply is delivered with each flood.

Biology

Humans live mostly in two dimensions and are most at home on the rain forest floor. In contrast, many organisms in the rain forest have evolved to use the vertical dimension provided by trees. Trees dominate the rain forest landscape and average about 40 metres in height. However, some reach 50, 60, or even 80 metres tall. Despite the great heights of these trees, many tropical rain forest species form very shallow root systems that grow through, over, and under the thin layer of organic matter on the forest floor. By having such shallow roots, these trees are able to absorb nutrients as soon as they are made available through the activity of the soil food web. Some plants have taken this approach to an extreme, growing roots up the stems of their neighbours. Such growth allows them to absorb the nutrients that are leached out of leaves as a consequence of the heavy rainfall. How can these giants of the rain forest grow so tall without a deep anchoring root system for structural support? Rather than anchors, many of these trees use **buttress roots**, which are equally effective in keeping them upright (fig. 2.34*a*). Buttress roots are large roots on all sides of a tree that occur above the soil surface, providing structural support rather than nutrient capture.

The diversity of rain forest trees is also impressive. One hectare (100 m $\times$ 100 m) of temperate forest may contain a few dozen tree species; 1 hectare of tropical rain forest may contain up to 300 tree species.

The three-dimensional framework formed by rain forest trees is festooned with other plant growth forms. The trees are trellises for climbing vines and growing sites for **epiphytes**, plants that grow on other plants (fig. 2.34*b*). The pools of water and foliage provided by epiphytes are also home to large populations of even more species of bacteria, fungi, arthropods, algae, plants, and small vertebrates.

Among the animals of the rain forest, it is the insects which are the most diverse of all. A single rain forest tree may support several thousand species of insects, many of which have not been described by scientists. Biologists now estimate that millions of undiscovered insect species may live in tropical rain forests, above and below ground.

(a)

(b)

Figure 2.34   (*a*) Large buttress roots in a tropical rain forest. (*b*) An epiphytic fern growing on a liana in Madagascar.

The rain forest is not, however, just a warehouse for a large number of dissociated species. Intricate relationships weave these species into a living green tapestry. Most rain forest plant species depend on animals, from bats and birds to butterflies and bees, to pollinate the orchids and other flowers for which the rain forest is famous. The plants produce a striking variety of fruit and many have their seeds dispersed by hungry animals. In the tropical rain forest there are plants that cannot live without particular species of ants, mites that make

their homes in the flowers of plants and depend on humming-birds to get them from flower to flower, and trees and vines that continuously compete for access to light.

Human Influences

People from all over the globe owe more to the tropics than is generally realized. Many of the world's staple foods, including maize (called corn in North America and Australia), rice, bananas, and sugarcane, and approximately 25% of all prescription drugs, were originally derived from tropical plants. Many more species, directly useful to humans, may await discovery. In addition, the tropics continue to harbour important genetic varieties of domesticated plant species. Unfortunately, tropical rain forests are fast disappearing. Without them, our understanding of the causes and maintenance of biological diversity will remain forever impoverished.

Humans have exploited tropical rain forests for thousands of years through a mixture of hunting and gathering and shifting agriculture. The hunter-gatherer cultures of rain forests, whether in Asia, Africa, or the Americas, have each used hundreds of species for everything from food and building materials to medicines. Today, we are destroying rain forest for timber, minerals, and short-lived agricultural profits. In response to demographic pressures from exploding human populations in tropical countries and economic pressures from developed countries, traditional systems of exploitation have given way to the bulldozer and chain saw.

Mountains: Islands in the Sky

We now shift our attention to mountains, even though they do not represent a specific biome. Instead, because of the environmental changes that occur with altitude, several biomes may be found on a single mountainside.

Everywhere, mountains capture the imagination as places of geological, biological, and climatic diversity and as places with a view (fig. 2.35). Mountains have long offered refuge for special flora and fauna and humans alike. Like oceanic islands, they offer unique insights into evolutionary and ecological processes.

Geography

Mountains are built by geological processes, such as volcanism and movements of the earth's crust that elevate and fold the earth's surface. These processes operate with greater intensity in some places than others, and so mountains are concentrated in belts where these geological forces have been at work (fig. 2.36). In the Western Hemisphere, these forces have been particularly active on the western sides of both North and South America, where a chain of mountain

Figure 2.35   Mount Logan, Yukon. Environmental conditions and organisms vary greatly from low to high elevations on mountains.

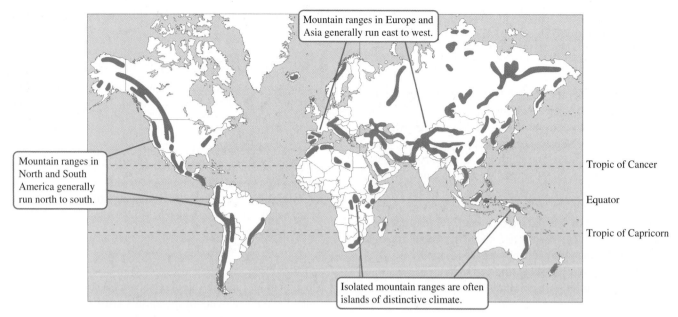

Figure 2.36   Mountain geography.

ranges extends from northern Alaska across western North America to Tierra del Fuego at the tip of South America. Ancient low mountain ranges occupy the eastern sides of both continents. In Africa, the major mountain ranges are the Atlas Mountains of northwest Africa and the mountains of East Africa that run from the highlands of Ethiopia to southern Africa like beads on a string. In Australia, the flattest of the continents, mountains extend down the eastern side of the continent. Eurasian mountain ranges include the Pyrenees, the Alps, the Caucasus, and of course, the Himalayas, the highest of them all.

Climate

On mountains, climates change from low to high elevation, but the specific changes are different at different latitudes. On mountains at middle latitudes, the climate is generally cooler and wetter at higher altitudes (fig. 2.37). In contrast, there is less precipitation at the higher elevations of polar mountains and on some tropical mountains. In other tropical regions, precipitation increases up to some middle elevation and then decreases higher up the mountain. On high tropical mountains, warm days are followed by freezing nights. The organisms on

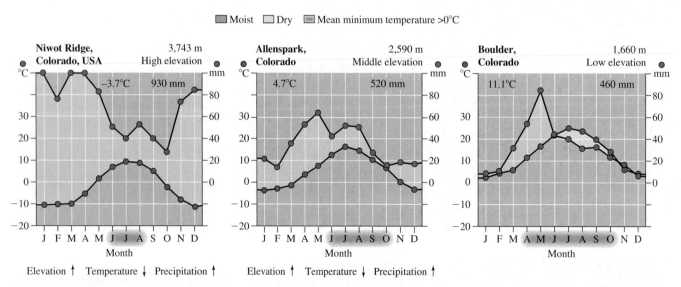

Figure 2.37   Mountain climates along an elevational gradient in the Colorado Rockies. Temperatures decrease and precipitation increases from low to high elevations in these mid-latitude mountains.

these mountains experience summer temperatures every day and winter temperatures every night. The changes in climate that occur up the sides of mountains have profound influences on the distribution of mountain organisms.

Soils

Mountain soils change with elevation and have a great deal in common with the various soils of each separate biome we have already discussed. However, some special features are worth noting. First, because of the steeper topography, mountain soils are generally well drained and tend to be thin and vulnerable to erosion. Second, persistent winds blowing from the lowlands deposit soil particles and organic matter on mountains, materials that can make a significant contribution to local soil building. In some locations in the southern Rocky Mountains, coniferous trees draw the bulk of their nutrition from materials carried by winds from the valleys below, not from local bedrock.

Biology

Climb any mountain that is high enough and you will notice biological and climatic changes. Whatever the vegetation at the base of a mountain, that vegetation will change as you climb and the air becomes cooler. The sequence of vegetation up the side of a mountain may remind you of the biomes we encountered on our journey from the poles to the equator. In the cool highlands of desert mountains in the southwestern United States, you can hike through spruce and fir forests much like those we encountered far to the north. However, what you see on these desert mountains differs substantially from boreal forests. These mountain populations have been isolated from the main body of the boreal forest for over 10,000 years; in the interim, some populations have become extinct, some teeter on the verge of extinction, while others have evolved sufficiently to be recognized as separate species or subspecies. On these mountains, time and isolation have forged distinctive gene pools and mixes of species.

The species on high equatorial mountains are even more isolated. Think for a moment of the geography of high tropical mountains: some in Africa, some in the highlands of Asia, and the Andes of South America. The high-altitude communities of Africa, South America, and Asia share very few species. On the other hand, despite differences in species composition, there are structural similarities among the organisms on these mountains (fig. 2.38). These similarities suggest there may be general rules for associating organisms with environments.

Human Influences

Because mountains differ in climate, geology, and biota (plants and animals) from the surrounding lowlands, they have been useful as a source of raw materials such as wood, forage for animals, medicinal plants, and minerals. Some of these uses, such as livestock grazing, are highly seasonal. In temperate regions, livestock are taken to mountain pastures during the summer and back down to the lowlands in winter.

(a)

(b)

Figure 2.38 Convergence among tropical alpine plants: (*a*) *Senecio* trees on Mount Kilimanjaro, Africa; (*b*) *Espeletia* in the Andes of South America.

Human exploitation of mountains has produced ecological degradation in many places and surprising balance in others. Increased human pressure on mountain environments has sometimes created conflict between competing economic interests, between recreation seekers and livestock ranchers, and even between groups of scientists. Because of their compressed climatic gradients and biological diversity, mountains offer living laboratories for the study of ecological responses to climatic variation.

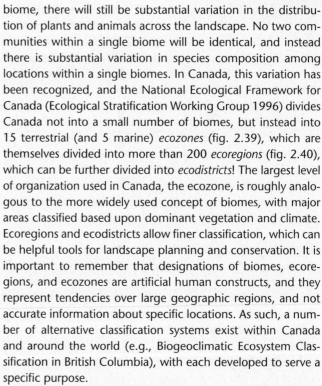

CONCEPT 2.3 REVIEW

1. Why do regions that contain high mountains tend to be more biologically diverse than regions without mountains?
2. Why are soils in the tropical rain forest generally depleted of their nutrients more rapidly compared to soils in the boreal forest?
3. Why do biomes differ in the relative amount of plant biomass that is found below ground? Why is most biomass in tundra and grasslands below ground?

ECOLOGICAL TOOLS AND APPROACHES

Biomes of Canada and Winter Ecology

As we first mentioned in chapter 1, the types of research questions ecologists are able to ask are often limited by the availability of research tools and influenced by different approaches to studying ecology. When new tools are developed, scientists are able to conduct new experiments and once again push back the limits of human understanding. Some of these new tools will involve new laboratory analyses, molecular methods, or remote sensing. Others will be more conceptual, based more upon novel approaches to testing questions. Great advances come when scientists develop new tools and gain new understanding. We will expand on these ideas in the Ecological Tools and Approaches sections of this book. In each chapter we will discuss different methods and approaches used by ecologists to test new research questions.

Knowledge of natural history is critical to ecology, allowing the scientist to have a broader understanding of the system in which they work. Rather than describe the tools needed to learn natural history (time, a notebook, and good binoculars), here we'll discuss how ecologists use knowledge of natural history to describe the ecological landscape of Canada, and how this may influence how ecologists approach their research. We will also discuss an often overlooked aspect of natural history—the winter ecology of species. With changes in global climates, it is becoming more apparent that understanding what species do in winter is going to have important impacts on what happens in the future.

Ecozones of Canada

In this chapter we described how different regions of the planet experience different climates, and how this is associated with the development of different biomes. No country contains all of the biomes of the world; instead, each is home to just a few. However, even if a country is home to a single biome, there will still be substantial variation in the distribution of plants and animals across the landscape. No two communities within a single biome will be identical, and instead there is substantial variation in species composition among locations within a single biomes. In Canada, this variation has been recognized, and the National Ecological Framework for Canada (Ecological Stratification Working Group 1996) divides Canada not into a small number of biomes, but instead into 15 terrestrial (and 5 marine) *ecozones* (fig. 2.39), which are themselves divided into more than 200 *ecoregions* (fig. 2.40), which can be further divided into *ecodistricts*! The largest level of organization used in Canada, the ecozone, is roughly analogous to the more widely used concept of biomes, with major areas classified based upon dominant vegetation and climate. Ecoregions and ecodistricts allow finer classification, which can be helpful tools for landscape planning and conservation. It is important to remember that designations of biomes, ecoregions, and ecozones are artificial human constructs, and they represent tendencies over large geographic regions, and not accurate information about specific locations. As such, a number of alternative classification systems exist within Canada and around the world (e.g., Biogeoclimatic Ecosystem Classification in British Columbia), with each developed to serve a specific purpose.

In figure 2.39 you can see how the ecozone framework allows for more specificity than the coarse tool of biomes. For example, consider the boreal biome, which would include the boreal shield ecozone, the boreal plain ecozone, and the boreal cordillera ecozone. The boreal shield is the largest ecozone in Canada and is influenced by the underlying bedrock. The boreal plains is considered a different ecozone due to a relative lack of influence by bedrock. These both differ from the boreal cordillera, which has substantial mountainous terrain and is influenced by weather patterns from the Pacific Ocean.

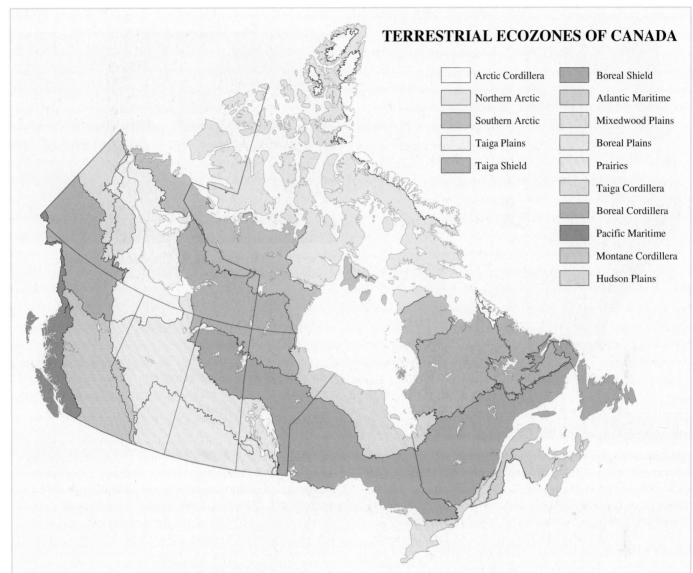

TERRESTRIAL ECOZONES OF CANADA

Arctic Cordillera
Northern Arctic
Southern Arctic
Taiga Plains
Taiga Shield
Boreal Shield
Atlantic Maritime
Mixedwood Plains
Boreal Plains
Prairies
Taiga Cordillera
Boreal Cordillera
Pacific Maritime
Montane Cordillera
Hudson Plains

Figure 2.39 The 15 terrestrial ecozones in Canada.

These differences have important consequences for the organisms that live within these three zones. An ecologist studying the boreal forest of Canada needs to take into account these differences in topography, soils, and vegetation to understand the ecology of a particular location. These basic differences in natural history can prove to be a critical step to understanding variations in ecological function among communities in a single biome. However, if a single country can have 15 ecozones, you can only imagine how many may be found across the globe, and thus the rough categories of biomes are critical for providing an overview of this variation. For larger-scale questions, broad divisions of biomes are helpful; for smaller-scale questions, a finer resolution is needed. A critical ecological tool is having the appropriate scale of natural history knowledge needed to answer your specific ecological question. It is equally critical to recognize that the designations given to an area are generally driven by climatic conditions. As climate changes throughout much of Canada, ecologists expect there

to be shifts in the boundaries of ecoregions throughout the country. For example, the northern limits of the boreal forest are expected to move even further north, and in many places tree and shrub expansion is already occurring. Though these changes are fast relative to historical rates of climatic shifts, they are still slow relative to an individual human lifetime, and thus though ecoregions will eventually need to be redrawn, this is many decades—or centuries—away.

Regardless of whether Canada is divided into a few biomes, more ecozones, or even more ecoregions, one thing is clear: compared to many other areas on the planet, Canada is cold and many areas receive substantial amounts of snow. As a result, one important tool of many Canadian ecologists is an understanding of the natural history of winter. Due to the importance of winter to the organisms that live in Canada, many aspects of winter ecology will be presented throughout the text. Here we provide the story of one species, the black-capped chickadee.

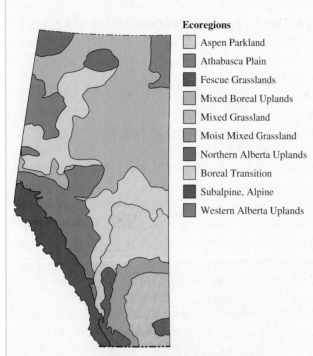

Ecoregions

☐ Aspen Parkland
☐ Athabasca Plain
☐ Fescue Grasslands
☐ Mixed Boreal Uplands
☐ Mixed Grassland
☐ Moist Mixed Grassland
☐ Northern Alberta Uplands
☐ Boreal Transition
☐ Subalpine, Alpine
☐ Western Alberta Uplands

Figure 2.40   Ecoregions of Alberta.

Winter Ecology of the Black-Capped Chickadee

As I sit at home in Edmonton writing this section in early December, it is –25°C. A relentless north wind makes for an effective temperature of –39°C and Environment Canada warns that exposed flesh can freeze in just 10 minutes. My neighbours dash from house to car, though they mainly stay inside. My children haven't had an outdoor recess all week, and it's hard to say whether it'll be the teachers or the kids who crack first. Yet even in this hostile environment, a chickadee (fig. 2.41) flies past my window. How can this be? It seems incredible that this tiny, 10 g bird can survive this temperature, let alone function. Looking closer at this little animal, we can learn a bit about how some animals are able to be active throughout a Canadian winter.

The black-capped chickadee, *Poecile atricapilla*, has a broad geographic range. It occurs throughout the temperate and deciduous biomes of North America, reaching as far north as the Yukon and the Northwest Territories in Canada. Even more amazing, the bird is a permanent resident of these areas, unlike the many human snowbirds that leave Canada for Florida and Texas when winter arrives. Like many resident species, chickadees have several morphological, physiological, and behavioural traits (chapter 5) that make it possible to survive and be active during extremely cold temperatures, temperatures that would cause many other animals to migrate, hibernate, or die. Morphologically, chickadees dress right; their feathers can maintain a temperature differential of nearly 40°C between their skin and the air. A round body shape, which chickadees share with marine mammals,

Figure 2.41   The black-capped chickadee is a permanent resident in biomes with harsh winter conditions.

muskoxen, and polar bears, conserves heat more effectively than a long elongated body.

Physiologically, chickadees do some very unusual things. Because chickadees store no more fat on their bodies than will carry them through a single winter night, they must forage voraciously on a combination of animals (mainly insect larvae) and plants (mainly seeds). But they can forage only during the day, and daylight during midwinter at the northern limit of their range consists of but a few hours of twilight. Chickadees conserve energy during long winter nights by huddling in tree cavities and permitting their body temperatures to drop by as much as 10°C while regulating this descent into nightly hypothermia with bouts of shivering. Ground squirrels, chipmunks, and bats hibernate to solve the problem of winter warmth, and a majority of bird species migrate to warmer areas. A few other birds migrate within Canada in their seasonal quest for food. Other species dig pits and dens beneath the snow. These small spaces, combining the warm body temperatures of winter animals and insulative properties of snow, can result in surprising warmth even in the depths of winter. But no other bird is known to use regulated hypothermia as a daily adaptation to cold.

Behaviourally, chickadees make the most of their foraging opportunities. Like tree squirrels, mice, and a few other bird species, chickadees cache food when temperatures are warm and retrieve it on colder days. They scatter these resources by depositing a single food item in each location, reducing their vulnerability to thieves, but also committing them to an endless and challenging game of Concentration to find their caches. Consequently, chickadees have phenomenal memories, comparable to that of a young child (unless, of course, you ask your child where he left his mittens and toque). Forgotten seeds may germinate the following spring. Much of the chickadee diet, particularly in winter, consists of insect larvae hidden under the bark of tree trunks and branches. For this reason, chickadees and other insectivores exert significant

effects on insect populations and limit the outbreaks of species like forest tent caterpillars.

As we see with the chickadee, winter places a variety of stresses on living organisms. In addition to the obvious risk of frozen tissues, there is limited food, water available only as ice, and for many, large numbers of hungry predators. Across Canada and the planet there is substantial variation in the climatic conditions that occur during winter. In some areas only a few months have average minimum temperatures above 0°C, while in other areas it barely freezes at all. The ecology that occurs during winter is of critical importance to the populations and communities of the many habitats. However, the world is changing and much of the north is getting warmer (chapter 23). How these changes will affect the natural history in Canada is unknown, and these discoveries await the next generation of ecologists.

SUMMARY

Natural history is helping with the difficult task of restoring tropical dry forest in Costa Rica. Natural history also formed the foundation upon which modern ecology developed. Because ecological studies continue to be built upon a solid foundation of natural history, this chapter is devoted to the natural history of terrestrial biomes. Biomes are distinguished primarily by their predominant vegetation and are associated with particular climates.

2.1 Uneven heating of the earth's spherical surface by the sun and the tilt of the earth on its axis combine to produce predictable latitudinal variation in climate.

Because the earth is a sphere, the sun's rays are most concentrated at the latitude where the sun is directly overhead. This latitude changes with the seasons because the earth's axis of rotation is not perpendicular to its plane of orbit about the sun but is tilted approximately 23.5° away from the perpendicular. The sun is directly overhead at the tropic of Cancer, at 23.5° N latitude during the northern summer solstice. During the northern winter solstice, the sun is directly overhead at the tropic of Capricorn, at 23.5° S latitude. The sun is directly overhead at the equator during the spring and autumnal equinoxes. During the northern summer, the Northern Hemisphere is tilted toward the sun and receives more solar energy than the Southern Hemisphere. During the northern winter, the Northern Hemisphere is tilted away from the sun and the Southern Hemisphere receives more solar energy.

Heating of the earth's surface and atmosphere drives atmospheric circulation and influences global patterns of precipitation. As the sun heats air at the equator, it expands and rises, spreading northward and southward at high altitudes. This high-altitude air cools as it spreads toward the poles, eventually sinking back to the earth's surface. Rotation of the earth on its axis breaks up atmospheric circulation into six major cells, three in the Northern Hemisphere and three in the Southern Hemisphere. These three circulation cells correspond to the trade winds north and south of the equator, the westerlies between 30° and 60° N or S latitude, and the polar easterlies above 60° latitude. These prevailing winds do not blow directly south because of the Coriolis effect.

As air rises at the tropics it cools, and the water vapour it contains condenses and forms clouds. Precipitation from these clouds produces the abundant rains of the tropics. Dry air blowing across the lands at about 30° latitude produces the great deserts that ring the globe. When warm, moist air flowing toward the poles meets cold polar air it rises and cools, forming clouds that produce the precipitation associated with temperate environments. Complicated differences in average climate can be summarized using a climate diagram.

2.2 Soil structure results from the long-term interaction of climate, organisms, topography, and parent mineral material.

Terrestrial biomes are built upon a foundation of soil, a vertically stratified and complex mixture of living and nonliving material. Most terrestrial life depends on soil, and much life occurs within soil. Soil structure varies continuously in time and space. Soils are generally divided into O (and LFH), A, B, and C horizons. The O and LFH horizons are made up of freshly fallen organic matter, including leaves, twigs, and other plant parts. The A horizon contains a mixture of mineral materials and organic matter derived from the O horizon. The B horizon contains clays, humus, and other materials that have been transported from the A horizon. The C horizon consists of weathered parent material.

2.3 The geographic distribution of terrestrial biomes corresponds closely to variation in climate, especially prevailing temperature and precipitation.

The major terrestrial biomes and climatic regimes are: *Tundra:* cold; low precipitation; short, soggy summers; poorly developed soils; permafrost; dominated by low vegetation and a variety of animals adapted to long, cold winters; migratory animals, especially birds, make seasonal use. *Boreal forest:* long, severe winters; climatic extremes;

moderate precipitation; infertile soils; permafrost; occasional fire; extensive forest biome, dominated by conifers. *Temperate forest:* moderate, moist winters; warm, moist growing season; fertile soils; high productivity and biomass; dominated by deciduous trees where growing seasons are moist, winters are mild, and soils fertile; otherwise dominated by conifers. *Temperate grassland:* hot and cold seasons; peak rainfall coincides with growing season; droughts sometimes last several years; fertile soils; fire important to maintaining dominance by grasses; historically inhabited by roving bands of herbivores and predators. *Mediterranean woodland and shrubland:* cool, moist winters; hot, dry summers; low to moderate soil fertility; organisms adapted to seasonal drought and

periodic fires. *Desert:* hot or cold; dry; unpredictable precipitation; low productivity but often high diversity; organisms well-adapted to climatic extremes. *Tropical savanna:* warm and cool seasons; pronounced dry and wet seasons; impermeable soil layers; fire important to maintaining dominance by grasses; still supports high numbers and diversity of large animals. *Tropical dry forest:* warm and cool seasons; seasonally dry; biologically rich; as threatened as tropical rain forest. *Tropical rain forest:* warm; moist; low seasonality; infertile soils; exceptional biological diversity and intricate biological interactions. *Mountains:* temperature, precipitation, soils, and organisms shift with elevation; mountains are climatic and biological islands.

REVIEW QUESTIONS

1. Daniel Janzen (1981a, 1981b) proposed that the seeds of the guanacaste tree were once dispersed by several species of large mammals that became extinct following the end of the Pleistocene about 10,000 years ago. There may have been other plant species with a similar relationship with large herbivorous mammals. How do you think the distributions of these plant species may have changed from the time of the extinctions of Pleistocene mammals until the introduction of other large herbivores such as horses? How might the introduction of horses about 500 years ago have affected the distribution of these species? How could you test your ideas?

2. Draw a soil profile for the area around your university. Indicate the principal layers, or horizons. Describe the characteristics of each layer.

3. Describe global patterns of atmospheric heating and circulation. What mechanisms produce high precipitation in the tropics? What mechanisms produce high precipitation at temperate latitudes? What mechanisms produce low precipitation in the tropics?

4. Use what you know about atmospheric circulation and seasonal changes in the Sun's orientation to Earth to explain the highly seasonal rainfall in the tropical dry forest and tropical savanna biomes. (Hint: Why does the rainy season in these biomes come during the warmer months?)

5. We focused much of our discussion of biomes on their latitudinal distribution. The reasonably predictable relationship between latitude and temperature and precipitation provides a link between latitude and biomes. What other geographic variable might affect the distribution of temperature and precipitation and, therefore, of biomes?

6. You probably suggested altitude in response to the previous question because of its important influence on climate. Some

of the earliest studies of the geographic distribution of vegetation suggested a direct correspondence between latitudinal and altitudinal variation in climate. Our discussion in this chapter stressed the similarities in climatic changes with altitude and latitude. What are some major climatic differences between high altitude at mid-latitudes and high altitude at high latitudes?

7. How is the physical environment on mountains at mid-latitudes similar to that in tropical alpine zones? How do these environments differ?

8. English and other European languages have terms for four seasons: spring, summer, autumn, and winter. This vocabulary summarizes much of the annual climatic variation at mid-latitudes in temperate regions. Are these four seasons useful for summarizing annual climatic changes across the rest of the globe? Look back at the climate diagrams presented in this chapter. How many seasons would you propose for each of these environments? What would you call these seasons?

9. Biologists have observed much more similarity in species composition among boreal forests and among areas of tundra in Eurasia and North America than among tropical rain forests or among Mediterranean woodlands around the globe. Can you offer an explanation of this contrast based on the global distributions of these biomes?

10. To date, which biomes have been the most heavily affected by humans? Which seem to be the most lightly affected? How would you assess human impact? How might these patterns change during the coming century?

11. Draw a climate diagram for the location of your university. Climate data for Canada can be found at the Environment Canada Web page (www.climate.weatheroffice.gc.ca/climateData/canada_e.html).

LIFE IN WATER

CHAPTER 3

CHAPTER CONCEPTS

3.1 **The hydrologic cycle exchanges water among reservoirs.**

Concept 3.1 Review

3.2 **The biology of aquatic environments corresponds broadly to variations in physical factors such as light, temperature, and water movements and to chemical factors such as salinity and oxygen.**

Ecology in Action: What Lies Below?

Concept 3.2 Review

Ecological Tools and Approaches: Reconstructing Lake Communities

Summary

Review Questions

The names that people around the world have given to our planet reveal a perspective consistent across cultures. Those names, whether in English (earth), French (*la terre*), Greek (*geos*), or Chinese (*diqiu*), all refer to land or soil, revealing that cultures everywhere hold a land-centred perspective. The Hawaiians, Polynesian inhabitants of the most isolated specks of land on earth, call the planet *ka honua,* an allusion to a level landing place or dirt embankment. This universal land-centred perspective may partly explain why portraits of earth transmitted from space are so stunning. Those images challenge our sense of place by portraying our planet as a shining blue ball, covered not by land but mostly by water (fig. 3.1).

From our perspective as terrestrial organisms, the aquatic realm remains an alien environment governed by unfamiliar rules. In the aquatic environment, life is often most profuse where conditions appear most hostile to us: along cold, wave-swept seacoasts, in torrential mountain streams during the depths of winter, in murky waters where rivers meet the sea. The aquatic world has particular importance for Canada, and this country is a leader in ecological research in freshwater and marine systems. Even in pop culture, there is recognition of how water shapes the landscape of Canada. Although the Ontario band, The Arrogant Worms, sings about Canada being full of "Rocks and Trees," they end their chorus with the word "Water." This should come as no surprise, as Canada is surrounded on three sides by oceans, is home to thousands of lakes and streams, and contains vast expanses of wetlands and peatlands. These environments are the source of natural beauty and substantial economic development, and are home to diverse flora and fauna. The goal of this chapter is to make this realm more familiar by taking a look at the natural history of aquatic environments.

Figure 3.1 From space, earth shows itself as a planet covered mostly by water.

3.1   The Hydrologic Cycle

The hydrologic cycle exchanges water among reservoirs. Over 70% of the earth's surface is covered by water. This water is unevenly distributed among aquatic environments such as lakes, rivers, and oceans. The oceans contain over 97% of the water in the biosphere, and the polar ice caps and glaciers contain an additional 2%. Less than 1% is freshwater in rivers, lakes, and actively exchanged groundwater. The situation on earth is indeed as Samuel Coleridge's ancient mariner saw it: "Water, water, everywhere, nor any drop to drink."

Even the small amount of freshwater that exists on the planet is not evenly distributed. Nearly 20% of the planet's freshwater is found in Canada, even though Canada contains only 7% of the world's landmass. Across the earth, over 65% of freshwater is found in glaciers and ice fields, and nearly 30% is groundwater. This leaves only a very small fraction of the planet's freshwater as surface waters (lakes and streams), upon which most of human society depends. As human populations continue to grow, the demands on existing freshwater reserves also increase. Many places are already beginning to realize that freshwater is not unlimited in supply.

The situation in Alberta is a good example of the increasing pressures being placed upon freshwater reserves. The mountains in western Alberta contain not only Jasper and Banff National Parks, but also many glaciers. These glaciers continue to contain vast amounts of freshwater, though for how long is unclear. Alberta's glaciers are retreating, and the days of riding in a buggy onto the Athabasca glacier are likely limited. Moving out of the mountains, we find the dry-mixed prairies (chapter 2) of southern Alberta. Though historically these were fields of native grasslands, they are now often agricultural fields dependent upon the water coming from the mountains to the west. In the north, hot water is pumped into the tar sands, allowing extraction of thick oil. As tar sand development increases, so too do pressures on the Athabasca river and other freshwater reserves. On top of all of this, Alberta continues a multi-decade long population boom. In 1970, Alberta was home to approximately 1.5 million residents. In 2012, over 3.5 million people lived here. This rate of population growth greatly outpaces Canada as a whole, and is a reflection of the energy boom(s) found throughout Alberta. The population growth increases the pressure on the government to follow the lead of other provinces and dam the few wild rivers that remain to generate hydro power and to divert water to support more strip malls, housing developments, and golf courses. Wetland and lake networks can slow water flows, remove pollutants, and permit groundwater recharge, but only if they persist on the landscape.

What happens within these freshwater ecosystems not only influences the ecology of these habitats, but will also have far-reaching consequences for human health, economic development, and population sustainability. But all is not lost. David Schindler (chapter 1) is once again arguing strongly for the need to protect the freshwater reserves of Alberta, and Sandra Postel from the Global Water Policy Project is working to increase global awareness of these problems. These

scientists, through their understanding of the natural history of aquatic environments, are helping governments achieve solutions before the water has run dry.

Because of changes to freshwater supplies and demands, the distribution of water across the biosphere is dynamic. The various aquatic environments such as lakes, rivers, and oceans plus the atmosphere, ice, and even organisms can be considered as "reservoirs" within the hydrologic cycle, places where water is stored for some period of time. The water in these reservoirs is renewed, or turned over at different rates. Figure 3.2 summarizes these exchanges of water among reservoirs, which as a whole is called the **hydrologic cycle**.

During the hydrologic cycle, water enters each reservoir either as precipitation or as surface or subsurface flow and exits as evaporation or flow. The hydrologic cycle is powered by solar energy, which drives the winds and evaporates water, primarily from the surface of the oceans. Water vapour cools as it rises from the ocean's surface and condenses, forming clouds. These clouds are then blown by solar-driven winds across the planet, eventually yielding rain or snow, the majority of which falls back on the oceans and some of which falls on land. The water that falls on land has several fates.

Some immediately evaporates and re-enters the atmosphere; some contributes to icefields and glaciers; some is consumed by terrestrial organisms; some percolates through the soil to become groundwater; and some ends up in lakes and ponds or in streams and rivers, which may eventually find their way back to the sea.

Reservoirs will be replenished at different rates, and ecologists often measure *turnover times*, the time required for the entire volume of a particular reservoir to be renewed. Reservoir size and rates of water exchange are two of the main determinants of turnover time, and thus turnover occurs at vastly different rates in the different reservoirs. Water in the atmosphere turns over about every nine days. The renewal time for river water, 12 to 20 days, is nearly as rapid. Lake renewal times are longer, ranging anywhere from days to centuries, depending on lake depth, area, and rate of drainage. But the biggest surprise is the renewal time for the largest reservoir of all, the oceans. With a renewal time of only 3,100 years, the total volume of the oceans, over 1.3 billion km³ of water, has turned over more than 30 times in the last 100,000 years, since the first *Homo sapiens* gazed out on the deep blue sea.

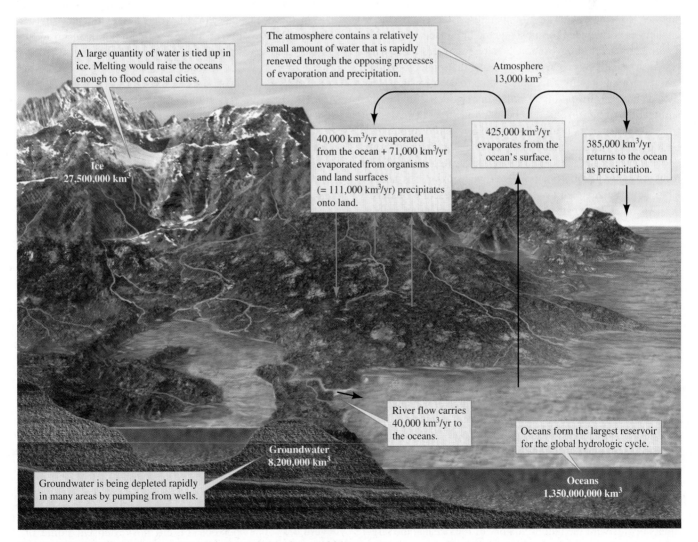

Figure 3.2   The hydrologic cycle (data from Schlesinger 1991)

CONCEPT 3.1 REVIEW

1. How will global warming affect the proportion of the earth's water that resides in the oceans?
2. How does the construction of dams for storing water affect the turnover time for water in rivers?
3. What aspects of the hydrological cycle are influenced most directly by changes in human population growth?

3.2 Life in Water and the Natural History of Aquatic Environments

The biology of aquatic environments corresponds broadly to variations in physical factors such as light, temperature, and water movements and to chemical factors such as salinity and oxygen. In chapter 2 we described a few of the hazards of life on land, including gravity, aridity, and stresses associated with high temperatures. In general, these challenges are reduced for most aquatic organisms. However, a whole other set of environmental stressors faces those who reside in aquatic systems. All organisms that undergo oxidative respiration require a reliable source of oxygen. In water, oxygen is generally dissolved, rather than gaseous. To prevent suffocation, organisms need to be able to extract that oxygen from the water (e.g., using gills), store oxygen for prolonged periods (e.g., marine mammals), or transport oxygen from above the water surface to their tissues below (e.g., specialized roots of many aquatic plants). Even when oxygen is accessible, being surrounded by water can itself present problems.

All natural water bodies consist of water, along with a number of dissolved minerals and gases. Similarly, all organisms contain substantial amounts of water, along with a number of dissolved minerals. Think back to introductory biology about what happens when two different concentrations of minerals are separated solely by a semi-permeable membrane (such as a plasma membrane). Water flows from areas of high solute concentrations to lower concentrations. As an organism living in water, this tendency of water to move along solute gradients presents unique problems if the internal solute concentrations differ from the water outside. Perhaps not surprisingly, there are a number of mechanisms by which organisms cope with this aquatic stress. Aquatic organisms also face challenges associated with temperature regulation, light availability, and access to nutrients and food. In this chapter we will discuss how different types of aquatic systems differ in the abiotic stressors. In section II, we discuss many of the unique traits possessed by organisms that allow them to cope with the sometimes harsh life of the water.

Our discussion of the natural history of aquatic environments begins with the natural history of the oceans, the largest aquatic environment on the planet. We continue our tour with environments found along the margins of the oceans, including kelp forests and coral reefs, the intertidal zone, and salt marshes. We then venture up rivers and streams, important avenues for exchange between terrestrial and aquatic environments. Finally, we consider the inland aquatic environments of lakes, bogs, and fens. As you will see, all but a few of these freshwater and marine systems are found in and around Canada.

The Oceans

The blue solitude of open ocean is something palpable. The only terrestrial biomes that evoke anything close to the feeling of this place are the "big sky" of the open prairies and the "sand sea" of deserts like the Namib. But there is a major difference between these terrestrial environments and the sea. On the open ocean, all is blue—blue sea stretching to the horizon, where it meets blue sky (fig. 3.3).

Experience with terrestrial organisms cannot prepare you for what you encounter in samples taken from the deep ocean. We dream of unknown extraterrestrial beings, some friendly and some monstrous, all with strange and shocking anatomy. We parade them through science fiction literature and films, while, unknown to most of us, creatures as odd and wonderful live in the deep blue world beyond the continental shelves. Figure 3.4 shows one of the species found in the deep sea—a female deep-sea anglerfish with her male partner.

Geography

The ocean covers over 360 million km^2 of earth's surface (70%) and consists of one continuous, interconnected mass of water. Depending upon your perspective, the water consists of either a single global ocean, or it is spread among five major oceans: the Arctic, Atlantic, Indian, Pacific, and southern oceans. Each of these oceans contains several smaller seas along its margins (fig. 3.5). The largest of the oceans,

Figure 3.3 The open ocean is the most extensive biome on the surface of the earth.

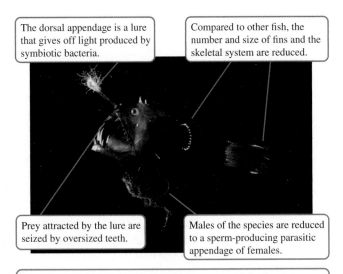

The dorsal appendage is a lure that gives off light produced by symbiotic bacteria.

Compared to other fish, the number and size of fins and the skeletal system are reduced.

Prey attracted by the lure are seized by oversized teeth.

Males of the species are reduced to a sperm-producing parasitic appendage of females.

Darkness, low food availability, and high pressures of the deep-sea environment have selected for organisms quite different from those typical of either shallow seas or the terrestrial environment. Only the females of this deep-sea anglerfish species are active predators.

Figure 3.4 Deep-sea anglerfish.

the Pacific, has a total area of nearly 180 million km^2 and extends from the Antarctic to the Arctic Sea. The second largest basin, the Atlantic, has a total area of over 106 million km^2 and extends nearly from pole to pole. The Indian Ocean covers 73 million km^2, and is bounded by southern Asia to the north, Africa to the west, and southeast Asia and Australia to the south. The Southern Ocean is confined to the Southern Hemisphere with an area of 20 million km^2, extending from Antarctica to 60°S latitude. The smallest of the world's oceans, the Arctic Ocean, covers a total of 14 million km^2 and is confined to the Northern Hemisphere. The Arctic Ocean is home to the seasonally open Northwest Passage connecting the Atlantic and Pacific oceans through Canada and the United States. A similar Northern Sea Route is seasonally open through Norway and Russia.

The Pacific is also the deepest ocean, with an average depth of over 4,000 m. The average depth of the Atlantic is about 3,500 m, while the average depth of the Arctic Ocean is only 1,000 m. Undersea mountains stud the floor of the deep sea, some isolated and some in long chains that run as ridges for thousands of kilometres. Undersea trenches, some of great depth and volume, rip through the seafloor. One such trench, the Marianas, in the western Pacific Ocean, is over 10,000 m deep—deep enough to engulf Mount Everest with 2 km to spare. The peak of Mauna Loa in Hawaii is a bit over 4,000 m above sea level, a modest height for a mountain. But Mauna Loa hides a secret below its sea apron. The base of Mauna Loa extends 6,000 m below sea level, making it, from base to peak, one of the tallest mountains on earth.

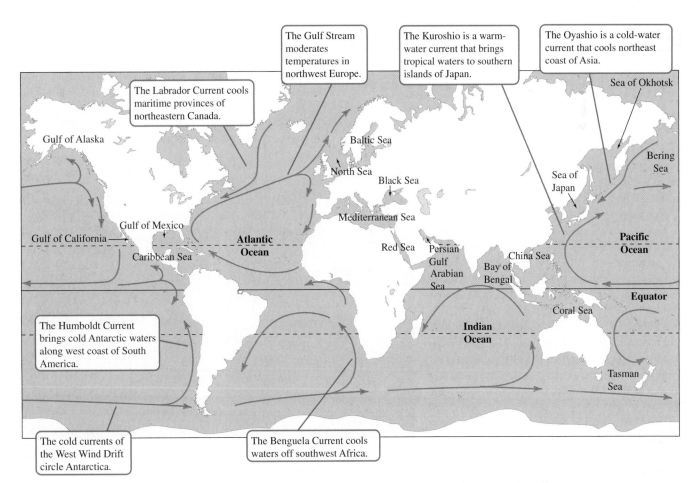

Figure 3.5 Oceanic circulation, which is driven mainly by the prevailing winds, moderates earth's climate.

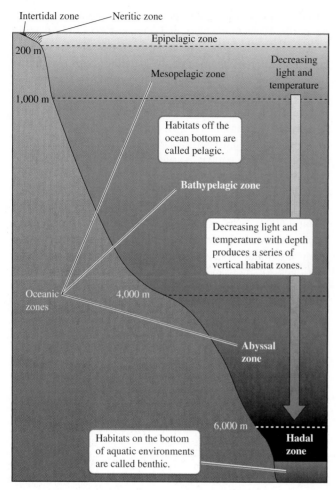

Figure 3.6 — Intertidal zone — Neritic zone — Epipelagic zone — 200 m — Mesopelagic zone — Decreasing light and temperature — 1,000 m — Habitats off the ocean bottom are called pelagic. — Bathypelagic zone — Decreasing light and temperature with depth produces a series of vertical habitat zones. — Oceanic zones — 4,000 m — Abyssal zone — 6,000 m — Hadal zone — Habitats on the bottom of aquatic environments are called benthic.

Figure 3.6 Vertical structuring of the oceans is associated with substantial variation in light and temperature with depth.

Structure

The oceans can be divided into several vertical and horizontal zones. The shallow shoreline under the influence of the rise and fall of the tides is called the **littoral**, or **intertidal**, **zone**. The **neritic zone** extends from the coast to the margin of the continental shelf, where the ocean is about 200 m deep. Beyond the continental shelf lies the **oceanic zone**. Vertically, the ocean is divided into several depth zones. The **epipelagic zone** is the surface layer of the oceans that extends to a depth of 200 m. The **mesopelagic zone** extends from 200 to 1,000 m, and the **bathypelagic zone** extends from 1,000 to 4,000 m. The layer from 4,000 to 6,000 m is called the **abyssal zone**, and finally the deepest parts of the oceans belong to the **hadal zone**. Habitats on the bottom of the ocean, and other aquatic environments, are referred to as **benthic**, while those off the bottom, regardless of depth, are called **pelagic**. Each of these zones supports a distinctive assemblage of organisms. Figure 3.6 sketches the general structure of the oceans.

Physical Conditions

Light

In the first 10 m below the surface, the marine environment is bright with all the colours of the rainbow; below 50 or 60 m it is a blue twilight. Even in the clearest oceans on the brightest days, the amount of sunlight penetrating to a depth of 600 m is approximately equal to the intensity of starlight on a clear night. That leaves, on average, about 3,400 m of deep black water receiving no meaningful direct solar input. Instead, the only light of the deep ocean is that produced by bioluminescent fish and invertebrates. Figure 3.7 compares the colours seen by a scuba diver in deep and shallow water to demonstrate the selective absorption of light by water. But why does the ocean tend to appear blue?

Approximately 80% of the solar energy striking the ocean is absorbed in the first 10 m. Most ultraviolet and infrared light is absorbed in the first few metres. Within the visible range, red, orange, yellow, and green light are absorbed more rapidly than blue light. In the terrestrial world, chlorophyll absorbs blue (and red) light in photosynthesis, while reflecting green light, and thus plants appear green. In the open ocean, algae are at low concentrations and very little of the blue light available is used in photosynthesis. Consequently, the open ocean appears blue.

Temperature

The sunlight absorbed by water increases the *kinetic state*, or velocity of motion, of water molecules. We detect this increased kinetic state as increased temperature. Because more rapid molecular motion decreases water density, warm water floats on cold water. As a consequence, surface water warmed by the sun floats on the colder water below. These warm and cold layers are separated by a **thermocline**, a layer of water through which temperature changes rapidly with depth. This layering of the water column by temperature, which is called *thermal stratification*, is a permanent feature of tropical seas. Temperate oceans are stratified only during the summer, and

(a) (b)

Figure 3.7 Changes in light quality with depth: (*a*) the rich colours on a shallow coral reef; (*b*) the blue of the deeper reef.

the thermocline breaks down as surface waters cool during fall and winter. At high latitudes, thermal stratification is only weakly, if ever, developed. As we shall see, these differences in thermal conditions at different latitudes have far-reaching consequences to the ecological functioning of the oceans.

At the ocean surface, average annual temperature and annual variation in temperature change with latitude but, at all latitudes, oceanic temperatures are much more stable than terrestrial temperatures. The lowest average oceanic temperature, about $-1.5°C$, is around the Antarctic. The highest average surface temperatures, a bit over $27°C$, occur near the equator. Maximum annual variation in surface temperature, approximately $7°C$ to $9°C$, occurs in the temperate zone above $40°$ N latitude. Near the equator, as the tropical rain forest, the total annual range in temperature, about $1°C$, approximately equals the daily range. The greatest stability in oceanic temperatures, however, is below the surface, where, at just 100 m depth, annual variation in temperature is often less than $1°C$.

Water Movements

If you are standing on the deck of a small boat off the coast of Labrador during a spring storm, you quickly learn to appreciate the movements of the ocean. The oceans are never still. Prevailing winds drive currents that transport nutrients, oxygen, and heat, as well as organisms, across the globe. These currents moderate climates, fertilize the surface waters off the continents, stimulate photosynthesis, and promote gene flow among populations of marine organisms. For example, wind-driven surface currents sweep across vast expanses of open ocean to create great circulation systems called **gyres** that move to the right (clockwise) in the Northern Hemisphere and to the left (counter-clockwise) in the Southern Hemisphere. The great oceanic gyres transport warm water from equatorial regions toward the poles, moderating climates at middle and high latitudes. A segment of one of these gyres, the Gulf Stream, moderates the climate of northwest Europe.

Even if you are standing in your boat under bright skies and on flat seas, the ocean remains in motion. In addition to surface currents, there are deepwater currents such as those produced as cooled, high-density water sinks at the Antarctic and Arctic and then moves along the ocean floor. Deep water may also be moved to the surface in a process called **upwelling**. Upwelling occurs along the west coasts of continents and around Antarctica, where winds blow surface water offshore, allowing colder water to rise to the surface. These various water movements are like undersea winds but with a difference: water is vastly more dense than air. How might this difference in density affect the anatomy, behaviour, and distributions of marine organisms?

Chemical Conditions

Salinity

The amount of salt dissolved in water is called **salinity**, and when an organism's internal salinity differs from the salinity of the surrounding water, that organism will be under osmotic stress. The degree of stress experienced will depend upon both its own chemical composition as well as that of the water in which it lives. Salinity varies with latitude and among the seas that fringe the oceans. In the open ocean, it varies from about 34 g of salt per kilogram of water (34‰ or parts per thousand) to about 36.5‰. The lowest salinities occur near the equator and above $40°$ N and S latitudes, where inputs of freshwater through snow and rainfall exceed evaporation, thereby diluting the salts in these oceans. The excess of precipitation over evaporation at these latitudes is shown by the climate diagrams for temperate forests, boreal forests, and tundra that we examined in chapter 2. The highest salinities occur in the subtropics at about $20°$ to $30°$ N and S latitudes, where precipitation is low and evaporation high—precisely those latitudes where we encountered deserts. Salinity varies a great deal more in the small, enclosed basins along the margins of the major oceans. The Baltic Sea, which is surrounded by temperate and boreal forest biomes and receives large inputs of freshwater, has local salinities of 7‰ or lower. In contrast, the Red Sea, which is surrounded by deserts, has surface salinities of over 40‰.

Despite considerable variation in total salinity, the relative proportions of the major ions (e.g., sodium [Na^+], magnesium [Mg^{+2}], and chloride [Cl^-]) remain approximately constant from one part of the ocean to another. This uniform composition, which is a consequence of continuous and vigorous mixing of the entire world ocean, underscores the connections between different regions of the world's oceans.

Oxygen

Oxygen is present in far lower concentrations and varies much more in the oceans than in aerial environments. A litre of air contains about 200 ml of oxygen at sea level, while a litre of seawater contains a maximum of 9 ml of oxygen. Oxygen concentrations are generally highest near the ocean surface, and then decrease progressively with depth down to approximately 1,000 m below the surface of the ocean. Below 1,000 metres, oxygen concentrations then increase as one travels deeper in the ocean. However, there are exceptions. Some marine environments, such as the deep waters in the Black Sea, are essentially devoid of oxygen.

Biology

There is a close correspondence between physical and chemical conditions and the diversity, composition, and abundance of oceanic organisms. For instance, because of the limited penetration of sunlight into seawater, photosynthetic organisms are limited to the brightly lighted upper epipelagic zone of the ocean (fig. 3.6). The most significant photosynthetic inhabitants of this zone, also called the **photic zone**, are microscopic organisms called **phytoplankton** that drift with the currents in the open sea. The small animals that drift with these same currents are called **zooplankton**. While there is no ecologically significant photosynthesis below the photic zone, there is no absence of deep-sea organisms. Fish, ranging from small bioluminescent forms to giant sharks, and invertebrates from tiny crustaceans to giant squid, prowl the entire water column. There is life even in the deepest trenches, below 10,000 m.

Linking the biotic and abiotic parts of the ocean ecosystem is a complex and extremely diverse set of microbial interactions.

Microbes are the unsung heroes of most ecological communities, and they will feature in critical points throughout this text. For every undergraduate who dreams about studying bacteria and fungi, there must be hundreds (thousands?) who want to work on dolphins, whales, polar bears, wolves, and butterflies. However, as you will see throughout this text, personal interest does not necessarily reflect ecological importance. In the ocean, these small organisms fill a variety of roles in the functioning of this ecosystem. They are key players in global carbon and nutrient cycles, as well as being food for yet more organisms. The exact role of this diverse group of species is only now being discovered, with many surprises likely to emerge. Because of the enormous size of the oceans, it is very likely that ocean microbes will drive global responses to climate change.

Most deep-sea organisms are nourished—whatever their place in the food chain—by organic matter fixed by photosynthesis near the surface. It was long assumed that the rain of organic matter from above was the *only* source of food for deep-sea organisms. Then, about two decades ago, the sea surprised everyone. There are entire biological communities on the seafloor that are nourished not by photosynthesis at the surface, but by chemosynthesis on the ocean floor (see chapter 7). These oases of life are associated with undersea hot springs and harbour many life forms entirely new to science. Figure 3.8 shows the great density of organisms found on the ocean floors near an undersea hydrothermal vent.

The deep ocean shines with the blue of pure water and is often called a "biological desert." This description suggests that the open ocean is an area nearly devoid of life—a wasteland, perhaps—that can be dismissed. While it is true that the average rate of photosynthesis per square metre of ocean surface is similar to that of terrestrial deserts, the oceans, because they are so vast, contribute approximately one-fourth of the total photosynthesis in the biosphere. This oceanic production constitutes a substantial contribution to the global carbon and oxygen budget. So why "desert"? Oceanic populations live at such low densities that there is little in the open ocean that can be economically harvested for direct human consumption. J. H. Ryther (1969) estimated that the open ocean contains less than 1% of the harvestable fish stocks. Most fish are found along the coasts. We can, however, appreciate the open ocean from other perspectives.

The open ocean is home, the only home, for thousands of organisms with no counterparts on land. The terrestrial environment supports 11 animal phyla, only one of which, Onychophora (velvet worms), is **endemic** to the terrestrial environment—that is, found in no other environments. Fourteen phyla live in freshwater environments, but none are endemic. Meanwhile, the marine environment, supports 28 phyla, 13 of which are endemic to the marine environment (fig. 3.9).

Does the greater diversity of phyla in the marine environment shown in figure 3.9 contradict our impression of high biological diversity in biomes such as the tropical rain forest? No. The terrestrial environment is extraordinarily diverse because there are many species in a few animal and plant phyla, especially arthropods and flowering plants. Still, the number of marine species may also be very high. J. F. Grassle (1991) estimated that the number of bottom-dwelling, or

Figure 3.8   Chemosynthesis-based community on the East Pacific Rise.

benthic, marine species may exceed 10 million, a level of species diversity that would rival that of the tropical rain forest.

Human Influences

Human impact on the oceans was once less than on other parts of the biosphere. For most of our history, the vastness of the oceans has been a buffer against human intrusions, but our influence is growing. The decline of large whale populations around Antarctica and elsewhere sounded a warning of what we can do to the open ocean system. The killing of whales has been reduced, but there are plans to harvest the great whales' food supply, the small planktonic crustaceans known as *krill*. Although we may find them less engaging than their predators, the large whales, these zooplankton may be more important to the life of the open ocean. Whales are not the only marine populations that have collapsed. Overfishing has led to great declines in commercially important fish stocks, such as the Grand Banks cod population. Many marine fish populations, which once seemed inexhaustible, are now all but gone and fishing fleets sit idle in ports all over the world.

Another threat to marine life in the open ocean is the dumping of wastes of all sorts, including nuclear, chemical, and general trash. For centuries, the open ocean has been a good example of "out of sight, out of mind," and has served as the repository for filth of all sorts. Though we learn in grade school the stories of European explorers traversing the open oceans, we also learned they typically returned home with treasure, not trash. Garbage was typically thrown into the oceans,

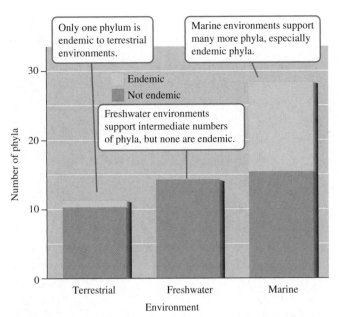

Only one phylum is endemic to terrestrial environments.

Marine environments support many more phyla, especially endemic phyla.

Freshwater environments support intermediate numbers of phyla, but none are endemic.

Endemic

Not endemic

Number of phyla

Terrestrial   Freshwater   Marine

Environment

Figure 3.9 Distribution of animal phyla among terrestrial, freshwater, and marine environments (data from Grassle 1991).

a grand tradition that continues to this day throughout much of the world's oceans. However, unlike the days of Columbus and Magellan, much of the ocean is no longer out of sight. There is a growing realization that dumping garbage does not eliminate the problem, instead it causes new ones. In recent years, chemical pollution of the sea has increased substantially, and chemical pollutants are accumulating in deep-sea sediments. The northern Pacific Ocean is home to the "Great Pacific Garbage Patch," also called the Pacific Trash Vortex. This is a cycling area of enormous size in which small debris (including many plastic fragments) and pollutants are trapped due to ocean currents. Similar garbage patches have been found in the Atlantic, and likely occur in other oceans throughout the world. Though floating debris can serve as home for a number of crustaceans, fish, and other marine organisms, few view the accumulation of trash in the world's oceans as a positive legacy of human inhabitation and exploration of the planet.

Beyond the horizon of the coasts of many countries lies another threat to both open ocean and near-shore environments—deep ocean petroleum extraction. Associated with oil extraction are leaks. Some of these will be small, some will be very large. Though few will see the leaks themselves, many regularly see the damage they have on coastal organisms. The impacts of oil leaks on the general ecology of open ocean species remains unclear. Simply moving oil extraction off-shore and out-of-sight does not reduce human impacts; instead, it just changes the manner in which they occur.

Shallow Marine Waters: Kelp Forests and Coral Gardens

The shallow waters along continents and around islands support marine communities of very high diversity and biomass. Imagine yourself snorkelling along a marine shore, beyond the intertidal zone. If you are at temperate latitudes and over a solid bottom, you are likely to swim through groves of brown seaweed called *kelp*. Along many coasts, kelp grows so tall,

over 40 m in some places, and in such densities that they resemble submarine forests (fig. 3.10).

If you snorkel in the tropics, you may come across a coral reef diverse in colour and texture. The colours on a coral reef rival that of any terrestrial biome (fig. 3.11).

Geography

The near-shore marine environment and its inhabitants vary with latitude. In temperate to subpolar regions, wherever there is a solid bottom and no overgrazing there are profuse growths of kelp. As you get closer to the equator, these kelp forests are gradually replaced by coral reefs. Coral reefs are confined to low latitudes between 30° N and S (fig. 3.12).

Are there any corals in Canada? Although coral reefs are restricted in their geographic distributions and only occur in relatively shallow water, there are many coral species that do not form reefs, live in deep oceans, and occur throughout the world. Deep-sea corals (fig. 3.13) have been known to exist for several centuries; however, more extensive exploration of the deep waters of the world is only now letting scientists learn about their biology and ecology (see Ecology in Action). Recent work suggests some corals may live more than 4,000 years, making them among the oldest living species on the planet (Roark et al. 2009). Unusually high levels of deep-sea coral diversity is found in the Sable Gully, located approximately 200 km off-shore of Nova Scotia. The gulley is a series of submarine canyons that occur well below 100 m. Interestingly, where coral diversity is high within the gully, so too is the diversity of other megafaunal species (Mortensen and Buhl-Mortensen 2005), suggesting these corals may provide many of the same ecological functions characteristic of the more familiar coral reefs of the tropical water.

Figure 3.10 A scene from a kelp forest off the west coast of North America. Like terrestrial forests, kelp forests are home to a diversity of organisms.

Figure 3.11   Coral reefs, such as this one in the Red Sea, support some of the most diverse assemblages of organisms on earth.

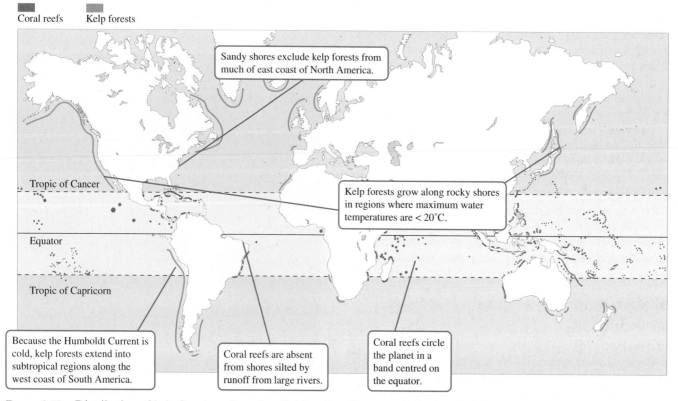

Coral reefs   Kelp forests

Sandy shores exclude kelp forests from much of east coast of North America.

Kelp forests grow along rocky shores in regions where maximum water temperatures are < 20°C.

Tropic of Cancer

Equator

Tropic of Capricorn

Because the Humboldt Current is cold, kelp forests extend into subtropical regions along the west coast of South America.

Coral reefs are absent from shores silted by runoff from large rivers.

Coral reefs circle the planet in a band centred on the equator.

Figure 3.12   Distribution of kelp forests and coral reefs (data from Barnes and Hughes 1988, after Schumacher 1976).

Figure 3.13   Examples of deep-sea corals found in the Sable Gully, 200 km off the coast of Nova Scotia.

Structure

Charles Darwin (1842a) was the first to place coral reefs into three categories: fringing reefs, barrier reefs, and atolls. **Fringing reefs** hug the shore of a continent or island. Barrier reefs, such as the Great Barrier Reef, which stretches for nearly 2,000 km off the northeast coast of Australia, stand some distance offshore. A **barrier reef** stands between the open sea and a lagoon. Coral **atolls**, which dot the tropical Pacific and Indian Oceans, consist of coral islets that have built up from a submerged oceanic island and ring a lagoon.

Distinctive habitats associated with coral reefs include the *reef crest*, where corals grow in the surge zone created by waves coming from the open sea. The reef crest extends to a depth of about 15 m. Below the reef crest is a *buttress zone*, where coral formations alternate with sand-bottomed canyons. Behind the reef crest lies the *lagoon*, which contains numerous small coral reefs, called *patch reefs*, and sea grass beds.

Beds of kelp, particularly those of giant kelp, have structural features similar to those of terrestrial forests. At the water's surface is the *canopy*, which may be more than 25 m above the seafloor. The *stems*, or *stipes*, of kelp extend from the canopy to the bottom and are anchored with structures called *holdfasts*. On the stipes and fronds of kelp grow numerous species of epiphytic algae and sessile invertebrates. Other seaweed species of smaller stature usually grow along the bottom, forming an understory to the kelp forest.

Physical Conditions

Light

Both seaweeds and reef-building corals grow only in surface waters, where there is sufficient light to support photosynthesis. The depth of light penetration sufficient to support kelp and coral varies with local conditions from a few metres to nearly 100 m.

Temperature

Temperature limits the distribution of both kelp and coral. Most kelp are limited to temperate shores, to those regions where temperatures may fall below 10°C in winter and rise to a bit above 20°C in summer. Reef-building corals are restricted to warm waters, to those regions where the minimum temperature does not fall below about 18°C to 20°C and average temperatures usually vary from about 23°C to 25°C. Reef-building corals are also sensitive to high temperatures, however, and temperatures above about 29°C are usually lethal.

Water Movements

Coral reefs and kelp beds are continuously washed by oceanic currents. These currents deliver oxygen and nutrients and remove waste products. The biological productivity of kelp beds and coral reefs may depend upon the flushing action of these currents. However, extremely strong currents and wave action, as during hurricanes, can detach entire kelp forests and flatten entire coral reefs built up over many centuries. Periodic disturbance is a characteristic of both the kelp bed and the coral reef, and both may require some abiotic disturbance for their long-term survival.

Chemical Conditions

Salinity

Coral reefs grow only in waters with fairly stable salinity. Heavy rainfall or runoff from rivers that reduces salinity below about 27% of seawater can be lethal to corals. Kelp beds appear to be more tolerant of freshwater runoff and grow well along temperate shores, where surface salinities are substantially reduced by runoff from large rivers.

Oxygen

Coral reefs and kelp beds occur where waters are well oxygenated.

Biology

Coral reefs face intense, and sometimes complex, biological disturbance. Periodic outbreaks of the predatory crown-of-thorns sea star, *Acanthaster planci*, which eats corals, have devastated large areas of coral reef in the Indo-Pacific region. In a Caribbean coral reef community, populations of a sea star relative, the sea urchin *Diadema antillarum*, eat both algae and corals. However, these urchins benefit the corals by reducing algal densities, thereby reducing the potential competition for space. Figure 3.14 shows one of these sea urchins on a coral reef in the Caribbean Sea.

Coral reefs and kelp beds are among the most productive and diverse of all ecological systems in the biosphere. Robert Whittaker and Gene Likens (1973) estimated that the rate of primary production on coral reefs and algal beds exceeds that of tropical rain forests. The centre of diversity for reef-building corals is the western Pacific and eastern Indian Oceans, where there are over 600 coral species and over 2,000 species of fish. By comparison, the western Atlantic Ocean

Figure 3.14 The sea urchin *Diadema* on a coral reef. Feeding by *Diadema* appears to play a key role in the interaction between reef-building corals and benthic algae.

supports about 100 species of corals. Biotic diversity on reefs is also impressive on a small scale. A single coral head may support over 100 species of polychaete worms (Grassle 1973) and over 75 species of fish (Smith and Tyler 1972).

Human Influences

Coral reefs and kelp forests are increasingly exploited for a variety of purposes. Tons of kelp are harvested for use as a food additive and for fertilizer. Fortunately, most of this harvest is replaced by rapid kelp growth. Corals, however, which are intensively harvested and bleached for decorations, do not grow quickly. The fish and shellfish of kelp forests and coral reefs have also been heavily exploited. Once again, it appears that coral reefs are more vulnerable. Some coral reefs have been so heavily fished, both for food and for the aquarium trade, that most of the larger fish are rare. Some especially destructive means of fishing are used on coral reefs, including dynamite and poisons. In the Philippines, over 60% of the area once covered by coral has been destroyed by these techniques during recent years. While an appreciation of the threats to rain forests grows, there is less said of the plight of the rain forest's marine cousin, the coral reef. There is some evidence that healthy coral reefs can buffer the effects of large waves as they approach shore. As a result, destruction of reefs in the water as a marine resource can have significant consequences for what happens to those who live near the water's edge.

ECOLOGY IN ACTION

What Lies Below?

Understanding the biodiversity of aquatic systems is just as important for society as is understanding the biodiversity of terrestrial systems (chapter 2). On land, we argued that soils were the biggest frontier for discovery of life on land. What about the world of water? Not too surprisingly, people's tendency to study those things more readily observable is not limited to the terrestrial world. We can watch "Shark Week" on TV, but I have yet to see an annual television event focused on microbes and the tiny animals of the world. Nonetheless, as we move from the surface of the ocean toward the sediment below, our understanding of basic natural history becomes as black as the water around us. There are obvious difficulties working in and around sediment and deep oceans, similar to those in soil ecology. The habitat is dark, organisms are difficult and expensive to reach, and many of the most common organisms are small and hard to see. Deep ocean studies are made even more difficult by extreme pressure differences, where simply bringing organisms up to the surface for study is often fatal to the organism. However, for those willing to take on these challenges, there is a great reward: a chance to explore a truly unknown world (fig. 3.15).

Our lack of understanding of deep waters and sediments is completely counter to their likely importance in the functioning of natural systems and global processes. Because of the expanse of the oceans, coupled with abundant underwater mountain ranges that increase the surface area of the ocean floor, ocean bottoms are the single most common habitat on the planet. As a result, changes to the activity of organisms on the ocean floor could impact global processes, including atmospheric composition and climate. One researcher who has dedicated his professional life to understanding the biology of the deep sea is Paul Snelgrove of Memorial University in Newfoundland. He has written extensively on the diversity and importance of ocean sediments as reservoirs of biodiversity and as a key player in global nutrient cycling (Snelgrove 1999, 2000). Because of the great cost of biodiversity research in open oceans, along with their great expanse and importance to Canada, research often is done through partnerships. For example, Snelgrove has been instrumental in the development of the CHONe (Canadian Healthy Oceans Network), a recent group focused on enabling collaborations among academia and government in an effort to use science to better inform management and protection of marine biodiversity (Snelgrove et al. 2012).

The level of biodiversity on the ocean floor is simply staggering. Estimates suggest somewhere between 1 million and

Figure 3.15 Some of the diversity found 145 m deep along a fjord wall at Hosie Islands, Barkley Sound, British Columbia. In the photo are glass sponges (*Aphrocallistes vastus*), fish, a variety of invertebrates in the sediment, and the manipulator arm of the remote operated vehicle, ROPOS. The green is fluorescein dye that the researcher squirted onto the sponges to test whether they were actively pumping sea water.

Taxon	Described Species	Estimated Total Species
Bacteria	500	Unknown. May be as high as 10^9
Fungi	600	2,000
Protists	3,000	30,000
Meiofauna	7,000	10^8
Macrofauna	87,000	725,000
Total	98,100	10^6–10^9

Figure 3.16 Described and estimated species diversity of organisms living in marine sediments. Meiofauna are organisms up to 1 mm in length, able to live between sand grains. Macrofauna are larger than 1 mm (data from Snelgrove 1999).

1 billion species live there, with less than 1% of these currently described (fig. 3.16). Even excluding the practically unknown diversity of bacteria, there could be millions of species yet to be discovered. Of the 13 animal phyla endemic to marine environments, all have species that live in, or on, marine sediment. Because of this diversity at deep branches in the evolutionary tree, understanding the diversity of this group of organisms can provide insights into fundamental process of animal ecology and evolution.

When we imagine the diversity of the ocean, it is often sharks, whales, and algae that come to mind. In reality, most species that live in the ocean are at the bottom, and many of these are barely visible to the naked eye. Since we have such a limited understanding of the types of organisms that live in ocean sediment, we have an even worse understanding of their natural history. For example, many deep ocean species have a free-living larval stage whose basic ecology may be fundamentally different from that of the adults. At a most basic level, it is unclear how these small creatures of the deep are able to settle in suitable habitats in which they can develop into sessile adults. Scientific understanding of the natural history of larval stages is even more limited than our understanding of the benthic adults.

The realization that a large bulk of the diversity in the oceans lies on the floor results in a very simple question. Why? It seems counter-intuitive that the bottom of the great

"desert" should hold such a wealth of diversity. Ecologists have proposed several theories, none of which have yet been fully supported (Grassle 1991). One possibility is that the deep ocean has a relatively stable environment (cold, dark, constant nutrient flow drifting down from the waters above), reducing the chance of severe climatic events that are often found in other habitats (such as drought, flooding, fire, and so on). Climatic stability may allow species with relatively small populations to persist, whereas they would go extinct in areas with more climatic disturbance. A second possibility could be simply that the deep ocean is expansive, and this large contiguous area could further allow species to persist, even at low densities, due to the potential size of the habitat range that is available. Further, within this seemingly homogenous area will be periodic localized disturbances (e.g., a whale carcass, animal burrows, sponge mats), which create a diversity of microhabitats upon which other species may specialize. In short, the mechanisms that generate diversity of deep oceans may be very similar to the mechanisms that generate diversity in other ecosystems. By studying areas that are poorly understood, we have the ability to test broader ecological theories about the factors that govern species distributions and abundance.

Just as scientists are now taking a closer look at the diversity of species in soils, efforts to explore the ocean floor are also underway. The Census of Marine Life (2010) is a worldwide initiative to catalogue the biological diversity of the world's oceans, with its first report released in 2010. Project Venus (Victoria Experimental Network Under the Sea, 2010) and Neptune Canada (2010) involve the construction and operation of permanent undersea laboratories on the ocean floor around Vancouver Island and into the deep ocean. This research infrastructure allows real-time imagery and monitoring of the local residents and environmental conditions and provides easy access to this data through the Internet. These projects are a critical step in improving the understanding of the natural history of the deep. Though we often think of the deep sea being a bottomless desert, it is not; all oceans have a bottom, and to many species, it is home.

A less direct, but potentially more widespread impact of people on these near-shore environments occurs to conditions in the water. Coral reefs are formed by a close interaction between the coral (phylum Cnidaria) and a variety of zooxanthellae (phylum Dinoflagellata). When these species are healthy, the hard exoskeletons associated with coral reefs are formed. However, a number of environmental triggers, including increased temperatures, light, and pollution, can cause a breakdown in this relationship, leading to *coral bleaching*. When bleaching begins, it can continue even if the initial stimuli is relaxed, potentially causing the death of large reefs.

Where Waves Meet Rocks: Intertidal Zones

The rise and fall of the tides make the shore one of the most dynamic environments in the biosphere. The intertidal zone is a magnet for the curious naturalist and one of the most convenient places to study ecology. Where else in the biosphere does the structure of the landscape change several times each day? Where else does nature expose entire aquatic communities for easy exploration? Where else are environmental and biological gradients so compressed? It should be no surprise that here in the intertidal zone, immersed in tide pools, salt spray, and the sweet smell of kelp, ecologists have found the inspiration and circumstance for some of the most elegant experiments and most enduring generalizations of ecology. The intertidal zone, the area covered by waves at high tide and exposed to air at low tides, has proved to be an illuminating window to the world. Figure 3.17 shows the tangle of diverse life that can be observed on a rocky shore during low tide.

Geography

Thousands of kilometres of coastline around the world have intertidal zones. It is significant to distinguish between exposed and sheltered shores. Battered by the full force of ocean waves, exposed shores support very different organisms from those found along sheltered shores on the inside of headlands or in coves and bays. A second important distinction is between rocky and sandy shores.

Structure

The intertidal zone can be divided into several vertical zones (fig. 3.18). The highest zone is called the *supratidal fringe*, or *splash zone*. The supratidal fringe is seldom covered by high tides but is often wetted by waves. Below this fringe is the intertidal zone proper. The upper intertidal zone is covered only during the highest tides, and the lower intertidal zone is uncovered only during the lowest tides. Between the upper and lower intertidal zones is the middle intertidal zone, which is covered and uncovered during average tides. Below the intertidal zone is the *subtidal zone*, which remains covered by water even during the lowest tides. As we shall see in the next two sections (Physical Conditions and Chemical Conditions), tidal fluctuation produces steep gradients of physical and chemical conditions within the intertidal zone.

Figure 3.17 A rocky shore at low tide, showing the diversity of life found within a small area.

Physical Conditions

Light

Intertidal organisms are exposed to wide variations in light intensity. At high tide, water turbulence reduces light intensity. At low tide, intertidal organisms are exposed to the full intensity of the sun. How might this variation in light intensity affect the distribution of photosynthetic organisms in the intertidal zone? How vulnerable are intertidal organisms to damage by sunlight, compared to organisms from other marine environments?

Temperature

Because the intertidal zone is exposed to the air once or twice each day, intertidal temperatures are always changing. At high latitudes, tide pools, small basins that retain water at low tide, can cool to freezing temperatures during low tides, while tide pools along tropical and subtropical shores can heat to temperatures in excess of 40°C. The dynamic intertidal environment contrasts sharply with the stability of most marine environments and presents substantial environmental challenges.

Water Movements

The two most important water movements affecting the distribution and abundance of intertidal organisms are the waves that break upon the shore and the tides. The tides vary in magnitude and frequency. Most tides are *semidiurnal*, that is, there are two low tides and two high tides each day. However,

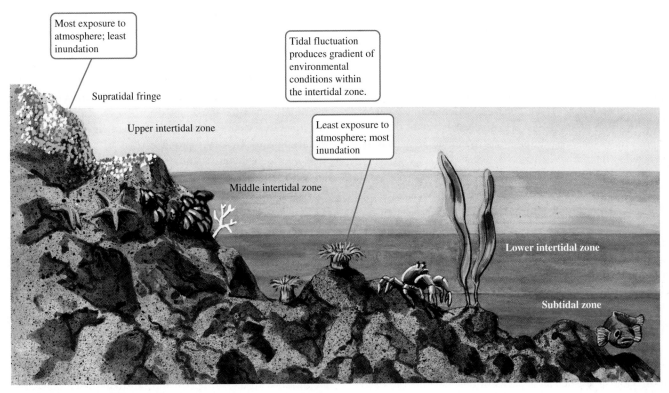

Figure 3.18   Intertidal zonation.

(a)   (b)

Figure 3.19   Hopewell (flowerpot) rocks at the Bay of Fundy at: (*a*) high tide; and (*b*) low tide.

in seas, such as the Gulf of Mexico and the South China Sea, there are *diurnal* tides, that is, a single high and low tide each day. The total rise and fall of the tide varies from a few centimetres along some marine shores to the world's largest tide of 15 m at the Bay of Fundy between Nova Scotia and New Brunswick (fig. 3.19).

The main tide-producing forces are the gravitational pulls of the sun and moon on water. Of the two forces, the pull of the moon is greater because, although the sun is far more massive, the moon is much closer. Tidal fluctuations are greatest when the sun and moon are working together, that is, when the sun, moon, and earth are in alignment, which happens at full and new moons. These times of maximum

tidal fluctuation are called **spring tides**. Tidal fluctuation is least when the gravitational effects of the sun and moon are working in opposition, that is, when the sun and moon, relative to earth, are at right angles to each other, as they are at the first and third quarters of the moon. These times of minimum tidal fluctuation are called **neap tides**. The size and geographic position of a bay, sea, or section of coastline determine whether the influences of sun and moon are amplified or damped and are responsible for the variations in tides from place to place.

Intertidal organisms have a lot to withstand, having to deal with the abiotic stressors encountered by both aquatic and terrestrial organisms. They face not only potential desiccation

from exposure to air during low tide, but also from the pounding of waves breaking on the seashore. The amount of wave energy to which intertidal organisms are exposed varies considerably from one section of coast to another; this variation affects the distribution and abundance of intertidal species. Exposed headlands are hit by high waves (fig. 3.20), and they are also subjected to strong currents, which are at times as strong as those of swift rivers. Coves and bays are the least exposed to waves, but even the most sheltered areas may be subjected to intense wave action during storms.

Chemical Conditions

Salinity

Salinity in the intertidal zone varies much more than in the open sea, especially within tide pools isolated at low tide. Rapid evaporation during low tide increases the salinity within tide pools along desert shores. Along rainy shores at high latitudes and in the tropics during the wet season, tide pool organisms can experience much reduced salinity.

Oxygen

Oxygen does not generally limit the distributions of intertidal organisms for two major reasons. First, intertidal species are exposed to oxygen-rich air at each low tide. Second, the water of wave-swept shores is thoroughly mixed and well oxygenated. An intertidal environment where oxygen availability may be low is in interstitial water within the sediments along

sandy or muddy shores, especially in sheltered bays, where water circulation is weak.

Biology

The inhabitants of the intertidal zone are adapted to an amphibious existence: partly marine, partly terrestrial. All intertidal organisms are adapted to periodic exposure to air, but some species are better equipped than others to withstand that exposure. This fact produces one of the most noticeable intertidal features, **zonation of species**. Some species inhabit the highest levels of the intertidal zone, are exposed by almost all tides, and remain exposed the longest. Others are exposed during the lowest tides only, perhaps once or twice per month, or even less frequently. On an even finer spatial scale, microtopography influences the distribution of intertidal organisms. Tide pools support very different organisms than sections of the intertidal zone from which the water drains completely. The channels in which seawater runs during the ebb and flow of the tides offer yet another habitat.

The substratum also affects the distribution of intertidal organisms. Hard, rocky substrates support a biota different from that on sandy or muddy shores. You can see an obvious profusion of life on rocky shores because most species are attached to the surface of the substratum (see fig. 3.17). Common species found in the rocky intertidal zone include sea stars, barnacles, mussels, and seaweeds. But even here, all is not obvious. Most organisms take shelter at low tide,

Figure 3.20   Storm waves pounding rocky headlands such as these in Newfoundland have an important influence on the distribution and abundance of intertidal organisms.

some among the fronds and holdfasts of kelp and others under boulders. There are even animals that burrow into and live inside rocks. As we shall see when we discuss competition in chapter 13 and predation in chapter 14, biological interactions make major contributions to the distributions of intertidal organisms.

On soft bottoms, some species wander the surface of the substrate, but most are burrowers and shelter themselves within the sand or mud bottom. To study the life of sandy shores you must separate organisms from sand or mud. Perhaps this is the reason why rocky shores have gotten more attention by researchers and why we know far less about the life of sandy shores. Beaches, like the open ocean, have been considered biological deserts. Careful studies, however, have shown that the intensity and diversity of life on sandy shores rivals that of any benthic aquatic community (MacLachlan 1983).

Human Influences

People have long sought out intertidal areas, first for food and later for recreation, education, and research. Shell middens, places where prehistoric people piled the remains of their seafood dinners, from Scandinavia to South Africa, are testimony to the importance of intertidal species to human populations for over 100,000 years. Today, each low tide still finds people all over the world scouring intertidal areas for mussels, oysters, clams, and other species. But the intertidal zone, which resists, and even thrives, in the face of twice daily exposure to air and pounding surf, is easily devastated by the trampling feet and probing hands of a few human visitors. Relentless exploitation has severely reduced many intertidal populations. The intertidal zone is also vulnerable to devastation by oil spills, which have damaged intertidal areas around the world.

Ocean–Land Transitions: Salt Marshes and Mangrove Forests

As we move from the ocean onto land, we find ecosystems that blend aspects of the terrestrial and aquatic environments. **Salt marshes** (fig. 3.21) and **mangrove forests** (fig. 3.22) are concentrated along low-lying coasts with sandy shores. In areas in which a river flows out into a sea we find an **estuary**, the part of the river where fresh- and saltwater merge. All of these areas are transitions between very different environments, and have a great deal in common physically, chemically, and biologically. Surrounded on three sides by oceans, a substantial portion of coastal Canada consists of salt marshes (fig. 3.23). Although people often associate salt marshes with warm climates, substantial salt marsh habitat exists in the arctic regions of Canada and the world. One such marsh, La Pérouse

Figure 3.21 A mixture of wetland habitats, including marshes and bogs, in Wapusk National Park, Manitoba. These types of habitats cover much of Canada's northern coast.

(a)   (b)

Figure 3.22   (*a*) The prop roots of mangroves provide a complex habitat for a high diversity of marine fish and invertebrates. (*b*) Many mangroves have aerial roots called pneumatophores, allowing the plant to acquire needed oxygen.

Bay, near Churchill, Manitoba, has been the summer home to a generation of ecologists exploring the impact that grazing geese have on this natural community.

Geography

Salt marshes, dominated by herbaceous vegetation, are concentrated along sandy shores from temperate to high latitudes. In tropical and subtropical latitudes, similar sandy shores will be filled instead by woody mangrove forests. Mangroves are associated with warmer climates mainly due to the sensitivity of mangroves to frost. Figure 3.23 maps the global distributions of salt marshes and mangrove forests.

Structure

Salt marshes generally include channels, called tidal creeks, that fill and empty with the tides. These meandering creeks can create a complex network of channels across a salt marsh (fig. 3.24). Fluctuating tides move water up and down these channels, or tidal creeks, once or twice each day. These daily movements of water gradually sculpt the salt marsh into a gently undulating landscape. Tidal creeks are generally bordered by natural levees. Beyond the levees are marsh flats, which may include small basins called *salt pans* that periodically collect water that eventually evaporates, leaving a layer of salt. This entire landscape is flooded during the highest

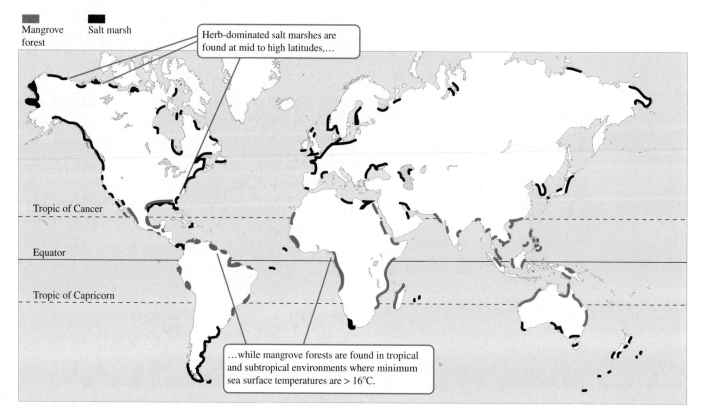

Figure 3.23   Salt marsh and mangrove forests (data from Chapman 1977, Long and Mason 1983).

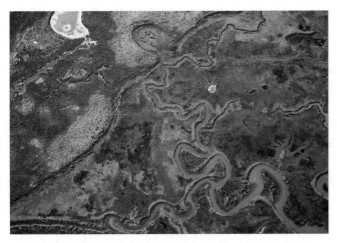

Figure 3.24 Viewing a salt marsh from the air reveals great structural complexity.

tides and drains during the lowest tides. A typical cross section of a salt marsh is shown in figure 3.25.

The mangrove trees of different species are usually distributed according to height within the intertidal zone. For instance, in mangrove forests near Rio de Janeiro, Brazil, the mangroves growing nearest the water belong to the genus *Rhizophora*. At this level in the intertidal zone, *Rhizophora* is inundated by average high tides. Above *Rhizophora* grow other mangroves such as *Avicennia*, which is flooded by the average spring tides, and *Laguncularia*, which is touched only by the highest tides. Figure 3.26 shows zonation within a mangrove forest.

Physical Conditions

Light

Estuaries, salt marshes, and mangrove forests experience significant fluctuations in tidal level. Consequently, the organisms in these environments are exposed to highly variable light conditions. They may be exposed to full sunlight at low tide and very little light at high tide. The waters of these areas are usually turbid because shifting currents, either from the

tides or rivers, keep fine organic and inorganic materials in suspension.

Temperature

Several factors make the temperatures of estuaries, salt marshes, and mangrove forests highly variable. First, because their waters are generally shallow, particularly at low tide, water temperature varies with air temperature. Second, the temperatures of seawater and river water may be very different. If so, the temperature of an estuary may change with each high and low tide. Salt marshes at high latitudes may freeze during the winter. In contrast, mangroves grow mainly along desert and tropical coasts, where the minimum annual temperature is about 20°C. The shallows in these environments can heat up to over 40°C.

Water Movements

Complex tidal currents flow in salt marshes and mangrove forests, where they are involved in ecological processes and also fragment and transport the litter produced by salt marsh and mangrove vegetation. Once or twice a day, high tides create saltwater currents that move up the estuaries of rivers and the channels within salt marshes and mangrove forests. Low tides reverse these currents and saltwater moves seaward. Tidal height may fluctuate far from where an estuary meets the sea. For example, tidal fluctuations occur over 200 km upstream from where the Hudson River flows into the sea. The vigorous mixing, in more than one direction, makes these transitional environments some of the most physically dynamic in the biosphere. Penetration of light and water movements vary over short distances and in the course of a day. This physical variability is reflected in highly variable chemical conditions.

Chemical Conditions

Salinity

The salinity of estuaries, salt marshes, and mangrove forests may fluctuate widely, particularly where river and tidal flow are substantial. In such systems, the salinity of seawater can

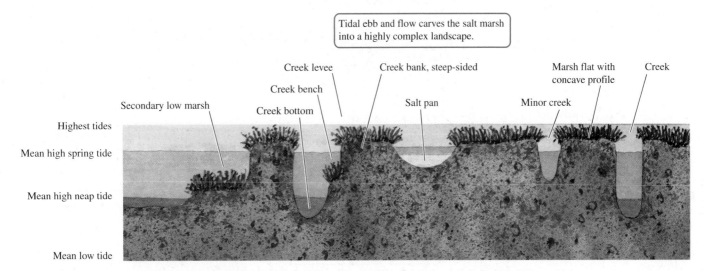

Figure 3.25 Salt marsh channels shown in cross section.

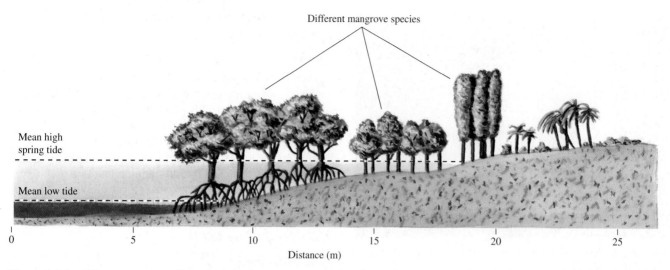

Different mangrove species

Mean high spring tide

Mean low tide

Distance (m)

Figure 3.26   Where mangrove diversity is high, mangrove species show clear patterns of vertical zonation relative to tidal level.

drop to nearly that of freshwater an hour after the tide turns. Because estuaries are places where rivers meet the sea, their salinity is generally lower than that of seawater. In hot, dry climates, however, evaporation often exceeds freshwater inputs and the salinity in the upper portions of estuaries may exceed that of the open ocean.

Tidal flow is not the only factor that can influence salinity; interactions between plants, animals, and water all play an important role. A major contributing factor to increased salinity is high rates of evaporation. Within a salt marsh, evaporation rates will tend to be highest in areas exposed to sun, and lower in areas with a cover of vegetation reducing direct exposure of the water to the sun. As a result, when plants grow, they often reduce soil salinity, allowing even more plant growth. Animals can influence this through high levels of grazing, which can reduce vegetation cover, increase evaporation, and increase soil salinity.

Estuarine waters are also often stratified by salinity, with lower-salinity, low-density water floating on a layer of higher salinity water, isolating bottom water from the atmosphere. On the incoming tide, seawater coming from the ocean and river water are flowing in opposite directions. As seawater flows up the channel, it mixes progressively with river water flowing in the opposite direction. Due to this mixing, the salinity of the surface water gradually increases down river from less than 1% to salinities approaching that of seawater at the river mouth (fig. 3.27).

Oxygen

In estuaries, salt marshes, and mangrove forests, oxygen concentration is highly variable and often reaches extreme levels. Decomposition of the large quantities of organic matter produced in these environments can deplete dissolved oxygen to very low levels, and isolation of saline bottom water from

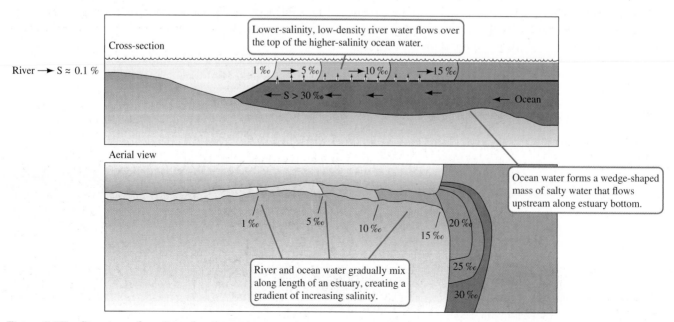

Cross-section

Lower-salinity, low-density river water flows over the top of the higher-salinity ocean water.

River → S ≈ 0.1 %

1 ‰ → 5 ‰ → 10 ‰ → 15 ‰

← S > 30 ‰ ← ← ← ← Ocean

Aerial view

Ocean water forms a wedge-shaped mass of salty water that flows upstream along estuary bottom.

1 ‰   5 ‰   10 ‰   15 ‰   20 ‰   25 ‰   30 ‰

River and ocean water gradually mix along length of an estuary, creating a gradient of increasing salinity.

Figure 3.27   Structure of a salt wedge estuary.

the atmosphere adds to the likelihood that oxygen will be depleted. At the same time, however, high rates of photosynthesis can increase dissolved oxygen concentrations to supersaturated levels. Again, the oxygen concentrations to which an organism is exposed can change with each turn of the tide.

Biology

The salt marshes of the world are dominated by grasses such as *Spartina* spp. and *Distichlis* spp., by glasswort, *Salicornia* spp., and by rushes, *Juncus* spp. The mangrove forest is dominated by mangrove trees belonging to many genera. The species that make up the forest change from one region to another; however, within a region, there is great uniformity in species composition.

Estuaries and salt marshes do not support a great diversity of species, but their primary production is very high. These are places where some of the most productive fisheries occur and where aquatic and terrestrial species find nursery grounds for their young. Most of the fish and invertebrates living in estuaries evolved from marine ancestors, but estuaries also harbour a variety of insects of freshwater origin. Estuaries and salt marshes also attract birds, especially water birds. In the mangrove forest, birds are joined by crocodiles and alligators, and, in the Indian subcontinent, by tigers.

Human Influences

Estuaries, salt marshes, and mangrove forests are extremely vulnerable to human interference. People want to live and work at the coast, but building sites are limited. One solution to the problem of high demand for coastal property and low supply has been to fill and dredge salt marshes, replacing wildlife habitat with human habitat (fig. 3.28). Throughout human history, villages have been established in these highly productive habitats. Because cities benefit from access to the sea, many, such as Boston, San Francisco, and London, have been built on estuaries. As a consequence, many estuaries have been polluted for centuries. The discharge of wastes depletes oxygen supplies, which physiologically stresses aquatic organisms. The discharge of organic wastes depletes oxygen directly as it decomposes, and the addition of nutrients such as nitrogen can lead to oxygen depletion by stimulating primary production. Heavy metals discharged into estuaries and salt marshes are incorporated into plant and animal tissues and have been, through the process of bioaccumulation, elevated to toxic levels in some food species. The assaults on estuaries and salt marshes have been chronic and intense, but the concern and interest of people are growing steadily.

Running Waters: Rivers and Streams

As we continue to head upstream and away from the brackish waters of estuaries, we find ourselves in the flowing freshwater of rivers and streams. Rivers such as the Nile, Tigris, Euphrates, St. Lawrence, Mekong, Ganges, Rhine, Mississippi, Missouri, Amazon, Seine, Zaire, Thames, and Rio Grande have been important in human history and economic development. The names of these rivers, and many others great and small,

Figure 3.28 A coastal Louisiana marsh in rapid transition to open water resulting from anthropogenic alteration. Dredging has created avenues for saline oceanic water to intrude and levees have slowed critical sediment deposition to maintain sediment elevations.

ring with a thousand images of history, geography, and poetry (fig. 3.29). The importance of rivers to human history, ecology, and economy is inestimable. However, river ecology has lagged behind the ecological study of lakes and oceans and is one of the youngest of the many branches of aquatic ecology.

Figure 3.29 The green of the meandering Nicholson River in northern Queensland, Australia contrasts sharply with the white salt pans in the surrounding landscape.

Geography

Rivers drain most of the landscapes of the world. When rain falls on a landscape, a portion of it runs off, either as surface or subsurface flow. Some of this runoff water eventually collects in small channels, which join to form larger and larger water courses until they form a network of channels that drains the landscape. A river basin is that area of a continent or island that is drained by a river drainage network, such as the Mississippi River basin in North America or the Congo River basin in Africa. Rivers eventually flow out to sea or to some interior basin like the Aral Sea or the Great Salt Lake. Some rivers, such as the Finke River in central Australia, do not flow into a lake or ocean but can dry out along the way. The Finke is one of the oldest rivers in the world and its waters naturally run dry in the Simpson Desert. River basins are separated from each other by watersheds, that is, by topographic high points. For instance, the peaks of the Rocky Mountains divide runoff from snowmelt. Water on the east side of the peaks flows to the Atlantic Ocean, while water on the west side flows to the Pacific Ocean. Figure 3.30 shows the distribution of the major rivers of the planet.

Structure

River, stream, creek, brook; you are certainly familiar with all of these words. Unfortunately, it is difficult to find agreement on the scientific differences among these terms. Part of this is because of the great complexity that is found when studying these features. Rivers and streams can be divided along three dimensions (fig. 3.31). They can be divided along their *lengths* into pools, runs, riffles, and rapids and, because of variation in flow, rivers can also be divided across their *widths* into wetted channels and active channels. In general, rivers are larger than the other groups, but much variability exists. Rather than worry about fine details of these terms, we focus here on ecologically important features. A wetted channel contains water even during low flow conditions. An active channel, which extends out from one or both sides of a wetted channel, may be dry during part of the year but is inundated annually during high flows. Outside the active channel is the **riparian zone**, a transition between the aquatic environment of the river and the upland terrestrial environment.

Rivers and streams can be divided *vertically* into the water surface, the water column, and the bottom, or benthic, zone. The benthic zone includes the surface of the bottom substrate and the interior of the substrate through depths at which substantial surface water still flows. Below the benthic zone is the **hyporheic zone**, a zone of transition between areas of surface water flow and groundwater. The area containing groundwater below the hyporheic zone is called the **phreatic zone**. Each part of a river or stream is a physically and chemically distinctive environment and each supports different organisms. Unique to stream and river environments is the constant and unidirectional flow of water. As a result, upstream processes generally have a stronger influence on downstream processes than vice versa. This asymmetry leads to a hierarchy of streams and rivers within a drainage network. Streams and rivers within a drainage network can be classified based on a system called **stream order** (fig. 3.32) developed by Arthur Strahler (1952). In this system, headwater streams are first order, while a stream formed by the joining of two first order streams is a second order stream. A third order stream results from the joining of two second order streams, and so on.

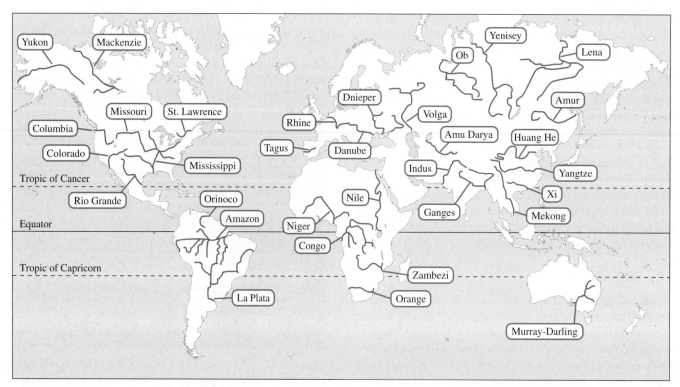

Figure 3.30   Major rivers throughout the world.

Figure 3.31   The three dimensions of stream structure.

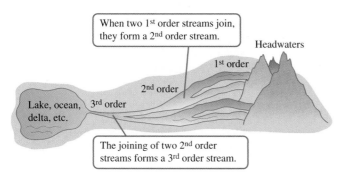

Figure 3.32   A drainage network can be described based upon stream orders.

Physical Conditions

Light

There are two principal aspects of light to consider in relation to rivers and streams: first, how far light penetrates into the water column; and second, how much light shines on the surface of a river. Streams and rivers vary considerably in water clarity. Generally, however, even the clearest streams are much more turbid than clear lakes or seas. The reduced clarity of rivers results from two main factors. First, rivers are in intimate contact with the surrounding landscape, and inorganic and organic materials continuously wash, fall, or blow into rivers. Second, river turbulence erodes bottom sediments

and keeps them in suspension, particularly during floods. The headwaters of rivers are generally shaded by riparian vegetation. Shading may be so thorough along some streams that there is very little photosynthesis by aquatic primary producers. The extent of shading decreases progressively downstream as stream width increases. In desert regions, headwater streams usually receive large amounts of solar radiation and support high levels of photosynthesis. Figure 3.33 contrasts the environments of headwater streams flowing through a forest and a desert.

Temperature

The temperature of rivers closely tracks air temperature but does not reach the extremes of terrestrial habitats. The coldest river temperatures, those of high altitudes and high latitudes, may drop to a minimum of 0°C. The warmest rivers are those flowing through deserts, but even desert rivers seldom exceed 30°C. The outflows of hot springs can be boiling in their upper reaches, but populations of thermophilic bacteria live in even the hottest of these.

Water Movements

What is notable about a river is the movement of water. Although the river as a whole moves continuously, there will be substantial variation in flow rates among microsites within the river. Some areas will have free-flowing water, while in other areas there may be standing water in pools.

(a)

(b)

Figure 3.33   Headwater streams in: (*a*) forested Great Smoky Mountains, Tennessee; and (*b*) Capital Reef National Park, Utah. The consumers in headwater streams draining forested lands generally depend on energy from the surrounding forest. Meanwhile desert streams are open to sunlight and support high levels of photosynthesis by stream algae, the source of most energy for desert-stream consumers.

These differences are obvious to anyone who canoes the rivers throughout Canada: as you attempt to navigate class IV rapids one minute, the next minute you look up to find your wet backpack and tent (that flew out of your canoe) sitting in a still pool at the side of the river. Currents in quiet pools may flow at only a few millimetres per second, while water in the rapids of swift rivers in a flood stage may flow at 6 m per second. Contrary to popular belief, the currents of large rivers may be as swift as those in the headwaters. These differences in flow rate can have significant effects on the species that live within the river.

The amount of water carried by rivers, which is called *river discharge*, differs a lot from one climatic regime to another. River flows are often unpredictable and "flashy" in arid and semiarid regions, where extended droughts may be followed by torrential rains. The flow in tropical rivers varies considerably. Many tropical rivers, which flow very little during the dry season, become torrents during the wet season. Some of the most constant flows are found in forested temperate regions, where, as we saw in chapter 2, precipitation is fairly evenly distributed throughout the year. Forested landscapes can damp out variation in flow by absorbing excessive rain during wet periods and acting as a reservoir for river flow during drier periods. Figure 3.34 compares the annual flows of rivers of moist temperate and semiarid climates.

It appears that the health and ecological integrity of rivers and streams depend upon keeping the natural flow regime for a region intact. Historical patterns of flooding have particularly important influences on river ecosystem processes, especially on the exchange of nutrients and energy between the river channel and the floodplain and associated wetlands. This idea, which was first proposed as the **flood pulse concept**, is supported by a growing body of evidence from research conducted on rivers on virtually every continent.

Chemical Conditions

Salinity

Water flowing across landscapes or through soils picks up dissolved materials. The amount of salt dissolved in river water reflects the history of leaching that has gone on in its basin. As we saw in chapter 2, annual rainfall is high in tropical regions. Consequently, many tropical soils have been leached of much of their soluble materials and it is in the tropics that the salinity of river water is often very low. Desert rivers generally have the highest salinities. Figure 3.35 shows that the salinity of river water from different regions may show 10- to 100-fold differences.

Oxygen

The oxygen content of river water is inversely correlated with temperature. Oxygen supplies are generally richest in cold, thoroughly mixed headwater streams and lower in the warm downstream sections of rivers. However, because the waters in streams and rivers are continuously mixed, oxygen is generally not limiting to the distribution of river organisms. The major exception to this generalization is in sections of streams and rivers receiving organic wastes from cities (wastes with high biochemical oxygen demand or BOD) and industry. Only organisms tolerant of low oxygen concentrations can inhabit these sections.

Biology

As in the terrestrial biomes, large numbers of species inhabit tropical rivers. The number of fish species in tropical rivers is much higher than in temperate rivers. For example, the Mississippi River basin, which supports one of the most diverse temperate fish faunas, is home to about 300 fish species. By contrast, the tropical Congo River basin contains about 669

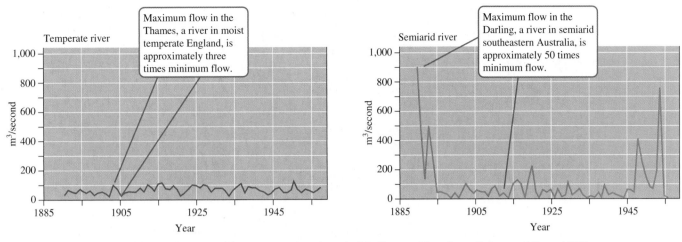

Figure 3.34   Annual flow of rivers in moist temperate and semiarid climates (data from Calow and Petts 1992).

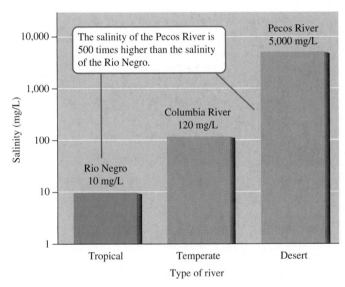

Figure 3.35   Salinities of tropical, temperate, and arid land rivers (data from Gibbs 1970).

species of fish, of which over 558 are found nowhere else. The most impressive array of freshwater fish is that of the Amazon River basin, which contains over 2,000 species.

The organisms of river systems change from headwaters to mouth. These patterns of biological variation along the courses of rivers have given rise to a variety of theories that predict downstream change in rivers and their inhabitants. One of these theories is the **river continuum concept** (Vannote et al. 1980). According to this concept, in temperate regions, leaves and other plant parts are often the major source of energy available to the stream ecosystem. Upon entering the stream, this coarse particulate organic matter (CPOM) is attacked by aquatic microbes, especially fungi. Colonization by fungi makes CPOM more nutritious for stream invertebrates. The stream invertebrates of headwater streams are usually dominated by two feeding groups: shredders (such as some caddisflies and amphipods), which feed on CPOM, and collectors (such as black fly larvae and other caddisflies), which feed on fine particulate organic matter (FPOM).

The fish in headwater streams are usually those, such as trout, that require high oxygen concentrations and cool temperatures.

The river continuum concept predicts that the major sources of energy in medium-sized streams will be FPOM washed down from the headwater streams and algae and aquatic plants. Algae and plants generally grow more profusely in medium streams because they are too wide to be entirely shaded by riparian vegetation. Because of the different food base, shredders make up a minor portion of the benthic community, which is dominated by collectors and grazers (such as snails and riffle beetles) on the abundant algae and aquatic plants. The fish of medium streams generally tolerate somewhat higher temperatures and lower oxygen concentrations than headwater fish.

In large rivers, the major sources of energy are FPOM and, in some rivers, phytoplankton. Consequently, the benthic invertebrates of large rivers are dominated by collectors, which make their living by filtering FPOM from the water column. In large rivers, there are also zooplankton. The fish found in large temperate rivers are those, such as carp and catfish, that are more tolerant of lower oxygen concentrations and higher water temperatures. Because of the development of a plankton community, plankton-feeding fish also live in large rivers. The major changes in temperate river systems predicted by the river continuum concept are summarized in figure 3.36.

Most of the invertebrates of streams and rivers live on or in the sediments; that is, most are benthic. These benthic organisms are influenced substantially by the type of bottom sediments. Stony substratum in the riffles and runs of rivers harbour fauna and flora that are different from those in sections with silt or sand bottoms mainly because of differences in the structure and stability of these bottom types. River ecologists have recently discovered that a great number and diversity of invertebrate animals live deep within the sediments of rivers in both the hyporheic and phreatic zones. These species may be pumped up with well water many kilometres from the nearest river. We know very little about the lives of these organisms. Once more, nature has yielded another surprise.

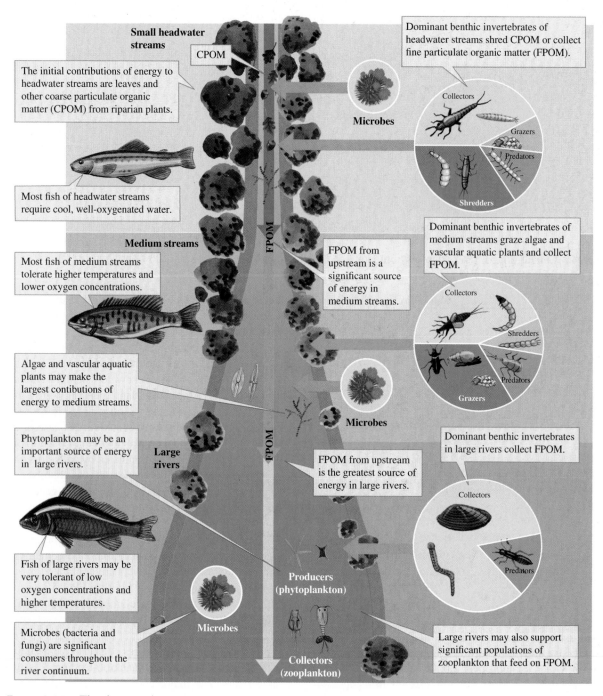

Small headwater streams

CPOM

The initial contributions of energy to headwater streams are leaves and other coarse particulate organic matter (CPOM) from riparian plants.

Dominant benthic invertebrates of headwater streams shred CPOM or collect fine particulate organic matter (FPOM).

Collectors

Grazers

Predators

Shredders

Microbes

Most fish of headwater streams require cool, well-oxygenated water.

Medium streams

Most fish of medium streams tolerate higher temperatures and lower oxygen concentrations.

FPOM

FPOM from upstream is a significant source of energy in medium streams.

Dominant benthic invertebrates of medium streams graze algae and vascular aquatic plants and collect FPOM.

Collectors

Shredders

Grazers

Predators

Algae and vascular aquatic plants may make the largest contibutions of energy to medium streams.

Microbes

Phytoplankton may be an important source of energy in large rivers.

Large rivers

FPOM

FPOM from upstream is the greatest source of energy in large rivers.

Dominant benthic invertebrates in large rivers collect FPOM.

Collectors

Predators

Fish of large rivers may be very tolerant of low oxygen concentrations and higher temperatures.

Producers (phytoplankton)

Microbes (bacteria and fungi) are significant consumers throughout the river continuum.

Microbes

Collectors (zooplankton)

Large rivers may also support significant populations of zooplankton that feed on FPOM.

Figure 3.36   The river continuum.

Human Influences

The influence of humans on rivers has been long and intense. Rivers have been important to human populations for commerce, transportation, energy, irrigation, and waste disposal. Because of their potential to flood, they have also been a constant threat. In the service of human populations, rivers have been channelized, poisoned, filled with sewage, dammed, filled with non-native fish species, and dried. One of the most severe human impacts on river systems has been the building of reservoirs. Reservoirs eliminate the natural flow regime—including flood pulses—alter temperatures, and impede the movements of migratory fish. Because of the rapid turnover of their waters,

however, rivers have a great capacity for recovery and renewal. The River Thames in England was severely polluted in the Middle Ages and remained so until recent times. During recent decades, great efforts have been made to reduce the amount of pollution discharged into the Thames, and the river has recovered substantially. The Thames once again supports a run of Atlantic salmon and gives hope to all the river conservationists of the world that their beleaguered rivers will recover.

Still Waters: Lakes and Ponds

In 1892, F. A. Forel defined the scientific study of lakes as the *oceanography of lakes*. On the basis of a lifetime of study,

Figure 3.37 The five Great Lakes lie between Canada and the United States and contain nearly 20% of the world's fresh surface water.

Forel concluded that lakes are much like small seas (fig. 3.37). Differences between lakes and the oceans are due, principally, to the smaller size of lakes and their relative isolation. Perhaps because they are cast on a more human scale, lakes have long captured the imagination of everyone from poets to scientists. For poets such as Henry David Thoreau (1854), they have been sources of inspiration and mirrors of inner truth. For scientists such as Stephen A. Forbes (1887), who wrote, "The lake as a microcosm," they have been mirrors of the outside world and microcosms of the ecological universe.

Geography

Lakes are simply basins in the landscape that collect water like so many rain puddles. Most lakes are found in regions worked over by the geological forces that produce these basins. These forces include shifting of the earth's crust (tectonics), volcanism, and glacial activity.

Globally, approximately 4.6 million km² of the planet's surface is covered by over 300,000,000 lakes (Downing et al. 2006). Most of the world's freshwater resides in a few large lakes. The Great Lakes of North America (fig. 3.37) together cover an area of over 245,000 km² and contain 24,620 km³ of water, approximately 20% of all the freshwater on the surface of the planet. An additional 20% of freshwater is contained in Lake Baikal, Siberia, the deepest lake on the planet (1,600 m), with a total volume of 23,000 km³. Much of the remainder is contained within the rift lakes of East Africa. Lake Tanganyika, the second deepest lake (1,470 m), alone has a volume of 23,100 km³, virtually identical to that of Lake Baikal. Aside from these few major lakes, there are millions of other lakes each of which is less than 1 km² in size. (Downing et al. 2006). Lakes are often concentrated in "lake districts" such as northern Minnesota, much of Scandinavia, and vast regions across north-central Canada and Siberia. Figure 3.38 shows the locations of some of the larger lakes.

Structure

Lake structure parallels that of the oceans but on a much smaller scale (fig. 3.39). The shallowest waters along the lake shore, where rooted aquatic plants may grow, is called the littoral zone. Beyond the littoral zone in the open lake is the **limnetic zone**. Lakes are generally divided vertically into three main depth zones. The **epilimnion** is the warm surface layer of lakes. Below the epilimnion is the thermocline, or **metalimnion**. The thermocline is a zone through which temperature changes substantially with depth, generally about 1°C per metre of depth. Below the thermocline are the cold dark waters of the **hypolimnion**. Each of these zones supports a distinctive assemblage of lake organisms.

Physical Conditions

Light

Lake colour ranges from the deep blue of the clearest lakes to yellow, brown, or even red. The colour, which depends on light absorption within a lake, is influenced by many factors, but especially lake chemistry, biological activity, and depth.

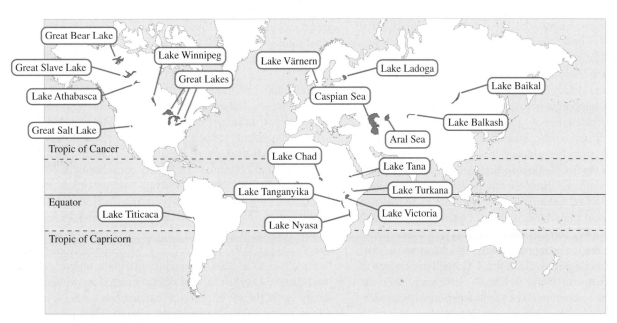

Figure 3.38 Distributions of some major lakes throughout the world.

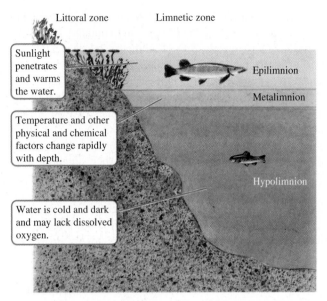

Littoral zone   Limnetic zone

Sunlight penetrates and warms the water.

Epilimnion

Metalimnion

Temperature and other physical and chemical factors change rapidly with depth.

Hypolimnion

Water is cold and dark and may lack dissolved oxygen.

Figure 3.39 Lake structure.

In shallow lakes where the surrounding landscape delivers large quantities of nutrients, primary production is high and phytoplankton populations reduce light penetration. These highly productive lakes are usually a deep green. When lakes receive high levels of dissolved organic compounds, such as humic acids leached from forest soils, productivity decreases. This shift is due to increased absorption of blue and green light by these compounds, reducing photosynthesis. This has the effect of moving lake colour to the yellow-brown end of the spectrum. In deep lakes where the landscape delivers low quantities of either nutrients or dissolved organic compounds, phytoplankton production is generally low and light penetrates to great depths. These deep lakes, such as Lake Superior, Lake Tahoe in California, and Crater Lake in Oregon, are nearly as blue as the open ocean.

Temperature

As in the oceans, many lakes become thermally stratified as they warm. Consequently, during the warm season they are substantially warmer at the surface than they are below the thermocline. Temperate lakes are stratified during the summer, while lowland tropical lakes may be stratified year round. As in temperate seas, thermal stratification breaks down in temperate lakes as they cool during the fall. Where climatic conditions cause lakes to freeze over in winter, lake area can strongly influence the severity of freezing on the organisms that live within the lake. Small lakes can freeze solid in cold winters, killing all vertebrates in a phenomenon often referred to as "fishkill." Larger lakes are more likely to form ice only on their surface, with liquid water remaining below. Where lakes form ice on the surface, the water immediately under the ice is approximately 0°C. Meanwhile, bottom water is a comparatively warm 4°C, the temperature at which the density of water is highest. In spring, once the ice has melted, temperate lakes spend a period without thermal stratification. As summer approaches, they gradually become stratified again. In high-elevation tropical lakes, a

thermocline may form every day and break down every night! This dynamic situation occurs on the same tropical mountains where, as we saw in chapter 2, terrestrial organisms experience winter temperatures every night and summer temperatures every day. As in the oceans, these patterns of thermal stratification determine the frequency and extent of mixing of the water column. The seasonal dynamics of thermal stratification and mixing in temperate lakes are shown in figure 3.40.

Water Movements

Wind-driven mixing of the water column is the most ecologically important water movement in lakes. As we have just seen, temperate zone lakes are thermally stratified during the summer, a condition that limits wind-driven mixing to surface waters above the thermocline. During winter on these lakes, ice forms a surface barrier that prevents mixing. In the spring and fall, however, stratification breaks down and winds drive vertical currents that can mix temperate lakes from top to bottom. These are the times when a lake renews oxygen in bottom waters and replenishes nutrients in surface waters. Like tropical seas, tropical lakes at low elevations are permanently stratified. Of the 1,400 m of water in Lake Tanganyika, for example, only about the upper 200 m is circulated each year. Tropical lakes at high elevations heat and stratify every day and cool sufficiently to mix every night. Patterns of mixing have profound consequences to the chemistry and biology of lakes.

Chemical Conditions

Salinity

The salinity of lakes is much more variable than that of the open ocean. The world average salinity for freshwater, 120 mg per litre (approximately 0.120‰), is a tiny fraction of the salinity of the oceans. Lake salinity ranges from the extremely dilute waters of some alpine lakes to the salt brines of desert lakes. For instance, the Great Salt Lake in Utah sometimes has a salinity of over 200‰, which is much higher than oceanic salinity.

Oxygen

Mixing and biological activities have profound effects on lake chemistry. Lakes of low biological production, which are called **oligotrophic**, are nearly always well oxygenated. Lakes of high biological production, which are called **eutrophic**, are often depleted of oxygen. Recall from chapter 1 that David Schindler and colleagues identified phosphorus pollution as a major cause of human-involved eutrophication. Oxygen depletion is particularly likely during periods of thermal stratification, when decomposing organic matter accumulates below the thermocline and consumes oxygen. In eutrophic lakes, oxygen concentrations may be depleted from surface waters at night as respiration continues in the absence of photosynthesis. Oxygen is also often depleted in winter, especially under the ice of productive temperate lakes. In tropical lakes, water below the euphotic zone is often permanently depleted of dissolved oxygen.

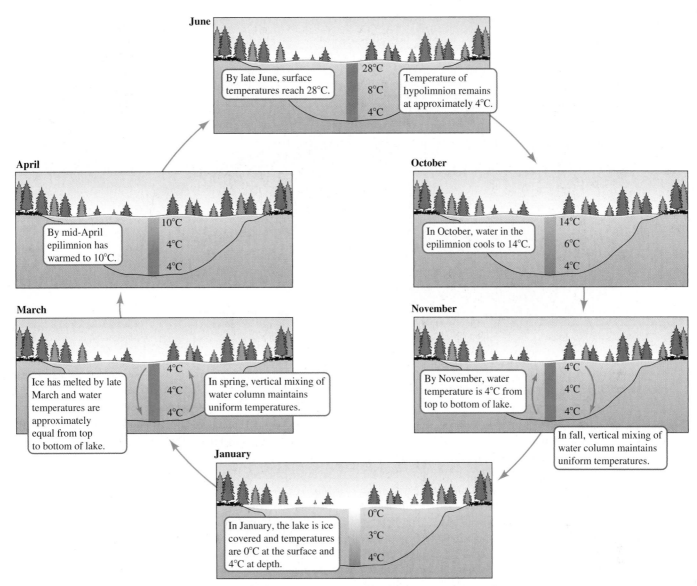

Figure 3.40   Seasonal changes in temperature in a temperate lake (data from Wetzel 1975).

Biology

In addition to their differences in oxygen availability, oligotrophic and eutrophic lakes also differ in factors such as availability of inorganic nutrients and temperature (fig. 3.41). Because aquatic organisms differ widely in their environmental requirements, oligotrophic and eutrophic lakes generally support distinctive biological communities. In temperate regions, oligotrophic lakes generally support the highest diversity of phytoplankton. These lakes are also usually inhabited by fish requiring high oxygen concentrations and relatively low temperatures, such as trout and whitefish. The benthic faunas of these lakes are rich in species and include the larvae of mayflies and caddisflies, small clams, and, along wave-swept shores, the larvae of stoneflies. Eutrophic temperate lakes, which tend to be warmer and, as we have seen, periodically depleted of oxygen, are inhabited by fish tolerant of high temperatures and low oxygen concentrations, such as carp and catfish, or fish that can breathe air in an emergency, such as gars and bowfins. The benthic invertebrate faunas of these lakes also tend to be tolerant

of low oxygen concentrations; for example, midge larvae and tubificid worms, common in such lakes, have hemoglobin that helps them extract oxygen from oxygen-poor waters.

Much less is known about the biology of tropical lakes, however a few generalizations are possible. Tropical lakes can be very productive. Also, their fish faunas may include a great number of species. Three East African lakes, Lake Victoria, Lake Malawi, and Lake Tanganyika, contain over 700 species of fish, approximately the number of freshwater fish species in all of the United States and Canada. All of western and central Europe and the former Soviet Union together contain only about 400 freshwater fish species. The invertebrates and algae of tropical lakes are much less studied, but it appears that the number of species may be similar to that of temperate zone lakes.

Human Influences

Human populations have had profound, and usually negative, influences on the ecology of lakes. In addition to examples of

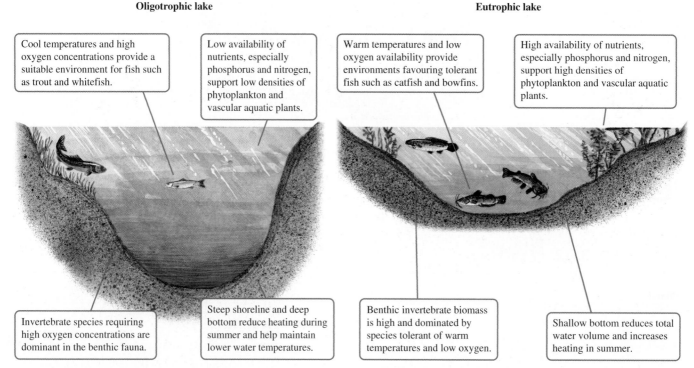

Oligotrophic lake

Cool temperatures and high oxygen concentrations provide a suitable environment for fish such as trout and whitefish.

Low availability of nutrients, especially phosphorus and nitrogen, support low densities of phytoplankton and vascular aquatic plants.

Invertebrate species requiring high oxygen concentrations are dominant in the benthic fauna.

Steep shoreline and deep bottom reduce heating during summer and help maintain lower water temperatures.

Eutrophic lake

Warm temperatures and low oxygen availability provide environments favouring tolerant fish such as catfish and bowfins.

High availability of nutrients, especially phosphorus and nitrogen, support high densities of phytoplankton and vascular aquatic plants.

Benthic invertebrate biomass is high and dominated by species tolerant of warm temperatures and low oxygen.

Shallow bottom reduces total water volume and increases heating in summer.

Figure 3.41   Oligotrophic and eutrophic lakes.

ecological degradation, however, are cases of amazing resilience and recovery—resilience in the face of fierce ecological challenge and recovery to substantial ecological integrity. Because lakes offer ready access to water for domestic and industrial uses, many human population centres have grown up around them. In both the United States and Canada, for example, large populations surround the Great Lakes. The human population around Lake Erie, one of the most altered of the Great Lakes, grew from 2.5 million in the 1880s to over 13 million in the 1980s. The primary ecological impact of these populations has been the dumping of astounding quantities of nutrients and toxic wastes into Lake Erie. By the mid-1960s, the Detroit River alone was dumping 1.5 billion gallons of waste water into Lake Erie each day. The Cuyahoga River, which flows through Cleveland before reaching the lake, was so fouled with oil in the 1960s that it would catch fire. In the face of such ecological challenges, much of Lake Erie, particularly the eastern end, was transformed from a healthy lake with a rich fish fauna to one that was, for a time, essentially an algal soup in which only the most tolerant fish species could live. With greater controls on waste disposal, the process of degradation began to reverse itself, and Lake Erie recovered much, but not all, of its former health and vitality by the 1980s.

Nutrients are not the only things that people put into lakes, however. Fish and other species are constantly moved around, either intentionally or unintentionally. For instance, the canals that were dug to connect the Great Lakes with each other and to bypass Niagara Falls inadvertently introduced two species of fish, the sea lamprey and the alewife, that seriously disrupted the biology of the lakes. Once in the Great Lakes, sea lampreys fed mainly on lake trout, lake herring, and chubs. This predation, combined with intense fishing,

devastated these commercially important fish populations. As these populations declined, alewife populations exploded. With exploding alewife populations came periodic and massive die-offs that littered beaches with tons of rotting fish. Massive efforts at controlling the sea lamprey by the United States and Canada have been reasonably successful.

These early introductions of fish into the Great Lakes were just a preview of future biological challenges, however. The rogues' gallery of introductions to the Great Lakes, which now includes species such as the zebra mussel, the river ruffe, and the spiny water flea, continues to grow, and there appears to be no end in sight. As figure 3.42 shows, 139 species of fish, invertebrates, plants, and algae had been introduced to the Great Lakes by 1990.

The population growth of many introduced species has been explosive, resulting in significant ecological and economic impacts. One such introduction was that of the zebra mussel, *Dreissena polymorpha*, a bivalve mollusc native to the drainages emptying into the Aral, Caspian, and Black Seas. Zebra mussels disperse by means of pelagic larvae but spend their adult lives attached to the substrate by means of byssal threads. Their pelagic larvae allows them to disperse at a high rate. Though they spread throughout western Europe by the early 1800s, zebra mussels were not recorded in North America until the late 1980s. In 1988, they were collected in Lake St. Clair, which connects Lake Huron and Lake Erie. In just three years, zebra mussels spread to all the Great Lakes and to most of the major rivers of eastern North America.

Locally, zebra mussels have established very dense populations within the Great Lakes. Shells from dead mussels have accumulated to depths of over 30 cm along some shores. Such dense populations threaten the native mussels of the

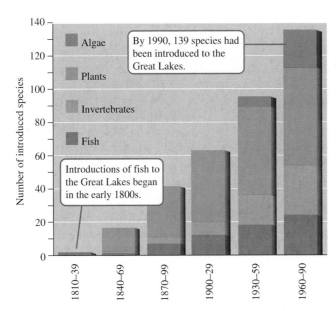

Figure 3.42   Cumulative number of species introduced to the Great Lakes (data from Mills et al. 1994).

Great Lakes with extinction. Zebra mussels are also fouling water intake structures of power plants and municipal water supplies, which may result in billions of dollars in economic impact. Just as progress is made in understanding the biology of the zebra mussels, the Great Lakes are now also threatened by the Quagga mussel, *Dreissena rostriformis*. Biologists are working furiously to document and understand the impact of these mussels and other species introduced in the Great Lakes. Meanwhile, the governments of Canada and the United States are taking steps to reduce the rate of biological invasion of the Great Lakes. As a consequence of such species, the Great Lakes have become a laboratory for the study of human-caused biological invasions (fig. 3.43).

Peatlands: Bogs and Fens

Throughout history, much of northern North America, western Europe, and the Siberian Lowlands have been covered in large expanses of peatlands. Words like moors, muskegs, and mires continue to be closely identified with the cultures of the British Isles. These areas have been of critical importance to early human populations as a source of fuel (peat bricks and coal) and forage (many berry-producing shrubs). The smell of burning peat is ingrained in the walls and whiskeys of Ireland and Scotland. But what exactly are peatlands? Wetland habitats come in two forms, those that form **peat**, and those that do not (fig. 3.44). Peat consists of partially decomposed plant material that builds up in certain poorly drained wetland habitats. We have already discussed several non–peat-forming wetlands, such as coastal marshes and mangroves. Here we discuss the two types of peat-forming wetlands, **bogs** and **fens** (fig. 3.45).

Geography

Peatlands occupy over 5% of the world's land base, with over 80% located in the high latitudes of the boreal and subarctic. Approximately 40% of the world's peatlands are found in North America, and over 15% of Canada's land base is peatland. Peatlands require significant water inputs, and thus are not found in the drier regions of the world. Although in chapter 2 we discussed the boreal forest as a terrestrial ecosystem, in a broader view the boreal region is a mixture of forest, bog, fen, and other wetland habitats.

Structure

The dominant feature of bogs and fens is a very well-developed layer of mosses and sedges, coupled with very low rates of decomposition. As a result, dead plant material accumulates, resulting in a buildup of peat. If water tables are stable, this process can continue for millennia, with peat deposits in some areas reaching more than 10 m in depth.

Bogs and fens differ as a function of the source of the water in the ecosystem. Bogs are found in depressions in the landscape, with precipitation being the only source of water into the system. Water levels tend to be about 50 cm below the surface. In contrast, fens are fed by both precipitation and by connections to ground or surface waters. Water levels tend to be at or near the surface.

(a)

(b)

Figure 3.43   Two invaders of the Great Lakes: (*a*) sea lamprey; and (*b*) zebra mussels. Invading species, such as these, have created ecological disasters in freshwater ecosystems around the globe.

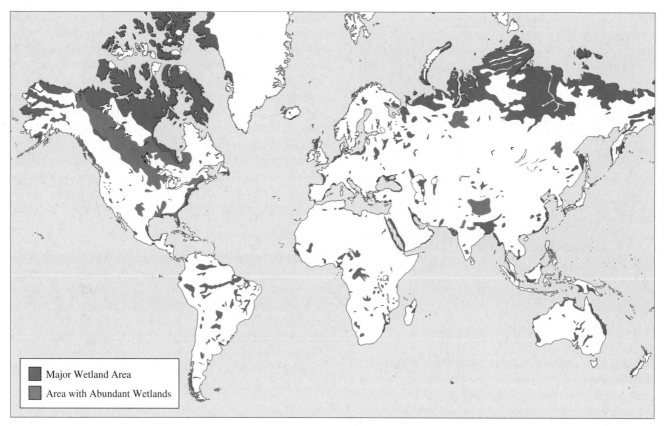

Figure 3.44 Global distribution of wetlands. Wetlands take different forms in different locations, including marshes, mangrove forests, bogs, and fens.

Because of the high water level, fens are typically flat. Bogs, however, often exhibit patterning of raised *hummocks* and lower *hollows* (see fig. 3.45*a*). The upper layers of hummocks are above the water table and thus are drier than the rest of the peatlands. As a result, hummocks are aerated, allowing root growth, and thus are home to a diversity of vascular plants. Only a very shallow segment of the peatland is photosynthetically active, with the majority of the depth of this system occupied by dead plant material.

Physical Conditions

Light

Light conditions can vary widely within and among peatlands. How much light hits the moss layer is influenced by the presence (or absence) of taller vascular plants, including trees. Bogs generally have a well-developed shrub layer, with only interspersed trees. Fens can be more variable, with some having few trees, and others having nearly full tree cover. In

(a)

(b)

Figure 3.45 Canada is home to substantial expanses of wetland habitats. Shown here are (*a*) a bog on the Labrador Coast, and (*b*) a fen North of Fort McMurray, Alberta.

general, the drier the area within a peatland, the greater the chance for vascular plant growth and reduced light reaching the moss layer. The water surrounding the mosses is generally dark due to high concentrations of chemicals that leach from the mosses and vascular plants, as well as large amounts of suspended particulates. As a result, there is limited light penetration below the moss layer, and limited algal growth.

Temperature

Peatlands occur when rates of decomposition are lower than rates of production, and when water inputs are greater (or equal to) outputs. If either of these conditions changes, peatland development is slowed, or will even cease. Temperature can have significant effects on both of these processes. All biological reactions are temperature dependent, and increasing temperatures will increase decomposition rates. Whether the increase in temperature will have a stronger effect on decomposition than production is unknown and likely site-specific. Increased temperatures will certainly increase evaporation rates, thereby reducing water outputs from these systems. At the same time, increased temperature may also alter water outputs through changes to plant transpiration rates. Because of the large amounts of stored carbon in peatlands across the planet, understanding the potential impact of global warming on the function of these systems is an active area of ecological research.

Water Movements

Relatively still waters are a prerequisite for bog and fen formation, and peat accumulation is only possible when water levels are stable over extended periods of time. If the water table lowers, large areas of the peatlands will often dry. This is a serious issue for many of the moss species in these communities, as they are generally not adapted for desiccation and require water for reproduction. At a larger scale, when peatlands dry out they are prone to fire, as if they were a pile of leaves thousands of years old. As a result of these factors, vertical water movement can prevent peatland formation and persistence on the landscape.

Similarly, rapid horizontal water movement reduces the likelihood of fen formation, and instead is more likely to produce non–peat-forming wetlands. Rapid water movement aerates the environment, increasing microbial growth and decomposition rates. It also "flushes" the system of a variety of chemicals produced by many of the mosses and vascular plant that would otherwise reduce decomposition. Physically, rapid water movement creates challenges for plant establishment and growth, which many species common to fens cannot overcome.

Chemical Conditions

Salinity

Salinity is not a major factor influencing the organisms that reside in bogs and fens. Instead, the productivity of these systems can be strongly influenced by pH. Bogs are uniformly acidic with pH < 4.5. This acidity is due to a lack of a source of basic ions that would be carried in moving waters. Fens vary in pH, with some being as acidic as bogs, while others are neutral or even basic. The pH of fens is strongly influenced by the chemical composition of the ground or surface waters that feed the community. In both bogs and fens, low pH greatly reduces decomposition, nutrient availability, and plant growth. Acidic fens are generally less productive than fens with a more neutral pH.

Oxygen

A dominant feature of bogs and fens is a water-logged anaerobic environment due to the high water levels. This lack of oxygen coupled with potentially low pH (all bogs) or high pH (all fens have pH higher than in bogs, some much higher, but others can have pH that approaches that observed in bogs) results in a greatly reduced microbial activity and limited decomposition. These water-logged "soils" also limit the growth of vascular plants, as roots need oxygen for respiration and survival. Higher oxygen levels would greatly alter the biology of these systems, likely converting them to a non–peat-forming wetland.

Biology

Despite the harsh chemical regime of many peatlands, they are home to a great number of plants and animals. The types of plants found vary widely across peatlands, with more productive areas dominated by trees and shrubs, and acidic areas having relatively few vascular plants. All peatlands include a dominant moss layer, consisting of many bryophyte species and associated microfauna.

One of the most recognizable features of many bog habitats is that they are home to a variety of carnivorous plants (fig. 3.46). Carnivory is a great example of a novel solution to a difficult situation. For a plant, nitrogen and other soil resources are essential for growth and reproduction (chapter 7). However, decomposition rates in bogs are extremely slow, and thus there is very little nitrogen available. It appears that there has been selection for unique methods of acquiring sources of nitrogen outside the soil environment. One of the more common types of carnivorous plants in bogs throughout North America is the pitcher plant. Inside the pitcher formed from modified leaves, the plants secrete a variety of enzymes that accelerate the decomposition of insects that get trapped inside. Further enhancing decomposition is

Figure 3.46 Carnivorous plants, such as this pitcher plant (*Sarracenia purpurea*) are commonly found in bog habitats.

a complex network of fungi and bacteria that live inside the pitchers. These plants are also home to a variety of spiders and other species, creating islands of diversity in a manner similar to the epiphytes that are common in tropical and temperate rain forests (chapter 2).

Animal life is not as diverse in peatlands as in other aquatic environments. The low calcium levels tend to reduce abundances of vertebrates and molluscs, though many transient species can be found passing through the area. Insect diversity and numbers are often very high in peatlands, particularly for species with aquatic larval stages.

Human Influences

The status of peatlands varies widely across the planet. Peat is mined throughout its range, with uses including that of a fuel source, a construction material, and as a raw ingredient to soils used in greenhouses and gardens across the globe. The process of mining peat can result in altered hydrology, which can lead to widespread drying and loss of the habitat. Mining has occurred on a larger scale over a longer time period throughout much of Europe, with the vast expanses of peatlands in North America generally removed from direct human influence.

However, much like the seemingly remote arctic tundra, being removed from most direct human influence does not mean peatlands are not facing widespread challenges. The most pressing concern is how peatlands will respond to climate changes. Altered precipitation or temperature regimes can both cause peatlands to expand (where it becomes wetter and cooler) or contract (where it becomes drier and

warmer). The loss of peatlands is of particular concern because they hold 30% of the world's soil carbon. Release of that carbon to the atmosphere through either increased decomposition rates or increased fire frequency may have significant implications for further climate change. Because of the potential for this positive feedback loop in the peatlands, they are currently a hotbed of activity for climate change researchers.

As we have seen in all of the habitats we explored in chapters 2 and 3, humans have significant influences on all areas of the planet, no matter how remote they may seem. Because of this, it is important to understand that current ecological processes occur in a world dominated by people. It is up to ecologists to determine how this influence will alter plant and animal distributions. This information will be critical for lawmakers and land managers in the development of strategies to protect the world's biological diversity.

CONCEPT 3.2 REVIEW

1. How are zebra mussels threatening populations of native mussels in Lake Erie?
2. Why is the prospect of global warming considered to be a serious threat to peatlands?
3. What ecological factors differ between lakes and marine habitats?

ECOLOGICAL TOOLS AND APPROACHES

Reconstructing Lake Communities

How can we put our knowledge of the natural history of aquatic life to work? A major question ecologists often face is whether a certain environmental factor will alter an aquatic community. To answer this, we first need a clear understanding of the species composition and abundances of the focal community under current environmental conditions. In the first chapter we described the experimental approach that David Schindler and colleagues at the Experimental Lakes Area have used to test the impacts fertilization, acidification, and a variety of other factors have had on lake communities. Here we will describe a different approach used by a number of researchers in Canada, including Roland Hall at the University of Waterloo and John Smol and colleagues at PEARL, the Paleoecological Environmental Assessment and Research Laboratory, based at Queen's University. The goal of these researchers is to provide the historical context to environmental change,

through detailed study of the paleoenvironmental record on lakes throughout the world. This is the field of paleolimnology, which is broadly defined as the scientific discipline that uses the biological, chemical, and physical information archived in lake sediment profiles to track past environmental changes. By understanding the historical patterns of variation in lake communities, the researchers can generate hypotheses about how environmental factors have shaped the communities we see now, and possibly predict what we will find in the future.

How to Reconstruct Past Communities

The fundamental research subject in most paleolimnological studies is the sediment core (fig. 3.47a). Suspended in the waters of all lakes are numerous microscopic organisms. When they die, many will sink down to the bottom. Some of these will then decompose, while many will leave

(a)

(b)

Figure 3.47   (*a*) A PEARL member collecting a sediment core while resting on the pontoon of a helicopter; (*b*) Two species of diatoms showing clearly distinct morphologies.

behind hard shells and crusts that get covered up by the continuing rain of detritus and dirt that falls from above. Sediments are continually accumulating, and the deeper you dig into them, the further back in time you move. The basic paleolimnological approach is to take a sediment core, divide it into many sections of differing depths, identify the approximate age of each depth, and identify the remains of the organisms and other paleolimnological information found at each depth. By putting this information together, a researcher can infer shifts in lake communities over long periods of time. The validity of this entire process depends upon two critical assumptions: (1) you can accurately determine the age of each depth, and (2) the species you are measuring in the sediment cores are unbiased indicators of past lake conditions.

Age

Sediment cores are generally removed from the lake bottom and divided into numerous thin segments. Each segment is then typically subjected to radioisotopic measurement to determine the approximate age of the cores. Accurate measures of age are highly dependent upon the ability of researchers in the field to take reliable and undisturbed sediment cores. Any significant mixing of sediment during the field sampling will invalidate countless hours of work and cost thousands of dollars. It is important to remember that even studies built upon high-tech analyses and microscopic imagery can fail if the most basic of methods are conducted poorly. Though one often associates the critical point of research being the "eureka" ideas of the scientist, in fact those breakthroughs can never occur without painstakingly accurate data collection gathered through countless hours of dedicated work in the field and in the lab.

Species Identification

Not all species that live in lakes will be suitable indicator species for paleolimnological studies. Good candidates will be species found in large numbers in the cores that also have hard bodies resistant to decomposition. One commonly used group of algal species are diatoms. Diatoms have hard silicate "shells" and are dominant members of the phytoplankton and periphyton (algae attached to submerged surfaces in shallow waters) in most aquatic communities. The shapes and sculpturing of the silicate structures are species specific, and patterns of abundance for individual species can be followed throughout the depth of the core (fig. 3.47*b*). With over 10,000 species of diatoms, one can observe shifts in the abundance of different species through time, rather than just the presence or absence of diatoms as a group. Additionally, the environmental conditions that are required for the growth of many diatom species are well studied, and thus if paleolimnologists find that a given diatom species was abundant during a particular time period, they are able to infer something about the likely lake conditions such as climate, pH, and nutrients during that time interval.

It is through linking species identification with basic knowledge about the natural history of these species that paleolimnologists are able to reconstruct lake conditions of times past. We will now explore an example that uses these research tools to address an ecological question.

Climate-Lake Linkages

Due to patterns of global water and air circulation and feedback among ice, snow, and the atmosphere, human-induced climate change is particularly pronounced in polar regions (Moritz et al. 2002). What is less well known is whether this warming is associated with broad ecological changes in arctic lakes (fig. 3.48). There is reason for concern, as primary production and nutrient cycling in arctic lakes are often limited by the short growth season. Increased temperatures could decrease ice cover, alter thermal stratification, and change nutrient cycling. All of these factors can influence the species composition of lakes, and thus there is reason to believe that rapid climate change in arctic areas has resulted in rapid ecological shifts.

John Smol and colleagues (Smol et al. 2005) tested the hypothesis that lakes that experienced more climate change will also have experienced greater change in species composition than lakes that have experienced less climate change. They were able to obtain data on temperature changes over the last 50 years in the area of their study lakes, but to determine how ecosystems have changed on longer time frames, before instrumental data were available, they had to use indirect approaches. The team turned to paleolimnology for the tools needed to obtain the biological data. Sediment cores were obtained from lakes that ranged in latitude from 58° N to 82° N, with each core divided by depths, and ages and species composition of diatoms and other hard-bodied organisms were determined. Within each core, they estimated the amount of change in species composition over time, which they report as beta-diversity. The higher the value of beta-diversity, the greater the change in species composition within the lake during the time interval represented in the sediment core. It is important to realize that species composition can change over time for reasons other than climate change. To provide a measure of the background level of change that occurs, Smol and colleagues used a group of 14 non-arctic lakes as a reference area.

Figure 3.49 shows that climate change has been most rapid at more northerly latitudes. It is also clear that

Figure 3.48 Two typical high arctic lakes on Ellesmere Island, Canada. Ice can remain in the centre of some lakes year round.

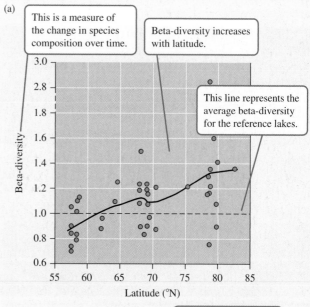

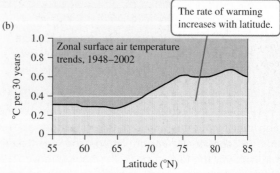

Figure 3.49 Change in (*a*) beta-diversity; and (*b*) air temperature as a function of latitude (data from Smol et al. 2005).

beta-diversity is higher at more northerly latitudes, suggesting that the rate of ecological change is associated with the rate of warming of a region. In fact, beta-diversity of 81% of the lakes north of the treeline was greater than that found in the reference lakes, while only 58% of the lakes south of the treeline had beta-diversity levels higher than the reference lakes.

These data are a good example of how describing a community in a rigorous scientific framework can lead to great insights into the basic ecology of systems. Although experimental approaches are useful for addressing many ecological questions, we must not forget that in many systems "natural experiments" have already occurred, with the results sitting at the bottom of a lake waiting to be collected.

SUMMARY

Humans everywhere hold a land-centred perspective of the planet. However, aquatic life is often most profuse where conditions appear most hostile to people, for example, along cold, wave-swept seacoasts, in torrential mountain streams, and in the murky waters where rivers meet the sea.

3.1 The hydrologic cycle exchanges water among reservoirs.

Of the water in the biosphere, the oceans contain 97% and the polar ice caps and glaciers an additional 2%, leaving less than 1% as freshwater. The turnover of water in the various reservoirs of the hydrologic cycle ranges from only nine days for the atmosphere to 3,100 years for the oceans.

3.2 The biology of aquatic environments corresponds broadly to variations in physical factors such as light, temperature, and water movements and to chemical factors such as salinity and oxygen.

The *oceans* form the largest continuous environment on earth. An ocean is generally divided vertically into several depth zones, each with a distinctive assemblage of marine organisms. Limited light penetration restricts photosynthetic organisms to the photic, or epipelagic, zone and leads to thermal stratification. Oceanic temperatures are much more stable than terrestrial temperatures. Tropical seas are more stable physically and chemically; temperate and high-latitude seas are more productive. Highest productivity occurs along coastlines. The open ocean supports large numbers of species and is important to global carbon and oxygen budgets.

Kelp forests are found mainly at temperate latitudes. *Coral reefs* are limited to the tropics and subtropics to latitudes between 30° N and S latitudes. Coral reefs are generally one of three types: fringing reefs, barrier reefs, and atolls. Kelp beds share several structural features with terrestrial forests. Both seaweeds and reef-building corals grow only in surface waters where there is sufficient light to support photosynthesis. Kelp forests are generally limited to areas where temperature ranges from about 10°C to 20°C, while reef-building corals are limited to areas with temperatures of about 18°C to 29°C. The diversity and productivity of coral reefs rival that of tropical rain forests.

The *intertidal* zone lines the coastlines of the world. It can be divided into several vertical zones: supratidal, high

intertidal, middle intertidal, and low intertidal. The magnitude and timing of the tides is determined by the interaction of the gravitational effects of the sun and moon with the configuration of coastlines and basins. Tidal fluctuation produces steep gradients of physical and chemical conditions within the intertidal zone. Exposure to waves, bottom type, height in the intertidal zone, and biological interactions determine the distribution of most organisms within this zone.

Salt marshes, *mangrove forests*, and *estuaries* occur at the transitions between freshwater and marine environments and between marine and terrestrial environments. Salt marshes, which are dominated by herbaceous vegetation, are found mainly at temperate and high latitudes. Mangrove forests grow in the tropics and subtropics. Estuaries are extremely dynamic physically, chemically, and biologically. The diversity of species is not as high in estuaries, salt marshes, and mangrove forests as in some other aquatic environments, but productivity is exceptional.

Rivers and *streams* are very dynamic systems and can be divided several ways into distinctive environments: longitudinally, laterally, and vertically. Periodic flooding has important influences on the structure and functioning of river and stream ecosystems. The temperature of rivers follows variation in air temperature but does not reach the extremes occurring in terrestrial habitats. The flow and chemical characteristics of rivers change with climatic regime. Current speed, distance from headwaters, and the nature of bottom sediments are principal determinants of the distributions of stream organisms.

Lakes are much like small seas. Most are found in regions worked over by tectonics, volcanism, and glacial activity, the geological forces that produce lake basins. A few lakes contain most of the freshwater in the biosphere. Lake structure parallels that of the oceans but on a much smaller scale. The salinity of lakes, which ranges from very dilute waters to over 200‰, is much more variable than that of the oceans. Lake stratification and mixing vary with latitude. Lake flora and fauna largely reflect geographic location and nutrient content.

Peatlands occur primarily in northern latitudes and contain large stores of partially decomposed plant material.

Bogs receive water only through precipitation, and have very low pH. Fens are fed both through precipitation as well as ground or surface waters, with pH varying among fens. In all peatlands, oxygen levels and microbial activity are low. As a result, decomposition rates are slower than production rates, allowing for the accumulation of peat. Peatlands face challenges through direct harvest, as well as indirectly through changes to global temperatures and precipitation patterns.

Paleolimnologists measure shifts in the composition of aquatic communities through time. Lake sediments are deposited continuously, and the remains of the hard-bodied organisms such as diatoms serve as a historical record of prior lake conditions. By comparing patterns in species turnover to recent records of changes in temperatures or other environmental factors, paleolimnologists are able to develop hypotheses about how lakes will respond to continued human influence in the future.

REVIEW QUESTIONS

1. Review the distribution of water among the major reservoirs of the hydrologic cycle. What are the major sources of freshwater? Explain why, according to some projections, availability of freshwater may limit human populations and activity.

2. The oceans cover about 360 million km² and have an average depth of about 4,000 m. What proportion of this aquatic system receives sufficient light to support photosynthesis? Make the liberal assumption that the photic zone extends to a depth of 200 m.

3. Below about 600 to 1,000 m in the oceans there is no sunlight. However, many of the fish and invertebrates at these depths have eyes. In contrast, fish living in caves are often blind. What selective forces could maintain eyes in populations of deep-sea fish? (Hint: Many species of deep-sea invertebrates are bioluminescent.)

4. Darwin (1842a) was the first to propose that fringing reefs, barrier reefs, and atolls are different stages in a developmental sequence that begins with a fringing reef and ends with an atoll. Outline how this process might work. How would you test your ideas?

5. How might a history of exposure to wide environmental fluctuation affect the physiological tolerances of intertidal species compared to close relatives in subtidal and oceanic environments? How might salinity tolerance vary among organisms living at different levels within the intertidal?

6. According to the river continuum model, the organisms inhabiting headwater streams in temperate forest regions depend mainly upon organic material coming into the stream from the surrounding forests. According to the model, photosynthesis within the stream is only important in the downstream reaches of these stream systems. Explain. How would you go about testing the predictions of the river continuum model?

7. How could you test the generalization that lake primary production and the composition of the biota living in lakes are strongly influenced by the availability of nutrients such as nitrogen and phosphorus? Assume that you have unlimited resources and that you have access to several lakes.

8. Biological interactions may also affect lake systems. How does the recent history of the Great Lakes suggest that the kinds of species that inhabit a lake influence the nature of the lake environment and the composition of the biological community?

9. Why are peatlands of particular interest to researchers who study climate change? What factors are likely to influence whether peatlands begin to release their vast stores of carbon into the atmosphere at a much faster rate?

10. What aspects of life in a bog may have favoured selection for carnivory in plants? Why are carnivorous plants relatively rare in all other types of communities, such as temperate forest, salt marshes, and even the tropical forest?

For more information on the resources available from McGraw-Hill Ryerson, go to **www.mcgrawhill.ca/he/solutions**.

EVOLUTION AND SPECIATION

CHAPTER 4

CHAPTER CONCEPTS

4.1 Phenotypic variation among individuals in a population results from the combined effects of genes and environment.

Concept 4.1 Review

4.2 Changes in gene frequency within a population can occur through both natural selection and random processes such as genetic drift.

Ecology In Action: Human-Induced Evolution

Concept 4.2 Review

4.3 Physical and ecological processes interact with selection and drift to produce new species.

Concept 4.3 Review

Ecological Tools and Approaches: Integrating Population Genetics and Ecology

Summary

Review Questions

The great diversity of organisms that live on the planet, and the even greater diversity of organisms that have gone extinct (chapter 23), are all the product of evolution and speciation. These organisms interact in countless ways with each other and their surroundings. The outcome of these ecological interactions influences an individual's survival and reproduction. These variations in survival and reproduction can lead to evolutionary changes, completing the circle. There would be no ecology without the species that are produced through evolution and speciation. At the same time, ecological interactions are the mechanism that allow for evolution by natural selection. This linkage has always influenced the research of both ecologists and evolutionary biologists; however in recent years new subdisciplines such as *community phylogenetics*, *ecological genomics*, and *conservation genetics* have emerged. Because evolution is central to ecology, it is important that students of ecology have a broad understanding of evolution. Therefore, evolutionary biology is integrated into all chapters and sections of this text. To understand the usage of evolutionary terms and concepts later in the text, we provide a general overview of key aspects of evolutionary biology in this chapter. We begin with a single person who fundamentally changed human understanding of the natural world.

Darwin's theory of evolution by natural selection, a unifying concept of modern biology, was crystallized by his observations in the Galápagos Islands. In mid-October of 1835, a small boat moved slowly from the shore of a volcanic island to a waiting ship. The boat carried a young naturalist who had just completed a month of exploring the group of islands known as the Galápagos, which lie on the equator approximately 1,000 km west of the South American mainland (fig. 4.1). As the seamen rowed into the oncoming waves, the naturalist, Charles Darwin, mused over what he had found on the island. His observations had confirmed expectations built on information gathered earlier on the other islands he had visited in the archipelago. Later Darwin recorded his thoughts in his journal, which he later published (Darwin 1839): "The distribution of the tenants of this archipelago would not be nearly so wonderful, if, for instance, one island had a mocking-thrush, and a second island some other quite distinct genus—if one island had its genus of lizard and a second island another distinct genus, or none whatever. . . . But it is the circumstance, that several of the islands possess their own species of the tortoise, mocking-thrush, finches, and numerous plants, these species having the same general habits, occupying analogous situations, and obviously filling the same place in the natural economy of this archipelago, that strikes me with wonder."

Darwin wondered at the sources of the differences among clearly related populations and attempted to explain the origin of these differences. He would later conclude that these populations were descended from common ancestors whose descendants had changed after reaching each of the islands. The ship to which the seamen rowed was the H.M.S. *Beagle*, halfway through a voyage around the world. The main objective of the *Beagle*'s mission, charting the coasts of southern

Figure 4.1   During his visit to the Galápagos Islands, Charles Darwin encountered many examples of plant and animal species that differed physically from one island to another. Shown here is the relatively small island of Fernandina and the nearby J-shaped Isabela Island.

South America, would be largely forgotten, while the thoughts of the young Charles Darwin would eventually develop into one of the most significant theories in the history of science. Darwin's wondering, carefully organized and supported by a lifetime of observation, would become the theory of evolution by natural selection, a theory that would transform the prevailing scientific view of life on earth and rebuild the foundations of biology. The theory of natural selection coupled with a strong understanding of natural history is a foundation of the science of ecology.

Darwin left the Galápagos Islands convinced that the various populations on the islands were gradually modified from their ancestral forms. In other words, Darwin concluded that the island populations had undergone a process of **evolution**, a process that changes populations of organisms over time. Though Darwin left the Galápagos convinced that the island populations had evolved, he had no mechanism to explain the evolutionary changes that he was convinced they had undergone. However, a plausible mechanism to produce evolutionary change in populations came to Darwin almost exactly three years after his taking leave of the Galápagos Islands. In October of 1838, while reading the essay on populations by Thomas Malthus, Darwin was convinced that during competition for limited resources, such as food or space, among individuals within populations, some individuals would have a competitive advantage. He proposed that the characteristics producing that advantage would be "preserved" and the unfavourable characteristics of other individuals would be "destroyed." As a result of this selection by the environment, those individuals with favourable characteristics would have

a greater chance of surviving and producing offspring than those individuals without those characteristics. Another way of saying this is that some traits will increase the **fitness** of the individual that possesses that trait, while other traits will decrease the fitness of an individual. A modern definition of fitness is "the relative genetic contribution of individuals to future generations," though Darwin was unaware of genetic mechanisms for his theory. Because selection can produce individuals with different fitness, populations will change over time. With this mechanism for change in hand, Darwin sketched out the first draft of his theory of natural selection in 1842. It would take him many years and many drafts before he honed the theory to its final form and amassed sufficient supporting information. The theory of **natural selection** can be summarized as follows:

1. More offspring are produced each generation than can be supported by the environment.

2. There is variation in physical, physiological, and behavioural traits among individuals in a population. Some of this variation is heritable (passed on to offspring).

3. Some traits will give some individuals an advantage over the other members of the population. Individuals who possess those traits will have a higher chance of surviving and reproducing than the other members of the population, increasing their fitness.

4. Traits that result in increased fitness will become more common within a population over subsequent generations.

Darwin (1859) proposed that differential survival and reproduction of individuals would produce changes in species populations that increase the fitness of individuals within that environment. Put another way, evolution can lead to **adaptations**. Adaptations are not something that an individual evolves out of need or desire, rather it is a trait that has been selected for through natural selection. Darwin now had a mechanism to explain the differences among populations that he had observed on the Galápagos Islands. Still, Darwin was aware of a major insufficiency in his theory. The theory of natural selection depended upon the passage of "advantageous" characteristics from one generation to the next. The problem was that the mechanisms of inheritance were unknown in Darwin's time. In addition, the prevailing idea at the time, blending inheritance, suggested that rare traits, no matter how favourable, would be blended out of a population, preventing change as a consequence.

As Darwin explored the Galápagos Islands, halfway around the world in central Europe a schoolboy named Johann Mendel was beginning an education that would eventually lead him to uncover the basic mechanisms of inheritance. Although Darwin and Mendel did not work together, their studies have been combined by later generations to form our modern understanding of evolution by natural selection (fig. 4.2).

Johann would be renamed Gregor Mendel when he joined the Augustinian order of monks that maintained a monastery near his birthplace. In a garden within the walls of the abbey,

Figure 4.2   The work of Charles Darwin forms the foundation for modern evolutionary theory.

Mendel would discover what Darwin's around-the-world voyage would not reveal. The two keys to Mendel's discoveries would be excellent training in mathematics and physics, from which he derived a sense of quantitative relationships, and the power of an experimental approach to the study of the natural world.

What did Mendel discover? Briefly, he uncovered what we now call "Mendelian genetics," including the fundamental concept of particulate inheritance. That is the concept that characteristics pass from parent to offspring in the form of discrete packets of information that we now call genes. Mendel also determined that genes come in alternative forms, which we term **alleles**. For instance, Mendel worked with alleles that led to traits such as round versus wrinkled seeds and tall versus short plants. In addition, he found that some alleles prevent the expression of other alleles. We call such alleles *dominant* and the alleles that they suppress *recessive*. Mendel's work also revealed the distinction between genotype and phenotype and the difference between homozygous and heterozygous genotypes. Mendel's work, which disclosed still other aspects of the laws of inheritance, laid a solid foundation for the science of genetics.

How did Mendel succeed, while so many others had failed? The sources of his success can be traced to his education and his own special genius. Mendel's education at the University of Vienna exposed him to some of the best minds working in the physical sciences and to an approach to science

that emphasized experimentation. His introduction to the physical sciences included a solid foundation in mathematics, including probability and statistics. As a consequence, Mendel could quantify the results of his experimental research.

Mendel chose to work with plants which could be maintained in the abbey garden. His most famous and influential work was done on the garden pea, *Pisum sativum.* Many domestic varieties of peas, which showed a great deal of physical variation, were available to Mendel. Rather than treat the phenotype as a whole, Mendel subdivided the organism into a set of manageable characteristics such as seed form, stem length, and so forth, which it turned out were controlled by individual genes. This analytical perspective of his study of organisms was probably another legacy of his training in the physical sciences. Finally, to his excellent education and genius, Mendel added a lot of hard work and perseverance.

Darwin and Mendel complemented each other perfectly and their unique visions of the natural world revolutionized biology. The synthesis of the theory of natural selection and genetics gave rise to modern evolutionary ecology, a very broad field of study. Here we examine several major concepts within that broad discipline.

4.1 Variation Within Populations

Phenotypic variation among individuals in a population results from the combined effects of genes and environment. Because phenotypic variation is the substrate upon which the environment acts during the process of natural selection, determining the extent and sources of variation within populations is one of the most fundamental considerations in evolutionary studies. Darwin's theory of natural selection sparked a revolution in thinking among biologists, who responded almost immediately by studying variation among organisms in all sorts of environments. The first of these biologists to conduct truly thorough studies of variation and to incorporate experimentation in their studies focused on plants.

Variation in a Widely Distributed Plant

Jens Clausen, David Keck, and William Hiesey, who worked at Stanford University in California, conducted some of the most widely cited studies of plant variation. Their studies provided deep insights into the extent and sources of morphological variation in plant populations, including both the influence of environment and genetics. Though this research group and its successors studied nearly 200 species, it is best known for its work on *Potentilla glandulosa*, or sticky cinquefoil (fig. 4.3) (Clausen, Keck, and Hiesey 1940).

Clausen and his research team worked with clones of several populations of *P. glandulosa*, which they grew in three main experimental gardens—one at Stanford near the coast at an elevation of 30 m, another in a montane environment at Mather at an elevation of 1,400 m in the Sierra Nevada, and a third garden in an alpine environment at Timberline at 3,050 m (fig. 4.4). By cloning lowland, mid-elevation, and alpine

Figure 4.3 *Potentilla glandulosa,* sticky cinquefoil, grows from sea level to over 3,000 m elevation and shows remarkable morphological variation along this elevational gradient.

plants and growing them in experimental gardens, Clausen, Keck, and Hiesey established experimental conditions that could reveal potential genetic differences among populations. In addition, because they studied the responses of plants from all populations to environmental conditions in lowland, mid-elevation, and alpine gardens, their experiment could demonstrate adaptation by *P. glandulosa* populations to local environmental conditions.

The growth response of *P. glandulosa* to environmental conditions at the three common garden sites is summarized in figure 4.4. Plant height differed significantly among sites, indicating an environmental effect on plant morphology. However, plants taken from the lowland, mid-elevation, and alpine plants responded differently to the three environments. While the mid-elevation and alpine plants attained their greatest height in the mid-elevation garden, the lowland plants grew the tallest in the lowland garden. The number of flowers produced by lowland, mid-elevation, and alpine plants also varied across the gardens.

Differences in response *among* and *within* clones of lowland, mid-elevation, and alpine *P. glandulosa* provide complementary information. Differences *among* clones, in growth and flower production, at the three common garden sites indicate genetic differences among lowland, mid-elevation, and alpine populations of *P. glandulosa*. Meanwhile, differences in growth and flower production *within* clones grown at the

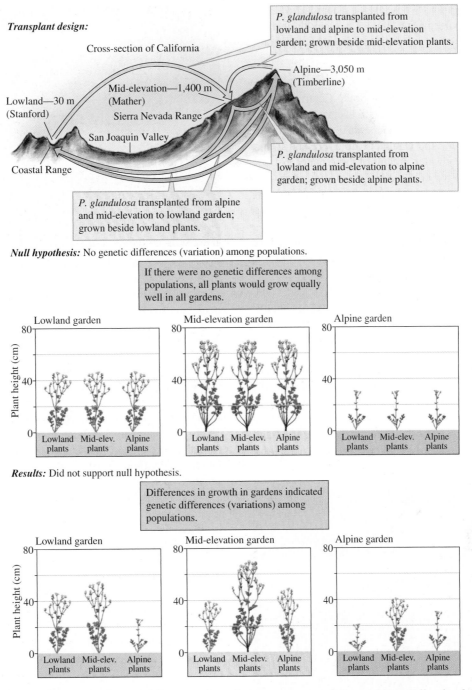

Transplant design:

Cross-section of California

P. glandulosa transplanted from lowland and alpine to mid-elevation garden; grown beside mid-elevation plants.

Alpine—3,050 m (Timberline)

Mid-elevation—1,400 m (Mather)

Lowland—30 m (Stanford)

Sierra Nevada Range

San Joaquin Valley

Coastal Range

P. glandulosa transplanted from lowland and mid-elevation to alpine garden; grown beside alpine plants.

P. glandulosa transplanted from alpine and mid-elevation to lowland garden; grown beside lowland plants.

Null hypothesis: No genetic differences (variation) among populations.

If there were no genetic differences among populations, all plants would grow equally well in all gardens.

Lowland garden   Mid-elevation garden   Alpine garden

Plant height (cm)

Lowland plants   Mid-elev. plants   Alpine plants

Results: Did not support null hypothesis.

Differences in growth in gardens indicated genetic differences (variations) among populations.

Lowland garden   Mid-elevation garden   Alpine garden

Plant height (cm)

Lowland plants   Mid-elev. plants   Alpine plants

Figure 4.4   A common garden approach to studying genetic variation among populations of *Potentilla glandulosa* (data from Clausen, Keck, and Hiesey 1940).

three elevations are the result of environmental differences among the common garden sites, not genetic differences. This is an example of **phenotypic plasticity**—variation among individuals in form, function, or physiology as a result of environmental influences.

Other observations by Clausen, Keck, and Hiesey indicate that the genetic variation among the plant populations was associated with adaptation to local environments. For instance, most lowland plants died during their first winter in the alpine garden and those that survived did not produce seeds. Alpine plants showed the opposite trends. They had

poor survival in the lowland garden and went dormant in winter, while the lowland plants remained active. In summary, the experiments of Clausen, Keck, and Hiesey demonstrated genetic differences among populations and adaptation to their natural environments. Ecologists call such locally adapted and genetically distinctive populations within a species **ecotypes**. Applying this term then, we can conclude that the lowland, mid-elevation, and alpine populations studied by Clausen, Keck, and Hiesey were ecotypes.

Using transplant and common garden approaches, ecologists have learned a great deal about genetic variation among

and within plant populations. These classical approaches, combined with modern molecular techniques, are rapidly increasing our knowledge of genetic variation in natural populations.

Variation in Alpine Fish Populations

The Alps rise out of the landscape of South Central Europe, forming a moist and cool high-elevation environment. The Alps' deep winter snows and glaciers make them the origin of four important rivers: the Danube, Rhine, Po, and Rhone rivers. Because the headwater streams of these rivers are cool, they became refuges for cold-water aquatic organisms following the last ice age. As temperatures of the surrounding lowlands began to warm at the end of the Pleistocene, approximately 12,000 years ago, aquatic species requiring cold water migrated to the headwaters of these rivers. The movement of cold-adapted aquatic species into the headwater streams and lakes of the glacial valleys that lace the Alps created clusters of geographically isolated populations (fig. 4.5). This isolation reduced movements of individuals between populations. With reduced gene flow, populations could diverge genetically. Such genetic divergence would increase the genetic variation among populations.

Morphological differences among populations of headwater fish species in the Alps have long suggested genetic differences among them. Nowhere has morphological variation among populations been better studied and documented than among the whitefish. Whitefish are relatives of the trout and salmon and are classified in the genus *Coregonus* (fig. 4.6).

Figure 4.6 Whitefish, *Coregonus* sp., are adapted to cold, highly oxygenated waters like their relatives the trout and salmon. Because they are valued food fish, whitefish have been intensively managed, particularly in the Central Alps.

Marlis Douglas and Patrick Brunner (2002) explored the genetic and phenotypic variation among populations of *Coregonus* in the Central Alps. Douglas and Brunner pointed out that ichthyologists have described 19 indigenous *Coregonus* populations from the Central Alps. However, there has been significant disagreement over the taxonomic status of these 19 populations. The classification of these populations ranges from that of a single variable species with 19 distinctive populations, to dividing the 19 populations into more than a dozen separate species.

The taxonomic status of *Coregonus* populations in the Central Alps is made more difficult by a 100-year history of intensive fisheries management. Douglas and Brunner review this history, which included raising *Coregonus* in hatcheries and moving fish between lakes. One of the main purposes of the study by Douglas and Brunner was to describe the genetic variation among the present-day populations of *Coregonus* to determine if there is evidence for significant genetic differences among historically recognized populations. A second purpose was to examine the genetic similarity between introduced *Coregonus* populations and the populations from which they were drawn. Using this information, Douglas and Brunner intended to offer suggestions for the management and conservation of *Coregonus* in the Central Alps.

Douglas and Brunner collected 907 *Coregonus* specimens from 33 populations in 17 lakes in the Central Alpine Region and used a mixture of anatomical and genetic features to characterize the fish. The anatomical features were the number of rays in the dorsal, anal, pelvic, and pectoral fins, the extent of pigmentation in these fins, and the number of gill rakers on the first gill arch. The study populations were characterized genetically using **microsatellite DNA**, tandemly repetitive nuclear DNA, 10 to 100 base pairs long (see Ecological Tools, this chapter).

Genetic analyses by Douglas and Brunner demonstrated a moderate to high level of genetic variation within all 33 study populations. They also found that genetic and morphological analyses distinguished the 19 historically recognized

Figure 4.5 Lake Lucerne, Switzerland, lies nestled in the heart of the Alps, where it provides an extensive cold-water habitat for aquatic organisms, including whitefish, *Coregonus*, populations.

Coregonus populations of the Central Alps. Genotypic differences among populations were sufficient to correctly assign individual fish to the indigenous population from which they were sampled with approximately a 71% probability. Fin ray counts correctly assigned fish to the 19 indigenous populations with a 69% probability, while pigmentation could identify them with a 43% probability. Combining genetic and phenotypic data increased the correct assignment of specimens to the populations from which they were drawn to 79%. Genetic analyses of the introduced *Coregonus* populations revealed their genetic similarity to the populations from which they were stocked. However, these analyses also showed that the introduced populations have differentiated genetically from their source populations.

The conclusion that Douglas and Brunner drew from these results was that the *Coregonus* of the Central Alps is made up of a highly diverse set of populations that show a high level of genetic differentiation. They suggest that these populations should be considered as "evolutionarily significant units." They further conclude that the distinctiveness of local *Coregonus* populations is sufficient so that they should be managed as separate units. Douglas and Brunner recommend that *Coregonus* should not be moved from one lake basin to another.

Phenotypic and genotypic variation are essential components to evolution by natural selection. However, genotypic variation within a species can itself alter interactions between species. We will come back to this idea in later chapters of the book, and now focus on the importance of heritability

Genetic Variation and Heritability

Darwin was aware that the only way natural selection can produce evolutionary change in a population is if the phenotypic traits upon which natural selection acts can be passed from generation to generation. In other words, evolution by natural selection depends upon the heritability of traits. We can define **heritability** of a trait—usually symbolized as h^2—in a broad sense as the proportion of total phenotypic variation in a trait, such as body size or eye colour, that is attributable to genetic variance. In equation form, heritability can be expressed as:

$$h^2 = V_G/V_P$$

Here V_G represents genetic variance and V_P represents phenotypic variance. (See Appendix A for how to calculate variance.) Many different factors contribute to the amount of phenotypic variance in a population, including both genetic effects and environmental influences. We will subdivide phenotypic variance into these two components: variance in phenotype due to genetic effects we will call V_G, and variance in phenotype due to environmental effects we will call V_E. There are several additional sources that can cause phenotypic variation (e.g., a genotype $\times$ environment interaction), though they are beyond the scope of this text. Subdividing V_P in the heritability equation given above produces the following:

$$h^2 = V_G/(V_G + V_E)$$

This expression for heritability has important implications, so let's examine it. First, consider the role of environmental

variance, V_E. Environment has substantial effects on many aspects of the phenotype of organisms. For instance, the quality of food eaten by an animal can contribute to the growth rate of the animal and to its eventual size. Similarly, the amount of light, nutrients, temperature, and so forth, affect the growth form and size of plants. So, when we consider a population of plants or animals, some of the phenotypic variation that we might measure will be the result of environmental effects, that is, V_E. However, we are just as familiar with the influence of genes on phenotype. For example, some of the variation in stature that we see in a population of animals or plants will generally result from genetic variation among individuals in the population, that is, V_G.

What our equation says is that the heritability of a particular trait depends on the relative sizes of genetic versus environmental variance. Heritability increases with increased V_G and decreases with increased V_E. Imagine a situation in which all phenotypic variation is the result of genetic differences between individuals and none results from environmental effects. In such a situation, V_E is zero and $h^2 = V_G/(V_G + V_E)$ is equal to $h^2 = V_G/V_G$ (since $V_E = 0$), which equals 1.0. In this case since all phenotypic variation is due to genetic effects, the trait is perfectly heritable. We can also imagine the opposite circumstance in which none of the phenotypic variation that we observe is due to genetic effects. In this case, V_G is zero and so the expression $h^2 = V_G/(V_G + V_E)$ also equals zero. Because all of the phenotypic variation we observe in this population is due to environmental effects, natural selection cannot produce evolutionary change in the population. Generally, heritability of traits falls somewhere in between these extremes in the very broad region where both environment and genes contribute to the phenotypic variance shown by a population. For instance, Peter Boag and Peter Grant (1978), the latter formerly a professor at McGill University, estimated bill width in the Galápagos finch *Geospiza fortis* to have a heritability of 0.95. By comparison, they estimated that bill length in the species has a heritability of 0.62. In a study of morphological variation in the water lily leaf beetle, a team of Dutch scientists (Pappers et al. 2002) found that body length and mandible width had heritabilities of between 0.53 and 0.83.

In the next section we will discuss how heritability and ecological interactions combine to cause evolution in natural populations.

CONCEPT 4.1 REVIEW

1. What is a fundamental evolutionary implication of the large amounts of genetic variation commonly found in natural populations?
2. What would you expect to see in figure 4.4 if alpine, mid-elevation, and lowland populations of *P. glandulosa* were not different genetically?
3. Can V_E be greater than V_G for a trait related to an organism's fitness? Explain.

4.2 Evolution

Changes in gene frequency within a population can occur through both natural selection and random processes such as genetic drift. In the previous sections of this chapter we have shown that phenotypic variation exists in natural populations, due to both environmental and genetic causes. Two scientists, George H. Hardy and Wilhelm Weinberg, have shown independently that under a set of stringent conditions (e.g., infinitely large populations, random mating, no selection), allelic variations in a gene will naturally be maintained within a population. This idea is called the **Hardy-Weinberg principle**, and serves as the starting point for a discussion of evolution. In this section, we will link our understanding of variation and heritability to two mechanisms of evolutionary change: natural selection and genetic drift.

The Process of Natural Selection

The basic concept of natural selection is that some heritable traits result in unequal fitness among individuals in a population. As a consequence, over time there is an increase in the frequency of individuals that possess these favourable traits. Although this idea is easy enough to grasp, natural selection does not take the same form everywhere and at all times. Natural selection can act against different segments of the population under different circumstances. Natural selection can accelerate changes in one population, and inhibit changes in another. We will begin our discussion of natural selection by describing the major forms of selection that occur in natural population, and then discuss the consequences on allelic frequencies.

Stabilizing Selection

One of the conclusions that we might draw from the discussion of genetic variability is that most populations have a high potential for evolutionary change. However, our observations of the natural world suggest that species can remain little changed for generation after generation. If the potential for evolutionary change is high in populations, why does it not always lead to obvious evolutionary change, at least in the short term? One form of natural selection, called **stabilizing selection**, can act to impede directional changes in populations.

Stabilizing selection acts against extreme phenotypes and as a consequence favours the average phenotype. Figure 4.7a pictures stabilizing selection, using a normal distribution of body size. Under the influence of stabilizing selection, individuals of average size have higher survival and reproductive rates, while the largest and smallest individuals in the population have lower rates of survival and reproduction. As a consequence of stabilizing selection, a population tends to sustain the same average phenotype over time while the frequency of extreme phenotypes can decrease. Stabilizing selection occurs where average individuals in a population are best adapted to a given set of conditions. If a population is well adapted to a given set of environmental circumstances, stabilizing selection may sustain the match between prevailing environmental conditions and the average phenotype within a population. However, stabilizing selection for a particular trait can be challenged by environmental change. In the face

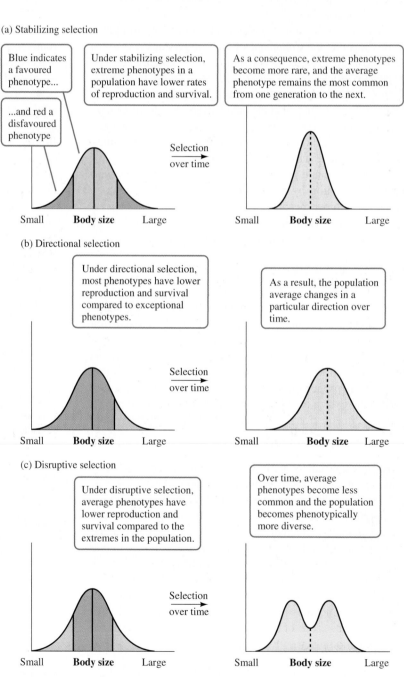

Figure 4.7   Three principle forms of natural selection: (*a*) stabilizing selection, (*b*) directional selection, and (*c*) disruptive selection.

of environmental change, the dominant form of selection may be directional.

Directional Selection

If we examine the fossil record or trace the history of well-studied populations over time, we can find many examples of how populations have changed in many characteristics. For instance, there have been remarkable changes in body size or body proportions in many evolutionary lineages. Such changes may be the result of **directional selection**.

Directional selection favours an extreme phenotype over other phenotypes in the population. Figure 4.7*b* presents an example of directional selection, again, using a normal distribution of body size. In this hypothetical situation, larger individuals in the population realize higher rates of survival and reproduction, while average and small individuals have lower rates of survival and reproduction. As a consequence of these differences in survival and reproduction, the average phenotype under directional selection changes over time. In the example shown in figure 4.7*b*, average body size increases with time. Directional selection occurs where one extreme phenotype has an advantage over all other phenotypes. However, there are circumstances in which more than one extreme phenotype may have an advantage over the average phenotype. Such a circumstance can lead to diversification within a population.

Disruptive Selection

There are populations that do not show a normal distribution of characteristics such as body size. In a normal distribution such as those depicted in figures 4.7*a* and 4.7*b*, there is a single peak, which coincides with the population mean. That is, the average phenotype in the population is the most common and all other phenotypes are less common. However, in some populations there may be two or more common phenotypes. In many animal species, for example, males may be of two or more discrete sizes. For example, it appears that in some animal populations, small and large males have higher reproductive success than males of intermediate body size. In such populations, natural selection seems to have produced a diversity of male sizes. One way to produce such diversity is through **disruptive selection**.

Disruptive selection favours two or more extreme phenotypes over the average phenotype in a population. In figure 4.7*c*, individuals of average body size have lower rates of survival and reproduction than individuals of either larger or smaller body. As a consequence, both smaller and larger individuals increase in frequency in the population over time. The result is a distribution of body sizes among males in the population with two peaks. That is, the population has many large males and many small males, but few of intermediate body size.

Figure 4.7*b* and 4.7*c* indicate change in the frequencies of phenotypes in the two hypothetical populations after a period of natural selection. This change depends on the extent to which genes determine the phenotype upon which natural selection acts.

Different types of selection (stabilizing, directional, and disruptive) can occur on different traits within a single population, or on a single trait in multiple populations. One factor that can also vary is the rate of evolution due to natural selection. As you can imagine, not all selective pressures are equally strong. Some traits will be lethal, resulting in strong selective pressures and rapid evolution. Others will be more subtle, requiring thousands of generations before any measurable shift in gene frequency can be found (fig. 4.8). Here we review studies that have explored evolution by natural selection in nature.

Stabilizing Selection for Egg Size among Ural Owls

Egg size, which affects offspring development and survival, influences successful reproduction by organisms ranging from sea urchins, lizards, and fish, to ostriches. Egg size can be highly variable within populations. For example, in a population of birds, the largest eggs produced can be over twice the size of the smallest. Pekka Kontiainen, Jon Brommer, Patrik Karrell, and Hannu Pietiäinen, of the Bird Ecology Unit at the University of Helsinki, Finland, studied heritability, phenotypic plasticity, and evolution of egg size in the Ural owl, *Strix uralensis* (Kontiainen et al. 2008). One of their key questions was how much of the variation in egg size in their study population is the result of genetic differences among females (heritability) and how much is the result of environmental influences (phenotypic plasticity).

The study team conducted their research on Ural owls in a 1,500 km² area in southern Finland from 1981 to 2005. The main prey species for the owls were field voles, *Microtus agrestis*,

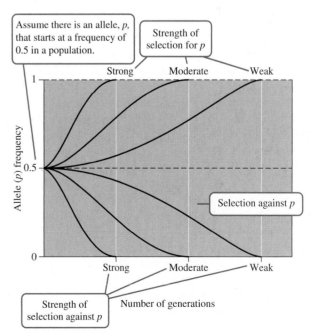

Figure 4.8 Variation in the rate of evolution as a function of the strength of selection, assuming genetic drift is not occurring.

Human-Induced Evolution

When we talk about evolution and natural selection, we often think about the Galápagos Islands and Darwin's finches, or other species responding to challenges in remote areas of the world. However, this view of evolution being something that happens only in the wilderness is not reflective of reality. Instead, there is reason to believe that humans are the greatest evolutionary force in the world (Palumbi 2001). Humans live, farm, fish, hunt, and build, placing direct selection pressure on populations of many species. Industrial emissions impact global biogeochemistry, resulting in nitrogen and toxin deposition in even the most remote corners of the globe. These direct and indirect changes to natural populations serve as strong evolutionary forces, upon which natural selection continues to act.

Evidence for evolution by natural selection is everywhere. For example, what does it mean when you hear that some disease-causing bacterium has developed antibiotic resistance? It means that at one point in time a species of bacteria could be killed by the application of some toxin (e.g., an antibiotic). Obviously, this puts an enormous directional selective pressure on the bacterial population, such that any individuals immune to that toxin will have a much higher fitness than those that are killed. As a result, the frequency of the genes that confer resistance increase within the population. This eventually reaches a point where the bacterial population consists primarily of individuals that cannot be killed by that particular antibiotic. This is evolution by natural selection, and it is a serious concern among medical professionals. Development of antibiotic resistance is widespread and rapid. The first evidence of resistance to a new antibiotic generally occurs within 10 years of the drug first being introduced (Palumbi 2001).

The underlying force of natural selection resulting in the evolution of resistance to poisons is also strong in plant and insect populations, with very negative consequences for agriculture. The introduction of new pesticides puts strong evolutionary pressures on insect populations, with natural selection favouring those individuals with resistance. Not surprisingly, resistance to insecticides quickly follows the introduction of new pesticides. Importantly, this happens both in conventional agriculture and in plants that have been genetically-modified to produce their own pesticides. Similar evolution occurs in weed populations that are regularly sprayed with herbicides. Soon after the introduction of a new poison, natural selection favours individuals who are resistant. The medical and agricultural worlds provide very clear examples of evolution in action, with humans as the dominant selective force. Similar patterns also occur outside of these highly managed systems. Here we will present examples from populations

(a)

(b)

Figure 4.9 Continued harvest of (*a*) cod and (*b*) mountain sheep by humans has caused evolutionary changes in maturation rates and horn lengths.

of Atlantic cod (*Gadus morhua*) and mountain sheep (*Ovis canadensis*).

The coasts of Labrador and Newfoundland have supported a commercial cod fishery for centuries (fig. 4.9a). In the late 1980s and early 1990s, this fishery collapsed, leading to an offshore fishing ban (see chapter 14 for a discussion of predator–prey dynamics). An international team of researchers from Canada, Austria, and Norway asked the question of whether the long-term harvest of cod caused any evolutionary response of these fish populations (Olsen et al. 2004).

Let us begin by asking what fish traits might be affected by commercial fishing activity. The most obvious is fish size. Larger fish are more likely to be caught in a net than smaller fish, and this can cause directional selection resulting in a reduction in average body size (Handford et al. 1977). In cod it takes several years before an individual is sexually mature. The greater the age of maturation, the greater the risk of mortality due to harvest prior to breeding. Being captured prior

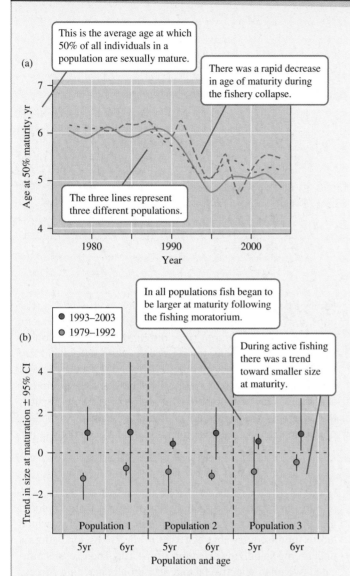

Figure 4.10 (*a*) Age of maturity of Atlantic cod decreased during the fishery collapse. (*b*) Evidence of maturation at smaller sizes during years with fishing than in the years following the moratorium (data from Olsen et al. 2004).

to breeding has an obviously greater negative consequence on an individual's fitness than if captured after breeding. As a result, we might expect sustained fishing to select for individuals who become sexually mature at a younger age and smaller size. Olsen and colleagues pored over the records of over 10,000 fish that were caught and measured between 1977 and 2002 in three populations off the coasts of Newfoundland and Labrador. In the early 1980s, 50% of the fish caught were sexually mature by age 6. During the fishery collapse, age of maturity had been reduced to age 5 (fig. 4.10). Although this is suggestive of evolution, this change could also be caused by a density-dependent response. In other words, by harvesting fish, the fish that remained may have

benefited from less competition for food and thus grew faster and were able to mature earlier. Olsen and his colleagues investigated the relationship between size and age of maturation. Under the density-dependent model, you would expect that the size at maturation would not change; instead the fish would simply get bigger faster. Olsen employed an elegant set of statistical analyses to suggest that it was evolution, and not density-dependence, driving the reduced age at maturity. Olsen found that during the years of fishing, there was a trend toward smaller size at maturation, while following the fishing moratorium, this was actually reversed. These results suggest that fishing put strong selective pressure for maturation at younger ages and smaller size, while the relaxation of fishing has resulted in selection for a return toward maturation at larger sizes.

We now turn our attention from the Atlantic ocean of eastern Canada to the Rocky Mountains of western Canada. Bighorn sheep live throughout the Rocky Mountains, and hunters pay thousands of dollars for a license allowing them to harvest an individual ram. Particularly desired by hunters are trophy rams; individuals which are particularly large with big horns (fig. 4.9*b*). David Coltman of the University of Alberta and colleagues from the Université de Sherbrooke, the Alberta Department of Sustainable Development, and the United States decided to explore the evolutionary consequences of trophy hunting in a population of bighorn sheep (Coltman et al. 2003). Coltman explored a dataset that contained the measurements of 192 harvested and unharvested rams between 1971 and 2002. This data set also contained information about the parents of all individuals, and thus patterns of paternity could be established. Both horn length and body size are heritable traits (h^2 = 0.69, 0.41 respectively), and larger values of both of these traits result in higher breeding values for those males. In other words, larger males with bigger horns are likely to sire more offspring than smaller males.

What might happen when hunters begin to kill those males with larger breeding values? As with cod, increased risk of mortality means that an individual is less likely to produce the number of offspring that he would in the absence of harvesting. As a result, the trait that used to confer a fitness advantage (size and horn length) now provides a fitness disadvantage and should become less common in the population through natural selection. This is in fact what Coltman and his colleagues found (fig. 4.11*a*); longevity decreased with horn-length breeding values, as did the number of paternities. Coltman also found that weight and horn-length breeding values decreased through the course of the study (fig. 4.11*b*). These results indicate that traits that historically conferred fitness benefits to males, such as enhanced size and larger horns, were becoming liabilities due to human-induced selection. What does this mean over the long-term? If these current trends continue, it is reasonable to expect to find this population dominated by smaller males with shorter horns.

(a)

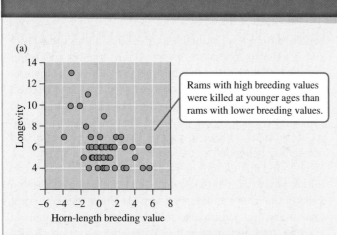

Rams with high breeding values were killed at younger ages than rams with lower breeding values.

(b)

Breeding values associated with weight and horn length have decreased over time.

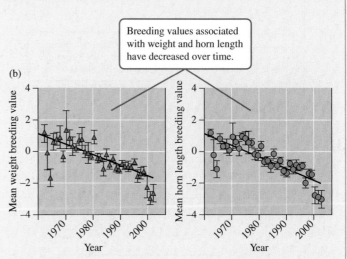

Figure 4.11 (*a*) Longevity decreases with increased horn-length breeding value of harvested rams. (*b*) Mean-weight and horn-length breeding values have decreased over the last 30 years of trophy hunting (data from Coltman 2003).

This may then decrease their attractiveness to hunters, relaxing this selection pressure. As you can see, evolution by natural selection is continuous.

All of these examples occurred through the intervention of people; however, the origin of selective pressures is irrelevant to the functioning of the mechanisms that cause evolution by natural selection to occur. What influences gene frequencies is whether there is a shift in the phenotype with the highest fitness, not why that shift has occurred. People can alter the fitness associated with different phenotypes in wild populations, and evolution occurs exactly as is predicted by theory. People cannot be thought of as distinct from the functioning of "natural" populations, for our actions alter the evolutionary trajectories of countless numbers of species. In fact, by understanding the evolutionary responses of different species to our actions, we may be better able to develop sustainable practices that decrease the likelihood of negative changes to natural population, such as fisheries collapses and loss of trophy rams.

and bank voles, *Clethrionomys glareolus*, which undergo regular population cycles in the study area, fluctuating in population density up to 50-fold over time. Because population fluctuations are not synchronized across large regions, some owl species in Finland lead nomadic lives, moving to areas where vole populations are on the increase and leaving areas where they are crashing. In contrast, Ural owls, which are monogamous, do not move in response to changing prey populations but stay in the pair's territory. Kontiainen and his colleagues describe them as "site tenacious."

During the course of their study, the research team made repeated size measurements of eggs laid by 344 female Ural owls in 878 clutches containing a total of nearly 3,000 eggs. The great variation in the owl's prey population combined with its site tenacity provided the research group with the opportunity to study the effects of the environment versus genetics on reproduction, including egg size. Based on measurements of eggs laid by 59 females in three phases of a vole population cycle (low, increasing, and decreasing), Kontiainen and his colleagues estimated that egg size is highly heritable in Ural owls, $h^2 = 0.60$. The finding that egg size is highly heritable was a critical element in their study, since it demonstrated that the trait is potentially subject to evolution by natural selection.

In other parts of the study, the research team explored the relationship of egg size to a variety of variables, which led to the discovery that egg size in the study population is undergoing stabilizing selection (fig. 4.12). Their results indicated two main selective factors: variation in hatching success and production of fledgling owls over a female's lifetime. The results showed that very small and very large eggs hatch at a lower rate compared to intermediate-sized eggs. Kontiainen and his colleagues also found that females that produced extremely small or large eggs produced fewer fledglings over the course of their lives, mainly because females producing eggs at the extremes of the size distribution had shorter reproductive lives. The result of these combined effects is stabilizing selection for egg size in this population of Ural owls. Elsewhere, ecologists have demonstrated directional selection in populations.

Evidence for Natural Selection: Rapid Adaptation by Soapberry Bugs to New Host Plants

Herbivores must overcome a wide variety of physical and chemical defences employed by their host. As a consequence, plants theoretically exert strong selection on herbivore physiology, behaviour, and anatomy. Nonetheless, few studies have documented the process of herbivore adaptation. A notable

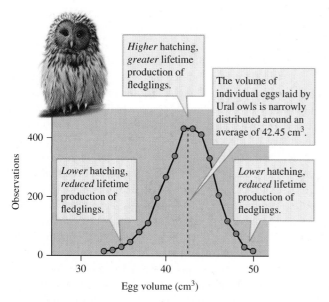

Figure 4.12 Stabilizing selection for egg volume in the Ural owl, *Strix uralensis.* Lower hatching rates by very small and very large eggs combined with reduced lifetime production of fledglings by female owls laying very small or very large eggs sustain stabilizing selection for egg volume in this population of Ural owls (data from Kontiainen et al. 2007).

exception is provided by studies of the soapberry bug and its evolution on new host plants.

The soapberry bug, *Jadera haematoloma,* feeds on seeds produced by plants of the family Sapindaceae. Soapberry bugs use their slender beaks to pierce the walls of the fruits of their host plants. To allow the bug to feed on the seeds within the fruit, the beak must be long enough to reach from the exterior of the fruit to the seeds. The distance from the outside of the fruit wall to the seeds varies widely among potential host species. As a result, there is likely strong selection within soapberry bug populations for beaks long enough to reach the seed of the particular species it feeds upon. If different bug populations feed upon different host plants, one would predict the average beak lengths to also differ among populations.

Scott Carroll and Christin Boyd (1992) reviewed the history and biogeography of the colonization of new host plants by soapberry bugs. Historically, soapberry bugs fed on three main host plants in the family Sapindaceae: the soapberry tree, *Sapindus saponaria* v. *drummondii,* in the south central region of the United States; the serjania vine, *Serjania brachycarpa,* in southern Texas; and the balloon vine, *Cardiospermum corindum,* in southern Florida. During the second half of the twentieth century, three additional species of the plant family Sapindaceae were introduced to the southern United States. The round-podded golden rain tree, *Koelreuteria paniculata,* from east Asia and the flat-podded golden rain tree, *K. elegans,* from southeast Asia are both planted as ornamentals, while the subtropical heartseed vine, *Cardiospermum halicacabum,* has invaded Louisiana and Mississippi. At some point after their introduction, some soapberry bugs shifted from their native host plants and began feeding on these introduced plant species.

Carroll and Boyd reconstructed the history of the colonization of the southern United States by new species of host plants and colonization of these new plants by soapberry bugs. Extensive historical museum collections of plants and insects allowed them to assemble the history of this host shift by an herbivorous insect. They were particularly interested in determining whether the beak length had changed in soapberry bugs that shifted from native to introduced host plants.

Figure 4.13 contrasts the fruit radius of native and introduced host plants in Florida and the south central United States. In Florida, the fruit of the native host plant *C. corindum* has a much larger radius than the fruit of the introduced *K. elegans* (11.92 mm versus 2.82 mm). In the south central United States, soapberry bugs shifting to introduced host plants faced the opposite situation. There, the fruit of the native *S. saponaria* has a smaller radius (6.05 mm) than the fruits of the introduced *K. paniculata* (7.09 mm) and *C. halicacabum* (8.54 mm).

Carroll and Boyd reasoned that if beak length was under natural selection to match the radius of host plant fruits, bugs

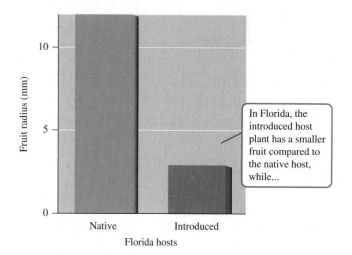

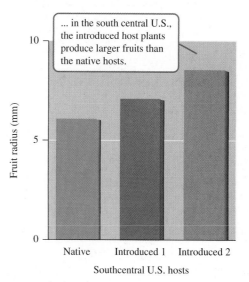

Figure 4.13 Comparison of the radius of fruits produced by native and introduced species of Sapindaceae (data from Carroll and Boyd 1992).

shifting to the introduced plants in Florida should be selected for reduced beak length, while those shifting to introduced hosts in the south central United States should be selected for longer beaks. Figure 4.14 shows the relationship between soapberry beak length and the radius of fruits of their host plants. As you can see, there is a close correlation between fruit radius and beak length.

At this point we should ask whether the differences in beak length observed by Carroll and Boyd might be developmental responses to the different host plants. In other words, are the differences in beak length due to genetic differences among populations of soapberry bugs, or were they induced by the different host plants? To test this, Carroll reared juvenile bugs from the various populations on alternative host plants. As it turns out, the differences in beak length observed in the field among bugs feeding on the various native and introduced host plants were retained in bugs that developed on alternative hosts. Here we have evidence for a genetic basis for interpopulational differences among soapberry bugs. Consequently, we can conclude that the differences in beak length documented by Carroll and Boyd were likely the result of natural selection for increased or decreased beak length.

Disruptive Selection in a Population of Darwin's Finches

As we have seen, the Galápagos Islands and their inhabitants played a key role in the development of Darwin's theory of evolution by natural selection. Darwin was particularly impressed by the variation in a group of 14 bird species now most commonly known as "Darwin's finches," or, less commonly, as "Galápagos finches." In the second edition of his journal recording his voyage on the *Beagle* (Darwin 1842b), Darwin suggests the influence of these birds on his thinking: "The most curious fact is the perfect gradation in the size of the beaks of the different species of *Geospiza* [a genus of Darwin's finches]—Seeing

this gradation and diversity of structure in one small, intimately related group of birds, one might really fancy that, from an original paucity of birds in this archipelago, one species had been taken and modified for different ends."

Darwin's musing anticipated the great contribution made by studies of his finches to our understanding of the evolutionary process. For instance, studies of the variation in beak size that caught Darwin's attention have revealed the importance of this trait to the feeding ecology of Darwin's finches. For instance, among species in the genus *Geospiza*, those with larger beaks are able to crack and feed on larger seeds. Studies of variation in beak size in populations of the medium ground finch, *Geospiza fortis*, have produced many notable discoveries. In a pioneering study of *G. fortis*, Peter Boag and Peter Grant (1978) showed that beak length, depth, and width are highly heritable, with heritability values of 0.62, 0.82, and 0.95, respectively. With this demonstration of heritability, Boag and Grant established a foundation for future evolutionary studies of beak size and form among Darwin's finches.

A recent study led by Andrew Hendry at McGill University provides one of the clearest and most complete examples of disruptive selection in a natural population. Andrew Hendry, Sarah Huber, Luis de León, Anthony Herrel, and Jeffrey Podos (2009) discovered that the *G. fortis* population at El Garrapatero, Santa Cruz Island, Galápagos, is dominated by two distinctive groups of individuals: those with small beaks and those with large beaks (fig. 4.15). Meanwhile, *G. fortis* with intermediate-sized beaks are relatively uncommon at El Garrapatero. Hendry and his colleagues uncovered the influences of disruptive selection in producing this distribution of beak sizes, when their studies revealed higher mortality, or possibly higher emigration, of birds with mid-sized beaks in this population. The researchers proposed that this higher mortality/emigration might be the result of either a lack of appropriate food for these birds and/or competition with the more abundant small- and large-beaked individuals in the population.

Ongoing studies have revealed important biological details, including the finding that disruptive selection on beak size at El Garrapatero is reinforced by nonrandom patterns of mate choice in the population. Nonrandom mating itself can be a source of evolutionary change in populations (see also chapter 8) because it violates one of the conditions for Hardy-Weinberg equilibrium. Darwin's finches choose mates at least partly on the basis of beak size and mating song. Since different species of Darwin's finches have beaks of different size and shape and sing different songs, individuals of different finch species rarely mate with each other. The *G. fortis* at El Garrapatero take this isolation one step further by mating preferentially within the population, with individuals choosing mates with similar-sized beaks. In other words, individuals in the population with small beaks mate preferentially with other small-beaked individuals, while large-beaked finches disproportionately choose mates that also have large beaks (de León et al. 2010). In addition, males in the population with different beak sizes

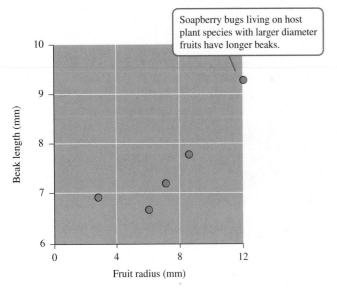

Soapberry bugs living on host plant species with larger diameter fruits have longer beaks.

Figure 4.14 Relationship between fruit radius and beak length in populations of native and introduced species of soapberry bugs (data from Carroll and Boyd 1992).

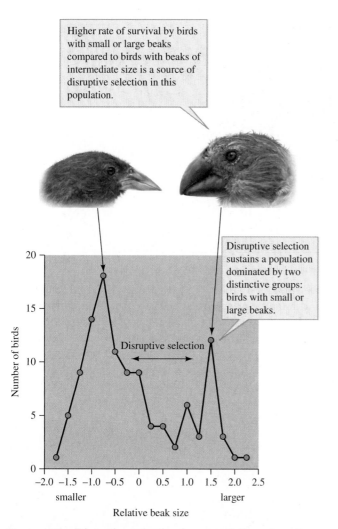

Figure 4.15 Disruptive selection in a population of medium ground finches, *Geospiza fortis*, at El Garrapatero, Santa Cruz Island, Galápagos (data from Hendry et al. 2009).

sing distinctive songs, which may reinforce nonrandom mating (Podos 2010). These recent studies have also shown that disruptive selection reinforced by nonrandom mate selection has produced genetic differences between small- and large-beaked *G. fortis* at El Garrapatero, which further underscores the evolutionary divergence between the two dominant beak morphs at that site.

Evolution Through Genetic Drift

While we may often think of evolutionary change as a consequence of predictable forces such as natural selection, which favour particular genotypes over others, allele frequencies also change as a consequence of random processes such as genetic drift. In fact, genetic drift occurs in all sexually reproducing populations at all times. However, the strength of drift and the resulting evolutionary change is much greater in small populations than in large ones. Here we will first discuss what genetic drift is, and then provide examples of how drift caused evolution in nature.

How Does Genetic Drift Occur?

Consider an individual that is heterozygous at a given locus (*Aa*). In the absence of any selection at this locus, one-half of the gametes produced will contain '*A*', and the other half will contain '*a*'. Now suppose this individual mates with another heterozygous individual, who also produces *A:a* gametes in a 1:1 ratio. If these two individuals produce an infinite number of offspring, this will result in genotypic frequencies of:

$$AA = 0.5(A) \times 0.5(A) = 0.25$$

$$Aa = 0.5(A) \times 0.5(a) + 0.5(a) \times 0.5(A) = 0.50$$

$$aa = 0.5(a) \times 0.5(a) = 0.25$$

The result contributed to the development of the Hardy-Weinberg principle, which states that in an infinitely large population mating at random in the absence of evolutionary forces, allele frequencies will remain constant over time. This principle is discussed in more depth online. The important point here is that in the absence of selection, gene frequencies in infinitely large populations will remain constant. In other words, without selection, genetic diversity will not be lost within a population.

However, what happens if two *Aa* individuals breed and produce only three offspring, rather than an infinitely large number of offspring? It should be immediately obvious that there is a problem. It is not possible to produce 25% *AA* offspring, 50% *Aa*, and 25% *aa* (the predictions of Hardy-Weinberg) when only three offspring are produced. As a result, the allelic frequencies among the offspring will not be exactly identical to the frequencies of the parents (1:1 *A:a*). This issue can be scaled up and extended to an entire population. Imagine that both '*A*' and '*a*' are present with a frequency of 0.5. With all individuals producing an infinite number of offspring, gene frequencies will not change from generation to generation. However, with a finite number of individuals producing a finite number of offspring, gene frequencies will change. This is evolution by genetic drift, and this is just as real a mechanism for evolution as is natural selection. In fact, genetic drift occurs on all loci within a genome, not only those upon which selection acts. A dominant factor that influences the rate of evolution due to genetic drift is population size, with drift causing more rapid evolutionary change in smaller populations (fig. 4.16). As we will discuss below, loss of genetic variation through drift is a significant concern for small populations, such as those often found in endangered species and on isolated habitats such as mountain tops and islands.

Genetic Drift in Chihuahua Spruce

One concern associated with human activities on the landscape is that reducing habitat availability will decrease the size of animal and plant populations to the point where genetic drift will reduce the genetic diversity.

Many natural populations have undergone fragmentation as a consequence of changing climates and natural habitat fragmentation. One of those is the Chihuahua spruce,

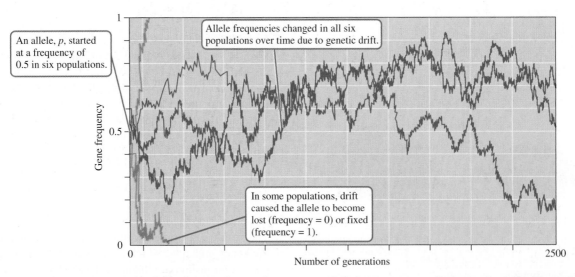

Figure 4.16   Random events cause allelic frequencies to change over time in a process called genetic drift. Here, three large populations (blue) and three small populations (green) each started with the frequency of an allele = 0.5. Even in the absence of selection, gene frequencies changed over time in all populations. However, the rate of change was much faster in the small populations. Note, too, that in the three small populations, random mating caused the allele to be lost in two populations and fixed in the third.

Picea chihuahuana, which is now restricted to the peaks of the Sierra Madre Occidental in northern Mexico. During the Pleistocene glacial period when the global climate was much cooler, spruce were found much farther south in Mexico and in more extensive populations. Today, all spruce populations in Mexico are restricted to small, highly fragmented areas of subalpine environment in the mountains of states of Chihuahua and Durango. On these high mountains, Chihuahua spruce live in an 800 km long band along the crest of the Sierra Madre Occidental at elevations between 2,200 and 2,700 m.

The Chihuahua spruce in the State of Chihuahua have been located and counted, with local populations ranging in size from 15 to 2,441 individuals. This situation presents itself as a natural experiment on the effects of population size and habitat fragmentation on genetic diversity in populations. The opportunity for such studies was pursued by a joint team of U.S. and Mexican scientists (Ledig et al. 1997). The researchers combined efforts to determine whether the Chihuahua spruce has lost genetic diversity as a consequence of reduced population size following climatic warming after the end of the last ice age. They were also interested in whether reduced genetic diversity may be contributing to continuing decline of the species and its potential for extinction.

Ledig and his colleagues found a significant positive correlation between population size and genetic diversity of their study populations. Figure 4.17 indicates that the smallest populations of Chihuahua spruce have much lower levels of genetic diversity than the largest populations.

It seems clear that drift is causing evolution and reducing genetic diversity in these populations of spruce. Many other researchers have shown similar patterns for other species of plants, as well as numerous species of animals. As we will see next, populations that colonize new areas are also likely to have low genetic diversity.

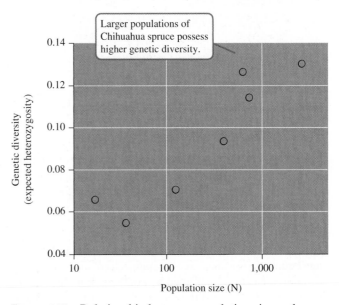

Figure 4.17   Relationship between population size and genetic diversity of Chihuahua spruce, *Picea chihuahuana*, populations (data from Ledig et al. 1997).

Founder Effect in Newfoundland Moose

The geographic range over which a species occurs changes through time. New populations establish for two principle reasons: (1) there is a change in climatic condition or habitat which allow a species to occupy a location that was previously uninhabitable for that species, and (2) individuals of a species colonize previously available but unoccupied (by that species) suitable habitat. In both cases, the initial outcome is the establishment of a very small population. As described above, small populations are most susceptible to genetic drift. The establishment of a new population, genetic drift, and low

genotypic diversity can lead to a **founder effect**. A founder effect can be defined as a decrease in genetic diversity associated with the formation of a new, small population. It is an extreme case of the effects of low population size on genetic diversity, and can be amplified through rapid genetic drift. An example of founder effects is provided by Hugh Broders, now at St. Mary's University, who led a team of researchers from Memorial University and the Newfoundland and Labrador Department of Forest Researcher and Agrifoods.

Moose, *Alces alces*, occur throughout the boreal forests of North America. Moose have lived in much of their range for thousands of years, while in other areas they are recent colonists. Broders reports that as of 1999, there were 150,000 moose in Newfoundland, with an additional 400,000 legally harvested since the late nineteenth century (Broders et al. 1999). This is not particularly surprising, until one learns that moose were historically absent from Newfoundland and Labrador, and that all of these moose are decedents of just three individuals brought over from Nova Scotia in 1878 and three individuals brought from New Brunswick in 1904 (Pimlott 1953). Cape Breton has historically had a moose population, until humans extirpated them through hunting. In 1947–48, 18 moose were brought in from Alberta to re-establish a Cape Breton population. Broders and his colleagues wanted to know what the effects of these small initial population sizes have been for the genetic diversity of moose.

To answer this question, Broders needed two things: (1) a way to measure genetic diversity within the recently established populations, and (2) other moose populations that could serve as a reference against which to compare observed genetic diversity. The rapid development of relatively inexpensive molecular tools has revolutionized the study of population genetics, leading to the development of the field of molecular ecology (see Ecological Tools and Approaches, this chapter). Broders was among the first to use these tools to address an issue of conservation concern, and he turned to microsatellites to quantify genetic diversity. Microsatellites are short, repeating sequences of DNA, also known as simple sequence repeats (SSR) and short tandem repeats (STR). For example, one microsatellite may be a sequence of the base pairs GTC (refer back to introductory biology!) repeated four times. The microsatellites used in ecological studies are generally non-coding, and thus not subject to selection. As a result, mutations will accumulate over time, resulting in different alleles within and between populations. More genetically diverse populations will have more individuals that are *heterozygous* at the microsatellite loci, while low genetic diversity will result in more *homozygosity* within the population.

Broders worked with hunters and wildlife officials in 11 regions in Alberta, Ontario, New Brunswick, Nova Scotia, and Newfoundland and Labrador to collect muscle samples from 563 moose. The researchers then extracted the DNA from these samples and used five polymorphic (multiple alleles) microsatellite loci to determine the genetic diversity of the different populations. There was strong evidence for a founder effect associated with the introduction of moose to Cape Breton and Newfoundland. Cape Breton moose had

14% less heterozygosity than the Alberta population, and the central Newfoundland population had 23% less heterozygosity than the New Brunswick population (fig. 4.18). These findings clearly show that colonization by few individuals comes at a cost of low genetic diversity. But what happens if these populations then serve as a source for yet another population? Broders was able to address this question as well, as individuals from the main Newfoundland population naturally colonized the Avalon Peninsula in SE Newfoundland. That daughter population had 30% less genetic diversity than the Newfoundland source population, and 46% less diversity than the original New Brunswick population (fig. 4.18).

Why should ecologist care about the genetic diversity of natural populations, and the effects of processes such as genetic drift and founder effects? Genetic diversity can impact the long-term sustainability of natural populations. Changes in climate, new diseases, and other stressors often require specific adaptations to allow individuals to cope. If a population is genetically homogenous, it is unlikely that novel solutions are lurking within the genomes of individuals, and thus the population is at greater risk of extinction as its environment changes. An example of the importance of genetic diversity can be found in the butterflies of Finland.

Genetic Diversity and Butterfly Extinctions

The landscape of Åland in southwestern Finland is a patchwork of lakes, wetlands, cultivated fields, pastures, meadows, and forest. Here and there in this well-watered landscape you can find dry meadows that support populations of plants, *Plantago lanceolata* and *Veronica spicata*, that act as hosts for

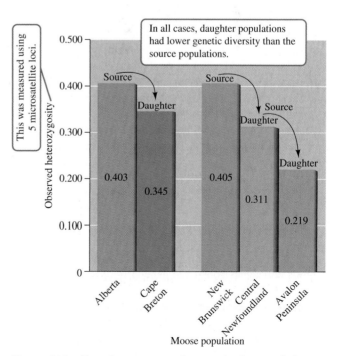

Figure 4.18 Founder events can be seen in the population genetics of moose in Newfoundland and Cape Breton. In both cases, daughter populations have lower genetic diversity than the source populations.

Figure 4.19 Long-term studies of the Glanville fritillary butterfly, *Melitaea cinxia*, have provided exceptional insights into the relationship between population size and genetic diversity.

the Glanville fritillary butterfly, *Melitaea cinxia* (fig. 4.19). The meadows where *Melitaea* lives vary greatly in size, and *Melitaea* population size increases directly with the size of meadows. Careful studies of these populations by Ilka Hanski, Mikko Kuussaari, and Marko Nieminen (1994) showed that small populations of *Melitaea* living in small meadows were most likely to go extinct.

Several factors likely influence the greater vulnerability of small populations to extinction. However, what role might genetic factors, especially reduced genetic variation, play in the vulnerability of small populations to extinction? Richard Frankham and Katherine Ralls (1998) point out that one of the contributors to higher extinction rates in small populations may be **inbreeding**. Inbreeding, which is mating between close relatives, is more likely in small populations. Combining already low genetic variation in small populations with a high rate of inbreeding has several negative impacts on populations, including reduced fecundity, lower juvenile survival, and shortened life span, and it further accelerates the loss of genetic diversity.

Ilik Saccheri and colleagues (1998) reported one of the first studies giving direct evidence that inbreeding contributes to extinctions in wild populations. Saccheri and his colleagues studied 1,600 dry meadows and found *Melitaea* in 524, 401, 384, and 320 of the meadows in 1993, 1994, 1995, and 1996, respectively. Over this period they documented an average of 200 extinctions and 114 colonizations of meadows annually. To determine the extent that genetic factors, especially inbreeding, may contribute to these local extinctions, Saccheri and his colleagues conducted genetic studies on populations of *Melitaea* in 42 of the meadows. Similar to what Broders and his colleagues did in their studies of moose, Saccheri and colleagues used microsatellite loci to estimate heterozygosity in the butterflies. Here, the researchers used the level of heterozygosity within each meadow population as an indicator of inbreeding, with low heterozygosity indicating high levels of inbreeding.

The results of the study indicated that influence of inbreeding on the probability of extinction was very significant. It turned out that the populations with the highest levels of inbreeding (lowest heterozygosity) had the highest probabilities of extinction. Saccheri and his colleagues found a connection between heterozygosity and extinction through effects on larval survival, adult longevity, and egg hatching. Females with low levels of heterozygosity produced smaller larvae, fewer of which survived to the winter dormancy period. Pupae of mothers with low heterozygosity also spent more time in the pupal stage, exposing them to greater attack by parasites. In addition, adult females with low heterozygosity had lower survival and laid eggs with a 24% to 46% lower rate of hatching. These effects have the potential to reduce the viability of local populations of *Melitaea* that are made up of individuals of low heterozygosity (low genetic variation), and increase their risk of local extinction.

We have seen how small population size and isolation can influence the genetic structure of populations of many kinds of organisms, including the Chihuahua spruce isolated in cool moist microenvironments in the mountains of Mexico and the Glanville fritillary, *Melitaea*, in the dry meadow environments of southwestern Finland. In situations like these, chance plays a significant role in determining the genetic structure of populations.

CONCEPT 4.2 REVIEW

1. If you observe no changes in gene frequencies in a population over several generations, can you conclude that the population is not subject to natural selection?
2. What factors can lead to low genetic diversity within a population?
3. Can a trait with no heritability ($h^2 = 0$) evolve? Explain.
4. What must have been true for beak length in soapberry bug populations before new species of soapberry plants were introduced into the United States?

4.3 Speciation

Physical and ecological processes interact with selection and drift to produce new species. Natural selection and genetic drift are two mechanisms that can cause dramatic changes in gene frequencies within a population. Such evolutionary changes have obvious implications for interactions among individuals within the larger ecological community. For example, selection toward larger body size in a predator may alter the intensity of predation experienced by the prey. What we have not yet discussed is what happens over even longer time scales, where large changes in gene frequencies can result in the evolution of a new species. Species are the raw material for all ecological interactions, and thus

any process that can alter the rate of speciation has significant ecological consequences. In this section we will discuss a variety of mechanisms that can cause speciation. However, before we can discuss how species evolve, we must first have an understanding of what we mean by species.

What Is a Species?

This at first may seem like a trivial question, but in fact this issue is at the heart of substantial disagreement among researchers. Originally, groups of individuals that shared similar morphologies were grouped together as members of a single species. This approach was championed by Carolus Linnaeus (later known as Carl von Linné), who is responsible for the Linnaean classification system that is currently used by many biologists. At the essence of this approach lies the concept of Platonic idealism in which there is a single truth that is unchanging. By extension, under the Linnaean system, species were discrete units that were constant through time.

Although this morphological approach is still widely used and is the principle form of species identification for amateur naturalists everywhere, it is not the definition of species most used by ecologists and evolutionary biologists. Instead, the most widely used definition of species is the **biological species concept**, presented by Ernst Mayr in 1942. Mayr defined species as "groups of actually or potentially interbreeding populations, which are reproductively isolated from other such groups" (Mayr 1942). This definition of species is not based upon arbitrary descriptions of morphology nor based upon patterns of occurrence. Instead, this is based upon a real (and measurable) ecological concept: reproductive isolation.

Even with this seemingly precise definition of species, we run into some troubles when we look at the population genetics of natural species. Over large geographic areas, an **ecocline** (or **cline**) will exist for some species. An ecocline is a gradual change in genotype and/or phenotype of a species over a large geographic area. Individuals of a species on opposite ends may appear quite different from each other; however, there is no specific location at which individuals "became" different. Other species may consist of a number of distinct ecotypes, a genetically identifiable subclass of a species that has evolved in response to local environmental conditions. If genetically distinct enough, ecotypes can eventually be designated as subspecies, or even separate species.

Although the biological species concept is the one most people are familiar with, and one that works well for organisms such as vertebrates and arthropods, it is a poor definition of species for many of the organisms that exist on the planet. Many bacteria, fungi, and even plants rarely interbreed, even within individuals from the same species. Instead, reproduction is often asexual. Additionally, many species readily form viable hybrids with individuals of other species. In these situations, the biological species concept breaks down. If a particular species of fungi consists of many genotypes, none of which ever interbreed, does this mean that each genotype is its own species? If individuals of different species are able to

produce a viable offspring just once, is that enough to declare them to be of a single species? There are no clear answers, though there are many alternative species concepts that are independent of reproduction. For example, the *phylogenetic species concept* defines species based upon evolutionary history and phylogenetic similarity. There is growing support for this concept. The increased focus on microbial organisms by ecologists, coupled with the increased availability of molecular methods, will likely allow this species concept to become more common over the next decade. A more exhaustive discussion of alternative species concepts is beyond the scope of this book. For now, we will simply pretend we never even asked the question, and instead try to distract you by talking about sex.

What Is Reproductive Isolation?

As you see from Mayr's definition of species, a critical requirement is reproductive isolation between populations. What is not clear, however, is how you go from having a single population of interbreeding individuals of a single species to two populations of reproductively isolated individuals, and thus two species. To answer this, we need to identify the mechanisms that can cause reproductive isolation.

Isolating mechanisms can be roughly categorized into two groups, pre- and postzygotic isolating mechanisms (fig. 4.20). Prezygotic isolating mechanisms are processes that prevent two individuals from forming a zygote. Postzygotic isolating mechanisms are equally efficient at maintaining species integrity, but they occur after a zygote has been formed.

How do two individuals actually produce a zygote? Though this is the sort of question discussed in grade 4 health class, discussion of sex may be equally relevant to university-level ecology students. Two individuals need to find each other, they both need to be sexually receptive at the same time, they need to engage in certain behaviours that allow for mating, their reproductive organs need to be compatible, and the sperm and egg need to be able to fuse. Things can go wrong at any of these steps, and thus there are a variety of possible prezygotic isolating mechanisms. Ecological isolation occurs when two individuals are physically separated,

Essential steps to producing offspring

	Step	Isolating Mechanism
Prezygotic	Find a mate	Ecological
	Both be fertile	Temporal
	Give & receive mating cue	Behavioural
	Mate & form zygote	Mechanical
Postzygotic	Zygote & embryonic development	Hybrid inviability
	Production of grandchildren	Hybrid sterility

Figure 4.20 Reproductive isolation can occur from a diversity of pre- and postzygotic isolating mechanisms.

such that they are unable to encounter each other. This could be as extreme as being isolated on different continents, or more subtle such as being restricted to different heights within a single forest canopy. Temporal isolation occurs when individuals are fertile at different times, such that even if they do encounter each other, they are not both producing viable gametes. Behavioural isolation is found in many animal species that require specific behaviours by one or both partners prior to mating (see chapter 9). Even if both individuals are fertile and appear in the same location, they may not mate if the proper behavioural cues have not been received by one or both individuals. Mechanical isolation can be as obvious as the two individuals having reproductive plumbing that simply does not fit together; you cannot get a square peg into a round hole. Mechanical isolation can also be more subtle, such as an inability of one plant's pollen tube to grow through the style of another, or if plants use different pollinators.

Suppose two individuals have made it through all of these potential isolating mechanisms and formed a zygote. There exist a variety of postzygotic isolating mechanisms that can be equally effective at preventing the production of a viable offspring. Hybrid inviability results if zygotic development is abnormal and the developing hybrid dies prior to sexual maturity. Hybrid sterility occurs if the hybrid develops normally, but is unable to produce viable gametes.

Figure 4.20 summarizes the steps that must occur for the production of a viable offspring. Evolution can cause changes anywhere along this pathway, and if these changes are of a sufficient magnitude, reproductive isolation can occur and lead to speciation. What factors influence the evolution of the isolating mechanisms?

What Causes Speciation?

The Hardy-Weinberg principle shows that under a certain set of restrictive assumptions, gene frequencies will not change over time. However, in real-world populations, both genetic drift and natural selection can cause significant shifts in gene frequencies. If this occurs for a trait that influences reproduction, reproductive isolation can occur. We generally divide speciation into three forms: allopatric, parapatric, and sympatric.

Allopatric, or *geographic*, **speciation** occurs when a single population becomes spatially subdivided into multiple subpopulations (fig. 4.21). How does a population become spatially subdivided? The most obvious example would be if a mountain range divides a previously contiguous area, and if it is impossible for individuals of a species to cross that divide. The appearance of a mountain or river may seem unlikely to occur in ecological timescales, but these events do occur in the deeper scales of geologic and evolutionary time. Faster processes of geographic isolation are also possible, such as the formation of a new river, island, or lake. A second form of speciation, **parapatric speciation**, occurs when a population expands into a new habitat within the pre-existing range of the parent species. For example, individuals of a forest-dwelling species may possess mutations that allow them to live within

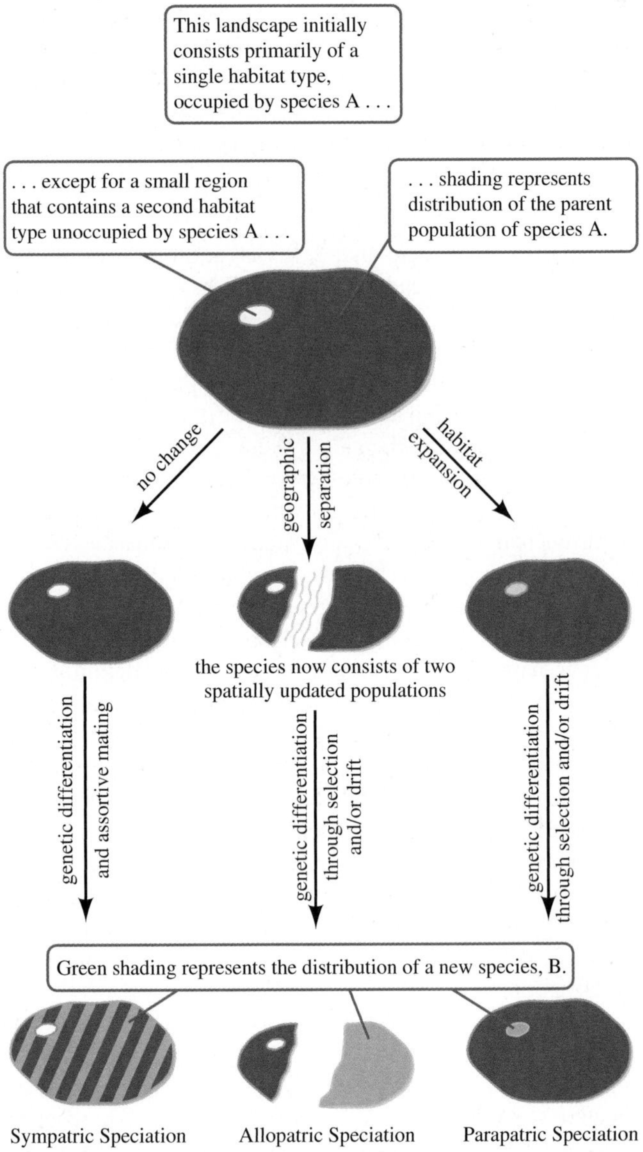

Figure 4.21 Speciation can be sympatric, allopatric, or parapatric. In all three cases, reproductive isolation among subpopulations needs to occur; however, the mechanisms that cause this isolation will differ.

the grassland areas on the landscape. If these subpopulations do not interbreed, reproduction isolation may evolve, leading to speciation.

In both allopatric and parapatric speciation, the evolution of reproductive isolation could occur through drift or natural selection. Since genetic drift is random, fluctuations in allele frequencies in subpopulations will be independent, and thus loss of genetic diversity through drift could lead to reproductive isolation. Alternatively, many geographic barriers may alter the local environment, or many new habitats within a landscape may contain a new microclimate. In such cases, there could be differential selective pressures on the subpopulations, and genetic differentiation could occur. If this influences a trait related to the production of a viable offspring, reproductive isolation and speciation can occur.

Sympatric speciation has historically been more controversial among ecologists and evolutionary biologists, with many believing it does not occur. In sympatric speciation, a single parent population forms genetically distinct subpopulations without any geographic barrier or spatial isolation (fig. 4.21). It is unlikely that genetic drift is important in sympatric speciation, and instead it is natural selection that drives this process. The most common model for sympatric speciation is that there exists disruptive selection for some trait (fig. 4.7), resulting in groups of individuals that differ greatly in phenotype even within a single population. If this is coupled with **assortative mating**, genetic differentiation can occur, leading to the evolution of reproductive isolation. What is assortative mating? In assortative mating, individuals may choose as mates individuals that are similar to themselves (positive assortative mating), or individuals that are different (negative assortative mating). It is positive assortative mating that is likely to lead to sympatric speciation. For example, if an insect chooses to mate only with individuals that feed upon the same host plant, there is the potential for genetic differentiation within the insect population based upon host plant selection.

In recent years, there has been renewed interest among evolutionary ecologists in understanding speciation and testing these models of speciation. This interest has been sparked in part because the development of readily available and inexpensive genetic tools has allowed the collection of data previously unavailable (see the Ecological Tools section). In addition, there is widespread interest in the fate of the world's biodiversity, and understanding the causes of speciation is just as important as understanding the causes of extinction. Next we will discuss two studies that are examples of current efforts in understanding whether ecological divergence can lead to reproductive isolation and speciation.

Reproductive Isolation and Ecological Divergence

Allopatric speciation through genetic drift is fairly easy to understand, and does not even require any ecology for it to occur! Instead, it simply requires a population to be split and random events can then cause reproductive isolation. In this section, we discuss issues more relevant to this book: how does ecology influence speciation?

Central to many models of speciation we have discussed is the idea that a diversity of habitats within the range of a species can lead to reproductive isolation. As subpopulations diverge ecologically, reproductive isolation and speciation may occur. This can be reworded into a testable prediction: Increased ecological divergence will be associated with increased reproductive isolation (fig. 4.22). Dan Funk and colleagues (Funk et al. 2006) decided to conduct a broad test of this prediction. They wanted to examine the widest number of species possible, and so dug through a variety of previously published data sets. Each data set contained pairs of closely related species, whose degree of pre- and postzygotic

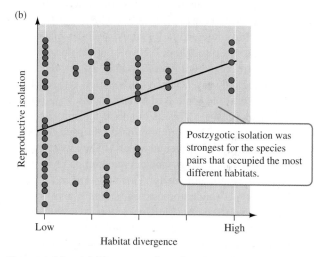
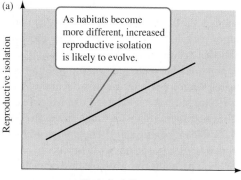

Figure 4.22 (*a*) Theory predicts that the strength of reproductive isolation should increase with increasing habitat divergence between closely related species. (*b*) This pattern was found for most groups of organisms by Funk et al. (2006), with the results from angiosperm plants presented here.

reproductive isolation was identified. Funk and colleagues then went through hundreds of additional studies and gathered information on the habitat that each species was generally found in, such as altitude, vegetation type, and moisture. The research team used a variety of statistical approaches to determine the average difference in habitats (divergence) between two species, and was able to conduct a series of regression analyses to determine whether habitat divergence was associated with reproductive isolation. In total, the data sets used contained over 500 species pairs, including plants, insects, birds, fish, and frogs. Using both parametric and nonparametric tests for correlations (Appendix A), they found that the more different the habitats were, the more reproductively isolated the pairs of related species were (fig. 4.22). This study lends support to a central prediction of several theories that suggest ecological interactions influence speciation by natural selection. Additional support for the role of natural selection in causing speciation comes from a team of researchers from Canada, Japan, and the United States (McKinnon et al. 2004).

One of the particularly strong examples of natural selection at work is the process of **parallel evolution**, in which species in similar habitats, but geographically isolated, evolve

similar traits. Genetic drift is a random process, and so it is unlikely to produce similar changes in isolated populations. Parallel speciation is a logical extension of this concept, in which the traits that result in reproductive isolation evolve similarly in populations subjected to similar conditions and selective pressures. Dolph Schluter and his lab at the University of British Columbia have conducted extensive research on this issue, focusing their efforts on small fish called sticklebacks (fig. 4.23; *Gasterosteus* spp.). There currently exists a diversity of *Gasterosteus* species, which occupy marine and freshwater habitats, with the freshwater species derived from the andadromous threespine stickleback (*Gasterosteus aculeatus*). Andadromous fish are those that migrate from the ocean into rivers, breeding in freshwater. This stickleback species is particularly interesting for study, as it has marine and stream populations throughout the world, often co-occurring. McKinnon and colleagues (2004) wanted to know to what extent ecological divergence plays in the early stages of speciation. To do this, they collected fish from marine and stream populations in Alaska, British Columbia, Iceland, Scotland, Norway, and Japan. They brought these fish back to the lab and placed them in experimental aquaria. They were particularly interested in knowing which combinations of individuals would, or would not, mate. Their experimental factors included ecotype (andadromous or stream) and location (same or different region). McKinnon and colleagues found a much greater level of mating compatibility between individuals of the same ecotype, regardless of whether they were from the same area or from areas separated by thousands of kilometres (fig. 4.24). In other words, reproductive isolation occurred based upon ecological differentiation, and not primarily geographic isolation.

What trait likely caused this result? It appears there has been divergent selection between habitats, resulting in the stream ecotypes being much smaller than the andadromous ecotypes. Additionally, there was strong evidence for size-assortative mating in which females were less likely to mate with males of very different sizes. As we discussed

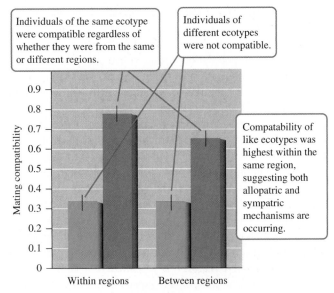

Figure 4.24   Mating compatibility between different ecotypes collected from populations located throughout the world (data from McKinnon et al. 2004).

previously, divergent selection coupled with assortative mating are expected to be preconditions for sympatric speciation. Overall, this study provides strong evidence that changes in the ecology of an organism can lead to reproductive isolation of sympatric populations. Additionally, because stream ecotypes were smaller than the andadromous ecotypes in numerous geographic regions, it suggests that similar habitats can apply similar evolutionary pressures, allowing for parallel evolution to occur.

These studies by Funk and McKinnon show that many of the assumptions and predictions made by current models of speciation through natural selection are supported by ecological data. We are a long way from understanding all of the conditions necessary for speciation to occur, leaving much opportunity for the next generation of ecologists. At the core of understanding speciation is the need to understand and identify genotypic and phenotypic variations within and across species. In the next section, we discuss many of the ecological tools that allow scientist to explore the genetic basis of variation.

Figure 4.23   The threespine stickleback (*Gasterosteus aculeatus*) has been used as a model organism for the study of evolutionary ecology.

CONCEPT 4.3 REVIEW

1. Reproductive isolation effectively eliminates many individuals as possible mates for each other. Is this likely to influence the fitness of the isolated individuals? Explain.
2. Allopatric, sympatric, and parapatric speciation can all occur in the same location at the same time. How?
3. What ecological processes are likely to speed up, or slow down, the rate of speciation?

ECOLOGICAL TOOLS AND APPROACHES

Integrating Population Genetics and Ecology

The molecular revolution has hit ecology, and it is now common for ecologists to use traditional field methods, advanced quantitative analyses, as well as molecular techniques to help them answer their research questions. The blending of molecular biology and ecology is most pronounced among evolutionary ecologists. These approaches have become so popular, and the answers to questions so important that new subdisciplines have been formed, including *molecular ecology* and *conservation genetics.*

We have already discussed a few studies that have used molecular methods to answer ecological questions, including Broder's studies of moose and Saccheri's studies of butterflies. In both cases, the researchers used one tool, *microsatellites,* to measure genetic diversity within a population. But exactly *why* are microsatellites (or some other DNA-based method) required to answer these questions? Prior to the molecular revolution, the best method to measure genetic variability within a population was to measure protein variability, or more specifically, *isozymes.* Isozymes are different forms of an enzyme caused by different gene sequences, and thus populations with more isozymes are ones that are more genetically diverse—at least for that protein. However, many sequence variations do not result in different isozymes, and thus there could be genetic diversity not measured by protein studies. In protein studies, the researcher is generally limited to measuring one or a small number of proteins. In DNA studies, the research can measure dozens of microsatellites, or even thousands of bases pairs if they are using gene sequences, both of which allow for enhanced detection of genetic variability. Finally, DNA studies require very small amounts of tissue, while protein studies require relatively large samples. Because of this, molecular methods allow ecologists to use samples from smaller organisms, or even just tufts of hair from larger organisms. For example, the grizzly bears of Glacier National Park are being counted and mapped using the DNA in hair that the bears leave on scratching trees and on baited hair traps (USGS 2000).

To obtain sufficient quantities of DNA for analysis, such as that contained within a hair follicle, biologists generally use one of two techniques to amplify the quantity of DNA present in a sample. DNA is usually cloned either by using bacteria and recombinant DNA technology, or it can be amplified by a procedure called polymerase chain reaction, or PCR (Hillis et al. 1996). During the PCR process, short, single-stranded DNA is used as primers for DNA synthesis. Each primer is highly specific for a given nucleotide sequence and can be used to amplify a specific locus or gene.

Once a sufficient quantity of DNA has been obtained, the sample may be analyzed in several ways. One commonly applied method uses **restriction enzymes**, enzymes produced naturally by bacteria to cut up foreign DNA. Restriction enzymes cut DNA molecules at particular places called **restriction sites**. Because restriction sites are determined by a specific sequence of base pairs on the DNA molecule, differences in number and location of restriction sites reflect differences in DNA structure. When exposed to a particular restriction enzyme, a given DNA molecule will be broken up into a series of DNA fragments of precise number and lengths. The number and lengths of DNA fragments, called **restriction fragments**, are determined by the number and location of restriction sites for a particular restriction enzyme. Therefore, if DNA samples from different organisms exposed to the same restriction enzyme yield different numbers and lengths of DNA fragments, we can conclude that those organisms differ genetically.

Restriction fragments are still used by ecologists, though they are losing popularity as newer, more powerful tools become available (and affordable). We have already discussed one such tool, microsatellites. As we mentioned, these are short repeating sequences of DNA. All species will have a large number of microsatellite loci, but not all will be useful to the ecologist. To measure genetic variability within a population, the ecologist needs to find microsatellite loci that are variable within the population, rather than loci that are fixed for all individuals. This process involves substantial lab work, though the publication of microsatellites for a given species are then a valuable research tool for other ecologists around the world.

An even more sensitive, though not yet as widely used, tool for measures of genetic variability are **single nucleotide polymorphisms**, or **SNPs** (pronounced "snips"). SNPs are a powerful tool as they represent single base pair changes within a region of DNA, rather than the presence/absence of an entire microsatellite allele, restriction fragment, or protein. The ability to detect single base pair differences is relatively new for ecologists, and has not yet been widely used. However, like all other aspects of molecular biology, the costs are rapidly decreasing and the power of SNPs will likely let them be more useful to ecologists in the near future.

The approach that gives the highest resolution picture of the genetic makeup of individuals and populations is **DNA sequencing**. Because sequencing reveals the sequence of nucleic acids along DNA molecules, this tool gives the ultimate genetic information. The number of DNA sequences described is increasing rapidly and our ability to interpret and compare DNA sequence data is also increasing at an impressive rate (Hillis et al. 1996). While the human genome project has assumed centre stage (DOE 2000), the genomes of hundreds of other species are also completely described, and many more will be soon. As we will show next, DNA sequencing is a valuable tool for ecologists, even when single genes, rather than the entire genome, are analyzed.

Species Identification

One area where molecular methods are strongly influencing ecological research is the ability to quickly and reliably identify species. In 2003, Paul Hebert of the University of Guelph suggested it would be possible to create a unique DNA "barcode" for species (Hebert et al. 2003). Just as actual barcodes allow anyone to rapidly determine information (e.g., price and identity) of any item in a grocery store, a DNA barcode could provide information about species. The basic idea is that each species contains sequences of DNA that are unique to it, and no other species on the planet. Hebert's idea has inspired scientists to make his vision a reality. The Biodiversity Institute of Ontario, located at the University of Guelph, is home to the Canadian Centre for DNA Barcoding, where they conduct the basic research needed to develop accurate barcodes. This centre works closely with others around the world through initiatives such as the Barcode of Life Initiative and the International Barcode of Life Project (fig. 4.25).

There are a variety of reasons why such efforts are urgently needed. First, accurate ecological studies often require species identification, and it simply is not practical to think each ecologist will also be an expert in species identification. This is particularly an issue for researchers of diverse groups, such as insects, bacteria, and fungi. In theory, the DNA barcode system would allow an ecologist to extract a DNA sequence for a specimen collected in the field, compare it to sequences in a large database, and find its species name. Such a database would be a significant help to ecological field studies. A second need for

DNA barcodes comes as the result of one of the great tragedies of modern scientific funding: a nearly worldwide decline in taxonomic expertise in universities and museums. Because of this, fewer and fewer people are able to accurately identify specimens collected in the field. If DNA barcodes existed for many taxonomic groups, there would be reduced demand for taxonomic experts. However, DNA barcodes are likely to be most effective when combined with continued support for taxonomy. For example, the barcode database is only as good as the data it contains. Taxonomists are needed to add new species, to verify existing records, and to provide guidance when molecular methods provide ambiguous results. Hebert's DNA barcodes are a great example of how continually developing molecular methods may fundamentally alter ecological research.

One complication of natural systems is that species boundaries are not always as discrete as we might imagine. Instead, species may breed with other species, resulting in fertile offspring. Here, molecular tools are also critical for ecologists, allowing them to understand the frequency and potential conservation concerns of gene flow among species.

When Species Boundaries Are "Fuzzy"

Hebert and his colleagues are using molecular methods to help identify species collected by scientists around the world. However, molecular methods have shone a light on a reality of nature—species boundaries are not always distinct, and individuals of different species can hybridize. Hybridization is the production of viable offspring from the mating to individuals

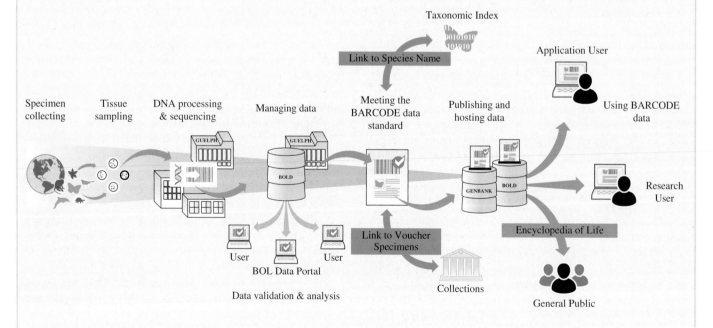

THE BARCODING PIPELINE

Figure 4.25   The Barcode of Life project (http://www.barcodeoflife.org/) is set up to process large numbers of samples from both fresh and preserved specimens. This project has the potential to help identify a large number of the unknown specimens ecologists obtain through field collections. (Consortium for the Barcode of Life, Smithsonian Institution)

of different species. If hybridizations are rare, one can typically ignore them as one-off events. However, if they are common in the wild, they present a significant challenge to the biological species concept. A related conservation concern is the introgression of genes from one species into another. Introgression is the movement of genes from one distinct gene pool into another. Over time, introgression can result in movement of specific traits from one group to another, or even a homogenization of the two gene pools. Ecologists are particularly concerned about introgression when the genes of domesticated species enter the gene pools of wild species. As you may realize, the best way to know whether hybridization and/or introgression has occurred is to study the DNA, and directly determine whether there has been a mixture of DNA among species.

James Mallet has published a review of studies that have documented hybridization among wild species (Mallet 2008). Though comprehensive lists of hybridization are not yet available for most taxonomic groups, Mallet was able to show that hybridization in the wild can be quite common (fig. 4.26). Up to 25% of the vascular plant species of Great Britain are documented to hybridize, and even 6% of the mammals of Europe have been shown to form viable hybrids. Mallet points out that hybridization can lead to speciation, and may be responsible for over 50% of the known diversity of vascular plants. At a minimum, these rates of hybridization suggest boundaries between species are more exact in most introductory biology textbooks than they are for wild populations. Ecologists need to be aware of the "fuzziness" of species boundaries, and be prepared for specimens that cannot be identified by barcode nor a taxonomic key. Hybrids can be found even among iconic species, such as polar bears. In 2006, a polar bear × grizzly

Taxon	Location	Fraction of species with hybrids (%)
Vascular Plants	Great Britain	25
Butterflies	Europe	16
Birds	Worldwide	9
Mammals	Europe	6

Figure 4.26 A survey of published reports suggest hybridization is common in the wild.

hybrid was shot and killed in the Northwest Territories. Though initial identifications were varied, molecular analyses confirmed its hybrid status. Another putative hybrid was shot as recently as Spring 2010. As climate change continues, grizzly bears are expected to become more common in the Arctic. Bears are not the only well known group of species to form hybrids. Coywolves, hybrids of coyote and wolves, appear to be quite common throughout eastern North America. More generally, sympatric ranges between species that can interbreed is likely to lead to increased rates of hybridization. Whether this will become frequent enough to lead to speciation, or to cause a breakdown of existing species designations, is not yet known.

A fundamental component of modern agri- and aquaculture is development of economically viable genetic stocks of the desired species, be they canola, wheat, or salmon. The genetic stocks can be produced through highly controlled breeding programs, as well as the deliberate introduction of novel genes to a species. One role of ecologists is to understand and determine whether these novel genes have escaped the farms and entered wild species. Once again ecologists turn to molecular methods, and unfortunately, such gene introgression is occurring in many locations of Canada. For example, a team of researcher from Agriculture and Agri-Food Canada have found a gene for herbicide tolerance has moved from a crop species, *Brassica napus* (Canola), into its wild relative, *Brassica rapa* (Warwick et al. 2008). Another team of researchers from Université Laval, the United States, and Norway have shown there is great potential for the introgression of genes from farm-raised Atlantic salmon, *Salmo salar*, into wild populations (Garant et al. 2003).

Though it was not ecologists who allowed such gene introgression to occur, it is ecologists to whom society is turning to determine the consequences of such gene flow, and whether anything can be done about it. The pictures of gene flow are not nearly as shocking as an open well at the bottom of the gulf of Mexico, but the implications may be even more far reaching, threatening both agriculture and the stability of species. The field of molecular ecology is rapidly evolving, providing better, less expensive methods at a rapid rate. These tools will be invaluable to this and future generations of ecologists.

SUMMARY

Although they did not work together, the twin visions of Darwin and Mendel revolutionized biology. The synthesis of the theory of natural selection and genetics gave rise to modern evolutionary ecology. Here we examine four major concepts within the area of population genetics and natural selection.

4.1 Phenotypic variation among individuals in a population results from the combined effects of genes and environment.

The first biologists to conduct thorough studies of phenotypic and genotypic variation and to incorporate experiments in their studies focused on plants. Clausen, Keck, and Hiesey explored the extent and sources of morphological variation in plant populations, including both the influences of environment and genetics. Molecular genetic studies, such as those conducted by Douglas and Brunner on whitefish populations in the Alps,

offer a powerful way of assessing the genetic variation in populations.

4.2 Changes in gene frequency within a population can occur through both natural selection and random processes such as genetic drift.

Natural selection can lead to changes in gene frequencies within populations (directional and disruptive selection), or can be a conservative force impeding change (stabilizing selection). These three forms of selection differ as a function of which phenotypes are favoured. In directional selection one extreme is favoured, in stabilizing selection the average phenotypes is favoured, and in disruptive selection, both extremes are favoured. In all types of selection, the rate of evolution increases with the strength of the selective force. There is abundant evidence from a variety of species showing that natural selection is a continuous process, occurring in extant species. Natural selection can cause shifts in feeding morphology associated with colonization of a new habitat as found in the studies of soapbugs. Evolution also occurs by the random process of genetic drift. Although drift occurs continuously in all populations, it is a greater evolutionary force in small populations, where chance events can impact a greater proportion of the individuals of the population. In populations of Chihuahua spruce, small populations were associated with lower levels of genetic diversity, attributed to loss through drift. A lack of genetic diversity is also associated with increased risk of local extinctions, as was found for populations of the Glanville fritillary butterfly.

4.3 Physical and ecological processes interact with selection and drift to produce new species.

Both natural selection and genetic drift can cause reproductive isolation to occur between populations of a single species. Reproductive isolation can occur at both prezygotic and postzygotic stages, through changes in location, timing, behaviour, morphology and physiology, and development pathways. Reproductive isolation is a necessary condition for speciation. Speciation can occur within a single location (sympatric speciation), when a population is geographically separated (allopatric speciation), or when a species extends into a new habitat (parapatric speciation). Increased habitat divergence is positively correlated with increased reproductive isolation, suggesting the current ecology of organisms can influence the likelihood of speciation. Ecological similarity can cause parallel evolution in geographically distinct populations, and assortative mating can lead to sympatric speciation.

The molecular revolution has allowed ecologists to ask more detailed questions about the nature of species and the movement of genes from one group to another. A number of tools are available, including the use of restriction fragments, microsatellites, and gene sequencing. These tools are being used to develop DNA barcodes, potentially leading to an easily accessible catalogue of biological diversity. The use of molecular methods has also revealed that species boundaries are not as discrete as commonly assumed. Hybridization rates can be very high, and many species show introgression of genes from captive into wild species.

REVIEW QUESTIONS

1. Contrast the approaches of Charles Darwin and Gregor Mendel to the study of populations. What were Darwin's main discoveries? What were Mendel's main discoveries? How did the studies of Darwin and Mendel prepare the way for the later studies reviewed in chapter 4?

2. How did the studies of phenotypic plasticity conducted by Douglas and Brunner complement the earlier studies of Clausen, Keck, and Hiesey?

3. What is genetic drift? Under what circumstances do you expect genetic drift to occur? Under what circumstances is genetic drift unlikely to be important? Does genetic drift increase or decrease genetic variation in populations?

4. Suppose you are a director of a captive breeding program for a rare species of animal, such as Siberian tigers, that are found in many zoos around the world but are increasingly rare in the wild. Design a breeding program that will reduce the possibility of genetic drift in captive populations.

5. Colonization of new habitat brings with it certain genetic risks. How can these risks be reduced if a large population, rather than a small population, establishes in a new area?

6. How might the distribution of beak sizes in the medium ground finch population differ from that shown in figure 4.15, if mate choice in the population was random with respect to beak size?

7. What are main advantages of using DNA-based methods in studies of genetic diversity relative to protein-based methods?

8. DNA barcoding will not be effective if traditional taxonomists no longer exist. Why?

9. Suppose you are in charge of constructing the harvesting rules for a large fishery. How could you use information on changes in body size and age of maturity as potential indicators of the effects of harvesting on the population? Would you expect to see different impacts of harvesting on these traits if you only harvest post-reproductive individuals?

10. Much like the case with Santa Claus, some people do not believe in sympatric speciation. What ecological conditions would make sympatric speciation more likely to occur? What evidence could an ecologist collect that would support, or refute, a claim that a particular species is the result of sympatric speciation?

For more information on the resources available from McGraw-Hill Ryerson, go to **www.mcgrawhill.ca/he/solutions**.

INDIVIDUALS

I n section II we discuss how individual organisms interact with their local surroundings. As a foundation for these discussions, we present the concepts of allocation and ecological trade-offs. Three dominant factors that influence individuals are temperature, water, and the need for energy and nutrients. An organism's physiology (chapters 5, 6, and 7) and behaviour (chapter 8) influence its ability to cope with its environment and neighbours. The total set of strategies, abilities, and limitations of an individual species is described as its life history, and will determine the shape of its niche (chapter 9).

Chapter 5   Temperature Relations

Chapter 6   Water Relations

Chapter 7   Energy and Nutrient Relations

Chapter 8   Behavioural Ecology

Chapter 9   Life Histories and the Niche

TEMPERATURE RELATIONS

CHAPTER 5

CHAPTER CONCEPTS

5.1 Macroclimate interacts with the local landscape to produce microclimatic variation in temperature.

Concept 5.1 Review

5.2 Adapting to one set of environmental conditions generally reduces fitness in other environments.

Concept 5.2 Review

5.3 Most species perform best in a fairly narrow range of temperatures.

Ecology In Action: Impacts of Stream Temperature on Salmon Recruitment

Concept 5.3 Review

5.4 Many organisms have evolved ways to compensate for variations in environmental temperature by regulating body temperature.

Concept 5.4 Review

5.5 Organisms exhibit a diversity of mechanisms to cope with extreme temperatures.

Concept 5.5 Review

Ecological Tools and Approaches: Climatic Warming and the Local Extinction of a Land Snail

Summary

Review Questions

Many organisms regulate the temperature of part of, if not their entire, body. For example, at least one plant of the arctic tundra regulates the temperature of its reproductive structures. Peter Kevan, of the University of Guelph, went to Ellesmere Island to study sun-tracking behaviour by arctic flowers. It was summer, there was little wind, and at 82° N latitude, the sun stayed above the horizon 24 hours each day. As the sun's position in the arctic sky changed, one of the common tundra flowers, *Dryas integrifolia* (fig. 5.1), tracked its movement across the sky.

Kevan found that by following the sun, *Dryas* increased the temperature of its flowers. Though the air temperature hovered around 15°C, the temperature of the *Dryas* flowers was nearly 25°C. Kevan discovered that the flowers act like small solar reflectors; their parabolic shape reflects and concentrates solar energy on the reproductive structures. He also observed that many species of small insects, attracted by their warmth, basked in the sun-tracking *Dryas* flowers, elevating their body temperatures as a consequence (fig. 5.1). *Dryas* depends on these insects to pollinate its flowers.

How do *Dryas* and its insect visitors benefit from their basking behaviours? How does cloud cover affect the temperature and sun-tracking behaviour of *Dryas* flowers? These are the kinds of questions addressed by Kevan (1975) and other ecologists who study the ecology of temperature relations, one of the most fundamental aspects of ecology. In the cold regions of the North, and more southerly hot deserts, shallow lakes and streams, and most everywhere in between, temperature is a major factor influencing the growth of individuals and the distributions of species.

Why are ecologists so concerned about how temperatures influence ecological interactions? Small differences in temperature can be associated with greatly altered performances of enzymes and organisms. Extreme temperatures can cause discomfort, reduced fitness, and even death. Long-term changes in temperature have set entire floras and faunas marching across continents, some species thriving, some holding on in small refuges, and others becoming extinct. Areas now supporting temperate species were at times tropical and at other times the frigid homes of reindeer and woolly mammoths. The dynamic environmental history of the earth has become more significant as we face the reality of rapidly rising global temperatures.

We defined ecology as the study of the relationships between organisms and their environments. In chapter 5 we examine the relationship between organisms and temperature, one of the most important environmental factors and one of the most relevant in the face of today's rapidly changing climate.

5.1 Microclimates

Macroclimate interacts with the local landscape to produce microclimatic variation in temperature. As we saw in chapter 2, temperatures are extremely variable across the planet in both space and time. For instance, which is warmer, Regina, Saskatchewan, or Tofino, British Columbia? The answer is going to depend first upon the question of "when"? Tofino is generally warmer than Regina in the winter, but cooler in the summer. This answer is also going to depend upon the answer of "where"? Are you standing on the open coastline of Tofino but under an aspen stand in Regina? As you will see in this section, the actual temperatures an individual encounters will be strongly influenced by the fine details of the local environment, and by the behaviour of the individual.

Microclimate is a fundamental aspect of environmental variation. What do we mean by macroclimate and microclimate? **Macroclimate** is what weather stations report and what we represented with climate diagrams in chapter 2. Macroclimate is determined by the global patterns of air and water circulation, and other forces, also described in chapters 2 and 3. **Microclimate** is climatic variation on a scale of a few kilometres, metres, or even centimetres, usually measured over short periods of time. You acknowledge macroclimate when you decide what clothes to pack on a summer camping trip; you acknowledge microclimate when you choose to stand in the shade on a summer's day or in the sun on a winter's day. Macroclimate and microclimate can be substantially different, and for organisms that live out their lives in very small areas, macroclimate may be less important than microclimate. Microclimate is influenced by landscape features such as altitude, aspect, vegetation, colour of the ground, and presence of boulders and burrows. The physical nature of water reduces temperature variation in aquatic environments.

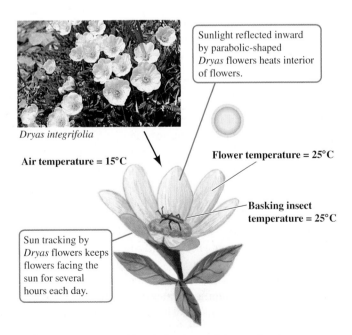

Dryas integrifolia

Sunlight reflected inward by parabolic-shaped *Dryas* flowers heats interior of flowers.

Air temperature = 15°C

Flower temperature = 25°C

Basking insect temperature = 25°C

Sun tracking by *Dryas* flowers keeps flowers facing the sun for several hours each day.

Figure 5.1   Sun-tracking behaviour of the arctic plant, *Dryas integrifolia*, heats the reproductive parts of its flowers, making them attractive to pollinating insects. This species is found in many Canadian arctic and alpine habitats.

Altitude and Aspect

As we saw in chapter 2, temperatures are generally lower at high elevations. Along the elevational gradient presented in

Figure 5.2   The north-facing slope at this site supports a Mediterranean woodland, while the vegetation on the south-facing slope is mainly grassland.

figure 2.37, average annual temperature is 11.1°C at 1,660 m compared to −3.7°C at 3,743 m. Lower average temperatures at higher elevations are a consequence of several factors. First, because atmospheric pressure decreases with elevation, air rising up the side of a mountain expands. The energy of motion (kinetic energy) required to sustain the greater movement of air molecules in the expanding air mass is drawn from the surroundings, which cool as a result. A second reason that temperatures are generally lower at higher elevations is that there is less atmosphere to trap and radiate heat back to the ground.

Topographic features such as hills, mountains, and valleys create microclimates that would not occur in a flat landscape. Mountains and hillsides create these microclimates by shading parts of the land. In the Northern Hemisphere, the shaded areas are on the north-facing sides, or *northern aspects*, of hills, mountains, and valleys, which face away from the equator. In the Southern Hemisphere, the *southern aspect* faces away from the equator.

You can see the effect of aspect, in miniature, around buildings. If you want to warm yourself on a sunny winter's day in the Northern Hemisphere, go to the south side of a building, to its southern aspect, which faces the equator. In the Southern Hemisphere, you would generally find the warmest spot on the north side of a building. Similarly, the northern and southern aspects of mountains and valleys offer organisms contrasting microclimates. The microclimates of north- and south-facing aspects of hillsides may support very different types of vegetation (fig. 5.2).

The greater density of oaks and shrubs on the north-facing slope shown in figure 5.2 is paralleled in miniature on north- and south-facing dune slopes in the Negev Desert, where north-facing slopes support a higher density of crust-forming mosses. A group of earth scientists from Hebrew University Jerusalem documented a possible physical basis for the differences in moss cover. Why? The north-facing dune slopes

are cooler: 7.8°C to 9.2°C cooler at midday in winter and 1.8°C to 2.5°C cooler at midday in summer (Kidron, Barzilay, and Sachs 2000). Further, north-facing slopes remain moist approximately 2.5 times longer than south-facing slopes following rainfall, suggesting both temperature and moisture interact to affect plant growth.

Vegetation and Ground Colour

Because they also shade the landscape, plants both create and respond to microclimates. Trees, shrubs, and *plant litter* (fallen leaves, twigs, and branches) produce ecologically important microclimates in many communities. For example, the desert landscape, which often consists of a mosaic of vegetation and bare ground, is also a patchwork of sharply contrasting thermal environments. Such a patchwork is apparent near Kemmerer, Wyoming, a cold desert much like the Gobi in Mongolia. Kemmerer can be bitterly cold in winter and blistering hot in summer. On one summer's day, Robert Parmenter and his colleagues (1989) measured the temperatures in various parts of the landscape. They found that while the temperature on bare soil soared to 48°C, a few metres away in plant litter under a tall shrub the temperature was only 21°C (fig. 5.3). Meanwhile, temperatures under low shrubs with less leaf area were a bit warmer but still not as hot as soil in the open. A small organism in this landscape could choose microclimates differing in temperature by 27°C!

Two additional factors that can affect temperature are the colour of the ground and the presence of any covering, such as vegetation or snow (fig. 5.4). Cover and colour influence microclimates through their effects on the local **albedo**, the reflectivity of the landscape. Objects that appear white reflect all visible colours and have a high albedo. Objects that appear black absorb all visible colours and have a low albedo. Vegetation is generally green, which means it absorbs some colours and reflects others, resulting in an albedo between white and black.

Albedos are not fixed properties of landscapes, and instead will change as local conditions change, resulting in changes in the local temperature. For example, snow cover reflects large amounts of light, resulting in a cooling effect (fig. 5.5). When snow melts, the underlying soil will generally have a lower albedo and absorb more light energy, causing local warming. As a result, any change in snow cover can have cascading effects on local temperatures. Over larger areas, decreased snow cover across much of the landscape, potentially associated with global climate change, has the potential to further enhance the warming that is currently occurring. In an era of changing climates, particularly in the snow-covered regions of the world, these changes in albedo are likely to have significant impacts on regional climate. Even more locally, small-scale human-induced changes, such as deforestation and transition from peatlands to forests, also alter albedo, with potentially cascading impacts on temperatures.

Soil surface in full sun heats to high temperatures.

Shading of soil surface by low shrubs lowers maximum temperatures.

A layer of leaf litter lowers maximum temperatures even more.

Greater leaf area and numerous twigs of tall shrubs intercept more light, creating the coolest temperatures.

| 48°C in bare soil away from shrubs | 29°C in litter under low shrub | 27°C in soil under low shrub | 21°C in litter under tall shrub | 23°C in soil under tall shrub |

Figure 5.3   Desert shrubs create distinctive thermal microclimates in the desert landscape (data from Parmenter, Parmenter, and Cheney 1989).

(a)   (b)   (c)

Figure 5.4   Ground cover and colour such as shown here in (*a*) white sand, (*b*) black sand, and (*c*) snow in Nunavut, alter the local albedo, causing altered microclimates. High albedos are found in white snow and white sand, with low albedos found in dark sand and other dark soils.

Presence of Boulders and Burrows

Many children soon discover that the undersides of stones harbour a host of organisms seldom seen in the open. This is partly because the stones create distinctive microclimates. E. B. Edney's classic studies (1953) of the seashore isopod *Ligia oceanica* documented the effect of stones on microclimate. Edney found that over the space of a few centimetres, *Ligia* could choose air temperatures ranging from 20°C in the open to 30°C in the air spaces under stones, which heated to between 34°C and 38°C.

Animal burrows also have their own microclimates, in which temperatures are usually more moderate than outside ambient conditions. For example, the Eurasian badger, *Meles meles*, constructs extensive burrows, called *setts*. In a study of temperatures inside and outside of several setts on farmland, Moore and Roper (2003) found that setts generally had average temperature fluctuations of less than 1°C each day, while surface temperatures generally varied by 9°C daily. Over an entire year, there was only a 10°C variation within setts, while more than 20°C variation outside. Moore and Roper also found that setts occupied by a badger were on average 2.5°C warmer than unoccupied setts, highlighting the fact that organisms themselves can alter their own microclimates.

Aquatic Temperatures

As we saw in chapter 3, air temperature generally fluctuates more than water temperature. However, though individual

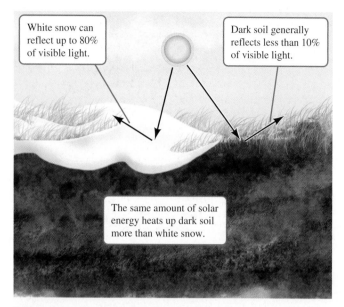

White snow can reflect up to 80% of visible light.

Dark soil generally reflects less than 10% of visible light.

The same amount of solar energy heats up dark soil more than white snow.

Figure 5.5 By reflecting most visible light, snow creates a much cooler microclimate than nearby bare ground.

locations are often thermally stable, differences in topography, distance to land, and chemical properties contribute to substantial spatial variation in microclimates within aquatic systems.

The thermal stability of the aquatic environment derives partly from the high capacity of water to absorb heat energy without changing temperature (a capacity called *specific heat*). This capacity is about 3,000 times higher for water than for an equal volume of air. It takes approximately 1 calorie of energy to heat 1 cm³ of water 1°C. For an equal volume of air, this temperature rise requires only about 0.0003 calories.

A second cause of thermal stability in aquatic environments is the large amount of heat absorbed by water as it evaporates (which is called the *latent heat of vaporization*). This amounts to approximately 584 calories per gram of water at 22°C and 580 calories per gram of water at 35°C. So, 1 g of water evaporating from the surface of a desert stream, a lake, or a tide pool at 35°C draws 580 calories of heat from its surroundings. From the definition of a calorie, this is enough energy to cool 580 g of water 1°C. The evaporation of even small amounts of water can result in significant cooling, and thus the water in a desert stream can be a cool relief to the hot temperature of the air.

A third cause of the thermal stability of aquatic environments is the heat energy that water gives up to its environment as it freezes (the *latent heat of fusion*). Water gives up approximately 80 calories as 1 g of water freezes because the energy of motion of water molecules decreases as they leave the liquid state and become incorporated into the crystalline latticework of ice. So, as 1 g of pond water freezes, it gives off sufficient energy to heat 80 g of water 1°C, thus slowing further cooling. The aquatic environments with greatest thermal stability are generally large ones, such as the open sea. These environments store large quantities of heat energy and daily fluctuations are often less than 1°C. Even the temperatures of small streams, however, usually fluctuate less than the temperatures of nearby terrestrial habitats (fig. 5.6).

There are, of course, limits to the thermal stability of aquatic systems. One of the most obvious examples is what you feel if you dive deep into a lake or ocean. Water temperatures generally decrease with depth, due in part to reduced penetration of solar radiation (chapter 3). Other factors besides

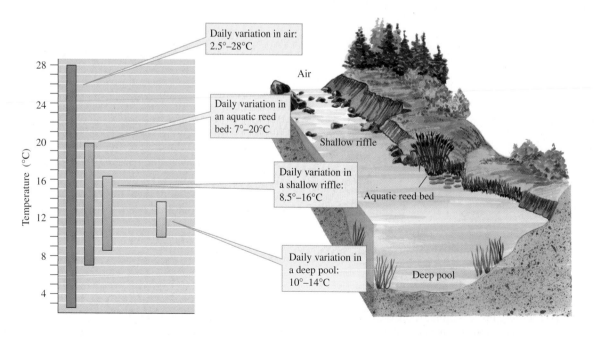

Figure 5.6 Aquatic microclimates: aquatic environments generally show less temperature variation compared to terrestrial environments (data from Ward 1985).

the physics of water and light can affect the temperature of aquatic environments. **Riparian vegetation**, vegetation that grows along rivers and streams, influences the temperature in streams in the same way that vegetation modifies the temperature of desert soils—by providing shade. Shading by riparian vegetation reduces temperature fluctuations by insulating the stream environment, with important consequences for the many animals that live within the stream (see Ecology in Action, this chapter).

Changes in temperature in aquatic environments will have two major consequences. First, there will be the direct effects of altered temperatures on the organisms living in the water (described later in the chapter). Second, and often of greater importance in aquatic systems, is the effect that changes in temperature have on the amount of dissolved oxygen in the water. Recall that in chapter 3, we emphasized that low oxygen levels were a hazard for organisms living in the water. Many aquatic organisms, such as most fish, use *dissolved oxygen*, rather than gaseous oxygen. Cold water holds more dissolved oxygen than warm water, and thus increases in water temperature can pose both a direct thermal stress as well as induce oxygen-limiting conditions for some aquatic species.

CONCEPT 5.1 REVIEW

1. What advantages might the warm microenvironments of *Dryas* flowers offer to the insects attracted to them?
2. Contrast the microclimates of the leaves and roots of a tree in the boreal forest in summer.
3. Why is thermal stability greater in large, rather than small, bodies of water?

5.2 Evolutionary Trade-Offs

Adapting to one set of environmental conditions generally reduces fitness in other environments. Imagine an organism that is not only capable of living in any environment, but thrives in all environments. In the language of evolution, such an organism would have high fitness across all environmental conditions. In everyday language, we might refer to such a life form as a "super" organism. Whatever we might call them, however, such life forms do not, as far as we know, exist. All known organisms are adapted to a limited range of environmental conditions, at least partially as a consequence of energy limitation.

The Principle of Allocation

All organisms have access to limited energy supplies. This simple idea has significant implications for our understanding of the ecology of individuals. We introduce the concept of

energy limitation here and will examine it again in chapter 7. One consequence of energy limitation is that energy allocated to one of life's functions, such as reproduction, defence against disease, or growth reduces the amount of energy available for other functions. Darwin appreciated the implications of energy limitation and included it in his writings. However, Richard Levins was the first to use a mathematical approach to analyze the evolutionary consequences of such trade-offs, which he referred to as the principle of allocation (Levins 1968). In his book *Evolution in Changing Environments,* Levins concluded that as a population adapts to a particular set of environmental conditions, its fitness (see chapter 4) in other environments is reduced.

Testing the Principle of Allocation

Demonstrating the evolutionary trade-offs proposed by the principle of allocation has been challenging. In fact, a direct test of the principle has been nearly 40 years in coming. The major difficulty with all such evolutionary questions is the time required for performing evolutionary experiments with living organisms. Albert Bennett and Richard Lenski solved this time problem by studying evolution of microbial populations (Bennett and Lenski 2007), which can go through hundreds of generations in a week. The central question of their work was whether adaptation to a low temperature (20°C) would be accompanied by a loss of fitness at a high temperature (40°C). Their working hypothesis was that they would observe just such a trade-off in fitness, a prediction that follows directly from Levins's principle of allocation.

Bennett and Lenski's experiments focused on 24 different lineages of the bacterium *Escherichia coli*. These lineages were derived from a single ancestral strain of *E. coli* that had been grown at 37°C (human body temperature) for 2,000 generations. Bennett and Lenski used this ancestral strain to establish six replicate populations at four temperature regimes: constant 32°C, 37°C, and 42°C, and daily alternation between 32°C and 42°C. They maintained these 24 populations at these temperatures for 2,000 generations, sufficient time for each population to adapt to its particular temperature regime. (Evolutionary research involving so many generations is only feasible with microbial populations, since they have short generation times. For example, the generation time for *E. coli* growing at 40°C is approximately 20 minutes!) Bennett and Lenski next used bacterial cells from each of their 24 populations to establish 24 new populations, which were all grown at 20°C for 2,000 generations, theoretically adapting to this relatively low temperature in the process.

To address their original question (Will adaptation to a low temperature [20°C] be accompanied by a loss of fitness at a high temperature [40°C]?), Bennett and Lenski compared the fitness of the low-temperature-selected line with the fitness of the ancestral line at 20°C and at 40°C. Their measure of fitness was the rate of population doubling of a selected line of *E. coli* compared to that of its ancestral line, when the two lines were grown together. Two major results stand out. First, the lines grown at 20°C had *higher* (positive) *fitness*

at 20°C temperature compared to their immediate ancestors. In other words, Bennett and Lenski showed that their lines grown at 20°C for 2,000 generations had indeed adapted to that lower temperature. However, the lines that had adapted to 20°C had, on average, *lower* (negative) *fitness* compared to their immediate ancestor, when grown at 40°C. Therefore, as predicted by the principle of allocation, selection for higher fitness at 20°C had been accompanied by an average loss in fitness at higher temperatures (fig. 5.7).

Bennett and Lenski's results provide the first direct experimental evidence in support of Levins's principle of allocation. This principle, in turn, offers an explanation for the observation that most organisms perform best under a limited range of environmental conditions, including thermal conditions.

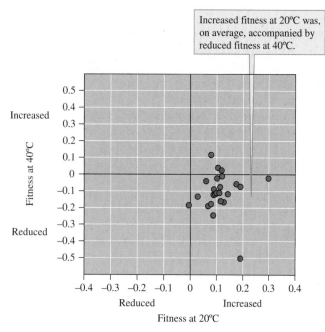

Figure 5.7 *Escherichia coli* grown at 20°C for 2,000 generations showed increased fitness at that temperature compared to ancestral lines, which were adapted to higher temperatures. However, they had reduced fitness at 40°C compared to ancestral lines (data from Bennett and Lenski 2007).

CONCEPT 5.2 REVIEW

1. If growing lines of *Escherichia coli* at 20°C for 2,000 generations increased their fitness at 20°C without reducing their fitness at 40°C, how would the distribution of points in figure 5.7 change?

2. If your research team obtained the hypothetical results described in question 1, what could you conclude about the principle of allocation?

5.3 # Temperature and Performance of Organisms

Most species perform best in a fairly narrow range of temperatures. Ecologists concerned with the ecology of individual organisms study how environmental factors, such as temperature, water, and light, affect the physiology and behaviour of organisms: how fast they grow; how many offspring they produce; how fast they run, fly, or swim; how well they avoid predators; and so on. We can group these phenomena and say that ecologists study how environment affects the "performance" of organisms. Victor Shelford was an influential ecologist active in the early 1900s who studied the link between species distributions and their physiology. His studies led him to propose the **law of toleration** (Shelford 1911): the abundance and distribution of an animal can be determined by the deviation between the local conditions (e.g., temperature) and the optimum set of conditions for a species. Shelford was among the first to explicitly link the ability of a species to tolerate local environmental conditions, and its range and abundance.

What led Shelford to this conclusion? He was able to recognize from his own research, and from that of others, that the performance of organisms generally varies as a function of differences in temperature, moisture, light, nutrient availability, and other environmental conditions. At extreme levels of any of these factors, many species are unable to survive. At severe levels, species may survive, but not thrive. At more moderate levels, growth and reproduction may be highest. In other words, the performance of most species is greatest in a fairly narrow range of environmental conditions (fig. 5.8).

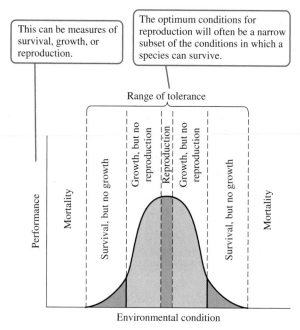

Figure 5.8 An individual's performance can be limited by environmental conditions, such as temperature. According to the law of toleration, species abundances will tend to be largest in areas with environmental conditions most similar to the performance optima for a species.

The entire range of conditions (e.g., temperature) over which a species is able to survive in is called its **range of tolerance**. What do you imagine will be the consequences for individuals living just on the edge of their range of tolerance?

Temperature and Animal Performance

Let's begin our discussion of temperature and an organism's overall performance by looking at a simpler situation: the influence of temperature on enzyme function. Because enzymes must match the shape of the substrate upon which they act, they must assume a specific shape for proper function. Most enzymes have a rigid, predictable shape at low temperatures, but rates of chemical reactions tend to be low at these low temperatures. Also, rigidity does not help an enzyme perform its function. Their functioning often depends upon flexibility, the ability to assume another shape after binding with the substrate. Enzymes have greater flexibility at higher temperatures, but excessively high temperatures destroy their shape. Temperatures at either extreme thus impair the functioning of enzymes.

Enzymes usually work fastest in some intermediate range of temperatures, where they retain both proper shape and sufficient flexibility. In other words, there is usually some optimal range of temperatures for most enzymes. How might you determine the optimal temperature for an enzyme? One way is to determine the minimum concentration of substrate required for an enzyme to work at a particular rate. If this concentration is low, the enzyme is performing well, that is, the enzyme has a high affinity for the substrate. The affinity of an enzyme for its substrate is one measure of its performance.

ECOLOGY IN ACTION

Impacts of Stream Temperature on Salmon Recruitment

The family Salmonidae consists of both trout and fish we generally refer to as salmon. Canada is home to many species of wild salmon, living in both the Atlantic and Pacific oceans (though some lakes are also home to salmon). Ecological research has identified that changes to the vegetation surrounding the spawning grounds of salmon can alter the thermal environment of the streams. These temperature changes have significant impacts on the health of individual salmon species, as well as commercial and recreational fishing.

Most species and populations of wild salmon are **anadromous**, meaning the adults live primarily in the ocean and then move into fresh waters to spawn. After the eggs hatch, the developing fry initially feed and grow in the streams, eventually migrating to the ocean. Adults have the tendency to return to their own birthing grounds to spawn, a fact that is both part of the mythology of salmon as well as a potential threat to their populations as industrial development grows around a number of previously isolated spawning grounds.

Salmon are important in Canada for a number of reasons. Culturally, the vision of these fish swimming in a clear coastal river, surrounded by a large and intact forest, is an image etched into the minds of generations of Canadians (fig. 5.9). Recreationally, salmon are valued by anglers, to the extent that many areas are regularly stocked with salmon with the desire by some to establish new populations, or at least provide anglers with more fish to catch. Finally, the harvest of wild salmon results in significant economic gains for British Columbia, though reduced salmon stocks are associated with a decrease in landings and value. At a recent peak in 2004, 386,000 tonnes of wild salmon were harvested, for a wholesale value of $220,000,000. In 2008, this decreased to 51,000

Figure 5.9   Many salmon spawning grounds, such as the Little Qualicum River in British Columbia, consist of water surrounded by forest.

tonnes landed for a value of $135,000,000 (Province of British Columbia 2010).

Because of these reasons, and others, there has been extensive research conducted on the factors that influence the health of wild salmon populations. One fact that has emerged is that a variety of human activities cause significant changes to the thermal environment of the spawning streams, with negative consequences for many populations.

Like all organisms, salmon have upper lethal temperatures, above which mortality occurs (fig. 5.8). These lethal upper temperatures vary among species and life-stage. However, the mature ocean-living stage is likely at limited risk from changes in temperature. Why? As you recall from earlier in

this chapter, the thermal properties of water reduce temperature variation relative to terrestrial habitats, and large bodies of water (oceans) exhibit less variation than small bodies of water (streams).

As a result, although the ocean-living stage of salmon may suffer other sources of mortality (e.g., fishing), its physiological ecology with respect to temperature is not of significant concern. In contrast, it is the egg and juvenile stages of salmon, both of which are found in streams, that appear to be most at risk due to human activity. The issue here is not just one of survival, but also one of reproduction. As we saw earlier in the chapter, there is generally a unimodal relationship between temperature and performance, with reproduction happening only in a narrow range of temperatures, even though survival can occur in a larger range (fig. 5.8). For example, Chinook Salmon have an upper lethal temperature of around 25°C, have zero growth above 19°C, an upper spawning threshold of 16°C, and exhibit maximum growth at around 15°C (McCullough 1999). In other words, increases in temperature do not have to kill a fish to put its population at risk, and even minor changes to stream temperatures can reduce, or prevent, reproduction. However, not all streams are equal, and they can vary greatly in size. Spawning grounds located in the smallest streams in the headwaters will be most sensitive to change. Why?

One factor that can influence stream temperature is logging activity. In small streams, trees often overhang the water, reducing light penetration to the water surface. If the vegetation is completely removed, there is a clear and immediate increase in stream temperature. For example, Steve MacDonald, of what is now called Fisheries and Oceans Canada, and his colleagues at Simon Fraser University, found that stream temperatures can be raised by 4°C–6°C, even five years after logging (MacDonald et al. 2003). The temperature changes can be in part mitigated by logging management practices, such as maintaining an unharvested buffer zone along the stream edge. However, MacDonald shows that trees in these buffers are very susceptible to wind damage, reducing their effectiveness over time.

Humans influence stream temperatures in a variety of other ways, including the construction of dams. Dams used to generate electrical power generally result in varied stream flows, depending upon the electrical needs at any point in time. As a result, there will be substantial variation in stream depths and temperatures, as a function of how much water is being released through a dam. At a scale even greater than individual dams and streams, changes to climate associated with global warming may be increasing stress for Atlantic salmon populations.

In Newfoundland, salmon rivers are closed to anglers on days in which river flow is low and river temperatures are high, out of concern that angling will further decrease the sustainability of Atlantic salmon populations. Brian Dempson and his colleagues at Fisheries and Oceans Canada found that the frequency of stream closures due to these "environmental" reasons has increased over the last decade (Dempson et al. 2001), suggesting an increase the in the frequency of warm waters that could put these fish populations at risk.

As an indicator of the importance of the thermal environment to the performance and survival of salmon, recent work by Erika Eliason and colleagues at the University of British Columbia, along with colleagues from Fisheries and Oceans Canada, has found evidence for physiological adaptation in sockeye salmon (Eliason et al. 2011). Specifically, Eliason and her team found that the optimal temperatures for a number of cardiac and aerobic measures varied as a function of the historical temperatures of migratory rivers. They suggest that continued increases in summer temperatures can result in further adaptations within populations. Interestingly, different populations appear to differ in their abilities to adapt to higher temperatures, with potential consequences for these fish in the future. As we found in chapter 4, wild populations are not static, but instead ecological interactions in a changing environment can cause local adaptation.

Salmon are but one example of a group of species whose abundance can be influenced by changes in temperature. The ideas of upper and lower lethal temperatures are not abstract ecological concepts, but instead are critical pieces of information needed to understand how species will respond to continued human-mediated changes. Indirect effects of human activity have significant consequences for a diverse set of species, and it is the role of many ecologists to understand why and to work with government and industry to develop solutions to reduce the risk to natural populations.

Peter Hochachka, formerly of the University of British Columbia, was one of Canada's leading zoologists. He had a diverse research program, with a particular emphasis on adaptational biochemistry. One line of his research program involved the influence of temperature on the activity of acetylcholinesterase, an enzyme produced at the synapse between neurons. This enzyme promotes the breakdown of the neurotransmitter acetylcholine to acetic acid and choline and so turns off neurons, a process critical for proper neural function. In one study, Baldwin and Hochachka (1970) found that rainbow trout, *Oncorhynchus mykiss*, produce two forms of acetylcholinesterase. One form has highest affinity for acetylcholine at 2°C, that is, at winter temperatures. However, the affinity of this enzyme for acetylcholine declines rapidly above 10°C. The second form of acetylcholinesterase shows highest affinity for acetylcholine at 17°C, at summer temperatures. However, the affinity of this second form of acetylcholinesterase falls off rapidly at both higher and lower temperatures. In other words, the optimal temperatures for the two forms of acetylcholinesterase are 2°C and 17°C (fig. 5.10).

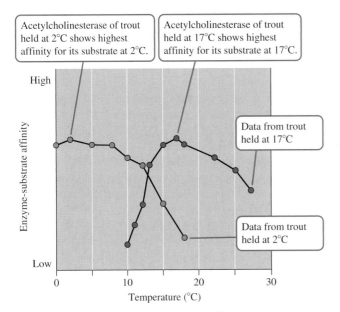

Acetylcholinesterase of trout held at 2°C shows highest affinity for its substrate at 2°C.

Acetylcholinesterase of trout held at 17°C shows highest affinity for its substrate at 17°C.

Data from trout held at 17°C

Data from trout held at 2°C

Figure 5.10 Enzyme activity is affected substantially by temperature (data from Baldwin and Hochachka 1970).

This influence of temperature on the performance of acetylcholinesterase makes sense if you consider the temperatures of the rainbow trout's native environment. Rainbow trout are native to the cool, clear streams and rivers of western North America. During winter, the temperatures of these streams hover between 0°C and 4°C, while summer temperatures approach 20°C. These environmental temperatures are similar to the temperatures at which the acetylcholinesterase of rainbow trout performs optimally.

Studies of reptiles, especially lizards and snakes, are offering additional insights into the influence of temperature on animal performance. Widely distributed species often offer the opportunity for studies of local variation in ecological relationships, including the influence of temperature on performance. For example, the eastern fence lizard, *Sceloporus undulatus*, is found across approximately two-thirds of the United States and into southern Canada, living in a broad diversity of climatic zones. Taking advantage of this wide range of environmental conditions, Michael Angilletta (2001) studied the temperature relations of *S. undulatus* over a portion of its range (fig. 5.11). In one of his studies, Angilletta determined how temperature influences metabolizable energy intake or MEI. He measured MEI as the amount of energy consumed (C) minus energy lost in feces (F) and uric acid (U), which is the nitrogen waste product produced by lizards. We can summarize MEI in equation form as:

$$MEI = C - F - U$$

Angilletta studied two populations from New Jersey and South Carolina, regions with substantially different climates. He collected a sample of lizards from both populations and maintained portions of his samples from both populations at 30°C, 33°C, and 36°C. Angilletta kept his study lizards in separate enclosures and provided them with crickets that he had weighed as food. Since he had determined the energy content of an average cricket, Angilletta was able to determine the

energy intake by each lizard by counting the number of crickets they ate and calculating the energy content of that number. He determined the energy lost as feces and uric acid by collecting all the feces and uric acid produced by each lizard and then drying and weighing this material. He estimated the average energy content of feces and uric acid using a bomb calorimeter.

The results of Angilletta's experiment, which are shown in figure 5.12, show clearly that MEI is highest in both populations of lizards at the intermediate temperature of 33°C. Note that the differences in performance indicated by this experiment were observed over a relatively small range of temperatures: from 30°C to 36°C. This result is consistent with the concept that most species perform best in a fairly narrow range of temperatures. Analogous influences of temperature on performance have also been well documented in plants.

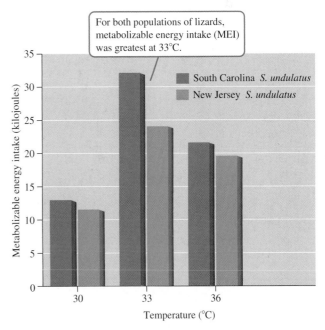

Figure 5.11 *Sceloporus undulatus*, the eastern fence lizard, is one of the most widely distributed lizard species in North America.

For both populations of lizards, metabolizable energy intake (MEI) was greatest at 33°C.

South Carolina *S. undulatus*
New Jersey *S. undulatus*

Figure 5.12 The rate of metabolizable energy intake by two populations of the eastern fence lizard, *Sceloporus undulatus*, peaks at the same temperature (data from Angilletta 2001).

Extreme Temperatures and Photosynthesis

One of the most fundamental characteristics of plants is their ability to photosynthesize. **Photosynthesis**, the conversion of light energy to the chemical energy of organic molecules, is the basis of the life of plants—their growth, reproduction, and so on—and the ultimate source of energy for most heterotrophic organisms.

Photosynthesis can be summarized by the following equation:

$$6\,CO_2 + 12\,H_2O \xrightarrow[\text{Chlorophyll}]{\text{Light}} C_6H_{12}O_6 + 6\,O_2 + 6\,H_2O$$

This equation indicates that as light interacts with chlorophyll, carbon dioxide and water combine to produce sugar and oxygen.

Extreme temperatures generally reduce photosynthetic rates. Figure 5.13 shows the influence of temperature on rate of photosynthesis by a moss from the boreal forest, *Pleurozium schreberi*, and a desert shrub, *Atriplex lentiformis*. The moss and the desert shrub both photosynthesize at a maximum rate over some narrow range of temperatures. Both plants photosynthesize at lower rates at temperatures above and below this range.

The results shown in figure 5.13 demonstrate that the moss and the shrub have substantially different optimal temperatures for photosynthesis. At 15°C, where the moss photosynthesizes at a maximum rate, the desert shrub photosynthesizes at about 25% of its maximum. At 44°C, where the desert shrub is photosynthesizing at its maximum rate, the moss would probably die. These physiological differences clearly reflect differences in the environments where these species live and seem to say something about their evolutionary histories.

Plant responses to temperature, as well as those of animals, can also reflect the short-term physiological adjustments called **acclimation**. Acclimation involves physiological, not genetic, changes in response to temperature; acclimation is generally reversible with changes in environmental conditions. Studies of *A. lentiformis* by Robert Pearcy (1977) demonstrate the effect of acclimation on photosynthesis. Pearcy located a population of this desert shrub in Death Valley and grew plants for his experiments from cuttings. By propagating plants from cuttings, he was able to conduct his experiments on genetically identical clones. The clones from the Death Valley plants were grown under two temperature regimes: one set in hot conditions of 43°C during the day and 30°C at night; the other set under cool conditions of 23°C during the day and 18°C at night.

Pearcy then measured the photosynthetic rates of the two sets of plants. The plants grown in a cool environment photosynthesized at a maximum rate at about 32°C. Those grown in a hot environment photosynthesized at a maximum rate at 40°C, a difference in the optimum temperature for photosynthesis of 8°C. Figure 5.14 summarizes the results of Pearcy's experiment. How can we be sure that the different responses to temperature shown by *A. lentiformis* grown under cool and hot conditions were due to physiological adjustments to their growing conditions and not to genetic differences between the plants? Remember that the experimental plants were clones grown from cuttings. Pearcy used clones so he could control for the effects of genes and uncover the effects of physiological adjustment through acclimation.

The physiological adjustments made by *A. lentiformis* correspond to what these plants do during an annual cycle. The plant is evergreen and photosynthesizes throughout the year, in the cool of winter and in the heat of summer. The physiological adjustments suggest that acclimation by *A. lentiformis*

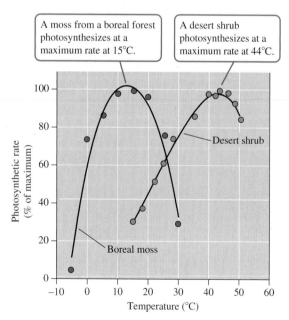

Figure 5.13   The optimal temperatures for photosynthesis by a boreal forest moss and a desert shrub differ substantially (data from Kallio and Kärenlampi 1975, Pearcy and Harrison 1974).

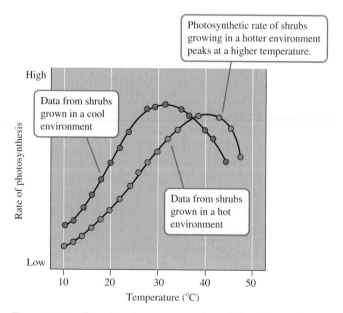

Figure 5.14   Growing the same species of shrub in cool versus hot environments altered their optimal temperature for photosynthesis. This change was a short-term physiological adjustment due to acclimation (data from Berry and Björkman 1980, after Pearcy 1977).

may shift its optimal temperature for photosynthesis to match seasonal changes in environmental temperature. Plants from cooler areas also acclimate in response to changing temperatures. These changes allow many boreal species to photosynthesize later into fall than could occur without acclimation. Cold acclimation appears more complex than warm acclimation, and includes altering lipid membrane saturation to maintain fluidity even in cold temperatures.

Temperature and Microbial Activity

Although often overlooked, microbes often control the flow of energy and nutrients in terrestrial and aquatic ecosystems. Changes in microbial activity have significant consequences for the other organisms that live alongside these organisms. It may come as no surprise that microbes can be extremely sensitive to changes in temperature.

Microbes appear to have adapted to all temperatures at which there is liquid water, from the frigid waters around the Antarctic to boiling hot springs. However, while each of these environments harbours one or more species of microbes, no known species thrives in all these conditions. All microbes that have been studied perform best over a fairly narrow range of temperatures. Let's look at two microbes that live in environments at opposite extremes of the aquatic temperature spectrum.

Richard Morita (1975) studied the effect of temperature on population growth among cold-loving, or **psychrophilic**, marine bacteria that live in the waters around Antarctica. He isolated and cultured one of those bacteria, *Vibrio* sp., in a temperature-gradient incubator. During the experiment, the temperature gradient within the incubator ranged from about −2°C to just over 9°C. The results of the experiment show that this *Vibrio* sp. grows fastest at about 4°C. At temperatures above and below this, its population growth rate decreases. As figure 5.15 shows, Morita recorded some growth in the *Vibrio*

population at temperatures approaching −2°C, however, populations did not grow at temperatures above 9°C. Morita has recorded population growth among some cold-loving bacteria at temperatures as low as −5.5°C.

Some microbes can live at very high temperatures. Microbes have been found living in all of the hot springs that have been studied. Some of these heat-loving, or **thermophilic**, microbes grow at temperatures above 40°C in a variety of environments. The most heat-loving microbes are the hyperthermophiles, which have temperature optima above 80°C. Some hyperthermophiles grow best at 110°C! Some of the most intensive studies of thermophilic and hyperthermophilic microbes have been carried out in Yellowstone National Park by Thomas Brock (1978) and his students and colleagues. One of the genera they have studied is *Sulfolobus*, a member of the microbial Domain Archaea, which obtains energy by oxidizing elemental sulfur. Jerry Mosser and colleagues (1974) used the rate at which *Sulfolobus* oxidizes sulfur as an index of its metabolic activity. They studied the microbes from a series of hot springs in Yellowstone National Park that ranged in temperature from 63°C to 92°C. The temperature optimum for the *Sulfolobus* populations ranged from 63°C to 80°C and was related to the temperature of the particular spring from which the microbes came. For instance, one strain isolated from a 59°C spring oxidizes sulfur at a maximum rate at 63°C. This *Sulfolobus* population oxidizes sulfur at a high rate within a temperature range of about 10°C (fig. 5.16). Outside of this temperature range, its rate of sulfur oxidation is much lower.

We have reviewed how temperature can affect microbial activity, plant photosynthesis, and animal performance. These examples demonstrate that most organisms perform best over a fairly narrow range of temperatures. Consider the effects of temperature on the performance of organisms relative to

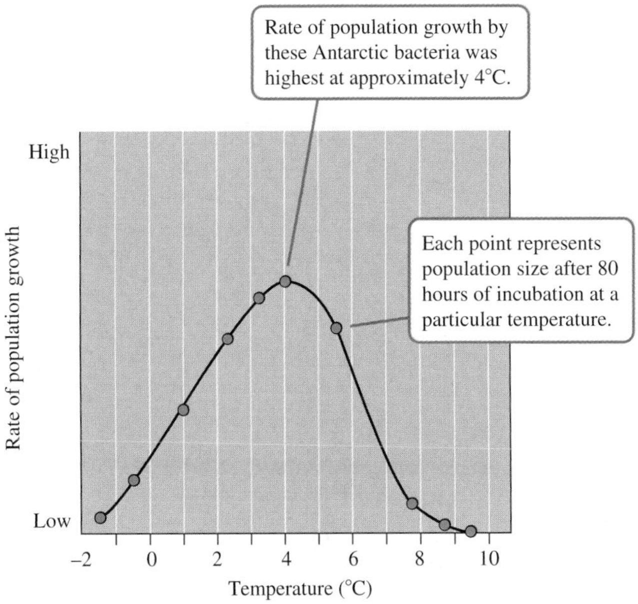

Figure 5.15 Antarctic bacteria have a very low optimal temperature for population growth (data from Morita 1975).

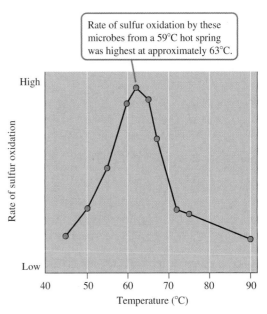

Figure 5.16 Hot spring microbes have a very high optimal temperature for population growth (data from Mosser et al. 1974).

our discussion of how temperatures can vary greatly over small distances. In addition, the climate diagrams presented in chapter 2 showed us that temporal variation in temperature can also be substantial. In the next section, we review how some organisms respond to variation in environmental temperatures.

CONCEPT 5.3 REVIEW

1. Signs of thermal stress in fish include swimming on their sides and swimming in spirals. Using what you know about temperature and acetylcholinesterase, explain.
2. How can we be sure that the two distinctive responses to temperature shown by *Atriplex lentiformis* were due to acclimation and not the result of genetic differences?
3. Will all species within a single habitat have similar temperature optima for a given ecological process, such as photosynthesis? Explain.

5.4 Regulating Body Temperature

Many organisms have evolved ways to compensate for variations in environmental temperature by regulating body temperature. So, how do organisms respond to the juxtaposition of thermal heterogeneity in the environment and their own fairly narrow thermal requirements? Do they sit passively and let environmental temperatures affect them as they will, or do they take a more active approach? Many organisms have evolved ways to regulate body temperatures.

Balancing Heat Gain Against Heat Loss

Organisms regulate body temperature by manipulating heat gain and loss. An equation, used by K. Schmidt-Nielsen (1983), can help us understand the components of heat that may be manipulated:

$$H_s = H_m \pm H_{cd} \pm H_{cv} \pm H_r - H_e$$

Here, H_s, the total heat stored in the body of an organism, is made up of H_m, heat gained from metabolism; H_{cd}, heat gained or lost through conduction; H_{cv}, heat lost or gained by convection; H_r, heat gained or lost through electromagnetic radiation; and H_e, heat lost through evaporation. These heat components represent ways that heat is transferred between an organism and its environment. **Metabolic heat**, H_m, is the energy released within an organism during the process of cellular respiration. **Conduction** is the movement of heat between objects in physical contact, as occurs when you sit on a stone bench on a cold winter's day; **convection** is the process of heat flow between a solid body and a moving fluid, such as wind or flowing water. During the process of

conduction or convection, H_{cd} and H_{cv}, the direction of heat flow is always from the warmer region to the colder.

Heat may also be transferred through electromagnetic radiation. This transfer of heat, H_r, is often called simply **radiation**. All objects above absolute zero, ($-273°C$), give off electromagnetic radiation, but the most obvious source in our environment is the sun. Curiously, we are blind to most of this because at sea level over half of the energy content of sunlight falls outside our visible range. Much of this radiation that we cannot see is in the infrared part of the spectrum. The electromagnetic radiation emitted by most objects in our environment, including our own bodies, is also infrared light. Infrared light is responsible for most of the warmth you feel when standing in front of a fire or that you feel radiating from the sunny side of a building on a winter's day. The chilling effect of standing outdoors under a clear, cold night sky with no wind is also mainly due to radiative heat flux, in this case from your body to the surroundings, including the night sky.

An organism may lose heat, H_e, through **evaporation**. In general, we need only consider the heat lost as water evaporates from the surface of an organism. The ability of water to absorb a large amount of heat as it evaporates makes cooling systems based on the evaporation of water very effective. Figure 5.17 summarizes the potential pathways by which heat can be transferred between an organism and the environment.

So how do these factors interact to determine body temperature, and how can organisms maintain a constant internal temperature? Not all species have constant body temperatures. These species, **poikilotherms**, have body temperatures that vary in response to changes in the external environment. In contrast, **homeotherms** maintain relatively constant internal temperatures even in the face of changing external

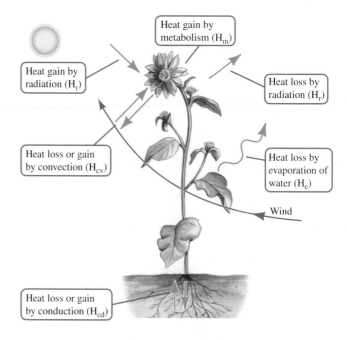

Figure 5.17 There are multiple pathways for heat exchange between organisms and the environment.

temperatures. A variety of physiological challenges are unique to each of these conditions. As we have discussed, individual enzymes generally have specific temperature optima. For homeotherms, stabilizing selection will favour enzymes with optima generally near the constant internal environment of the organism (and selection will favour a body temperature near enzyme optima!). For poikilotherms, internal temperatures are variable and thus stabilizing selection is unlikely to be operating. Instead, many poikilotherms have redundant enzyme systems for critical functions, each with different temperature optima. Can you imagine any energetic cost associated with maintaining redundant systems? If so, why aren't all species homeotherms?

The answer is that homeothermy also has costs associated with the mechanisms that organisms use to maintain constant body temperatures. Some organisms, such as humans, are **endotherms**. Endotherms rely heavily on internally derived metabolic heat energy, H_m, to elevate internal temperatures over external temperatures. Endothermic birds and mammals use metabolic energy to heat most of their bodies, while some endothermic fish and insects selectively heat critical organs. For endotherms, lowering the body temperature is generally more difficult than raising the body temperature, though it can be achieved through mechanisms such as panting, sweating, and altered body hair and feather positioning (increasing energetic losses through convection, conduction, evaporation, and radiation). As a result of the limited effectiveness of the cooling mechanisms relative to the warming mechanism, most endotherms are able to survive at ambient temperatures well below their set body temperatures while at only a limited range of temperatures above their set body temperature. In other words, endotherms tend to live closer to the upper end of their range of tolerance than the lower end.

Ectotherms are able to control their body temperatures through the use of external sources of energy, manipulating predominantly H_{cd}, H_{cv}, H_r, and H_e. Ectotherms will often use behaviour to control their internal temperatures. For example, many reptiles can be found laying still on roads, rocks, and other exposed objects early in the morning. Why? This behaviour exposes their body to the sun, resulting in an elevated temperature. Later in the day, these same animals will often be found in crevices, cracks, or underground, preventing their body temperature from reaching a lethal point. Clearly, being an ectotherm will "cost" less energy than being an endotherm. Why then are not all species ectotherms? One answer may come to you if you consider how rarely you actually see snakes, lizards, and other terrestrial ectotherms being active.

There is a great natural diversity in temperature relations between organisms and their environments. It is because of this diversity of nature that the old terms of *cold-blooded* and *warm-blooded* are frustratingly inaccurate. For example, the behavioural changes of many ectotherms are so effective that they are actually homeotherms, at least for part of the day. Ectotherms of the deep ocean are also homeotherms, as the lack of change in the external temperatures results in a lack of change in body temperatures. Some endotherms, such as many hummingbirds, maintain constant body temperatures during the day, and then are poikilothermic during the night. Let's now take a closer look at how plants and animals thermoregulate.

Temperature regulation presents both plants and ectothermic animals with a similar problem. Both groups of organisms rely primarily on external sources of energy. Despite the much greater mobility of most ectothermic animals, the ways in which plants and ectothermic animals solve these problems are similar.

Temperature Regulation by Plants

What sorts of environments are best for studying temperature regulation by plants? Plant ecologists have typically concentrated their studies in extreme environments, such as the tundra and desert, where the challenges of the physical environment are great and where ecologists believed they would find the most dramatic adaptations.

Arctic and Alpine Plants

Cold environments present a variety of unique challenges to plants: freezing can destroy their vascular systems, enzymatic reactions are slower under cold conditions, and staying warm has significant consequences for plant fitness. How do plants meet these challenges? They, like plants from other environments, use morphology, physiology, and behaviour to alter heat exchange with the environment. So how do plants thermoregulate in cold conditions?

We can ignore H_m, metabolic energy, as most plants produce only a small quantity of heat by metabolism. Evaporative cooling (H_e) is not relevant as plants in these locations are faced with challenges for warming, not cooling. We thus start with the equation:

$$H_s = H_{cd} \pm H_{cv} \pm H_r$$

To stay warm, arctic and alpine plants have two main options: increase their rate of radiative heating, H_r, and/or decrease their rate of convective cooling, H_{cv}. It appears that many have evolved to do both and, as a result, can heat up to temperatures far above air temperature. Natural selection has favoured arctic and alpine plants with dark pigments that absorb light. These dark pigments increase radiative heat gain, H_r. Arctic and alpine plants, such as the *Dryas integrifolia* (see fig. 5.1), also increase their H_r gain by orienting their leaves and flowers perpendicular to the sun's rays. In addition, many plants increase their H_r gain from the surroundings by assuming a "cushion" growth form that "hugs" the ground. The ground often warms to temperatures exceeding that of the overlying air and radiates infrared light, which can be absorbed by cushion plants. Cushion plants can also gain heat from warm substrate through conduction, H_{cd}.

The cushion growth form also reduces convective heat loss, H_{cv}, in two main ways. First, growing close to the ground gives them some shelter from the wind. Second, the compact, hemispherical growth form of cushion plants reduces the ratio of surface area to volume, which slows the movement of air through the interior of the plant. Reduced surface area also reduces the rate of radiative heat loss.

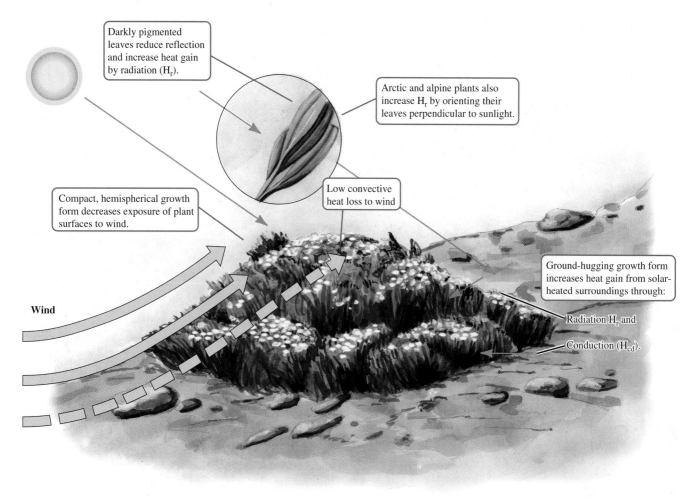

Darkly pigmented leaves reduce reflection and increase heat gain by radiation (H_r).

Arctic and alpine plants also increase H_r by orienting their leaves perpendicular to sunlight.

Compact, hemispherical growth form decreases exposure of plant surfaces to wind.

Low convective heat loss to wind

Ground-hugging growth form increases heat gain from solar-heated surroundings through:

Radiation H_r and

Conduction (H_{cd}).

Wind

Figure 5.18   Arctic and alpine cushion plant form and orientation increases heat gain from sunlight and the surrounding landscape and conserves any heat gained.

Figure 5.18 summarizes the processes involved in thermal regulation by a cushion plant. As a consequence of these processes, cushion plants are often warmer than the surrounding air and plants with other growth forms. For example, Yngvar Gauslaa (1984) has documented the thermal consequences of the cushion growth form. He found that while the temperature of plants with an open growth form closely matches air temperature, the temperature of cushion plants can be more than 10°C higher than air temperature.

Lohengrin Cavieres and colleagues in Chile have studied the effects of cushion plants on other species, finding strong evidence that the impacts of this growth form extend well beyond the individual plant (Cavieres et al. 2002). Though figure 5.18 is drawn to suggest that cushion plants grow as individuals, separated from neighbours, the reality in Chile, Canada, and anywhere such plants exist is quite different. Next time you find yourself in an alpine system, look closely at the cushion plants and you will find a number of other species growing in the small gaps among branches, or at least closely nearby. Why? Most plants benefit from a reduction in thermal stress. Even if a plant does not itself possess the specific adaptations of a cushion plant, it can benefit from growing in close proximity to such a plant. In such a close survey in a Chilean system, Cavieres found more species occurred within the "cushion" of *Bolax gummifera* than nearby but outside the cushion (figure 5.19). Even more, the relative difference increased with altitude, such that a greater proportion of species were found inside the cushion at the more thermally stressful higher altitudes. This is a great example of *facilitation*, a form of ecological interaction whereby one species gains a benefit from the presence or actions of another.

Desert Plants

Now that we see the main challenges for arctic plants, what do desert species encounter? The desert environment challenges plants to avoid overheating; that is, plants are challenged to reduce their heat storage, H_s. How do desert plants meet this challenge? For the most part they do everything opposite to what we saw in arctic and alpine locations. Additionally, evaporative cooling of leaves, which would increase heat loss, H_e, is not a workable option because desert plants usually have inadequate supplies of water. So, for a plant in a hot desert environment, our equation for heat balance reduces to:

$$H_s = H_{cd} \pm H_{cv} \pm H_r$$

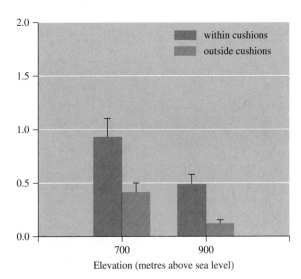

Figure 5.19 In a Chilean alpine system, many other species appear to benefit from presence of a cushion plant (Cavieres et al. 2002).

To avoid heating, plants in hot deserts have three main options: decreasing heating by conduction, H_{cd}; increasing rates of convective cooling, H_{cv}; and reducing rates of radiative heating, H_r. Many desert plants place their foliage far enough above the ground to reduce heat gain by conduction. Many desert plants have also evolved very small leaves and an open growth form, adaptations that give high rates of convective cooling because they increase the ratio of leaf surface area to volume and the movement of air around the plant's stems and foliage. Some desert plants have low rates of radiative heat gain, H_r, because they have evolved reflective surfaces. As we observed in chapter 2, many desert plants have light-coloured leaves, rather than the dark green leaves associated with boreal forest plants. This lighter colouring is often obtained by covering their leaves with a dense coating of white plant hairs. These hairs reduce H_r gain by reflecting visible light, which constitutes nearly half the energy content of sunlight.

We can see how natural selection has resulted in the adaptation of plants to different temperature regimes by comparing species in the genus *Encelia*, which are distributed along a temperature and moisture gradient from the coast of California to Death Valley. James Ehleringer (1980) showed that the leaves of the coastal species, *Encelia californica*, lack hairs entirely and reflect only about 15% of visible light. He also found that two other species that grow part way between the cool coast regions and Death Valley produce leaves that are somewhat pubescent (hairy) and reflect about 26% of visible light. The desert species, *Encelia farinosa*, produces two sets of leaves, one set in the summer and another when it is cooler. The summer leaves are highly pubescent and reflect more than 40% of solar radiation. What do you think the cool season leaves are like? If you predict that they are much less pubescent than summer leaves, you are correct. Why is that? We know the benefits of leaf pubescence. What might be some costs? (Hint: What do plants do with visible light other than heat up?)

Plants can also modify radiative heat gain, H_r, by changing the orientation of leaves and stems. Many desert plants

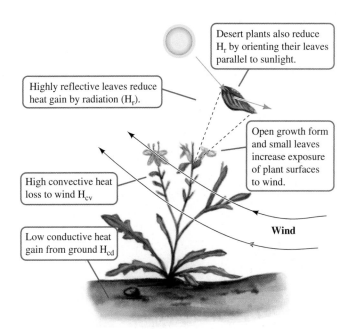

Figure 5.20 The form and orientation of desert plants reduces heat gain from the environment and facilitates cooling.

reduce heating by orienting their leaves parallel to the rays of the sun or by folding them at midday, when sunlight is most intense. Figure 5.20 portrays the main processes involved in heat balance in desert plants.

Temperature Regulation by Ectothermic Animals

Like plants, the vast majority of animals, including fish, amphibians, reptiles, and invertebrates of all sorts, use external sources of energy to regulate body temperature. These ectothermic animals use means analogous to those used by plants, including variations in body size, shape, and pigmentation. The obvious difference between plants and ectothermic animals is that the animals have more options for using behaviour to thermoregulate. Yet, as we shall see, the difference between the behaviour of these animals and that of plants is more a matter of degree than of kind.

Lizards

The eastern fence lizard, *Sceloporus undulatus*, is an ectotherm that regulates its body temperature by behaviours such as basking in the sun to warm its body or seeking shade to cool (fig. 5.21). Research by Michael Angilletta showed that the rate of metabolizable energy intake is maximized at a temperature of 33°C (see fig. 5.12). Knowing this, he studied the relationship between this optimal temperature and the preferred temperature of *S. undulatus*. Angilletta (2001) explored this relationship in the laboratory and the field. In the laboratory, he placed *S. undulatus* from New Jersey and South Carolina in a temperature gradient that ranged from 26°C at one end to 38°C at the other end. He determined preferred temperature early each morning by quickly measuring the body temperature of

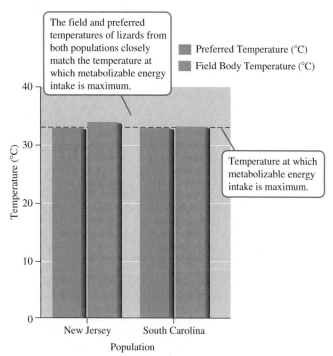

Figure 5.21 label box: The field and preferred temperatures of lizards from both populations closely match the temperature at which metabolizable energy intake is maximum.

Legend: Preferred Temperature (°C) / Field Body Temperature (°C)

Label box: Temperature at which metabolizable energy intake is maximum.

y-axis: Temperature (°C)

x-axis: New Jersey   South Carolina
Population

Figure 5.21 Two populations of the eastern fence lizard, *Sceloporus undulatus*, both regulate their body temperatures to match closely the temperature of maximum metabolizable energy intake (data from Angilletta 2001).

each lizard. Body temperature would indicate where each lizard had been in the temperature gradient, that is, its "preferred" temperature. In the field, Angilletta examined thermoregulation by measuring the body temperatures of active individuals.

The results of Angilletta's study provide strong evidence for a correspondence among preferred temperature, thermoregulation, and optimal temperatures in *S. undulatus* (fig. 5.21). Lizards from New Jersey and South Carolina had virtually identical preferred temperatures: 32.8°C versus 32.9°C, respectively. The body temperatures found by Angilletta in the field were also very similar. The body temperatures of *S. undulatus* measured in the field in New Jersey averaged 34.0°C, while the body temperatures of *S. undulatus* taken in South Carolina averaged 33.1°C. As shown in figure 5.21, both preferred temperatures determined in the laboratory and the body temperatures of *S. undulatus* measured in the field are very close to the temperature that maximizes metabolizable energy intake by these lizards. The following example shows that effective thermoregulation by ectotherms is not limited to lizards.

Grasshoppers: Some Like It Hot

Many grasshoppers also bask in the sun, elevating their body temperature to 40°C or even higher. R. I. Carruthers and his colleagues (1992) described how some species of grasshoppers even adjust their capacity for radiative heating, H_r, by varying the intensity of their pigmentation during development. When reared at low temperatures, these species appear to compensate by developing dark pigmentation; at higher developmental temperatures, they produce less pigmentation (fig. 5.22). How would changing pigmentation in response to developmental temperatures affect thermoregulation by these grasshoppers?

Label box: Grasshoppers reared at low temperatures develop dark pigmentation that is highly absorbent of visible light.

Label box: Grasshoppers reared at high temperatures develop reflective, light pigmentation.

Figure 5.22 Rearing temperatures influence the pigmentation of the clear-winged grasshopper.

Because grasshoppers reared at low temperatures develop darker pigmentation, they increase their potential for H_r gain. Because those reared at high temperatures develop lighter pigmentation, they reduce their potential for H_r gain.

The clear-winged grasshopper, *Camnula pellucida*, is found in grasslands throughout North America, including those of the southwest United States, southern Canada, and even up into the Yukon. Needless to say, this species experiences a great diversity of climates. During early morning, *Camnula* orients its body perpendicular to the sun's rays and quickly heats to 30°C to 40°C. Given the opportunity, young *Camnula* will maintain a body temperature around 38°C to 40°C, very close to its optimal temperature for development. In the laboratory, *Camnula* is able to elevate its body temperature to 12°C above air temperature and maintain it within a very narrow range (±2°C) for many hours.

Temperature Regulation by Endothermic Animals

Do endothermic animals thermoregulate differently than the other organisms we have discussed? Endotherms use all the anatomical and behavioural tricks used by other organisms to manipulate heat exchange with the environment. So, our basic equation for temperature regulation, $H_s = H_m \pm H_{cd} \pm H_{cv} \pm H_r - H_e$, still applies but with some changes in the relative importance of the terms. Most significantly, endotherms rely a great deal more on metabolic heat, H_m, to maintain constant body temperature.

Environmental Temperature and Metabolic Rates

P. F. Scholander and his colleagues (1950) studied thermoregulation in several endothermic species by monitoring metabolic rate while exposing them to a range of temperatures. The range of environmental temperatures over which the metabolic rate

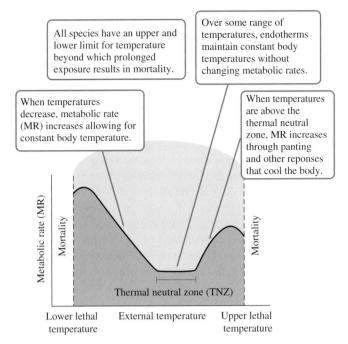

All species have an upper and lower limit for temperature beyond which prolonged exposure results in mortality.

When temperatures decrease, metabolic rate (MR) increases allowing for constant body temperature.

Over some range of temperatures, endotherms maintain constant body temperatures without changing metabolic rates.

When temperatures are above the thermal neutral zone, MR increases through panting and other reponses that cool the body.

Figure 5.23 In response to changing external temperatures, endotherms vary metabolic rates to maintain a constant body temperature.

of a homeothermic animal does not change is called its **thermal neutral zone** (figure 5.23). When environmental temperatures are within the thermal neutral zone of an endothermic animal, its metabolic rate stays steady at resting metabolism. An endotherm's metabolic rate will rapidly increase to two or even three times resting metabolism if the environmental temperature falls below or rises above the thermal neutral zone.

What causes metabolic rates to rise when environmental temperatures are outside the thermal neutral zone? We can use

humans as a model for the responses of endotherms generally. At low temperatures, we start shivering, which generates heat by muscle contractions. We also release hormones that increase our metabolic rate, the rate at which we metabolize our energy stores, which are mainly fats. Increasing metabolic rate increases the rate at which we generate metabolic heat, H_m. At high temperatures, heart rate and blood flow to the skin increase. This increased blood flow transports heat from the body core to the skin, where an evaporative cooling system based on sweating accelerates unloading of heat to the external environment. Many large endotherms, such as horses and camels, also cool by sweating. Other endotherms do not sweat but evaporatively cool by other means: dogs and birds pant, and marsupials and rodents moisten their body surfaces by salivating and licking.

The breadth of the thermal neutral zone varies a great deal among endothermic species. Scholander and his colleagues suggested that differences in the width of the thermal neutral zone defines two groups of organisms: tropical species, with narrow thermal neutral zones, and arctic species, with broad thermal neutral zones. The researchers pointed out that the narrow thermal neutral zone of *Homo sapiens* is similar to that of several species of rain forest mammals and birds. Meanwhile, arctic species, such as the arctic fox, have impressively broad thermal neutral zones.

Since the normal body temperature of most endotherms varies from about 35°C to 40°C, it is no surprise that this range of temperatures falls within the thermal neutral zone of both tropical and arctic species. What distinguishes tropical and arctic species is the great tolerance that arctic species have for cold. For instance, the arctic fox can tolerate environmental temperatures down to at least −40°C without showing any increase in metabolic rate. Meanwhile the metabolic rate of some tropical species begins to increase when air temperature falls below 29°C. Figure 5.24 contrasts the thermal neutral zones of some arctic and tropical species.

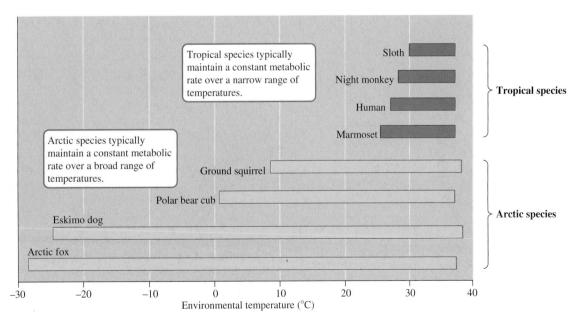

Figure 5.24 Temperature and the thermal neutral zone of arctic and tropical mammals. Bars indicate the range of temperatures over which metabolic rate does not change for each species (data from Scholander et al. 1950).

From evolutionary and ecological perspectives, the important point of this discussion is that thermoregulation outside the thermal neutral zone costs energy that could be otherwise directed toward reproduction. How might such energetic costs affect the distribution and abundance of organisms in nature? This is one of the central questions of ecology.

Aquatic Animals

Now let's turn to thermoregulation by aquatic endotherms, where the aquatic environment limits the possible ways organisms can regulate their body temperatures. Why is that? First, as we have seen, the capacity of water to absorb heat energy without changing temperature is about 3,000 times that of air. Second, conductive and convective heat losses to water are much more rapid than to air, over 20 times faster in still water and up to 100 times faster in moving water. Thus, the aquatic organism is surrounded by a vast heat sink. The potential for heat loss to this heat sink is very great, particularly for gill-breathing species that must expose a large respiratory surface directly to the environment to extract sufficient oxygen from water. In the face of these environmental difficulties, only a few aquatic species are truly endothermic.

Aquatic birds and mammals, such as penguins, seals, and whales, can be endothermic in an aquatic environment for two major reasons. First, they are all air breathers and do not expose a large respiratory surface to the surrounding water. Second, many endothermic aquatic animals, including penguins, seals, and whales, are well insulated from the heat-sapping external environment by a thick layer of fat, while others, such as the sea otter, are insulated by a layer of fur that traps air. The parts of these animals that are not well insulated, principally appendages, are outfitted with *countercurrent heat exchangers*, vascular structures that reduce the rate of heat loss to the surrounding aquatic environment. Figure 5.25

diagrams the structure and functioning of a countercurrent heat exchanger in the flipper of a dolphin.

The lateral swimming muscles of endothermic fish, such as tuna and white sharks, are also well supplied with blood vessels that function as countercurrent heat exchangers. These heat exchangers heat cool arterial blood as it carries oxygen to the lateral swimming muscles, and by the time this blood delivers its supply of oxygen and nutrients it has been heated to the same temperature as the active muscles. On the return trip, the heat in this warm blood is used to heat the newly arriving blood and so, when blood exits the swimming muscles, it is again approximately the same temperature as the surrounding water. The countercurrent heat exchangers of tuna are efficient enough at conserving heat that these fish can elevate the temperature of their swimming muscles up to 14°C above the temperature of the surrounding water. The anatomy of the countercurrent heat exchanger in bluefin tuna muscles is presented in figure 5.26.

Francis Carey and his colleagues (Carey 1973) implanted devices that would measure and transmit the temperature of the muscles of bluefin tuna and of the surrounding water. Their tracking boat could usually follow a released fish carrying a temperature-sensing implant for a few hours, which provided enough time to collect data that revealed a great deal about their temperature relations. As one of the monitored fish swam through water varying in temperature from 7°C to 14°C, the temperature of its swimming muscles remained a constant 24°C. These results, shown in figure 5.27, demonstrate that bluefin tuna can maintain a remarkably constant muscle temperature even in the face of substantial variation in water temperature. More recent work has shown that other organs of bluefin tuna, such as the stomach, vary in temperature much more than do the swimming muscles (Stevens et al. 2000).

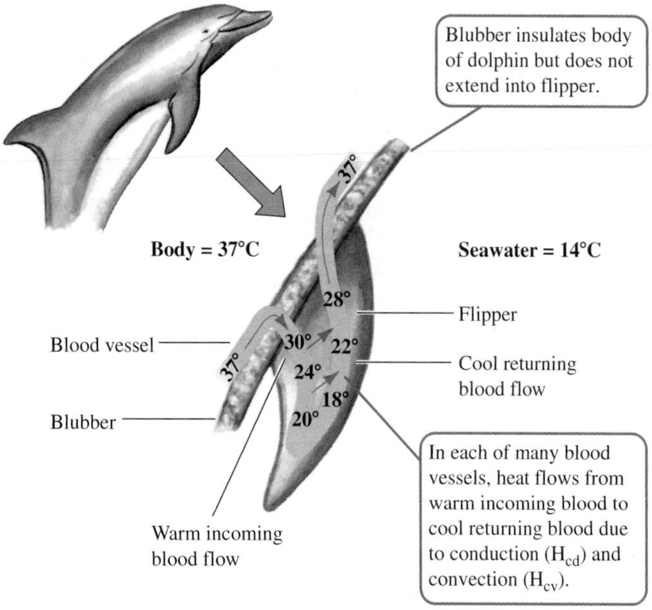

Figure 5.25 Countercurrent heat exchange in dolphin flippers promotes conservation of body heat.

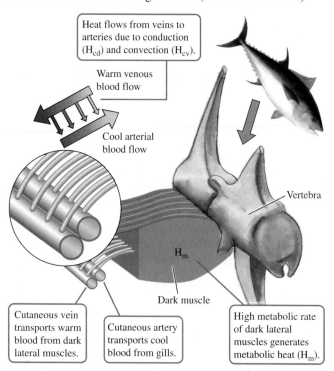

Heat flows from veins to arteries due to conduction (H_{cd}) and convection (H_{cv}).

Warm venous blood flow

Cool arterial blood flow

Vertebra

H_m

Dark muscle

Cutaneous vein transports warm blood from dark lateral muscles.

Cutaneous artery transports cool blood from gills.

High metabolic rate of dark lateral muscles generates metabolic heat (H_m).

Figure 5.26 Countercurrent heat exchange in the lateral muscles of bluefin tuna.

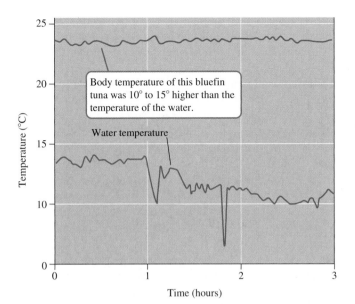

Figure 5.27   The muscle temperature of an actively swimming bluefin tuna is elevated above that of the surrounding ocean water (data from Carey 1973).

Now, let's move from the sea and the giant bluefin tuna, which can reach up to 1,000 kg, to land, where we find some of the smallest endotherms. Many terrestrial insects have evolved the capacity to heat their flight muscles.

Warming Insect Flight Muscles

Have you ever gone outside on a cool fall or spring morning when few insects were active and yet met with bumblebees visiting flowers? Were you surprised? While you may have taken the meeting for granted, these early morning forays by bumblebees require some impressive physiology. Most insects use external sources of energy to heat their bodies, but there are some notable exceptions. Bumblebees maintain the temperature of their thoraxes, which house the flight muscles, at 30°C to 37°C regardless of air temperature (Heinrich 1979). Because they can warm their flight muscles, bumblebees can fly when environmental temperatures are as low as 0°C. A number of other insects use metabolic heat, H_m, to warm their flight muscles, including large nocturnal moths, which were the subject of some of the earliest studies of endothermic insects.

Bernd Heinrich (1993) has spent a great deal of his professional life studying thermoregulation by insects. Some of the inspiration that launched this work came to him when he was a graduate student recording the body temperatures of moths in the highlands of New Guinea. Heinrich relates how as he captured moths flying to a sheet illuminated by a lantern, air temperatures were about 9°C. Despite these low temperatures, some of the larger moths captured had thoracic temperatures of 46°C, 9°C higher than Heinrich's own body temperature. It was at this point that he became convinced that some insects can thermoregulate by endothermic means. However, you do not have to travel to the highlands of New Guinea to meet endothermic insects. Some of Heinrich's most elegant studies of thermoregulation have been done on moths from temperate latitudes.

Studies of temperature regulation by moths began in the early 1800s. Many of these studies were focused on moths of the family Sphingidae, the sphinx moths. Sphinx moths are convenient insects for study because many reach impressive sizes, large enough to be mistaken for hummingbirds. Heinrich's dissertation focused on thermoregulation by the sphinx moth *Manduca sexta*, whose large green caterpillars feed on a wide variety of plants, including tobacco and tomato plants. *M. sexta* is among the larger sphinx moths and weighs 2 to 3 g—which is heavier than some hummingbirds and shrews, the smallest of the birds and mammals.

Since the nineteenth century, researchers have been aware that active sphinx moths have elevated thoracic temperatures. These early researchers also knew that temperature increases within the thorax were due to activity of the flight muscles contained within the thorax that vibrated the wings. Later researchers discovered that during flight, the muscles responsible for the upstroke of the wings, and those responsible for the downstroke contracted sequentially. However, during preflight warm-up, the upstroke and downstroke muscles contracted nearly simultaneously. Consequently, the wings of a moth warming its flight muscles only vibrated. Once warmed up and actively flying, sphinx moths maintained a relatively constant thoracic temperature over a broad range of environmental temperatures. This was evidence that sphinx moths thermoregulate.

You can see that a lot was known before Heinrich began his dissertation research. However, a significant problem remained: no one knew how sphinx moths accomplished thermoregulation. Phillip Adams and James Heath (1964) proposed that the moths thermoregulate by changing their metabolic rate in response to changing environmental temperatures. In terms of our equation for thermoregulation, Adams and Heath proposed that the moths increased H_m when environmental temperatures fell, and decreased H_m when environmental temperatures rose.

Several observations led Heinrich to propose an alternative hypothesis, however. He proposed that active sphinx moths have a fairly constant metabolic rate and so generate metabolic heat, H_m, at a constant rate. Heinrich also proposed that sphinx moths thermoregulate by changing their rates of heat loss to the environment. In terms of our equation for thermoregulation, the moths *decrease* their rate of cooling by convection and conduction when environmental temperatures fall, and when temperatures rise, sphinx moths *increase* their cooling rates.

Heinrich tested his hypothesis with a series of pioneering experiments that demonstrated *M. sexta* cools its thorax by using its circulatory system to transport heat to the abdomen. In other words, the blood of these moths acts as a coolant. In his first experiment, he immobilized a moth and heated its thorax with a narrow beam of light while monitoring the temperature of the thorax and abdomen. Because it was narrow, the light beam increased radiative heat gain, H_r, of the thorax only. Heinrich used the beam to simulate metabolic heat

production by the flight muscles. He observed that the thoracic temperature of these heated moths stabilized at about 44°C. Meanwhile, their abdominal temperatures gradually increased.

These results indicated that heat within the thorax was transferred to the abdomen. Heinrich proposed that blood flowing from the thorax to the abdomen was the means of heat transfer. To confirm this, he conducted a second experiment. He tied off blood flow to the thorax using a fine human hair. With this blood flow stopped, flying moths overheated and stopped flying. Instead of stabilizing at 44°C, the thoracic temperatures approached the lethal limit of 46°C. An interesting debate between two groups of researchers with competing hypotheses was decided by two decisive experiments, which are summarized by figure 5.28.

Endothermic insects were a surprise to many biologists. The existence of endothermic plants was even more surprising.

Temperature Regulation by Thermogenic Plants

Roger Knutson (1974, 1979) visited a marsh on a cold February day in northeast Iowa. There he saw eastern skunk cabbage, *Symplocarpus foetidus*, emerging from the frozen landscape. Each plant was surrounded by a melted circle in the snow. It appeared as though the skunk cabbage had generated enough heat to melt its way through the snow. Knutson returned the next day with a thermometer and so began a research project that produced some surprising observations of thermoregulation by plants.

Almost all plants are poikilothermic ectotherms. However, plants in the family Araceae use metabolic energy to heat their flowers. Some of the temperate species in this mostly tropical family use this ability to protect their inflorescences from freezing and to attract pollinators. One of the most studied of these temperate species is the eastern skunk cabbage, which lives in the deciduous forests of eastern North America including much of eastern Canada. This skunk cabbage blooms from February to March, when air temperatures vary between −15°C to 15°C. During this period, the inflorescence of the plant, which weighs from 2 to 9 g, maintains a temperature 15°C to 35°C above air temperature. As Knutson observed, this temperature is warm enough so that *S. foetidus* can melt its way through snow. The plant's inflorescences can maintain these elevated temperatures for up to 14 days. During this period, it functions as an endothermic organism.

How does the skunk cabbage fuel the heating of its inflorescence? It has a large root in which it stores large quantities of starch. Some of this starch is translocated to the inflorescence, where it is metabolized at a high rate, generating large quantities of heat in the process. This heat, besides keeping the inflorescence from freezing, may help attract pollinators.

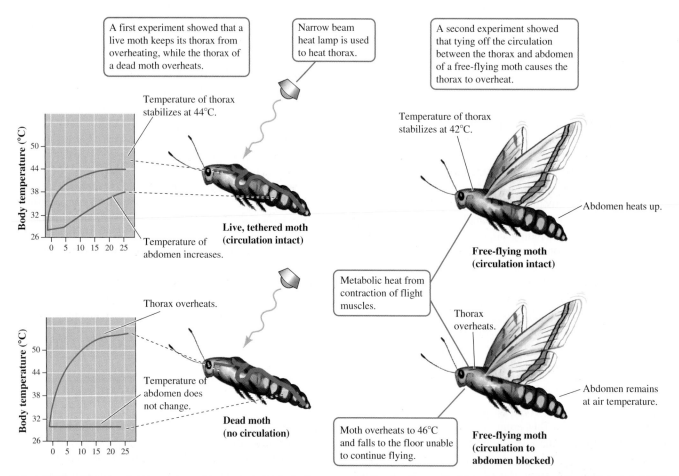

Figure 5.28 The circulatory system plays a central role in thermoregulation by the moth, *Manduca sexta* (data from Heinrich 1993).

Various pollinators are attracted to both the warmth and the sweetish scent given off by the plant. Some of the biology of this interesting plant is summarized in figure 5.29.

The inflorescence of the skunk cabbage maintains a high respiratory rate, equivalent to that of a small mammal of similar size. However, its metabolic rate is not constant. The plant adjusts its metabolic rate to changes in environmental temperatures. The metabolic rate increases with decreasing temperature, which increases the rate of metabolic heat production. By adjusting its metabolic rate, the plant can maintain its inflorescence at a similar temperature despite substantial variation in environmental temperature (fig. 5.30).

In this section, we have considered how various organisms regulate their body temperatures by using external sources of energy, internal sources of energy, or both. Thermoregulation is possible where organisms face temperatures within their range of tolerance. However, organisms do not always respond to variation in environmental temperatures by thermoregulating. In many circumstances, they use various means to survive extreme environmental temperatures, as we shall discuss next.

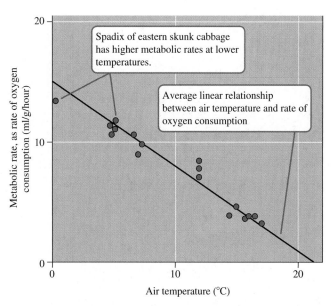

Figure 5.30 Air temperature has a clear influence on the metabolic rate of eastern skunk cabbage (data from Knutson 1974).

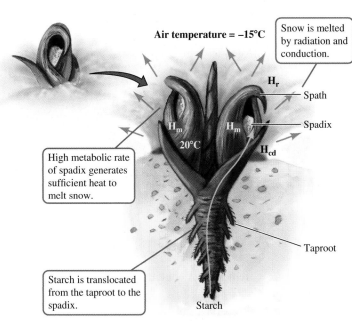

Figure 5.29 Eastern skunk cabbage, an endothermic plant, can melt its way up through spring snow cover (data from Knutson 1974).

CONCEPT 5.4 REVIEW

1. Why would selection likely act against the production of light pigmentation and white hairs on the leaf surface of arctic plants?
2. Can behavioural thermoregulation be precise? What evidence supports your answer?
3. Why are all endothermic fish relatively large?

5.5 # Surviving Extreme Temperatures

Organisms exhibit a diversity of mechanisms to cope with extreme temperatures. Think of an environment that is either very cold or very hot, perhaps a −40°C winter day in the boreal forest. For certain, you are likely to notice less obvious biological activity on that day than you will in the same location in the middle of the summer. However, even that cold winter day is not devoid of life. In this section we will discuss strategies that have evolved that allow species to survive extreme temperatures.

When we use the term extreme, it is necessary to understand that this is a relative term, and what is extreme to one species may in fact be quite comfortable to another. We use the term to indicate temperatures well beyond the range of tolerance for most species (fig. 5.8). For example, although many species of spruce trees are able to survive at temperatures as low as −80°C, most scientists would agree that that is an extreme temperature. Or put another way, few ecologists would themselves choose to work outside under such conditions! Extreme conditions can last for a day, a week, or months, with different strategies existing for all of these scenarios. One thing that is common in response to extreme temperatures is that relatively simple solutions, such as panting, increasing hair cover, or other minor behavioural and physiological changes, can help an organism cope for short periods of time. However, individually these options are likely not quite enough to allow for survival over longer time periods. Instead, dramatic environmental conditions have resulted in the evolution of equally dramatic ecological responses. Here we examine some of the more common responses to extreme temperatures, particularly responses to extreme cold (fig. 5.31).

Figure 5.31   Plants and animals exhibit a variety of adaptations to surviving extreme winter conditions.

Death

You may not consider death to be a particularly adaptive response to extreme conditions, but in fact it is a common strategy used by many organisms. Why? To answer this we must first return to the idea of energy budgets, a topic we mentioned earlier in this chapter. All organisms have a certain amount of energy based upon what they eat (or photosynthesize). This can be represented in a pie diagram, with the size of the pie representing the total amount of available energy to the organism (fig. 5.32). For a given organism at a given point in time, the size of the pie is fixed, and energy spent on one biological process cannot also be spent on another process. The main types of energy expenditure for all organisms (plants, animals, microbes, etc.) can be broken down into four general groups: growth, maintenance, activity, and reproduction (fig. 5.32). Growth consists of all the energy needed to build new tissues and organs; maintenance represents the basal metabolic costs of simply staying alive; reproduction costs include the production of reproductive organs (e.g., flowers), mechanisms of mate attraction (e.g., nectar, showy plumage), and the development of offspring; and activity costs include the extra energy required to move, eat, defend territories, and most anything else that organisms do when they are not asleep or dormant. The relative size of each of these slices of pie will differ among species. For example, endotherms will have much larger maintenance costs than will ectotherms.

How does this relate to extreme environments? One strategy for surviving harsh conditions can be increased energy expenditures for maintenance (e.g., increasing metabolic rate, construction of freeze-resistant tissues, etc.), resulting in less energy available for other activities, such as reproduction.

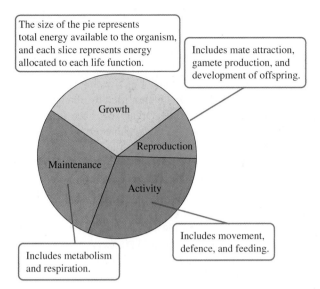

The size of the pie represents total energy available to the organism, and each slice represents energy allocated to each life function.

Includes mate attraction, gamete production, and development of offspring.

Includes movement, defence, and feeding.

Includes metabolism and respiration.

Figure 5.32 Pie diagrams can be used to represent energy budgets for organisms.

For many other organisms, natural selection has favoured a solution that involves minimal investment in maintenance and maximal investment in reproduction. What types of organisms do this? "Annual" plants and many insects are among the more common examples. What does being "annual" actually mean for plants? It means that an individual completes its life cycle within a single year. As it turns out, the adult life-stage generally dies just prior to the more extreme temperatures, which would be winter for most parts of Canada.

A reasonable question to ask is if extreme conditions kill the adults of a particular species, how is it possible to find that same species in the same location the following year? The solution to this problem lies in the realization that many species or organisms have different life-stages that have inherently different morphologies and ranges of tolerance. For example, each seed of a flowering plant is a living, breathing organism (with its own very small energy pie); it is not an inert piece of the soil. Pause to consider this for a minute. How many lives are you killing when you grind wheat to make a loaf of bread? How about when you eat a single strawberry, with all of those seeds exposed on the outer surface of the fruit? Although most seeds are unable to withstand the grinding abilities of grain mills or your teeth, many seeds do have seed coats and other protective tissues that allow them to withstand environmental conditions that would kill them as adults. As a result, when spring arrives, these seeds are able to germinate, grow, and reproduce, until the arrival of winter again causes their death as well. Protective structures and coatings are also found in the eggs and early instars of many insects, spores of many fungi, and cell walls of many bacteria (organisms you also regularly consume; intentionally or not).

Migration

The boreal forest comes alive in the spring and summer with the arrival of countless bird species that winter in the more temperate climates to the south. There are over 300 bird species in the boreal forest and it is estimated that over 90% of these migrate south as winter approaches. These species result in an estimated 3 billion breeding adults and 5 billion migrating individuals (adults and offspring) each year. Needless to say, migration is a common method of coping with extreme temperatures! Small animals, with large surface area:volume ratios are at particular risk from extreme temperatures, and thus it is not surprising that many small songbirds fly south each winter.

Extreme shifts in temperature drive the migration of many other species as well, including the Monarch butterfly, which summers in southern Canada and throughout the United States, wintering in the mountains of Mexico. A question to consider: why don't these birds and butterflies stay in their "winter" homes all year long? The answer will lie in the specific costs and ability to withstand extreme temperatures for each species. In general, we would expect species to migrate when the fitness costs of staying through the extreme conditions are greater than the costs of migration.

Resistance

The third general strategy for coping with extreme weather conditions is possession of traits that allow the individual to tolerate extreme temperatures. Individuals that find themselves in harsh temperatures and do not possess specialized traits (or either of the two strategies described above), are destined to become evolutionary losers—producing fewer and lower-quality offspring than their neighbours that are adapted to life under extreme conditions. Across plant and animal species there exists substantial variation in an organism's ability to survive and thrive under low temperature conditions. Many tropical plant species die when temperatures reach a relatively warm 5°C, while white spruce is able to survive temperatures as low as −80°C! Because of this variation, the minimum temperature that is reached during the winter months (chapter 2) sets the northern limit of the range of many species (chapter 10). What do you think might happen to the ranges of such temperature-limited species under global warming? Books can (and have!) be written about the specialized traits that allow some species to thrive where others die. Here are a few of the more common adaptations to extreme temperatures.

Fur, Fat, and Feathers

Here is the problem. Imagine you are a homeothermic endotherm living in the Arctic, and you will stay active during the winter. As the air temperature decreases, you will need to increase your basal metabolic rate to maintain your body temperature. However, this process uses substantial energy reserves, leaving less energy available for other activities. What do you do? One effective strategy is to increase the insulative properties of your body, which has the result of decreasing your energy lost by radiation. Many mammals do this by depositing a subcutaneous layer of fat at the onset of winter, as well as increased production of body hair (fur). The fat often serves two roles. First, it provides increased stored energy that can be used to pay for the increased metabolic rates often associated with winter. Second, increased fat

decreases heat loss through radiation while also decreasing the rate at which the body cools down. Fur, and feathers in birds, also enhance the thermal properties of the organism by trapping warm air near the body.

Acclimation

Early in the chapter we described the idea of acclimation, and explained that exposure to mild cold (or heat) causes physiological changes in many species. Acclimation is a critical adaptation for many species that live in extreme environments. This may best be shown by the numerous studies conducted by C.J. Weiser and the laboratory of cold hardiness at the University of Minnesota. It was Weiser and his colleagues who identified the importance of winter temperatures to setting the northern limit of many plant species (Sakai and Weiser 1973). Weiser also found that for many species, the lower lethal temperature (i.e., killing temperature) decreases as winter approaches (Weiser 1970). For example, *Cornus stolonifera*, red-osier dogwood, will die if exposed to temperatures near freezing in July or August. However, that same species can withstand temperatures below −30°C in November (Weiser 1970). Clearly, acclimation to cold plays an important role in allowing species to live in extreme environments.

Inactivity, Tolerance, and Avoidance

A simple way to avoid extreme environmental temperatures is to seek shelter during the hottest or coldest times of the day. We have already seen one example of this behaviour. During the cold nights of the tropical alpine zone, *Liolaemus* lizards take shelter in burrows, where temperatures are several degrees warmer than on the surface. This form of behavioural response is common among many organisms, including reptiles, amphibians, and many insects, and it is equally effective in avoiding cold as well as excessive heat. As we have seen with badger setts, being belowground is an effective way of hiding from potential extreme surface temperatures.

Going underground is not always an option in cold climates, where the ground itself is frozen solid. Instead, many species take relief from the cold air by forming burrows within the snow. Fresh snow is an extremely good insulator, even better than the glass wool used in the walls of many modern homes (Marchand 1996)! As the snow ages and becomes more compact, it also becomes a poorer insulator. This process is very similar to what we see with fur and feathers. These are great insulators for animals when they are full of air, but if the fur becomes matted down and compressed, its insulative properties also are reduced. With a deep enough snow pack (generally more than 20 cm), ground temperatures can hover near zero, even if air temperatures are well below that value. This warm refuge serves as a critical way that many small mammals, unable to add substantial fat or fur, are able to survive in the north. The insulative properties of snow are also of great importance to people that live and travel in extreme temperatures.

Not all species will, or can, move to warmer microclimates, and instead their bodies will be exposed to subzero temperatures for at least some part of the winter. Having ice inside of one's body is not a particularly attractive notion, as ice crystals can rip apart cells and tissues, destroying critical organs in the process. However, freezing is not inevitable, even when temperatures are below zero. Why? You may recall from introductory chemistry that water freezes at 0°C only under very stringent conditions. The freezing point of water is actually quite variable, and is modified by changes in pressure and solute concentration. Organisms have little control over atmospheric pressure, but they can exert significant control over the solute concentration of the intra- and extracellular fluids, in effect manipulating them to become anti-freeze agents. As a result, many plants, insects, and polar marine fish are able to avoid having critical tissues destroyed by ice formation, even when temperatures are below zero.

A more extreme solution is found in a variety of ectotherms of northern areas: freeze tolerance. A number of species of turtles, snakes, and frogs are able to survive extreme temperatures because they allow their bodies to freeze, rather than spending substantial amounts of energy on the avoidance-of-freezing strategy dominant among endotherms. One of the best known examples is the wood frog, *Rana sylvatica.* The wood frog is found in forests over a broad geographic range, from above the Arctic Circle down into the Appalachian Mountains. It is found as far east as the Maritime provinces and west into Alaska. In a review of freezing tolerance in ectothermic vertebrates, Kenneth and Janet Storey of Carleton University describe many of the freezing features of this remarkable animal (1992). Wood frogs can survive more than 10 days, frozen, with body temperatures of −6°C. During this time, over 60% of the body fluids can be frozen solid (fig. 5.33). There is evidence of acclimation for freezing, with frogs in the fall having higher freezing-survival than do frogs of the spring. During the freezing, heart beat slows to around 4 beats/min, and then stops once the frog has frozen. The heart starts again within an hour of the body temperature reaching more than 3°C.

How can these frogs do this? Freeze tolerance requires several critical adaptations. One of the most important is the

Figure 5.33   Wood frogs can survive freezing during cold winter months.

presence of ice-nucleating compounds. These can be proteins, minerals, or microbes that initiate and control extracellular ice formation, the opposite effect to the one we found for the anti-freeze agents with the freeze-avoidance strategy, above. Without these nucleating compounds, ice formation would either be non-existent or, worse, would occur in a haphazard manner within the body, causing serious tissue damage. A second critical adaptation is the presence of high levels of cryoprotectants, such as glucose. Rapid synthesis of glucose in the liver by wood frogs occurs immediately following ice crystallization on the body surface. The glucose is distributed to cells throughout the body where it reduces cell damage. The exact mechanisms involved remain unclear. A third critical adaptation in wood frogs is that prior to freezing, much of the extracellular fluids are removed from critical organs and stored in the lymphatic system and coelom. A few jagged ice crystals in these locations are less likely to cause significant damage.

Reducing Metabolic Rate

The last group of physiological adaptations to extreme temperatures are likely the most familiar to you, and all involve reducing an organism's metabolic rate. One of the great difficulties for many organisms that live in areas of extreme temperatures is that even if they are able to survive exposure to the conditions, there is little available food. As a result, their maintenance costs (e.g., metabolism) will be greater than their entire energy budget, and thus substantial weight loss and/or mortality may ensue. There is nothing an animal can do about whether its food items are available or not; however, the maintenance cost of the organism can be controlled. Many organisms enter periods in which they reduce their metabolic rates, thereby reducing their energy demands.

Hummingbirds depend upon a diet of nectar and insects to maintain a high metabolic rate and a body temperature of about 39°C. When food is abundant, they maintain these high rates throughout the day and night. However, when food is scarce and night temperatures are cold, they may enter a state of torpor (fig. 5.34). **Torpor** is a state of self-induced hypothermia that generally lasts for only a few hours. In torpor, metabolic rates are reduced and core body temperatures are lowered, saving energy. During torpor, the hummingbird's body temperature may drop to between 12°C and 17°C. F. L. Carpenter and colleagues (1993) estimated that Rufous hummingbirds that maintain full body temperature all night metabolized 0.24g of fat. In torpor, these birds used only 0.02g of fat, an energy savings of over 90%.

Torpor can also be found among some mammal species. Mark Brigham, of the University of Regina, has been investigating the use of torpor by a diversity of organisms over the last several decades. He and colleagues (Willis et al. 2005) have shown that big brown bats, *Eptesicus fuscus*, can experience substantial drops in body temperature (fig. 5.35). They found that the bats generally entered torpor as soon as the ambient temperature went below the lower limit of the thermal neutral zone. As a result, although these bats are mammals, there was only a very narrow range of temperatures in which they maintained constant body temperatures.

Torpor generally only lasts for a few hours. Prolonged states of reduced metabolic activity are common in many other species. If this occurs mainly in winter, it is called **hibernation**; if in summer, it is called **estivation**. During hibernation, the body temperature of arctic ground squirrels may drop to 2°C. The metabolic rates of hibernating marmots may fall to 3% of the levels seen during active periods. During estivation, the metabolic rates of long-neck turtles may fall to 28% of their normal metabolic rate. Such reductions in metabolism allow individuals to survive long arctic and alpine winters, or hot and dry periods in the desert, during which they must rely entirely on stored energy reserves. Without this reduction

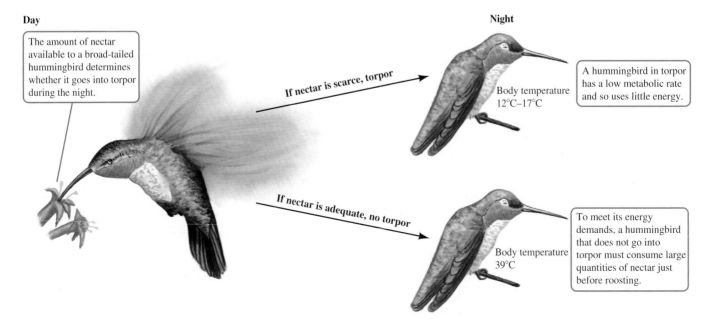

Day

The amount of nectar available to a broad-tailed hummingbird determines whether it goes into torpor during the night.

If nectar is scarce, torpor

If nectar is adequate, no torpor

Night

Body temperature 12°C–17°C

A hummingbird in torpor has a low metabolic rate and so uses little energy.

Body temperature 39°C

To meet its energy demands, a hummingbird that does not go into torpor must consume large quantities of nectar just before roosting.

Figure 5.34   The availability of nectar affects whether broadtailed hummingbirds enter torpor at night.

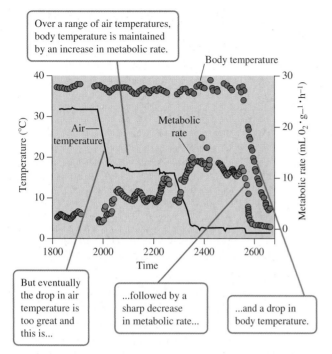

Over a range of air temperatures, body temperature is maintained by an increase in metabolic rate.

But eventually the drop in air temperature is too great and this is...

...followed by a sharp decrease in metabolic rate...

...and a drop in body temperature.

Figure 5.35 Some mammals, such as the big brown bat, can enter torpor. The graph describes the metabolic recording in one evening for one nonreproductive big brown bat (*Eptesicus fuscus*). Metabolic rate is measured as net O_2 consumption, V_{O2} (data from Willis et al. 2005).

in metabolism, metabolic costs would be too great for their energy budget and mortality would occur.

Temperature relations are a significant factor influencing the ecology of a diversity of species across the globe. This branch of ecology is attracting increased attention within the scientific community, fuelled by concerns about the ecological consequences of global warming, a topic we discuss in depth in chapter 23. In the Ecological Tools and Approaches section, we look at how studies of temperature relations and climatic warming are helping to explain the local extinction of a species.

CONCEPT 5.5 REVIEW

1. How can death be considered an evolutionarily successful strategy for coping with extreme temperatures?
2. Do plants and animals have similar or completely different mechanisms for dealing with extreme temperatures? Explain.
3. Why don't hummingbirds save energy by going into torpor at night even when food supplies are abundant? In other words, what would be a possible disadvantage of routine, nightly torpor?

ECOLOGICAL TOOLS AND APPROACHES

Climatic Warming and the Local Extinction of a Land Snail

One of the most powerful ecological tools is the ability to study single locations over extended periods of time. Many organisms grow slowly, reproduce even more slowly, and exhibit changes in population size at what seems to be a snail's pace. Understanding how thermal factors alter the population size of a given organism requires a long study. Unfortunately, most agencies that fund ecological research guarantee funds for only a short period of time, typically 1 to 5 years. As a result, ecologists are learning a lot about ecological processes that occur in less than five years. However, ecologists are used to finding ways to address longer problems, and the creativity to do so is itself an essential research tool of an ecologist. Here we discuss how only a long-term study could have solved a mystery of local extinctions.

Between 1906 and 1908, a graduate student named G. Bollinger (1909) studied land snails in the vicinity of Basel, Switzerland. Eighty-five years later, Bruno Baur and Anette Baur (1993) carefully resurveyed Bollinger's study sites near Basel for the presence of land snails. In the process, they found

that at least one snail species, *Arianta arbustorum*, had disappeared from several of the sites. This discovery led the Baurs to explore the mechanisms that may have produced extinction of these local populations.

A. arbustorum is a common land snail in meadows, forests, and other moist, vegetated habitats in northwestern and central Europe. The species lives at altitudes up to 2,700 m in the Alps. The Baurs report that the snail is sexually mature at 2 to 4 years and may live up to 14 years. Adult snails have shell diameters of 16 to 20 mm. The species is hermaphroditic. Though individuals generally mate with other *A. arbustorum*, they can fertilize their own eggs. Adults produce one to three batches of 20 to 80 eggs each year. They deposit their eggs in moss, under plant litter or in the soil. Eggs generally hatch in 2 to 4 weeks, depending upon temperature. The egg is an especially sensitive stage in the life cycle of land snails. *A. arbustorum* often lives alongside *Cepea nemoralis*, a land snail with a broader geographic distribution that extends from southern Scandinavia to the Iberian peninsula.

How did the Baurs document local extinctions of *A. arbustorum*? If you think about it a bit, you will probably realize that it is usually easier to determine the presence of a species than its absence. If you do not encounter a species during a survey, it may be that you just did not look hard enough. Fortunately, the Baurs had over 13 years of experience doing field work on *A. arbustorum* and knew its natural history well. For instance, they knew that it is best to search for the snails after rainstorms, when up to 70% of the adult population is active. Consequently, the Baurs searched Bollinger's study sites after heavy rains. They concluded that the snail was absent at a site only after two, 2-hour surveys failed to turn up either a living individual or an empty shell of the species.

The Baurs found *A. arbustorum* still living at 13 of the 29 sites surveyed by Bollinger near Basel. Eleven of these remaining populations lived in deciduous forests and the other two lived on grassy riverbanks. However, the Baurs could not find the snail at 16 sites. Eight of these sites had been urbanized, which made the habitat unsuitable for any land snails because natural vegetation had been removed. Between 1900 and 1990, the urbanized area of Basel had increased by 500%. However, the eight other sites where *A. arbustorum* had disappeared were still covered by vegetation that appeared suitable. Four of these sites were covered by deciduous forest, three were on riverbanks, and one was on a railway embankment. These vegetated sites also supported populations of five other land snail species, including *C. nemoralis*.

What caused the extinction of *A. arbustorum* at sites that still supported other snails? The Baurs compared the characteristics of these sites with those of the sites where *A. arbustorum* had persisted. They found no difference between these two groups of sites in regard to slope, percent plant cover, height of vegetation, distance from water, or number of other land snail species present. The first major difference the Baurs uncovered was in altitude. The sites where *A. arbustorum* was extinct have an average altitude of 274 m. The places where it survived have an average altitude of 420 m. The places where the snail had survived were also cooler.

A thermal image of the landscape taken from a satellite showed that surface temperatures in summer around Basel ranged from about 17°C to 32.5°C. Surface temperatures where *A. arbustorum* had survived averaged approximately 22°C, while the sites where the species had gone extinct had surface temperatures that averaged approximately 25°C. The sites where the snail was extinct were also much closer to very hot areas with temperatures greater than 29°C. Figure 5.36 is based on the Baurs' thermal image of the area around Basel and shows where the snail was extinct and where it persisted.

The Baurs attributed the higher temperatures at the eight sites where the snail is extinct to heating by thermal radiation

from the urbanized areas of the city. Buildings and pavement store more heat than vegetation. In addition, the cooling effect of evaporation from vegetation is lost when an area is built over. Increased heat storage and reduced cooling make urbanized landscapes thermal islands. Heat energy stored in urban centres is transferred to the surrounding landscape through thermal radiation, H_r.

The Baurs documented higher temperatures at the sites near Basel where *A. arbustorum* is extinct and identified a well studied mechanism that could produce the higher temperatures of these sites. However, are the temperature differences they observed sufficient to exclude *A. arbustorum* from the warmer sites? The researchers compared the temperature relations of *A. arbustorum* and *C. nemoralis* to find some clues. They concentrated their studies on the influence of temperature on reproduction by these two snail species.

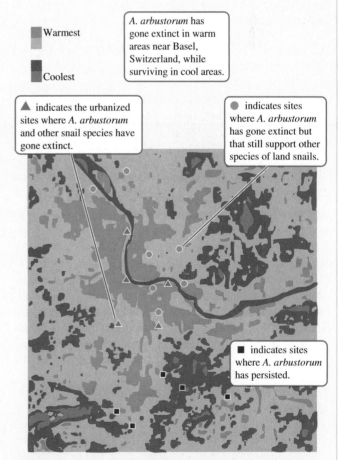

Figure 5.36   Relative surface temperatures and patterns of extinction and persistence by the snail *Arianta arbustorum* around Basel, Switzerland (data from Baur and Baur 1993).

The eggs of each species were incubated at four temperatures—19°C, 22°C, 25°C, and 29°C. Notice that these temperatures fall within the range measured by the satellite image (fig. 5.36). The eggs of both species hatched at a high rate at 19°C. However, at higher temperatures, their eggs hatched at significantly different rates. At 22°C, less than 50% of *A. arbustorum* eggs hatched, while the eggs of *C. nemoralis* continued to hatch at a high rate. At 25°C, no *A. arbustorum* eggs hatched, while approximately 50% of the *C. nemoralis* eggs hatched. At 29°C, the hatching of *C. nemoralis* eggs was also greatly reduced. Figure 5.37 summarizes the results of this hatching experiment.

The results of this study show that the eggs of *A. arbustorum* are more sensitive to higher temperatures than are the eggs of *C. nemoralis.* This greater thermal sensitivity can explain why *A. arbustorum* is extinct at some sites, while *C. nemoralis* survived. These results also suggest that climatic warming can lead to the local extinction of species. As we face the prospect of warming on a global scale, studies of temperature relations will assume greater importance. In chapter 6, we look at a related topic, water relations.

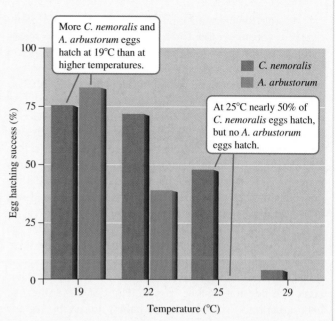

Figure 5.37   Temperature and hatching success of two snail species; the eggs of *Arianta arbustorum* are sensitive to high temperatures (data from Baur and Baur 1993).

SUMMARY

5.1 Macroclimate interacts with the local landscape to produce microclimatic variation in temperature.

The sun's uneven heating of the earth's surface and earth's permanent tilt on its axis produce macroclimate. Macroclimate interacts with the local landscape—mainly albedo, altitude, aspect, vegetation, colour of the ground, and small-scale structural features such as boulders and burrows—to produce microclimates. For the individual organism, macroclimate may be less significant than microclimate. The physical nature of water limits temperature variation in aquatic environments.

5.2 Adapting to one set of environmental conditions generally reduces fitness in other environments.

The principle of allocation, which is supported by research on bacterial populations, proposes that evolutionary trade-offs are inevitable, since organisms have access to limited amounts of energy.

5.3 Most species perform best in a fairly narrow range of temperatures.

The influence of temperature on the performance of organisms begins at the molecular level, where extreme temperatures impair the functioning of enzymes. Rates of photosynthesis and microbial activity generally peak in a narrow range

of temperatures and are much lower outside of this optimal temperature range. How temperature affects the performance of organisms often corresponds to the current distributions of species and their evolutionary histories.

5.4 Many organisms have evolved ways to compensate for variations in environmental temperature by regulating body temperature.

Temperature regulation balances heat gain against heat loss. Plants and ectothermic animals use morphology and behaviour to modify rates of heat exchange with the environment. Birds and mammals rely heavily on metabolic energy to regulate body temperature. The physical nature of the aquatic environment reduces the possibilities for temperature regulation by aquatic organisms. Most endothermic aquatic species are air breathers. Some organisms, mainly flying insects and some large marine fish, improve performance by selectively heating parts of their anatomy. The energetic requirements of thermoregulation may influence the geographic distribution of species.

5.5 Organisms exhibit a diversity of mechanisms to cope with extreme temperatures.

Many species are unable to live in extreme temperatures, restricting their range. For some species, the adult stages of many organisms will die during extreme events, while an

alternative life-stage, such as seeds, persist during these periods. Other species avoid extreme temperatures through regular migrations to more moderate climates. For species that stay year-round in extreme environments, maintaining a positive energy budget is difficult. Energy budgets can be described by pie diagrams, with trade-offs in allocation between growth, maintenance, reproduction, and activity. Increasing insulative properties of the organism through fur, fat, and feathers reduces heat loss through radiation. Moderate microclimates can often be found underground or beneath deep snow pack, reducing the need for elevated metabolic rates. Many animals enter a state of torpor, reducing metabolic rates during periods of inactivity. Periods of reduced metabolic rates can also persist for several months. If this occurs mainly in winter, it is called hibernation. In summer, it is called estivation. Energy savings from reducing metabolic rates allow organisms to live in environments even when resources are periodically scarce and temperatures are extreme.

Long-term studies of populations of land snails around Basel, Switzerland, have documented local extinctions of these land snails. These extinctions are attributable to habitat destruction and climatic warming. The results of these studies suggest that climatic warming can lead to the local extinction of species. As we face the prospect of climatic warming at a global scale, studies of temperature relations will assume greater importance.

REVIEW QUESTIONS

1. Many species of plants and animals that are associated with boreal forests also occur on mountains far to the south of the boreal forests. Using what you have learned about microclimates, predict how aspect and elevation would influence their distributions on these southern mountains.

2. Imagine a desert beetle that uses behaviour to regulate its body temperature above 35°C. How might this beetle's use of microclimates created by shrubs, burrows, and bare ground change with the season?

3. Figure 5.10 shows how temperature influences the activity of acetylcholinesterase in rainbow trout. Assuming that the other enzymes of rainbow trout show similar responses to temperature, how would trout swimming speed change as environmental temperature increases above 20°C?

4. The Ecological Tools and Approaches section reviews how the studies of Bruno Baur and Anette Baur (1993) have documented the local extinction of the land snail *Arianta arbustorum*. Their research also shows that these extinctions may be due to reduced egg hatching at higher temperatures. Do these results show conclusively that the direct effect of higher temperatures on hatching success is responsible for the local extinctions of *A. arbustorum*? Propose and justify alternative hypotheses. Be sure you take into account all of the observations of the Baurs.

5. Butterflies, which are ectothermic and diurnal, are found from the tropical rain forest to the Arctic. They can elevate their body temperatures by basking in sunlight. How would the percentage of time butterflies spend basking versus flying change with latitude? Would the amount of time butterflies spend basking change with daily changes in temperature?

6. Some plants and grasshoppers in hot environments have reflective body surfaces, which make their radiative heat gain, H_r, less than it would be otherwise. If you were to design a beetle that could best cope with thermal challenges associated with living on snow, what colour would it be? If these beetles were white, what would that tell us about the relative roles of thermoregulation and predation pressure in determining beetle colour? What does this example imply about the ability of natural selection to "optimize" the characteristics of organisms?

7. In most of the examples discussed in chapter 5, we saw a close match between the characteristics of organisms and their environment. However, natural selection does not always produce an optimal, or even a good, fit of organisms to their environments. To verify this you need only reflect on the fact that most of the species that have existed are now extinct. What are some of the reasons for a mismatch between organisms and environments? Develop your explanation using the environment, the characteristics of organisms, and the nature of natural selection.

8. Why do species exhibit different strategies for coping with extreme temperatures? Why hasn't evolution resulted in all species doing the "right" thing under these conditions?

9. Draw energy budgets using pie diagrams for a typical endotherm and ectotherm. What aspects of these budgets likely represent the largest energy expenditure? Which type of organism likely has more food intake and a larger overall energy budget?

10. Many animals huddle together in extreme cold. What is the possible energetic benefit of this behaviour? Under what climatic conditions is huddling likely to be disadvantageous?

WATER RELATIONS

CHAPTER 6

CHAPTER CONCEPTS

6.1 Concentration gradients influence the movement of water between an organism and its environment.
Concept 6.1 Review

6.2 Terrestrial plants and animals regulate their internal water by balancing water acquisition against water loss.
Ecology In Action: Dams, Flows, and Cottonwoods
Concept 6.2 Review

6.3 Marine and freshwater organisms use complementary mechanisms for water and salt regulation.
Concept 6.3 Review
Ecological Tools and Approaches: Using Stable Isotopes to Study Water Uptake by Plants
Summary
Review Questions

arm temperatures do not directly cause significant harm to most organisms. However, increased temperatures can lead to high rates of water loss, which can be lethal. Water plays a central role in the lives of all organisms in all habitats, though water acquisition and conservation are particularly critical for desert organisms. As a consequence, many ecologists studying the water relations of organisms have focused their attention on desert species. An example is found in the Sonoran Desert cicada, *Diceroprocta apache.* Even when air temperature in the shade hovers around 46°C and the ground surface temperature is over 70°C, the buzz of cicada can be heard. All other animals take refuge from the desert heat, as these temperatures cause rapid water loss and dehydration. Aside from the cicada, the desert can be quiet, with the exception of an ecologist trying to understand how the cicada copes with these extreme conditions.

Eric Toolson knows a lot about cicadas, and he has learned to associate the call of *Diceroprocta* with the hottest hours of the day, when air temperatures often exceeded the lethal limit for the species. Toolson wanted to understand how this species could be active in temperatures that would cause dehydration for most others. We might ask the same question of Toolson himself. How did he maintain a body temperature of approximately 37°C in this desert heat? Humans cool by sweating, and to keep from becoming dehydrated, Toolson drank a lot of water. This enabled him to maintain sufficient internal water and continue to evaporatively cool by sweating. But what about the cicada that did not have a bottle of water?

Did the cicada conserve water and keep cool by using small, shady microclimates in the mesquite tree from which it called? Did the cicada somehow manage to evaporatively cool? This seems unlikely, since biologists have long assumed that insects are too small and vulnerable to water loss to do so. If *Diceroprocta* did evaporatively cool, how did it avoid desiccating in the desert heat? Figure 6.1 summarizes the physical conditions under which *Diceroprocta* lives that inspired Toolson and his colleagues to study its ecology (Toolson 1987, Toolson and Hadley 1987).

Before we discuss the ecology of these desert cicadas, we need to introduce some background information. Water and life on earth are closely linked, with most organisms consisting of between 50% and 90% water. Life on earth originated in salty aquatic environments and is built around biochemistry within an aquatic medium. To survive and reproduce, organisms must maintain appropriate internal concentrations of water and dissolved substances. To maintain these internal concentrations, organisms must balance water losses to the environment with water intake. How organisms maintain this water balance is called their water relations, which is the subject of chapter 6, and it will be intimately intertwined with temperature relations, the subject of chapter 5.

Figure 6.1   An ecological puzzle: the cicada, *Diceroprocta apache,* is active when air temperatures would appear to be lethal for the species.

The problem of maintaining proper water balance is especially strong for those organisms, such as *Diceroprocta,* that live in arid terrestrial environments. A parallel challenge faces organisms that live in aquatic environments with a high salinity. However, most organisms, in nearly all habitats, must expend some energy to maintain their internal pool of water.

6.1   Water Availability

Concentration gradients influence the movement of water between an organism and its environment. The tendency of water to move down concentration gradients and the magnitude of those gradients between an organism and

its environment determine whether an organism tends to lose or gain water from the environment. To understand the water relations of organisms, we must understand the basic physical behaviour of water in terrestrial and aquatic environments.

In chapter 2, we saw that water availability on land varies tremendously among biomes, from the tropical rain forest with abundant moisture throughout the year to hot deserts with year-round drought. In chapter 3, we reviewed the considerable variation in salinity among aquatic environments, ranging from the diluted waters of tropical rivers to hypersalined lakes. The majority of aquatic environments fall somewhere between these extremes. Salinity, as we shall see, reflects the relative "aridity" of aquatic environments.

In snow-covered areas such as the arctic tundra and boreal forests, water availability can be particularly variable within a single year. As we saw in chapter 2, tundra habitats can be dry, with less than 200 mm precipitation a year, or relatively moist, with over 500 mm per year. Such variability also occurs in the boreal forest. One dominant feature of these colder habitats is that whatever precipitation falls can remain frozen for much of the year, making it unusable by most resident organisms until snowmelt. Even within Canada there is substantial geographic variation in both the average duration and average maximum snow depth (fig. 6.2). Notice that in the far north there are relatively few days without snow cover each year. As a consequence, liquid water is available to support growth and activity for only short periods of each year. Throughout most of Canada, however, snowmelt generally results in moist soils in the spring, and water is not generally limiting to spring and early summer plant growth. Water may become more limiting during the summer, depending upon the amount of rainfall that is received.

These broad comparisons across biomes ignores the substantial variation faced by individual organisms within their microclimates—microclimates such as those experienced by a desert animal that lives at an oasis, where it has access to abundant moisture, or a rain forest plant that lives in the forest canopy where it is exposed to full tropical sun and drying winds. As with temperature, to understand the water relations of an organism we must consider its microclimate. We begin with a simple question facing all individuals: How much water is there?

Water Content of Air

For organisms living on land, the answer to this question will depend upon how much water is found in the air that surrounds them. As we saw when we reviewed the hydrologic cycle in chapter 3, water

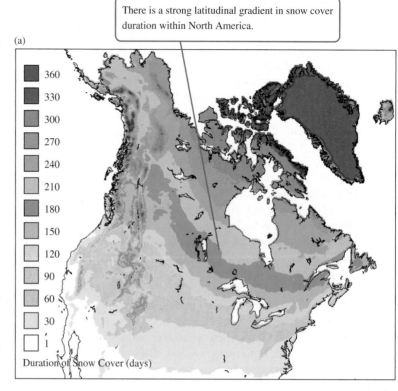

(a)

■	360
■	330
■	300
■	270
■	240
■	210
■	180
■	150
■	120
■	90
■	60
■	30
□	1

Duration of Snow Cover (days)

> There is a strong latitudinal gradient in snow cover duration within North America.

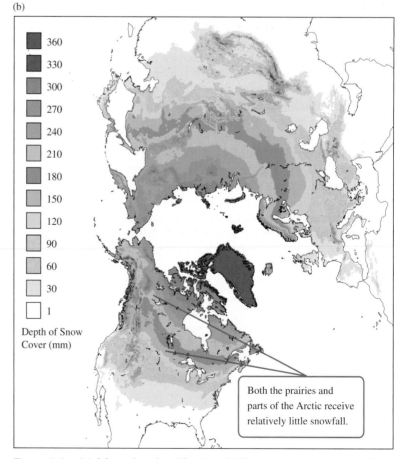

(b)

■	360
■	330
■	300
■	270
■	240
■	210
■	180
■	150
■	120
■	90
■	60
■	30
□	1

Depth of Snow Cover (mm)

> Both the prairies and parts of the Arctic receive relatively little snowfall.

Figure 6.2   (*a*) Mean duration (days) and (*b*) average maximum depth (mm) of snow cover throughout northern latitudes.

vapour is continuously added to air as water evaporates from the surfaces of oceans, lakes, and rivers. On land, evaporation also accounts for much of the water lost by organisms. The potential for such evaporative water loss depends upon the temperature and water content of the air around the organisms. As the amount of water vapour in the surrounding air increases, the water concentration gradient from organisms to the air is reduced and the rate at which organisms lose water to the atmosphere decreases.

We know how temperature is measured, but how is the water content of air measured? The quantity of water vapour in the air can be expressed in relative terms. Since air rarely contains all the water vapour it can hold, we can use its degree of saturation with water vapour as a relative measure of water content. The most familiar measure of the water content of air relative to its content at saturation is **relative humidity**, defined as:

$$\text{Relative humidity} = \frac{\text{Water vapour density}}{\text{Saturation water vapour density}} \times 100$$

The actual amount of water in air is measured directly as the mass of water vapour per unit volume of air. This quantity, the *water vapour density*, is the numerator in the relative humidity equation and is given either as milligrams of water per litre of air (mg H_2O/L) or as grams of water per cubic metre of air (g H_2O/m^3). The quantity of water vapour that air can potentially hold is its *saturation water vapour density*, the denominator in the relative humidity equation. Saturation water vapour density changes with temperature and, as you can see from the orange curve in figure 6.3, warm air can hold more water vapour than cold air.

A visual demonstration of this difference in water holding capacity of air as a function of temperature is seen each winter. Why exactly can you see your breath on a cool winter morning? As an endotherm, your breath will be a fairly consistent temperature of approximately 37°C. Additionally, the function of gas exchange in our lungs is dependent upon the alveoli being saturated with water. As a result, our breath is generally at 100% relative humidity, which at body temperature results in over 40 g/m^3 of water leaving our bodies upon exhalation. What happens when that wet, hot air leaves your body? If the humidity of the air is less than 100%, some of the water in your breath will be absorbed by the surrounding air. However, if the air temperature is low, such as 0°C, it will hold substantially less water (5 g/m^3 at 0°C). This means the remaining 35 g/m^3 cannot enter the air, and instead condenses into a cloud, and you see your breath.

One of the most useful ways of expressing the quantity of water in air is in terms of the pressure it exerts. If we express the water content of air in terms of pressure, we can use similar units to consider the water relations of organisms in air, soil, and water. We usually think in terms of *total atmospheric pressure*, the pressure exerted by all the gases in air, but you can also calculate the partial pressures due to individual atmospheric gases such as oxygen, nitrogen, or water vapour. We call this last quantity **water vapour pressure**. At sea level, atmospheric pressure averages approximately

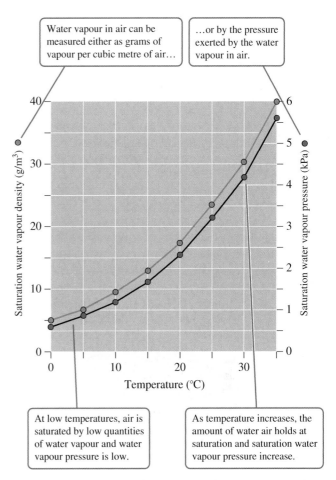

Figure 6.3   The relationship between air temperature and two measures of water vapour saturation of air.

760 mm of mercury, the height of a column of mercury supported by the combined force (pressure) of all the gas molecules in the atmosphere. The international convention for representing water vapour pressure, however, is in terms of the pascal (Pa), where 1 Pa is 1 Newton of force per square metre. Using this convention, 760 mm of mercury, or one atmosphere of pressure, equals approximately 101,300 Pa, 101.3 kilopascals (kPa), or 101 megapascals (MPa = 10^6 Pa).

The pressure exerted by the water vapour in air that is saturated with water is called **saturation water vapour pressure**. As the black curve in figure 6.3 shows, this pressure increases with temperature and closely parallels the increase in saturation water vapour density shown by the red curve. Why are the two curves so similar? They are similar because the amount of pressure exerted by a gas, in this case water vapour, is directly proportional to its density.

We can also use water vapour pressure to represent the *relative* saturation of air with water. We calculate this measure, called the **vapour pressure deficit (VPD)**, as the difference between the actual water vapour pressure and the saturation water vapour pressure at a particular temperature. In warm moist environments, air is near saturation and VPD is low. In warm dry environments, relative humidity will be lower and VPD is higher. In terrestrial environments, water flows from organisms to the atmosphere at a rate influenced by the

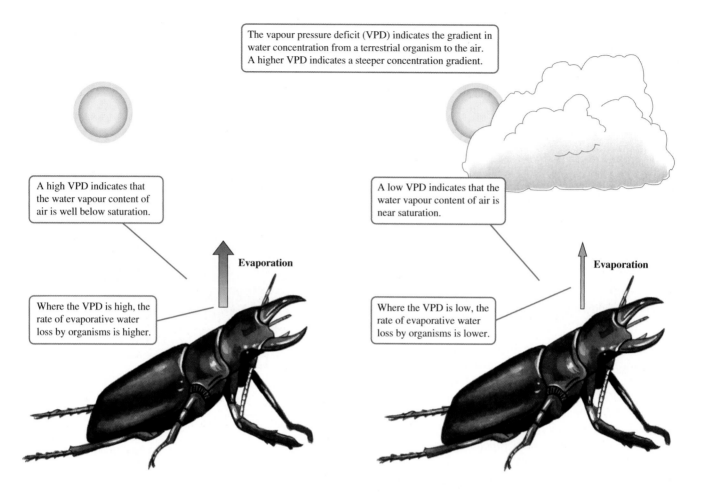

The vapour pressure deficit (VPD) indicates the gradient in water concentration from a terrestrial organism to the air. A higher VPD indicates a steeper concentration gradient.

A high VPD indicates that the water vapour content of air is well below saturation.

A low VPD indicates that the water vapour content of air is near saturation.

Evaporation

Evaporation

Where the VPD is high, the rate of evaporative water loss by organisms is higher.

Where the VPD is low, the rate of evaporative water loss by organisms is lower.

Figure 6.4   The potential for evaporative water loss by terrestrial organisms increases with increased vapour pressure deficit.

vapour pressure deficit of the air surrounding the organism. Figure 6.4 shows the relative rates of water loss by an organism exposed to air with a low versus high VPD. Again, one of the most useful features of VPD is that it is expressed in units of pressure, generally kilopascals.

Water Movement in Aquatic Environments

In aquatic environments, water moves down its concentration gradient. It may sound silly to speak of the amount of water in an aquatic environment but, as we saw in chapter 2, all aquatic environments contain dissolved substances. These dissolved substances dilute the water. While oceanographers and limnologists (those who study bodies of freshwater) generally focus on salt content, or salinity, here we take the opposite point of view—a focus on water. Though this will be "backwards" for those that first learned the principles of water and solute movement in limnology and oceanography courses, this point of view allows us to build a consistent perspective for considering water relations in air, water, and soil throughout this chapter.

From this perspective, pure H_2O is the most concentrated. Slightly less concentrated will be freshwater, which is itself more concentrated than the oceans. The oceans, in turn, contain more water per litre than do saline lakes such as the Dead Sea or the Great Salt Lake. The relative concentration of water in each of these environments strongly influences the biology of the organisms that live in them.

The body fluids of all organisms contain water and solutes, including inorganic ions and amino acids. We can think of aquatic organisms and the environment that surrounds them as two aqueous solutions separated by a selectively permeable membrane. If the internal environment of the organism and the external environment differ in concentrations of water and salts, these substances will tend to move down their concentration gradients. This movement of solutes is called **diffusion**. We give the movement of water across a semipermeable membrane a special name, **osmosis**, where water moves from areas of high water concentration to low water concentration. As a point of clarification, if you were hoping you could learn ecology through "osmosis" by placing this text under your pillow at night and having all the nuggets of knowledge move into your brain, you are woefully incorrect. Osmosis refers specifically to the movement of water. As long as knowledge moves in the form of particles, then the "under pillow" method is an example of diffusion (particles of ecological knowledge moving from high concentration in the text to low concentration in the brain of the student needing to sleep on a textbook).

In the aquatic environment, water moving down its concentration gradient produces osmotic pressure. Osmotic

pressure, like vapour pressure, can be expressed in pascals. The strength of the osmotic pressure across a semipermeable membrane, such as the gills of a fish, depends upon the difference in water concentration across the membrane. Larger differences, between organism and environment, generate higher osmotic pressures.

Aquatic organisms generally live in one of three environmental circumstances. Organisms with body fluids containing the same concentration of water as the external environment are **isosmotic**. Organisms with body fluids with a higher concentration of water (lower solute concentration) than the external medium are **hypoosmotic** and tend to lose water to the environment. Those with body fluids with a lower concentration of water (higher solute concentration) than the external medium are **hyperosmotic** and are subject to water flooding inward from the environment. In the face of these osmotic pressures, aquatic organisms must expend energy to maintain a proper internal environment. How much energy the organism must expend depends upon the magnitude of the osmotic pressure between them and the environment and the permeability of their body surfaces. Figure 6.5 summarizes the movement of water and salts into and out of isosmotic, hyperosmotic, and hypoosmotic organisms.

Water Movement Between Soils and Plants

Plants play a critical role in the global hydrological cycle (chapter 3). You may recall from introductory biology that plants take up liquid water from the soil, move it through their vascular tissues, and transpire it through stomata into the atmosphere as water vapour. It is estimated that on a global scale, 10% of the water vapour in the atmosphere is there due to plant transpiration. Any change in transpiration rates could have significant consequences for cloud cover and groundwater reserves. For example, Nicola Gedney and colleagues (2006) explored the possible reasons why freshwater runoff has increased by approximately 3% throughout the twentieth century. Using a series of simulation models, they found the largest contributor is likely decreased transpiration of plants due to increased atmospheric CO_2 concentrations. This reduction in transpiration is thought to have increased annual global runoff by 2,000 km^3, with many potential ecological and societal consequences. We will discuss the links between CO_2 and transpiration in chapter 7, but first we must better understand transpiration itself.

On land, water flows from the organism to the atmosphere at a rate influenced by the VPD of the air surrounding the organism. In the aquatic environment, water may flow either to or from the organism, depending on the relative concentrations of water and solutes in body fluids and the surrounding medium. But here too, water flows down its concentration gradient. As shown in figure 6.6, water moving from the soil through a plant and into the atmosphere flows down a gradient of **water potential**. We can conceptualize water potential as the capacity of water to do work. Flowing water has the capacity to do work such as turning the water wheel of a water mill or the turbines of a hydroelectric plant. The capacity of water to do work depends upon its free energy content. Water

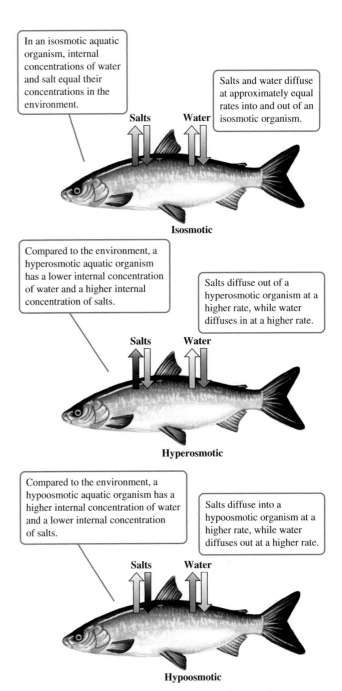

In an isosmotic aquatic organism, internal concentrations of water and salt equal their concentrations in the environment.

Salts and water diffuse at approximately equal rates into and out of an isosmotic organism.

Salts   Water

Isosmotic

Compared to the environment, a hyperosmotic aquatic organism has a lower internal concentration of water and a higher internal concentration of salts.

Salts diffuse out of a hyperosmotic organism at a higher rate, while water diffuses in at a higher rate.

Salts   Water

Hyperosmotic

Compared to the environment, a hypoosmotic aquatic organism has a higher internal concentration of water and a lower internal concentration of salts.

Salts diffuse into a hypoosmotic organism at a higher rate, while water diffuses out at a higher rate.

Salts   Water

Hypoosmotic

Figure 6.5   Water and salt regulation by isosmotic, hyperosmotic, and hypoosmotic aquatic organisms.

flows from positions of higher to lower free energy. Under the influence of gravity, water flows downhill from a position of higher free energy, at the top of the hill, to a position of lower free energy, at the bottom of the hill.

In the previous section, "Water Movement in Aquatic Environments," we saw that water flows down its concentration gradient, from locations of higher water concentration (hypoosmotic) to locations of lower water concentration (hyperosmotic). The measurable "osmotic pressure" generated by water flowing down these concentration gradients shows that water flowing in response to osmotic gradients has the capacity to do work. Which has a higher free energy

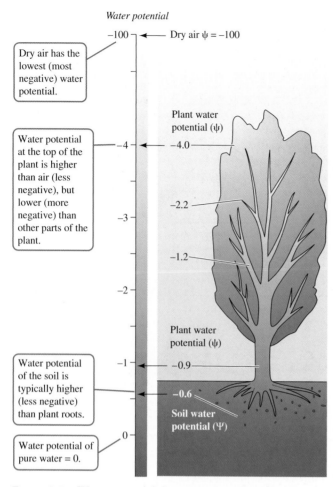

Water potential

Dry air has the lowest (most negative) water potential.

Water potential at the top of the plant is higher than air (less negative), but lower (more negative) than other parts of the plant.

Water potential of the soil is typically higher (less negative) than plant roots.

Water potential of pure water = 0.

Dry air $\psi = -100$

Plant water potential (ψ)   −4.0

−2.2

−1.2

Plant water potential (ψ)   −0.9

−0.6
Soil water potential (Ψ)

Figure 6.6 Water potential decreases (becomes more negative) as you move from soil to plant to atmosphere (data from Wiebe et al. 1970).

content, pure water or seawater? Since osmotic flow would be from pure water to seawater and water flows from high to low free energy, pure water must have higher free energy content than seawater. We measure water potential, like vapour pressure deficit and osmotic pressure, in pascals, usually megapascals (MPa = Pa $\times$ 10^6). By convention, water potential is represented by the symbol Ψ (Psi), and the water potential of pure water at one atmosphere of pressure is set at 0. If the water potential of pure water is 0, then the water potential of a solution, such as seawater, must be negative (i.e., < 0).

In nature, water potential is generally negative. Why is that? This must be so since all water in nature, even rainwater, contains some solute or occupies spaces where matric forces (see following) are significant. So, gradients of water potential in nature are generally from less negative to more negative water potential. This convention takes a bit of getting used to. Once familiar, however, the convention is useful for representing and thinking about the water relations of plants. Figure 6.6 shows that water is flowing down a gradient of water potential that goes from a slightly negative water potential in the soil through the moderately negative water potentials of the plant to the highly negative water potential of dry air.

Now let's look at some of the mechanisms involved in producing a gradient of water potential such as that shown in figure 6.6. We can express the water potential of a solution as:

$$\Psi = \Psi_{solutes}$$

$\Psi_{solutes}$ is the reduction in water potential due to dissolved substances, which is a negative number.

Within small spaces, such as the interior of a plant cell or the pore spaces within soil, other forces, called **matric forces**, are also at work. Matric forces are a consequence of water's tendency to adhere to the walls of containers such as cell walls or the soil particles lining a soil pore. Matric forces lower water potential. The water potential for fluids within plant cells is approximately:

$$\Psi_{plant} = \Psi_{solutes} + \Psi_{matric}$$

In this expression, Ψ_{matric} is the *reduction* in water potential due to matric forces within plant cells. For most plants species, matric forces are very low and thus this term is often ignored. At the level of the whole plant, another force is generated as water evaporates from the surface of leaves into the atmosphere. Evaporation of water from the surfaces of leaves generates a negative pressure, or tension, on the column of water that extends from the leaf surface through the plant all the way down to its roots. This negative pressure reduces the water potential of plant fluids still further.

So, the water potential of plant fluids is affected by solutes, matric forces, and the negative pressures exerted by evaporation. Consequently, we can represent the water potential of plant fluids as:

$$\Psi_{plant} = \Psi_{solutes} + \Psi_{matric} + \Psi_{pressure}$$

Here again, $\Psi_{pressure}$ is the *reduction* in water potential due to negative pressure created by water evaporating from leaves.

Thus, for most species, plant physiological ecologists view water potential in plants as:

$$\Psi_{plant} = \Psi_{solutes} + \Psi_{pressure}$$

Because soils are the immediate source of water for plants, and because water in the soil influences microbial growth and nutrient cycling, it is important to also understand the factors that control water potential in the soil.

In plants, matric forces were small, and solute and pressure forces were strong. The opposite is the case for soils, with the solute content of soil water near zero, minimal pressure forces, and strong soil matric forces. Thus for soils:

$$\Psi_{soil} \cong \Psi_{matric}$$

Matric forces vary considerably from one soil to another, depending primarily upon soil texture and pore size. Coarser soils with larger pore sizes, such as sands and loams, exert lower matric forces, while fine clay soils, with smaller pore sizes, exert higher matric forces. So, while clay soils can hold a higher quantity of water compared to sandy soils, the higher matric forces within clay soils bind that water more tightly.

As long as the water potential of plant tissues is less than the water potential of the soil, $\Psi_{plant} < \Psi_{soil}$, water flows from the soil to the plant.

The higher water potential of soil water compared to the water potential of roots induces water to flow from the soil into plant roots. As water enters roots from the surrounding soil, it joins a column of water that extends from the roots through the water-conducting cells, or xylem, of the stem to the leaves. Hydrogen bonds between adjacent water molecules bind the water molecules in this water column together. Consequently, as water molecules at the upper end of this column evaporate into the air at the surfaces of leaves, they exert a tension, or negative pressure, on the entire water column. This negative pressure further reduces the water potential of plant fluids and helps power uptake of water by terrestrial plants. Figure 6.7 summarizes the mechanisms underlying the flow of water from soil to plants.

As plants draw water from the soil, they soon deplete the water held in the larger soil pore spaces, leaving only water held in the smaller pores. Within these smaller soil pores matric forces are greater than in the larger pores. Consequently, as soil dries, soil water potential becomes more and more negative and the remaining water becomes harder and harder to extract.

This section has given us a basis for considering the availability of water to organisms living in terrestrial and aquatic environments. Let's use the foundation we have built here to explore the water relations of organisms on land and in water. To survive and reproduce, organisms must maintain appropriate internal concentrations of water and dissolved substances. As a consequence, in the face of variation in water availability, organisms have been selected to regulate their internal water.

CONCEPT 6.1 REVIEW

1. Why are the two curves shown in figure 6.3 so similar?
2. Which has a higher free energy content, pure water or seawater?
3. Why is water potential in nature generally negative?

6.2   Water Regulation on Land

Terrestrial plants and animals regulate their internal water by balancing water acquisition against water loss. When organisms first moved into the terrestrial environment, they faced two major water-related challenges: potentially massive losses of water to the environment through evaporation, and reduced access to replacement water. Many adaptations helped terrestrial organisms meet these challenges and acquire the capacity to regulate their internal water content.

To understand water regulation, physiological ecologists use a series of equations to summarize the main determinants of water content, or water potential, within an organism. Although the processes that govern water movement in plants, animals, microbes, and soils are conceptually similar, the notation used by scientists in each subdiscipline is not. Further, different components will be more important for some taxa than others. For consistency here, we use a single form of notation which emphasizes general concepts rather than using subdiscipline-specific notation.

We can summarize water regulation by terrestrial animals as:

$$W_i = W_d + W_f + W_a - W_e - W_s$$

This says simply that the internal water of an animal (W_i) results from a balance between water acquisition and water loss. The major sources of water are:

W_d = water taken by drinking

W_f = water taken in with food

W_a = water absorbed from the air

The avenues of water loss are:

W_e = water lost by evaporation

W_s = water lost with various secretions and excretions including urine, mucus, and feces

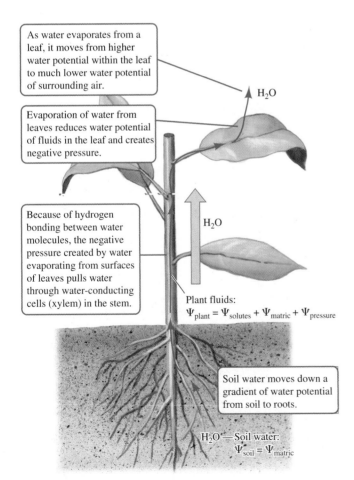

As water evaporates from a leaf, it moves from higher water potential within the leaf to much lower water potential of surrounding air.

Evaporation of water from leaves reduces water potential of fluids in the leaf and creates negative pressure.

Because of hydrogen bonding between water molecules, the negative pressure created by water evaporating from surfaces of leaves pulls water through water-conducting cells (xylem) in the stem.

H_2O

H_2O

Plant fluids:
$\Psi_{plant} = \Psi_{solutes} + \Psi_{matric} + \Psi_{pressure}$

Soil water moves down a gradient of water potential from soil to roots.

H_2O — Soil water:
$\Psi_{soil} = \Psi_{matric}$

Figure 6.7 Mechanisms of water movement from soil through plants to the atmosphere.

We can summarize water regulation by terrestrial plants in a similar way:

$$W_i = W_r + W_a - W_t - W_s$$

The internal water concentration of a plant (W_i) results from a balance between gains and losses, where the major sources of water for plants are:

W_r = water taken from soil by roots

W_a = water absorbed from the air

The major ways that plants lose water are:

W_t = water lost by transpiration

W_s = water lost with various secretions including nectar, and tissue loss including fruit, seeds, and senescent leaves and roots

The main avenues of water gain and loss by terrestrial plants and animals are summarized in figure 6.8. The figure presents a generalized picture of the water relations of terrestrial organisms. However, organisms in different environments face different environmental challenges and they have evolved a wide variety of solutions to those problems. Let's now look at the diverse ways in which terrestrial plants and animals regulate their internal water.

Water Acquisition by Animals

Many small terrestrial animals can absorb water from the air. Most terrestrial animals, however, satisfy their need for water either by drinking or by taking in water with food. In moist climates there is generally plenty of water, and, if water becomes scarce, the mobility of most animals allows them to go to sources of water to drink. In deserts, animals that need abundant water must live near oases. Those that live out in the desert itself, away from oases, have evolved adaptations for living in arid environments.

Some desert animals acquire water in unusual ways. Coastal deserts such as the Namib Desert of southwest Africa receive very little rain but are bathed in fog. This aerial moisture is the water source for some animals in the Namib. One of these, a beetle in the genus *Lepidochora* of the family Tenebrionidae, takes an engineering approach to water acquisition. These beetles dig trenches on the face of sand dunes to condense and concentrate fog. The moisture collected by these trenches runs down to the lower end, where the beetle waits for a drink. Another tenebrionid beetle, *Onymacris unguicularis*, collects moisture by orienting its abdomen upward. Fog condensing on this beetle's body flows to its mouth. Figure 6.9 shows this beetle's unique means of obtaining drinking water. *Onymacris* also takes in water with its food. Some of this water is absorbed within the tissues of the food.

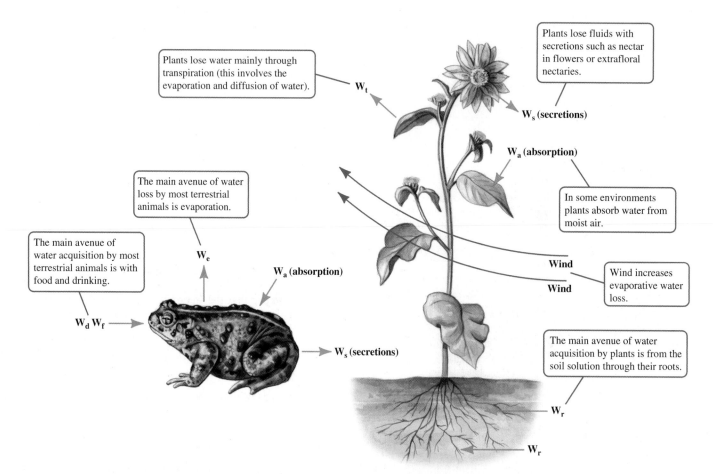

Plants lose fluids with secretions such as nectar in flowers or extrafloral nectaries.

Plants lose water mainly through transpiration (this involves the evaporation and diffusion of water). W_t

W_s (secretions)

W_a (absorption)

In some environments plants absorb water from moist air.

The main avenue of water loss by most terrestrial animals is evaporation.

W_e

W_a (absorption)

Wind

Wind

Wind increases evaporative water loss.

The main avenue of water acquisition by most terrestrial animals is with food and drinking.

$W_d \, W_f$

W_s (secretions)

The main avenue of water acquisition by plants is from the soil solution through their roots.

W_r

W_r

Figure 6.8 Terrestrial plants and animals can be characterized by analogous pathways for water gain and loss.

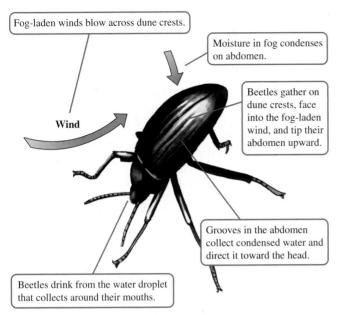

Fog-laden winds blow across dune crests.

Moisture in fog condenses on abdomen.

Beetles gather on dune crests, face into the fog-laden wind, and tip their abdomen upward.

Wind

Grooves in the abdomen collect condensed water and direct it toward the head.

Beetles drink from the water droplet that collects around their mouths.

Figure 6.9   Some beetles of the Namib Desert can harvest sufficient moisture from fog to meet their needs for water.

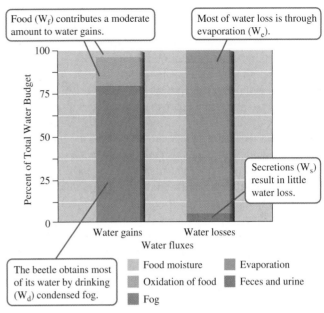

Food (W_f) contributes a moderate amount to water gains.

Most of water loss is through evaporation (W_e).

Secretions (W_s) result in little water loss.

The beetle obtains most of its water by drinking (W_d) condensed fog.

Food moisture — Evaporation
Oxidation of food — Feces and urine
Fog

Figure 6.10   Water budget of the desert beetle, *Onymacris unguicularis* (data from Cooper 1982).

The remaining water is produced when the beetle metabolizes the carbohydrates, proteins, and fats contained in its food. We can see the source of this "metabolic water" if we look at an equation for oxidation of glucose:

$$C_6H_{12}O_6 + 6\,O_2 \rightarrow 6\,CO_2 + 6\,H_2O$$

As you can see, cellular respiration liberates the water that combined with carbon dioxide during the process of photosynthesis (see chapter 5). The water released during cellular respiration is called **metabolic water**.

Paul Cooper (1982) estimated the water budget for free ranging *Onymacris* from the Namib Desert near Gobabeb. He estimated the rate of water intake by this beetle at 49.9 mg of H_2O per gram of body weight per day. Of this total, 39.8 mg came from fog, 1.7 mg came from moisture contained within food, and 8.4 mg came from metabolic water. The rate of water loss by these beetles, 41.3 mg of H_2O per gram per day, was slightly less than water intake. Of this total, 2.3 mg were lost with feces and urine, and 39 mg by evaporation. The water budget of the beetle studied by Cooper is shown in figure 6.10.

While *Onymacris* gets most of its water from fog, other small desert animals get most of their water from their food. Kangaroo rats of the genus *Dipodomys* are found throughout the arid regions of Canada, United States, and Mexico. This group of rodents possess traits that allow them to avoid needing to drink at all, and instead they can survive entirely on metabolic water. Knut Schmidt-Nielsen (1964) showed that the approximately 60 ml of water gained from eating 100 g of barley makes up for the water a Merriam's kangaroo rat, *D. merriami*, loses in feces, urine, and evaporation while metabolizing the 100 g of grain! The 100 g of barley contains only 6 ml of absorbed water, that is, water that can be driven off by drying. The remaining 54 ml of water is released as

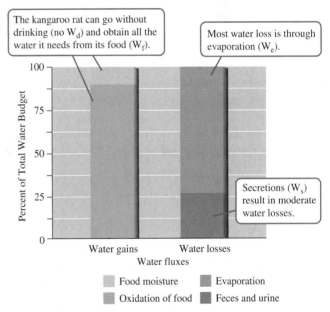

The kangaroo rat can go without drinking (no W_d) and obtain all the water it needs from its food (W_f).

Most water loss is through evaporation (W_e).

Secretions (W_s) result in moderate water losses.

Food moisture — Evaporation
Oxidation of food — Feces and urine

Figure 6.11   Water budget of Merriam's kangaroo rat *Dipodomys merriami* (data from Schmidt-Nielsen 1964).

the animal metabolizes the carbohydrates, fats, and proteins in the grain. The importance of metabolic water in the water budget of Merriam's kangaroo rat is pictured in figure 6.11.

While animals generally obtain most of their water by drinking or with their food, these options are not available to plants. Though many plants can absorb some water from the air, most get the bulk of their water from the soil through their roots.

Water Acquisition by Plants

Plants in dry climates generally grow relatively more, and deeper, roots than do plants in moist climates. The tap roots of some desert shrubs can extend up to 30 m down into the soil,

giving them access to deep groundwater. Roots may account for up to 90% of total plant biomass in deserts, grasslands, and tundra. In contrast, roots in coniferous forests typically constitute only about 25% of total plant biomass.

You do not have to compare forests and deserts, however, to observe differences in root architecture. R. Coupland and R. Johnson (1965) compared the rooting characteristics of plants growing in the dry mixed grasslands of western Canada. During their study, they carefully excavated the roots of over 850 individual plants, digging over 3 m deep to trace some roots. They found that many species have lower root biomass and higher aboveground biomass in moist microclimates within the temperate grassland biome than in the drier areas. For instance, the roots of *Artemesia frigida* grow over 120 cm deep on dry sites; on moist sites, its roots grow only to a depth of about 60 cm (fig. 6.12). These deeper roots often help plants from dry environments extract water from deep within the soil profile.

Many people have followed the up on the work of Coupland, excavating root systems around the world. Jochen Schenk and Robert Jackson (2002) conducted an analysis of 475 root profile, studies from 209 geographic localities (see fig. 6.12 for an example of such a study). In over 90% of the 475 root profiles, at least 50% of roots were in the top 0.3 m of the soil and at least 95% of roots were in the upper 2 m (fig. 6.13). However, they also found pronounced geographic differences in rooting depth. Rooting depth increased from 80° to 30° latitude, that is from arctic tundra to Mediterranean woodlands and shrublands and deserts (chapter 2). However, there were no clear trends in rooting depth in the tropics. Consistent with our present discussion, Schenk and Jackson found that deeper rooting depths occur mainly in water-limited ecosystems.

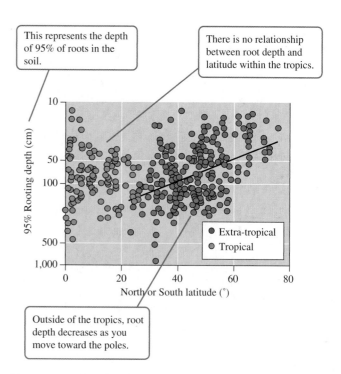

Figure 6.13   Rooting depth varies across a broad geographical gradient (data from Schenk and Jackson 2002).

Water Conservation by Plants and Animals

Another way to balance a water budget is by reducing water losses. One of the most obvious ways to cut down on water losses is by waterproofing to reduce evaporation. Many terrestrial plants and animals cover themselves with a fairly waterproof "hide" impregnated with a variety of waterproofing waxes. However, some organisms are more waterproof than others, and rates of evaporative water loss vary greatly from one animal or plant species to another.

Why do the water loss rates of organisms differ? One reason is that species have evolved in environments that differ greatly in water availability. As a consequence, selection for water conservation has been more intense in some environments than others. Species that evolved in warm deserts are generally much more resistant to desiccation than relatives that evolved in moist tropical or temperate habitats. In general, populations that evolved in drier environments lose water at a slower rate. For instance, turtles from wet and moist habitats lose water at a much higher rate than do desert tortoises (fig. 6.14). As the following example shows, the water loss rates of even closely related species can differ substantially.

Neil Hadley and Thomas Schultz (1987) studied two species of tiger beetles in Arizona that occupy different microclimates. *Cicindela oregona* lives along the moist shoreline of streams and is active in fall and spring. In contrast, *Cicindela obsoleta* lives in the semiarid grasslands of central and southeastern Arizona and is active in summer. The researchers suspected that these differences in microclimate select for differences in waterproofing of the two tiger beetles.

Hadley and Schultz studied the waterproofing of the tiger beetles by comparing the amount of water each species lost while

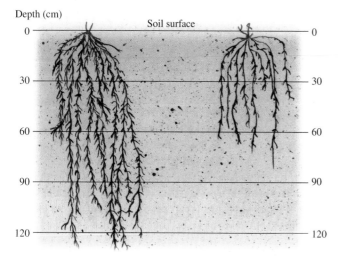

Figure 6.12   Soil moisture influences the extent of root development by this desert forb (data from Coupland and Johnson 1965).

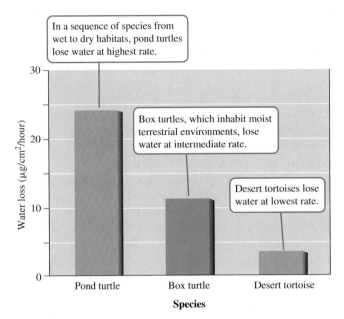

Figure 6.14   Rates of water loss by two turtles and a tortoise indicate an inverse relationship between the dryness of the habitat and water loss rates (data from Schmidt-Nielsen 1969).

held in an experimental chamber. They pumped dry air through the chamber at a constant rate and maintained its temperature at 30°C. They weighed each beetle at the beginning of an experiment and then again after 3 hours in the chamber. The difference between initial and final weights gave them an estimate of the water loss rate of each beetle. By determining water loss for several individuals of each species, they estimated the average water loss rates for *C. oregona* and *C. obsoleta*. Hadley and Schultz found that *C. oregona* loses water two times as fast as *C. obsoleta* (fig. 6.15). In other words, the species from the drier microclimate, *C. obsoleta*, appears to be more waterproofed.

Waterproofing of the cuticles of terrestrial insects is usually provided by hydrocarbons. Hydrocarbons include organic compounds such as lipids and waxes. Because of their influences on waterproofing, Hadley and Schultz analyzed the cuticles of the two species of tiger beetles for their hydrocarbon content. They found that the concentration of hydrocarbons in the cuticle of *C. obsoleta* is 50% higher than in the cuticle of *C. oregona* (fig. 6.16). In addition, the two species differ in the percentages of cuticular hydrocarbons that are saturated with hydrogen. Fully saturated hydrocarbons are much more effective at waterproofing. One hundred percent of the hydrocarbons in the cuticle of *C. obsoleta* are saturated. In contrast, only 50% of the cuticular hydrocarbons of *C. oregona* are saturated. These results support the hypothesis that *C. obsoleta* loses water at a lower rate because its cuticle contains a higher concentration of waterproofing hydrocarbons.

Merriam's kangaroo rats conserve water sufficiently that they can live entirely on the moisture contained within their food and on "metabolic water" (see fig. 6.11). This capacity is assumed to be an adaptation to desert living. Over long periods of time, as the American Southwest became increasingly arid, the ancestors of today's Merriam's kangaroo rats were subject to natural selection that favoured a range of adaptations to dry environments, including water conservation. However, Merriam's kangaroo rat is a widespread species that lives from 21° N latitude in Mexico to 42° N latitude in northern Nevada. Over this large geographic range, Merriam's kangaroo rat populations are exposed to a very broad range of environmental conditions.

Intrigued by their large geographic range and exceptional adaptation to desert living, Richard Tracy and Glenn Walsberg studied three populations of Merriam's kangaroo rats across a

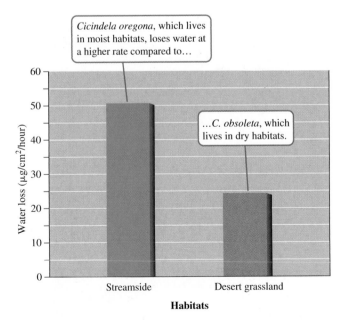

Figure 6.15   A tiger beetle species from a moist habitat lost water at a higher rate than one from a dry habitat (data from Hadley and Schultz 1987).

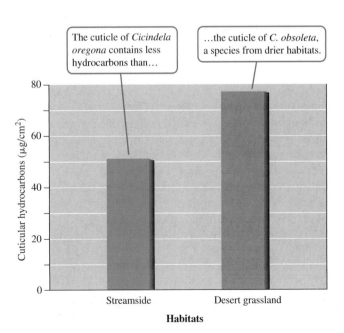

Figure 6.16   The cuticles of tiger beetles from dry habitats tend to contain a higher concentration of waterproofing hydrocarbons compared to tiger beetles from moist habitats (data from Hadley and Schultz 1987).

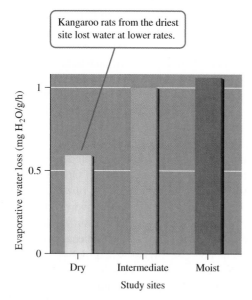

Kangaroo rats from the driest site lost water at lower rates.

Figure 6.17 Water loss rates by Merriam's kangaroo rats from across a moisture gradient suggest adaptation to local climate by each of the populations (data from Tracy and Walsberg 2001).

climatic gradient. Their main objective was to determine if different populations of Merriam's kangaroo rat vary in their degree of adaptation to living in dry environments (Tracy and Walsberg 2000, 2001, 2002). The three populations studied live in southwest Arizona near Yuma, central Arizona, and north-central Arizona, at elevations of 150 m, 400 m, and 1200 m respectively. Mean annual maximum temperatures at the study sites are 31.5°C, 29.1°C, and 23.5°C, and mean annual precipitation at the three sites is 10.6 cm, 33.6 cm, and 43.6 cm. The differences in climates at the three study sites are reflected in the vegetation. The habitat at the driest site consists of sand dunes with scattered shrubs; the intermediate site is a desert shrubland; and the vegetation at the moist site consists of a pinyon-juniper woodland.

One of the main questions asked by Tracy and Walsberg was whether rates of evaporative water loss would differ among the Merriam's kangaroo rats at dry, intermediate, and moist sites. The results of this study showed clear differences among the study populations. The mean rate of evaporative water loss at the dry site was 0.69 mg of water per g per hour, compared to 1 mg H_2O/g/h and 1.08 mg H_2O/g/h at the intermediate and moist sites respectively (fig. 6.17). Tracy and Walsberg expressed the rate of water loss by the kangaroo rats on a per gram basis because the kangaroo rats from the three sites differ significantly in size. The average mass of individuals from the moist site was approximately 33% greater than the mass of rats from the dry site. In additional studies, Tracy and Walsberg found that acclimating animals to laboratory conditions did not eliminate the differences in water conservation among populations. In other words, even after being kept in the laboratory under controlled conditions, Merriam's kangaroo rats from the driest study site continued to lose water at a lower rate. The evidence from these studies supports the conclusion that these three populations differ in their degree of adaptation to desert living.

Animals adapted to dry conditions have many other water conservation mechanisms besides waterproofing. These mechanisms include producing concentrated urine or feces with low water content, condensing and reclaiming the water vapour in breath, and restricting activity to times and places that decrease water loss.

Plants have also evolved a wide variety of means for conserving water, which result in different water use efficiencies (WUE). WUE is defined as the biomass of plant tissue produced per gram of water used, and this value will vary among species. The WUE of a plant depends in part on its leaf area relative to its root area or length. Plants with more leaf surface per length of root tend to lose more water. Compared to plants from moist climates, arid land plants generally have less reduced leaf area : root area ratios, and correspondingly higher water use efficiencies. Many plants reduce leaf area over the short term by dropping leaves in response to drought. Some desert plants produce leaves only in response to soaking rains and then shed them when the desert dries out again. These plants reduce leaf area to zero in times of drought. Figure 6.18 shows one of these plants, the ocotillo of the Sonoran Desert of North America.

(a)

(b)

Figure 6.18 Changing leaf area: (*a*) following rainfall ocotillo plants of the Sonoran Desert develop leaves and flower; (*b*) during dry periods they lose their leaves and blossoms.

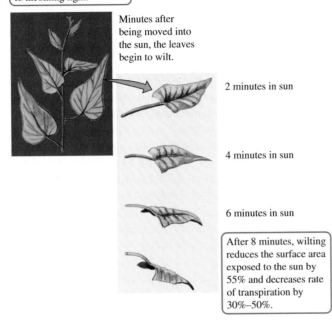

In a shaded portion of a greenhouse, the leaves of the rain forest plant are unwilted and fully exposed to incoming light.

Minutes after being moved into the sun, the leaves begin to wilt.

2 minutes in sun

4 minutes in sun

6 minutes in sun

After 8 minutes, wilting reduces the surface area exposed to the sun by 55% and decreases rate of transpiration by 30%–50%.

Figure 6.19   Temporary wilting by this rain forest plant decreases rates of water loss (data from Chiariello et al. 1987).

Other plant adaptations that conserve water include thick leaves, which have less transpiring leaf surface area per unit volume of photosynthesizing tissue than thin leaves do; few stomata on leaves rather than many; structures on the stomata that impede the movement of water; dormancy during times when moisture is unavailable; and alternative, water-conserving pathways for photosynthesis. (We discuss these alternative pathways for photosynthesis in chapter 7.)

We should remember that plants and animals in terrestrial environments other than deserts also show evidence of

selection for water conservation. For instance, Nona Chiariello and her colleagues (1987) discovered an intriguing example of adjusting leaf area in the moist tropics. *Piper auritum*, a large-leafed, umbrella-shaped plant, grows in clearings of the rain forest. Because it grows in clearings, the plant often faces drying conditions during midday. However, it reduces the leaf area it exposes to the midday sun by wilting. Wilting at midday reduces leaf area exposed to direct solar radiation by about 55% and leaf temperature by up to 4°C to 5°C. These reductions decrease the rate of transpiration by 30% to 50%, which is a substantial water savings. The behaviour of this tropical rain forest plant reminds us that even the rain forest has its relatively dry microclimates, such as the forest clearings where *P. auritum* grows. The rapidity of *P. auritum*'s wilting response is shown in figure 6.19.

Organisms balance their water budgets in numerous ways. Some rely mainly on water conservation. Others depend upon water acquisition. However, every biologist who studies organisms in their natural environment knows that nature is marked by diversity and contrast. To sample nature's variety, let's review the variety of approaches to desert living.

As in the example with *P. auritum*, plants have developed adaptations to cope with periodic water stress; however, these adaptations are often at odds with human needs. For example, although closing stomata reduces water loss and is likely to be a favoured strategy over evolutionary time, closing stomata also ceases photosynthesis (for most plants; see chapter 7), which is bad news for a farmer trying to grow a crop. Because of this evolutionary solution to short-term water stress, many agricultural fields are irrigated through the dry summer months, particularly in the southern prairies. As we saw from Steward Rood's work, changes in stream flow—for whatever purpose—will influence other habitats within the broader prairie landscape. How plants deal with water stress, and how humans rely on plants for survival, has changed the face of the prairies over the last century. This struggle continues as human consumption of water continues to rise, and climate change increases rates of evaporation and alters precipitation patterns.

ECOLOGY IN ACTION

Dams, Flows, and Cottonwoods

The western prairies of North America are often viewed as flat and dry expanses of unending fields of grasses. However, cutting through these areas are rivers and streams, often flowing out from the Rocky Mountains. Along these rivers we find a completely different type of habitat, a wetter riparian area dominated by trees (fig. 6.20). Standing on the bank of a river in the prairies, you will find yourself in floodplain forests, underneath the shade provided by the Cottonwoods (*Populus* spp.). When you walk just a few hundred metres away, these species are nowhere to be found. Floodplain forests are oases in the prairie

for many native animals as well as livestock. They are home to species of plants, insects, fungi, and other organisms not found in the drier regions of the prairie landscape, and thus these forests are critical to both maintenance of biodiversity and to the economic health of the dry prairies of western North America. However, over the last several decades there has been a severe decline in cottonwood abundances throughout the west, raising great concerns. To try to understand why this decline has occurred, and to see if the pattern can be reversed, we turn to the work of Stewart Rood of the University of Lethbridge.

(a)

(b)

(c)

Figure 6.20 (*a*) Cottonwood forests along the Old Man River in southern Alberta; (*b*) a flood on the Old Man River; (*c*) bands of Cottonwood trees of different ages, each established during different river floods.

We begin by trying to understand why Cottonwoods are restricted to riparian habitats, rather than being distributed broadly throughout the prairie itself. Cottonwoods tend to be early colonizers of bare riparian areas, providing a critical service of stream-bank stabilization (Rood et al. 2003). Isotopic analyses (see the Ecological Tools and Approaches section later in this chapter) indicate that Cottonwoods predominantly use **alluvial groundwater** (water that comes from a surface stream) rather than deeper ground water, at least during dry periods of the summer (Rood et al. 2003).

As a result of this reliance on surface waters, these plants are very sensitive to drought. The trees respond very quickly to reduced water availability through altered hormonal levels, stomatal closures (to reduce evaporation), and decreased photosynthesis (Rood et al. 2003). Over longer periods, drought leads to reduced growth and increased plant mortality. One of the unique aspects of cottonwood water relations is that they are particularly prone to **cavitation**. In cavitation, air bubbles form in the xylem, effectively breaking the chain of water from roots to leaves. Once cavitation occurs in the xylem, those cells no longer have the ability to move water, and thus cavitation can render large parts of the vascular tissue useless for these trees. In summary, Cottonwoods colonize bare riparian soil, use predominately shallow waters, and are uniquely sensitive to drought. These factors can explain why we do not find Cottonwoods in the driest parts of the prairies. However, what would explain why they are declining from areas that are traditionally the wettest parts of the landscape?

To answer this, we begin with a look at long-term trends in river flows heading east and west from the Rocky Mountains (Rood et al. 2005b). Rood and his colleagues collected data from a variety of existing long-term data sets of flows through 31 river reaches, with data collected upstream of any dams (we will get to dams shortly!). After adjusting for global climatic cycles (chapter 23), they found significant flow declines in 15 of the 31 river reaches. On average, rivers had a 0.22%/year flow reduction, with some Albertan rivers showing a recent decline as high at 0.5%/year. As we discussed in chapter 5, decreased water levels result in increased stream temperatures, with a variety of potential consequences for fish and other animals that live within the streams. Based upon what we know about Cottonwoods, their reliance on surface waters means reduced stream flows also puts them at increased risk of mortality and reduced growth. These changes in stream flows occurred upstream of dams, and thus are likely caused by large-scale climatic changes (e.g., global warming). However, direct human activity is putting additional pressures on these forest floodplain habitats.

Some activities, such as clearing forest for housing or agricultural development or harvesting trees for fuel and money, cause obvious negative consequences for riparian habitats that do not take any scientific understanding to understand. Instead we will discuss a more subtle and widespread challenge to these systems: dams. By design, dams modify stream flows, often with the intent of reducing flooding events and protecting property and infrastructure. Interestingly, even if dams provide a constant rate of river flow, cottonwood forests seem to decline. In other words, there is more than just water relations driving the loss of these forests. Rood and colleagues have explored the impacts of dams on riparian forests, and have found ways to work with dam operators to help restore these challenged riparian areas (Rood et al. 2005b).

As you may recall, Cottonwoods colonize bare and wet ground. Where is that bare ground found on the landscape? It is found along rivers after floods. Floods can rip out existing trees, cause severe erosion to stream beds, and leave large deposits of

organic material on large expanses of the prairie. Over timescales of decades and centuries, floods are common to the rivers of the west, and are most frequent during the early summer months. Cottonwood reproduction is suited to this fairly regular occurrence, with seed dispersal and seedling establishment following the summer floods. If a dam prevents flooding, it can also prevent successful establishment of Cottonwoods. But how can you reconcile flood prevention with cottonwood preservation? Rood has been part of many restoration projects where he works with dam operators to help allow for flood events without putting human infrastructure at risk. These projects have resulted in dramatic recruitment of Cottonwoods along both the Old Man and St. Mary rivers in Alberta (fig. 6.20).

The work of Rood and his colleagues is a wonderful example of how knowledge about the ecology of an organism, coupled with an understanding of the abiotic environment, can be used to address issues of societal concern. Without understanding how extreme water events influence cottonwood regeneration, it would be difficult to understand how to prevent further population declines. Rood has shown that ecologists can directly impact environmental decisions, in this case by helping to develop a new method of flow management from dams. However, floodplain forests still face the challenge of reduced flows even upstream of the dams, likely due to changes in global climate. It will be up to the next generation of ecologists to help solve this issue.

Dissimilar Organisms with Similar Approaches to Desert Life

On the surface, camels and saguaro cactus appear entirely different (fig. 6.21). If you look deeper into their biology, however, you find that they take very similar approaches to balancing their water budgets. Both the camel and the saguaro cactus acquire massive amounts of water when water is available, store water, and conserve water.

The camel can go for long periods in intense desert heat without drinking, up to six to eight days in conditions that would

kill a person within a day. During this time, the animal survives on the water stored in its tissues and can withstand water losses of up to 20% of its body weight without harm. For humans, a loss of about 10% to 12% is near the fatal limit. When the camel has the opportunity, it can drink and store prodigious quantities of water, up to one-third of its body weight at a time. Such consumptions of water by humans is generally also fatal.

Between opportunities to drink, the camel is a master of water conservation. One way it conserves body water is by reducing its rate of heat gain. Like overheating tiger beetles (see chapter 5), the camel faces into the sun, reducing the body

(a)

(b)

Figure 6.21 Two desert dwellers, (*a*) saguaro cactus, and (*b*) camel; as different as they are, they seem to show parallel adaptations to desert environments.

The saguaro reduces heat gain by exposing only tops of its trunk and branches to the midday sun.

The trunk and branch tips are shaded and insulated with a high density of spines, which reduces heat gain.

The camel does not store water in its hump but fat, which is a source of metabolic water.

The camel reduces heat gain by facing into the sun.

The camel is covered with dense hair, which reduces heat gain.

Water is stored in the massive trunk and arms.

The saguaro reduces water loss by transpiration by keeping stomates closed and allowing its temperature to rise.

When water is available, both the saguaro and camel take in massive quantities.

The camel reduces evaporative water loss by not sweating and allowing body temperature to rise.

Figure 6.22   Dissimilar organisms with similar approaches to desert living.

surface it exposes to direct sunlight. In addition, its thick hair insulates it from the intense desert sun, and rather than sweating sufficiently to keep its body temperature down, the camel allows its body temperature to rise by up to 7°C. This reduces the temperature difference between the camel and the environment and so decreases the rate of additional heating. Reduced heating translates into reduced water loss by evaporation.

The saguaro cactus takes a similar approach. The trunk and arms of the plant act as organs in which the cactus can store large quantities of water. During droughts, the saguaro draws on these stored reserves and so can endure long periods without water. When it rains, the saguaro, like a camel at an oasis, can ingest great quantities of water, but instead of drinking, the saguaro gets its water through its dense network of shallow roots. These roots extend out in a roughly circular pattern to a distance approximately equal to the height of the cactus. For a 15 m tall saguaro, this means a root coverage of over 700 m² of soil.

The saguaro also reduces its rate of evaporative water loss in several ways. First, like other cacti, it keeps its stomata closed during the day when transpiration losses would be highest. In the absence of transpiration, in full sun, the internal temperature of the saguaro rises to over 50°C, which is among the highest temperatures recorded in plants. However, as we noted for the

camel, higher body temperature can be an advantage because it reduces the rate of additional heating. The saguaro's rate of heating is also reduced by the shape and orientation of its trunk and arms. At midday, when the potential for heating is greatest, the saguaro exposes mainly the tips of its arms and trunk to direct sunlight. However, the tips of the saguaro's arms and trunk are insulated by a layer of plant hairs and a thick tangle of spines, which reflect sunlight and shade the growing tips of the cactus.

The parallel approaches to desert living seen in saguaro cactuses and camels are outlined in figure 6.22. Now let's examine two organisms that live in the same desert but have very different water relations.

Two Arthropods with Opposite Approaches to Desert Life

Though both are arthropods and may live within a few metres of each other, cicadas and scorpions take sharply contrasting approaches to living in the desert. The scorpion's approach is to slow down, conserve, and stay out of the sun. Scorpions are relatively large and long-lived arthropods with very low metabolic rates. A low rate of metabolism means that they can subsist on low rations of food and lose little water during

While Sonoran Desert cicada sings from the branches of a mesquite tree during a midsummer's afternoon...

...the scorpion spends the day in its burrow near the base of the tree.

Scorpions emerge from their burrows at night, when temperatures are lower.

The low temperature and high humidity of the burrow reduces water loss.

Waterproofed cuticle also reduces evaporative water loss.

A low metabolic rate reduces respiration and further decreases water loss.

Figure 6.23 These two desert arthropods, a scorpion and a cicada, have evolved very different approaches to living in the desert.

respiration. In addition, scorpions conserve water by spending most of their time in their burrows, where the humidity is higher than at the surface. They come out to feed and find mates only at night, when it is cooler. In addition, desert scorpions are well waterproofed; hydrocarbons in their cuticles seal in moisture. With this combination of water-conserving characteristics, scorpions can easily satisfy their need for water by consuming the moisture contained in the bodies of their arthropod prey. Figure 6.23 summarizes the habits of desert scorpions.

In comparison to desert scorpions, the cicada's approach to desert living may seem out of place. As we saw in the introduction to this chapter, the Sonoran Desert cicada, *Diceroprocta apache*, is active on the hottest days, when air temperature is near its lethal limit. How can *Diceroprocta* do this and not die? The solution to this puzzle begins with a study by James Heath and Peter Wilkin (1970). These researchers observed that just before sunrise, *Diceroprocta* perches on large branches of mesquite trees, *Prosopis juliflora*, where it feeds on the fluids in the tree's xylem. As the sun rises, the cicadas move from their feeding sites to leaves and twigs exposed to full sun. They remain motionless on these perches until midmorning, when the temperature rises above 35°C. At this high temperature, birds and wasps, the main predators of the cicadas, seek shelter from the heat.

As their predators retire to the shade, the cicadas reach their peak of activity. When body temperature reaches 39°C, they shift their position to the shade of large mesquite branches, where the males sing. If the temperature does not rise above 40°C, they sing throughout midday. However, when air temperature reaches 48°C, *Diceroprocta* will sit quietly from about 1:00 to 3:00 p.m., and then resume singing.

Heath and Wilkin found that singing *Diceroprocta* have a body temperature considerably below the temperature of the surrounding air. They also found that the temperature close to the surface of the branches where the cicadas perch is cooler than other potential perches. Heath and Wilkin concluded that the cicadas keep cool by remaining in these small patches of cool air on the shady sides of large branches. They suggested that these cool microclimates are too small to be exploited by birds, the chief predators of *Diceroprocta*.

Are cool microclimates the only means of thermoregulation used by *Diceroprocta*? A study of another cicada by two graduate students suggested that *Diceroprocta* might evaporatively cool. Stacy Kaser and Jon Hastings (1981) found evidence of evaporative cooling by *Tibicen duryi*, which lives in the same region as *Diceroprocta* but at higher elevations, where it feeds on the xylem fluids of pinyon pine trees, *Pinus edulis*. Kaser and Hastings found that the abdominal temperature of *Tibicen* remained lower than air temperature when air temperature rose above 36°C. The cicadas were able to maintain these reduced abdominal temperatures as long as they had access to xylem fluids. However, when Kaser and Hastings denied their access to water, their abdominal temperatures rose. Though never observed before, these results suggested that *Tibicen* is capable of evaporative cooling.

These observations led to a series of investigations and papers by Eric Toolson and Neil Hadley that showed conclusively that cicadas, including *Diceroprocta*, are capable of evaporative cooling. In one of these studies, Eric Toolson (1987) collected *Diceroprocta* from a mesquite tree and placed them in an environmental chamber. The chamber temperature was kept at 45.5°C; however, *Diceroprocta* was able to maintain its body temperature at least 2.9°C lower. Since the cicadas within the chamber did not have access to any cool

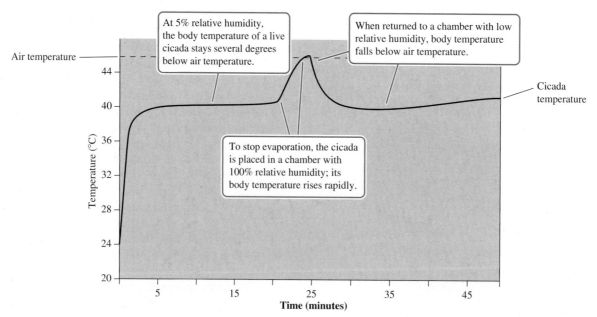

Figure 6.24   A laboratory experiment verified evaporative cooling by the cicada, *Diceroprocta apache* (data from Toolson 1987).

microclimates, Toolson concluded that they must be evaporatively cooling. To verify this hypothesis, he placed cicadas in the environmental chamber and then raised the relative humidity to 100%. At 100% relative humidity, the body temperatures of the cicadas quickly increased to the temperature of the environmental chamber. When Toolson reduced relative humidity to 0%, the cicadas cooled approximately 4°C within minutes. The results of this experiment are outlined in figure 6.24.

How do the results of Toolson's experiment support the hypothesis of evaporative cooling? Remember that air with a relative humidity of 100% contains all the water vapour it can hold. Consequently, by raising the humidity of the air surrounding the cicadas to 100%, Toolson shut off any evaporative cooling that might be taking place. When he reintroduced dry air, he created a gradient of water concentration from the cicada to the air and evaporative cooling resumed.

Toolson's results are consistent with the hypothesis that *Diceroprocta* evaporatively cools but does not demonstrate that capacity directly. Consequently, Toolson and Hadley (1987) conducted observations to make a direct demonstration. First, they placed a live *Diceroprocta* in an environmental chamber with a humidity sensor just above its cuticle. If *Diceroprocta* evaporatively cools, then this sensor would detect higher humidity as the temperature of the environment was increased. This is exactly what occurred. As the temperature was increased from 30°C to 43°C, the rate of water movement across the cicada's cuticle increased in three steps. When Toolson and Hadley increased the temperature from 37°C to 39°C, water loss increased from 5.7 to 9.4 mg H_2O per square centimetre per hour. At 41°C, water loss increased from 9.4 to 36.1 mg H_2O per square centimetre per hour, and at 43°C, water loss increased from 36.1 to 61.4 mg H_2O per square centimetre per hour. These results are graphed in figure 6.25.

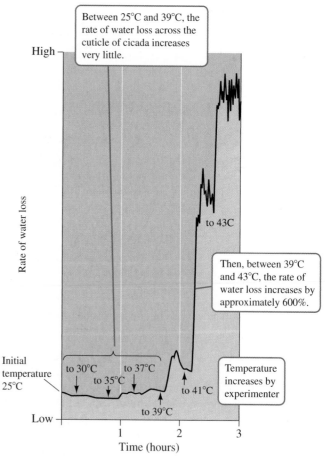

Figure 6.25   High temperatures induce massive rates of water loss by the cicada, *Diceroprocta apache* (data from Toolson and Hadley 1987).

The rate of water loss by *Diceroprocta* is among the highest ever reported for a terrestrial insect. How does water cross

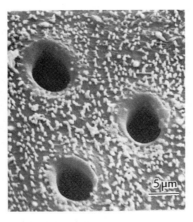

Figure 6.26 (*a*) Magnified view of *D. apache* outlining three areas with high densities of small pores; (*b*) dorsal pores under high magnification.

the cuticle of this cicada at such a high rate? Toolson and Hadley searched the cuticle of *Diceroprocta* for avenues of water movement. They found three areas on the dorsal surface with large pores that might be involved in evaporative cooling (fig. 6.26). When they plugged these pores, *Diceroprocta* could no longer cool itself. In summary, Toolson and Hadley verified a previously unknown phenomenon, evaporative

cooling by cicadas, and carefully demonstrated the underlying mechanisms.

So, it turns out that these cicadas can sing in the hottest hours of the desert day because they sweat! *Diceroprocta* is able to maintain this seemingly impossible lifestyle because it has tapped into a rich supply of water. Cicadas are members of the order Homoptera and distant relatives of the aphids. Like aphids, cicadas feed on plant fluids. So, though the cicada lives in the same macroclimate as the scorpion, it has tapped into a totally different microclimate. The cicada's scope for water acquisition is extended up to 30 m deep into the soil by the tap roots of its mesquite host plant, *P. juliflora*. *Diceroprocta* can sustain high rates of water loss through evaporation, high W_e, because it is able to balance these losses with a high rate of water acquisition, high W_d. Figure 6.27 illustrates how *Diceroprocta* uses mesquite trees to get access to deep soil moisture.

Sometimes, similar organisms employ radically different approaches to balancing their water budgets. Sometimes, organisms of very different evolutionary lineages employ functionally similar approaches. In short, the means by which terrestrial organisms balance water acquisition against water loss are almost as varied as the organisms themselves. Similar variation occurs among aquatic organisms.

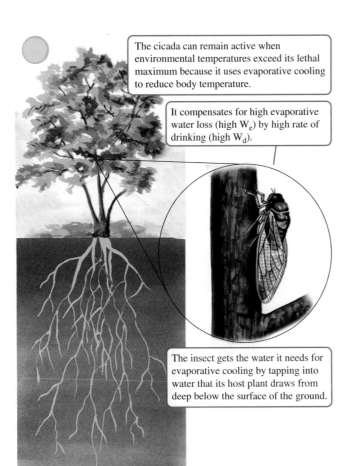

The cicada can remain active when environmental temperatures exceed its lethal maximum because it uses evaporative cooling to reduce body temperature.

It compensates for high evaporative water loss (high W_e) by high rate of drinking (high W_d).

The insect gets the water it needs for evaporative cooling by tapping into water that its host plant draws from deep below the surface of the ground.

Figure 6.27 An ecological puzzle solved.

CONCEPT 6.2 REVIEW

1. The tiger beetle *Cicindela oregona* has a distribution that extends from Arizona through the temperate rain forests of Alaska. Why should the amounts of cuticular hydrocarbons vary geographically among populations of *C. oregona*?
2. During severe droughts, some of the branches of shrubs and trees die, while others survive. How might losing some branches increase the probability that an individual plant will survive a drought?
3. How are water and temperature regulation related in many terrestrial organisms?

6.3 Water and Salt Balance in Aquatic Environments

Marine and freshwater organisms use complementary mechanisms for water and salt regulation. As we mentioned before, we continue here our discussion on water relations from the perspective of "water," rather than "solutes." Though this is reversed to traditions in limnology and oceanography, doing so allows us to more clearly draw comparisons among the different sections of this chapter.

Aquatic organisms, like their terrestrial kin, regulate internal water, W_i, by balancing water gain against water loss.

We can represent water regulation in aquatic environments by modifying our equation for terrestrial water balance to:

$$W_i = W_d - W_s \pm W_o$$

Drinking, W_d, is a ready source of water for aquatic organisms. Secretion of water with urine, W_s, is an avenue of water loss. By osmosis, W_o, an aquatic organism may either gain or lose water, depending on the organism and the environment.

Marine Fish and Invertebrates

Most marine invertebrates maintain an internal concentration of solutes equivalent to that in the seawater around them. What does the animal gain by remaining isosmotic with the external environment? The isosmotic animal does not have to expend energy overcoming an osmotic gradient. This strategy is not without costs, however. Though the total concentration of solutes is the same inside and outside the animal, there are still differences in the concentrations of some individual solutes. These concentration differentials can only be maintained by active transport, which consumes some energy.

Sharks, skates, and rays generally elevate the concentration of solutes in their blood to levels slightly hyperosmotic to seawater. However, inorganic ions constitute only about one-third of the solute in shark's blood; the remainder consists of the organic molecules urea and trimethylamine oxide (TMAO). As a consequence of being slightly hyperosmotic, sharks slowly gain water through osmosis, that is, W_o is slightly positive. The water that diffuses into the shark, mainly across the gills, is pumped out by the kidneys and exits as urine. Sodium, because it is maintained at approximately two-thirds its concentration in seawater, diffuses into sharks from seawater across the gill

membranes and some sodium enters with food. Sharks excrete excess sodium mainly through a specialized gland associated with the rectum called the salt gland. The main point here is that sharks and their relatives reduce the costs of osmoregulation by decreasing the osmotic gradient between themselves and the external environment (fig. 6.28).

In contrast to most marine invertebrates and sharks, marine bony fish have body fluids that are strongly hypoosmotic to the surrounding medium. As a consequence, they lose water to the surrounding seawater, mostly across their gills. Marine bony fish make up these water losses by drinking seawater. However, drinking adds to salt influxes through their gills. The fish rid themselves of excess salts in two ways. Specialized "chloride" cells at the base of their gills secrete sodium and chloride directly to the surrounding seawater, while the kidneys excrete magnesium and sulfate. These ions exit with the urine. The urine, because it is hypoosmotic to the body fluids of the fish, represents a loss of water. However, the loss of water through the kidneys is low because the quantity of urine is low.

The larvae of some mosquitoes in the genus *Aedes* live in saltwater. These larvae meet the challenge of a high-salinity environment in ways analogous to those used by marine bony fish. Like marine bony fish, saltwater mosquitoes are hypoosmotic to the surrounding environment, to which they lose water. Saltwater mosquitoes also make up this water loss by drinking large amounts of seawater, up to 130% to 240% of body volume per day. This would even impress a camel! While this prodigious drinking solves the problem of water loss, it imports another: large quantities of salts that must be eliminated. Saltwater mosquitoes secrete these salts into the urine using specialized cells that line the posterior rectum. Here, saltwater mosquitoes do something that marine bony fish

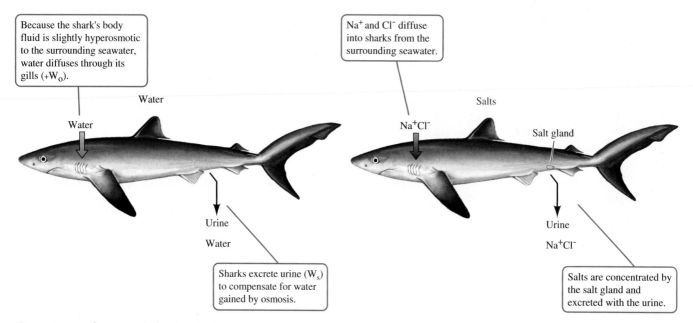

Figure 6.28   Osmoregulation by sharks.

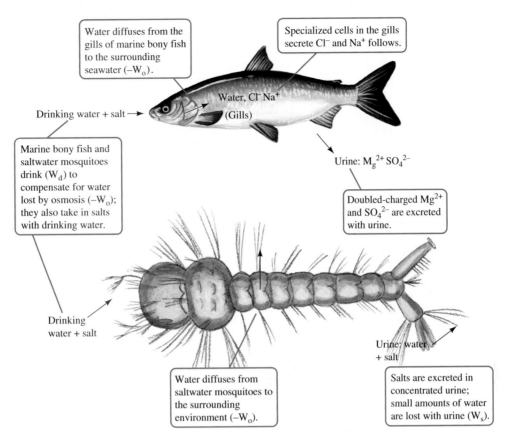

Water diffuses from the gills of marine bony fish to the surrounding seawater $(-W_o)$.

Specialized cells in the gills secrete Cl^- and Na^+ follows.

Drinking water + salt →

Water, Cl^- Na^+ (Gills)

Marine bony fish and saltwater mosquitoes drink (W_d) to compensate for water lost by osmosis $(-W_o)$; they also take in salts with drinking water.

Urine: Mg^{2+} SO_4^{2-}

Doubled-charged Mg^{2+} and SO_4^{2-} are excreted with urine.

Drinking water + salt

Urine: water + salt

Water diffuses from saltwater mosquitoes to the surrounding environment $(-W_o)$.

Salts are excreted in concentrated urine; small amounts of water are lost with urine (W_s).

Figure 6.29 Osmoregulation by marine fish and saltwater mosquitoes.

cannot: they excrete a urine that is hyperosmotic to their body fluids, which reduces water loss through the urine. The parallels in water and salt regulation by marine bony fish and saltwater mosquitoes are outlined in figure 6.29.

Freshwater Fish and Invertebrates

Freshwater bony fish face an environmental challenge opposite to that faced by marine bony fish. Freshwater fish are hyperosmotic; they have body fluids that contain more salt and less water than the surrounding medium. As a consequence, water floods inward and salts diffuse outward across their gills. Freshwater fish excrete excess internal water as large quantities of dilute urine. They replace the salts they lose to the external environment in two ways. Chloride cells at the base of the gill filaments absorb sodium and chloride from the water, while other salts are ingested with food.

Like freshwater fish, freshwater invertebrates are hyperosmotic to the surrounding environment. Freshwater invertebrates must expend energy to pump out the water that floods their tissues. They also expend energy by actively absorbing salts from the external environment. However, the concentration of solutes in the body fluids of freshwater invertebrates ranges from between about one-half and one-tenth that of their marine relatives. This lower internal concentration of solutes reduces the osmotic gradient between freshwater and the outside environment and so reduces the energy freshwater invertebrates must expend to osmoregulate.

Freshwater mosquito larvae are a good model for osmoregulation by freshwater invertebrates. The larvae of approximately 95% of mosquito species live in freshwater, where they face osmotic challenges very similar to those faced by freshwater fish. Like freshwater fish, mosquito larvae must solve the twin problems of water gain and ion loss. In response, they drink very little water. They conserve ions taken with the diet by absorbing them with cells that line the midgut and rectum, and they secrete a dilute urine. Freshwater mosquito larvae replace the ions lost with urine by actively absorbing Na^+ and Cl^- from the water with cells in their anal papillae. Freshwater mosquitoes and fish use totally different structures to meet nearly identical environmental challenges. Figure 6.30 compares water and salt regulation by freshwater fish and mosquitoes.

Living with Variable Salinity Levels

The examples we have provided give an overview of the mechanisms by which plants and animals are able to cope with water stress that occurs due to low precipitation, extended periods of snow cover, or living in either fresh or

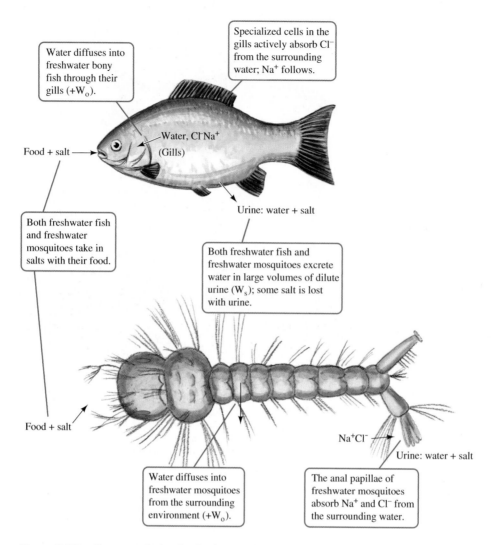

Water diffuses into freshwater bony fish through their gills ($+W_o$).

Specialized cells in the gills actively absorb Cl^- from the surrounding water; Na^+ follows.

Food + salt

Water, Cl^-Na^+ (Gills)

Both freshwater fish and freshwater mosquitoes take in salts with their food.

Urine: water + salt

Both freshwater fish and freshwater mosquitoes excrete water in large volumes of dilute urine (W_s); some salt is lost with urine.

Food + salt

Na^+Cl^-

Urine: water + salt

Water diffuses into freshwater mosquitoes from the surrounding environment ($+W_o$).

The anal papillae of freshwater mosquitoes absorb Na^+ and Cl^- from the surrounding water.

Figure 6.30 Osmoregulation by freshwater fish and mosquitoes.

salt water. However, many organisms experience great variability in salinity over the course of their lifetime. As we described in chapters 2 and 3, unique abiotic conditions are found where the ocean meets the land. The organisms that live within estuaries, salt marshes, and intertidal zones experience periods of high and low salinity, temperature, and water levels depending upon the lunar cycle and local climatic conditions. These organisms typically have a high tolerance (chapter 5) to high salt levels, and may be able to acclimatize (chapter 5) to changing conditions. However, salt is a powerful stressor for plants, and you will typically see only a few species able to live under the highest salinity levels; more species are able to persist where this stressor is less pronounced. One of the most interesting examples of organisms that live in variable salinity come not from the plants growing along an estuary, but from the fish that hatch and spawn in fresh water yet spend most of their life living in salt water.

We first introduced anadromous fish in chapter 5. As you may recall, many species of salmon and other fish (fig. 6.31) migrate twice in their lives, first from their freshwater hatching

grounds into the ocean, and then back into the freshwater habits when they spawn. This process requires a number of fairly complicated traits, including the ability to remember and navigate, tolerance of variable temperature regimes and food items, and the ability to cope with both hypo- and hypersaline conditions.

It may come as no surprise that understanding the detailed physiology of salmon is of great interest to researchers throughout the world, as these fisheries are highly valuable. Changing salinity levels triggers a number of hormonal responses in anadromous fish, resulting in changes in the gill proteins which regulate internal osmolarity (McCormick 2001). Continued exposure to new salinity levels results in a degree of acclimation, allowing the fish to live in its new environment. A more detailed explanation of how these fish are able to cope with such variable salinities is beyond the scope of this book. However, the pattern of the environment presenting a number of abiotic stressors, and some species possessing specific traits allowing them to mitigate the effects of these stressors is a common theme in the study of physiological ecology.

Figure 6.31 A diverse array of fish spend part of their lives in the ocean, and other parts in freshwater, including (*a*) sea lamprey (*Petromyzon marinus*), (*b*) steelhead trout (*Oncorhynchus mykiss*), (*c*) Atlantic sturgeon (*Acipenser oxyrinchos*), and (*d*) sockeye salmon, (*Oncorhynchus nerka*).

In chapter 6 we have reviewed the water relations of individual organisms. The relationship between individual organisms and the environment is a fundamental aspect of ecology. However, ecologists are also concerned with levels of organization above the individual, such as the ecology of populations or of entire biomes. The following example in the Ecological Tools and Approaches section shows how an understanding of the water relations of individual organisms is helping ecologists study the distribution of biomes across a continent.

CONCEPT 6.3 REVIEW

1. Why do isosmotic marine invertebrates expend less energy for osmoregulation compared to hypoosmotic marine fish?
2. The body fluids of many freshwater invertebrate species have very low internal salt concentrations. What is the benefit of such diluted internal fluids?

ECOLOGICAL TOOLS AND APPROACHES

Using Stable Isotopes to Study Water Uptake by Plants

To fully understand the ecology of an individual plant or the dynamics of an entire landscape, ecologists need information about what happens below the earth's surface as well as about surface structure and processes. However, ecologists have produced much more information about the surface realm than about the subsurface, the domain of soil microbes, burrowing animals, and roots. As we discussed in chapter 2, many

ecologists have worked very hard to fill this gap in our knowledge, and once again a major contributor to progress in ecology has been the development of new tools. One of the most important of those is **stable isotope analysis**, which involves the analysis of the relative concentrations of stable isotopes, such as the stable isotopes of carbon ^{13}C and ^{12}C, in materials. Stable isotope analysis is increasingly used in ecology to study the flow of energy and materials through ecosystems (Dawson et al. 2002). For instance, stable isotope analysis has proved a very powerful tool in studies of water uptake by plants. To understand the applications of this analytical tool, we need to know a little about the isotopes themselves and about their behaviour in ecosystems.

Stable Isotope Analysis

Most chemical elements include several stable isotopes, which occur in different concentrations in different environments or differ in concentration from one organism to another. Stable isotopes of hydrogen include ^{1}H and ^{2}H, which is generally designated as D, an abbreviation of deuterium. Stable isotopes of carbon, for example, include ^{13}C and ^{12}C; stable isotopes of nitrogen include ^{15}N and ^{14}N; and stable isotopes of sulfur include ^{34}S and ^{32}S. The relative concentrations of these stable isotopes can be used to study the flow of energy and materials through ecosystems because different parts of the ecosystem often contain different concentrations of the light and heavy isotopes of these elements.

Different organisms contain different ratios of light and heavy stable isotopes because they use different sources of these elements, because they preferentially use (fractionate) different stable isotopes, or because they use different sources *and* fractionate. For instance, the lighter isotope of nitrogen, ^{14}N, is more likely to be excreted than is ^{15}N by organisms during protein synthesis. As a consequence of this preferential excretion of ^{14}N, an organism becomes relatively enriched in ^{15}N compared to its food. Therefore, as materials pass from one trophic level to the next, tissues become richer in ^{15}N. The highest trophic levels within an ecosystem contain the highest relative concentrations of ^{15}N, while the lowest trophic levels contain the lowest concentrations. Stable isotope analysis can also measure the relative contribution of C_3 and C_4 plants to a species' diet. This is possible because C_4 plants are richer in ^{13}C than are C_3 plants. Other processes affect the relative concentrations of stable isotopes of sulfur. Because different sources of water often have different ratios of D to ^{1}H, for example, shallow soil moisture versus deep soil moisture, hydrogen isotope analyses have been valuable aids to identifying where plants acquire their water.

The concentrations of stable isotopes are generally expressed as differences in the concentration of the heavier isotope relative to some standard. The units of measurement are differences ($\pm$) in parts per thousand ($\pm$ ‰). These differences are calculated as:

$$\delta X = \left(\frac{R_{sample}}{R_{standard}} - 1 \right) \times 10$$

where:

$$\delta = \pm$$

X = the relative concentration of the heavier isotope, for example, D, ^{13}C, ^{15}N, or ^{34}S in ‰

R_{sample} = the isotopic ratio in the sample, for example, D:^{1}H, ^{13}C:^{12}C, or ^{15}N:^{14}N

$R_{standard}$ = the isotopic ratio in the standard, for example, D:^{1}H, ^{13}C:^{12}C, or ^{15}N:^{14}N

The reference materials used as standards in the isotopic analyses of hydrogen, nitrogen, carbon, and sulfur are the D:^{1}H ratio in Standard Mean Ocean Water, the ^{15}N:^{14}N ratio in atmospheric nitrogen, the ^{13}C:^{12}C ratio in PeeDee limestone, and the ^{34}S:^{32}S in the Canyon Diablo meteorite.

The ecologist measures the ratio of stable isotopes in a sample and then expresses that ratio as a difference relative to some standard. If $\delta X = 0$, then the ratios of the isotopes in the sample and the standard are the same; if $\delta X = -X$ ‰, the concentration of the heavier isotope is lower (e.g., ^{15}N) in the sample compared to the standard, and if $\delta X = +X$ ‰, the concentration of the heavier isotope is higher in the sample compared to the standard. The important point here is that these isotopic ratios are generally different in different parts of ecosystems. Therefore, ecologists can use isotopic ratios to study the structure and processes in ecosystems. Here is an example of how hydrogen isotope ratios have been used to study the uptake of water by plants in a natural ecosystem. We will discuss other uses of stable isotopic analyses in later chapters.

Using Stable Isotopes to Identify Plant Water Sources

The laboratory of James Ehleringer has taken a leadership role in the development of stable isotope analysis as a tool for assessing water relations among plants and within ecosystems (e.g., Ehleringer et al. 2000). In an early study, Ehleringer and several colleagues (Ehleringer et al. 1991) used deuterium:hydrogen (D:^{1}H) ratios, or δD, to explore the use of summer versus winter rainfall by various plant growth forms in the deserts of southern Utah. They could use δD to determine the relative utilization of these two water sources since summer rains are relatively enriched with D and winter rains are relatively depleted of D. The δD of summer and winter rains in southern Utah at the time of Ehleringer's study were −25 ‰ and −90 ‰ respectively (fig. 6.32).

Ehleringer measured δD in the xylem fluid of several plant growth forms during spring, when soil moisture at all rooting depths would be predominantly from winter precipitation; and summer, when summer precipitation would be present as moisture in surface soils and winter precipitation would predominate at deeper soil layers. Ehleringer and his research team found that a succulent, several herbaceous perennials, and several woody perennials used winter moisture in the spring (fig. 6.32). However, when summer rains fell, the succulent species shifted entirely to using soil moisture from

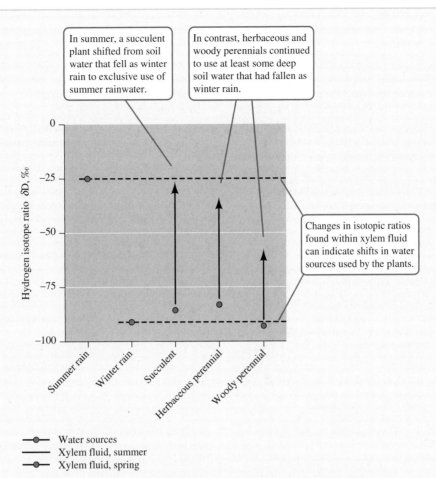

Figure 6.32   Stable isotope analysis identified the water sources used by three groups of desert plants during the spring and summer (data from Ehleringer et al. 1991). In the figure, the lower dashed line corresponds to the isotopic ratio found in winter rain, while the upper dashed line corresponds to the isotopic ratio found in summer rain.

summer rains that were stored mainly at shallow soil depths. Meanwhile herbaceous and woody perennials continued to use significant amounts of deeper soil moisture that fell the previous winter. So, stable isotope analysis opens a window to the water relations of plants that would not be accessible without this innovative tool.

SUMMARY

6.1 Concentration gradients influence the movement of water between an organism and its environment.
The most familiar relative measure of the water content of air is relative humidity, defined as water vapour density divided by saturation water vapour density multiplied by 100. On land, the tendency of water to move from organisms to the atmosphere can be approximated by the VPD of the air.

Vapour pressure deficit is calculated as the difference between the actual water vapour pressure and the saturation water vapour pressure.

In the aquatic environment, water moves down its concentration gradient from solutions of higher water concentration and lower salt content (hypoosmotic) to solutions of lower water concentration and higher salt content (hyperosmotic).

This movement of water creates osmotic pressure. Larger osmotic differences, between organism and environment, generate higher osmotic pressures.

In the soil–plant system, water flows from areas of higher water potential to areas of lower water potential. The water potential of pure water, which by convention is set at zero, is reduced by adding solute and by matric forces, the tendency of water to cling to soil particles and to plant cell walls. Typically, the water potential of plant fluids is determined by a combination of solute concentrations and matric forces, while the water potential of soils is determined mainly by matric forces. In saline soils, solutes may also influence soil water potential. Water potential, osmotic pressure, and VPD can all be measured in pascals (newtons/m^2), a common currency for considering the water relations of diverse organisms in very different environments.

6.2 Terrestrial plants and animals regulate their internal water by balancing water acquisition against water loss.

Water regulation by terrestrial animals is summarized by $W_i = W_d + W_f + W_a - W_e - W_s$, where W_d = drinking, W_f = taken in with food, W_a = absorption from the air, W_e = evaporation, and W_s = secretions and excretions. Water regulation by terrestrial plants is summarized by $W_i = W_r + W_a - W_t - W_s$, where W_r = uptake by roots, W_a = absorption from the air, W_t = transpiration, and W_s = secretions and reproductive structures. Some very different terrestrial plants and animals, such as the camel and saguaro cactus, use similar mechanisms to survive in arid climates. Some organisms, such as scorpions and cicadas, use radically different mechanisms. Comparisons such as these suggest that natural selection is opportunistic.

6.3 Marine and freshwater organisms use complementary mechanisms for water and salt regulation.

Marine and freshwater organisms face exactly opposite osmotic challenges. Water regulation in aquatic environments is summarized by: $W_i = W_d - W_s \pm W_o$, where W_d = drinking, W_s = secretions and excretions, W_o = osmosis. An aquatic organism may either gain or lose water through osmosis, depending on the organism and the environment. Many marine invertebrates reduce their water regulation problems by being isosmotic with seawater. Some freshwater invertebrates also reduce the osmotic gradient between themselves and their environment. Sharks, skates, and rays elevate the urea and TMAO content of their body fluids to the point where they are slightly hyperosmotic to seawater. Marine bony fish and saltwater mosquito larvae are hypoosmotic relative to their environments, while freshwater bony fish and freshwater mosquito larvae are hyperosmotic.

While the strength of environmental challenge varies from one environment to another, and the details of water regulation vary from one organism to another, all organisms in all environments expend energy to maintain their internal pool of water and dissolved substances.

Stable isotope analysis, an important new tool in ecology, involves the analysis of the relative concentrations of stable isotopes in materials. Examples of stable isotopes include the stable isotopes of hydrogen ^2H (which is usually symbolized by D, referring to deuterium) and ^1H, and the stable isotopes of carbon, ^{13}C and ^{12}C. Stable isotope analysis has proved a very powerful tool in studies of water uptake by plants. For example deuterium : hydrogen (D : ^1H) ratios, or δD, have been used to quantify the relative use of summer versus winter rainfall by various plant growth forms in the deserts of southern Utah.

REVIEW QUESTIONS

1. Cottonwood regeneration is dependent upon periodic flooding. How can land managers use this information to maintain stable cottonwood populations?

2. Distinguish between vapour pressure deficit, osmotic pressure, and water potential. How can all three phenomena be expressed in the same units of measure: pascals?

3. Leaf water potential is typically highest just before dawn and then decreases progressively through midday. Should lower leaf water potentials at midday increase or decrease the rate of water movement from soil to a plant? Assume soil water potential is approximately the same in early morning and midday. Are the water needs of the plant greater in early morning or at midday?

4. Compare the water budgets of the tenebrionid beetle, *Onymacris*, and the kangaroo rat, *Dipodomys*, shown in figures 6.10 and 6.11. Which of these two species obtains most of its water from metabolic water? Which relies most on condensation of fog as

a water source? In which species do you see greater losses of water through the urine?

5. In the Sonoran Desert, the only insects known to evaporatively cool are cicadas. Explain how cicadas can employ evaporative cooling while hundreds of other insect species in the same environment cannot.

6. Many desert species are well waterproofed. Evolution cannot, however, eliminate all evaporative water loss. Why not? (Hint: Think of the kinds of exchanges that an organism must maintain with its environment.)

7. While we have concentrated in chapter 6 on regulation of water and salts, most marine invertebrates are isosmotic with their external environment. What is a potential benefit of being isosmotic?

8. Review water and salt regulation by marine and freshwater bony fish. Which of the two is hypoosmotic relative to its

environment? Which of the two is hyperosmotic relative to its environment? Some sharks live in fresh water. How should the kidneys of marine and freshwater sharks function?

9. Some plants in the tropics use wilting as a mechanism to decrease internal water potentials and thus increase water uptake. However, many plants in temperate and boreal regions also wilt on hot summer days. Does wilting have a similar physiological effect on these plants from different regions, or are different mechanisms of water uptake operating in different parts of the world?

10. Jochen Schenk and Robert Jackson (2002) have shown that outside of the tropics, rooting depth decreases as you move toward the poles. Use what you have learned in other chapters about the biomes in each region of the globe to provide a potential explanation for this pattern.

For more information on the resources available from McGraw-Hill Ryerson, go to **www.mcgrawhill.ca/he/solutions**.

ENERGY AND NUTRIENT RELATIONS CHAPTER 7

CHAPTER CONCEPTS

7.1 Organisms use one of three main sources of energy: solar radiation, organic molecules, or inorganic molecules.

Concept 7.1 Review

7.2 The rates at which organisms can take in energy and nutrients are limited.

Concept 7.2 Review

7.3 Natural selection will influence how organisms feed, and this process can be understood through the use of optimal foraging theory.

Concept 7.3 Review

Ecology In Action: Using Ecological Knowledge to Predict C$_4$ Plant Distributions in a Changing World

Ecological Tools and Approaches: Bioremediation—Using the Trophic Diversity of Bacteria to Solve Environmental Problems

Summary

Review Questions

The need to capture and consume energy and nutrients is ubiquitous among organisms. Unique solutions to this need have emerged through natural selection, and can be seen everywhere in nature. A scorpion fish lies half buried in the sand near the edge of a coral reef; the only clues to its presence are movements of its gill covers. Its head looks so much like an algae-covered stone that several tiny shrimp gather over it and swim lazily in the current. A small fish on the nearby reef sees the shrimp and darts over to feed on them. The scorpion fish opens its mouth and swallows the small fish in a lightning-quick movement. However, before the scorpion fish can settle back into the sand, a green moray eel, nearly 2 m long, darts from the reef, grabs the scorpion fish with its razor-sharp teeth, and swallows it (fig. 7.1).

A plant with broad leaves and a slender stem grows in the half light of the boreal forest floor. It is difficult to understand how it can live in such dim light. However, as you watch, a small ray of sunlight pierces through a hole in the forest canopy and shines on one of the plant's leaves. The photosynthetic machinery rapidly adjusts to the intense light, and for a few minutes the plant uses the energy of the tiny sunfleck. Whether on coral reefs, forests, or abandoned urban lots, organisms engage in an active search for, and capture of,

Figure 7.1 The moray eel meets its energy and nutrient needs by being an effective predator.

energy and nutrients. The energy used by different organisms comes in the form of light, organic molecules, or inorganic molecules. Nutrients are the raw materials an organism must acquire from the environment to build the organic and inorganic compounds critical to life. Because different organisms acquire energy and nutrients in diverse ways, we organize our discussion under the umbrella of three major concepts.

7.1   Energy Sources

Organisms use one of three main sources of energy: solar radiation, organic molecules, or inorganic molecules. Undergraduate students are often taught about biological diversity by grouping organisms on the basis of shared evolutionary histories. This approach allows for focused lectures on specific taxa such as vertebrate animals, insects, coniferous trees, and orchids. Such an approach is a useful way to understand the diversity of life, but it is not a particularly helpful way to understand ecological interactions. An alternative way of grouping organisms is based upon functional similarities among species, such as the means by which organisms obtain energy—that is, by their **trophic (feeding) biology**. Organisms that use inorganic sources of both carbon and energy are called **autotrophs** ("self-feeders") and are of two types, **photosynthetic** and **chemosynthetic**. Photosynthetic autotrophs use carbon dioxide (CO_2) as a source of carbon and solar radiation in the form of light as a source of energy. This group includes the plants, photosynthetic protists, and photosynthetic bacteria. These taxa have independent evolutionary histories, but share a key aspect of their ecology: the means by which they acquire energy. Chemosynthetic autotrophs use inorganic molecules as a source of carbon and energy. This group contains a large diversity of chemosynthetic bacteria. **Heterotrophs** ("other-feeders") are organisms that use organic molecules both as a source of carbon and as a source of energy. The heterotrophs include bacteria, fungi, protists, animals, and parasitic plants.

Prokaryotes show more trophic diversity than the other major biological groupings (fig. 7.2). Prokaryotes, which have cells with no membrane-bound nucleus or organelles, include both bacteria and the **archaea**. The archaea are prokaryotes distinguished from bacteria on the basis of structural, physiological, and other biological features. Though first discovered in association with extreme environments, the archaea are now known to be widely spread in the biosphere, particularly in the oceans. The protists are either photosynthetic or heterotrophic, most plants are photosynthetic, and all fungi and animals are heterotrophic. In contrast, the prokaryotes include photosynthetic, chemosynthetic, and heterotrophic species, making them, as a group, the most trophically diverse organisms in the biosphere.

Some of the most ecologically significant discoveries of prokaryotic trophic diversity have come from studies of marine prokaryotes. For instance, Oded Béjà and Edward Delong and their research team discovered a new type of energy production from light, involving bacterial **rhodopsin** (Béjà et al. 2000). Rhodopsins are light-absorbing pigments found in animal eyes and in the bacteria and archaea. The rhodopsin in

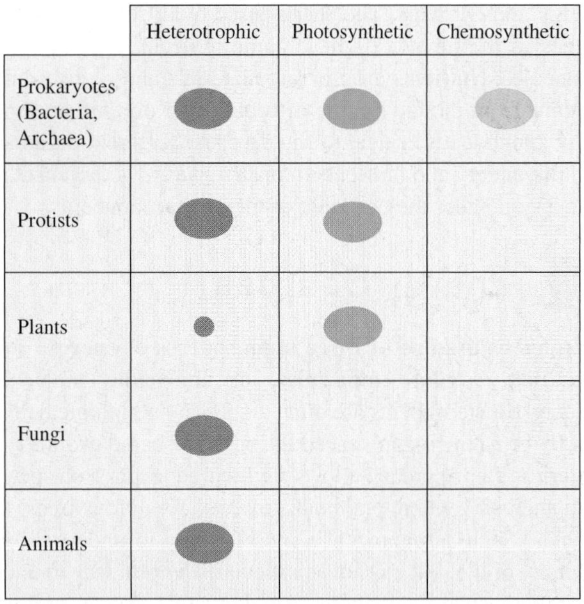

	Heterotrophic	Photosynthetic	Chemosynthetic
Prokaryotes (Bacteria, Archaea)	⬤	⬤	⬤
Protists	⬤	⬤	
Plants	•	⬤	
Fungi	⬤		
Animals	⬤		

Figure 7.2 A plot of trophic diversity across the major groups of organisms. The highest trophic diversity is found among the prokaryotic bacteria and archaea, while the least trophic diversity is found among fungi and animals.

bacteria and archaea performs a variety of functions, including that of a proton pump involved in ATP synthesis, that is, in the production of energy. Further study by Béjà, Delong, and their research team (Béjà et al. 2001) has shown that bacterial rhodopsin is widespread through the oceans. In one particularly intriguing aspect of their study, they found that the light sensitivity of bacterial rhodopsin appears adapted to local variations in light quality. For instance, bacterial rhodopsin from deep clear waters absorbs light most strongly within the blue range of the visible spectrum, while that from shallow coastal waters absorbs most strongly in the green range (chapter 3). These discoveries, along with others (e.g., Kolber et al. 2000, Béjà et al. 2002), are rapidly revolutionizing our understanding of how the biosphere works.

Photosynthesis

The Solar-Powered Biosphere

As we saw in chapters 2 and 3, solar energy powers the winds and ocean currents, and annual variation in sunlight intensity drives the seasons. In chapter 5, we also discussed how organisms use sunlight to regulate body temperature. Here, building on those discussions, we look at light from the sun as a source of energy for photosynthesis.

Light propagates through space as a wave, with all the properties of waves such as frequency and wavelength. When light interacts with matter, however, it acts not as a wave but as a particle. Particles of light, called *photons*, bear a finite quantity of energy. Longer wavelengths, such as *infrared light*, carry less energy than shorter wavelengths, such as *visible* and *ultraviolet light.*

Infrared radiation is very important for temperature regulation by organisms. As we saw in chapter 5, many organisms

alter their behaviour to either increase or decrease the absorption and retention of this heat energy, allowing them to modify their body temperatures. This works because the main effect of infrared light on matter is to increase the motion of whole molecules, which we measure as increased temperature. However, infrared light does not carry enough energy to drive photosynthesis. At the other end of the solar spectrum, ultraviolet light carries so much energy that it breaks the covalent bonds of many organic molecules and can destroy the complex biochemical machinery of photosynthesis. Between these extremes of solar radiation wavelengths is the light we (humans) can see, so-called visible light. Visible light is better referred to as **photosynthetically active radiation**, or **PAR**, and contains wavelengths of solar radiation between about 400 and 700 nm. These wavelengths carry sufficient energy to drive the light-dependent reactions of photosynthesis (see below) but not so much as to destroy organic molecules. PAR makes up about 45% of the total energy content of the solar spectrum at sea level, infrared light accounts for approximately 53%, and ultraviolet light most of the remainder.

Measuring PAR

Ecologists quantify PAR as **photon flux density (PFD)**, the number of photons striking a square metre surface each second. The number of photons is expressed as micromoles (μmol), where 1 mole is Avogadro's number of photons, 6.023×10^{23}. To give you a point of reference, a PFD of about 4.6 μmol per square metre per second equals a light intensity of about 1 watt per square metre. PAR in Edmonton on a clear summer day can reach 1800–2000, while the values can exceed 2400 near the equator. In your classroom, PAR is likely < 100, even with all the lights turned on. Measuring light as photon flux density makes sense ecologically because chlorophyll absorbs light as photons.

Light changes in quantity and quality with latitude, the seasons, the weather, and with the time of day. In addition, landscapes, water, and even organisms themselves change the amount and quality of light. For example, in aquatic environments (see chapter 3), only the superficial euphotic zone receives sufficient light to support photosynthetic organisms. The amount of light penetrating the depths of aquatic systems is influenced by many factors, including the amount of particles suspended in the water. Increased particle density (and thus reduced light penetration) can come from the runoff associated with melting glaciers, disturbed sediments, and even chemicals leached from the leaves and roots of the surrounding vegetation. Depending upon water clarity, the **euphotic zone** (the part able to support photosynthesis), can range in depth from a few metres to about 100 m. In addition to changes in the quantity of light that penetrates through the water column, there are shifts in the spectral composition of light due to selective absorption of certain wavelength of light by plant pigments, and physical influences of the water itself.

As in the sea, sunlight changes as it shines through vegetation on land. A mature temperate or boreal forest can reduce the total quantity of light reaching the forest floor to about 1% to 2% of the amount shining on the forest canopy (fig. 7.3).

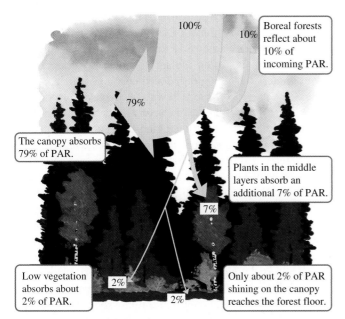

100%

10%

Boreal forests reflect about 10% of incoming PAR.

79%

The canopy absorbs 79% of PAR.

Plants in the middle layers absorb an additional 7% of PAR.

7%

Low vegetation absorbs about 2% of PAR.

2%

2%

Only about 2% of PAR shining on the canopy reaches the forest floor.

Figure 7.3 Photosynthetically active radiation (PAR) diminishes substantially with passage through the canopy of a boreal forest (data from Larcher 1995, after Kairiukstis 1967).

However, forests also change the quality of sunlight. Within the range of photosynthetically active radiation, leaves absorb mainly blue and red light and transmit mostly green light with a wavelength of about 550 nm. As in the deep sea, the organisms on the forest floor live in a kind of twilight. Only here, the twilight is green. We will discuss how plants respond to altered light quality in chapter 13, Competition.

Alternative Photosynthetic Pathways

During photosynthesis, the photosynthetic pigments of plants, algae, or bacteria absorb light and transfer their energy to electrons. Subsequently, the energy carried by these electrons is used to synthesize ATP and NADPH. This process generally requires complex photosystems and only occurs in the light. Perhaps it comes as no surprise that these reactions are commonly referred to as "light reactions." These molecules, in turn, serve as donors of electrons and energy for the synthesis of sugars. This second stage also generally occurs in the light, though is not directly dependent upon light. These reactions go by a number of names, including the Calvin cycle reactions. Through these two sets of reactions, photosynthetic organisms convert the electromagnetic energy of sunlight into energy-rich organic molecules. Within photosynthetic organisms, different biochemical pathways carry out this energy conversion.

Biologists often speak of photosynthesis as "carbon fixation," which refers to the reactions in which CO_2 becomes incorporated into a carbon-containing acid. In the photosynthetic pathway used by most plants and all algae, the CO_2 first combines with a five-carbon compound called *ribulose bisphosphate*, or *RuBP*. The product of this initial reaction, which is catalyzed by the enzyme RuBP carboxylase (RUBISCO), is *phosphoglyceric acid*, or *PGA*, a three-carbon acid. This photosynthetic pathway is usually called **C_3 photosynthesis** and the plants that employ it are called C_3 plants (fig. 7.4).

To fix carbon, plants must open their stomata to let CO_2 into their leaves, but as CO_2 enters, water exits. Water vapour flows out faster than CO_2 flows in. The movement of water is more rapid because the gradient in water concentration from the leaf to the atmosphere is much steeper than the gradient in CO_2 concentration from the atmosphere to the leaf. In C_3 plants, there is another factor that contributes to a low rate of CO_2 uptake: RUBISCO has a low affinity for CO_2. Relatively high rates of water loss are generally not a problem for plants that live in cool, moist conditions, but in hot, dry climates,

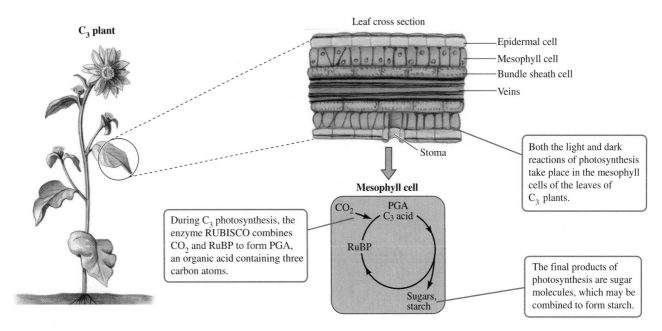

C_3 plant

Leaf cross section

Epidermal cell
Mesophyll cell
Bundle sheath cell
Veins

Stoma

Both the light and dark reactions of photosynthesis take place in the mesophyll cells of the leaves of C_3 plants.

Mesophyll cell

During C_3 photosynthesis, the enzyme RUBISCO combines CO_2 and RuBP to form PGA, an organic acid containing three carbon atoms.

CO_2
PGA
C_3 acid
RuBP
Sugars, starch

The final products of photosynthesis are sugar molecules, which may be combined to form starch.

Figure 7.4 C_3 photosynthesis.

high rates of water loss can close the stomata and shut down photosynthesis (see chapter 6).

In arid environments, two alternative photosynthetic pathways have repeatedly evolved, both of which separate (in space or time) the initial fixation of carbon from the light-dependent reactions. In C_4 **photosynthesis**, carbon fixation and the light-dependent reactions of photosynthesis occur in separate cells (fig. 7.5). C_4 plants fix CO_2 in mesophyll cells by combining it with *phosphoenolpyruvate*, or *PEP*, to produce an acid. This initial reaction, which is catalyzed by PEP carboxylase, concentrates CO_2. Because PEP carboxylase has a high affinity for CO_2, C_4 plants can reduce their internal CO_2 concentrations to very low levels. Low internal concentration of CO_2 increases the gradient of CO_2 from atmosphere to leaf, which in turn increases the rate of diffusion of CO_2 inward. Consequently, compared to C_3 plants, C_4 plants need to open fewer stomata to deliver sufficient CO_2 to photosynthesizing cells. By having fewer stomata open, C_4 plants conserve water.

In C_4 plants, the acids produced during carbon fixation diffuse to specialized cells surrounding a structure called the **bundle sheath**. There, deeper in the leaf, the four-carbon acids are broken down to a three-carbon acid and CO_2. C_4 photosynthesis also benefits plants by reducing, or even eliminating, **photorespiration**. Although RUBISCO is a carboxylase (it binds CO_2 to RuBP), it can also serve as an

oxygenase, binding O_2 to RuBP. When this happens, RuBP is partly broken down and a CO_2 molecule is released from the plant, a process known as photorespiration. Needless to say, release of CO_2 from a plant is counter to the needs of photosynthesis, resulting in reduced energetic efficiency and increased water loss associated with needing to keep stomata open longer. One of the major factors influencing the rate of photorespiration is the concentration of O_2 relative to that of CO_2, with increased photorespiration in a relatively oxygen-rich and carbon dioxide-poor atmosphere.

If RUBISCO is both an oxygenase and a carboxylase, why don't C_4 plants, which still contain RUBISCO, photorespire? Quite simply, their unique morphology segregates RUBISCO into the bundle sheath cells. By doing this, plants put this enzyme in an area of high CO_2 concentration (remember, it is transported out of the mesophyll cells), and low O_2 concentrations. Why are the bundle sheath cells of lower O_2 concentration than the mesophyll? In large part because the O_2 generated by the light reactions of photosynthesis occurs in the mesophyll and not the bundle sheath cells. The impacts of atmospheric oxygen and carbon dioxide levels will have strong selective forces on plant photosynthesis and evolution, something we will discuss more in the Ecology In Action section of this chapter. It is interesting to notice that C_4 plants appear to have evolved primarily during periods of low atmospheric CO_2

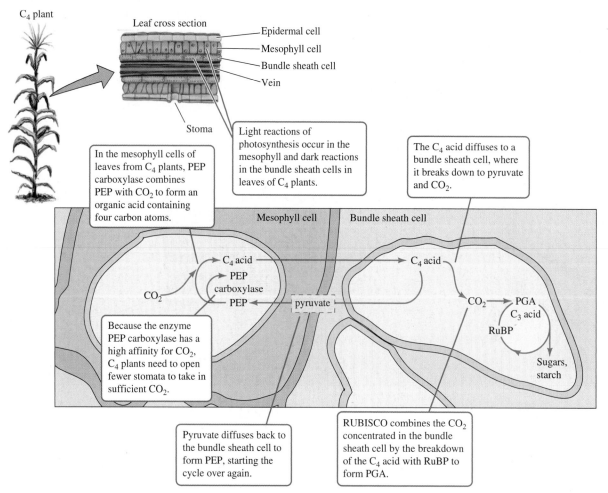

Figure 7.5 C_4 photosynthesis.

(Sage 2004). Review C_3 and C_4 photosynthesis (figs. 7.4 and 7.5) before considering the third major photosynthetic pathway.

CAM (crassulacean acid metabolism) **photosynthesis** is largely limited to succulent plants in arid and semiarid environments. In both C_3 and C_4 plants, the light-dependent and Calvin cycle reactions all occur during the day. In CAM photosynthesis, carbon fixation typically takes place at night, when lower temperatures reduce the rate of water loss during CO_2 uptake. CAM plants fix carbon by combining CO_2 with PEP to form four-carbon acids. These acids are stored until daylight, when they are broken down into pyruvate and CO_2, which then enters the C_3 photosynthetic pathway (fig. 7.6). In CAM plants, all these reactions take place in the same cells. While CAM plants do not normally show very high rates of photosynthesis, their water use efficiency, as estimated by the mass of CO_2 fixed per kilogram of water used, is higher than that of either C_3 or C_4 plants.

Separating initial carbon fixation from the other reactions reduces water losses during photosynthesis: C_3 plants lose from about 380 to 900 g of water for every gram (dry weight) of tissue produced. C_4 plants lose from about 250 to 350 g of water per gram of tissue produced, while CAM plants lose approximately 50 g of water per gram of new tissue. The differences in these numbers give us one of the reasons C_4 and CAM plants do well in hot, dry environments.

Whether the pathway of carbon fixation is CAM, C_3, or C_4, plants and photosynthetic algae and bacteria capture energy from sunlight and carbon from CO_2. These photosynthesizers package this energy and carbon in organic molecules. The photosynthesizers and other autotrophs opened the way for the evolution of organisms that could get their energy and carbon from organic molecules. And this new trophic level did indeed evolve.

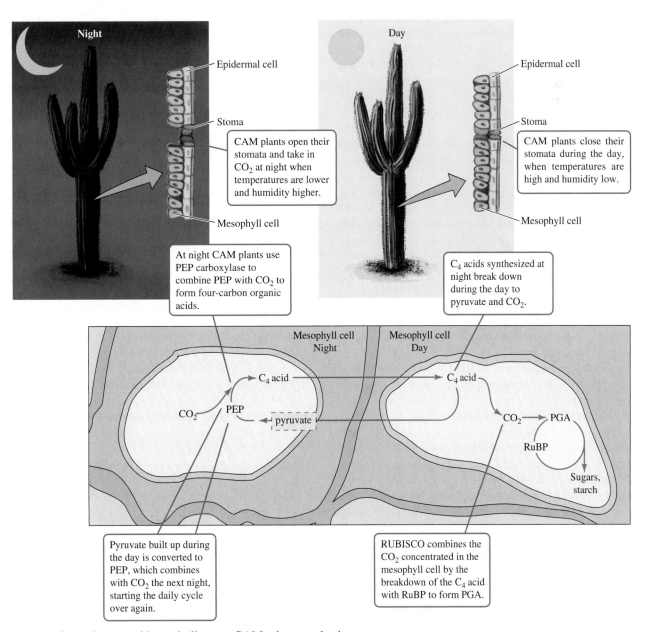

Figure 7.6   Crassulacean acid metabolism, or CAM, photosynthesis.

Chemical Composition and Nutrient Requirements

We can get some idea of the nutrient requirements of organisms by examining their chemical composition. The chemical composition of nearly all organisms is quite similar, with just five elements (carbon [C], oxygen [O], hydrogen [H], nitrogen [N], and phosphorus [P]) making up 93% to 97% of the biomass of plants, animals, fungi, and bacteria on the planet. Although the chemicals that build all organisms are very similar, the relative abundances of these chemicals are not. Of these four groups, plants are the most chemically distinct, containing low concentrations of phosphorus and nitrogen. The nitrogen content of plant tissues averages about 2%, while it is typically 5%–10% in fungi, animals, and bacteria. Vertebrate animals typically have a high demand for calcium and phosphorus to support the growth and maintenance of a mineral-rich internal skeleton, while demand for these elements is typically reduced among invertebrate species. Fast-growing organisms require relatively more nutrient-rich resources to support their higher allocation to tissue building compared to those with slower growth rates. Thus, how an organism allocate elements has consequences for its elemental requirements.

Ecologists use the principles of stoichiometry, which means literally "measuring chemical elements," to study the relationships between ratios of elements in a food resource to those ratios in an organism eating that food resource. Such studies are the subject of **ecological stoichiometry**, which concerns the balance of multiple chemical elements in ecological interactions, for example, the balance of multiple chemical elements between plants and the herbivores that consume them. Ecologists often express the relative nitrogen content of whole organisms or tissues as the ratio of carbon to nitrogen (C:N ratios). The C:N ratio of plants averages about 25:1, which is substantially higher than the C:N ratios of animals, fungi, and bacteria, which average approximately 5:1 to 10:1 (fig. 7.7). Differences in C:N ratios among tissues or among organisms significantly influence what organisms eat, how rapidly consumers reproduce, and how rapidly organisms decompose. If nitrogen is an essential building block of proteins and nucleic acids, and the food of herbivores (plants) contains relatively little nitrogen, you may begin to recognize an ecological puzzle. How can an herbivore create a C:N ratio of 10:1 if it only eats food that has a 25:1 ratio?

Getting enough nitrogen is not the only nutritive challenge for organisms, as there are dozens of elements other than C, O, H, N, and P found in the tissues of organisms. Essential plant nutrients include potassium (K), calcium (Ca), magnesium (Mg), sulfur (S), chlorine (Cl), iron (Fe), manganese (Mn), boron (B), zinc (Zn), copper (Cu), and molybdenum (Mo). Most of these nutrients are also essential for other organisms. Some organisms require additional nutrients. For instance, animals also require sodium (Na) and iodine (I), and diatoms require silica (Si).

Plant leaves capture the energy found in sunlight with pigments and obtain carbon from the air through stomata. The other essential nutrients are captured mainly from the soil through plant roots. As a result, plants obtain different

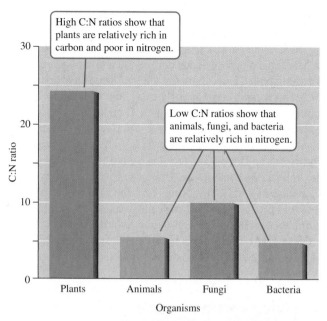

Figure 7.7 On average, the ratio of carbon to nitrogen is much higher in terrestrial plants than in other major groups of organisms (data from Spector 1956).

essential resources through different organs (leaves versus roots), which results in potential energetic conflicts associated with foraging for these different resources. In contrast, most consumers obtain both the energy they require and essential nutrients with the food they consume with their mouth (or similar organ), resulting in comparatively simpler foraging strategies. We will discuss these differences in plant and animal foraging later in this chapter, but now turn to the energy and nutrient relations of heterotrophs.

Heterotrophs

Heterotrophic organisms use organic molecules both as a source of carbon and as an energy source. They depend, ultimately, on the carbon and energy fixed by autotrophs. Heterotrophs have evolved numerous ways of feeding. This trophic variety has stimulated ecologists to invent numerous terms to describe the ways heterotrophs feed, including browsers, grazers, detritivores, and omnivores. A full list of the trophic categories proposed by ecologists would be impossibly long and not especially useful to this discussion. So, we will concentrate on three major categories of consumers: **herbivores**, organisms that eat living plants; **carnivores**, organisms that mainly eat living animals; and **detritivores**, organisms that feed on nonliving organic matter. Herbivores, carnivores, and detritivores must solve fundamentally different problems to obtain adequate supplies of energy and nutrients.

Detritivores

Often the first images related to the consumption of organic matter that come to mind will be something like a pack of wolves on the hunt, or a herd of elk grazing in the mountains. As beautiful as these images may be, they do not reflect the reality that most biomass produced on this planet is consumed after it dies,

not while it is alive. Feeding upon these dead tissues are not the charismatic organisms that typically star in nature shows, but instead primarily small-bodied insects, fungi, and bacteria. As a result, detritivores control the movement of energy and nutrients in most ecosystems. As we discussed in chapter 2, the natural history of soil-living organisms is relatively poorly understood, and many species remain to be discovered (see figure 2.8 for some images of soil organisms). Instead of focusing on detailed biology of species taxa, here we will discuss some of the common constraints facing this group of organisms.

To understand the feeding of detritivores, it is critical to first recognize that animals are rare on this planet when compared to the biomass of non-animal species. The vast majority of biomass contained in living organisms is found in plants, bacteria, and fungi. As a result, one of the most dominant food sources for detritivores will be dead plants and plant parts.

A central problem faced by detritivores is that dead plants are rich in carbon and energy, but very poor in nitrogen. In other words, dead logs are great for the campfire, but not for serving as dinner. Dead plant litter is in fact of lower quality (where quality refers to N content) than living plants (fig. 7.8), which are themselves low in N relative to the organisms that feed upon them (fig. 7.7). Why might dead leaves contain less N than living leaves, even before detritivores have attacked these leaves? Nitrogen, unlike light energy, can be recycled within a plant. It also is often the most limiting nutrient for plant growth in natural systems. As a result, there has often been strong selection acting on plants to increase their **nitrogen use efficiency (NUE)**. NUE represents how much plants are able to grow per unit of nitrogen. One mechanism to improve NUE is to reabsorb nitrogen contained in plant organs, such as leaves, before the leaves are dropped from the plant, leaving a very nitrogen-poor substrate for the detritivores.

Detritivores face three main problems related to feeding: the search, the handling, and the quality of the food they consume. Individual organisms, be they a snail, mite, or fungus, first need to find a potential food item. Once found, that item needs to be captured, consumed, and digested. Upon digestion, the quality of the food impacts an organism's need to continue foraging, or to allocate time and energy for a different activity. For detritivores, body size influences both the microhabitat in which they are able to live as well as a species' ability to find and handle food. Across species, detritivore body sizes range from less than one micrometre for some bacteria to over two metres for some giant earthworms. Because of the importance size plays in influencing the feeding ecology of these species, terrestrial detritivores are often classified by their size, and not solely their taxonomic affiliation (fig. 7.9). The smallest of the detritivorous animals (microfauna) live primarily within the film of water that adheres to soil particles. The slightly larger mesofauna tend to be found in larger pore spaces within the soil, while the macrofauna such as earthworms are able to create habitat through their movement. In addition to creating pore spaces in the soil, these larger classes of detritivores are also active in converting large fragments of litter (e.g., dead leaves) into small fragments, facilitating the feeding of the smaller detritivores.

Due to the relatively high abundance of plants in most communities, the abundance of food is not usually limiting to the growth of detritivorous species. Instead, the abiotic environment and chemical composition of the dead material have more direct impacts. In particular, limited soil moisture greatly reduces the activity and growth of the smaller detritivores, particularly the microfauna that live within water films. As for most ectotherms (chapter 5), increased soil temperatures will increase body temperatures and enzymatic activity of detritivores; however, if this is coupled with reduced soil moisture, many species will become dormant or will move to cooler and moister areas within the soil (i.e., shaded, deeper, etc.). Finally, tissues with lower C:N ratios will result in increased detritivore growth and activity relative to tissues with high C:N ratios. Like all other organisms, detritivores have preferred food sources, which not surprisingly will tend to be leaves, fruits, dead animals, and other sources of relatively high concentrations of nitrogen.

Herbivores

While a herd of elk grazing in the foothills of Alberta or a sea turtle munching on sea grass in a tropical lagoon may suggest a life of ease, this image does not accurately represent the life of an herbivore. To only a slightly less severe extent than detritivores, herbivores face substantial problems related to nutritional chemistry. A hint of the difficulties faced by herbivores comes when we realize that cattle have multiple stomachs, many insects have specific enzymes that detoxify their food, and the gut lengths of vertebrate herbivores are generally longer than the gut lengths of vertebrate carnivores.

Most plant tissues contain a great deal of carbon but low concentrations of nitrogen (fig. 7.7). Additionally, herbivores are often faced with a variety of physical and chemical defences that make plants more difficult to eat, less nutritious, and potentially lethal. We will explore the details of plant defence strategies in chapter 14. Here we focus on

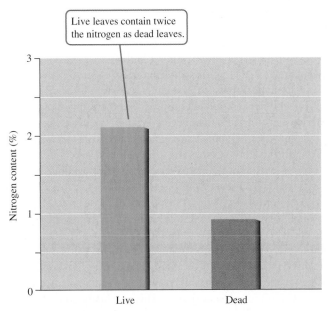

Live leaves contain twice the nitrogen as dead leaves.

Figure 7.8   Nitrogen content of live and dead leaves (data from Killingbeck and Whitford 1996).

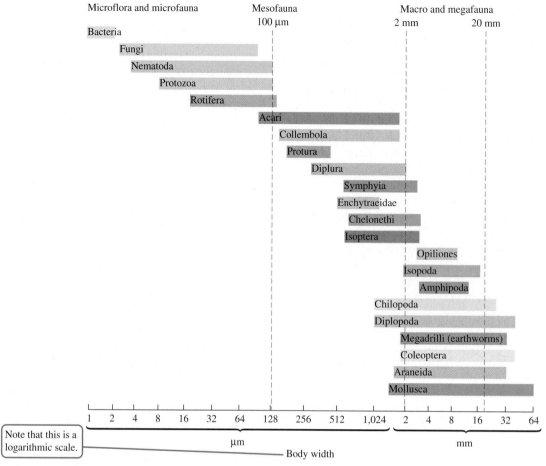

Figure 7.9 Detritivores are often classified according to their body size as microflora, microfauna, mesofauna, macrofauna, and megafauna (data from Swift et al. 1979).

the nutritional challenges that herbivores face in consuming plants: a low quality and potentially toxic food source.

As with detritivores, herbivores come in a variety of shapes and sizes (fig. 7.10). The size of food (e.g., litter fragment) that a detritivore eats is often strongly related to its size. This relationship does not hold up for herbivores, where individuals of greatly different sizes may all eat the same parts of the same plant. For example, when you commit the herbivorous act of biting into an apple, you are likely aware of the chance that a smaller herbivore, the larvae of the codling moth (*Carpocapsa spp.*), may itself already be consuming that fruit. You may be less aware that on the surface of that fruit a variety of mites, aphids, and other insects may have been, or still are, consuming the same apple. In other words, a single part of a plant can be a food for animals of dramatically different sizes. If you were instead to consume a different part of a plant, such as plant leaves in a salad, you once again will likely be consuming a diversity of animals along with the plant tissue. Many of these animals were likely themselves busily eating away before you ruthlessly put them and their host plant into your salad bowl. These herbivores include other species of aphids, leafhoppers, caterpillars, beetles, mites, and ants. Aside from the small herbivores that were hoping to share your lunch, there may also have been deer and rabbits snacking in your garden before you arrived. We can learn many

things from these examples. First, the idea that a person could ever create a diet completely devoid of the consumption of living animals is, well, not biologically plausible. Second, the differences in the species composition of the herbivores found on different plant tissues are not just random events. Instead, different plant tissues are structurally and chemically dissimilar, even within a single plant. Because of these differences, you will find adaptations among herbivores as a function of what they eat, even if they differ greatly in size.

Herbivores must overcome a variety of chemical and physical defences presented by plants before they are able to derive nutrition from their vegetarian diet. For example, the use of cellulose and lignin to strengthen plant tissues increases the C:N ratios of these tissues (fig. 7.11), decreasing their value to herbivores as a food source—or even preventing small mouthparts of many insects from penetrating the plant tissue. Even if the lignin and cellulose are ingested, most animal species do not possess the enzymes needed to fully digest these compounds. As a result, the time and energy spent feeding upon these plant tissues returns reduced energetic gains due to the relative unsuitability of the food source, even for herbivores. One of the central difficulties with a vegetarian diet is the high C:N ratio of plant tissues. This has likely contributed to there being relatively few species that specialize on feeding on the least nutritious of plant parts—bark, roots, and stem

Figure 7.10 Herbivores of greatly different sizes can feed upon the same plant tissues. Though here we can see an elk feeding upon the plants underneath, not seen is a multitude of smaller organisms likely feeding in and upon the same tissues.

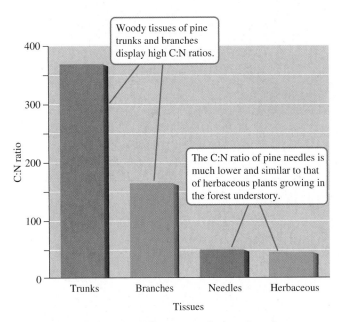

Woody tissues of pine trunks and branches display high C:N ratios.

The C:N ratio of pine needles is much lower and similar to that of herbaceous plants growing in the forest understory.

Figure 7.11 C:N ratios differ a great deal among the tissues of pines and between the woody tissues of pines and those of herbaceous plants on the forest floor (data from Klemmedson 1975).

tissues—at least in comparison to the diversity of species that feed on leaves, fruits, and seeds. This pattern is roughly analogous to the relatively low diversity of species we find in environments with harsh environmental conditions (chapter 22). Nonetheless, many species do survive eating only (well, at least primarily!) plant tissues. How do animals overcome the problem of consuming food that contains such high C:N ratios?

One way of looking at a vegetarian diet is as a search for rare essential nutrients, commonly hidden within a sea of carbon. For animals that eat whole tissues (as opposed to fluid feeders like aphids), an essential first step will be in the physical disintegration of the ingested food. This can be a bird crushing a seed in its beak, or repeated bouts of chewing by large ungulates. This process increases the surface area exposed to digestive enzymes and liberates nutrients from the confines of the plant cell walls. Animals that eat relatively hard plants will tend to have stronger mouthparts than those that eat softer plant tissues. Different herbivores possess different physiological mechanisms to detoxify the potentially harmful chemicals found within their food, once it reaches their guts. This could be as simple as having an alkaline pH to neutralize some compounds, to more elaborate adaptations such as mixed function oxidases (MFOs), which catalyze oxidizing reactions to detoxify a variety of compounds. The gut of many herbivores is also home to a diverse collection of microbial **symbionts**. These bacteria, fungi, and protists are able to digest cellulose and other complex plant compounds, converting them into new microbes. The host, in turn, digests the dead microbes, which can be the source of over 50% of the available N absorbed by ungulates. Many herbivores also make behavioural choices that allow them to eat better food, either through increased nutrient content or reduced toxicity. Some of these examples will be discussed in chapter 8 (Behavioural Ecology) and chapter 14 (Herbivory and Predation).

Despite the diversity of adaptations found among herbivores for coping with a high C:N ratio food source, plants remain a relatively poor food for most animals. As a result, individual animals generally need to consume large amounts of material, with only a small proportion of the ingested food being fully digested. For example, feces and urine of domestic cattle generally represent over 80% of the weight of their ingested food. In other words, most of what a large herbivore puts into its mouth simply comes out at the other end. There is a reason why your parents tell you that roughage will help clean you out!

As you might imagine, being eaten by an herbivore is not generally a beneficial event for an individual plant, and should act as a strong selective force. In fact, chemists have identified thousands of toxins from a diversity of plant species widely implicated in deterring herbivory. In chapter 14, we will explore the evolutionary implications of this form of plant-animal interactions, and will discuss a variety of aspects of an ever-escalating arms race.

Carnivores

In contrast to detritivores and herbivores, carnivores consume prey that are nutritionally rich, and with a chemical composition similar to themselves. However, just as selection has favoured plant defences against herbivory, so too has selection favoured prey defences against predators. In chapter 14 we will discuss a variety of specific adaptations that are common to prey species and help reduce predation. Here we focus on the predator. Just like detritivores and herbivores, carnivores vary greatly in size, and include predatory nematodes, mites, beetles, birds, and mammals (fig. 7.12).

In contrast to the wildly variable C:N ratios within the tissues of an individual plant (fig. 7.11), there is very little variation in C:N ratios across different animal species. As a result, different prey species available to a single carnivore are fairly similar in nutrient content, and thus changes in diet composition have relatively minor nutritional impacts on carnivores. Consequently, there can be substantial variation in

Figure 7.12   Predators come in a diversity of shapes and sizes.

the diets of individual carnivores within a single population of carnivores, as well as variation among populations across the entire range a particular species occupies.

Erin Urton and Keith Hobson of the University of Saskatchewan used stable isotopic analyzes to determine the dietary composition of wolves and other mammals in a study area centred around Prince Albert National Park (PANP) in central Saskatchewan (Urton and Hobson 2005). You may recall from chapter 6 that different biological processes discriminate among the different isotopes of common elements, such as carbon and nitrogen, resulting in unique isotopic signatures. A variety of ecological processes result in different isotopic signatures for different plant species. Because of this, and their own unique biochemistry, herbivores that consume different plant species end up with unique isotopic signatures.

Urton and Hobson collected hair samples for 18 mammal species, and subjected them to isotopic analysis. As you can see in figure 7.13*a*, these species differ greatly in their isotopic signatures, even though they all were collected from a single study site in central Saskatchewan. You may even notice that most of the carnivore species are relatively enriched in ^{15}N and ^{13}C compared to the herbivorous species. Perhaps more surprising is that they found substantial variation in the isotopic signatures of individual wolves, both within and among different areas of the study site (fig. 7.13*b*). Wolves are pack hunters, and thus the assumption would be they have similar diets and thus little variation in isotopic signatures among individuals. Instead, Urton and Hobson found that the variation among individual wolves was similar to that found in other generalist carnivores, such as coyotes and bears. One potential explanation is that the boreal forest and aspen parkland, where this study was conducted, has a relatively rich diversity of potential prey sources, and thus there is substantial opportunity for choice in dietary composition among individuals. Despite the broad taxonomic diversity of the prey that makes up the diets of these wolves, they are all fairly similar in terms of their carbon, nitrogen, and phosphorus content. As a result, selection on carnivores often acts not on the nutritional rewards given by a particular prey, but instead on the ability and efficiencies of carnivores to catch and consume different prey.

Because predators must catch and subdue their prey, they often select prey by size, a behaviour that ecologists call **size-selective predation**. Because of this, prey size is often correlated with predator size, especially among solitary predators. One such predator, the puma, or mountain lion, *Felis concolor*, ranges from the Canadian Yukon to the tip of South America. Puma size changes substantially along this latitudinal gradient. Mammals make up over 90% of the puma's diet, and large mammals, especially deer, are its main prey in the northern part of its range in North America. However, Augustin Iriarte and his colleagues (1990) found that as pumas decrease in size southward, the average size of their prey also decreases (fig. 7.14). In the tropics, pumas feeds mainly on medium and small prey, especially rodents. Then, as pumas again increase in size south of the equator, large mammals form an increasing portion of their diet. Why should different-sized pumas feed on different-sized prey? One reason is that large prey may be difficult to subdue and may even injure

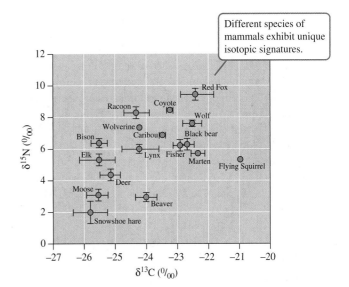

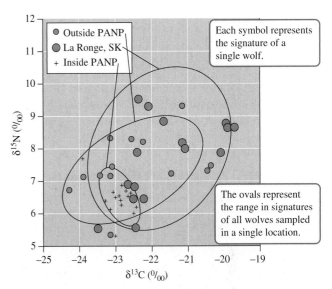

Figure 7.13   (*a*) Mammal species from central Saskatchewan differ in nitrogen isotopic signatures. (*b*) There is also variation in isotopic signatures among individuals wolves, even within single locations in and around Prince Albert National Park and La Ronge, Saskatchewan (data from Urton and Hobson 2005).

the predator, while very small prey may be difficult to find or catch. As we shall see later in this chapter, size-selective predation may also have an energetic basis.

Now let's turn from typical heterotrophs, such as wolves and pumas, to organisms that obtain their energy from inorganic molecules. These are the chemosynthetic autotrophs. Though less familiar to most of us, chemosynthesis may be one of the world's oldest professions.

Chemosynthetic Autotrophs

In 1977, a routine dive by a small submersible carried scientists exploring the Galápagos rift to a grand discovery. Their discovery changed our view of how a biosphere can be structured. Ecologists had long assumed that photosynthesis provides the

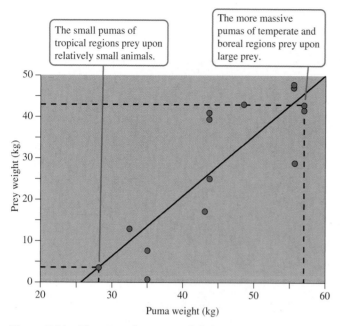

The small pumas of tropical regions prey upon relatively small animals.

The more massive pumas of temperate and boreal regions prey upon large prey.

Figure 7.14 The size of pumas and their prey change with latitude (data from Iriarte et al. 1990).

energy for nearly all life in the sea. However, these scientists came across a world based upon an entirely different energy source, energy captured by chemosynthesis. The world they discovered is inhabited by giant worms up to 4 m long with no digestive tracts, by filter-feeding clams, and by carnivorous crabs tumbling over each other in tangled abundance (chapter 3). These organisms live on nutrients discharged by deep-sea volcanic activity through an oceanic rift, a crack in the seafloor. Interconnected systems of rifts extend tens of thousands of kilometres along the seafloor. Subsequent explorations have confirmed that chemosynthetic communities exist at many points of volcanic discharge along the seafloor.

The autotrophs upon which these submarine oases depend are chemosynthetic bacteria. Some of the most common are sulfur oxidizers, bacteria that use CO_2 as a source of carbon and get their energy by oxidizing elemental sulfur, hydrogen sulfide, or thiosulfite. The submarine volcanic vents with which these organisms are associated discharge large quantities of sulfide-rich warm water. The sulfur-oxidizing bacteria that exploit this resource around the vents are of two types: free-living forms and those that live within the tissues of a variety of invertebrate animals, including the giant tube worms (fig. 7.15). Other communities dependent upon sulfur-oxidizing

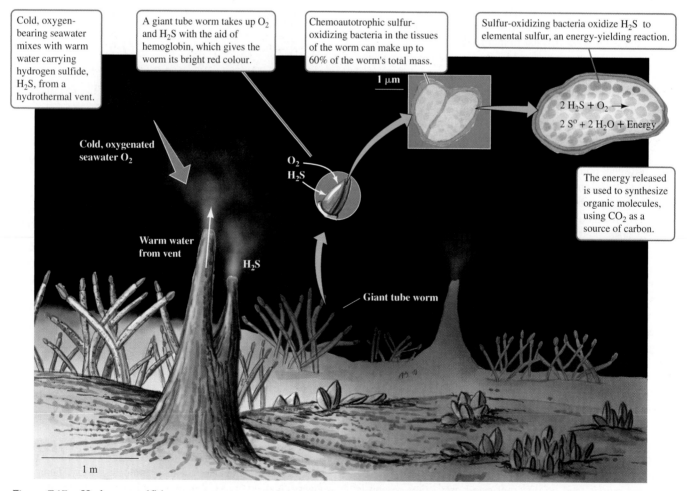

Cold, oxygen-bearing seawater mixes with warm water carrying hydrogen sulfide, H_2S, from a hydrothermal vent.

A giant tube worm takes up O_2 and H_2S with the aid of hemoglobin, which gives the worm its bright red colour.

Chemoautotrophic sulfur-oxidizing bacteria in the tissues of the worm can make up to 60% of the worm's total mass.

Sulfur-oxidizing bacteria oxidize H_2S to elemental sulfur, an energy-yielding reaction.

Cold, oxygenated seawater O_2

Warm water from vent

H_2S

O_2
H_2S

1 μm

$$2 H_2S + O_2 \longrightarrow 2 S^o + 2 H_2O + Energy$$

The energy released is used to synthesize organic molecules, using CO_2 as a source of carbon.

Giant tube worm

1 m

Figure 7.15 Hydrogen sulfide as an energy source for chemoautotrophic bacteria in the deep sea.

bacteria have been discovered in thermal vents in deep fresh-water lakes, in surface hot springs, and in caves.

Other chemosynthetic bacteria oxidize ammonium nitrite iron (Fe^{2+}), hydrogen (H_2), or carbon monoxide (CO). Of these, the nitrifying bacteria, which oxidize ammonium to nitrite and nitrite to nitrate, are undoubtedly among the most ecologically important organisms in the biosphere. Figure 7.16 summarizes one of the energy-yielding reactions exploited by nitrifying bacteria. The importance of these bacteria is due to their role in cycling nitrogen. As we saw earlier in this chapter, nitrogen is a key element in the chemical makeup of individual organisms. It also plays a central role in the economy of the entire biosphere. In the Ecological Tools and Approaches section of this chapter, we will see how bacteria can be used to remediate polluted areas.

Mixotrophy and Omnivory

In this chapter we have presented species as if each has only a single way of capturing energy. Though this will be true for many species, others are able to exploit more than one source of carbon. One group of organisms that you are likely familiar with are the **omnivores**. These species are able to gain energy from, and regularly consume, both plant and animal matter. Humans are well known examples of omnivores, with teeth suited both for biting (incisors) and grinding (molars).

Grizzly bears are another example, and are able to include berries, roots, small mammals, and fish in their diets.

A similar group of organisms, though less well known and studied, are the **mixotrophs**. Mixotrophic species are able to gain energy both from photosynthesis and from consuming organic or inorganic compounds. A variety of algae, bacteria, and protist species are mixotrophs. One of the best examples of mixotrophy in the wild comes from Quebec. David Bird and Jacob Kalff, both from McGill University, determined that four common species of the lake alga, *Dinobryon* (fig. 7.17), consumed substantial amounts of bacteria (Bird and Kalff 1986). In a detailed study testing the feeding rates of different planktonic species, they found *Dinobryon* could consume bacteria at a rate similar to non-photosynthetic predators, such

Figure 7.17   Algal species of the genus *Dinobryon* not only photosynthesize, but are also efficient predators of bacteria.

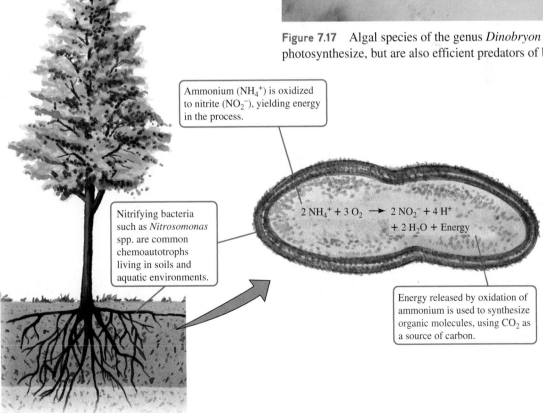

Ammonium (NH_4^+) is oxidized to nitrite (NO_2^-), yielding energy in the process.

Nitrifying bacteria such as *Nitrosomonas* spp. are common chemoautotrophs living in soils and aquatic environments.

$$2\,NH_4^+ + 3\,O_2 \longrightarrow 2\,NO_2^- + 4\,H^+ + 2\,H_2O + Energy$$

Energy released by oxidation of ammonium is used to synthesize organic molecules, using CO_2 as a source of carbon.

Figure 7.16   Ammonium as an energy source for chemoautotrophic bacteria in soil.

as rotifers. Further, they estimate that under low light conditions, up to 50% of the carbon obtained by the alga comes from feeding upon bacteria, rather than photosynthesis! There is likely a very large number of very small organisms that are mixotrophs, though like the small species found in the soil, this remains a black hole of ecological research.

Another group of organisms that occupy an unusual trophic position are the carnivorous plants. Less than 1000 species of vascular plants fall into this group, with fewer than 50 occurring in North America. Canada is home to several species of carnivorous plants, including bladderworts, sundews, and pitcher plants. These species tend to be restricted to aquatic (bladderworts) or low nitrogen environments, such as bogs and fens. Predation results in significant increases in the nitrogen these plants are able to capture.

As you can see, the trophic diversity among organisms is great. However, at least one ecological characteristic is shared by all organisms, regardless of the trophic group to which they belong—all organisms take in energy at a limited rate.

CONCEPT 7.1 REVIEW

1. What are the principle similarities between how photosynthetic, chemoautotrophic, and heterotrophic organisms capture energy from their "food" sources?
2. Why can many different sizes of herbivores consume a single leaf when it is alive, while there is strong size bias in which detritivores can consume that same leaf when it dies?
3. How can stable isotopes be used to infer variation in diet composition of carnivores?

7.2 Energy and Nutrient Limitation

The rates at which organisms can take in energy and nutrients are limited. Imagine that at the start of tomorrow's lecture, your professor enters the room with an enormous bag of loonies: in fact, as you can likely tell by the high-end fashions worn by most of us profs (please note tongue firmly in cheek), this is a magical bag that is able to generate an unlimited supply of money. One by one, your professor calls students up to the bag, and you are given 2 minutes to take as many loonies as you can. How many will you take? The answer will vary among students, but assuming you did not try to steal the bag itself, it will always be less than infinity. In other words, even when presented with the opportunity for unlimited intake (loonie acquisition), your actual rate of intake is limited. You can only move your hands so quickly and you can only hold so many loonies before they begin to spill out of your hands and pockets. Such physical and physiological limitations on consumption are common to all species, even in the presence of an unlimited supply of resources (light, prey, etc.).

Limits on the potential rate of energy and nutrient intake by animals have been demonstrated by studying how feeding rate increases as the availability of food increases. Limits on rates of energy intake by plants have been demonstrated by studying how photosynthetic rate responds to photon flux density.

Photon Flux and Photosynthetic Response Curves

Plant physiologists generally test the photosynthetic potential of plants in environments that are ideal for the particular species being studied. These environments have abundant nutrients and water, normal concentrations of oxygen and carbon dioxide, ideal temperatures, and high humidity. If you gradually increase the intensity of light shining on plants growing under these conditions, that is, if you increase the photon flux density, the plants' rates of photosynthesis gradually increase and then level off. At low light intensities, photosynthesis increases linearly with PFD. At intermediate light intensities, photosynthetic rate rises more slowly. Finally, at high light intensity, but well below that of full sunlight, photosynthesis levels off. Organisms that show this type of photosynthetic response curve include terrestrial plants, lichens, planktonic algae, and benthic algae.

The photosynthetic response curves of different plant species generally level off at different maximum rates of photosynthesis. This rate in figure 7.18 is indicated as P_{max}. A second difference among photosynthetic response curves is the PFD, or **irradiance**, required to produce the maximum rate of photosynthesis. The irradiance required to saturate photosynthesis is shown in figure 7.18 as I_{sat}. A third difference among photosynthetic response curves is the **light**

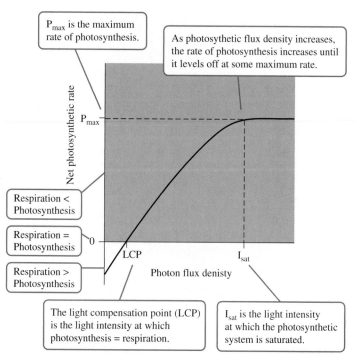

P_{max} is the maximum rate of photosynthesis.

As photosythetic flux density increases, the rate of photosynthesis increases until it levels off at some maximum rate.

Respiration < Photosynthesis

Respiration = Photosynthesis

Respiration > Photosynthesis

The light compensation point (LCP) is the light intensity at which photosynthesis = respiration.

I_{sat} is the light intensity at which the photosynthetic system is saturated.

Figure 7.18 A graphical representation of a "typical" photosynthetic response curve.

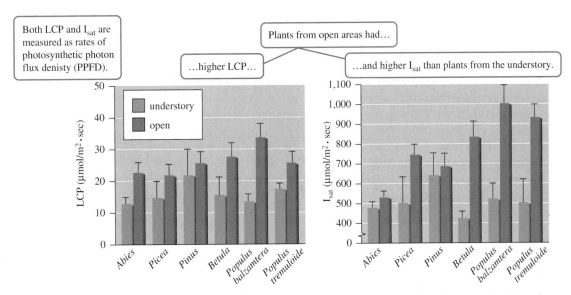

Both LCP and I_{sat} are measured as rates of photosynthetic photon flux denisty (PPFD).

Plants from open areas had…

…higher LCP…

…and higher I_{sat} than plants from the understory.

Figure 7.19   LCP and I_{max} were higher in open habitats than understory habitats for six boreal tree species (data from Landhausser and Lieffers 2001).

compensation point, or LCP. As you can see in figure 7.18, the light response curve does not pass through the origin of the graph, and instead there will be a positive x-intercept and negative y-intercept. What do these values represent? The x-intercept is the LCP, and indicates the amount of light necessary for the plant to have a zero net production of O_2. Remember that plants, like all eukaryotic organisms, undergo oxidative respiration, and thus are continually consuming oxygen. The LCP represents the amount of light necessary for the rate of photosynthesis to equal the rate of respiration. If more light is available, the plant is producing more sugars than it consumes. If less light is available, the plant is in trouble, as it is spending more sugars than it is producing.

Differences in photosynthetic response curves have been used to divide plants into "sun" and "shade" species. The response curves of plants from shady habitats suggest selection for efficiency at low light intensities. The photosynthetic rate of shade plants levels off at lower light intensities, and they are often damaged by intense light. However, at very low light intensities, shade plants usually have higher photosynthetic rates than sun plants.

The ability of seedlings to tolerate shade has important consequences for regenerating forests following the death of canopy trees. Victor Lieffers and Simon Landhausser, of the University of Alberta, have conducted extensive research into the physiological ecology of the trees of the boreal forest. In one study (Landhausser and Lieffers 2001), they grew seedlings of six species of common boreal forest trees in either the natural forest understory (shade) or in an adjacent sunny site (open). They then measured the light response curves of all the plants over two years (fig. 7.19). For nearly all species, the plants grown under open conditions had higher rates of maximum photosynthesis (P_{max}), saturated photosynthesis at higher levels of irradiance (I_{max}), and higher light compensation points than the same species grown in the shade (fig. 7.20). This result should indicate a few things. First, this

is a clear example of acclimation, as discussed in chapter 5. For most species, continued growth under high light conditions allowed them to more efficiently exploit that resource than did growth under low light conditions. Second, this is also an example of phenotypic plasticity, where a single individual has the potential to express a variety of alternative phenotypes (e.g., high or low LCP) depending upon its local environment. Finally, you may also notice that there is a

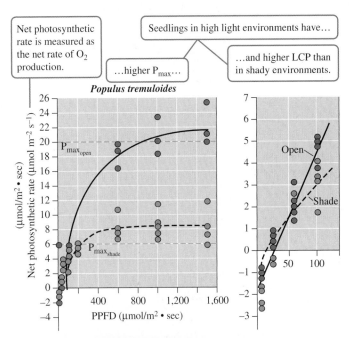

Net photosynthetic rate is measured as the net rate of O_2 production.

Seedlings in high light environments have…

…higher P_{max}…

…and higher LCP than in shady environments.

Figure 7.20   Light response curve for one tree of the boreal forest (data from Landhausser and Lieffers 2001). Orange dots correspond to shade plants and blue to plants in the open. The figure on the right is an enlargement of the lower left part of the figure on the left, allowing improved visualization of the LCP differences among sun and shade plants.

physiological trade-off occurring. Increasing P_{max} is generally associated with an increase in the plant's LCP. In other words, plants that adapted to use high light levels are poorly suited to growing under low light levels. Landhausser and Lieffers have shown that such trade-offs can exist among species from a single habitat. Even more extreme differences can occur from species from different habitats.

Whether a shade or sun plant, photosynthetic response curves eventually level off. In other words, the rate at which photosynthetic organisms can take in energy is limited. As we shall now see, animals also take in energy and nutrients at a limited rate.

Food Density and Animal Functional Response

If you gradually increase the amount of food available to a hungry animal, its rate of feeding increases and then levels off. This relationship between food availability and feeding rate is called the **functional response**. Ecologists use graphs to describe functional responses. C. S. Holling, a former professor of Zoology at the University of British Columbia, (1959) described three types of functional responses. Though all three forms level off at a maximum feeding rate at high prey densities, they differ in the shape of the curve at low and intermediate prey densities (fig. 7.21).

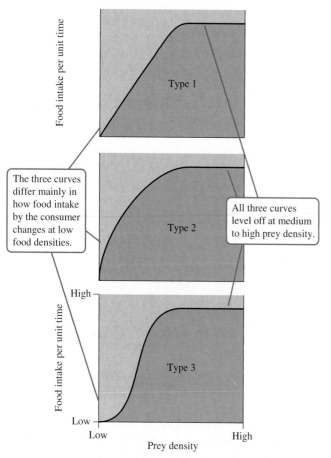

The three curves differ mainly in how food intake by the consumer changes at low food densities.

All three curves level off at medium to high prey density.

Figure 7.21 Three theoretical response curves describe the relationship between prey density and feeding rate.

Type 1 functional responses are those in which feeding rate increases linearly (as a straight line) as food density increases and then levels off abruptly at some maximum feeding rate. The only animals that are known to have type 1 functional responses are consumers that require little or no time to process their food; for example, some filter-feeding aquatic animals that feed on small prey.

In a type 2 functional response, feeding rate at first rises linearly at low food densities, rises more slowly at intermediate food densities, and then levels off at high densities. At low food densities, feeding rate appears limited by how long it takes the animal to find food. At intermediate food densities, the animal's feeding rate is partly limited by the time spent searching for food and partly by the time spent handling food. "Handling" refers to such activities as cracking the shells of nuts or snails, removing distasteful scent glands from prey, and chasing down elusive prey. At high food density, an animal does not have to search for food at all and the feeding rate is determined almost entirely by how fast the animal can handle its food. At these very high densities, the animal, in effect, has "all the food it can handle."

The type 3 functional response is S-shaped. At low food densities, type 3 functional response curves increase more slowly than during either type 1 or type 2 functional response curves. Food intake then rises steeply at intermediate food densities, eventually levelling off at higher densities. What mechanisms may be responsible for the more complicated shape of the type 3 functional response? At low densities, food organisms may be better protected from predators because they occupy relatively protected habitats, or "safe sites." In addition, animals often ignore uncommon foods, focusing most of their attention on more abundant foods. Animals may also require some learning to exploit food at a maximum rate. At low food densities, the animals may not have sufficient exposure to a particular food item to fully develop their searching and handling skills. Holling's research provided a theoretical basis for later empirical studies of animal functional response.

Of the hundreds, perhaps thousands, of functional response curves described by ecologists, the most common is the type 2 functional response. For example, John Gross and colleagues (1993) conducted a study of the functional responses of 13 mammalian herbivore species. The researchers manipulated food density by offering each herbivore various densities of fresh alfalfa, *Medicago sativa*. The rate of food intake was measured as the difference between the amount of alfalfa offered to an animal at the beginning of a trial and how much was left over at the end. Gross and his colleagues ran 36 to 125 feeding trials for each herbivore species for a total of over 900 trials. Every species of herbivore examined, from moose to lemmings to prairie dogs, showed a type 2 functional response. Figure 7.22 shows the type 2 functional response shown by moose, *Alces alces*.

Gross and his colleagues worked in a controlled experimental environment. Do consumers in natural environments also show a type 2 functional response? To answer this question, let's examine the functional response of wolves, *Canis lupus*, feeding on moose. François Messier of the University

of Saskatchewan (1994) examined the interactions between moose and wolves in North America. He focused on areas where moose are the dominant large prey species eaten by wolves. When moose density in various regions was plotted against the rate at which they are killed by wolves, the result was a clear type 2 functional response (fig. 7.23), similar to what we saw for moose feeding on plants.

Type 2 functional responses are remarkably similar to the photosynthetic response curves shown by plants (see fig. 7.20) and have the same implications. Even if you provide an animal with unlimited food, its energy intake eventually levels off at some maximum rate. This is the rate at which energy intake is limited by internal rather than external constraints. What conclusions can we draw from this parallel between plants and animals? We can conclude that even under ideal conditions, organisms as different as wolves, moose, and the plants eaten by moose take in energy at a limited rate. As we shall now see, limited energy intake is a fundamental assumption of optimal foraging theory.

CONCEPT 7.2 REVIEW

1. In type 3 functional response, what mechanisms may be responsible for low rates of food intake—compared to type 1 and type 2 functional response—at low food densities?
2. Why are plants such as mosses living in the understory of a dense forest, which show higher rates of photosynthesis at low irradiance, unable to live in environments where they are exposed to full sun for long periods of time?
3. What conclusion can we draw from the parallel between photosynthetic response curves in plants and functional response curves of animals?

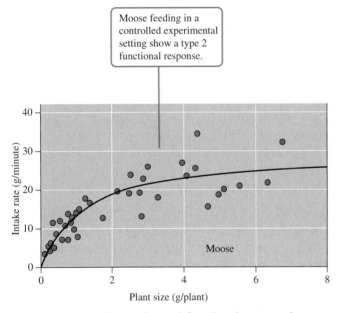

Figure 7.22 An observed type 2 functional response by moose (data from Gross et al. 1993).

Moose feeding in a controlled experimental setting show a type 2 functional response.

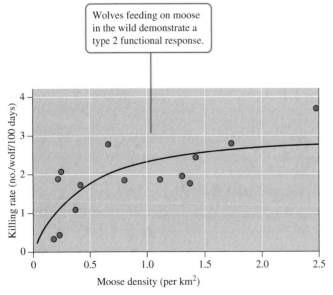

Wolves feeding on moose in the wild demonstrate a type 2 functional response.

Figure 7.23 An observed type 2 functional response by wolves (data from Messier 1994).

7.3 Energy and Nutrient Capture

Natural selection will influence how organisms feed, and this process can be understood through the use of optimal foraging theory. Evolutionary ecologists predict that if organisms have limited access to resources (e.g., nutrients, energy), and if these resources limit fitness, then natural selection is likely to favour individuals within a population that are more effective at acquiring the limiting resources. This prediction spawned an area of ecological inquiry called **optimal foraging theory**. Optimal foraging theory assumes that if energy supplies are limited, organisms cannot simultaneously maximize all of life's functions; for example, allocation of energy to one function, such as growth or reproduction, reduces the amount of energy available to other functions, such as defence. Similarly, there will be a trade-off of time allocation for most organisms. For example, a prairie dog that is feeding upon grasses cannot simultaneously stand guard, on the look-out for hawks high above. As a consequence, there must be compromises between competing demands. This inevitable conflict between energy allocations has been called the principle of allocation, and this is the basis for the energy budgets presented in figure 5.32. These budgets can be expanded to include "time" as a resource, resulting in "time-energy budgets." Here, however, we focus on energy, nutrients, and foraging.

Optimal foraging theory attempts to model how organisms feed as an optimizing process, a process that maximizes or minimizes some quantity. In some situations, the environment may favour individuals that assimilate energy or nutrients at a high rate (e.g., some filter-feeding zooplankton and short-lived weedy annual plants growing in disturbed habitats). In other situations, selection for minimum water loss

appears much stronger (e.g., cactus and scorpions in the desert). Optimal foraging theory attempts to predict what consumers will eat, and when and where they will feed. Early work in this area concentrated on animal behaviour. More recently, the acquisition of energy and nutrients by plants has also been investigated as forms of foraging behaviour. It is important to recognize that optimal foraging theory is not a single "grand" idea, but instead is a general approach to understanding behaviour. We will discuss two aspects, movement among patches and diet selection.

Movement Among Patches

One of the initial ideas of optimal foraging theory that drew the attention of many researchers was the **marginal value theorem**, proposed by Eric Charnov (1976). How do we know this theory, over 35 years old, has been influential and is worth continuing to teach in an introductory ecology course? Over 1,700 papers have cited Charnov's initial study, making it one of the most frequently cited papers in ecology. Ever. The value of Charnov's contribution can be seen in the simplicity of the question he asked, and the elegance of the answer he provided.

Charnov was interested in understanding how long an individual organism should forage in a single location before moving to a new location. He imagined a world in which food items were organized into patches, such as Saskatoon berries on a bush or flowers on a plant. Some patches will have lots of food, and others few. The question that Charnov wanted to answer was, when should an animal abandon the patch where it is currently feeding and move to a new one? He recognized that when an individual first reaches a patch, consumption rates will be at their maximum, as there is lots of food remaining in the patch. However, as they consume the food, the rate of intake will slow, as it will take longer to find the remaining food items. Using a series of equations, Charnov was able to predict that the optimal time to leave a patch was dependent upon both the time it would take to move to a new patch, qualities of a patch, and aspects of the foraging environment. In general, one should stay in a patch longer if transit time to a new patch is high (fig. 7.24), if the environment is generally low in food items, or if a selected patch is particularly high value.

The marginal value theorem has been tested hundreds of times in a diversity of species. Though its predictions do not hold for all organisms under all conditions, it remains a central concept in understanding how animals move among food patches in a heterogeneous world. Another productive avenue of research has been to use optimal foraging theory to predict the composition of animal diets.

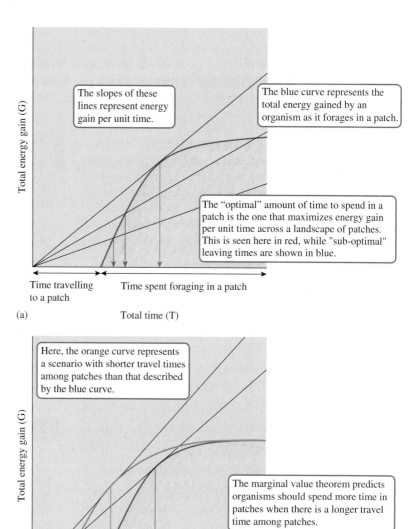

Figure 7.24 A graphical representation of the marginal value theorem. The x-axis represents the total time spent foraging, which includes both travel to a patch and time spent in a patch. The y-axis represent the total amount of energy gained by the organism as a function of time spent foraging. (*a*) The rate of energy gain can be calculated as the slope of G/T. This value is maximized at the point where a line drawn from the origin is tangential to the gain curve. The optimal time to spend in the patch is determined by the value of the x-axis directly below the point of intersection. (*b*) Here we see two possible scenarios, short travel times (orange) and longer travel time (blue). The optimal foraging strategy is to spend less time in a single patch when travel times are shorter.

Diet Composition

When ecologists determine what prey a consumer might eat, they try to identify the prey attributes that may affect the rate of energy intake by the predator. One of the most important factors is the abundance of a potential food item. All things being equal, a more abundant prey item yields a larger energy return than an uncommon prey. In optimal foraging studies, prey abundance is generally expressed as the number of the

prey encountered by the predator per unit of time, N_e. Another prey attribute is the amount of energy, or costs, expended by the predator while searching for prey, C_s. A third characteristic of potential prey that could affect the energy return to the predator is the time spent processing prey in activities such as cracking shells, fighting, removing noxious scent glands, and so forth. Time spent in activities such as these are summarized as handling time, H. Ecologists ask, given the searching and handling capabilities of an animal and a certain array of available prey, do animals select their diet in a way that yields the maximum rate of energy intake? We can rephrase this question mathematically by incorporating the terms for prey encounter rate, N_e, searching costs, C_s, and handling time, H, into a model.

One of the most basic questions that we might ask about feeding by a predator concerns the number of prey items that should be included in its diet. Put another way, what mix of prey can a predator consume that will maximize its energy intake, while minimizing the time it spends feeding? Should it feed upon the common, but low nutritive value prey items? How about the rare, but high quality items? Maybe it should simply be a generalist, eating everything it can find. As you may recognize, the answer to this question is going to depend on the specific costs and benefits of consuming each prey type.

Early work on this question was published by MacArthur and Pianka (1966) and Charnov (of marginal value fame!; 1973) and several others. We can represent the rate of energy intake of a predator as E/T, where E is energy and T is time. Earl Werner and Gary Mittelbach (1981) modelled the rate of energy intake for a predator feeding on a single prey species as follows:

$$\frac{E}{T} = \frac{N_{e1}E_1 - C_s}{1 + N_{e1}H_1}$$

In this equation, N_{e1} is the number of prey 1 encountered per unit of time. E_1 is the energy gained by feeding on an individual of prey 1 minus the costs of handling. Cs is the cost of searching for the prey. H_1 is the time required for "handling" an individual of prey 1. Once again, this equation expresses the net rate at which a predator takes in energy when it feeds on a particular prey species.

What would be the rate of energy intake if the predator fed on two types of prey? The rate is calculated as follows:

$$\frac{E}{T} = \frac{(N_{e1}E_1 - C_s) + (N_{e2}E_2 - C_s)}{1 - N_{e1}H_1 + N_{e2}H_2}$$

This is an extension of the first equation. Here, we have added encounter rates for prey 2, N_{e2}, the energetic return from feeding on prey 2, E_2, and the handling time for prey 2, H_2. The searching costs, Cs, are assumed to be the same for prey 1 and prey 2.

The rate of energy intake by a predator feeding on several prey can be represented as:

$$\frac{E}{T} = \frac{\sum_{i=1}^{n} N_{ei}E_i - C_s}{1 + \sum_{i=1}^{n} N_{ei}H_i}$$

Here, Σ means "the sum of" and i equals 1, 2, 3, etc., to n, where n is the total number of prey. Remember that this equation gives an estimate of the rate of energy intake. The question that optimal foraging theory asks is whether organisms feed in a way that maximizes the rate of energy intake, E/T.

Optimal foraging theory predicts that a predator will feed exclusively on prey 1, ignoring other available prey, when:

$$\frac{N_{e1}E_1 - C_s}{1 + N_{e1}H_1} > \frac{(N_{e1}E_1 - C_s) + (N_{e2}E_2 - C_s)}{1 + N_{e1}H_1 + N_{e2}H_2}$$

This expression says that the rate of energy intake is greater if the predator feeds only on prey 1. If the predator feeds on both prey species, the rate will be lower.

Optimal foraging theory predicts that predators will include a second prey species in their diet when:

$$\frac{(N_{e1}E_1 - C_s) + (N_{e2}E_2 - C_s)}{1 + N_{e1}H_1 + N_{e2}H_2} > \frac{N_{e1}E_1 - C_s}{1 + N_{e1}H_1}$$

In this case, feeding on two prey species gives the predator a higher rate of energy intake than if it feeds on one. The general prediction is that predators will continue to add different types of prey to their diet until the rate of energy intake reaches a maximum. This is called **optimization**.

Now let's get back to our basic question: Do animals select food in a way that maximizes their rate of energy intake? Testing such a prediction requires a great deal of information. Fortunately, mathematical models such as this one help focus experiments and observations on a few key variables.

Foraging by Bluegill Sunfish

Some of the most thorough tests of optimal foraging theory have been conducted on the bluegill sunfish, *Lepomis macrochirus*. The bluegill is a medium-sized fish native to eastern and central North America, where it inhabits a wide range of freshwater habitats, from small streams to the shorelines of small and large lakes. Bluegills feed mainly on benthic and planktonic crustaceans and aquatic insects, prey that differ in size and habitat and in ease of capture and handling. Bluegills often choose prey by size, feeding on organisms of certain sizes and ignoring others. This behaviour is convenient because it gives the ecologist a relatively simple measure to describe the composition of the available prey and the composition of the theoretically optimal diet.

Werner and Mittelbach used published studies to estimate the amount of energy expended by bluegills while they search for (C_s) and handle prey. They used laboratory experiments to estimate handling times (H) and encounter rates (N_e) for various prey. For these laboratory experiments, they constructed approximations of the places where bluegills forage in nature—open water, sediments, and vegetation. These model habitats were constructed in large aquaria and stocked with some of the important prey of bluegills: damselfly larvae, midge larvae, and *Daphnia*. These experiments showed that encounter rates increase as fish size, prey size, and prey density increase, and that handling time depends on the relative

sizes of predator and prey. Small bluegills require a relatively long time to handle large prey, while large bluegills expend little time handling small prey.

The energy content of prey was calculated by measuring the lengths of prey available in lakes and ponds; prey length was converted to mass, and then mass was converted to energy content using published values. With this information, Werner and Mittelbach characterized the prey available in Lawrence Lake, Michigan, and then estimated the diet that would maximize the rate of energy intake. They then sampled the bluegills of Lawrence Lake and examined their stomach contents to see how closely their diet approximated the diet predicted by optimal foraging theory.

The upper graph in figure 7.25 shows the size distribution of potential prey in vegetation in Lawrence Lake. The middle graph shows the composition of the optimal diet as predicted by the optimal foraging model just presented. Finally, the bottom graph shows the actual composition of the diets of bluegills from Lawrence Lake. Bluegills feeding in vegetation selected prey that were uncommon and larger than average. The match between the optimal diet and the prey that bluegills in Lawrence Lake actually ate seems uncanny. A similar match was obtained for bluegills feeding on zooplankton in open water.

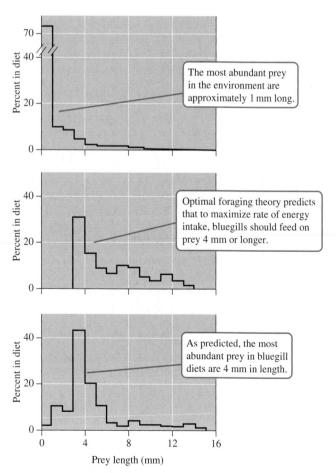

Figure 7.25 Optimal foraging theory predicts composition of bluegill sunfish diets (data from Werner and Mittelbach 1981).

Werner and Mittelbach found that optimal foraging theory provides reasonable predictions of prey selection by natural populations of bluegills. Ecologists studying plants have developed an analogous predictive framework for foraging by plants.

Optimal Foraging by Plants

Do plants forage? When we think of foraging, fish, elk, wolves, and squirrels often come to mind. But in its most basic sense, foraging is simply the search for and acquisition of resources, something that all organisms do, including plants. The more interesting question then is not whether plants forage (they do), but instead are plants able to exhibit some form of optimality, similar to what we saw with the sunfish? At first, this idea may seem absurd; complex neurological pathways are an essential component of optimal foraging, right? No. First, the argument that natural selection favours effective resource capture due to the constraints of the principle of allocation are valid for all organisms whose fitness is limited by energy. Evolution should favour phenotypes that are most efficient in resource capture, and select against those that are less efficient. Second, we think of behaviour in a certain way, in large part because we are mammals and have only a single frame of reference. However, there is more than one way to express behaviour related to foraging, and not all of them require neurons, muscles, and movement. We will look here at foraging decisions made by vascular plants.

How do plants forage? Quite simply, they put their resource-capturing organs (leaves and roots) in the locations that have the resources. Selection should favour plants that put those organs in areas of high resource availability and not in areas of low resource availability. This would be very similar to selection favouring a squirrel that feeds in areas of high acorn abundance, while selecting against those that only forage in areas where there is no food to be had! The critical difference between the plant and animal example is that many animals are mobile, and can move their whole self from one research patch to another. Plants (and some animals) are sessile, and thus they forage not by moving the individual, but instead by either growing different organs, or placing their organs in different locations.

We will start our investigation at the whole plant level. We can simplify plants by dividing them into two parts: (1) shoots, which acquire light, and (2) roots, which acquire mineral resources and water. Using economic theory, Arnold Bloom and colleagues (Bloom et al. 1985) suggested that plants will adjust their allocation of energy to growth in such a way that all resources are equally limited. This idea is itself related to Liebig's law of the minimum, in which Justus von Liebig postulated that plant growth will be limited by the scarcest essential resource, rather than the total amount of resources available to a plant. Therefore, Bloom reasoned that if light limits plant growth, plants would invest more energy in growth of shoots and less in roots. If instead soil resources are more limiting than light, plants would be expected to increase root growth relative to shoot growth.

There have been numerous experimental tests of these predictions. Most experiments generally consist of growing a certain species of plant under high and low nutrient conditions. After a given period of time, the plant is harvested and root and shoot biomass are weighed. In one **meta-analysis**, Heather Reynolds and Carla D'Antonio (1996) found that in 75% of the 206 cases they surveyed, plants had relatively less root growth under high nitrogen conditions than under low nitrogen conditions. This result was further supported by an experiment by Nichole Levang-Brilz and Mario Biondini (2002) in which they found root:shoot ratios of 62% of the 55 species they tested decreased when nitrogen was added to the soil. These studies show that across a large number of species, plants do alter their relative production of roots and shoots in response to the relative abundance of mineral resources, in a manner consistent with optimal foraging theory. In chapter 13, we will also provide an example of how plants alter shoot growth in response to reduced light availability. Although altering root:shoot ratios themselves are one means by which plants can adjust their foraging strategy to the match local conditions, it is not a particularly precise one. Instead, you could imagine that within the soil surrounding an individual plant, there will be some patches of soil that are enriched in nutrients relative to the rest of the area, perhaps due to urination by a local herbivore. These enriched patches are likely short lived, either washed away in the rain or exploited by the surrounding plants. If these patches are common in natural systems, selection may have favoured mechanisms for their exploitation—something more elegant than the blunt hammer approach of altered root:shoot ratio.

M.C. Drew, of Letcombe Laboratory in England, conducted the first of what would lead to many studies on the ability of plants to alter their root growth in response to small-scale variation in nutrient distributions (Drew 1975). Drew grew barley plants in pots filled with sand, through which he continuously irrigated a nutrient solution. In a very clever experimental design, Drew divided the pots into three vertical compartments, and was able to give different parts of the root system different levels of nutrients (fig. 7.26). What he found was striking. Plants grew roots relatively uniformly in response to a uniform distribution of nutrients, while they proliferated roots in zones of high nutrients compared to zones of low nutrients. In other words, plants were able to alter the distribution of their foraging organs in response to differences in the distribution of resources! This is a form of optimal foraging.

Since Drew's study, ecologists have been working furiously to determine how widespread this phenomenon is, and whether it has any general ecological consequences. A critical step in this process has been the documentation that most natural communities are inherently heterogeneous in soil nutrient distributions, a finding summarized by Martin Lechowicz and Graham Bell of McGill University (Lechowicz and Bell 1991). They show that in many natural communities, nutrient levels can vary by orders of magnitude within the rooting zone of an individual plant. This indicates that the potential

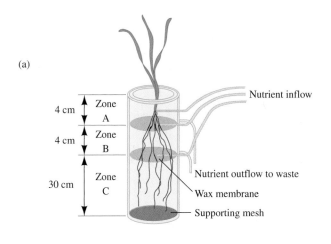

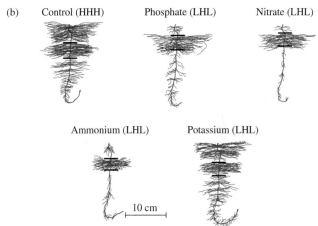

Figure 7.26 Drew (1975) manipulated nutrient levels in different zones of soil. Plants responded by non-uniform root growth.

for evolution of foraging in plants exists, as the selective environment favouring precise root placement is likely widespread. At the same time, there have been countless numbers of experiments using a large number of plant species replicating Drew's basic design, though generally varying nutrients horizontally, rather than vertically. In a recent paper by one of this book's authors and a former graduate student, Steve Kembel, we attempted to summarize this literature (Kembel and Cahill, 2005). We compiled data for over 125 plant species and subjected them to a meta-analysis. On average, plants placed approximately twice as many roots in areas of high nutrient availability than in areas of low nutrient availability. Additionally, most species were significantly larger when grown in heterogeneous soil than when grown under uniform conditions. In short, most plants can forage, and when given the opportunity to do so, they perform better than under uniform conditions.

One interesting result from this study was that monocots, such as grasses, are generally less precise foragers than are dicots, such as sunflowers. Why might this be? Work by Scott Wilson and colleagues at the University of Regina provides one possible answer. They found that root densities are higher and distributed more uniformly in grasslands

than in forested areas (Partel and Wilson 2002). They speculated that this results in more uniform resource distribution in grasslands than in forests. It is possible then, that any selective advantage of "optimal foraging" among grasses is reduced, as in their natural habitat they do not experience a particularly patchy world. However, these findings are all very new, and much more work needs to be conducted. The study of plant behaviour and foraging ecology is a rapidly growing field, and much of this work is being conducted in Canada.

CONCEPT 7.3 REVIEW

1. According to optimal foraging theory, under what conditions should a predator add a new prey species to its diet?
2. Do patterns of feeding by bluegills include any evidence that these consumers ignore certain potential prey?
3. What ecological conditions likely favour the evolution of optimal foraging in plants?

ECOLOGY IN ACTION

Using Ecological Knowledge to Predict C_4 Plant Distributions in a Changing World

C_3 and C_4 plants possess different photosynthetic pathways (figs. 7.4 and 7.5), and as a result perform differently under different temperature and moisture conditions. This interaction between plant physiology and abiotic conditions has profound implications for population growth and the geographic distribution of plants. For example, there currently exists a clear latitudinal gradient in the distribution of C_4 plants, with C_4 plants representing an increasing proportion of the local flora as you move away from the poles and toward the equator (fig. 7.27). But the world is changing. Local and global climates are being rapidly modified through

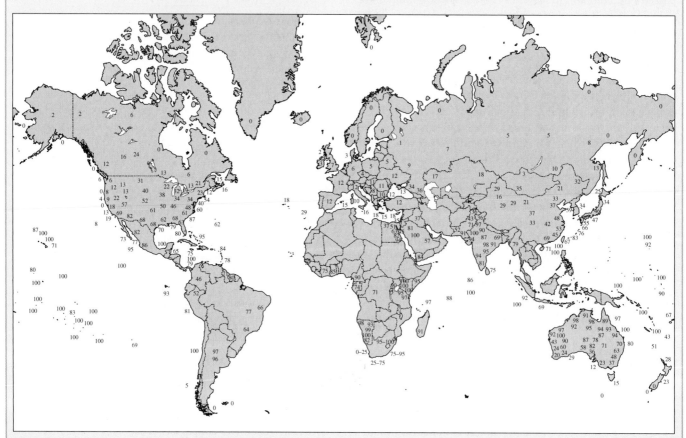

Figure 7.27 Percentage representation of C_4 grasses in grass flora from different regions of the world (data from Sage 1999).

a variety of human activities, causing changes to temperatures, precipitation, and evapotranspiration in the soil (see chapter 23 for more discussion about climate change). A shift in local climate can exert selective pressures on the species that reside within the local community. For a plant, a debate over the causes of climate change is irrelevant to the potential selective forces associated with increased atmospheric temperatures and altered precipitation. Here we will show how a strong understanding of physiological ecology can provide insights into questions of global concern. Specifically, we will address how increased temperatures may impact global distributions of C_4 plants.

Rowan Sage at the University of Toronto is a world leader in understanding the ecology of C_4 plants. Sage has blended a variety of disciplines in his work, including evolution, physiology, chemistry, ecology, and atmospheric sciences. By having such a diverse set of tools, Sage is able to address the question of how climate change may impact C_3 and C_4 plants from a more holistic perspective than could specialists in any of these individual disciplines. C_4 plants represent a relatively small fraction of the world's diversity, only 7,500 of the estimated 250,000 species of land plants (Sage 1999), with the vast majority being grasses and sedges. However, in many warm climates, C_4 plants are dominant, while decreasing in abundance as you move toward the poles or up in elevation. C_4 plants are responsible for approximately 25% of all plant growth on the planet (Sage and Kubien 2003), and include species of critical agronomic importance such as corn. We have already discussed explanations for why C_4 plants can outperform C_3 plants in bright warm conditions, but what is less clear is why they get outperformed in cooler environments. In other words, what is the cost of C_4 photosynthesis? Recent work by Sage and colleagues (Kubien et al. 2003) suggest that the architecture of C_4 leaves has resulted in reduced RUBISCO concentrations. Under hot conditions, this is not an issue, as high levels of RUBISCO in C_3 plants also result in high levels of photorespiration, reducing C_3 efficiency. However, photorespiration is reduced under cooler conditions, and the reduced levels of RUBISCO appear to limit rates of photosynthesis in C_4 plants. In other words, there appears to be a fundamental trade-off where the photosynthetic machinery is either optimized for warm or for cool conditions. What then happens when the world becomes hotter?

In analyzing current C_4 distributions, midsummer temperature is a strong correlate of C_4 plant abundance in North America, where C_4 plants are unlikely to occur if midsummer temperatures go below 10°C (fig. 7.28), or if average midsummer temperatures are below 13°C (Sage and Kubien 2003). From all of this information, it is obvious then that an increase in temperatures will result in a range expansion of C_4 plants, right? Not necessarily. It is here that we must step back and

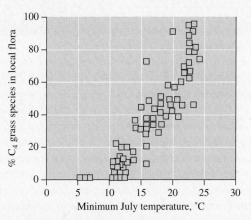

Figure 7.28   Relationship between midsummer temperature and the relative abundance of C_4 plants in North America (data from Wan and Sage 2001).

realize that an increase in global temperature is relatively meaningless to an individual plant, or even a particular species. What matters much more is what degree of change is found in a given locality, and during what time of year this change occurs. Sage and Kubien (2003) summarize current warming trends, and point out that many of the predictions regarding climate change suggest the greatest changes will occur in the winter, rather than the summer. This would actually result in an extended cool-growing season, favouring C_3, not C_4, plants! Even if warming does occur in the summer, if this is coupled with increased aridity, that could effectively shut down summer growth, leaving only spring and fall (the cooler seasons) for growth, again favouring C_3 plants. However, if precipitation also increases during the warmer summers, then this should increase C_4 growth at the expense of C_3 plants. In short, without detailed information about the exact climatic conditions a particular location is likely to experience, it will be difficult to predict the likely impact on plant distributions. This is even without considering there are other factors at play, including fire frequency, light, CO_2 levels, and many more.

It is clear that Sage and others are not yet able to conclusively say what will happen to plants with climate change, but you should be able to see that scientists are actively working on these questions. Questions of global patterns are particularly difficult to answer, as they require integrating many disciplines, as well as numerous interacting variables (e.g., temperature, water, etc.). Work by Sage, and others, provides examples that the most effective ecologists will possess a deep understanding the basic biology of the organisms they study. Global questions are not answered solely by describing patterns, but instead they require an understanding of the functional mechanisms that generate the patterns.

ECOLOGICAL TOOLS AND APPROACHES

Bioremediation—Using the Trophic Diversity of Bacteria to Solve Environmental Problems

Imagine yourself in the centre of a densely populated region with thousands of leaky gasoline tanks or complex mine wastes contaminating the groundwater. How would you solve these environmental problems? Where would you turn for help? Increasingly, we are turning to nature's own cleanup crew, the bacteria. Here we describe how an understanding of nutritional and energetic ecology can itself serve as a research tool. Environmental managers are taking advantage of the exceptional trophic diversity of bacteria to perform a host of environmental chores.

Leaking Underground Storage Tanks

Gasoline and other petroleum derivatives are stored in underground storage tanks all over the planet. Those that leak are a serious source of pollution. Maribeth Watwood and Cliff Dahm (1992) explored the possibility of using bacteria to clean up soils and aquifers contaminated by leaking storage tanks. The first step in their work was to determine if there are naturally occurring populations of bacteria that can break down complex petroleum derivatives such as benzene.

Watwood and Dahm collected sediments from a shallow aquifer that contained approximately 8.5×10^8 bacterial cells per gram of wet sediment. Of these, 6.55×10^4 bacterial cells per millilitre were capable of living on benzene as their only source of carbon and energy. By exposing sediments from the aquifer to benzene for six months, the researchers increased the populations of benzene-degrading bacteria approximately 100 times.

How rapidly can these bacteria break down benzene? Watwood and Dahm found that with no prior exposure, bacterial populations could break down 90% of the benzene in their test flasks within 40 days (fig. 7.29). Exposing sediments to benzene prior to their tests increased the rate of breakdown.

Briefly, this study demonstrated that naturally occurring populations of bacteria can rapidly break down benzene leaking from underground storage tanks. This study suggests that these bacteria will eventually clean up the organic contaminants from leaking gasoline storage tanks without manipulation of the environment. However, in the next example, environmental managers found that they had to manipulate the environment to stimulate the desired bacterial cleanup of a contaminant.

Cyanide and Nitrates in Mine Spoils

Many gold mines were abandoned when they could not be mined profitably with the mining technology of the nineteenth and early twentieth centuries. Then, in the 1970s,

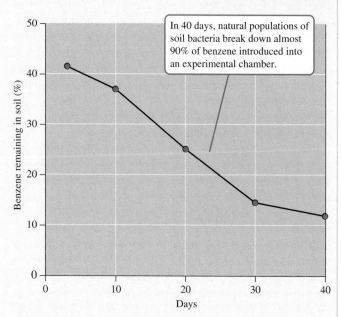

In 40 days, natural populations of soil bacteria break down almost 90% of benzene introduced into an experimental chamber.

Figure 7.29 Benzene breakdown by soil bacteria (data from Watwood and Dahm 1992).

techniques were developed to economically extract gold from low-grade ores. One of the main extraction techniques was to leach ore with cyanide (CN). Dissolved CN forms chemical complexes with gold and other metals. The solution containing gold-bearing CN can be collected and the gold and CN removed by filtering the solution with activated charcoal.

This new method of mining solved a technical problem but contaminated soils and groundwater. When the leaching process is finished, the leached ore is stored in piles; however, much CN remains. Several kinds of bacteria can break down CN and produce NH_3. This NH_3 can, in turn, be used by nitrifying bacteria as an energy source, producing NO_3. Thus, leaching gold-bearing ores and subsequent microbial activity can contaminate soil and groundwater with CN, a deadly poison, and with nitrate, another contaminant.

Carleton White and James Markwiese (1994) studied a gold mine that had been worked with the CN leaching process. The leached ores from the mine were gradually releasing CN and NO_3 into the environment. The researchers looked to bacteria to solve this environmental problem. They first documented the presence of CN degraders by looking for bacterial growth in a diagnostic medium. This medium contained CN as the only source of carbon and nitrogen. Using this growth medium, White and Markwiese estimated that each gram of ore contained approximately 10^3 to 10^5 cells of organisms capable of growing on, and breaking down, CN.

The leached ores presented bacteria with a rich source of nitrogen in the form of CN and NO_3, but the ores contained little organic carbon. White and Markwiese predicted that adding a source of carbon to the residual ores would increase the rate at which bacteria break down CN and reduce the concentration of NO_3 in the environment. Why should adding organic molecules rich in carbon increase bacterial use of nitrogen in the environment? Look back at figure 7.7, which shows that bacteria have a carbon:nitrogen ratio of about 5:1. In other words, growth and reproduction by bacteria require about five carbon atoms for each nitrogen atom.

White and Markwiese tested their ideas in the laboratory. In one experiment, they added enough sucrose to produce a C:N ratio of 10:1 within leached ores. This experiment included two controls, both of which contained leached ores without sucrose. One of the controls was sterilized to kill any bacteria. The other control was left unsterilized.

Bacteria in the treatments containing sucrose broke down all the CN within the leached ore in 13 days. Meanwhile, only a small amount of CN was broken down in the unsterilized control and no CN was broken down in the sterilized control (fig. 7.30). Why did the researchers include a sterilized control? The sterilized control demonstrated that nonbiological processes were not responsible for the observed breakdown of CN.

Figure 7.30 shows that adding sucrose to the residual ore stimulates the breakdown of CN. However, remember that this process ultimately leads to the production of NO_3. Does adding sucrose to eliminate CN lead to the buildup of NO_3, trading one pollution problem for another? No, it does not. In another experiment, White and Markwiese (1994) showed that adding sucrose also stimulates uptake of NO_3 by heterotrophic bacteria and fungi. These organisms use organic molecules, in this case sucrose, as a source of energy and carbon and NO_3 as a source of nitrogen. The nitrogen taken up by bacteria and fungi becomes incorporated in biomass as

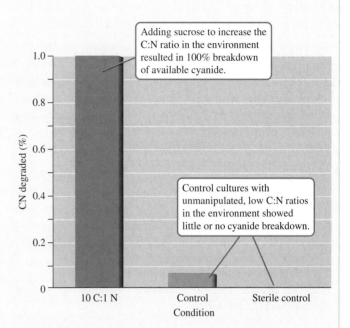

Figure 7.30 Manipulating C:N ratios to stimulate breakdown of cyanide (CN) (data from White and Markwiese 1994).

complex organic molecules. Nitrogen in this form is recycled within the microbial community and is not a source of environmental pollution.

White and Markwiese recommended that sucrose be added to leached gold-mining ores to stimulate breakdown of CN and uptake of NO_3 by bacteria. This environmental cleanup project was successful because the researchers were thoroughly familiar with the energy and nutrient relations of bacteria and fungi. Another key to the project's success was the great trophic diversity of bacteria. Bacteria will likely continue to play a great role as we address some of our most vexing environmental problems.

SUMMARY

7.1 Organisms use one of three main sources of energy: solar radiation, organic molecules, or inorganic molecules. Photosynthetic plants and algae use CO_2 as a source of carbon, and light, of wavelengths between 400 and 700 nm, as a source of energy. Light within this band, which is called photosynthetically active radiation, or PAR, accounts for about 45% of the total energy content of the solar spectrum at sea level. PAR can be quantified as photosynthetic photon flux density, generally reported as μmol per square metre per second. Among plants, there are three major alternative photosynthetic pathways, C_3, C_4, and CAM. C_4 and CAM plants are more efficient in their use of water than are C_3 plants and have reduced rates of photorespiration. Heterotrophs use organic molecules both as a source of carbon and as a source of energy. Herbivores, carnivores, and detritivores face fundamentally different trophic problems. Herbivores feed on plant tissues, which often contain a great deal of carbon but little nitrogen. Herbivores must also overcome the physical and chemical defences of plants. Detritivores feed on dead plant material, which is even lower in nitrogen than living plant tissues. Carnivores consume prey that are nutritionally rich but may be hard to capture. Chemosynthetic autotrophs, which

consist of a highly diverse group of chemosynthetic bacteria, use inorganic molecules as a source of energy. Bacteria are the most trophically diverse organisms in the biosphere.

7.2 The rates at which organisms can take in energy and nutrients are limited.

The relationship between photon flux density and plant photosynthetic rate is called photosynthetic response. Plants from sunny habitats have high maximum photosynthetic rates that level off at high irradiance and high light compensation points. The lowest maximum rates of photosynthesis and LCP occur among plants from shady environments. The relationship between food density and animal feeding rate is called the functional response. The shape of the functional response is generally one of three types. The forms of photosynthetic response curves and type 2 animal functional responses are remarkably similar. Energy limitation is a fundamental assumption of optimal foraging theory.

7.3 Natural selection will influence how organisms feed, and this process can be understood through the use of optimal foraging theory.

Evolutionary ecologists predict that if organisms have limited access to energy, natural selection is likely to favour individuals that are more effective at acquiring energy and nutrients. Many animals select where they feed and what they eat in a way that appears to maximize the rate at which they capture energy. Plants allocate energy to roots versus shoots in a way that increases their rate of intake of the resources that limit their growth. In environments rich in light but poor in nutrients, plants tend to invest more energy in the growth of roots. Within a root system, root distributions will vary vertically and horizontally as a function of resource distributions.

The trophic diversity of bacteria, which is critical to the health of the biosphere, can also be used as a tool to address some of our most challenging waste disposal problems. Bacteria can be used to clean up soils and aquifers polluted by petroleum products such as benzene, and eliminate the pollution caused by some kinds of mine waste. The success of these projects requires that ecologists understand the energy and nutrient relations of bacteria. Bacteria will likely continue to play a great role as we address some of our most vexing environmental problems.

REVIEW QUESTIONS

1. Why don't plants use highly energetic ultraviolet light for photosynthesis? Would it be impossible to evolve a photosynthetic system that uses ultraviolet light? Does the fact that many insects see ultraviolet light change your mind? Would it be possible to use infrared light for photosynthesis? (Photosynthetic bacteria tap into the near-infrared range.)

2. In what kinds of environments would you expect to find the greatest predominance of C_3, C_4, or CAM plants? How can you explain the co-occurrence of two, or even all three, of these types of plants in one area? (Think about the variations in microclimate that we considered in chapters 5 and 6.)

3. What are the relative advantages and disadvantages of being an herbivore, detritivore, or carnivore? What kinds of organisms were left out of our discussions of herbivores, detritivores, and carnivores? Where do parasites fit? Where do *Homo sapiens* fit?

4. Design a planetary ecosystem based entirely on chemosynthesis. You might choose an undiscovered planet of some distant star or one of the planets in our own solar system, either today or at some distant time in the past or future.

5. What kinds of animals would you expect to have type 1, 2, or 3 functional responses? How should natural selection for better prey defence affect the height of functional response curves? How should natural selection for more effective predators affect the height of the curves? What net effect should natural selection on predator and prey populations have on the height of the curves?

6. The rivers of central Portugal have been invaded, and densely populated, by the Louisiana crayfish, *Procambarus clarki*,

which looks like a freshwater lobster about 12 to 14 cm long. The otters of these rivers can easily catch and subdue these crayfish. Use the model for prey choice:

$$\frac{E}{T} = \frac{\sum_{i=1}^{n} N_{ei}E_i - C_s}{1 + \sum_{i=1}^{n} N_{ei}H_i}$$

Explain why the diets of the otters of central Portugal would shift from a highly diverse menu, which includes fish, frogs, water snakes, birds, and insects, to a diet dominated by crayfish. For the crayfish, assume low handling time, very high encounter rates, and high energy content.

7. The data of Iriarte and colleagues (1990) suggest that prey size may favour a particular body size among pumas. However, this variation in body size also correlates well with latitude; the larger pumas live at high latitudes. Consequently, this variation in body size has been interpreted as the result of selection for efficient temperature regulation. Homeothermic animals are often larger at high latitudes, a pattern called Bergmann's rule. Larger animals, with lower surface area relative to their mass, would be theoretically better at conserving heat. Smaller animals, with higher surface area relative to their mass, would be theoretically better at keeping cool. So what determines predator size? Is predator size determined by climate, predator–prey interactions, or both? Design a study of the influence of the environment on the size of homeothermic predators.

8. How is plant allocation to roots versus shoots similar to plant regulation of temperature and water? (We discussed these topics in chapters 5 and 6.) Consider discussing these processes under the more general heading of homeostasis. (Homeostasis is the maintenance of a relatively constant internal environment.)

9. If herbivores are able to optimally forage, why do they not more efficiently extract resources from their food? Why has natural selection allowed for the majority of the biomass ingested by herbivores to be passed through the digestive system without being fully digested?

10. Is a plant putting roots in a resource rich patch, but not in a low resource patch, the same as a predator foraging in an area of high prey density but not in an area of low prey density? Is intelligence necessary for behaviour? Why or why not?

For more information on the resources available from McGraw-Hill Ryerson, go to **www.mcgrawhill.ca/he/solutions**.

BEHAVIOURAL ECOLOGY

CHAPTER 8

CHAPTER CONCEPTS

8.1 Natural selection favours those behaviours that increase the inclusive fitness of individuals.

Concept 8.1 Review

8.2 The evolution of sociality is generally accompanied by cooperative feeding, defence of the social group, and restricted reproductive opportunities.

Ecology In Action: Human–Wildlife Conflict

Concept 8.2 Review

8.3 Mate choice by one sex and/or competition for mates among individuals of the same sex can result in selection for particular traits, a process called sexual selection.

Concept 8.3 Review

Ecological Tools and Approaches: Using Game Theory to Understand Behaviour

Summary

Review Questions

During a short swim over a coral reef, you can observe a diversity of interactions among individuals of many species. At dusk, you may see a school of fish move steadily toward an opening in the reef, heading into the open sea for a night of feeding. Approached underwater, the edge of the school looks like a giant translucent curtain stamped with the silhouettes of thousands of seemingly identical fish. Their colouration, countershaded dark above and silvery below, highly coordinated movements, and great numbers give the fish within the school some protection from predators. Though seabirds and fish attack the school as it makes its way, only a small proportion of the schooling fish are eaten.

Meanwhile, along the reef, damselfish are distributed singly on territories. The damselfish retain possession of their patches of coral rubble, living coral, and sand by patrolling the boundaries and driving off any fish attempting to intrude. At certain times, some territory-holding males are joined by females, where they court and deposit eggs and sperm on the nest site prepared by the male.

Higher along the reef face a male bluehead wrasse mates with one of the females that live within his territory (fig. 8.1). In contrast to the male with his blue head, black bars, and green body, the female is mostly yellow with a large black spot on her dorsal fin. As the blueheaded male extrudes sperm to fertilize the eggs laid by the female, small males similar in colour to the female streak by the mating pair, discharging a cloud of sperm along the way. Some of the female's eggs will be fertilized by the large territorial blueheaded male, while others will be fertilized by the sperm discharged by the smaller yellow streakers. We thus see two types of reproductive behaviour, even within this single species: dominance and sneakiness. Close observation of natural history guides behavioural ecologists in their studies of how such behaviours evolve, and the relative cost and benefits of such different strategies.

Such intriguing behaviours occur all around us. In coral reefs, forests, soils, lakes, and streams, we find interactions among members of the same species that are as significant to the long-term success of the individual organism as are its interactions with temperature, food, or the quantity and quality of available water. We will see that elaborate behaviours occur not only in the large vertebrates with which we are most familiar, but also invertebrates, plants, and even microbes. Cognition is critical for us to express behaviour, but it is critical to remember than not all species are similar to us. There is no value in trying to "think like a plant," even though they too are able to choose mates or forage non-randomly for food (chapter 7).

Perhaps given the breadth of organisms that express behaviour, it may come as no surprise that the field of behavioural ecology is also very broad. Its origins are found in the close observations of animals both in the wild and captivity: natural history and animal husbandry. The scientific study of behaviour is typically called *ethology*, a subdiscipline of zoology heavily influenced by the pioneering work of Konrad Lorenz in the twentieth century. When aspects of behaviour are integrated into ecological questions, we enter the domain of behavioural ecologists. For example, a behavioural ecologist may study the movement behaviour of a grizzly bear as it walks through a landscape. What aspects of the habitat make it stop, turn, or go faster? Such information is critical for conservation efforts, as well as the placement of hiking trails in ways that minimize human–wildlife conflict! Thus, behavioural ecology is much more than simply trying to "think like a bear."

In general, behavioural ecologists study the relationships between organisms and environment that are mediated by behaviour (fig. 8.2). We have already discussed many aspects of behavioural ecology in the preceding chapters, such as optimal foraging and movements associated with temperature and water regulation. In this chapter we will explore the theoretical underpinning of behavioural ecology. We will also study issues associated with group living, and how natural selection can favour cooperation rather than competition. We will then discuss sex and mating systems, combining evolutionary, ecological, and behavioural information to study a process Darwin called sexual selection. Behavioural ecology consists of many more topics than can be presented here, and issues of behaviour will be woven throughout our later chapters on species interactions such as competition, predation, and disease. Here we present three central concepts to this fascinating field of ecology, which in combination form the framework of chapter 8.

8.1   Evolution and Behaviour

Natural selection favours those behaviours that increase the inclusive fitness of individuals. In chapter 4 we presented the central aspects of Darwin's theory of natural selection, including the idea that if a given trait had a heritable component, and that alternative expressions of that trait resulted in differential fitness among individuals, then the frequency of that trait would increase within the population. A critical aspect of this theory is that selection acts upon *individuals*, which can cause evolution within *populations*.

When we think of natural selection, we often imagine traits such as beak size, seed number, and body size being associated with fitness and serving as the raw materials upon which selection can act. We don't usually think of behaviour.

Figure 8.1   Bluehead wrasse males with yellow females of the species. If the blueheaded male is removed from a territory, the largest female in the territory can change to a fully functional blueheaded male within days.

Figure 8.2 Organisms exhibit a diversity of behaviours, which include (clockwise from upper left), foraging and vigilance, mate selection, heat regulation, and herding.

However, a variety of commonly observed behaviours have genetic bases. One of the clearest examples of this comes from collaboration by researchers at the University of Toronto, University of Illinois at Urbana-Champaign, and the Université de Bourgogne (Ben-Shahar et al. 2002). The team of researchers was interested in the genetic control of foraging in honey bees. In honey bee colonies, worker bees work in the hive when they are young (e.g., brood care), and forage when they are older (two to three weeks later). This represents a fundamental shift in behaviour of individuals over the course of their life. The timing of this switch is not fixed, but can be influenced by needs within and external to the hive. How does this switch occur? The researchers focused on a single gene, *for*, which codes for a specific protein kinase, PKG. They found that mRNA expression was significantly higher in foraging bees than bees that remained at work in the hive. When the researchers experimentally increased PKG levels, the bees switched to foraging behaviour sooner

than untreated bees. In other words, simply increasing the abundance of a single protein, coded for by a single gene, can cause a dramatic change in bee behaviour. There are numerous other examples of genetic control of behaviour, including foraging decisions of zebra finches (Lemon 1993), anti-predator movement patterns in *Daphnia* (DeMeester 1993), and even anti-competitor growth in tobacco plants (Schmitt et al. 1995). In total, these studies provide examples that complex behaviours can have a genetic basis, and that cognitive "choice" is not the sole determinant of how an organism behaves.

What is the evolutionary basis for this variation in behaviour as a function of bee age? It is unknown; however, there is reason to believe that certain behaviours are more *adaptive* under some circumstances than others. For example, bees that are active foragers before the hive is constructed, or before plants are producing nectar, are likely less fit than bees that do not forage until later. Thus foraging and hive building

behaviours are both adaptive behaviours; however, their value is dependent upon local conditions (the presence or absence of nectar and a suitable hive). One of the great findings in behavioural ecology over the last 50 years has been that the adaptive value of a given trait is often contingent upon the specific environmental conditions that an organism faces. The idea that *either* nature *or* nurture causes individuals to act a certain way is great for sales in the media, but is sadly out of date among biologists. In other words, a squirrel exposing itself to predation risk by a hawk for a food reward makes more sense as (1) the value of the reward increases, (2) the hunger level of the squirrel increases, and (3) the probability of predation decreases. So, if we see a squirrel run after some nuts when hawks are visible, it is not fair to say that the "nature" of the squirrel is to be inherently risky; instead the squirrel possesses the ability to *either* run after the food *or* not. Evolution may fine tune this process by setting the threshold for risk taking higher or lower depending upon local conditions, creating *intraspecific* variation in behaviours. You may recall from chapter 4 that if these variations in behaviour are related to mating, they could even serve as effective isolating mechanisms leading to speciation.

At a larger level, we can see *interspecific* differences in behaviour. For example, Laurence Packer, of York University, has studied the evolution of sociality and nest architecture among several species of closely related bees (Halictidae; Packer 1991). These species are known to vary greatly in behaviour, with social bee species forming large colonies each year, some species being completely solitary, and others forming a perennial colony. What was unknown was whether these interspecific differences were the result of multiple (and random) evolutionary events, or if instead there was a general pattern to the evolution of the behaviours. After constructing a phylogeny for his eight study species, Packer mapped the known behaviours against it. The results were striking: in this group, social behaviour was an ancestral trait, with solitary behaviour recently derived. Packer's work was among the first to show that some interspecific variation in behaviour is likely the result of evolution, and like the more commonly studied physical traits such as beak size, behaviour can be passed on to daughter species.

There is certainly evidence that species and individuals vary in behaviour. We also know that individuals will alter their behaviour depending upon local conditions (do you always order the same food from every restaurant?). Such variation can rapidly overwhelm us, and it is helpful to have a broader theoretical framework on which we can base our discussion of behavioural ecology.

Inclusive Fitness and Types of Behaviour

Before we go any further in our discussion of behaviour, it is necessary for us to have a broader understanding of fitness, called **inclusive fitness**. The concept of inclusive fitness was developed by William D. Hamilton (1964). He proposed that an individual's inclusive, or overall, fitness is determined by its own survival and reproduction, plus the survival and reproduction, of individuals with whom the individual shares genes. Under some conditions, individuals can increase their inclusive fitness by helping increase the survival and reproduction of genetic relatives that are not offspring. Because this help is given to relatives, or kin, the evolutionary force favouring such behaviour is called **kin selection**.

Using the concept of inclusive fitness, Hamilton explored the potential evolutionary consequences of different forms of social interactions. He classified all social interactions into four main classes, and argued that natural selection will favour certain types of behaviour, and select against others (fig. 8.3). Specifically, Hamilton views social relations as an interaction between a "donor" and a "recipient." A donor performs a given action, such as sings a song, removes parasites from another, or displays a threat. The recipient is the individual who recognizes the given behaviour. Hamilton classified all behaviours as having a potential negative or positive effect on the fitness of the two participants. Using this model, we see that two sets of behaviours, *altruism* and *spitefulness*, have negative fitness consequences for the donor, and as a result, natural selection should select against these behaviours. In contrast, *cooperation* and *selfishness* have positive fitness consequences for the donor, and should be favoured by natural selection.

Although it may be tempting to argue that all observed behaviours are inherently adaptive and the result of natural selection, this approach is negatively referred to as *adaptationist*. Adaptationist stories in ecology are similar to Kipling's *Just So Stories*, such as "How the Camel Got His Hump." In these stories, Kipling provided fanciful "mechanisms" that generated the patterns we observe in nature, such as hump-backed camels. Modern behavioural ecologists are well aware of the adaptationist trap, and they recognize that many behaviours are evolutionarily neutral, neither selected for nor against. As a result, behavioural ecologists are not content to simply suggest an evolutionary consequence of a behaviour, but instead actively work to test whether selection actually occurs. A related issue is that for natural selection to occur, there needs to be a large heritable component to a

		Fitness Consequences to Recipient	
		+	−
Fitness Consequences to Donor	+	Cooperation	Selfishness
	−	Altruism	Spite

Figure 8.3 Hamilton (1964) proposed that social interactions can be classified into four groups based upon the potential fitness consequences for the donor and recipient of any given interaction.

given behaviour. This in no way suggests that all behaviours need to have a genetic component; instead, only those behaviours that could be influenced by natural selection must have a genetic basis.

An additional concern is that according to Hamilton's classification, some behaviours, like altruism, should not persist, as they would be selected against. However, we can go out into a variety of systems and see animals exhibiting behaviours that put them in immediate bodily harm, yet appear to prevent harm in others. This behaviour can be shown repeatedly within a species, strongly suggesting a genetic basis. In other words, we can see altruism, and we believe it can have a genetic basis. How can this be reconciled with Hamilton's ideas that altruism should be selected against?

Altruism and Natural Selection

Since 1989, a team of researchers from the University of Alberta, McGill University, and Guelph University have been making detailed studies of a red squirrel population in the Yukon as part of the Kluane Red Squirrel Project. The three principle investigators, Stan Boutin, Murray Humphries, and Andrew McAdam, along with a legion of graduate and undergraduate students, have kept meticulous notes of every squirrel birth and death in the population. The research team employs both observational and molecular methods to determine the relatedness of different individuals in the population, providing a detailed pedigree of the population. One day in the field, Jamie Gorrell, a graduate student at the University of Alberta, was up in a tree checking on the squirrel nests. He noticed that one nest had an extra baby—one female squirrel had adopted the offspring of another squirrel. Needless to say, Jamie wanted to figure out what was going on. Jamie and his colleagues (Gorrell et al. 2010) soon realized their larger data set contained five different instances of adoption (fig. 8.4). Using Hamilton's classifications, an altruistic act is one that benefits the recipient but harms the donor, and these should

Figure 8.4 Some red squirrels adopt the offspring of related individuals, a likely example of kin selection promoting the evolution of an altruistic act.

not be common in nature. What conditions would allow a squirrel to adopt the offspring of another? It turns out, behavioural ecologists have a number of explanations to the puzzle posed by altruism in nature.

One of the earliest sets of explanations for altruism came from V. C. Wynne-Edwards (1962), who argued in favour of group selection as a means to explain many observed phenomenon. In Wynne-Edwards' presentation of **group selection**, he argued that individuals may act counter to their own personal interests for the betterment of the group. For instance, an organism may reduce its reproductive rate to prevent a population from exhausting its resources. This line of thinking was rapidly attacked by many scientists (Williams 1966, Smith 1964) as being inherently adaptationist without any consistency with current evolutionary understanding. They were very effective in moving discussions of altruism toward a gene-centred, rather than group-centred level. However, over the last 40 years, the evidence has accumulated that group selection can occur in some special circumstances (Wade 1977). It has been rebranded under the term "*multilevel selection*," and its role in the evolution of altruism is still debated. Perhaps more importantly than whether group selection can exist is that ecologists have uncovered a number of other causes of altruism: kin selection, manipulation, and reciprocal altruism.

We now turn our attention to the more widely accepted idea that kin selection can promote altruism. We know that we each received 50% of our genes from each of our two biological parents. From a parental point of view, this means that each offspring they have is equivalent to approximately 50% of their own genetic material. The **coefficient of relationship** can be determined for any two individuals. It will be 25% between grandparent and grandchild, 12.5% between great-grandparent and great-grandchild, 50% between full siblings, and 25% between half-siblings. Have you figured out the pattern? There is a reduction of 50% in the coefficient in relationship for every additional connection between any two related individuals. So what? From an inclusive fitness point of view, if a sister had the choice to save the lives of her two siblings at the expense of her own life, her inclusive fitness would be equal regardless of what behaviour she chose. However, selection would favour her heroic act of self-sacrifice if she were able to save three siblings, or two siblings and a cousin, or any other combination of relatives whose coefficients of relationship sum to more than 1. However, most behaviours do not result in certain death for the donor, nor certain survival for the recipient, and so the costs and benefits of an action to one's fitness is generally less than one. Hamilton (1964) formalized the situation under which a particular behaviour would be advantageous as:

$$\frac{\text{Cost}}{\text{Benefit}} < \text{Coefficient of Relationship}$$

In this model, selection would favour a given behaviour only if the inclusive fitness gains exceed the inclusive fitness costs. The obvious question to ask is whether this really happens.

Some of the best examples that kin selection can be important in altruistic behaviours come from studies of prairie dogs and ground squirrels. A variety of species of the small rodents of the Sciuridae family will produce alarm calls when a predator is visible. These alarm calls are often loud noises associated with the individual taking an upright and aggressive posture. Work by David Wilson and James Hare of the University of Manitoba shows that for at least one species, the Richardson's ground squirrel, the vigilant animal can use an ultrasonic call to alert others to impending threat (Wilson and Hare 2004)! In a classic study of Belding's ground squirrels, Paul Sherman found that individuals displaying alarm calls increased the likelihood of themselves being attacked, but also increased the ability of others to escape predation (Sherman 1977). Importantly, the probability of an individual making an alarm call was higher when close relatives were nearby than when less closely related (or unrelated) individuals were nearby.

Jamie Gorrell was aware of the importance of kin selection as he investigated his puzzling case of squirrel adoption high in the trees of a Yukon forest. Using microsatellites (chapter 4), the research team was able to confirm that the adopted squirrels were related to the females that adopted them. Further, because they had detailed information on the costs associated with having more babies in a nest (e.g., less food available for the other babies and thus reduced survival of natal litter), as well as the potential gains through inclusive fitness, Gorrell and his colleagues were able to determine if Hamilton's rule was satisfied. In all cases, the models predicted that adoption resulted in increased fitness for the adoptive mother, providing a possible solution to his puzzle. However, in some cases altruism can also occur even without benefits to the donor. As we show next, sometimes an individual can be tricked into being altruistic.

The Brown-headed Cowbird (*Molothrus ater*) has a rather interesting mechanism for incubating its eggs and rearing its young. It is an obligate **brood parasite**, meaning that a female must lay her eggs in the nests of birds of other species. The host birds then keep the parasitic bird's eggs warm and feed the hatchling until it can fledge from the nest. Based on the principle of allocation we discussed in chapters 5 and 7, you can see an obvious problem. If the host bird gives food and thermal energy to this parasitic bird, less will be available for its own offspring, reducing its own fitness. In other words, why would these host birds perform this altruistic act? The short answer to this question is that this is an example of *manipulation*, where the song sparrow does not appear to possess any obvious means to prevent this from occurring. In a study at Delta Marsh, the field station associated with the University of Manitoba, Todd Underwood and Spencer Sealy added artificial objects of different shapes to nests of American robins and Gray catbirds (Underwood and Sealy 2006), two species that are commonly parasitized by Brown-headed Cowbirds (fig. 8.5). The researchers found that although cowbirds eggs are significantly more spherical than their host eggs, spherical test "eggs" were only slightly more likely to be rejected by host birds than the control "eggs" (fig. 8.6). In other words, although the researchers could measure a

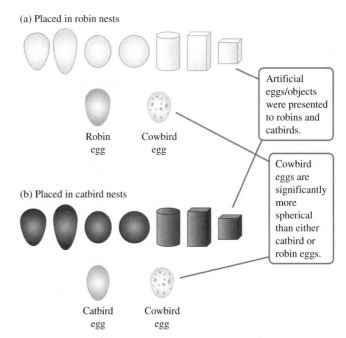

Figure 8.5   Differently shaped objects were placed in the nests of robins and catbirds (Underwood and Sealy 2006).

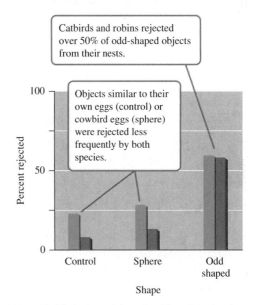

Figure 8.6   Catbirds (purple) and robins (blue) reject objects shaped similarly to cowbird eggs at the same frequency as objects shaped similarly to their own eggs (data from Underwood and Sealy 2006).

significant difference in shape between cowbird and host eggs, the host birds apparently could not, and thus cowbirds induce altruism through manipulation of the reproductive biology of their hosts. James Smith and Peter Arcese (1994), from the University of British Columbia, have measured the potential fitness consequences of cowbird parasitism on a song sparrow population on an island off the coast of British Columbia. In a 16-year study, they found the presence of a cowbird egg in a sparrow nest reduced the number of sparrows that fledged from the nest by 79%, though this was reduced to 27% when

food was experimentally added. Sparrows were also more likely to fledge no sparrows from nests when parasitized than when they were not parasitized. In short, having a cowbird egg in your nest is bad news to your fitness, though obviously you are doing the cowbird a nice favour. This form of altruism persists in nature because the host cannot do anything about it. Such an example highlights the need to avoid attributing fitness benefits to all observed behaviours.

We will provide one final explanation for altruism, which is **reciprocal altruism**. Under this model, individuals do not have to be related to each other for altruism to be evolutionarily stable. Instead, this model is based upon recognition and experience, and is also called *tit-for-tat*. We will discuss this idea in depth in the Ecological Tools and Approaches section at the end of this chapter. In brief, this idea says that natural selection will favour altruistic behaviours to unrelated individuals if that individual will repay in kind at some point in the future. The reciprocal act does not need to be immediate (that would be cooperation, not altruism), but it does need to occur with a high degree of certainty.

In this section we have provided a general background into how natural selection can influence behaviour. We find that initially counterintuitive actions, such as altruism, can also be the result of natural selection, as long as we allow ourselves to think more broadly about who benefits, why, when, and whether there is even any choice. We will now continue with more examples of how selection can influence behaviour, with a focus on group living.

CONCEPT 8.1 REVIEW

1. If a researcher is interested in understanding the evolution of a behaviour, why does it matter if that behaviour has a genetic basis? Does a genetic basis of a behaviour necessarily mean the behaviour will always be expressed?
2. What is the difference between inclusive fitness as discussed in this chapter, and fitness, as defined in chapter 4?
3. What conditions are likely necessary for the evolution of altruistic behaviours in a species?

8.2   Sociality

The evolution of sociality is generally accompanied by cooperative feeding, defence of the social group, and restricted reproductive opportunities. A fundamental change in relationships among individuals within a population takes place when individuals begin living in groups, such as colonies, herds, or schools. Cooperation generally involves exchanges of resources between individuals or various forms of assistance, such as defence of the group against predators, and altruism among ground squirrels. Group living and cooperation signal the beginnings of **sociality**. The degree of sociality in a species

ranges from acts as simple as mutual grooming or group protection of young, to highly complex, stratified societies such as those found in colonies of ants or termites. This more complex level of social behaviour is called **eusociality**. Eusociality is generally thought to include three major characteristics: (1) individuals of more than one generation living together, (2) cooperative care of young, and (3) division of individuals into sterile, or nonreproductive, and reproductive castes.

Because individuals in social species often appear to have fewer opportunities to reproduce compared to individuals in nonsocial species, the evolution of sociality has drawn a great deal of attention from ecologists. The apparent restriction of reproductive opportunities that comes with sociality appears to challenge the idea that the fitness of an individual is determined by the number of offspring it produces. How does sociality challenge this concept of fitness? The challenge emerges from the observation that in many situations, individuals in social species do not reproduce themselves, while helping others in the population to reproduce. How can we explain such behaviour that on first glance appears to be self-sacrificing? It can be argued that such behaviour should be quickly eliminated from populations. However, since eusocial species such as bees and ants have survived for millions of years, behavioural ecologists have assumed that in some circumstances, the benefits of sociality must outweigh the costs.

In our quest for such understanding, where should we begin the accounting of costs and benefits? David Ligon (1999) pointed the way when he wrote, "Most, if not all, of the important issues relevant to cooperative-breeding systems are. . .related to the costs and benefits of sociality." Following Ligon's suggestion, the case histories begin with cooperative breeders.

Cooperative Breeders

Approximately 100 species of birds and several species of mammals such as wolves and African lions engage in **cooperative breeding**. Cooperative breeders live in groups, with many adults cooperating during the process of producing and/or rearing offspring. Such cooperation extends to offspring that are not their own. Help may include defending the territory or the young, preparing and maintaining a nest or den, or feeding young. Since the young that receive the care are not the offspring of the helpers, one of the most basic questions that we can ask about these breeding systems is why do helpers help? In other words, what benefits do helpers gain from their cooperation? As we saw in the example of adoption of red squirrels, one potential gain could be an increase in their own inclusive fitness. For instance, although the young being helped are not their own young, this does not necessarily mean they are completely unrelated.

A second reason offered to explain the evolution of cooperative breeding is that helping may improve the helper's own probability of successful reproduction. Because helping gives the helper experience in raising young, helping may increase the helper's chances of successfully raising young of its own and recruiting helpers of its own. Here we review one intensely studied species where several benefits of cooperative breeding have been demonstrated.

African Lions

Craig Packer and Anne E. Pusey have studied cooperation among African lions in the Serengeti (Packer and Pusey 1982, 1983, 1997, Packer et al. 1991). Their studies have revealed a great deal of complexity in lion societies. Female lions live in groups of related individuals called prides (fig. 8.7). Prides of female lions generally include three to six adults but may contain as many as 18 or as few as one. In addition to adult females, prides also include their dependent offspring and a coalition of adult males. Male coalitions may be made up of closely related individuals or of unrelated individuals.

Within lion societies, one can observe many forms of cooperation. Female lions nurse each other's cubs, cooperate when hunting large, difficult-to-kill game such as zebra and buffalo, and cooperatively defend their pride's territory against encroaching females. However, the most critical form of cooperation among females is their group defence of the young against infanticidal males. These attacks on the young generally take place as a male coalition is displaced by another invading coalition. While a single female lion has little chance in a fight against a much larger male lion, cooperating females are often successful at repelling attacking males. Males, in turn, cooperate in defending the territory against invading males that threaten the young they have sired, and against threats from other predators such as hyenas. The challenge for the ecologist has been to determine whether these various forms of cooperation can be reconciled with evolutionary theory.

Since the females in lion prides are always close relatives, their cooperative behaviour can be readily explained within the conceptual framework of kin selection. As females cooperate in nursing or defending young against males, they contribute to the growth and survival of their own offspring or to those of close kin. Cooperative hunting and sharing the kill also contribute to the welfare of offspring and close relatives.

Figure 8.7   African lions are highly social predators.

All these contributions add to the inclusive fitness of individual females.

In contrast, because male coalitions are sometimes made up of close relatives and sometimes not, cooperation within coalitions has represented a greater challenge to evolutionary theory. However, Packer and colleagues (Packer et al. 1991) discovered that the rules associated with the formation and behaviour of coalitions are also consistent with predictions of evolutionary theory. Single males have virtually no chance of claiming and defending a pride of female lions. Therefore they must form coalitions with other males. This represents a type of ecological constraint on viable choices open to males. If males form a coalition with brothers and cousins, cooperative behaviour that increases the production and survival of offspring of the coalition will increase an individual male's inclusive fitness. However, a male within a coalition with unrelated males must produce some offspring of his own or he is merely increasing the fitness of others at the expense of his own fitness.

ECOLOGY IN ACTION

Human–Wildlife Conflict

It is easy to understand how one could be drawn into the world of behavioural ecology. The blend of ecology, evolution, and physiology presents a continuous intellectual challenge. Even more, many of the behaviours one observes in the wild are mirrored by members of our own species. But there is another more practical benefit of this line of research: helping develop strategies to reduce human–wildlife conflict.

Each year, tens of thousands of conflicts occur between people and wildlife throughout Canada. The "problem wildlife" involved in these interactions are often killed, resulting in large numbers of potentially preventable animal deaths across Canada, North America, and the world. At the same time, a number of these conflicts also kill or injure people,

again potentially preventable casualties associated with animal behaviour. Sources of human–wildlife conflict are diverse and range from traffic collisions and crop damage by ungulates, to home invasions by polar bears, to birds flying into jet engines. The frequency of such encounters are increasing globally as humans expand population centres and industrial activity into formerly remote areas, and as transportation networks become even more heavily used. Some conflicts concern hyper-abundant and human-habituated animals in urban areas, such as geese in parks and coyotes in trash cans. Habituated animals have little fear of people and congregate in urban areas because they can avoid wary predators and feed on the rich resources provided by human

garbage and horticultural practices. Everyone is familiar with the pirating gulls (*Larus* species) of the fast food restaurant parking lot, but most do not consider this behaviour to be a problematic source of conflict. However, your perception may change if you are tasked with cleaning up their mess every day, or if we start talking about larger species with sharp teeth and claws.

Over each of the last 14 years in British Columbia, there has been an average of over 9,500 complaints about grizzly and black bears near humans. Over this time period there has also been an average of about eight people killed or injured per year by bears, 900 of the complaint bears killed per year, and another 175 bears captured and relocated each year (BC Ministry of Environment, pers. comm.). The magnitude of complaints received each year indicates that people are quite concerned about having these large animals near where they live and work. As these numbers also indicate, these concerns result in a very large number of animal deaths.

Can behavioural ecologists use their knowledge to reduce human–wildlife conflict, finding solutions that both maintain the physical safety of people while also allowing animals to be wild? Here we discuss the work of Colleen St. Clair, of the University of Alberta, who has studied human–wildlife conflict in Alberta and British Columbia for over 15 years. Her study organisms are varied, and have included birds, grizzly and black bear, coyote, cougar, and elk. As an example of her work, we turn to Banff National Park. Elk (*Cervus elaphus*) are prone to habituation in mountainous urban areas. Their large size and aggressive behaviour create opportunity for injury, and Banff reported an average of seven contact charges between elk and humans each year in the 1990s (G. Peers, Warden, Banff National Park, pers. comm.). Most of these occurred in or near the townsite of Banff, which is situated in the highly productive Bow Valley in the heart of the spectacular rocks and ice that make up most of the park. Solving the problem of habituated elk in Banff and elsewhere is difficult. Translocated animals typically return to their capture sites or die in their new locations. Killing habituated animals is unpalatable to many people, and disrupts the social structure of the animal populations. Approaching the problem by focusing on the habituated behaviour appears to offer some promise for a lasting solution. Working in conjunction with Banff Park biologists and wardens, St. Clair and her MSc student, Elsabé Kloppers, sought to reduce conflicts by teaching habituated elk to be more wary of people.

To achieve this, they designed an experiment that used 24 radio-collared elk, which allowed daily monitoring of movement and behaviour (fig. 8.8). Sixteen elk were assigned to one of two "predator-resembling chase treatments." The remaining eight animals were designated as controls; captured, handled, and monitored, but not chased. In both chase treatments, the researchers used repeated (up to 10 times)

(a)

(b)

(c)

Figure 8.8 (*a*) Elk in Banff; (*b*) human-based conditioning treatment; (*c*) dog-based conditioning treatment (Kloppers et al. 2005).

chase sequences during the winter, each of which lasted 15 minutes. One chase treatment used researchers and wardens wielding guns with cracker and screamer shells to chase elk away from the town core (ecologists have the coolest jobs!). The second chase treatment included hiring a professional dog handler to get border collies to emulate wolf hunting behaviour as they herded the elk out of town. Realistic predator simulation appeared to be important; a pilot study indicated that the silent hunting style of the collies initiated a flight responses by the elk, while hunting associated with barking by New Zealand huntaways resulted in charges by the elk! Both types of chases provided what psychologists would term *aversive conditioning*, a form of operant learning. Operant learning may be positive or negative and occurs whenever an animal learns to associate an unconditioned stimulus (e.g.,

noisy cracker shells and chasing) with a conditioned stimulus (e.g., the appearance of a human on foot). The principle of allocation (chapter 7) should favour learning that minimizes energetic costs and maximizes foraging gains. We will discuss more of the "ecology of fear" in chapter 14.

After conditioning, the treated elk fled from approaching humans when they were at greater distances, tended to spend more time being vigilant, and foraged farther from the town perimeter relative to the control elk (fig. 8.9; Kloppers et al. 2005). Interestingly, some aspects of the strength of the conditioning effects were strongest when wolves were not very active and less effective when they were present.

Overall, aversive conditioning appears to work as a means of reducing elk–human conflict; elk are much less common now in the townsite and there has been only one contact charge in the initial four years since it was implemented, while the treatments were maintained. Both dogs and humans are still used, but the guns (which were offensive to tourists) have been replaced with equally-effective hockey sticks (yes, hockey sticks).

This study is an example of how the concepts of behavioural ecology have clear and direct conservation and management implications. The research team demonstrated that these animals can learn to avoid humans through conditioning, even without receiving an actual physical deterrent or being captured and translocated. St. Clair and her lab are using aversive conditioning and other methods to dissuade black bears from consuming garbage in Whistler and grizzly bears from being hit by trains in Banff, to encourage habituated elk to reinstate traditional migratory routes, and to understand the movement patterns of coyote in an urban landscape. She also leads the large "Research on Avian Protection Project" (RAPP) whose focus is to increase bird protection associated with the large tailings ponds created in the process of tar sand development. The scale of the "ponds" is significant, covering 176 square kilometres in 2010 (Alberta Environment and Sustainable Resource Development 2013). St. Clair's RAPP project began through a court-ordered creative sentence applied to Syncrude for ineffectively preventing the landing and thus increasing the mortality of migratory birds in 2008. The ongoing work integrates toxicology, bird physiology, behaviour, and ecology. Though not as exciting as cracker guns, and the outcome of the work has important implications for Canada.

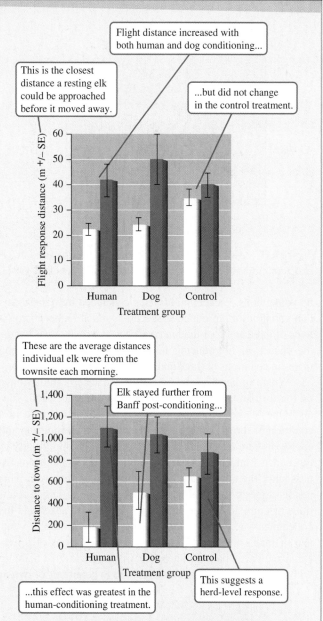

Figure 8.9 Flight response distance and elk location were influenced by avoidance conditioning in Banff townsite (data from Kloppers et al. 2005). White bars correspond to measures taken before treatments were imposed and purple bars are measures post-treatment.

The first question we should ask is, do all males within a coalition have an equal opportunity to reproduce? If all males within a coalition have an equal probability of reproducing, then forming coalitions with unrelated males is easier to reconcile with evolutionary theory. However, if there is significant variation in reproductive opportunities within coalitions, then cooperating with unrelated males is more difficult to reconcile with theories predicting that individuals will attempt to maximize

their inclusive fitness. It turns out that the probability of a male siring young depends on his rank within a coalition and on coalition size. As shown in figure 8.10, males in coalitions of two sire a relatively similar proportion of the young produced by the pride. In addition, these proportions are close to the proportions sired by the two top ranked males in coalitions of three and four. However, the third ranked males in coalitions of three and the third and fourth ranked in coalitions of four sire almost

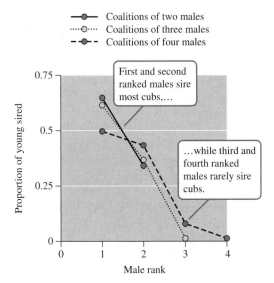

Figure 8.10 Male lion rank and proportion of cubs sired in male coalitions of different sizes (data from Packer et al. 1991).

no young lions. Packer and his team concluded from these data that variation in reproductive success is much higher in coalitions of three and four than in coalitions of two. In other words, the chance of reproducing is less evenly distributed among males in coalitions of three and four than in coalitions of two.

What implications do the results of Packer's studies have on the formation of coalitions containing unrelated individuals? One of the implications is that an unrelated male in a coalition of three or more runs the risk of investing time and energy in helping maintain a pride without an opportunity to reproduce himself and without improving his inclusive fitness since the other coalition members are not relatives. This result suggests that males should avoid joining larger coalitions of unrelated males, and this is just what Packer and his colleagues found (fig. 8.11). Figure 8.11 shows the percentage of males with unrelated partners in coalitions of different sizes. These patterns show clearly that males that team up with unrelated individuals mostly do so in coalitions of two or

three. Larger coalitions of four to nine individuals are almost entirely made up of relatives. What are the implications of these data? They suggest that males avoid joining larger coalitions unless the coalition consists of relatives. Such a strategy avoids the risk of helping without gaining in inclusive fitness.

In summary, cooperation among African lions appears to be a response to environmental conditions that require cooperation for success. Packer and Pusey (1997) captured the situation facing African lions in a fascinating article titled, "Divided We Fall: Cooperation Among Lions." To survive, reproduce, and successfully raise offspring to maturity, African lions must work in cooperative groups. The lone lion has no chance of meeting the ecological challenges presented by living on the Serengeti in lion society with its aggressive prides and invasive and infanticidal male coalitions. However, as we have seen, within the constraints set by their environments, African lions appear to behave in a way that contributes positively to their overall fitness.

While the complexities of African lion societies have taken decades to uncover, they pale beside the intricacies of life among eusocial species such as bees, termites, and ants. Let's explore eusociality in some animal populations to get some insights into the evolution of these complex social systems.

Eusocial Species

Probably the most thoroughly studied of eusocial species are the ants. Ants and their complex behaviours have attracted the attention of people from the earliest times and appear in the oldest writings such as the Bible and the classical writings of ancient Greece. Such written records were likely predated by older folktales. Bert Hölldobler and Edward O. Wilson (1990) pointed out that many of the earliest accounts of ants focused on ant species that make their living by harvesting seeds. These seed-harvesting species were serious agricultural pests around the Mediterranean Sea, and their dependence on grains paralleled remarkably the economy of the human populations of the region.

One of the most socially complex groups of ants are the leafcutters (fig. 8.12). The 39 described species of leafcutter

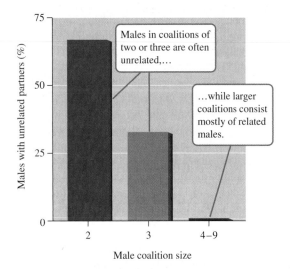

Figure 8.11 Relatedness and size of male coalitions among African lions (data from Packer et al. 1991).

Figure 8.12 Leafcutter ants carrying leaf fragments back to the nest where they will be processed to create a substrate for growing the fungi that the ants eat. Smaller ants riding on leaf fragments offer protection from aerial attack by parasitoid flies.

ants, which belong to two genera, are found only in the Americas, from the southern United States to Argentina. Leafcutter ants make their living by cutting and transporting leaf fragments to their nest, where the leaf material is fragmented and used as a substrate upon which to grow fungi. The fungi provide the primary food source for leafcutter ants.

Among the various species of leafcutter ants, some of the most thoroughly studied are species belonging to the genus *Atta*. *Atta* species live mainly in tropical Central and South America. However, at least two species reach as far north as Arizona and Louisiana in the United States. Leafcutter ants are important consumers in the tropical ecosystems, where they move large amounts of soil and process large quantities of leaf material in their nests. The nests of leafcutter ants can attain great size. For instance, the nests of *A. sexdens* can include over 1,000 entrance holes and nearly 2,000 occupied and abandoned chambers. In one excavation of an *A. sexdens* nest (cited in Hölldobler and Wilson 1990), researchers estimated that the ants had moved more than 22 m³ of soil, which weighed over 40,000 kg. Within this nest, the occupants had stored nearly 6,000 kg of leaves. Mature nests of *A. sexdens* contain a queen, various numbers of winged males and females, which disperse to mate and found colonies elsewhere, and up to 5 to 8 million workers.

Leafcutter ants live in social groups in which individuals are divided among **castes** that engage in very different activities. We can define a caste as a group of physically distinctive individuals that engage in specialized behaviour within the colony. E. O. Wilson (1980) studied how labour is divided among castes of ants in a laboratory colony of *A. sexdens* that he established and studied over a period of eight years. During this period, Wilson carefully catalogued the behaviours of individual colony members. Because the colony lived in a closed series of clear plastic containers, their behaviour could be studied easily. In addition to recording behaviours, Wilson also estimated the sizes of individuals engaging in each behaviour by measuring their head widths to the nearest 0.2 mm. He made his estimates visually by comparing an ant to a standard array of preserved *A. sexdens* specimens of known size.

When Wilson compared the leafcutter ant *A. sexdens* with three non-leafcutter ant species, he found that the leafcutter ants included a larger number of castes and engaged in a wider variety of behaviours (fig. 8.13). Wilson identified a total of 29 distinctive tasks performed by the leafcutter ants compared to an average of 17.7 tasks performed by the three other species. He found that the division of labour within the *A. sexdens* colony was mainly based on size. Possibly because of the large number of specialized tasks that need to be performed by leafcutter ants, they have one of the most complex social structures and one of the greatest size ranges found among the ants. Within *A. sexdens* colonies, the head width of the largest individuals (5.2 mm) is nearly nine times the head width of the smallest individuals (0.6 mm). On the basis of size, Wilson identified four castes within his leafcutter colony. However, because the tasks performed by some of the size classes change as they age, Wilson discovered three additional temporal or developmental castes for a total of seven castes

within the colony, compared to an average of three castes in the non-leafcutter ant species he studied.

As a consequence of this great variation, someone watching a trail of leafcutter ants bring freshly cut leaf fragments back to their nest is treated to a rich display of size and behavioural diversity. While medium-sized ants carry the leaf fragments above their heads, the largest ants line the trail like sentries, guarding against ground attacks on the column of ants carrying leaf fragments. Very small ants ride on many of the leaf fragments, protecting the ant carrying a leaf fragment from aerial attacks by parasitic flies. Meanwhile, other size classes of leafcutters performing behaviours associated with processing leaves, tending larvae, and maintaining fungal gardens remain hidden in the nest. It was the activity of these smaller individuals that Wilson's laboratory colony was able to reveal so clearly.

Aside from leafcutter ant, there are many other eusocial animals, including the only eusocial mammal, the naked mole rat.

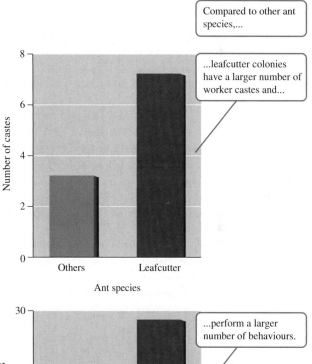

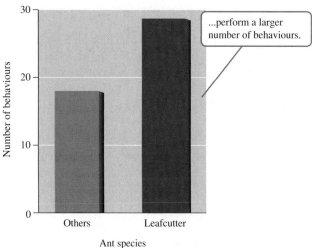

Figure 8.13 Comparison of the number of castes and number of behaviours in a colony of leafcutter ants, *Atta sexdens,* and in colonies of three other ant species (data from Wilson 1980).

Careful study has revealed some remarkable parallels in the structures of naked mole rat and leafcutter ant societies. The social behaviour of naked mole rats was first reported by Jennifer Jarvis (Jarvis 1981). Her study was based on more than six years of observation and experimentation with colonies of naked mole rats that she had established in the laboratory.

The social organization of the colony appeared more similar to an ant colony than to any other mammal population known. Within a colony of naked mole rats, one female and only a few males breed. This group of reproductive individuals functions basically as a queen and her mates, while all of the rest of the colony is nonreproductive. Behavioural ecologists have found that life in a naked mole rat colony centres on the queen and her offspring, and the queen's behaviour appears to maintain this focus. She is the most active member of the colony and literally pushes her way around the colony. By physically pushing individuals, she appears to call them to action when there is work to be done or when the colony is threatened and needs defending. The aggressiveness of the queen also appears to maintain her dominance over other females in the colony and prevent them from coming into breeding condition. If the queen dies or is removed from the colony, one of the other females in the colony will assume the role of queen. If two or more females compete for the position of queen, they may fight to the death during the process of establishing the new social hierarchy.

In contrast to leafcutter ant colonies, where all workers are females, both males and females work in naked mole rat colonies. Jarvis found that work is divided among colony members, as in leafcutter ant colonies, according to size. However, in contrast to leafcutter ants, colonies of naked mole rats include only two worker size classes, small and large. Small workers are the most active. Small workers excavate tunnels, build the nest, which is deeper than most of the passage ways, and line the nest with plant materials for bedding. In addition, small workers also harvest food, mainly roots and tubers, and deliver it to other colony members, including the queen, for feeding. Since they spend most of their time sleeping, the role of large nonbreeders was unclear for some time. However, eventually researchers working in the field were able to observe these large nonbreeders in action. It turns out that the large workers, as in ant colonies, are a caste specializing in defence. If the tunnel system is breached by members of another colony, the large nonbreeders move out quickly from their resting places to defend the colony from the invaders, literally throwing themselves into the breach. Eventually the large nonbreeders push up enough soil to wall off the intruders. However, they may be most important in defending against snakes, the most dangerous predators of naked mole rats. When confronted with a snake, the large nonbreeders will try to kill the snake or spray it with soil until it is driven off or buried.

Evolution of Eusociality

Despite their distinctive evolutionary histories and other biological differences, the studies of Wilson and Jarvis suggest interesting parallels in the organizations of leafcutter ant and naked mole rat colonies (fig. 8.14). Similarities include division of labour within colonies based on size, with smaller workers specializing in foraging, nest maintenance, and excavation of extensive burrow systems. Meanwhile, larger workers in both species specialize in defence. In addition, reproduction in both species is limited to a single queen and her mates. These areas of convergence in social organization between such different organisms may help shed light on the forces responsible for the evolution of eusociality. Such comparisons form the basis of the comparative method.

What factors may have been important in the evolution and maintenance of naked mole rat and leafcutter ant sociality? Kin selection may play a role. Leafcutter ants, along with other Hymenoptera, such as bees and wasps, have an inheritance system called **haplodiploidy**. The term haplodiploid refers to the number of chromosome sets possessed by males and females. In haplodiploid systems, males develop from unfertilized eggs and are haploid, while females develop from fertilized eggs and so are diploid. One of the consequences of haplodiploidy is that worker ants within a colony can be very similar genetically. In an ant colony where there is a single queen that mated with a single male, the workers will be more related to each other than they would be to their own offspring. W. D. Hamilton (1964) was the first to point out that under these conditions, the average genetic similarity among workers would be 75%, while their relationship with any offspring they might produce would be 50% (fig. 8.15).

What is the source of this high degree of relatedness? The queen mates only during her mating flight and stores the sperm she receives to fertilize all the eggs she lays to produce daughters. If she mates with a single male, since he is haploid, all her daughters will receive the same genetic information from their male parent. As a consequence, the 50% of the genetic makeup that workers receive from their male parent will be identical. In addition, workers will share an average of 25% of their genes through those that they receive from the queen, yielding an average genetic relatedness of 50% + 25% = 75%. The important point here is that the activity of workers promotes the production of closely related individuals, their sisters, an activity that should be favoured by kin selection.

Because naked mole rat colonies are relatively closed to outsiders, the individuals within each colony, like the workers within leafcutter ant colonies, are also very similar genetically. Paul Sherman, Jennifer Jarvis, and Stanton Braude (1992) reported that approximately 85% of matings within a colony of naked mole rats are between parents and offspring or between siblings. As a consequence of these matings between close relatives, the relatedness between individuals within a colony is about 81%, suggesting that kin selection may be involved in the maintenance of nonreproductive helpers in colonies of naked mole rats.

What factors other than kin selection may have contributed to the evolution of eusociality? Many factors have been

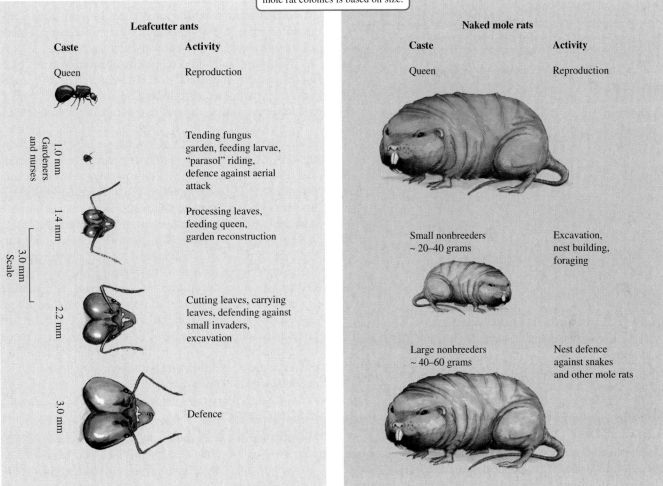

Figure 8.14   Division of labour among castes of leafcutter ants, *Atta sexdens,* and naked mole rats, *Heterocephalus glaber.* Ant sizes are head widths of workers typically engaged in each activity (data from Wilson 1980, Jarvis 1981, and Sherman, Jarvis, and Braude 1992).

implicated. While researchers working on ants and other social Hymenoptera have emphasized the potential importance of kin selection, studies of cooperative-breeding vertebrate species have emphasized ecological constraints. What sorts of ecological common constraints are faced by leafcutter ants and naked mole rats? One of the most obvious is the work associated with the creation, maintenance, and defence of extensive burrow systems. The more social organisms are studied, the less likely it has become that one or a few simple mechanisms will be adequate to explain their evolution. However, the results of studies such as those of Wilson and Jarvis should encourage continued careful comparative studies as a means for eventual understanding of the evolution of sociality. In the application of the comparative method, species such as the leafcutter ant *A. sexdens* and naked mole rats function as invaluable tools.

We have only discussed a few aspects of sociality, completely ignoring equally important and interesting studies related to herding and other behaviours. Many of these topics will be presented in chapter 14. Others, unfortunately, are beyond the scope of this text. Here, we now turn our attention to sex.

CONCEPT 8.2 REVIEW

1. What are the evolutionary implications of the fact that larger coalitions of male lions consist almost entirely of close relatives?
2. Among the ants and other eusocial Hymenoptera, why would kin selection favour workers that helped rear sister workers rather than their own offspring?
3. What are the two major ecological challenges favouring colony living shared by leafcutter ants and naked mole rats?

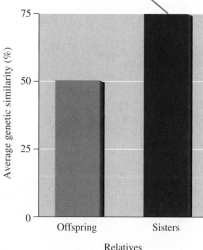

As a consequence of haplodiploidy, ant workers may be more similar genetically to their sister workers than they would be to their own offspring.

Figure 8.15 Average genetic similarity between ant workers and sisters (other workers) versus their offspring if they reproduced.

8.3 Mating Systems and Mate Choice

Mate choice by one sex and/or competition for mates among individuals of the same sex can result in selection for particular traits, a process called sexual selection. From a human perspective, sexual reproduction appears to be the norm. However, asexual reproduction is common among many groups of organisms such as bacteria, fungi, protozoans, plants, and even some vertebrates. Questions about the evolutionary costs and benefits of sexual and asexual reproduction are fascinating—but are also beyond the scope of this text. In this section, we focus on the behaviour of sexually reproducing species.

Most described species of plants and animals include male and female functions, even if these same individuals are also able to reproduce asexually. The male and female functions can be distributed among individuals in a variety of ways, or **sex types**. The most obvious to us is the relatively boring condition of each individual being a single sex (male or female). The **females** are the sex that produces larger, and typically more energetically expensive gametes (eggs or ova), while the **males** produce smaller, and typically less costly gametes (sperm or pollen). Other species have more complicated sex types, which can include **hermaphrodites**, in which an individual is able to perform both male and female reproductive functions. Hermaphroditism is found in over 75% of all flowering plant species, and also occurs in a variety of fish species. Individuals can be instantaneous hermaphrodites, in which they perform male and female function at the same time, or sequential

hermaphrodites, in which the individual changes sex over the course of its life. In plants, individual flowers within a single plant can be hermaphrodites, or the different sexes can occur on different flowers on the same plant. In short, nature produces a diversity of sex types much richer than the simple male and female combinations found in the human species.

Not surprisingly, the complexity of nature was the basis for research into the evolution of different reproductive strategies. Once again, we visit the work of Eric Charnov, here in collaboration with J. Maynard Smith and James Bull (1976). These scientists addressed several fundamental questions related to the evolution of sex in a classic paper titled "Why Be a Hermaphrodite?" The authors identified three conditions that should favour a hermaphroditic population over one with separate sexes: (1) low mobility, which limits the opportunities for male-to-male competition; (2) low overlap in resource demands by female and male structures and functions, such as in plants where pollen production often occurs much earlier than seed and fruit maturation; and (3) sharing of costs for male and female function, for instance in insect-pollinated plants where attractive flowers promote both male and female reproductive success. In this section we will explore several evolutionary and behavioural patterns associated with sex in a diversity of species. We begin by describing the overall social interactions that commonly are found in groups of reproductive individuals, and then end with discussing the evolutionary implications of sexual preferences.

Mating Systems

The first step in understanding the social interactions of individuals related to sexual reproduction is to be able to describe the sex types that naturally occur, and are fertile within a population. This task is relatively straightforward for most species, and can be accomplished though basic skills in natural history (chapters 2 and 3). The next step is more difficult, and requires more expertise in behavioural ecology—understanding the social structure of populations in relation to sex. Do individuals mate with multiple individuals, or do they appear to mate with just one? Do all individuals in a population have equal access to mates, or are fertile mates a guarded resource? Are putative fathers actually genetically related to the young they help rear, or has the male been cuckolded? These are questions answered by understanding **mating systems**—the social sexual structure of a population. Though both plants and animals have a diversity of interesting mating systems, we focus here on those of animals.

We are likely most familiar with **monogamy**, at least in concept. In monogamous mating systems, one male and one female have an exclusive relationship, at least for some duration of time. However, because two individuals have a *pair-bond* does not necessarily mean that all offspring from the female of the pair were sired by the male. Instead, nature is full of examples of males engaged in seemingly monogamous relationships being *cuckolded*. We do not need to go far to find an example. Genetic tests have become common in many human societies, both as a means to identify pre-natal health concerns, and to determine paternity in situations where this

is in doubt. As a result, there have been a number of studies published describing measured rates of non-paternity in human population across the planet, and these were recently summarized by Kermyt Anderson (Anderson 2006).

Anderson divided the published studies into two groups: situations in which the putative father had high levels of certainty in his paternity, and situations in what there was a low degree of certainty. We all can likely imagine the situations in which certainty would be low, but what about those where certainty is high? These studies came from families that volunteered for genetic screening for other research projects, or for reasons unrelated to concerns about fidelity. Anderson asked the simple question: what is the actual non-paternity rate for these different groups? He found that when fathers were "certain" they were the fathers, they were wrong nearly 2% of the time (fig. 8.16). In cases of disputed certainty, the offspring was unrelated to the putative father nearly 30% of the time. Interestingly, these median values did not substantially vary across the planet—they were as consistent in Canada and the United States as they were in other parts of the world (figure 8.16), suggesting these may be background rates of infidelity across many human cultures. What the "true" level of non-paternity is for the human species is impossible to estimate, as we are currently lacking reliable measures of cross-cultural "certainty" levels. What does appear true, however, is that when paternal certainty is questioned, it is frequently—but not always—for good cause. This issue has significant implications, as a common feature of many species is for "fathers" to reduce investment in offspring when paternal certainty is questioned.

To help separate paternity from investment, animal behavioural ecologists often refer to two types of monogamy—*social monogamy* and *genetic monogamy*. Songbirds are frequently seen in socially monogamous relationships during the nesting season, where one male and one female will share a nest and rear any offspring produced by that female. It was traditionally assumed that such provision of resources from the male was due to him being the father of these offspring. In fact, the very influential avian ecologist David Lack estimated that 93% of passerines are monogamous in their mating (Lack 1968). However, a recent review of rates of non-paternity in passerines suggest that despite the appearance of fidelity based upon social monogamy, over 90% of species actually show evidence for a lack of genetic monogamy (Griffith et al. 2002)! Needless to say, one never quite knows what is going on behind closed doors, or at least within the nest high in the tree.

If many mating systems are not truly monogamous, then what are they? Many species exhibit different types of **promiscuity**, in which individuals may have multiple sexual partners. Promiscuous mating systems can be further defined as **polygyny**, **polyandry**, and **polygynandry**, which describe, respectively, systems in which one male mates with multiple females while each female mates (putatively) with just one male; one female mates with multiple males while each male mates (putatively) with just one female; and groups of multiple males and multiple females who mate with each other. Of these, polygyny appears most common among vertebrates, polyandry occurs among species of diverse taxa including insects, frogs, birds, fish, and mammals, and polygynandry is quite rare, apparently restricted to a few species of primates. Regardless of the exact mating system of a species, males and females will end up choosing specific individuals as their mates. The social interactions involved here can cause interesting evolutionary changes.

Sexual Selection

As is often the case, we begin with Darwin (1871), who proposed that the social environment, particularly the mating environment, could exert significant influence on the characteristics of organisms. He was particularly intrigued by the existence of what he called "secondary sexual characteristics," the origins of which he could not explain except by the advantages they gave to individuals during competition for mates. Darwin used the term *secondary sexual characteristics* to mean characteristics of males or females not directly involved in the process of reproduction. Some of the traits that Darwin had in mind were "gaudy colors and various ornaments...the power of song and other such characters." How do we explain the existence of characteristics such as the antlers of male deer, the bright peacock's tail, or the gigantic size and large nose of the male elephant seal? To explain the existence of such secondary sexual characteristics, Darwin proposed a process that he called **sexual selection**. Sexual selection results from differences in reproductive rates among individuals as a result of differences in their mating success.

Sexual selection is thought to be important under two circumstances. The first is where individuals of one sex compete among themselves for mates, which results in a process called **intrasexual selection**. For instance, when male mountain sheep or elephant seals fight among themselves for dominance or mating territories, the largest and strongest generally

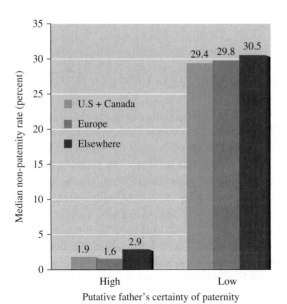

Figure 8.16 Non-paternity rates varied as a function of whether the father had high or low confidence in whether they were the fathers of "their" offspring.

win such contests. In such situations, the result is often selection for larger body size and more effective weapons such as horns or teeth. Since this selection is the result of contests within one sex, it is called intrasexual selection.

Sexual selection can also occur when members of one sex consistently choose mates from among members of the opposite sex on the basis of some particular trait. Because two sexes are involved, this form is called **intersexual selection**. Examples of traits used for mate selection include female birds choosing among potential male mates based on the brightness of their feather colours or on the quality of their songs. Darwin proposed that once individuals of one sex begin to choose mates on the basis of some anatomical or behavioural trait, sexual selection would favour elaboration of the trait. For instance, the plumage of male birds' colour might become brighter over time or their songs more elaborate or both.

However, how much can sexual selection elaborate a trait before males in the population begin to suffer higher mortality due to other sources of natural selection, such as that exerted by predators? Darwin proposed that sexual selection will continue to elaborate a trait until balanced by other sources of natural selection, such as predation. Since Darwin's early work on the subject, research has revealed a great deal about how organisms choose mates and the basis of sexual selection. An excellent model for such studies is the guppy, *Poecilia reticulata.*

Mate Choice and Sexual Selection in Guppies

It would be difficult for experimental ecologists interested in mate choice and sexual selection to design a better experimental subject than the guppy (fig. 8.17). Guppies are native to the streams and rivers of Trinidad and Tobago, islands in the southeastern Caribbean, and in the rivers draining nearby parts of the South American mainland. The waters inhabited by guppies range from small clear mountain streams to murky lowland rivers. Along this gradient of physical conditions, guppies also encounter a broad range of biological

Figure 8.17 A colourful male guppy courting a female guppy: what are the influences of mate selection by female guppies and natural selection by predators?

situations. In the headwaters of streams above waterfalls, guppies live in the absence of predaceous fish or with the killifish *Rivulus hartii*, which preys mainly on juveniles and is not a very effective predator on adult guppies. In contrast, guppies in lowland rivers live with a wide variety of predaceous fish, including the pike cichlid, *Crenicichla alta*, a very effective visual predator of adult guppies.

Male guppies show a broad range of colouration both within and among populations. What factors may produce this range of variation? It turns out that female guppies, if given a choice, will mate with more brightly coloured males. However, brightly coloured males are attacked more frequently by visual predators. This trade-off between higher mating success by bright males but greater vulnerability to predators provides a mechanistic explanation for variation in male colouration among different habitats. The most brightly coloured male guppies are found in populations exposed to few predators, while those exposed to predators, such as the pike cichlid, are much less brightly coloured (Endler 1995). Thus the colouration of male guppies in local populations may be determined by a dynamic interplay between natural selection exerted by predators and by female mate choice.

While field observations are consistent with a trade-off between sexual selection due to mate choice and natural selection due to predation, the evidence would be more convincing with an experimental test. John Endler (1980) performed such a test in an exemplary study of natural selection for colour pattern in guppies. This work has proven to be a classic study of experimental ecology, showing evolutionary shifts over short periods of time.

Experimental Tests

Endler performed two experiments, one in artificial ponds in a greenhouse at Princeton University (fig. 8.18) and one at field sites (fig. 8.19). For the greenhouse experiments, Endler constructed 10 ponds designed to approximate pools in the streams of the Northern Range in Trinidad. Four of the ponds were of a size (2.4 m × 1.2 m × 40 cm) typical of the pools inhabited by a single pike cichlid in smaller streams. During the final phase of the experiment, Endler placed a single pike cichlid in each of these ponds. The six other ponds were similar in size (2.4 m × 1.2 m × 15 cm) to stream pools in the headwaters which contain approximately six *Rivulus*. Endler eventually placed six *Rivulus* in four of these ponds and maintained the other two ponds with no predators as controls. What did Endler create with this series of pools and predator combinations? These three groups of ponds represented three levels of predation: high predation (pike cichlid), low predation (*Rivulus*), and no predation.

However, before introducing predators, Endler established similar physical environments in the pools and stocked them with carefully chosen guppies. He lined all ponds with commercially available dyed gravel, taking care to put the same proportions of gravel colours in each of the ponds. The gravel he used in all ponds was 31.4% black, 34.2% white, 25.7% green, plus 2.9% each of blue, red, and yellow. One

Experimental conditions

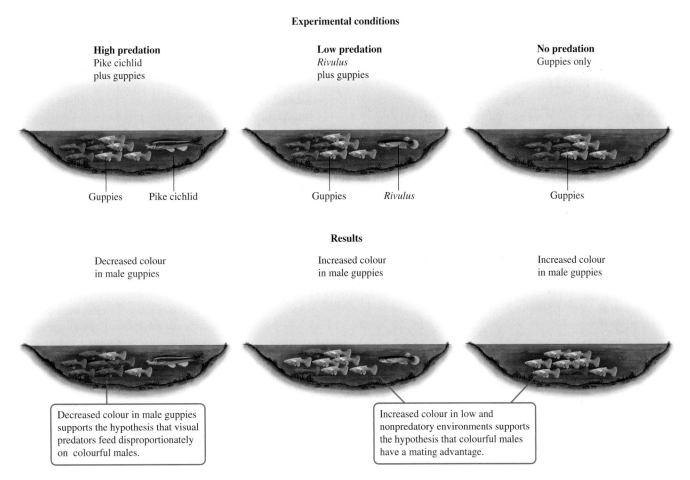

Figure 8.18 Summary of greenhouse experimental design and results (information from Endler 1980).

of the most critical elements of the experiment was to standardize the background colours across all of the ponds, as the influence of prey colour on vulnerability to predators depends on the background against which the prey is viewed by visual predators. Endler stocked the experimental pond with 200 guppies, which were descended from 18 different populations in Trinidad and Venezuela. By drawing guppies from so many populations, Endler ensured that the experimental populations would include a substantial amount of colour variation.

Endler's second experiment was conducted in the field within the drainage network of the Aripo River (fig. 8.19), where he encountered three distinctive situations within a few kilometres. Within the mainstream of the Aripo River, guppies coexisted with a wide variety of predators, including pike cichlids, which provided a "high predation" site. Upstream from the high predation site, Endler discovered a small tributary that flowed over a series of waterfalls near its junction with the mainstream. Because the waterfalls prevented most fish from swimming upstream, this tributary was entirely free of guppies but supported a population of the ineffective predator *Rivulus*. This potential "low predation" site provided an ideal situation for following the evolution of male colour. The third site, which was a bit farther upstream, was a small tributary that supported guppies along with *Rivulus*. This third site

gave Endler a low predation reference site for his study. Endler captured 200 guppies in the high predation environment, measured the colouration of these guppies, and then introduced them to the site lacking guppies. Six months later the introduced guppies and their offspring had spread throughout the previously guppy-free tributary. Finally, two years or about 15 guppy generations after the introduction, Endler returned and sampled the guppies at all three study sites.

The results of the greenhouse and field experiments supported each other. As shown in figure 8.20, the number of coloured spots on male guppies increased in the greenhouse ponds with no predators and with *Rivulus*, but decreased in the high predation ponds containing pike cichlids. Figure 8.21, which summarizes the results of Endler's field experiment, compares the number of spots on males in high predation and low predation stream environments with guppies transferred from the high predation environment to a low predation environment. Notice that the transplanted population converged with the males at the low predation reference site during the experiment. In other words, when freed from predation, the average number of spots on male guppies increased substantially. This result, along with the results of the greenhouse experiment, supports the hypothesis that predation reduces male showiness in guppy populations.

Experimental design

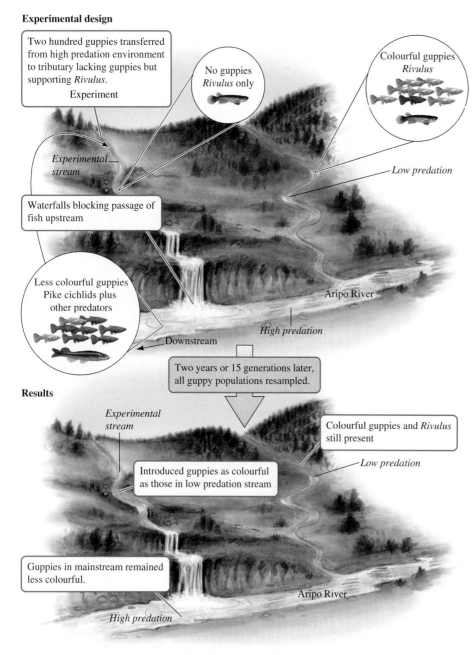

Two hundred guppies transferred from high predation environment to tributary lacking guppies but supporting *Rivulus*.
Experiment

No guppies
Rivulus only

Colourful guppies
Rivulus

Experimental stream

— *Low predation*

Waterfalls blocking passage of fish upstream

Less colourful guppies Pike cichlids plus other predators

Aripo River

Downstream

High predation

Two years or 15 generations later, all guppy populations resampled.

Results

Experimental stream

Colourful guppies and *Rivulus* still present

Introduced guppies as colourful as those in low predation stream

— *Low predation*

Guppies in mainstream remained less colourful.

Aripo River

High predation

Figure 8.19   Field experiment on effects of predation on male guppy colouration (information from Endler 1980).

Research by many other researchers supports the impact of predators on male ornamentation. However, the observation that male colourfulness increased in the absence of predators or in the presence of weak predation both in the field and the laboratory invites explanation. Why did male colour increase rather than just remain static? The observed changes imply that colourful males enjoy some selective advantage. That advantage appears to result from how female guppies choose their mates.

Mate Choice by Female Guppies

What cues do female guppies use to choose their mates? Anne Houde (1997), who summarized the findings of numerous studies, found that several male traits were associated with greater mating success. The weight of the evidence supports the conclusion that male colouration contributes significantly to male mating success. Colour characteristics that have been shown to confer a male mating advantage include "brightness," number of red spots, number of blue spots, iridescent area, total pigmented area, and carotenoid or orange area. These results appear to account for the increase in male colourfulness observed by Endler in the absence of predation or in the presence of low predation pressure. That is, female preference for more colourful males gave them greater fitness in the absence of strong predation. As a consequence, male colourfulness increased in the study populations in low predation or no predation environments. Male behaviour, especially their rate of making courtship displays, has also been found associated with increased male mating success.

Astrid Kodric-Brown (1993) studied whether competitive interactions among males contribute to variation in male mating success. She obtained guppies for her behavioural experiments from stock John Endler had originally collected from the Aripo and Paria Rivers in Trinidad. Males and females used in the behavioural experiments were reared separately. Males were kept in 95-litre aquaria in populations consisting of 10 males and 20 females. Meanwhile virgin females were reared in all-female groups of sisters until they were six months old. During this period they had no visual contact with males. Both males and females were fed a standardized diet and maintained at the same temperatures and exposed to the same numbers of hours of dark and light.

From her stock populations, Kodric-Brown chose 59 pairs of males with contrasting colours and 59 females. To test female preference, she placed a single female into the central chamber of a test tank and each member of a male pair in the side chambers flanking the central chamber. Screens covering glass partitions prevented visual contact between males and females initially. After 10 minutes of acclimation by the guppies, Kodric-Brown removed the screens. Once the screens were removed, males would usually begin courtship displays and the female would inspect the males through the glass partition. Kodric-Brown recorded the behaviour of

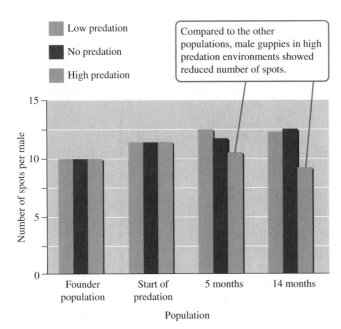

Figure 8.20   Results of greenhouse experiment, which exposed populations of guppies to no predation, low predation (killifish), and high predation (pike cichlid) environments (data from Endler 1980).

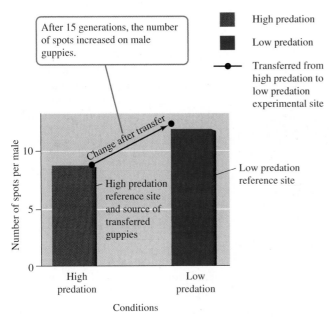

Figure 8.21   Results of field experiment involving transfer of guppies from high predation site to site with killifish, a fairly ineffective predator (data from Endler 1980).

males and females in the display tank for 10 minutes, recording the time and the rates at which males displayed, and the amount of time the female spent within 5 cm of the glass partition of each male. She designated the male that the female spent the most time with as the preferred or attractive male and the male with which the female spent less time as the nonpreferred or unattractive male.

After this initial 10-minute period during which females indicated their preferences, Kodric-Brown removed the glass partitions separating the guppies, allowing interactions among the males and the female. Kodric-Brown observed that males engaged in agonistic interactions, such as chasing and nipping, in over 94% of mating trials, which gave her a basis for determining which males were behaviourally dominant and which were subordinate. Kodric-Brown recorded the interactions between the two males and between the males and the female until 5 minutes after a copulation. After a mating trial, the female was moved to a rearing tank where she eventually gave birth. The offspring from each female were raised separately. To establish paternity, male offspring were raised to maturity, when they expressed their full colouration, which is inherited from their fathers.

The results of Kodric-Brown's experiments indicate that reproductive success was determined by a combination of male attractiveness and male dominance status. Female mate preference, which was determined when the guppies had visual contact only, was highly correlated with subsequent male mating success (fig. 8.22). The males that attracted females when viewed through the glass partition subsequently sired a greater percentage of broods than did unattractive males. Approximately 67% of the broods were sired by attractive males compared to 33% that were sired by unattractive males. However, it appears that male dominance status also contributes to male reproductive success. Among unattractive males that sired broods, 87.5% were dominant. The conclusion that reproductive success is determined by a combination of competition between males and female choice is reinforced by the

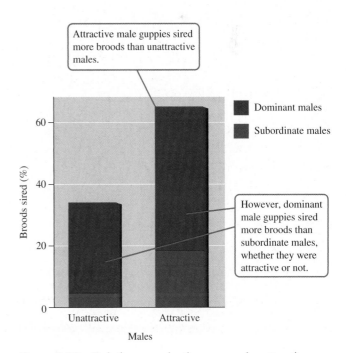

Figure 8.22   Relative reproductive success by attractive versus unattractive and dominant versus subordinate male guppies (data from Kodric-Brown 1993).

low reproductive success by males that were neither attractive nor dominant. These males, which lacked the apparent advantages associated with either dominance or attractiveness, sired only 4% of the broods. The result indicates that reproductive opportunities are highly restricted for these males.

The characteristics associated with male mating success among guppies are often correlated. Kodric-Brown observed that attractive males tended to be dominant, court more, and have more and brighter orange and iridescent spots. These characteristics are closely associated with a male's anatomy and physiology. Let's look now at a mating system where male and females are engaged in significant sexual conflict.

Sexual Conflict Among Water Striders

Sex isn't free. Although one can immediately recognize the potential reproductive benefits of sex, there are a variety of potential costs. One of the most obvious is the risk of sexually transmitted diseases, which can cause significant damage to the genitalia and reproductive machinery of plant and animal species. Needless to say, being castrated by a fungus that was acquired through sex is not good for one's fitness (well, except for the fitness of the parasite!). There are, however, much more subtle costs of sex, most of which return us to the principle of allocation we discussed in chapters 5 and 7. Mating takes time, and depending upon the details of the species involved, it can also require expenditure of significant amounts of energy. During mating, an individual is unable to perform other tasks, such as foraging, defending, or even

finding an alternative (more suitable) mate. In some cases, these costs are shared equally by both males and females. In other cases, there is *sexual conflict,* in which there is asymmetry between the sexes in the potential evolutionary costs and benefits of any particular mating event. Locke Rowe, of the University of Toronto, along with a diverse group of colleagues, has conducted extensive theoretical and empirical studies of sexual conflict, with particular emphasis on water striders.

Water striders (Heteroptera) are commonly found on the surfaces of slow flowing bodies of fresh water (fig. 8.23) throughout North America. Their graceful appearance moving across the water surface is in sharp contrast to their mating system. Conflict between the sexes at mating is visually apparent, with males chasing and grasping females in an attempt to mate. More often than not, the female escapes from the male, and mating does not occur. However, if the male grabs hold, there is a vicious struggle in which significant energy is spent and both sexes are at a greatly increased risk of predation. Only occasionally does the male maintain hold, and mating occurs (Rowe et al. 1994). The classic explanation for such conflict has been that in water striders, females are able to retain viable sperm for about 10 days, and thus repeated mating is unnecessary to achieve full fertilization for the female. In contrast, males are more likely to sire more offspring if they are the last male to mate with a female rather than the first, and thus selection should favour male promiscuity. However, Rowe and colleagues have pointed out that this classic explanation is lacking an explanation for the female behaviour, in that these mating events are not neutral for the females, but instead are actually detrimental to their fitness. This physical conflict also results in evolutionary conflict between the sexes.

In a review of the literature, Rowe and colleagues suggest two key costs of mating for the female: (1) reduced female skating speed while carrying a male reduces foraging efficiency, and (2) mating females are at increased predation risk due to slower speed. As might be expected, sexual selection appears to have resulted in the evolution of a variety of physical and behavioural adaptations that mitigate the level of resistance in females. At the heart of this is the realization that both resisting and submitting to mating pose energetic and fitness costs to the female. As a result, evolution should favour strategies in females that minimize the costs of these two detrimental options. As you might expect, the "solution" to this problem will be dependent upon the

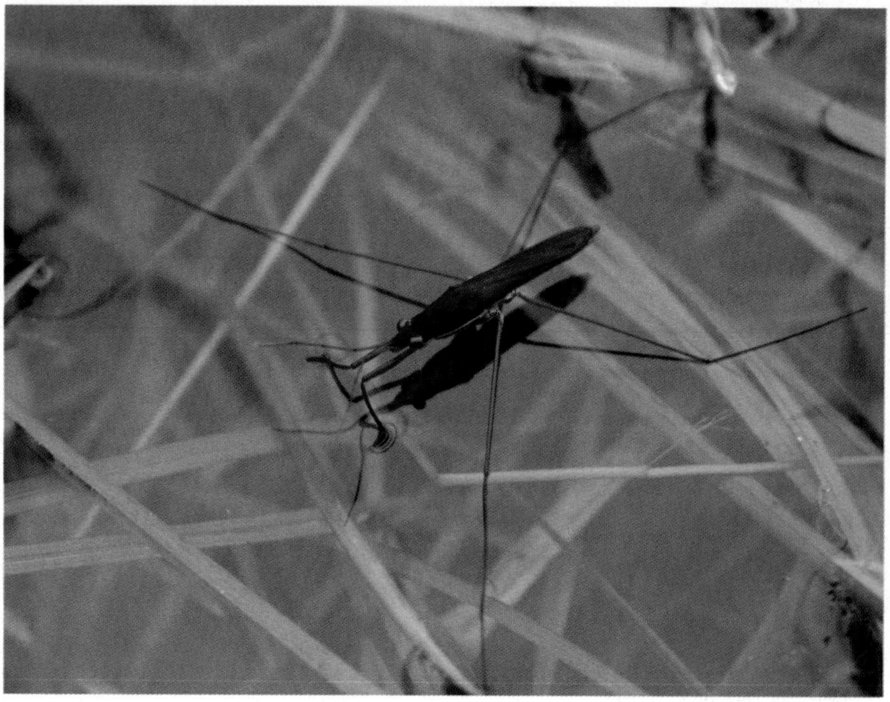

Figure 8.23   Water striders serve as a model organism for the study of sexual conflict between males and females.

local environmental conditions around a particular female and her population. For example, females of some species tend to spend more time hiding in vegetation when males are present than when they are absent. Though this decreases her ability to forage, this cost is likely less than she would incur during a mating struggle.

Over longer periods, sexual conflict can have significant evolutionary consequences. In a study combining comparative and experimental approaches, Goran Arnqvist and Locke Rowe (2002) have found evidence that sexual conflict has caused the **co-evolution** of male and female armaments (clasping and anti-clasping appendages) in water striders. Female armaments increase the efficacy of resistance and male armaments increase the ability of males to overcome this resistance. Coevolution can be defined as a reciprocal evolutionary interaction between two or more species (or evolving groups, such as males and females). In coevolution, genetic change in one group results in genetic change in another, with this process repeating over time.

Arnqvist and Rowe studied 15 species of water striders, paying particular attention to the unique morphologies of the males and females that allow them to clasp (males), or prevent clasping (females). Males and females of all species were subjected to a barrage of morphological measurements, from which the researchers were able to measure the degree of armaments of each sex of each species. They used ordination procedures (see appendix 1) to collapse these measures into fewer dimensions to facilitate interpretation. They coupled the morphological measures with behavioural observation, whereby they placed males and females of a particular species in an artificial pond and observed mating behaviours. They reasoned that it is not the total amount of armaments of the males and females that will influence the duration and outcome of mating attempts by the males, but instead it will be the relative difference in armaments between the sexes that drives mating (or escape) success. This is exactly what their data showed. The outcome of mating attempts was not related to the absolute amount of arms found in a species, but instead was determined by the relative differences between the sexes. When males were more heavily armed, mating occurred most frequently. When females were more heavily armed, mating was rarer. It is not difficult to see how sexual selection will then favour the evolution of increased armaments in the sex that is at a relative disadvantage.

We now turn our attention to plants. Though many undergraduates are surprised even to learn that plants have sex, the behavioural ecology of mating by plants is even more complex than that found among animals.

Nonrandom Mating Among Wild Radish

Wild radish grows as an annual weed in California where it can be commonly seen along roadways and in abandoned fields (fig. 8.24). The seeds of wild radish germinate in response to the first winter rains of California's Mediterranean climate (chapter 2) and the plants flower by January. Flowering may continue to late spring or early summer, depending on the length of the wet season. During their flowering season, wild radishes are pollinated by a wide variety of insects, including honeybees, syrphid flies, and butterflies. Wild radish flowers have both male (**stamens**) and female (**pistils**) parts and produce both pollen and ovules. However, a wild radish plant cannot pollinate itself, a condition called **self-incompatibility**. Because they must mate with other

Figure 8.24   The wild radish, *Raphanus sativus*, has become a model for studying the mating behaviour of plants.

plants, a researcher working on wild radish can more easily control matings between plants.

Diane Marshall has used the many advantages offered by wild radish, such as its rapid growth to maturity and self-incompatibility, to explore the topic of mate selection in plants. Marshall and Michael Folsom (1992) listed a number of other characteristics of wild radish that make it convenient for study. For instance, its fruits contain several seeds, which allows the possibility of multiple paternity of offspring. However, the seeds are not so numerous that the researcher is overwhelmed by a vast number of seeds. In addition, each plant produces numerous flowers, allowing the possibility of several kinds of matings per plant and several replications of each mating experiment on the same plant. The seeds, which weigh about 10 mg, are also a convenient size for handling and weighing. Finally, there is sufficient genetic variation among individual radish plants to identify the male parent of each seed using electrophoresis of isozymes (see Ecological Tools and Approaches in chapter 4).

The insects that pollinate wild radish generally arrive at flowers carrying pollen from several different plants, and as a consequence a wild radish plant typically has about seven mates. Under these circumstances of multiple mates, Marshall asked whether siring offspring is a random process. In other words, do the seven mates of a typical wild radish plant have an equal probability of fertilizing the available ovules? The alternative, nonrandom mating, would suggest the potential for mate choice and sexual selection. What mechanisms might produce nonrandom mating among wild radish? Nonrandom mating could result from maternal control over the fertilization process, competition among pollen, or a combination of the two processes. If it does occur in plants, nonrandom mating establishes the conditions necessary for sexual selection in plants. However, as Marshall and Folsom (1991) pointed out, though sexual selection is well documented in animals, its occurrence among plants was a controversial and open question.

While the existence of sexual selection in plants was controversial, nonrandom mating was well documented. Marshall and her colleagues have repeatedly demonstrated nonrandom mating in wild radish. For instance, Marshall (1990) carried out greenhouse experiments that showed nonrandom mating among three maternal plants and six pollen donors. In this experiment, Marshall mated three seed parents or maternal plants with six pollen donors, the plants that would act as sources of pollen to pollinate the flowers of the seed plants.

Marshall used the six pollen donors to make 63 kinds of crosses, six single donor crosses plus 57 mixed donor crosses, on each maternal plant. Her crosses included all possible mixtures of pollen from one to six donors. Plants were pollinated in the greenhouse by hand. All pollinations were performed on freshly opened flowers in the morning when the temperature was cool enough for researchers to work comfortably. Pollen was collected by tapping flowers lightly on the bottom of small petri dishes from an equal number of flowers of each pollen donor. Pollen was then mixed and applied to the stigmas of flowers on the maternal plant using forceps wrapped in tissue. Sufficient pollen was applied to cover each stigma. Because

each cross was replicated from two to 20 times depending on the type of cross, the total number of pollinations performed on each plant was 300. This is a good example of the unique opportunities for experimental work offered by plants.

One of the ways that Marshall assessed the possibility of nonrandom mating was through performance of pollen donors. She estimated pollen donor performance in three ways: (1) number of seeds sired in mixed pollinations, (2) positions of seeds sired, and (3) weight of seeds sired. The results of this analysis are shown in figure 8.25. What

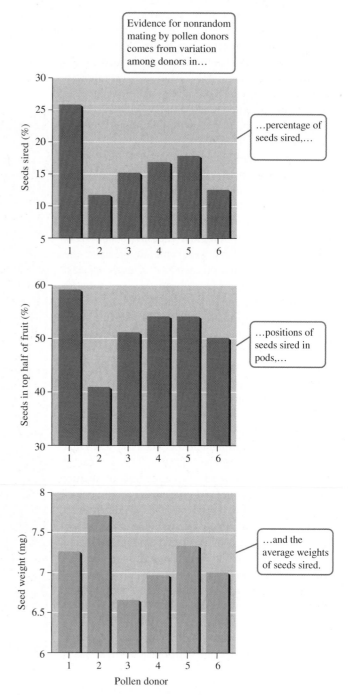

Figure 8.25 Evidence for unequal mating success among wild radish pollen donors in a greenhouse environment (data from Marshall 1990).

would you expect to see in figure 8.25 if performance was equal across pollen donors? If performance was equal, the heights of the bars would be approximately equal for all pollen donors. However they are not, and figure 8.25 indicates clearly that pollen donors vary widely in their performance. In other words, mating in this experiment was nonrandom.

Because Marshall conducted her 1990 study under greenhouse conditions, we might ask whether nonrandom mating also occurs under field conditions. In other words, could the nonrandom mating she documented have been an artefact of greenhouse conditions? Marshall and Ollar Fuller (1994) designed a study to address this question. Why might nonrandom mating be limited to the greenhouse environment? Marshall and Fuller point out that the harsh and variable environments to which plants are exposed in nature might mean that the condition of the maternal plant may be of overwhelming importance in determining the amount of seed produced, the weight of seeds, and so forth. Under such conditions, nonrandom pollination, which produces differences in seed weight in the greenhouse, might be undetectable and biologically insignificant.

Marshall and Fuller chose four maternal plants and grew their offspring in a field setting. Three other maternal lineages, (A, B, and C) were chosen to act as pollen donors. In the field, the maternal plants were covered with fine mesh nylon bags until the experimental pollinations were completed. Using the forceps and tissue method described earlier, Marshall and Fuller performed several kinds of hand pollinations, including mixed pollinations using pollen from all three pollen donors. Once the hand pollinations were completed, the nylon mesh bags were removed from the flowers.

The result of this experiment provided clear support for nonrandom mating in the field population. Figure 8.26 shows that during the mixed pollen donor pollinations, pollen donor C1 (56.5%) sired a much greater proportion of seeds compared to pollen donors A1 (24.8%) and B1 (18.7%). This finding suggests that the nonrandom matings observed in prior greenhouse pollination studies were not an artefact of greenhouse conditions.

Additional work by Marshall and her colleagues (Marshall et al. 1996) suggests that competition between pollen grains may contribute to nonrandom mating in wild radish populations. They used three maternal plants in these crosses, which they crossed with seven pollen donors (A, B, C, D, E, F, Z). The maternal plants were pollinated with pollen from single donors and from pairs of donors. The paired pollinations (A + B, C + D, etc.) were done in two ways. In one set of experiments, the pollen from the two donors was mixed as in the previous experiments described earlier. Because the two pollen types were in physical contact with each other in these "mixed" pollinations, this method of pollinating increased the opportunity for interaction between pollen types. In the second set of experiments, the pollen of the two donors used was not mixed. Each was applied to adjacent halves of the stigma, the tip of the pistil that acts as a pollen-receptive area. Since the two pollen types did not contact each other in these "adjacent" pollinations, there was a reduced chance that they would interact. Pollen response to these conditions was measured as the

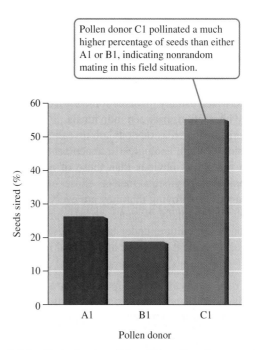

Figure 8.26 Variation in wild radish pollen donor mating success in a field environment (data from Marshall and Fuller 1994).

percentage of pollen that germinated within 90 minutes of pollination. Reduced percentage of germination would indicate lower pollen responsiveness and the possibility of inhibition of pollen response, either through pollen to pollen interactions or through maternal tissue effects expressed through the stigma.

Some of the results of this experiment are shown in figure 8.27. The percentage of pollen that germinated after 90 minutes was essentially the same in the single donor and adjacent pollinations. Meanwhile, the rate of germination when

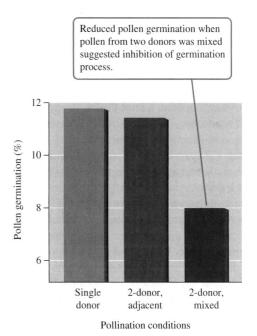

Figure 8.27 Competition between pollen from different donors (data from Marshall et al. 1996).

that the rewards and costs are fixed (at least within a population)? The variable that can change is p, the frequency of Hawks. We can thus use the two equations:

$$\text{Hawk} = p \cdot (0.5 \cdot R - 0.5 \cdot C) + (1 - p) \cdot R$$

$$\text{Dove} = p \cdot 0 + (1 - p) \cdot (0.5 \cdot R)$$

We can then set Hawk = Dove:

$$p \cdot (0.5 \cdot R - 0.5 \cdot C) + (1 - p) \cdot R = p \cdot 0 + (1 - p) \cdot (0.5 \cdot R)$$

And solve for p:

$$p = R/C$$

What does this mean? We already know that if rewards are greater than costs ($R > C$), the ESS will be a Hawk-only world, and $p = 1$. If instead rewards are less than costs, then p will be less than one. For example, if $R = 50$ and $C = 100$, then the mixed ESS solution will be Hawks at a frequency of $50/100 = 0.5$. In other words, in this game, with those values for R and C, the ESS is a population that consists of equal numbers of Hawks and Doves. If R and C were 50 and 75, respectively, then the mixed ESS solution would be $50/75$, Hawks = $p = 2/3$.

Our Hawk–Dove example shows that determining the relative fitness of individual actions will be dependent upon the frequency of other behaviours in the population, as well as the costs and rewards of a given action. A population consisting of only Doves results in the highest average fitness of individuals, but it is the least stable in this game—susceptible to invasion by Hawks regardless of the values of the reward and costs of fighting. Remember from chapter 4 that selection does not act on the absolute fitness of individuals, but instead on the relative differences in fitness among individuals within a population. Natural selection does not work toward a goal of maximizing fitness in a population; instead it simply favours those with the highest relative fitness.

These games can be expanded in a variety of ways, including adding costs of display for the Doves or costs of fighting for Hawks (independent of injury), and can include additional behaviours. Next we discuss a few examples of how researchers are using game theory to address real ecological questions.

Game Theory in Modern Ecology

In a collaboration between researchers at the University of Otago and the Université du Québec à Montréal (Poulin and Vickery 1995), game theory was used to explore cleaning symbioses. Many organisms engage in cooperative behaviours regarding the removal of dead tissue and parasites. These interactions include birds removing ticks from the backs of large ungulates, and wrasses removing parasites from other fish on coral reefs. Many of these interactions are spectacular to watch, such as wrasses that move in and out of the jaws of much larger fish, without any apparent risk of predation. However, there is ample opportunity for cheating by both parties. The cleaners could easily feed upon living tissue and blood of the host, while the host itself could feed upon the cleaners. Poulin and Vickery explored the conditions under which cheating may become favoured. A major influence for both cleaners and clients was the relative fitness value of being cleaned (or eating parasites) versus eating the cleaner (or the client). In other words, if the value of R is high, relative to the alternative food source, honesty is an ESS. You may recognize this has some similarities to our discussion of optimal foraging in chapter 7.

Dubois and Giraldeau (2005), also from the Université du Québec à Montréal, discuss the strengths and weaknesses of using the Hawk–Dove game to model the defence of resources by animals. They explain that the classic game theory model says that when the cost of defence is low, there should be increased aggression and defence of resources. However, they are able to expand this original model and show that aggression is itself going to be dependent upon the spatial distribution of resources, predation risk, the density of individuals in a population, and the value of the resources themselves. They demonstrate that animal behaviour extends well beyond simple interactions between two individuals, and to truly understand how individuals will interact it is essential to also understand the landscape in which they will compete. In other words, behaviour is displayed by individuals, but is done in response to a diversity of simultaneously interacting factors. These ideas will be more fully explored in chapter 21, Landscape Ecology.

It may surprise you that the conditional behavioural strategies that can be modelled by game theory can also apply to plants. Recall from chapter 7 that plants are very flexible in where they put their roots in response to varied nutrient levels in the soil. Not surprisingly, one of the determinants of root placement is the *choices* made by other plants, as we will explore in chapter 13. Mordechi Gersani (2001) and his colleagues explored the ESS of the "choice" faced by plants: do you put your roots near other plants to try and take all of their resources, or do you put your roots away from plants, "sharing" resources among all? Their model produced an outcome similar to the traditional Hawk–Dove model, where the ESS appears to be increased root allocation when neighbours are present, causing an increase in competition and a reduction in the absolute number of seeds (fitness) produced. Although there is currently much controversy surrounding experimental work testing these ideas (Schenk 2006), the study by Gersani and colleagues shows that the usefulness of game theory extends well beyond the realm of animals.

SUMMARY

The behaviour of organisms and their social relations can frequently directly impact the reproductive contribution of individuals to future generations, a key component of fitness. The field of behavioural ecology blends understanding of physiology, evolution, and ecology. Many patterns observed in nature are difficult to understand without a firm grounding in behavioural ecology.

8.1 Natural selection favours those behaviours that increase the inclusive fitness of individuals.

Many behaviours have a genetic basis, and are thus at least partially heritable. As a result, there is the potential for natural selection to influence not only phenotype, but also social relations. Critical to understanding the adaptive value of different behaviours is the concept of inclusive fitness, which accounts for the similarity in genetic composition of closely related individuals. By using this broader view of fitness, seemingly maladaptive behaviours such as altruism can be favoured through natural selection, through a process called kin selection. In kin selection, individuals are more likely to perform a given behaviour if the potential benefit to their inclusive fitness is greater than the cost. Not all behaviours among individuals are altruistic, and instead selection can also favour selfishness. For example, brood parasites such as the cowbird are often successful in inducing altruistic acts from their host by manipulating pre-existing behaviours and limitations. Natural selection does not necessarily favour the "nicest" behaviours, only the most effective. Cooperation can occur among individuals when there is a *tit-for-tat* arrangement in which each individual is assured of cooperation from the other. In this scenario, altruism can occur even among unrelated individuals and without manipulation.

8.2 The evolution of sociality is generally accompanied by cooperative feeding, defence of the social group, and restricted reproductive opportunities.

The degree of sociality in a social species ranges from acts as simple as mutual grooming or group protection of young, to highly complex, stratified societies such as those found in colonies of ants or termites. This more complex level of social behaviour, which is considered to be the pinnacle of social evolution, is called eusociality. Eusociality is generally thought to include three major characteristics: (1) individuals of more than one generation living together, (2) cooperative care of young, and (3) division of individuals into sterile, or nonreproductive, and reproductive castes. Cooperation among African lions appears to be a response to environmental conditions that require cooperation for success. To survive, reproduce, and successfully raise offspring to maturity, African lions must work in cooperative groups of females, which are called prides, and of males, which are called coalitions.

8.3 Mate choice by one sex and/or competition for mates among individuals of the same sex can result in selection for particular traits, a process called sexual selection.

Species vary greatly in the combination of sex types that they contain, ranging from hermaphrodites to single sexes, with nearly all possible alternatives found somewhere in nature. Sex types are arranged into different mating systems, depending upon the social interactions among individuals. Sexual selection results from differences in reproductive rates among individuals as a result of differences in their mating success. Sexual selection is thought to work either through intrasexual selection, where individuals of one sex compete with each other for mates, or intersexual selection, when members of one sex consistently choose mates from among members of the opposite sex on the basis of some particular trait.

In some species, such as water striders, the immediate fitness consequences of mating will differ between males and females, resulting in sexual conflict. Repeated mating is not inherently beneficial for female striders, as it can increase predation risk, reduce foraging time, and is redundant if they already contain enough sperm for fertilization of their eggs. However, male striders gain benefit from being the last to mate with a given female. As a result, natural selection has resulted in an escalating arms race in morphologies that allow the male to clasp the females, and allow the females to escape. The relative difference in armaments between the sexes greatly influences the outcome of mating attempts.

Experimental evidence supports the hypothesis that the colouration of male guppies in local populations is determined by a dynamic interplay between natural selection exerted by predators, under which less-colourful males have higher survival, and by female mate choice, which results in higher mating success by more colourful males. Studies of mating in the wild radish indicate nonrandom mating and suggest interference competition among pollen from different pollen donors.

Game theory is an essential theoretical tool for behavioural ecologists. Understanding the relative fitness of behaviours is often difficult because their values are dependent upon the actions of others. By imagining behavioural interactions as a game, it is possible to determine which behaviour is evolutionary stable, and resistant to invasion by alternative behaviours. In the Hawk–Dove game, a world of Doves results in the highest absolute fitness, but is easily invaded by a Hawk. The ESS will be a mixture of Hawks and Doves, with the frequency of each being a function of the costs and benefits of each strategy. Game theory has been applied to a variety of situation in behavioural ecology, including defence of resources among both plants and animals, as well as cleaner–client relationships.

REVIEW QUESTIONS

1. The introduction to chapter 8 included sketches of the behaviour and social systems of several fish species. Using the concepts that you have learned in the chapter, revisit those examples and predict the forms of sexual selection occurring in each species.

2. One of the basic assumptions of the material presented in chapter 8 is that the form of reproduction will exert substantial influence on social interactions within a species. How might interactions differ in populations that reproduce asexually versus ones that engage in sexual reproduction? How might having separate sexes versus hermaphrodites affect the types of social interactions within a population? How should having several forms of one sex, for example, large and small males, influence the diversity of behavioural interactions within the population?

3. Is altruism likely to become a common trait within a species if there is no fitness benefit (in either short- or long-term) to the individual performing the altruistic act? Why?

4. Endler (1980) pointed out that though field observations are consistent with the hypothesis that predators may exert natural selection on guppy colouration, some other factors in the environment could be affecting variation in male colour patterns among guppy populations. What other factors, especially physical and chemical factors, might affect male colours and should each influence male colour?

5. Examine figure 8.22. While most of the male guppies that successfully mated were dominant, a substantial proportion of attractive males that sired broods were subordinate. How might we interpret this reproductive success by attractive but subordinate males? What might these results indicate about the potential influence of female choice on mating success among male guppies?

6. Locke Rowe and colleagues have explored sexual conflict between male and female water striders. What ecological and environmental conditions are likely to result in sexual conflict in other species?

7. The results of numerous studies indicate nonrandom mating among plants at least under some conditions. These results lead to questions concerning the biological mechanisms that produce these nonrandom matings. How might the maternal plant control or at least influence the paternity of her seeds? What role might competition between pollen determine in the nonrandom patterns observed?

8. The details of experimental design are critical for determining the success or failure of both field and laboratory experiments. Results often depend on some small details. For instance, why did Jennifer Jarvis wait one year after establishing her laboratory colony of naked mole rats before attempting to quantify the behaviour of the laboratory population? What might have been the consequence of beginning to quantify the behaviour of the colony soon after it was established?

9. Behavioural interactions are often difficult to study because an individual's behaviour can be dependent upon the behavioural responses of other individuals of the same and different species. How does this differ from the physiological responses of organisms to their abiotic environment? How does game theory allow behavioural ecologists to develop theory to understand these social interactions?

10. Choose a problem in the behavioural ecology of social relations, formulate a hypothesis, and design a study to test your hypothesis. Take two approaches. In one approach use field and laboratory experiments to test your ideas. In the second design, develop a study that uses the comparative method.

LIFE HISTORIES AND THE NICHE   CHAPTER 9

CHAPTER CONCEPTS

9.1 Because all organisms have access to limited energy and resources, there are fundamental trade-offs in how these can be allocated between survival, offspring number, and offspring size.

Ecology In Action: How Life Histories Influence Extinction Risk

Concept 9.1 Review

9.2 The great diversity of life histories observed in nature can be classified on the basis of a few common characteristics.

Concept 9.2 Review

9.3 The fundamental niche reflects the environmental requirements of species, while the realized niche also includes interactions with other species.

Concept 9.3 Review

Ecological Tools and Approaches: Using Life-History Information as Indicators of Biological Effects of Climate Change

Summary

Review Questions

Different species living side-by-side differ in a number of important ways. They may reproduce at vastly different rates, have lifetimes that differ by several orders of magnitude, and produce offspring of substantially different sizes. Some may reproduce asexually, some produce sexually. For some, offspring may disperse and live independently, while others may grow as an interconnected network of genetically identical "individuals." Despite these fundamental differences in aspects of their biology, co-occurring species have something in common—the ability to live and reproduce under similar environmental conditions.

We can imagine sitting by a stream on a sunny day in the Great Bear Rainforest along British Columbia's central coast (fig. 9.1). We are cooled by the deep shade cast by the giant Western Red Cedar tree, *Thuja plicata*. Bathed in fog during the summer, soaked by rain during fall, winter, and spring, these photosynthesizing giants have lived for centuries.

On this summer morning, while we choose which lure to cast into the water in the hopes of a fresh lunch, we see a female mayfly along with thousands of others of her species shedding their larval exoskeletons as they transform from their aquatic stage to their flying stage. As a larva, the mayfly had lived in the stream for a year. Her adult stage lasts just this one day, during which she mates, deposits her eggs in the stream, and then dies. As the mayflies swarm, some will be eaten by birds nesting in trees that grow along the stream, some will be caught by bats that roost among the giant cedars, and some will be eaten by the fish that they had successfully eluded for a year of larval life. Looking across the water, we see trout flashing as they swim to the surface to consume the adult mayflies that linger too long. We tie on our mayfly lure, wade into the water, and cast away.

Cedar, mayfly, fish, and humans all have lives intertwined in a web of ecological connections, but which differ greatly in scale and timing. While the cedar produces seeds numbering in the millions over a lifetime that will stretch for centuries, the mayfly will spend a year in the stream and then emerge to lay eggs that will number in the hundreds. The trout's spawn will number in the thousands, deposited over the several years of her life. Meanwhile, humans typically produce just a few children, each requiring significant investments of time and energy for decades—even longer for those parents with university-aged offspring still living at home! Despite the differences in how these four species live their life, they all are able to find this part of British Columbia suitable for growth and reproduction.

The story we have just told is rich in natural history, and is underlain with many critical ecological concepts. In the previous chapters of this section we focused on how organisms deal with isolated environmental and social conditions. However, individuals never encounter these factors in isolation, and instead natural selection acts upon all of these factors simultaneously. Because of limited amounts of energy, resources, and genetic variation, not all organisms are able to cope with all potential combinations of environmental conditions. Instead, for each species there will be a limited set of conditions suitable for growth and reproduction. That

Figure 9.1   The Great Bear Rainforest is a lush region of coastal British Columbia.

combination of suitable conditions is a species' **niche**, and we might expect to find a species occupying areas of the landscape in which environmental conditions match the species' niche requirements. However, even species with overlap in niche requirements may differ greatly in important factors such as the number and size of offspring they are able to produce, the timing of first reproduction, and patterns of survival. These sorts of questions fall within the domain of those who study **life histories**. Chapter 9 presents several concepts from these two central aspects of ecology.

9.1 Trade-offs

Because all organisms have access to limited energy and resources, there are fundamental trade-offs in how these can be allocated between survival, offspring number, and offspring size. In 1976, Stephen Stearns was a graduate student at the University of British Columbia. During the process of deciding what project he wanted to tackle for his Ph.D. thesis, he wrote a paper entitled "Life-History Tactics: A Review of the Ideas," published in the *Quarterly Review of Biology*.

This paper was the first synthesis of the ideas in life history, and by itself, created a field of research that would shape the careers of many researchers yet to come. As a sign of how influential Stearns was, and continues to be, this paper has been cited over 1,800 times by other scientists. To put this in perspective, if a single paper is cited 100 times, it is generally considered an influential paper. Few scientists create a field of research; even fewer do it while still a graduate student.

In chapters 5–7, we discussed how trade-offs in energy allocation influence an organism's ability to cope with abiotic stressors, such as low water availability or extreme temperatures. However, the principle of allocation is just as important in influencing how an organism allocates energy within a given segment of its energy budget, such as reproduction. For example, producing large offspring costs more energy than producing an equal number of small offspring. If the amount of energy an organism has available to allocate to reproduction is limited, there is an inevitable trade-off between offspring number and offspring size. Perhaps an individual increases its energetic allocation to reproduction, allowing it to produce many large offspring. Has this individual avoided a trade-off? No. That increased allocation to reproduction must come at the cost of reduced allocation to some other life function, such as growth rate or "maintenance." As a result, though this organism may breed, it is likely to either have reduced growth or increased risk of mortality. Understanding trade-offs serves as the foundation of the study of life histories. In this section, we explore a few of the many trade-offs that structure life histories.

Size and Number of Offspring

Fish Egg Size and Number

Because of their great diversity (more than 20,000 existing species) and the wide variety of environments in which they live, fish offer many opportunities for studies of life history. Fish show more variation in many life-history traits than any other group of animals (Winemiller 1995). For instance, the number of offspring they produce per brood ranges from the one or two large live young produced by Mako sharks, to the 600,000,000 eggs per clutch laid by the ocean sunfish. However, many variables other than offspring number and size change from sharks to sunfish. Therefore, more robust patterns of variation can be obtained by analyzing relationships within closely related species, such as within families or genera.

Tom Turner and Joel Trexler investigated life-history variation among populations of darters, small freshwater fish in the perch family, Percidae (Turner and Trexler 1998). They were particularly interested in determining the relationship between egg size and egg number, also known as **fecundity**. Fecundity is simply the number of offspring produced by an organism. Darters are small, streamlined benthic fish that live in rivers and streams throughout eastern and central North America, including Canada. Male darters are usually strikingly coloured during the breeding season (fig. 9.2). Darters consist of 174 species in three genera within the family

Figure 9.2   Darters such as this male greenside darter form a diverse and distinctive subfamily of fish within the perch family, native only to North America.

Percidae, making them one of the most species-rich groups of vertebrates in North America. Despite the fact that the darters as a whole live in similar habitats and have similar anatomy, they vary widely in their life histories. The genera most similar to the ancestors of the darters, *Crystallaria* (one species) and *Percina* (38 species), are larger and produce more eggs than species in the genus *Etheostoma* (135 species). However, even species within the genus *Etheostoma* vary substantially in their life histories.

Turner and Trexler sampled 64 locations on streams and rivers in the Ohio, Ozark, and Ouachita Highlands regions of Ohio, Arkansas, and Missouri, the heart of freshwater fish diversity in North America and one of the most diverse temperate freshwater fish faunas on earth. Of the darters they collected at these locations, they chose 15 species for detailed study, five in the genus *Percina* and 10 *Etheostoma* species. Overall, the species ranged in length from 44 to 127 mm; the number of mature eggs that they produced ranged from 49 to 397; and the size of eggs produced by the study species varied from 0.9 to 2.3 mm in diameter. Turner and Trexler found that these variables were interrelated. For example, larger darter species produce larger numbers of eggs (fig. 9.3). Further, darters that produce larger eggs produce fewer eggs (fig. 9.4), suggesting a trade-off between offspring size and number.

Similar relationships have been found among other vertebrates, leading ecologists to view the negative relationship between offspring size and number as a general rule structuring animal life histories. That by itself is interesting, but the pattern itself leads to new questions. For example, how do these differences in life histories relate to other ecological processes, such as gene flow? Turner and Trexler proposed that gene flow would be higher among populations producing more numerous smaller eggs, that is, among populations with higher fecundity.

Turner and Trexler found a negative relationship between egg size and gene flow, but a strong positive relationship of gene flow with the number of eggs produced by females (fig. 9.5). That is, populations of darter species that produce many small eggs showed less variation in genetic diversity across the study region than did populations that produce fewer larger eggs.

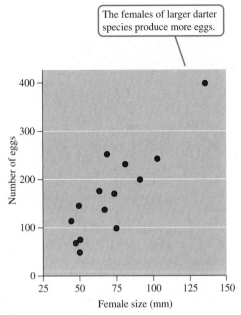

Figure 9.3 Relationship between female darter size and number of eggs (data from Turner and Trexler 1998).

How do differences in egg size and number translate into differences in gene flow among populations? It turns out that the larvae of darters that hatch from larger eggs are larger when they hatch. These larger larvae begin feeding at an earlier age on prey that live on the streambed, and spend less time drifting with the water current. Consequently, larvae hatching from larger eggs disperse shorter distances and therefore carry their genes shorter distances. As a result, populations of species producing fewer larger eggs will be more isolated genetically from other populations. Because of their greater isolation, such populations will differentiate genetically more rapidly compared to populations of species that produce many smaller larvae that disperse longer distances.

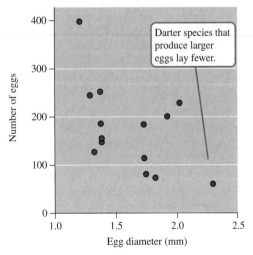

Figure 9.4 Relationship between the size of eggs laid by darters and the number of eggs laid (data from Turner and Trexler 1998).

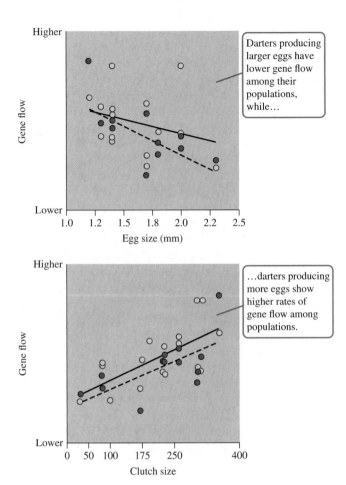

Figure 9.5 Relationship between egg size and egg number and gene flow in darter species. Solid lines and purple dots represent estimates by one genetic method, and dashed lines and green dots by a second method (data from Turner and Trexler 1998).

Turner and Trexler's study not only provides a case history consistent with the generalization that there is a trade-off between offspring size and number, it also reveals some of the consequences of that trade-off. For example, because larger offspring will travel shorter distances before feeding than smaller offspring, populations of species that produce large offspring will be more genetically distinct than the species with small offspring. Genetic differentiation is a necessary precursor to speciation events (chapter 4), and thus this most basic of life-history trade-offs: offspring size and number, has the potential to influence macro evolutionary processes, such as variation in speciation rates.

Ecologists have found parallel relationships among terrestrial plants, involving seed number and size.

Seed Size and Number in Plants

Like fish, plants vary widely in the number of offspring they produce, ranging from those that produce many small seeds to those that produce a few large seeds (fig. 9.6). The sizes of seeds produced by plants range over 10 orders of magnitude, from the tiny seeds of orchids that weigh 0.000002 g to the giant double coconut palm with seeds that weigh up to

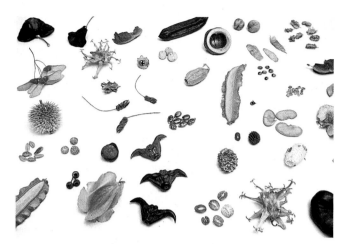

Figure 9.6   A small sample of the great diversity of seed sizes and shapes.

27,000 g. While some orchids are known to produce billions of seeds, coconut palms produce small numbers of huge seeds. At this scale it is clear that there is a trade-off between seed size and seed number. While there are complexities that must be accounted for (Harper et al. 1970), botanists long ago described a negative relationship between seed size and seed number (Stevens 1932). Figure 9.7 shows the relationship between average seed mass and the number of seeds per plant among species in four families of plants: daisies (Asteraceae), grasses (Poaceae), mustards (Brassicaceae), and beans (Fabaceae). In all four families, species producing larger numbers of seeds on average produce fewer seeds.

In the darter example, we saw that dispersal and off-spring size were related. Is that also the case in plants? Mark Westoby, Michelle Leishman, and Janice Lord (1996) conducted a study that included the seeds of 196 to 641 species of plants from five different regions. Three of their study regions were in Australia: New South Wales, central Australia, and Sydney; one was in Europe: Sheffield, United Kingdom; and one was in North America: Indiana Dunes National Lakeshore. By including the plants on three different continents, Westoby, Leishman, and Lord increased their chances of discovering patterns of general importance.

Westoby and his coauthors recognized six dispersal strategies. They classified seeds with no specialized structures for dispersal as unassisted dispersers. If seeds had hooks, spines, or barbs, they were classified as **adhesion-adapted**. Meanwhile, seeds with wings, hairs, or other structures that provide air resistance were assigned to a wind-dispersed category. Animal-dispersed seeds in the study included ant-dispersed, vertebrate-dispersed, and scatterhoarded. Westoby, Leishman, and Lord classified seeds with an **elaiosome**, a structure on the surface of some seeds generally containing oils attractive to ants, as ant-dispersed. Seeds with flesh or with an **aril**, a fleshy covering of some seeds that attracts birds and other vertebrates, were classified as vertebrate-dispersed. Finally they classified as **scatterhoarded** those seeds known to be gathered by mammals and stored in scattered caches or hoards.

Plants that disperse their seeds in different ways tend to produce seeds of different sizes (fig. 9.8). Plants that they had classified as unassisted dispersers produced the

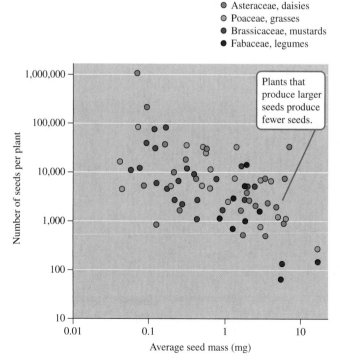

Figure 9.7   Relationship between seed mass and seed number (data from Stevens 1932).

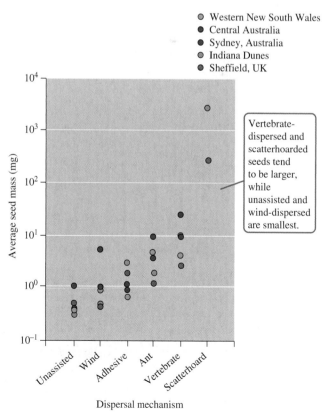

Figure 9.8   Plant dispersal mechanism and seed mass (data from Westoby et al. 1996).

smallest seeds, while wind-dispersed seeds were slightly larger. Adhesion-adapted seeds were of intermediate size, while the various types of animal-dispersed seeds were largest. Within the animal-dispersed seeds, ant-dispersed seeds were larger than the adhesion-adapted seeds, vertebrate-dispersed seeds typically even larger, and scatterhoarded were the largest by far. Westoby and his team point out that between 21% and 47% of the variation in seed size in the five floras included in their study is accounted for by a combination of growth form and mode of dispersal. Other analyses indicated different **plant growth forms** were associated with different sized seeds. For example, climbing plants tended to have very heavy seeds, while grasses tended to have small seeds (Westoby et al. 1996).

The relationships between seed size and both growth form and dispersal mode were consistent across widely separated geographic regions. However, even within dispersal mode and growth form groups, there remained substantial unexplained variation in seed size among plants in all regions. Once again, we see that studies of life-history variation can lead to new questions. For example, what are the factors that maintain variation in seed size? To maintain such variation, there must be advantages and disadvantages of producing either large or small seeds. What are those advantages and disadvantages?

Jakobsson and Eriksson (2000) investigated the relationship between seed size and recruitment among 50 plant species living in the meadows of their study region, using a field experiment. At their field sites, Jakobsson and Eriksson planted the seeds of each species in 14 small 10 × 10 cm plots. Each plot was sown with 50 to 100 seeds of the study species. They left half of the study plots undisturbed, while the other plots were disturbed before planting

by scratching the soil surface and removing any accumulated litter. Of the 50 species of seeds planted, the seeds of 48 species germinated and those of 45 species established recruits. Though plants recruited to both undisturbed and disturbed plots, the number of recruits was generally higher in disturbed plots. Further, eight species of plants recruited only on disturbed plots.

What role did differences in seed size play in the rate of recruitment by different species? Jakobsson and Eriksson calculated recruitment success in various ways. The simplest measure of recruitment success was to divide the total number of recruits by the total number of seeds of a species that they planted, giving the proportion of seeds sown that produced recruits. While 45 of 50 species established new recruits in the experimental plots, the rate at which they established varied widely among species from approximately 5% to nearly 90%. Differences in seed size explained much of the observed differences in recruitment success among species (fig. 9.9). On average, larger seeds, which produce larger seedlings, were associated with a higher rate of recruitment. It appears that by investing more energy into a seed, the maternal plant increases the probability that her offspring would successfully establish itself. This advantage associated with large seed size is probably very important in environments such as the grasslands studied by Jakobsson and Eriksson, where competition with established plants is likely to be high. Such maternal investment is likely not necessary, or is even wasteful, in areas with low competition. For example, smaller seeds may have more success in colonizing newly disturbed locations. Thus both small and large seeds can provide fitness benefits under different ecological conditions, and thus one expects to find substantial variation in this life-history trait among species.

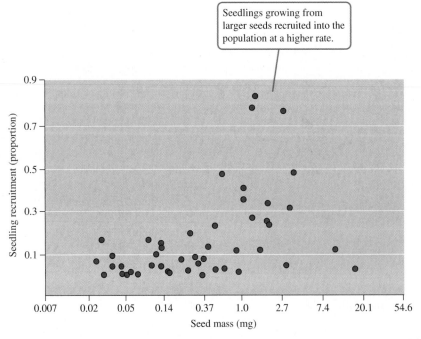

Seedlings growing from larger seeds recruited into the population at a higher rate.

Figure 9.9   Seed mass and recruitment rates in grassland plants (data from Jakobsson and Eriksson 2000).

As we can see from these examples in fish and plants, there is broad evidence for an offspring size vs. offspring number trade-off. But more important than simply quantifying that pattern is the realization that this trade-off has significant implications for other aspects of the ecology and evolution of these species.

In addition to showing variation in the number and sizes of offspring produced, organisms also show a great deal of variation in the age at which they begin reproducing. They also differ greatly in the relative amount of energy they allocate to reproduction versus growth and maintenance. Ecologists have observed patterns in age of reproductive maturity and relative investment in reproduction among species that support some broad generalizations.

Adult Survival and Reproductive Allocation

Reproductive effort is the allocation of energy, time, and other resources to the production and care of offspring. Within an individual, reproductive effort involves trade-offs with other needs of the organism, including allocation to growth and maintenance. Because of these trade-offs, allocation to reproduction may reduce the probability that an organism will survive. However, delaying reproduction also involves risk. An individual that delays reproduction runs the risk of dying before it can reproduce. Consequently, evolutionary ecologists have predicted that variation in mortality rates among adults will be in association with variation in the age of first reproduction, or age of reproductive maturity. Specifically, they have predicted that where adult mortality is higher, natural selection will favour early reproductive maturity; and where adult mortality is low, natural selection is expected to favour delaying reproductive maturity.

Variation Among Species

The relationship between mortality, growth, and age at first reproduction or reproductive maturity has been examined in a large number of organisms. Early work, which concentrated on fish, shrimp, and sea urchins, suggested linkages between mortality or survival, growth, and reproduction. Richard Shine and Eric Charnov (1992) explored life-history variation among snakes and lizards to determine whether generalizations developed through studies of fish and marine invertebrates could be extended to another group of animals living in very different environments (fig. 9.10).

Shine and Charnov (yes, the same Charnov from chapter 8) began their presentation with a reminder that, in contrast to most terrestrial arthropods, birds, and mammals (including humans), many animals continue growing after they reach sexual maturity. In addition, most vertebrate species begin reproducing before they reach their maximum body size. As a result, the energy budgets of these other vertebrate species, such as fish and reptiles, are different before and after sexual maturity. Before these organisms reach sexual maturity, energy acquired by an individual is allocated to one of two competing demands: maintenance and growth. However,

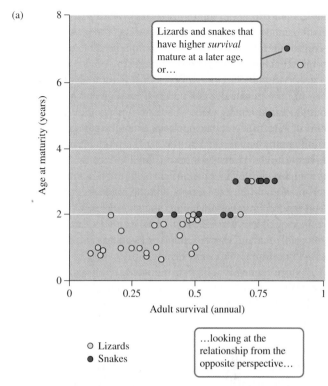

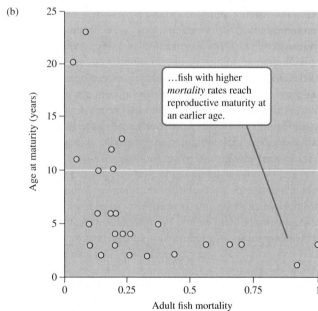

Figure 9.10 Relationship between (*a*) adult survival among lizards and snakes and (*b*) adult fish mortality and age of reproductive maturity (data from Shine and Charnov 1992 and Gunderson 1997).

after reaching sexual maturity, limited energy supplies are allocated to three functions: maintenance, growth, and reproduction. Because they have fewer demands on their limited energy supplies, individuals delaying reproduction until they are older will grow faster and reach a larger size. Because of the increase in reproductive rate associated with larger body size (see fig. 9.3), deferring reproduction would lead to a higher reproductive rate. However, where mortality rates are

high, deferring reproduction increases the probability that an individual will die before reproducing. These relationships suggest that mortality rates will play a pivotal role in determining the age at first reproduction.

Shine and Charnov gathered information from published summaries on annual adult survival and age at which females mature for several species of snakes and lizards. The annual rate of adult survival among snakes in their data set ranged from approximately 35% to 85% of the population, while age at reproductive maturity ranged from 2 to 7 years. Meanwhile, the annual rate of lizard survival ranged from approximately 8% to 67% of the population, and their age at first reproduction ranged from a little less than 8 months to 6.5 years. The results of Shine and Charnov's study showed clearly that as survival of adult lizards and snakes increases, their age at maturity also increases (fig. 9.10*a*).

More recent analyses of the relationship between adult mortality rate and age at maturity among fish species provide additional support for the prediction that high adult survival leads to delayed maturity. Donald Gunderson (1997) explored patterns in adult survival and reproductive effort among several populations of fish. The life-history information Gunderson summarized in his analysis included mortality rate, estimated maximum length, age at reproductive maturity, and reproductive effort. Gunderson estimated reproductive effort as each population's **gonadosomatic index**, or **GSI**. GSI was taken as the ovary weight of each species divided by the species body weight and adjusted for the number of batches of offspring produced by each species per year. For example, because the northern anchovy spawns three times per year, the weight of its ovary was multiplied by 3 for calculating its GSI. Meanwhile, the ovary weight for dogfish sharks, which reproduce only every other year, was divided by 2.

The fish included in Gunderson's analysis ranged in size from the Puget Sound rockfish, which reaches a maximum size of approximately 15 cm, to northeast Arctic cod that reaches a length of 130 cm. The age at maturation among these fish species ranges from 1 year in northern anchovy populations to 23 years in dogfish shark populations. Like Shine and Charnov, his results show a clear relationship between adult mortality and age of reproductive maturity (fig. 9.10*b*). These results support the idea that natural selection has acted to adjust age at reproductive maturity to rates of mortality experienced by populations.

Gunderson's analysis also gives information on variation in reproductive effort among species. His calculations of GSI spanned more than a 30-fold difference, from a value of 0.02 for the rougheye rockfish to 0.65 for the northern anchovy. What do these numbers mean? Reproductive effort is expressed as a proportion of body weight. Converting these proportions to percentages, we can say that the yearly allocation to reproduction by the rougheye rockfish is approximately 2% of its body weight, while the northern anchovy allocates approximately 65% annually! When Gunderson plotted GSI against mortality rates (fig. 9.11), the results supported the prediction from life-history theory that species

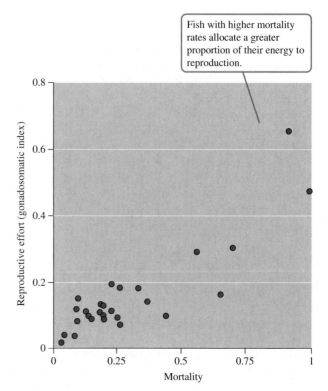

Fish with higher mortality rates allocate a greater proportion of their energy to reproduction.

Figure 9.11 Relationship between adult fish mortality and reproductive effort as measured by the gonadosomatic index or GSI (data from Gunderson 1997).

with higher mortality would show higher relative reproductive effort.

Variation Within Species

To this point in our discussion we have emphasized life-history differences between species. However, even within a species one can find variation in critical aspects of life history. Once again, some of the best examples come from ecologists studying fish.

Mart Gross, of the University of Toronto, has conducted a number of studies that provide understanding of how intraspecific variation in life histories can lead to alternative behaviours among salmonoid fish, particularly the Coho salmon, *Oncorhynchus kisutch* (e.g., Gross 1985, 1991). We have discussed salmon many times in this book, particularly in the context of their moving between fresh and saltwater habitats (chapter 6). However, these organisms also exhibit substantial plasticity in their life histories, resulting in important consequences for mating behaviour.

Female Coho salmon typically reach sexual maturity after 18 months in the ocean, at which time they return to their birth stream, spawn, and die. Males are more variable. Some will mature after 18 months in the ocean, while others mature at smaller body sizes after only 6 months at sea. These alternative life histories are commonly referred to as the "hooknose" (6 month) and "jack" (18 month) forms of male Coho salmon (fig. 9.12). The developmental decision to mature at an early or late stage is irreversible, and appears dependent

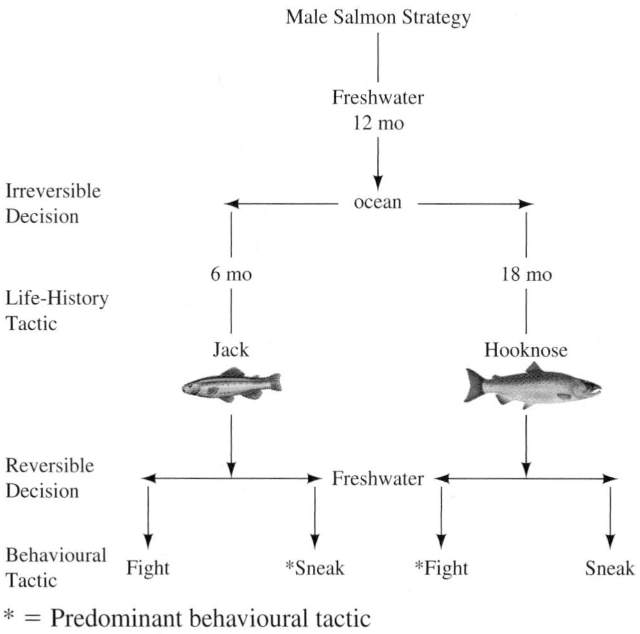

Male Salmon Strategy

Freshwater
12 mo

Irreversible
Decision — ocean —

6 mo ⟷ 18 mo

Life-History
Tactic

Jack   Hooknose

Reversible
Decision — Freshwater —

Behavioural
Tactic   Fight   *Sneak   *Fight   Sneak

* = Predominant behavioural tactic

Figure 9.12 Male Coho salmon exhibit two alternative life-history strategies. "Jack" forms mature earlier and at small sizes, while "hooknose" mature later and bigger. These life histories are associated with different mating behaviours (redrawn from Gross, 1991).

upon a number of environmental, genetic, and size-related factors. In general, fry that grow rapidly are larger as juveniles and are more likely to become jacks, while the slower growing individuals tend to become hooknose. In addition to differences in size at sexual maturity, individual salmon have options when it comes to mating strategies.

There are two alternative mating behaviours available to both jacks and hooknose: "sneaking" and "fighting" (fig. 9.12). Fighters will typically fight for proximity to a desired female who is about to spawn, while sneakers will try to fertilize the female's eggs while other males are engaged in fighting. (I have opted to take the high-road and not insert a joke here.)

One of the key questions Gross was interested in understanding is why both hooknose and jack forms coexist within a population. The answer to this question appears to be that hooknose and jack forms have roughly equivalent lifetime fitness, such that both can be evolutionary stable strategies (chapter 8). How is this possible? By observing males of different sizes, Gross (1985) was able to determine that both very small males and very large males had roughly equal success in getting close to females, while intermediate sized males were rarely able to get near a female. As you likely imagined, large fish were very good at fighting, and generally were successful in fights. Small fish were poor fighters, but good at hiding, and thus were successful in sneaking. Intermediate sized fish were too large to sneak, yet too small to successfully fight, and thus

they rarely were able to get near females. As a result of these effects of size on behavioural outcomes, Coho salmon are experiencing disruptive selection (chapter 4) on the key life-history trait of age of sexual maturity. As long as conditions remain constant, these two alternative forms should coexist within the population. However, Gross (1991) points out that conditions are not constant, and commercial and recreational anglers disproportionally harvest the larger hooknose fish. Removing the largest fish from the population should decrease the size at which fighting is a successful strategy. This in turn could lead to changes in the frequencies of jacks in subsequent populations (Gross 1991).

Gross's work demonstrates that alternative life histories can coexist within a population, and that behavioural strategies are intimately tied to the fitness of individuals. If the costs or benefits of alternative aspects of a life-history change (e.g., increased mortality from anglers at larger size), this could result in natural selection toward alternative life-history traits. Additional support for the idea of viewing life histories not as an end point that characterizes a species, but instead as a delicate evolutionary balance among costs and benefits associated with multiple traits, comes from a comparative study of several populations of the pumpkinseed sunfish, *Lepomis gibbosus* (fig. 9.13).

Kirk Bertschy and Michael Fox of Trent University (1999) studied the influence of adult survival on pumpkinseed sunfish life histories. One of the major objectives of their study was to test the prediction of life-history theory that increased adult survival, relative to juvenile mortality, favours delayed maturity and reduced reproductive effort. They selected five populations of pumpkinseed sunfish living in five lakes from a group of 27 lakes in southern Ontario. The lakes were similar in area and depth and small enough that Bertschy and Fox had a reasonable chance of estimating mortality rates and variation in other life-history characteristics.

Figure 9.13 Male pumpkinseed sunfish, *Lepomis gibbosus*, build their nests in the shallows of lakes and ponds. They guard their nests against intrusions by other males and attempt to attract females of their species to deposit eggs within them.

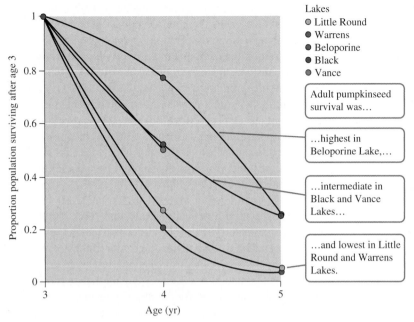

Figure 9.14 Pumpkinseed sunfish survival after age three years in five small lakes (data from Bertschy and Fox 1999).

Bertschy and Fox estimated life-history characteristics from annual samples of approximately 100 pumpkinseed sunfish taken from shallow waters in each of the five study lakes. They made several measurements on each individual in their samples, including their age (by counting annual rings in scales), weight (to the nearest 0.1 g), length (in mm), sex, and reproductive status. Because female reproductive effort is largely restricted to egg production while male reproductive effort includes activities such as territory guarding and nest building, Bertschy and Fox studied reproductive traits in females only. A female was considered mature if her ovaries contained eggs with yolk. Bertschy and Fox represented female reproductive effort using the gonadosomatic index, GSI, as we described previously.

Bertschy and Fox used mark and recapture surveys to estimate the number of adult pumpkinseed sunfish and the age structure of pumpkinseed populations in each of the study lakes. These surveys, which were conducted each year from 1992 to 1994, gave a basis for estimating rates of adult survival for each age in each lake's population. The lowest rate, or probability, of adult survival was 0.19, while the highest was 0.65. In other words, the proportion of adults surviving from one year to the next ranged from approximately 1 adult out of 5 (0.19) to about 2 adults out of 3 (0.65). This variation among lakes produced striking differences in the pattern of survival (fig. 9.14).

Juvenile survival was estimated by counting the number of pumpkinseed nests and then collecting all the larval fish in a sample of nests. The number of nests in the study lakes varied from 60 to over 1,000; the number of larval fish produced ranged from approximately 100,000 to over a million. Using their estimate of the number of larvae produced and the number of three-year-old fish in the same lake, Bertschy and Fox estimated juvenile survival. Juvenile survival to adulthood in

the study lakes ranged from 0.004, or about 4 out of 1,000 larvae, to 0.016, or about 16 out of 1,000 larvae. Because they were interested in the relative rates of adult and juvenile survival, Bertschy and Fox represented survival in their study lakes as the ratio of adult to juvenile survival probabilities. Figure 9.15 shows that this ratio ranged widely among study lakes from a low of 10.6 to 116.8, a tenfold difference among lakes.

Bertschy and Fox found significant variation in most life-history characteristics across their study lakes. Pumpkinseed sunfish matured at ages ranging from 2.4 to 3.4 years in the different study lakes, and they showed reproductive investments (gonadosomatic indexes or GSI) ranging from 6.9% to 9.3%. The relationship between survival rate and age at maturity found by Bertschy and Fox suggests that populations with higher adult survival mature at a greater age (fig. 9.16). The correlation between survival rate and age at maturity was not high enough to be statistically significant; however, the relationship between adult survival and reproductive effort was very clear and highly significant (fig. 9.17). The patterns of life-history variation across the pumpkinseed populations studied by Bertschy and Fox support the theory that where adult survival is lower relative to juvenile survival, natural selection will favour allocating greater resources to reproduction.

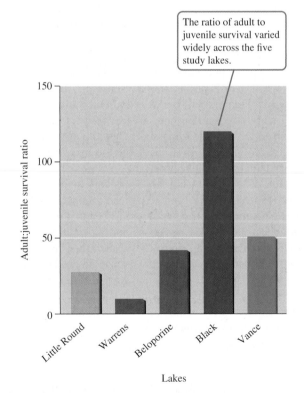

Figure 9.15 Ratio of adult to juvenile survival in pumpkinseed sunfish populations in five small lakes (data from Bertschy and Fox 1999).

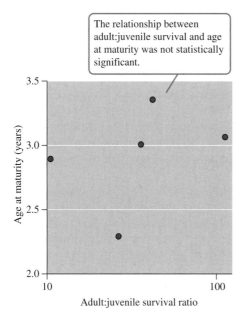

Figure 9.16   Adult:juvenile survival ratios and age at reproductive maturity in populations of pumpkinseed sunfish (data from Bertschy and Fox 1999).

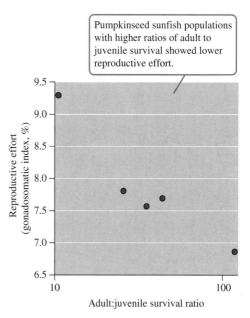

Figure 9.17   Adult:juvenile survival ratio and reproductive effort as measured by the gonadosomatic index or GSI (data from Bertschy and Fox 1999).

ECOLOGY IN ACTION

How Life Histories Influence Extinction Risk

The extinction of species is an issue of concern in Canada and around the world. Ecologists are on the forefront of research into understanding the causes and consequences of extinction, and are providing ideas for how to protect the species that remain. The immediate causes of species loss are, in a broad sense, well known and often referred to as the "evil quartet": over-exploitation, habitat loss, competition with introduced species, and trophic dependency leading to cascading chains of extinction (Diamond 1984). All of these topics will be discussed in later chapters of the book.

Although we often hear about a global biodiversity crisis, not all species are equally likely to go extinct, even when faced with the same environmental challenges (fig. 9.18). In later chapters we will discuss aspects of how human activities impact population dynamics and viability of a diversity of species. We will also discuss how the Species at Risk Act may be used to help protect some species in Canada. Here, we ask a different question: what aspects of a species' life history increase its susceptibility to extinction? There are a few motives for asking this question. On a practical level, John Reynolds (2003), of Simon Fraser University, has pointed out that because the money available for conservation programs is very limited, having some easily measurable life-history trait, or set of traits, would help managers determine which species should become priorities for recovery. On a more fundamental

level, understanding functional linkages between life history and population growth and extinction is a worthy scientific goal, one likely to result in a variety of unintended benefits.

Andy Purvis of Imperial College and his colleagues have been leaders in research to understand how the biology of different species interacts with human-mediated changes to cause increased extinction risks. Purvis and colleagues (2000) summarized and tested eight hypotheses gathered from the literature. Here we will focus on one of these. As we have seen throughout this chapter, there are a variety of trade-offs associated with reproduction, and many life-history traits appear to be able to be classified into groupings, representing different strategies (this will be explored more fully later in the chapter). One of the initial hypotheses about extinction risk has been that species that have "slow" life histories will be more at risk than those with "fast" life histories. What do we mean by a slow life history? We mean species that have slow growth rates, reach sexual maturity only late in life, breed infrequently and in small numbers, and have similar life-history traits. Purvis and colleagues tested this hypothesis by collecting these life-history traits from previously published studies for Carnivora and Primate mammals. Measures of extinction risk were also collected from the literature, specifically the International Union for the Conservation of Nature and Natural Resources Red List.

For the carnivores, extinction risk increased with gestation length and age of sexual maturity, supporting the "slow life history" hypothesis. However, these traits were not related to extinction risk in primates. For primates, increased size rather than species-specific life-history traits influenced extinction risk. Purvis and colleagues suggest that primates actually do not exhibit substantial variation in life history independent of size, and thus they question the meaning of that particular result. Purvis and colleagues also present substantial data to show that it is not just size and life-history that influence extinction risk, but that other factors such as the geographical range of a species (larger reduces risk), trophic level (higher increases risk), and population density (larger decreases risk) are also important. You may recognize that many of these factors are likely correlated, for example high rates of reproduction likely lead to higher population densities, and due to energetic trade-offs, small body size. Their study highlights that biology matters when it comes to extinction. Although the results of their study may not seem particularly surprising, never before have these ideas been so rigorously tested and explored. Having a degree of certainty in the validity of scientific ideas and conclusions is critical to the ability of ecologists to provide useful information and guidance to policy makers.

The importance of recognizing the inherent interspecific variation in extinction risk can be seen in another paper by Purvis and colleagues (Cardillo et al., 2004). In this study, they build upon the model they developed to predict extinction risk for Carnivora in the previously described study (Purvis et al. 2000). However, this time they also included predicted changes to the population densities of people in Africa as a case study. To do this, they first added the variable of current human population densities to their model, allowing them to include both biological (e.g., life history, geographic range, etc.) and a surrogate for human-mediated disturbance (population density) into a single model. When they did this, they found that biological factors are better predictors of extinction risk than is human population density alone. This finding is most pronounced in areas of high population density, where the biology of the species explains over 80% of the variation in extinction risks! In other words, to predict which species are at risk for extinction in areas of high human densities, you need to understand the basic biology of the local species.

In a nice addition to their study, they then changed their measures of population density to demographic projections extending to 2030. By doing this, they were able to predict which species will become at risk, or will increase their level of risk. Such a predictive approach to conservation biology has great potential to help managers respond to conservation needs before they happen, rather than continue in a state of repair. The work by Purvis and his colleagues is a great example of how ecology can be used to address real problems of local and global concern.

Figure 9.18   These species are all at risk of extinction. Species with "slow" life histories, and species that live in or on endangered species, are at increased risk of extinction.

The link between life history and extinction risk is not limited to life on land, but also holds for the chondrichthyans (sharks, rays, chimaeras) of the oceans. Nicholas Dulvy, of Simon Fraser University, is a leader in understanding the linkages among population dynamics, life histories, and conservation biology of these always interesting groups of organisms. In a recent review, Dulvy and Forrest (2010) found there was a significant negative relationship between the body length of a shark species and its population growth. Underlying this are a number of familiar life-history trade-offs: smaller species reproduce earlier and die younger than larger species. These life-history characteristics make smaller sharks generally more resilient to fishing pressures than larger species (Dulvy and Forrest 2010). It may thus be of little surprise that the large pelagic sharks of the open ocean are the most threatened (Dulvy and Forrest 2010).

Although the public generally sees images of these large carnivores and primates in the media, they represent just a small fraction of the species on the planet, and only a segment of the species at risk of extinction. Many species are dependent upon others for survival, such as butterfly larvae that feed on only a few plant species, and host-specific parasites. What happens to the butterfly or parasite if its only host species goes extinct? Unless it is immediately able to expand the breadth of its niche to include other hosts, it, too, is doomed. As a result, species that have very specific niche requirements, dependent upon other species, are exposed to increased extinction risk. An international team of researchers, including Heather Proctor of the University of Alberta, decided to determine whether the potential for these "species coextinctions"

were of sufficient magnitude to warrant concern (Koh et al. 2004). To address this question, the research team developed a model that calculated the probability of a species going extinct if its host went extinct. To make these numbers meaningful, they compiled information from the literature describing the host-specificity of these "affiliate" species. The model then weighted both the probability of the host going extinct (as some species are more at risk than others), and whether the affiliate had multiple possible hosts. In their database, they had records of nearly 400 host extinctions of plants, fish, birds, and mammals. Their model estimates that around 200 extinctions of affiliate species such as beetles, mites, butterflies, and monogeneans (flukes) were unreported. For the nearly 8,500 host species that are currently endangered, their model estimates that there are another 6,000 affiliate species at risk! In short, their research clearly indicates that aspects of a species' niche, in this case host-specificity, can contribute to a species' risk of extinction.

Although this talk of extinction is often disheartening, particularly when we realize how many species are overlooked by scientists and the media, it is also very important. Extinctions are real, and are happening at an extremely high rate. If we wish to reduce these rates, at least in cases where humans are contributing to the risk, it is essential that we understand how human disturbances and species' biology interact. Work by ecologists studying life histories and niches can augment governmental protections and recovery programs, providing our society with the greatest hope of reducing the permanent ecological and evolutionary changes associated with extinctions.

Genetic Control of Life History

Variation in life-history traits, such as the relationship between adult and juvenile survival, can be due to differences in both the ecological and the environmental conditions faced by individuals and populations. However, this environmentally induced variation can only influence evolution if there is also a genetic, and heritable, component to life-history variation among individuals within and between populations (chapter 4). David Innes, of Memorial University of Newfoundland, has published extensively on one of the most fundamental aspects of life history: sexual versus asexual reproduction. As you will see, his work has clearly shown that aspects of life history can be influenced by both environmental and genetic factors.

Daphnia pulex (fig. 9.19) is a small crustacean commonly referred to as a water flea (Crustacea: Cladocera) that is common in lakes, ponds, and temporary water bodies throughout the world. The reproductive cycle of *D. pulex* is a bit more complicated than what we find in most vertebrate species. There exist two forms of *D. pulex*: the first is similar to most species of *Daphnia* and reproduces by *cyclical*

parthenogenesis. In this form of reproduction, individuals create *diploid* eggs through *mitosis*, rather than producing *haploid* eggs through *meiosis*, as is the norm for vertebrates. The diploid eggs develop into offspring, resulting in genetic clones of the mother water flea. Since these offspring are clones of their mom, they must be all be females, right? No. *D. pulex* has environmental sex determination, with the eggs developing into females at low population density and males at high population density. As a result, a single female is able to produce genetically identical males and females! Occasionally, these females will undergo meiosis, producing haploid diapausing (resting) eggs that require fertilization by the males to develop. However, a second form of *D. pulex* also exists in which individuals reproduce only through *obligate* parthenogenesis. These clones produce diapausing eggs through mitosis, not meiosis, and thus have no haploid aspect to their life cycle. In a very elegant study, David Innes and his former postdoctoral supervisor, Paul Hebert (chapter 4; formerly at the University of Windsor) exploited this variation in life history to explore the genetic basis of obligate parthenogenesis in *D. pulex* (Innes and Hebert 1988).

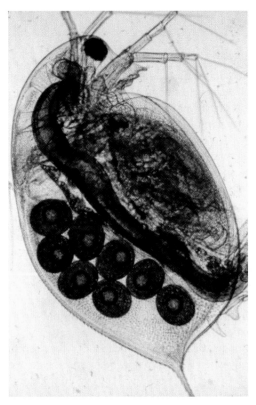

Figure 9.19 Different forms of *Daphnia pulex* can be either sexually reproducing or obligately parthenogenetic. This female is developing a brood of parthenogenetic eggs.

Innes and Hebert grew cultures of several clones collected from natural populations throughout Ontario, Illinois, Michigan, and Iowa. They then took males from an obligately parthenogenetic clone and mated them with females from a cyclically parthenogenetic clone. In total, they conducted 19 such crosses, resulting in 102 hybrid clones. Innes and Hebert collected the diapausing eggs that were produced by 10 of these hybrids. Why the focus on the diapausing eggs? If you recall, the diapausing eggs are produced through mitosis for the clones that use obligate parthenogenesis and meiosis for the clones that use cyclical parthenogenesis. By looking at protein variations of the individuals that emerged from the diapausing eggs, Innes and Hebert were able to infer the mode of reproduction. Those eggs derived from mitosis would have uniform protein patterns, indicating obligate parthenogenesis, while those derived from meiosis would show variation, indicating cyclical parthenogenesis. What they found was quite striking: four hybrids reproduced by obligate parthenogenesis like their father, while six hybrids reproduced by cyclical parthenogenesis like their mother. In other words, although all of the mothers reproduced by cyclical parthenogenesis at the start of the experiment, mating with the males derived from obligate parthenogenesis causes a switch in reproductive behaviour in approximately ½ of the hybrids!

Clearly the males contained genes that suppressed meiosis, indicating this extremely fundamental aspect of life history may be under relatively simple genetic control, at least in this species. A related study with the cyclical parthenogens

explored variation in the ability to produce males under high levels of crowding (Innes and Dunbrack 1993). Over ⅓ of the clones they tested lacked this ability to produce males. When male-producing lines were mated with themselves, nearly all offspring could also produce males. However, when male-producing lines were mated with non–male-producing females, over 50% of the outcrossed progeny were unable to produce males. Once again, these results are strongly suggestive of basic genetic control of this aspect of reproduction in *D. pulex*.

There are numerous examples from a diverse array of other plant, bacterial, and animal species, also showing genetic influences on life history. Because of the heritability of life-history traits, natural selection can result in evolution, altering the basic parameters of how a species lives, grows, and reproduces. Ecology and evolution are linked, and this is rarely made more clear than in the study of life histories.

As we explored the relationship between offspring size and number and the influence of mortality on the timing of maturation and reproductive effort, we have accumulated a large body of information on life histories. We have also seen that aspects of life history are genetically variable within a species, and subject to selection and evolution. Let's step back now and try to organize that information to make it easier to think about life-history variation in nature.

CONCEPT 9.1 REVIEW

1. Why did Westoby, Leishman, and Lord (1996) include five floras on three continents in their study?
2. What is a main difference between the study by Bertschy and Fox (1999) and that of Gunderson (1997)?
3. What are the evolutionary implications of life-history traits that are, or are not, influenced by an individual's genotype?

9.2 Life-History Classification

The great diversity of life histories observed in nature can be classified on the basis of a few common characteristics. While classification systems never capture the full diversity of nature, they make working with the often bewildering variety of nature much easier. It is important to bear in mind when using classification systems, however, that they are an abstraction from nature and that most species fall somewhere in between the extreme types. Thus these classification schemes should be used to organize the variety that exists in nature, and not to assign a classification to every species.

r and K Selection

One of the earliest attempts to organize information on the great variety of life histories that occur among species was under the heading of *r* and K selection (MacArthur and Wilson

1967). The terms *r* and K selection refer to parameters of population growth models that will be described in depth in chapter 12, and only briefly here. *r* represents a measure of population growth rate, with larger values corresponding to populations that are growing rapidly. K represents the maximum sustainable size of a population, such that habitats with larger K values could contain larger populations than areas with smaller K values. Robert MacArthur and E. O. Wilson adopted these population growth parameters as ways of describing variation in life histories among species. They suggest that for some species, selection will favour those life-history traits that cause increases in growth rates, so called "*r*-selected" species. MacArthur and Wilson suggested that *r* selection would be strongest in species often colonizing new or disturbed habitats, with high levels of disturbance leading to ongoing *r* selection. In contrast, they proposed that in other species, selection will act upon life-history traits important for when habitats are "full" of a population. These "K-selected" species are likely to have life-history traits that favour efficient utilization of resources such as food and nutrients, rather than maximizing growth rates. They envisioned that K selection would be most prominent in those situations where species populations are near the "carrying capacity" of the habitat much of the time.

Eric Pianka (1970, 1972) developed the concept of *r* and K selection further in two important papers. Pianka pointed out that *r* selection and K selection are the endpoints on a continuous distribution and that most organisms are subject to forms of selection somewhere in between these extremes. In addition, he correlated *r* and K selection with attributes of the environment and of populations. He also listed the population characteristics that each form of selection favours. Following MacArthur and Wilson, Pianka predicted that while *r* selection should be characteristic of variable or unpredictable environments, fairly constant or predictable environments should create conditions for K selection. Figure 9.20 summarizes Pianka's proposed contrast in population characteristics favoured by *r* versus K selection.

Pianka's detailed analysis clarified the sharp contrast between the two selective extremes represented by *r* and K selection by revealing biological details. The most fundamental contrasts are of course between potential growth rates, *r*, which should be highest in *r*-selected species, and competitive ability, which should be highest among K-selected species. In addition, according to Pianka, development should be rapid under *r* selection and relatively slow under K selection. Meanwhile, early reproduction and smaller body size will be favoured by *r* selection, while K selection favours later reproduction and larger body size. Pianka predicted that reproduction under *r* selection will tend toward a single reproductive event in which many small offspring are produced. This type of reproduction, which is called **semelparity**, occurs in organisms such as annual weeds and salmon. In contrast, K selection should favour repeated reproduction, or **iteroparity**, of fewer larger offspring. Iteroparity, which spaces out reproduction over several reproductive periods during an organism's lifetime, is the type of reproduction seen in most perennial plants and most vertebrate animals. Pianka's contrast puts a name on and fleshes out the comparison we developed in the Ecology In Action example in this chapter, where "small and fast organisms," analogous to *r*-selected species, were less likely to be at an extinction risk than ones that were "large and slow," analogous to K-selected species (fig. 9.21).

Figure 9.21   The deer mouse and the African elephant represent extremes among mammals of *r* versus K selection.

Characteristics favoured by *r* versus K selection		
Population attribute	***r* selection**	**K selection**
Potential of population growth rate, *r*	High	Low
Competitive ability	Not strongly favoured	Highly favoured
Development	Rapid	Slow
Reproduction	Early	Late
Body size	Small	Large
Reproduction	Single, semelparity	Repeated, iteroparity
Offspring	Many, small	Few, large

Source: After Pianka 1970.

Figure 9.20

The ideas of *r* and *K* selection helped greatly as ecologists and evolutionary biologists attempted to think more systematically about life-history variation and its evolution. However, ecologists who found that the dichotomy of *r* versus *K* did not include a great deal of known variation in life histories have proposed alternative classifications.

Plant Life Histories

r and *K* strategies are a useful shorthand for talking about groups of correlated life-history traits for all taxa. However, some organisms, such as plants, may be better described using a different shorthand. Phil Grime (1977, 1979) proposed that variation in environmental conditions has led to the development of distinctive strategies or life histories among plants. The two variables that he selected as most important in exerting selective pressure on plants were the intensity of disturbance and abiotic stress. Grime also argues that competition can exert strong pressures on plants, and that competition should be relatively more important when stress and disturbances are low. Grime contrasted four extreme environmental types, which he characterized by combinations of disturbance intensity and stress intensity. Four environmental extremes envisioned by Grime were: (1) low disturbance–low stress, (2) low disturbance–high stress, (3) high disturbance–low stress, and (4) high disturbance–high stress. Drawing on his extensive knowledge of plant biology, Grime suggested that plants occupy three of his theoretical environments, but that there is no viable strategy among plants for the fourth environmental combination, high disturbance–high stress.

Grime next described plant strategies, or life histories, that match the requirements of the remaining three environments. His strategies were ruderal, stress-tolerant, and competitive (fig. 9.22). **Ruderals** are plants that live in highly disturbed habitats and that may depend on disturbance to persist in the face of potential competition from other plants. Grime summarized several characteristics of ruderals that allow them to persist in habitats experiencing frequent and intense **disturbance**, which he defined as any mechanisms or processes that limit plants by destroying plant biomass. One of the characteristics of ruderals is their capacity to grow rapidly and produce seeds during relatively short periods between successive disturbances. This capacity alone would favour persistence of ruderals in the face of frequent disturbance. However, ruderals also invest a large proportion of their biomass in reproduction, producing large numbers of seeds that are capable of dispersing to new habitats made available by disturbance. The term ruderal is sometimes used synonymously with the term "weed." Animals that are associated with disturbance, have high reproductive rates, and are good colonists, are also sometimes referred to as ruderals.

Grime (1977) began his discussion of the second type of plant life history, stress-tolerant, with a definition of **stress** as ". . . external constraints which limit the rate of dry matter production of all or part of the vegetation." In other words, stress is induced by environmental conditions that limit the growth of all or part of the vegetation. What environmental conditions might create such constraints? Our discussions in

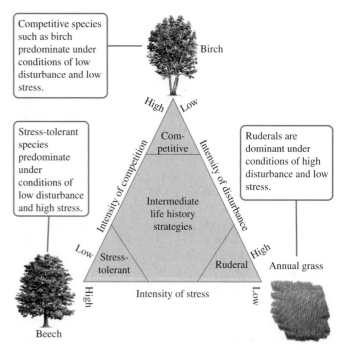

Figure 9.22 Grime's classification of plant life-history strategies (after Grime 1979).

chapters 5, 6, and 7, where we considered temperature, water, and energy and nutrient relations, provide several suggestions. Stress is the result of extreme temperatures, high or low; extreme hydrologic conditions, too little or too much water; or too much or too little light or nutrients. Because different species are adapted to different environmental conditions, the absolute levels of light, water, temperature, and so forth that constitute stress will vary from species to species. In addition, conditions that induce stress will vary from biome to biome. For instance, the amount of precipitation leading to drought stress is different in rain forest and desert, or the minimum temperatures inducing thermal stress are different in tropical forest compared to boreal forest.

The important point that Grime made, however, was that in every biome, some species are more tolerant to the environmental extremes that occur than other species. These are the species that he referred to as "stress-tolerant." Stress-tolerant plants are those that live under conditions of high stress but low disturbance. Grime proposed that, in general, stress-tolerant plants grow slowly; are evergreen; conserve fixed carbon, nutrients, and water; and are adept at exploiting temporary favourable conditions. In addition, stress-tolerant plants are often unpalatable to most herbivores. Because stress-tolerant species endure some of the most difficult conditions a particular environment has to offer, they are there to take advantage of infrequent favourable periods for growth and reproduction.

The third plant strategy proposed by Grime is a competitive life history. In Grime's classification, competitive plants occupy environments where disturbance intensity is low and the intensity of stress is also low. Under conditions of low stress and low disturbance, plants have the potential to grow

well. As they do so, however, they eventually compete with each other for resources, such as light, water, nutrients, and space. Grime's model predicts that the plants living under such circumstances will be selected for strong competitive abilities.

In presenting the initial model, we have emphasized the extreme strategies that represent each of the corners of "Grime's triangle." However, Grime recognized that life histories in nature will fall along a continuum of these axes, and thus the middle of the triangle represents intermediate plant strategies.

How does Grime's system of classification compare with the *r* and *K* selection contrast proposed by MacArthur and Wilson and Pianka? Grime proposed that *r* selection corresponds to his ruderal strategy of life history, while *K* selection corresponds to the stress-tolerant end of his classification. Meanwhile, he placed the competitive life-history category in a position intermediate between the extremes represented by *r* selection and *K* selection. However, while attempting this reconciliation of the two classifications, Grime suggested that a linear arrangement of life histories with *r* selection and *K* selection occupying the extremes fails to capture the full variation shown by organisms. He suggested that more dimensions are needed and, of course, Grime's triangular arrangement (fig. 9.22) adds another dimension. The factors varying along the edges of Grime's triangle are intensity of disturbance, stress, and competition. Other ecologists have

also recognized the need for more dimensions in representing life-history diversity.

Opportunistic, Equilibrium, and Periodic Life Histories

In a review of life-history patterns among fish, Kirk Winemiller and Kenneth Rose (1992) proposed a classification of life histories based on some of the aspects of population dynamics. They drew particular attention to survivorship especially among juveniles, fecundity or number of offspring produced, and generation time or age at maturity.

Winemiller and Rose start with the concept of trade-offs. Their trade-offs are among fecundity, survivorship, and age at reproductive maturity. Using variation in fish life histories as a model, Winemiller and Rose proposed that life histories should lie on a semitriangular surface as shown in figure 9.23. They called the three endpoints on their surface "opportunistic," "equilibrium," and "periodic" life histories. The opportunistic strategy, by combining low juvenile survival, low numbers of offspring, and early reproductive maturity, maximizes colonizing ability across environments that vary unpredictably in time or space. It is important to keep in mind, however, that while the absolute reproductive output of opportunistic species may be low, the percentage of their energy budget allocated to reproduction is high. Winemiller and Rose's equilibrium strategy combines high

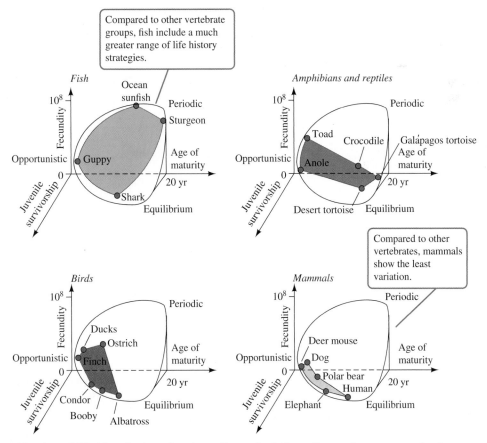

Figure 9.23   Classification of life histories based on juvenile survival, fecundity, and age at reproductive maturity (after Winemiller and Rose 1992).

juvenile survival, low numbers of offspring, and late reproductive maturity. Finally, the periodic strategy combines low juvenile survival, high numbers of offspring, and late maturity. Among fish, periodic species tend to be large and produce numerous small offspring. By producing large numbers of offspring over a long life span, periodic species can take advantage of infrequent periods when conditions are favourable for reproduction.

It is difficult to map the exact correspondence of Winemiller and Rose's classification of life-history strategies to either the r–K continuum of MacArthur and Wilson and Pianka or the triangular classification of plant life histories developed by Grime. For instance, opportunistic species share characteristics with r-selected and ruderal species. However, opportunistic species differ from the typical r-selected species because they tend to produce small clutches of offspring. The equilibrium strategy, which combines production of high juvenile survival, low numbers of offspring, and late reproductive maturity, approaches the characteristics of typical K-selected species. Winemiller and Rose point out, however, that many fish classified as "equilibrium" are small, while typically K-selected species tend toward large body size (see fig. 9.21). Periodic species are not captured by the linear r to K selection gradient. Meanwhile, the periodic and equilibrium species in Winemiller and Rose's classification share some characteristics with Grime's stress-tolerant and competitive species, but differ in other characteristics.

Thus far in this review of systems for life-history classification, we have focused on just three of the many that have been proposed. Even with just these three, however, translation from one classification to another is difficult. What are the sources of these differences in perspective? One of the

sources is that different ecologists have worked with different groups of organisms. While MacArthur and Wilson's system was built after years of work on birds and insects, respectively, Pianka had worked mainly with lizards. Grime's classification was built on, and intended for, plants. Finally, the perspective of Winemiller and Rose was influenced substantially by their work with fish. Because these ecologists worked with such different groups of organisms, it is not surprising that their classifications of life histories do not overlay precisely.

However, it may be that the analysis by Winemiller and Rose has laid the foundation for a more general theory of life histories. By basing their classification system on some of the most basic aspects of population ecology, Winemiller and Rose (1992) established a common currency for representing and analyzing life-history information for any organism. By plotting life-history variation among vertebrate groups on the same axes using the same variables, figure 9.24 demonstrates differences in the amount of life-history variation between the groups. Notice that fish show the greatest variation and mammals the least, while birds and reptiles and amphibians include intermediate levels of variation.

Lifetime Reproductive Effort and Relative Offspring Size: Two Central Variables?

In response to the various attempts to classify life histories, Eric Charnov, with Robin Warne and Melanie Moses, (Charnov 2002, Charnov et al. 2007) developed a new approach to life-history classification. In his most recent attempts at life-history classification, Charnov has focused his attention on mammals, altricial birds, and lizards. His goal has been to develop a

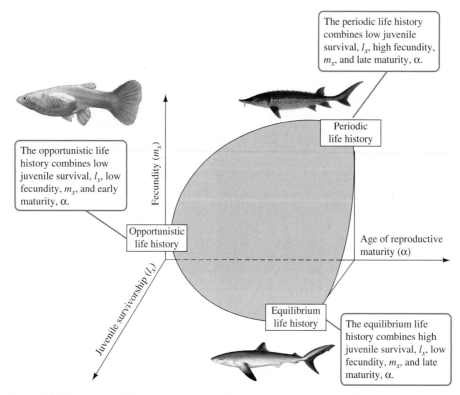

The periodic life history combines low juvenile survival, l_x, high fecundity, m_x, and late maturity, α.

The opportunistic life history combines low juvenile survival, l_x, low fecundity, m_x, and early maturity, α.

Fecundity (m_x)

Juvenile survivorship (l_x)

Age of reproductive maturity (α)

Opportunistic life history

Periodic life history

Equilibrium life history

The equilibrium life history combines high juvenile survival, l_x, low fecundity, m_x, and late maturity, α.

Figure 9.24 Variation in life histories within vertebrate animals (after Winemiller 1992).

classification free of the influences of size and time that would facilitate the exploration of life-history variation within and among groups of closely related taxa. Why remove the influences of size and time? Our discussion of *r* and K selection underscored the relationship between size of organisms and timing of life-history features. The influences of size and timing are responsible for many of the obvious life-history differences among species of closely related taxa, for instance, the differences among large and small mammal species, such as between a deer mouse and an African elephant. By removing size and time effects, we may be able to more clearly detect life-history differences among evolutionary lineages.

Charnov's approach was to take a few key life-history features and convert them to dimensionless numbers. One of his variables was relative size of offspring. He created this dimensionless variable by dividing the mass of offspring at independence from the parent, I, by the adult mass at first reproduction, m. The result, I/m, is the size of offspring expressed as a proportion of adult body mass. While it is clear that an elephant is larger at independence than is a mouse at the same life stage, Charnov's approach allows us to determine whether one is relatively larger than the other. A young, newly independent mouse may represent as large a proportion of its parent's mass as a young elephant. The second measure was proportion of adult body mass allocated to reproduction per unit time, C, multiplied by the adult life span, E, which gives us an estimate of the fraction of adult body mass allocated to reproduction over a life span. As we have seen, higher reproductive effort is associated with shorter adult life span, so Charnov reasoned their product might be similar for closely related taxa. Charnov chose these two dimensionless numbers (I/m and C•E) for two particular reasons. First, R_0, the net reproductive rate, is a measure of an individual's fitness in populations that are not growing. Second, R_0 can be rewritten solely in terms of these two numbers and the chance of surviving to adulthood.

For his initial classification of life histories, Charnov chose three groups of well-studied organisms: mammals, lizards, and altricial birds. Altricial birds are those birds, ranging from sparrows to eagles, that are born helpless and depend entirely on parental care to mature to independence. One of the striking results of using Charnov's dimensionless analysis is that while there is little variation within mammals, lizards, or birds, there are substantial differences among these groups of animals. Figure 9.25 shows that the birds have the highest I/m (essentially 1, since they raise their young to adult size) and C•E values. In contrast, lizards and mammals share the *same* C•E value but differ a lot in I/m (0.1 vs. 0.3).

Previous classifications of life histories have revealed substantial variation within taxa, such as mammals and fish (see fig. 9.24). In contrast, Charnov's classification, by removing the influences of time and size, allows us to see the great similarities within these groups and reveals the substantial differences among them. Figure 9.26 shows the results of plotting the average values of I/m and C•E for mammals, lizards, and altricial birds. The striking separation of these taxa within the two dimensional plane of the graph suggests that mammals, lizards, and birds have life histories that are

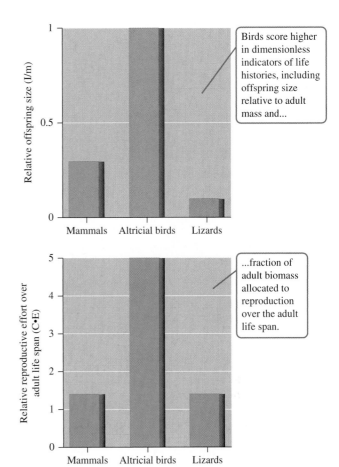

Figure 9.25 Comparison of life-history features of mammals, altricial birds, and lizards (data from Charnov 2002, Charnov et al. 2007).

fundamentally different. But notice that lizards and mammals do not differ in the value of C•E, only I/m.

This analysis is only the beginning, however, since it raises many unanswered questions. Charnov wonders where bats will appear in his life-history plane, since they raise their offspring to nearly adult size. He also raises a question about precocial birds, such as pheasants and quail, whose offspring are independent at a very small size. In terms of life history, will bats be more like altricial birds, while precocial birds are more like mammals? Then there are the hundreds of thousands of vascular plants to consider.

The knowledge of species' life histories revealed by the studies of life-history ecologists has produced a subdiscipline of ecology rich in both theory and biological detail. In the challenges that lie ahead as we work to conserve endangered species, both theory and detailed knowledge of the life histories of individual species will be important. For instance, life-history information is playing a key role in the conservation of riparian forests across western North America.

In this chapter we have seen how simple energetic trade-offs can produce life-history strategies. We have also seen how some ecological factors tend to be associated with certain life-history strategies, while other conditions will favour alternative strategies. In chapters 5–7 we learned that species

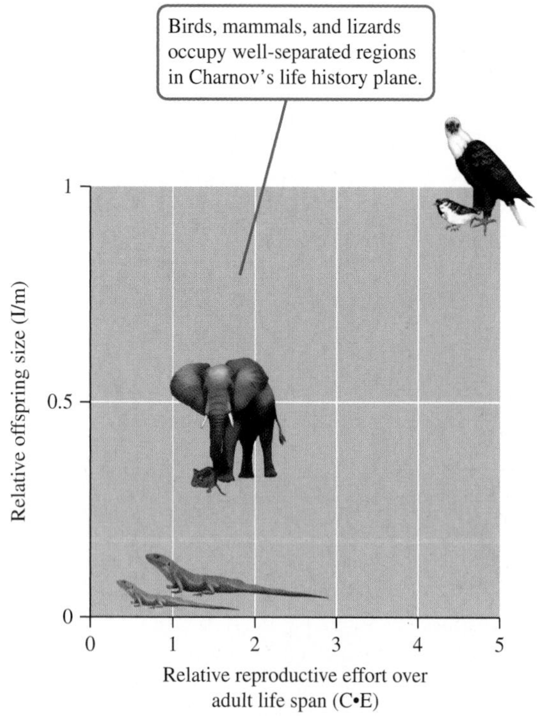

Birds, mammals, and lizards occupy well-separated regions in Charnov's life history plane.

Figure 9.26 A planar classification of lizard, mammal, and altricial bird life histories based on two numbers, I/m and C•E, reveals much more variation between than within taxa, although lizards and mammals share the same average C•E value (data from Charnov 2002, Charnov et al. 2007).

vary greatly in their ability to cope with diverse energetic and environmental challenges, and that this too was governed by the theory of allocation. In the next section we will begin to put the puzzle together, and describe one of the most important concepts in ecology, the *niche*.

CONCEPT 9.2 REVIEW

1. Mart Gross demonstrated that successful mating behaviours can be influenced by life-history traits, such as size at sexual maturity. How will selection favour or disfavour the jack and hooknose life histories if anglers remove large numbers of hooknose males?

2. If a concept, such as *r* and *K* selection, does not fully represent the richness of life-history variation among species, can it still be valuable to science?

3. Where would you place the following plant species in Grime's and in Winemiller and Rose's classifications of life histories? The plant species lives in an environment where it has access to plenty of water and nutrients, but is subject to disturbance by flooding and wind. An average individual produces several million seeds per year and may live several centuries. However, ideal conditions for reproduction by the species occurs only once or twice per decade.

Fundamental and Realized Niches

The fundamental niche reflects the environmental requirements of species, while the realized niche also includes interactions with other species. In chapters 5–8, we discussed how individual factors such as temperature, water availability, and food resources can have significant implications for the evolution and ecology of organisms. Although species vary greatly in their adaptations to these environmental factors, one commonality is that most adaptations require energy. A common theme through the chapters of section II has been the *principle of allocation*, in which allocation of energy to one aspect of the energy budget means there is less energy to allocate for other uses. This idea is a unifying concept in ecology, and is never more apparent than in discussions of life histories and the niche.

The word "niche" has been in use a long time. Its earliest and most basic meaning was that of a recessed place in a wall where one could set or display items. For the last century, however, ecologists have given a broader meaning to the word. To the ecologist, the niche summarizes the factors that influence the growth, survival, and reproduction of a species. If conditions in a given location fall outside of the conditions of even a single dimension of the niche, the species will be unable to persist.

The niche concept was developed independently by Joseph Grinnell (1917, 1924) and Charles Elton (1927), who use the term *niche* in slightly different ways. In his early writings, Grinnell's idea of the niche focused on the influences of the physical environment, while Elton's earliest concept included both biological interactions and abiotic factors. However their thinking and emphasis may have differed, it is clear that the views of these two researchers had much in common and that our present concept of the niche rests squarely on their pioneering work.

It was G. Evelyn Hutchinson (1957) who crystallized the niche concept, stimulating the work of a generation of ecologists. In his seminal paper entitled simply, "Concluding Remarks," Hutchinson defined the niche as an *n-dimensional hypervolume*, where *n* equals the number of environmental factors important to the survival and reproduction of a species. Hutchinson called this hypervolume, which specifies the values of the *n* environmental factors permitting a species to survive and reproduce, the **fundamental niche** of the species (fig. 9.27). The fundamental niche defines the physical conditions under which a species might live, in the absence of interactions with other species. This should sound vaguely familiar, as this is simply a multivariate extension of the range of tolerance that was discussed in chapter 5. In chapter 5, we discussed how all organisms will have a range of environmental conditions (e.g., temperature) in which they perform well, poorly, or not at all. Each axis of the *Hutchinsonion* niche is made of different environmental parameters, each with its own range of tolerance. The niche itself consists of the hypervolume, which is defined by the overlapping tolerance zones of each axis (fig. 9.27). Importantly, the niche is *not* a

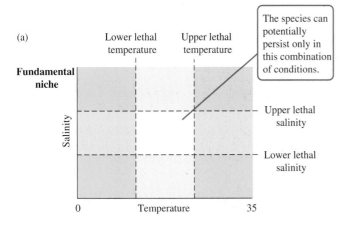

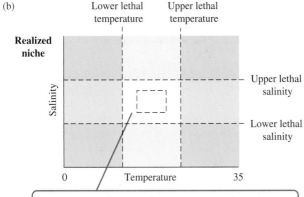

Figure 9.27 Two dimensions of a (*a*) fundamental niche, and (*b*) realized niche of a hypothetical species. The niches of most species will be defined by a larger number of dimensions.

physical location, but instead it is an abstract representation of the environmental conditions necessary for a species to potentially survive. In this regard, the ecological use of the word *niche* has moved away from its original meaning as a hole in a wall. As will be shown in later chapters, understanding the fundamental niche of a species can provide great insight into the habitats and locations one may find a species. Incorporating the knowledge with information about life-history traits can provide further information about not only where a species may live, but whether it will thrive or wither away.

Hutchinson's contribution to the niche concept extends beyond the fundamental (i.e., Hutchinsonian) niche. Hutchinson recognized that interactions among species, such as competition, may restrict the environments in which a species actually can persist, and he referred to these more restricted conditions as the **realized niche**. This too makes sense given our discussion of the range-of-tolerance concept in chapter 5. Although species may be able to survive across a broad range of temperatures (or another environmental factor), its performance is likely greatest only in a narrow subset of this range. It is here where it can compete most

effectively, while at the edge of its thermal range it is more likely to be displaced. As a result, the fundamental niche represents the maximal niche size of an organism, while the realized niche will be smaller.

Do you think it is possible to completely measure Hutchinson's *n*−dimensional hypervolume niche for any species? Probably not, since there are so many environmental factors that potentially influence fitness. Fortunately, it appears that niches are determined mostly by a few environmental factors, and so ecologists are able to apply a simplified version of Hutchinson's comprehensive concept.

The Feeding Niches of Galápagos Finches

As we saw in chapter 7, availability of suitable food significantly affects the evolution, survival, and reproduction of many animals. Among the most well-studied animals are the Galápagos finches. Because the kinds of food used by birds is largely reflected by the form of their beaks, Peter Grant (1986) and his colleagues were able to represent the feeding niches of Galápagos finches by measuring their beak morphology. For instance, differences in beak size among small, medium, and large ground finches translate directly into differences in diet. The large ground finch, *Geospiza magnirostris*, eats larger seeds; the medium ground finch, *G. fortis*, eats medium-sized seeds; while the small ground finch, *G. fuliginosa*, eats small seeds (fig. 9.28).

The size of seeds that can be eaten by Galápagos finches can be estimated by simply measuring the depths

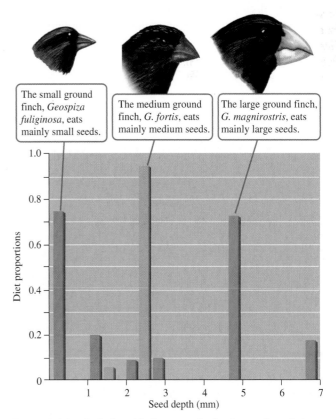

Figure 9.28 Relationship between body size and seed size in Galápagos finch species (data from Grant 1986).

of their beaks. Studies of seed use by *G. fortis* on Daphne Major showed clearly that even within species, beak size affects the composition of the diet. Within this population, individuals with the deepest beaks fed on the hardest seeds, while individuals with the smallest beaks fed on the softest seeds (fig. 9.29).

These studies show that beak size provides significant insights into the feeding biology of Galápagos ground finches. Since food is the major determinant of survival and reproduction among these birds, beak morphology gives us a very good picture of their niches. However, the niches of other kinds of organisms are determined by entirely different environmental factors. Let's consider the niche of a dominant species in salt marshes.

The importance of beak size to seed use was also demonstrated by the effects of a 1977 drought on the *G. fortis* population of Daphne Major. During the drought, mortality did not fall equally on all segments of the population. As seeds were depleted, the birds ate the smallest and softest seeds first, leaving the largest and toughest seeds (fig. 9.30). In other words, following the drought not only were seeds in short supply, the remaining seeds were also tougher to crack. Because they could not crack the remaining seeds, mortality fell most heavily on smaller birds with smaller beaks. Consequently, at the end of the drought, the *G. fortis* population on Daphne Major was dominated by larger individuals that had survived by feeding on hard seeds (fig. 9.31).

The Habitat Niche of a Salt Marsh Grass

Biologists discovered *Spartina anglica* approximately one century ago, as a new species produced by **allopolyploidy**

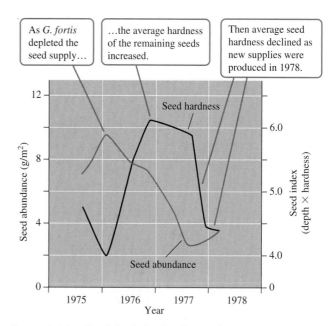

Figure 9.30   Seed depletion by the medium ground finch, *Geospiza fortis,* and average seed hardness (data from Grant 1986).

(fig. 9.32). Allopolyploidy is a process of speciation initiated by hybridization of two different species. *S. anglica* arose initially as a cross between *S. maritima,* a European species, and *S. alterniflora,* a North American species. At least one of these hybrid plants later doubled its chromosome number, making it capable of sexual reproduction, and produced a new species: *S. anglica.* From its centre of origin in Lymington,

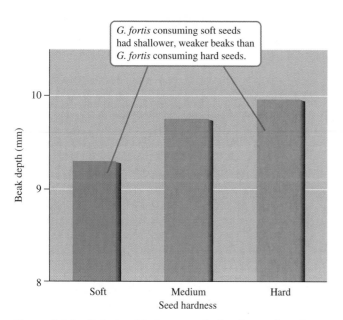

Figure 9.29   Relationship between the hardness of seeds eaten by medium ground finches, *Geospiza fortis,* and beak depth (data from Boag and Grant 1984b).

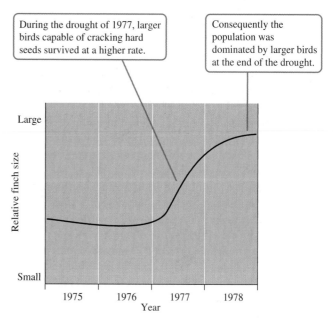

Figure 9.31   Selection for larger size among medium ground finches, *Geospiza fortis,* during a drought on the island of Daphne Major (data from Grant 1986).

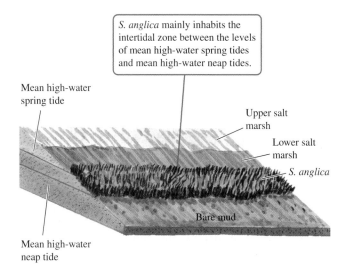

Figure 9.32   The salt marsh grass *Spartina anglica* originated on the coast of England as a hybrid of European and North American species of salt marsh grasses and has since spread to salt marshes in many parts of the world.

S. anglica mainly inhabits the intertidal zone between the levels of mean high-water spring tides and mean high-water neap tides.

Mean high-water spring tide

Upper salt marsh

Lower salt marsh

S. anglica

Bare mud

Mean high-water neap tide

Figure 9.33   The niche of *Spartina anglica* is related to tidal fluctuations.

Hampshire, England, *S. anglica* spread northward along the coasts of the British Isles. During this same period, it colonized the coast of France and was widely planted elsewhere in northwest Europe as well as along the coasts of New Zealand, Australia, and China. The Chinese population of this salt marsh grass, established from only 21 plants in 1963, grew to cover 36,000 ha by 1980. *S. anglica* is extensively planted for stabilizing mud-flats because it is more tolerant of periodic inundation and water-saturated soils than most other salt marsh plants. This environmental tolerance is reflected in the distribution of the plant in northwestern Europe, where it generally inhabits the most seaward zone of any of the salt marsh plants.

The local distribution of *S. anglica* in the British Isles is well predicted by a few physical variables related to the duration and frequency of inundation by tides and waves. The lower and upper intertidal limits of the grass are mainly determined by the magnitude of tidal fluctuations during spring tides. Where tidal fluctuations are greater, both the lower and upper limits are higher up on the shore. However, throughout its British range, the grass generally occupies the intertidal zone between mean high-water *spring tides* and mean high-water *neap tides* (fig. 9.33). Spring tides occur during new and full moons, when the tidal fluctuations are greatest. Neap tides occur during the first and third quarter phases of the moon and result in the smallest amount of tidal variation (see chapter 3). A second factor that determines the local distribution of *S. anglica* is the **fetch** of the estuary. The fetch of a body of water is the longest distance over which wind can blow and is directly related to the maximum size of waves that can be generated by wind. All other factors being equal, larger waves occur on estuaries with greater fetch. The larger the

fetch, the higher *S. anglica* must live in an estuary to avoid disturbance by waves.

The upper limit of *S. anglica*'s distribution within the intertidal zone is also negatively correlated with latitude. In northerly locations within the British Isles, the grass does not occur quite as high in the intertidal zone as it does in the south. What factors might restrict the distribution at northern sites? One factor we should consider is that *S. anglica* is a C_4 plant.

The knowledge of species life histories and the concept of the niche have created subdisciplines of ecology rich in both theory and biological detail. In the challenges that lie ahead as we work to conserve endangered species, both theory and detailed knowledge of the life histories and the limits of a species fundamental niche will be important. For instance, changes in life-history parameters are signalling biological impacts of climate change.

CONCEPT 9.3 REVIEW

1. How do trade-offs influence both the shape of a niche and the form of a species' life-history strategy?
2. Why can't the realized niche be larger than a species' fundamental niche?
3. If niches do not represent actual locations on a map, and instead represent a set of conditions necessary for survival, how could an ecologist measure the niche of a species?

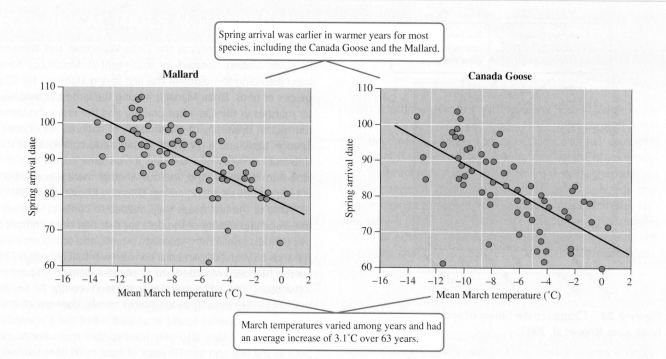

> Spring arrival was earlier in warmer years for most species, including the Canada Goose and the Mallard.

Mallard

Canada Goose

> March temperatures varied among years and had an average increase of 3.1°C over 63 years.

Figure 9.35   Arrival dates of migratory birds is related to temperature at Delta Marsh in Manitoba (data from Murphy-Klassen et al. 2005).

This study by the research team at the University of Manitoba clearly shows how both current temperatures and general background changes can impact phenology. Across 63 years, there was an increase in temperature, associated with an overall earlier arrival of spring migrants. However, within that time period there were warm and cold years, and the actual date of arrival was highly variable. Overall, birds come to Delta Marsh when it warms up, and if the average temperature continues to increase, we will see birds even earlier in the future. That is, of course dependent upon the assumptions that there are not opposite pressures in the wintering range of these species, that their prey species arrive earlier as well, and that their timing of breeding also accelerates. In other words, although at first glance it may appear that seeing birds a bit earlier is a nice thing (who doesn't like to see birds?), it is important to remember that all species are connected to other species through a network of ecological interactions. All cylinders need to be firing in synch for an organism to meet its niche requirements, and as climate changes, the certainty of this synchronization for some species is less clear. In the last example we will discuss how climate change has influenced one other fundamental aspect of life histories, reproduction.

Reproduction

The tufted puffin, *Fratercula cirrhata* (fig. 9.36), breeds only on cliffs and islands of the North Pacific. They are found as far south as California, though the only large breeding colony south of Alaska is on Triangle Island off the coast of British Columbia. This breeding colony is the largest in Canada, and several colony-wide reproductive failures have been

Figure 9.36   A tufted puffin, *Fratercula cirrhata*, on Triangle Island off the Coast of British Columbia.

documented. A team of researchers from Simon Fraser University, University of British Columbia, University of Alberta, and the Canadian Wildlife Service decided to test whether climate change was in part responsible for these reproductive failures of this emblematic species of the North.

The researchers recognized that the factor of potentially greatest importance to the birds was not temperature on the island, but instead, sea-surface temperature (SST) in the area. Why? Puffins are near the top of the food chain, feeding upon fish which themselves feed upon phyto- and zooplankton. Increased SST can influence the growth of these small planktonic species, which the researchers reasoned could have cascading effects on the puffins. To test whether SST was related to breeding success, the authors dug into a

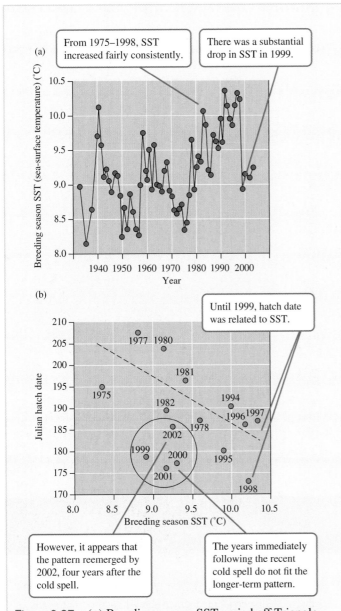

(a)

From 1975–1998, SST increased fairly consistently.

There was a substantial drop in SST in 1999.

(b)

Until 1999, hatch date was related to SST.

1977 1980

1981

1975

1982

1994

1996 1997

1978

2002

1999 2000

1995

2001

1998

However, it appears that the pattern reemerged by 2002, four years after the cold spell.

The years immediately following the recent cold spell do not fit the longer-term pattern.

Figure 9.37 (*a*) Breeding-season SST varied off Triangle Island; (*b*) for much of the record, breeding-season SST was correlated with the hatch date of puffin chicks.

66-year database of SST near the island, and a 28-year database of breeding and fledging success on the island. Since 1940 there has been substantial variation in SST during puffin breeding season (fig. 9.37), with an overall increase of 0.9°C over 66 years. You can notice from figure 9.37 that there was a steady increase in SST from about 1975–1998. From 1999–2002, there was substantial cooling. During the period of warming (1975–1998), there was a significant relationship between SST and the hatch date of chicks (fig. 9.37). However, when the dates from the cooling period were included, there was no overall relationship between SST and hatch date! The research team also found that SST was related to nestling growth rates and overall fledging

success. Both of these factors peaked at intermediate levels of breeding-season SST.

Clearly the picture on puffins is not as clear as in the prior examples, but this complexity is likely what we will find for many other species in natural areas. It appears that within a single year, SST impacts the likelihood of fledging success and the growth rates of the young birds. That this relationship peaks at intermediate values is consistent with what we know about physiological ecology, where most processes have an optimum temperature, or range of temperatures. In this case, the researchers believe it is not the birds specifically that are responding to temperature, but instead they are responding to fish that are responding to plankton. More difficult to understand is the relationship between fledging date and SST, and why those "cool" years do not follow the longer pattern. The researchers believe that the birds have some capacity to manipulate when they breed, but that there is a lag in this response. If you look closely at figure 9.37, you will notice that the hatch dates in 2002 fall right onto the longer-term trend. The researchers suggest it may have taken the birds several years to respond to the large temperature drop that occurred in 1999. They point out that although it appears that temperature is playing a role in the breeding success, and failure, of this species, there remain many unanswered questions.

The issue of lags in response is important, and it suggests that some phenological shifts are less likely to change rapidly than others. So far, most of the changes we have discussed regarding phenology and climate change have appeared to be behavioural and physiological changes. Can climate change cause evolutionary changes in populations, which then influence their life history? Or, does climate change happen at a speed much greater than natural selection, meaning that only those species that are phenotypically plastic are able to cope with the changing environment? A team of researchers from McGill University, University of Alberta, and the Université du Québec à Rimouski decided to test these questions (Réale et al. 2003; Berteaux et al. 2004).

The North American red squirrel (*Tamiasciurus hudsonicus*), is found in much of the forested areas of North America. The research team decided to focus on one phenological measure, the parturition date (timing of birth). Prior work indicated that parturition dates are in part heritable, with an $h^2 = 0.16$ (chapter 4). Additionally, parturition dates generally coincide with food abundance and shifts in spring weather. These factors make it a good candidate for the study of the evolutionary consequences of climate change. The focal population they used was located near Kluane Lake, in the Yukon. The entire population has been studied for years, with all individuals tagged and reproductive activity monitored from 1989–2001. Because the researchers had tracked the maternity of all squirrels, they were able to estimate how much of the observed phenotype (parturition dates) was heritable, and how much was phenotypic plasticity (see chapter 4 for a review of these terms). During this period, spring temperatures increased

by nearly 2°C, and the number of spruce cones available for feeding by the squirrels increased by 35%. Parturition dates also changed, becoming earlier by two weeks in just ten years (fig. 9.38). Through their understanding of the maternity of the squirrels in their population, they were able to show that nearly 15% of the shift in parturition dates was due to selection on this trait. The rest of the variation was due to phenotypic plasticity and other unidentified factors. This study is important in showing that yes, natural selection can result in phenological shifts of critical life-history parameters over very short periods of time. In other words, although most species have some phenotypic plasticity to climate, prolonged climate change is likely to cause evolutionary shifts in natural populations. In fact, as the researchers have shown, for some species, it already has.

As you can see from the studies we have presented here, there is substantial evidence that climate change is impacting natural populations in biologically significant ways. Shifts in phenology are being used as a climatic fingerprint, providing some of the first biological evidence that change not only might occur, but has in fact already occurred. As ecologists continue to develop the methods needed to detect the importance of climate change, it is certain we will learn much more about how biology and the abiotic environment interact to influence life histories and niches. Only through continued research will society be able to mitigate some of

the negative consequences of these changes, helping protect species that otherwise may be in peril due to human activities.

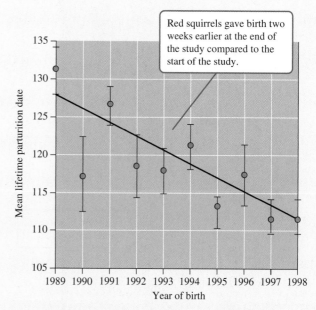

Figure 9.38   Parturition dates became earlier during the course of the study for red squirrel. (Data from Réale et al. 2003.)

SUMMARY

A niche represents the set of conditions in which a species could survive. Life history consists of the adaptations of an organism that influence aspects of their biology, such as the number of offspring it produces, its survival, and its size and age at reproductive maturity. This chapter presents concept discussions bearing on some of the central concepts of niches and life history.

9.1 Because all organisms have access to limited energy and resources, there are fundamental trade-offs in how these can be allocated between survival, offspring number, and offspring size.

Turner and Trexler found that larger darter species produce larger numbers of eggs. Their results also support the generalization that there is a trade-off between offspring size and number. On average, darters that produce larger eggs produce few eggs. They found a strong positive relationship between gene flow among darter populations and the number of eggs produced by females, and a negative relationship between egg size and gene flow. Plant ecologists have also found a negative relationship between sizes of seeds produced by plants and the number of seeds they produce. Westoby, Leishman,

and Lord found that plants of different growth form and different seed dispersal mechanisms tend to produce seeds of different sizes. Larger seeds, on average, produce larger seedlings that have a higher probability of successfully recruiting, particularly in the face of environmental challenges such as shade and competition.

Where adult survival is lower, organisms begin reproducing at an earlier age and invest a greater proportion of their energy budget into reproduction. Where adult survival is higher, organisms defer reproduction to a later age and allocate a smaller proportion of their resources to reproduction. Shine and Charnov found that as survival of adult lizards and snakes increases, their age at maturity also increases. Gunderson found analogous patterns among fish. In addition, fish with higher rates of mortality allocate a greater proportion of their biomass to reproduction. In other words, they show higher reproductive effort. These generalizations are supported by comparisons both between and within species. Male Coho salmon display jack and hooknose life-history strategies, each of which is typically associated with a particular mating strategy. Pumpkinseed sunfish allocate greater energy, or biomass, to reproductive

effort where adult pumpkinseed survival is lower. Many life-history traits, such as sexual reproduction in *Daphnia pulex*, can be inherited traits subject to evolutionary pressures.

9.2 The great diversity of life histories observed in nature can be classified on the basis of a few common characteristics.

One of the earliest attempts to organize information on the great variety of life histories that occur among species was under the heading of *r* selection and K selection. *r* selection refers to the per capita rate of increase, *r*, and is thought to favour higher population growth rate. *r* selection is predicted to be strongest in disturbed habitats. K selection refers to the carrying capacity in the logistic growth equation and is envisioned as a form of natural selection favouring more efficient utilization of resources such as food and nutrients. Grime described plant strategies, or life histories, that match the requirements of three environments: (1) low disturbance–low stress, (2) low disturbance–high stress, (3) high disturbance–low stress. His plant strategies matching these environmental conditions were competitive, stress-tolerant, and ruderal. Based on life-history patterns among fish, Kirk Winemiller and Kenneth Rose proposed a classification of life histories based on survivorship especially among juveniles, fecundity or number of offspring produced, and generation time or age at maturity. By basing their classification system on some of the most basic aspects of population ecology, Winemiller and Rose established a common currency for representing and analyzing life-history information for any organism.

9.3 The fundamental niche reflects the environmental requirements of a species, while the realized niche also includes interactions with other species.

The niche concept was developed early in the history of ecology and has had a prominent place ever since. Hutchinson developed the concepts of the *fundamental niche*, the physical conditions under which a species might live in the absence of other species, and the *realized niche*, the more restricted conditions under which a species actually lives as the result of interactions with other species. While a species' niche is theoretically defined by a very large number of biotic and abiotic factors, Hutchinson's *n*-dimensional hypervolume, the most important attributes of the niche of most species, can often be summarized by a few variables. For instance, the niches of Galápagos finches are largely determined by their feeding requirements, while the niche of a salt marsh grass can be defined by tidal levels.

Eric Charnov developed a new approach to life-history classification free of the influences of size and time that facilitates the exploration of life-history variation within and among groups of closely related taxa. Charnov's classification, based on relative offspring size, I/m, relative reproductive life span, E/α, and reproductive effort per unit adult mortality, C•E, suggests that mammals, fish, and altricial birds have life histories that are substantially different.

Life-history information is being used to find evidence that climate change is having effects on natural populations. The search for a climate fingerprint has centred around shifts in phenology, the timing of life events. There is substantial evidence that spring events, such as bud break and mating, are occurring earlier in areas of increased temperature. These changes occur in a diversity of taxa and are the result of phenotypic plasticity, behavioural responses, and natural selection.

REVIEW QUESTIONS

1. Researchers have characterized the niches of Galápagos finches by beak size (which correlates with diet) and the niches of salt marsh grasses by position in the intertidal zone. How would you characterize the niches of sympatric canid species such as red fox, coyote, and wolf in North America? What characteristics or environmental features do you think would be useful for representing the niches of arctic plants?

2. The discussion of seed size and number focused mainly on the advantages associated with large seeds. However, research by Westoby, Leishman, and Lord has revealed that the plants from widely separated geographic regions produce a wide variety of seed sizes. If this variation is to be maintained, what are some of the advantages associated with producing small seeds?

3. Under what conditions should natural selection favour production of many small offspring versus the production of a few well provisioned offspring?

4. The studies by Shine and Charnov (1992) and Gunderson (1997) addressed important questions of concern to life-history ecologists and their work provided robust answers to those questions. However, the methods they employed differed substantially from those used in most of the studies discussed in this and other chapters. The chief difference is that both relied heavily on data on life histories published previously by other authors. What was it about the nature of the problems addressed by these authors that constrained them to use this approach? In what types of studies would it be most appropriate to perform a synthesis of previously published information?

5. Much of our discussion of life-history variation involved variation among species within groups as broadly defined as "fish," "plants," or "reptiles." However, the work of Bertschy and Fox revealed significant variation in life history within species. In general, what should be the relative amount of variation within a species compared to that among many species? Develop your discussion using relative amounts of genetic variation upon which natural selection might act. You might review the sections discussing the evolutionary significance of genetic variation in chapter 4.

6. Using what you know about the trade-off between seed number and seed size (e.g., fig. 9.7) and patterns of variation among plants, predict the relative number of seeds produced by the various plant growth forms and dispersal strategies listed on figure 9.8.

7. Apply Winemiller's model to plants. If you were to construct a strictly quantitative classification of plant life histories using Winemiller and Rose's approach, what information would you need about the plants included in your analysis? How many plant species would you need to have an idea of how variation in their life histories compares with those of animals (e.g., as in fig. 9.24)? Try to reconcile Grime's plant classification with the scheme offered by Winemiller and Rose. Where are they similar? How are they different?

8. David Innes demonstrated that sexual vs. asexual reproduction in *Daphnia pulex* could be altered depending upon the life-history traits possessed by the parents. Pick another species or organism and a different life-history trait. Design a study that will allow you to determine whether this aspect of life history is heritable. Why does this issue of heritability matter?

9. Climate change consists of variation in many factors other than temperature. How might shifts in precipitation patterns impact phenology for the plants and animals of the prairies? How about for the wetter temperate forest?

10. Will species be able to adjust to climate changes, resulting in no altered risks of extinctions? What factors influence these abilities?

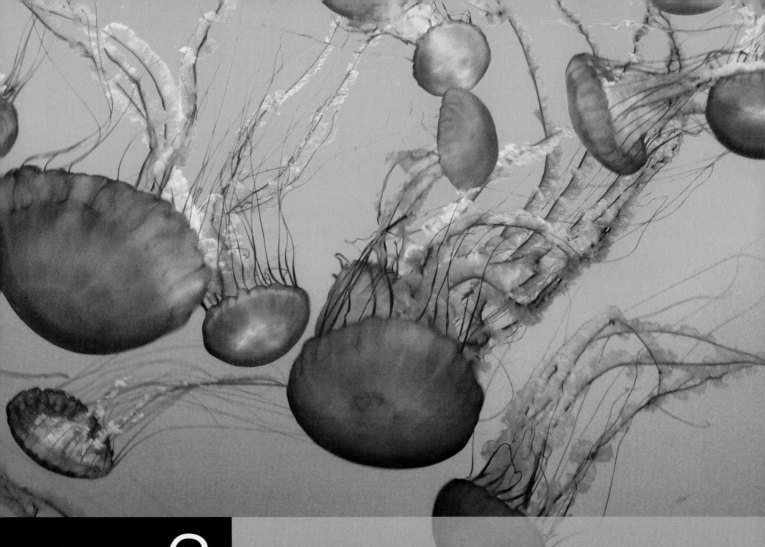

SECTION 3 POPULATION ECOLOGY

In section III we discuss the properties and dynamics of populations. Population ecology is at the interface between physiological ecology (section II), and community and landscape level processes (sections IV and V). We begin by describing the geographic distribution of populations and species (chapter 10). We then discuss different ways of quantifying population structure (chapter 11), and conclude this section by exploring major factors that influence population growth, and the models ecologists use to describe these changes (chapter 12).

Chapter 10 Distribution and Abundance of Populations and Species
Chapter 11 Population Structure
Chapter 12 Population Dynamics and Growth

DISTRIBUTION AND ABUNDANCE
OF POPULATIONS AND SPECIES

CHAPTER

10

CHAPTER CONCEPTS

10.1 The physical environment limits the geographic distribution of species.
Concept 10.1 Review

10.2 Dispersal can alter species distributions and local population densities.
Concept 10.2 Review

10.3 Some populations, called metapopulations, consist of interconnected subpopulations.
Concept 10.3 Review

10.4 On small scales, individuals within populations are distributed in patterns that may be random, regular, or clumped; on larger scales, individuals within a population are clumped.
Ecology In Action: Using Ecology to Protect Threatened Species
Concept 10.4 Review

10.5 Population density declines with increasing organism size.
Concept 10.5 Review

10.6 Commonness and rarity of species are influenced by population size, geographic range, and habitat tolerance.
Concept 10.6 Review
Ecological Tools and Approaches: Estimating Abundance

Summary
Review Questions

The distributions and dynamics of populations vary widely among species. While some populations contain only dozens of individuals within a highly restricted distribution, other populations number in the billions of individuals, ranging over vast areas of the planet.

Standing on a headland in Nunavut overlooking the Arctic Ocean, a group of students spots a breeding colony of Arctic terns, *Sterna paradisaea* (fig. 10.1*a*). The population is of mixed sexes, with both males and females defending the nest site from potential threats. These birds are particularly aggressive, as one student with a camera learned as he walked just a bit too close. When winter comes in the north, this entire population will fly to feeding grounds in the south, reaching the coast of Antarctica. Each bird, even the young fledglings, makes this round trip of over 18,000 km each year. In the process, these birds see more daylight and have the longest regular migration of any species on the planet.

While several students are watching the birds, others observe a small herd of muskox, *Ovibos moschatus*, grazing on a variety of plants in a nearby river valley (fig. 10.1*b*). Even a casual observer recognizes that these animals have traits that allow them to withstand extremely cold temperatures. Most obvious is their fur coat, with numerous thick guard hairs nearly reaching the ground. These guard hairs are water repellent and help protect the insulative properties of the finer undercoat. On a closer inspection, it appears this herd consists of only males, many of whom are engaged in competition, trying to achieve a dominant position within the herd. In winter, these animals do not leave the Arctic. Instead, they form herds consisting of both sexes, and move to higher elevations. In these winter grounds, they find less snow, allowing them to more easily find suitable forage for grazing.

Arctic terns and muskox, as different as they may appear, lead parallel lives. As climatic conditions change, and food becomes more scarce or harder to find, the entire population moves to a new area. Although the distance travelled differs between the species, the causes of migration are similar. However, as the students continue to look at the landscape, well after these animals have moved on, they realize the more abundant organisms on the landscape, numerous plant and lichen species, do not migrate at all. The students are able to find hundreds of species of clubmosses, lichens, ferns, mosses, and flowering plants within just a short distance of their base camp. Even more dramatic, although the colony of terns appeared large with tens of thousands of birds present, that is just a pittance compared to the millions of individual plants that are present around the students on the tundra.

With these examples, we begin to consider the ecology of populations. Ecologists usually define a **population** as a group of potentially interbreeding individuals of a single species inhabiting a specific area. A population of plants or animals might occupy a mountaintop, a river basin, a coastal marsh, or an island, all areas defined by natural boundaries. Just as often, the populations studied by biologists occupy artificially defined, but societally important, areas such as a particular country or park. The areas inhabited by populations

(a)

(b)

Figure 10.1   (*a*) During their annual migration, the entire population of Arctic terns moves from the Arctic Ocean in the northern summer to as far south as Antarctica in the southern summer. (*b*) Muskox populations remain in the Arctic all year, though they migrate to higher elevations in the winter to avoid deep snow.

range in size from the few cubic centimetres occupied by the bacteria in a rotting apple to the millions of square kilometres occupied by a population of migratory terns. A population studied by ecologists may consist of a highly localized group of individuals representing a fraction of the total population of a species, or it may consist of all the individuals of a species across its entire range.

Many attributes of populations are determined by interactions between the physiological ecology of a species and the biotic and abiotic conditions that individuals in a population encounter. Because of this, population ecology serves as a bridge between physiological and community ecology, topics discussed in other sections of this book. Ecologists study populations for a number of reasons. First, like all levels of ecological organization, detailed understanding of natural populations can provide insight into the general processes that drive ecological interactions. However, population-level interactions serve as the foundation for many resource-based economies, and thus there are often strong societal pressures to understand population dynamics. Just hearing the words "cod fishery," "zebra mussel," or "mountain pine beetle," sends shudders down the spines of many Canadians. At the

core of the economic crises involving these species have been issues related to population ecology. Population ecologists provide valuable insight into the understanding and possible control of numerous species that cause economic, aesthetic, and functional harm to Canada's natural resources. Population ecology is also at the centre of many studies of species at risk, with recovery plans often constructed to allow for the recovery of threatened populations. Finally, one of the greatest pressures faced by many plant and animal species around the planet has at its heart a shift in the population of a single species—the exponential growth of human populations.

All populations share several characteristics. The first is its distribution. The distribution of a population includes the size, shape, and location of the area (or volume) it occupies. A population is also characterized by the number of individuals within it and their **density**; the number of individuals per unit area. Population density can be further refined as either **absolute density** or **ecological density**. Absolute density is what most scientists refer to when they simply say "density" (as we will do in this chapter), and it is the number of individuals of a population per unit area (e.g., number of musk ox per square kilometre). Ecological density incorporates the concept of the niche (chapter 9), in that not all of the conditions found within a given area will contain the niche requirements of a particular species. For example, within a large tract of land in the tundra, there will be areas suitable for musk ox grazing, and rocky areas that do not support suitable plant growth. The ecological density of the musk ox would be the number of individuals per unit suitable habitat.

Additional characteristics of populations—their age distributions, sex ratios, birth and death rates, immigration and emigration rates, and rates of growth—are the subject of chapters 11 and 12. In chapter 10, we focus on three population characteristics: distribution, abundance, and dispersal.

10.1 Distribution Limits

The physical environment limits the geographic distribution of species. A major theme in chapters 4 to 8 is that natural selection has resulted in the evolution of physiological, morphological, and behavioural characteristics that enable individuals to compensate for environmental variation. In chapter 9 we saw how these characteristics were driven in part by a series of trade-offs, resulting in a diversity of life histories and niches. Here we move from our understanding of the conditions that organisms need to persist and thrive, to understanding the locations in which those conditions are found. You may recall from chapter 9 that the niche represents the multidimensional set of conditions necessary for a species to persist. The niche is an abstract concept, and not a tangible trait or specific location on the landscape. However, across a landscape there will be variability in environmental conditions, prey distributions, and other critical axes of the niche. Thus the conditions defined by a species' niche will only be found in specific locations, and therefore species should only be able to be found on the landscape in locations where conditions fall within those required by a species' niche. Thus, one determining factor of

the geographic distribution of a species will be the underlying distribution of biotic and abiotic conditions in combination with a species' niche requirements.

While there are few environments on earth without life, no single species can tolerate the full range of earth's environments—not even cockroaches! For each species some environments are too warm, too cold, too saline, or unsuitable in other ways, and thus conditions will eventually be outside those described by the niche. As we saw in chapter 7, organisms take in energy at a limited rate. When a species occupies habitat that contains conditions on the edge of those found within the species' niche, the metabolic costs of compensating for environmental stressors will take up a greater part organism's energy budget (e.g., thermoregulation). Partly because of these energy constraints, the physical environment places limits on the distributions of populations. Let's now turn to some actual species and explore the factors that limit their distributions.

Kangaroo Distributions and Climate

The Macropodidea includes the kangaroos and wallabies, which are some of the best known of the Australian animals. However, this group of large-footed mammals includes many less familiar species, including rat kangaroos and tree kangaroos. While some species of macropods can be found in nearly every part of Australia, no single species ranges across the entire continent.

G. Caughley and his colleagues (1987) found a close relationship between climate and the distributions of the three largest kangaroos in Australia (fig. 10.2). The eastern grey kangaroo, *Macropus giganteus*, is confined to the eastern third of the continent. This portion of Australia includes several biomes (see chapter 2). Temperate forest grows in the southeast and tropical forests in the north. Mountains, with their varied climates, occupy the central part of the eastern grey kangaroo's range. The climatic factor that distinguishes these varied biomes is little seasonal variation in precipitation or dominance by summer precipitation. The western grey kangaroo, *M. fuliginosus*, lives mainly in the southern and western regions of Australia. Most of the western grey kangaroo's range coincides with the distribution of the temperate woodland and shrubland biome in Australia. The climatically distinctive feature of this biome is a predominance of winter rainfall. Meanwhile, the red kangaroo, *M. rufus*, wanders the arid and semiarid interior of Australia. The biomes that cover most of the red kangaroo's range are savanna and desert (chapter 2). Of the three species of large kangaroos, the red kangaroo occupies the hottest and driest areas.

As a group, the distributions of these three large kangaroo species cover most of Australia. However, as you can see in figure 10.2, none of these species lives in the northernmost region of Australia, an area throughout which tropical forests are common. Caughley and his colleagues explain that these northern areas are probably too hot for the eastern grey kangaroo, too wet for the red kangaroo, and too hot in summer and too dry in winter for the western grey kangaroo. However, they are also careful to point out that these limited

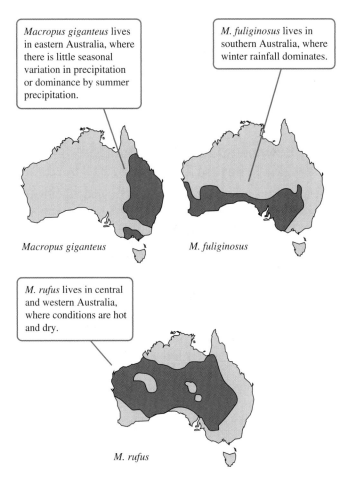

Macropus giganteus lives in eastern Australia, where there is little seasonal variation in precipitation or dominance by summer precipitation.

M. fuliginosus lives in southern Australia, where winter rainfall dominates.

Macropus giganteus

M. fuliginosus

M. rufus lives in central and western Australia, where conditions are hot and dry.

M. rufus

Figure 10.2   Climate and the distributions of three kangaroo species (data from Caughley et al. 1987).

distributions may not be determined by climate directly. Instead, the kangaroo may possess the physiological traits needed to survive under those conditions, but they may yet be limited due to lack of food production or suitable habitat. Climate also affects the incidence of parasites, pathogens, and competitors that can further restrict the realized niche of species.

Regardless of how the influences of climate are played out, the relationship between climate and the distributions of species can be stable over long periods of time. The distributions of the eastern grey, western grey, and red kangaroos have been stable for at least a century. In the next example, we discuss a species of beetle that appears to have maintained a stable association with climate for tens of thousands of years.

A Tiger Beetle of Cold Climates

The tiger beetle *Cicindela longilabris* lives at higher latitudes and higher elevations than just about any other species of tiger beetle in North America. *C. longilabris* is distributed from the Yukon Territory in northwestern Canada to the Atlantic provinces of eastern Canada (fig. 10.3). This northern band of beetle populations coincides with the distribution of northern temperate forest and boreal forest in North America (chapter 2).

C. longilabris also lives as far south as Arizona and New Mexico. However, these southern populations are confined to high mountains, where *C. longilabris* is associated with montane coniferous forests. As we saw in chapter 2, these high mountains have a climate similar to that of boreal forest.

Ecologists suggest that during the last glacial period, *C. longilabris* lived far south of its present range limits. Then with climatic warming and the retreat of the glaciers, the tiger beetles followed their preferred climate northward and up in elevation into the mountains of western North America (fig. 10.3). As a consequence, the beetles in the southern part of this species' range live in isolated mountaintop populations. This hypothesis is supported by the fossil records of many beetle species.

Intrigued by the distribution and history of *C. longilabris*, Thomas Schultz, Michael Quinlan, and Neil Hadley (1992) set out to study the environmental physiology of widely separated populations of the species. Populations separated for many thousands of years may have been exposed to significantly different environmental regimes, and natural selection could have produced significant physiological differences among populations (think about the processes that can lead

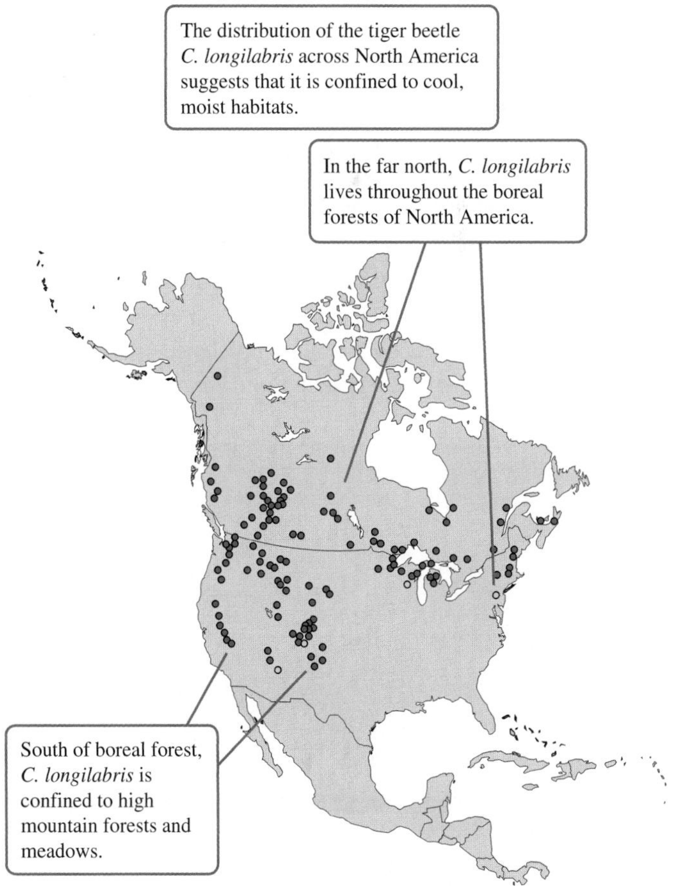

The distribution of the tiger beetle *C. longilabris* across North America suggests that it is confined to cool, moist habitats.

In the far north, *C. longilabris* lives throughout the boreal forests of North America.

South of boreal forest, *C. longilabris* is confined to high mountain forests and meadows.

Figure 10.3   A tiger beetle, *Cicindela longilabris*, confined to cool environments. Physiological studies conducted on populations are indicated by yellow dots (data from Schultz et al. 1992).

to allopatric speciation (chapter 4). The researchers compared the physiological characteristics of beetles from populations of *C. longilabris* from Maine, Wisconsin, Colorado, and northern Arizona (fig. 10.3). Their measurements included water loss rates, metabolic rates, and body temperature preferences.

Schultz and his colleagues found that the metabolic rates of *C. longilabris* are higher, and its preferred temperatures lower, than those of most other tiger beetle species. These differences support the hypothesis that *C. longilabris* is adapted to the cool climates of boreal and montane forests. In addition, the researchers found that none of their measurements differed significantly among populations of *C. longilabris*. Figure 10.4 illustrates the remarkable similarity in preferred body temperature shown by foraging *C. longilabris* from populations separated by as much as 3,000 km and, perhaps, by 10,000 years of history. These results support the

generalization that the physical environment limits the distributions of species. It also suggests that those limits may be stable for long periods of time.

Here we find widely separated populations possessing very similar physiological tolerances. In the next example, we will find species that occur very close together may have very different physiological limits.

Distributions of Barnacles Along an Intertidal Exposure Gradient

The marine intertidal zone presents a steep gradient of physical conditions from the shore seaward (fig. 3.18). As we saw in chapter 3, the organisms high in the intertidal zone are exposed by virtually every tide, while the organisms that live at lower levels in the intertidal zone are exposed by the lowest tides only. Exposure to air differs at different levels within the intertidal zone. Organisms that live in the intertidal zone have evolved different degrees of resistance to drying, a major factor contributing to zonation among intertidal organisms (chapter 3).

Barnacles, one of the most common intertidal organisms (fig. 10.5), show distinctive patterns of zonation within the intertidal zone. For example, Joseph Connell (1961a, 1961b) described how along the coast of Scotland, adult *Chthamalus stellatus* are restricted to the upper levels of the intertidal zone, while adult *Balanus balanoides* are limited to the middle and lower levels (fig. 10.6). What role does resistance to drying play in the intertidal zonation of these two species? Unusually calm and warm weather, combined with very low tides, gave Connell some insights into this question. In the spring of 1955, warm weather coincided with calm seas and very low tides. As a consequence, no water reached the upper intertidal zone occupied by both species of barnacles. During this period, *Balanus* in the upper intertidal zone suffered much higher mortality than *Chthamalus* (fig. 10.7). Meanwhile, *Balanus* in the lower intertidal zone showed normal rates of mortality. Of the two species, *Balanus* appears to be more vulnerable to desiccation. Higher rates of desiccation may exclude this species of barnacle from the upper intertidal zone.

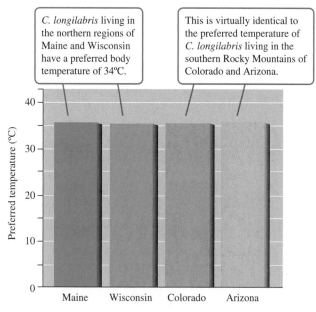

> *C. longilabris* living in the northern regions of Maine and Wisconsin have a preferred body temperature of 34°C.

> This is virtually identical to the preferred temperature of *C. longilabris* living in the southern Rocky Mountains of Colorado and Arizona.

Figure 10.4 Uniform temperature preference across an extensive geographic range (data from Schultz et al. 1992).

(a)   (b)

Figure 10.5 (*a*) *Chthamalus stellatus* and (*b*) *Balanus balanoides* occur in different zones within intertidal regions. Ecologists have studied these species extensively, leading to insights into the processes that govern species distributions.

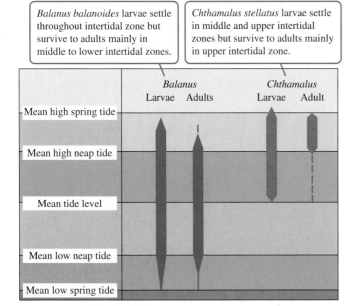

Balanus balanoides larvae settle throughout intertidal zone but survive to adults mainly in middle to lower intertidal zones.

Chthamalus stellatus larvae settle in middle and upper intertidal zones but survive to adults mainly in upper intertidal zone.

Figure 10.6 Distributions of two barnacle species within the intertidal zone (data from Connell 1961a, 1961b).

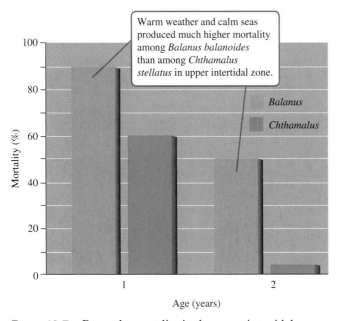

Warm weather and calm seas produced much higher mortality among *Balanus balanoides* than among *Chthamalus stellatus* in upper intertidal zone.

Figure 10.7 Barnacle mortality in the upper intertidal zone (data from Connell 1961a, 1961b).

Vulnerability to desiccation, however, does not completely explain the pattern of intertidal zonation shown by *Balanus* and *Chthamalus*. What excludes *Chthamalus* from the lower intertidal zone? Though the larvae of this barnacle settle in the lower intertidal zone, the adults rarely survive there. Connell explored this question by transplanting adult *Chthamalus* to the lower intertidal zone and found that transplanted adults survive very well in the lower intertidal zone. If the physical environment does not exclude *Chthamalus* from the lower intertidal zone, what does? It turns out that this species is excluded from the lower intertidal zone by competitive interactions with *Balanus*. We discuss the mechanisms by which this competitive exclusion is accomplished in chapter 13.

These barnacles remind us that the environment consists of more than just physical and chemical factors. An organism's environment also includes biological factors. In many situations, biological factors may be even more important than physical factors in determining the distribution and abundance of some species. Often the influences of biological factors remain hidden, however, because of the difficulty of demonstrating them. In ecology, we must usually probe deeper to see beyond outward appearances, as Connell did when he transplanted *Chthamalus* from the upper to the lower intertidal zone. The influence of biological factors, such as competition, predation, and disease, on the distribution and abundance of organisms is a theme that enters our discussions frequently in the remainder of this book, especially in chapters 13, 14, and 15.

Now that we have considered factors limiting the distributions of individuals, let's consider the patterns of distribution of individuals within their habitat. We begin by considering three basic patterns of distribution.

CONCEPT 10.1 REVIEW

1. How might climate change influence the distribution of a species?
2. What role does life history play in determining how a species responds to changes in the biotic or abiotic environment?

10.2 Dispersal

Dispersal can alter species distributions and local population densities. The seeds of plants disperse with wind or water or may be transported by a variety of mammals, insects, or birds. Adult barnacles may spend their lives attached to rocks, but their larvae travel the high seas on far-ranging ocean currents. A host of other sessile marine invertebrates, algae, and many highly sedentary reef fish also disperse widely as larvae. Some young spiders spin a small net that catches winds and carries them for distances up to hundreds of kilometres. Young mammals and birds often disperse from the area where they were born and may join other local populations. As a consequence of movements such as these (fig. 10.8), the population ecologist trying to understand local population structure must consider dispersal *into* (**immigration**) and *out of* (**emigration**) the local population. As we will discuss later in this chapter, dispersal of individuals allows for the persistence of metapopulations, and has important consequences for natural communities. It is important to recognize that dispersal is different from migration. Migration is the seasonal movement of individuals from one location to another, while dispersal is (typically) a permanent exodus from one population into another. The causes and consequences of these differences are significant, though beyond the scope of this text.

Despite its importance, dispersal is one of the least-studied aspects of population ecology. Its study is clearly a difficult undertaking. One of the richest sources of information

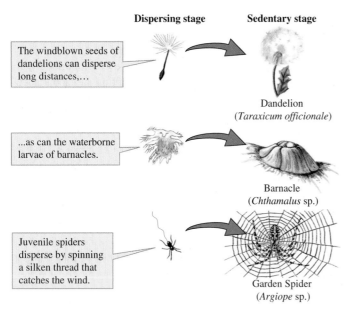

Figure 10.8 Dispersing and sedentary stages of organisms.

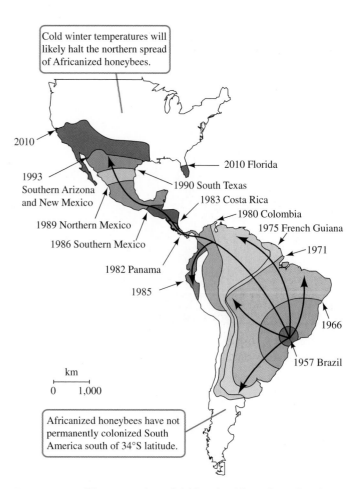

Figure 10.9 The expansion of Africanized bees from South America through Central and North America, 1956 to 2008 (data from Winston 1992, USDA Agricultural Research Service 2011).

on dispersal and some of the clearest examples come from studies of expanding populations.

Dispersal of Expanding Populations

Expanding populations are those that are in the process of increasing their geographic range. Why should this type of population provide us with some of the best records of species dispersal? The appearance of a new species in an area is quickly noted and recorded, especially if the species impacts the local economy or human health or safety. For instance, the expansion of Africanized bees through South and North America is well documented (fig. 10.9). The legendary aggressiveness of these bees ensures that their dispersal into an area does not escape notice for long.

Honeybees, *Apis melifera*, evolved in Africa and Europe, where their native range extends from tropical to cold, temperate environments. Across this extensive environmental range, this species has differentiated into a number of locally adapted subspecies. In an attempt to improve the adaptability of managed honeybees to their tropical climate, Brazilian scientists imported queens of the African subspecies *Apis melifera scutellata* in 1956. These queens mated with the European honeybees used by Brazilian beekeepers, producing what we now call Africanized bees.

Africanized honeybees differ in several ways from European honeybees. Temperate and tropical environments have apparently selected for markedly different behaviour and population dynamics. Natural selection by a high diversity and abundance of nest predators has probably produced the greater aggressiveness shown by Africanized bees. The warmer climate and greater stability of nectar sources eliminates the advantages of storing large quantities of honey and maintaining large colonies for survival through the winter. Most important to this discussion of dispersal, Africanized honeybees produce swarms that disperse to form new colonies at a much higher rate than do European honeybees.

High rates of colony formation and dispersal have caused a rapid expansion of Africanized honeybees through South and North America. Their rate of dispersal has ranged from 300 to 500 km per year. Within 30 years, Africanized honeybees occupied most of South America, all of Central America, and most of Mexico. The estimated number of wild colonies of these bees in South America alone is 50 to 100 million. Africanized bees reached southern Texas in 1990, and southern Arizona and New Mexico in 1994. The honeybees stopped spreading southward through South America by about 1983, stopping at about 34° S latitude. However, they continue to spread northward through North America and will continue to do so until stopped by cold climates. Population ecologists predict that Africanized honeybees will reach the northern limit of their distribution within North America sometime early in the twenty-first century. What is likely to halt the northern spread of this species? Cold winter temperatures appear to fall outside the range of tolerance for this species (chapter 5), and thus environmental conditions in northern North America generally do not overlap with the niche requirements of this species (chapter 9).

How does this rate of expansion by African honeybees compare to rates of expansion by other populations? Figure 10.10, which summarizes rates of dispersal for a variety

of mammals and birds, shows that rates of dispersal differ by three orders of magnitude. While some species, such as Africanized bees, spread at rates of tens or hundreds of kilometres per year, others disperse only a few hundred metres per year. This is about the same rate at which North American trees expanded their distributions following the retreat of the glaciers.

Range Changes in Response to Climate Change

In response to climate change following retreat of the glaciers northward in North America beginning about 16,000 years ago, organisms of all sorts began to move northward from their ice age refuges. Temperate forest trees have left one of the best preserved records of this northward dispersal. In chapter 1 we saw how Margaret Davis was able to show the migration of tree species through well-preserved pollen records in lake sediment. For example, the northward advance of maple and hemlock is shown in figure 10.11.

Figure 10.11 illustrates a number of ecologically significant messages. Though the distributions of maple and hemlock overlap today, they did not during the height of the last ice age. In addition, maple colonized the northern part of its present range from the lower Mississippi Valley region, while hemlock colonized its present range from a refuge along the Atlantic coast. The two trees dispersed at very different rates. Of the two species, maple dispersed faster, arriving at the northern limits of its present-day range about 6,000 years ago. In contrast, hemlock did not reach the northwestern limit of its present distribution until 2,000 years ago.

The pollen preserved in lake sediments indicates that forest trees in eastern North America spread northward following the retreat of the glaciers at the rate of 100 to 400 m (0.1–0.4 km) per year. This rate of dispersal is similar to that of some large mammals, such as the North American elk. However, it is 1/1,000 the dispersal rate of Africanized bees across South, Central, and North America.

It is easy to take some comfort from the work of Davis, in that trees are able to move large distances over relatively

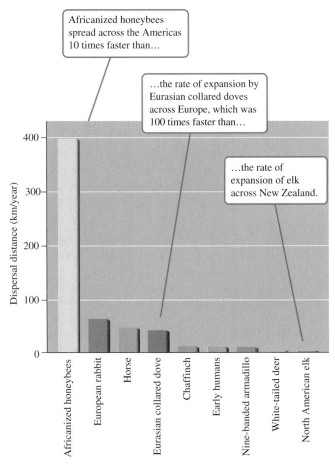

Figure 10.10 Rates of expansion by animal populations (data from Caughley 1977, Hengeveld 1988, Winston 1992).

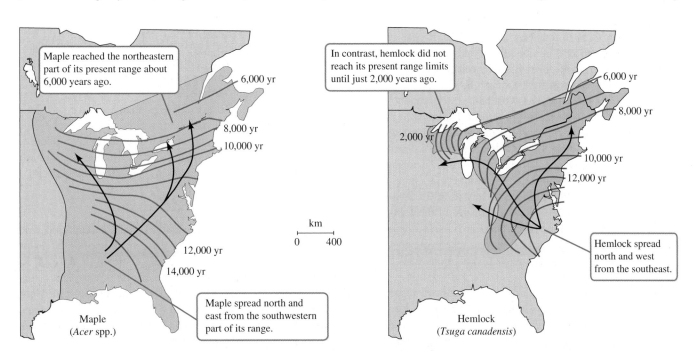

Figure 10.11 The northward expansion of two tree species in North America following glacial retreat (data from Davis 1981).

short periods of time in response to climate change. As we will discuss in depth later in this book, the planet is facing another period of rapid climatic change, which should cause many populations to find themselves in inhospitable conditions. In theory, dispersal will allow species ranges to move along with the climate. However, since the last ice age, there has been substantial human alteration of the landscape. It remains unclear to what extent these alterations will prevent, or slow down, the migration of plant and animal species in response to the current climate change that many parts of the planet are experiencing.

The previous examples concern dispersal by populations in the process of expanding their ranges. Significant dispersal also takes place within established populations whose ranges are not changing. Movements within established ranges can be an important aspect of local population dynamics. We will consider two examples.

Dispersal in Response to Changing Food Supply

Predators show several kinds of responses to variation in prey density. In addition to the functional response we discussed in chapter 7, C. S. Holling (1959) also observed **numerical responses** to increased prey availability. Numerical responses are changes in the density of predator populations in response to increased prey density. Holling studied populations of mice and shrews preying on insect cocoons and attributed the numerical responses he observed to increased reproductive rates. He commented that "because the reproductive rate of small mammals is so high, there was an almost immediate increase in density with increase in food." However, some other predators, with much lower reproductive rates, also show strong numerical responses. These numerical responses to prey density are almost entirely due to dispersal.

In some years, northern landscapes are alive with small rodents called voles, of the genus *Microtus*. Go to the same place during other years and it may be difficult to find any voles. In northern latitudes, vole populations usually reach high densities every three to four years. Between these peak times, population densities crash. Population cycles in different areas are not synchronized, however. In other words, while vole population density is very low in one area, it is high elsewhere.

Erkki Korpimäki and Kai Norrdahl (1991) conducted a 10-year study of voles and their predators. The study began in 1977 during a peak in vole densities of about 1,800 per square kilometre and continued through two more peaks in 1982 (960/km^2) and 1985–86 (1,980 and 1,710/km^2). The researchers estimated that between these population peaks, vole densities per square kilometre fell to as low as 70 in 1980 and 40 in 1984. During this period, the densities of the European kestrel, *Falco tinnunculus*, short-eared owls, *Asio flammeus*, and long-eared owls, *Asio otus*, closely tracked vole densities (fig. 10.12). How do kestrel and owl populations track these variations in vole densities?

What mechanisms produce the numerical responses by kestrels and owls to changing vole densities? Look at figure 10.12 for a clue. The peaks in raptor densities in 1977, 1982, and 1986 match the peaks in vole densities

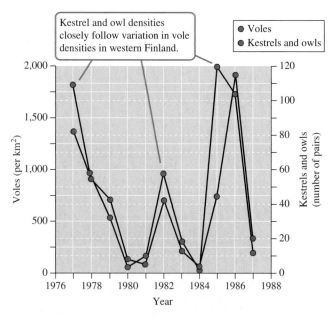

Figure 10.12   Dispersal and numerical response by predators (data from Korpimäki and Norrdahl 1991).

almost perfectly. If reproduction was the source of numerical response by kestrels and owls, there would have been more of a delay, or time lag, in kestrel and owl numerical response. From this close match in numbers, Korpimäki and Norrdahl proposed that kestrels and owls must move from place to place in response to local increases in vole populations.

Is there any supporting evidence for high rates of movement by kestrels and owls? Korpimäki (1988) marked and recaptured 217 kestrels, a large proportion of their study population. Because European kestrel populations have an annual survival rate of 48% to 66%, he predicted a high rate of recapture of the marked birds. However, only 3% of the female and 13% of the male kestrels were recaptured. These very low rates of recapture indicated that kestrels were moving out of the study area. From their data, Korpimäki and Norrdahl concluded that the hawks and owls in western Finland are nomadic, moving from place to place in response to changing vole densities. These studies documented the contribution of dispersal to local populations of kestrels and owls. Earlier in this section, we saw how studies of expanding populations have shed light on the contribution of dispersal to local population density and dynamics. Many other local populations are strongly influenced by dispersal. One of the environments in which dispersal has a major influence on local populations is in streams and rivers.

Dispersal in Rivers and Streams

One of the most distinctive features of the stream and river environment is *current*, the downstream flow of water. What effect does current have on the lives of stream organisms? As you may recall from chapter 3, the effects of current are substantial and influence everything from the amount of oxygen in the water to the size, shape, and behaviour of stream organisms. In this section, we stop and consider how stream populations are affected by current.

Let's begin with a question. Why doesn't the flowing water of streams eventually wash all stream organisms, including fish, insects, snails, bacteria, algae, and fungi, out to sea? All stream dwellers have a variety of characteristics that help them maintain their position in streams. Some fish, such as trout, are streamlined and can easily swim against swift currents, while other fish, like sculpins and loaches, avoid the full strength of currents by living on the bottom and seeking shelter among or under stones. Microorganisms resist being washed away by adhering to the surfaces of stones, wood, and other substrates. Many stream insects are flattened and so stay out of the main force of the current, while others are streamlined and fast-swimming.

Despite these means of staying in place, stream organisms do get washed downstream in large numbers, particularly during flash floods, or **spates**. To observe this downstream movement of organisms, put a fine or medium mesh net in a stream or river. You will soon capture large numbers of stream insects and algae along with fragments of leaves and wood. If you place some of the organic matter washed into your net under a microscope, you will find all sorts of microorganisms. Stream ecologists refer to this downstream movement of stream organisms as **drift**. Some drift is due to displacement of organisms during flash floods. However, some is due to the active movement of organisms downstream.

Whatever its cause, stream organisms drift downstream in large numbers. Why doesn't drift eventually eliminate organisms from the upstream sections of streams? Karl Müller (1954, 1974) hypothesized that drift would eventually wash entire populations out of streams unless organisms actively moved upstream to compensate for drift. He proposed that stream populations are maintained through a dynamic interplay between downstream and upstream dispersal that he called the **colonization cycle**. The colonization cycle is a dynamic view of stream populations in which upstream and downstream dispersal, as well as reproduction, have major influences on stream populations (fig. 10.13).

Many studies support Müller's hypothesized colonization cycle, especially among aquatic insects. As larvae, aquatic insects disperse upstream as well as downstream by swimming, crawling, and drifting. Because of continuous dispersal, which

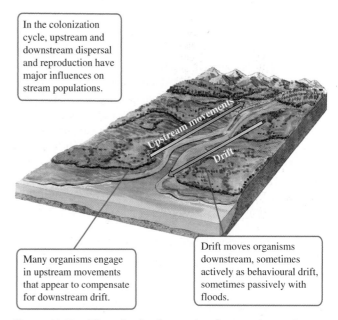

In the colonization cycle, upstream and downstream dispersal and reproduction have major influences on stream populations.

Many organisms engage in upstream movements that appear to compensate for downstream drift.

Drift moves organisms downstream, sometimes actively as behavioural drift, sometimes passively with floods.

Figure 10.13 The colonization cycle of stream invertebrates.

reshuffles stream populations, new substrates put into streams are quickly colonized by a wide variety of stream invertebrates, algae, and bacteria. Most of these dynamics are difficult to observe because they occur too quickly, within the substratum, or at night, or they involve microorganisms impossible to observe directly without the aid of a microscope. However, a snail that lives in a tropical stream in Costa Rica provides a well-documented example of the colonization cycle.

The Rio Claro flows approximately 30 km through tropical forest on the Osa Peninsula of Costa Rica before flowing into the Pacific Ocean. One of the most easily observed inhabitants of the Rio Claro is the snail *Neritina latissima*, which occupies the lower 5 km of the river. The eggs of *Neritina* hatch to produce free-living planktonic larvae that drift down to the Pacific Ocean. After the larvae metamorphose into small snails they re-enter the Rio Claro and begin moving upstream in huge migratory aggregations of up to 500,000 individuals (fig. 10.14). These aggregations move slowly and may take up to one year to reach the upstream limit of the population.

(a)

(b)

Figure 10.14 (*a*) A close-up *Neritina latissima*. (*b*) A wave of migrating *Neritina* snails in the Rio Claro, Costa Rica.

The population of *Neritina* in the Rio Claro consists of a mixture of migrating and stationary subpopulations, with exchange between them. Individual snails migrate upstream for some distance and then leave the migrating wave and enter a local subpopulation. At the same time, individuals from the local subpopulation enter the migratory wave and move upstream. Thus, individuals move upstream in steps and immigration continuously adds to local subpopulations, while emigration removes individuals. Because an organism that is visible to the naked eye does all this in a clear stream, and does it at a snail's pace, we are provided with a unique opportunity to observe that dispersal can strongly influence local population density. Dispersal dynamics, though difficult to study, deserve greater attention.

How can information on population dynamics be used to address environmental problems? For instance, how would you go about evaluating the possible effects of a potential pollutant on natural populations? Making such a judgment is usually not as simple as it might sound. If a toxin kills everything in its path, at virtually all detectable concentrations, the situation is clear enough, but often the effects of pollutants are not so obvious. One of the most promising approaches to assessing the impact of pollutants is to study their effects on population dynamics.

CONCEPT 10.2 REVIEW

1. Why might a species like Africanized honeybees be less threatened by climate change than maple trees?
2. Some ecologists who have hung clear plastic sheets (coated with adhesive capable of trapping flying insects) from river bridges have found that the side of the sheets facing downstream traps more adult aquatic insects than the upstream-facing side. Explain.

10.3 Metapopulations

Some populations, called metapopulations, consist of interconnected subpopulations. Populations of many species occur not as a single, continuously distributed population but in spatially isolated patches, with significant exchange of individuals among patches. A group of subpopulations living on such patches connected by exchange of individuals among patches make up a **metapopulation**. Why are some populations divided into subpopulations and other populations able to persist as single integrated population?

Metapopulations develop due to interactions between the biology of the species of interest and the landscape upon which it lives. For example, some species have very specific habitat requirements, such as a butterfly that can only oviposit on certain meadow plants. If meadows exist as large and continuous areas, then you would also expect the butterfly

population to be large and continuous. However, if the meadows are only found as small patches of land surrounded by forest, agricultural fields, or other habitat unsuitable for this butterfly, then you would expect this species to form small populations in these meadows. If the biology of the organism allows for dispersal of individuals from one meadow to another, this then forms a metapopulation. Other species may have historically existed as a large, connected population, with changes to the landscape causing fragmentation (chapter 21) and the development of metapopulations. For example, much of northern Alberta has historically consisted of a large expanse of undisturbed boreal forest. Decades of oil and gas development has created a checkerboard appearance in many regions, with the forest divided by roads, pipelines, logging, and other human activities (fig. 10.15). As human development of formerly intact areas continues, more species are potentially facing the fragmentation of their habitat and populations (chapter 21).

Regardless of the mechanism that is causing small populations to exist within proximity to each other, the critical issue relevant to metapopulations is whether individuals are able to disperse from one population to another. If dispersal does not occur, then several small and unconnected populations occur on the landscape. If dispersal is common, these small populations can be viewed as subpopulations of a larger metapopulation. More information about the characteristics of metapopulations can be found in figure 10.6.

Butterflies commonly live within metapopulations, and are among the best studied taxa. For example, the Glanville fritillary butterflies, *Melitaea cinxia*, we observed in chapter 4 live in meadows scattered through the landscape of southern Finland (see chapter 4) and form a metapopulation. Scattered suitable habitats are a common cause of metapopulations, coupled with the ability of individuals to move among habitats. We will find another example in the alpine meadows of the Rocky Mountains.

Figure 10.15   Large regions of the Boreal forest in Alberta have been divided into a grid due to industrial development, such as oil and gas extraction.

Metapopulations are complex networks of movement and residency that have important consequences for species abundances, extinctions, and gene flow. Here are a few essential points about metapopulations:

1. Metapopulations are a population of subpopulations.
2. The subpopulations are connected by movement of individuals from one subpopulation to another.
3. Any subpopulation can go extinct and be re-colonized repeatedly over time.
4. The risk of subpopulation extinction is generally greatest for small subpopulations, which usually occur in small patches on the landscape.
5. Density-dependent and density-independent population dynamics (chapters 11, 12) occur within each subpopulation.

Figure 10.16   Metapopulations share several characteristics.

A Metapopulation of an Alpine Butterfly

Once population biologists began to include the concept of metapopulations in their thinking, they found them everywhere. Butterflies have been well represented in studies of metapopulations. One of these butterflies is the Rocky Mountain Parnassian butterfly, *Parnassius smintheus* (figure 10.17). The range of *P. smintheus* extends from northern New Mexico along the Rocky Mountains to southwest Alaska. Along this range, *P. smintheus* caterpillars feed mainly on the leaves and flowers of stonecrop, *Sedum* sp., in areas of open forest and meadows. Because of their tie to a narrow range of host plants, *P. smintheus* populations are often distributed among the habitat patches occupied by their host plant, appearing to form metapopulations.

One such metapopulation was studied by Jens Roland, Nusha Keyghobadi, and Sherri Fownes of the University of Alberta in Edmonton (Roland et al. 2000). Roland, Keyghobadi, and Fownes focused their attention on a series of 20 alpine meadows on ridges in the Kananaskis region of the Canadian Rocky Mountains. The study meadows ranged in area from about 0.8 ha to 20 ha. While some meadows were adjacent to each other, others were separated by up to 200 m of coniferous forest. The host plant of *P. smintheus* in the study meadows was the lanceleaf stonecrop, *Sedum lanceolatum*.

A combination of fire suppression and global warming appears to be decreasing the size of alpine meadows and increasing their isolation from each other by intervening forest. In 1952, the study meadows averaged approximately 36 ha in area. By 1993, the average area of these meadows had declined to approximately 8 ha, a decrease in area of approximately 77%. These changes motivated the research team of Roland, Keyghobadi, and Fownes to study the influences of meadow size and isolation on movements of *P. smintheus* during the summers of 1995 and 1996.

The research team used mark and recapture techniques (see Ecological Tools and Approaches) to estimate population size in each meadow and to follow their movements.

Butterflies were hand netted and marked on the hind wing with a three-letter identification code, using a fine-tipped permanent marker (fig. 10.17*a*). The team recorded the sex of *P. smintheus* captured and its location within 20 m. Upon recapture, dispersal distance of an individual was estimated as the straight line distance from its last point of capture.

Roland, Keyghobadi, and Fownes marked 1,574 *P. smintheus* in 1995 and 1,200 in 1996. Of these marked individuals, they recaptured 726 in 1995 and 445 in 1996. Over the course

(a)

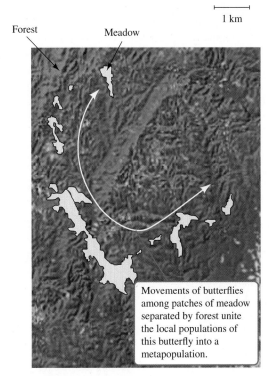

(b)

Figure 10.17   (*a*) Jens Roland and colleagues marked (notice the QMC on the wing) and recaptured many Rocky Mountain Parnassian butterflies to understand metapopulation dynamics for this species. Because this species is tied to meadows and open forest where its larval host plants grow, *P. smintheus* lives in scattered subpopulations connected by dispersal. (*b*) A metapopulation of the Rocky Mountain Parnassian butterfly, *Parnassius smintheus*. (after Matter et al. 2009).

of the study, the size of *P. smintheus* populations in the 20 study meadows ranged from 0 to 230. The average movement distance by males and females in 1995 was approximately 131 m. In 1996, the average movement distances of males and females was 162 m and 118 m respectively. The maximum dispersal distance for a butterfly in 1995 was 1,729 m and in 1996 the maximum dispersal distance was 1,636 m. Most of the movements determined by recaptures were the result of dispersal within meadows. In 1995, 5.8% of documented dispersal movements were from one meadow to another, and in 1996 dispersal between meadows accounted for 15.2% of total recaptures.

One of the questions posed by Roland and colleagues was how meadow size and population size might affect dispersal by *P. smintheus*. As shown in figure 10.18, average butterfly population size increased with meadow area. It turned out that butterflies are more likely to leave small populations than large populations. Butterflies leaving small populations generally immigrate to larger populations. The results of this study indicate that as alpine meadows in the Rocky Mountains decline in area, due in part to climatic warming, populations of *P. smintheus* will become progressively more compressed into fewer and fewer small meadows, perhaps disappearing entirely in parts of their range.

In the last two discussions, we have reviewed patterns of distribution within populations. We have seen that those patterns vary from one population to another and may depend upon the scale at which ecologists make their observations. Now we turn from patterns of spatial variation within populations to compare the average densities of different populations. Is there any way to predict the average population density of populations? While it is not possible to make precise predictions, the following examples show that population densities are very much influenced by organism size.

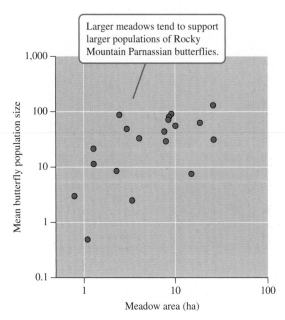

Figure 10.18 The relationship between meadow area and the size of Rocky Mountain Parnassian butterfly, *Parnassius smintheus*, populations. With forest encroachment into alpine meadows in the Rocky Mountains, populations of *P. smintheus* will likely decline.

CONCEPT 10.3 REVIEW

1. How can you determine whether the population of a species you are studying is a single population, or a connected subpopulation of a larger metapopulation?
2. If a subpopulation of a metapopulation collapses to a population size of zero individuals, does the entire metapopulation crash? Why or why not?

10.4 Distribution Patterns

On small scales, individuals within populations are distributed in patterns that may be random, regular, or clumped; on larger scales, individuals within a population are clumped. We have just considered how the environment interacts with the niche, resulting in geographic limits to the distribution of species. When you map the distribution of a species, you are highlighting the range of the species (see figs. 10.2 and 10.6). In other words, your map shows where individuals of the species live and where they are absent. Knowing a species' range, as defined by presence and absence, is useful, but it says nothing about how the individuals that make up the population are distributed in the areas where they are present. Are individuals randomly distributed across the range? Are they regularly distributed? As we shall see, the distribution pattern observed by an ecologist is strongly influenced by the scale at which a population is studied.

Ecologists refer frequently to large-scale and small-scale phenomena. What is "large" or "small" depends on the size of organism or other ecological phenomenon under study. For this discussion, **small scale** refers to distances of no more than a few hundred metres, over which there is little environmental change significant to the organism under study. **Large scale** refers to areas over which there is substantial environmental change. In this sense, large scale may refer to patterns over an entire continent or patterns along a mountain slope, where environmental gradients are steep. The area being studied, or over which an ecological process or population occurs, is also referred to as the *spatial extent*, which can be directly measured (e.g., square metres) or described qualitatively (e.g., large or small scale). Though we will not discuss it here, it is important to recognize that there is also variation in the temporal extent of a study or process. Let's begin our discussion with patterns of distribution observed at small spatial scales.

Distributions of Individuals on Small Scales

Three basic patterns of distribution are observed on small scales: random, regular, or clumped. A **random distribution** is one in which individuals within a population have an equal chance of living anywhere within an area. A **regular distribution** is one in which individuals are uniformly spaced. In a **clumped distribution**, individuals have a much higher probability of being found in some areas than in others (fig. 10.19).

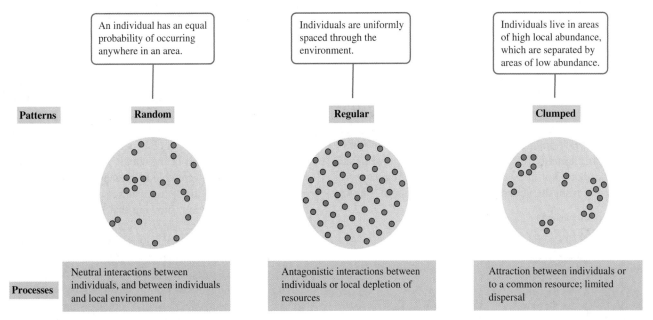

Figure 10.19   Random, regular, and clumped distributions.

These three basic patterns of distribution are produced by the kinds of interactions that take place between individuals within a population, by the structure of the physical environment, and by a combination of interactions and environmental structure. Individuals within a population may *attract* each other, *repel* each other, or *ignore* each other. Mutual attraction creates clumped, or aggregated, patterns of distribution. Clumped distributions can also occur if individuals produce offspring that fail to disperse far from the parents. Regular patterns of distribution are produced when individuals avoid each other or claim exclusive use of a patch of landscape. Neutral responses contribute to random distributions.

The patterns created by social interactions may be reinforced or reduced by the structure of the environment. An environment with patchy distributions of nutrients, nesting sites, water, and so forth also fosters clumped distribution patterns. An environment with a uniform distribution of resources and frequent, random patterns of disturbance (or mixing) tends to reinforce random or regular distributions. Let's now consider factors that influence the distributions of some species in nature.

Distributions of Tree Species on Vancouver Island

Both competition among individuals (chapter 13) and local environmental conditions can influence the spatial distribution of individuals within a population. These factors may also interact, such that competition may be more, or less, important under some environmental conditions than other levels. As a result, discerning the mechanisms that cause spatial patterns in natural populations can be a challenge. A team of researchers from Canada and Germany decided to tackle this issue, and to try to understand what factors influenced the small-scale distribution of trees in a Douglas-fir forest (fig. 10.20) on Vancouver Island, British Columbia (Getzin et al. 2006).

They chose as a study site a set of forest stands on southeastern Vancouver Island. These stands differed in age,

Figure 10.20   The small-scale distribution of different tree species in a Douglas-fir forest is determined by both biotic and abiotic interactions.

ranging from old-growth (254 years old) to relatively young (39 years old). The research team mapped the locations and species identity of all the dead and living trees in several plots within each stand (fig. 10.21). They were primarily interested in three species: Douglas-fir (*Pseudotsuga menziesii*), western hemlock (*Tsuga heterophylla*), and western redcedar (*Thuja plicata*). If competition was important in structuring these populations, they predicted that trees in clumps were more likely to suffer greater mortality than more widely dispersed trees. As a result of mortality related to competition, they predicted that the distribution of trees should become more regular over time (moving from the young stand to the old stand). Strong

influences of local site characteristics would likely be seen as clumped distributions being maintained through time. Why? Trees of a given species would only be found in areas that have the necessary site conditions for its survival and growth, and these conditions are not expected to move over time.

At the smallest spatial scales, trees tended to be clumped together, suggesting influence of the local habitat. However, there was a positive correlation between spatial aggregation and competition. For all three species, the highest levels of aggregation were found in the stands for which competition was strongest! They were able to measure competition as the relationship between the distance of a tree to its nearest neighbour and its growth rate, showing that the closer other trees were, the slower the tree grew. When competition was greatest varied among species, but in general strong competition did not necessarily result in regular distribution of plants.

Why did these surprising results occur? One possible explanation is that although competition was strong and significantly reduced plant growth rates, it was not strong enough to kill them. In other words, competition should impact spatial patterns if it kills the plants involved (or, if looking at animal populations, it would need to cause the animals to either die or leave the area). An additional possibility is that clumped trees may somehow facilitate the growth of the other trees (chapter 15), thereby mitigating the negative consequences of competition. Finally, within the large data set that Getzin and colleagues generated was another clue to the answer. For one species, western hemlock, spatial distributions of the trees were more regular post-mortality than pre-mortality, a result consistent with competition. This suggests that the factors that influence spatial distributions of individuals within a population are going to vary among species. Although we use generalizations frequently, it is important to realize that different species have their own niches, and these differences may have important ecological consequences.

Below Ground Distributions of Desert Shrubs

As we have seen in the forests of British Columbia, competition between plants may alter the distribution of individuals within a population. However, in many systems competition among plants will be predominantly below ground (chapter 13) for resources such as water and nitrogen. How do researchers study these sorts of below-ground interactions? For a classic example, we turn to the work of Jacques Brisson and James Reynolds (1994) describing the root distributions of creosote bush, *Larrea tridentata*. These researchers carefully excavated and mapped the distributions of 32 creosote bushes in the Chihuahuan Desert. They proposed that if creosote bushes compete, their roots should grow in a way that reduces overlap with the roots of nearby individuals.

The excavated creosote bushes occupied a 4 m by 5 m area near Las Cruces, New Mexico. The creosote bush was the only shrub within the study plot. Their roots penetrated to only 30–50 cm, the depth of a hardpan calcium carbonate deposition layer. Because they did not have to excavate to great depths, Brisson and Reynolds were able to map more root systems than previous researchers. Still, their excavation and mapping of roots required two months of intense labour.

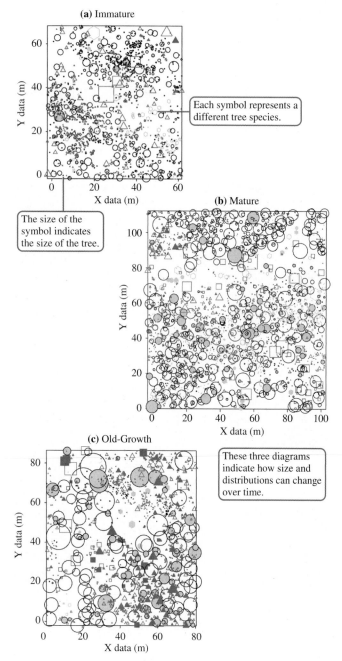

(a) Immature

Each symbol represents a different tree species.

The size of the symbol indicates the size of the tree.

(b) Mature

(c) Old-Growth

These three diagrams indicate how size and distributions can change over time.

Figure 10.21   The spatial distribution of trees in three separate stands of different ages on Vancouver Island (data from Getzin et al. 2006). Differences among stands are assumed to indicate changes through time.

The complex pattern of root distributions uncovered confirmed the researchers' proposal: Creosote bush roots grow in a pattern that reduces overlap between the roots of adjacent plants (fig. 10.22*a*). We can make the root distributions of individual plants clearer by plotting their perimeters only. Figure 10.22*b* shows the hypothetical distributions of creosote bushes with circular root systems, while figure 10.22*c* shows their actual root distributions. Notice that the root systems of creosote bushes overlap much less than they would if they had circular distributions. Brisson and Reynolds conclude that competitive interactions with neighbouring shrubs influence the distribution of creosote bush roots.

As we have seen, numerous factors can influence both the above and below-ground distributions of plants. In the following section, we find distributions are predominantly clumped.

Distributions of Individuals on Large Scales

We have considered how individuals within a population are distributed on a small scale. Now let's step back and ask how individuals within a population are distributed on a larger scale over which there is significant environmental variation.

Bird Populations Across North America

Terry Root (1988) mapped patterns of bird abundance across North America using the "Christmas Bird Counts." These bird counts provide one of the few data sets extensive enough to study distribution patterns across an entire continent. Christmas Bird Counts, which began in 1900, involve annual counts of birds during the Christmas season. The first Christmas Bird Count was attended by 27 observers, who counted birds in 26 localities—two in Canada and the remainder in 13 states of the United States. In the 1985–86 season, 38,346 people participated in the Christmas Bird Count. The observers counted birds in 1,504 localities throughout the United States and much of Canada. In the 2008–2009 season, 59,813 observers recorded 65,596,663 birds in 2,124 localities! Included in these numbers were 2,836,595 birds spotted by 11,059 observers in 361 localities in

Canada. Of all the locations across the planet, the one with the greatest number of participants was Edmonton, Alberta. Despite the cold winter weather, 409 people spent part of the winter holiday in Edmonton counting birds. This annual count continues to produce a unique record of the distribution and population densities of wintering birds across most of a continent.

Root's analysis centres around a series of maps that show patterns of distribution and population density for 346 species of birds that winter in the United States and Canada. Although species as different as swans and sparrows are included, the maps show a consistent pattern. At the continental scale, bird populations have clumped distributions. Clumped patterns occur in species with widespread distributions, such as the American crow, *Corvus brachyrhynchos*, as well as in species with restricted distributions, such as the fish crow, *C. ossifragus*. Though the winter distribution of the American crow includes most of the continent, the bulk of individuals in this population are concentrated in a few areas. These areas of high density, or "hot spots," appear as orange dots in figure 10.23*a*. For the American crow population, hot spots are concentrated along river valleys, especially the Cumberland, Mississippi, Arkansas, Snake, and Rio Grande. Away from these hot spots, the winter abundance of American crows diminishes rapidly.

The fish crow population, though much more restricted than that of the American crow, is also concentrated in a few areas (fig. 10.23*b*). Fish crows are restricted to areas of open water near the coast of the Gulf of Mexico and along the southern half of the Atlantic coast of the United States. Within this restricted range, however, most fish crows are concentrated in a few hot spots—one on the Mississippi Delta, another on Lake Seminole west of Tallahassee, Florida, and a third in the everglades in southern Florida. Like the more widely distributed American crow, the abundance of fish crows diminishes rapidly away from these centres of high density.

Why do these bird species, and many others, demonstrate such clumped distributions? There can be many explanations, including predation, disease, and dispersal; however,

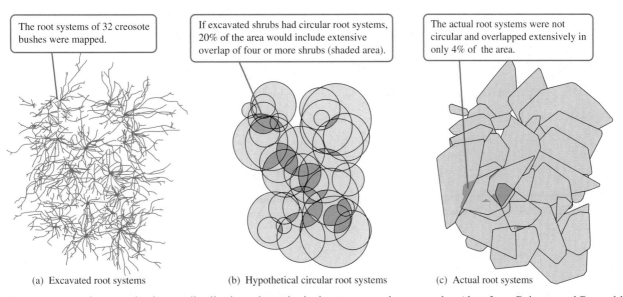

The root systems of 32 creosote bushes were mapped.

If excavated shrubs had circular root systems, 20% of the area would include extensive overlap of four or more shrubs (shaded area).

The actual root systems were not circular and overlapped extensively in only 4% of the area.

(a) Excavated root systems   (b) Hypothetical circular root systems   (c) Actual root systems

Figure 10.22   Creosote bush root distributions: hypothetical versus actual root overlap (data from Brisson and Reynolds 1994).

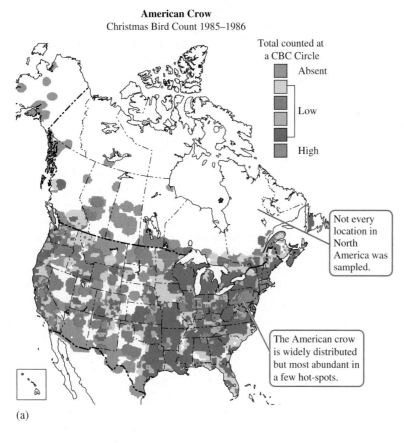

American Crow
Christmas Bird Count 1985–1986

Total counted at
a CBC Circle

Absent

Low

High

Not every location in North America was sampled.

The American crow is widely distributed but most abundant in a few hot-spots.

(a)

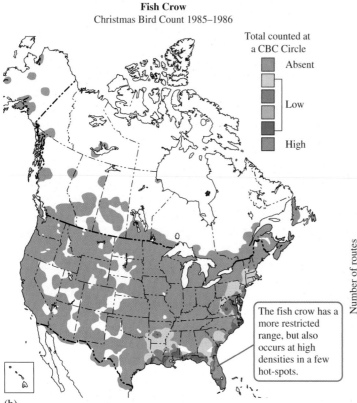

Fish Crow
Christmas Bird Count 1985–1986

Total counted at
a CBC Circle

Absent

Low

High

The fish crow has a more restricted range, but also occurs at high densities in a few hot-spots.

(b)

Figure 10.23 (*a*) Winter distribution of the American crow, *Corvus brachyrhynchos*. (*b*) Winter distribution of the fish crow, *C. ossifragus* (data from National Audubon Society).

a common explanation again returns us to the niche concept (chapter 9). Because environmental conditions vary across geographic areas, only certain locations will have the combination of necessary environmental conditions for a given species. When the environmental conditions of a specific location match the optimum growth conditions described by a species' niche, one would expect that species to potentially thrive. When conditions are near the survival thresholds for some niche axes, one would expect reduced growth and population sizes.

Might bird populations have clumped distributions only on the wintering grounds? James H. Brown, David Mehlman, and George Stevens (1995) analyzed large-scale patterns of abundance among birds across North America during the breeding season, the opposite season from that studied by Root. In their study these researchers used data from the Breeding Bird Survey, which consists of standardized counts by amateur ornithologists conducted each June at approximately 2,000 sites across the United States and Canada under the supervision of the Fish and Wildlife Services of the United States and the National Wildlife Research Centre run by the Canadian Wildlife Service. For their analyses, they chose species of birds whose geographic ranges fall mainly or completely within the eastern and central regions of the United States, which are well covered by study sites of the Breeding Bird Survey.

Like Root, Brown and his colleagues found that a relatively small proportion of study sites yielded most of the records of each bird species. That is, most individuals were concentrated in a fairly small number of hot spots. For instance, the densities of red-eyed vireos are low in most places (fig. 10.24).

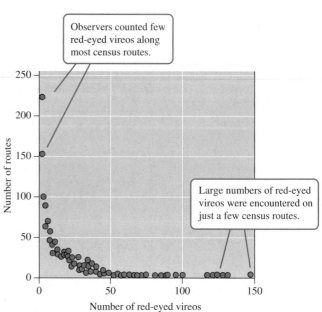

Observers counted few red-eyed vireos along most census routes.

Large numbers of red-eyed vireos were encountered on just a few census routes.

Figure 10.24 Red-eyed vireos, *Vireo olivaceus*, counted along census routes of the Breeding Bird Survey (data from Brown, Mehlman, and Stevens 1995).

Clumped distributions were documented repeatedly. When the numbers of birds across their ranges were totalled, generally about 25% of the locations sampled supported over half of each population. By combining the results of Root and Brown and his colleagues, we can say confidently that at larger scales, bird populations in North America show clumped patterns of distribution. In other words, most individuals within a bird species live in a few hot spots, areas of unusually high population density.

Brown and his colleagues propose that these distributions are clumped because the environment varies and individuals aggregate in areas where the environment is favourable. What might be the patterns of distribution for populations distributed along a known environmental gradient? Studies of plant populations provide interesting insights.

Plant Abundance Along Moisture Gradients

Several decades ago, Robert Whittaker gathered information on the distributions of woody plants along moisture gradients in several mountain ranges across North America. This work has since proven to be a foundation of ecology. As we saw in chapter 2, environmental conditions change substantially with elevation. These steep environmental gradients provide a compressed analog of the continental-scale gradients to which the birds studied by Root and Brown and his colleagues were presumably responding.

Let's look at the distributions of some tree species along moisture gradients in two of the mountain ranges studied by Whittaker. Robert Whittaker and William Niering (1965) studied the distribution of plants along moisture and elevation gradients in the Santa Catalina Mountains of southern Arizona. These mountains rise out of the Sonoran Desert near Tucson, Arizona, like a green island in a tan desert sea. Vegetation typical of the Sonoran Desert, including the saguaro cactus and creosote bush, grow in the surrounding desert and on the lower slopes of the mountains. However, the summit of the mountains is topped by a mixed conifer forest. Forests also extend down the flanks of the Santa Catalinas in moist, shady canyons.

There is a moisture gradient from the moist canyon bottoms up the dry southwest-facing slopes. Whittaker and Niering found that along this gradient, the Mexican pinyon pine, *Pinus cembroides*, is at its peak abundance on the uppermost and driest part of the southwest-facing slope (fig. 10.25). Along the same slope, Arizona Madrone, *Arbutus arizonica*, reaches its peak abundance at middle elevations. Finally, Douglas-firs, *Pseudotsuga menziesii*, are restricted to the moist canyon bottom. Mexican pinyon pines, Arizona Madrone, and Douglas-fir are all clumped along this moisture gradient, but each reaches peak abundance at different positions on the slope. These positions appear to reflect the different environmental requirements of each species.

Whittaker (1956) recorded analogous tree distributions along moisture gradients in the Great Smoky Mountains of eastern North America. Again, the gradient was from a moist valley bottom to a drier southwest-facing slope. Along this moisture gradient, hemlock, *Tsuga canadensis*, was concentrated in the moist valley bottom and its density decreased rapidly upslope

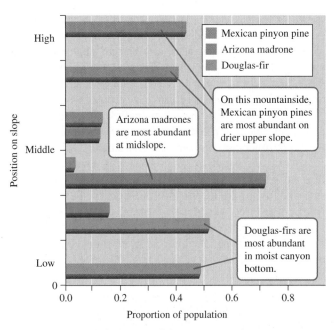

Figure 10.25   Abundances of three tree species on a moisture gradient in the Santa Catalina Mountains, Arizona (data from Whittaker and Niering 1965).

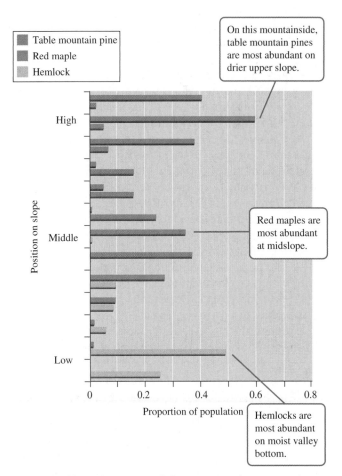

Figure 10.26   Abundance of three tree species on a moisture gradient in the Great Smoky Mountains, Tennessee (data from Whittaker 1956).

(fig. 10.26). Meanwhile red maple, *Acer rubrum*, grew at highest densities in the middle section of the slope, while table mountain pine, *Pinus pungens*, was concentrated on the driest upper sections. As in the Santa Catalina Mountains of Arizona, these tree distributions in the Great Smoky Mountains reflect the moisture requirements of each tree species.

The distribution of trees along moisture gradients seems to resemble the clumped distributional patterns of birds across the North American continent, but on a smaller scale. All species of trees discussed here showed a highly clumped distribution along moisture gradients, and their densities decreased substantially toward the edges of their distributions. In other words, like birds, tree populations are concentrated in hot spots. As we shall see in the next concept discussion, some populations are subdivided into separate subpopulations that exchange individuals over time.

CONCEPT 10.4 REVIEW

1. How could you test the hypothesis that low overlap in the root systems of creosote bush populations is the result of ongoing competition, and not due to variation in underlying soil nutrient distributions?

2. Why do population densities generally decline as you move from the centre to the edge of a species' range?

ECOLOGY IN ACTION

Using Ecology to Protect Threatened Species

In the media we often hear reports of species on the verge of extinction, and of government efforts underway to protect remaining populations. The laws protecting these species vary widely among countries; in Canada, we have the Species at Risk Act (SARA). By November, 2006, there were 389 species formally listed and given legal protection in Canada under SARA (Environment Canada 2006; fig. 10.27). But what exactly does this mean? Who actually makes this determination, what happens after such a designation is made, and what role does ecology play in this process?

As stated in the summary of SARA itself, "The purposes of this enactment are to prevent Canadian indigenous species, subspecies and distinct populations of wildlife from becoming extirpated or extinct, to provide for the recovery of endangered or threatened species, to encourage the management of other species to prevent them from becoming at risk" (Species at Risk Act Public Registry 2007). To achieve these goals there are two important steps: (1) the identification of species at risk, and (2) the development and implementation of a recovery and/or protection plan. Both of these steps require substantial research into understanding issues such as species distributions and the causes of changes to population size.

Decisions about at-risk designations involve substantial deliberation among an independent body of experts, the Committee on the Status of Endangered Wildlife in Canada (COSEWIC). In 2006, COSEWIC consisted of 30 members, including: governmental members from the wildlife agencies of each of the 13 territories or provinces; members from four federal agencies (Canadian Wildlife Service, Parks Canada, Department of Fisheries and Oceans, and the Federal Biodiversity Partnership); and nongovernmental representatives, including three science members, nine members from the

Figure 10.27   Species currently endangered in Canada include (*a*) the Burrowing Owl, *Athene cunicularia*; (*b*) Taylor's Checkerspot, *Euphydryas editha taylori*; (*c*) Aurora trout, *Salvelinus fontinalis timagamiensis*; and (*d*) the Western spiderwort, *Tradescantia occidentalis*.

Species Specialist Subcommittees, and one co-chair from the Aboriginal Traditional Knowledge Subcommittee. COSEWIC makes decisions about whether the best science and traditional knowledge support a case for listing a particular species

as endangered. It is then up to the Minister of the Environment to act upon that recommendation. However, listing many species can present significant economic and political challenges, and thus despite recommendations based upon sound ecological science, not all species recommended for listing by COSEWIC are listed by the Minister of the Environment. In other words, science and politics both influence the legal status of species in Canada.

The first step in giving a species an at-risk designation is for COSEWIC to become aware of a potential threatened species. This is not a trivial undertaking, considering that there are over 70,000 known wild species in Canada. These efforts are assisted by biologists at the provincial, territorial, and federal governmental levels who regularly assess a number of species, forwarding species of concern to COSEWIC. Additional inputs on species for consideration can come from nongovernmental organizations and private citizens. Assessments are based mainly on changes in abundance and distribution of the species in Canada using quantitative benchmarks based upon those elaborated by the International Union for the Conservation of Nature (IUCN). Factors that get considered include species range, population size, rates of population decline, habitat fragmentation, and the existence of current or expected threats to the species (e.g., introduced species, disease, habitat destruction, etc.).

Although only species thought to be at risk are brought to COSEWIC, upon further study of the data, the committee often finds that not all of these species are actually at risk. For example, by April 2006, COSEWIC had evaluated 727 species (COSEWIC 2006). Of these, 157 (22%) were found to be not at risk, meaning the best science to date suggests that these species will continue to persist without special protection. An additional 41 species (5%) were deemed "data-deficient," which means there are not enough data available to make a sound scientific recommendation for or against protection. The remaining 529 species (73%) were recommended for listing by COSEWIC. However, you may recall from the beginning of this section that by November 2006, only 389 species were actually listed under SARA. What happened to the other 140 species COSEWIC recommend for listing? Some are in the pipeline, and are simply experiencing expected delays within the government. Others, however, are intentionally not listed by the Minister of the Environment.

The Minister of the Environment has the ability to make non-science-based discretionary decisions that reflect concerns about potential economic or political implications of a listing. In contrast to the Endangered Species Act in the United States, Canada's SARA does not provide the opportunity for private citizens to appeal such discretionary decisions. Although SARA does provide some protections, it is a substantially weaker act than is in place in the United States.

A team of researchers including Arnie Mooers from Simon Fraser University, Laura Prugh from the University of British Columbia, Marco Festa-Bianchet from the Université de Sherbrooke, and Jeff Hutchings from Dalhousie University, have published a study investigating evidence for political bias in which species were given legal protection under SARA (Mooers et al. 2007). The team explored all decisions regarding listing of species as at-risk made by the Minister of Environment between 2004–2006. During this period, COSEWIC recommended listing 186 species, of which 30 were not listed by the Minister. Analyses indicated that only 17% of the COSEWIC-recommended fish and mammals species harvested by humans were listed, while 93% of the non-harvested species were given legal protection. These results were particularly evident for marine fish, where nearly all of the recommended species were denied listing. The researchers note that the one marine fish that was listed, the green sturgeon, *Acipenser medirostri*, has a "disagreeable taste" and there is no commercial fishery. A second bias appeared in a reluctance to list northern species. None of the 10 species that occurred in Nunavut recommended for listing by COSEWIC were listed, and in general only 28% of northern species were listed, compared to 90% of non-northern species. Clearly science only plays a partial role in the protection of species in Canada, with politics getting the final say.

Despite evidence of politics influencing the decision to protect some species, other species do end up with legal protection. Being at risk can take several forms, from the most extreme being already extinct (no longer found anywhere) or extirpated (no longer found in Canada, but found in other countries), to less extreme forms of risk such as endangered (facing imminent extirpation or extinction), threatened (likely to become extinct or extirpated unless actions are taken), and of special concern (may become threatened without actions being taken). Once a species has been listed, a recovery plan is developed that is designed to meet the unique needs of that species. Actions can include harvest moratoriums, captive breeding programs, control of competing or predating species, translocation of individuals to enhance existing or establish new populations, and education programs that promote changes in land use. These efforts are made through the cooperation of government agencies, a variety of nongovernmental organizations, scores of local volunteers, and with the help of landowners and industrial stakeholders. Although not every species will be able to be successfully recovered, several populations of several protected species have improved.

For example, the Swift Fox (*Vulpes velox*) is a small fox found in southern Alberta and Saskatchewan. It was listed as extirpated in 1978. Between 1983 and 1997, foxes were reintroduced, resulting in a population of 279 foxes in the wild in Canada in 1999, and the species was thus downgraded to endangered. The populations appear to be continuing to grow, and though this species is still endangered, there has been improvement over the last several decades. There are

other successes, such as the downlisting of the red-shouldered hawk from special concern to not-at-risk as populations increase, and populations of peregrine falcon continue to grow. For all listed species, continued monitoring to assess the effectiveness of recovery efforts is critical, with the eventual hope to be able to de-list recovered species.

Although being listed as "at risk" provides legal protection to many species, it is important to recognize that we do not have good data on all species in Canada. For example, it is widely acknowledged that there is currently a bias in data collection toward vertebrates. In fact, over 60% of the species brought forward to COSEWIC have been vertebrates, with only 2% being insects, even though vertebrates make up only a small fraction of Canada's biodiversity. These biases mean that many inconspicuous species likely at risk are unprotected. Yet these species can be extremely important to ecosystem function and have equal ethical rights for consideration under COSEWIC

guidelines. It is also important to recognize that species do not recognize political boundaries. Many of the species of concern in Canada are abundant and have healthy populations in the United States. Thus Canada represents the northern edge-of-range for many otherwise common species. One argument suggests that edge populations are particularly valuable as they may hold unique genotype. An alternative argument suggests that approaches to conservation should transcend national borders, taking into consideration the full spatial extent of a species' distribution.

It is the job of future generations of ecologists to learn more about the biodiversity of Canada and other locations in the world, and to decide the best path forward. One thing is clear—without dedicated intervention by ecologists, species extinction rates would be higher than they currently are. Only through continued ecological research is there any hope to preserve a diverse world for future generations.

10.5   Organism Size and Population Density

Population density declines with increasing organism size.
If you estimate the densities of organisms in their natural environments, you will find great ranges. Bacterial populations in soils or water can exceed 10^9 individuals per cubic centimetre. Phytoplankton densities often exceed 10^6 individuals per cubic metre. Populations of large mammals and birds can average considerably less than one individual per square kilometre. What factors produce this variation in population density? One factor appears to be body size. In general, population densities decrease with increasing body size of individuals.

While it makes sense that small organisms generally live at higher population densities than larger ones, quantifying the relationship between body size and population density provides valuable information. Measuring the relationship between body size and population density for a wide variety of species reveals different relationships for different groups of organisms. Differences in the relationship between size and population density can be seen among major groups of animals.

Animal Size and Population Density

John Damuth (1981) produced one of the first clear demonstrations of the relationship between body size and population density. He focused his analysis on herbivorous mammals, ranging from small rodents with a mass of about 10 g, to rhinoceros, with a mass well over 10^6 g. Meanwhile, average population density ranged from about 0.1 individual (10^{-2}) per 1 km^2 to about 10,000 (10^4) per 1 km^2. As figure 10.28 shows, the population density of 307 species of herbivorous mammals decreases with increased body size.

Building on Damuth's analysis, Robert Peters and Karen Wassenberg (1983), of McGill University, explored the relationship between body size and average population density for a wider variety of animals, including terrestrial invertebrates, aquatic invertebrates, mammals, birds, and poikilothermic vertebrates. In their study they included animals that ranged in mass from 10^{-11} to nearly 10^3 kg. For these same species, population density ranged from nearly 10^{12} individuals per square kilometre to fewer than 1 individual per square kilometre. Peters and Wassenberg, like Damuth, found that population density decreased with increased body size.

If you look closely at the data in figure 10.29, however, it is clear that there are differences among the animal groups. First, aquatic invertebrates of a given body size tend to have higher

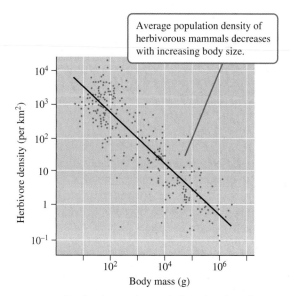

Average population density of herbivorous mammals decreases with increasing body size.

Figure 10.28 Body size and population density of herbivorous mammals (data from Damuth 1981).

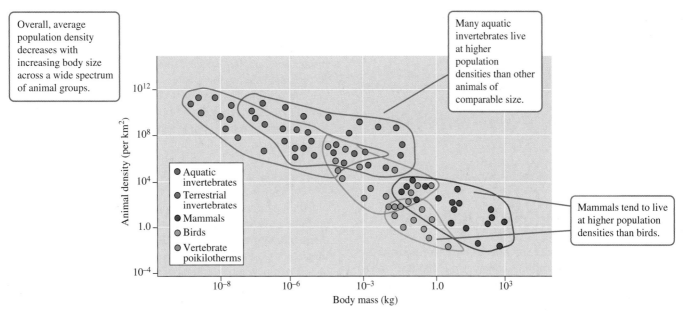

Figure 10.29   Animal size and population density (data from Peters and Wassenberg 1983).

population densities than terrestrial invertebrates of similar size. Second, mammals tend to have higher population densities than birds of similar size. These differences suggest that although there appears to be a general ecological principle of decreasing population densities with increasing body size, taxonomic differences influence the specific shape of this relationship.

The general relationship between animal size and population density has held up under careful scrutiny and reanalysis. Plant ecologists have found a qualitatively similar relationship in plant populations, as we see next.

Plant Size and Population Density

James White (1985) summarized the relationship between size and density for a large number of plant species spanning a wide range of plant growth forms (fig. 10.30).

The pattern in figure 10.30 illustrates that as in animals, plant population density decreases with increasing plant size. However, the biological details underlying the size–density relationship shown by plants are quite different from those underlying the size–density patterns shown by animals. The different points in figures 10.28 and 10.29 represent different species of animals. A single species of tree, however, can span a very large range of sizes and densities during its life cycle. Even the largest trees, such as the giant sequoia, *Sequoia gigantea*, start life as small seedlings. These tiny seedlings can live at very high densities. As the trees grow, density declines progressively until the mature trees live at low densities. We discuss this process, which is called *self-thinning*, in chapter 13. Thus, the size–density relationship changes dynamically within plant populations and also differs significantly between populations of plants that reach different sizes at maturity. Despite differences in the underlying processes, the data summarized in figure 10.30 indicate a predictable relationship between plant size and population density.

The value of such an empirical relationship, whether for plants or animals, is that it provides a standard against which we can compare measured densities and gives an idea of expected

population densities in nature. For example, suppose you go out into the field and measure the population density of some species of animal. How would you know if the densities you encounter are unusually high, low, or about average for an animal of the particular size and taxon? Without an empirical relationship such as that shown in figures 10.29 and 10.30 or a list of species densities, it would be impossible to make such an assessment. One question that we might attempt to answer with a population study is whether a species is rare. As we shall see next, rarity is a more complex consideration than it might seem at face value.

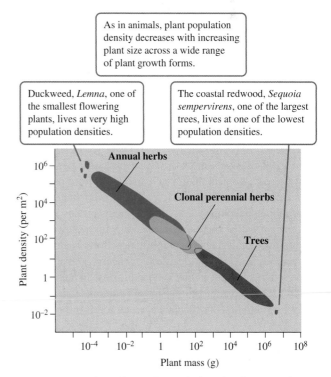

Figure 10.30   Plant size and population density (data from White 1985).

CONCEPT 10.5 REVIEW

1. What are some advantages of Damuth's strict focus on herbivorous mammals in his analysis of the relationship between body size and population density?
2. How might energy and nutrient relations explain the lower population densities of birds compared to comparable sized mammals?

10.6 Commonness and Rarity

Commonness and rarity of species are influenced by population size, geographic range, and habitat tolerance. Viewed on a long-term, geological timescale, populations come and go and extinction seems to be the inevitable punctuation mark at the end of a species' history. However, some populations seem to be more vulnerable to extinction than others. What makes some populations likely to disappear, while others persist? At the heart of the matter are patterns of distribution and abundance. Species that are rare even in the absence of human activity seem to be more vulnerable to extinction. Species for whom human activity causes loss of habitat, introduction of new competitors and predators, or harvest for economic gain may be particularly at risk.

The loss of species diversity is a global issue, and has generated a number of global responses. One of most important first steps in reducing species extinction rates is a scientifically grounded catalogue of species at risk across the planet. The International Union for the Conservation of Nature (IUCN) is a large group of researchers from across the world, including over 1,000 members in 140 countries. As a group, they have published the "Global Species Assessment" (Baillie et al. 2004), describing the global distribution of species determined to be at risk of extinction. They estimate a minimum of 15,000 known species are threatened with extinction, though the vast majority of known species (97%) do not have sufficient data for a scientifically rigorous assessment. Although vertebrates tend to be well studied, little information is available for organisms that live in aquatic systems, those that live in particularly species-rich locations (e.g., tropical rainforests), and those from particularly species-rich taxonomic groups (e.g., fungi, invertebrates, plants). Thus, although ecologists can identify many species at risk, we also recognize that there are many more for whom sufficient data are just not available. Complicating efforts is a realization that rarity by itself is not a cause for concern, as many species can persist indefinitely at low population sizes. To help prioritize species for conservation efforts, and to better understand extinction, we need to first understand the seven forms of rarity.

Seven Forms of Rarity and One of Abundance

Deborah Rabinowitz (1981) devised a classification of *commonness* and *rarity*, based on combinations of three factors: (1) the geographic range of a species (*extensive* versus *restricted*),

(2) habitat tolerance (*broad* versus *narrow*), and (3) local population size (*large* versus *small*). Habitat tolerance is related to the range of conditions in which a species can live. For instance, some plant species can tolerate a broad range of soil texture, pH, and organic matter content, while other plant species are confined to a single soil type. As we shall see, tigers have broad habitat tolerance; however, within the tiger's historical range in Asia lives the snow leopard, which is confined to a narrow range of conditions in the high mountains of the Tibetan Plateau. Small geographic range, narrow habitat tolerance, and low population density are all attributes of rarity.

As shown in figure 10.31, there are eight possible combinations of these factors, seven of which include at least one attribute of rarity. The most abundant species and those least threatened by extinction typically have extensive geographic ranges, broad habitat tolerances, and large local populations at least somewhere within their range. Some of these species, such as starlings, Norway rats, and house sparrows, are associated with humans and are considered pests. However, many species of small mammals, birds, and invertebrates not associated with humans, such as the deer mouse, *Peromyscus maniculatus*, or the marine zooplankton, *Calanus finmarchicus*, also fall into this most common category.

Ecologists exploring the relationship between size of geographic range and population size have found that they are not independent. Instead, there is a strong positive correlation between the two variables for most groups of organisms. In other words, species abundant in the places where they occur are generally widely distributed within a region, continent, or ocean, while species living at low population densities generally have small, restricted distributions. The positive relationship between range and population density was first brought to the attention of ecologists by Ilka Hanski (Hanski 1982) and James H. Brown (Brown 1984). Kevin Gaston (Gaston 1996, Gaston et al. 2000) points out that in the two decades since the early work by Hanski and Brown, ecologists have found a positive relationship between range and population density for many groups, including plants, grasshoppers, scale insects, hoverflies, bumblebees, moths, beetles, butterflies, birds, frogs, and mammals. Several mechanisms have been proposed to explain the positive relationship between local abundance and range size. Many of the explanations focus on breadth of environmental tolerances and differences in metapopulation dynamics. However, as Gaston and his colleagues point out (Gaston et al. 2000) there is still no consensus on the most likely explanations.

Most species are uncommon; seven combinations of range, tolerance, and population size each create a kind of rarity. As a consequence, Rabinowitz referred to "seven forms of rarity." Let's look at species that represent the two extremes of Rabinowitz's seven forms of rarity.

Rarity I: Extensive Geographic Range, Broad Habitat Tolerance, and Small Local Population

The sight and sound of a peregrine falcon, *Falco peregrinus* (figure 10.32), in full dive at over 200 km per hour is a sight few will ever forget. However, though the peregrine has a geographic range that circles the Northern Hemisphere and broad habitat tolerance, is uncommon throughout its range, and thus

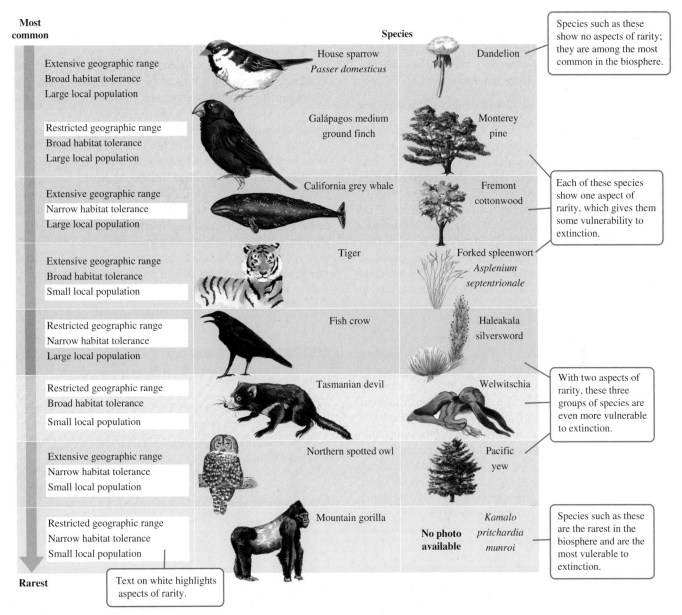

Most common

Species

Extensive geographic range Broad habitat tolerance Large local population	House sparrow *Passer domesticus*
Restricted geographic range Broad habitat tolerance Large local population	Galápagos medium ground finch
Extensive geographic range Narrow habitat tolerance Large local population	California grey whale
Extensive geographic range Broad habitat tolerance Small local population	Tiger
Restricted geographic range Narrow habitat tolerance Large local population	Fish crow
Restricted geographic range Broad habitat tolerance Small local population	Tasmanian devil
Extensive geographic range Narrow habitat tolerance Small local population	Northern spotted owl
Restricted geographic range Narrow habitat tolerance Small local population	Mountain gorilla

Dandelion — Species such as these show no aspects of rarity; they are among the most common in the biosphere.

Monterey pine

Fremont cottonwood — Each of these species show one aspect of rarity, which gives them some vulnerability to extinction.

Forked spleenwort *Asplenium septentrionale*

Haleakala silversword

Welwitschia — With two aspects of rarity, these three groups of species are even more vulnerable to extinction.

Pacific yew

Kamalo pritchardia munroi No photo available — Species such as these are the rarest in the biosphere and are the most vulerable to extinction.

Rarest

Text on white highlights aspects of rarity.

Figure 10.31 Commonness, rarity, and vulnerability to extinction.

Figure 10.32 The peregrine falcon, *Falco peregrinus*, has a broad geographic range, but occurs in low population densities.

rarely seen. Apparently, this one attribute of rarity was enough to make the peregrine vulnerable to extinction. The falcon's feeding on prey containing high concentrations of DDT, which produced thin eggshells and nesting failure, drove the peregrine to the brink of extinction. Populations have since recovered (or are recovering), due to control of the use of DDT, strict regulation of the capture of the birds, captive breeding, and reintroduction of the birds to areas where local populations had become extinct.

Rarity II: Extensive Geographic Range, Large Local Population, and Narrow Habitat Tolerance

When Europeans arrived in North America and visited what is now the midwestern United States, the rivers harboured an abundant, widely distributed but narrowly tolerant fish, the harelip sucker, *Lagochila lacera*. This fish was found in streams across most of the east-central United States and was abundant enough that early ichthyologists cited it as one of the commonest and most valuable food fish in the region. However, the harelip sucker had narrow habitat requirements; restricted to large pools with rocky

bottoms in clear, medium-sized streams about 15 to 30 m wide. This habitat was eliminated by the silting of rivers that followed deforestation and by the erosion of poorly managed agricultural lands. The last individuals of this species collected by ichthyologists came from the Maumee River in northwestern Ohio in 1893.

Extreme Rarity: Restricted Geographic Range, Narrow Habitat Tolerance, and Small Local Population

Species that combine small geographic ranges with narrow habitat tolerances and low population densities are the rarest of the rare. This group includes species such as the mountain gorilla, the giant panda, and the California condor. Species showing this extreme form of rarity are clearly the most vulnerable to extinction. Many island species have these attributes, so it is not surprising that island species are especially vulnerable. Of the 171 bird species and subspecies known to have become extinct since 1600, 155 species were restricted to islands. Of the 70 species and subspecies of birds known to have lived on the Hawaiian Islands, 24 are now extinct and 30 are considered in danger of extinction.

Organisms on continents that are restricted to small areas, have narrow habitat tolerance, and have a small population size are also vulnerable to extinction. Examples of populations in such circumstances are common. More than 20 species of plants and animals are confined to about 200 km^2 of mixed wetlands and upland desert in California called Ash Meadows. The Ash Meadows stickleaf, *Mentzelia leucophylla*, inhabits an area of about 2.5 km^2 and has a total population size of fewer than 100 individuals. Another plant, the Ash Meadows milkvetch, *Astragalus phoenix*, has a total population of fewer than 600 individuals. Human alteration of Ash Meadows appears to have caused the extinction of at least one native species, the Ash Meadows killifish, *Empetrichthys merriami*.

Amazingly, there are species with ranges even more restricted than those of Ash Meadows, California. In 1980, the total population of the Virginia round-leaf birch, *Betula uber*, was limited to 20 individuals in Smyth County, Virginia. Until recently the total habitat of the Socorro isopod, *Thermosphaeroma thermophilum*, of Socorro, New Mexico, was limited to a spring pool and outflow with a surface area of a few square metres. Meanwhile, a palm species, *Pritchardia munroi*, which is found only on the island of Maui in the Hawaiian Islands, has a total population in nature of exactly one individual!

Examples such as these fill books listing endangered species. In nearly all cases, the key to a species' survival is increased distribution and abundance. One of the most fundamental needs for managing species, endangered or not, is making accurate estimates of population size. Some of the conceptual and practical issues that population ecologists must consider when censusing a population are the subject of the Ecological Tools and Approaches section.

CONCEPT 10.6 REVIEW

1. How can the type of rarity displayed by a particular species influence its risk of going extinct? In other words, do low population sizes and restricted ranges present equal risks for extinction?
2. How does the life history influence whether a species will be common, or rare? Which types of life histories are more prone to restricted ranges? Small population sizes?

ECOLOGICAL TOOLS AND APPROACHES

Estimating Abundance

The abundance of organisms and how abundance changes in time and space are among the most fundamental concerns of ecology. These factors are so basic that some authors define ecology as the study of distribution and abundance of organisms. Because abundance is so important, ecologists should understand how to estimate it for a wide variety of organisms. Accurate estimates of abundance are critical for the management of many species, such as those at-risk or those of economic value. Accurate measures are also a critical tool for ecologists to use in understanding the underlying biology of populations. Knowing how abundant an organism is can tell us whether its population is growing, declining, or stable. However, to estimate the abundance of species, the ecologist must contend with a variety of practical challenges and conceptual subtleties. Some of these are discussed here.

One of the first challenges that an ecologist wanting to estimate population sizes will face is the diverse array of methods available (fig. 10.33). Some of these differences will be cultural (yes, even scientists are influenced by cultural norms!), while most of these differences will be driven by the demands of the species being sampled. Sessile organisms, such as plants and many intertidal invertebrates, are among the simplest groups to sample, as they do not have the nasty habit of walking away. For these groups, ecologists will often lay down a quadrat of a known size, and simply count the number of individuals that occur in that space. By using many quadrats, ecologists are able to estimate population densities. Flying organisms can be a bit trickier, and generally require either a lure, such as a pheromone trap for moths or coloured traps for bees, or they can be caught mid-flight using a mist net (for

Figure 10.33 Shown here are students conducting ecological research in a diversity of field sites in Alberta. Different focal taxa and geographic locations require diverse methodologies.

small birds) or a sweep net (for insects). Mammals are generally trapped, though larger, more dangerous mammals often need to be chemically immobilized. Though we may be most familiar with using traps and mist-nets to catch animals in the summer months (chapter 11), the winter can be an effective time of year to measure population sizes of many animals. Any ecologist with even a basic understanding of natural history will understand that measures of populations based only on summer numbers are likely less informative than those that include winter data, at least for species that are active and resident year round. How, though, does an ecologist measure populations in winter?

In much of Canada, the ground is snow covered and much of the vegetation has died back during winter (chapter 5). As a result, large animals have relatively few places to hide, and can be easily identified and counted from the air. Ecologists regularly use surveys in helicopters and fixed-wing aircraft to estimate population sizes of large mammals such as elk over large expanses of land. Small animals, such as insects, can still be caught directly during winter. Subnivean traps can be placed below the snow to trap small animals that are active in the warm space between the ground and the surface of the snow (chapter 5).

Population sizes can also be estimated using a number of indirect measures based upon evidence of animal activity, rather than direct capture or observation. By counting tracks in snow of animals such as wolves, accurate estimates of local activity and population size can be constructed. These measures can be made even more accurate by including pellet/dung counts and using molecular methods to identify individuals within the population (chapter 4). Other animals, such as hare, leave tell-tale signs of their presence through unique damage left on the stems of the browse they leave behind. A much more thorough discussion of population sampling is beyond the scope of this textbook, but could be found in ecology labs and advanced ecology courses at your university.

A number of other factors complicate sampling, including spatial heterogeneity in species distributions, the physical size of the organisms, and rarity. Aquatic organisms present a whole set of additional complications, given they are much better at surviving under water than is the student attempting to sample them. Below we provide a more detailed description of some sampling methods used on some aquatic species.

Estimating Whale Population Size

In 1989, the journal *Oceanus* published a table that listed the estimated sizes of whale populations. The table included the following note: "All estimates. . . are highly speculative." Why is it difficult to provide firm estimates of whale population size? Briefly, whales live at low population densities and may be distributed across vast expanses of ocean. They also spend much time submerged and move around a great deal. As large as they are, you cannot count all the whales in the ocean. Instead, marine ecologists rely on population estimation. Each method of estimation has its own limitations and uncertainties.

One method used to estimate population sizes of elusive animals involves marking or tagging some known number of individuals in the population, releasing the marked individuals so they will mix with the remainder of the population, and then sampling the population at some later time. The ratio of marked to unmarked individuals in the sample gives an estimate of population size. The simplest formula expressing this relationship is the Lincoln-Peterson index:

$$M/N = m/n$$

where:

   M = the number of individuals marked and released
   N = the actual size of the study population

m = the number of marked individuals in a sample of the population
n = the total number of individuals in the sample

The major assumption of the Lincoln-Peterson index is that the ratio of marked to unmarked individuals in the population as a whole equals the ratio of marked to unmarked individuals in a sample of the population. If this is approximately so, then the population size is estimated as:

$$N = Mn/m$$

However, on average, the Lincoln-Peterson index overestimates population size. To reduce this tendency to overestimate, N. Bailey (1951,1952) proposed a corrected formula:

$$N = \frac{M(n + 1)}{m + 1}$$

Some of the assumptions of mark and recapture studies are:

- All individuals in the population have an equal probability of being captured.
- The population is not increased by births or immigration between marking and recapture.
- Marked and unmarked individuals die and emigrate at the same rates.
- No marks are lost.

Although real populations rarely meet all these assumptions, mark and recapture estimates of population size are often the best estimates available.

Whale populations have been studied using mark and recapture techniques for some time. In the early days of whale population studies, population biologists marked whales by shooting a numbered metal dart into their blubber. Refined mark and recapture methods do not require artificially marking or capturing whales. In the "marking" phase of newer procedures, a whale is photographed and its distinguishing marks are identified. These photographs, along with information such as where the photograph was taken and whether the whale was accompanied by an offspring, are catalogued for future reference. In the "recapture" phase the whale is photographed at a later date and identified from previous photos. This method is called *photoidentification*.

For more than two decades, Steven Katona (1989) has used photoidentification to study the humpback whales, *Megaptera novaeangliae*, of the North Atlantic (fig. 10.34). Humpback whales are particularly rich in individual marks, especially on the tail or flukes. This is convenient for photographic studies because humpback whales generally raise their flukes above the water before they dive. This behaviour, called "fluking," exposes the flukes to the photographer and reveals potentially unique markings (fig. 10.35).

Using photographs of these marks, Katona and his colleagues have produced the North Atlantic Humpback Catalog, which includes photographs of more than 4,000 individual whales. The photographs included in the catalogue, along with information on where each photograph was taken, whether the whale was accompanied by an offspring, and

Figure 10.34 A humpback whale, *Megaptera novaeangliae.*

(a)

(b)

Figure 10.35 Unique markings identify individual humpback whales. A humpback whale called "Siphon," #700, photographed in Frenchman Bay, Maine: (*a*) in 1995 and (*b*) in 1993.

other available observations, are curated for future reference. This photographic record is an invaluable source of information for determining the migration routes, feeding grounds, breeding grounds, and size of the North Atlantic humpback whale population (fig. 10.36).

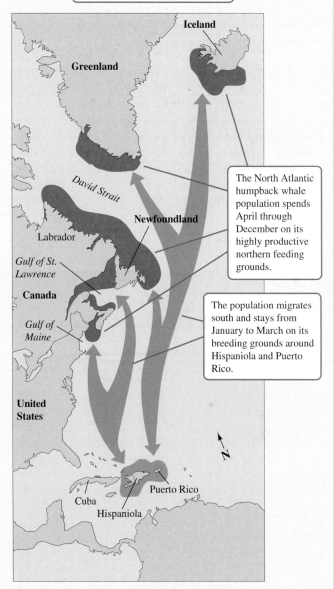

> Mark and recapture estimates based on photographs place the current population of humpback whales in the North Atlantic at about 5,000.

> The North Atlantic humpback whale population spends April through December on its highly productive northern feeding grounds.

> The population migrates south and stays from January to March on its breeding grounds around Hispaniola and Puerto Rico.

Figure 10.36 Photoidentification and the North Atlantic humpback whale population.

From 1979 to 1986, Scott Baker, Janice Straley, and Anjanette Perry (1992) photographed and identified 257 humpback whales along the coast of southeastern Alaska. In one part of their study the researchers used photoidentification to estimate the number of humpback whales in Frederick Sound, Alaska. In their first sampling period, from July 31 to August 3, 1986, the team photographed and identified 72 humpback whales. In a second sampling period, from August 29 to September 1, 1986, they photographed and identified 78 humpback whales. Of the 78 whales photographed in the

second sampling period, 56 were photographed for the first time, while 22 had also been photographed during the first sampling period. These 22 whales were the "recaptures." We can use these data and the corrected Lincoln-Peterson index to estimate the total number of whales in Frederick Sound from August 29 to September 1, 1986:

$$N = M (n + 1)/m + 1 = 72 (78 + 1)/22 + 1 = 247$$

In other words, Baker and his colleagues estimated that there were 247 humpback whales in Frederick Sound during the time of their study. Population estimates such as this are very important for monitoring the state of populations. In addition, photographic studies provide information on movements, calving intervals, and survival because photoidentified whales can go on yielding information throughout their lives.

In another study, population ecologists photographed and identified the entire population of 325 killer whales in Puget Sound and around Vancouver Island, revealing information about births, deaths, and the size of the population. An advance in this research approach is the use of computerized image analysis to help identify and match photos of whales. While not providing all the information necessary for conserving and managing whale populations, photographic studies are clearly making an important contribution.

Though it may be more challenging physically, the process of counting whales is much like counting many other kinds of animals such as humans, lynxes, trout, or lady beetles. However, ecologists must use different methods to estimate the abundance of organisms that have a more variable growth form or differ greatly in size. The best way to learn the different ways to study natural populations is to get some experience in the field. Spending a summer chasing whales, counting butterflies, and walking through forests is not a horrible way to earn a living.

SUMMARY

Ecologists define a population as a group of individuals of a single species inhabiting an area delimited by natural or human-imposed boundaries. Population studies hold the key to solving practical problems, such as saving endangered species, controlling pest populations, or managing fish and game populations. All populations share a number of characteristics. Chapter 10 focused on two population characteristics: distribution and abundance.

10.1 The physical environment limits the geographic distribution of species.

While there are few environments on earth without life, no single species can tolerate the full range of earth's environments. For instance, there is a close relationship between climate and the distributions of the three largest kangaroos in Australia. The tiger beetle *Cicindela longilabris* is limited to cool boreal and mountain environments. Large- and small-scale variation in temperature and moisture limits the distributions of certain plants. However, differences in the physical environment only partially explain the distributions of some species, a reminder that biological factors constitute an important part of an organism's environment.

10.2 Dispersal can alter species distributions and local population densities.

The contribution of dispersal to local population density and dynamics is demonstrated by studies of expanding populations of species such as Africanized bees in the Americas. Climate changes can induce massive changes in the ranges of species. As availability of prey changes, predators may disperse, which increases and decreases their local population densities. Stream organisms actively migrating upstream or drifting downstream increase densities of stationary and migrating populations by immigrating and decrease them by emigrating.

10.3 Some populations, called metapopulations, consist of interconnected subpopulations.

Populations of many species occur not as a single continuously distributed population, but in spatially isolated patches with significant exchange of individuals among patches. A group of subpopulations living on such patches connected by exchange of individuals among patches make up a metapopulation, such as is found for the Rocky Mountain Parnassian butterfly, *Parnassius smintheus*, in Alberta, Canada.

10.4 On small scales, individuals within populations are distributed in patterns that may be random, regular, or clumped.

Patterns of distribution can be produced by the social interactions within populations, by the structure of the physical environment, or by a combination of the two. Social organisms tend to be clumped; territorial organisms tend to be regularly spaced. An environment in which resources are patchy also fosters clumped distributions. The distribution of trees in a Douglas-fir forest changes as the forest ages and varies among species. **On larger scales, individuals within a population are clumped.** In North America, populations of both wintering and breeding birds are concentrated in a few hot spots of high population density. Clumped distributions are also shown by plant populations living along steep environmental gradients on mountainsides.

10.5 Population density declines with increasing organism size.

In general, animal population density declines with increasing body size. This negative relationship holds for animals as varied as terrestrial invertebrates, aquatic invertebrates, birds, poikilothermic vertebrates, and herbivorous mammals. Plant population density also decreases with increasing plant size. However, the biological details underlying the size–density relationship shown by plants are quite different from those underlying the size–density patterns shown by animals. A single species of tree can span a very large range of sizes and densities during its life cycle. The largest trees start life as small seedlings that can live at very high population densities. As trees grow, their population density declines progressively until the mature trees live at low densities.

10.6 Commonness and rarity of species are influenced by population size, geographic range, and habitat tolerance.

Rarity of species can be expressed as a combination of extensive versus restricted geographic range, broad versus narrow habitat tolerance, and large versus small population size. The most abundant species and those least threatened by extinction combine large geographic ranges, wide habitat tolerance, and high local population density. All other combinations of geographic range, habitat tolerance, and population size include one or more attributes of rarity. Rare species are vulnerable to extinction. Populations that combine restricted geographic range with narrow habitat tolerance and small population size are the rarest of the rare, and are usually the organisms most vulnerable to extinction.

The abundance of organisms and how abundance changes in time and space are among the most fundamental concerns of ecology. To estimate the abundance of species, the ecologist must contend with a variety of practical challenges and conceptual subtleties. Mark and recapture methods are useful in the study of populations of active, elusive, or secretive animals. Mark and recapture techniques, which use natural distinguishing marks, are making an important contribution to the study of populations of whales. Ecologists studying organisms, such as corals, algae, and sponges or many types of terrestrial plants, that differ a great deal in size and form, often estimate abundance as coverage, the area covered by a species. Population size can be estimated in the winter for many species using a variety of methods that take advantage of the snow. Patterns of distribution and abundance are ultimately determined by underlying population dynamics.

REVIEW QUESTIONS

1. Spruce trees, members of the genus *Picea*, occur throughout the boreal forest and on mountains farther south. For example, spruce grow in the Rocky Mountains south from the heart of boreal forest all the way to the deserts of the southern United States and Mexico. How do you think they would be distributed in the mountains that rise from the southern deserts? In particular, how do altitude and aspect (see chapter 5) affect their distributions in the southern part of their range? Would spruce populations be broken up into small local populations in the southern or the northern part of the range? Why?

2. What kinds of interactions within an animal population lead to clumped distributions? What kinds of interactions foster a regular distribution? What kinds of interactions would you expect to find within an animal population distributed in a random pattern?

3. How might the structure of the environment, for example, the distributions of different soil types and soil moisture, affect the patterns of distribution in plant populations? How should interactions among plants affect their distributions?

4. Suppose one plant reproduces almost entirely from seeds and its seeds are dispersed by wind, and a second plant reproduces asexually, mainly by budding from runners. How should these two different reproductive modes affect local patterns of distribution seen in populations of the two species?

5. Suppose that in the near future, the fish crow population in North America declines because of habitat destruction. Now that you have reviewed the large-scale distribution and abundance of the fish crow, devise a conservation plan for the species that includes establishing protected refuges for the species. Where would you locate the refuges? How many refuges would you recommend?

6. Use the empirical relationship between size and population density observed in the studies by Damuth (1981) (see fig. 10.28) and Peters and Wassenberg (1983) (see fig. 10.29) to answer the following: For a given body size, which generally has the higher population density, birds or mammals? On average, which lives at lower population densities, terrestrial or aquatic invertebrates? Does an herbivorous mammal twice the size of another have on average one-half the population density of the smaller species? Less than half? More than half?

7. Outline Rabinowitz's classification (1981) of rarity, which she based on size of geographic range, breadth of habitat tolerance, and population size. In her scheme, which combination of attributes makes a species least vulnerable to extinction? Which combination makes a species the most vulnerable?

8. Can the analyses by Damuth (1981) and by Peters and Wassenberg (1983) be combined with that of Rabinowitz (1981) to make predictions about the relationship of animal size to its relative rarity? What two attributes of rarity, as defined by Rabinowitz, are not included in the analyses by Damuth and by Peters and Wassenberg?

9. Suppose you have photoidentified 30 humpback whales around the island of Oahu in one cruise around the island. Two weeks later you return to the same area and photograph all the whales you encounter. On the second trip you photograph a total of 50 whales, of which 10 were photographed previously. Use the Lincoln-Peterson index with the Bailey correction to estimate the number of humpback whales around Oahu during your study.

10. Outline Müller's (1954, 1974) colonization cycle. If you were studying the colonization cycle of the freshwater snail *N. latissima*, how would you follow colonization waves upstream? How would you verify that these colonization waves gain individuals from local populations and also contribute individuals to those same local populations?

For more information on the resources available from McGraw-Hill Ryerson, go to **www.mcgrawhill.ca/he/solutions**.

POPULATION STRUCTURE

CHAPTER 11

CHAPTER CONCEPTS

11.1 A survivorship curve summarizes the pattern of survival in a population.
Ecology in Action: Unintended Consequences of Ecological Research
Concept 11.1 Review

11.2 The age distribution of a population reflects its history of survival, reproduction, and potential for future growth.
Concept 11.2 Review

11.3 Population sex ratios can change depending upon the relative fitness of different sexes within a population.
Concept 11.3 Review
Ecological Tools and Approaches: Using Population Structure to Assess the Impact of Human-Mediated Change
Summary
Review Questions

n chapter 10, we discussed how populations were distributed on the landscape. In this chapter, we will look at the underlying **population structure** found within individual populations. Population structure can be defined by a number of factors, including patterns of mortality, age distributions, sex ratios, and dispersal. Uncovering these patterns within natural populations requires extended field studies, and population ecology has a tradition of combining understanding gained through natural history with the rigour central to scientific study. One example of this approach comes from a family living in remote regions of Alaska over 50 years ago.

Adolph Murie is a foundational figure in population ecology, and one of the first wildlife biologists in North America. As a young man, Adolph travelled through northern Alaska with his brother Olaus, who was investigating caribou populations (fig. 11.1). After several years in the backcountry, Adolph returned to finish his undergraduate degree, and then earned a Ph.D. from the University of Michigan. Adolph's largest contributions to science came when he returned to Alaska with his wife Louise, daughter Gail, and son Jan. His detailed understanding of natural history, combined with his scientific training, allowed him to understand populations in a way that had not yet been achieved for many North America species. Adolph published many books and papers during his career, including *The Wolves of Mount McKinley* (Murie 1944), and *A Naturalist in Alaska* (Murie 1961).

One of Adolph's greatest works was in his detailed study and observations of interactions among wolves and sheep. As Adolph Murie watched, a grey wolf, *Canis lupus*, ran downhill toward a herd of 20 Dall sheep, *Ovis dalli*. As the wolf approached, the herd of white sheep split into two bands. One band circled the wolf and ran up the slope, while the other ran downhill. In response, the wolf stopped. The two bands of sheep also stopped, only 30 to 40 m away from the wolf. Suddenly the wolf sprinted after the lower band, but they easily outran him on the steep terrain. Again, the sheep and the wolf stopped and rested. After an hour, the wolf broke the stalemate and again charged the lower band. The sheep avoided

Figure 11.2   The Dall sheep, *Ovis dalli*, a mountain sheep of far northern North America, was the subject of one of Murie's classic studies of survivorship within natural populations.

him, circling the wolf and rejoining the other half of their herd. A few minutes later the wolf abandoned the hunt, trotting away as the herd of Dall sheep watched from the ridge above (fig. 11.2).

Despite this particular wolf's failure, wolves kill enough Dall sheep to cause some people to suggest that wolf populations should be reduced to protect the sheep. Fifty years later, a similar argument about the impacts of wolves on ungulate numbers is now being made about threatened populations of woodland caribou, *Rangifer tarandus caribou*, in Alberta and a number of other species throughout Canada. One of the reasons Adolph Murie was so influential was his ability to use his knowledge of the natural history of the entire system to develop novel scientific studies, rather than focus only on a single interaction between a predator and its prey. One example of Murie's work came when he was hired by the U.S. National Park Service to study the interactions between wolves and Dall sheep in what was then Mount McKinley National Park (now Denali National Park), Alaska. The main purpose of his study (Murie 1944) was to determine whether wolves kill enough sheep to justify the call for reducing the wolf population. This was a very controversial issue at the time, as hunters, naturalists, scientists, and politicians were all interested in wolves and sheep (Rawson 2001). What was needed, and what Murie provided, was sound science to help direct a management strategy.

Murie adopted several methods for his studies. As we described above, he directly observed wolves and sheep. He also indirectly studied their interactions by tracking wolves through winter snow to find their kills. The tracks left a record of wolf interactions with their prey. Where wolves had killed Dall sheep, they often left the skulls, which provided a record as rich as the telltale tracks. Murie could age and sex the sheep based upon the skulls by the size of the horns. The teeth provided an indication of the sheep's general condition; worn teeth were a sign of poor nutrition and weakness. A careful

Figure 11.1   Olaus and Adolph Murie were influential in the development of the field of wildlife ecology.

search of Mount McKinley National Park yielded a sample of 608 sheep skulls, which Murie used to explore the causes and age of death. The skulls showed Murie that death within the Dall sheep population fell mainly on the very young and the very old. Most sheep in the population could, as his direct observations had shown, avoid attack by wolves. Today, studies of mortality and predation risk would also include GPS-collared individuals, allowing researchers to study movement patterns and unique information not available just a few decades ago.

Adolph Murie's studies of wolves and Dall sheep represent one aspect of population structure, the description of the patterns of mortality among individuals within a population. However, population structure includes many more topics, and these too have been studied by a Murie out in the field. However, now we see Jan Murie, son of Adolph Murie and Professor Emeritus at the University of Alberta, studying ground squirrels in southern Alberta. From his experiences living with his family in remote Alaska, Jan recognized the scientific value of detailed observations of individuals over time. Through live-trapping and detailed observation, Murie and his colleagues were better able to understand the structure of Columbian ground squirrel populations, *Spermophilus columbianus* (Boag and Murie 1981; Murie 1985). In one study, Murie and his colleague Dave Boag found that populations of adult ground squirrels consistently contained more females than males, even though populations of juveniles were balanced between sexes (Boag and Murie 1981). This bias could be explained by observing the dynamics of the juvenile males. Males dispersed more often and farther from the natal population than females, with some moving over 6 km away. Mortality of males, both juvenile and adult, was also higher than females (Boag and Murie 1981), resulting in adult populations with unbalanced sex ratios.

Although separated by 40 years, thousands of kilometres, and studying different species, both Jan Murie and his father focused on critical aspects of population structure. For all populations, the patterns of distribution and abundance we studied in chapter 10 result from a dynamic balance between rates of birth, death, immigration, and emigration. In this chapter we will explore these topics in more depth, providing the foundation for understanding how populations will change over time, the topic of chapter 12.

It is difficult to keep track of everything going on in populations. Distributions may expand and contract. Numbers may increase for some time and then fall precipitously. A new population of a previously unrecorded species may suddenly appear in an area, persist for a season or a decade, and then disappear. Estimating characteristics such as survival and birthrates requires a great deal of information. Numbers of individuals alone, which may range from dozens to millions, can overwhelm the population ecologist. In addition, individuals of different ages and sexes may make different contributions to population dynamics and so must be followed separately. To organize our exploration of population dynamics, we first consider patterns of survival in populations and then age and sex distributions.

11.1 Patterns of Survival

A survivorship curve summarizes the pattern of survival in a population. One of the most fundamental descriptions of a population is the pattern of mortality and survival among individuals. Patterns of survival vary a great deal from one species to another and, depending on environmental circumstances, can vary within a single species. Some species produce young by the millions, which, in turn, die at a high rate. Other species produce few young and invest heavily in their care, resulting in high rates of juvenile survival. Still other species show intermediate patterns of reproductive rate, parental care, and juvenile survival. In response to practical challenges of discerning patterns of survival, ecologists use bookkeeping devices called **life tables** that list the births, the survivorship, and the deaths, or *mortality*, in populations. In this chapter we will focus on the mortality component of life tables; births will be added in chapter 12, allowing for estimation of population growth rates.

Estimating Patterns of Survival

There are three main ways of estimating patterns of survival within a population. The first and most reliable way is to identify a large number of individuals that are born at about the same time and keep records on them from birth to death. In this context, a group born at the same time is called a **cohort**, and a life table made from data collected in this way is called a **cohort life table**. The cohort studied might be a group of plant seedlings that matured at the same time, or all the lambs born into a population of mountain sheep in a particular year.

While understanding and interpreting a cohort life table may be relatively easy, obtaining the data upon which a cohort life table is based is not. Imagine yourself lying face down in a meadow counting thousands of tiny seedlings of an annual plant. You must mark their locations and then come back every week for six months until the last member of the population dies. Or, if you are studying a moderately long-lived species, such as a barnacle or a perennial herb like a buttercup, imagine checking the cohort repeatedly over a period of several years. If your study organism is a mobile animal such as a whale or falcon, or one that bites like a polar bear or cobra, the problems multiply. If your species is very long-lived, such as a giant sequoia, such an approach is impossible within a single human lifetime. When it is difficult or impossible to follow individuals through time, population biologists usually resort to other techniques.

A second way to estimate patterns of survival in wild populations is to go into the field for a narrow window of time and record the age at death of a large number of individuals. This method differs from the cohort approach because the individuals in your sample are born at different times. This method produces a **static life table**. The table is called *static* because the method involves a snapshot of survival within a population during a short interval of time. Estimating the age of death can be difficult, and its accuracy is critical to the value of the data generated with this approach. The most accurate method would

be to tag individuals when they are born and then recover the tags after death. However, this is not practical in most circumstances, and instead the ecologist may somehow estimate the age of dead individuals. For instance, mountain sheep can be aged by counting the growth rings on their horns. There are also growth rings on the carapaces of turtles, in the trunks of trees, and in the "stems" of soft or hard corals.

A third way of determining patterns of survival is from the **age distribution**. An age distribution consists of the proportion of individuals of different ages within a population. You can use an age distribution to estimate survival by calculating the difference in proportion of individuals in succeeding age classes. This method, which also produces a static life table, assumes that the difference in numbers of individuals in one age class and the next is the result of mortality. What are some other major assumptions underlying the use of age distributions to estimate patterns of survival? This method assumes that a population is neither growing nor declining, and that it is not receiving new members from the outside or losing members because they migrate away. Since most of these assumptions are often violated in natural populations, a life table constructed from this type of data tends to be less accurate than a cohort life table. Static life tables are often useful, however, since they may be the only information available for many populations.

High Survival Among Young Individuals

As we saw in the introduction, Adolph Murie studied patterns of survival among Dall sheep in what is now Denali National Park, Alaska. Murie estimated survival patterns by collecting the skulls of 608 sheep that had died from various causes. He determined the age at which each sheep in his sample died by counting the growth rings on their horns and by studying tooth wear.

Figure 11.3 summarizes the survival patterns for Dall sheep based on Murie's sample of skulls. The upper portion of the figure shows the static life table that Murie constructed. The first column lists the ages of the sheep, the second column lists the number surviving in each age class, and the third column lists the numbers dying in each age class. Notice that although Murie studied only 608 skulls, the numbers in the table are expressed as numbers per 1,000 individuals. This adjustment to 1,000 individuals is standard in population ecology, and is made to ease comparisons with other populations. The upper portion of figure 11.3 also shows how to translate numbers of deaths into numbers of survivors.

The major assumption of this study is that the proportion of skulls in each age class represents the typical proportion of individuals dying at that age. For example, the proportion of skulls found belonging to sheep younger than age 1 was 199/1,000. But what if skulls of younger individuals are harder to find or weather faster than skulls of older individuals? This would mean that the ecologist's estimate that 19.9% of sheep die in their first year of life is lower than the actual value. Similarly, if the skulls of older individuals were harder to find or decay faster than skulls of younger individuals, then the estimate of 19.9% would be higher than the true risk of mortality in this population. Although the assumption that the rate of skull capture is exactly equal to the proportion of

individuals that generally die during the first year may not be strictly true, the pattern of survival that emerges probably gives a reasonable picture of survival in the population, particularly when the sample is as large as Murie's.

Plotting number of survivors per 1,000 births against age produces the **survivorship curve** shown in the lower portion of figure 11.3. A survivorship curve shows patterns of life

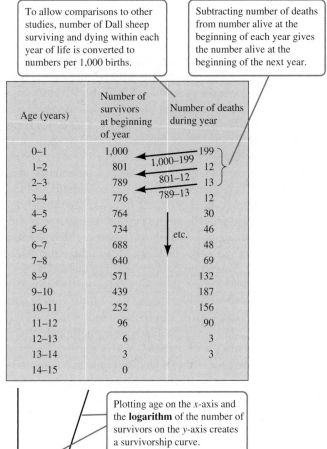

To allow comparisons to other studies, number of Dall sheep surviving and dying within each year of life is converted to numbers per 1,000 births.

Subtracting number of deaths from number alive at the beginning of each year gives the number alive at the beginning of the next year.

Age (years)	Number of survivors at beginning of year	Number of deaths during year
0–1	1,000	199
1–2	801	12
2–3	789	13
3–4	776	12
4–5	764	30
5–6	734	46
6–7	688	48
7–8	640	69
8–9	571	132
9–10	439	187
10–11	252	156
11–12	96	90
12–13	6	3
13–14	3	3
14–15	0	

1,000–199
801–12
789–13
etc.

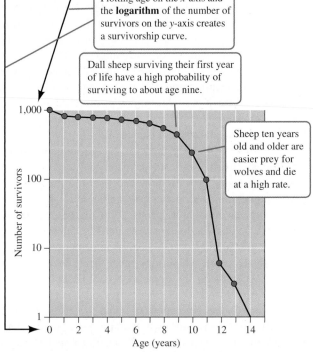

Plotting age on the *x*-axis and the **logarithm** of the number of survivors on the *y*-axis creates a survivorship curve.

Dall sheep surviving their first year of life have a high probability of surviving to about age nine.

Sheep ten years old and older are easier prey for wolves and die at a high rate.

Figure 11.3 Dall sheep: from life table to survivorship curve (data from Murie 1944).

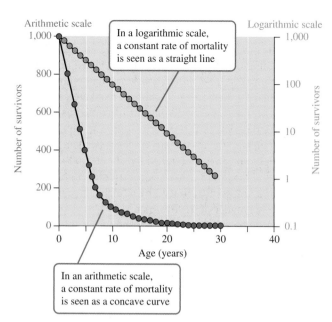

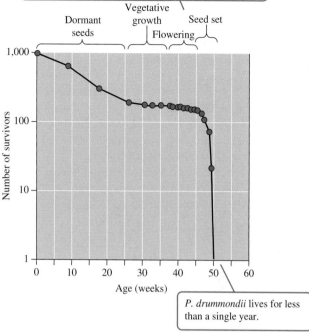

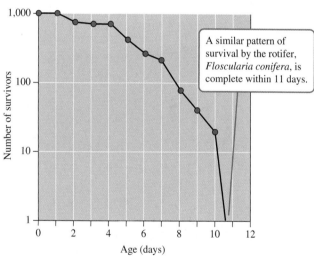

Figure 11.4 In this hypothetical population, 20% of individuals at the start of a given age class die prior to their next birthday. Using a logarithmic scale, the resulting survivorship curve is a straight line, while in the arithmetic scale the line is curved. As a result, the use of a logarithmic scale makes it easier to quickly understand mortality patterns in populations.

Figure 11.5 High rates of survival among the young and middle-aged in plant and rotifer populations (data from Leverich and Levin 1979, *top*, and Deevey 1947, *bottom*).

and death within a population. You will notice that the y-axis of the survivorship curve is presented in a logarithmic scale. Why is this, and what happens if we use the arithmetic, rather than logarithmic scale? First, it is important to understand why ecologists draw survivorship curves in the first place. Survivorship curves let us quickly determine whether mortality rates for a given population change with age by simply observing whether the resulting line is linear, or if it curves. If we used the arithmetic scale, changes in slope would occur even without changes in survivorship rates (fig. 11.4). In the logarithmic scale, a straight line indicates that mortality rates do not change as a function of an individual's age.

Notice in figure 11.3 that in this population of Dall sheep, the survivorship curve has two areas where the slope is relatively steep: during the first year and during the period between 9 and 13 years. The increased steepness of the slope during those periods indicates that juvenile mortality and mortality of the aged are high in this population, while mortality in the middle years is relatively lower than these other age classes. The overall pattern of survival and mortality among Dall sheep is much like that for a variety of other large vertebrates, including red deer (*Cervus elaphus*), African buffalo (*Syncerus caffer*), and humans. The key characteristics of survival among these populations are relatively high rates of survival among the young and middle-aged and high rates of mortality among the older members.

This pattern of survival has also been observed in populations of annual plants and small invertebrate animals. Notice in figure 11.5 that patterns of survival in a population of a plant, *Phlox drummondii*, and a rotifer, *Floscularia conifera*,

are remarkably similar to that of Dall mountain sheep. Following an initial period of higher juvenile mortality, mortality is relatively low for a period, and then mortality is high among older individuals. In the *Phlox* population, however, this pattern of survival is played out in less than 1 year and in the rotifer population in less than 11 days. Thus, species of dramatically different longevities can express similar patterns of mortality. The notion of "young" and "old" will be relative to the life span of the organism being studied.

Survival patterns can be quite different in other species. In the next example, mortality is not delayed until old age, but occurs at approximately equal rates throughout life.

Constant Rates of Survival

The survivorship curves of many species are nearly straight lines. In these populations, individuals die at approximately the same rate throughout life. This pattern of survival has been commonly observed in birds, such as the American robin, *Turdus migratorius*, and the white-crowned sparrow, *Zonotrichia leucophrys nuttalli* (fig. 11.6). While birds are commonly known for showing a linear pattern of survival, many other taxa do as well. For instance, figure 11.6 also shows the same pattern of survival for a population of the northern water snake *Nerodia sipedon*. Though the water snake has a high rate of mortality during the first year of life, thereafter, survival follows a straight line.

As we shall see next, some organisms die at a much higher rate as juveniles than we have seen in any of the populations we have considered to this point.

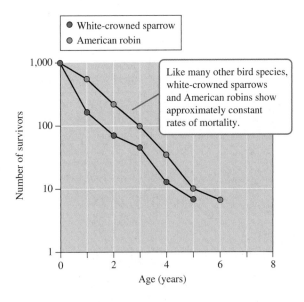

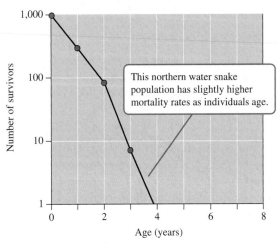

Figure 11.6 Constant rates of survival in sparrows and robins (data from Deevey 1947, Baker et al. 1981, *top*). Water snakes have higher juvenile survival rates than older individuals (Brown and Weatherhead 1999, *bottom*).

Low Survival Among Young Individuals

Some organisms produce large numbers of young with very high rates of mortality. The eggs produced by marine fish such as the mackerel, *Scomber scombrus*, may number in the millions. Out of 1 million eggs laid by a mackerel, more than 999,990 die during the first 70 days of life either as eggs, larvae, or juveniles. Survival rates are similar in populations of the prawn *Leander squilla* off the coast of Sweden. For every 1 million eggs laid by *Leander*, only about 2,000 individuals survive the first year of life. This period of high mortality among young prawns is followed by a fairly constant mortality over the remainder of the life span.

Similar patterns of survival are shown by other marine invertebrates and by fish and by plants that produce immense numbers of seeds. One of these plants is *Cleome droserifolia*, a desert shrub. Local populations of approximately 2,000 plants produce almost 20 million seeds each year (Hegazy 1990). Of these, approximately 12,500 seeds germinate and produce seedlings. Only 800 seedlings survive to become juvenile plants. Figure 11.7 traces this pattern of survival by *Cleome* expressed as survivors per million seeds. For each 1 million seeds produced, about 39 survive to the age of one year, a survival rate of only 0.0039%. Survival in this desert plant population contrasts sharply with that seen in Dall sheep. The striking difference in patterns of survival between populations such as *Cleome*, birds such as the American robin, and large mammals such as Dall sheep led early population biologists to propose a classification of survivorship curves.

Three Types of Survivorship Curves

Based on studies of survival by a wide variety of organisms, population ecologists have proposed that most survivorship curves fall into three major categories (fig. 11.8a). A

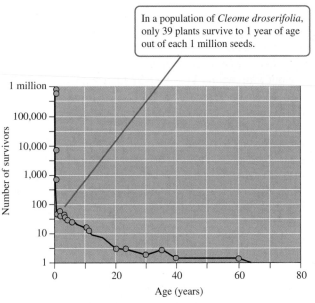

Figure 11.7 A high rate of mortality, and thus low survival, among the young of a perennial plant population (data from Hegazy 1990).

relatively high rate of survival among young and middle-aged individuals followed by a high rate of mortality among the aged is known as a **type I survivorship curve**. Constant rates of survival throughout life produce the straight-line pattern of survival known as a **type II survivorship curve**. A **type III survivorship curve** is one in which a period of extremely high rates of mortality among the young is followed by a relatively high rate of survival.

How well does this classification of survivorship represent natural populations? A team of researchers, including Phil Currie, the renowned paleontologist from the University of Alberta, have recently summarized survivorship curves for several familiar vertebrate taxa (figure 11.8b; Erickson et al. 2006). Included in the table is the hypothesized type I survivorship curve of North American tyrannosaurs. Just as Adolph Murie has been able to infer patterns of survivorship from estimating the age of death from the skulls of sheep, so too has Currie been able to infer age of mortality from found bones. The only difference is that the bones Currie works with are substantially older, but the underlying ecological models and analyses are exactly the same. Consequently, though these extinct dinosaurs lived over 60 million years ago, they appear to demonstrate the same ecological patterns found in species today.

From figure 11.8b, you will see that most populations do not conform perfectly to any one of the three basic types of survivorship, but show virtually every sort of intermediate form of survivorship between the curves. Even single species can show considerable variation in survivorship from one environment to another. For example, while human survivorship generally follows a type I survivorship curve, in difficult environments, human survivorship approaches a type II

curve. This variation in patterns of human survival prompted G. Evelyn Hutchinson (1978) to muse: "One can only conclude that sometimes man is constrained to die randomly like a bird, but in other circumstances he may aspire to as ripe an old age as that of a wild sheep or an African buffalo." If survivorship can be so variable within species, what good are these idealized, theoretical survivorship curves? Their most important value, like most theoretical constructs, is that they set boundaries that mark what is possible within populations. Survivorship curves can be thought of as the "Coles Notes" of understanding patterns of mortality in natural populations. They do not include all of the fine details found in nature, but instead they serve as useful summaries of survival patterns within populations.

We now turn to the age distributions of populations, a topic closely related to survivorship.

CONCEPT 11.1 REVIEW

1. How do static and cohort life tables differ from each other? Under what conditions would you choose to construct one over the other?
2. Female cottonwood trees produce millions of seeds each year. Does this information give you a sound basis for predicting their survivorship pattern?
3. How would human mortality patterns have to change for our species to shift from type I to type II survivorship?

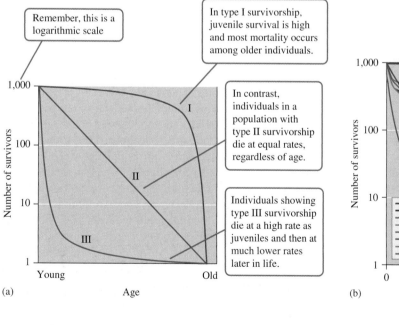

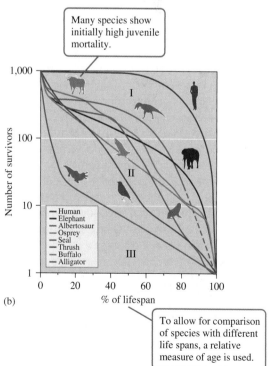

Figure 11.8 Three types of survivorship curves. (*a*) Idealized forms. (*b*) Comparisons among some familiar vertebrates (modified from Erickson et al. 2006).

ECOLOGY IN ACTION

Unintended Consequences of Ecological Research

When we look at life tables and other measures of populations, it is easy to forget that each data point often represents an actual organism that an ecologist located, measured, marked, and released back into the wild (chapter 10). The numbers of organisms that are marked in a given year can be amazingly high. For example, the United States and Canada have a joint effort coordinated by the Bird Banding Laboratory (BBL) to catch, band, and release birds. Recaptures and recoveries are used for a variety of population measures (chapter 10). Over 1,000,000 birds are banded annually in North America, and since the BBL program began in 1908, over 60,000,000 birds have been banded. Of these, a total of about 3,000,000 birds (5%) have been recovered or recaptured. Population studies of other species also involve the capture and release of large numbers of individuals.

Because the biology of species differ so greatly, so too do the methods of capture and release. Many birds are caught in fine "mist-nets" installed within flight paths. Birds are removed from the nets by hand, measured, and a small band is placed on one leg. Many large mammals are caught by being followed with a helicopter and then shot with a tranquilizer. Marking can involve tattooing, insertion of tags around ears or other body parts, and in some cases, the removal of a tooth for age determination. Lizards and frogs have historically been captured in snares and pitfall traps with marking involving "toe-clipping," in which the ecologist snips off various combinations of toes to give each animal a unique pattern of remaining digits. With increased technological advances over the last several decades, many organisms are outfitted with VHF (very high frequency) or GPS (global positioning systems) telemetry devices that can be inserted internally or attached externally. So what? Do ecologists need to concern themselves with the effects of these methods on their organisms?

Yes, and many ecologists have been concerned for quite some time. In Canada, all research on vertebrates, and on some invertebrates, requires formal approval by Animal Care Committees. These procedures are not trivial, and they require the researcher to fully describe the research protocols that will be used, the justification for the need for these protocols and the steps that will be taken to minimize stress, the number of animals handled, and the risk of physical harm to the animals and researchers. Failure to show due diligence during the study can result in significant penalties, including the loss of funding, inability to publish, and a variety of more severe disciplinary actions. Aside from these "sticks" associated with animal welfare and scientific research, and the associated ethical considerations they are designed to protect, ecologists are increasingly concerned about their activities based upon scientific grounds.

Concerns are generally raised on two issues: (1) immediate harm to individuals during the capture and marking process, and (2) longer-term harm through altered physiology and/or morphology. For example, capture and handling can cause significant stress to animals. When this is coupled with inadequate training, chance events, and other factors, trapping and handling can lead to mortality in a variety of species. Although exact numbers of capture-related deaths are difficult to find in the literature, mortality rates in excess of 2% for large mammals due to capture and handling have been suggested to be of concern (Arnemo et al. 2006).

Due to the magnitude of some mark-recapture efforts, large numbers of animals may be adversely affected. For example, one study in Australia suggested a 1% rate of mortality associated with mist-nests and bird banding (Recher et al. 1985). If we assume this value to be constant, then banding activity in North America alone may cause the death of over 10,000 birds annually, and 600,000 birds since 1908. Though these numbers are dwarfed in comparison to mortality associated with habitat loss, power lines, and other human-mediated causes, it is important to recognize that trapping and handling of animals does cause mortality. When these activities are on a large scale like the BBL, the numbers of deaths due to research activity will also be large. Aside from immediate mortality, some organisms will continue to show negative consequences of capture and handling for days, weeks, or years after the capture event. For example, toe-clipping can reduce the clinging ability of an arboreal lizard (Bloch and Irschick 2005), outfitting marine birds with transmitters reduces their foraging efficiency (Wilson et al. 1986), capturing butterflies alters their subsequent behaviour (Singer and Wedlake 1981), and even repeated measures of plants can alter rates of herbivory (Cahill et al. 2001). Few studies have determined the impacts of marking on population dynamics, with one main exception.

Gauthier-Clerc and colleagues (2004) investigated the impact of flipper bands on populations of King Penguins (fig. 11.9). Due to the shape of penguin ankles, leg bands that are commonly used for songbirds cannot be used, and instead bands are placed on penguin flippers. Gautier-Clerc and colleagues identified and followed 100 adult King Penguins (*Aptenodytes patagonicus*) in a colony of 25,000 breeding pairs for five years. To 50 of these birds they attached standard flipper tags. To the other 50 birds they inserted a transponder tag below each bird's skin. They also buried antennae under paths between the water and the colony, which recorded each time individual birds crossed the paths. Over five years, the 50 banded birds produced 28 chicks, while the unbanded birds produced 54 chicks. Additionally,

Figure 11.9   Flipper tags have been used extensively in the study of penguin population dynamics.

each year the banded birds arrived to the breeding colony several days later than unbanded birds, which may have negative consequences for mate selection. In a related study in which researchers inserted transponders into 300 chicks (their prior results led them to conclude it would be unethical to place flipper bands on any more penguins), they found survival rates nearly twice as high as those in published studies that used banded chicks (Gauthier-Clerc et al. 2004). Taken together, these data strongly suggest banding penguins can have significant negative consequences for the fitness of the banded birds, as well as altering the structure of the population being studied.

This all may sound familiar to the Heisenberg Uncertainty Principle, in which Werner Heisenberg (1927) suggested that you cannot simultaneously know the speed and location of an electron, as the act of measuring one alters the value of the other. Ecologists are recognizing that they are not invisible monitors of the natural world, and the very act of conducting ecological research causes changes in the behaviour of natural systems. Does this mean we should stop doing ecological research or that all field work is inherently flawed and unethical? Of course not, as the costs associated with not studying many ecological questions can be higher than the impacts of the research itself. Ecologists have become more aware of these issues, and studies documenting unintended consequences are being published in high profile journals and receiving extensive media coverage. This encourages other scientists to test the effects of the methods they use, and helps us develop less invasive methods. For example, many GPS-recording devices, transponders, and other attachments have greatly decreased in size, which should reduce the stress associated with wearing the device. Ecologists are also improving the use of non-invasive methods, further reducing the potential for harm to the study organisms. For example, genetic approaches can allow researchers to follow individual organisms not by recording the number on an ear tag, but by using DNA samples from hair snags or fecal collections, reducing the need for live-captures. At the same time, technological advances are reducing the cost of many recording devices that can be attached to animals, resulting in a proliferation of studies that place measuring devices on wild animals themselves. Wilson and McMahon (2006) have called for the development of a framework to establish acceptable practices for ecologists. Such a step is a clear sign that ecologists are working to reduce unnecessary harm to study organisms.

All research activity results in unintended and potentially confounding effects. However, it is important to remember that many of the questions that ecologists are addressing have the potential to positively impact the health and sustainability of numerous wild populations. It is unfortunate that the process of study causes mortality of some individuals; however, without these studies even larger numbers of individuals are likely at risk. Ecologists work hard to minimize these negative effects, both because it is ethically sound and because it provides better data.

11.2   Age Distribution

The age distribution of a population reflects its history of survival, reproduction, and potential for future growth. Population ecologists can tell a great deal about a population by studying its age distribution. Age distributions indicate periods of successful reproduction, periods of high and low juvenile and adult survival, whether the older individuals in a population are being replaced by younger individuals, and whether population is declining. By studying the history of a population through describing its age distribution, population ecologists can make predictions about its future.

Stable and Declining Tree Populations

In 1923, R. B. Miller published data on the age distribution of a population of white oak, *Quercus alba*, in a mature forest in Illinois. In his study, Miller first determined the relationship between the age of a white oak and the diameter of its trunk. To do this, he measured the diameters of 56 trees of various sizes and then took a core of wood from their trunks. By counting the annual growth rings from each of the cores, he could determine the ages of the trees in his sample. With the relationship between oak age and diameter in hand, Miller used diameter to estimate the ages of hundreds of trees.

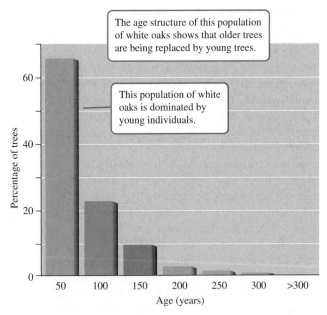

Figure 11.10 The age distribution of a white oak, *Quercus alba*, population in Illinois (data from Miller 1923).

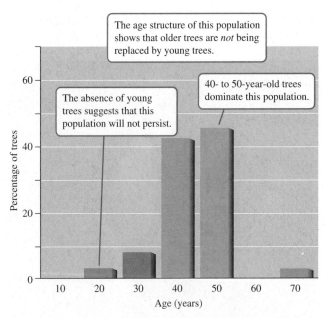

Figure 11.11 The age distribution of a population of Rio Grande cottonwoods, *Populus deltoides* ssp. *wislizenii*, near Belen, New Mexico (data from Howe and Knopf 1991).

Most white oaks in Miller's study forest were concentrated in the youngest age class of 1 to 50 years, with progressively fewer individuals in the older age classes (fig. 11.10). In other words, the age distribution of white oak in this forest was biased toward the young trees. What might we infer from this age distribution? The age distribution suggests that reproduction is sufficient to replace the oldest individuals in the population as they die.

The age distribution of this white oak population contrasts sharply with the age distributions of populations of Rio Grande cottonwoods, *Populus deltoides* ssp. *wislizenii*. The most extensive cottonwood forests remaining in the southwestern United States grows along the Middle Rio Grande in central New Mexico. However, studies of age distributions indicate that these populations are declining. In contrast to the white oak population in Illinois, the Rio Grande cottonwood population is dominated by older individuals. Older trees are not being replaced by younger trees. At the study site, here has been no successful reproduction for over a decade (fig. 11.11).

Why have Rio Grande cottonwoods failed to reproduce? As we discussed in chapter 6, regeneration by cottonwoods depends upon seasonal floods, which play two key roles. First, floods create areas of bare soil without a surface layer of organic matter and without competing vegetation. Floods also keep these areas of bare soil moist until cottonwood seedlings can grow their roots deep enough to tap into the shallow water table. The annual rhythm of seed bed preparation and seeding has been interrupted by the construction of dams on the Rio Grande.

The age distributions of tree populations change over the course of many decades or centuries. Meanwhile, other populations can change significantly on much shorter timescales. One of these dynamic populations has been thoroughly studied on the Galápagos Islands.

Shifting Age Distributions in a Variable Climate

Here we return to the work of Rosemary and Peter Grant (chapter 9), and discuss how changes in climate can cause shifts in aspects of population structure, including age distributions (Grant and Grant 1989). One of the Grants' most thorough studies focused on the large cactus finch, *Geospiza conirostris*. The study took place on the island of Genovesa, which lies in the northeastern portion of the Galápagos archipelago, approximately 1,000 km off the west coast of South America. The Galápagos Islands have a highly variable climate, which is reflected in the highly dynamic populations of the organisms living on the islands, including populations of the large cactus finch.

The age distributions of the large cactus finch during 1983 and 1987 show that the population can be very dynamic (fig. 11.12). The 1983 age distribution shows a fairly regular distribution of individuals among age classes, suggesting frequent years of successful reproduction. However, although there were many 5-year-olds and many 7-year-olds, there were no 6-year-old individuals in the population. A missing age group in a population can often be sign that some environmental factor had an unusual influence during a certain time period. In this case, the gap is due to a drought in 1977, during which no finches reproduced. Now, compare the 1983 and 1987 age distributions. The distributions contrast markedly, though they are for the same population separated by only four years! Such a dramatic change in population structure is a clear sign that something important changed during this time period.

The 1977 gap is still present in the 1987 age distribution and another has been added for two- and three-year-old finches. This second gap is the result of two years of reproductive failure during a drought that persisted from 1984 to 1985. Another difference is that the 1987 age distribution is

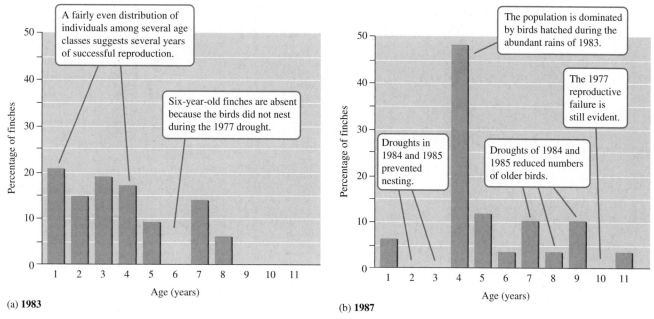

Figure 11.12 The age distribution of a population of large cactus finches, *Geospiza conirostris*, on the island of Genovesa in the Galápagos Islands during 1983 (*a*) and 1987 (*b*) (data from Grant and Grant 1989).

dominated by four-year-old birds that were fledged during 1983. The 1983 class dominates because wet weather that year resulted in very high production of food that the finches depend upon for reproduction. The 1987 age distribution also shows evidence of high mortality among older finches, perhaps associated with the 1984–85 drought. Whatever the cause of these declines, the reproductive output of this population of large cactus finches is dominated by birds hatched in one exceptionally favourable year, 1983. This long-term study of the large cactus finch population of Genovesa Island demonstrates the responsiveness of population age structure to environmental variation.

In this section, we have seen that an age distribution tells population ecologists a great deal about the dynamics of a population, including whether a population is growing, declining, or approximately stable. Looking even more closely at populations, we can find differences among populations in the relative frequency of different sexes within the populations. In the next section we will find these differences are often the result of natural selection.

CONCEPT 11.2 REVIEW

1. Can a healthy population that is not in danger of extinction have an age structure that shows years of reproductive failure?
2. The last major natural reproduction by Rio Grande cottonwoods, which produced the large number of 40- and 50-year-old trees documented by Howe and Knopf (1991), occurred before the last major dam was built on the river. Is there any evidence for reproductive failure before that dam was built?

11.3 ## Sex Ratios

Population sex ratios can change depending upon the relative fitness of different sexes within a population. By studying patterns of mortality and age distributions, ecologists are able to understand many processes that are occurring within populations. Another pattern of population structure that can help ecologists learn about the factors influencing natural populations is the relative frequency of alternative sex types (chapter 8) within a population. Sexual reproduction is widespread among plant and animal species, and there can be strong evolutionary advantages to sexual recombination. However, if we look closely at sex types in the populations of many species, we find a puzzling pattern: although species and populations differ in many attributes such as population growth rates and size, males and females are frequently found in approximately equal numbers. As a result, many populations of many species have 1:1 **sex ratios** (fig. 11.13). Sex ratios can be defined as the relative frequency of each sex type (e.g., male, female) in a population. What factors influence the sex ratio of a population?

Fisher (1930) was among the first to suggest that sex ratios could be the result of natural selection. The logic he used was elegant in its simplicity. Imagine a population that had 100 individuals, one of which was female, and 99 of which were male. Some of you may find such a scenario attractive, while others most assuredly would not. Nonetheless, this hypothetical scenario can inform our understanding of how natural selection influences sex ratios. Let us take away the complication of mate choice, and assume that mating is random among individuals, but that each male can only mate with one female (and vice versa). In this scenario of a 1:99 sex ratio, the lone female will most assuredly be able to

(a)   (b)

Figure 11.13   (*a*) Male and (*b*) female individuals of the banded Uromastyx, *Uromastyx flavofasciata*, are different colours. Most natural populations of animals have equal numbers of males and females.

mate, while the males will experience strong competition for access to the female. As a result, the parents of the female will have a high fitness (as they will have grandchildren), while the parents of nearly all the males will have zero fitness (no grandchildren). If the ability to produce males or females has at least some additive genetic variance (chapter 4), then the relative frequency of female-producing individuals will increase in subsequent generations. As the relative frequency of females approaches a 1:1 sex ratio, the fitness benefit for producing females instead of males decreases. If the population contains more females than males, then the selection will favour the production of sons, and not daughters. This process is a form of **frequency-dependent selection**, where the relative fitness of producing males or females is not inherent in the gender of the offspring itself, but instead is dependent upon the relative frequency of both alternative phenotypes. Through this process of frequency-dependent selection, populations should reach equilibrium at approximately a 1:1 sex ratio.

Although we do not generally consider the gender of one's offspring as a factor under evolutionary control, there is substantial research identifying a variety of specific genes and processes that increase or decrease the likelihood of producing males or females. The most obvious examples are in cases of environmental sex determination where species lack sex chromosomes (e.g., XY), and instead the gender of an offspring is determined by the environmental conditions in which the embryo develops. Those conditions can be under parental control. For example, the sex of many reptile species is determined by the temperature of incubation of the egg during the middle trimester of development. This is controlled in many species by changes in nest construction and egg burial depth. In other species, the relatively motility of "male" and "female" sperm differs, potentially contributing to the likelihood of a male producing male or female offspring. In other species, including some human populations, infanticide can be biased among the sexes, such that

either male or female offspring are more likely to be cared for and reared than the alternative gender. In other words, many species have a variety of mechanisms by which parents are able to influence the likelihood of raising male or female offspring.

Although Fisher's theoretical model may be useful in explaining the many populations that do have 1:1 sex ratios, it fails to explain the many populations that have biased sex ratios. This issue has not escaped the attention of many biologists over the last several decades, and here we will discuss just a few of the mechanisms that can cause unequal sex ratios. First, differential mortality of the sexes can cause sex ratios to vary among age classes within a population. For example, in human populations across the world there is a bias toward males at birth (Central Intelligence Agency 2007), with 1.07 males born for every female. However, for people older than 65, there is a female bias, with 0.78 males remaining alive to every female. Across all age classes, the sex ratio is 1.01:1, very close to Fisher's theoretical prediction of 1:1.

Second, for many species, the body sizes of the different sexes are different, even at birth. As a result, so too is the energetic cost of producing a son or a daughter. In general, natural selection will favour producing more individuals of the least costly sex, such that if males cost twice as much to produce as females, the population sex ratio should be female-biased. Fisher's model assumed that all individuals had an equal probability of mating, but as we saw in chapter 8, there are many mating systems found in plant and animal species where this assumption is not met. For example, in harem-forming systems, dominant males generally receive more than an equal share of mating opportunities, while subordinate males receive few, if any, opportunities. If only the biggest and healthiest males become dominant in a population, then there should be selection against producing small sons, but not against producing smaller females (nearly all females will mate regardless of size in most harem mating systems). This can then result

in increased costs in producing males relative to females (as described above), or instead it could result in only the healthiest females producing sons. In both scenarios, sex ratios should be female biased. Finally, in the introduction to this chapter, Dave Boag and Jan Murie described female-biased sex ratios in a ground squirrel population (Boag and Murie 1981). This was caused both by increased mortality experienced by the males, as well as an increased tendency of the males, but not females, to disperse away from their natal population.

CONCEPT 11.3 REVIEW

1. Is frequency-dependent selection likely to influence the sex ratio of individual populations, or the average ratio among all populations of a species? Why?
2. How can a sex ratio of 2:1 males:females be stable? Is such a skewed sex ratio an indication of extinction risk for a population?

ECOLOGICAL TOOLS AND APPROACHES

Using Population Structure to Assess the Impact of Human-Mediated Change

As we describe throughout the book, humans are modifying the landscape and environment in a number of ways. These changes have no impact on populations of many species, and substantial impacts on others. One impact of humans that is difficult to see directly is associated with the production of pollutants associated with industrialization. As we show below, some ecologists are using shifts in population structure of flagship species as a tool to indicate and draw awareness to ongoing ecological change.

Many scientists are studying the effects of sublethal concentrations of pollutants (concentrations too low to kill within a short period of time) on the population biology of a diverse set of organisms. Recently, there has been increased attention given to the potential of pollution to impact organisms located in arctic habitats. At first glance, it is difficult to understand why researchers in the Arctic would be concerned about pollutants, as the Arctic is far removed from areas of high industrial development. However, as we saw in chapters 2 and 3, global patterns of air and water movement bring large quantities of pollutants to these seemingly isolated areas. Of particular concern is the movement of persistent organic pollutants (POPs), such as polychlorinated biphenyls (PCBs), and heavy metals, such as mercury (Hg). POPs are able to volatize in warmer southern latitudes and move north through global air circulation. As these POPs reach colder air, they condense and become redeposited in the Arctic, resulting in high pollutant concentrations in arctic communities (Barrie et al. 1997). Similar effects are found in alpine communities (Blais et al. 1998), where the POPs carried in warm air from lower elevations condense in the cool air at higher elevations. POPs are particularly troublesome because they are hydrophobic, and thus they tend to accumulate rapidly in biological (i.e., fatty) tissues. These compounds can be ingested or absorbed at higher rates than they can be excreted or detoxified. As a result, toxin concentrations gradually increase within an individual through

the process of **bioaccumulation.** If the contaminated individuals are consumed (e.g., when a seal eats a fish), the predator gains both the nutritive value and toxin load of its prey. Because bioaccumulation has resulted in the prey item having elevated toxin levels compared to its environment, the levels in the predator will become even greater, through a process called **biomagnification.** This process continues up the food chain, where the top predators have very high concentrations of pollutants due to the consumption of prey items with lower levels of pollutant concentrations. Arctic food webs generally include species with particularly high fat reserves (e.g., seal, walrus, etc.), making them particularly prone to accumulation of POPs. These pollutants enter the systems of all individuals that consume polluted prey species. For example, PCB concentrations in human breast milk of individuals from Inuit communities can be much higher than those found in southern areas where PCBs are actually used and produced (Dewailly et al. 1989). There is some thought that this is related to processes of bioaccumulation and biomagnification. A detailed discussion of the potential effects of pollution in the north on human populations is beyond the scope of this text, and we will instead focus on the potential, and documented, impacts on non-human populations.

One of the central themes running through the ecological study of pollution is the attempt to connect the effects of pollutants on animal physiology with their effects on populations. An energy balance equation provides the key to bridging physiological and population ecology:

Energy assimilated = Respiration + Excretion + Production

In this equation, the amount of energy assimilated by an animal equals the sum of that expended in respiration, the amount of energy excreted (perspiration, urination, defecation, etc.), and the amount of energy available for production. This production energy is the amount of energy that an organism can use for growth and reproduction.

How does this equation connect the physiological effects of pollutants with their effects on populations? The connection derives from the principle of allocation we have already discussed in the text. The principle of allocation assumes that energy supplies available to organisms are limited, and predicts that any increase in the allocation of energy to any one of life's functions decreases the amount of energy available to other functions. In terms of our energy balance equation, if an organism is exposed to a toxin that induces physiological stress, energy expended in respiration generally increases. This increased respiration includes energy expended to excrete the toxin, to convert the toxin into a non-toxic chemical form, and to repair cellular damage caused by the toxin. The important point is that the processes that increase the energy spent for respiration decrease the energy available for growth and reproduction. This trade-off between reproduction and respiration provides the bridge between physiological and population ecology.

Now that we understand the reasons why pollutants might alter mortality or other aspects of population structure, what information is needed to determine whether such effects are actually occurring? Three critical pieces of information are needed: (1) identification of a pollutant in a population of interest, (2) evidence that observed concentrations have a negative physiological effect on individual performance, and (3) evidence that the level of pollutants in all individuals in the population will alter population parameters.

POPs and heavy metals have been found in the blood and tissues of a disappointingly large number of wild species (Gamberg et al. 2005; Evans et al. 2005; Braune et al. 2005); however, documenting causal effects of these pollutants on aspects of population structure can be logistically difficult. It is in trying to meet criteria numbers 2 and 3 where desired scientific information comes into conflict with scientific ethics and the difficult logistics associated with field work in remote locations.

As we discussed in chapter 1, experiments are very useful tools for determining the direct effects of a factor of interest. For example, if we wanted to understand the impacts of PCBs on polar bears, the scientifically cleanest approach would be a controlled experiment in which different individuals are exposed to different amounts of PCBs and the resulting changes measured. This is exactly the approach routinely used in toxicology labs, though typically centred on model species such as lab mice and rats. It is not a viable option for many wild species for a variety of reasons, including naturally low population densities, where removing individuals for study could put the population at risk, the inability of many species to thrive in captivity, and the extreme expenses associated with large-scale and long-term experiments. Instead, in the study of pollution in wild species, a correlative approach is generally used in which correlations are found between factors (such as PCB levels in individuals and their fertility) and causality is inferred. So what have ecologists learned about pollutants in

Figure 11.14   Polar bears feed upon a number of marine mammals. They are currently at the centre of international efforts to understand the impact of bioaccumulation and biomagnification on marine mammal populations in the Arctic.

northern and alpine populations over the last few decades? To address this issue we will focus on one well-studied and dramatic example, the polar bear, *Ursus maritimus* (fig. 11.14).

Polar bears are the largest extant land predator, and are at the top of the food chain in the Arctic. Males often weigh more than 450 kg, and females generally weigh less than 400 kg. Polar bears can be found throughout the Arctic, with their range limited to areas where sea-ice persists for much of the year. Ringed seals are their primary food source, and polar bears tend to preferentially consume the fatty tissues over the protein. This preference for consuming fat makes sense from an evolutionary perspective, given that nearly 50% of the calories of a seal are in the fat tissues, but it poses a potential risk due to the accumulation of lipophilic POPs. As a result, the bears preferentially consume the parts of the seal that contain the highest levels of pollutants. Additionally, these levels of pollutants are magnified in the seals as they themselves consume fish and other prey items that contain pollutants. By understanding the basic aspects of the ecology of this species and the system, it is reasonable to believe that this species is particularly at risk for detrimental effects of pollution on its population dynamics. So what have ecologists learned?

Over the last several decades, teams of researchers from Canada, Russia, Norway, Sweden, and the United States have been investigating POP impacts on polar bears. A variety of POPs, including PCBs and pesticides, have been found in tissue samples of polar bears from many populations (Verreault et al. 2005).

There were complex spatial patterns in terms of which populations had high levels of specific compounds, though in general PCB concentrations were higher in the eastern populations from Svalbard, Norway, and Eastern Greenland than from the western populations of Alaska. Even within a single population there is substantial variation in PCB concentrations among individuals.

Olsen et al. (2003) conducted a study to explore potential causes of this variation in which they tagged 54 female polar bears from around Svalbard with transmitters to monitor bear movement. At the end of the study, they found that the size of the home range of individual bears was the strongest predictor of total PCB levels found within the bear, with bears with larger home ranges having higher PCB levels. Why might this be the case? Going back to our theory of allocation, if an animal is moving a lot, it either needs to burn existing fat reserves for energy, or it needs to eat more food, both of which can influence the amount of PCBs found in the blood. By eating more food, the animal may simply be consuming more pollutants contained in their prey, and the authors believe that was likely occurring in their study. However, what happens when an animal burns fat for energy? Lipophilic compounds previously stored in the fat, such as PCBs, become liberated, and can now affect the physiology of the animals. These results show that not only can regional differences in pollutant levels cause large-scale gradients in PCB concentrations, but the behaviour of individual animals can influence their own pollutant levels. If PCBs reduce an individual's fitness, do you think natural selection would favour larger or smaller home range sizes?

Now that we have established that POPs are found in wild polar bear populations, what evidence is there that they have any physiological effect on the bears? Polar bear females, like all mammals, feed their cubs milk postpartum. Where does the energy for that milk come from? In large part, it comes from the stored fat reserves. In this process, PCBs and other POPs are liberated, and high concentrations of these pollutants are found in the milk itself (Polischuk 2002). Not all cubs will survive, and there is some evidence that the POP concentrations in the milk of mothers whose cubs were lost are higher than the POP concentrations of mothers who kept their cubs (Polischuk 2002). This provides us with a hint that there may be a reproductive cost to POP concentrations on cub survival. However, without a decisive experiment, it is difficult to refute alternative explanations, and more research is needed.

Other studies by Lie et al. (2004, 2005) suggest that PCBs and other POPs can negatively impact the immune system of adult bears. In these studies, the authors captured bears in Canada and Norway and measured their POP levels and collected blood samples for in vitro immunological assays (e.g., lymphocyte proliferation). They also gave the bears immunizations for a variety of compounds such as influenza virus, and upon recapture they measured antibody levels. They found that for many variables, the level of immune response was negatively correlated with the level of PCBs in the bear. In other words, it appears that high PCB concentrations can increase the risk of infection of polar bears. If infection is a natural cause of mortality for these bears, then this again suggests that POPs pollution can negatively impact population dynamics.

The final piece of this puzzle requires us to see if there is a link between POPs and population dynamics, and here the data are fairly sparse. The best study to date comes from Andy Derocher, at the University of Alberta, and his colleagues (Derocher et al. 2003). They measured POP contents in polar bear blood samples that were collected and stored from the Svalbard population in 1967, and then related those values to observed patterns in population age distributions. In 1973, hunting of polar bears was banned in Svalbard, and in the absence of pollutants, populations were expected to show growth during the last 30 years. During this same time period, Derocher et al. (2003) found an increase in PCBs, potentially posing an increased stress to this population. By measuring the age distribution of individuals within the Svalbard population, they found there were fewer older females (>16 year) compared to other polar bear populations where hunting is also restricted. Additionally, this age distribution more closely resembles a Canadian population, which is managed for maximal harvest yet experiences relatively little pollution. These data suggest that although the Svalbard population has grown following the hunting ban, its rate of growth is well below that expected, and mortality and decreased reproduction associated with pollution is a likely contributing factor.

In this example, Derocher and colleagues used age distributions to identity a population-level consequence of a human-mediated activity, the release of POP into the atmosphere. In a separate study (Derocher et al. 1997) Derocher was able to show how other human activities could influence sex ratios within populations of polar bears in Western Hudson Bay. Derocher and his colleagues examined a long-term data set on this population of bears, including information on every bear that was hunted, killed due to human-wildlife conflict (chapter 9), sent to a zoo, or died during handling associated with research (Ecology in Action, this chapter). Between 1966 and 1992, an average of 41.9 bears were removed from the population each year by humans, the vast majority of which were part of a regulated harvest by Inuit peoples (fig. 11.15). At least 2/3 of the animals harvested or killed as problem animals were male, while those sent to zoos or killed during handling had a slight tendency to be female. Derocher and colleagues (1997) suggest that this male-biased harvest contributes to this population having a strongly female-biased sex ratio (over 60% female by the end of the study). However, they also point out that this level of a biased sex ratio is not necessarily detrimental to the long-term prospects of this population, as the mating system of this species is such that all females are likely to mate, even if there are fewer males.

What you can see in these studies is not the end product of decades of research, which have resulted in a firm and certain conclusion, but instead, a view of what science-in-progress looks like. There are hints humans can alter aspects

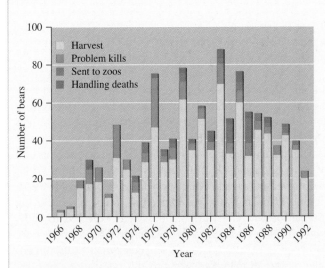

Figure 11.15   Over nearly 30 years, humans removed many polar bears for a variety of reasons, from a population in northern Canada.

of population structure of these long-lived organisms, through direct management and long-term poisoning of the environment. However the data are not completely firm. There are great scientists hard at work trying to fill in the missing pieces,

but the inherent difficulty in working with large and dangerous animals in very remote locations under often brutal conditions makes this a very expensive and slow process. However, these are important questions being addressed, with significant implications for this species. It is only through continued work by future ecologists that we can hope to further unravel these and related questions.

The implications of the work of these researchers goes well beyond the effects of particular pollutants on particular animal species. Their results suggest that organisms that are seemingly isolated from industrial development and large human population centres are connected through global patterns of water and air circulation, and through the actions of indigenous peoples. Their work also raises concern in the context of global warming, which is placing additional stresses on many species of the north. How these populations will respond to multiple stressors remains the future work of ecologists. It is also significant that this research at the population level is rooted in phenomena at the level of the individual organism. This successful bridging between physiological and population ecology suggests that similar connections exist between the population level and higher organizational levels that we examine in the later sections of the book.

SUMMARY

11.1 A survivorship curve summarizes the pattern of survival in a population.

Patterns of survival can be determined either by following a cohort of individuals of similar age to produce a cohort life table, or by determining the age at death of a large number of individuals or the age distribution of a population to produce a static life table. Life tables can be used to draw survivorship curves, which generally fall into one of three categories: (1) type I survivorship, in which there is low mortality among the young but high mortality among older individuals; (2) type II survivorship, in which there is a fairly constant probability of mortality throughout life; and (3) type III survivorship, in which there is high mortality among the young and low mortality among older individuals.

11.2 The age distribution of a population reflects its history of survival, reproduction, and potential for future growth.

Age distributions indicate periods of successful reproduction, high and low survival, and whether the older individuals in a population are replacing themselves or if the population is declining. Population age structure may be highly complicated in variable environments, such as that of the Galápagos

Islands. Populations in highly variable environments may reproduce episodically.

11.3 Population sex ratios can change depending upon the relative fitness of different sexes within a population.

Many populations contain approximately equal numbers of males and females. This balanced sex ratio can be the result of frequency-dependent selection, in which there should be selection favouring the rarer sex. In species in which there are complicated mating systems, sex-dependent survivorship differences, or differential costs associated with producing offspring of each gender, sex ratios can diverge from 1:1.

Ecologists are studying the impacts of pollutants on the population dynamics of many species in arctic communities. Working with wild species imposes constraints on the methods available to physiological and population ecologists, and correlative rather than experimental approaches are often used. Pollutants can alter population-level processes by changing the physiology of individual organisms. The results of this research suggest that variation in population growth rates for some species can be an indicator for pollutant levels, though much more research is needed before making broad conclusions.

REVIEW QUESTIONS

1. Compare cohort and static life tables. What are the main assumptions of each? In what situations or for what organisms would it be practical to use either?

2. Of the three survivorship curves, type III has been the least documented by empirical data. Why is that? What makes this pattern of survivorship difficult to study?

3. Population ecologists have assumed that populations of species with very high reproductive rates, those with offspring sometimes numbering in the millions per female, must have a type III survivorship curve even though very little survivorship data exist for such species. Why is this a reasonable assumption? In general, what is the expected relationship between reproductive rate and patterns of survival?

4. Draw hypothetical age structures for growing, declining, and stable populations. Explain how the age structure of a population with highly episodic reproduction might be misinterpreted as indicating population decline. How might population ecologists avoid such misinterpretations?

5. C. S. Holling (1959) observed predator numerical responses to changes in prey density. He attributed the numerical responses to changes in the reproductive rates of the predators. Discuss how dispersal could be responsible for such phenomena.

6. Persistent organic pollutants have the potential to greatly impact the population dynamics of many species of the arctic and alpine environments. Why are species so far removed from industry at risk from an industrial pollutant? Draw a hypothetical graph relating the levels of PCBs you would expect in a polar bear population as a function of latitude, and explain why.

7. Which aspects of our understanding of the impacts of POPs on polar bear populations came from manipulative experiments, and which came from correlative studies? What are the strengths and weaknesses of each approach?

8. Suppose you measure the sex ratio of a population and find 1.2 males per female. Is this an indication of a skewed sex ratio? What additional information would you seek to help determine whether this result is due to chance events or due to stabilizing selection?

For more information on the resources available from McGraw-Hill Ryerson, go to **www.mcgrawhill.ca/he/solutions**.

POPULATION DYNAMICS AND GROWTH

CHAPTER 12

CHAPTER CONCEPTS

12.1 Population size changes as a function of birth rates, death rates, immigration, and emigration. These processes may be either density independent or density dependent.

Concept 12.1 Review

12.2 A life table combined with a fecundity schedule can be used to estimate net reproductive rate (R_0), geometric rate of increase (λ), generation time (T), and per capita rate of increase (r).

Concept 12.2 Review

12.3 In the presence of abundant resources, populations can grow at geometric or exponential rates.

Concept 12.3 Review

12.4 If resources become limited, population growth rate slows and eventually stops; this is known as logistic population growth.

Concept 12.4 Review

Ecology In Action: Fisheries

Ecological Tools and Approaches: The Human Population

Summary

Review Questions

Given suitable environmental conditions, populations will grow rapidly. Each spring, in temperate seas and lakes around the planet, populations of diatoms explode as these single-celled organisms survive, mature, and reproduce. Populations of zooplankton respond to the "spring blooms" of diatoms, on which they feed, by increasing their own numbers (fig. 12.1). Later in the annual cycle, the numbers of individuals in the diatom and zooplankton populations decrease, responding to decreases in sunlight and nutrients and increases in competition and predation. Populations are dynamic—increasing, decreasing, and responding to changes in the biotic and abiotic environments.

In chapter 12 we examine the factors that determine rates and patterns of population growth. We will look at population growth in the presence of abundant resources, growth where resources are limiting, and how the environment can act to change birth and death rates within populations. Understanding the processes that influence changes to population size, and being able to predict future population sizes, are fundamental goals of population ecologists. The accuracy of

(a)

(b)

Figure 12.1 Lake plankton populations undergo explosive population growth each spring in mid- and high-latitude lakes as a result of favourable environmental conditions. Shown here are (*a*) diatoms and (*b*) a copepod.

these predictions has significant economic and conservation implications. Many organisms are harvested for food, fun, or profit. As we will discuss in this chapter, harvest quotas are often determined through a combination of information derived from ecological models, as well as political and economic considerations. In chapter 10 we discussed species rarity, and Canada's Species At Risk Act. A critical aspect of this federal law was the development of recovery plans designed to increase the population sizes of threatened species. Once again, ecological models of population growth form the foundation of many of these plans.

In this chapter we discuss two approaches to understanding populations. One approach uses mathematics to model population growth. The second approach focuses on studies of laboratory and natural populations. Our knowledge of population growth has progressed through an interplay between modelling and observations of actual populations. We begin with a general discussion of the factors that can affect population growth.

12.1 BIDE (Birth, Immigration, Death, Emigration) Dynamics

Population size changes as a function of birth rates, death rates, immigration, and emigration. These processes may be either density independent or density dependent. In this chapter we will present a number of equations that describe population growth under different conditions. It is easy to let the numbers and equations obscure the underlying biology, and it is easy to become overwhelmed by equations. However, at its core, understanding how populations change over time is very simple, as there are only four factors that can cause a population to change in size: births of new individuals, immigration into the population, deaths, and emigration out of the population.

Population biologists use the term *birth* to refer to any process that produces new individuals in the population. In populations of most species of birds, fish, and reptiles, births are usually counted as the number of eggs laid. In plants, the number of births may be the number of seeds produced or the number of shoots produced during asexual reproduction. In bacteria, the birth rate is measured as the rate of cell division. Immigration and emigration are the consequence of dispersal, a topic discussed in chapter 10. Death is (both inevitable) and self-evident, and was discussed in chapter 11.

As a group, the number of births, immigrants, deaths, and emigrants that occur within a population over some time span are described as the BIDE dynamics (pronounced *bye-dee*). BIDE dynamics can explain changes in the size of all populations on this planet, and likely any others. This can be seen by constructing a simple equation:

$$N_{t+1} = N_t + B + I - D - E$$

In this equation, N_{t+1} is the size of a population at some future time (one time step in the future), and N_t is the size of the population at time *t*. The time interval, "+1," may be

one year, day, hour, or second, depending upon the biology of the organism of interest and the personal preference of the ecologist. B, I, D, and E represent the number of individuals that were born, immigrated, died, or emigrated during this time interval. If the number of individuals born plus those that immigrate is greater than the number of individuals that die plus those that emigrate, the population grows. If it is less, the population decreases. This is the essence of understanding population dynamics, and it is no different than understanding any other system of accounting.

Although this equation is a useful way to determine whether population size is changing over time, complexity arises when we want to compare differences among populations, or to understand why changes are occurring. The first step in making these comparisons is to recognize the difference between **per capita rates** of birth, death, immigration, and emigration, and the *total number* of individuals that are born, die, immigrate, or emigrate. A per capita rate is the rate of some ecological process (e.g., births) divided by the number of individuals in a population. For example, in a population of 100 individuals that produces 10 offspring during a time interval, the per capita birth rate would be 0.10 offspring per individual per time interval. By using per capita rates, we can modify the above equation as:

$$N_{t+1} = N_t + N_t b + N_t i - N_t d - N_t e$$

which can be further rewritten as:

$$N_{t+1} = N_t + N_t(b + i - d - e)$$

where b, i, d, and e represent per capita birth, immigration, death, and emigration rates respectively. Per capita rates allow us to understand how and why population size changes over time. For example, simply multiplying each of these four per capita rates by the total number of individuals in a population allows us to determine the magnitude of population change. If we want to understand differences in population growth among populations or changes in growth rates over time, we again need to focus on per capita rates. One factor that frequently alters per capita rates is the density of a population.

Density Dependence and Density Independence

Most of us could recite an impressive list of factors that can affect the size of populations. Such lists generally include food, competitors, shelter, rainfall, disease, floods, and predators—a mixture of abiotic and biotic factors. Ecologists have long been concerned with the effects of factors such as these on populations. Out of this concern came a long period of debate between the champions of the importance of abiotic factors in limiting population growth and those who argued for the importance of biotic factors as growth-limiting factors. Because the effects of some factors, such as competition, disease, and predation, are often influenced by population density, biotic factors are typically referred to as **density-dependent factors** (fig. 12.2b). Meanwhile, abiotic factors, such as floods and extreme temperature, can exert their influences independently of population density and are often called **density-independent factors** (fig. 12.2a).

Figure 12.2 illustrates what we mean by density independence and dependence for two processes that influence population growth: per capita birth rates and per capita death rates. In figure 12.2a, b and d are constant over the entire range of population sizes (N), which in words indicates that per capita birth and death rates are *independent* of population size. In figure 12.2b, per capita birth rates decrease and per capita death rates increase as population size increases, indicating that the rate of each of these processes is *dependent* upon population size.

Although in these examples we drew both processes as either density independent or both as density dependent, in natural populations it is possible to have one process dependent and the other independent. It is also possible that immigration and emigration may be density dependent. For example, offspring may be more likely to disperse from their natal habit (e.g., emigrate) at high population densities than at low population densities. Although immigration and emigration are important for population dynamics, we will focus on birth and death rates throughout the remainder of this chapter. These rates are most easily measured, most often used, and allow us to calculate a number of critical measures of population growth. Before that, however, let us explore some evidence for density dependence and independence in a natural population.

Figure 12.2 Per capita rates of births and deaths as a function of population size with (*a*) density independence and (*b*) density dependence. Note that in *b*, we drew both birth and death rates as being density dependent. However, it is not uncommon to find that only one may be density dependent and the other density independent within natural populations. Additionally, though not drawn, both immigration and emigration rates may also be either density dependent or density independent.

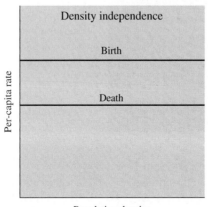

(a)

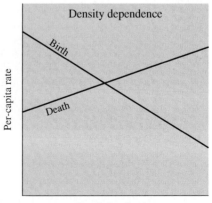

(b)

Roughly categorizing abiotic factors as having density-independent effects and biotic factors as having density dependent effects on populations is a useful first approximation. However, many ecologists were (and are) quick to point out that abiotic factors can also influence populations in a density-dependent fashion. For instance, think of the effect of an unusually cold period on mortality. At low population density, most of the individuals may be able to find sheltered sites, and thus mortality may be low. However, at high population densities, a larger proportion of the population will inhabit less sheltered sites, and so mortality rate in the population may be greater at high population density than at low population density. Similarly, biotic factors such as disease can affect populations in a density-independent way—for example, the virulent pathogen, Dutch elm disease, causes total mortality in infected populations regardless of their local density. The significance of biotic and abiotic factors on populations has been well demonstrated by studies of Galápagos finches.

Environment and Birth and Death Among Galápagos Finches

We return to the Galápagos Islands and the studies of Peter and Rosemary Grant (chapters 9 and 11). Here we focus on long-term records describing highly variable rainfall, responsive plant populations, and abiotic effects on birth and death rates in these finches (fig. 12.3).

In 1976, Peter Boag was a graduate student working with Peter Grant at McGill University. Now a professor at Queen's University, Boag began his research career with detailed studies of Darwin's finches. Among his early studies was one of the populations of Darwin's finches inhabiting Daphne Major, an island of only 0.4 km² situated in the middle of the Galápagos Archipelago (Boag and Grant 1984*b*). This study has since become a classic study integrating population biology, ecology, and evolution. At its heart is solid field study in which Boag counted the numbers of birds found on islands. The numerically dominant finch on Daphne Major at the beginning of the study was the medium ground finch, *Geospiza fortis*, with about

1,200 individuals. In 1977, a drought struck the Galápagos Islands, and by the end of the year the population of *G. fortis* had fallen to about 180 individuals. This decrease represents a decline in population size of about 85% in just one year.

Though a few birds may have emigrated to other nearby islands, most of this population decline was due to starvation. During the drought, the plants that normally produce an annual crop of seeds upon which the finches depend for food failed to do so. From 1977 to 1982, the population of *G. fortis* on Daphne Major averaged about 300 individuals. Then in 1983, about 10 times the average amount of rainfall fell and the population grew to about 1,100 individuals (fig. 12.4). This population growth was due to an increased birth rate as a consequence of an abundance of seeds that the adult finches eat and an abundance of caterpillars that the finches feed to their young (fig. 12.5). As you can see, *G. fortis* populations declined in 1977 because deaths due to starvation far exceeded births. However, the situation was reversed in 1983, when, in the presence of abundant food, the number of births greatly exceeded the number of deaths.

Over this same period, Rosemary Grant and Peter Grant (1989) were studying a population of the large cactus finch, *Geospiza conirostris*, on Genovesa, a small, highly isolated island in the extreme northeastern portion of the Galápagos Archipelago. The study continued from 1978 to 1988, long enough for the researchers to observe the effects of two droughts and two wet periods on reproductive biology. In this population of cactus finches, there was a positive correlation between the number of clutches of eggs laid by birds and the total annual rainfall (fig. 12.6). This study also showed how wet and drought cycles and cactus finches affect populations of prickly pear cactus.

Rainfall, Cactus Finches, and Cactus Reproduction

The Galápagos finches harvest a variety of foods from several species of prickly pear cactus. Two species of finches, *Geospiza scandens* and *G. conirostris*, are well-known specialists on cacti. The Grants documented several ways in which these finches make use of cacti, including (1) opening flower buds in the dry season to eat pollen, (2) consuming nectar and pollen from mature flowers, (3) eating a seed coating called the

(a)

(b)

Figure 12.3   The abundant rains of 1983 (*a*) greatly increased plant growth on the Galápagos Islands compared to (*b*) periods of lower rainfall.

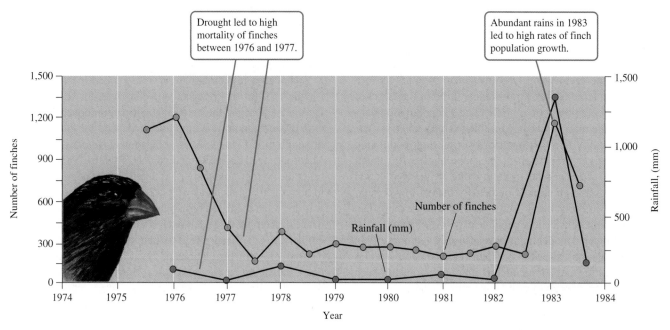

Figure 12.4   Rainfall and the medium ground finch, *Geospiza fortis*, population of Daphne Major Island (data from Gibbs and Grant 1987).

aril, (4) eating seeds, and (5) eating insects from rotting cactus pads and from underneath bark. In return, the finches disperse some cactus seeds and pollinate cactus flowers.

Finches also damage many cactus flowers, however. When they open flower buds or partially opened flowers, they snip the style and destroy the stigmas. As a consequence, the ovules of these flowers cannot be fertilized and they do not produce seeds. The Grants found that up to 78% of a population of flowers can be damaged in this way. These activities, which take place during the wet season, may reduce the seeds available to finches during the dry season.

Opuntia helleri, one of the main sources of food for cactus finches on Genovesa Island, was negatively impacted by the El Niño of 1983. This El Niño damaged the cacti in three ways: (1) Many *O. helleri* simply absorbed so much water that their roots could no longer support them and they were blown over by wind; (2) *O. helleri* on sea cliffs were bathed in salt spray during the many storms that hit the island during 1983, which may have produced osmotic stress (see chapter 6); and (3) increased rainfall stimulated growth by a fast-growing vine that smothered many *O. helleri* (fig. 12.7). Though outright mortality of the cactus was not common, flower and fruit production was severely reduced for several years.

Reduced reproductive output by *O. helleri* was at least partly due to the activities of the cactus finches on Genovesa. The stigma snipping behaviour of cactus finches was especially

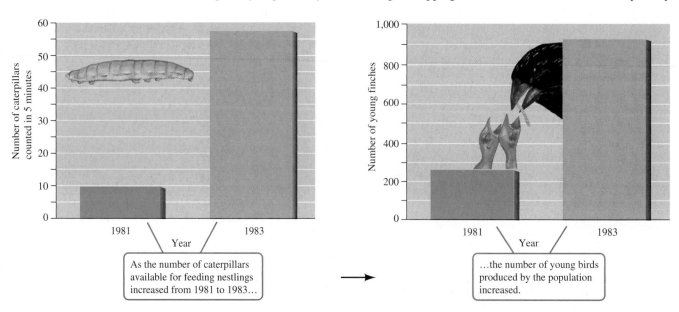

Figure 12.5   Availability of caterpillars and number of fledglings of medium ground finches on Daphne Major (data from Gibbs and Grant 1987).

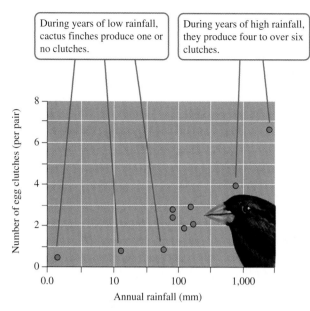

During years of low rainfall, cactus finches produce one or no clutches.

During years of high rainfall, they produce four to over six clutches.

Figure 12.6   Relationship between annual rainfall and the number of egg clutches produced by large cactus finches, *Geospiza conirostris*, on Genovesa Island (data from Grant and Grant 1989).

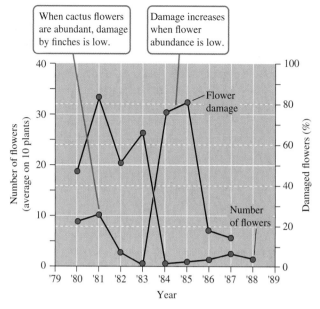

When cactus flowers are abundant, damage by finches is low.

Damage increases when flower abundance is low.

Figure 12.8   Cactus flower abundance on Genovesa Island and extent of flower damage by large cactus finches (data from Grant and Grant 1989).

damaging during the drought years of 1984 and 1985. In normal years stigma damage is mainly confined to the early part of the wet season from January to March. During the extremely wet 1983 season there was very little damage to the stigmas of cactus flowers. However, during the drought years of 1984 and 1985, up to 95% of stigmas were snipped (fig. 12.8). This extensive damage to flowers helped delay recovery of flower and fruit production until 1986, when another El Niño brought heavy rains to the Galápagos Islands.

Populations of Galápagos finches and their food plants are an instructive model of how the environment can affect birth and death rates. Sometimes, as when the cactus fell because they were engorged with water during the El Niño of 1983, the effect of the physical environment is clear and direct. Sometimes, as when *G. fortis* starved in response to

reduced seed supplies during the drought of 1977, the effect of the physical environment on a population is clearly mediated through a biological resource (in this case, seeds). In other cases, such as reduced fruit production by *O. helleri* on Genovesa, populations respond to a complex mixture of abiotic (drought) and biotic (damage by finches) factors that are themselves interrelated. The message to remember from these detailed studies is that both biotic and abiotic factors have important influences on birth and death rates in populations and that their effects are often tightly interconnected. In the examples just presented, environmental variation essentially changed the carrying capacity (K) of the environment for Galápagos finch populations. In section II, we have focused on how various aspects of the physical environment affect the performance of organisms, including their reproductive performance. In chapters 13, 14, and 15 of section IV we will consider at length how biological interactions affect populations. Let's now explore how ecologists measure birth and death rates in natural populations.

Figure 12.7   High rainfall during the El Niño of 1983 caused increased mortality of the cactus *Opuntia helleri* on Genovesa Island.

CONCEPT 12.1 REVIEW

1. Why can BIDE dynamics be said to govern population growth of all populations on the planet?
2. Why are abiotic factors often considered to have density-independent effects on per capita rates births, death, immigration, and emigration?
3. Why might medium ground finch population responses to short-term, episodic increases in rainfall differ from their responses to increases in rainfall lasting for years or decades?

12.2 Rates of Population Change

A life table combined with a fecundity schedule can be used to estimate net reproductive rate (R_0), geometric rate of increase (λ), generation time (T), and per capita rate of increase (r). Now that we understand what processes can be involved in causing population sizes to change over time, we need to understand how an ecologist can actually measure these rates in natural populations. We can then use that information to predict changes in population growth. To do this, we return to chapter 11, where we introduced *life tables* as a means to demonstrate age-specific mortality. Here we will expand life tables to also include birth rates.

Tracking birth rates in a population is similar to tracking survival rates. In a sexually reproducing population, the population biologist needs to know the average number of births per female for each age class and the number of females in each age class. In practice, the ecologist counts the number of eggs produced by birds or reptiles, the number of fawns produced by deer, or the number of seeds or sprouts produced by plants. The numbers of offspring produced by parents of different ages are then tabulated. The tabulation of birthrates for females of different ages in a population is called a **fecundity schedule**. It may seem a bit surprising that population biologists primarily focus on the reproduction of females, rather than both males and females. However, for most species it is quite simple to determine maternity, while as we discussed in chapter 8, paternity can be more difficult to establish. As a result, though information

on paternity would improve population modelling, high-quality paternity data is often difficult and expensive to obtain, and so most population ecologists focus on female reproduction.

Once a fecundity schedule is obtained, it can be combined with the other information in a life table and used to estimate several important characteristics of populations. To a population ecologist, one of the most important things to know is whether a population is growing or declining.

Estimating Rates for a Short-Lived Plant

Figure 12.9 combines survivorship with seed production by the plant *P. drummondii*. The first column, x, lists age intervals in days. The second column, n_x, lists the number of individuals in the population surviving to each age interval. The third column, l_x, lists survivorship, the proportion of the population surviving to each age x. The fourth column, m_x, lists the average number of seeds produced by each individual in each age interval. Finally, the fifth column, $l_x m_x$, is the product of columns 3 and 4.

Let us first explore the first two columns, x and n_x. For this species, the ecologist has chosen to uses days as the time interval of interest. Why not months or years? You will notice that in the 355–362 age class, there are no surviving individuals ($n_x = 0$). Even without seeing this species grow, we have been able to learn it is an annual plant species, completing its life cycle in less than one year—and thus years would have been a poor choice for age intervals. Looking more closely, you will notice that the all of the mortality of the individuals occurs in a very narrow age-window,

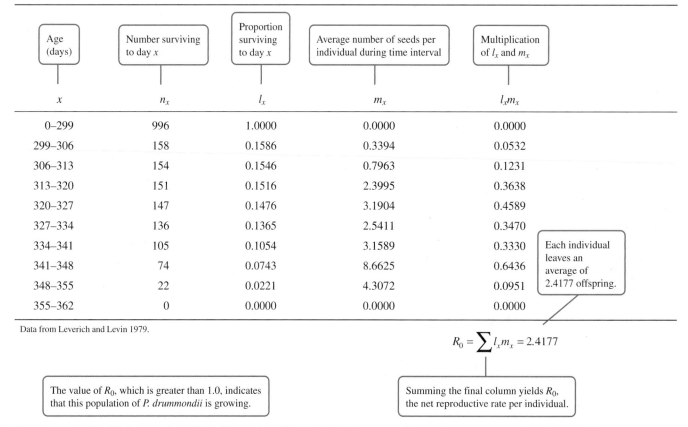

Age (days)	Number surviving to day x	Proportion surviving to day x	Average number of seeds per individual during time interval	Multiplication of l_x and m_x
x	n_x	l_x	m_x	$l_x m_x$
0–299	996	1.0000	0.0000	0.0000
299–306	158	0.1586	0.3394	0.0532
306–313	154	0.1546	0.7963	0.1231
313–320	151	0.1516	2.3995	0.3638
320–327	147	0.1476	3.1904	0.4589
327–334	136	0.1365	2.5411	0.3470
334–341	105	0.1054	3.1589	0.3330
341–348	74	0.0743	8.6625	0.6436
348–355	22	0.0221	4.3072	0.0951
355–362	0	0.0000	0.0000	0.0000

Each individual leaves an average of 2.4177 offspring.

Data from Leverich and Levin 1979.

$$R_0 = \sum l_x m_x = 2.4177$$

The value of R_0, which is greater than 1.0, indicates that this population of *P. drummondii* is growing.

Summing the final column yields R_0, the net reproductive rate per individual.

Figure 12.9   Combining survivorship with seed production by *P. drummondii* to estimate net reproductive rate, R_0

between ages 299 and 362—a span of only 63 days. Thus, using months as an age interval would be too coarse a measure to understand the age-specific processes that are occurring. Let us now turn to the other columns in this life table.

We have already used the data in column 3, l_x, to construct the survivorship curve for this species (see fig. 11.5). Now, let's combine those survivorship data with the seed production for *P. drummondii*, m_x, to calculate the **net reproductive rate**, R_0. The calculations of reproductive rates in this section assume that birth rates and death rates for each age class in a population are constant and that the population under study has a **stable age distribution**. In a population with a stable age distribution, the proportion of individuals in each of the age classes is constant. In general, the net reproductive rate is the average number of offspring produced by an individual in a population during its lifetime or per generation. In the case of the annual plant *P. drummondii*, the net reproductive rate is the average number of seeds left by an individual. You can calculate the net reproductive rate from figure 12.9 by adding the values in the final column. The result is:

$$R_0 = \sum l_x m_x = 2.4177$$

To calculate the total number of seeds produced by this population during the year of study, multiply 2.4177 by 996, which was the initial number of plants in this population. The result, 2,408, is the number of seeds that this population of *P. drummondii* will begin with the next year.

Since *P. drummondii* has pulsed reproduction, we can estimate the rate at which its population is growing with a quantity known as the **geometric rate of increase**, λ. The geometric rate of increase is the ratio of the population size at two points in time:

$$\lambda = \frac{N_{t+1}}{N_t}$$

In this equation, N_{t+1} is the size of the population at some future time and N_t is the size of the population at some earlier time (fig. 12.10). The time interval t may be years, days, or

hours; which time interval you use to calculate the geometric rate of increase for a population depends on the organism and the rate at which its population grows.

Let's calculate λ for the population of *P. drummondii*. What time interval should we use for our calculation? Since *P. drummondii* is an annual plant, the most meaningful time interval would be one year. The initial number of *P. drummondii* in the population, N_t, was 996. The number of individuals (seeds) in the population at the end of a year of study was 2,408. This is the number in the next generation, which is N_{t+1}. Therefore, the geometric rate of increase for the population over the period of this study was:

$$\lambda = \frac{2,408}{996} = 2.4177$$

This is the same value we got for R_0. But, before you jump to conclusions, you should know that R_0, which is the number of offspring per female per generation, does not always equal λ. In this case, λ equalled R_0 because *P. drummondii* is an annual plant with pulsed reproduction. Consequently, parents always die before their offspring germinate, and thus the generations are discrete and non-overlapping. If a species has overlapping generations and continuous reproduction, R_0 will usually not equal λ. How long do you think this plant can continue to reproduce at the rate of λ, or $R_0 = 2.4177$? Not long, as you will see later in this chapter. Before we do that, let's do some calculations for organisms with overlapping generations.

Estimating Rates When Generations Overlap

The population of the northern water snake, *Nerodia sipedon*, whose mortality we examined in figure 11.6, contrasts with the *P. drummondii* population in various ways. Let's examine some of the details of this snake and study to better understand life tables. The data presented in figure 12.11 were collected in a marsh near Queen's University Biological Station in Ontario. Snakes were captured, marked, and recaptured regularly over a period of nine years. Approximately 70% of adult females will breed in any particular year. In contrast to annual plants, individual snakes do not die following breeding, and thus there is overlap in survival among generations (parents and children coexist). Further complicating matters, individuals can mate multiple times in their life. Females are not generally sexually mature until age four, and even then larger females tend to produce larger litters than smaller females. Across all ages and sizes of females that do breed, the average litter size is 19.7 offspring. Multiplying the proportion of females that breed (0.7) by the average litter size (19.7), gives us an estimate of the average number of offspring produced by an adult (reproductively mature) female each year: 13.79. On average, half of these offspring will be male, and half will be female. However, as previously mentioned, population biologists generally keep track of only females, and thus we are concerned here with only the production of daughters. Since the sex ratio in this population is 1:1, we multiply 13.79 by 0.50 to calculate the number of daughters per adult female per year in the population: 6.9. However, if you look at figure 12.11, you will not find the value 6.9 listed under the m_x column. Why? Because 6.9 is

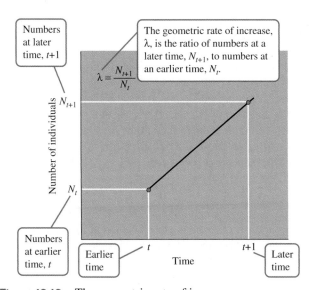

Figure 12.10   The geometric rate of increase.

x (years)	l_x	m_x	$l_x m_x$	$x l_x m_x$
0	1.0000	0	0	0
1	0.4000	0	0	0
2	0.1640	0	0	0
3	0.1000	0	0	0
4	0.0640	5.5400	0.3547	1.4188
5	0.0307	6.7600	0.2078	1.0388
6	0.0148	7.8100	0.1152	0.6913
7	0.0071	8.8900	0.0629	0.4406
8	0.0034	9.1000	0.0309	0.2474
9	0.0016	9.2400	0.0151	0.1357

Source: Table based on Brown and Weatherhead 1999, CJ277:1358-1366 (Survival of northern water snakes).

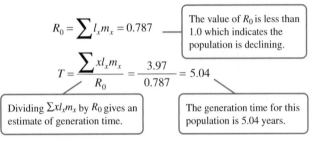

$$R_0 = \sum l_x m_x = 0.787$$

The value of R_0 is less than 1.0 which indicates the population is declining.

$$T = \frac{\sum x l_x m_x}{R_0} = \frac{3.97}{0.787} = 5.04$$

Dividing $\sum x l_x m_x$ by R_0 gives an estimate of generation time.

The generation time for this population is 5.04 years.

Figure 12.11 Calculating net reproductive rate, R_0, and generation time, T, for a population of the northern water snake, *Nerodia sipedon*. (Table based on Brown and Weatherhead 1999.)

an average value across all adult females, while in this snake population older females tended to be larger than younger females, and also produced more offspring per litter.

Figure 12.11 includes the life table information used to construct figure 11.6 plus the fecundity information estimated during the study. The sum of $l_x m_x$ provides an estimate of R_0, the net reproductive rate of females in this population. In this case, $R_0 = 0.787$. We can interpret this number as the average number of daughters produced by each female in this population over the course of her lifetime. If this number is correct, the mothers in this population are not producing enough daughters to replace themselves. What value of R_0 would suggest a stable snake population? In a stable population, R_0 would be 1.0, which means that each female would replace just herself during her lifetime. In a growing population, such as the population of *Phlox*, R_0 would be greater than 1.0.

Population ecologists are also interested in several other characteristics of populations. One of those is the **generation time**, **T**, which is the average age at which a female gives birth to her offspring. Or put another way, a population's generation time represents the average time it takes to go from egg to egg, seed to seed, and so forth. We can use the information in figure 12.11 to calculate the average generation time for the northern water snakes of Barb's Marsh as:

$$T = \frac{\sum x l_x m_x}{R_0}$$

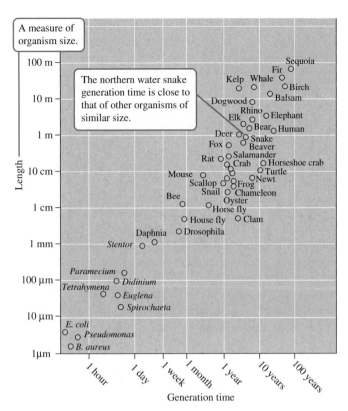

A measure of organism size.

The northern water snake generation time is close to that of other organisms of similar size.

Figure 12.12 Size and generation time (data from Bonner 1965).

In this equation, x is age in years. To calculate T, sum the last column and divide the result by R_0. The result shows that the average generation time is 5.04 years.

How could you tell if 5.0 years is an unusually long or short generation time? Figure 12.12 plots the generation time against body size for a broad range of organisms. As we saw for population density in chapter 10, there is a significant positive correlation between body size and generation time. The largest organisms tend to have the longest generation times and the smallest have the shortest. While this relationship might not be particularly surprising, its consistency across such a wide range of organisms is impressive. In addition, the relationship is not restricted to a narrow taxon such as herbivorous mammals. John Bonner (1965) found the trend shown in figure 12.12 is rooted in the bacteria and extends all the way to the largest organisms in the biosphere, the giant sequoia, *Sequoia gigantea*. Humans and water snakes lie somewhere in the middle range of the distribution.

Knowing R_0 and T allows us to estimate r, the **per capita rate of increase** for a population:

$$r = \frac{\ln R_0}{T}$$

(ln is the base of the natural logarithms). We can interpret r as per capita birth rate minus per capita death rate: $r = b - d$. Using this method, the estimated per capita rate of increase for the northern water snake population is:

$$r = \frac{\ln 0.787}{5.04} = -0.048$$

The negative value of r in this case indicates that birth rates are lower than death rates and the population is declining. A value of r greater than 0 would indicate a growing population, and a value equal to 0 would indicate a stable population. While there are ways to make more accurate estimates of r, this method is accurate enough for our discussion.

In this section we have seen how a life table combined with a fecundity schedule can be used to estimate net reproductive rate, R_0, geometric rate of increase, λ, generation time, T, and per capita rate of increase, r. We will next use r to model population growth.

CONCEPT 12.2 REVIEW

1. Suppose that you are managing a population of an endangered species that has been reduced in numbers throughout its historic range, and that your goal is to increase the size of the population. What values of R_0 would meet your management goals?
2. Both R_0 and r indicate that the water snake population at Barb's Marsh is in decline. Is there any way that this population could persist, without human intervention, for many generations even with such negative indicators?
3. Life tables can be intimidating. Imagine you found another population of water snakes that had the same l_x values as in figure 12.11, but whose m_x values were doubled for each age class. Recalculate r.

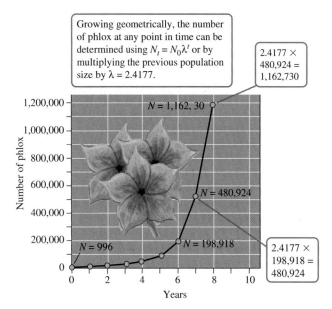

Figure 12.13 Geometric growth by a hypothetical population of *Phlox drummondii*.

12.3 Geometric and Exponential Population Growth

In the presence of abundant resources, populations can grow at geometric or exponential rates. Suppose a population had access to abundant resources, such as food, space, nutrients, and so forth. Imagine that birth, death, immigration, and emigration rates are all density independent, and births are much greater than deaths. How fast could it grow? Imagine a plant, animal, or bacterial population reproducing at its maximum reproductive rate and experiencing relatively little mortality. What would be the resulting pattern of population growth (think back to the BIDE equation)? Regardless of the species you choose, the pattern will be the same. A population growing at its maximum rate will add a few new individuals at first, and then increasingly more at each later time step. In other words, population growth accelerates, producing a characteristic *J-shaped curve* (fig. 12.13). This is the outcome of density independence, if per capita emigration and death rates are continually lower than the rates of birth and immigration (fig. 12.2a).

When growing at their maximum rates, some populations are said to grow *geometrically* and others *exponentially*. We examine what causes these two ways of modelling population growth in this section.

Geometric Growth

Because it is an annual plant, populations of *Phlox drummondii* grow in discrete annual pulses. Populations of insects that produce a single generation a year also grow in pulses. Growth by any population with pulsed reproduction can be modelled as **geometric population growth**, in which successive generations differ in size by a constant ratio.

We can use the population of *Phlox* studied by Leverich and Levin (1979) to build a model of geometric population growth. You may recall that we calculated a geometric rate of increase, $\lambda = N_{t+1}/N_t$, for this population of 2.4177 (figure 12.9). At the end of that discussion, we asked rhetorically how long the *Phlox* population could continue growing at this rate. Let's address that question here.

We can compute the growth of a population of organisms whose generations do not overlap by simply multiplying λ times the size of the population at the beginning of each generation. The initial size of the population studied by Leverich and Levin was 996 and the number of offspring produced by this population during their year of study was:

$$N_1 = N_0 \times \lambda, \text{ or } 996 \times 2.4177 = 2{,}408$$

Now let's repeat this calculation for a few generations. The population size at the beginning of the next generation, N_2, would be $N_1 \times \lambda$. However, because

$$N_1 = N_0 \times \lambda, N_2 = N_0 \times \lambda \times \lambda, \text{ or } N_0 \times \lambda^2,$$

which is

$$996 \times 2.4177 \times 2.4177 = 5{,}822.$$

At the third generation, N_3,

$$N_0 \times \lambda^3 = 14{,}076$$

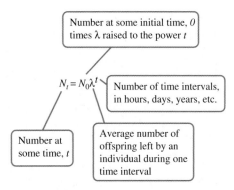

Figure 12.14 Anatomy of the equation for geometric population growth.

and in general, the size of a population growing geometrically at any time, t, can be modelled as:

$$N_t = N_0\lambda^t$$

In this model, N_t is the number of individuals at any time t, N_0 is the initial number of individuals, λ is the geometric rate of increase, and t is the number of time intervals or generations. The interpretation of this model and the definitions of each of its terms are summarized in figure 12.14. We can use this model to project the future size of our hypothetical *Phlox* population. Notice in figure 12.13 that in only 8 years the population has grown from 996 to 1.16×10^6, to over 1 million individuals. By 16 years, the population would be over a billion, by 24 years the population would top 1 trillion individuals, and by year 40 it would increase to over 10^{18}, or 1 billion billion individuals.

We can get a feeling for how large this hypothetical *Phlox* population would be by calculating how much space the growing population would occupy. Since the *Phlox* population studied by Leverich and Levin was from Texas, let's confine our hypothetical population to North America and scale population growth against the area of the North American continent, which is about 24 million km^2. Assuming a uniform density across the continent, by 32 years our population would reach a density of nearly 80 million individuals per square kilometre, or about 80 individuals per square metre across the entire continent, from southern Mexico to northern Canada and Alaska. Eight years later, the density would be nearly 90,000 individuals per square metre!

There are many reasons why this exercise is unrealistic, and we would reasonably expect density to alter birth and death rates. This population would soon be so dense that plants would die because they lacked sufficient nutrients, light, and water; and the population would soon spread beyond the physical climates to which *P. drummondii* is adapted. In other words, we would expect per capita death rates to increase with density, and likely per capita birth rate to decrease, due to reduced access to energy and food with which one could produce offspring. However, out of this unrealistic exercise comes an important fact about the natural world. Natural populations have a tremendous capacity for increase, and geometric population growth cannot be maintained in any population for very many generations. You may also recognize how this

realization influenced the development of the theory of natural selection (chapter 4). It is apparent that populations cannot grow without bounds for extended periods of time, and thus the relative performance of individuals within a population will have strong influences on their overall fitness.

Now let's consider population growth by organisms such as bacteria, forest trees, and humans, which have overlapping generations. Because growth by these populations can be continuous, the geometric model is usually not appropriate.

Exponential Growth

Continuous population growth in an unlimited environment can be modelled as **exponential population growth**:

$$\frac{dN}{dt} = rN$$

The exponential growth equation (fig. 12.15) expresses the rate of population growth, dN/dt, which is the change in numbers of individuals with change in time, as the per capita rate of increase, r, times population size, N. The exponential model is appropriate for populations with non-pulsed reproduction because it represents population growth as a continuous process. In the exponential model, r is a constant, while N is a variable. Therefore, as population size, N, increases, the rate

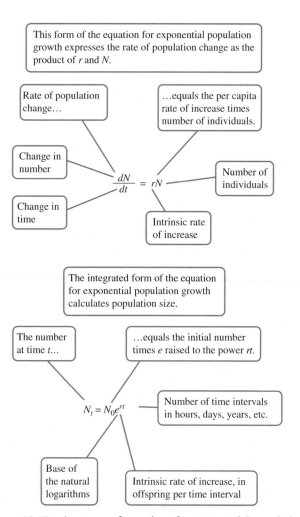

Figure 12.15 Anatomy of equations for exponential population growth. The first equation is the derivative of the second.

of population increase, *dN/dt*, gets larger and larger. The rate of increase gets larger because the constant *r* is multiplied by a larger and larger population size, *N*. Consequently, during exponential growth, the rate of population growth increases over time.

For a population growing at an exponential rate, the population size at any time *t* can be calculated as:

$$N_t = N_0 e^{rt}$$

In this form of the exponential growth model, N_t is the number of individuals at time *t*, N_0 is the initial number of individuals, *e* is the base of the natural logarithms, *r* is the per capita rate of increase, and *t* is the number of time intervals. Notice that this form of the exponential model of population growth is virtually the same as our equation for geometric growth but with e^r taking the place of λ. The two forms of the exponential growth equation are presented and explained in figure 12.15.

Exponential Growth in Nature

Some of the assumptions of the exponential growth model, such as a constant rate of per capita increase, may seem a bit unrealistic. Do populations in nature ever grow at an exponential rate? The answer is a qualified yes. Natural populations may grow at exponential rates for relatively short periods of time in the presence of abundant resources.

Exponential Growth by Tree Populations

As we saw in chapters 1 and 10, as the last ice age was ending, tree populations in the Northern Hemisphere followed the retreating glaciers northward. Ecologists have documented these movements by studying the sediments of lakes, where the pollen of wind-pollinated tree species is especially abundant. The appearance of pollen of a tree species in the lake sediment is a record of its establishment near the lake. The date of each establishment can be determined using carbon-14 concentration to determine the age of organic matter along a sediment profile.

Pollen records have also been used to estimate the growth of several post-glacial tree populations in Britain. K. Bennett (1983) estimated population sizes and growth by counting the number of pollen grains of each tree species deposited within lake sediments. By counting the number of pollen grains per square centimetre deposited each year, Bennett was able to reconstruct changes in tree population densities in the surrounding landscape. This approach is a bit different from going out in a forest and estimating population density directly by counting trees. What is the main assumption of this method? Bennett's assumption was that the rate of pollen deposition is proportional to the size of tree populations around a lake. This assumption, which seems reasonable, leads to an interesting picture of growth by postglacial tree populations in the British Isles. Populations of the tree species studied grew at exponential rates for 400 to 500 years following their initial appearance in the pollen record. Figure 12.16 shows the exponential increase in abundance of Scots pine, *Pinus sylvestris*, which first appeared in the pollen record of the study lake about 9,500 years ago.

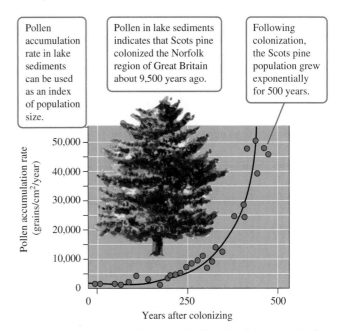

> Pollen accumulation rate in lake sediments can be used as an index of population size.

> Pollen in lake sediments indicates that Scots pine colonized the Norfolk region of Great Britain about 9,500 years ago.

> Following colonization, the Scots pine population grew exponentially for 500 years.

Figure 12.16   Exponential growth of a colonizing population of Scots pine, *Pinus sylvestris* (data from Bennett 1983).

Figure 12.17   Whooping cranes in the breeding grounds found within Wood Buffalo National Park, Alberta.

Conditions for Exponential Growth

Natural populations of organisms as different as diatoms, birds, and trees can grow at exponential rates. However, as different as these organisms are, the circumstances in which their populations grow at exponential rates have a great deal in common. All begin their exponential growth in favourable environments at low population densities. The trees studied by Bennett began at low densities because they were invading new territory previously unoccupied by the species. Spring blooms of planktonic diatoms are also the result of exponential population growth in response to seasonal increases in nutrients and light.

The whooping crane provides another example of exponential growth following protection and careful management (fig. 12.17). Hunting and habitat destruction had reduced the population of whooping cranes to 15 individuals by 1941–42.

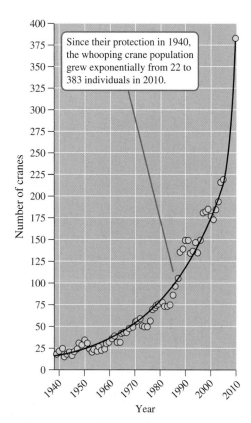

Figure 12.18 Hunting and habitat destruction reduced the whooping crane, which is endemic to North America, to a single natural population. Protection and intensive management of this population has led to its dramatic recovery (data from USFWS 2010).

At that time it was known that this remnant population of whooping cranes wintered on the Texas Gulf Coast, but its northern breeding grounds were unknown. It was later discovered that they breed in Wood Buffalo National Park in Canada. Under full protection and careful management in both Canada and the United States, the migratory whooping crane population has grown exponentially from 22 individuals in 1942 to 383 birds in 2010 (fig. 12.18). However, continued tar sands development in northern Alberta may present risk to these populations by the loss of suitable habitat, potential impacts on migratory pathways, and the creation of large tailings ponds. However, as a species protected by the Migratory Bird Treaty, there are significant legal consequences for inadequate protection of this species.

These examples suggest that exponential population growth may be very important to populations during the process of establishment in new environments; during exploitation of transient, favourable conditions; and during the process of recovery from some form of exploitation. However, as we saw with *P. drummondii*, geometric or exponential growth cannot continue indefinitely. In nature, population growth eventually slows and population sizes level off.

Slowing of Exponential Growth

The collared dove, *Streptopelia decaocto*, expanded beyond its historical range into western Europe during the latter half of the twentieth century. As the bird spread into new territory,

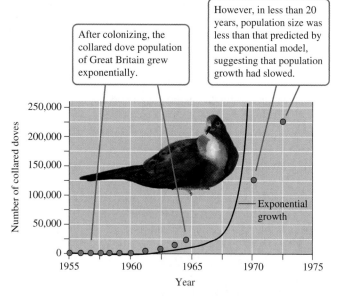

Figure 12.19 Exponential growth of the collared dove population of Great Britain (data from Hengeveld 1988).

its populations grew at exponential rates for a decade or more. For instance, from 1955 to 1972, the expanding population in the British Isles followed a typical exponential curve (fig. 12.19). However, if you examine figure 12.19 closely, you will see evidence that the rate of growth by the collared dove population began to slow by 1970.

The pattern for the collared dove indicates that its population grew at a higher rate from 1955 to 1964, and then, between 1965 and 1970, its rate of population growth began to slow. This slowdown suggests that between 1965 and 1970, this invading population was approaching some environmental limits. Environmental limitation is generally associated with density dependence, and is incorporated into another model of population growth called **logistic population growth**.

CONCEPT 12.3 REVIEW

1. What was the major assumption underlying Bennett's (1983) use of pollen deposited in lake sediments to estimate the postglacial population size of Scots pine?
2. Why do many populations of exotic species, such as zebra mussels in the Great Lakes or Eurasian collared doves in Europe, often grow at exponential rates for some time following their introduction into a new environment?
3. African annual killifish live in temporary pools, where their populations survive the dry season as eggs that lie dormant in the mud, developing and hatching only when the pools fill each wet season. In contrast, the guppy, a common aquarium fish, lives in populations consisting of mixed-age classes in which reproduction occurs year-round. Which model of population growth, exponential or geometric, would be most appropriate for each of these fish species?

12.4 Logistic Population Growth

If resources become limited, population growth rate slows and eventually stops; this is known as logistic population growth. Exponential growth cannot continue indefinitely. Resource limitation, competitors, predators, pathogens, and other factors all act to reduce the rate of population growth. As we will see, the basic models of exponential growth can be modified to represent these biotic influences on population growth. One challenge that nearly all populations will encounter is a limited supply of resources, and that is the topic we use here to demonstrate how exponential models of population growth can be expanded to include other ecological interactions.

Eventually, populations run up against environmental limits to further increase. The effect of the environment on population growth is reflected in the shapes of population growth curves. As population size increases, growth rate eventually slows and then ceases as population size levels off. This pattern of growth produces a **sigmoidal**, or "*S-shaped*," **population growth curve** (fig. 12.20). The population size at which growth stops is generally called the **carrying capacity**, or **K**, which is the number of individuals of a particular species that the local environment can support. What causes K to exist? Since

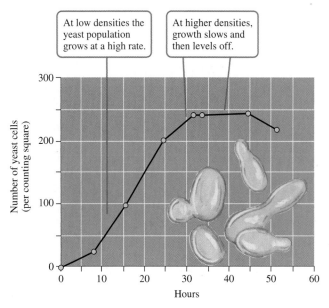

Figure 12.21   Sigmoidal growth by a population of the yeast *Saccharomyces cerevisiae* (data from Gause 1934).

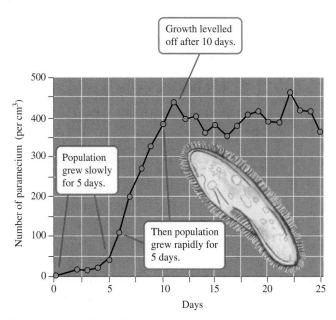

Figure 12.22   Sigmoidal growth by a population of *Paramecium caudatum* (data from Gause 1934).

the only factors that can affect population growth are births, deaths, immigration, and emigration, we should have a good idea. In general, K is reached when per capita birth + immigration rates equal per capita death + emigration rates. However, immigration and emigration are generally low relative to births and deaths, and are excluded from the models we are discussing here. Thus, with density dependence, carrying capacity is the outcome of per capita birth rates equalling per capita death rates, resulting in zero net population growth (fig. 12.20).

Sigmoidal growth curves have been observed in a wide variety of populations. In the course of his laboratory experiments, G. F. Gause (1934) obtained sigmoidal growth curves for populations of several species of yeast (fig. 12.21) and protozoa (fig. 12.22). Similar patterns of population growth

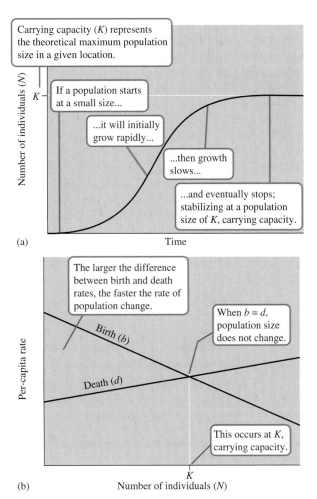

Figure 12.20   (*a*) Sigmoidal, or logistic, population growth results from environmental limitation on population size acting in a (*b*) density-dependent manner.

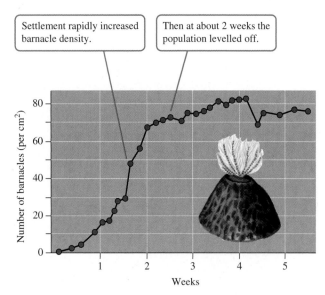

Settlement rapidly increased barnacle density.

Then at about 2 weeks the population levelled off.

Figure 12.23   Settlement by the barnacle *Balanus balanoides* in the intertidal zone (data from Connell 1961*a*, 1961*b*).

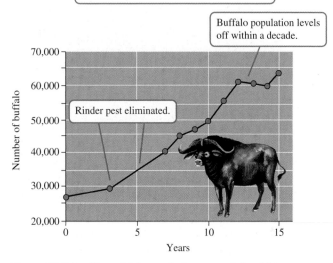

When rinder pest, a disease of cattle and their relatives, was eliminated from the Serengeti, the buffalo population began to grow.

Buffalo population levels off within a decade.

Rinder pest eliminated.

Figure 12.24   Sigmoidal population growth by African buffalo, *Syncerus caffer*, on the Serengeti Plain (data from Sinclair 1977).

have been recorded for other populations, including barnacles (fig. 12.23) and African buffalo (fig. 12.24).

What causes these populations to slow their rates of growth and eventually stop growing at carrying capacity? The idea behind the concept of carrying capacity is that a given environment has a fixed supply of food, space, light, or other limiting resources, and thus can only support so many individuals of a particular species. For the barnacles studied by Connell (1961*a*, 1961*b*), carrying capacity was largely determined

by the amount of space available on rocks for attachment by new barnacles. For African buffalo, Tony Sinclair of the University of British Columbia found carrying capacity depends upon the amount of grass available as food (Sinclair 1977). Yeast feed on sugars and produce alcohol. As the density of a population of yeast increases, their environment contains less and less sugar and more and more alcohol, which is toxic to them. So, yeast populations are eventually limited by their own waste products. For most species, carrying capacity is likely determined by a complex interplay among factors such as food, parasitism, disease, and space. While we can discuss these factors in a general way, the mathematical models of population biology help us to discuss population processes in a more precise way.

The logistic model was proposed to account for the patterns of growth shown by populations as they begin to deplete environmental resources. Population ecologists built the logistic growth model by modifying the exponential growth model:

$$dN/dt = r_{max}N$$

Notice that here, the per capita rate of increase, r, has a subscript $_{max}$. The subscript indicates that this is the *maximum* per capita rate of increase, achieved by a species under ideal environmental conditions, where birth rates, death rates, and age structure are constant. The per capita rate of increase attained under such circumstances, r_{max}, is called the **intrinsic rate of increase**. When we calculated the rate of increase from a life table earlier in this chapter, we determined r, the *realized* or *actual* per capita rate of increase. As we saw, realized r may be positive, zero, or negative, depending on environmental conditions. Because natural populations are usually subject to factors such as disease, competition, and so forth, the actual per capita rate of increase, realized r, is generally less than r_{max}. It is this maximum value, r_{max}, that is used in this section, as opposed to realized value of r that was used previously.

The exponential model of population growth can be modified to produce a model in which population growth is sigmoidal. The simplest way to do this is to add an element that slows growth as population size approaches carrying capacity, K:

$$\frac{dN}{dt} = r_{max}N\left[\frac{K-N}{K}\right]$$

The inventor of this equation for sigmoidal population growth, P. F. Verhulst, called it the **logistic equation** (Verhulst and Quetelet 1838). Rearranging the logistic equation shows more clearly the influence of population size, N, on rate of population growth:

$$\frac{dN}{dt} = r_{max}N\left(\frac{K-N}{K}\right) = r_{max}N\left(\frac{K}{K}-\frac{N}{K}\right) = r_{max}N\left(1-\frac{N}{K}\right)$$

In the logistic equation, the rate of population growth, dN/dt, slows as population size increases because the difference, $(1 - N/K)$, becomes a smaller and smaller value as N approaches K. Imagine a population in which N is very low, while K is very high. What impact would $(1 - N/K)$ have on population growth? Very little. Now imagine that N equals K.

In this case, $(1 - N/K) = 0$, and population growth will stop. Therefore, as population size increases, the logistic growth rate becomes a smaller and smaller fraction of the exponential growth rate. When $N = K$, population growth ceases. By taking the integral of this equation (fig. 12.25) we can calculate population size at a given time period.

The ratio N/K has been called the "environmental resistance" to population growth. As the size of a population, N, gets closer and closer to carrying capacity, environmental factors increasingly impede further population growth.

In the logistic growth model, the *realized* per capita rate of increase, which is $r = r_{max}(1 - N/K) = r_{max} - r_{max}(N/K)$, depends upon population size. Therefore, when population size, N, is very small, the per capita rate of increase is approximately r_{max}. As N increases, however, realized r decreases until N equals K. At that point, realized r is zero.

The relationship between realized r and population size in the logistic model, which follows a straight line, is shown in figure 12.26. If, according to the logistic equation, per capita growth rates are highest at low population sizes, when will population growth itself be greatest? Or, put another way, at what population size will the largest number of individuals be added during a given time interval? We know the answer cannot be at population sizes above K, as that results in either zero or negative population growth (fig. 12.26). What about at the other extreme, when population sizes are very low? Under these conditions, r, the realized per capita growth rate (the value that we measured in the life tables of chapter 11), is at its highest point, equal to r_{max} (fig. 12.26). However, because the population size is low, although the population is growing rapidly on a per capita basis, it is not increasing rapidly in absolute numbers. Instead, the growth rate of a population, dN/dt, is influenced both by population size, N, and the realized per capita growth rate. If a population is demonstrating logistic growth, dN/dt is greatest when $N = K/2$ (fig. 12.27).

When working with mathematical models, it is always useful for the ecologist to keep the biology behind the model firmly in mind. A mathematical model is only a formal description of an idea. It's not magic, it's not law, it's just an idea.

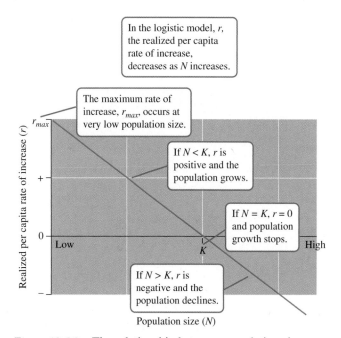

Figure 12.26   The relationship between population size, N, and realized per capita rate of increase, r, in the logistic model of population growth.

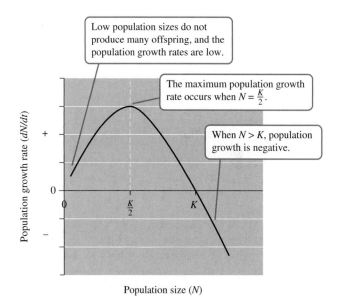

Figure 12.27   Relationship of population growth rate, dN/dt, as a function of population size, N, in the logistic model of population growth.

These equations can be very helpful in trying to understand and predict changes in population sizes. In the case of models of population growth, we should remember that r is the difference between birth and death rates in a population. Let's think about figure 12.20 from this perspective. At very low population size, the per capita birth rate, b, greatly exceeds the per capita death rate, d. As population size increases, the logistic model assumes that per capita birth rates will decrease and per capita death rates will increase. Then, when population size reaches carrying capacity, or K, $b = d$ and since $b - d = 0$, population growth stops.

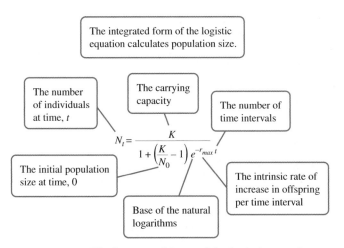

Figure 12.25   The integrated form of the logistic equation.

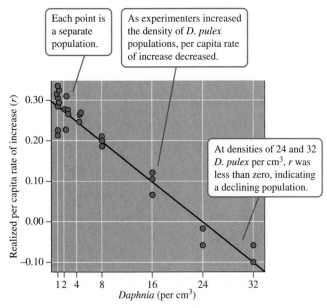

Each point is a separate population.

As experimenters increased the density of *D. pulex* populations, per capita rate of increase decreased.

At densities of 24 and 32 *D. pulex* per cm³, *r* was less than zero, indicating a declining population.

Figure 12.28   Relationship of density to per capita rate of increase in populations of *Daphnia pulex* (data from Frank et al. 1957).

The response of per capita rate of increase by *Daphnia pulex*, a water flea, to population density closely matches the assumptions of the logistic growth model. When *D. pulex* are grown at densities ranging from 1 to 32 individuals per cubic centimetre, *r* decreases with increasing population size (fig. 12.28). As assumed by the logistic growth model, per capita rate of increase was highest at the lowest population densities. Per capita rate of increase was positive in *D. pulex* populations with densities of 16 individuals per cubic centimetre or lower. However, at densities of 24 and 32 individuals per cubic centimetre, per capita rate of increase was negative.

Ultimately the environment limits the growth of populations by modifying birth and death rates. In the following Ecology in Action section, we examine in detail a few examples of environmental effects on population growth.

CONCEPT 12.4 REVIEW

1. Interpret the pattern of population growth shown by figure 12.23 in terms of the information given in figure 12.26, and discuss the relationship between population size and *r*.
2. How could you test the hypothesis that carrying capacity for the *Paramecium* population shown in figure 12.22 was set by the availability of their main food—yeast cells?
3. Why might a manager of an exploited population, such as a commercially important fish, want to keep fish population size near one-half *K* and not much lower?

ECOLOGY IN ACTION

Fisheries

Commercial fishing has a long history in Canada, serving as the economic and social foundation of many communities on the Atlantic, Pacific, and Northern coasts, as well as many inland communities that rely on freshwater fisheries. In 2006, the economic value of seafood harvested by Canadian marine fisheries was in excess of two billion dollars ($Cdn) annually, with over 80% of that coming from the Atlantic fisheries. However, Atlantic fish harvests have declined from around 1.2 million tonnes annually in the late 1980s to about 850,000 tonnes annually in the early 2000s. Hidden within these numbers are harvests of a diversity of species, some of which have shown dramatic declines in population sizes over a relatively short time period. For example, the cod harvest in Newfoundland and Labrador declined from approximately 250,000 tonnes (valued at approximately $133 million) in 1990 to 20,000 tonnes (valued at approximately $27 million) in 2002. Clearly these changes carry significant challenges for the local and national economies. Underlying collapses of fisheries are big changes in the population dynamics of species of commercial interest. We begin here with a general discussion of fisheries management, and the potential influence that ecologists can have in the collection and interpretation of data. We will then provide a more detailed analysis of the Atlantic Cod fishery collapse off the coast of Newfoundland and Labrador.

What is a fishery? A fishery includes fish, fishers, the marketplace, local communities, and other related industries. Fisheries are themselves embedded into natural ecosystems that influence the population dynamics of the fish, and they are influenced by local and national governments. A principle goal of sustainable fishery management is to provide the maximum long-term economic return while also maintaining a stable fish population. Successful fisheries will combine sound ecological and scientific knowledge with accurate local knowledge, helping to construct appropriate governmental policies that provide incentives to protect the resource while also allowing for the economic viability of communities and industry. This is not an easy task, and over the last 50 years, 366 of the world's 1519 fisheries have experienced a collapse (Mullon et al. 2005),

and many more fisheries are likely to collapse in the upcoming decades. Daniel Pauly and Johanne Dalsgaard from the University of British Columbia, along with colleagues from the Philippines, have documented that over the last several years there has been a global move to "fish down the food chain" (Pauly et al. 1998). In a survey of catches from fisheries across the globe, they found that there has been a shift away from large piscivorous fish toward small planktivorous fish and invertebrates. This pattern is likely due to rapid population declines of the "desired" species, causing a shift in the fishing effort toward fish that historically did not support commercial fisheries. Global changes in fishing efforts suggest a general failure in managing these "renewable" resources. Why? Critical to the management of a sustainable fishery is a sound understanding of the ecology of the species of interest, and knowledge of the factors that influence population growth. It also is dependent upon governments and individuals choosing to maintain long-term sustainability, even at the cost of short-term profits. This is complicated by the fact that many marine species migrate through the territorial waters of many countries, and thus international cooperation is often necessary. Global politics is a bit beyond the scope of this book, and instead we limit ourselves to a simpler question: What does ecological theory and population ecology tell us about sustainable harvest levels?

If we believe that a population is following the logistic growth curve, then we already know a few pieces of information that may help us manage the fishery. Although there are countless numbers of fishery models currently in use (Caddy 1999), we will talk about the most basic idea of the **maximum sustainable yield, MSY**. MSY represents the maximum harvest (catch) of a population that can occur without decreasing population growth rates (fig. 12.29). In an ideal population, such as one that follows the very simple and easy to understand logistic model of population growth, MSY is achieved when harvests maintain population densities at $N = K/2$. Why this value? When $N = K/2$, population growth rates are highest (fig. 12.27)! If harvests are greater than that, then dN/dt is reduced because there are relatively few individuals in the population left to reproduce. If harvest rates are reduced N below $K/2$, density-dependent factors will reduce per capita reproduction (fig. 12.26), and thus population growth rates are suppressed. It is important to recognize that MSY is generally higher than the **optimum sustainable yield, OSY** (fig. 12.29). OSY incorporates economics of harvesting as well as population growth rates, with the OSY being at the point which maximizes the difference between total revenue and total costs. The exact shape of the cost and revenue curves will depend on the value of the fish, as well as the type of equipment and intensity of harvest.

This all sounds so simple, yet why do fisheries so frequently collapse? We need to remember that fisheries are set within a social context, and the actions of individuals and governments are not necessarily those that will result in a sustainable harvest. In many cases, local economic pressures to maximize economic

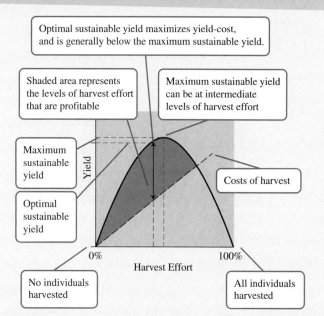

Figure 12.29 By integrating harvest intensity, costs, yields, and population growth, fishery managers can develop predictions of maximum and optimal sustainable yields.

returns over the short-term, even at the risk of fishery collapse, can place significant political pressures to set harvest targets that are not biologically justified. At the same time, the logistic growth model has a variety of assumptions built into it, which if not true, means the resulting predictions are also not true. For example, to calculate dN/dt, you need actual numbers for r, K, and N, and these are not necessarily easy to get for large populations of deep ocean fish. Inaccurate assessments of these measures, or of age of maturity, generation time, and sample size can result in equally inaccurate predictions of MSY and OSY. Additionally, mathematical models of population growth are simply that, models. Sometimes, despite the best efforts of population biologists, the models that are constructed are simply wrong for a given species of interest. When this is the case, even accurate measures of population parameters will result in inaccurate predictions of population dynamics. Taking into consideration that faulty data, misguided governmental decisions, selfish behaviour, and incomplete ecological knowledge can all lead to fishery collapses, it may be less surprising that many of the world's fisheries are not particularly healthy. We end this section with one specific example, the recent collapse of cod (*Gadus morhua*) fisheries off the coast of several Atlantic Provinces in eastern Canada.

During the late 1980s and early 1990s there was a dramatic collapse in cod fisheries off the coasts of Nova Scotia and Newfoundland and Labrador (fig. 12.30), leading to a fishing moratorium declared in the early 1990s. Particularly striking about this collapse was that the decades prior showed relatively little variation in harvests. This fishery is rapidly becoming a model for study among ecologists, with the exact reasons

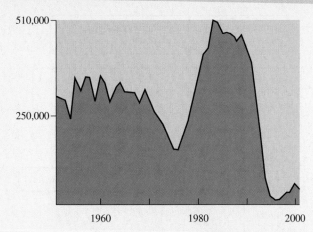

Figure 12.30   A 50-year time series of harvest of Atlantic cod in Canada.

behind the collapse still an issue of intense social debate. The central question for ecologists to answer is whether this collapse was the result of natural events (e.g., shifting habitats, altered climate, increase in natural predation rates, etc.), or if it was due to overexploitation through commercial fishing.

The population density of cod has historically been measured by recording the catch rate. This methodological choice is based upon the assumption that there is a linear relationship between fish population density and catch rate (proxy measure). Figure 12.30 clearly shows that catch rates were constant just prior to the fishery collapse. Does this mean that the population densities were themselves constant? Jeffrey Hutchings (1996) suggests otherwise, and instead argues that the data suggest that population densities off the coast of Newfoundland and Labrador were decreasing since the middle 1980s, and thus the apparent sudden collapse had longer-term biological explanations. Hutchings found that the cod population appears to have become more clumped as fishing mortality increased and population size decreased throughout the 1980s. By focusing fishing efforts primarily in areas of high fish density, commercial catch rates did not decrease substantially, even though the underlying fish population was experiencing a substantial decline. The idea of the population becoming more clumped assumes there is a fitness benefit to cod

for being part of a group, such as increased foraging success, predator avoidance, or increased mating success. Another risk of relying on catch rates as a measure of population size is that technical advances in fishing can cause increases in catch rates even when the underlying population is declining.

It is difficult to overestimate the political and social sensitivities to the idea that fishing caused the collapse of the cod fishery, and it is important to point out there exist several other hypotheses. Here we briefly discuss one of the more commonly discussed hypotheses, the idea that the fishery collapse was due to increased predation by seals, rather than fishing. During Fu and colleagues at the Department of Fisheries and Oceans conducted a set of mathematical analyses designed to determine the relative impacts of several factors on the collapse of a cod population off the coast of Nova Scotia (2001). Of particular interest was the role of seals, which are natural predators of the Atlantic cod. The researchers simulated the effects of seal on cod populations by developing a population growth model for the fish. More specifically, this model accounted for different sources of mortality and rates of increase in different age classes. In their analyses, they manipulated the values given to the different parameters to determine the overall sensitivity of cod populations to each value. They found no evidence that predation by seals was strong enough to cause the initial population collapse. However, they found that the intensity of seal predation has increased since 1993, and seals may in part be responsible for a failure of this fish population to recover.

Understanding the population dynamics of natural populations can have significant consequences for many local communities. There can be competing pressures between maximizing instantaneous rates of harvest and providing good stewardship of a long-term sustainable fishery. Responding to all of the actions taken by people are the fish, whose population growth and evolutionary trajectories will be a direct function of changes in birth and death rates. Ecologists are essential to any hopes of reducing the pressures put on natural fisheries throughout the world. Without accurate data and scientific understanding of population growth, there will be no hope for maintaining healthy fish stocks as human populations continue to grow, placing even higher demands on wild fish stocks.

ECOLOGICAL TOOLS AND APPROACHES

The Human Population

Most of the environmental concerns expressed by human society trace their origins to the effects of the human population itself on the environment. Therefore, it is very important that students of ecology be familiar with the history, current state, and

projected growth of human populations. This knowledge serves as a critical tool in understanding the root cause of many ecological issues students may be called upon to fix in the future. Let's use some of the conceptual tools we discussed in chapters 10

and 11 and in this chapter to review patterns of human distribution and abundance, population dynamics, and growth.

Distribution and Abundance

One of the most distinctive features of the human population is its distribution. Our species is virtually everywhere. We occupy all the continents—even the Antarctic includes a population of scientists and support staff—and most oceanic islands. What other species, except those dependent upon humans, is so ubiquitous? Except for the Antarctic population, the current distribution of humans did not require modern technological advances. People with stone-age technology nearly reached the present limits of our distribution over 10,000 years ago. Colonization of only the most isolated oceanic islands had to await the development of sophisticated navigational techniques by the Polynesians and Europeans.

Like other populations, human populations are highly clumped at large scales (see chapter 10). In 2011, 60.3% of the global population, or about 4.2 billion people, were concentrated in Asia (fig. 12.31). In turn, most Asians live in two countries, China and India, the most populous countries on the planet. The remainder of the human population is spread across Africa (15.0%), Europe (10.6%), North America (6.7%), and South and Central America and the Caribbean

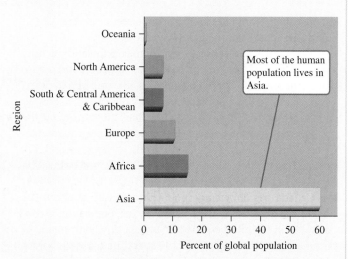

Figure 12.31   Distribution of the human population by region in 2011 (data from the U.S. Bureau of the Census, International Data Base 2011).

(6.9%). The remainder (0.5%) live in Oceania (Australia, New Zealand, and scattered oceanic islands).

Within continents, human populations attain their highest densities in eastern, southeastern, and southern Asia. Other areas of high population density include western and central Europe, northern and western Africa, and eastern and western North America. The patterns shown in figure 12.32

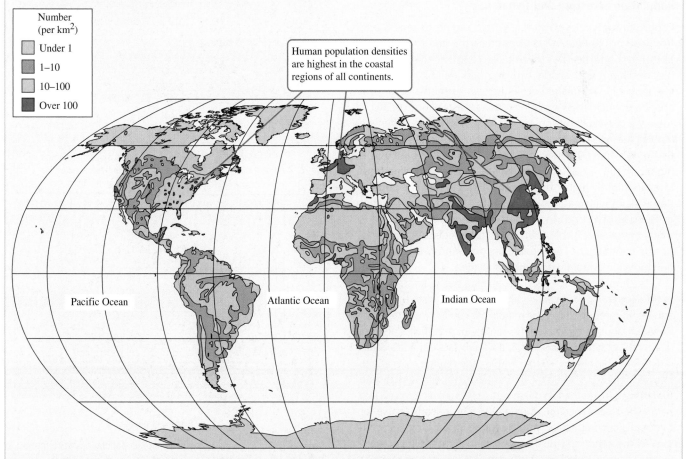

Figure 12.32   Variation in human population density (data from the United Nations Population Information Network).

suggest that the highest human population densities are in coastal areas and along major river valleys.

There is even more variation in human population density if viewed on a smaller scale. Within Asia, Singapore has a population density of over 6,900 persons per square kilometre, while Mongolia has a population density of only 2 persons per square kilometre. This is slightly less than the density on the continent of Australia, which is 2.8 persons per square kilometre. Within Europe, The Netherlands harbours nearly 500 persons per square kilometre, while Greece has population densities of about 80 per square kilometre. In North America, Canada has an average population density of about 3.7 people per square kilometre. However, this population is concentrated in the southern part of the country, with nearly ¾ of the population living within 200 km of the southern border with the United States. Within Canada, population densities are lowest in Nunavut (0.02 people per square kilometre) and highest in Prince Edward Island (24.5 people per square kilometre). In contrast, the United States has an average population density of about 30 per square kilometre. This ranges from nearly 450 people per square kilometre in New Jersey to less than 1 person per square kilometre in Alaska. Again, on a large scale, human populations are highly clumped and as a consequence, population density is highly variable. Other aspects of human populations also vary a great deal.

Population Structure and Dynamics

Population dynamics vary widely from region to region and from country to country. Let's examine the age distributions, birth rates, and death rates of three countries that have stable, declining, and rapidly growing populations. As we saw in chapter 11, population ecologists can surmise a great deal about a population by examining its age distribution. In 2011, there were over 34 million people living in Canada. When we look at the age structure of Canada, we see an age distribution that is approximately the same width near its base as it is higher up (fig. 12.33a). Across all age classes, Canadian birth rates are slightly higher than death rates, and thus the population is slightly increasing. Compare this distribution with that of Hungary. The age distribution of Hungary's population is much narrower at its base, which indicates a declining population. In contrast, the very broad base of Rwanda's age distribution indicates a rapidly growing population.

The impressions we get by examining the age distributions of these three countries are confirmed if we calculate their birth and death rates. In 2011, the annual per capita birth rate, b, of Canada's population was 0.010, slightly higher than Canada's death rate, d, which was 0.0.008. If we subtract Canada's death rate from its birth rate (0.010 − 0.008), the result is a per capita rate of increase, r, of 0.002. In contrast, Hungary's birth rate (0.010) was lower than its death rate (0.013), which results in a per capita rate of increase, r, of −0.003. This negative value for r confirms our impression that Hungary's population is declining. At the other end of the population dynamics spectrum, Rwanda's population has a birth rate that is over two times its

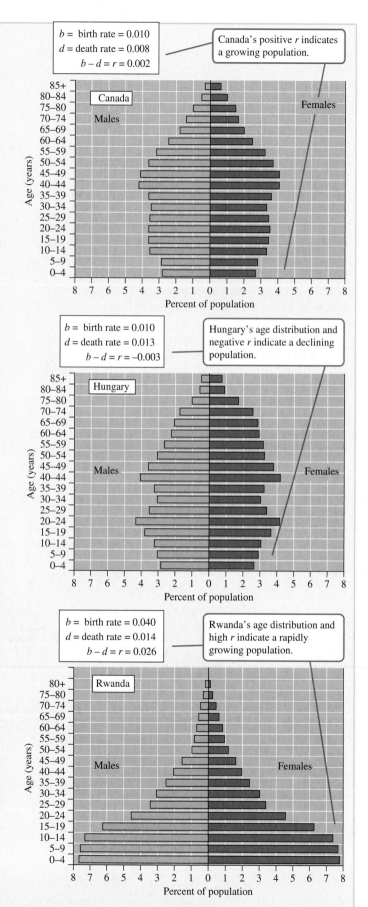

b = birth rate = 0.010
d = death rate = 0.008
$b - d = r = 0.002$

Canada's positive r indicates a growing population.

b = birth rate = 0.010
d = death rate = 0.013
$b - d = r = -0.003$

Hungary's age distribution and negative r indicate a declining population.

b = birth rate = 0.040
d = death rate = 0.014
$b - d = r = 0.026$

Rwanda's age distribution and high r indicate a rapidly growing population.

Figure 12.33 Age distributions for human populations in countries with stable, declining, and rapidly growing populations (data from the U.S. Bureau of the Census, International Data Base 2011).

death rate. As a consequence, this country's annual per capita rate of increase is 0.026, which is strongly positive growth. Let's move from these estimates of the present rates of change to examine the longer-term population trends in these countries.

Population Growth

Figure 12.34 presents the historical and projected populations of Canada, Hungary, and Rwanda. In 1950, the population of Rwanda was only 18% that of Canada's population and approximately 25% that of Hungary's population. Rwanda's population exceeded that of Hungary by the year 2010, and is projected to be 65% that of Canada's population in 2050.

How is the global human population changing? While the populations of many developed countries are either stable or declining, those of most developing countries are growing, and the trend for the entire global population is continued growth. While the rate of growth has begun to slow, the global population is expected to exceed 9 billion by the middle of the twenty-first century (fig. 12.35).

There are signs that global population growth is slowing. While the global population continues to grow, it is not now growing exponentially. The *rate* of global population growth has declined substantially over the past 40 years, as shown in figure 12.35*b*. The size of the global population is not rising as steeply as it once was and is projected to level off sometime after the middle of the twenty-first century. Figure 12.35*b* also displays the proximate cause of this levelling off in population size, a decline in annual growth of the global population. The

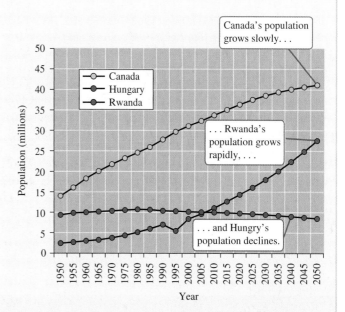

Figure 12.34 Historical and projected human populations of countries with growing, declining, and stable populations (data from the U.S. Bureau of the Census, International Data Base 2011).

rate of annual growth by the global population rose steadily from 1950 to 1957, and then took a sharp dip during a major famine in China that lasted from 1958 to 1961, resulting in the deaths of an estimated 16 to 33 million Chinese. Annual

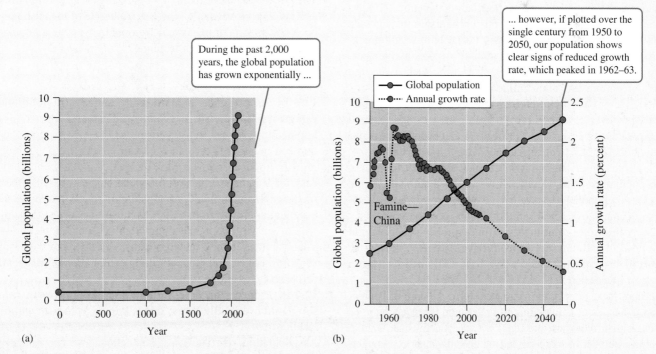

Figure 12.35 Temporal perspectives on global population growth: (*a*) Exponential growth during the past 2,000 years is evident, but (*b*) the past 40 years have been a period of slowing growth by the global human population; growth is projected to continue to slow over the next half century (data from the United Nations Population Information Network and the U.S. Bureau of the Census, International Data Base 2008).

growth rate, which peaked from 1962 to 1963 at 2.19%, has been decreasing in the four decades since, reaching 1.15% in 2008. The global growth rate is projected to decline to less than 0.5% by 2050. However, this is a projection based on current conditions and recent dynamics of the global and regional populations. Since rates of growth in human populations are currently very dynamic, projections of future global population sizes are being adjusted frequently. During the past five years, most of these adjustments have produced lowered estimates of future global population size. However, while the cost that the present human population exacts upon the global environment is already substantial (see chapter 23), size alone is insufficient for estimating the environmental impact of a population. Such impact results from a combination of population size and per capita resource consumption. If you factor in resource use, populations of developed countries, on average, use natural resources at a rate eight times higher than the populations of developing countries (WWF 2006). One of the greatest environmental challenges of the twenty-first century will be to establish a sustainable global population, and good ecological data and theory will be critical to our prospects for success.

SUMMARY

12.1 Population size changes as a function of birth rates, death rates, immigration, and emigration. These processes may be either density independent or density dependent.

Changes in population size can only occur through changes in the number of births, deaths, immigrants, and emigrants within a population. These BIDE processes provide a useful framework for understanding population dynamics. Underlying these factors are ecological mechanisms that include biotic factors such as food, disease, competitors, and predators, and abiotic factors such as rainfall, floods, and temperature. Because the effects of biotic factors, such as disease and predation, are often influenced by population density, biotic factors are often referred to as density-dependent factors. Meanwhile, abiotic factors such as floods and extreme temperature can exert their influences independently of population density and so are often called density-independent factors. Both abiotic and biotic forces have important influences on populations. The significant effects of biotic and abiotic factors on populations have been well demonstrated by studies of Galápagos finches and their major food sources.

12.2 A life table combined with a fecundity schedule can be used to estimate net reproductive rate (R_0), geometric rate of increase (λ), generation time (T), and per capita rate of increase (r).

Because these population parameters form the core of population dynamics, it is important to understand their derivation as well as their biological meaning. Net reproductive rate, R_0, the average number of offspring left by an individual in a population, is calculated by multiplying age-specific survivorship rates, l_x, times age-specific birthrates, m_x, and summing the results:

$$\sum l_x m_x$$

The geometric rate of increase, λ, is calculated as the ratio of population sizes at two successive points in time. Generation time is calculated as:

$$T = \frac{\sum x l_x m_x}{R_0}$$

The per capita rate of increase, r, is related to generation time and net reproductive rate. The per capita rate of increase may be positive, zero, or negative depending on whether a population is growing, stable, or declining.

$$r = \frac{ln R_0}{T}$$

12.3 In the presence of abundant resources, populations can grow at geometric or exponential rates.

Population growth by organisms with pulsed reproduction can be described by the geometric model of population growth. Population growth that occurs as a continuous process, as in human or bacterial populations, can be described by the exponential model of population growth. Examples of exponential growth from natural populations suggest that this type of growth may be very important to populations during establishment in new environments, during recovery from some form of exploitation, or during exploitation of transient, favourable conditions.

12.4 If resources become limited, population growth rate slows and eventually stops; this is known as logistic population growth.

As population size increases, population growth eventually slows and then ceases, producing a sigmoidal, or S-shaped, population growth curve. Population growth stops when populations reach a maximum size called the carrying capacity, the number of individuals of a particular population that the

environment can support. Sigmoidal population growth can be modelled by the logistic growth equation, a modification of the exponential growth equation that includes a term for environmental resistance. In the logistic model, per capita growth rates decrease linearly with increasing population density. In contrast, the growth rate of the population itself, dN/dt, shows a unimodal relationship with density, with maximal population growth when $N = K/2$. Population growth is a function both of per capita growth rates and population size. Research on laboratory populations indicates that zero population growth at carrying capacity can be due to a variety of combinations of reduced birth rates and increased death rates.

The present state of the human population can be examined using the conceptual tools of population biology discussed in chapters 10, 11, and 12. Though humans live on every continent, their population density differs by several orders of magnitude in different regions. In 2008, 60.6% of the global population, or about 4 billion people, were concentrated in Asia. The remainder of the human population was spread across Africa (14.3%), Europe (10.9%), North America (7.9%), South America (5.8%), and Oceania (0.5%). Population densities in different regions vary from less than 1 person per square kilometre to nearly 7,000 persons per square kilometre. While the populations of some countries are stable and some are declining, the global population is expected to continue growing past the year 2050. One of the greatest environmental challenges of the twenty-first century will be to establish a sustainable global human population.

REVIEW QUESTIONS

1. For what types of organisms is the geometric model of population growth appropriate? For what types of organisms is the exponential model of population growth appropriate? In what circumstances would a population grow exponentially? In what circumstances would a population not grow exponentially?

2. In chapters 10, 11, and 12 we have presented a number of mathematical models that describe natural populations. Why are models used extensively in population biology? How can models enhance, or hinder, understanding of the underlying concepts of population biology?

3. How do you build the logistic model for population growth from the exponential model? What part of the logistic growth equation produces the sigmoidal growth curve?

4. In question 3, you thought about how the logistic growth equation produces a sigmoidal growth curve. Now, let's think about nature. What is it about the natural environment that produces sigmoidal growth? Pick a real organism living in an environment with which you are familiar and list the things that might limit the growth of its population.

5. What is the relationship between per capita rate of increase, r, and the intrinsic rate of increase, r_{max}? In chapter 11, we estimated r from the life tables and fecundity schedules of two species. How would you estimate r_{max}?

6. Both abiotic and biotic factors influence birth and death rates in populations. Make a list of abiotic and biotic factors that are potentially important regulators of natural populations.

7. Population biologists may refer to abiotic factors, such as temperature and moisture, as density-independent because such factors can affect population processes independently of local population density. At the same time, biotic factors, such as disease and competition, are called density-dependent factors because their effects may be related to local population density. Explain how abiotic factors can influence populations in a way that is independent of local population density. Explain why the influence of a biotic factor is often affected by local population density. Now, explain how the impact of an abiotic factor may also be affected by the local population density, that is, may behave at least partly as a density-dependent factor.

8. What factors will determine the earth's carrying capacity for *Homo sapiens*? Explain why the earth's long-term (thousands of years) carrying capacity for the human population may be much lower than the projected population size for the year 2050. Now argue the other side. Explain how the numbers projected for 2050 might be sustained over the long term.

9. What role can ecologists play in developing a sustainable fishery? Does the source of harvest mortality (e.g., seals vs. people) have differential impacts on population growth and/or evolution?

INTERACTIONS

Interactions among species can take a variety of forms, and can have varying effects on an organism's fitness, population dynamics, and community structure. In this section we explore several types of ecological interactions common in natural and managed systems: competition, predation, herbivory, mutualism, disease, and parasitism. These topics build on our understanding of populations (section III), and are critical to our ability to understand how communities are structured, the topic of section V.

Chapter 13 Competition

Chapter 14 Herbivory and Predation

Chapter 15 Mutalism, Parasitism, and Disease

COMPETITION

CHAPTER 13

CHAPTER CONCEPTS

13.1 Individuals can compete with other individuals, of their own and of different species, in a number of different ways.
Concept 13.1 Review

13.2 Field and mesocosm studies show that resource limitation and competition are widespread.
Concept 13.2 Review

13.3 Mathematical and laboratory models provide a theoretical foundation for studying competitive interactions in nature.
Concept 13.3 Review

13.4 Competition can have significant effects on species coexistence and the direction of evolution.
Ecology In Action: The Role of Competition in Forest Management
Concept 13.4 Review
Ecological Tools and Approaches: Identifying the Mechanisms by Which Plants Compete
Summary
Review Questions

Walk outside to your nearest park, sit down, and watch. What organisms do you see, and what are they doing? When I take my lunch down to Emily Murphy Park near my office in Edmonton, what I mostly see are plants (fig. 13.1). Unless you have chosen a coastal bluff, the odds are pretty good that you, too, see mostly plants. Most communities are dominated, in numbers and biomass, by these primary producers, and thus they are the most obvious living members of most ecological systems. As you look more closely at the plants that surround you, you recognize that light levels near the soil are much lower than those above the tallest plants, as each plant absorbs and reflects the light that hits its leaves. The taller trees are getting more than a fair share of the light, casting deep shade on those below, while the smaller plants are unable to cast shade on those above. As I am in a city park, I choose not to bring a shovel and observe the plant roots, but I can imagine that if I had, I would find a big tangle of roots, with no obvious distinction between the tallest and smallest plants. All of these plants are accessing a shared pool of resources, and when one plant takes up a nitrate molecule, no other plant is able to acquire that same molecule. Though some of us have difficulty looking beyond the plants (and thus we become plant ecologists!), I force myself to be patient, and look hard to see other organisms in the park.

Off to one side I find the reproductive structures of several species of fungi. These mushrooms could be quite tasty, or deadly, and as I have several book deadlines to meet, I choose not to find out. I know, however, that these mushrooms are the reproductive structures of fungi that form intimate associations with the roots of the surrounding trees. The trees provide carbon to the fungi in the form of sugars, and receive mineral resources from the fungi. The balance sheet is not always even, and this exchange may favour one of the participants, neither, or both players of this ecological game may gain benefit.

As I continue to observe the inherently interesting sessile organisms of the park, I can't help but notice some things moving all around me. Beetles and ants crawl on and in the soil, carrying parts of plants, aphids full of honeydew, and a number of other items. A mule deer is off in the distance browsing on a small shrub, and high above a red-tailed hawk is circling in its hunt for a vole. I know that Edmonton grew up as an outpost for trappers, and along the river's edge live beavers, otter, coyotes, and other species that survive by killing others.

In the trees above, I see holes drilled by woodpeckers, some now filled by cavity-nesting birds. I also see bird nests, hear the chattering of those incessant chickadees, and see a magpie scare away most anything that it encounters. Everywhere I look I see one organism somehow influencing the lives of others.

The species in this park are related, not through immediate taxonomic bonds, but through a diverse array of ecological interactions. Some are exploitative, such as the predator who consumes prey; some are competitive, such as the tall tree shading the small plant; and others are likely neutral, such as the tree that is home to the nests of many birds. Ecologists, like all scientists, like to create order in the face of chaos, and we can arrange the diversity of ecological interactions into a grid based upon the costs and benefits of an interaction to each participation (fig. 13.2).

How does figure 13.2 relate to the interactions I observed in the park? Competition, the subject of this chapter, was the most obvious interaction when I first entered the park. By shading each other and by having tangled roots systems, the plants took light and soil resources away from each other, resulting in a "−, −" interaction. The hawk eating a vole and the deer browsing on a shrub both gain energy from their food, while their food is harmed. These "+, −" interactions are forms of exploitation, and will be the focus of chapter 14. Mutualisms are the subject of chapter 15. An example of these "+, +" interactions are the fungi that provide nutrients to their host trees, while receiving sugars in return.

Though these three interactions are the ones we discuss most in this book, **commensalism**, **neutralism**, and **amensalism** are all also common in natural systems. The trees in the park provided a home for the bird nest. This interaction comes at no cost to the tree, but great benefit to the bird, and is an example of commensalism (+, 0). Amensalisms are less well studied, and many may be a form of competition. For example, if we focus only on light and ignore soil resources, we can find amensalism among the trees. The tall trees which cast deep shade, yet are not shaded themselves, are harming another while not receiving harm or help from those beneath (−, 0). Another example would be the mule deer we observed chewing on the shrub. The consumption of the shrub was exploitation, but what about the path the deer created to get to its food source? In walking through the tall grasses, it trampled many down, causing harm to the grasses. In return, those grasses neither helped nor harmed the deer, and thus this too is an amensalism. Neutralisms are the vanilla ice-cream of community ecology. Species regularly come into contact with other species, passing by without more than a sniff or a wave. These "0, 0" interactions may be common, but they are likely hard to get research funding support to study!

Figure 13.1 A diversity of ecological interactions occur in all natural systems, such as those found in Emily Murphy Park in Edmonton, Alberta.

		What effect does the interaction with species A have on species B?		
		Positive (+)	Neutral (O)	Negative (−)
What effect does the interaction with species B have on species A?	Positive (+)	Mutualism	Commensalism	Exploitation (e.g., predation, parasitism, herbivory)
	Neutral (O)	—	Neutralism	Amensalism
	Negative (−)	—	—	Competition

Figure 13.2   Ecological interactions can be roughly characterized based upon the impacts of those interactions on each of the participants.

Having now provided an overview of types of interactions that occur in natural systems, we focus our attention on just one: competition. We begin by describing what exactly is meant by competition.

13.1 Forms of Competition

Individuals can compete with other individuals, of their own and of different species, in a number of different ways. Careful observation and experimentation reveals competition among species in nature. For example, along coral reefs off the north coast of Jamaica, damselfish guard small territories of less than 1 m² (fig. 13.3). These territories are dispersed regularly across the reef and contain most of the resources upon which the damselfish depend: nooks and crannies for shelter against predators, tended patches of fast-growing algae for food, and in the territories of males, an area of coral rubble kept clean for spawning. The damselfish constantly patrol and survey the borders of their territories, vigorously attacking any intruder that presents a threat to their eggs and developing larvae, or to their food supply. Not all members of the population have a territory, and some damselfish live in marginal areas around the territorial members, wandering from one part of the reef to another.

If you create a vacancy on the reef by removing one of the damselfish holding a territory, other damselfish appear within minutes to claim the vacant territory. Some of the new arrivals are threespot damselfish like the original resident, and some are cocoa damselfish, which generally live a bit higher on the reef face. These new arrivals fight fiercely for the vacated territory. The damselfish chase each other, nip each other's flanks, and slap each other with their tails. The new resident, which may have driven off a half dozen rivals, is usually another threespot damselfish.

This example demonstrates several things. First, individual damselfish maintain possession of their territories through ongoing competition with other damselfish, and this competition takes the form of *interference competition* (chapter 8), which involves direct aggressive interactions between individuals. Second, though it may not appear so to the casual observer, there is a limited supply of suitable space for damselfish territories, a condition that ecologists call **resource limitation**. Here, the limited resource is space on the reef, rather than a direct limitation of food items.

Third, the threespot damselfish engage in both **intraspecific competition**, competition with members of their own species, and **interspecific competition**, competition between individuals of different species.

The effects of competition on the fitness of the competitors are not necessarily the same for all individuals. Instead, competitive effects can be asymmetric, with some individuals harmed (the losers), while others (the winners) are not, or at least less severely harmed. Competition is not always as dramatic as fighting damselfish, nor is it always resolved so quickly. In the white pine forests of New Hampshire, tree roots grow throughout the soil taking up nutrients and water as they provide support. In 1931, J. Toumey and R. Kienholz designed an experiment to determine whether the activities of these tree roots suppress the activities of other plants. The researchers cut a trench, 0.92 m deep, around a plot 2.74 m by 2.74 m in the middle of the forest. In so doing, they cut 825 roots, which removed potential competition by these roots for soil resources. They also established control plots on either side of the trenched plot, and then watched as the results of their experiment unfolded. The experiment continued for eight years, with the plot retrenched every two years, cutting over 100 roots each time. By retrenching, the researchers maintained their experimental treatment, suppression of potential root competition.

Figure 13.3   Territorial reef fish can compete intensely for space.

In the end, this eight-year experiment yielded results as dramatic as those with the damselfish. Vegetative cover on the section of forest floor that had been released from root competition was 10 times that present on the control plots. Apparently the roots of white pines exert interspecific competition for limited supplies of nutrients and water that is strong enough to suppress the growth of forest floor vegetation (fig. 13.4). In addition, the growth of young white pines was much greater within the trenched plots than in the control plots, demonstrating that considerable intraspecific competition was occurring.

In both the forest floor and damselfish examples, individuals are competing for limited resources. A critical difference is that the damselfish compete by actively attacking other individuals, in the hopes of preventing access to the desired resource contained on the reef. In the forest example, the plants are not competing by preventing access to the soil nutrients and water. Instead, competition occurs when some individuals acquire these resources before other individuals are able to capture the resources. The damselfish demonstrate interference competition, while the plants demonstrate **exploitative competition** (fig. 13.5). Both plants and animals are able to demonstrate exploitative and interference competition, depending upon the details of the specific competitive interaction.

Ecologists have long thought that competition is pervasive in nature, and in many circumstances competitive interactions can affect fitness and evolution of species. In the

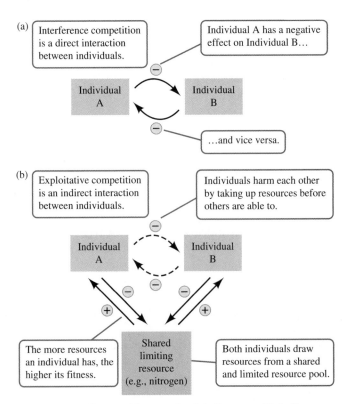

Figure **13.5** Competition can be (*a*) direct, or (*b*) indirect interaction among individuals of the same or different species.

next section, we provide some evidence that competition for resource occurs in diverse communities, with often predictable consequences.

Figure **13.4** Competition in a forest can be as intense as competition on a coral reef. However, much of the competition in a forest takes place underground, where the roots of plants compete for water and nutrients.

CONCEPT 13.1 REVIEW

1. Competitive interactions among co-occurring individuals can be either direct or indirect. What aspects of how individuals compete determine whether the competition is direct or indirect?
2. How does the logistic model of population growth explicitly assume intraspecific competition is occurring?

13.2 Evidence of Competition in Natural Systems

Field and mesocosm studies show that resource limitations and competition are widespread. In chapter 12, we saw that slowing population growth at high densities produces a sigmoidal, or S-shaped, pattern in which population size levels off at carrying capacity. Our assumption in that discussion was that intraspecific competition for limited resources plays a key role in slowing population growth at higher densities. In fact,

the effect of intraspecific competition was explicitly included in the model of logistic population growth as $(K-N)/K$. But is competition truly widespread in natural systems? If so, then we should be able to observe it most commonly among individuals of the same species, individuals with identical or very similar resource requirements.

Intraspecific Competition in Plant Populations

The development of a stand of plants from the seedling stage to mature individuals suggests competition for limited resources. Each spring as the seeds of annual plants germinate, their population density often numbers in the thousands per square metre. However, as the season progresses and individual plants grow, population density declines. This same pattern occurs in the development of a stand of trees. As the stand of trees develops, more and more biomass is composed of fewer and fewer individuals. In populations of long- or short-lived plants, this process is often referred to as **self-thinning**. Importantly, this term does not imply the plants are actively eliminating themselves from the population to benefit the others which remain. Instead, self-thinning indicates that even in the absence of outside agents (e.g., people with chainsaws!), the number of individual plants found within a stand decreases as the average size of the plants within the stand increases. Driving this process is competition.

Self-thinning results from intraspecific competition for limited resources. As a local population of plants develops, individual plants take up increasing quantities of nutrients, water, and space for which some individuals compete more successfully than others. The losers in this exploitative competition are unable to continue to grow, and many die. Consequently, intraspecific competition results in lower population densities over time. As the population is thinned, it is composed of fewer and fewer large individuals.

One way to represent the self-thinning process is to plot total plant biomass (the sum of the biomasses of all individuals in the population) against population density. If we plot the logarithm of total plant biomass against the logarithm of population density, the slope of the resulting line is often around $-\frac{1}{2}$. In other words, there is an approximately one-unit increase in total plant biomass with each two-unit decrease in population density. What does this mean? In plant populations that undergo self-thinning (such as occurs after students plant trees in recently logged areas), as the population ages, population density declines more rapidly than biomass increases. We can visualize this process by understanding figure 13.6. Here, we imagine four populations, given the unique names of A, B, C, and D. In all cases, self-thinning would be indicated by a movement from the right of the graph (high density) toward the left (lower density), over time. Population A begins at a low population density. Over time, there is an increase in population biomass, as indicated by the upward pointing arrow. However, due to the low density, there is no intraspecific competition, no change in population density, and thus no self-thinning. Population B starts at slightly higher population density. As the plants grow, there is an increase in population

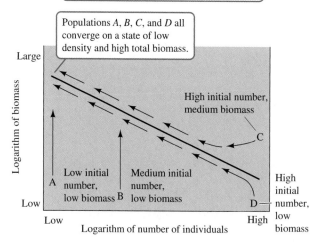

Figure 13.6   Self-thinning in plant populations (data from Westoby 1984).

biomass, as indicated by the upward arrow. However, at some point the population hits the self-thinning line, with its $-\frac{1}{2}$ slope. At that point, there is continued increase in population biomass, but this is associated with a decrease in population density. This is indicated by arrow pointing up and to the left, and indicates that intraspecific competition occurred. Populations C and D both start at higher densities, and thus self-thinning occurs more rapidly. Note that population C starts above the self-thinning line. Analogous to what is described in the logistic model of population growth (chapter 12) when a population starts above the carrying capacity of the habitat, the self-thinning model predicts a rapid decrease in population density and biomass.

Another common way to represent the self-thinning process is to plot the average weight of individual plants in a population against density (fig. 13.7). The slope of the line in such plots typically averages around $-\frac{3}{2}$. Because self-thinning by many plant species is close to this value, this relationship has come to be called the $-\frac{3}{2}$ **self-thinning rule**. The self-thinning rule was first proposed by K. Yoda and colleagues (1963) and amplified by White and Harper (1970).

Recent analyses have shown that self-thinning in some plant populations deviates significantly from the $-\frac{3}{2}$ (or $-\frac{1}{2}$ for biomass-numbers) slope. However, regardless of the precise trajectory followed by different plant populations, self-thinning of plant populations has been demonstrated repeatedly. The important points, from the perspective of our present discussion, is that self-thinning occurs and appears to be the consequence of intraspecific competition for limited resources. Additionally, the self-thinning law appears to apply to most plant species tested, suggesting this is a very generalizable phenomenon. Resource limitation has also been demonstrated in experiments on intraspecific competition within animal populations.

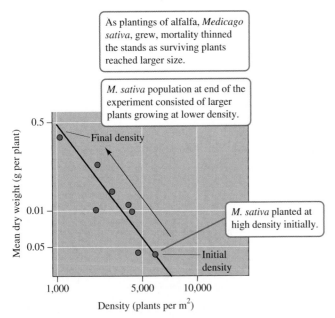

Figure 13.7 Self-thinning in populations of alfalfa, *Medicago sativa* (data from White and Harper 1970).

Intraspecific Competition Among Planthoppers

Even though competition is common among many organisms, that does not mean competition is common for all. For example, ecologists have often failed to demonstrate that insects, particularly herbivorous insects, necessarily compete for limiting resources, and instead other factors limit their populations. However, one group of insects in which competition has been repeatedly demonstrated are the Homoptera, including the leafhoppers, planthoppers, and aphids. Robert Denno and George Roderick (1992), who studied interactions among planthoppers (Homoptera, Delphacidae), attribute the prevalence of competition among the Homoptera to their habit of aggregating, to rapid population growth, and to the mobile nature of their food supply, plant fluids.

Denno and Roderick demonstrated intraspecific competition within populations of the planthopper *Prokelisia marginata*, which lives on the salt marsh grass *Spartina alterniflora* along the Atlantic and Gulf coasts of the United States. The population density of *P. marginata* was controlled by enclosing the insects with *Spartina* seedlings at densities of 3, 11, and 40 leafhoppers per cage, densities that are within the range at which they live in nature. At the highest density, *P. marginata* showed reduced survivorship, decreased body length, and increased developmental time (fig. 13.8). These signs of intraspecific competition were probably the result of reduced food quality at high leafhopper densities. Plants heavily populated by planthoppers show reduced concentrations of protein, chlorophyll, and moisture. Therefore, competition between these leafhoppers was probably the result of limited resource supplies. However, as demonstrated in the following example, interference competition may occur in the absence of obvious resource limitation.

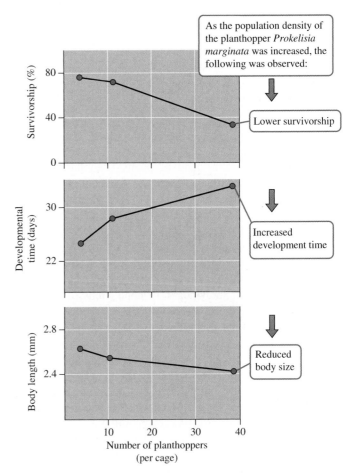

Figure 13.8 Population density and planthopper performance (data from Denno and Roderick 1992).

Interference Competition Among Song Sparrows

Peter Arcese (1987) conducted a field study on Mandarte Island, British Columbia, to determine how male song sparrows, *Melospiza melodia*, defend their territories. These sparrows are primarily monogamous. Starting at age one, males set up territories in which they sing and present visual displays to attract females as potential mates. However, appropriate space for territories is limited, and many males are left without established territories (around 20% of males on this island). These males, called *floaters*, live within the territories of other males, rarely singing or perching on visually obvious branches. In other words, they generally hide, waiting for the territorial male to die and thus allowing them to take over the territory, or they challenge the territorial male in the hope of winning the contest and claiming the territory. When a territorial male sees a floater intruding in his territory, there is a rapid and obvious response of a song followed by a chase, a very clear example of interference competition.

For 10 years prior to Arcese's study, the sparrows on this island had been extensively studied, with every bird individually marked. Arcese and his field crew then spent 294 hours over the course of two years observing the behaviour of many floaters and territorial males. Of particular interest to Arcese

were intrusions by the floaters into the territories of other males, and whether some territorial males were more likely to be intruded upon than others. This question is similar to our discussion of how the strength of exploitative competition can vary with some factors, such as resource availability. Here, however, Arcese was trying to determine what factors influence intraspecific interference competition. Prior research and theories suggested that territory size, male age, and male health may all influence the likelihood of an intrusion by a floater.

Intrusion pressure was not related to territory size, nor was it related to the presence of fertile females in the territory. Instead, there was a strong relationship between the age of the territory owner and intrusion pressure (fig. 13.9). These sparrows typically live up to four years, and both the youngest and the oldest males were most likely to be challenged by floaters. These intrusions appeared to come at a real cost to the resident males, as the youngest and oldest males held on to their territories for a shorter duration than two- and three-year-old males. In many cases the physical chase that ensued resulted in broken limbs or other injuries, often followed by the presumed death of the previously territorial male. In looking in more detail at the data, Arcese was also able to determine that those males that lost their territory often had a broken limb or other physical handicap, and were more likely to show weight loss (a sign of poor health) than males that retained their territories. The one-year-olds did not generally show physical handicaps, and instead Arcese reasoned that they were less experienced and less able to defend a territory than slightly older males.

Overall, Arcese's field study shows that interference competition can occur in a natural setting, with potentially strong consequences for the competing individuals. He also shows that, like exploitative competition, a variety of factors can influence the strength of competition experienced by

different individuals in the population. In this case, it appears that the floating males were choosing to challenge the weakest and most inexperienced males, while generally avoiding the stronger males. These results show that for some organisms, behavioural choices also can influence competitive interactions. Next we will provide a more general discussion of evidence for competition in natural systems.

Is Competition a Common Ecological Interaction?

So far we have presented several specific examples of competition observed in natural communities. However, it is important to recognize that Darwin himself focused our attention on the potential importance of competition to the ecology and evolution of natural species, and thus this issue has been the subject of substantial research effort. There have been literally thousands of ecological studies conducted, and the study of competition has gone through several phases. There was an early theoretical phase (see next section), followed by work with laboratory models, which was in turn followed by intensive observation and experimentation in the field. At the same time, there has been persistent questioning about the basic assumption that competition is an important force in nature. Here we will first discuss some of the results from large reviews of the literature, and then will follow with an example of a manipulative field experiment.

In the early 1980s, there was a very basic question unanswered in ecology: is competition common in natural populations? Two of the first analyses designed to provide a broad test of this question were by Thomas Schoener (1983) and Joseph Connell (1983), both of whom reviewed the evidence provided by field experiments. Schoener reviewed over 150 experiments on interspecific competition, and reported that competition was found in 90% of the studies and among 76% of the species. Connell reviewed 527 experiments on 215 species, and found evidence of interspecific competition in about 40% of the experiments and about 50% of the species. Why is there such a difference in these results? One reason is that the researchers analyzed different groups of studies and used different criteria for including studies in their analyses. This idea is supported by Jessica Gurevitch and her colleagues (1992), who analyzed field experiments published during the 1980s. She found that although competition had a very strong and negative impact on biomass in general, there was substantial variation among taxa and trophic level. Despite the differences found in these studies, the best evidence to date shows that competition is an important force in the lives of many organisms in natural systems. However, the data also indicate that competition is not omnipresent, and instead is just one of many factors that can influence population dynamics, species distributions, and an individual's fitness.

Many of the questions about whether competition plays an important role in natural populations were raised by animal ecologists. As you will see in later chapters (section V), animals are generally rare on the landscape relative to plants, and direct encounters between individuals are not as frequent in comparison to a plant living its life rooted next to another.

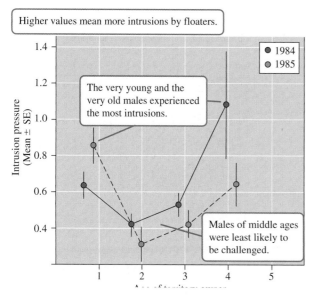

Figure 13.9 Intrusion pressure by floaters varies as a function of the age of the territorial male (data from Arcese 1987).

Plants generally grow in very close proximity to their neighbours, and their leaves and roots likely interact for their entire lives. The impact of these interactions can be obvious, as any gardener knows if they don't pull weeds from their strawberry beds. So for plant ecologists, the big question about competition was not in whether it occurred, but rather whether competition is strongest when resources are rare or when resources are common.

This debate originated with Phil Grime, who developed one of the theories of plant life history strategies we discussed in chapter 9. Grime (1973) argued that competition among plants will be unimportant in unproductive areas, areas of low resource availability and little plant growth. Edward Newman (1973), and later David Tilman (1987), disagreed with this position, and argued that competition will be important at both high and low resource availability. What will differ, they hypothesized, is that in unproductive environments competition will be primarily belowground, while in productive environments competition will be predominantly above-ground (fig. 13.10). Of course, is it really too surprising that people that study competition for a living are often themselves embroiled in competitive encounters?

Throughout the 1980s and early 1990s, numerous experiments were designed to resolve this debate, generally with conflicting results. One concern was that most relevant experiments were conducted over a relatively small spatial scale, and thus differences observed could have been due to site-specific differences. Richard Reader, of the University of Guelph, initiated an ambitious study to try to finally resolve what had been a long-standing and very combative debate amongst ecologists. Reader assembled a team of 20 researchers located throughout the world (Canada, United States, the Netherlands, Sweden, and Australia). The team conducted identical experiments at each of 12 study sites, allowing a broad test of the research question (Reader et al. 1994). To minimize variation among sites, they used similar types of communities (grasslands and abandoned fields) in all locations, and they chose sites that had naturally occurring variation in productivity (an indirect measure of resource availability). Within each site they laid out a number of plots from which they either removed the neighbouring vegetation by spraying an herbicide, or left the neighbouring vegetation intact. They then transplanted one individual of the species *Poa pratensis* (Kentucky bluegrass) into every plot, measuring its growth over the course of the season. This sort of design is called a *focal plant study*, in which measures are taken from a specific individual within each plot (the transplanted bluegrass seedlings).

The strength of competition can be measured in several ways, but is most widely reported as some function of the growth of the focal plants when neighbours were present relative to their growth when neighbours were removed. Using this relative measure of competition, Reader and his colleagues found no evidence that competition varied in intensity along this intercontinental productivity gradient (fig. 13.11). They also found that within their study there was substantial variation in the relationship between competition and productivity among study sites, and the results changed slightly if they used a different method of measuring competition. These findings support Reader's initial motivations for this unprecedented study in plant ecology—to investigate whether site- and experiment-specific variation might obscure

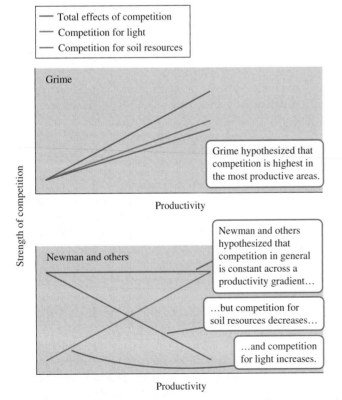

Figure 13.10 Contrasting theories about the relationship between plant competition and productivity.

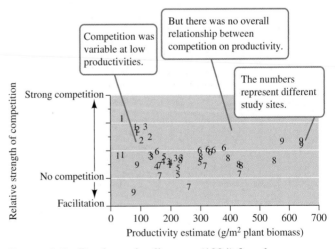

Figure 13.11 Reader and colleagues (1994) found no evidence that the strength of competition varied as a function of habitat productivity. Note that the different numbers in the graph indicate data drawn from the twelve study sites, and that there are often multiple samples per site.

any overall patterns which are, or are not, occurring. This study continues to serve as an outstanding example of how large-scale collaborative work can be used to address issues of particular conflict in the ecological literature.

We have now provided several examples of several different forms of competition occurring in natural systems. To understand the ecological significance of these findings, it will be helpful to take a step back and explore the underlying predictions and expectations that come from competition theory.

CONCEPT 13.2 REVIEW

1. The self-thinning rule appears to apply to most species of plants; however, whether the slope is closer to $-\frac{3}{2}$ or $-\frac{1}{2}$ depends upon species. What factors about a species' biology are likely to influence the slope of the relationship between plant density and average plant weight?
2. Richard Reader and his colleagues (1994) found no overwhelming evidence that, across a broad geographic gradient, competition among plants varied as a function of productivity. How is it possible that even when resources vary, competition may stay constant?

13.3 Mathematical and Laboratory Models

Mathematical and laboratory models provide a theoretical foundation for studying competitive interactions in nature. Ecologists have used both mathematical and laboratory models to explore the ecology of competition. Models are generally much simpler than the natural circumstances the ecologist wishes to understand, and thus can lead to an understanding of key principles. Though modelling sacrifices realism, its simplicity offers a degree of control that ecologists would not have in most natural settings.

In this section we will present an influential approach to modelling competition that is an extension of the logistic equation. In our experiences teaching ecology to literally thousands of students over the years, we appreciate that models can be intimidating. However, with patience and practice, a deeper understanding of ecology will emerge. Another benefit to taking the time to understand the following material is that we will present similar models in both chapters 14 and 15, so you might as well learn it now!

Modelling Interspecific Competition

Models of competition typically try to predict one thing: how do competitors influence population growth rates? If we go back to the exponential growth models presented in chapter 12, we see what happens when a population grows without any restriction. One "brake" to this unrealistic situation was

introduced in the model of logistic population growth by including a term for intraspecific competition, $\frac{K-N}{K}$. This approach to modelling competition is quite simple: take a model we already know (e.g., exponential growth), and add a new term (e.g., representing intraspecific competition). We will now take this approach one step further, and add an additional term representing *interspecific* competition.

Lotka–Volterra Model of Interspecific Competition

The first person to modify the logistic equation to incorporate interspecific competition as an additional brake on population growth was Vito Volterra (1926). Volterra's specific interest was to develop a theoretical basis for explaining changes in the composition of a marine fish community in response to reduced fishing during World War I. Alfred Lotka (1932a) independently repeated Volterra's analysis and extended it using graphics to represent changes in the population densities of competing species during competition. Because of their independent efforts and the great importance of their findings, ecologists have named the resulting equations the "Lotka–Volterra Model of Competition."

Let's retrace the steps of Lotka's and Volterra's modelling exercise, beginning with the logistic model for population growth discussed in chapter 12:

$$\frac{dN}{dt} = r_{max}N\left(\frac{K-N}{K}\right)$$

The logistic equation is great when we have a single species, but by definition interspecific competition involves multiple species. The first step then is to express the population growth of multiple species of potential competitors with multiple equations. Here, we will limit our discussion to two species, though this model can be expanded to include more species. Subscripts 1 and 2 refer to model parameters that are characteristic of species 1 or 2 respectively. The basic logistic equation describes change in population growth of species 1 as

$$\frac{dN_1}{dt} = r_{max1}N_1\left(\frac{K_1-N_1}{K_1}\right)$$

and change in population growth of species 2 as

$$\frac{dN_2}{dt} = r_{max2}N_2\left(\frac{K_2-N_2}{K_2}\right)$$

where N_1 and N_2 are the population sizes of species 1 and 2, K_1 and K_2 are their carrying capacities, and r_{max1} and r_{max2} are the intrinsic rates of increase for species 1 and 2. In these models, population growth slows as N increases due to increased intraspecific competition. The relative level of intraspecific competition can expressed as the ratio of current population size to carrying capacity, either N_1/K_1 or N_2/K_2. The assumption here is that resource supplies will diminish as population size increases due to intraspecific competition for resources. We can continue that logic, and assume that resource levels can also be reduced by interspecific competition.

This is where the math gets a bit more complicated, but it is important to understand that the logic is simple: the logistic

equation works by including a brake on population growth that represents *intraspecific* competition. Lotka and Volterra added an additional brake to represent the effects of *interspecific* competition. The way they achieved this was by introducing new terms called **competition coefficients**, which we define below. The resulting equations are:

$$\frac{dN_1}{dt} = r_{max1}N_1 \left(\frac{K_1-N_1-\alpha_{12}N_2}{K_1}\right)$$

and

$$\frac{dN_2}{dt} = r_{max2}N_2 \left(\frac{K_2-N_2-\alpha_{21}N_1}{K_2}\right)$$

In these equations, the rate of population growth of a species is reduced both by intraspecific competition and interspecific competition. The effect of interspecific competition is incorporated into the Lotka–Volterra model by introducing the terms $-\alpha_{12}N_2$ and $-\alpha_{21}N_1$. The terms α_{12} and α_{21} are the competition coefficients and express the interspecific competitive effects of species 1 and species 2. To understand this model, it is important to understand exactly what these competition coefficients represent.

α_{12} is the effect that one individual of species 2 has on the rate of population growth of species 1, while α_{21} is the effect of one individual of species 1 on the rate of population growth of species 2. In other words, these coefficients describe the *per capita* effects of species 2 on the population growth of species 1, and the *per capita* effects of species 1 on the population growth of species 2. For example, if $\alpha_{12} = 3$, this means that one individual of species 2 has a *per capita* effect on the population growth of species 1 equivalent to 3 individuals of species 1. If, on the other hand, $\alpha_{12} = 0.5$, then the competitive effect of one individual of species 2 on the population growth of species 1 is equivalent to one-half of an individual of species one. By multiplying α_{12} and α_{21} by N_2 and N_1 respectively, we move away from *per capita* effects and measure population level effects of one species on another.

There is another way of looking at competition coefficients. Why does the logistic equation cause a reduction in population growth? Let us imagine a scenario in which $r_{max1} = 0.5$, $K_1 = 200$, and $N_1 = 50$. What would dN_1/dt equal if only intraspecific competition were occurring?

$$\frac{dN_1}{dt} = 0.5 * 50 \left(\frac{200-50}{200}\right) = 18.75$$

In this scenario, species 1 would increase at a rate of 18.75 individuals per unit time. Now let us add interspecific competition by assuming $\alpha_{12} = 3$ and $N_2 = 25$. As you see below, the competition coefficients translate the population size of one species into "population equivalents" of its competitor, based upon its effectiveness as a competitor.

$$\frac{dN_1}{dt} = 0.5*50 \left(\frac{200-50-(3*25)}{200}\right) = 25\left(\frac{200-50-75}{200}\right)$$

$$= \left(\frac{200-125}{200}\right) = 9.375$$

In this example, the presence of an interspecific competitor reduced population growth of species 1 from 18.75 to 9.375 individuals per unit time. This happened because the 25 individuals of species 2 were equivalent to 75 individuals of species 1 in the numerator of the brake in the logistic equation. The next step is to move from solving the equations for specific combinations of parameter values, and toward understanding what general patterns emerge across all possible combinations of parameters. It is here that we find the true value of theory.

Under most circumstances, the Lotka–Volterra model predicts that interspecific competition will cause the local extinction (population size = 0) of one of the two species. We will develop this prediction of *competitive exclusion* more thoroughly in the next section. Although exclusion is often predicted, species coexistence can also occur, particularly if interspecific competition is weaker than intraspecific competition for both species. How do we know this? How can you use this theory to predict that species will co-exist under some conditions, while not under other conditions? The answer to this question involves a bit of mathematical rearrangement, and we begin by determining the conditions under which the population growth of both species is zero.

Populations of species 1 and 2 stop growing when:

$$\frac{dN_1}{dt} = r_{max1}N_1 \left(\frac{K_1-N_1-\alpha_{12}N_2}{K_1}\right) = 0$$

and

$$\frac{dN_2}{dt} = r_{max2}N_2 \left(\frac{K_2-N_2-\alpha_{21}N_1}{K_2}\right) = 0$$

We can exclude the $r_{max}N$ situations outside the bracket as not being relevant scenarios, and instead focus on the numerator inside the bracket. Why? If N or $r_{max} = 0$ for either species, it is already extinct! Remember, r_{max} represents the *maximum potential* population growth rate, and all extant populations must at some point have had positive growth. Therefore we can further simplify the biologically meaningful conditions at which population growth rates will equal 0 to:

$$(K_1-N_1-\alpha_{12}N_2) = 0 \text{ and } (K_2-N_2-\alpha_{21}N_1) = 0$$

Or, further rearranging these equations, we predict that population growth for the two species will stop when:

$$N_1 = K_1 - \alpha_{12}N_2 \text{ and } N_2 = K_2 - \alpha_{21}N_1$$

Here is some good news: the resulting equations describe two straight lines ($y = $ (slope)(x) + y-intercept). In the first equation, the population size of species 1 (N_1) is our y-value, the effects of species 2 on species 1 (α_{12}) is the slope, the population size of species 2 (N_2) is the x-value, the carrying capacity of species 1 is the y-intercept (the value of y when $x = 0$), and K_1/α_{12} is the x-intercept (the value of x when $y = 0$). The second equation has a similar form. We will start by graphing these lines, and giving them a special name, **isoclines of zero population growth**. (fig. 13.12).

At every point along these lines, population growth is stopped:

$$\frac{dN_1}{dt} = 0 \text{ and } \frac{dN_2}{dt} = 0$$

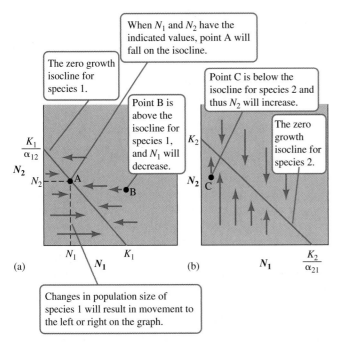

Figure 13.12 Graphical representation of the isoclines of zero population growth derived from the Lotka–Volterra competition models for (*a*) species 1 and (*b*) species 2. To better understand the next step (fig. 13.13), N_1 and N_2 (the population sizes of species 1 and 2) are the x- and y-axes for both panels.

Above an isocline of zero growth, the population of a species is decreasing ($\frac{dN}{dt} < 0$); below it the population is increasing ($\frac{dN}{dt} < 0$).

You will notice in figure 13.12 that N_1 is always on the x-axis, and N_2 is always on the y-axis. This is the conventional way of drawing these isoclines, and will make understanding

exclusion and coexistence easier. For now, it is important to remember that changes in population size of species 1 are indicated by left/right movement and changes in species 2 are indicated by up/down movement. *Highlight this in your notes, as forgetting this point is among the most common student mistakes in interpreting these graphs.*

The isoclines of zero growth show how the environment can be filled up or, in other words, show the relative population sizes of species 1 and species 2 that will deplete the critical resources. Looking at the isocline of zero growth for species 1, at one extreme species 1 completely fills the environment and species 2 is absent. This occurs where $N_1 = K_1$. At the other extreme, the environment is saturated entirely by species 2, while species 1 is absent. This occurs where $N_2 = K_1/\alpha_{12}$. In between these extremes, the environment is saturated with a mixture of species 1 and 2. The graph of the isocline for zero growth for species 2 can be interpreted in a similar way.

In figure 13.13, we combine these two graphs, and there are four possible arrangements of the isoclines. Putting the isoclines of zero growth for the two species on the same axis allows us to predict if one species will exclude the other or whether the two species will coexist. The precise prediction depends upon the relative orientation of the two isoclines. The Lotka–Volterra model predicts that one species will exclude the other when the isoclines do not cross. If the isocline for species 1 lies above that of species 2, species 1 will eventually exclude species 2. This exclusion occurs because all growth trajectories lead to the point where $N_1 = K_1$ and $N_2 = 0$ (fig. 13.13*a*). Figure 13.13*b* portrays the opposite situation in which the isocline for species 2 lies completely above that of species 1 and species 2 excludes species 1. In this case, all trajectories of population growth lead to the point where $N_2 = K_2$ and $N_1 = 0$.

Coexistence is possible only in the situations in which the isoclines cross. However, only one of the two such situations

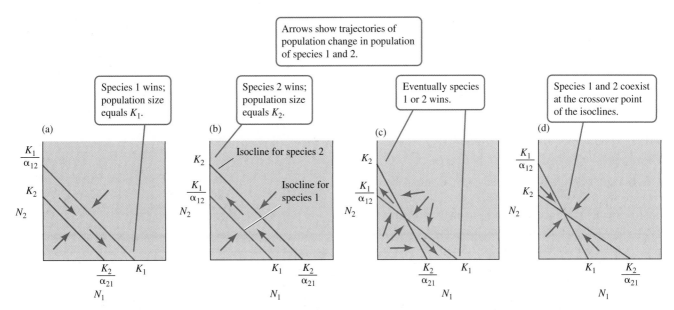

Figure 13.13 The orientation of isoclines for zero population growth and the outcome of competition according to the Lotka–Volterra competition model.

leads to stable coexistence. Figure 13.13*c* shows the situation in which coexistence is possible at the point where the isoclines of zero population growth cross, but this coexistence is unstable. In this situation, $K_1 > K_2/\alpha_{21}$ and $K_2 > K_1/\alpha_{12}$ and most population growth trajectories lead either to the points where $N_1 = K_1$ and $N_2 = 0$, or to where $N_2 = K_2$ and $N_1 = 0$. The populations of species 1 and 2 may arrive at the point where the lines cross, but any variation that moves the populations off this point eventually leads to exclusion of one species by the other. Figure 13.13*d* represents the only situation that predicts stable coexistence of the two species. In this situation, $K_2/\alpha_{21} > K_1$ and $K_1/\alpha_{12} > K_2$ and all growth trajectories lead to the point where the isoclines of zero growth cross. No matter what population sizes of species 1 and 2 you start with, they will always end up at the point where the isoclines cross.

What is the biological meaning of saying that all growth trajectories lead to the point where the isoclines of zero growth cross? What this means is that the relative abundances of species 1 and 2 will eventually arrive at the point where the isoclines cross, a point where the abundances of both species are greater than zero. In this situation, each species is limited more by members of their own species than they are by members of the other species. In other words, the Lotka–Volterra model predicts that species coexist when intraspecific competition is stronger than interspecific competition.

The Lotka–Volterra model is but one of many different models that describe competitive interactions among species. An alternative theoretical framework was presented by David Tilman (Tilman 1982), commonly referred to as the "resource-ratio" model. The main difference between these two modelling approaches is that Lotka–Volterra's model does not include any biological mechanism, and instead is based simply upon changes in population sizes. In other words, it does not include the resources that are actually the subject of competition. Tilman's model is substantially more explicit in terms of resource supply and uptake, and is easily expanded to address competition under different conditions. However, a detailed description of his model is beyond the scope of this text. In the simplified version of his model, he finds a result very similar to that of Lotka and Volterra: when interspecific competition is weaker than intraspecific competition, species tend to coexist. This is a central finding of competition theory and it is supported by the results of laboratory experiments on interspecific competition.

Laboratory Models of Competition

Experiments with Paramecia

G. F. Gause (1934) was among the first to use laboratory experiments to test the major predictions of the Lotka–Volterra competition model. Among the most well-known of Gause's experimental subjects were paramecia: small, freshwater, ciliated protozoans. Since protozoans are small, they can be kept in large numbers in a small space, and some of their natural habitats are fairly well simulated by laboratory aquaria. In addition, paramecia feed on microorganisms that can be easily cultured in the laboratory and provided in whatever concentration desired by the experimenter.

In one of his most famous experiments, Gause studied competition between two species: *Paramecium caudatum* and *P. aurelia*. He wanted to know whether one of these two species would drive the other to extinction if grown together in microcosms where they were forced to compete with each other for a limited food supply. In other words, would you get competitive exclusion or coexistence?

Gause demonstrated resource limitation by growing pure populations of *P. caudatum* and *P. aurelia* in the presence of two different concentrations of their food, the bacterium *Bacillus pyocyaneus*. If food supplies limit the growth of laboratory populations of these paramecia, what kind of population growth would you expect them to show? As you probably expect, Gause observed sigmoidal growth with a carrying capacity at both full- and half-strength concentrations of the food supply (fig. 13.14). When grown in the presence of a full-strength concentration of food, the carrying capacity of *P. aurelia* was 195. When food availability was halved, the carrying capacity of this species was reduced to 105. *P. caudatum* showed a similar response to food concentration, with carrying capacity of 137 and 64 under high and low resource conditions. The nearly one-to-one correspondence between food level and the carrying capacities of these two species provides evidence that when grown alone, the carrying capacity was determined by intraspecific competition for food. These results set the stage for Gause's experiment to determine whether interspecific competition for food, the limiting resource in this system, would lead to the exclusion of one of the competing species.

When grown together, *P. aurelia* survived, while the population of *P. caudatum* quickly declined (fig. 13.15).

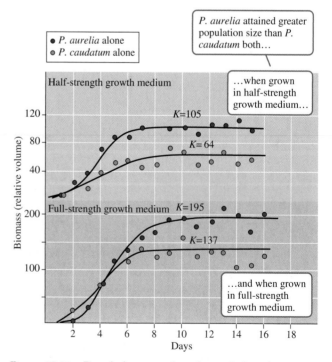

Figure 13.14 Population growth and population sizes attained by *Paramecium aurelia* and *P. caudatum* grown separately (data from Gause 1934).

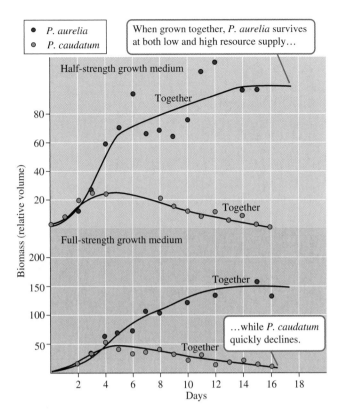

Figure 13.15   Population growth and population sizes attained by *Paramecium aurelia* and *P. caudatum* grown together.

The difference in results obtained at the two food concentrations support the conclusion that competitive exclusion results from competition for food. At full-strength food concentrations, the decline in the *P. caudatum* population approached exclusion by 16 days, but exclusion was not complete. In contrast, at a half-strength food concentration, *P. caudatum* was entirely eliminated by day 16. What does this contrast in the time to exclusion suggest about the influence of food supply on competition? It suggests that reduced resource supplies increase the intensity of competition.

Competitive Exclusion Principle and Mechanisms of Coexistence

The results of Gause and the predictions of Lotka and Volterra contributed to the development of the **competitive exclusion principle**, which in its simplest form states that "complete competitors cannot coexist" (Hardin 1960). What does this actually mean? Quite simply, it states that if two species that are nearly identical in their basic ecology (feeding, nesting, etc.) come into competition, one of them will persist while the second will go locally extinct. This idea has become a central tenet in ecological theory. However, like all theories, the world is full of exceptions. For example, if you go for a walk in a field, you may find 20 different species of plants all growing within a metre of where you are standing. These plants may appear similar, all needing light, nitrogen, and water, and yet they appear to coexist. As we will see in later chapters, one obvious explanation is that competition is not occurring

in all communities, and thus competitive exclusion should not occur. For example, in many communities the struggle for existence of individuals within a population may be primarily with extreme environmental conditions, rather than interspecific competitors. Populations may also be limited through predation and disease (chapters 14 and 15), rather than competition. Even with these exceptions, we can still find a large number of situations where species coexist *and* competition is occurring among the species. How is this possible if the competitive exclusion principle is true? For the last several decades, ecologists have tried to determine what mechanisms allow for the coexistence of competing species. Many potential mechanisms have been proposed and demonstrated in the literature; here we will discuss only a few.

In the Lotka–Volterra equations, stable coexistence can occur when interspecific competition is low relative to intraspecific competition. What does this mean in the context of the competitive exclusion principle? In short, species are unlikely to cause the extinction of similar species if they don't compete very strongly with them. This leads to the first of our potential mechanisms of coexistence: *spatial heterogeneity in the strength of competition*. As we saw in Gause's work, the speed with which *P. caudatum* went extinct was a function of the amount of food provided. If we think more broadly and consider two species that have overlapping distributions across a landscape, we could imagine that in some areas resources will be limiting, and in other areas resources may be abundant. A requirement of exploitative competition is that resources must be limiting, and thus in areas of high resource abundance competition will be low or non-existent, and the species can coexist. In areas of lower resources, competition may be more intense and one species will go locally extinct. The heterogeneity in resources and competition can allow for coexistence on the landscape, even if not within every single patch on the landscape.

Varied resource levels are not the only factor that can cause variation in the strength of competition. Instead, we could imagine that disease, predation, herbivory, extreme climatic conditions, and countless of other factors all will influence population growth, densities, behaviour, and ultimately the strength (or lack thereof) of competition. If there is heterogeneity on the landscape in any of these factors, we can then expect species coexistence in some locations, even if they compete strongly elsewhere on the landscape.

Species coexistence can also occur even if competition is everywhere, if there is *variation in competitive ability within a species*. The Lotka–Volterra model assumes that the competition coefficients are fixed values for each species. However, this is not always the case, and often many factors influence competitive abilities, including local environmental conditions and even the genotype of the individuals engaged in competition. Why might climate alter a species' competitive ability? As we discussed in section II, there are trade-offs in the ability to perform different physiological and ecological functions, including competitive ability. In 1954, Thomas Park published a classic laboratory study demonstrating the role that variation in the local microclimate can have on competitive outcomes.

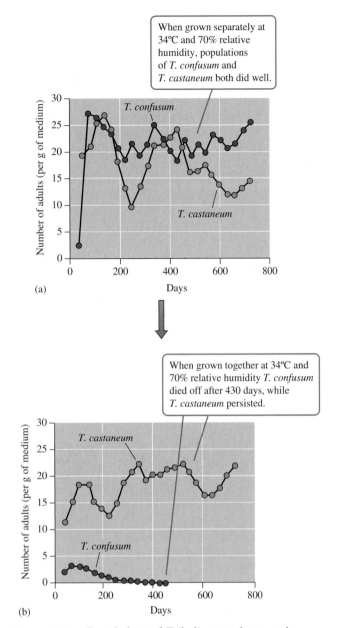

Figure **13.16** Populations of *Tribolium confusum* and *T. castaneum* grown (*a*) separately and (*b*) together at 34°C and 70% relative humidity (data from Park 1954).

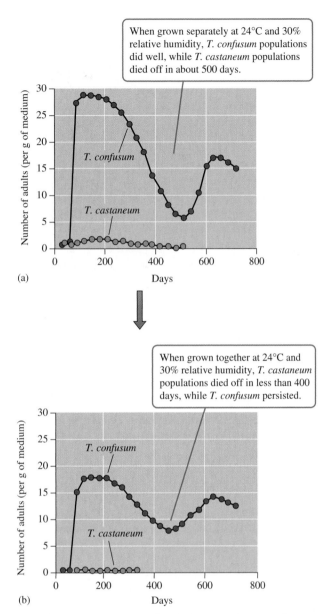

Figure **13.17** Populations of *Tribolium confusum* and *T. castaneum* grown (*a*) separately and (*b*) together at 24°C and 30% relative humidity (data from Park 1954).

Tribolium beetles infest stored grains and grain products. Since all of the life stages of *Tribolium* live in finely milled flour, small containers of flour provide all the environmental requirements necessary to sustain a population, and thus *Tribolium* are ideal subjects of laboratory research. Thomas Park (1954) worked extensively on interspecific competition between two species, *T. confusum* and *T. castaneum*, under varied levels of temperature and humidity. Under hot (34°C) and wet (70% RH) conditions, and without competition, both species were able to maintain populations for the duration of the experiment (fig. 13.16*a*). However, when grown together under these conditions, *T. castaneum* usually caused competitive exclusion of *T. confusum* (fig. 13.16*b*). In contrast, cool-dry conditions generally favoured *T. confusum*, with *T. castaneum* going extinct under these conditions even without competition (fig. 13.17).

These results demonstrate that competitive outcomes can be influenced by altered climatic conditions. If such variation exists in natural setting (think about the temperature and humidity differences you experience sitting under a tree versus sitting in an open field), then coexistence should occur across the landscape.

A third mechanism of coexistence is the idea of *competitive equivalence*. We have so far been assuming that under some conditions, one species is able to displace another, causing competitive exclusion. But in some situations species may be completely equal in their competitive abilities, such that the outcome of competition is not predictable. Although individually one species may win or lose a competitive contest, on average across a landscape, these species should win and lose an approximately equal number of times. As a result, coexistence in the landscape should occur.

The final mechanism of coexistence we will discuss here is that of *non-equilibrium conditions.* Competitive exclusion is not instantaneous, and instead is a process that may take many generations to occur. Both Gause and Park found that for fast-growing species, exclusion took weeks or even years to occur. What this means is that prior to exclusion, coexistence occurred; it just wasn't stable. In many communities, the environment may be variable and unlikely to ever allow population dynamics to reach equilibrium. At the same time, we must keep in mind that competition can alter the fitness of the individuals that are competing, and this may cause an evolutionary response. Most models of competition, such as Lotka–Volterra, are based upon the assumption that competitive ability is a fixed trait of a species. Park has shown how this isn't true when you have variation in climate. Next we will discuss how competition can cause evolutionary changes, which may themselves promote coexistence.

CONCEPT 13.3 REVIEW

1. *Paramecium aurelia* and *P. caudatum* coexisted for a long period before competitive exclusion when fed full-strength food compared to when they were fed half that amount. What does this contrast in time suggest about the role of food supply on competition between these two species?
2. Competitive exclusion can, but does not necessarily, occur when species interact. How can competitive equivalence among species prevent exclusion?
3. Using the isoclines in figures 13.13*a* and 13.13*b*, is there any way that predation on one of the two competing species could alter the outcome of competition?

13.4   Competition and Niches

Competition can have significant effects on species coexistence and the direction of evolution. Species have both fundamental and realized niches (chapter 9). The fundamental niche represents the range of conditions under which a species has the capacity to survive, while the realized niche represents the conditions under which that species is typically found. One of the dominant factors causing realized niches to be smaller than fundamental niches is interspecific competition. As we discussed above, a species' competitive ability may vary with environmental conditions, and we might expect a species to be a most effective competitor only under a narrow set of environmental conditions (perhaps near the performance optima; chapter 5). As a result, competition can have short-term ecological effects on species' distributions by restricting them to realized niches, likely only those conditions under which it is an effective competitor. Under most conditions, these changes will be restricted to the ranges of individual populations based upon resource

distributions (ecological shifts). However, in some circumstances, competitive interactions may be strong and pervasive enough to produce an evolutionary response, causing a change in the dimensions of the fundamental niche. In this section, we explore the evidence for the effects of competition in structuring both the realized and fundamental niches of natural populations.

Niches and Competition Among Plants

A. Tansley (1917) conducted one of the first experiments to test whether competition was responsible for the separation of two species of plants on different soil types. In the introduction to his paper, Tansley pointed out that while the separation of closely related plants had long been attributed to mutual competitive exclusion, it was necessary to perform manipulative experiments to demonstrate that this interpretation is correct. That is exactly what Tansley did to account for the mutually exclusive distributions of *Galium saxatile* and *G. sylvestre* (now *G. pumilum*), two species of small perennial plants (fig. 13.18). In the British Isles, *G. saxatile* is largely confined to acidic soils and *G. sylvestre* to basic limestone soils.

Tansley conducted his experiment at the Cambridge Botanical Garden from 1911 to 1917, where seeds of the two species of plants were sown in planting boxes (i.e., a **mesocosm**) of acidic and basic soils. The seeds were sowed in single-species plantings and in mixtures of the two species, similar to the experiments of Gause and Park. Both species germinated on both soil types, in both single- and mixed-species plantings (fig. 13.19). Both *Galium* species established healthy populations on both soil types when grown by themselves, and these single-species plantings persisted to the end of the six-year study. This indicates that both soil types occur within the *fundamental niche* of both species, and thus observed differences in species distribution cannot be explained purely by physiological limitation. However, as the

Figure 13.18   These two species of bedstraw grow predominately on different soil types: *Galium saxatile* (shown here) grows mainly on acidic soils, while *G. sylvestre* (*G. pumilum*) grows mainly on basic limestone soils.

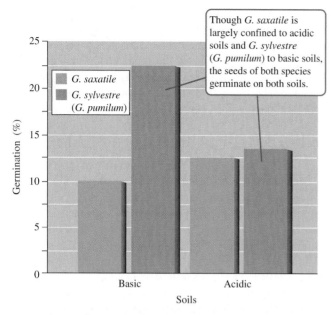

Though *G. saxatile* is largely confined to acidic soils and *G. sylvestre* (*G. pumilum*) to basic soils, the seeds of both species germinate on both soils.

Figure 13.19   Percentage seed germination by *Galium saxatile* and *G. sylvestre* in basic calcareous soils and acidic peat soil (data from Tansley 1917).

two species grew in mixed plantings, Tansley observed clear competitive dominance by each species on the soil type in which each species typically grows.

On limestone soils, *G. sylvestre*, the species naturally found on limestone soils, overgrew and eliminated *G. saxatile*, the acidic soil species, by the end of the first growing season. On acidic soils, the relationship was reversed and *G. saxatile* was competitively dominant but competitive exclusion was not completed. Growth by both species was so slow on the acidic soils that it took until the end of the six-year experiment for *G. saxatile* to completely cover the planting boxes containing acidic soils, a density attained by *G. sylvestre* on limestone soils in just one year. Tansley was one of the first ecologists to use experiments to demonstrate the influence of interspecific competition on the niches of species. The fundamental niche of both species of *Galium* included a wider variety of soil types than they inhabit in nature. The results of this experiment suggest that interspecific competition restricts the realized niche of each species to a narrower range of soil types.

Niche Overlap and Competition Between Barnacles

The barnacles *Balanus balanoides* and *Chthamalus stellatus* are restricted to predictable bands in the intertidal zone. We saw in chapter 10 that adult *Chthamalus* along the coast of Scotland are restricted to the upper intertidal zone, while adult *Balanus* are concentrated in the middle and lower intertidal zones. Joseph Connell's observations (1961a, 1961b) indicate that *Balanus* is limited to the middle and lower intertidal zones because it cannot withstand the longer exposure to air in the upper intertidal zone. However, physical factors only partially explain the distribution of *Chthamalus*. Connell

noted that larval *Chthamalus* readily settle in the intertidal zone below where the species persists as adults, but that these colonists die out within a relatively short period. In the course of field experiments, Connell discovered that interspecific competition with *Balanus* plays a key role in determining the lower limit of *Chthamalus* within the intertidal zone.

Because barnacles are sessile, small, and grow in high densities, they are ideal for field studies of survivorship. Their exposure at low tide is an additional convenience for the researcher. Connell established several study sites from the upper to the lower intertidal zones where he kept track of barnacle populations by periodically mapping the locations of every individual barnacle on glass plates. He established his study areas and made his initial maps in March and April of 1954, before the main settlement by *Balanus* in late April. He divided each of the study areas in half and kept one of the halves free of *Balanus* by scraping them off with a knife. Connell determined which half of each study site to keep *Balanus*-free by flipping a coin.

By periodically remapping the study sites, Connell was able to monitor interactions between the two species and the fates of individual barnacles. The results showed that in the middle intertidal zone, *Chthamalus* survived at higher rates in the absence of *Balanus* (fig. 13.20). *Balanus* settled in densities up to 49 individuals per square centimetre in the middle intertidal zone and grew quickly, crowding out the second species in the process. In the upper intertidal zone, removing *Balanus* had no effect on survivorship by the second species because the population density of *Balanus* was too low to compete seriously. Connell's results provide direct evidence that *Chthamalus* is excluded from the middle intertidal zone by interspecific competition with *Balanus*.

How does interspecific competition affect the niche of *Chthamalus*? In the absence of *Balanus*, it can live over a broad zone from the upper to the middle intertidal zones. Using the terminology of Hutchinson (1957), we can call this broad range of physical conditions the fundamental niche of *Chthamalus*. However, competition largely restricts *Chthamalus* to the upper intertidal zone, a more restricted range of physical conditions constituting the species' realized niche (fig. 13.21).

Does variation in interspecific competition completely explain the patterns seen by Connell? At the lowest levels in the lower intertidal zone, *Chthamalus* suffered high mortality even in the absence of *Balanus*. What other factors might contribute to high rates of mortality by *Chthamalus* in the lower intertidal zone? Experiments have shown that this species can withstand periods of submergence of nearly two years, so it seems that it is not excluded by physical factors. It turns out that the presence of predators in the lower intertidal zone introduces complications that we will discuss in chapter 14 when we examine the influences of predators on prey populations.

Competition and the Niches of Small Rodents

One of the most ambitious and complete of the many field experiments ecologists have conducted on competition among rodents focused on desert rodents in the Chihuahuan Desert

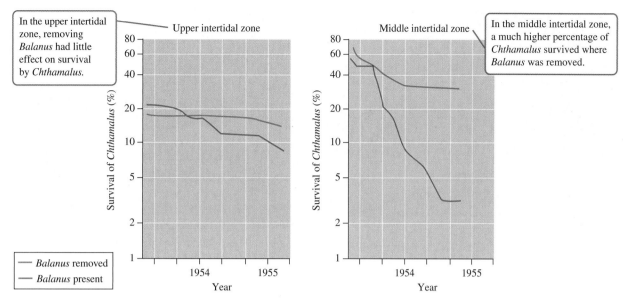

In the upper intertidal zone, removing *Balanus* had little effect on survival by *Chthamalus*.

Upper intertidal zone

Middle intertidal zone

In the middle intertidal zone, a much higher percentage of *Chthamalus* survived where *Balanus* was removed.

— *Balanus* removed
— *Balanus* present

Figure 13.20   A competition experiment with barnacles: removal of *Balanus* and survival by *Chthamalus* in the upper and middle intertidal zones (data from Connell 1961a, 1961b).

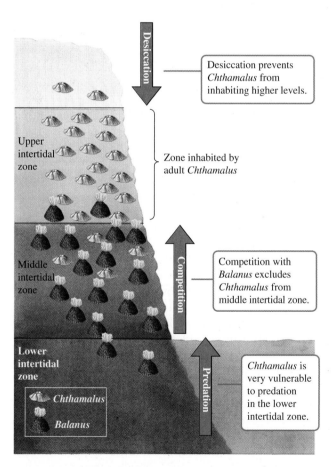

Desiccation prevents *Chthamalus* from inhabiting higher levels.

Zone inhabited by adult *Chthamalus*

Competition with *Balanus* excludes *Chthamalus* from middle intertidal zone.

Chthamalus is very vulnerable to predation in the lower intertidal zone.

Figure 13.21   Environmental factors restricting the distribution of *Chthamalus* to the upper intertidal zone.

Figure 13.22   Aerial photo showing the placement of 24 study plots, each 50 m by 50 m, in the Chihuahuan Desert near Portal, Arizona (courtesy of J. H. Brown).

near Portal, Arizona. This experiment, conducted by James H. Brown and his students and colleagues (Munger and Brown 1981, Brown and Munger 1985), is exceptional in many ways. First, it was conducted at a large scale; the 20 hectare study

site includes 24 study plots each 50 m by 50 m (fig. 13.22). Second, the experimental trials have been well replicated, both in space and in time. Third, the project has been long term; it began in 1977 and is ongoing. These three characteristics

Figure 13.23   Two species of granivorous rodents living in the Chihuahuan Desert: (*a*) the kangaroo rat, *Dipodomys* spp., a large granivore; (*b*) a pocket mouse, *Perognathus* sp., a small granivore.

combine to demonstrate subtle ecological relationships and phenomena that would not otherwise be apparent.

The rodent species living on the Chihuahuan Desert study site can be divided into groups based upon size and feeding habits. Most members of the species are **granivores**, rodents that feed chiefly on seeds. The large granivores consist of three species of kangaroo rats (fig. 13.23*a*) in the genus *Dipodomys*—*D. spectabilis*, 120 g; *D. ordi*, 52 g; and *D. merriami*, 45 g. In addition, the study site is home to four species of small granivores (fig. 13.23*b*)—*Perognathus penicillatus*, 17 g; *P. flavus*, 7 g; *Peromyscus maniculatus*, 24 g; *Reithrodontomys megalotis*, 11 g—and two species of small insectivorous rodents—*Onychomys leucogaster*, 39 g; and *O. torridus*, 29 g. Many of these species have very broad distributions, found throughout parts of Canada, the United States, and Mexico.

In one experiment, Brown and his colleagues set out to determine whether large granivorous rodents (*Dipodomys* spp.) limit the abundance of small rodents on their Chihuahuan Desert study site. They also wanted to know whether the rodents might be competing for food. The researchers addressed their questions with a field experiment in which they enclosed 50 m by 50 m study plots with mouse-proof fences. The fences were constructed with wire mesh with 0.64 cm openings, which were too small for any of the rodent species to crawl through. They also buried the fencing 0.2 m deep so the mice couldn't dig under it, and they topped the fences with aluminum flashing so the mice couldn't climb over it. This may sound like a lot of work, but to answer their questions, the researchers had to control the presence of rodents on the study plots.

The researchers next cut holes 6.5 cm in diameter in the sides of all the fences to allow all rodent species to move freely in and out of the study plots. With this arrangement in place, the rodents in the study plots were trapped live and marked once a month for 3 months. Following this initial monitoring period, the holes on four of eight study plots were

reduced to 1.9 cm, small enough to exclude *Dipodomys* but large enough to allow free movement of small rodents. Brown and his colleagues refer to these fences with small holes as semipermeable membranes, since they allow the movement of small rodents but exclude *Dipodomys*, the large granivores in this system.

If *Dipodomys* competes with small rodents, how would you expect populations of small rodents to respond to its removal? The density of small rodent populations should increase, right? If food is the limiting resource, would you expect granivorous and insectivorous rodents to respond differently to *Dipodomys* removal? The researchers predicted that if competition among rodents is mainly for food, then small granivorous rodent populations would increase in response to *Dipodomys* removal, while insectivorous rodents would show little or no response.

The results of the experiment were consistent with the predictions. During the first three years of the experiment, small granivores were approximately 3.5 times more abundant on the *Dipodomys* removal plots compared to the control plots, while populations of small insectivorous rodents did not increase significantly (fig. 13.24).

The results presented in figure 13.24 support the hypothesis that *Dipodomys* spp. competitively suppress populations of small granivores. But would they do so again in response to another experimental manipulation? We cannot be certain unless we repeat the experiment. That's just what Edward Heske, James H. Brown, and Shahroukh Mistry (1994) did. In 1988, they selected eight other fenced study plots that they had been monitoring since 1977, installed their semipermeable barriers on four of the plots, and removed *Dipodomys* from them. The result was an almost immediate increase in small granivore populations on the removal plots (fig. 13.25). By reproducing the major results of the first experiment, this second experiment greatly strengthens the case for competition between large and small granivores at this Chihuahuan Desert site.

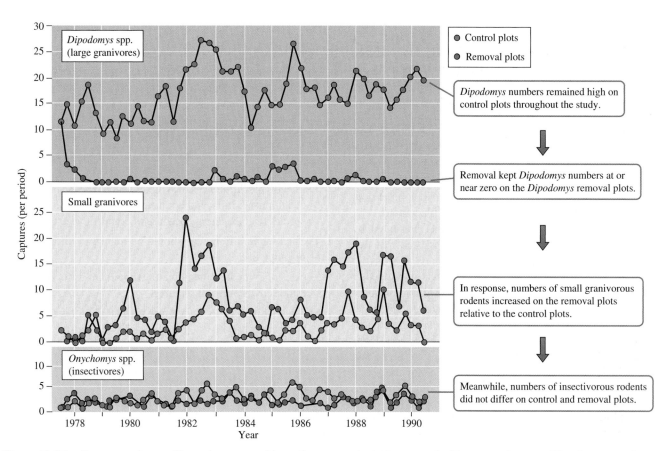

Figure 13.24 Responses by small granivorous and insectivorous rodents to removal of large granivorous *Dipodomys* species (data from Heske, Brown, and Mistry 1994).

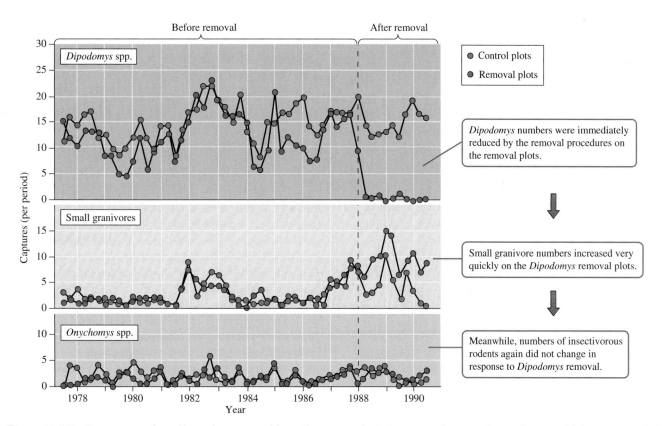

Figure 13.25 Responses of small granivorous and insectivorous rodents to a second removal experiment, which was preceded by several years of study before initiating *Dipodomys* removal (data from Heske, Brown, and Mistry 1994).

Character Displacement

Because competition can reduce an individual's fitness, it can exert selective pressure within a population. If this pressure is strong enough, it can cause evolutionary changes, including (1) selection favouring improved competitive abilities and increasing the rewards of competition to the "winners," or (2) selection favouring reduced niche overlap and reduced competition (and thus the cost of competition). We discuss some traits associated with good competitors in the next section. Here we will focus on the issue of evolution toward niche divergence (reduced niche overlap) in the face of competition, an evolutionary process called **character displacement**.

The idea of character displacement was presented by Brown and Wilson in 1956, where they suggested that two species that live apart (allopatric) may be nearly identical in form and function, though when these species live together (sympatric) competition will cause the evolution of some meaningful differences between them. Although the idea that evolution can cause a reduction in competition seems to be a modest proposal, it resulted in a prolonged and often inflammatory debate among ecologists. At the core of the debate were broad concerns that competition was being used as a mechanism to explain observed patterns without sufficient data. These issues were presented most succinctly in a paper by Joseph Connell (1980) in which he criticized the invoking of the "Ghost of Competition Past." He pointed out that just because one observes morphological differences between sympatric species does not prove that competition caused those differences. Connell's paper, and others, contributed to

concerns about whether there was truly any strong evidence for character displacement in natural systems. To help resolve this issue, Dolph Schluter and John McPhail (1992) compiled a list of criteria that would be necessary to vigorously show that character displacement has occurred:

1. Chance should be ruled out as an explanation for the differences in phenotypes among allopatric and sympatric populations.
2. Phenotypic differences must have a genetic basis.
3. Phenotypic differences in sympatry should be the outcome of evolutionary shifts, and not just the inability of similar-sized species to coexist (e.g., because of competitive exclusion).
4. Phenotypic differences should be related to differences in resource use.
5. Sites of sympatry and allopatry should not differ in food or major environmental features.
6. There should be evidence that similar phenotypes actually compete for food.

You can see how difficult demonstrating character displacement can be, and you can see the rigours of doing good, strong science. We will end this section with one of the best examples of character displacement, the threespine stickleback. You may remember this species from chapter 4 in our discussion of sympatric speciation. Character displacement and speciation are related topics, and so it should come as no surprise that the same researcher, Dolph Schluter of the University of British Columbia, is investigating both phenomena.

ECOLOGY IN ACTION

The Role of Competition in Forest Management

Competition is not an abstract scientific concept with little relevance to broader society; instead, the effects of competition on the growth of economically important species can result in economic losses in the millions, and maybe even billions, of dollars. The economics of competition have not escaped the attention of farmers, ranchers, fishers, and foresters. Modifying the strengths of intra- and interspecific competition is often an integral aspect of resource management. Canada is home to numerous researchers studying the impacts of competition on crop production and developing management strategies to reduce the economic cost of this ecological process. For example, Paul Cavers of Western University links population ecology and the study of interspecific competition by focusing his research on understanding how weed species use temporal dispersal (a seed bank) to escape competition from crop plants. His work also explores how crop litter may suppress future weed growth. There are numerous other

examples of ecological research being applied to agricultural systems; however, here we will focus on another important "crop" grown in Canada: trees.

Approximately 50% of the Canadian land base is covered by forests and woodlands (402 million hectares). On a global scale, Canada is home to nearly 30% of the world's boreal forest and about 10% of all global forests. Within Canada, approximately 680,000 hectares of forest were harvested in 2008, with a total value of nearly $24 billion ($Cdn) (Canada, Natural Resources Canada 2010). In short, Canada is home to a large reserve of forests, and the harvest of this area makes a significant contribution to the national and local economies. The impacts of forestry on local communities are also important, providing jobs to nearly 500,000 people. At the same time, logging activities dramatically alter the landscape, both through logging itself as well as through construction of roads and movement of large heavy equipment, causing habitat fragmentation. Forests are also home to countless numbers of

species in addition to the commercially desired trees. These can include other harvested species, such as deer and moose, and the much more diverse and abundant group of non-harvested species. These understory plants, mosses, insects, birds, mammals, fungi, and other species represent a large proportion of Canada's biodiversity.

Forests provide much more than wood, and there is often conflict between continued expansion of the forest industry and the conservation of existing forests. The realities of Canadian society are such that forest activities are likely to continue for the foreseeable future, and thus forest biologists and ecologists are actively working on ways to both minimize the environmental damage associated with logging and increase potential economic returns. This research has led to changes in tree planting programs, minimization of soil disturbance, reduced road development, and changes in the methods used for harvesting timber. Our understanding of succession in the boreal forest, a topic we discuss in chapter 18, greatly influences these efforts. Here we focus on efforts to increase yields in regrowth forests (forests that have been logged). In theory, the overall footprint of logging activity can be kept smaller if we are able to increase the yields from the areas we currently harvest. Competition plays an important role in determining yields by causing a reduction in the harvestable biomass in Canada's forests.

To understand the impact of competition in stand development and forestry, it is first important to understand what an area that has been recently logged looks like (fig. 13.26). The removal of the tall over-story trees causes a dramatic increase in light reaching the soil floor, and the dead roots and leaf litter often result in a flush of nutrients. In other words, conditions are ideal for the establishment of large numbers of *r*-selected, ruderal species (chapter 9). At the same time, forestry practices often involve a replanting effort, generally with economically desirable tree species. As you can imagine, it would be very easy for the ruderal species to rapidly overtake the plantings, causing high tree mortality and slower wood production. In other words, competition by "weeds" can kill and stunt trees desired by the forest industry, causing a loss of wood production and economic benefit. We use the term "weed" for a specific reason. **Weeds** are species that a person does not want in a certain location at a certain point in time. If our goal is to maximize harvestable biomass of trees, then species that reduce this are undesired weeds. However, if our

Figure 13.26   Open space is found in a Lodgepole pine stand after thinning.

goal is instead to maximize biodiversity, then those same species would be desired as they contribute to species diversity, and thus would not be called weeds. In other words, a weed is a human designation of a species based upon what people want; it is not an inherent characteristic of a species.

Foresters have learned how to use the self-thinning law to increase harvestable biomass from forests. Rather than waiting for the trees and other plants to shade out the smaller individuals, unwanted plants can be managed through a variety of practices including herbicide application, grazing, burning, and other methods of weed removal. All of these practices cost money, and it is thus not surprising that several long-term studies are testing whether vegetation management practices (i.e., reducing interspecific competition) result in increased tree growth and economic benefit. Responses can be large. Full removal of neighbouring vegetation increased growth of Lodgepole pine 150% over 15 years in British Columbia; Balsam fir in New Brunswick increased 250% after 28 years; and White spruce in Ontario increased by up to 90% over 30 years (Wagner et al. 2006).

Whether these increases in yield offset the cost of the vegetation management itself depends upon market conditions (e.g., price of timber, labour costs, etc.), and is beyond the scope of ecology. What is clear is that applying knowledge of ecological processes such as competition can have significant impacts on the harvest and management of Canada's natural resources.

Numerous species of closely related sticklebacks (*Gasterosteus aculeatus* complex) live in small lakes. Some sympatric species appear to exhibit character displacement such that one species feeds on benthic organisms in the littoral zone, with the second species feeding on planktonic species in the littoral zone. These species are morphologically dissimilar, with the benthic species having few, short gill rakers and a wide gape, and the limnetic species having many, long gill rakers and a narrow gape (fig. 13.27). Prior work indicates

that these phenotypes improve efficiency at capturing specialized food items. What is particularly interesting is that when these species live allopatrically, they demonstrate intermediate phenotypes (fig. 13.27) and feed in both the littoral and benthic zones. Knowing these pieces of natural history, it becomes easy to understand why Schluter would believe this to be a potential case of character displacement. But is it? To answer this, we will work through the list of criteria that Schluter published.

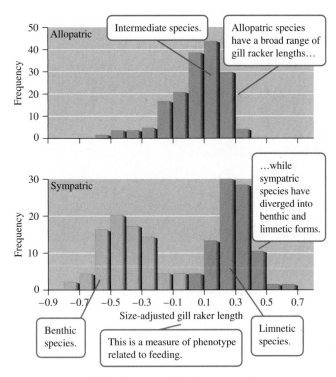

Figure 13.27   With character displacement, phenotypes differ among allopatric and sympatric populations (data from Schluter and McPhail 1992).

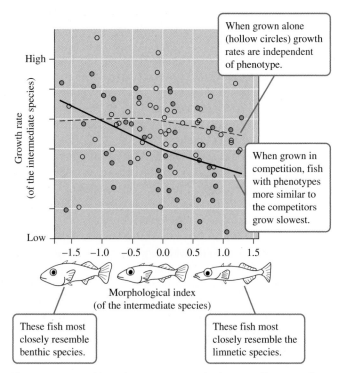

Figure 13.28   Growth rates among the intermediate species of Stickleback varied as a function of phenotype and the presence of a competitor species (data from Schluter 1994).

Detailed work on these populations has shown that the phenotypic variations found between sympatric and allopatric populations are greater than expected by chance (Schluter and McPhail 1992), that these phenotypes have a heritable component, and that the phenotype influences feeding. To address the remaining three issues (#3, #5, #6), Schluter (1994) designed an elegant experiment in which he controlled environmental conditions (eliminating the concern of #5), tested whether there was competition for food (#6), and tested whether there was directional selection due to sympatry (#3). Schluter reasoned that a prediction of character displacement would be that if you put an intermediate species in the same pond as a limnetic species, there should be directional selection on the intermediate species towards a benthic form. In other words, those individuals of the intermediate form that were most similar to its competitor (the limnetic species) would have lower fitness than those individuals that were most dissimilar to the competitor.

To see if this actually occurred, Schluter constructed two experimental ponds on the campus of the University of British Columbia. He divided each pond in half, placing individuals of the intermediate species into both halves of both ponds. On one half of each pond, he also added individuals of a limnetic species. After three months, he harvested all the remaining fish and was able to measure growth rates. Overall growth rates were negatively correlated with fish density, suggesting competition was occurring. Additionally, as predicted by theory, individuals of the intermediate species that most resembled the competitor species had the

lowest growth rates (fig. 13.28). Since these fish all grew under identical environmental conditions, this directional selection cannot be due to any factor other than competition, providing very clear and convincing evidence that competition can cause evolutionary shifts in populations over short ecological timescales.

In the final section of this chapter, we will look below the level of the population and investigate some of the mechanisms organisms use in competition. It is one thing to talk about competition as a process that has occurred, but what traits actually confer competitive advantage, and how would an ecologist know?

CONCEPT 13.4 REVIEW

1. What do you think would have happened to the *Galium sylvestre* on acidic soil if Tansley had continued his experiment for a few more years?

2. What does the increase in small granivore populations but the lack of response by populations of insectivorous rodents suggest about the nature of competition between rodents in Brown's Arizona study area?

3. Why do phenotypic differences among populations need to be partly heritable to believe character displacement may have occurred?

ECOLOGICAL TOOLS AND APPROACHES

Identifying the Mechanisms by Which Plants Compete

Discussions of competition often centre on the consequences of competition, such as reduced fitness, altered population dynamics and distributions, or changes in community structure. However, there is another side of competition that ecologists explore, and this is the study of the mechanisms by which individuals actually compete. This research is most actively pursued by plant ecologists, and we will explore two case studies in which the researchers were trying to identify the factor(s) that influence competitive ability in plants. You will see that experiments are a critical tool when you want to understand the mechanisms or interactions among individuals. You will also see that many types of experiments can be used to address similar research questions.

Size Does Matter

One of the pioneers in the study of mechanisms of competition among plants is Paul Keddy, formerly of the University of Ottawa. For the past several decades, he and a large number of students and post-docs have published a series of papers designed to understand which plant traits are most closely associated with competitive ability in plants. When Keddy began his work, the standard experimental approach was to choose one or just a few species and study them very intensely. The hope was that by understanding the specific ecology of one species, you would gain an understanding of many species. However, by using this approach the literature rapidly filled with a series of special cases without a clear understanding of general processes across large numbers of taxa. Keddy understood that to make truly broad generalizations about the relationship between plant traits and competitive abilities, he would need to develop a unique methodological approach.

Keddy, along with graduate student Connie Gaudet (Gaudet and Keddy 1988), developed a comparative method in which they could study large numbers of species simultaneously. In their study, they chose 44 species of plants found in the wetlands near the campus of the University of Ottawa. One of the first problems they faced was deciding how to conduct an experiment from which they could determine a standard measure of competitive performance. If they used two species, this would be easy, as they would simply need to put these plants together in a pot, or grow them individually. With three species, it is still manageable; pair-wise contests result in only three competition treatment (species A vs. B, A vs. C, B vs. C). However, the number of pair-wise contests is equal to $N(N - 1)/2$, where N is the number of species used. With 44 species, this would result in 946 different competition treatments. Clearly this was not feasible, no matter how many undergraduate assistants they hired! Gaudet and Keddy instead used what is now called a *phytometer.* They chose one species, *Lythrum salicaria,* which would compete against all 44 species. By measuring the growth of the phytometer against the different competitors, they could then establish which species were strong competitors and which were weak. In other words, if *Lythrum* was small in a pot, it was against a strong competitor. It if was large, it was against a weak competitor. By using this approach, Gaudet and Keddy were able to reduce the size of the experiment from 946 treatments to 44. This was a major advance in competition studies, and is widely used today.

Now that they had measures of competitive ability, they needed a way to determine which plant traits were most likely the cause of enhanced competitive ability. To assess this, they measured a variety of traits of each of their study species, such as above and below ground biomass, height, leaf shape, canopy diameter, etc. Using a multiple regression analysis (appendix A), they were able to explain most of the variation in competitive abilities of the species (74%) using their measures of plant traits. In other words, if they knew what a plant looked like (quantitatively), they were fairly accurate in predicting its competitive ability. Looking at the traits individually, plant biomass was most strongly associated with competitive ability (fig. 13.29), with the largest plants being the best competitors.

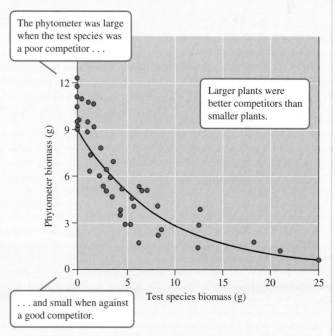

Figure 13.29 Results of Gaudet and Keddy's experiment investigating the relationship between plant traits and competitive ability.

Numerous studies have been conducted since Gaudet and Keddy. Plant size remains one of the major correlates of competitive ability in plants. However, as we see in the next example, size is not the only weapon available to plants.

Perceiving One's Environment Allows for Adaptation

As we saw in section II, plants exhibit a diverse set of mechanisms that allow them to adapt to changes in their abiotic environment. They do not simply "sit and take it," but instead are able to change their morphologies and physiologies to be better suited to the specific microenvironment they find themselves rooted in. From an evolutionary perspective, this makes sense, as selection will favour those genotypes (plants or animals) with the highest fitness within a population. Using the same logic, there is no reason to believe that plants should just suffer the consequences of competition, with no evolutionary response. Instead, if competition is strong, it should favour a response by the competing plants. Such a response is obvious to see when animals compete, as you can see one bird attacking another, but what can plants do? The major difference in responses between plants and mobile animals is that plants respond by altered morphology, while many animals respond with movement. However, both approaches can be adaptive and can have a genetic basis. Johanna Schmitt and her students have published a series of papers describing one response in plants: shade avoidance.

Many plants exhibit an interesting trait: in response to low light levels, they grow taller than they would under high light conditions. More specifically, many plants are not just responding to low light levels, but instead they are responding primarily to light that has low levels of red wavelengths (relative to far-red wavelengths). Why? First we can ask, what makes leaves green? Leaves are green because chlorophyll reflects green light, absorbing red and blue. That means that light that travels through a leaf will have a lower R:FR ratio than light that has not passed through another plant. This physical fact results in a signal that many plants are able to perceive: if low R:FR light hits their leaves, that means a neighbouring plant is above them. This is potentially really bad news for the plant, and a very common response is for the lower plant to grow tall quickly, trying to overtop its neighbour. This process is mediated through the phytochrome system, which is extremely sensitive to changes in R:FR ratios and influences a variety of aspects of plant growth and development. Theory predicts that plants that exhibit this shade avoidance response have the potential to access direct sunlight at the top of the canopy, while plants that are unable to exhibit this response are likely doomed to subordinate status where they will receive very little light. Although this response is well documented, and the logic behind its adaptive advantage makes sense, Schmitt realized that tests to determine whether it actually was an adaptive behavioural response were lacking.

Schmitt and colleagues (1995) reasoned that support for the adaptive hypothesis would require demonstrating that elongated plants have higher fitness in a dense stand than unelongated plants in a dense stand. However, Schmitt immediately reached an impasse: if all plants in a population elongate in response to being part of a dense stand, there is no way of measuring the fitness of short and tall individuals! Schmitt and her colleagues devised a novel solution, and were among the first researchers to incorporate transgenic plants in ecological research. Schmitt and her colleagues developed two transgenic strains of tobacco, *Nicotiana tabacum*, in which they inserted a gene from oats, which greatly reduces the shade avoidance response. By doing this, they produced plants that even in deep shade were unable to elongate, and thus she could now begin her experiment. The experimental design was very straightforward, growing plants at low and high density in both monocultures and mixtures. As expected, the transgenic plants exhibited a reduced shade avoidance response at high density. After the plants had experienced significant competition for light, the transgenic plants were smaller than the wild type plants when grown at high density. As we know from Keddy's work, reduced size could further reduce a plant's competitive ability. Small size is also commonly associated with reduced survival and fecundity, and thus this reduction in size likely is a demonstration of a real fitness cost of not possessing the shade avoidance response.

These results support the adaptive hypothesis. Even more importantly, the creative experimental design by Schmitt and her colleagues shows that by blending molecular biology with traditional approaches in ecology, researchers are able to find answers to questions that previously were impossible to address.

SUMMARY

Species exhibit a diversity of interactions with other species in natural systems. Species interactions can be roughly characterized based upon the effects of these interactions on each of the participants. Competition is a form of interaction in which all individuals are harmed.

13.1 Individuals can compete with other individuals, of their own and of different species, in a number of different ways.

Competition is generally divided into *intraspecific competition*, competition between individuals of the same species, and

interspecific competition, competition between individuals of different species. Competition can take the form of interference competition, which consists of direct aggressive interactions between individuals, or exploitative competition, in which individuals interact indirectly through use of a shared and limiting resource.

13.2 Field and mesocosm studies show resource limitation and competition are widespread.

Experiments under field and semi-natural conditions (mesocosms) show that competition occurs outside of the laboratory. Growing plant populations can experience self-thinning in which the average plant size varies with plant density. Resource competition among leafhoppers also varies with population density, and results in reduced survivorship and growth of the competing individuals. A field study with song sparrows shows that even in the absence of a clear limiting resource, interference competition can occur, with individual birds choosing to enter or avoid competitive encounters due to the relative experience and health of their potential competitor. Several large reviews show that competition is widespread in natural systems, but is not omnipresent. Plant ecologists have investigated the roles of resource availability and habitat productivity on the strength of competition, and have developed contrasting models. An intercontinental field experiment was conducted to try to provide a critical test, lending support to the idea that competition is strong across a broad resource gradient.

13.3 Mathematical and laboratory models provide a theoretical foundation for studying competition in nature.

Lotka and Volterra independently expanded the logistic model of population growth to represent interspecific competition. In the Lotka–Volterra competition model, the growth rate of species depends both upon numbers of conspecifics and numbers of the competing species. In this model, the effect of one species upon another is summarized by competition coefficients. In general, the Lotka–Volterra competition model predicts coexistence of species when interspecific competition is less intense than intraspecific competition. Competitive exclusion of one species by another is a common outcome of laboratory experiments. However, changes to experimental conditions can impact the outcome of competition, enhancing the possibility of coexistence. Observations in nature suggest the competitive exclusion principle is not inviolate. Competition theory suggests that competing species can coexist if there is spatial heterogeneity in resources or in the strength of competition, if there is variation in competitive abilities within a species or equivalence in competitive ability among species, or if the natural system is not at equilibrium.

13.4 Competition can have significant effects on species coexistence and the direction of evolution.

Field experiments involving a diversity of organisms have demonstrated that competition can restrict the niches of species to a narrower set of conditions than they would otherwise occupy in the absence of competition. Natural selection can lead to divergence in the niches of competing species, a phenomenon called character displacement. Stringent requirements for a definitive demonstration of character displacement have limited the documented number of cases. However, studies like those of the threespine stickleback indicate that character displacement does occur under natural condition. After many decades of work on competition, we can conclude that competition is a common and strong force operating in nature, but not always, and not everywhere.

Due to the potential importance of competition to ecologists, foresters, farmers, fishers, ranchers, and other members of society, it is not surprising the study of competition continues to be a major focus of attention by ecologists. At the core of resolving genuine scientific and societal issues in science is a strong scientific method and creative experimental designs. Ecologists have incorporated theory, laboratory studies, observations, and experiments to develop a body of knowledge about competition. Continued improvements are gained through novel approaches such as using phytometers in comparative studies and the incorporation of transgenic plants to address ecological questions. Continued expansion of research methodologies will allow for improved understanding of this topic, which is central to much of ecology and society.

REVIEW QUESTIONS

1. How can the results of greenhouse experiments on competition help us understand the importance of competition among natural populations? How can a researcher enhance the correspondence of results between greenhouse experiments and the field situation?

2. Explain how self-thinning in field populations of plants can be used to support the hypothesis that intraspecific competition is a common occurrence among natural plant populations.

3. Explain why species that overlap a great deal in their fundamental niches have a high probability of competing. Now explain why species that overlap a great deal in their realized niches and live in the same area probably do not compete significantly.

4. Draw the four possible ways in which Lotka's (1932a) isoclines of zero growth (see fig. 13.13) can be oriented with respect to each other. Label the axes and the points where the isoclines intersect the horizontal and vertical axes. Explain how each situation represented by the graphs leads to either competitive exclusion of one species or the other or to stable or unstable coexistence.

5. How was the amount of food that Gause (1934) provided in his experiment on competition among paramecia related to carrying capacity? In Gause's experiments on competition, *P. aurelia* excluded *P. caudatum* faster when he provided half the amount of food than when he doubled the amount of food. Explain.

6. Discuss how mathematical theory, laboratory models, and field experiments have contributed to our understanding of the ecology of competition. List the advantages and disadvantages of each approach.

7. One of the conclusions that seems justified in light of several decades of studies of interspecific competition is that competition is a common and strong force operating in nature, but not always and not everywhere. List the environmental circumstances in which you think intraspecific and interspecific competition would be most likely to occur in nature. In what circumstances do you think competition is least likely to occur? How would you go about testing your ideas?

8. The study of competition has been filled with contentious debates among researchers, such as was seen in the study of character displacement. Schluter and McPhail (1992) compiled a list of criteria that would be necessary to convincingly show character displacement had occurred. Develop a similar list of criteria to convincingly show that competition is a strong influence on the current distribution of any particular species.

9. The study of competition can increase economic benefits associated with forestry. This, in turn, has the potential to increase forest activity by making previously marginal forests economically viable for harvest. What role do ecologists have in deciding how their results are used by industry and science, and should ecologists advocate specific policy positions?

10. Discuss potential reasons why we observe competitors coexisting in natural systems when the competitive exclusion principle predicts this should not occur.

HERBIVORY AND PREDATION

CHAPTER 14

CHAPTER CONCEPTS

14.1 Herbivory is a widespread ecological interaction, and has caused the evolution of a diversity of plant defence strategies.

Ecology In Action: Invasive Species and Exploitative Relationships

Concept 14.1 Review

14.2 Prey populations are influenced by food availability, by consumption by predators, and by non-consumptive effects of predators.

Concept 14.2 Review

14.3 The population consequences of exploitative relationships can be explored with theoretical models.

Concept 14.3 Review

14.4 Prey populations can persist in the presence of predators through the use of refugia and a diversity of defence strategies.

Concept 14.4 Review

Ecological Tools and Approaches: Evolution and Exploitation

Summary

Review Questions

361

In nature, the consumer eventually becomes the consumed. A willow tree grows during the summer months, consuming mineral resources and water, while utilizing the energy from the sun to produce new tissues and biomass. A moose browses on the twigs and buds of the willow, here shown barely protruding above the deep snow of midwinter (fig. 14.1). With each mouthful, the moose reduces the mass of the willows and adds to the growing energy store in its own large and complex stomach, energy stores that the moose will need to maintain its internal body temperature through the cold winter. Then, a familiar scent catches the moose's attention, and startled, it runs off.

Suddenly, the clearing where the moose had been feeding is a blur of bounding forms dashing headlong in the direction the moose has gone—a pack of wolves in pursuit of its own meal. The moose has experienced this chase many times, each time successfully getting away. This time, the moose isn't so fortunate, and after a fierce struggle the wolves settle in to feed.

Some of the strongest ecological interactions in natural systems are based upon *exploitation* of one organism by another. Here we find the herbivore (moose) benefiting from the exploitation of the willow, and the predator (wolf) benefiting from the exploitation of the moose. But we must remember that predators do more than just consume their prey. Even when they are unsuccessful in the hunt, they may change the behaviour of their potential prey, increase stress hormones, and produce significant consequences when the prey escapes from the chase. These too are the effects of exploitative interactions.

In chapters 2 and 3 we described the different species that lived in different parts of the planet. Throughout section II, we continued a focus on species as we described the niche and adaptations that allow species to inhabit different parts of the world. However, there is another way of looking at the diversity on the planet, one based on interactions rather than taxonomic affiliation. There are somewhere on the order of 350,000 species of photosynthetic plants, and some unknown number of autotrophic bacteria. Combined, these make up just a tiny fraction of the life on the planet, which means that most species obtain essential resources through some sort of exploitative relationship with other species. It is perhaps then no surprise that ecologists have focused on many aspects of these exploitative relationships, using terms like plant–animal interactions, tri-trophic interactions, predator–prey, herbivore–host, disease–host, and others to describe the branch of ecology in which they work.

Predation and herbivory are not the only forms of exploitative relationships we have encountered. Recall from chapter 8 that some social interactions were manipulative, such as the cowbirds that lay eggs in the nests of other species. Parasitic interactions in general are considered exploitative, and they, along with a closely related form of interaction called mutualism, will be discussed in chapter 15. Competition, the subject of chapter 13, occurs due to common exploitation of a limiting resource, such as the willows' consumption of soil nitrate. In exploitative relationships, one participant exploits another, which is different than competition, where all participants exploit a shared pool of resources. As you will see, this is much more than a subtle difference in wording.

Let's consider some of the most common types of exploitation. *Herbivores* consume live plant material but do not usually kill plants. Common herbivores include caterpillars, aphids, and ungulates. **Predators** kill and consume other organisms. Typical predators are animals that feed on other animals—wolves that eat moose, snakes that eat mice, and people that eat cattle.

As clear as all these definitions may seem, they are fraught with semantic problems. Once again, we are faced with capturing the full richness of nature with a few restrictive definitions. For instance, not all predators are animals; a few are plants, some are fungi, and many are protozoans. When an herbivore kills the plant upon which it feeds, should we call it a predator? If an ant eats a seed, thereby killing a baby plant, is it an herbivore or a predator? If an herbivore does not kill its food plants, would it be better to call it a parasite? The point of these questions is not to argue for more terminology, but to argue for fewer, less restrictive terms. Let's recognize the diversity and continuous variation facing the ecologist, put the restrictive definitions aside for the moment, and recognize what is common to all these interactions: **exploitation** of one organism at the expense of another. We begin by discussing one of the most common ecological interactions, herbivory.

14.1 Herbivory and Plant Defence

Herbivory is a widespread ecological interaction, and has caused the evolution of a diversity of plant defence strategies. The effect of a successful predation event to a prey is pretty obvious: death. The effect of an act of herbivory on the host plant is less clear. Herbivory rarely immediately kills a plant, and following the departure of the herbivore, many

Figure 14.1 This moose exploits the twigs and buds of woody plants for the food it needs to survive a cold northern winter. Eventually, wolves may prey upon the moose for their own survival.

plants appear to recover very well. Under some conditions, herbivory may actually stimulate plant growth. However, to find out what typically happens, Christine Hawkes and Jon Sullivan (2001) decided to comb through the extensive literature on herbivory and determine whether there were any general patterns. They summarized a total of 81 cases in which growth or reproduction were measured on plants grown with and without herbivory under experimental conditions. When averaged across all species, they found that herbivory typically harms plants through reduced plant growth and reproduction. However, the exact effects of herbivory varied among plant species, with monocots (e.g., grasses) generally increasing their growth rates following herbivory when nutrients were abundant. So, although herbivory is detrimental for a "typical" plant, there will be times in which herbivory may stimulate growth. We will discuss this unexpected outcome of herbivory next.

Snow Goose Grazing and a Sub-Arctic Salt Marsh

Until his death in 2009, Bob Jefferies, of the University of Toronto, was a global leader in the study of the ecological consequences of herbivory in natural systems. For decades Jeffries brought a team of students to the sub-arctic wetlands at La Pérouse Bay, Manitoba (chapter 3). La Pérouse Bay is at the northern limit of the boreal forest, just east of Churchill, Manitoba. These wetlands are the summer home to large numbers of herbivores, whose feeding behaviour has the ability to change the landscape. When we think of herbivores, it is often images of bison, caterpillars, and deer that come to mind. However, in La Pérouse Bay and other wetlands of the North, geese are the dominant herbivores, having the potential to completely devegetate areas (fig. 14.2).

Within La Pérouse Bay, there is a large expanse of marsh dominated by two plant species, *Puccinellia phryganodes* and *Carex subspathacea*. These two species alone make up nearly 95% of all plant biomass in the marsh, and thus changes in their growth indicate changes in the overall biomass production of this community. In 1979–80 there were approximately 4,000 nesting pairs of snow geese, along with many more non-breeding geese. The birds graze heavily, often leaving only 1–2 cm of vegetation unclipped (Cargill and Jefferies 1984). One of the first questions that Jefferies and his colleagues asked was quite simple: what is the effect of this grazing on the growth of these plant species? As he was to find out over several decades of research, the answer isn't as simple as "negative." To understand why, we need to better understand how Jefferies and his colleagues addressed this question.

To determine the effects of geese grazing on plant growth, Jeffries created areas of the marsh that were protected from the herbivores. By building a series of 5 × 5 m *exclosures* out of wood and chicken wire, they were able to keep geese out of their study plots. Some of these exclosures were temporary, and some were permanent, allowing them to determine both the short and longer-term consequences of grazing on plant growth. They then measured plant biomass inside and outside the exclosures over the course of the growing season for two years.

(a)

(b)

Figure 14.2 (*a*) Geese are the dominant herbivores in many northern wetlands, such as this marsh at La Pérouse Bay, Manitoba. (*b*) Exclosures can be used to experimentally manipulate grazing intensity.

No one was surprised when they found grazing reduced aboveground biomass (fig. 14.3). In other words, at any point in time, there was more **standing biomass** in the ungrazed plots than the grazed plots. Standing biomass is a measure of how much plant biomass is found at a specific point in time, per unit area. What was surprising, however, was when they added up all the biomass production from the plots over the entire summer, taking into account the amount of biomass the geese ate, the grazed plots actually had higher *primary productivity* (chapter 1) than the ungrazed ones (fig. 14.3)! Primary productivity is a measure of plant growth per unit area, per unit time, and here we represent it as cumulative plant growth. Jefferies found that herbivory increased plant productivity, even though standing biomass was reduced. This is an example of **overcompensation**, where growth following herbivory is greater than growth without herbivory. This concept should be vaguely familiar to you, as it is similar to the idea that populations that follow the logistic growth curve will have higher population growth rates (analogous to productivity) at intermediate population densities than when population size (analogous to standing biomass) is larger, such as equal to carrying capacity (chapter 12).

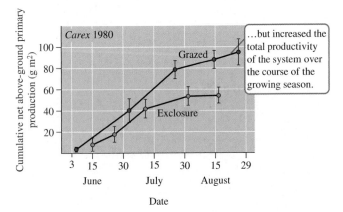

Grazing reduced the amount of plant biomass found at any point in time . . .

...but increased the total productivity of the system over the course of the growing season.

Figure 14.3 Grazing decreased standing biomass, but increased productivity of a sub-arctic wetland (data from Cargill and Jefferies 1984).

Despite this similarity to the logistic growth model, overcompensation seems very counterintuitive. How can plant productivity increase when plants are being consumed? Jefferies and his students have explored this issue, finding this pattern is much more complex than it first appears. David Hik (now at University of Alberta) and Jefferies conducted an experiment designed to understand why overcompensation occurs (Hik and Jefferies 1990). Researchers quickly zeroed in on three ideas that could influence plant recovery. (1) Not all grazing is of the same potential impact to the plant. Minor grazing could be beneficial if herbivores consumed dead/dying parts of the plant, increasing light availability to the rest of the plant. At high levels of herbivory, however, herbivores may consume the whole plant, with negative impact. (2) Grazers don't only eat, they also defecate. As a result, the geese may be converting nitrogen into a form that plants can take up, stimulating growth. (3) Plants may be more vulnerable to grazing at different times of the year, and early-season grazing may give plants the most opportunity to recover.

Hik and Jefferies conducted a series of experiments where they manipulated the duration of grazing, removed feces from the experimental plots (yes, that couldn't have been fun!), and altered the timing of herbivory. To do this, they used *enclosures*, rather than exclosures. The difference here is that they added geese inside the enclosures, permitting them to graze

for known durations during different times of year, thereby controlling the level of herbivory experienced by the plants. To manipulate nutrient remobilization, they removed feces by hand from several plots. They found that overall productivity increased in response to light grazing and when feces were present. This response was greatest early in the summer, and absent later. When the plants were grazed heavily, growth was reduced. When feces were removed, growth was reduced. When herbivory happened late in the season, plants couldn't recover. In short, overcompensation only occurred if a very narrow set of conditions were met. If these conditions were not met, herbivory reduced primary productivity.

One may think of this as a nice story about the balance of nature, and how these geese are able to coexist with their food resources, increasing the production of the food they depend upon, with all members living happily ever after. Unfortunately, no matter what we might have learned from the movie *Avatar*, nature doesn't work like that. The "balance" that may have once existed between the geese and their food has now mostly collapsed. Peter Kotanen, from the University of Toronto, and Jefferies have shown that there has been a significant shift in the dynamics of this plant–animal interaction in much of the sub-arctic wetland (Kotanen and Jefferies 1997). At the heart of this change has been rapid population growth of geese; the numbers of breeding pairs of lesser snow geese at La Pérouse Bay increased from less than 2,000 in 1968 to over 20,000 in 1990. This population growth has a variety of causes, though it is primarily driven by decreased mortality on the geese's wintering grounds in the United States, due to increased food availability in agricultural fields and reduced hunting activity. As you might imagine, this population growth has resulted in an increase in the intensity of grazing in the breeding grounds. Knowing what we do through the work of Hik and Jefferies, it should come as no surprise that during this period there has been nearly a 65% decrease in the abundances of *Puccinellia* and *Carex*, two of the dominant plant species. In their place have emerged carpets of moss, plants the geese do not eat, and large expanses of completely devegetated soil (fig. 14.4). In other words, changes in human

Figure 14.4 Rapid population growth of geese has resulted in extensive areas of La Pérouse Bay becoming devegetated.

behaviour and agricultural practices thousands of kilometres away have significant consequences for a very local ecological interaction.

These studies by Jefferies and his colleagues show that herbivory isn't inherently bad for plant growth. Instead, its effects will depend upon a variety of issues such as nutrient relations, plant phenology, and the intensity of the grazing event. Next we show, in a different system, how the same issues can impact the food resources available for the herbivore.

An Herbivorous Stream Insect and Its Algal Food

Exploitative interactions have the potential to influence prey and host populations. Gary Lamberti and Vincent Resh (1983) studied the influence of an herbivorous stream insect on the algal and bacterial populations upon which it feeds. The herbivorous insect was the larval stage of the caddisfly (order Trichoptera), *Helicopsyche borealis*. This insect inhabits streams across most of North America and is most notable for the type of portable shelter it builds as a larva. The larvae cement sand grains together to form a helical portable home that looks just like a small snail shell. In fact, the species was originally described as a freshwater snail. Larval *Helicopsyche* graze on the algae and bacteria growing on the exposed surfaces of submerged stones. This feeding habit requires that *Helicopsyche* spend considerable time out in the open, where it would be far more vulnerable to predators were it not for its case.

Lamberti and Resh found that larval *Helicopsyche* grow and develop through the summer and fall, attaining densities of over 4,000 individuals per square metre in Big Sulphur Creek, California. At this density, they make up about 25% of the total biomass of benthic animals. A consumer that reaches such high population densities clearly has the potential to reduce the density of its food supply. Lamberti and Resh got an indication of the potential of *Helicopsyche* to influence its food supply in a preliminary experiment. In this first experiment they placed unglazed ceramic tiles (15.2 cm × 7.6 cm) on the bottom of the creek and observed the colonization of these artificial substrates by algae and *Helicopsyche* over a period of seven weeks.

Algae rapidly colonized the tiles, reaching peak density two weeks after the tiles were placed in Big Sulphur Creek. The *Helicopsyche* population reached its highest density one week later. Algal biomass decreased from week two to week five of the study and then rose again during the last two weeks, as *Helicopsyche* numbers declined. These results (fig. 14.5) suggest that the caddisfly larvae depleted their food supply. However, Lamberti and Resh could not be certain. Why is that? First, there are many other benthic invertebrates living in Big Sulphur Creek, some of which might be depleting the algal populations. Second, physical factors could have changed during the seven weeks of the study, and these changes could have produced the fluctuations in both algal and *Helicopsyche* populations. This initial experiment provided valuable indications but was not a definitive test.

In a follow-up study, the researchers used an exclusion experiment to test for the effect of *Helicopsyche* on its food supply. They placed unglazed ceramic tiles in two 3-by-6

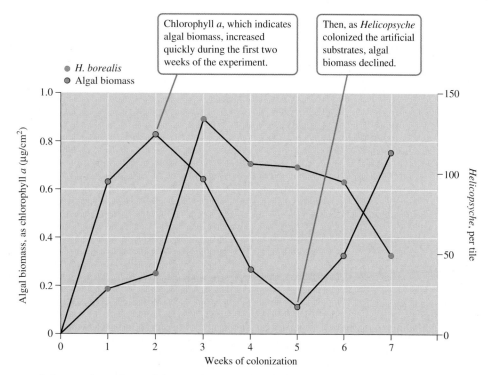

Figure 14.5   Biomass of algae and numbers of the grazing caddisfly *Helicopsyche borealis* (data from Lamberti and Resh 1983).

grids of 18 tiles each. One grid was placed directly on the stream bottom, while the other was placed on a metal plate supported by an upside-down J-shaped metal bar. This arrangement, which raised the tiles 15 cm above the bottom but still 35 cm below the stream surface, allowed colonization of tiles by algae and most invertebrates, while preventing colonization by *Helicopsyche*. *Helicopsyche* could not colonize the tiles because their heavy snail-shaped case confines them to the stream bottom. To reach the tiles, *Helicopsyche* would have to crawl up the J-shaped support bar, out of the water, and then back down, while most other invertebrates could colonize by either drifting downstream with the current or by swimming to the raised tiles. Lamberti and Resh coated the above-water parts of the bar with an adhesive to prevent adult *Helicopsyche* from crawling down to the tiles to deposit their eggs. This design was effective at excluding *Helicopsyche* while allowing large numbers of other invertebrates to colonize the raised tiles.

The results of this experiment show that *Helicopsyche* reduces the abundance of its food supply. Figure 14.6 shows that the tiles without *Helicopsyche* supported higher abundances of both algae and bacteria. The large effect of *Helicopsyche* on its food supply is apparent from paired photos of the experimental and control tiles at the beginning and the end of the experiment (fig. 14.7).

Herbivory is common in terrestrial and aquatic systems across the planet. Given that herbivory is widespread and generally has negative consequences for the plant, it should come as no surprise that natural selection has favoured a variety of traits that allow plants to defend themselves. The idea that plants are passive recipients of whatever ecological challenges they face is woefully out of date. As you will see next, a diversity of defences are actively and passively employed by plants.

Plant Defences

Plants are not passive creatures that simply exist to be eaten by others. These organisms are subject to natural selection, just like every other living thing on this planet. If being eaten reduces the reproductive output and/or survival of an organism, there can be selection for traits that result in the individual either being less likely to be eaten (*resistance*) or that reduce the harm associated with being eaten (*tolerance*). For example, imagine there is a caterpillar that can eat only one species of plant. When it finds the plant, it will consume a large portion of the leaves, reducing the plant's photosynthetic capacity and potential to produce seeds. Some aspects of this interaction are likely related to genotype, and with genetic variation in the plant population, there can be variation in the fitness consequences of this association. Some plants may produce a toxin that reduces feeding, others may grow smaller and be harder to find, while still others may produce leaves of low nutritive value, decreasing the cost of replacement. These are examples of possible adaptations that increase the resistance to exploitation or increase the ability of the organism to tolerate exploitation. As you might recognize, these changes would then have impacts on the herbivore, potentially resulting in a co-evolutionary response (See Ecological Tools and Approaches).

In this section we will discuss common mechanisms of plant defence. We will also discuss some evolutionary consequences

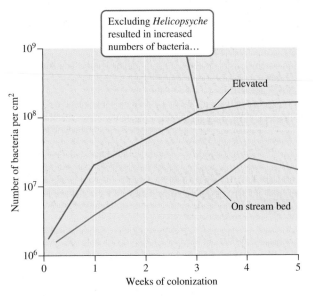

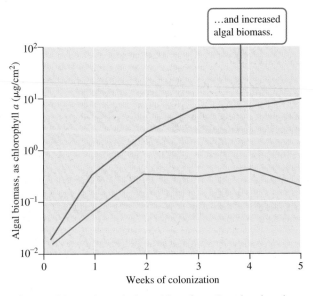

Figure 14.6 Influence of excluding *Helicopsyche borealis* on abundance of bacteria and algae (data from Lamberti and Resh 1983).

(a)

(b)

Figure 14.7   Effects of excluding *Helicopsyche borealis* on benthic algal biomass: (*a*) two sets of tiles at the beginning of experiment; exclusion tiles in foreground; (*b*) same tiles five weeks into the experiment.

of long-term herbivore–host relationships, further demonstrating that ecological interactions have the potential to profoundly alter species, populations, and communities.

Warning colouration (see later in the chapter) is common among animals, but it is generally absent among the leaves of plants. Why don't plants colour their leaves to warn herbivores that dangers may lie within? Wouldn't plants be better off scaring away an herbivore then letting that animal take even one bite? Certainly plants have the capacity to produce different colours, as various pigments are critical to attracting pollinators to assist with plant reproduction. The most obvious explanation for why such pigments tend to be restricted (or at least most abundant) in flowers has to do with photosynthesis. Plants use chlorophyll to absorb most of the light used in photosynthesis, and this pigment reflects green light, absorbing reds and blues. To reduce chlorophyll content (to allow some red and blue reflection) would reduce

photosynthetic capacity, likely causing a greater loss of fitness than would be experienced by some degree of herbivory. However, just because plants don't use colouration as a warning doesn't mean that they are just sitting there waiting to be eaten. In fact, many plants are simply bad food for many animals.

We have already discussed how plants have high C:N ratios (chapter 7), resulting in a low nutritive value for animals that need nitrogen for growth and reproduction. Maintaining relatively low-value leaves may itself be seen as one defence against herbivores, though certainly herbivory is not the only cause of a plant's C:N ratios. One consequence of poor nutrition in any given leaf is that for an herbivore to obtain sufficient nitrogen for their own growth, they will need to consume large amounts of plant tissues. As a result, herbivores are forced to come in contact with many other defences employed by the plants.

ECOLOGY IN ACTION

Invasive Species and Exploitative Relationships

One of the most ecologically damaging activities that humans regularly engage in is the intentional and accidental release of organisms into novel habitats. These activities occur through the introduction of new horticultural plants, in ballast water released near shore, as contaminants to imported agricultural products, and as simple stowaways in our cars and backpacks as we leave our houses for cottages or decide to see how long it really takes to travel from St. John's to Nanaimo. Most of these **introduced** (i.e., **exotic** or **non-native**) **species** will quickly flounder before they establish a sustainable population. Perhaps the new home is too hot, too cold, or too crowded. Others will establish and maintain small populations, being simply another minor component of a complex ecological system. In fact, nearly one-third of all vascular plant species in Canada are non-native. A small subset of introduced species will not only establish populations, but rapidly expand, reducing the abundance and diversity of the pre-existing native species. These **invasive species** are an issue of global concern (Mack et al. 2000). Ecologists throughout the world are actively pursuing research designed to understand both the causes of species invasion and potential ways to control their spread.

What allows introduced species to establish in novel habitats? What allows some introduced species to become invasive and spread? In a classic view of ecological systems, ecologists have often thought of all species as being essential components to the system, where bending one part will cause bends elsewhere. In this model, the community was also viewed as closed, where all the available niches were full and competitive exclusion (chapter 13) would keep out new species. We realize now that this model was woefully incorrect. Introduced species are able to establish in nearly every ecological community across the planet. How is this possible? Why don't the regular processes of exploitation and resource limitation keep these species in check? We will discuss here the "enemy release hypothesis," one of several explanations for the spread of species into new communities.

One of the interesting findings that researchers have uncovered is that many species that spread in novel habitats are typically relatively minor members of the community in their native environments. The enemy release hypothesis suggests that at home, population growth is reduced due to exploitation. In new habitats, these species do not bring with them their native predators and herbivores, nor are they eaten extensively by the predators and herbivores in their new home, and thus their populations grow, restricted only by resources. Making things even worse is that with enemy release, organisms may grow a bit bigger and have increased vigour, making them better able to compete with the native

organisms. In other words, by not bringing along their pests, these new species do not suffer the costs of exploitation, and may actually accrue the benefit of increased competitive ability. But does this really occur?

Peter Kotanen (see earlier in this chapter) and his colleague Anurag Agrawal were skeptical of this idea. They conducted a large field experiment at the Koffler Scientific Reserve at Jokers Hill, about an hour away from campus (Agrawal and Kotanen 2003). They planted seeds of 30 plant species into a ploughed field, measuring rates of herbivory on each plant at the end of the growing season. Making this study particularly well-designed is that these species were divided into different pairs of congeneric species, such that within each pair, one species was native to Joker's Hill and its congener was introduced. By using this taxonomic pairing, they controlled for a variety of confounding effects that could be associated with differences among species. In contrast with the enemy release hypothesis, they found that leaf damage by herbivores was about 40% higher on exotic species compared to their native relatives! Importantly, they also found that overall levels of herbivory were low (around 6% leaf damage). They suggest that not only is the pattern opposite to that which was predicted, the low magnitude of leaf damage suggests that herbivory itself is not a significant stressor on most of the species they tested. In other words, if herbivory doesn't hurt plants too much, being released from herbivory is not likely to be of much benefit.

A similar result was found by Michael Stastny while he was an undergraduate student with Elizabeth Elle of Simon Fraser University (Stastny et al. 2005). They conducted an experiment in Switzerland with the plant *Senecio jacobaea* that is native to much of Europe. *Senecio* has been introduced and has become invasive to rangelands throughout North America, Australia, and New Zealand. The researchers were interested in whether the genotypes that invaded new habitats were less susceptible to damage by the specialist herbivore, *Longitarsus jacobaeae*, a flea beetle (fig. 14.8), than the genotypes commonly found in the native habitat. To do this, they collected seed from eight populations of *Senecio* from their introduced and native ranges. The plants were then planted into a meadow in Switzerland, where *Senecio* and *Longitarsus* naturally occur. They measured herbivory and growth of the plants throughout the growing season. They found that the introduced genotypes grew larger, had greater reproductive output, *and* were eaten more than the native genotypes. These results also are not consistent with the enemy release hypothesis, and instead suggest that invasive genotypes are likely to be larger and better competitors than native ones. The researchers suggest that the increased vigour of the introduced species allows them to tolerate the increased levels of

(a)

Figure 14.8
(a) Senecio jacobaea;
(b) Longitarsus jacobaeae.

(b)

effects are changes to species other than the intended invasive target. It may come as no surprise that there is substantial divide amongst ecologists as to whether biocontrol is an environmentally responsible, or reckless, idea (Louda et al. 2003). On one side, proponents of biocontrol programs point out that once an agent is identified, it is inexpensive to use, self-replicates, and reduces the need to use potentially toxic compounds. There is also substantial evidence that biocontrol can be effective in reducing populations of many species.

In a recent review of the effects of herbivores on plant population growth, John Maron and Elizabeth Crone (formerly of the University of Calgary) report that biocontrol agents have a seven times stronger negative effect on plant population growth than do native herbivores (Maron and Crone 2006). Clearly, biocontrol agents can be effective in reduced plant growth. However, there are serious ecological risks associated with using biocontrol agents (Louda et al. 2003), including: (1) substantial evidence indicating that relatives of the target species are also likely to be attacked, including endangered native species; (2) biocontrol agents can have undesired cascading effects on the trophic dynamics of ecological communities; and (3) in many cases, exploitation is not of a magnitude sufficient to cause declines in abundance of the invasive species. In other words, if, as in the examples above, enemy release is not the driver of a species' spread, it is unlikely that the introduction of an enemy will slow it down. Finally, there is often a difference of goals, with many biocontrol agents designed to tackle agricultural pests, where success is measured as reduction in weed densities and increased crop yield, while many ecologists are concerned about what happens when these organisms spread outside the fields and into native communities.

Understanding the causes of species invasion, as well as mechanisms of control, is a critical issue for the current and next generation of ecologists. By identifying which aspects of a species' life history limits, or encourages, population growth, one may be able to design more appropriate control measures. However, it is clear that the world isn't as simple as saying that enemies control growth. The outcome of one interaction is dependent upon other interactions, and only by understanding these connections can we hope to learn how to control species invasion.

herbivory, which, as in the Agrawal and Kotanen study, are thought not to be of a magnitude great enough to reduce fitness. This is another example of the importance of both understanding the diversity of ecological interactions that individuals encounter, and not assuming that increased levels of herbivory will necessarily reduce plant fitness.

These findings have very significant implications for the management of invasive species in natural and managed systems. Invasive species can be managed in a variety of ways, including ignoring them, mechanical removal (i.e., weeding), herbicides, and **biocontrol**. Biocontrol is the deliberate introduction of some agent (herbivore, pathogen, etc.) that will exploit an invasive species, reducing its population size. You can see that the ideas presented in this chapter lend some support to this approach: under some conditions, exploitation can reduce population growth. However, you likely also recognize that information in this chapter raises significant questions about how effective these programs will be, and whether there will be any **nontarget effects**. Nontarget

Many plants also possess a variety of morphological defences, such as thorns, which deter herbivores (fig. 14.9). These defences are generally small and non-lethal—an irritant rather than a real risk to the large herbivores they deter. Why do thorns reduce herbivory? As we discussed previously (chapter 7), animals engage in some sort of optimal foraging in which they increase energy (or nutrition) uptake per unit time. To eat a thorny plant, the animal will need to move its head and body more precisely, which slows down the rate of feeding. It may be more energetically advantageous for the animal to keep walking and find a less prickly bush than to stop walking and feed

slowly. In other words, thorns work as defences because plants are able to use animal behaviour to their own advantage.

Although morphological defences are widespread among plants, plants also contain a variety of chemical defences that can be roughly divided as (1) toxins, and (2) digestion-reducing substances. Toxins are chemicals that kill, impair, or repel most would-be herbivores. The compounds are widely used by humans as medicines, and include such compounds as cocaine, morphine, digitalis, and others. Digestion-reducing substances are generally phenolic compounds, such as tannins, that bind to plant proteins and inhibit their breakdown

Figure 14.9 Herbivores must overcome the wide variety of physical and chemical defences evolved by plants.

by digestive enzymes. This in turn further reduces the value of plants as food for the herbivore. Humans are familiar with tannins as the bitter taste one gets when eating an unripe banana, or as the dark colouration in a cup of Earl Grey tea.

Chemists have isolated thousands of toxins from plant tissues, and the list continues to grow. The great variety of plant toxins defies easy description and generalization. However, one interesting pattern is that more tropical plants contain toxic alkaloids than their temperate counterparts. Despite these higher levels of chemical defence, herbivores appear to remove approximately 11%–48% of leaf biomass in tropical forests, while only about 7% in temperate forests. These higher levels of herbivore attack on tropical plants suggest that natural selection for chemical defence is more intense in tropical plant populations. However, clearly no defence is perfect.

Plant chemical defences often work against some herbivores, but not all. The tobacco plant uses nicotine, a toxic alkaloid, to repel herbivorous insects, most of which die immediately upon ingestion. However, several insects specialize in eating tobacco plants and manage to avoid the toxic effects of nicotine. Unfortunately, humans do not fall into this group of specialist insects, and thus the health consequences of regular ingestion of this toxic plant are readily apparent. Some of the specialist insects avoid such harm by excreting nicotine, while others convert it to nontoxic molecules. Similarly, toxins and repellents produced by plants in the cucumber family repel most herbivorous insects but attract the spotted cucumber beetle. This beetle is a specialist that feeds mainly on members of the cucumber family. Some specialized herbivores go even further by using plant toxins as a source of nutrition. Even more amazing is that some species, such as the Monarch butterfly and the dogbane leaf beetle, are able to sequester plant toxins, using these as chemical deterrents against their own natural enemies, such as predators.

As we have seen with competition and foraging, plants are able to alter their physiology and morphology in response to changes in their environment, such as the deposition of a nutrient patch or the presence of a competitor. Plants show similar plasticity in response to herbivores. Many morphological and

chemical defences are **constitutive defences**, produced continuously, independent of what happens to a plant. Many, however, are also **induced defences**, where concentrations of defensive chemicals (or even morphological defenses) increase rapidly in response to the first indication of herbivore damage. Such induced defences make sense in the context of the theory of allocation, where allocating energy and limited resources to defences when insects are not around seems maladaptive. It seems likely that the benefit of producing constitutive or induced defences will depend upon the likelihood of a plant being attacked.

The world may appear green to us, but to herbivores only some shades of green are edible. Plant defences and the adaptations of herbivores that overcome those defences are complex.

CONCEPT 14.1 REVIEW

1. How can geese cause an increase in productivity but a decrease in standing biomass in La Pérouse Bay?
2. In many natural communities there are numerous herbivorous species that feed simultaneously. How did Lamberti and Resh determine the specific effects of *Helicopsyche* on algal biomass?
3. Plants can possess traits that make them resistant to herbivores, or tolerant of herbivory. Are the same plant traits likely to confer both of these abilities? Why?

14.2 Impacts of Predators on Prey Populations

Prey populations are influenced by food availability, by consumption by predators, and by non-consumptive effects of predators. In the previous section we saw how herbivores can affect the plants they feed upon, with the plants also impacting the herbivores. In this section we move to understanding the interactions between predators and their prey. We will begin with an overview of a landmark experiment led by Canadian researchers. We then discuss more general aspects of both the effects predators can have on prey populations, including both consumptive and non-consumptive effects. We now look to the north, where the population sizes of many animals appear to cycle, sparking decades of ecological research on predation.

Cycles of Abundance in Snowshoe Hares and Their Predators

Population cycles are well documented for a wide variety of animals living at high latitudes, including lemmings, voles, muskrats, red fox, arctic fox, ruffed grouse, and porcupines. We have already seen (in chapter 11) how periodic outbreaks of voles lead to local increases in the abundance of avian

Figure 14.10 Lynx–hare interactions have served as a model system for the study of the effects of predation on population dynamics.

predators due to *numerical responses* by owls and hawks (Korpimäki and Norrdahl 1991), and in chapter 12 we talked about how Adolph Murie was hired to determine what effect wolves were having an Dall Sheep populations in Alaska. There has been a long history in ecology of studying how predation would alter prey populations.

One of the best-studied cases of animal population cycles is that of the snowshoe hare, *Lepus americanus*, and the lynx, *Lynx canadensis*, one of the snowshoe hare's chief predators (fig. 14.10). The population cycles of these two species are especially well documented because the Hudson Bay Company kept trapping records during most of the eighteenth, nineteenth, and twentieth centuries. Drawing on this unique historical record, ecologists were able to estimate the relative abundances of Canada lynx and snowshoe hare over a period of about 200 years. That record, shown in figure 14.11, demonstrates a remarkable match in the cycles of the two populations.

The regularity of the pattern struck the imagination of many ecologists, and several hypotheses were proposed to explain these and other cycles among northern populations. One of the first ideas was from Charles Elton (1924), who thought the system was driven by plants, not predators. He proposed that variation in intensity of solar radiation, associated with sunspot cycles, altered plant growth, directly affecting snowshoe hares, and that lynx populations then responded to the changing abundance of the snowshoe hare, their main prey. The sunspot hypothesis was rejected by D. MacLulich (1937) and P. Moran (1949), who showed that sunspot cycles do not match snowshoe hare population cycles.

The second group of hypotheses, which Lloyd Keith (1963) referred to as "overpopulation theories," suggested that periods of high population growth are followed by (1) decimation by disease and parasitism, (2) physiological stress at high densities leading to increased mortality as a consequence of nervous disorders, and (3) starvation due to reduced quantity and quality of food at high population densities. An alternative to the overpopulation hypothesis was that population cycles are driven by predators. According to this hypothesis, predators increase in number in response to increasing prey availability and then eventually reduce prey populations.

Keith observed that none of these hypotheses completely accounts for population cycles in snowshoe hare and other northern populations. He went on to say, "the 10-year cycle is not likely to become better understood by further theorizing. Clearly the present need is for comprehensive long-term investigations by a diversified team of specialists." As you will see, population cycles of predators and prey occur through a number of co-occurring mechanisms.

The Role of Food Supply

Snowshoe hares live in the boreal forests of North America, an area dominated by a variety of coniferous and deciduous trees (chapter 2). Within the boreal forest, snowshoe hares associate with dense growths of understory shrubs, which provide both cover and winter food, the most critical portion of the snowshoe hare's food supply.

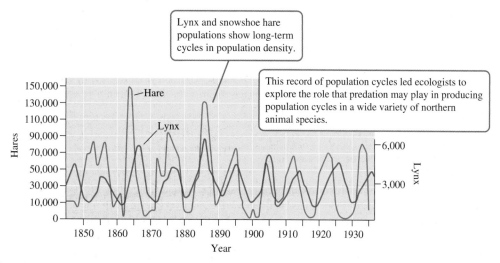

Figure 14.11 Historical fluctuations in lynx and snowshoe hare populations based on the number of pelts purchased by the Hudson Bay Company (data from MacLulich 1937).

Hares can "breed like rabbits," with estimated geometric rate of increases (chapter 11) during the growth phase of a hare population cycle averaging as high as 2.0. In other words, snowshoe hare populations can double in size each generation. As a result of potentially high growth rates, snowshoe hares have the potential to reduce the quantity and quality of their food supply.

Local population densities are highly dynamic. Keith cites 100-fold fluctuations in snowshoe hare densities in some areas and found 10- to 30-fold fluctuations to be common. Snowshoe hares spend the long northern winter (six to eight months) browsing on the buds and small stems of shrubs and tree saplings. The most nutritious portions of these shrubs and trees are the small stems (< 4–5 mm diameter). Over the winter, each hare requires about 300 g of these stems each day. In some areas, however, snowshoe hares have been observed to remove over 1,500 g of food biomass per day. Feeding at these rates, one population of snowshoe hares reduced food biomass from 530 kg per hectare in late November to 160 kg per hectare by late March. Many ecologists have demonstrated food shortages during winters of peak snowshoe hare density.

Snowshoe hares also influence the quality of their food supply. Feeding by snowshoe hares induces chemical defences in their food plants, like those we discussed previously in this chapter. Shoots produced after browsing contain elevated concentrations of terpene and phenolic resins, defensive chemicals that repel mammals. Elevated concentrations of plant defensive chemicals can persist for up to two years after browsing by hares, reducing *usable* food supplies for the hare during the population decline.

The Role of Predators

The long historical record of lynx population cycles may have distracted ecologists from the fact that lynxes are only one of several predators that feed on snowshoe hares. Other major predators of snowshoe hares include goshawks, *Accipiter gentilis*, great horned owls, *Bubo virginianus*, mink, *Mustela vison*, long-tailed weasels, *Mustela frenata*, red foxes, *Vulpes vulpes*, and coyotes, *Canis latrans*. Populations of these predators are known to cycle synchronously with snowshoe hare populations. Though the lynx is a specialist on snowshoe hares, the diet of a generalist predator such as the coyote may also depend heavily on snowshoe hares. This is particularly true when snowshoe hare populations are at peak density. Arlen Todd and Lloyd Keith (1983) report that snowshoe hares made up 67% of the coyote diets in central Alberta. Ecologists have estimated that predation by this diverse group of predators may account for 60% to 90% of snowshoe hare mortality during peak densities.

Research by a team of ecologists from British Columbia, Alaska, the Yukon, Alberta, and Argentina (O'Donoghue et al. 1997, 1998) provides clear evidence of *functional* and *numerical responses* to increased hare densities. You may recall from chapter 7 that a functional response relates the density of prey (x-axis) to the feeding rate of a predator (y-axis). O'Donoghue and colleagues found that lynx killed more hares when hare

numbers were declining, while coyotes showed higher predation rates when the hare population was increasing. Further, lynx show a clear type 2 functional response to increasing hare densities, reaching a maximum predation rate of 1.2 hares per day (per lynx). This maximum occurs at intermediate hare densities, such that further increases in hares have no effect on how many hares an individual lynx can predate. In contrast, over the range of hare densities they observed, coyote show type 1 functional response, with a predation rate of 2.3 hares per day (per coyote) at the highest hare densities. Even at that level, the coyote functional response showed no signs of levelling off. At high hare densities, coyote and lynx predation rates greatly exceeded their daily energetic needs. Coyotes killed more hares early in the winter, caching many and retrieving them later in the season.

In chapter 10 we first mentioned *numerical responses*, which describe how predator populations increase in relation to prey population increases. Increases in predator populations can be due to two major mechanisms: (1) movement of more predators into areas where more prey are found (i.e., immigration rates increase), and (2) increased reproductive rates of predators due to increases food availability (i.e., birth rates increase). O'Donoghue and his colleagues found both coyote and lynx demonstrated significant numerical responses to hare populations, with six- to sevenfold more predators present when hares were at high density than at low hare density. As both per-capita feeding rates and predator population sizes increase with increasing hare densities, O'Donoghue and colleagues demonstrate there is great potential for lynx and coyote to have strongly negative effects on high-density snowshoe hare populations.

In summary, several decades of research provided evidence that both predation and food can make substantial contributions to snowshoe hare population cycles (Haukioja et al. 1983, Keith 1983, Keith et al. 1984). The food availability and predation hypotheses are complementary, not mutually exclusive, alternatives. As hare populations increase, they reduce the quantity and quality of their food supply. Reduced food availability, which leads to starvation and weight loss, would itself likely produce population decline. This potential decline is ensured and accelerated by high rates of mortality due to predation. As hare population density is reduced, predator populations decline in turn, plant populations recover, and the stage is set for another increase in the hare population. This scenario was tested through a series of long-term experiments.

Experimental Test of Food and Predation Impacts

Charles J. Krebs, now an emeritus professor at the University of British Columbia, along with several colleagues from UBC, University of Alberta, and the University of Toronto (Krebs et al. 1995) conducted a large-scale, long-term experiment designed to sort out the tangle of conflicting evidence regarding the impacts of food and predation on snowshoe hare population cycles. Over a period of eight years, Krebs and colleagues conducted one of the most ambitious field experiments

to date. This project is on the scale of the large experiments conducted by David Schindler at the experimental lakes area (chapter 1), and will certainly be remembered by ecologists as a project of grand objectives and strong science. As a sign of the scope of the project, the main findings of the study are best absorbed as a book (Krebs, Boutin, and Boonstra 2001), rather than simply a series of individual papers.

What do we mean by a large experiment? In this study, each experimental plot was a 1 km² block of undisturbed boreal forest near Kluane, Yukon. In total they used nine such blocks, each separated from other experimental blocks by a minimum of 1 km. Three blocks served as controls, and were left unmanipulated. To test whether food availability limited hare densities, hares were given unlimited supplemental food in two experimental blocks during the entire period of the study. To test whether plant tissue quality limited hare numbers, the researchers applied a nitrogen-potassium-phosphorus fertilizer from the air to two of the experimental blocks. To explore the role of predators on hare numbers, they built electric fences around two of the 1 km² blocks, which excluded mammalian predators (but not hawks and owls). One of these predator reduction blocks also received supplemental food. The fences on both predator reduction areas (8 km of fence) had to be checked every day through the winter, when temperatures would sometimes dip as low as −45°C. Krebs' research team maintained these experimental conditions through one full cycle of snowshoe hare numbers. Due to maintenance requirements (and limited budget) of such a large project, they could not replicate the predator reduction and predator reduction + food experimental manipulations.

During the eight years of the experiment, the researchers observed an increase in hare numbers to a peak, followed by a decline on all the study plots, regardless of the treatments imposed. However, the treatments had diverse effects on the magnitude and duration of these peaks. For example, fertilizer application increased plant growth, but did not increase the numbers of snowshoe hares. However, hare numbers increased substantially in the food addition, predator reduction, and predator reduction + food addition plots. Averaged over the peak and decline phases of the study, reducing predators doubled hare density, adding food tripled hare density, and excluding predators and adding food increased hare density to 11 times that of the control plots (fig. 14.12). Krebs and his colleagues found that these higher hare densities were the result of both increased per-capita rates of survival and reproduction.

After approximately 70 years of research, we can conclude that the population cycle of snowshoe hares is the result of an interaction between three trophic levels: the hares, the plants upon which they feed, and the predators that feed upon them. In other words, different forms of exploitation interact to create the cycles of hares that have puzzled scientists for decades.

Krebs and colleagues (2001) point out that to understand the controls on hare numbers, researchers have had to work with all three trophic levels simultaneously. In addition, the critical experiment had to be done on a large scale and in

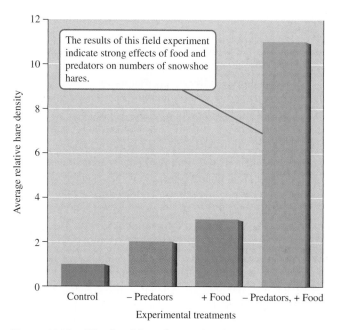

Figure 14.12   The densities of snowshoe hares averaged from the peak in hare density through the period of declining density observed during the study. Hare densities are expressed relative to the densities on the control plots where no experimental manipulation was applied (data from Krebs et al. 1995, 2001).

the field. Still, this experiment leaves a number of questions unanswered, such as why does artificial rabbit food increase hare densities but increased natural food (plants) does not? Perhaps an even more interesting set of questions comes when one recognizes that predators do much more to prey than kill them. Fear itself matters.

Non-Consumptive Effects of Predators: The Ecology of Fear

I may be unusual in a number of respects, but I would imagine that if I were a hare munching away on my favourite type of willow and were to see a lynx running toward me, a number of things would likely happen. First, I would "drop pellets," and then I would run, hop, bounce, or whatever it is hares do. At least some of the time I and my fellow hares would escape, with the lynx going away hungry. At other times while feeding I may again see a lynx on the hunt, this time chasing other hares in the population, rather than myself. That, too, is likely to get my heart rate up, and get me moving away. Such a situation is not unique to imaginary anthropomorphized hares, and instead appears to be widespread among prey. Even when predation is successful, predators only kill and consume a fraction of the entire prey population. As a result, the direct **consumptive effects of predation** influence only a small number of prey at any particular point in time. Consumptive effects of predation are the direct effects that predators have on prey populations through the capture and consumption of living prey. This is what Lord Alfred Tennyson was commenting on in his famous line, "nature, red in tooth and

claw" (Tennyson, "In Memoriam A.H.H.," canto 56). But predators do much more than kill, and there is evidence that **nonconsumptive effects of predation** have significant consequences on prey population dynamics.

Nonconsumptive effects of predators are those changes to the prey that occur as a consequence of predators being present, even when the prey are not killed. These changes include shifts in morphological traits, stress-physiology, and altered behaviour. Because it is easy to imagine how we ourselves would feel when chased by a predator, or even when knowing predators are around, the study of these nonconsumptive effects of predation is commonly referred to as "the ecology of fear." This phrase was first applied to natural systems by Joel Brown and colleagues (Brown et al. 1999), and has led to a renewed interest in predator–prey dynamics. Though we have no idea whether prey actually feel fear, we do know that the presence of a predator causes biologically significant effects on prey populations. A team of researchers, including Peter Abrams of the University of Toronto and Larry Dill of Simon Fraser University, have called on textbook authors to include this material in discussions of predator–prey interactions (Peckarsky et al. 2008). And so, not wanting to disappoint these colleagues, we now return to the snowshoe hare and look more closely at the effects of predators.

Rudy Boonstra, of the University of Toronto, was interested in whether the hares exhibited stress in response to predators, and whether this could influence population cycling. Boonstra and colleagues (Boonstra et al. 1998) worked within the larger lynx-hare experiment described above, focusing primarily on the hares during the decline phase of their population cycle. During this population decline, nearly every hare in the control plots that died was killed by a predator, suggesting that most hares see predators occasionally, and thus "fear" is likely rampant throughout the hare population. The research team recognized that stress can cause predictable physiological responses, often indicated by shifts in blood cortisol levels and general shifts in hormonal physiology. Over time, prolonged stress can lead to changes in a number of factors related to fitness, including reproduction rate and survival (fig. 14.13). To test this, the research team collected blood samples from hares during different years of the decline (early versus late) and from the plots with predators and those without.

The results Boonstra found were convincing. Blood cortisol levels were higher in hares when predation rates were high than in a year with lower predation. They were also higher in plots in which predators were present than when predators were experimentally removed. In other words, hares were exhibiting the physiological signature of stress, due to the presence of predators, well before they died. Boonstra had evidence that this chronic stress had negative impacts on the hares, as female hares exposed to predators had reduced reproductive rates, among other changes (Boonstra et al. 1998). These results suggest that in addition to the consumptive effects that predators would have on hare populations, these non-consumptive effects would cause an even faster drop in hare populations. In other words, the predators seem to be causing both increases

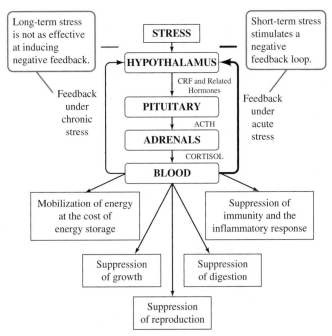

Figure 14.13 Mammals possess a number of physiological pathways related to stress. One example is the hypothalamic-pituitary-adrenal feedback system, commonly associated with "fight or flight" responses. Under acute (short-term) stress there are a series of physiological changes starting in the hypothalamus that lead to changes in blood chemistry and short-term effects on other body processes. Chronic stress (long-term) results in a breakdown in this feedback system, with potentially negative fitness consequences (from Boonstra et al. 1998).

in hare per-capita rates of mortality *and* decreases in per-capita birth rates. Evidence of non-consumptive effects of predators on prey have now become common in the literature, in both terrestrial and aquatic system.

Tiger sharks are a top predator of marine mammals though much of their range, including Shark Bay, Australia (fig. 14.14*b*). Larry Dill and a team of students from Simon Fraser University, along with colleagues around the world, have been studying what role fear may be playing in the behavioural decisions of the shark's potential prey. One common prey are dugongs, *Dugong dugon*, large herbivorous mammals that feed upon seagrass beds (fig. 14.14*a*). Dill and his colleagues found that dugongs altered the location of where they feed as a function of the density of tiger sharks (Wirsing, Heithaus, and Dill 2007). When sharks were relatively absent, the dugongs were more likely to occupy shallow areas of high seagrass density. However, when tiger sharks were more abundant, the dugongs increased their use of the deeper areas, even though food availability was lower. Dill and his colleagues suggest the dugongs are faced with a food vs. safety trade-off, yet another example of a non-consumptive effect of predators.

How important are these non-consumptive effects in general? Surely the direct effects of predators eating prey must be more important in determining prey population dynamics

(a)

(b)

Figure 14.14 Dugongs (*a*) adjust their foraging behaviour as a function of whether or not tiger sharks (*b*) are hunting in the area.

than the indirect effects associated with stress and altered foraging. Not necessarily, though substantially more research is needed. Evan Preisser and colleagues conducted a recent meta-analysis comparing the relative effects of consumptive and non-consumptive effects of predators on prey populations (Preisser et al. 2005). In studies that measured both effects, non-consumptive effects were, on average, approximately equal in magnitude as the more commonly studied consumptive effects. Or put another way, the vast majority of research in predator–prey interactions has focused on one organism eating another. It appears that what happens to those animals not (yet) eaten is just as important if one wants to understand prey population dynamics. There is substantial research to be done, and great opportunities for the next generation of ecologists.

Understanding prey population dynamics is a critical goal of many branches of ecology, with significant societal implications. To do this requires generalization beyond specific cases studies. To achieve this, ecologists again turn to theoretical and laboratory studies for help.

14.3 Predator–Prey Dynamics in a Mathematical Model

The population consequences of exploitative relationships can be explored with theoretical models. As we discussed in chapter 13, mathematical and laboratory models offer ecologists the opportunity to manipulate variables that they cannot control in the field, in an attempt to understand underlying principles about ecological interactions. For example, the Lotka–Volterra competition model contributed to the identification of the competitive exclusion principle and described necessary conditions for species coexistence. As discussed above, predator–prey dynamics in natural systems often cycle through time. If we rip away the specific details of individual systems, can models provide a general explanation for these coupled predator–prey dynamics?

We will begin this section similarly to chapter 13, by viewing predation as a potential "brake" that limits the growth rate of prey. Once again, we find Lotka (1925) and Volterra (1926) independently developing a mathematical solution to the problem of population cycles. Both researchers built their models based on observations of interactions among natural populations. Lotka was impressed by the reciprocal oscillations of populations of moth and butterfly larvae and the parasitoids that attack them. Volterra was inspired by the response of marine fish populations to cessation of fishing during World War I. Volterra observed that the response of fish populations was uneven. Predaceous fish, particularly sharks, increased in abundance, while the populations upon which they fed decreased. This reciprocal change in numbers suggested that predators have the potential to reduce the abundance of their prey. In this single observation, Volterra somehow saw the potential for predator–prey population cycles. With these observations in mind, Lotka and Volterra set out to build mathematical models that would produce the cycles that they thought occurred in nature. It is worth mentioning at the start that in contrast to other models we have presented, the parameters of the Lotka–Volterra predator–prey models are represented by different letters by nearly every researcher and textbook author. We emphasize the key to learning ecological

models is to understand the concepts they represent, rather than focusing solely on the equation. If concepts are learned, then you will be able to understand the model even if different letters are used in different situations. Here we refer to the prey as "H" (you could think "herbivore") and the predator as "P." This model also applies to host–pathogen interactions (chapter 15), though we limit discussion here to predator–prey dynamics.

We start by describing what factors might influence the population growth of the prey. The basic Lotka–Volterra predator–prey model assumes that in the absence of predators, prey populations grow at an exponential rate:

$$\frac{dN_h}{dt} = r_h N_h$$

Here, N_h represents prey population size (h could stand for host, or herbivore) and r_h represents the prey's per capita growth rate (r_{max}). You should see something unusual here, in that this model assumes there is no intraspecific competition among the prey. How do we know this? The base of the equation is the exponential, rather than the logistic, model of population growth. Instead of intraspecific competition, Lotka and Volterra suggested that the prey's population size will be limited by its predators through the inclusion of another set of parameters:

$$\frac{dN_h}{dt} = r_h N_h - b N_h N_p$$

In the Lotka–Volterra model, exponential growth by the host (prey) population is opposed by deaths due to predation, which is represented by $-b N_h N_p$. Again, N_h is the number of hosts, and N_p is the number of predators. The new term, b, is the capture efficiency of the prey by the predators. So, we have one part of the equation describing how many prey are created as a function of per capita prey growth rates multiplied by the number of prey, and a second part that describes how many prey are killed by predators as the product of the frequency of encounters between predator and prey ($N_h N_p$) and the proportion of those encounters that result in prey death (b).

The Lotka–Volterra model assumes that the rate of growth by the predator population is determined by the rate at which it converts the hosts it consumes into offspring (new predators) minus the predator's per capita mortality rate:

$$\frac{dN_p}{dt} = cb N_h N_p - d_p N_p$$

Here again, N_h and N_p are the numbers of hosts and predators respectively. The rate at which the predators convert hosts into offspring is $cb N_h N_p$. This term is the product of the number of prey killed by the predator as described in the prior equation ($b N_h N_p$) multiplied by a new term, c. c represents a conversion factor of how many dead prey it takes to create one new predator. For example, if five prey need to be consumed to create one new predator, $c = 0.20$. The growth rate of the predator population is opposed by predator deaths, $d_p N_p$, where d_p represents the per-capita death rate of the predators. Once again, Lotka and Volterra have assumed no intraspecific competition among the predators, as per-capita death rates are a

constant. Thus in these models, prey densities are determined by predator numbers along with some constants, and predator densities are determined by prey densities, along with some constants. The Lotka–Volterra predator–prey model is summarized in figure 14.15.

Now let's reflect on the behaviour of this model. To do this, we will follow the same approach as in chapter 13, and solve these coupled equations at the point of equilibrium, when dN_h/dt and dN_p/dt each equal 0. This results in:

$$dN_h/dt = 0 \text{ when } 0 = r_h N_h - b N_h N_p$$

This can be reduced and rearranged such that prey population growth will be zero when:

$$N_p = r_h/b$$

And for the predator:

$$dN_p/dt = 0 \text{ when } 0 = cb N_h N_p - d_p N_p$$

This can be reduced and rearranged such that predator population growth will be zero when:

$$N_h = d_p/cb$$

You may recognize what we have just done. We now have the ability to draw the zero-growth isoclines for the predator and

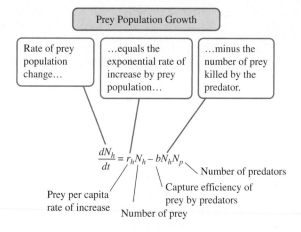

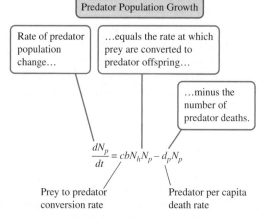

Figure 14.15 Anatomy of the Lotka-Volterra equations for predator–prey population growth.

prey populations (fig. 14.16). These graphs represent the conditions under which either predator or prey populations are predicted to change based upon the Lotka–Volterra model. We can combine these onto a single graph, and make predictions about the dynamics of the coupled systems (fig. 14.17).

Figure 14.17 represents the only solution for this model when both predators and prey have populations densities > 0. We can see in this figure the basis for population cycles. Because the host population grows at an exponential rate, its population growth accelerates with increasing population size. However, this tendency to grow faster and faster with increasing N_h is opposed by exploitation. As N_h increases, the rate of exploitation, bN_hN_p, also increases. Consequently, in the Lotka–Volterra model, reproduction by the host is translated immediately into destruction of prey by the predator. In addition, increased predation, bN_hN_p, is translated directly and immediately into more predators by cbN_hN_p. Increased numbers of predators increase the rate of exploitation since increasing N_p increases bN_hN_p. Growth of the predator population eventually reduces the prey population, which in turn

leads to declines in the predator population. So, like the prey, exploiter success carries the seeds of its own destruction.

These reciprocal effects of host and exploiter produce oscillations in the two populations, which we can represent in two ways. In figure 14.18a, population oscillations are presented as we looked at them in snowshoe hare and lynx populations (see fig. 14.11), while figure 14.18b gives an alternative representation. The time axis has been eliminated and the two remaining axes represent the numbers of predators and hosts. When we plot population data in this way, we see that the Lotka–Volterra model produces oscillations in predator and prey populations that follow an elliptical path whose size depends upon the initial sizes of host and prey populations. Whatever the ellipse size, however, the host and prey populations just go round and round on the same path forever.

The prediction of eternal oscillations on a very narrowly defined path is obviously unrealistic. Another unrealistic assumption is that neither the host nor the exploiter populations are subject to carrying capacities. Another is that changes in either population are instantaneously translated into responses in the other population. This model also does not allow for any non-consumptive effects. Despite these unrealistic assumptions, Lotka and Volterra made valuable contributions to our understanding of predator–prey systems. They showed that simple models with a minimum of assumptions produce reciprocal cycles in populations of predator and prey analogous to those that can occur in natural populations. They demonstrated that exploitative interactions themselves can, in theory, produce population cycles without any influences from an outside force such as climatic variation. Other researchers have taken their basic models and expanded them, allowing for more biological realism. One of the great uses of a simple model is the ability to expand them, allowing researchers to test whether the addition of more biological complexity alters our basic understanding of biological processes.

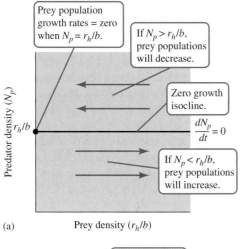

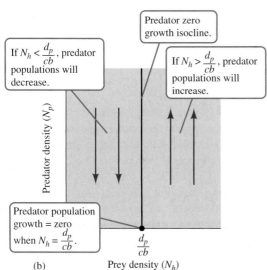

Figure 14.16 Zero-growth isoclines for (*a*) prey and (*b*) predator populations derived from the Lotka–Volterra predator–prey model.

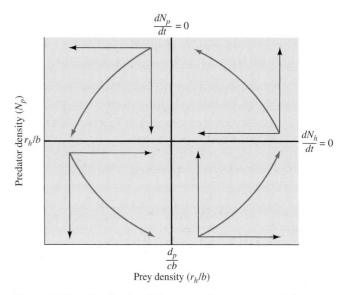

Figure 14.17 The Lotka–Volterra predator–prey model predicts cycling of predator and prey populations.

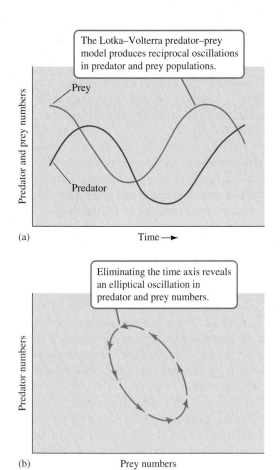

The Lotka–Volterra predator–prey model produces reciprocal oscillations in predator and prey populations.

(a)

Eliminating the time axis reveals an elliptical oscillation in predator and prey numbers.

(b)

Figure 14.18   A graphical view of the Lotka–Volterra predator–prey model (data from Gause 1934).

Although there has been some success in laboratory models to reproduce Lotka–Volterra type oscillations, most attempts have failed. Instead, most laboratory experiments have led to extinction of the predator or prey population in a fairly short period of time. To sustain oscillations even for a short period the prey had to have some sort of protection from the predators.

CONCEPT 14.3 REVIEW

1. How can we tell that the Lotka-Volterra predator–prey model does not include intraspecific competition?
2. If no natural population exactly follows the predictions of the Lotka-Volterra model, what is its value?
3. What are the key differences between the Lotka-Volterra competition and predator–prey models?

14.4   Predator Avoidance

Prey populations can persist in the presence of predators through the use of refugia and a diversity of defence strategies. Despite all of the potential negative effects predators can have on prey populations, we do find a world in which

potential prey exists. Here, we will discuss an evolutionary solution involving animal display, and then we discuss *refugia*, situations in which members of an exploited population have some protection from predators. Let us begin by taking a closer look at some of the potential prey that exist in the natural world.

Animal Display

Most prey species are masters of defence, one of the most basic means of which is *camouflage*. Quite simply, predators can not eat prey they can not find. The efficiency of this defence can be astounding, as shown by Bernd Heinrich (1984) in a study of predatory bald-faced hornets. The hornets hunt other insects by flying rapidly among the plants in their environment and pouncing on objects that may be prey. Because their prey are well camouflaged, the hornets often pounce on inanimate objects. Heinrich was able to observe 260 pounces by hornets. About 70% of these were directed at inanimate objects, such as bird droppings and brown spots on leaves. Another 20% were directed at insects, such as bumblebees and other wasps, insects too well defended to be prey. Only 7% of the pounces were on potential insect prey! The hornets managed to capture two of these, a moth and a fly. Heinrich's observations indicate bald-faced hornets have a prey capture rate of less than 1%!

Not all prey species are hidden to predators, and instead many prey are coloured to be extremely visually apparent. This can be seen in the striking colours displayed by many butterflies, snakes, and nudibranchs. How can prey persist with such colouration? Many of these animals are toxic. Prey that carry a threat to predators often advertise that fact, usually by being brightly coloured or conspicuous in some other way. The conspicuous colours, or **aposematic colouration**, of many distasteful or toxic animals warn predators that "feeding on me may be hazardous to your health." However, such a signal is not perfect. For example, one of the authors of this text (J.C.) enjoyed catching butterflies as a young boy. I recall well the bright sunny day that I decided the Monarch just looked so beautiful that I promptly licked its wings for a taste. Needless to say, the Monarch was advertising truthfully: its colouration is associated with a variety of foul tasting compounds. Lest you think that I am the sole potential predator of species with aposematic colouration, many predatory species need to learn to associate colouration with toxicity. Only for a subset of species is this "knowledge" an innate trait of the species. The curious predator is not the only potential threat to species with warning colouration.

In **Batesian mimicry**, a harmless (nontoxic) species will exhibit colouration similar to that of a noxious species that lives in the same area. For example, king snakes mimic the poisonous coral snakes, Viceroy butterflies mimic the noxious Monarch butterfly, and syphid flies mimic stinging bees. Batesian mimics elude predation not through the actual ability to defend themselves from attack, but instead by using the learned (and innate) abilities of predators to associate harm with particular colours and patterns. What do you imagine might happen if in a given community the frequency of mimics exceeds the frequency of actually toxic models?

Müllerian mimicry is also common, and can enhance the learning by potential predators associated with aposematic colouration. Müllerian mimics are *all* toxic/noxious, and share similar colouration. For example, you may have noticed that many stinging flies, wasps, and bees, three distantly related groups of taxa, have superficially similar appearances that include yellow and black stripes. These are Müllerian mimics. One likely advantage of similar colouration is that potential predators are likely to encounter toxic/noxious organisms with similar colouration more frequently than if only one species has such colouration. As a result, it is thought that Müllerian mimicry systems enhance the rate at which predators learn to associate a particular colour/pattern with risk, thereby reducing predation risk for these species. However, you may have noticed that some flies share the same colouration, yet do not sting. These are Batesian mimics of Müllerian mimics (fig. 14.19).

Refuges and Prey Persistence

Although some prey species are able to avoid predation through appearance, many are not. Nonetheless, these prey can be found on the landscape, co-occurring with a diversity of potential predators. However, recreating co-existence between predator and prey in a lab setting has proven to be surprisingly difficult. Gause (chapter 13) was among the first to realize that creating Lotka–Volterra oscillations in the lab was a challenge. He established a simple system involving *Paramecium caudatum* and one of its predators, another aquatic protozoan called *Didinium nasutum*. When Gause grew these organisms together, *Didinium* quickly consumed all the *Paramecium* (fig. 14.20), and thus there was no coexistence. Gause responded by putting some sediment on the bottom of his microcosm to provide a refuge for *Paramecium*. In this case, once *Didinium* had eaten all of the *Paramecium* not hiding in bottom sediments, it starved and became extinct. Following the disappearance of *Didinium* and the removal of predation pressure, the population of *Paramecium* quickly increased. Here, a simple refuge for the prey population led to extinction of the predator.

Gause was only able to maintain oscillations in predator–prey populations if he periodically restocked the populations from his laboratory cultures. In this experiment, the microcosm contained no refuges for *Paramecium*, but every three days Gause would take one of each organism from his pure laboratory cultures and add them to the experimental microcosm. Using these periodic immigrations he was able to produce Lotka–Volterra-type predator–prey oscillations (see fig. 14.20).

(a)

(b)

Figure 14.19   (*a*) Poisonous Müllerian (a stinging bee), and (*b*) nonpoisonous Batesian (a non-stinging hoverfly) mimics.

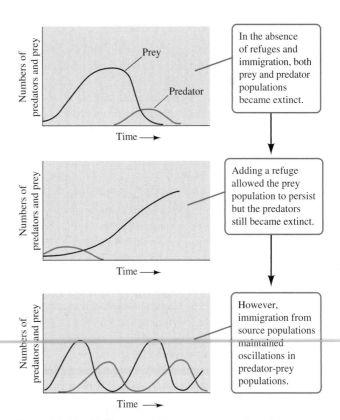

Figure 14.20   Refuges and the persistence of predator–prey oscillation in laboratory populations of prey (*Paramecium caudatum*) and predators (*Didinium nasutum*) (data from Gause 1934).

Are these experimental requirements entirely artificial or do they correspond with anything we already know about natural populations? Gause's experimental results match many of our observations in natural populations. In chapter 10, we saw that on larger scales, populations show clumped distributions. Most species are much more common in some parts of their range than in others. Then in chapter 11, we saw how dispersal is an important contributor to population dynamics and that some local populations are maintained entirely by dispersal from other areas. Some biologists have combined observations such as these to hypothesize the existence of population sources and population sinks—local populations maintained by immigration from source populations. In Gause's experiment, the laboratory cultures were population hot spots, or sources, while the microcosms where predator and prey interacted were population sinks. The requirements of Gause's experiment are also consistent with the results of later experiments.

C. Huffaker (1958) set out to test whether Gause's results could be reproduced in a situation in which the predator and prey are responsible for their own immigration and emigration among patches of suitable habitat. Huffaker chose the six-spotted mite, *Eotetranychus sexmaculatus*, a mite that feeds on oranges, as the prey and the predatory mite *Typhlodromus occidentalis*, which attacks *E. sexmaculatus*, as the predator. Huffaker's experimental setups, or "universes" as he called them, consisted of various arrangements of oranges, or combinations of oranges and rubber balls, separated by partial barriers to mite dispersal consisting of discontinuous strips of petroleum jelly.

An important point of natural history is that the predatory mite had to crawl to disperse from one orange to another, while the herbivorous mite can disperse either by crawling or by "ballooning," a means of aerial dispersal. A mite balloons by spinning a strand of silk that can catch wind currents. Huffaker gave the herbivorous mite the chance to balloon by providing small wooden posts that could serve as launching pads and by having a fan circulate air across his experimental setup.

While Huffaker's simpler experimental universes did not produce predator–prey oscillations, his most elaborate setup of 120 oranges did. These oscillations spanned several months (fig. 14.21). Huffaker observed three oscillations that spanned about six months. They were maintained by the dispersal of predator and prey among oranges in a deadly game of hide-and-seek, in which the prey managed to keep ahead of the predator for three full oscillations. These results are similar to those obtained by Gause, but we need to remember that Huffaker did not directly manipulate dispersal. In Huffaker's experiment, both predator and prey moved from patch to patch under their own power.

Lotka (1932b) recognized the importance of refuges and incorporated them into his mathematical theory of predator–prey relations. The starting point for his discussion were the Lotka–Volterra predator–prey equations that we discussed previously:

$$\frac{dN_h}{dt} = r_h N_h - b N_h N_p \text{ and } \frac{dN_p}{dt} = cb N_h N_p - d_p N_p$$

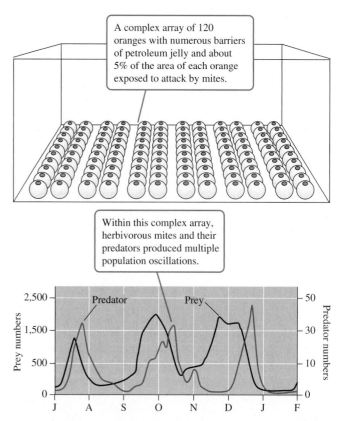

A complex array of 120 oranges with numerous barriers of petroleum jelly and about 5% of the area of each orange exposed to attack by mites.

Within this complex array, herbivorous mites and their predators produced multiple population oscillations.

Figure 14.21 Environmental complexity and oscillations in laboratory populations of an herbivorous mite and a predatory mite (data from Huffaker 1958).

The part of this equation that provided the starting point for Lotka's discussion was *b*, the capture or consumption rate of the predator. Lotka pointed out that while it may be reasonable to assume that *b* is a constant for a particular environment, its value should change from one environment to another if the environments differ structurally, particularly if there is a difference in the availability of refuges in the two environments. Specifically, *b* should be lower where the prey or hosts have access to more refuges. This refinement of the Lotka–Volterra predator–prey model anticipated recent theoretical analysis of the role that refuges and spatial diversity in general play in the persistence of predator–prey and parasite–host systems. While Lotka's analysis concentrated on physical refuges that could shelter terrestrial prey, he recognized the wide variety of forms that refuges could take. He pointed out, for instance, that flight is a refuge for birds from terrestrial predators.

Exploited Organisms and Their Wide Variety of "Refuges"

Space

Most of our discussion has focused on what we might call "spatial" refuges, places where members of the exploited population have some protection from predators. Many forms of spatial refuge are familiar: burrows, trees, air, water (if faced with terrestrial predators), and land (if faced with aquatic

predators). However, some spatial refuges differ in subtle ways from other areas.

St. John's wort, *Hypericum perforatum*, persists in refuges in the face of attacks by the beetle *Chrysolina quadrigemina*, one of the chief enemies of *Hypericum* in the Pacific Northwest region of the United States. *Hypericum* was introduced into areas along the Klamath River around 1900, and its population quickly grew to cover about 800,000 hectares by 1944. Following the release of the beetles, the area covered by St. John's Wort was reduced to less than 1% of its maximum coverage. This remnant population of the plant was concentrated in shady habitats, where, though it grows more poorly than in sunny areas, it is protected from the beetles, which avoid shade.

Protection in Numbers

Living in a large group provides a type of refuge. Aside from the potential of social groups to intimidate would-be predators, numbers alone can reduce the probability of an individual prey or host being eaten. We can make this prediction based solely on the work of C. S. Holling (1959) on the responses of predators to prey density. Holling is a fellow of the Royal Society of Canada, and has worked at the University of British Columbia and the Department of the Environment for the Canadian government. His research on predator–prey relationships has been central to the theoretical understanding of this ecological process. In chapter 5 we looked at the functional responses of several predators and herbivores. Briefly, predator functional response results in an increasing rate of food intake as prey density increases. Eventually, however, the predator's feeding rate levels off at some maximum rate. In chapter 11, we looked at numerical response, a second component of predator response to prey density that results in increased predator density as prey density increases. As with functional response, the numerical response eventually levels off at the point where further increases in prey density no longer produce increased predator density.

Now let's put functional response and numerical response together to predict the predator's **combined response** to increased prey density. We can combine the two responses by multiplying the number of prey eaten per predator times the number of predators per unit area:

$$\frac{\text{Prey consumed}}{\text{Predator}} \times \frac{\text{Predator}}{\text{Area}} = \frac{\text{Prey consumed}}{\text{Area}}$$

By dividing the prey consumed per unit area by the population density of the prey, we can determine the percentage of the prey population consumed by the predator. If we plot the percentage of the prey consumed against prey density over a broad range of prey densities, the prediction is that the percentage of the prey population consumed will be lower at high prey densities (fig. 14.22).

Why should the percentage of the prey consumed by the predator decline at high prey densities? The answer to this question, which may not be obvious at first, lies in the predator functional and numerical responses. We see this effect

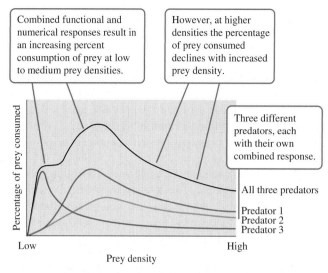

Figure 14.22   Prey density and the percentage of prey consumed due to combined functional and numerical responses (data from Holling 1959).

because both numerical and functional responses level off at intermediate prey densities; that is, beyond a certain threshold, further increases in prey density do not lead to either higher predator densities or increased feeding rates. Meanwhile, the density of the prey population continues to increase and the proportion of the prey eaten by predators declines. This work by Holling suggests that prey can reduce their individual probability of being eaten by occurring at very high densities. It appears that this defensive tactic, called **predator satiation**, is employed by a wide variety of organisms, from insects and plants to marine invertebrates and African antelope.

Predator Satiation by an Australian Tree

A great number of trees flower and produce seeds synchronously over large areas, including bamboo, pine, beech, and oak. This phenomenon of synchronous widespread seed and fruit production is called **masting**. Daniel Janzen (1978) proposed that a major selective force favouring the production of mast crops is seed predation. You may recall Janzen from chapter 1, when we highlighted his work in tropical rainforests. He suggested that mast crops may lead to satiation of seed predators, allowing some seeds to escape predation, germinate, and successfully establish.

Many Australian trees in the genus *Eucalyptus* disperse their seeds in large numbers following forest fires. Trees produce seeds each year, but most remain stored in closed seed capsules that are retained on the tree. Following a fire, a massive, synchronized release floods the forest floor with seeds.

Synchronous seed release by *Eucalyptus* may be a defence against seed predators, but which ones? The chief seed predators in Australian forests appear to be ants. We usually think of Australia as the continent of kangaroos and koalas, but the region could be just as well known for its ants. Australia harbours a tremendous diversity of ants. For instance, while North American deserts support about 160 species of ants, the deserts of Australia contain an estimated 2,000 species and the continent

as a whole may harbour nearly 4,000 species. The ants in Australian forests have been reported to prevent forest regeneration by removing up to 80% of the seeds broadcast by foresters.

D. O'Dowd and A. Gill (1984) used field experiments to determine whether synchronous seed dispersal by *Eucalyptus* might be a means to reduce seed losses to ants. They set up study plots in two forests of Australian alpine ash, *Eucalyptus delgatensis*, a gigantic tree found in the Australian Alps and Tasmania, where it commonly grows 50 to 60 m in height. One of the study sites was to serve as a reference site and the second as an experimental site. *E. delgatensis* constituted nearly 90% of the tree biomass at both study sites. The researchers monitored a number of physical and biological variables at the control and experimental sites and then set a controlled, high-intensity fire at the experimental site. The area burned was approximately 98 hectares; 93% of the trees were killed.

The results of O'Dowd and Gill's field experiments support their hypothesis that synchronous seed dispersal by *Eucalyptus* reduces losses of seeds to ants. As expected, the fire stimulated the release of massive numbers of seeds. During the three weeks following the fire, seed fall was approximately 405 fertile seeds per square metre, compared with a peak seed fall of 10 seeds per square metre per week at the control site, which was not burned. The fire also seemed to stimulate ant activity. Prior to the fire, researchers trapped an average of 176 ants belonging to 14 species each week. After the fire, the number of ants trapped each week rose to an average of 680 individuals belonging to 23 species. Despite this strong numerical response, the rate at which ants removed seeds dropped following the fire. The rate of seed removal from seed trays at the experimental site dropped from an average of about 65% per week during the five weeks prior to the fire to an average of about 14% per week during the five weeks following the fire. This result is consistent with the predator satiation hypothesis proposed by O'Dowd and Gill and is consistent with Holling's prediction of reduced predator combined response at high prey densities.

So, what does O'Dowd and Gill's experiment tell us? We know that *E. delgatensis* stores seeds in closed seed capsules, that these seeds are released synchronously following intense fires, and that a substantial proportion of these seeds escape predation even in the face of strong numerical response by seed-eating ants. Is this information sufficient to conclude that the apparent predator satiation strategy of *E. delgatensis* provides an effective "refuge" from predation? It seems that we should also know whether greater seed survival is translated into greater seedling establishment, an evolutionary bottom line. O'Dowd and Gill also showed that seedling establishment was greater on the burned experimental plot than on the control plot (fig. 14.23). About 1.5 years after the experimental fire, seedling survival at the experimental site was approximately two individuals per square metre, or 20,000 individuals per hectare. This seems a respectable level of reproductive success for trees that could eventually reach 50 to 60 m in height. Predator satiation also provides protection to many kinds of insects, but nowhere is this more apparent than among the cicadas.

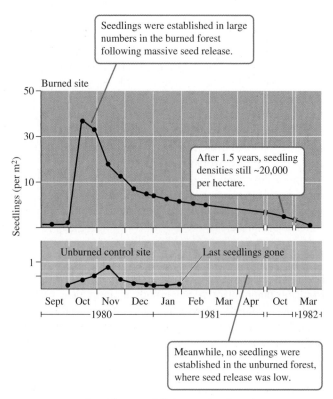

Figure 14.23 Seedling establishment by *Eucalyptus delgatensis* at burned and unburned sites (data from O'Dowd and Gill 1984).

Predator Satiation by Periodical Cicadas

Periodical cicadas, *Magicicada* spp., emerge as adults once every 13 years in the southern part of their range in North America, and once every 17 years in the northern part of their range. Though these insects emerge only once every 13 or 17 years in any particular area, virtually every year sees a brood emerging somewhere in eastern North America. An emergence of periodical cicadas produces a sudden flush of singing insects whose density can approach 4×10^6 individuals per hectare, which translates into a biomass of 1,900 to 3,700 kg of cicadas per hectare, the highest biomass of a natural population of terrestrial animals ever recorded.

Periodical cicadas are insects of the order Homoptera, which includes the leafhoppers and aphids. Like their relatives, cicadas make their living by sucking the fluids of plants. Cicadas spend either 13 or 17 years of their life as nymphs underground, where they feed on the xylem fluids in roots. When mature, nymphs dig their way to the soil surface, where they shed their nymphal skin and emerge as winged adults. Among periodical cicadas, this emergence is so synchronized that millions of adults emerge over a period of only a few days. Following emergence, males fly to the treetops where they sing the mating songs to which females are attracted. After they mate, females lay their eggs in living twigs of shrubs and trees. When the nymphs hatch in about six weeks, they immediately drop to the ground and burrow down to a root, where they begin to feed, moving around very little for the next 13 or 17 years. A mass emergence of periodical cicadas, one of the

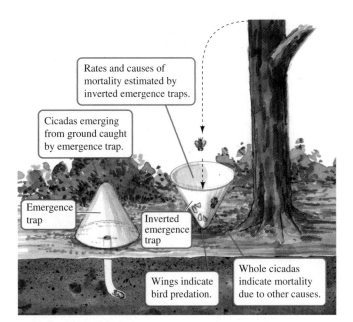

Figure 14.24 Estimating cicada population size and predation rates by birds.

most memorable biological phenomena nature has to offer, appears aimed at predator satiation.

Kathy Williams and her colleagues (1993) tested the effectiveness of predator satiation in a population of 13-year periodical cicadas in northwest Arkansas. They monitored emergence of cicadas using conical emergence traps constructed of plastic mesh and inverted their traps to measure predation rates (fig. 14.24). Nymphs emerging from the ground below the traps could be counted to estimate the numbers of emerging nymphs. Then, as adult cicadas died from a variety of factors, including physical factors, senescence, and pathogens, they fell from the trees to the ground, where some were caught in the inverted traps. Because the major predators were birds, predation rates could be estimated because birds discard

the wings of cicadas as they feed upon them. The wings falling into the inverted traps gave an estimate of predation rates.

Patterns of mortality and predation rates relative to population size support the predator satiation hypothesis. Williams and her colleagues estimated that 1,063,000 cicadas emerged from their 16 hectares study site and that 50% of these emerged during four consecutive nights. Cicada abundance peaked in late May and then declined rapidly during the first two weeks of June. Part of this decline was due to mortality from severe thunderstorms during the first week of June. Figure 14.25 shows that losses due to birds were low throughout the period of peak cicada abundance and then climbed to 100% as cicada populations declined during June. These results indicate that the predator satiation tactic was sufficiently effective to reduce cicada losses to birds to only 15% of the total population.

Size as a Refuge

We first encountered size-selective predation in chapter 7 among bluegills, *Lepomis macrochirus*, and pumas, *Felis concolor*. However, many other organisms select their prey by size. In fact, average prey size shows a significant correlation with predator size across taxa ranging from lizards to small mammals. The reason for size selective predation among such a diverse array of organisms is that prey capture and consumption are mechanical problems. As we saw in chapter 7, size can influence the time required to handle prey and therefore the rate of energy intake. The bottom line is that for a given predator, some prey are simply too large to be profitable and so are not attacked.

Now let's look at size from the perspective of the prey. If large individuals are ignored by predators, then large size may offer a form of refuge. An obvious example is the African savanna. While a variety of predators may attack the calves of elephants or rhinoceros, the same predators avoid the adults, which have been observed to kill adult lions (fig. 14.26). On a smaller scale, Robert Paine (1976) found that the sea star

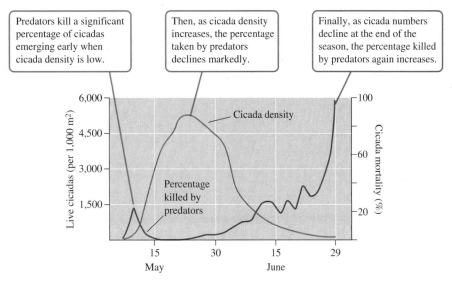

Figure 14.25 Cicada population density and their percent mortality due to predation (data from Williams et al. 1993).

Figure 14.26 Large size can provide a refuge from predators. While young African elephants may be vulnerable to predation by African lions, mature elephants are not.

Pisaster ochraceus does not consume the largest individuals in populations of one of its chief prey species, the mussel *Mytilus californianus.* Figure 14.27 shows that the maximum size of mussels eaten by sea stars is a function of sea star size. Notice that most of the successful predation observed by Paine involved small- to medium-sized sea stars attacking mussels less than 11 cm long. Most sea stars cannot eat the largest mussels, and the largest sea stars that can were limited to a few areas of coastline in the study area. What this means is that if a mussel can manage to escape predation long enough to reach 10 to 12 cm in length, it will be immune from attack by most sea stars. When Paine removed the sea stars from an area of the intertidal zone, resident mussels survived at higher rates and therefore grew to a larger average size (fig. 14.28). When Paine allowed sea stars to recolonize the area, many of the mussels were large enough that they effectively escaped predation by sea stars. This result has implications that reach far beyond higher survival within a single prey population.

If predators pass up prey above a particular size threshold, might natural selection favour organisms that project a "large" body size to some would-be predators? It appears that some aquatic insects have been selected to do just that. Barbara Peckarsky (1980, 1982) observed that mayflies in the family Ephemerellidae would stand their ground in the face of a foraging predatory stonefly. In fact, they would not only stand their ground, they would curve their abdomens over their backs and point the tips of their abdominal cerci into the face and antennae of a stonefly, a behaviour Peckarsky called a "scorpion" posture (fig. 14.29). Usually a stonefly greeted in this way does not attack. While many other stream ecologists had seen this behaviour in ephemerellidae mayflies, Peckarsky was the first to suggest that the scorpion posture was a defensive tactic in which the mayfly projected a larger image to a tactile, size-selective predator.

Why should a large stonefly avoid large ephemerellid mayflies? Large ephemerellids have been observed attacking stoneflies trying to prey on them, and so like lions that avoid rhinoceros, stoneflies that avoid ephemerellids may be

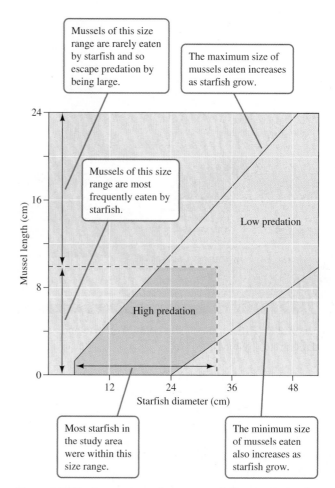

Figure 14.27 Large mussels are eaten infrequently by the sea star *Pisaster ochraceus* (data from Paine 1976).

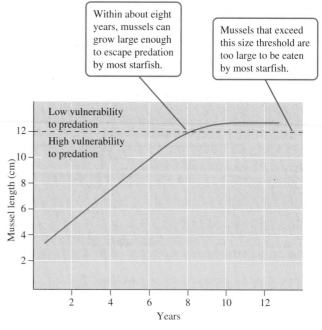

Figure 14.28 Growth by mussels in an intertidal area from which the sea star, *Pisaster ochraceus*, was excluded (data from Paine 1976).

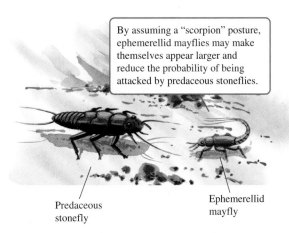

By assuming a "scorpion" posture, ephemerellid mayflies may make themselves appear larger and reduce the probability of being attacked by predaceous stoneflies.

Predaceous stonefly

Ephemerellid mayfly

Figure 14.29 Posturing by an ephemerellid mayfly confronted by a predaceous stonefly.

protecting themselves from injury. Most ephemerellids, however, present no danger to large predaceous stoneflies, so self-protection only partially answers our question. For the bulk of encounters between stoneflies and ephemerellid mayflies, large apparent size would probably indicate low profitability, low E/T in terms of optimal foraging theory (see chapter 7), and send the predator looking for a prey that would yield a higher energy return. It may be that the display by ephemerellids is not a bluff, however, since they require an

exceptionally long handling time for a prey of their size. The scorpion posture of ephemerellids may be a case of "truth in advertising." As you will see in the next section, organisms possess a variety of mechanisms of defence against predators and herbivores.

In the next section, we will explore how scientists are beginning to understand the evolutionary consequences of this widespread ecological interaction.

CONCEPT 14.4 REVIEW

1. O'Dowd and Gill demonstrated that the release of large numbers of seeds by *Eucalyptus delgatensis* allows a substantial number of seeds to escape predation by ants. Is this information sufficient to conclude that the apparent predator satiation of *Eucalyptus delgatensis* provides an effective "refuge" from ant predation?
2. Why should there be strong selection on periodical cicadas for highly synchronous emergence?
3. Why should a large predaceous stonefly avoid ephemerellid mayflies that assume a scorpion posture to project a large appearance?

ECOLOGICAL TOOLS AND APPROACHES

Evolution and Exploitation

Research in ecology can take place at a variety of spatial and temporal scales. At the shortest and smallest scales, an ecologist might be interested in understanding which predator consumes the eggs of nesting birds in a single field. Another ecologist may be interested in understanding how nest predation influences population dynamics. At an even broader scale may be a study showing how nest predation and egg production vary across a landscape. At a deeper time scale may be the evolutionary ecologist studying how predation alters selective pressures on nesting birds, resulting in evolutionary shifts in nesting strategy. At an even broader scale may be the scientist trying to understand how evolutionary shifts in nesting strategies could cause an evolutionary shift in foraging practices of a predator. Seemingly simple ecological questions can be addressed in a variety of ways using a diversity of research tools.

In this section we focus on aspects of the evolutionary ecology of exploitation. We will show how studying interactions over longer time scales reveals new insights about interactions. It is difficult to understand the ecology of exploitation

without also understanding its evolutionary causes and consequences, and thus sometimes significant advances come not through the development of a new research technology, but instead through the adoption of different conceptual approaches to a single research question. Specifically, we will discuss two issues related to exploitation: (1) does exploitation place selective pressures on organisms, and (2) how do prolonged periods of exploitation alter evolutionary trajectories? In these studies you will see how molecular methods can enhance an ecologist's ability to answer research questions.

Selection

Does predation cause selective pressure and evolutionary responses in prey populations? The answer to this question is dependent upon a variety of factors. For example, is predation common or rare within a population? If rare, then few individuals will likely experience predation risk, and thus it would be difficult for predation to cause an evolutionary response. If it is common, then there is the possibility for natural selection to favour genotypes that are either better protected or

better able to avoid predation, and evolution could occur. If predation is extremely strong, it may be possible for evolution to not only occur, but to occur rapidly. Showing evolutionary change requires being able to measure the genotypic composition of a population over several generations. For slow-growing species, generation times can be on the order of decades, and thus it isn't practical for a single researcher to actually document evolutionary shifts in ecological time scales. However, for fast-growing species, ecologists may be able to observe many generations within a single year, and thus studies documenting evolutionary shifts in response to predation are possible.

Justin Meyer, of the University of Ottawa, and colleagues at Cornell University tested the evolutionary effects of predation using rotifer-algal microcosms as their experimental system (fig. 14.30). **Microcosms** are small models of natural systems that allow experimental manipulation. Meyer and his colleagues use a particular type of microcosm, called a *chemostat*, that allows for continuous population growth of small-bodied organisms, such as the algae and rotifers used here (Meyer et al. 2006). Chemostats are generally maintained at constant temperatures and nutrient levels, and consist of glass beakers or vials that allow for flow-through of waste and nutrients. These microcosms are obviously poor approximations of the complexity of the natural world; however, their strength as research tools lies in their ability to let researchers focus on very specific questions. In this case, Meyer was able to address the impact of predation on algal evolution, independent of changes in nutrients and population growth rates.

Meyer chose a single predatory rotifer, *Brachionus calyciflorus*, and a single algal species, *Chlorella vulgaris*, as focal species. The rotifer is considered a predator, as it consumes the entire single-celled algae. Because Meyer was interested in understanding evolution, it was critical that he be able to show shifts in gene frequencies of the algal population over time. To do this, he used nine distinct strains of the algae, each of which he was able to distinguish using microsatellite markers (chapter 4). The experimental design was rather straightforward: Meyer placed two of the algal strains in the chemostat, added the rotifer, and then sampled the populations daily. The results were dramatic. After 30 days of predation, the algal populations consisted almost exclusively of only one of the two clones, even though both were present at the start (fig. 14.31). This is a shift in gene frequency within a population, and this is evolution. But why did this happen? Why did one clone consistently outperform the other in the presence of this predator?

There appears to be a trade-off in the competitive ability of these algal clones when grown without predation, and their ability to defend against predation. Those clones that grew fastest when alone also grew slowest when a rotifer was present. Such a trade-off makes sense in the view of the theory of allocation (chapter 7), where allocation to one ecological ability (e.g., competitive ability), likely results in less energy available for allocation to other traits (e.g., defence). The trade-off may also exist if morphological defences to predation harden cell walls or have some other physical effect of possible growth rates. What was the nature of the defence? Both clones were consumed with equal frequency by the rotifers, indicating the "defended" clone did not deter predation. Instead, the defended clone had a much higher probability of still being alive after passage through the rotifer gut than did the "competitive" clone. In other words, the competitive clone was digested when consumed, while the defended clone was not. This is a fairly effective defence against predation! It may come as no surprise that the clone that dominated the populations after 30 days of predation was the defended clone, while the competitive clone neared extinction when grown with the predator.

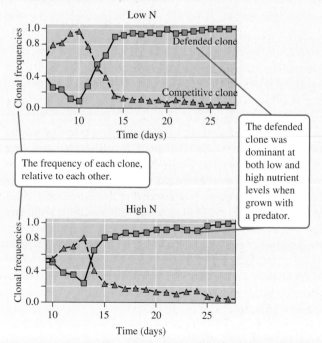

The frequency of each clone, relative to each other.

The defended clone was dominant at both low and high nutrient levels when grown with a predator.

Figure 14.31 Changes in relative frequency of two clones of algae in the presence of a predatory rotifer.

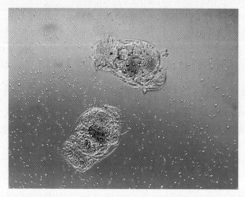

Figure 14.30 The rotifer, *Brachionus calyciflorus*, is a large predator that consumes the smaller algae, *Chlorella vulgaris*.

Meyer's study is an example of how strong levels of predation can cause rapid evolution. In this case, one genotype nearly went extinct after only 30 days of predation. This example also highlights the role that trade-offs can play in maintaining genetic diversity and thus altering ecological interactions. One might expect areas lacking rotifers to be dominated by competitive algal lines, while areas with rotifers to be dominated by well-defended clones. However, this evolutionary response by the prey should impact the predators too. Clearly, a rotifer that is unable to digest its prey will be at a selective disadvantage relative to a rotifer that is able to overcome this prey defence. In this next section, we explore these potential evolutionary feedbacks.

Evolutionary Dynamics
Co-evolution

As we can see from Meyer's example, predators can cause evolution in prey. If this can cause a reciprocal evolutionary response in the predator populations, this would be an example of co-evolution. The study of co-evolution in exploitative relationships has been an active area of research for evolutionary ecologists. At the base of this research lie two alternative models for co-evolution: Red Queen and Stable Cycling.

Red Queen

In 1973, Leigh van Valen suggested that over geological time, the probability of a taxanomic family going extinct does not change. This finding was a bit surprising, as we know that there is substantial evolution occurring within families over this timescale, and yet there appears to be no "improvement" in the extinction levels with time. This finding highlights the fact that evolution is not directional, nor does it reach an end state. Instead, natural selection is a continuous process. Van Valen viewed species interactions as analogous to an "evolutionary arms race" in which all members are actively changing (through evolution), with each adaptation leading to a counter-adaptation. The idea of an evolutionary arms race was named the "Red Queen Hypothesis" by van Valen, after the line from Lewis Carroll's book, *Through the Looking Glass* in which the Red Queen says, "It takes all the running you can do, to keep in the same place." This has been applied extensively to predator–prey and herbivore–host dynamics, suggesting that the reason there hasn't been a "winner" to these exploitative interactions is because both participants are involved in a complex co-evolutionary dance.

One prediction of the Red Queen hypothesis is that prey/plant defences and predator/herbivore countermeasures should become increasingly sophisticated and complex over evolutionary times. The idea is of an arms race, and it is likely not by chance that this terminology was coined during the cold war between the United States and the Soviet Union. Although there are examples supporting the idea of an arms race for some exploitative interactions, there are other examples where no such escalation occurs. Does this mean co-evolution is not occurring? Not necessarily. John Thompson (1994) has presented an alternative model for co-evolution, one based on *stable cycling*, rather than escalation, of the phenotypes of the interacting species.

Stable Cycling

At the heart of stable cycling is frequency dependent selection (chapter 4), and the idea that different populations will have different dominant genotypes, resulting in a *geographic mosaic* of the genotypes and phenotypes of the interacting species across the species' distributions. In general, the argument for stable cycling is that some defences and countermeasures will be controlled by single genes. For instance, a given allele may cause a particular shape and toxicity of a certain plant chemical defence, while a different allele may cause a different shape and toxicity. The ability of an insect to detoxify a particular compound may be dependent upon having the allele that produces the correct detoxification enzyme for the particular plant defence that it experiences. For example, let's suppose the plant toxin produced by the allele T_1 at the T locus could be detoxified by the insect enzyme produced by the allele E_1 at the E locus.

Now suppose that all plants in a population had the same allele, T_1, and that there were different genotypes of herbivores that had enzymes that ranged from E_1 to E_5. What should happen to gene frequencies in the population of the herbivore? Natural selection should favour those herbivores that have E_1, as they will be able to eat the plant. But let's not stop here. If this happens, this means that the herbivore population will soon become full of individuals that are E_1, which means that nearly every herbivore would be able to eat this plant. What should now happen to the plant population? Well, any new mutant that produces any other form of the defence, perhaps T_2, will be at a selective advantage and increase in frequency. This in turn reduces the fitness of herbivores that have E_1, and increases that of those with E_2. As you can see, this can go on forever. What is most important is that this is co-evolution without escalation. This process can occur independently in each population of the plant and herbivore, such that across the landscape there is a mosaic of dominant phenotypes in each population.

These ideas are supported by a variety of field and lab studies, showing that there will not be a "single" answer to how co-evolution works in natural systems. Instead, these insights from evolution help ecologists understand that exploitative interactions are dynamic. We end this section by looking at a slightly deeper time-scale, asking what could happen if exploitative interactions continue to exist for many generations.

Speciation

Although only a fraction of insect species are described in science, a current estimate suggests that there are around 5–10 million insect species, with perhaps 35%–40% of these

being plant-eating, or **phytophagous**, species (Ødegaard 2000). The number of phytophagous insect species alone is greater than the total number of birds, fish, and mammal species combined (9,000 species of birds, 20,000 species of fish, and 4,500 species of mammals). This level of diversity has led many researchers to wonder whether there is something about the herbivore–host interaction that could cause such high levels of diversity. Of particular interest was the realization that although many insects are **generalists**, feeding upon a diverse set of host plants, other species are **specialists**, feeding upon a more restricted diet—perhaps limited to even a single plant species. Could this specialization lead to speciation?

When people began to explore this issue, it soon became apparent that a single species of insect could form **host races**, genetically distinct subpopulations that are differentiated as a function of the host species. For example, *Rhagoletis pomonella*, the apple maggot, forms two main host races. One of these feeds upon the common apple, while a second feeds upon a related species, the hawthorn. Such differentiation may be the first step in the evolution of isolating mechanisms that could lead to sympatric speciation (chapter 4). What is unclear, however, is how common such differentiation is among herbivores. Unfortunately, broad surveys of large numbers of species have not yet been conducted, and there is not yet enough information to make a conclusive statement. However, Steve Heard at the University of New Brunswick and colleagues in Iowa used a different approach, leading them to conclude that host differentiation may, in fact, cause the levels of diversity we see.

Heard and colleagues decided to address this question in a novel way (Stireman et al. 2005). Rather than focus in-depth on a single insect species, they instead chose two common host plants (*Solidago altissima* and *S. gigantea*), and looked at many of the herbivore species that feed upon these plants. These two plant species are ideal for such a study, as they are found growing together over most of southern Canada and the United States, and thus there is substantial opportunity for host-race formation. They found nine common herbivores, which include leaf-feeding beetles and gall-forming midges, flies, and moths (fig. 14.32). To test for divergence, they collected insects from both plant species throughout much of Canada and the United States. They flash froze the insects in the field, allowing them to later sequence segments of mitochondrial DNA. Divergence was then estimated by looking at the differences in sequences for a given species as a function of its two hosts. In other words, was a particular insect species genetically homogeneous or genetically distinct across the two plant species?

They found that four of their nine insect species showed evidence of genetic divergence among host plants. This high number supports the idea that variation among host species can lead to genetic specialization, which could be the first step toward speciation. In a follow-up study, the authors

Figure 14.32   (*a*) Adult moths oviposit within stems of *Solidago*, forming (*b*) galls. (*c*) Within the galls are the developing larvae of the moths.

show that such differentiation is not limited to the plant and herbivore, but can also extend to the parasitoids of the herbivores (Stireman et al. 2006). They again sampled a broad geographic range, this time focusing exclusively on the common gall-forming insects of these plant species. Many of these insects will themselves serve as host to a variety of parasitoid species. Again using genetic analysis, Heard and his colleagues were able to show that the parasitoid populations themselves were genetically differentiated as a function of the plant species their host insect was feeding upon, even though the parasitoid had no direct interactions with the plant itself. They suggest that host-race formation can cascade to these top predators, potentially contributing to increased diversity for them as well.

The studies by Heard and colleagues leave many questions unanswered, such as what about the other 100 species of insects that feed on these plants? What are the mechanisms? When did this occur? Heard and colleagues readily acknowledge their study is not the end to the story, but instead just the beginning. Continued research by them, and by the next generation of ecologists, will lead to more answers, and of course, even more questions. By combining ecology, evolution, field work, and genetic analysis, details of exploitation are being unveiled that could never before be seen.

SUMMARY

Predator–prey and host–herbivore interactions are two common forms of exploitation that occur among species. These interactions increase the fitness of one member at the expense of the other, and can have significant consequences on population dynamics and evolutionary trajectories.

14.1 Herbivory is a widespread ecological interaction, and has caused the evolution of a diversity of plant defence strategies.

Most plants experience some degree of herbivory during their life. Feeding by herbivores typically has negative fitness consequences for the plant and positive benefits for the consumer. However, light grazing by geese can cause overcompensation in a subarctic salt marsh, while heavy grazing by the same geese can cause reductions in plant growth. Herbivorous stream insects can control the density of their algal and bacterial food. Plants often contain numerous morphological and chemical defences that deter feeding or cause illness in the herbivore if consumed. Some of these defences will be constitutive, while others will be induced following an attack.

14.2 Prey populations are influenced by food availability, by consumption by predators, and by non-consumptive effects of predators.

Populations of a wide variety of predators and prey show highly dynamic fluctuations in abundance ranging from days to decades. A particularly well-studied example of predator–prey cycles is that of snowshoe hares and their predators, which have been shown to result from the combined effects of the snowshoe hares on the food and of the predators on the snowshoe hare population. In addition to direct consumptive effects on prey populations, predators can significantly impact prey populations through non-consumptive effects. The study of these effects is commonly referred to as the "ecology of fear." By altering stress physiology of hares, lynx can cause reduced health and reproduction of the hares that have not been killed, with implications for future population growth. In a large meta-analysis, such non-consumptive effects appear to be at least as important in determining prey population dynamics as are consumptive effects.

14.3 The population consequences of exploitative relationships can be explored with theoretical models.

Mathematical models of predator–prey interactions by Lotka and Volterra suggest that exploitative interactions themselves can produce population cycles without any influences from outside forces such as weather. This model assumes no intraspecific competition is occurring and that prey population growth is limited only by predation. Though these assumptions are unrealistic, this model is a useful starting point for understanding general principles related to predator–prey population dynamics.

14.4 Prey populations can persist in the presence of predators through the use of refugia and a diversity of defence strategies.

Prey need a way to avoid predators, or else their populations will tend to crash. Many animal species are Batesian mimics, in which they display the warning colouration that is associated with a toxic model species. Other animal species are Müllerian mimics, in which there has been convergence toward a common warning colouration for unrelated toxic species, such as the black and yellow stripes of stinging insects. Another method of avoiding predation is the use of refugia. The refuges that promote the persistence of hosts and prey include secure places to which the exploiter has limited access. However, living in large groups can be considered as a kind of refuge since it reduces the probability that an individual host or prey will be attacked. It appears that predator satiation is a defensive tactic used by a wide variety of organisms, from rain forest trees to temperate insects. Growing to large size can also represent a kind of refuge when the prey species is faced by size-selective predators. Size is used as a refuge by prey species ranging from stream insects and intertidal invertebrates to the rhinoceros.

Exploitative interactions can cause evolution in the prey species. For example, predatory rotifers caused an algal population to consist primarily of well-defended genotypes, even though these genotypes grew more slowly when the predators were absent. These evolutionary changes can also influence the predator species, resulting in co-evolution. The Red Queen hypothesis and Stable Cycling are two models of co-evolution regularly used to describe exploitative relationships. Populations of herbivores can become genetically subdivided if they feed upon multiple host species. This could be the first step toward sympatric speciation, and may contribute to the large number of phytophagous insect species that exist on the planet.

REVIEW QUESTIONS

1. Predation is one of the processes by which one organism exploits another. Others are herbivory, parasitism, and disease. What distinguishes each of these processes, including predation, from the others? We can justify discussing these varied processes under the heading of exploitation because each involves one organism making its living at the expense of another. By what "currency" would you measure that expense (e.g., energy, fitness)?

2. Researchers have suggested that predators could actually increase the population density of a prey species heavily

infected by a pathogenic parasite (Hudson et al. 1992). Explain how predation could lead to population increases in the prey population.

3. Explain the roles of food and predators in producing cycles of abundance in populations of snowshoe hare. Populations of many of the predators that feed on snowshoe hares also cycle substantially. Explain population cycles among these predator populations.

4. What contributions have laboratory and mathematical models made to our understanding of predator–prey population cycles? What are the shortcomings of these modelling approaches? What are their advantages?

5. We included spatial refuges, predator satiation, and size in our discussions of the role played by refuges in the persistence of exploited species. How could time act as a refuge? Explain how natural selection could lead to the evolution of temporal refuges.

6. Joseph Culp and Gary Scrimgeour (1993) studied the timing of feeding by mayfly larvae in streams with and without fish. These mayflies feed by grazing on the exposed surfaces of stones, where they are vulnerable to predation by fish, which in the streams studied are size-selective feeders and feed predominantly during the day. In the study streams without fish, both small and large mayflies have a slight tendency to feed during the day, but feed at all hours of the day and night. In the streams with abundant fish populations, small mayflies fed around the clock, while large mayflies fed mainly at night. Explain these patterns in terms of time as a refuge and size-selective predation.

7. The growth of all populations must be controlled by some factor. What factors are potentially limiting to population growth? How can ecologists figure out which factors are operating on a particular population at any given point in time?

8. Batesian mimics confer an advantage from the toxicity of the model species, yet do not incur any of the energetic costs associated with the actual production of the toxic chemical. Why do the Batesian model species allow this to happen?

9. Having induced, rather than constitutive, plant defences seems like a very cost-effective mechanism to protect oneself against attack. However, many plant species contain constitutive defences. Why?

10. Snow geese can cause either positive or negative changes in the growth of their food plants, depending upon the intensity of grazing. When grazing is most severe, a variety of low-growing moss species become dominant. Why aren't these moss species dominant when grazing is light? How can grazing alter competitive interactions among these plant species?

11. Ecological interactions, such as exploitation, can have significant evolutionary consequences, such as host-race formation. To understand this, it is critical that researchers be able to blend techniques from different disciplines, such as evolutionary biology and ecology. Are ecology and evolution truly distinct disciplines, or do they look at similar questions, but in different time scales?

MUTUALISM, PARASITISM, AND DISEASE

CHAPTER 15

CHAPTER CONCEPTS

15.1 There is great diversity in the types of parasitic and mutualistic interactions that exist, defying easy generalization.

Concept 15.1 Review

15.2 Basic ecological principles can be applied to our understanding of disease, and the population dynamics of pathogens can be predicted using a compartmental model.

Concept 15.2 Review

15.3 Many forms of interactions can switch from parasitic to mutualistic, depending upon the specific conditions of the local environment.

Ecology In Action: Impacts of Mycorrhizae on Forest Sustainability

Concept 15.3 Review

15.4 Theory predicts that mutualism will evolve where the benefits of mutualism exceed the costs.

Concept 15.4 Review

Ecological Tools and Approaches: Mutualism and Humans

Summary

Review Questions

n chapters 13 and 14 we discussed a variety of interactions that were primarily negative for at least one participant, such as the plant that is shaded by taller plants above, or the moose eaten by a wolf. Here we continue our discussion of exploitation but expand it to include both disease and situations where multiple individuals exploit each other. We again emphasize that the human desire to classify interactions as either negative or positive does not represent the true variation found in nature. Instead, there is great complexity in the effects of exploitative interactions on all participants, and the *mutualist–parasite continuum* is the main theme of this chapter.

At one end of this continuum are parasites, organisms that live in or on the tissues of their host, drawing resources from their host. Similarly, pathogens live inside their host, often inducing disease. The negative consequences to the host and positive benefits to the parasite/pathogen are obvious, and they can be viewed as simple exploitative relationships similar to predation and herbivory. However, other organisms, such as the epiphytes of chapter 2, are able to live on their host, causing no apparent harm. Some fungi live in plant tissues, consuming plant resources with no apparent effect on plant growth. Many scavenger fish follow sharks and other predators, consuming food that otherwise would be left behind, again without apparent harm to the predators. All of these *commensal* interactions (chapter 13) are neutral for at least one participant. Then, at the other extreme, there are interactions in which both participants benefit, such as the butterfly that feeds upon nectar and the flower that receives pollination services. In this chapter, we continue to explore the rich variety of exploitative interactions, and how the relative costs and benefits of a particular interaction will be dependent on the specifics of the interaction.

Positive interactions among species are common in nature. We are familiar with the plant–pollinator interaction (fig. 15.1), but there are many more. For example birds and fish that remove the parasites of other animals (chapter 8) gain food for themselves and reduce the parasite load for the host. We often refer to lichens as a singular organism, though it is actually an intimate relationship between fungi and algae, with the fungi providing housing and nutrient capture and the algae photosynthesizing to produce sugars. Below ground there exists a world of partnerships as well. The roots of most plants are intimately connected with fungi in associations called **mycorrhizae**. The fungal hyphae extend far from the roots of the plant, increasing the capacity of the plant to forage for nutrients. Also located in the mycorrhizae are specialized structures that allow the fungi to draw large amounts of sugars from the plant.

There are many critical differences among the interactions described above. Some, such as mycorrhizae and lichens, involve **symbiotic relationships**. Symbiosis involves organisms that live in close proximity to each other. In contrast, the birds that visit the flowers spend most of their lives far from the flowers, and thus are part of a **nonsymbiotic relationship**.

Mycorrhizae, lichen, and pollinators are a few examples of **mutualisms**, interactions between individuals of different species that have a net benefit both partners. Not all mutualisms are alike, and the differences have important

Figure 15.1 Hummingbirds feeding on nectar transfer pollen from flower to flower.

consequences for the ecology of the species involved in the interactions. Some species, such as pollinating birds, can live without their mutualistic partners, and so the relationship is called a **facultative mutualism**. Other species are so dependent upon the mutualistic relationship that they cannot live in its absence, such as many species of mycorrhizal fungi. Such relationships are **obligate mutualisms**.

Historically, the study of mutualisms has fallen well behind that of predator–prey interactions, though in recent years ecologists have realized that this bias in research greatly skewed our understanding of the natural world. Mutualisms are widespread, involve large numbers of individuals and species, and have great impacts on population dynamics and community organization. Without mutualisms, the biosphere would be entirely different. For example, without mutualisms we can erase the Great Barrier Reef, the largest biological structure on earth. The deep sea would have not luminescent fish or invertebrates, and the deep sea life around ocean floor hydrothermal vents would not exist (chapter 7). On land, there would be no orchids, sunflowers, apples, or other animal-pollinated plants and produce. No bumblebees, hummingbirds, or monarch butterflies would be left. Many wind pollinated plants, such as conifers and grasses, would exist; however, over 90% of these form mycorrhizae, and what they would look like without these below-ground mutualists is unclear. Even if the grasses remained, the large herbivores such as bison, elephants, and camels, and even the smaller rabbits and caterpillars, would not. They have a variety of mutualistic relationships with microbes in their guts that allow them to eat plants. If we remove predators from a system, there will be some shifts in population dynamics. If we remove mutualists, natural systems as we know them would quickly disappear.

The effect mutualisms have on extant life is even greater than we might expect. Lynn Margulis and René Fester (1991) have amassed convincing evidence that all eukaryotes, both heterotrophic and autotrophic, originated as mutualistic

associations between different organisms. Eukaryotes are apparently the product of a mutualistic relationship so ancient that the mutualistic partners have become cellular organelles (e.g., mitochondria and chloroplasts) whose mutualistic origins long went unrecognized. Consequently, without mutualisms, all eukaryotes—from *Homo sapiens* to protists—would be gone.

In this chapter, we will review what is known about parasitism and mutualism, and show why many ecologists are moving away from the idea that exploitation and mutualism are fundamentally different types of interactions. Instead, there is an increasing understanding that exploitation and mutualisms are simply different extremes on a continuum of possible interactions. We will begin with a discussion of the diversity of interactions that are found in nature.

15.1 Complex Interactions

There is great diversity in the types of parasitic and mutualistic interactions that exist, defying easy generalization. Most species on the planet are host to at least one species of specialist parasite, and several species of generalist parasites. As a result, most species on the planet are parasites (and small). However, not all interactions between species are inherently exploitative, or even competitive. Instead, there also exist a variety of mutualistic relationships among species. It is impossible to present the full diversity of these interactions in a single section of a chapter, and instead we present just a few examples that demonstrate the variability that exists in nature.

Control: Behaviour Modification by Parasites

A number of parasites alter the behaviour of their hosts in ways that benefit transmission and reproduction of the parasite. Acanthocephalans, or spiny-headed worms, change the behaviour of amphipods, small aquatic crustaceans, in ways that make it more likely that infected amphipods will be eaten by a suitable vertebrate host. Janice Moore (1983, 1984a, and 1984b) studied a parasite–host interaction involving an acanthocephalan, *Plagiorhynchus cylindraceus*, a terrestrial isopod or pill bug, *Armadillidium vulgare*, and the European starling, *Sturnus vulgaris*. In this interaction, the pill bug serves as an intermediate host for *Plagiorhynchus*, which completes its life cycle in the starling (fig. 15.2).

At the outset of her research, Moore predicted that *Plagiorhynchus* would alter the behaviour of *Armadillidium.* She based this prediction on several observations. One was the relative frequency of infection of *Armadillidium* and starlings by *Plagiorhynchus*. Field studies had demonstrated that even where *Plagiorhynchus* infects only 1% of the *Armadillidium* population, over 40% of the starlings in the area were infected. Some factor was enhancing rates of transmission to the starlings, and Moore predicted that it was altered host behaviour. Moore thought that the size of *Plagiorhynchus* might also be a factor. At maturity, the infective cystacanth stage of *Plagiorhynchus* grows to about 3 mm, a substantial fraction of the internal environment of an 8 mm pill bug!

Moore brought *Armadillidium* into the laboratory and established two populations: an uninfected control group

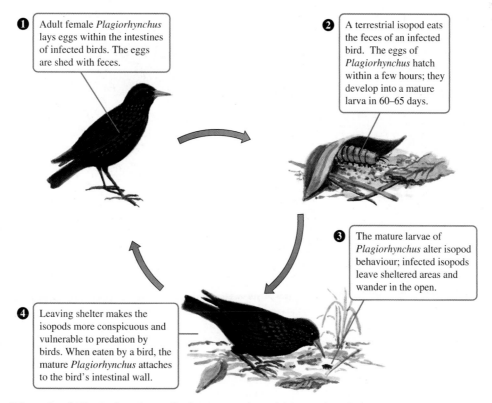

❶ Adult female *Plagiorhynchus* lays eggs within the intestines of infected birds. The eggs are shed with feces.

❷ A terrestrial isopod eats the feces of an infected bird. The eggs of *Plagiorhynchus* hatch within a few hours; they develop into a mature larva in 60–65 days.

❸ The mature larvae of *Plagiorhynchus* alter isopod behaviour; infected isopods leave sheltered areas and wander in the open.

❹ Leaving shelter makes the isopods more conspicuous and vulnerable to predation by birds. When eaten by a bird, the mature *Plagiorhynchus* attaches to the bird's intestinal wall.

Figure 15.2 The life cycle of *Plagiorhynchus cylindraceus*, an intestinal parasite of birds.

and an infected experimental group. After three months, the *Plagiorhynchus* in the infected populations matured to the cystacanth stage. At this point Moore mixed the infected and uninfected populations.

Moore found that *Plagiorhynchus* alters the behaviour of *Armadillidium* in several ways. Infected *Armadillidium* spend less time in sheltered areas and more time in low-humidity environments and on light-coloured substrates. These changes in behaviour would increase the time an *Armadillidium* spends in the open, where a bird could easily see it. In other words, infected *Armadillidium* behave in a way that increases the probability of discovery by foraging birds.

A critical step in this research was to determine whether the changed behaviour of infected *Armadillidium* translates into their being eaten more frequently by wild birds. Moore collected the arthropods that starlings feed to their nestlings and from these collections estimated the rate at which they delivered *Armadillidium*—about one every 10 hours. Using this delivery rate and the proportion of the *Armadillidium* population infected by *Plagiorhynchus* (about 0.4%), she was able to predict the expected rate of infection among starling nestlings if the adults capture *Armadillidium* at random from the natural population. The proportion of infected nestlings was 32%, about twice the rate of infection predicted if starlings fed randomly on the *Armadillidium* population. These results support Moore's hypothesis that the altered behaviour of infected *Armadillidium* increases their probability of being eaten by starlings.

Moore emphasized that *Plagiorhynchus* does not just alter *Armadillidium's* behaviour, but alters its behaviour in a particular way—in a way that increases the rate at which the final host of the parasite, starlings, is infected. As you might expect, parasites can have impacts on host population dynamics.

Infestation: Ghost Moose and Winter Ticks

Moose, *Alces alces*, are found throughout most of Canada (fig. 15.3*d*), and are the subject of many myths, legends, and stories. One of the more common stories is about the "ghost moose," white moose seen walking across the landscape (fig. 15.3*b*). Bill Samuel, of the University of Alberta, has studied these "ghost" moose, and has been able to show the cause: winter ticks (Samuel 2004).

Dermacentor albipictus is a tick that can feed on a variety of hosts, including moose, elk, and white-tailed deer (fig. 15.3*c*). Winter ticks are unique compared to all other ticks in Canada in that the larval, nymph, and adult stages feed upon the blood of a single host. This is in contrast to parasites such as *Plagiorhynchus* described above, which alternates between isopod and avian hosts during different stages of its own development. *Dermacentor albipictus* are found throughout most of the southern range of moose in North America (fig. 15.3*d*). Although these ticks are large relative to other ticks, reaching 1.5 cm in length as a blood-engorged adult, their size is dwarfed in comparison to an adult moose standing nearly 2 m in height. How is it possible that this little parasite can cause

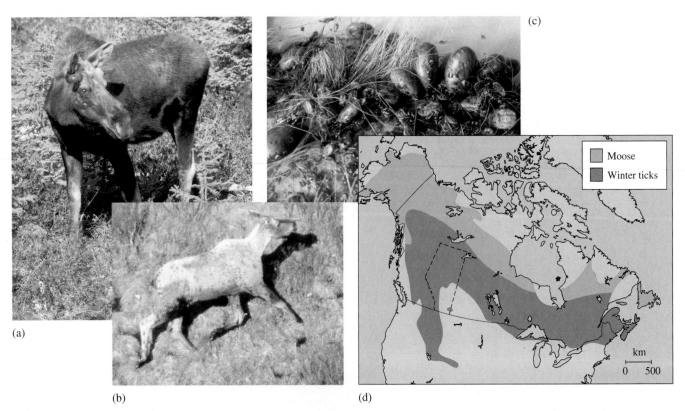

Figure 15.3   (*a*) With few ticks, moose retain a brown coat; (*b*) at high numbers of ticks, moose self-groom, destroying the winter coat of hair and giving the whitish image of a "ghost" moose; (*c*) winter ticks can occur at extremely high densities on the skin of a moose; (*d*) the ranges of winter ticks and moose overlap over much of Canada and the northern United States.

a dramatic shift in the appearance and health of this large animal? Think of Gulliver's encounters with the diminutive Lilliputians (Swift 1726). The answer lies primarily in numbers.

Over the years, Samuel and his students examined the hides of hundreds of moose collected in the winter. On 214 hides collected from western Canada, there was an average of 33,000 winter ticks per moose, with 3% of the moose having in excess of 100,000 ticks. As a point of reference, 50,000 ticks correspond to approximately 3.0 ticks per cm^2 on a calf moose (Samuel 2004). Samuel compared tick densities on co-occurring hosts in Elk Island National Park, Alberta, and found tick densities to be more than 25 times greater on moose than elk, deer, or bison. In other words, these ticks infest this particular host, even though other hosts are available in the area.

The consequences of this infestation can be severe. Using estimates on the amount of blood that individual female ticks can consume, Samuel (2004) made some rough calculations about blood loss. He estimated that naturally occurring tick densities consume approximately 17% of the blood volume of a bull moose, 11% of the blood volume of cows (though this is during the last trimester of pregnancy), and 58% of the blood volume of calves. Aside from blood loss, high densities of these parasites cause a behavioural shift in the moose—increased grooming.

Grooming of moose includes biting and licking, scratching with hind hooves, and rubbing against trees. In a study of captive moose, Samuel found tick-infested moose groom up to two hours each day in March through April, the period in which the ticks are most actively feeding. In contrast, tick-free moose groom less than five minutes per day. The direct outcome of this high level of grooming is hair loss (Mooring and Samuel 1999). The "ghost" moose have broken off the dark outer portion of their hair on over 80% of the body surface, exposing the white-coloured lower portion, giving rise to an overall whitish appearance.

Knowing what you do about the theory of allocation and physiological ecology (section II), it should be readily apparent that increased expenditure of energy to replace blood, increased time spent grooming, and decreased insulative properties of the coat likely increase stress and reduce the health of infested individuals. For nearly a century, ticks have been seen as reducing the strength of moose, and a likely source of mortality. Samuel (2004) lists a variety of accounts throughout Canada linking moose die-offs to tick numbers. Within Elk Island National Park, moose and tick numbers seem to track in synch (fig. 15.4), similar to what we saw with predator–prey dynamics in chapter 14. In figure 15.4, the average number of ticks found on moose appears to be tightly linked to the number of moose present the previous year. This is similar to the number of predators responding to the number of potential prey available. We now turn to a different example, and show that parasites can not only alter behaviour, but also influence the outcome of competitive interactions.

Interactions: Predation, Parasitism, and Competition

During their work on competition among flour beetles, Thomas Park and his colleagues (Park 1948, Park et al. 1965) uncovered one of the very first examples of competitors eating

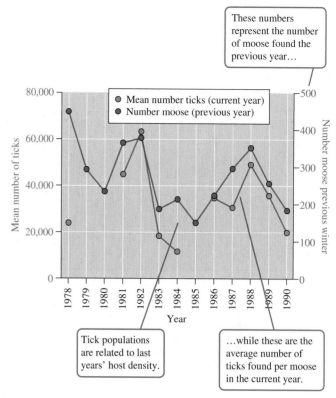

Figure 15.4   Relationship between average number of ticks on a moose and moose population sizes in Elk Island National Park, Alberta (data from Samuel 2004).

each other. As we saw in chapter 13, the outcome of competition between *Tribolium castaneum* and *T. confusum* depended upon temperature and moisture. It turns out that the presence or absence of a protozoan parasite of *Tribolium*, *Adelina tribolii*, also influences the competitive balance between flour beetle species. The effects of this parasite are also entangled with predation among the flour beetles and cannibalism, which we might think of as a form of intraspecific exploitation.

Of the two species, *T. castaneum* is the most cannibalistic; however, it preys on the eggs of *T. confusum* at an even higher rate than it cannibalizes its own eggs. In light of its predatory behaviour, it is not surprising that *T. castaneum* eliminated *T. confusum* in 84% of 76 competition experiments spanning a period of about 10 years. This predatory strategy works best, however, in the absence of *Adelina*.

Several biologists before Park had noted that *Adelina* caused sickness and death among *Tribolium* populations. It was Park, however, who demonstrated that *Adelina* reduces the density of *Tribolium* populations and can alter the outcome of competition between *T. confusum* and *T. castaneum*. *Adelina* strongly reduces the population density of *T. castaneum* populations but has little effect on *T. confusum* populations. In the absence of the parasite, *T. castaneum* won 12 of 18 competitive contests against *T. confusum*. When the parasite was included, however, *T. confusum* won 11 of 15 contests (fig. 15.5). In other words, parasitism can completely reverse the outcome of competitive interactions between species. We now move to an example where having one species live within and on the host confers benefits to the host.

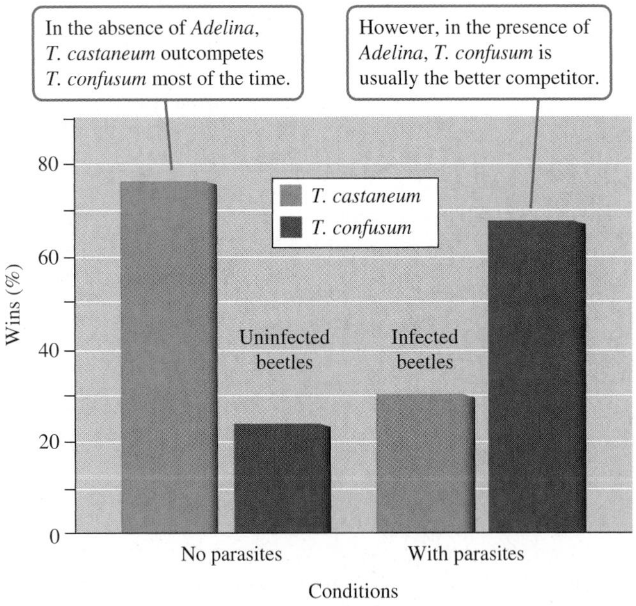

In the absence of *Adelina*, *T. castaneum* outcompetes *T. confusum* most of the time.

However, in the presence of *Adelina*, *T. confusum* is usually the better competitor.

Figure 15.5   The influence of the protozoan parasite *Adelina tribolii* on competition between the flour beetles *Tribolium castaneum* and *T. confusum* (data from Park 1948).

Figure 15.6   Split thorn of a bullshorn acacia, revealing a nest of its ant mutualists.

Protection: Ants and Bullshorn Acacia

Writing about the natural history of mutualism, Daniel Janzen (1985) included "plant–ant protection mutualisms" as one of his general categories of mutualism. Janzen (1966, 1967a, 1967b) himself is responsible for studying one of the best known of these mutualisms, the obligate mutualism between ants and swollen thorn acacias in Central America. The ants mutualistic with swollen thorn acacias are members of the genus *Pseudomyrmex* in the subfamily Pseudomyrmecinae. This subfamily of ants is dominated by species that have evolved close relationships with trees, and show several characteristics that Janzen suggested are associated with arboreal living. They are generally fast and agile runners, have good vision, and forage independently. The *Pseudomyrmex* spp. associated with swollen thorn acacias, or "acacia-ants," are also aggressive toward vegetation and animals contacting their home tree, maintain large colony sizes, and exhibit 24-hour activity outside of the nest. This combination of characteristics means that any herbivore attempting to forage on an acacia occupied by acacia-ants is met by a large number of fast, agile, and highly aggressive defenders.

Worldwide, the genus *Acacia* includes over 700 species. Distributed throughout the tropical and subtropical regions around the world, acacias are particularly common in drier tropical and subtropical environments. The swollen thorn acacias, which form obligate mutualisms with *Pseudomyrmex* spp., are restricted to the New World, where they are distributed from southern Mexico, through Central America, and into Venezuela and Columbia in northern South America. Across this region, swollen thorn acacias occur mainly in the lowlands up to 1,500 m elevation in areas with a dry season of one to six months. Swollen thorn acacias show several

characteristics related to their obligate association with ants, including enlarged thorns with a soft, easily excavated pith; year-round leaf production; enlarged foliar nectaries; and leaflet tips modified into concentrated food sources called Beltian bodies. The thorns provide living space for ants, while the foliar nectaries provide a source of sugar and liquid. Beltian bodies are a source of oils and protein. Resident ants vigorously guard these resources against encroachment by nearly all comers, including other plants.

Janzen's detailed natural history of the interaction between bullshorn acacia and ants suggests interactions of mutual benefit to both partners (fig. 15.6). Newly mated *Pseudomyrmex* queens move through the vegetation searching for unoccupied seedlings or shoots of bullshorn acacia. When a queen finds an unoccupied acacia, she excavates an entrance in one of the green thorns or uses one carved previously by another ant. The queen then lays her first eggs in the thorn and begins to forage on her newly-acquired home plant. She gets nectar for herself and her developing larvae from the foliar nectaries and gets additional solid food from the Beltian bodies. Over time, the number of workers in the new colony increases, and the queen shifts to a mainly reproductive function.

Ants protect acacias from attack by herbivores and competition from other plants. Workers have several duties, including foraging for themselves, the larvae, and the queen. One of their most important activities is protecting the home plant. Workers will attack, bite, and sting nearly all insects they encounter on their home plant or any large herbivores, such as deer and cattle, that attempt to feed on the plant. They will also attack and kill any vegetation encroaching on the home tree. Workers sting and bite the branches of other plants that come in contact with their home tree or that grow near its base. These activities keep other plants from growing near the base of the home tree and prevent other trees, shrubs, and vines from shading it. Consequently the home plant's access to light and soil nutrients is increased.

Once a colony has at least 50 to 150 workers, which takes about nine months, they patrol the home plant day and night.

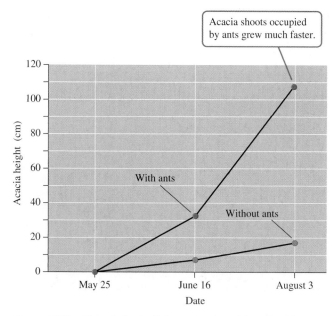

Figure 15.7 Growth by bullshorn acacia with and without resident ants (data from Janzen 1966).

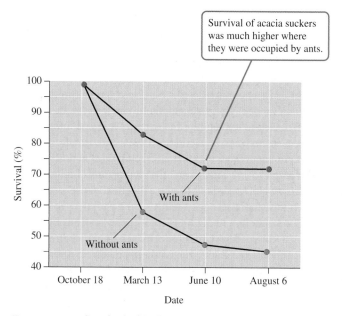

Figure 15.8 Survival of bullshorn acacia shoots with and without resident ants (data from Janzen 1966).

Eventually, colonies grow so large that they occupy all the thorns on the home tree and may spread to neighbouring acacias. The queen, however, generally remains on the shoot that she colonized originally. When the colony reaches a size of about 1,200 workers, it begins producing a more or less steady stream of winged reproductive males and females, which fly off to mate. The queens among them may eventually establish new colonies on other bullshorn acacias or one of the other Central American swollen thorn acacias.

While much of the natural history of this mutualism was known at the time Janzen conducted his studies, no one had experimentally tested the strength of its widely supposed benefits. Janzen took his work beyond natural history to experimentally test for the importance of ants to bullshorn acacias. It was clear that the ant needs swollen thorn acacias, but do the acacias need the ants? Janzen's experiments concentrated on the influence of ants on acacia performance. He also tested the effectiveness of the ants at keeping acacias free of herbivorous insects. Janzen removed ants from acacias by clipping occupied thorns or by cutting out entire shoots with their ants. He then measured the growth rate, leaf production, mortality, and insect population density on acacias with and without ants.

Janzen's experiments demonstrated that ants significantly improve plant performance. Differences in plant performance were likely the result of increased competition with other plants and increased attack by insects faced by acacias without their tending ants. Suckers growing from stumps of acacias occupied by ants lengthened at seven times the rate of suckers without ants (fig. 15.7). Suckers with ants were also more than 13 times heavier than suckers without ants, and had more than twice the number of leaves and almost three times the number of thorns. Suckers with ants also survived at twice the rate of suckers without ants (fig. 15.8).

What produces the improved performance of acacias with ants? One factor appears to be reduced populations of herbivorous insects. Janzen found that acacias without ants had more herbivorous insects on them than did acacias with ants (fig. 15.9). Janzen's experiments provide strong evidence that bullshorn acacias need ants nearly as much as the ants need the acacia.

Construction: Zooxanthellae and Corals

Because of the importance of mutualism in the lives of reef-building corals, it appears that the ecological integrity of coral

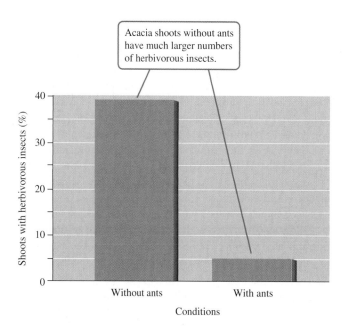

Figure 15.9 Ants and the abundance of herbivorous insects on bullshorn acacia (data from Janzen 1966).

reefs depends upon mutualism. Coral reefs show exceptional productivity and diversity. Recent estimates put the number of species occurring on coral reefs at approximately one-half million, and coral reef productivity is among the highest of any natural ecosystem. As we saw in chapter 3, the paradox is that this overwhelming diversity and exceptional productivity occurs in an ecosystem surrounded by nutrient-poor tropical seas. The key to explaining this paradox lies with mutualism; in this case, between reef-building corals and unicellular algae called zooxanthellae, members of the phylum Dinoflagellata. Most of these organisms are free-living unicellular marine and freshwater photoautotrophs. Together, these organisms create the foundation ecosystem.

Zooxanthellae live within coral tissues at densities averaging approximately 1 million cells per square centimetre of coral surface. Like plants, zooxanthellae receive nutrients from their animal partner. In return, the coral receives organic compounds synthesized by zooxanthellae during photosynthesis.

One of the most fundamental discoveries concerning the relationship between corals and zooxanthellae is that the release of organic compounds by zooxanthellae is controlled by the coral partner. Corals induce zooxanthellae to release organic compounds with "signal" compounds, which alter the permeability of the zooxanthellae cell membrane. Zooxanthellae grown in isolation from corals release very little organic material into their environment. However, when exposed to extracts of coral tissue, zooxanthellae immediately increase the rate at which they release organic compounds. This response appears to be a specific, chemically mediated communication between corals and zooxanthellae. Zooxanthellae do not respond to extracts of other animal tissues, and coral extracts do not induce leaking of organic molecules by any other algae that have been studied.

Corals not only control the secretion of organic compounds by zooxanthellae, they also control the rate of zooxanthellae population growth and population density. In corals, zooxanthellae populations grow at rates 1/10 to 1/100 the rates observed when they are cultured separately from corals. Corals exert control over zooxanthellae population density through their influence on organic matter secretion. Normally, unicellular algae show balanced growth, growth in which all cell constituents, such as nitrogen, carbon, and DNA, increase at the same rate. However, zooxanthellae living in coral tissues show unbalanced growth, producing fixed carbon at a much higher rate than other cell constituents. Moreover, the coral stimulates the zooxanthellae to secrete 90% to 99% of this carbon, which the coral uses for its own respiration. Carbon secreted and diverted for use by the coral could otherwise be used to produce new zooxanthellae, which would increase population growth.

What benefits do the zooxanthellae get out of their relationship with corals? The main benefit appears to be access to higher levels of nutrients, especially nitrogen. Corals feed on zooplankton, which gives them a means of capturing nutrients, especially nitrogen and phosphorus. When corals metabolize the protein in their zooplankton prey, they excrete ammonium as a waste product. L. Muscatine and C. D'Elia (1978) showed that coral species such as *Tubastrea aurea* that do not harbour zooxanthellae continuously excrete

ammonium into their environment, while corals such as *Pocillopora damicornis* do not excrete measurable amounts of ammonia (fig. 15.10). What happens to the ammonium

(a)

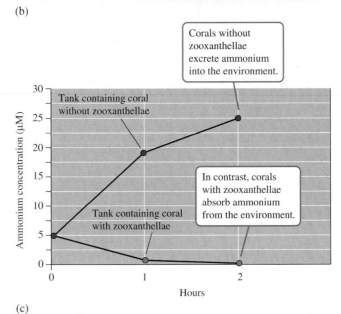

(b)

(c)

Corals without zooxanthellae excrete ammonium into the environment.

Tank containing coral without zooxanthellae

In contrast, corals with zooxanthellae absorb ammonium from the environment.

Tank containing coral with zooxanthellae

Figure 15.10 (*a*) *Tubastrea aurea* does not harbour zooxanthellae, while (*b*) *Pocillopora damicornis* does. (*c*) Harbouring zooxanthellae by corals reduces ammonium flux compared to corals without zooxanthellae (data from Muscatine and D'Elia 1978).

produced by *Pocillopora* during metabolism of the protein in their zooplankton prey? Muscatine and D'Elia suggested that this ammonium is immediately taken up by zooxanthellae as the coral excretes it. In addition to internal recycling of the ammonium produced by their coral partner, zooxanthellae also actively absorb ammonium from seawater. By absorbing nutrients from the surrounding medium and leaking very little back into the environment, corals and their zooxanthellae gradually accumulate substantial quantities of nitrogen. So, as in tropical rain forest, large quantities of nutrients accumulate on coral reefs and are retained in living biomass.

CONCEPT 15.1 REVIEW

1. Many parasites cause their hosts to alter their behaviour. What impact can this have on the parasite's ability to complete its life cycle?
2. Winter ticks are small relative to the size of their hosts. Even with this size disparity, there is reason to believe they can increase moose mortality. Why?
3. There is a big difference between describing an interaction and experimentally showing that the interaction has a potential fitness consequence. Why were Janzen's experiments effective in demonstrating that mutualisms do exist under natural conditions?

15.2 Ecology of Disease

Basic ecological principles can be applied to our understanding of disease, and the population dynamics of pathogens can be predicted using a compartmental model. Diseases are atypical conditions in living organisms that cause some sort of physiological impairment. Diseases can be caused by a number of factors, including genetic abnormalities, exposure to toxins, and a diversity of other organisms. Here we focus on diseases caused by other organisms.

Why, in a textbook of ecology, is a section devoted to disease? There are two answers. First, humans are not the only species to contract diseases. Instead, diseases alter the fitness of individuals and serve as a brake restraining population growth of many, if not all, species. Second, the pathogens that cause disease are themselves living organisms, just like the caribou, pine trees, and whales that are more often associated with ecology. Although there are certainly debates about what types of pathogens are alive (e.g., bacteria, fungi, etc.) and which are not (e.g., prions, viruses, etc.), this debate is irrelevant to applying ecological principles to our understanding of disease. Instead, it is important to recognize that natural selection is not dependent upon life to operate. As you may recall from chapter 4, evolution by natural selection requires traits to be heritable (the pathogen must be able to reproduce or replicate), and there need to be different levels of fitness (rates of reproduction or

replication) among genotypes (or heritable units). This applies to viruses as well as it applies to wolves.

What influences the population size of pathogens? Some factors will be processes within its host (e.g., immune response, competition with other pathogens), and others will occur outside the host (e.g., transmission rates). Those heritable traits in the pathogen that increase its fitness (e.g., increase transmission) will tend to increase in frequency, while those that reduce fitness will tend to be selected against. The core mechanism of this, as with natural selection in general, is ecology.

Diseases differ greatly in a number of critical life-history parameters, with significant implications for the growth of the agents that cause disease, as well as host populations. As you will see, the efficiency with which disease-causing agents are transferred from host to host has important implications for the population dynamics of the host. Transmission can be *direct*, such as through touching an infected individual, or *indirect*, such as when an uninfected individual touches a surface that has become infected. Diseases also differ as a function of whether they are horizontally or vertically transmitted. **Horizontal transmission** is the transfer of diseases among different individuals of the same generation, such as the spread of H1N1 flu virus through university campuses. **Vertical transmission** is the transfer of a disease from parent to offspring. The differences in transmission, as well as a number of other factors that influence the spread and growth of disease, will influence the host populations. At the core, these differences are life-history differences among different disease-causing agents. Studying the interactions between disease and host is simply another form of exploitative ecological interactions. Understanding disease is the domain of ecology.

Taking an ecological approach to understanding disease also provides insights that may be helpful in reducing the spread of disease through population of concern, be they human or wildlife. In an influential paper entitled "The Dawn of Darwinian Medicine," evolutionary biologists George Williams and Randolph Nesse (1991) argued that human health could be better improved by understanding the evolutionary and ecological basis of disease. How so?

Quite simply, the goal of disease management programs is to reduce the spread of the disease among the host population. Some of our population management decisions (such as many medical treatments) may reduce pathogen growth rates, while others may not. In human populations, public health interventions (e.g., immunizations, quarantine) are expensive and invasive to individuals. As a result, there is a great desire to only apply such measures if there is evidence they will be effective in reducing the spread of disease within the population. You may recall from chapters 12–14 that ecologists have developed a number of models to study population dynamics. It should then come as no surprise that these models have been modified for application to the study of disease.

To understand disease models, we first need to understand what factors actually influence the population growth of diseases. Though disease is widespread across all species, here we focus on humans.

Compartmental Models

In chapter 12 we introduced the concept that populations, given unlimited resources and no enemies, would grow exponentially. However, natural populations rarely encounter such conditions, and instead a variety of ecological processes serve as brakes to population growth. Limited resources cause intraspecific competition within a population, a process that can be modelled with the logistic model. Interspecific competition was added to that model in chapter 13, and predator–prey dynamics used a similar modelling framework in chapter 14.

Although there is conceptual similarity among competition, predation, and disease in terms of their effects in reducing population growth, the ecology of disease has a number of specific differences that require a new modelling framework. One unique aspect of disease is that there are two scales at which pathogen populations can grow: pathogen levels within the body of a single host (e.g., viral load) and the number of new hosts a pathogen is able to colonize. As you will see, it is often the rate of spread to new hosts that most severely limits the spread of disease, rather than the population size of disease-causing agents within a single host. Because of the population-level importance of transmission, this life-history characteristic of the disease-causing agent is often a main target of vaccination and quarantine programs. The modern approach to understanding the impacts of disease on host populations was presented in a foundational paper by Roy Anderson and Robert May (1979).

At the core of this modelling approach are a series of "compartments" that represent different subpopulations of the host, connected through a series of arrows and parameters that represent disease transmission, recovery, and mortality (fig. 15.11). This modelling approach is an elegant way of showing how these basic aspects of pathogen population growth are connected to host population dynamics, allowing researchers to address questions of great public concern. But what exactly is being represented, and how can these be used?

In the centre of figure 15.11 are three compartments: susceptible, infected, and immune. These compartments represent different subpopulations of the hosts. This may seem vaguely familiar, as we discussed subpopulations in the section describing metapopulations (chapter 10). In fact, the math underlying both compartmental models and many of the traditional metapopulation models is nearly identical. The core difference is that here, subpopulations represent individuals that differ not in location (as in metapopulation models), but instead in health status with respect to the disease of interest. Susceptible hosts are those individuals in the population that have the potential to acquire the disease. Infected hosts already have the disease, and thus are no longer susceptible. Some individuals may have acquired immunity, either naturally through recovery, or through an intervention such as a vaccination program. In either case, immune individuals are a discrete subpopulation.

What determines the size of each of these subpopulations? Though we are focused on disease, we cannot forget the basic factors that influence population dynamics of all populations: births, immigration, deaths, and emigrations. For simplicity, we

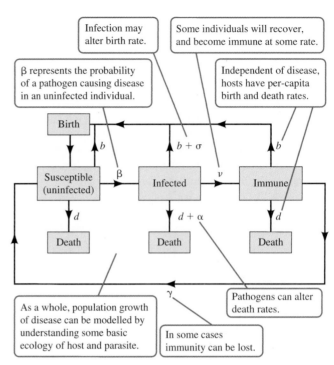

Figure 15.11 A compartmental model of the population growth of a disease-causing organism (data from Anderson and May 1979).

will ignore immigration and emigration in figure 15.11, though these can be added if needed. Each of the host compartments is connected to another compartment labelled "death." These represent the number of susceptible, infected, and immune individuals that die. All individuals have a background per-capita mortality rate, d. Infected individuals may die at a higher rate (depending upon the disease), and thus we can modify their mortality rate to be $d + \alpha$, where α represents the change in per-capita mortality associated with the disease, generally called *virulence* of the pathogen. Highly virulent pathogens cause the presentation of many symptoms in the host, and can lead to high rates of mortality. Pathogens with low virulence may result in hosts that are asymptomatic, with very low rates of mortality. It is worth considering this issue a bit more, from the perspective of the pathogen. All else being equal, what is likely to confer the greatest fitness to a pathogen, high or low virulence? If a pathogen quickly kills its host, it has less time to find a new host, and thus its growth rate is likely lower than a pathogen whose host persists longer. In other words, high rates of virulence are often counter to the best interests, evolutionarily, of a disease. In fact, many diseases become less virulent over time, likely due to natural selection within the pathogen's population.

All subpopulations of hosts also exhibit a background per-capita birth rate, here represented as b. This rate may be altered in infected individuals through the addition of another term, σ (negative values would indicate reduced birth rates of infected individuals). It this model, all newborn individuals enter the susceptible subpopulation, indicating horizontal disease transmission. If a vertically transmitted disease was being modelled, births from individuals within

infected subpopulation would go directly into the infected subpopulation.

Missing from the model at this point is the likelihood of individuals transitioning directly among the three main subpopulations. The probability of a susceptible individual becoming infected will be a function of the ability of the pathogen to move from one host to another. Some pathogens are particularly good at this, and have very high transmission rates, ß, while others are less efficient at this, and have lower transmission rates. Pathogens with a high ß will move quickly through a host population and will tend to have, at least for a short time, a high population growth rate. Depending upon the disease and the population being modelled, some infected individuals will recover and gain immunity, thereby entering the immune subpopulation. Here, that occurs at a rate *v*. Depending upon the disease, immunity may decay over time, resulting in some individuals in the immune subpopulation moving into the susceptible subpopulation at a rate γ.

Once a compartmental model is constructed, each of these parameters can be estimated. This allows the ecologists (or public health officials) to determine the likely progression of the disease through populations, and most importantly, assess the potential impacts of any health interventions on the size of each subpopulation. Next we show how these models can be used to prepare for a potential disease, to evaluate the merits of human interventions after a disease has already passed, and to try and cause the extinction of a disease.

Preparing for an Eventual Zombie Attack

The idea of a zombie eating one's brain casts fear into the hearts of most people. Though these reanimated corpses (fig. 15.12*a*) have been seen with even greater frequency than Sasquatch and Nellie, the public has made surprisingly few evidence-based attempts to determine the best course of action in the case of an outbreak. This lack of preparedness is particularly surprising given the increased frequency with which zombies are featured in movies (fig. 15.12*b*). Making the reasonable assumption that movies reflect reality, the rapid increase in zombie-based movies in the last 10 years suggests there is great concern among the general public of having their brains eaten by an infectious, undead creature. Fortunately, a team of researchers at Carleton University and the University of Ottawa have spent some of their federal research dollars (NSERC) to develop compartmental models involving zombie attacks (Munz et al. 2009). The goal of this research was to determine the effectiveness of alternative human interventions in the face of a zombie outbreak. This work is both critically important to the long-term survival of our species, as well as a helpful example of how compartmental models can be used to understand the impacts of disease on human (and non-human) populations.

Munz and his colleagues begin with a basic model (fig. 15.13) that includes three classes of humans: susceptible (S), zombie (Z), and removed (R). The first two classes are obvious, while the last class represent humans that have died. Because of the possibility that these individuals could be reanimated and converted into zombies, they need to be included in the model.

(a)

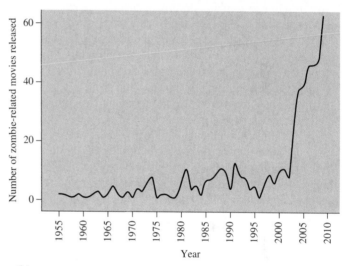

(b)

Figure 15.12   (*a*) Zombies are a common theme in movies. However, (*b*) the number of zombie movies released each year has recently accelerated. Is an attack imminent? If so, ecological models are critical when preparing for zombie outbreaks.

In this basic model (fig. 15.13), susceptibles are converted to zombies at a rate ß and die of natural causes at a rate *d*. For zombies, some encounters with susceptibles may be lethal (when either their brain or head is removed), and

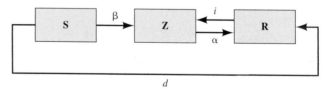

Figure 15.13   A compartmental model describing the potential interactions between humans and zombies. The boxes represent susceptible, zombie, and removed subpopulations, while the arrows represent rates of movement of individuals from one subpopulation to another (from Munz et al. 2009).

they are removed from the population at rate α. Humans in the removed class will be resurrected as zombies at a rate i (analogous to per-capita immigration).

By parameterizing this model, Munz was able to determine that the unfortunate outcome for humans will be their eradication (fig. 15.14). So what are humans to do? By adding additional terms, Munz was able to assess the impacts of three potential human interventions: (1) quarantine, (2) a cure, and (3) aggressive eradication of zombies. Quarantines slowed down eradication of humans, but could not prevent them. A cure was modelled by adding a term from zombie to susceptible, representing the rate of moving out of the zombie compartment. This model predicts a stable coexistence between humans and zombies, though humans would remain in very low densities. The only effective intervention Munz and colleagues could model was a rapid and aggressive response to zombies, destroying them as resources allow. Under this model, there would be a series of increasingly effective attacks against zombies, representing the ability of humans to learn and strategize with experience. In this model, additional terms of "mortality" are added for the zombies, and Munz et al. predict zombies can be eradicated.

What we learn from this example is two things: (1) When zombies attack, act aggressively rather than wait for a cure; and (2) compartmental models are very easily modified to represent the specific disease of interest. By doing so, researchers can predict the impacts of public health interventions. As we see next, this approach also allows researchers to assess and evaluate past events.

Quarantine During a SARS Outbreak

Severe acute respiratory syndrome, SARS, was first reported in November 2002 in China. SARS has a high mortality rate, killing about 15% of those infected, and up to 50% of elderly individuals who contract the disease. SARS spread from China, reaching 32 countries, killing over 750 people, and infecting

over 7,000 more (Gumel et al. 2004). In 2003, there was a SARS outbreak in the greater Toronto area, killing 44 people. At that time, vaccines had yet to be successfully developed for SARS. Isolation and quarantine of individuals suspected of having SARS were used as a means of reducing the spread of the disease. Isolation means separating sick individuals from people who are healthy. Quarantine also involves separating people who have been exposed to the illness, even if they are not presenting any symptoms of the disease. As you may recognize, isolation and quarantine disrupt the lives of many people, and thus should only be implemented if they are likely to improve public health. Troy Day, of Queen's University, along with colleagues from the University of Manitoba, the University of New Brunswick, the University of British Columbia, the University of Victoria, York University, several Canadian health groups, and other researchers in the United States, used compartmental models to determine the effectiveness of isolation and quarantine during the SARS outbreak (Gumel et al. 2004). As you might imagine, this model is a bit more complicated than the hypothetical examples we have already discussed.

The research team developed a compartmental model, consisting of six potential subpopulations (fig. 15.15): susceptible, asymptomatic, quarantined, symptomatic, isolated, and recovered. They parameterized their model using data from the SARS outbreaks in Toronto, Hong Kong, Singapore, and Beijing. Using a variety of mathematical equations, they were then able to explore which of the parameters of the model most strongly influences the spread of the disease in these populations. They found that isolation, if rigorously applied, can be effective in reducing the rate of spread of SARS. However, if isolation is not complete, then mortality rates will increase unless quarantine is also implemented. Of critical concern is the timing of implementation of isolation and quarantine. For example, their model suggests that delaying an isolation and quarantine program around Toronto

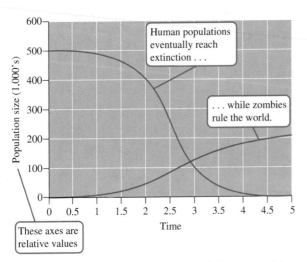

Figure 15.14 If humans do not mount a defence, zombies are predicted to eradicate human populations (from Munz et al. 2009).

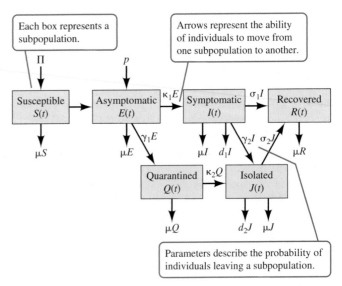

Figure 15.15 A compartmental model was constructed to determine the effectiveness of isolation and quarantine during the SARS outbreak of 2003.

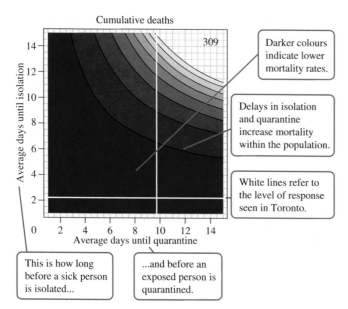

Cumulative deaths

309

Darker colours indicate lower mortality rates.

Delays in isolation and quarantine increase mortality within the population.

White lines refer to the level of response seen in Toronto.

This is how long before a sick person is isolated...

...and before an exposed person is quarantined.

Figure 15.16 Delays in isolation and quarantine would have increased mortality due to SARS during the 2003 outbreak in Toronto.

Infection	R_0	H^*(%)
Diphtheria	6–7	85
Malaria	5–100	80–99
Measles	12–18	83–94
Mumps	4–7	75–86
Pertussis	12–17	92–94
Polio	5–7	80–86
Rubella	6–7	83–85
Smallpox	5–7	80–85

* H is defined as the minimum percent of the population that needs to be immunized for herd immunity to occur.

Figure 15.17 Estimated population of growth rates (R_0) and herd immunity thresholds (H) for some common human diseases (adapted from Paul E. M. Fine, *Herd Immunity: History, Theory, Practice, Epidemiologic Reviews*, Vol. 15, No. 2. Copyright © 1993 by The Johns Hopkins University School of Hygiene and Public Health.)

by only five days would have led to an additional 16 deaths. The overall importance of speed-of-response can be seen in figure 15.16, which shows the predicted mortality results as a function of the average number of days before individuals are isolated or quarantined in the greater Toronto area.

The results from this team's research demonstrate that fast responses by the health care system can be critical in reducing mortality of SARS. Next we show that vaccination programs may also be effective in reducing the spread of disease in human populations.

Using Vaccination to Provide Herd Immunity

Why do humans spend billions of dollars annually on immunization programs? There are two main answers. At the individual level, people are concerned about individuals they know contracting a variety of diseases, many of which have very significant negative consequences for individual health. However, many of the diseases that we currently vaccinate for are actually rare in Canada, though that was certainly not always the case. What is the point in vaccinating for a rare disease, one that even an unvaccinated individual is unlikely to contract?

By understanding the ecology of diseases, the answer should come as no surprise. Vaccination programs provide a significant benefit to public health through modifying the growth rates of diseases. At the extreme, a very effective vaccination program can lead to negative pathogen population growth rates, such that the pathogen goes extinct in that host population (e.g., Canada). At that tantalizing point, **herd immunity** has been achieved and a great public health objective has been met. Why does this work? Let us go back to our basic compartmental model (fig. 15.11). How would we account for vaccination? A simple solution would be to include a new arrow linking the susceptible subpopulation

with the immune subpopulation. By moving previously susceptible hosts to an "immune" subpopulation, vaccination will reduce the number of potential hosts for the pathogen, with direct negative consequences for the rate of pathogen growth.

Unfortunately, herd immunity is unlikely to be achieved for every population of every disease. What types of diseases do you think are more likely to be effectively controlled? The answer can be found in figure 15.17, which provides population growth rates (R_0) and the estimated percent of a population that would need to be vaccinated to confer herd immunity. Pathogens with naturally low levels of transmission have low population growth rates, and are the most susceptible to vaccination programs. It may then be no surprise that polio, with a relatively low R_0, has been eradicated throughout many countries by using aggressive vaccination programs. It is important to recognize that this happened not because every person in a population was vaccinated, but instead because the rates of vaccination were high enough to cause negative population growth of the disease. In contrast, measles has a very high R_0, and is unlikely to ever be eliminated through vaccination.

In the next section we move back to the more traditional organisms studied by ecologists, and begin to explore the mutualist–exploiter continuum.

CONCEPT 15.2 REVIEW

1. Why is life not a necessary condition for application of ecological models of population growth to diseases?
2. Describe the similarities and differences between quarantine and vaccination as means to reduce the spread of a disease in a human population.
3. Why is herd immunity hard to achieve for diseases with high transmission rates?

Mutualist–Exploiter Continuum

Many interactions can switch from parasitic to mutualistic depending upon the specific conditions of the local environment. So far in this chapter we have seen what appears to be a very static portrayal of parasitic and mutualistic interactions. Similarly, we have presented examples that generally involve few individuals, such as the ant–acacia mutualism, where there are highly specialized adaptations that link species. Although this view is helpful in contrasting different types of ecological interactions, they give a skewed perspective of the complexity that actually exists in nature. To understand that mutualism and parasitism are actually different points on a continuum of possible ecological interactions, we must first recognize that most mutualistic interactions are facultative, not obligatory. Additionally, the more common mutualisms generally involve sets of species, rather than single species pairs, such as the ant–acacia example. Two examples we will discuss here, pollination and mycorrhizae, are typical of the complexity of mutualisms. Only in rare exceptions can a single flower be pollinated by a single animal; instead, most animal-pollinated flowers can be serviced by a diversity of insects (fig. 15.18). Similarly, insects are not usually dependent upon a single plant host for nectar or other food, but instead often have a broad selection to choose from. The fact that multi-species interactions are involved, rather than the simpler idea of one-to-one interactions, has required ecologists to take a fresh look at mutualistic and exploitative interactions. We begin, once again, with natural selection.

Recall from chapter 8 that altruism and cooperation required stringent conditions to be evolutionarily stable. There is strong selection against an individual decreasing its fitness, as cheaters in the population would gain benefits from others, while expending no cost. This same logic applies to facultative mutualisms. Individuals are selected most strongly based upon traits that increase their own fitness, not the fitness of others. If an individual in the population "donates" a portion of its fitness to an unrelated individual (here of a different species), and receives less than that amount in return, that behaviour will be selected against. Mutualisms are not "friendly" interactions that occur among species, but instead are exploitative interactions that happen to be reciprocal. In these examples, we highlight that interactions can switch from parasitic to neutral to mutualistic depending upon which species are participating, the local environmental conditions, and even the energetic status of the individuals involved.

Pollination: Optimal Foraging vs. Pollen Movement

Let us imagine pollination for a minute. Most of us will picture a sunny summer day, a field of flowers, and bees moving from one to the next, fertilizing the plants and in turn, receiving nectar from the flowers. We can, however, look at it another way. Plants that undergo sexual reproduction have a problem: they cannot move. As a result, they are unable to actively pursue potential mates, and instead require a **pollen vector** to move pollen from the anther to a stigma. In many cases, this pollen vector is abiotic, such as the wind moving the pollen of grasses and many boreal and temperate tree species. Other plant species use a biotic pollen vector, such as bees, flies, ants, birds, butterflies, or even small mammals. It is this group of "animal-pollinated" plants that we will discuss here.

From the plant's perspective, traits that (1) increase visitation rates by pollinators, (2) enhance rates of pollen deposition, and (3) ensure that pollen moves from one individual to another individual of the same species at a minimum energetic cost, should all be favoured by natural selection. Let us now look at it from the perspective of a pollinator, perhaps a bee. The bee is not interested in pollination; instead it is searching for food while trying to spend the minimum amount of energy foraging (chapter 5). Traits that help the bee locate food efficiently and reduce handling time will be favoured. This presents a problem. For the bee, it is best to fly from one flower to another on a single plant, as this will reduce travel time. Additionally, the bee should spend very little time on

Figure 15.18 Mutualisms, such as those that occur among plants and pollinators, generally involve large numbers of species. Here are three pollinators of *Camas quamash*, a plant found throughout southwestern Canada.

each flower, just taking the nectar and leaving. Unfortunately, for the plant, it is best if the bee visits very few flowers on a single plant (or else there is a good chance of inbreeding), and spends some time at each flower (ensuring pollen deposition). We clearly see that the mutualism of pollination is the outcome of conflicting exploitative interactions: the plants need sex, the bees need food. I don't think this is what parents have in mind when they teach their children about the "birds and the bees."

These conflicts of interest have been extensively studied and show how the evolutionary self-interest of members of mutualistic associations drives these exploitative interactions. Let us first consider an example of a non-obligate pollination mutualism, and the issue of how long flowers "should" stay open. Plant species vary greatly in how long their flowers stay open, with some lasting a few hours, others several weeks. Why? Tia-Lynn Ashman, a former post-doc of Daniel Schoen at McGill University, has addressed this issue in a series of papers (Ashman and Schoen 1994, 1997). She began by developing a model based upon the potential costs and benefits of keeping flowers open for different lengths of time.

What does a plant gain from having its flowers open? Only when open is there a chance that a pollinator will bring or remove pollen, and thus the male and female function of the plant is dependent upon the flower being open. But this lasts only to a point. Although not all pollen is removed during a single visit by a pollinator, nor all ovules generally fertilized, the fitness gained from subsequent visits by a pollinator is likely less than that gained on the first visit. In other words, there are diminishing returns from staying open longer (fig. 15.19). At the same time, there are a variety of

costs associated with keeping flowers open, such as increased evaporation of nectar, increased respiration costs, and even increased risk of acquiring a sexually transmitted disease. The shapes of the cost and benefit curves will vary among species, but the point is the same. Maintaining open flowers is a balance between potential rewards and costs. In experimental work, they showed that seed set decreases when flowers are fertilized long after opening as opposed to soon after opening (Ashman and Schoen 1997), supporting their model. From the pollinator perspective, having the plant close flowers is not in the insect's best interest but is a perfectly understandable "selfish" behaviour of the plant, one that is likely favoured by natural selection. Any thoughts as to what selective pressures this would place on the pollinators?

The costs and benefits of mutualisms to each partner are variable, even within an obligate mutualism. John Addicott, of the University of Calgary, has spent decades unravelling details of the obligate mutualism occurring between the Yucca plant and its pollinator, the Yucca moth. Yuccas are a group of species (*Yucca* spp.) common throughout the dry areas of the western United States, also existing as small populations in southern Alberta, and are common to gardens throughout Canada. Yuccas are pollinated by specialist moths (*Tegeticula* spp.). This is a highly specialized system where neither the plant nor moth can complete their life cycle without the other (fig. 15.20).

We begin in spring, when the moths emerge from cocoons in the soil and quickly mate. The gravid females fly to a nearby Yucca plant, which is now in bloom. The moth enters the flower, and picks many packets of pollen. Using specialized appendages, she forms the pollen into a ball and carries it with her out of the flower. She flies to a new flower, and lays her eggs in its ovary. She then moves to the stigma of the flower and inserts the pollen ball, ensuring fertilization of the ovules of the plant. The moth larvae emerge from their eggs, consuming many of the developing seeds within the Yucca fruit. Fall eventually arrives, and the fruits split open, releasing whatever seeds were not consumed. The fruit falls to the ground, and soon the moth larvae will crawl out, go below ground, and form a cocoon, repeating this cycle in the spring. Some Yucca–Yucca moth pairs are species specific, some Yuccas can be pollinated by a few species of the moth, and some moths can pollinate a few species of Yucca. However, Yucca can not be pollinated by anything other than Yucca moths, and these moths can not complete their life cycle without Yucca plants.

You may recognize in this description that there are a variety of places where cheating could happen. Why does the plant use a pollinator that eats its babies? Why does the moth take the time to pollinate the plant? Why don't the larvae eat all the seeds? Why doesn't the plant just drop the fruit that are being eaten? Over the years, Addicott and his students have been able to learn much about this system.

One of his initial discoveries was that though most Yucca and Yucca moth associations are similar in terms of their general mode of operation, there is substantial variation in the potential costs and rewards of this mutualism among Yucca

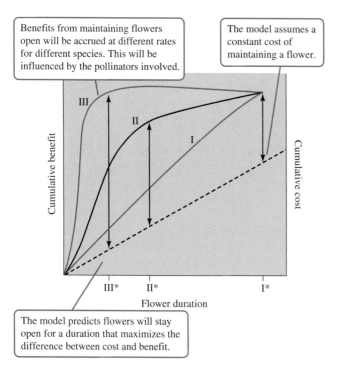

Benefits from maintaining flowers open will be accrued at different rates for different species. This will be influenced by the pollinators involved.

The model assumes a constant cost of maintaining a flower.

The model predicts flowers will stay open for a duration that maximizes the difference between cost and benefit.

Figure 15.19 Cost-benefit analyses can be helpful in trying to understand mutualisms, such as the optimal time for a plant to keep its flowers open.

(a)

(b)

Figure 15.20 (*a*) *Yucca baccata* in full flower; (*b*) a Yucca moth, *Tegeticula altiplanella*, ovipositing on a Yucca flower.

species. One measure of the benefit of this mutualism to the plant is the ratio of viable seeds to available ovules (the female structures that become seeds with fertilization). A ratio of 1.0 would indicate that all ovules developed into seeds (maximal benefit), a ratio of 0.5 would indicate that half the ovules developed into seeds, and a ratio of 0.0 would indicate that there were no mature seeds (no benefit). Across populations, Addicott (1986) found the benefits to the plant ranged from 0.36 to 0.60, a substantial degree of variability. This variability was caused by variation among populations and species in the probability of certain parts of the fruit being occupied by larvae, and by variation in the level of feeding of larvae. He found that many fruit were unoccupied by larvae (they likely died during development), resulting in high seed set, while other fruits had many larvae (and low seed set). This variation highlights that even this elaborate obligate mutualism is dynamic, and the costs and benefits vary in natural systems.

Feeding by pollinators is not the only risk to the Yucca plant. The morphology of the moth greatly influences its ability to place pollen on the stigma, and the morphology of the plant's reproductive structures influences the ability of the moth to successfully lay her eggs. Variation in these traits can lead to cheating, receiving benefit from the mutualistic partner, while not providing a service in return. In fact, upon closer examination of several species, Addicott (1996) found that cheating was common in the Yucca–Yucca moth system. After capturing a number of female Yucca moths, he was able to show that a number of the females of this "mutualist" species were lacking the specialized appendages necessary to move pollen! These females continued to lay their eggs in the ovules of the Yucca ovary, but did not display any of the behaviour associated with pollen ball formation and deposition.

As it turns out, these cheaters are not rare, and can represent 30% of all larvae in the fruits of at least five Yucca species. Needless to say, such cheaters represent an increased cost for these Yucca species, one for which no apparent reward is obtained. This is a further example of how the field of ecology has moved away from viewing mutualism as associated species that "do things" for each other, to seeing mutualisms as cases of reciprocal exploitation. There are a number of questions left unanswered. How common can cheaters be in a population before Yucca populations decline? Do cheater females lay eggs in flowers they know have been pollinated by other moths? If not, how do her offspring get fed?

Cheaters are not unique to the obligate mutualism of Yucca and the Yucca moths. The next time you are in a field full of flowers, sit down and look closely. You will likely see many animals, ants, flies, wasps, bees, beetles, and bugs, moving in and out of the flowers. Some of these will be carrying or leaving pollen, but many of these will not. Instead, they are called **nectar robbers**, who exploit an energy-rich resource (nectar) while providing no pollination services. This exploitation is not limited to insects, and plants too deceive their pollination "partners." A variety of orchid species produce flowers similar in shape, size, and odour to reproductively receptive female wasps, inducing pseudocopulation by male wasps. These males land on the flowers and "mate," taking away and depositing pollen in the process. Clearly the plant benefits from these services provided by the wasp. I will leave it to your own imagination as to whether the plant is providing a service or instead taking advantage of the wasp.

Pollination services are of enormous economic importance in Canada, contributing millions of dollars annually to the economy as a critical aspect to the successful production of many agricultural crops. At the core of this critical agricultural process is a very familiar ecological theme, exploitation. What we learn in ecology does not just apply to our national parks and wilderness areas. These processes affect our lives every day. We see in this next example that exploitation is common in another interaction that involves plants, mycorrhizae.

Mycorrhizae: Nutrient Gain vs. Carbon Gain

The study of mutualisms has largely centred on interactions between plants and other organisms. This is in part because plants are the dominant life form on land. It would be no exaggeration to say that the integrity of the terrestrial portion of the biosphere depends upon plant-centred mutualisms. However, there is another reason so much research has been done on plant mutualisms: plants make very good experimental subjects. Researchers can often learn much more, more quickly, by being able to experimentally alter environmental conditions and thus the potential costs and benefits of associations, and plants are ideally suited for this. We thus continue our discussion on mutualisms, once again involving plants, but now move from the colourful flowers and diverse pollinators to a less well-understood web of interactions in the soil.

The fossil record shows that mycorrhizae arose early in the evolution of land plants, perhaps as long as 400 million years ago. Over evolutionary time, a relationship between plants and some fungi evolved in which mycorrhizal fungi provide plants with greater access to inorganic nutrients while feeding off the root exudates of plants. The two most common types of mycorrhizae are (1) **arbuscular mycorrhizal fungi (AMF)**, in which the mycorrhizal fungus produces **arbuscules**, sites of exchange between plant and fungus; **hyphae**, fungal filaments; and **vesicles**, fungal energy storage organs within root cortex cells, and (2) **ectomycorrhizae (ECM)**, in which the fungus forms a mantle around roots and a netlike structure around root cells (fig. 15.21). Mycorrhizae are especially important in increasing plant access to phosphorus and other immobile nutrients (nutrients that do not move freely through soil).

Mycorrhizae and the Water Balance of Plants

Mycorrhizal fungi appear to improve the ability of many plants to extract soil water. Edie and Michael Allen (1986) studied how mycorrhizae affect the water relations of the grass *Agropyron smithii* by comparing the leaf water potentials of plants with and without mycorrhizae. Figure 15.22 shows that *Agropyron* with mycorrhizae maintained higher leaf water potentials than those without mycorrhizae. This means that when growing under similar conditions of soil moisture, the presence of mycorrhizae helped the grass maintain a higher water potential. Does this comparison show that mycorrhizae are directly responsible for the higher leaf water potential observed in the mycorrhizal grass? No, it does not.

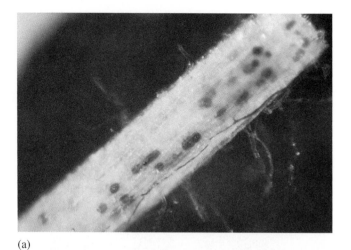

(a)

(b)

Figure 15.21 Mutualistic associations between fungi and plant roots: (*a*) arbuscular mycorrhizal fungus stained so that fungal structures appear blue; and (*b*) ectomycorrhizae, which give a white fuzzy appearance to these roots.

These higher water potentials may be an indirect effect of greater root growth resulting from the greater access to phosphorus provided by mycorrhizae.

Plants with greater access to phosphorus may develop roots that are more efficient at extracting and conducting water; mycorrhizal fungi may not be directly involved in the extraction of water from soils. Kay Hardie (1985) tested this hypothesis directly with an ingenious experimental manipulation of plant growth form and mycorrhizae. First, she grew mycorrhizal and nonmycorrhizal red clover, *Trifolium pratense*, in conditions in which their growth was not limited by nutrient availability. These conditions produced plants with similar leaf areas and root:shoot ratios. Under these carefully controlled conditions, mycorrhizal red clover showed higher rates of transpiration than nonmycorrhizal plants.

Hardie took her study one step further by removing the hyphae of mycorrhizal fungi from half of the red clover with mycorrhizae. She controlled for possible side effects of this manipulation by using a tracer dye to check for root damage and by handling and transplanting all study plants, including those in her control group. Removing hyphae significantly reduced

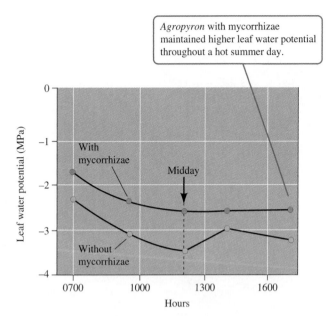

Figure 15.22 Influence of mycorrhizae on leaf water potential of the grass *Agropyron smithii* (data from Allen and Allen 1986).

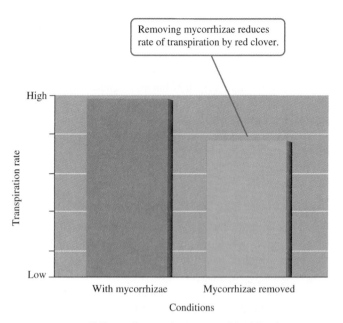

Figure 15.23 Effect of removing mycorrhizal hyphae on rate of transpiration by red clover (data from Hardie 1985).

rates of transpiration (fig. 15.23), indicating a direct role of mycorrhizal fungi in the water relations of plants. Hardy suggests that mycorrhizal fungi improve water relations of plants by giving more extensive contact with moisture in the rooting zone and provide extra surface area for absorption of water.

So far, it seems that plants always benefit from mycorrhizae. That may not always be the case. Environmental conditions may change the flow of benefits between plants and mycorrhizal fungi.

Nutrient Availability and the Mutualistic Balance Sheet

Mycorrhizae supply inorganic nutrients to plants in exchange for carbohydrates, but not all mycorrhizal fungi deliver nutrients to their host plants at equal rates. The relationship between fungus and plant ranges from mutualism to parasitism, depending on the environmental circumstance and mycorrhizal species or even strains within species.

Nancy Johnson (1993) performed experiments designed to determine whether fertilization can select for less mutualistic mycorrhizal fungi. Before discussing her experiments, we have to ask what would constitute a "less mutualistic" association. In general, a less mutualistic relationship would be one in which there was a greater imbalance in the benefits to the mutualistic partners. In the case of mycorrhizae, a less mutualistic mycorrhizal fungus would be one in which the fungal partner received an equal or greater quantity of photosynthetic product in trade for a lower quantity of nutrients.

Johnson pointed out that there are several reasons to predict that fertilization would favour less mutualistic mycorrhizal fungi. The first is that plants vary the amount of soluble carbohydrates in root exudates as a function of nutrient availability. Plants release more soluble carbohydrates in root exudates when they grow in nutrient-poor soils and decrease

the amount of carbohydrates in root exudates as soil fertility increases. Consequently, fertilization of soils should favour strains, or species, of mycorrhizal fungi capable of living in a low-carbohydrate environment. Johnson suggested that the mycorrhizal fungi capable of colonizing plants releasing low quantities of carbohydrates will probably be those that are aggressive in their acquisition of carbohydrates from their host plants, perhaps at the expense of host plant performance. She addressed this possibility using a mixture of field observations and greenhouse experiments.

In the first phase of her project, Johnson examined the influence of inorganic fertilizers on the kinds of mycorrhizal fungi found in soils. She collected soils from 12 experimental plots in a field on the Cedar Creek Natural History Area in central Minnesota that had been abandoned from agriculture for 22 years. Six of the study plots had been fertilized with inorganic fertilizers for eight years prior to Johnson's experiment, while the other six had received no fertilizer over the same period.

Johnson sampled the populations of mycorrhizal fungi from fertilized and unfertilized soils and showed that the composition of mycorrhizal fungi differed substantially. Of the 12 mycorrhizal species occurring in the samples, unfertilized soil supported higher densities of three mycorrhizal fungi, *Gigaspora gigantea*, *G. margarita*, and *Scutellospora calospora*, while fertilized soil supported higher densities of one species, *Glomus intraradix*. Spores of *G. intraradix* accounted for over 46% of the spores recovered from fertilized soils, but only 27% of the spores from unfertilized soils.

Johnson used greenhouse experiments to assess how these differences in the composition of mycorrhizal fungi might affect plant performance. She chose big bluestem grass, *Andropogon gerardii*, as a study plant for these experiments because it is native to the Cedar Creek Natural History Area and is well adapted to the nutrient-poor soils of the area. Seedlings of *Andropogon* were planted in pots containing sand.

Johnson also added a composite sample of other soil microbes living in the soils of the fertilized and unfertilized study plots.

To each pot Johnson added a mycorrhizal "inoculum" of 30 g of soil of one of three types: (1) a fertilized inoculum consisting of 15 g of soil from fertilized study plots mixed with 15 g of sterilized unfertilized soil, (2) an unfertilized inoculum consisting of 15 g of soil from unfertilized study plots mixed with 15 g of sterilized fertilized soil, or (3) a non-mycorrhizal inoculum consisting of 30 g of a sterilized composite from the soils of fertilized and unfertilized study plots. The first two inocula acted as a source of mycorrhizal fungi for colonization of *Andropogon*. The design of Johnson's experiment is summarized in figure 15.24.

Why did Johnson create her inocula by mixing sterilized and unsterilized soils from the fertilized and unfertilized study areas? She did so to control for the possibility that some nonbiological factor such as trace nutrients in one of the two soil types might have a measurable effect on plant performance. The completely sterilized inoculum acted as a control to assess the performance of plants in the absence of mycorrhizae. Why did Johnson's control consist of sterilized composite soil from all the study areas? Again, she had to guard against the possibility that the soils themselves without mycorrhizal fungi might affect plant performance.

Pots were next assigned to one of four nutrient treatments in which Johnson (1) added no supplemental nutrients (None), (2) added phosphorus only (+P), (3) added nitrogen only (+N), or (4) added both nitrogen and phosphorus (+N +P). The sand from the Cedar Creek Natural History Area contained a fairly low concentration of nitrogen but considerably higher concentrations of phosphorus. Nutrient additions were adjusted so that the supplemented treatments offered nitrogen and phosphorus concentrations comparable to those of the topsoil in the fertilized study plots.

Johnson harvested five replicates of each of the treatments at two points in time: at 4 weeks, when *Andropogon* was actively growing, and at 12.5 weeks, when the grass was fully grown. At each harvest she measured several aspects of plant performance: plant height, shoot mass, and root mass; and at 12.5 weeks she also recorded the number of inflorescences per plant.

At 12.5 weeks, shoot mass was significantly influenced by nutrient supplements and by whether or not plants were mycorrhizal, but not by the source of the mycorrhizal inoculum (fig. 15.25). Shoot mass was greatest in the double nutrient supplement treatment (+N +P), somewhat lower in the nitrogen supplement (+N), and very low in the other two treatments (None and +P). Figure 15.25*a* also indicates a definite influence of mycorrhizae on performance. Shoot mass was significantly greater for mycorrhizal plants across all nutrient treatments.

Nutrient supplements and mycorrhizae also significantly influenced root:shoot ratios (fig. 15.25*b*). As we saw in

Question: Does fertilizing soil select for less mutualistic mycorrhizal fungi?

Experimental Design

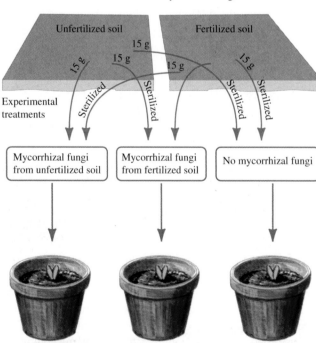

Figure 15.24   Testing the effects of long-term fertilizing on interactions between mycorrhizal fungi and plants on agricultural lands.

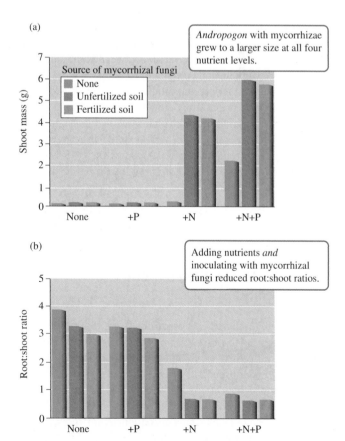

Figure 15.25   Effect of nutrient additions and mycorrhizae on the grass *Andropogon gerardii* (data from Johnson 1993).

chapter 7, plants invest differentially in roots and shoots depending on nutrient and light availability. It also appears that variation in investment is aimed at increasing supplies of resources in short supply. For instance, in nutrient-poor environments, many plants invest disproportionately in roots and consequently have high root:shoot ratios, which decline with increasing nutrient availability. The results of Johnson's experiments are consistent with this generalization. Root:shoot ratios were highest in the treatments without nitrogen supplements (None and +P) and lowest in the treatments with nitrogen supplements (+N and +N +P). In other words, higher plant investment in roots in the low-nitrogen treatments suggests greater nutrient limitation than in the high-nitrogen treatments.

In summary, Johnson's study produced two pieces of evidence that bear on the question posed at the outset of her study: Can fertilization of soil select for less mutualistic mycorrhizal fungi? First, in the early stages of her experiment, *Andropogon* inoculated with fertilized soil had lower shoot mass than those inoculated with unfertilized soil. Second, *Andropogon* inoculated with unfertilized soils produced more inflorescences than did *Andropogon* inoculated with fertilized soils. In other words, *Andropogon* inoculated with mycorrhizal fungi from unfertilized soils showed faster shoot growth as young plants. These results suggest that plants receive more benefit from association with the mycorrhizal fungi from unfertilized soils. Johnson's simultaneous studies of the mycorrhizal fungi indicate the mechanisms producing these patterns. It appears that altering the nutrient environment does alter the mutualistic balance sheet, an influence of potential importance to agricultural practice.

John Klironomos, from the University of Guelph, has also delved into the complex world of plant–fungal interactions. He found that the form of interaction between plants and fungi is even more variable and complex than people had imagined. Klironomos asked a very important question: Are AMF generally mutualists, or parasites? In an elegantly simple experiment, he subjected individual plants of 64 plant species to one of two treatments: Plants were planted in a greenhouse pot with either propagules of one species of AMF (*Glomus etunicatum*), or sterile soil (Klironomos 2003). He used ten

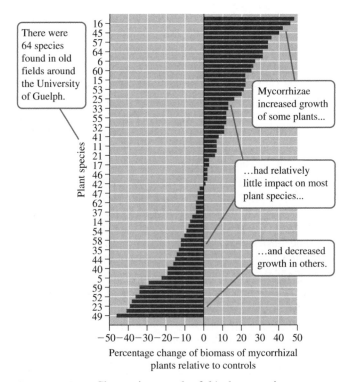

Figure 15.26   Change in growth of 64 plant species as a function of the presence or absence of a mycorrhizal fungal species (data from Klironomos 2003).

replicates of each plant species × AMF combination, resulting in 1,280 pots. After 16 weeks, he measured plant biomass, comparing growth with and without AMF. The results were dramatic (fig. 15.26). The growth of most species did not differ between the AMF and sterile soil treatments! In other words, this relationship was generally neutral—not mutualistic nor parasitic. However, for some species the interaction was strongly parasitic, and others strongly beneficial. Across this broad range of species, Klironomos found a broad range of plant responses. Ecological interactions, like mycorrhizae, fall along a continuum of effect for the partners. Understanding why requires us to look a bit at the evolution of mutualisms.

ECOLOGY IN ACTION

Impacts of Mycorrhizae on Forest Sustainability

As we have discussed, mycorrhizae have the potential to impact a plant's life positively or negatively, and the position along the mutualism–exploitation continuum depends upon the exact costs and benefits at any particular time. This issue has enormous implications for agriculture and forestry, and here we will discuss two examples in which mycorrhizal interactions may have significant consequences for forest regeneration and community composition.

Suzanne Simard, of the University of British Columbia, has studied the ecology of ectomycorrhizae and their potential impact on forest dynamics extensively. Forest dynamics are an important issue for the forest industry, and having a detailed understanding of the factors that influence regeneration can be of broad economic importance. One of the interesting aspects of mycorrhizae is that many of the fungi involved are generalists, able to colonize the roots of different species of plants. This aspect of fungal biology is not restricted to pots in

Figure 15.27   A number of tree species can be interconnected by mycorrhizal fungi in the forests of British Columbia.

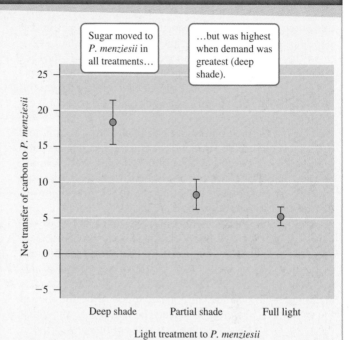

Figure 15.28   Sugar can move from one individual to another through mycorrhizal connections (data from Simard et al.1997).

a greenhouse, but also can occur in the field, where you can regularly find one individual fungus associated with the roots of many individuals of plant species—simultaneously. Simard developed an elegant design to test whether these shared connections could result in sugar moving toward or away from some plants (Simard et al. 1997). In other words, could some plants partially parasitize others through these shared mycorrhizal connections? Her study used three focal species, *Betula payrifera*, *Pseudotsuga menziesii*, and *Thuja plicata* (fig. 15.27), all of which are important to the forestry industry of British Columbia. Simard planted young plants of these three species together in forest soil, and after some time, fed the leaves of the plants with ^{13}C or ^{14}C. Why did she use these tracers? To follow the carbon. For example, if she fed *Betula* with ^{13}C, but found ^{13}C in the other plants, that would tell her the carbon moved. But does that mean it moved through hyphae? No. It is certainly possible that the carbon went from the leaves,

to the roots, and then entered the soil as dead roots, or root exudate. Part of the elegance of her design is that she included *Thuja* in her study. This species does not share fungal species with *Betula* and *Pseudotsuga*, and so the amount of labelled carbon in *Thuja* would indicate how much passed through the plants to the soils, with any excess found in the other species coming through mycorrhizal connections.

Why did she use two tracers in this study? She was not interested in simply whether carbon moved from one plant to another (as prior studies have shown it could); instead she wanted to find whether there was *net* movement from one plant to another. Net movement, if it occurs, would indicate parasitism by the recipient on the host, and would be quite a surprise to many forest biologists! So, in a single trial she would feed *Betula* with one tracer and *Pseudotsuga* with the other. In her analyses, she was particularly interested in knowing the net movement of sugars into, or out of, *Pseudotsuga*. Net movement could be measured as the difference in tracer concentrations between *Pseudotsuga* and *Betula*. For instance, if *Betula* was labelled with ^{13}C and *Pseudotsuga* with ^{14}C, net movement would be the difference between the ^{14}C found in *Betula* and the ^{13}C found in *Pseudotsuga*.

What did Simard find? There was very little tracer in *Thuja*, indicating the plant-to-soil pathway was not likely important. However, there was substantial net movement of sugars to *Pseudotsuga*, indicating it was exploiting *Betula*! Even more interesting, the amount of parasitism expressed increased when she shaded *Pseudotsuga* (fig. 15.28), reaching up to 6% of its entire carbon budget. Why would *Betula* feed

this unrelated host? We can once again return to our understanding of mutualisms as reciprocal exploitation. Not everything that happens in such an interaction is "good" for each member; instead, the net effect is positive. So, in this example it is possible that the potential benefit *Betula* receives from this mutualism with the fungus is greater than the costs of feeding other plants. But there is also an alternative explanation. Perhaps *Pseudotsuga* simply cannot do anything about it, and that at this point in the evolution of this interaction, the parasite is winning! We cannot lose site of the fact that parasites, be they fungal or plant, are also subject to natural selection, and will certainly evolve traits that allow them to circumvent the defence systems of the host organisms.

John Klironomos, of the University of Guelph, has evidence that ectomycorrhizae may also serve as parasites to some living animals (Klironomos and Hart 2001). Klironomos found that one species of fungus, *Laccaria bicolor*, was able to infect the small soil-dwelling arthropod, *Folsomia candida* (a springtail). This infection appears to kill large numbers of the springtails. By using ^{15}N tracers, he was able to show that the nitrogen in the springtails was moved into new tissue in seedlings of *Pinus strobus*. In other words, this ectomycorrhizal fungus is a predator to the springtail, and a mutualist to the tree! Similar results were not found for a second species of fungus, suggesting that even within mycorrhizal fungi there is substantial variation in the mechanisms by which resources are captured.

So what does this mean for forests sustainability? The answer to that question is unknown. Many ecologists continue to work in this area, with a growing realization that it is much more complicated than simply saying mycorrhizae are "good" for the forests. Although there may be some feeding going on through mycorrhizae, it remains unclear whether that is greater than the negative effects of competition for light and nutrients. In other words, resource sharing is yet another type of interaction among species, one that happens in addition to the other forms of interaction we have already discussed. Because of the enormous potential impact on forest regeneration, it is fair to say we will hear more of this story in the years to come.

CONCEPT 15.3 REVIEW

1. What similarities do nectar robbers and "cheating" Yucca moths share? What risk may they encounter if they represent a large proportion of the insects that visit the host flowers?
2. Explain why plants and pollinators have competing interests about how long flowers should be kept open.
3. Why should selection favour mycorrhizal fungi that are "less mutualistic" when soil nutrients are high?

15.4 Evolution of Mutualism

Theory predicts that mutualism will evolve where the benefits of mutualism exceed the costs. We have reviewed several complex mutualisms both on land and in marine environments. There are many others, every one a fascinating example of the intricacies of nature. Ecologists not only study the present biology of those mutualisms, but also seek to understand the conditions leading to their evolution and persistence. We have also seen evidence that interactions are not fixed in time, but can vary according to changes in local conditions. Theoretical analyses point to the relative costs and benefits of a possible relationship as a key factor in the evolution of mutualism.

Modelling of mutualisms has generally taken one of two approaches. The earliest attempts involved modifications of the Lotka–Volterra equations to represent the population dynamics of mutualism. The alternative approach has been to model mutualistic interactions using cost-benefit analysis to explore the conditions under which mutualisms can evolve and persist. In chapters 13 and 14, where we discussed models of competition and predation, we focused on the population dynamic approach to modelling species interactions. Here, we concentrate on cost-benefit analyses of mutualism.

Kathleen Keeler (1981, 1985) developed models to represent the relative costs and benefits of several types of mutualistic interactions. Among them are two of the mutualistic interactions we discussed in this chapter: ant–plant protection mutualisms and mycorrhizae. Keeler's approach requires that we consider a population polymorphic for mutualism containing three kinds of individuals: (1) *successful mutualists*, which give and receive measurable benefits to another organism; (2) *unsuccessful mutualists*, which give benefits to another organism but, for some reason, do not receive any benefit in return; and (3) *nonmutualists*, neither giving nor receiving benefit from a mutualistic partner. The bottom line in Keeler's approach is that for a population to be mutualistic, the fitness of successful mutualists must be greater than the fitness of either unsuccessful mutualists or nonmutualists. In addition, the combined fitness of successful and unsuccessful mutualists must exceed that of the fitness of nonmutualists. If these conditions are not met, Keeler proposed that natural selection will eventually eliminate the mutualistic interaction from the population.

In general, we can expect mutualism to evolve and persist in a population when and where mutualistic individuals have higher fitness than nonmutualistic individuals.

Keeler represented the fitness of nonmutualists as:

$$w_{nm} = \text{fitness of nonmutualists}$$

(Fitness has been traditionally represented by the symbol w and though it might be clearer to use another symbol, such as f, the traditional symbol is used here.) Keeler represents the fitness of mutualists as:

$$w_m = pw_{ms} + qw_{mu} \qquad (1)$$

where:

p = the proportion of the population consisting of successful mutualists

w_{ms} = the fitness of successful mutualists

q = the proportion of the population consisting of unsuccessful mutualists

w_{mu} = the fitness of unsuccessful mutualists.

We can represent Keeler's conditions for the evolution and persistence of mutualism as:

$$w_m > w_{nm} \qquad (2)$$

or

$$pw_{ms} + qw_{mu} > w_{nm} \qquad (3)$$

Keeler predicts that mutualism will persist when the combined fitness of successful and unsuccessful mutualists exceeds the fitness of nonmutualists. Why do we have to combine the fitness of successful and unsuccessful mutualists? Remember that both confer benefit to their partner, but only the successful mutualists receive benefit in return.

The analysis is more convenient if we think of these relationships in terms of **selection coefficients (s)**, the relative selective costs associated with being either a successful mutualist, an unsuccessful mutualist, or a nonmutualist:

$$s = 1 - w \text{ and } w = (1 - s).$$

Using selective coefficients, Keeler expressed the selective cost of being a successful mutualist, an unsuccessful mutualist, or a nonmutualist as:

$$s_{ms} = (H)(1 - A)(1 - D) + IA + ID \qquad (4)$$

$$s_{mu} = (H)(1 - D) + IA + ID \qquad (5)$$

$$s_{nm} = H(1 - D) + ID \qquad (6)$$

where:

H = the proportion of the plant tissue damaged in the absence of any defences

D = the amount of protection given to the plant tissues by defences other than ants (e.g., chemical defences); so, $1 - D$ is the amount of tissue damage that would occur in spite of these alternative defences

A = the amount of herbivory prevented by ants (so, again, $1 - A$ is the amount of herbivory that occurs in spite of ants)

IA = the investment by the plant in benefits extended to the ants

ID = investment in defences other than ants

Using these selective coefficients, we can express Keeler's conditions for evolution and persistence of the ant-plant mutualism as:

$$p(1 - s_{ms}) - q(1 - s_{mu}) > 1 - s_{nm}$$

into which Keeler substituted the relationships given in equations (4), (5), and (6). By simplifying the resulting equation, she produced the following expression of benefits relative to costs:

$$p[H(1 - D) A] > I_A$$

Facultative Ant–Plant Protection Mutualisms

Keeler applied her cost-benefit model to facultative mutualisms involving plants with extrafloral nectaries and ants that feed at the nectaries and provide protection to the plant in return. Her model is not appropriate for obligate mutualisms like that between swollen thorn acacias and their mutualistic ants, but instead applies to situations in which both the plant and ant can live without its partner. In addition, Keeler wrote her model from the perspective of the plant side of the mutualism. Let's step through the general model and connect each of the terms with the ecology of facultative plant–ant protection mutualisms.

In this model, w_{ms} is the fitness of a plant that produces extrafloral nectaries and that successfully attracts ants effective at guarding it, while w_{mu} is the fitness of a plant that produces extrafloral nectaries but that has not attracted enough ants to mount a successful defence. For example, these plants may be too far from an ant nest. In addition, Keeler includes the fitness of nonmutualistic plants, w_{nm}, which would be the fitness of individuals of a plant that does not produce extrafloral nectaries. Are there such individuals in natural populations? We do not know, but that is not the point. The reason Keeler includes nonmutualists in her model is to provide an assessment of the potential costs and benefits of such a strategy against which she can weigh the mutualistic strategy. This is analogous to the approach used in game theory in chapter 8.

Keeler's model represents potential benefits to the host plant as:

$$p[H(1 - D) A]$$

where:

p = the proportion of the plant population attracting sufficient ants to mount a defence

Keeler's model represents the plant's costs of mutualism as:

$$I_A = n[m + d (a + c + h)]$$

where:

n = the number of extrafloral nectaries per plant

m = the energy content of nectary structures

d = the period of time during which the nectaries are active

a = costs of producing amino acids in nectar

c = costs of producing the carbohydrates in nectar

h = costs of providing water for nectar

Again, Keeler's hypothesis is that for mutualism to persist, benefits must exceed costs. In terms of her model:

$$p[H(1 - D)A] > I_A$$

This model proposes that for a facultative ant–plant mutualism to evolve and persist, the proportion of the plant's energy budget that ants save from destruction by herbivores must exceed the proportion of the plant's energy budget that is invested in extrafloral nectaries and nectar.

The details of Keeler's model offer insights into what conditions may produce higher benefits than costs. First, and most obviously, I_A, the proportion of the plant's energy budget invested in extrafloral nectaries and nectar, should be low. This means that plants living on a tight energy budget, for example, those living in a shady forest understory, should be less likely to invest in attracting ants than those living in full sun. Higher benefits result from (1) a high probability of attracting ants, p; (2) a high potential for herbivory, H; (3) low effectiveness of alternative defences, D; and (4) highly effective ant defence, A.

The task for ecologists is to determine how well these requirements of the model match the values of these variables in nature. By finding the conditions under which mutualisms are or are not most likely to occur, ecologists can begin to unravel the complexity of interactions that occur in the natural world.

CONCEPT 15.4 REVIEW

1. Suppose you discover a mutant form of plant that does not produce extrafloral nectaries. What does Keller's theory predict concerning the relative fitness of these mutant plants and the typical ones that produce extrafloral nectaries?
2. According to Keller's theory, under what general conditions would the mutant, lacking extrafloral nectaries, increase in frequency in a population and displace the typical plants that produce extrafloral nectaries?

ECOLOGICAL TOOLS AND APPROACHES

Mutualism and Humans

Mutualism has been important in the lives and livelihood of humans for a long time. Historically, much of agriculture has depended upon mutualistic associations between species and much of agricultural management has been aimed at enhancing mutualisms, such as nitrogen fixation, mycorrhizae, and pollination to improve crop production. Agriculture itself has been viewed as a mutualistic relationship between humans and crop and livestock species. However, there may be some qualitative differences between agriculture as it has been generally practised and mutualisms among other species. How much of agriculture is pure exploitation and how much is truly mutualistic remains an open question. Here we discuss how understanding the ecology of mutualisms can help us understand some human behaviours.

There is, however, at least one human mutualism that fits comfortably in this chapter, a mutualism involving communication between humans and a wild species with clear benefit to both. This mutualism joins the traditional honey gatherers of Africa with the greater honeyguide, *Indicator indicator* (fig. 15.29). Honey gathering has long been an important aspect of African cultures, important enough that there are scenes of honey gathering in rock art painted over 20,000 years ago (Isack and Reyer 1989). No one knows how long humans have gathered honey in Africa, but it is difficult to imagine the earliest hominids resisting such sweet temptation. Whenever honey gathering began, humans have apparently had a capable and energetic partner in their searches.

The Honeyguide

Honeyguides belong to the family Indicatoridae in the order Piciformes, an order that also includes the woodpeckers. The family Indicatoridae includes a total of 17 species, 15 of which are native to Africa. Honeyguides have the unusual habit of feeding on waxes of various sorts—most feed on beeswax and insects. Of the 17 species of honeyguides, only the greater honeyguide, *I. indicator*, is known to guide humans and a few other mammals to bees' nests.

Figure 15.29   The greater honeyguide, *Indicator indicator.*

The greater honeyguide is found throughout much of sub-Saharan Africa. It avoids only dense forests and very open grasslands and desert, and its distribution corresponds broadly with the distributions of tropical savanna and tropical dry forest. Like all of the honeyguides, the greater honeyguide is a brood parasite that, like cuckoos, lays its eggs in the nests of other birds. This way of life is reflected in the early morphology of nestling honeyguides, which retain "bill hooks" on their upper and lower bills for the first 14 days of life that they use to lacerate and kill their nest mates. However, nests sometimes contain two honeyguide nestlings, so apparently there is some mechanism by which nestlings of the same species can coexist. After the deaths of their nest mates, honeyguide nestlings receive all the food brought by their foster parents, which continue to feed young honeyguides until they are completely independent, approximately 7 to 10 days after leaving the nest.

Greater honeyguides are capable of completely independent life without mutualistic interactions with humans, so we would classify their mutualism as facultative. Living independently, honeyguides feed on beeswax, and on the adults, larvae, pupae, and eggs of bees. They also feed on a wide variety of other insects. Greater honeyguides show highly opportunistic feeding behaviour and sometimes join flocks of other bird species foraging on the insects stirred up by large mammals. The most distinguishing feature of the greater honeyguide, however, is its habit of guiding humans and ratels, or honey badgers, to bees' nests.

Guiding Behaviour

The first written report of the guiding behaviour of *I. indicator* was authored in 1569 by João Dos Santos, a missionary in the part of East Africa that is now Mozambique. Dos Santos first noticed honeyguides because they would enter the mission church to feed upon the bits of beeswax on candlesticks. He went on to describe their guiding behaviour by saying that when the birds find a beehive, they search for people and attempt to lead them to the hive. He noted that the local people eagerly followed the birds because of their fondness for honey, and he observed that the honeyguide profits by gaining access to the wax and dead bees left after humans raid the hive. Dos Santos's report of this behaviour was confirmed by other European visitors to almost all parts of Africa for the next four centuries. However, it was not until the middle of the twentieth century that the mutualism of honeyguides with humans was examined scientifically. The foundation work of these studies was that of H. Friedmann (1955), who reviewed and organized the observations of others, including those of Dos Santos, and who conducted his own extensive research on the honeyguides of Africa.

Friedmann's report of some of the African legends surrounding the greater honeyguide suggests that a wide variety of African cultures prescribed rewarding the bird for its guiding behaviour and that native Africans recognized the need for reciprocity in their interactions with honeyguides. One proverb reported by Friedmann was, "If you do not leave anything for the guide [*I. Indicator*], it will not lead you at all in the future." Another proverb stated more ominously, "If you do not leave anything for the guide, it will lead you to a dangerous animal the next time." Friedmann also observed that many African cultures forbid killing a honeyguide and once "inflicted severe penalties" for doing so. These observations suggest long association between humans and honeyguides and that the association has been consciously mutualistic on the human side of the balance sheet.

The mutualistic association between humans and honeyguides may have developed from an earlier association between the bird and the ratel, or honey badger, *Mellivora capensis*. The honey badger is a powerful animal, well equipped with strong claws and powerful muscles to rip open bees' nests, that readily follows honeyguides to bees' nests. The honey badger, though secretive, has been observed often following honeyguides while vocalizing. African honey gatherers also vocalize to attract honeyguides, and Friedmann reported that some of their vocalizations imitate the calls of honey badgers.

The most detailed and quantitative study of this mutualism to date is that of H. Isack of the National Museum of Kenya and H.-U. Reyer of the University of Zurich (Isack and Reyer 1989), who studied the details of the interaction of the greater honeyguide with the Boran people of northern Kenya. The Boran regularly follow honeyguides and have developed a penetrating whistle that they use to attract them. The whistle can be heard over 1 km away, and Isack and Reyer found that it doubles the rate at which Boran honey gatherers encounter honeyguides. If they are successful in attracting a honeyguide, the average amount of time it takes to find a bees' nest is 3.2 hours. Without the aid of a honeyguide, the average search time per bees' nest is about 8.9 hours. This is an underestimate of the true time, however, since Isack and Reyer did not include days in which no bees' nests were found in their analysis. The benefit of the association to the bird seems apparent from Isack and Reyer's analysis, since they report that 96% of the nests to which the Boran were guided would have been inaccessible to the birds without human help.

The greater honeyguide attracts the attention of a human by flying close and calling as it does so. Following this initial attention-getting behaviour, the bird will fly off in a particular direction and disappear for up to one minute. After reappearing, the bird again perches in a conspicuous spot and calls to the following humans. As the honey gatherers follow, they whistle, bang on wood, and talk loudly to "keep the bird interested." When the honey gatherers approach the perch from which the honeyguide is calling, the bird again flies off, calling and displaying its white tail feathers as it does so, only to reappear at another conspicuous perch a short time later. This sequence of leading, following, and leading is repeated

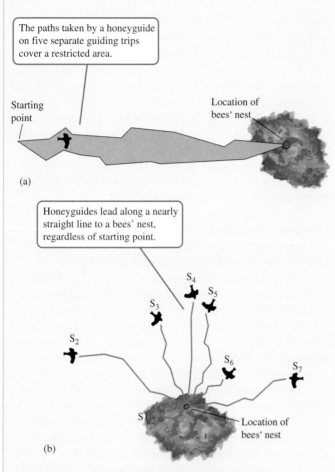

The paths taken by a honeyguide on five separate guiding trips cover a restricted area.

Starting point

Location of bees' nest

(a)

Honeyguides lead along a nearly straight line to a bees' nest, regardless of starting point.

S₄
S₅
S₃
S₂
S₆
S₇
S₁
Location of bees' nest

(b)

Figure 15.30   Paths taken by honeyguides leading people to bees' nests (data from Isack and Reyer 1989).

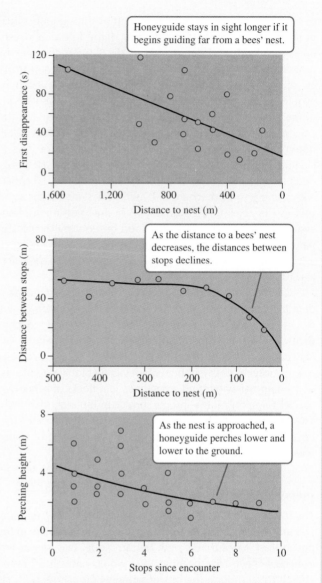

Honeyguide stays in sight longer if it begins guiding far from a bees' nest.

First disappearance (s)

Distance to nest (m)

As the distance to a bees' nest decreases, the distances between stops declines.

Distance between stops (m)

Distance to nest (m)

As the nest is approached, a honeyguide perches lower and lower to the ground.

Perching height (m)

Stops since encounter

Figure 15.31   Changes in behaviour of the honeyguide as it nears a bees' nest (data from Isack and Reyer 1989).

until the bird and the following honey gatherers arrive at the bees' nest.

Isack, who is a Boran, interviewed Boran honey gatherers to determine what information they obtained from honeyguides. The main purpose of the study was to test assertions by the honey gatherers that the bird informs them of (1) the direction to the bees' nest, (2) the distance to the nest, and (3) when they arrive at the location of the nest. The data gathered by Isack and Reyer support all three assertions.

Honey gatherers reported that the bird indicated direction to the bees' nest on the basis of the direction of its guiding flights. One method used by Isack and Reyer to test how well flight direction indicated direction was to induce honeyguides to guide them from the same starting point to the same known bees' nest on five different occasions. Figure 15.30a shows the highly restricted area covered by these five different guiding trips. Another approach was to induce the bird to guide them to a bees' nest from seven different starting points (fig. 15.30b). The result was a consistent tendency by the bird to lead directly to the site of the bees' nest.

The Boran honey gatherers said that three variables decrease as distance to the nest decreases: (1) the time the

bird stays out of sight during its first disappearance following the initial encounter, (2) the distance between stops made by the bird on the way to the bees' nest, and (3) the height of the perch on the way to the nest. Data gathered by Isack and Reyer support all three statements (fig. 15.31).

The honey gatherers also report that they can determine when they arrive in the vicinity of a bees' nest by changes in the honeyguide's behaviour and vocalizations (fig. 15.32). Isack and Reyer observed several of these changes. While on the path to a bees' nest, a honeyguide emits a distinctive guiding call and will answer human calls by increasing the frequency of the guiding call. On arriving at a nest, the honeyguide perches close to the nest and gives off a special "indication" call. After a few indication calls, it remains silent

Figure 15.32 Vocal communication between honeyguides and humans.

and does not answer to human sounds. If approached by a honey gatherer, a honeyguide flies in a circle around the nest location before perching again nearby.

Isack and Reyer observe that their data do not allow them to test other statements by the Boran honey gatherers, including that when bees' nests are very far away (over 2 km), the honeyguide will "deceive" the gatherers about the real distance to the nest by stopping at shorter intervals. Isack and Reyer add, however, that they have no reason to doubt these other statements, since all others have been supported by the data they were able to collect. What these data reveal is a rich mutualistic interaction between wild birds and humans. It remains unclear how widely mutualisms alter human behaviour. Using ecological tools and methods of study may provide further insights into the social biology of people.

SUMMARY

Many interactions between individuals are difficult to classify, and range along a continuum of exploitation and mutualism. Mutualisms, interactions between individuals that benefit both partners, are common in nature, and form the foundation of most of life as we know it within the biosphere. Mutualisms can be divided into those that are facultative, where species can live without their mutualistic partners, and obligate, where species are unable to complete their life cycle without their partner.

15.1 There is great diversity in the types of parasitic and mutualistic interactions that exist, defying easy generalization.

Despite the ubiquity of mutualistic interactions, most species on the planet are parasites. The specific interactions between parasites and hosts and between mutualistic partners are extremely diverse. Many pathogens alter behaviour of their hosts in ways that increase the transmission rate of the pathogen. Such changes can have negative consequences for the host, such as increased predation rates and altered competitive abilities. Some parasites, such as winter ticks, can infest their hosts, causing shifts in appearance, behaviour, and likely population dynamics. Other interactions appear to benefit both partners, such as the obligate mutualism that occurs between ants and Acacia trees. Acacia trees provide food and housing for ants, which provide protection from herbivores and potential competitors for the tree. The mutualism between zooxanthellae and corals results in the construction of the foundation of an entire ecosystem, coral reefs. The zooxanthellae live within their animal partners (the coral), receiving nutrients from the coral while returning organic compounds for the coral to synthesize.

15.2 Basic ecological principles can be applied to our understanding of disease, and the population dynamics of pathogens can be predicted using a compartmental model.

Disease can be viewed as an exploitative interaction between a host and a pathogen. Population growth of the disease can be modelled by the use of a compartmental model. One key

parameter is the transmission rate of the disease, which is a measure of how efficiently an infected host can infect a susceptible member of the population. Virulence is a measure of how symptomatic an infection is, along with any increased mortality. Population growth of a disease is highest when transmission rates are high and virulence low, and natural selection often favours decreased virulence over time. Humans can use these models to control the growth of disease within human populations. For example, having basic ecological measures of SARS can lead to evaluation of the effectiveness of isolation and quarantine programs. Basic ecological data on common human diseases allows public health professionals to design vaccination programs to provide herd immunity to the target population.

15.3 Many interactions can switch from parasitic to mutualistic, depending upon the specific conditions of the local environment.

Although many mutualisms appear as though individuals are doing things "for each other," mutualisms are better viewed as reciprocal exploitation. Most mutualisms are facultative, and the net effect can be parasitic, neutral, or mutualistic, depending on the specific environmental conditions and species involved. For example, plants modify flower longevity to maximize their own fitness, even though this comes at the cost of reduced foraging opportunities for their "partners," the pollinators. Even in the obligate mutualism of Yucca–Yucca moths, the costs and benefits of the interaction can vary greatly among populations. Many of populations contain high densities of cheater phenotypes of the moths, which do not possess the physical ability to pollinate their host plants. Pollination services are of great importance to the economy of Canada, and to the sustainability of natural systems. This interaction is based upon an exploitative interaction that is generally reciprocal.

Mycorrhizae are another form of mutualism involving plants, also with enormous economic importance.

Mycorrhizae, which are mostly either vesicular-arbuscular mycorrhizae or ectomycorrhizae, are important in increasing plant access to water, nitrogen, phosphorus, and other nutrients. In return for these nutrients, mycorrhizae receive energy-rich photosynthate. Experiments have shown that the balance sheet between plants and fungi can be altered by nutrient availability, and that the net effects of mycorrhizae on plant growth vary greatly among plant species. These results further emphasize the idea that interactions fall along a continuum of net effects.

15.4 Theory predicts that mutualism will evolve where the benefits of mutualism exceed the costs.

Keeler built a cost-benefit model for the evolution and persistence of facultative plant–ant protection mutualisms in which the benefits of the mutualism to the plant are represented in terms of the proportion of the plant's energy budget that ants protect from damage by herbivores. The model assesses the costs of the mutualism to the plant in terms of the proportion of the plant's energy budget invested in extrafloral nectaries and the water, carbohydrates, and amino acids contained in the nectar. The model predicts that the mutualism will be favoured where there are high densities of ants and potential herbivores and where the effectiveness of alternative defences are low.

Humans have developed a variety of mutualistic relationships with other species, but one of the most spectacular is that between the greater honeyguide and the traditional honey gatherers of Africa. In this apparently ancient mutualism, humans and honeyguides engage in elaborate communication and cooperation with clear benefit to both partners. The mutualism offers the human side a higher rate of discovery of bees' nests, while the honeyguide gains access to nests that it could not raid without human help. Careful observations have documented that the honeyguide informs the honey gatherers of the direction and distance to bees' nests as well as of their arrival at the nest.

REVIEW QUESTIONS

1. Why do scientists view mutualisms as one point along an exploitation–mutualism continuum? Why can some interaction switch from parasitic to mutualistic?

2. Why don't individuals "do things for each other," even if at a cost to their own fitness? Simard's studies with mycorrhizae suggest that in some cases this may occur. How can you reconcile your understanding of ecology and natural selection with her finding that one tree feeds unrelated individuals of another species?

3. Outline the experiments of Johnson (1993), which she designed to test the possibility that artificial fertilizers may select for less mutualistic mycorrhizal fungi. What evidence does Johnson present in support of her hypothesis?

4. Explain how mycorrhizal fungi may have evolved from ancestors that were originally parasites of plant roots. Is there any evidence that present-day mycorrhizal fungi may act like parasites to plants or animals? Be specific.

5. Janzen (1985) encouraged ecologists to take a more experimental approach to the study of mutualistic relationships. Outline the details of Janzen's own experiments on the mutualistic relationship between swollen thorn acacias and ants.

6. Explain how human diseases can be viewed as an ecological interaction. What benefits may come from using ecological models to describe population growth of a pathogen? Is medicine connected to ecology?

7. How are the coral-centred mutualisms similar to the plant-centred mutualisms we discussed in this chapter? How are they different? The exchanges between mutualistic partners in both systems revolve around energy, nutrients, and protection. Is this an accident of the cases discussed or are these key factors in the lives of organisms?

8. Outline the benefits and costs identified by Keeler's (1981, 1985) cost-benefit model for facultative ant–plant mutualism.

From what perspective does Keeler's model view this mutualism? From the perspective of plant or ant? What would be some of the costs and benefits to consider if the model was built from the perspective of the other partner?

9. How could you change the Lotka–Volterra model of competition we discussed in chapter 13 into a model of mutualism? Would the resulting model be a cost-benefit model or a population dynamic model?

10. Outline how the honeyguide–human mutualism could have evolved from an earlier mutualism between honeyguides and honey badgers. In many parts of Africa today people have begun to abandon traditional honey gathering in favour of keeping domestic bees and have also begun to substitute refined sugars bought at the market for the honey of wild bees. Explain how, under these circumstances, natural selection might eliminate guiding behaviour in populations of the greater honeyguide. (In areas where honey gathering is no longer practised, the greater honeyguide no longer guides people to bees' nests.)

For more information on the resources available from McGraw-Hill Ryerson, go to **www.mcgrawhill.ca/he/solutions**.

SECTION 5 — COMMUNITIES AND ECOSYSTEMS

In this section we move beyond specific interactions among individuals and local environmental conditions and discuss broader topics in community and ecosystem ecology. In chapter 16 we discuss what communities are, how ecologists describe them, and how community structure & genetic diversity influences ecological function. In chapter 17 we show how species interactions can influence community assembly. In chapter 18 we discuss how disturbances influence communities, causing changes to species interactions resulting in a process of succession. We end this section with chapters 19 and 20, in which we describe ecosystems, with an emphasis on the flow of energy and the cycling of elements such as carbon and various nutrients among the biotic and abiotic components of these systems.

Chapter 16 Community Structure and Function

Chapter 17 Species Interactions and Community Structure

Chapter 18 Disturbance, Succession, and Stability

Chapter 19 Production and Energy Flow

Chapter 20 Nutrient and Elemental Cycling

COMMUNITY STRUCTURE AND FUNCTION

CHAPTER 16

CHAPTER CONCEPTS

16.1 A combination of the number of species and their relative abundance defines species diversity.

Concept 16.1 Review

16.2 Species diversity is higher in complex environments.

Concept 16.2 Review

16.3 Ecological functions performed by communities are dependent upon community structure.

Concept 16.3 Review

Ecology In Action: Indicators of Human Impacts

16.4 Genetic variation of species within a community influences ecological function.

Concept 16.4 Review

Ecological Tools and Approaches: Sampling Communities

Summary

Review Questions

ifferent areas within the same geographic region may differ substantially in the number of species they support. Vast areas of flat or gently sloping land in the hot deserts of North America are often dominated by a single species of shrub, the creosote bush, *Larrea tridentata*. While grasses and forbs grow in the spaces between these shrubs, creosote bushes make up most of the biomass in these systems. In some areas, you can travel many kilometres and see only subtle changes in a landscape dominated by this single species (fig. 16.1).

The uniformity of the creosote flats contrasts sharply with the diversity of other places in these hot deserts (fig. 16.2). For instance, a rich variety of plant species cover Organ Pipe National Monument in southern Arizona. Here grow ocotillo, consisting of several slender branches 2 to 3 m tall originating from a common base, palo verde trees with green bark and tiny leaves, and mesquite, which reach the size of medium-sized trees. In addition, there are cacti such as the low-growing prickly pears and the shrub-like teddy bear chollas. The most striking are the column-shaped squat barrel cactus, the organ pipe cactus, with its densely packed slender columns, and the saguaro, a massive cactus that towers over all the other plant species. Among these larger plants also grow a wide variety of small shrubs, grasses, and forbs.

The creosote flats, dominated by one species of shrub, convey an impression of great uniformity. The vegetation of Organ Pipe National Monument, consisting of a large number of species of many different growth forms, gives the impression of high diversity. The ecologist is prompted to ask, what factors control this difference in diversity? Digging deeper, the ecologist may also ask whether these diversity differences have any functional consequences for the efficiency of delivery of ecological services upon which people, and other species, rely. In chapters 13 to 15 we focused on competition, predation, mutualism, and disease, primarily between pairs of species. In this section, we consider patterns and processes that involve a larger number of species. A **community** is an association of potentially interacting species inhabiting some defined area, at some particular scale, over some particular span of time. Communities generally consist of many species that potentially interact in all of the ways discussed in chapters 13 to 15. At the same time, species within a community must continue to cope with the abiotic environment, and thus the issues discussed in chapters 5 to 9 also influence the patterns we observe, and the functions we measure, within communities.

Before immersing ourselves in the complexity of ecological communities, let us first ask a simple question: If we understand population ecology, why do we need to bother measuring communities? Isn't it possible to simply scale-up from single populations and pairwise interactions to a general understanding of more diverse communities? The short answer is no, or at least not often. Due to high levels of diversity, complexity, and indirect interactions among co-occurring species, it is very difficult—if not impossible—to understand the behaviour of communities by simply scaling up from understanding individual populations. Or put another way, understanding population-level processes is critical to understanding population-level patterns. However, this is not sufficient for understanding communities.

An even more important explanation as to why ecologists study communities is because many of the most urgent environmental pressures and issues of societal concern, in Canada and abroad, occur at the community level. For example, we are in the midst of a massive loss of global biodiversity (chapter 23), due to numerous anthropogenic causes. As species are lost from a community, there is both the potential for a loss of **ecological function** as well as potential for increased invasion by non-native species, with additional negative consequences. As we will discuss in this chapter, communities (and ecosystems), perform a number of ecological functions that result in the delivery of services critical to human society. These include the basic requirements of human society, such as biomass production (i.e., food, fuel, building materials), water filtration, and nutrient cycling. As we will discuss in this chapter, properties of the community influence the ability of a community to perform different functions.

A key starting point in the study of communities to define what is meant by **community structure.** This concept

Figure 16.1 Desert landscape dominated by the creosote bush, *Larrea tridentata.*

Figure 16.2 Species-rich Sonoran Desert landscape.

includes attributes such as the number of species, the relative abundance of species, and the kinds of species comprising a community. Not surprisingly, ecologists have developed a number of metrics to help translate concepts into measurable variables, allowing for comparisons and understanding. This is similar to ecologists describing population structure through differences in sex ratios, ages, and numbers of individuals. As with most topics in ecology, measures of the community are scale-dependent, and this is particularly important when discussing patterns of diversity. Additionally, although society typically focuses on species diversity, ecologists do not. Instead, there is growing recognition that other forms of diversity, including genetic diversity, have substantial impact on ecological function.

We begin this chapter by discussing some general patterns observed in communities and some means by which ecologists are able to quantify community structure.

16.1 Species Abundances and Diversity

A combination of the number of species and their relative abundance defines species diversity. What is diversity? This seemingly simple question can prove extraordinarily complex to answer. To begin to simplify this, we will focus on biological diversity, rather than social and abiotic aspects of diversity. This, however, still leaves us with many options. Diversity could represent variation in genotypes among individuals, differences in the physical structure of communities (e.g., low-growing peatland vs. tall forest), variation in the types of organisms found (mites, springtails, plants, etc.), or perhaps variation in the species that are found in a community. It is this latter form of diversity, **species diversity,** that community ecologists study most frequently and which we discuss first. However, it is important to recognize that species diversity represents just one type of diversity that can be found in a single community and other forms of diversity (e.g., genotypic) are also important.

The number of species found within a community, called **species richness,** is one of the most fundamental aspects of community structure. It is such a common measure in ecology that it even has a standard abbreviation, *s.* How does one calculate this metric? Though in theory it is as simple as going into a community and counting the unique number of species observed, there are a few complications. On the technical side, determining what is a species is straightforward for vertebrates, but is complicated for other taxa, such as bacteria (ask your local microbial ecologist why!). Even when one has a working concept of "species," counting species is not always easy (see Ecological Tools), particularly when the species are cryptic or as-of-yet unidentified to science. An additional concern is that the spatial scale at which one measures diversity will influence the results obtained. Consequently, ecologists typically refer to three scales of diversity: alpha, beta, and gamma. The differences among these can be described using Canada's Aspen Parkland region as an example (fig. 16.3).

In the Prairie provinces, the Aspen Parkland is an ecological tension zone, situated between the boreal forest to the north, and grasslands to the south. Within the Parkland, one will find aspen stands, complete with forest understory plants and forest-dwelling animals. However, these forests tend to be restricted towards the wetter areas (e.g., lowlands and north-facing slopes), while patches of grassland, complete with the expected complement of plant and animal species, are found in the drier upland areas. Combined, this region is a savanna habitat, with the relative mixture of grassland and forest community types a function of precipitation, fire history, and grazing activities. So, what is its diversity?

If we measured the diversity of the entire region (or at least some defined area), we would measure forest and grassland communities, along with some shrubland and wetland patches. Such measures would indicate *gamma diversity.* If instead we were to measure only the diversity of the grassland, or forest, or shrubland, or wetland areas, we would measure *alpha diversity.* In other words, alpha diversity is a measure of local diversity, while gamma diversity is a measure of regional or landscape diversity. *Beta diversity* has traditionally be viewed as a measure of the differences among communities within the region or landscape, such that it could be calculated as β = gamma/alpha (Whittaker 1972). However, beta diversity can have other meanings and metrics within community ecology (Anderson et al. 2010); though in general it represents a measure of variation in diversity among locations.

Regardless of what type of diversity is being measured, it is rare for an ecologist to measure all species found within a location, and instead we typically work with taxonomically restricted groups of organisms. For example, vascular or non-vascular plants, mammals, butterflies, beetles, or birds. Some community ecologists restrict their focus even more by studying **guilds.** A guild is a group of organisms that all make their living in a similar way. Examples include the seed-eating animals in the boreal forest, the fruit-eating birds in a tropical rain forest,

Gamma diversity is the total diversity found within the entire area, which includes all habitat types.

Beta diversity is a measure of how different patches are from each other. This habitat has high *beta* diversity.

Alpha diversity is the diversity found within a small area, such as a patch of forest or grassland.

Figure 16.3 Aspen Parkland regions, such as that found outside Edmonton, consist of forest and grassland patches. As is true for all habitat types, the scale of interest influences one's estimate of diversity.

or the filter-feeding invertebrates in a stream. Some guilds consist of closely related species, while others are taxonomically diverse. For instance, the fruit-eating birds on many South Pacific islands consist mainly of pigeons, while the seed-eating guild in the boreal forest includes mammals, birds, and ants.

Studying all species or a restricted group, ecologists quickly realized that within natural systems there is substantial variation in the population sizes of each species within a community. Early ecologists soon discovered repeating patterns in the relative abundances of species in natural communities, allowing them to propose there were some general rules governing community structure.

Patterns of Species' Abundances

One of first patterns ecologists observe when studying a new community is whether or not there is evidence of **dominance** by one or a few species. A species is *dominant* when it substantially more common than the other species in the community. Decades of study have routinely shown that within most communities, most species are moderately abundant; few are very abundant or extremely rare. This property is so fundamental that George Sugihara (1980) referred to it as "minimal community structure."

Often, dominance will be visually obvious, as most individuals will tend to be of a single (or few) species. Such was the case with the creosote bush in the example at the start of this chapter. However, dominance can also occur within the more cryptic parts of a community, such as among mycorrhizal fungi, ants, and herbivorous insects. The actual measurement of dominance can be done using a variety of means, including counting individuals, estimating biomass, or estimating basal area occupied by sessile organisms (e.g., barnacles on a rocky shore). These different forms of measurement can be important, depending on what questions the ecologist is asking. For example, a forester is likely most interested in whether a single species dominates a stand of trees by biomass rather than as a count of individuals. Some species, such as the trembling aspen that grows throughout much of the boreal forest, are clonal, spreading partly through asexual reproduction as they spread across the landscape. For such species counts of individuals are intellectually challenging, and ecologists often rely on measures such as basal area or biomass. Regardless of what part of the community you measure, and the exact units of measurement you use, ecological dominance can have important implications for natural communities. If most individuals within a community are a single species, then that particular species will drive most interactions within that community. Thus if an ecologist, or society, is interested in the functions that a community provides (e.g., wood production, food, recreation), then understanding dominance helps explain whether these functions are likely the result of many, or few species.

Looking at whole communities, and not just the dominant species, we find that there tend to be regularities in the relative abundance of species in communities that hold whether you examine plants in a forest, moths in that forest, or algae inhabiting a nearby stream. If you thoroughly sample groups of organisms such as these, you will come across a few abundant species

and a few that are very rare. Most species in most communities will be moderately abundant. This pattern was first quantified by Frank Preston (1948, 1962a, 1962b), who carefully studied the relative abundance of species in collections and communities. Preston worked throughout the Canadian Prairies, and his "distribution of commonness and rarity" among species is one of the best documented patterns in natural communities.

Preston focused on understanding the abundances of different species in relative, rather than absolute, terms. For example, describing one species as twice as abundant as another, rather than as having 200 vs. 100 individuals. This form of comparison is well suited to logarithmic scales, specifically log base 2. In this way, Preston was able to graph the frequency distributions of number of species of a given relative abundance, with each level on the x-axis corresponding to twice the number of individuals as the previous level. When the relative abundance of species were plotted in this way he consistently obtained results like those shown in figure 16.4. Figure 16.4*a* shows the relative abundance of 86 species of birds breeding

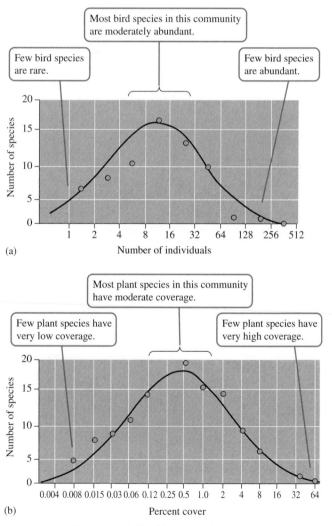

Figure 16.4 Lognormal distributions of (*a*) forest birds, and (*b*) desert plants (data from Whittaker 1965, Preston 1962a). Note that in both graphs, the x-axis is scaled to log2. Thus, each step from left to right is a doubling of population size.

near Westerville, Ohio, over a 10-year period (Preston 1962a). Notice that few species were represented by over 64 individuals or by a single individual. Figure 16.4*b* shows the relative abundance of desert plants. Robert Whittaker (1965) plotted these abundances using coverage rather than numbers of individuals, which accords well with our discussions in chapter 10 of how to represent the relative abundance of plants. Notice that few plant species were represented by more than 8% cover or less than 0.15% cover. Most species had intermediate coverage.

Both of these data sets show the most distinctive feature of Preston's distributions, that is, they are approximately bell-shaped, or normal. Since abundance is plotted on a log scale, Preston's curves are called lognormal distributions. However, in many cases, only a portion of a bell-shaped curve is apparent, suggesting variations to Preston's distribution. For instance, in figure 16.5*b*, a sample of moths from Lethbridge, Alberta, comes closer to a complete curve than does figure 16.5*a*, a sample of moths from Saskatoon, Saskatchewan. Preston suggested that much of the difference between the two curves results from a difference in sample size. While the sample of moths from Saskatoon contained approximately 87,000 individuals belonging to 277 species, the sample from Lethbridge contained an incredible 303,251 individuals belonging to 291 species. If the sample from Saskatoon had contained 300,000 individuals, it would have likely contained more species, producing a more complete lognormal curve.

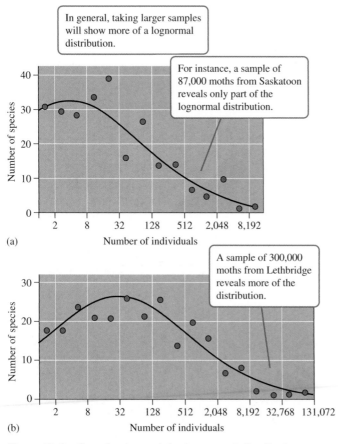

(a)

(b)

Figure 16.5 Sample size and the lognormal distribution (data from Preston 1948). As in the prior figure, the x-axis is scaled to log2.

Ecologists have found that the more you sample a community, the more species you will find. Common species show up in even small samples, but a great deal of sampling effort is needed to capture the rare species. As a result, our typical sampling schemes result in an under-representation of the rare species that live within natural communities. This is unfortunate, as more and more ecologists are realizing that rarity is itself common among species in a community. Thus, in order to have an accurate estimate of these species-abundance patterns, ecologists need to conduct substantial sampling.

So, how do ecologists explain the lognormal distribution of commonness and rarity? Robert May (1975) proposed that the lognormal distribution is the product of many random environmental variables acting upon the populations of many species. In other words, the lognormal distribution is a statistical expectation. Is the lognormal distribution just a mathematical artifact or does it reflect important biological processes? George Sugihara (1980) suggested that the lognormal distribution is a consequence of the species within a community subdividing niche space, and this alone could result in there being relatively few very abundant species. However, regardless of its origins, the lognormal distribution is important because it allows us to predict the distribution of abundance among species. As you see next, species abundances and species richness can be combined to describe other patterns of community structure.

An Integrative Index of Species Diversity

Previously, we discussed species richness as one measure of diversity. However, ecologists typically define species diversity on the basis of two factors: (1) species richness, and (2) the relative abundance of the different species within a community, or **species evenness.** Evenness can be thought of as the inverse of *dominance* as we described it the prior section. A community that is "even" is one without an obviously dominant species. The influence of species richness on community diversity is clear. A community with 20 species is obviously less diverse than one with 80 species. The effects of species evenness on diversity are more subtle but easily illustrated.

Figure 16.6 contrasts two hypothetical forest communities. Both forests contain five tree species, so they have equal levels of species richness. However, community *b* is more diverse than community *a* because its species evenness is higher. In community *b*, all five species are equally abundant, each comprising 20% of the tree community. In contrast, 84% of the individuals in community *a* belong to one species, while each of the remaining species constitutes only 4% of the community. In other words, community *a* is dominated by a single species. As a result, when walking through the two forests you would almost certainly form an impression of higher species diversity in community *b*, despite equal levels of species richness in the two forests.

This issue is of critical importance to understanding and describing communities. Diversity is generated though an increase in the number of species *and* through an increase in the evenness among those species. Different factors can affect species numbers and evenness, and these two measures of diversity may themselves differentially affect other community and ecosystem processes. Because of the importance of this issue,

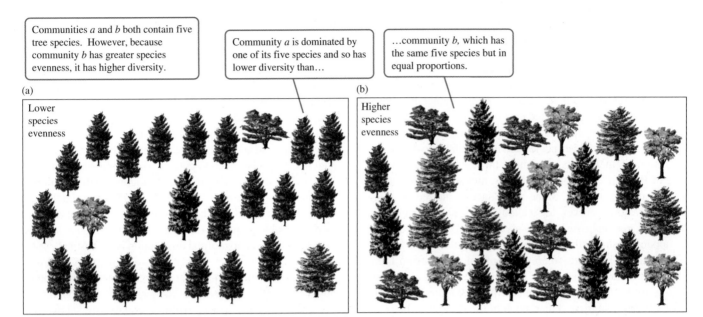

Communities a and b both contain five tree species. However, because community b has greater species evenness, it has higher diversity.

Community a is dominated by one of its five species and so has lower diversity than...

...community b, which has the same five species but in equal proportions.

(a) Lower species evenness

(b) Higher species evenness

Figure 16.6   Species evenness and species diversity.

it should come as no surprise that these measures of diversity have been incorporated into a single index of diversity.

Getting ecologists to agree on the best index for species diverse is slightly more difficult than herding cats. A quick search through the literature will yield a diversity of indices seemingly as great as the diversity of the species they are intended to describe. These indices go by the names of Simpson's index (Edward, not Homer), Margalef's index, and Brillouin's index of diversity to name just a few. These indices all share a core trait: their values depend upon levels of species richness and evenness. Here we apply one of the more widely used indices, the Shannon–Wiener index, to our hypothetical forest communities.

The Shannon–Wiener index is:

$$H' = -\sum_{i=1}^{s} p_i \log_e p_i$$

where:

H' = the value of the Shannon–Wiener diversity index

p_i = the proportion of the ith species

$\log_e$ = the natural logarithm of p_i

s = the number of species in the community

To calculate H', determine the proportions of each species in the study community, p_i, and the $\log_e$ of each p_i. Next, multiply each p_i times $\log_e p_i$ and sum the results for all species from species 1 to species s, where s = the number of species in the community:

$$\sum_{i=1}^{s}$$

Since this sum will be a negative number, the Shannon–Wiener index calls for taking its opposite:

$$-\sum_{i=1}^{s}$$

The minimum value of H' is 0, which is the value of H' for a community with a single species, and increases as species richness and species evenness increase.

Figure 16.7 shows how to calculate H' for our two hypothetical forest communities. The different values of H' for

Calculating species diversity (H′) for two hypothetical communities of forest trees

Community a					*Community* b				
Species	Number	Proportion (p_i)	$\log_e p_i$	$p_i \log_e p_i$	Species	Number	Proportion (p_i)	$\log_e p_i$	$p_i \log_e p_i$
1	21	0.84	−0.174	−0.146	1	5	0.20	−1.609	−0.322
2	1	0.04	−3.219	−0.129	2	5	0.20	−1.609	−0.322
3	1	0.04	−3.219	−0.129	3	5	0.20	−1.609	−0.322
4	1	0.04	−3.219	−0.129	4	5	0.20	−1.609	−0.322
5	1	0.04	−3.219	−0.129	5	5	0.20	−1.609	−0.322
Total	25	1.00		−0.662	Total	25	1.00		−1.610

$$H' = -\sum_{i=1}^{s} p_i \log_e p_i = 0.662$$

$$H' = -\sum_{i=1}^{s} p_i \log_e p_i = 1.610$$

Figure 16.7   Calculating species diversity (H') for two hypothetical communities of forest trees.

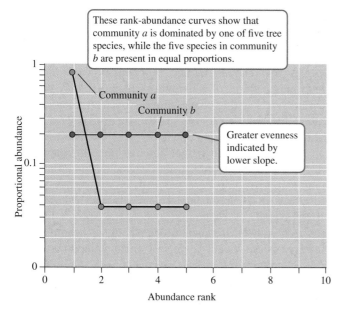

Figure 16.8 Rank-abundance curves for two hypothetical forests.

the two communities reflect the difference in species evenness that we see when we compare the two forests depicted in figure 16.6. H' for community b, the community with higher species evenness, is 1.610, while H' for community a is 0.662.

The Shannon–Wiener index is one way to get a snapshot of the diversity of the community, capturing aspects of both the number and evenness of species. However, sometimes an ecologist may be interested in these two components of diversity individually. There are many metrics used to measure evenness, including Pielou's J. Not surprisingly, this index is named after the Canadian ecologist Evelyn Pielou. Pielou was influential in developing mathematical tools to answer questions in community ecology. Her influence in the field is in part evidenced by the Statistical Ecology section of the Ecological Society of America naming an annual award given to graduate students in her honour. Pielou's measure of evenness, J, is key to many studies of biodiversity. The simplicity of the measure itself is evidence of the elegance of Pielou's research, as J is developed and supported by a large body of mathematical research in information science (Pielou 1966), yet has been presented in a very usable form. Simply:

$$J = \frac{H'}{H_{max}}$$

where:

H' = the value of the Shannon–Wiener diversity index

H_{max} = the total possible H for the number of species in the sample

H_{max} is calculated by assuming all individuals in a sample are evenly distributed among the species contained in the sample. For example, if there were five species ($s = 5$), then you

would assume each has a p_i of 0.20, and calculate H accordingly. As Pielou shows, H_{max} will equal log s, and thus you can rewrite the equation for evenness as:

$$J = \frac{H'}{\log s}$$

By this equation, as evenness increases, J approaches 0. By using these equations, both evenness and species richness can be directly measured, providing ecologists with more tools for understanding communities. As you will see next, we can also use a graphical approach to contrast communities.

Rank-Abundance Curves

We can portray the relative abundance, dominance, and diversity of species within a community by plotting the relative abundance of species against their rank in abundance. The resulting **rank-abundance curve** provides us with important information about a community, information accessible at a glance. Figure 16.8 plots the abundance rank of each tree species in communities a and b (see fig. 16.6) against its proportional abundance. The rank-abundance curve for community b shows that all five species are equally abundant, while the rank-abundance curve for community a shows its dominance by the most abundant tree species.

Figure 16.9 shows rank-abundance curves for the understory vegetation found in burned and unburned forests just north of Thunder Bay, Ontario (Lamb et al. 2003). These data were collected by Eric Lamb, now at the University of Saskatchewan, while he was a graduate student at Lakehead University. Lamb wanted to determine the effects of forest burning on plant diversity, so he measured the diversity and abundance of vegetation in areas that were burned about four years prior to data collection,

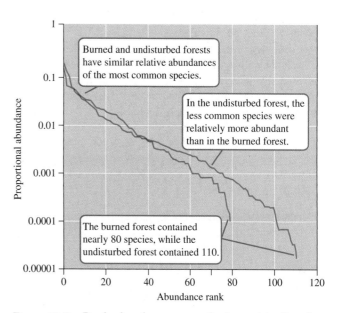

Figure 16.9 Rank-abundance curves for burned (red) and undisturbed (blue) forests near Thunder Bay, Ontario (data courtesy of E. Lamb).

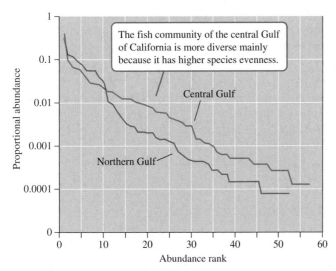

The fish community of the central Gulf of California is more diverse mainly because it has higher species evenness.

Figure 16.10   Rank-abundance curves for two reef fish communities in the Gulf of California (data from Molles 1978, Thomson and Lehner 1976, and courtesy of D. A. Thomson and C. E. Lehner 1976).

and in areas with no recent history of fire. From the rank-abundance curve, you can see the undisturbed forests contained 110 species, while the burned forest only held 79. Additionally, you will notice that although the proportional representation of the common species was similar in both forest types, the less common species were found at a lower abundance in the burned forests than the undisturbed forests.

Two reef fish communities from the Gulf of California further demonstrate the usefulness of rank-abundance curves (fig. 16.10). Using these curves, one is quickly able to see the two reef fish communities contained similar numbers of species (52 vs. 57) but differed substantially in species evenness. The community of the central Gulf of California showed a more even distribution of individuals among species.

Combined, the great usefulness of rank-abundance curves is they allow ecologists to visually describe dominance and diversity patterns within a single community, or when comparing communities. Often, such visual representations are more useful than numerical summaries.

CONCEPT 16.1 REVIEW

1. Why do smaller samples result in only part of the bell-shaped curve that is characteristic of the lognormal distribution?
2. What do measures of evenness describe about community structure that cannot be captured by measures of species richness?
3. Describe the differences between alpha and gamma diversity.

Environmental Complexity and Species Diversity

Species diversity is higher in complex environments. Describing patterns of community structure is only the first step in understanding communities. As scientists rather than natural historians, ecologists strive to understand what causes the observed patterns in community structure, and why they can vary among locations and through time. In chapter 17, we will discuss the role of species interactions in influencing community structure. Here, we focus on a more basic issue: the effects of environmental complexity and heterogeneity on the diversity of communities. In general, species diversity increases with environmental complexity or heterogeneity. However, aspects of environmental structure important to one group of organisms may have no effect on other groups. Consequently, you must know something about the ecological requirements of species to predict how environmental structure affects their diversity. In other words, you must know something about niches and natural history to understand ecological processes.

Structural Complexity, the Niche, and Bird Species Diversity

As we have discussed throughout the text (chapters 8 and 13), the fundamental niche is the multi-dimensional set of conditions an organism needs to survive. However, competitors can cause the exclusion of a species under some sets of conditions, and thus the realized niche will tend to represent a smaller set of suitable conditions than that described by the fundamental niche. Over time we might expect competition to decrease, either due to competitive exclusion or an evolutionary response (e.g., character displacement). In either case, the competitive exclusion principle leads us to predict that coexisting species will have different niches. As we saw in chapter 1, that is what Robert MacArthur (1958) found when he examined the ecology of five species of warblers that live together in the forests of northeastern North America.

What does MacArthur's study of warbler niches have to do with the influence of environmental complexity on species diversity? MacArthur's results suggest that since these species forage in different vegetative strata, the vertical structure of the vegetation may influence their distributions. He explored this possibility on Mount Desert Island, Maine, where he measured the relationship between volume of vegetation above 6 m and the abundance of warblers (fig. 16.11). The number of warbler species at the study sites increased with forest stature. The study sites with greater volume of vegetation above 6 m supported more warbler species. In other words, MacArthur found that warbler diversity increased as the stature of the vegetation increased. These results formed the foundation of later studies of how foliage height diversity influences bird species diversity.

MacArthur was one of the first ecologists to quantify the relationship between species diversity and environmental heterogeneity. He quantified the diversity of species and the complexity of the environment using the Shannon–Wiener index, H'. He measured environmental complexity as foliage height diversity, which increased with the number of vegetative layers and with an even distribution of vegetative biomass among three vertical layers, 0 to 0.6 m, 0.6 to 7.6 m, and > 7.6 m. MacArthur's foliage height diversity, like species diversity, increases with richness (the number of vegetative layers) and evenness (how evenly vegetative biomass is distributed among layers).

Robert MacArthur and John MacArthur (1961) measured foliage height diversity and bird species diversity in 13 plant communities in northeastern North America, Florida, and Panama. The vegetative communities included in their study ranged from grassland to mature deciduous forest, with foliage height diversity that ranged from 0.043 to 1.093. Plant communities with greater foliage height diversity supported more diverse bird communities (fig. 16.12). MacArthur and his colleagues went on to study the relationship between foliage height diversity and bird species diversity in a wide variety of temperate, tropical, and island settings, from North America to Australia. They again found a positive correlation between foliage height diversity and bird species diversity. The combined weight of the evidence from North and Central America and Australia suggests that the relationship is not one of chance but reflects something about the way that birds in these environments subdivide space.

How is environmental complexity related to the diversity of other organisms besides birds? Ecological studies have shown positive relationships between structural complexity and species diversity for many groups of organisms, including mammals, lizards, plankton, arthropods, marine gastropods, reef fish, and many other groups of animals. How does environmental complexity affect diversity of plants?

Niches, Heterogeneity, and the Diversity of Algae and Plants

The existence of approximately 300,000 species of terrestrial plants presents a multitude of opportunities for specialization by animals. Consequently, high plant diversity can explain much of animal diversity. However, how do we explain the diversity of primary producers? G. Evelyn Hutchinson (1961) described what he called "the paradox of the plankton." He suggested that communities of phytoplankton present a paradox because they live in relatively simple environments (the open waters of lakes and oceans) and compete for the same nutrients (nitrogen, phosphorus, silica, etc.), yet many species can coexist without competitive exclusion. This situation seemed paradoxical because it appears to violate the competitive exclusion principle. Hutchinson argued that much of the paradox could be explained by taking into consideration the substantial heterogeneity in abiotic conditions and resource distributions, even though the essential resources needed by the planktonic species remain constant. The diversity of terrestrial plants presents a similar paradox, and it too can be (partly) explained by focusing on species' niches and environmental heterogeneity.

The Niches of Algae and Terrestrial Plants

The niches of algae appear to be defined by their nutrient requirements, and this was most clearly elucidated by David Tilman (1977). This name may sound familiar, as

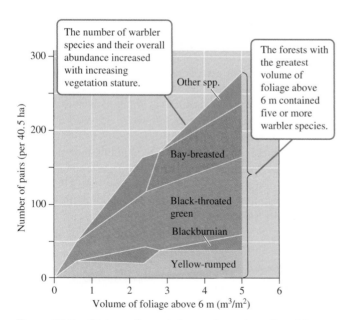

Figure 16.11   Stature of vegetation and number of warbler species (data from MacArthur 1958).

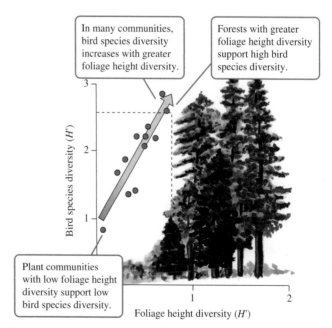

Figure 16.12   Foliage height diversity and bird species diversity (data from MacArthur and MacArthur 1961).

we discussed his resource-based model of competition in chapter 13. Tilman conducted a set of 76 long-term competition experiments on freshwater diatoms. His work is important not only in showing competitive exclusion, but also in showing sets of conditions that allowed coexistence of diatom species. Exclusion or coexistence depended not upon the absolute amount of essential resources in the environment, but instead it depended upon the ratio of two nutrients, silicate, SiO_2^{-2}, and phosphate, PO_4^{-3}.

When Tilman grew the diatoms *Asterionella formosa* and *Cyclotella meneghiniana* by themselves, they each were able to establish and maintain stable populations at all resource ratios and flow rates (representing the rate of nutrient turnover). When grown together, the outcome of Tilman's experiments depended upon the ratio of silicate to phosphate (fig. 16.13). At high ratios (representing an abundance of Si relative to P) *Asterionella* eventually excluded *Cyclotella*. At lower ratios the two species coexisted. At the lowest ratio, *Cyclotella* was numerically dominant over *Asterionella*.

How can we explain Tilman's results? It turns out that *Asterionella* takes up phosphorus at a much higher rate than does *Cyclotella*. Tilman reasons that at high ratios of silicate to phosphate, *Asterionella* is able to deplete the environment of phosphorus and consequently eliminate *Cyclotella*. However, when ratios are low, silicate limits the growth rate of *Asterionella* and it cannot deplete phosphate. Consequently, when ratios are low, *Asterionella* cannot exclude *Cyclotella*. At these low ratios, silicate limits the growth rate of *Asterionella*, while phosphate limits the growth rate of *Cyclotella*. Consequently, in the presence of low ratios of silicate to phosphate, the two diatoms coexist.

What do the results of Tilman's experiments have to do with the relationship of environmental complexity to species diversity? A general prediction from his work is that as Si/P ratios go from high to low, the abundance of *Cyclotella* relative to *Asterionella* should increase. To test whether his predictions were consistent with reality, Tilman (1977) was able to access data on water samples taken from Lake Michigan. Among samples, Si:P ratios ranged from approximately 600 to 1. The relative abundance of *Cyclotella* changed as predicted: from nearly absent at high Si:P ratios, and nearly 100% at lower ratios. Thus, Tilman's landmark work clearly shows that heterogeneity in resource ratios, one form of environmental complexity, has important consequences for community structure.

Effects of Environmental Heterogeneity on Terrestrial Plants

Light, water, and a diversity of nutrients are essential for plant growth, and plant responses to different levels of these resources form the dominant niche axes for most terrestrial plant species. However, unlike structural complexity, it is not visually obvious to the research the degree to which resources vary within a community. As it turns out, there is substantial variation, at a diversity of spatial scales, with impacts on plant growth and community structure.

G. Robertson and a team of researchers (1988) quantified variation in nitrogen and moisture across an abandoned agricultural field. Their study site was located in southeast Michigan, on the E. S. George Reserve, a 490 hectare natural area maintained by the University of Michigan. Farmers cleared the field of its original oak-hickory forest and plowed the land sometime before 1870. Crop raising continued on the field until the early 1900s, when most of the land was converted to pasture. Then in 1928, the cattle were removed and the nature reserve was established.

Robertson and his colleagues focused their measurements on a 0.5 hectare (69 m × 69 m) subplot within the old field in which they measured several soil variables, including nitrate concentration and soil moisture, at 301 sampling points. This large number of sampling points over a small area provided sufficient data to construct a detailed map of soil properties. Figure 16.14 shows considerable patchiness in both nitrate and moisture. Both variables show at least tenfold differences across the study plot. In addition, nitrate concentration and moisture do not appear to correlate well with each other; hot spots for nitrogen were not necessarily hot spots for moisture. The researchers concluded that soil conditions show sufficient spatial variability to affect the structure of plant communities. Since this initial study by Robertson, many other ecologists have found similar results in a diversity of communities, ranging from dry grasslands to wet forests. Now let's examine how spatial heterogeneity in these resources may affect the distribution and diversity of plants.

Influences of Environmental Heterogeneity on the Diversity of Forest Sedges

Graham Bell, Martin Lechowicz, and Marcia Waterway of McGill University teamed up to identify the factors that influence the distribution of sedges in the deciduous forests of

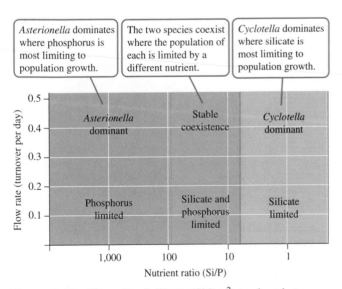

Figure 16.13   The ratio of silicate (SiO_2^{-2}) to phosphate (PO_4^{-3}) and competition between the diatoms *Asterionella formosa* and *Cyclotella meneghiniana* (data from Tilman 1977).

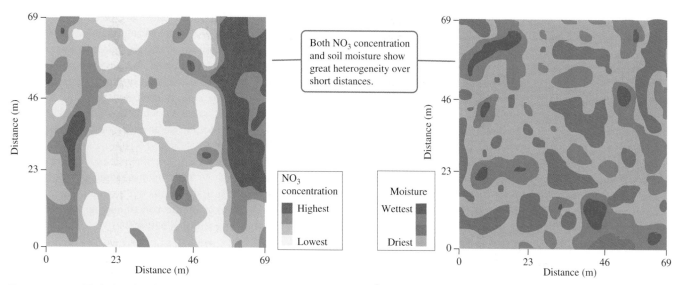

Both NO$_3$ concentration and soil moisture show great heterogeneity over short distances.

Figure 16.14 Variation in nitrate (NO$_3$) and soil moisture in a 4,761 m^2 area in an old agricultural field (data from Robertson et al. 1988).

Quebec (Bell et al. 2000; fig. 16.15). The research team chose to focus on sedges, more specifically the genus *Carex,* as there are more *Carex* species in forest and wetland habitats of these northern areas than any other genus of seed plant. Additionally, there are over 500 species of *Carex* in North America, and over 50 are found within the 1,000 hectare study site used by the research team. In other words, this is an ideal group of organisms to explore the linkages between heterogeneity and diversity.

One of the difficulties that ecologists face when trying to identify whether heterogeneity influences diversity is to figure out what to measure. We have already discussed a variety of measures for diversity, such as species number and evenness, but what about heterogeneity? We have seen that many animal ecologists measure heterogeneity and complexity as a

Figure 16.15 McGill University's Gault Nature Reserve on Mont-Saint-Hilaire, Quebec.

function of the plant community, and many plant ecologists measure complexity as heterogeneity in nutrient distributions. In all these cases it has been a person choosing a specific factor to measure, and then trying to relate variation in that factor to diversity. However, from our discussions of niches (chapter 9), it is clear that niches are multidimensional, and the performance of individuals is influenced by multiple co-occurring factors. So, what if researchers choose the wrong factor for their study? How can they be certain they are choosing the most important niche axes? Bell, Lechowicz, and Waterway (2000) used a very ingenious method to get around this problem. They decided to let the plants "speak" for themselves.

The research team went into the forest and collected several healthy individuals of 11 *Carex* species. These plants grow by forming numerous *ramets,* genetically identical modules of the plant. The team separated each individual into its ramets, planted those individually, and ended up with a large number of clones for each of their 11 species. They then went back to the field and laid out three 1,000 m transects, planting one individual of each species every 10 m. By ensuring they only used a single genetic individual of a given plant species on a single transect, they could say that any variation in performance of the plants they found was due to environmental, not genetic, influences. Very clever, and once again wonderful evidence as to why plants make such excellent study organisms for ecological research.

After a year, the research team went back to their sites and recorded which plants were alive, and which had died. As you can see in figure 16.16, there was substantial variation in the number of survivors at each position along the three transects. In addition to the number of survivors, the researchers recorded the identity of the survivors. Why? Just because five species may have survived at each of two locations does not necessarily mean it was the same five species. Shifts in

the **species composition** of a community, even without shifts in species richness, would indicate a shift in community structure.

What does this variation in survival (and composition) indicate? Since the use of clones allowed the research team to rule out genetic factors, they can conclude that there was biologically meaningful variation in the environment for these species. The next question is whether this variation was actually related to species diversity. To test this, the researchers first applied a variety of statistical procedures allowing them to quantify the variation in performance among the species in the different locations. They were then able to use a variety of regression analyses to relate environmental heterogeneity found among nearby sites to the number of species in those sites. In general, they found that environmental variation between sites increased with the distance between sites. More interestingly, as environmental variation increased among sites, there was also increased variation in how each of the 11 species performed. In other words, as environmental heterogeneity increased, so too did the variability in species responses.

This supports the idea that species have different niches, and that different factors will more strongly influence different species. This also supports the experimental approach the research team took: not measuring a single environmental factor, but instead looking for variation in responses in the plants themselves. Finally, the researchers found that overall species diversity in their plots increased with environmental heterogeneity (fig. 16.17), providing an answer to the initial question of this study.

The work here by Bell, Lechowicz, and Waterway provides an example of how focusing on a single group of diverse species, *Carex,* can reveal patterns of community structure. In the next section, we explore the role of another factor in altering community composition: disturbance.

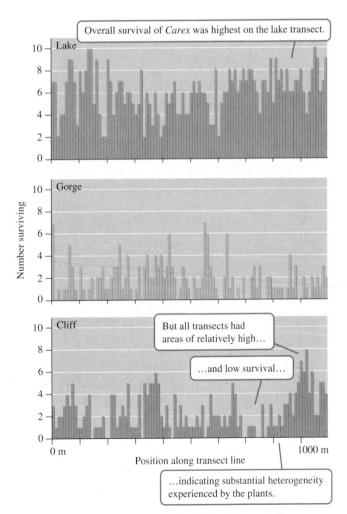

Figure 16.16   Plant survival varied along three 1000 m transects in a deciduous forest in Quebec (data from Bell et al. 2000).

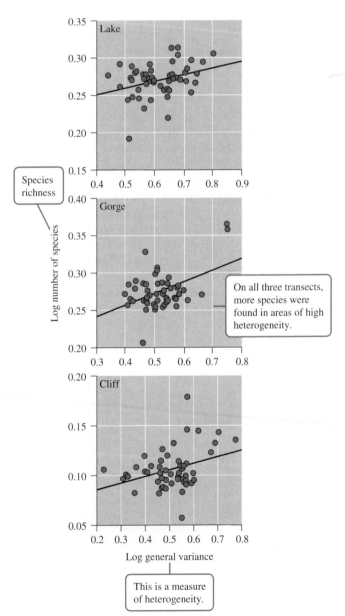

Figure 16.17   The diversity of forest sedges increased with increased environmental heterogeneity (data from Bell et al. 2000).

CONCEPT 16.2 REVIEW

1. Does Tilman's finding that *Asterionella* and *Cyclotella* exclude each other under certain conditions but coexist under other conditions violate the competitive exclusion principle?
2. Suppose you discover that the fish species inhabiting small isolated patches of coral reef use different vertical zones on the reef face—some species live down near the sand, some live a bit higher on the reef, and some higher still. Based on this pattern of zonation, can you predict how reef structure should affect the diversity of fish living on such reefs?
3. Why did Bell et al. (2000) use plants as indicators of heterogeneity rather than rely on measures of abiotic variables such as light and nitrogen?

16.3 Functional Consequences of Diversity

Ecological functions performed by communities are dependent upon community structure. Globally, there is significant concern about the rapid rate of biodiversity loss, often associated with human disturbances. This concern arises for many reasons, including aesthetic, moral, and even functional grounds. It is this latter issue, the impact of loss of biodiversity on ecological function and the delivery of **ecological services** that we discuss here. Ecological services represent the processes and resources provided by ecological systems that are of value to humans. These processes and resources are typically called ecological functions, and examples include biomass production, nutrient cycling, water filtration, carbon sequestration, recreation, and pollination of crops. The essential point here is that community and ecosystems have functions, which result in services. If function is diminished, then so too is the quality of the service. Thus, independent of any moral or aesthetic argument, humans benefit directly from healthy ecological systems. As we will discuss in chapter 23, these benefits are beginning to be included in development plans, emphasizing the potential economic value.

Ecosystem function and the delivery of services does not imply intent by the ecosystem; instead, the function is a natural by-product of ecological and biogeochemical interactions within the ecosystem. Some of these functions will directly impact humans. For example, if a large wetland along a coastal region buffers tidal surges, then the loss of that ecosystem service (tidal dissipation) costs humans through risk of personal and property damage. A grassland that produces substantial amounts of plant matter has the potential to be more economically viable for a rancher than one that produces little. In other words, the ecological services provided by ecological systems directly alter the economic well-being

and personal safety of humans. As a result, there is substantial interest in understanding what factors control the efficiency of ecosystem services, so that some processes can be protected or even augmented to enhance or restore the delivery of these services. We begin our discussion by focusing on species diversity, and its impact on the delivery of ecosystem services.

Impacts of Biodiversity on Delivery of Ecological Services

Let us imagine a number of hypothetical communities that fall within some landscape. As we all love learning about plants, let us focus only on plant diversity, and a key ecological function, biomass production. Why biomass production? Quite simply, plant biomass = food, fuel, and habitat (be they buildings for us or homes for other species). We notice that some of our hypothetical plant communities contain large numbers of plant species, some few, and some an intermediate number. What relationship between species diversity and biomass production is to be expected?

In recent years there has been an explosion of research activity trying to answer this question. These studies have taken place in the computer lab, the greenhouse, and in the field. The standard experimental design is to grow "synthetic communities" of varying levels of diversity. To achieve this, the researcher typically decides on some overall pool of species (i.e., gamma diversity among all experimental plots). Each plot is then assigned some varying combination of numbers of species from this pool, thereby varying alpha diversity among plots (fig. 16.18). After some period of time, the researcher measures ecological function in the plots, using regression or other analyses to determine the form of the relationship between diversity and function. Peter Reich and colleagues (including David Tilman, mentioned previously in this chapter), have synthesized the results of two such experiments (Reich et al. 2012).

BioDIV and BioCON are two independent experiments established in a Minnesota grassland in the 1990s (fig. 16.18), and each have run for over a decade. Each experimenter set his species pool to 16, though there were some differences in which species were used in each experiment. The results obtained between these two studies are striking (fig. 16.19). In both experiments, not only did biomass production increase with increased species diversity, but the magnitude of this diversity effect grew stronger the longer the experiment ran. As strong as these results are, there are some important limitations. First, gamma diversity for each was only 16, while the true gamma diversity for the surrounding grassland area is well over 100. Second, the maximum diversity within each plot was limited to 16, a value lower than the maximum diversity of equally sized areas in the surrounding grassland. Third, though these experiments were run independently of each other, they do share species and are in similar geographic areas, and thus do not represent completely independent tests. What is needed to address the generality of the effects of diversity of ecological function would be additional studies in geographically diverse

Figure 16.18   Aerial and close-up views of a large biodiversity experiment in Cedar Creek, Minnesota. Each of the 342 plots is 13 × 13 m in size, with measurements taken only on the innermost 9 × 9 m.

locations, with independent species pools. Fortunately, such data are available.

As a sign of the increased importance this topic has gained over the years, there were fewer than five experiments investigating biodiversity–function relationships in 1995, and

about 40 just ten years later in 2004. Patricia Balvanera and colleagues have synthesized the findings from 103 studies, allowing us to draw some general conclusions (Balvanera et al. 2006).

Across the studies they sampled, increased plant diversity caused a significant increase in primary production (fig. 16.20), consistent with Reich's (2012) results. Interestingly, the effects of plant diversity manipulation were not limited to the plants. Increased plant diversity also caused an increase in insect herbivore biomass and enhanced litter decomposition in most studies in which they were measured. Though plant diversity increased herbivore biomass, there was little continuing effect on the biomass of the predators that eat the herbivores (fig. 16.20). These findings are a clear indication that aspects of community structure, such as plant species diversity, impact the functioning of the local community. It is also important to note that not all members of the community have the same effects on every ecological service. For instance, manipulating the diversity of the herbivores, rather than the plants, has no impact on primary production (fig. 16.20). In contrast, manipulating the diversity of mycorrhizal fungi has nearly as large an impact on primary production as does manipulating the plants directly! These findings are a clear example that ecological processes impact, and are impacted by, a diversity of ecological interactions. Due to the functional importance of diversity, we will return to this point throughout many later chapters in the book.

What Causes Diversity-Function Relationships?

The consistency with which different research groups find functional benefits of species diversity suggests there are some general mechanisms at play. There are three main mechanisms proposed to explain how biodiversity could enhance productivity (or other ecological functions), though there remains substantial debate regarding which mechanisms are most prominent (van Ruijven and Berendse 2005).

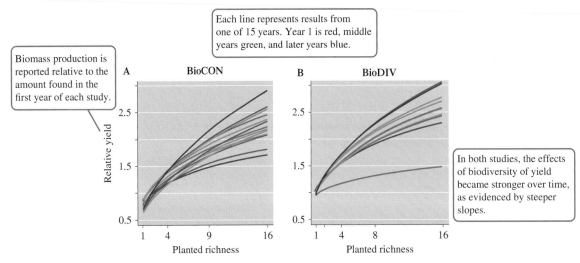

Figure 16.19   The effects of species diversity on biomass production became stronger over time in two parallel experiments (BioCON and BioDIV) in a Minnesota grassland (data from Reich et al. 2012).

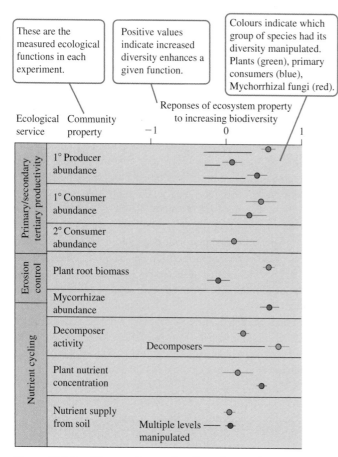

These are the measured ecological functions in each experiment.

Positive values indicate increased diversity enhances a given function.

Colours indicate which group of species had its diversity manipulated. Plants (green), primary consumers (blue), Mychorrhizal fungi (red).

Figure 16.20 Changes in species diversity can impact a number of ecological functions and services (data from Balvanera et al. 2006).

The first mechanism, *complementarity*, comes from niche theory (chapter 9). The basic logic is that a given ecological service will be highest/fastest in a community in which all resources/microenvironments are being exploited or occupied. If a single species has a single niche, then one might expect it only to be able to exploit a fraction of the potential niche space that might be available in a location that has multiple microhabitats. Similarly, a single species may have limited growth (e.g., shallow roots), or narrow diet, thereby consuming only a fraction of the available food/resources within a community. Consequently, though the habitat has the potential to host multiple species without competitive exclusion, alpha diversity is too low to allow for full exploitation of the environment. However, as new species are added, some will have different niche requirements and the ability to exploit different microhabitats, coexisting without exclusion. As a result, more of the niche space and resources in the community gets exploited, and ecological function should increase. This can continue as you add species, until all niche space and resources are exploited, at which point there should be no increased function due to increased addition of species.

A second mechanism of diversity effects is *facilitation*. In this model some species enhance the growth of others, perhaps by reducing soil salinity or modifying the thermal environment. Bradley Cardinale and colleagues (2002) have conducted an elegant study showing evidence for this mechanism in relation to diversity effects among aquatic suspension feeders. Larval caddisflies are common occupants of streams around the world (fig. 16.21), and as suspension feeders they extract food from moving water. Cardinale and his colleagues were interested in understanding how the diversity of caddisflies influenced the roughness of the moving water, and its subsequent effects on feeding rates. To test this, they constructed artificial streams into which they allowed either 18 individuals of one species, or six individuals of each of three species of caddisflies to colonize. You might note that this experimental design resulted in variation in both species number and evenness among the two treatments. Overall, they found the capture of suspended particulate matter by the caddisflies was 66% higher in the mixed species treatment than in the single species treatments. However, this does not indicate whether the cause was facilitation or complementarity. Digging deeper, Cardinale and his colleagues investigated the feeding rate of each species, when alone and when in mixture. The complementarity hypothesis would not predict feeding rate of a given species to vary as a function of species number, as it is based upon the idea that different species consume different resources and/or occupy different microhabitats. However, the facilitation hypothesis does predict that the presence of one species can enhance the function (e.g., feeding rate) of another. That is exactly what Cardinale found. For two of the three species in their study, feeding rate was significantly higher in the mixed species treatment relative to the single species treatment (fig. 16.22). Why? Feeding rates of suspension feeders are strongly influenced by flow rates of the water and here, feeding rate was higher with increased flow rate. Single species assemblages resulted in slower overall flow (rougher water) than the multispecies treatment. Thus, diversity here altered water movement, causing changes in feeding.

A third means by which biodiversity can enhance ecological function is through the *sampling effect*, also called species selection. This mechanism is based upon the idea

Figure 16.21 Caddisfly larvae are filter feeders, inhabiting streams around the world.

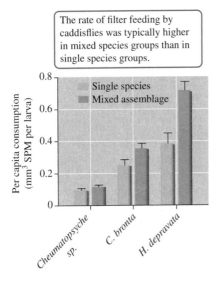

The rate of filter feeding by caddisflies was typically higher in mixed species groups than in single species groups.

Figure 16.22 For two of three species of caddisflies, per capita feeding rates were higher in mixed species assemblages than when single species grew alone (from Cardinale et al. 2002).

that species differ in their inherent rates of delivery of some ecological service. For example, some plant species are more productive than others; some microbes result in faster nitrogen cycling than others. As the number of species in a community increases, the odds of the community containing at least one species with enhanced function increases, resulting in an overall pattern of increased function with increased diversity. Thus, sampling is not a benefit of diversity itself, as much as increased odds of having the most productive species.

Although these three mechanisms have been presented as distinct, there is no reason to expect them to be exclusionary.

In fact, a number of statistical tools exist allowing researchers to quantify what proportion of an observed diversity effect is due to the different mechanisms. For example, Cardinale estimated that 17% of his observed responses were due to species selection, while the remaining 83% were due to a combination of complementarity and facilitation (Cardinale 2005). Reich and his colleagues (2012) were able to show that complementarity effects increased in strength over time for both the BioCON and BioDIV studies; selection effects did not.

It is also important to remember that diversity of a given taxonomic group can have simultaneous impacts on many ecological services, and these may result in positive feedback. For example, within the BioCon study (Reich et al. 2012), species diversity increased soil fertility, with the magnitude of these effects growing over time. Thus, not only did plant diversity increase plant biomass through increased complementarity of the plant species, but it also resulted in increased microbial activity, leading to more nitrogen in the soil and further enhancing plant growth. Or put another way, communities are complex and interconnected biological systems; changing one component, such as biodiversity, can have functional consequences throughout the system. As we see next, species diversity is not the only level of complexity that is functionally important.

CONCEPT 16.3 REVIEW

1. What are ecological services, and how do they relate to the structure of communities?
2. Why is species selection a statistical, rather than biological, mechanism to explain diversity–function relationships?
3. How does complementarity relate to niche theory?

ECOLOGY IN ACTION

Indicators of Human Impacts

A running theme of this book has been a discussion of impacts humans are having in natural systems, and how ecologists are using a data-driven approach to reduce, mitigate, and recover from the environmental harm that comes from anthropogenic activities. When focused on a single species, the work of the ecologist is often relatively straightforward (even if politically charged). For example, to set quotas for harvest of cod requires a detailed understanding of cod populations; to decide whether hunters can go after grizzly bears requires good data on bear populations. In neither case does the information the ecologist provides to government necessarily require a detailed description of the entire community

and all the species found within it. However, suppose one wanted different types of questions answered, such as: Following a disturbance, how do we know a wetland has recovered to a natural state?, or, Is a particular human activity reducing the ecological integrity of a location? These questions are decidedly more difficult to answer, as they require comparisons among communities (i.e., populations of many species) as opposed to changes in the population of only one species (e.g., cod or grizzlies). Here, we discuss a few examples of how ecologists are able to simplify the data needed to answer these questions, making answers more accessible for government and those in need of assessing change.

Ecological "integrity," "intactness," and "health" are all terms commonly used in government documents and regulation, both as things to protect as well as goals for recovery following development. However, to a scientist these are awfully squishy concepts—they are easy to conceptualize, but difficult to quantify. For example, imagine a forest with thousands of species of plants and animals. How do we know if it is intact or not? We could perhaps compare one forest with another, but do we need to measure the populations of thousands of species? Later in the book we will discuss some ways ecologists do compare diverse communities (e.g., ordinations); however, here we focus on finding a simpler answer. Why? From a regulatory perspective, measuring entire systems is very expensive because it requires detailed taxonomic expertise and substantial sampling over multiple seasons, if not years or decades. Consequently, ecologists frequently identify indicators as a rapid means of assessing human impacts and the condition of ecological communities. An indicator can be any species or group of species whose abundance or condition is representative of the overall condition of the community or ecosystem. You may immediately see the potential benefits; with an accurate indicator, a measure of ecological integrity or health may be obtained by measuring only a small component of a complex system.

Not all species can serve as effective indicators, and a poor choice has significant societal, economic, and environmental consequences. In an influential paper, Université de Moncton ecologists, Marc-André Villard and his former graduate student, Vincent Carignan, suggest valuable indicators will possess a number of characteristics (Carignan and Villard 2002). For example, the characteristics have the ability to provide early warnings of impending change, are relatively inexpensive to measure, and can be accurately measured by non-specialists. However, they also highlight several potential limitations to the value of some indicators. For example, ecological theory suggests that no two species are likely to share the same niche, and thus no two species likely respond exactly the same when conditions change. Species with shorter generation times likely show effects of disturbance faster than do species with slower generation times, and thus a slowly changing indicator may underestimate degradation of ecological integrity. In addition, an indicator likely has a limited range of conditions over which it responds, a range narrower than the potential degree of human influence. Further, good indicators need to respond as quickly to positive change in the environment as they do to negative change, otherwise the impacts of environmental improvements may not be properly assessed. Here we offer two examples of how indicators are being used in Canada to (1) measure urban pollution, and (2) to monitor wetland recovery associated with oil sands development.

Using Lichens to Estimate Vehicular Pollution

Lichens rarely get any love (fig. 16.23). They are small, excruciatingly difficult to identify, and often appear more as a

Figure 16.23   Trees are home to a diversity of lichens.

background in a nice photo rather than the point of focus. Despite popular indifference, they are both biologically intriguing (they are the product of a mutualism between a fungus and an alga, or a cyanobacterium), and they are well known to be very sensitive to air pollution. Critical to water and nutrient balance in lichens is the ability to absorb essential resources directly from air and water. They do not have filtration systems found in vascular plants, nor detoxification pathways common in insects. Consequently, pollutants that harm biological systems often have rapid and pronounced effects on lichens. That's bad news for lichens, but great news for someone searching for indicators of pollution. Though lichens have been used as indicators of pollution for decades in many locales (Conti and Cecchetti 2001), their response specifically to vehicular pollution has not been well understood. Two ecologists from Carleton University have recently published a study to help fill this knowledge gap (Coffey and Fahrig 2012).

Heather Coffey and her MSc supervisor, Lenore Fahrig, conducted a survey of 420 trees within Ottawa, measuring lichen abundance and species richness on each. The sites were distributed throughout the city and included areas that varied in vehicular pollution, moisture, and colonization potential by new propagules. For use as an indicator of pollution, Coffey and Fahrig reasoned that measures of lichen abundance and/or richness need not be *influenced* only by pollution. Instead, pollution needs to have a stronger effect than abiotic factors such as moisture. Overall, they identified 18 macrolichen species, three of which were found in nearly all sites. At a given site, the

total abundance of lichens was most strongly (and negatively) influenced by vehicular pollution within 300 m of the location measured. As expected, local moisture and availability of colonization sources were also important (and positive), though their influence was low relative to vehicular pollution. In contrast, though macrolichen species richness was also negatively influenced by vehicular pollution, richness was most strongly influenced by moisture and the availability of colonization sources.

Combined, these results support the use of lichens as indicators of very localized levels of vehicular pollution. For use as an indicator, their results suggest species level identification is not needed, which is very good news. More specifically, with only minor training, individuals could rapidly (and inexpensively) measure lichen cover. For those of you interested in finding a simple research project, you might consider testing the generality of Coffey and Fahrig's results near your school!

Wetlands and Oil Sands

As you may have heard, there is a bit of oil sands development occurring in Alberta. Much of this oil extraction involves surface mining, rather than the classic image of oil wells and pumps. The vast majority of the oil sands reserves of Alberta occur within the boreal forest, and more specifically, areas covered by wetlands. Rebecca Rooney (now at the University of Waterloo), and her former PhD supervisor, Suzanne Bayley (from the University of Alberta), have recently published a study proposing a few indicator species to help set targets for reclamation (Rooney and Bayley 2011).

Rooney and Bayley (2011) point out that due to a variety of regulations, companies involved in surface mining are not required to restore the landscape; instead reclamation activities must return the landscape to an equivalent land capability. Though there is substantial debate over what exactly that means, there is no doubt that there will be (and currently is) substantial effort towards wetland reclamation following surface mining (fig. 16.24). Though several companies have conducted reclamation activities, specific targets have not been set by the government. Consequently, it is unclear when reclamation is done—a frustrating situation for industry,

Figure 16.24   Reclamation activities attempt to return the landscape to equivalent land capability.

conservation groups, and everyone involved in development. Rooney and Bayley set out to help define targets for wetland reclamation in this region.

The researchers measured the vegetation in 63 wetlands, 25 of which were reclaimed and 38 of which were undisturbed and represented the best case for that region. As these were wetlands, simply laying out transects and walking a path was not an option. Instead, key research gear included kayaks and a rake—the latter allowing them to sample the submerged vegetation.

Across all sites, they identified 26 species. Using a variety of complex statistical approaches (e.g., ordination), they were able to identify seven types of wetlands, each of which could be described by a single indicator species. Of these seven wetland types, two of them (marsh and marsh-fen) were most typical among the undisturbed sites, and Rooney and Bayley suggest represent suitable targets for reclamation. Unfortunately, all 25 of the reclaimed wetlands do not resemble either of these targets, and instead most closely resemble the five alternative wetland types, each of which is rare among undisturbed wetlands. Thus, though substantial reclamation activity is underway, data to date suggest the community types being reclaimed differ from those common on the undisturbed landscape. Whether this still meets the requirement of "equivalent land capability" is unclear, and that answer will require measures of large numbers of potential ecological services.

16.4 | Genetic Diversity and Ecological Processes

Genetic variation of species within a community influences ecological function. You may have noticed that discussions of evolution have been generally lacking throughout this chapter, at least in contrast to its more thorough integration into previous sections of the text. Such omission is not limited to this book alone, but instead fairly reflects the traditional approach used by ecologists in describing communities. In the

last decade, however, there has been rapid growth in research devoted to integrating evolutionary biology and community ecology. Here we will focus on the functional importance of genetic diversity.

Functional Consequences of Genetic Diversity in Communities

Population biologists have long recognized the value of genetic diversity among their species of interest. For example, it is a general tenet in conservation biology that genetic

variation is critical to the long-term viability of populations (e.g., Lacy 1997). The value of genetic diversity is also clear from agricultural studies. For example, in a classic study investigating the effects of genetic diversity within rice crops and the spread of a devastating crop disease, mixed-genotype plantings (in contrast to traditional genetic monocultures) were so effective at reducing disease that fungicide application was not needed (Zhu et al. 2000). However, it has been relatively recently that community ecologists have been able to show functional consequences of the genetic diversity of the species within a community. We begin with a study that asks a simple question: Does community structure depend upon the genetic diversity of the species within the community?

Rosemary Booth and Phil Grime (2003) designed an elegant experiment to address the question of whether the diversity of the plants within the community influenced plant community structure. Why plants? Aside from the fact that Grime is one of the most influential ecologists over the last hundred years, and plants are his area of expertise, plants make excellent subjects for studies of genetic diversity. Most plant species have the ability to be cloned, either from single cells or through cuttings. Consequently, by taking one individual (of a single genotype) and using effective horticultural skills, one is able to rapidly cultivate many individuals (still of a single genotype). By repeating this procedure on different individuals, one can generate multiple individuals of a number of different genotypes. This is the research equipment needed in any study in which genetic diversity needs to be known and manipulated. In contrast, it is very hard to clone animals, and nearly all university ethics boards would not be keen in reading a proposal in which one takes cuttings in an attempt to try!

The experiment Booth and Grime conducted was straightforward in its approach. They used 36 experimental communities into which they planted the same 16 individuals of each of 11 plant species. However, these 36 communities were each assigned one level of genetic diversity: low, intermediate, and high. In the low diversity treatment, each of the 16 individuals of a single species were all of the same genotype. In the intermediate treatment, the used four individuals of each of four genotypes per species. In the highest diversity treatment, all 16 individuals were of different genotypes. Thus, this experimental design allowed Booth and Grime to manipulate genetic diversity while keeping species richness and evenness constant.

To allow the plants time to interact and work out any competitive differences, they measured community composition over five years. Over the course of the experiment, there was an overall drop in the Shannon-Weiner index, due to both species loss and increased dominance (fig. 16.25); both of these are common in long-term mesocosm experiments. Of more interest is the effect of genetic diversity at the end of the study: increased genetic diversity resulted in higher community diversity, by reducing the overall rate of species loss. Or put another way, just as genetic diversity of a single species leads to increased viability of that population, increased genetic diversity of species appears to lead to increased species diversity within a community. Why? Genotypes likely

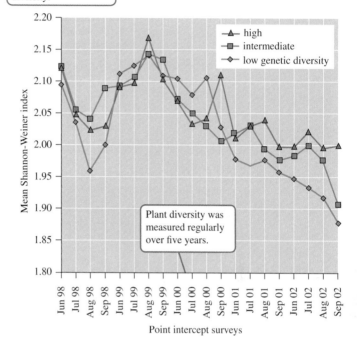

Figure 16.25 Changes in diversity over time, as a function of the genetic diversity of species (from Booth and Grime 2003).

differ in how they acquire resources, where they put the roots and leaves, and their susceptibility to competition and other processes. This is the same as saying an individual's genotype influences the exact form of an individual's niche, and how it occupies habitat. Therefore, genetic diversity should lead to niche complementarity, similar to that previously described for species diversity.

The effects of plant genetic diversity are not restricted to impacts on the plants alone. Instead, as part of a connected ecological system they can cascade to impact herbivores, and to the predators of the herbivores. This was most clearly shown by meticulous work by Greg Crutsinger, now at the University of British Columbia (Crutsinger et al. 2006), while he was a graduate student in eastern United States.

Common throughout much of eastern North America are abandoned agricultural fields in various stages of succession (chapter 18). In many cases, species of *Solidago* (Goldenrod) can become dominant, serving as food and foraging ground for a diversity of insect herbivores and predators. To tease apart the impacts of genetic diversity of this dominant plant on a number of aspects of the community, Crutsinger cultivated clones of 21 genotypes of *Solidago altissima*. He then planted 12 individuals from a total of 1, 3, 6, or 12 genotypes into 1 m² plots in a field. Thus, all plots started with the same number of species (one), the same number of plants (12), but different numbers of genotypes (1–12). As a result, any differences at the end of the study can be attributed to differences in genetic diversity.

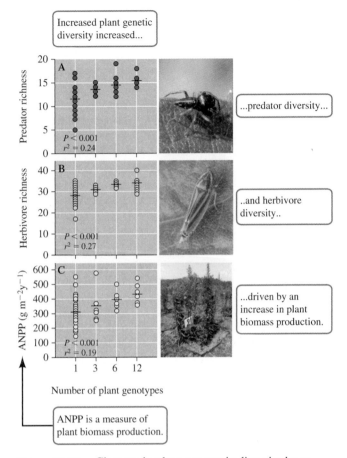

Figure 16.26 Changes in plant genotypic diversity have cascading effects of herbivore and predator diversity (from Crutsinger et al. 2006).

Arthropods *loved* his research plots—so much so that Crutsinger and his crew counted 36,997 individuals from over 130 species in his plots over the course of a single growing season! However, arthropods seemed to prefer the high diversity plots, as Crutsinger counted over 25% more individuals in the 12-genotype plots than in the genetic monocultures (Crutsinger et al. 2006). This increase in arthropod diversity was due to increases in both herbivores and predators, as their diversities each increased with increases in plant diversity (fig. 16.26). Why? One possible contributor to increased insect abundance was the observed 36% increase in plant abundance with increased plant genetic diversity (fig. 16.26). In other words, genetic diversity led to increased plant growth, which could have caused increased herbivore and predator abundances. However, what led to increased plant growth? Once again, niche complementarity and sampling effects are likely explanations. It is comforting when a single set of theories can be used to explain a diversity of results! Importantly, it is also possible that complementarity was occurring among the arthropods, though future studies would be needed to know why they may have been using different components of niche space and/or habitat.

CONCEPT 16.4 REVIEW

1. Why might genetic diversity impact processes at the community level?
2. Why are plants so often used in studies of genetic diversity?

ECOLOGICAL TOOLS AND APPROACHES

Sampling Communities

At the heart of community ecology is the need to accurately and reliably measure the composition of a community. This may seem to be a trivially easy task, as we all know that ecology professors simply go out into the field, lay down a few transects or plots, write down a few numbers, and then return home ready to devise a difficult exam for the undergraduates in their introductory courses. Except for that last part, this is a woefully inaccurate overview of how community ecology is actually done, and takes no account of the numerous pitfalls that lie along the way.

In the previous section, we discussed the growing recognition of how important genetic diversity can be within natural communities. In chapter 4, we described new innovations in molecular biology, and how these tools were revolutionizing ecological research. Few areas of ecology are more influenced

by the adoption of molecular tools than studies involving genetic diversity. However, as do most ecologists of my generation, I will put further discussion of the specific ways diversity is measured aside. Instead, the focus here is on species.

The question of how many species are found in a community is one of the most fundamental questions an ecologist can ask. With increasing threats to biodiversity, species richness is also one of the most important community attributes we might measure. Estimates of species richness are critical for determining areas suitable for conservation, for diagnosing the impacts of environmental change on a community, or for identifying critical habitat for rare and threatened species. However, determining species richness of an actual community is not simple. Sound estimates require a carefully designed, standardized sampling program and great accuracy

when collecting and handling the data. This section will focus on several fundamental aspects of study design.

One of the positions that Evelyn Pielou advocated was that advancement in ecology would come through integration of models, lab studies, and data-rich studies from the field. Mathematical ecology would then serve a critical role in "processing large bodies of observational data in such a way that interesting regularities, hitherto buried from sight, become apparent" (Pielou 1977). This approach by Pielou is important in that it emphasizes a link between question development (modelling, lab studies) and testing in real-world conditions (field studies confronted with statistics). Over the decades, ecologists have grappled with developing the appropriate research methods that provide society not only with large volumes of data, but more importantly, with large volumes of high quality and accurate data. In chapter 1 we presented a general overview of the scientific method. Here we explore some of the issues that ecologists face when they work at that point between research idea and statistical analysis (fig. 16.27).

Where, When, Who, and How Much?

It is impossible to conduct accurate field work in community ecology unless you know how to identify species. It is really

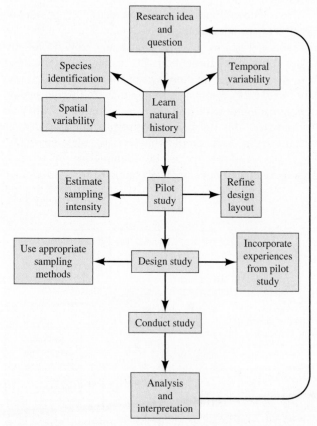

Figure 16.27   Much time and effort occurs between the development of a research idea and the statistical analysis of the data.

that simple—inaccurate identifications of birds, bats, butterflies, bears, and beetles result in meaningless data and a large waste of time and money. It is beyond the scope of this book to describe how to identify species, but we can lead you in a few directions: (1) get outside and look around—closely, (2) take courses in systematics and biodiversity from your college or university, and (3) get back outside and apply your knowledge. Accurate species identification is a very hard skill to acquire, particularly for species-rich groups. Nonetheless, it is the foundation of real-world ecology.

When conducting ecological studies, you will need to make a reference collection of your specimens that you (ideally) deposit in a local museum. This will serve as a valuable reference for future researchers who may want to return to your locations and conduct new studies. It also serves as a backup plan for your identification errors, as others will know what species you sampled, even if you misidentified them.

Once you are able to accurately identify the species in your area, a critical next step in doing community ecology is knowing exactly where and when you should sample. For some projects, this may be trivially easy. For example, if you are contracted to measure the number of native plant species growing in your parents' flower garden, and there is only one weekend left before you return to campus for the fall term, then this study has clearly defined boundaries, in both space and time. However, suppose your contract was to measure the number of plant species found in gardens throughout your home town. If you live in a very small town, with only a handful of gardens, it is possible that you would be able to measure every single garden and get an actual count of species richness. However, suppose you lived in Windsor, Ontario. It simply is not possible to measure every garden over the entire summer, let alone your last weekend home. Instead, you will need to sub-sample. Additionally, because the growing season in Windsor is longer than a single weekend, there is going to be variation in which species you see at different points of the year, and thus sampling only in the fall is likely inadequate to measure the actual diversity of the system. Measuring only in that one weekend may result in a failure of fulfilling your contractual obligations.

Timing

We will first discuss a few issues related to deciding when and how often you should sample. In general, you want to sample with a frequency that allows you to accurately identify all species that are likely present. What that frequency is will depend upon the organisms. For example, you likely only want to sample for flying insects during the months and times of day that they are active. If you are working with plants, there is little value in sampling during the winter months throughout much of the Northern hemisphere. However, some regions around the world are too hot to support plant growth during the summer, and thus are best surveyed during the winter. Some groups of organisms are likely to have little change in species composition over their period of activity (e.g., small

mammals over summer), while others may change substantially. As a result, you will need to sample high-turnover taxa more frequently than low-turnover taxa. For example, Elise Bolduc and her colleagues at McGill University sampled the diversity of ground-dwelling spiders in vineyards in southern Quebec (Bolduc et al. 2005). Their data show that the abundances of five of the more common species vary greatly over the summer months, and thus if they used a single snapshot of the community, they would have missed several of these species (fig. 16.28). It is clearly important to sample when your species are active! At the same time, you do not want to oversample your community, as this would be wasted effort, costing you money, loss of time, and even increasing risk to your study populations for little scientific value (chapter 9). Whether the right frequency means you should sample once a week, once a month, or once a year will depend on the organisms you work with; once again having a strong basis in natural history is critical to doing good ecological research.

Location

Deciding where to sample poses difficulties similar to deciding when to sample. If all species were distributed evenly across a community, the life of a field ecologist would be quite simple, as we could simply throw down a quadrat and what we would find would be representative of every other location in the community. The real world, however, is much more heterogeneous. As we have discussed throughout the text, different species have different niche requirements, and even more restricted realized niches, and thus only a narrow set of locations within a community are likely suitable for growth for any particular species. As a result, even if we placed two quadrats down on the forest floor, separated only by 1–2 m, and

measured the diversity of plant species in each, there is a very good chance we would not find identical results. If we assume that it is not possible to sample every square inch of the forest floor, we need to instead use sub-samples. Where do we lay them? How many do we use?

Let's suppose we have the time, energy, and budget to sample the vegetation of only 100 m^2 of a 10 hectare forest community, or 0.1% of the actual community. How do we decide what size of plots we should use, and where do we lay them? (It is worth noting that many ecological questions can also be measured using plotless sampling techniques, though that is beyond the scope of this text). The most basic consideration given to determining the size of study plots is the size of the organisms you are going to study. Plots need to be larger than many individuals of all the species you are measuring. In other words, you can use a 50 × 50 cm plot if you are measuring mosses, but not if you are measuring trees. Second, your plot size needs to be small enough that you can accurately measure all the individuals within the plot. For organisms such as mosses that are very small, large plots result in substantial error. You learn the appropriate size of plot for your system through experience and through conversations with graduate students and professors. However, even then a solid grounding in natural history is again critical to good ecological research.

We will now suppose that you are focusing your work on the diversity of understory seedlings, and you have decided that plots of 1 × 1 m are most appropriate. How do you distribute those plots throughout the community? You have three main choices: random, systematic, and stratified random (fig. 16.29). Random is simply that. You use a random number generator to develop XY coordinates for each of your 100 samples. This will give a completely unbiased sample (which is good), sometimes (which is bad). Why only sometimes? We know that species distributions are not typically random, or at least not completely random. Some species are

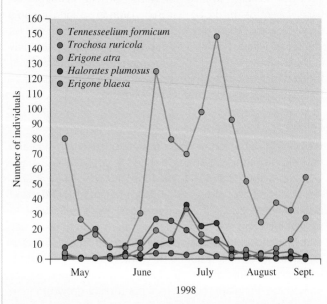

Figure 16.28   The abundances of five co-occurring species of spiders can vary greatly over the summer (data from Bolduc et al. 2005).

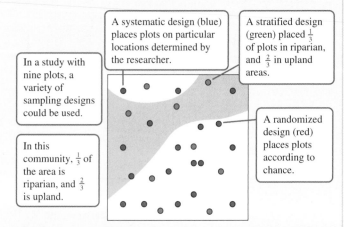

Figure 16.29   Systematic, random, and stratified sampling in a community.

going to be found only in some locations, particularly those that have very narrow niche requirements. When you randomly assign plots to locations, the plots may—by chance—aggregate in certain areas of the community. It is important to recognize that random is not the same as even. Random distributions of plots work best in communities that do not have any obvious major subcommunities within them. For instance, random plot assignments might work well in a homogeneous forest, but not one that has a stream going through it, as you would expect differences in species composition as a function of distance to the stream. The potential negative effects of random plot placement are greatest when you are using relatively few plots.

So does this mean that we should generally place our plots in certain places, using instead some sort of systematic plot design? No. Systematic designs can come in a variety of flavours. One design would be to place plots in areas that the researcher knows are important areas of diversity. This will obviously bias the results and the study, as the areas sampled are not representative of the entire area. In the wrong hands, such a biased design could be used to either artificially inflate or deflate measures of biodiversity of a single community, even if the data collected within each plot is accurate. It is because of this reason that scientists pay particular attention to the details of study designs in their own work, as well as that of others. However, there is another form of systematic plot layout that is sometimes used, and that is to spread plots out evenly over the community. For example, in this study you could devise a grid with 100 evenly spaced intersections, sampling in each location. This design introduces a new bias, one that is based upon the natural distribution of the organisms in the system. If the organisms are distributed according to any particularly spatial pattern, then superimposing any new spatial pattern (e.g., a grid) imposes a new bias! For example, imagine that competition for light results in a recurring pattern of tall tree—small tree—tall tree—small tree. Sampling on a grid that overlays a regular spatial pattern will cause a biased sample, overestimating the number of either large or small trees. As a result, systematic designs are generally avoided, unless substantial prior research is available showing such underlying patterns do not exist.

The final design, and one that is often used, particularly when only a few plots are available, is the stratified random design. This approach takes the best parts of both the randomized and systematic design, without falling prey to their statistical traps. Quite simply, suppose you are working in a forest that has riparian and upland habitats, and you think that these subcommunities will contain different species. You can stratify your study into two parts, upland and riparian, and then you assign plots to those strata in proportion to their abundance on the landscape. For example, if 30% of the area was riparian, you would assign 30 of your 100 plots to riparian, and the remaining 70 to upland. Within a given strata, you would randomly locate those 30 (or 70) plots. This design is very commonly used, and works best when a community is subdivided into a few strata, allowing for many plots within each.

The Need for Pilot Studies

In this section we have only touched upon a few of the common issues field ecologists encounter when they attempt to sample communities. There exist many more problems that we have not yet even touched upon. For example, how do we know when we have sampled enough? In other words, when is sampling the same plot for longer worse than sampling a new plot for a shorter duration? Even more basic is the issue of species identification. How do we know we are right in the names we are assigning to our samples? Without a high level of accuracy in that most basic of skills, much of the time and money spent on a project is wasted.

How does one acquire those skills? Practice and patience. There is no substitute for actual field experience if you want to become a field researcher. The idea of natural history being important in ecology is not because all ecologists are granola eating (I hate granola) relics of the sixties (I was only alive for 23 days of the 1960s). Rather, natural history is important because a sound understanding of the system that you will explore is critical to the development of a sound experimental design. Pilot studies are "first tries" of projects and experiments. With limited scope, money, and time, they give you an opportunity to refine your identification skills, sampling protocols, and statistical analyses. They are critical to ecology. So, do you want to do a field study? Then stop spending all your free time sitting in the library discussing Sartre and Heidegger, and get to the field!

SUMMARY

A *community* is an association of interacting species inhabiting some defined area. Examples of communities include the plant community on a mountainside, the insect community associated with a particular species of tree, or the fish community on a coral reef. Community ecologists often restrict their studies to groups of species that all make their living in a similar way. Animal ecologists call such groups *guilds*, while plant ecologists use the terms *life-form* and *functional groups*. The field of community ecology concerns how the environment influences community structure, including the relative abundance and diversity of species, the subjects of this chapter.

16.1 A combination of the number of species and their relative abundance defines species diversity.

Diversity can be measured at different scales. *Alpha* diversity represents the most local scale, while *gamma* diversity represents a landscape scale. *Beta* diversity indicates the variability among locations within the landscape. In natural communities, most species are moderately abundant; few are very abundant or extremely rare. Frank Preston (1948) graphed the abundance of species in collections as distributions of species abundance, with each abundance interval twice the preceding one. Preston's graphs were approximately bell-shaped curves and are called lognormal distributions. Lognormal distributions, which describe the relative abundance of organisms ranging from algae and terrestrial plants to birds, may result from many random environmental variables acting upon the populations of a large number of species or may be a consequence of how species subdivide resources. Regardless of the underlying mechanisms, the lognormal distribution is one of the best-described patterns in community ecology.

Two major factors define the diversity of a community: (1) the number of species in the community, which ecologists usually call *species richness*, and (2) the relative abundance of species, or *species evenness*. One of the most commonly applied indices of species diversity is the Shannon–Wiener index:

$$H' = -\sum_{i=1}^{s} p_i \log_e p_i$$

Species evenness is generally measured with Pielou's J. The relative abundance and diversity of species can also be portrayed using *rank-abundance curves*. Accurate estimates of species richness require carefully designed sampling programs.

16.2 Species diversity is higher in complex environments.

Robert MacArthur (1958) discovered that five coexisting warbler species feed in different layers of forest vegetation and that the number of warbler species in North American forests increases with increasing forest stature. Various investigators have found that the diversity of forest birds increases with increased foliage height diversity. Heterogeneity in physical and chemical conditions across aquatic and terrestrial environments can account for a significant portion of the diversity among planktonic algae and terrestrial plants. Heterogeneity in forests is positively associated with the diversity of *Carex* communities.

16.3 Ecological functions performed by communities are dependent upon community structure.

Ecological communities perform a number of functions, such as nutrient cycling and biomass production. These functions result in the delivery of services of value to people. Changes in the structure of natural communities can influence the efficiency of these ecological processes, and thus have societal impact. One of the most well studied examples is the relationship between species diversity and plant biomass production, where increased plant diversity usually causes increased biomass production. Similar patterns have been found for other species, and trophic groups. Underlying these patterns are explanations based upon niche theory (complementarity), species interactions (facilitation), and probability theory (sampling).

16.4 Genetic variation of species within a community influences ecological function.

Similar to the patterns found for species diversity–function relationships, recent studies are finding significant ecological consequences of genetic diversity for community-level functions. Again, by studying plants, ecologists have discovered that increased genetic diversity can lead to increased plant diversity. Additionally, these effects of plant diversity can impact herbivore and predator diversity, highlighting the complexity of natural systems. The integration of genetics and evolutionary biology is a rapidly growing area within ecology.

Studies in community ecology are complicated by variation in the distributions of species in both space and time. A common strategy when addressing real-world issues is to try and find species, or groups of species, that can serve as indicators of overall community condition. However, in all studies of community ecology, appropriate study designs require detailed knowledge of the natural history of the study system and the organisms that live within it. It is critical to consider aspects of the timing and frequency of measurements, as well as the shape, number, and distribution of study plots. Designs not founded in an understanding of the study system are likely to result in biased findings. In order to learn how to conduct field research, it is critical to do field research.

REVIEW QUESTIONS

1. What is the difference between a community and a population? What are some distinguishing properties of communities? What is a guild? Give examples. What is a plant life-form? Give examples.

2. Draw a typical lognormal distribution. Include properly labelled horizontal (x) and vertical (y) axes. You can use the lognormal distributions included in chapter 16 as models.

3. Suppose you are a biologist working for an international conservation organization concerned with studying and conserving biological diversity. On one of your assignments you are sent out to explore the local biotas of several regions. As part of your survey work you are to take large quantitative samples of the copepods of the North Atlantic, the butterflies of central New Guinea, and the ground-dwelling beetles of southwest Africa. Using the lognormal distribution, predict the patterns of relative abundance of species you expect to see within each of these groups of organisms.

4. What are species richness and species evenness? How does each of these components of species diversity contribute to the value of the Shannon–Wiener diversity index (H′)? How do species evenness and richness influence the form of rank-abundance curves?

5. Why is it important that the ecologist be familiar with the niches of study organisms before exploring relationships between environmental complexity and species diversity?

6. Communities in different areas may be organized in different ways. For instance, C. Ralph (1985) found that in Patagonia in Argentina, as foliage height diversity increases, bird species diversity decreases. This result is exactly the opposite of the pattern observed by MacArthur (1958) and others reviewed in chapter 16. Design a study aimed at determining the environmental factors determining variation in bird species diversity across Ralph's Patagonian study sites.

7. The study of diversity–function relationships has been led predominantly by plant ecologists. However, this does not mean these patterns do not apply to vertebrates or other taxa. Given the constraints associated with working with vertebrates, design a study to test whether guilds of seed-eating birds show facilitation in mixed species assemblages.

8. Suppose you are being paid to increase the long-term biomass production of a field. How would you determine whether it is economically important to take into consideration plant species and genotypic diversity in your management?

9. You have been contracted to determine the diversity of the species of your favourite group of organisms in your favourite part of the world. Money is tight, and you can only sample 1% of the area of your study community. Design a sampling protocol that is most likely to give an unbiased estimate of the number of species in the community. How would you know if you are right?

10. Draw hypothetical landscapes in which (a) beta diversity is low but gamma diversity is high, and (b) alpha diversity is high and beta diversity is high.

For more information on the resources available from McGraw-Hill Ryerson, go to **www.mcgrawhill.ca/he/solutions**.

SPECIES INTERACTIONS AND COMMUNITY STRUCTURE

CHAPTER 17

CHAPTER CONCEPTS

17.1 A food web summarizes the feeding relationships in a community.

Concept 17.1 Review

17.2 Strong competitors can alter community structure.

Concept 17.2 Review

17.3 The activities of a few keystone species may control the structure of communities.

Ecology in Action: Keystone Species, Ecosystem Engineers, and Conservation Biology

Concept 17.3 Review

17.4 Mutualists can act as keystone species.

Concept 17.4 Review

Ecological Tools and Approaches: Humans as Keystone Species

Summary

Review Questions

446

So far in this book we have presented a number of isolated facts: mutualisms, herbivory, parasitism, and competition are some of the ways species can interact; population growth can be exponential or regulated; species richness and evenness are two measures of biodiversity. However, if we want to understand *why* we see the patterns in communities that are commonly described, we need to integrate this information. We began such integration in chapter 16 with our discussion of the *intermediate disturbance hypothesis*. In this chapter we explore more explicitly how complex interactions among diverse groups of species result in changes in community structure.

Feeding relationships provide some of the most visually obvious examples of interactions in communities. For example, we can see around the Antarctic waters krill, shrimp-like crustaceans named *Euphausia superba*, feeding upon large numbers of diatoms. The krill are themselves prey to many other species, including crabeater seals, penguins, seabirds, many fish and squid, as well as the large baleen whales that migrate to these waters (fig. 17.1). The krill-eating fish and squid are eaten by other predators, including emperor penguins, other fish, and Weddell and Ross seals. These seals are themselves fed upon by leopard seals, and all of these are fed upon by orcas. How do we go beyond this verbal description to one that more accurately summarizes these feeding relationships? This question is at the heart of one of the earliest approaches to studying communities, descriptions of who eats whom. Since the beginning of the twentieth century, ecologists have meticulously described the feeding relationships of hundreds of communities, each producing a tangle of relationships called a **food web**. These summaries of feeding interactions within a community can reveal many basic aspects of community structure, serving as a portrait of a community.

Food webs, however, are just one example of a larger category of **ecological networks**. An ecological network is a description of the interactions that occur among co-occurring species in a community. They can be thought of as describing a community not based upon taxonomic affiliation, but instead based upon some ecological process in which the

organisms participate. Ecological networks are typically divided into three main categories, *trophic networks*, *host–parasitoid networks*, and *mutualistic networks*. Trophic networks describe interactions based upon feeding relationship, such as the food web described above. Host–parasitoid networks describe the interconnectedness of host and their parasites, diseases, and parasitoids. Mutualistic networks focus on interactions such as pollination and mycorrhizae, and emphasize that most mutualisms involve many species and differing degrees of specialization.

Networks are complicated, but only because communities themselves are complicated. Fortunately, with close study a number of general patterns and principles emerge. One approach to identifying the key mechanisms that drive community structure is to determine whether any **community assembly rules** are occurring in a given location. Community assembly rules can occur within or across trophic levels, and describe the processes that limit or promote coexistence. Though originally presented as a very specific set of rules that governed what species could, or could not co-occur (Cody and Diamond 1975), assembly rules are now typically used in a more general way (Weiher and Keddy 1999).

Ecological interactions can cause predictable patterns, many of which can be described through the use of networks and the creation of assembly rules. In this chapter we will explore this complexity of nature, and describe some aspects of how species interactions influence community structure. We first return to feeding relationships to describe what one type of ecological network looks like.

17.1 Ecological Networks Across Trophic Boundaries: Food Webs

A food web summarizes the feeding relationships in a community. The trophic networks described by food webs are difficult to construct, but when done well, serve as a bridge between community and ecosystem ecology. They incorporate aspects of the biology of the organism, as well as describing the direction of movement of energy and resources within, or even between, communities. Here we focus on the underlying biology of food webs, leaving the study of energy and nutrient flow for later chapters.

The earliest food webs concentrated on simplified communities. In 1927, Charles Elton pointed out that the number of well-described food webs, which he called food cycles, could be counted on the fingers of one hand. One of the first of those food webs described the feeding relations on Bear Island off the coast of Northern Norway in the high Arctic (fig. 17.2). Summerhayes and Elton (1923) studied the feeding relations there because they believed that the high Arctic, with few species and thus reduced complexity, would be the best place to begin the study of food webs.

Summerhayes and Elton used a food web to present the feeding relations on Bear Island in a single picture. The primary producers in the Bear Island food web are terrestrial plants and

Figure 17.1 A marine food web in action: feeding baleen whales and birds.

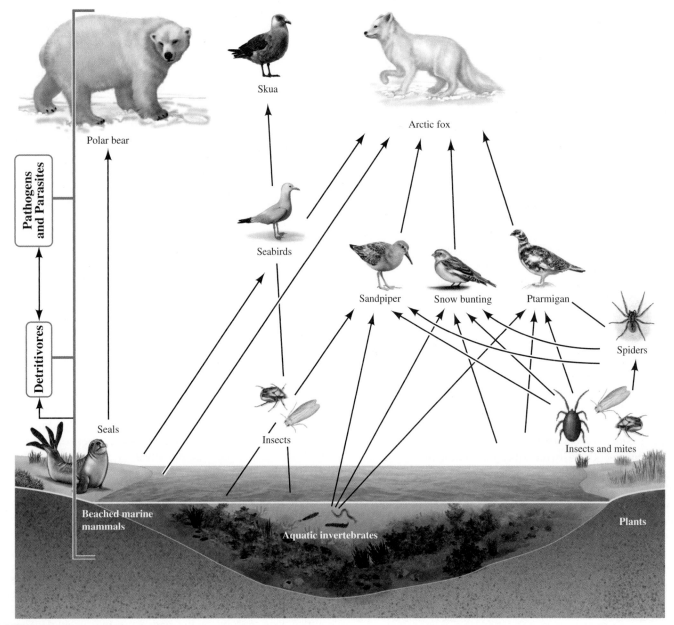

Figure 17.2   Simple food web of an arctic island. *Note:* The indication of detritivores and pathogens was not part of Elton's original food web. They are added to indicate that parasites, pathogens, and detritivores feed on organisms of all trophic levels.

aquatic algae. These primary producers are fed upon by several kinds of terrestrial and aquatic invertebrates, which are in turn consumed by birds. The birds on Bear Island are attacked by arctic foxes. Arctic foxes also feed on marine mammals that have washed up onto the beaches, and on the dung of polar bears. The polar bears of Bear Island subsist on a diet of seals and beached marine mammals. Seabirds harvest food from the sea around Bear Island but enter the Bear Island food web because they are attacked by foxes, feed on beached marine animals and on the freshwater invertebrates of Bear Island, and contribute dung that fertilizes the primary producers of the island.

In recent years, there has been growing recognition that even though food webs are cartoons of just one type of interaction among species (feeding), most published food webs are woefully incomplete even in accomplishing that simplified task. The failures tend to occur in the same place—an overemphasis on the larger organisms in the system. Though polar bear and arctic fox are beautiful animals, that alone does not make them more important to understanding food webs than the less charismatic insects, algae, and microbes with which they co-occur. Another group of researchers (Hodkinson and Coulson 2004) decided to look more closely at the food web of a high Arctic island, finding a diversity of interactions lacking from the web of Elton (fig. 17.2). One of the major additions of this web is the inclusion of soil organic matter, decomposers, and detritivores. Everything dies eventually, and the energy they contain does not simply leave the system, instead it becomes food. Or put another way, most of the feeding that

occurs in even this simple system is hidden from view, occurring in and on the soil.

As we will discuss in more depth in chapters 19 and 20, most biomass in a community is consumed only after death, and not as a predation or herbivory event. Missing from the classic cartoons of most food webs is a large proportion of the biological diversity on the planet, and the links that connect the bulk of biomass to its consumers. This is another example of the oversight that has resulted in a historical bias against understanding those things that are small, and those things that occur in the soil and sediments of the world (chapters 2 and 3). The sad reality of the state of ecology is that the ecology of parasites, pathogens, microbes, and other small consumers is woefully understudied. These disciplines in ecology will remain open areas of research for enterprising students for decades to come. Because our understanding of the details of these aspects of food webs is so incomplete, we must ignore them for now, coming back to decomposition in chapters 19 and 20. But first we show that even when we do ignore this aspect of feeding relationships, there still exists great complexity in food webs.

Detailed Food Webs Reveal Great Complexity

One study by Kirk Winemiller (1990), who described the feeding relations among freshwater fish, gives a hint of the great complexity of many food webs. Winemiller studied the aquatic food webs at two locations in the savannas, or llanos, of Venezuela and at two other sites in the lowlands of Costa Rica. His study sites supported from 20 to 88 fish species. One of Winemiller's least species-rich study sites was a medium-sized stream called Caño Volcán. This stream flows through the piedmont of the Andes and supports 20 fish species.

Winemiller represented the food webs at his study sites in various ways. In some he only included the common fish species whose aggregate abundance comprised 95% of

the individuals in his collections. These common-fish webs excluded many rare species. Winemiller also constructed food webs that excluded the weakest trophic links, those comprising less than 1% of the diet.

Let's look at the results from Caño Volcán, the simplest fish community. Figure 17.3a shows that even when only the ten most common fish at Caño Volcán are included in the food web, it remains remarkably complex. The most comprehensible of Winemiller's food webs, though still complex, were those that focused on the strongest trophic links only (fig. 17.3b). In addition to simplifying food web structure, focusing on the strongest feeding relationships identifies and emphasizes the more biologically significant trophic interactions.

Feeding Relationships: Cross Community Boundaries

Ralph Bird published a paper in 1930 entitled *Biotic Communities of the Aspen Parkland of Central Canada*. Bird travelled throughout the Parkland region (chapter 16) and provided the first detailed survey of the feeding relationships among species in each of the major community types of the parkland: prairie, Aspen forest, and willow stands (fig. 17.4). We have presented the original hand-drawn versions of these food webs, as presented in Bird's papers, to give a sense of the level of care and detail that was necessary to publish such monumental work during the early years of the discipline of ecology. There are several things that are important to point out in these figures. First, the number of connections in each community does not appear to be particularly troublesome, and certainly a level of complexity a competent scientist should be able to handle. However, you may notice that these webs do not usually list all of the species involved, but instead list guilds and functional groups. In particular, the smaller organisms, such as snails, insects, spiders, etc., are lumped together, while the vertebrates are separated by species.

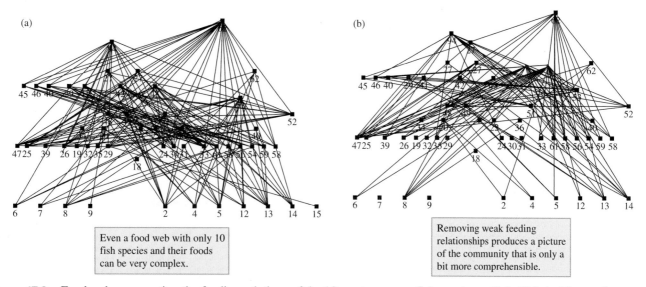

Even a food web with only 10 fish species and their foods can be very complex.

Removing weak feeding relationships produces a picture of the community that is only a bit more comprehensible.

Figure 17.3   Food web representing the feeding relations of the 10 most common fish species at Caño Volcán, Venezuela, (*a*) with all feeding—relationships represented and (*b*) with weak feeding relationships excluded (data from Winemiller 1990).

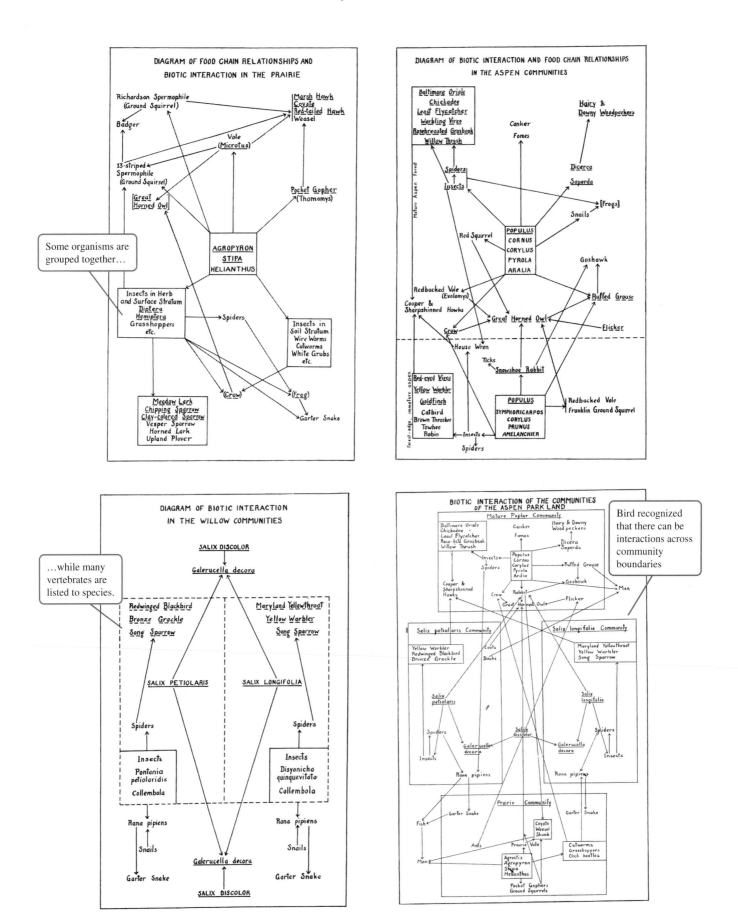

Figure 17.4   Biotic interactions within and among three Aspen Parkland community types, drawn by Bird (1930).

Why? Obviously this is in large part because of historical patterns of taxonomic bias toward larger organisms. Can you imagine what these would look like if Bird used the level of detail shown in Winemiller's food webs?

Aside from convenience, there may be a biological basis for only identifying a subset of complex food webs. In many cases, some connections between species will be more important in influencing community structure and ecological function than others. In other words, some species may be substitutable in terms of the overall community structure, while other species may be critical by themselves. However, here, the lumping of species was not based upon experiments that can test for such strong or weak effects.

In addition to providing food webs for each of the three communities common within the Parkland savanna, Bird also drew the connections he observed among species in different communities (fig. 17.4). This is critical, as it shows that as early as 1930 ecologists were recognizing that community boundaries are fuzzy, and that there can be direct interactions of species among communities. This issue has recently received substantially more attention among ecologists, and it is now recognized that feeding relations across communities (e.g., streams and forests) can play a substantial role in energy and nutrient cycles (chapters 19 and 20).

Before we return to the idea that some interactions are likely more functionally important in influencing community structure than others, let's first return to the idea of competition. Similar to what we see for feeding relations, there can be predictable linkages of competition across species. From this emerge a number of assembly rules, which under certain circumstances better enable us to understand community structure. Here we try to understand community within a single trophic group, focusing on the role of competition.

CONCEPT 17.1 REVIEW

1. What are the main advantages of including only strong linkages in a food web?
2. What was the primary way by which Bird simplified the food web representing the interactions of species in the Aspen Parkland?
3. Why are parasites and detritivores generally left out of food webs, and what impact does this have on ecological understanding?

17.2 Community Assembly: Competitive Asymmetries

Strong competitors can alter community structure. In chapter 13, we discussed competition, describing many of the potential effects it could have on populations and species coexistence. We also talked about the most extreme impact

of competition in a community: competitive exclusion. Under a narrow set of conditions, the competitive exclusion principle leads to an assembly rule: functionally identical species sharing a limited resource cannot coexist. However, we know that this rule does not always apply, as a number of ecological mechanisms do allow for competing organisms to coexist (chapter 13). This leaves us a bit unclear about whether competition can actually influence community structure. In this section we provide several examples in which competition has clear effects on community structure.

Competition and Diversity

What should happen to species diversity within a community if the strength of competition increases over time? The answer to this question is going to be dependent upon whether species are similar in their competitive abilities (competitive equivalence), or instead if communities contain **competitive hierarchies**. A competitive hierarchy is a very simple idea: some species are consistently better competitors than other species, and thus species can be ranked in the order of their competitive abilities. For example, if there were four species in a community (A, B, C, and D), and if a competitive hierarchy existed, then you could rank their competitive abilities as A > B > C > D. You may notice that this hierarchy is also transitive (think back to introductory algebra!), meaning that if A > B and B > C, then A > C. This is the most extreme possible version of a hierarchy, and one could imagine others such as A > B = C > D. Regardless of the details of the rankings, the implications of hierarchies and transitivity for community structure are broad. If there is no competition in the community then a hierarchy is irrelevant and competitive exclusion will not occur. Similarly, if intransitivity occurs (such that a complete hierarchy is not formed), species coexistence can also occur, even if competition is strong (Laird and Schamp, 2006). However, if competition is strong, and transitivity occurs, then in the above example A, B, and C will start to squeeze species D out, potentially causing it to be lost from the community. If competition continues to increase, the community may lose species C, and perhaps even B, resulting in a community consisting only of species A. In other words, if the species of a community differ consistently in their competitive abilities, then increased competition should cause a drop in species diversity. That sure sounds like an assembly rule! Does it actually occur?

Competitive Hierarchies

We once again turn to plants. We do this for several reasons. The first is practical: plant ecologists have a long history of studying competition, and thus much of the best data on the impacts of competition on community structure was collected by plant ecologists. The second reason is more conceptual: as we discussed in chapter 16, the diversity of animals in a community often varies as a function of the heterogeneity of the plants. As a result, changes to plant community structure due to competition can cause changes in animal community structure, even if the animals themselves are not competing with each other. This critical issue is often overlooked when examining the impact of competition on community structure.

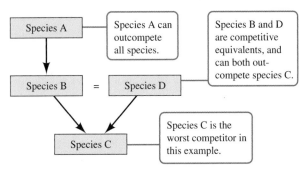

Figure 17.5 Competitive relationships among species can be displayed in a manner similar to that of food webs.

Bill Shipley, of the Université de Sherbrooke, has spent many years combining mathematical and community ecology. He has been quite interested in the importance of competitive hierarchies in plant communities. In fact, he contributed to the initial concept of competitive transitivity (Keddy and Shipley 1989) which he then refined (Shipley 1993). In his 1993 paper, Shipley developed an analytical method allowing one to test whether competitive relationships among plants are, or are not, transitive. At that time, Shipley was able to find ten published studies of matrices that recorded the competitive relationships (analogous to trophic networks described by food webs; fig. 17.5) of different species of plants. In nine of ten cases, relationships were transitive, supporting the idea that competition has the potential to alter plant community structure.

As we will see next, the idea of competitive hierarchies can be combined with the theory of allocation (chapter 7) and an understanding of physiological ecology (chapters 5 and 6), leading to a theory that could be helpful in explaining the distribution of plant species along environmental gradients.

Centrifugal Organization of Species

Paul Keddy, formerly of the University of Ottawa, developed the concept of "centrifugal organization of plant communities."

In the freshwater wetlands in Ontario he kept observing a repeating pattern: much of the area would be dominated by a single genus of grass, *Typha*, while many other species could be found nearby in small patches of much higher diversity (fig. 17.6). What caused these reoccurring patterns in this system? Answering this question has served as the foundation of research for many students and postdocs from the Keddy lab, many of whom continue their research in plant community ecology in universities and government agencies throughout North America. The combined work of Keddy and former lab members including Scott Wilson, Lauchlan Fraser, Evan Weiher, Connie Gaudet, Bill Shipley, and Irene Wisheu resulted in an innovative approach to understanding community organization, one that extends far beyond the wetlands of Ontario.

The theory of centrifugal organization of species is most thoroughly explained in a 1992 paper by Irene Wisheu and Paul Keddy entitled *Plant Competition and Centrifugal Organization of Plant Communities: Theory and Test*. The theory is based upon the idea of that both core and peripheral habitats exist within a landscape. The core habitat is the prime real estate in the community, with few abiotic stresses, lots of resources, and few pests or pathogens. In short, the core habitat meets the requirements of the fundamental niche for nearly all species of the community (fig. 17.7). However, because species differ in competitive abilities, and there exists a competitive hierarchy in this system; not all species will be able to occupy the core habitat. Instead, the core habitat will be dominated by the best competitor, which in these wetlands is *Typha*. But why do you find so many other species in this system?

As we discussed in chapter 16, the world is a heterogeneous place. Some places will freeze up and be subjected to frequent ice scouring. Other areas will be sandy and low in nutrient content. Others will be near beaver dams and subjected to repeated flooding. Some will be exposed to brackish water and have saline soils. In the theory of centrifugal organization of species diversity, Keddy makes the assumption that plants require specific adaptations to perform well under these less-than-ideal

(a)   (b)

Figure 17.6 Areas of differing productivity and diversity in a wetland. (*a*) Typha dominates core habitats, while (*b*) a diversity of species live in peripheral habitats.

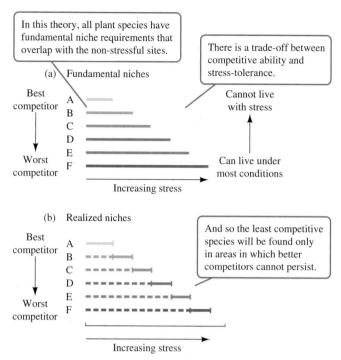

Figure 17.7 Competitive hierarchies form the basis of the theory of centrifugal organization of plant communities (data from Wisheu and Keddy 1992).

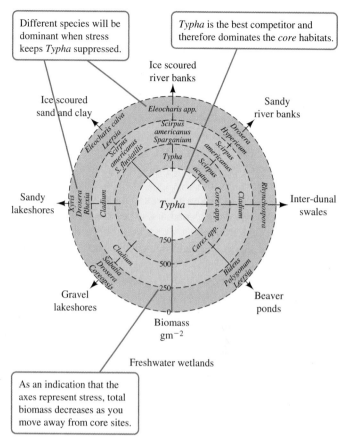

Figure 17.8 Centrifugal organization of the biotic and abiotic factors that influence community structure within a freshwater wetland (data from Wisheu and Keddy 1992, originally from Moore et al. 1989). Note that this diagram is a representation of a set of concepts, rather than a specific map of a specific wetland.

conditions. He further assumes that not all plants are able to perform at their optimum under all environmental conditions, and instead there will exist trade-offs between competitive ability and the ability to cope with the different types of environmental stresses. As we saw in our discussion of life histories (chapter 9), this assumption is quite reasonable.

As a result of these trade-offs, Keddy argues that you will find the competitively inferior species occupying areas that are dominated by these stresses, as under those conditions they either are able to outcompete *Typha*, or competition itself no longer occurs. Each community will have its own set of stress gradients along which stress-competition trade-offs will occur, and Keddy would expect a predictable arrangement of species along each of those gradients. These gradients can be arranged graphically (fig. 17.8), with the core habitat in the centre, and each stress gradient radiating out. If you have a detailed understanding of the species of the system, you can then include likely species found along each of these gradients. Once this is developed, you could then go out to a community, identify what stressors are, or are not, occurring in a given location, and then see whether you find the species you expect to occur. In other words, this relatively simple model of community organization, based in the ideas of competition and theory of allocation, is a powerful tool to explain observed patterns of species occurrence.

Of course, this model is just one of many possible models to explain species distributions, and it has built into it several assumptions. For example, species hierarchies and trade-offs between competitive ability and stress tolerance are key aspects of the model. There will certainly be examples of communities where these assumptions are not met, and thus this

model would not apply. However, there are other communities, such as the wetlands that Keddy has studied, that seem to be very well described by this model (Wisheu and Keddy 1992), and thus it is an important tool to help ecologists understand how species interactions can alter community structure.

But the story does not end here. Although feeding relations and competitive interactions can both influence community structure, we need to recognize that these processes do not occur in isolation of each other. Instead, organisms will potentially need to deal with prey, predators, and competitors simultaneously. As we will see in the next section, interactions between feeding relations and competition can be critical to structuring some communities.

CONCEPT 17.2 REVIEW

1. Why are the effects of competition on community structure dependent upon whether competitive hierarchies are transitive or non-transitive?
2. Explain how the theory of allocation is an important aspect of Keddy's theory of centrifugal organization of plants.

17.3 # Community Assembly: Keystone Species

The activities of a few keystone species may control the structure of communities. Robert Paine (1966, 1969) proposed that the feeding activities of a few species have disproportionately strong influences on community structure. He called these **keystone species**. Paine's keystone species hypothesis emerged from a chain of reasoning. First, he proposed that predators might keep prey populations below their carrying capacity. Next, he reasoned the potential for competitive exclusion would be low in populations kept below carrying capacity. Finally, he concluded that if keystone species reduce the likelihood of competitive exclusion, their activities would increase the number of species that could coexist in communities. In other words, Paine predicted that some predators may increase species diversity due to reduced competition among the prey species. The idea of keystone species is an important one, and a great deal of ecological research has resulted in a clearer understanding of what being a keystone species entails.

Food Web Structure and Species Diversity

Paine began his studies by examining the relationship between overall species diversity within food webs and the proportion of the community represented by predators. He cited studies that demonstrated that as the number of species in marine zooplankton communities increases, the proportion that are predators also increases. For instance, the zooplankton community in the Atlantic Ocean over continental shelves includes 81 species, 16% of which are predators. In contrast, the zooplankton community of the Sargasso Sea contains 268 species, 39% of which are predators. Paine set out to determine if similar patterns occur in marine intertidal communities.

Paine described a food web from the intertidal zone at Mukkaw Bay, Washington, which lies in the north temperate zone at 49° N. This food web is typical of the rocky shore community along the west coast of North America (fig. 17.9) including regions of the BC coast. The base of this food web consists of algae and phytoplankton. However, Paine was particularly interested in nine dominant intertidal invertebrates: two species of chitons, two species of limpets, a mussel, three species of acorn barnacles, and one species of gooseneck barnacle. Paine pointed out that *Pisaster*, a starfish, commonly consumes two other prey species in other areas, a snail and another bivalve, bringing the total food web diversity to 13 species. Ninety percent of the energy consumed by the middle level predator, *Thais*, consists of barnacles. Meanwhile the top predator, *Pisaster*, obtains 90% of its energy from a mixture of chitons (41%), mussels (37%), and barnacles (12%).

Paine also described a subtropical food web (31° N) from the northern Gulf of California, a much richer web that included 45 species. However, like the food web at Mukkaw Bay, Washington, the subtropical web was topped by a single predator, the starfish *Heliaster kubinijii* (fig. 17.9). However, six predators occupy middle levels in the subtropical web, compared to one middle level predator at Mukkaw Bay.

Because four of the five species in the snail family Columbellidae are also predaceous, the total number of predators in the subtropical web is 11. These predators feed on the 34 species that form the base of the food web. Despite the presence of many more species in this subtropical web, the top predator, *Heliaster*, obtains most of its energy from sources similar to those used by *Pisaster* at Mukkaw Bay. *Heliaster* obtains 74% of its energy directly from a mixture of bivalves, herbivorous gastropods, and barnacles.

Paine found that as the number of species in his intertidal food webs increased, the proportion of the web represented by predators also increased. As Paine went from Mukkaw Bay to the northern Gulf of California, overall web diversity increased from 13 species to 45 species, a 3.5-fold increase. However, at the same time, the number of predators in the two webs increased from 2 to 11, a 5.5-fold increase. According to Paine's predation hypothesis, this higher proportion of predators produces higher predation pressure on prey populations, which in turn promotes the higher diversity in the Gulf of California intertidal zone.

Does this pattern confirm Paine's predation hypothesis? No, it does not. First, Paine studied a small number of webs—not enough to make broad generalizations. Second, while the patterns described by Paine are consistent with his hypothesis, they may be consistent with a number of other hypotheses. To evaluate the keystone species hypotheses, Paine needed a direct experimental test.

Experimental Removal of Starfish

For his first experiment, Paine removed the top predator from the intertidal food web at Mukkaw Bay and monitored the response of the community. He chose two study sites in the middle intertidal zone that extended 8 m along the shore and 2 m vertically. One site was designated as a control and the other as an experimental site. He removed *Pisaster* from the experimental site and relocated them in another portion of the intertidal zone. Each week Paine checked the experimental site for the presence of *Pisaster* and removed any that might have colonized since his last visit.

Paine followed the response of the intertidal community for two years. Over this interval the diversity of intertidal invertebrates in the control plot remained constant at 15, while the diversity within the experimental plot declined from 15 to 8, a loss of 7 species. This reduction in species diversity supported Paine's keystone species hypothesis. However, if this reduction was due to competitive exclusion, what was the resource over which species competed?

The most common limiting resource in the rocky intertidal zone is space. Within three months of removing *Pisaster* from the experimental plot, the barnacle *Balanus glandula* occupied 60% to 80% of the available space. One year after Paine removed *Pisaster*, *B. glandula* was crowded out by mussels, *Mytilus californianus*, and gooseneck barnacles, *Pollicipes polymerus*. Benthic algal populations also declined because of a lack of space for attachment, indicating that algae and animals compete for the same resources. The herbivorous chitons and limpets also left, due to a lack of space and a shortage

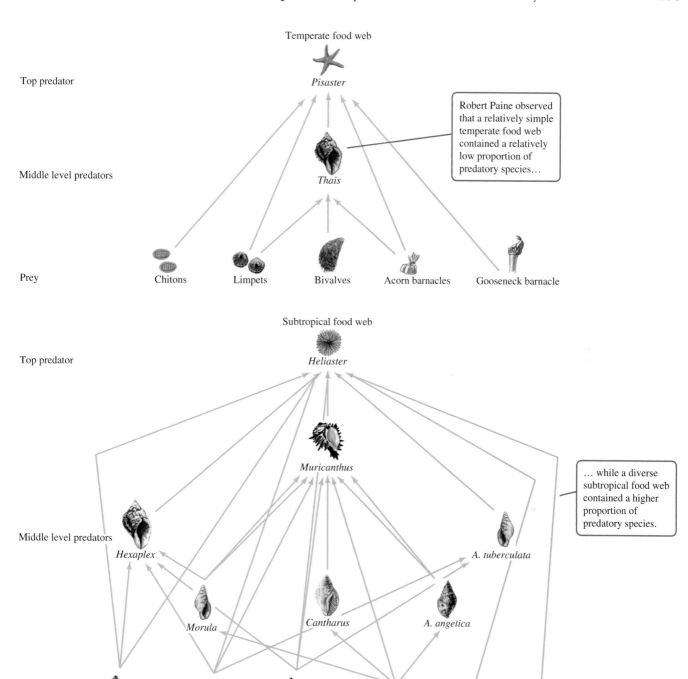

Figure 17.9 Roots of the keystone species hypothesis: does a higher proportion of predators in diverse communities indicate that predators contribute to higher species diversity? Algae and phytoplankton are not included in these diagrams.

of food. Sponges were also crowded out and a nudibranch that feeds on sponges also left. After five years, the *Pisaster* removal plot was dominated by two species: the mussel, *M. californianus*, and the gooseneck barnacle, *P. polymerus.*

This experiment showed that *Pisaster* can act as a keystone species. When Paine removed this relatively rare predator from his study plot, the community structure changed dramatically. As we see next, keystone effects occur in other systems as well.

Fish as Keystone Species in River Food Webs

Mary Power (1990) tested the possibility that fish can significantly alter the structure of food webs in rivers. She conducted her research on the Eel River in northern California, where most precipitation falls during October to April, sometimes producing torrential winter flooding. During the summer, however, the flow of the Eel River averages less than 1 m^3 per second.

In early summer, the boulders and bedrock of the Eel River are covered by a turf of the filamentous alga *Cladophora* (fig. 17.10). However, the biomass of the algae declines by midsummer and what remains has a ropy, prostrate growth form and a webbed appearance. These mats of *Cladophora* support dense populations of larval midges in the fly family

(a)

(b)

Figure 17.10   Seasonal changes in biomass and growth form of benthic algae in the Eel River, California: (*a*) in early summer, June 1989; (*b*) in late summer, August 1989.

Chironomidae. One chironomid, *Pseudochironomus richardsoni*, is particularly abundant. *Pseudochironomus* feeds on *Cladophora* and other algae and weaves the algae into retreats, altering their appearance in the process.

Chironomids are eaten by predatory insects and the young (known as *fry*) of two species of fish: a minnow called the California roach, *Hesperoleucas symmetricus*, and three-spined sticklebacks, *Gasterosteus aculeatus*. These small fish are eaten by young steelhead trout, *Oncorhynchus mykiss*. Steelhead and large roach eat predatory invertebrates, and large roach also feed directly upon benthic algae. These interactions form the Eel River food web pictured in figure 17.11.

Power asked whether or not the two top predators in the Eel River food web, roach and steelhead, significantly influence web structure. She tested the effects of these fish on food web structure by using 3 mm mesh to cage off 12 areas 6 m^2 in the riverbed. The mesh size of these cages prevented the passage of large fish but allowed free movement of aquatic insects and stickleback and roach fry. Power excluded fish from six of her cages and placed 20 juvenile steelhead and 40 large roach in each of the other six cages. These fish densities were within the range observed around boulders in the open river.

Significant differences between the exclosures and enclosures soon emerged. Algal densities were initially similar; however, enclosing fish over an area of streambed significantly reduced algal biomass (fig. 17.12). In addition, the *Cladophora* within cages with fish had the same ropy, webbed appearance as *Cladophora* in the open river.

How do predatory fish decrease algal densities? The key to answering this question lies with the Eel River food web (fig. 17.11). Predatory fish feed heavily on predatory insects, young roach, and sticklebacks. Lower densities of these smaller predators within the enclosures decreased predation

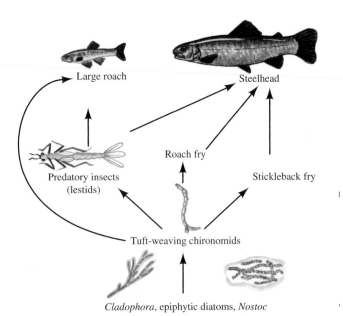

Figure 17.11   Food web associated with algal turf during the summer in the Eel River, California.

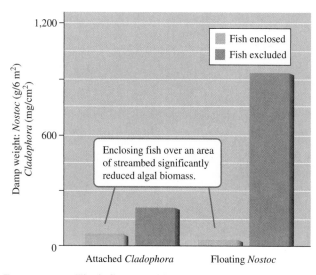

Figure 17.12 The influence of juvenile steelhead and California roach on benthic algal biomass in the Eel River (data from Power 1990).

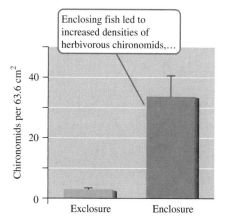

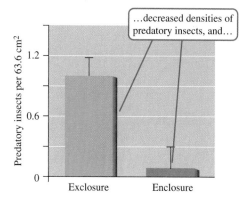

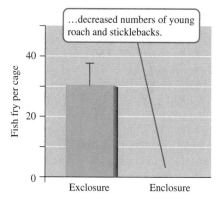

Figure 17.13 Effect of juvenile steelhead and roach on numbers of insects and young (fry) roach and sticklebacks (data from Power 1990).

on chironomids. Higher chironomid density increased the feeding pressure of these herbivores on algal populations. This explanation is supported by Power's estimate that enclosures contained lower densities of predatory insects and fish fry and higher densities of chironomids (fig. 17.13). By enclosing and excluding fish from sections of the Eel River, Power demonstrated that fish act as keystone species in the Eel River food web.

All of the examples that we have discussed so far have been aquatic. Do terrestrial communities also contain keystone species? An increasing body of evidence indicates that they do, and we have already discussed several terrestrial keystone species throughout this text, such as the geese in arctic wetland habitats and their role in herbivory (chapter 14). As you may recall, under moderate rates of grazing, plant growth actually increased, while in response to high levels of grazing there was a drop in production as only herbivory-resistant species were able to survive. This is a clear example of how one form of species interaction (grazing) can strongly influence community organization. Ecologists quickly came up with a long list of species they deemed were keystone. It quickly became apparent that an explicit definition was needed.

Refining the Definition of Keystone Species

Many studies of food webs and keystone species have been done since Robert Paine's classic study of the intertidal food web. The studies have revealed a great deal of biological diversity, which has prompted biologists to ask what traits characterize keystone species. This reflection is necessary, as the term *keystone species* has often been applied to indicate a species a person felt was important, as opposed to any specific scientific basis for this designation. To avoid the possibility that the term may become so inclusive that it becomes

meaningless, a conference was organized to address the specific definition of *keystone species*, with the results summarized in figure 17.14 (Power et al. 1996).

Keystone species are those that, despite low biomass and relative abundance in a community, exert strong effects on the structure of the communities they inhabit. In other words, keystone species are species whose effects on community structure are disproportionate to their abundance in the community. Important to this definition is the recognition that keystone species are not dominant members of communities (in terms of biomass or abundance), even if their actions or interactions dominate the direction of community assembly.

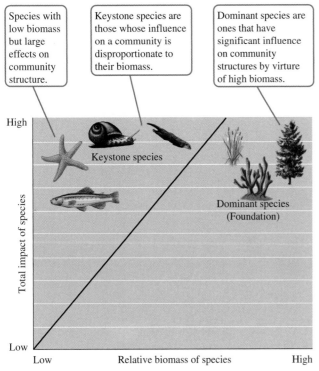

Species with low biomass but large effects on community structure.

Keystone species are those whose influence on a community is disproportionate to their biomass.

Dominant species are ones that have significant influence on community structures by virtue of high biomass.

High

Total impact of species

Keystone species

Dominant species
(Foundation)

Low

Low   Relative biomass of species   High

Figure 17.14   What is a keystone species (data from Power et al. 1996)?

(a)   (b)

Figure 17.15   (*a*) The activity of beavers (*b*) can cause significant hydrological changes. Thus, beavers can have strong impacts as ecosystem engineers.

Keystone species are not the only ones that can have strong impacts on how a community is structured. We see next that the actions of some organisms, even common ones, physically create the conditions necessary for communities to be formed. We begin with the humble beaver.

Ecosystem Engineers: Impacts of Beavers on Forest Communities

Castor canadensis, the North American beaver, is found throughout most of Canada and the United States (fig. 17.15). Beavers have been commercially exploited for their pelts, which has caused population crashes in part of their range, particularly in the southern and central United States. Across North America reintroductions and legislative protections have resulted in increases in population densities over the last several decades. As you may recognize, beavers are not quite like most other rodent species, and as a result, they can have pronounced impacts on the structure of communities in which they live.

Beavers fall into a very select grouping of species, generally referred to as **ecosystem engineers** (Jones et al. 1994). Ecosystem engineers are species who, by the nature of their activities, maintain and/or create new habitats for themselves and/or other species. For example, the coral-forming species of chapter 15 are a "poster-child" of ecosystem engineers. Without those species, coral reefs simply would not exist.

Beavers cut down a variety of trees near the edges of streams and other water bodies, forming dams. These dams cause flooding, the formation of ponds, and increase the amount of riparian area on the landscape. In the resulting

ponds, the beavers build lodges. The reasons for this behaviour are not completely clear, though it is thought that the isolation provides some protection from predators and increased access to food sources. It is, however, important to recognize that because beavers have effects on natural communities to a much greater extent than would be predicted based upon their relative abundance in a community, this familiar animal also counts as a keystone species, and thus you are more familiar with these ecological concepts than you may think. In contrast, the species that literally make up a coral reef are extremely abundant (within their community), and though they are certainly ecosystem engineers, we would not also refer to them as keystone species. Jargon aside, what exactly are the impacts of beavers on natural communities?

There are two locations of primary impact, the stream and the surrounding terrestrial area. Putting up a dam, or more likely a series of dams, alters rates of stream flow and drainage, and can alter various aspects of the biogeochemical cycles (Naiman et al. 1994). The flooding and alteration of stream flow can change stream temperatures (Rosell et al. 2005). As we discussed in chapter 5, changes in water temperature can have significant effects on the growth of many aquatic organisms, and thus can alter community structure. However, the effects of beavers are not consistent from location to location, and instead are dependent upon local issues of water quality, acidity, and level of beaver activity (Rosell et al. 2005). Even with this variability it is no surprise that the activity of beavers causes widespread changes to the aquatic communities in which they reside. What may be less obvious, however, is that beavers can also have strong effects on the terrestrial communities.

Noble Donkor, of the University of Alberta, and John Fryxell, of the University of Guelph, explored the impacts of beaver on the vegetation in Algonquin Provincial Park, Ontario (Donkor and Fryxell 1999). They chose for their study 15 ponds, each less than 2 hectares in area, that had one

active beaver lodge within it. They laid out several transects extending away from the pond and into the surrounding forest, along which they recorded beaver-cut stumps and the size and identity of woody vegetation.

In total, they found 1,841 tree stems cut by beaver, consisting of 20 plant species. However, 78% of the cut stems belonged to only six species (speckled alder, beaked hazel, red maple, trembling aspen, white birch, and beaked willow). Not surprisingly, the greatest proportion of stem cuts was found near the edge of the pond (fig. 17.16). As a result, there is a sharp herbivory gradient from near the water's edge to the intact forest. Donkor and Fryxell found that along this gradient, there was a unimodal relationship between species richness and distance (fig. 17.16), with maximum species diversity at an intermediate distance from the edge of the pond. This should look familiar, as this is exactly the prediction one would make based upon the intermediate disturbance hypothesis and altered competitive interactions. However, the interpretation in this case is not quite as clear. Although certain plant species were most often cut down by beavers, these preferred tree species were also quick to re-sprout following cutting, and thus were not necessarily underrepresented near the water's edge. Instead, the effects of beaver near the water's edge is likely to increase the abundance of plant species that can tolerate cutting. Deeper into the forest, there is less beaver activity, and thus these areas tend to be dominated by species that are good competitors for light or other resources.

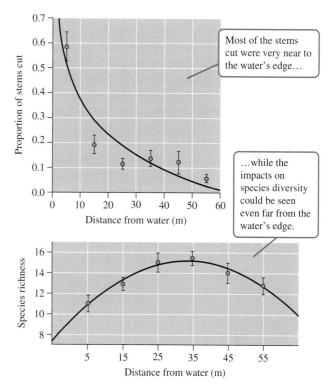

Figure 17.16 The intensity of exploitation and species richness both varied as a function of distance from the edge of a pond containing beavers (data from Donkor and Fryxell 1999).

ECOLOGY IN ACTION

Keystone Species, Ecosystem Engineers, and Conservation Biology

The impacts of keystone species and ecosystem engineers on community structure have been of great interest to conservation biologists for many years, both in terms of conservation efforts and reintroduction of extirpated species. The logic behind such approaches is simple: if a natural community is maintained through the activities of only a few species, then removal of those species will cause a shift in community structure. As a result, conservation efforts to protect populations of those critical species should protect the overall structure of the community. Similarly, if human activities have caused the loss of a keystone or engineer within a community, reintroduction of that species should restore critical ecological services and community structure. Right? The real world is not nearly that simple.

Tony Sinclair, of the University of British Columbia, argues in favour of viewing many large mammals as potential keystone species structuring communities (Sinclair 2003). However, he also acknowledges that there are difficulties in deciding what is, and what is not, a keystone species. For

example, exactly how much does a community need to change by the introduction or removal of a species to consider that a critical species? Is 10% enough, 50%, 95%? Further, what do you actually measure? Species richness? Evenness? Biomass production? What trophic levels must be affected for a species to be keystone? For instance, if you add a predator, is it a keystone if that addition causes a decline in prey numbers, or does the effect have to continue on to the plants, decomposers, and soil systems? Further, when we look more closely, the default assumption that large animals are keystone is often not supported by data. Instead, the use of the keystone idea is often applied in conservation biology without consistency.

The potential advantage of focusing on keystone species in conservation efforts is also supported by Daniel Simberloff (1998). Simberloff argues that many historical approaches to conservation schemes (e.g., using umbrella, flagship, and indicator species—all terms you may have learned in other classes) are ineffective and/or not well supported by actual data. Similarly, he argues that a current trend toward

ecosystem management has dangers in that the management goals are often vague, focusing on processes such as nutrient cycling rather than protection of actual species. Simberloff suggests instead that research should be focused toward identifying keystone species and groups of species in natural communities. He readily acknowledges that not all communities will have such members, but in those that do, conservation efforts can be highly focused, and potentially effective. Here we describe one example of how ecologists used the keystone species concept for a conservation goal: the reintroduction of wolves into Yellowstone National Park in the United States.

After 70 years of absence, grey wolves were reintroduced to Yellowstone National Park in the United States in 1995 (fig. 17.17). There were countless reasons justifying this reintroduction, including the argument that bringing back a top predator of this system should restore keystone processes and alter many aspects of the community. More specifically, wolves were expected to alter predation pressures on a dominant herbivore (elk), which in turn would alter plant community organization. In other words, this single species (wolf) is viewed as keystone to the Yellowstone system. It is now over 15 years since the initial reintroduction, and data are available to begin to determine whether wolves are in fact keystone in this community.

A team of researchers from the United States and the University of Alberta followed a number of radio-collared elk in Yellowstone, recording their locations as a function of both wolf densities in the area and a number of habitat characteristics (Mao et al. 2005). Mao and her coauthors found that elk population sizes changed very little over the course of the study, suggesting that wolves are not having major impacts on the total numbers of these large mammals. However, wolves are impacting where and when elk feed. In the summer months, elk primarily occupied areas of low wolf density, suggesting a behavioural response to predators. This may sound familiar, as it is another example of the non-consumptive effects of predators on prey populations (chapter 14). Though few elk died through predation, the ecology of fear altered whole populations. Once again, the main effect of predators may not be mortality of individual prey, but more subtle behavioural shifts. However, Mao found that the story was even more complicated.

In the winter elk were found in high wolf density areas, indicating the effects of wolves on elk movement are season-dependent. Mao and her coauthors argue that in the summer, food for elk is relatively abundant, and they are able to choose to feed in areas of low predator numbers. In the winter, food is scarce and the luxury to choose to feed in areas without predators does not occur. Instead, the elk need to feed wherever they find food.

Although Mao found that wolves influence elk behaviour, these results lend only limited support to the idea that wolves act as a keystone species. Clearly, if wolves alter where elk feed, this has the potential to alter plant communities. However, because habitat shifts as a function of wolves only occur part of the year, and it does not appear that elk numbers were suppressed by wolves, this study does not conclusively show keystone effects. We now turn to another study where there is more evidence of such effects.

Ripple and Beschta (2006) investigated the effects of wolf reintroduction on the height of a common group of riparian plant species in Yellowstone, willows (*Salix* spp.). Willows are of particular interest in this system because they serve as browse for elk, and are habitat for a variety of bird species. As a result, a change in *Salix* would be an indication of potential keystone effects of wolves in this system. Ripple and Beschta analyzed a variety of photographs of *Salix* stands prior to wolf reintroduction, and compared them to measured sizes following reintroduction. In upland habitats, wolves had no apparent effects of willow heights, while in lowland sites, the results were quite dramatic. In the river valley populations, nearly all willow stands increased in height following wolf reintroduction, and this was related to a decrease in the frequency of browsing by elk. Recolonization by wolves has also recently been shown to impact the diversity of understory plants in the Great Lakes region (Callan et al. 2013). Though such effects are slow, there is growing evidence that these top predators can impact even the bottom of food webs. Interestingly, the impacts of wolves may also extend into other aspects of the food web.

There is some evidence to suggest that wolf activity also results in an increase in the amount of carrion available for scavengers, primarily during the winter months (Wilmers et al. 2003). This temporal subsidy by the wolves may provide a steadier food supply for the guild of scavengers, which may become more important in the face of climate changes in this system (Wilmers and Getz 2005). However, whether this temporal subsidy actually alters scavenger population sizes has not yet been demonstrated, and is critical to interpreting

Figure 17.17   A wolf on the hunt in Yellowstone National Park.

the importance of these changes in the context of a keystone species.

As we have already discussed, a species is not viewed as keystone in a community if it simply alters some interactions (e.g., removes some prey, is food for some animals), but instead is a keystone if its impacts are large relative to the organism abundance in the system. The research to date suggests that wolves could serve a keystone role in Yellowstone (Beschta and Ripple 2009), but is not yet conclusive. Fortunately, the wolves of Yellowstone are quite well established, and continued research by ecologists in this system will be able to provide an answer to whether wolves are important restoration tools that serve keystone roles, or whether desire by people to reintroduce them should be based upon other arguments, independent of any potential keystone effects.

The concept of keystone species and ecosystem engineers has implications for the management and restoration of natural areas. However, there are also many examples where the addition of what was perceived to be a keystone species did not actually alter communities. There is a growing realization that some changes to communities may be so severe that simple restoration efforts such as a species reintroduction will be insufficient to restore the community. It is important to recognize that even if a species is not found to be keystone, it does not mean reintroductions are not warranted. Instead, it means that using these concepts as the basis for reintroduction may not be appropriate in all cases. There is much research yet to be done investigating the details of when individual species may, or may not, alter community structure.

Diversity is likely highest at intermediate distances from the water's edge as this is the location where both the cutting-tolerant and competitively dominant species are likely to be found. It is also important to recognize that the beavers are creating soggy conditions for terrestrial plants near the water's edge, and this itself could contribute to reduced growth (or absence) of some species, as those conditions may be outside of their niche requirements. Regardless of the mechanism of effect, the fact that beavers' activity can cause variation in species composition clearly makes them a keystone species in this system.

The legacy of beaver dams extends well beyond the life of the dams themselves. Eventually, all beaver dams will be abandoned, and some time after that they lose structural integrity. When these dams "break," the stored water flows back into the streams, exposing land previously covered by water, initiating forest succession. The impacts of beavers can be seen for decades, even if the individual dams last only a few years.

So far we have focused primarily on negative interactions among species, and their role in structuring communities. However, much more happens in communities than killing, fighting, and cutting down trees. As we discuss next, mutualisms and mutualistic networks are can also play critical roles in determining community structure.

CONCEPT 17.3 REVIEW

1. Paine discovered that intertidal invertebrate communities of higher diversity include a higher proportion of predator species. Did this pattern confirm Paine's predation hypothesis?
2. How can beavers alter the growth of plants they do not eat?
3. What is the difference between a keystone and a dominant species (see figure 17.14)?

17.4 Mutualistic Keystones

Mutualists can act as keystone species. While our earlier discussions of keystone species have emphasized the roles of predators as keystone species, many other kinds of organisms can act as keystone species. Returning to the classification of Power and colleagues shown in figure 17.14, the only requirements for keystone status is that the species in question have relatively low biomass in the community and a high impact on community structure. Increasingly, ecologists are discovering that many mutualistic species meet these requirements.

A Cleaner Fish as a Keystone Species

Many species of fish on coral reefs clean other fish of ectoparasites. This relationship, which involves the cleaner fish and its clients, has been shown to be a true mutualism. One of the most widely distributed cleaner fish in the Indo-Pacific region is the cleaner wrasse, *Labroides dimidiatus*. The feeding activity of cleaner wrasses is intense. Alexandra Grutter of the University of Queensland, Australia, has shown that a single cleaner wrasse can remove and eat 1,200 parasites from client fish per day. She also performed experiments (Grutter 1999) that documented that fish on reefs without cleaner wrasses harbour approximately four times the number of parasitic isopods as those living on reefs with cleaner wrasses.

What effect might cleaning activity by *L. dimidiatus* have on the diversity of fish on coral reefs? This is the question addressed with a series of field experiments by Redouan Bshary of the University of Cambridge. Bshary studied the effects of cleaner wrasses on reef fish diversity at Ras Mohammed National Park, Egypt (Bshary 2003). The study area consists of a sandy bottom area approximately 400 m

from shore, dotted with reef patches, in water depths from 2 to 6 m. Bshary chose 46 reef patches separated from other patches by at least 5 m of sandy bottom. He identified and counted the fish species present during dives on these reefs and noted the presence or absence of cleaner wrasses on each reef patch. Bshary recorded 29 natural disappearances or appearances of cleaner wrasses during his study. In addition, he performed experimental removals of cleaner wrasses from reefs and introductions of these cleaners to reef patches where there were none.

Bshary followed the responses of the fish community to natural disappearances and experimental removals and natural colonization and experimental introductions. In doing so, he gained insights into the influence of these tiny mutualists on reef fish diversity. Figure 17.18 summarizes the responses of fish communities on reef patches four months following the natural or experimental addition or removal of cleaner wrasses. Bshary observed a median reduction in fish species richness of approximately 24% where cleaner wrasses disappeared or were removed. Where cleaner wrasses were added, either naturally or experimentally, he observed a median increase in fish species richness of 24%. Bshary's results indicate that the cleaner wrasse acts as a keystone species on the coral reefs of the Red Sea. Mutualists that act as keystone species have also been found on land.

Seed Dispersal Mutualists as Keystone Species

It appears that ants that disperse seeds have a significant influence on the structure of plant communities in the species-rich fynbos of South Africa. Caroline Christian (2001) observed that native ants disperse 30% of the seeds in the shrublands of the fynbos. The plants attract the services of these dispersers with food rewards on the seeds called elaiosomes. However, the Argentine ant, *Linepithema humile* (fig. 17.19), which does not disperse seeds, has invaded these shrublands. Christian documented how the invading Argentine ants have displaced (as they have in other regions) many of the native ant species in the fynbos. In addition, she discovered that the native ant species most impacted by Argentine ant invasion are those species most likely to disperse larger seeds.

Seed-dispersing ants are important to the persistence of fynbos plants because they bury seeds in sites where they are safe from seed-eating rodents and from fire. Fires are characteristic of Mediterranean shrublands such as the fynbos, and seeds are the only life stage of many fynbos plants to survive fires. Consequently, ant dispersal is critical to the survival of many plant species. In a comparison of seedling recruitment following fire, Christian found substantial reductions in seedling recruitment by plants producing large seeds in areas invaded by Argentine ants (fig. 17.20). Meanwhile, small-seeded plants, whose dispersers are less affected by Argentine ants, showed no reduction in recruitment following fire. Christian's results, like Bshary's, reveal the influence of mutualists acting as keystone species within the communities they occupy. Other studies are revealing the importance of other mutualists, such as pollinators and mycorrhizal fungi, as keystone species.

One of the things you may have noticed in several of the examples we have provided about keystone species is that not every case was actually a single species! Instead, studies often referred to some group of species, such as insect-eating birds or seed-dispersing ants, as providing ecological services which, if disrupted, can greatly alter natural communities. The issue of whether species, or guilds/functional groups, are most critical for ecosystem function is a topic of much debate among ecologists, and we will discuss it in later chapters. We end this chapter instead with a discussion

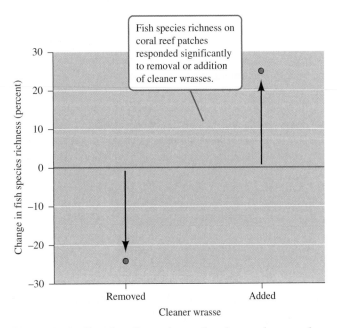

Figure 17.18   Results of experimental and natural removals or additions of cleaner wrasses. *Labroides dimidiatus*, to reef patches in the Red Sea (data from Bshary 2003).

Figure 17.19   The Argentine ant, *Linepithema humile*, has invaded and disrupted ant communities in many geographic regions. In the fynbos of South Africa, invading Argentine ants are displacing keystone ant species, which threatens the exceptional plant diversity of the fynbos.

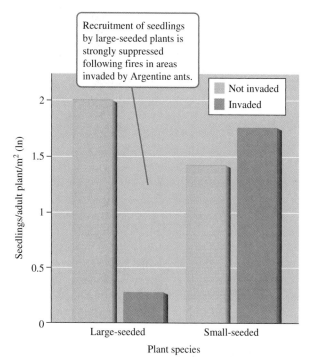

Recruitment of seedlings by large-seeded plants is strongly suppressed following fires in areas invaded by Argentine ants.

Figure 17.20   A comparison of recruitment of seedlings following fire in areas invaded by Argentine ants and areas not invaded shows the effects of the displacement of native seed-dispersing ants by Argentine ants (data from Christian 2001).

of one more type of keystone species, humans. Humans are nearly everywhere on the planet, and to ignore their impact on community structure would greatly hinder our ecological understanding.

CONCEPT 17.4 REVIEW

1. Bshary studied changes in fish species richness in response to both natural and experimental removals and additions of the cleaner fish *Labroides dimidiatus* (see fig. 17.18). Why did he not just focus on the response of fish species richness to natural additions and removals of the cleaner fish?
2. In many regions native pollinator insects seem to be declining. Why is this a cause for concern among conservationists and ecologists?

ECOLOGICAL TOOLS AND APPROACHES

Humans as Keystone Species

People have long manipulated food webs both as a consequence of their own feeding activities and by introducing or deleting species from existing webs. In chapter 4, we described how human harvesting of some species (e.g., Dall Sheep) could alter their evolutionary trajectories. Chris Darimont, of the University of Victoria, along with colleagues from Calgary and California, found such changes were widespread across species (Darimont et al. 2009). Across 40 systems in which humans harvested some species (e.g., hunting, commercial fisheries, etc.), they found a 300% increase in phenotypic changes in the harvested species relative to systems in which the species were not harvested. These changes were most pronounced for size and life-history traits. Clearly human harvesting has strong impacts on individuals and the direction of evolution. But what happens to the community if the species being harvested are keystone? Either consciously or unwittingly, people have, themselves, acted as keystone species in communities. In this section we show how critical evaluation of some human activities can provide further information about the function of natural communities.

The Empty Forest: Hunters and Tropical Rain Forest Animal Communities

The current plight of the tropical rain forest is well known. However, Kent Redford (1992) points out that with few exceptions, most studies of human impact on the tropical rain forest have concentrated on direct effects of humans on vegetation, mainly on deforestation. Redford expands our view by examining the effects of humans on animals. The picture that emerges from this analysis is that humans have so reduced the population densities of rain forest animals in many areas that they no longer play their keystone roles in the system, a situation Redford calls ecologically extinct.

Redford estimated that subsistence hunting, a major source of protein for many rural people, results in an annual death toll of approximately 14 million mammals and 5 million birds and reptiles within the Brazilian Amazon. He estimated further that commercial hunters, seeking skins, meat, and feathers, kill an additional 4 million animals annually. Consequently, the total take by hunters within the Brazilian Amazon is approximately 23 million individual animals. However, this figure underestimates the total number of animal deaths,

since many wounded animals escape from hunters only to die. Including those fatally wounded animals that escape, Redford places the annual deaths within the Brazilian Amazon at approximately 60 million animals.

Hunters generally concentrate on a small percentage of larger bird and mammal species, however. For instance, Redford estimated that at Cocha Cashu Biological Station in Manu National Park, located in the Amazon River basin in eastern Peru, hunters concentrate on 9% of the 319 bird species and 18% of the 67 mammal species. Because hunters generally concentrate on the larger species, this small portion of the total species pool makes up about 52% of the total bird biomass and approximately 75% of the total mammalian biomass around Manu National Park (fig. 17.21).

As impressive as all these numbers are, there remains a critical question: Do hunters reduce the local densities of the birds and mammals they hunt? The answer is yes. Redford estimated that moderate to heavy hunting pressure in rain forests reduces mammalian biomass by about 80% to 93% and bird biomass by about 70% to 94%.

There may be cause for concern, however, that goes beyond the losses of these immense numbers of animals. As you might expect, many large rain forest mammals and birds may act as keystone species. If so, their decimation will have effects that ripple through the entire community. The first to suggest a keystone role for the large animals preferred by rain forest hunters was John Terborgh (1988), who presented his hypothesis in a provocative essay titled, *The Big Things That Run the World*.

Terborgh's hypothesis has been supported by a variety of studies. He observed that in the absence of pumas and jaguars on Barro Colorado Island, Panama, medium-sized mammal species are over ten times more abundant than in areas still supporting populations of these large cats. R. Dirzo and A. Miranda (1990) compared two forests in tropical southern Mexico, one in which hunting had eliminated most of the large mammals and one in which most of the large mammals were still present. The comparison was stark. In the absence of large mammals such as peccaries, jaguars, and deer, the researchers found forests carpeted with undamaged plant seedlings and piled with uneaten and rotting fruits and nuts, signs of a changing forest. Such observations prompted Redford to warn, "We must not let a forest full of trees fool us into believing all is well." Tropical rain forest conservation must also include the large, and potentially keystone, animal species that are vulnerable to hunting by humans. However, we must also recognize that importance in a community does not mean a species needs to be big.

Ants and Agriculture: Keystone Predators for Pest Control

In 1982, Stephen Risch and Ronald Carroll published a paper describing how the predaceous fire ant, *Solenopsis geminata*, acts as a keystone predator in the food web of the corn-squash agroecosystem in southern Mexico. While natural enemies had been used to control insect pests for some time, Risch and Carroll put these efforts into a community context. They drew conceptual parallels between biological control of insects with natural enemies and studies of the influences of keystone species, citing studies of the influences of herbivores on plant communities and the effects of predators on intertidal communities. In their own experiments, Risch and Carroll demonstrated how predation by *Solenopsis* in the corn-squash agroecosystem reduces the number of arthropods and the arthropod diversity (fig. 17.22). This study showed how *Solenopsis* could act as a keystone species to the benefit of the agriculturist.

The conceptual breakthrough represented by the work of Risch and Carroll is impressive. However, their work had been anticipated 1,700 years earlier, by farmers in southern China. H. Huang and P. Yang (1987) cite Ji Han, who, in AD 304, wrote *Plants and Trees of the Southern Regions* in which he included the following:

The Gan (mandarin orange) is a kind of orange with an exceptionally sweet and delicious taste . . . In the market, the natives of Jiao-zhi [southeastern China and North Vietnam] sell ants stored

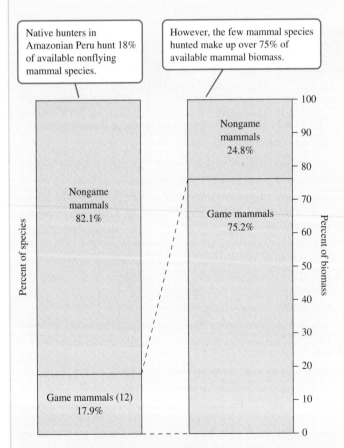

Native hunters in Amazonian Peru hunt 18% of available nonflying mammal species.

However, the few mammal species hunted make up over 75% of available mammal biomass.

Percent of species

Nongame mammals 82.1%

Game mammals (12) 17.9%

Percent of biomass

Nongame mammals 24.8%

Game mammals 75.2%

Figure 17.21   Highly selective hunting by Amazonian natives (data from Redford 1992).

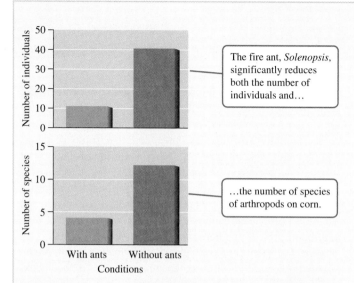

Figure 17.22 Effect of *Solenopsis geminata* on the arthropod populations on corn (data from Risch and Carroll 1982).

in bags of rush mats. The nests are like thin silk. The bags are all attached to twigs and leaves, which, with the ants inside the nests, are for sale. The ants are reddish-yellow in color, bigger than ordinary ants. In the south, if the Gan trees do not have this kind of ant, the fruits will be damaged by many harmful insects and not a single fruit will be perfect.

Now, 17 centuries after the observations of Ji Han, we know this ant as the citrus ant, *Oecophylla smaragdina*. The use of this ant to control herbivorous insects in citrus orchards was unknown outside of China until 1915. In 1915, Walter Swingle, a plant physiologist who worked for the U.S. Department of Agriculture, was sent to China to search for varieties of oranges resistant to citrus canker, a disease that was devastating citrus groves in Florida. While on this trip, Swingle came across a small village where the main occupation of the people was growing ants for sale to orange growers. The ant was the same one described by Ji Han in AD 304.

Oecophylla is one of the weaver ants, which use silk to construct a nest by binding leaves and twigs together. These ants spend the night in their nest. During the day, the ants spread out over the home tree as they forage for insects. Farmers place a nest in a tree and then run bamboo strips between trees so that the ants can have access to more than one tree. The ants will eventually build nests in adjacent trees and can colonize an entire orchard.

The ants harvest protein and fats when they gather insects from their home tree, but they have other needs as well. They also need a source of liquid and carbohydrates, and they get these materials by cultivating *Homoptera*, known as soft-scale insects or mealy bugs, which produce nectar. The ants and soft-scale insects have a mutualistic relationship in which the ants transport the insects from tree to tree and protect them

from predators. In return the ants consume the nectar produced by the soft-scale insects. Because of this mutualism with the soft-scale insect, which can itself be a serious pest of citrus, several early agricultural scientists expressed skepticism that *Oecophylla* would be an effective agent for pest control in citrus. They suggested that the use of this ant could produce infestations by soft-scale insects.

Despite these criticisms, all Chinese citrus growers interviewed insisted that *Oecophylla* is effective at pest control and that the damage caused by soft-scale insects is minor. Research done by Yang appears to have solved this apparent contradiction. Comparing orange trees treated with chemical insecticides to those protected by *Oecophylla*, Yang recorded higher numbers of soft-scale insects in the trees tended by ants. However, these higher numbers did not appear to cause serious damage to the orange trees. When Yang inspected the soft-scale insects closely, he found that they were heavily infested with the larvae of parasitic wasps. He also found that the ants did not reduce populations of lacewing larvae and ladybird beetles, predators that feed on soft-scale insects. Huang and Yang concluded that *Oecophylla* is effective at pest control because while it attacks the principal, larger pests of citrus, it does not reduce populations of other predators that attack the smaller pests of citrus, such as soft-scale insects, aphids, and mites.

The association between *Oecophylla* and citrus trees seems similar to that between ants and acacias (see chapter 15). There is a difference, however. Humans maintain *Oecophylla* as a substantial component of the food web in citrus orchards. Not only have specialized farmers historically cultivated and distributed the ants, *Oecophylla* must also be protected from the winter cold. The ant cannot survive the winter in southeast China in orange trees. Consequently, farmers must generally provide shelter and food for the ants during winter.

The labour and expense of maintaining these ants through the winter may be reduced by mixed plantings of orchard trees. Farmers in Shajian village in the Huaan district of southeast China have successfully maintained *Oecophylla* over the winter in mixed plantings of orange and pomelo trees. During winter the ants are mostly in pomelo trees, which are larger and have thicker foliage than orange trees, characteristics that reduce cooling rates on winter nights. In this situation, farmers do not have to add new nests of *Oecophylla* each spring. Gradually, the ant has become integrated into the mixed citrus and pomelo orchards and requires little special care from the farmers.

The farmers of southeast China have employed *Oecophylla* as a keystone species in a complex citrus-based food web for a long time. However, the results would not be the same with just any ant species. The citrus growers required a species that acts in a particular way. One wonders how long farmers of the region had experimented with this species before Ji Han wrote his account of their activities in AD 304.

SUMMARY

Community structure will be influenced by a diversity of interactions, all of which may be occurring simultaneously. A description of the patterns of species interactions in a community is called an *ecological network*. Different ecological interactions can result in predictable *assembly rules* that govern the structure of communities. Different ecological processes can interact among themselves, with potentially large consequences for the relative abundances of the component species.

17.1 A food web summarizes the feeding relationships in a community. The earliest work on food webs concentrated on simplified communities in areas such as the Arctic islands. However, researchers such as Charles Elton (1927) soon found that even these so-called simple communities included very complex feeding relations. Ralph Bird (1930) showed that an added level of complexity exists when members of one community feed upon species primarily found in a different community. This work emphasizes that communities do not have discrete boundaries, and that species connections can be very broad. Missing from most studies of food webs are parasites, pathogens, and decomposers.

17.2 Strong competitors can alter community structure. Some communities will contain competitive hierarchies, in which certain species are continually able to suppress the abundance of other species. In such systems, competition can greatly limit species diversity, with the competitively subordinate species being excluded from the community. Paul Keddy combined the ideas of competitive hierarchies and the theory of allocation when he developed the theory of centrifugal organization of species. In this theory, core habitats are occupied by dominant competitors, while poorer competitors will be found in more stressful satellite habitats. The presence of the poorer competitors occurs because they are better able to deal with other stressors in the environment than are the dominant competitors.

17.3 The activities of a few keystone species may control the structure of communities. Robert Paine (1966) proposed that the feeding activities of a few species have inordinate influences on community structure. He predicted that some predators may increase species diversity by reducing the probability of competitive exclusion. Manipulative studies of predaceous species have identified many keystone species, including starfish and snails in the marine intertidal zone and fish in rivers. On land, birds exert substantial influences on communities of their arthropod prey. Some keystone species, such as beavers, may also be ecosystem engineers. This designation is given to organisms whose activities result in the construction of a novel habitat. Keystone species are those that, despite low biomass, exert strong effects on the structure of the communities they inhabit.

17.4 Mutualists can act as keystone species. Experimental studies have shown that cleaner fish, species that remove parasites from other fish, act as keystone species on coral reefs. Removing cleaner fish produces a decline in reef fish species richness. Ants that disperse plant seeds in the fynbos of South Africa have been shown to have major influences on plant community structure. Where invading ants have displaced the mutualistic dispersing ants, the plant community suffers a decline in species richness following fires. Other mutualistic organisms that may act as keystone species include pollinators and mycorrhizal fungi.

Humans have acted as keystone species in communities. People have long manipulated food webs both as a consequence of their own feeding activities and by introducing or deleting species from existing food webs. In addition, many of these manipulations have been focused on keystone species. Hunters in tropical rain forests have been responsible for removing keystone animal species from large areas of the rain forests of Central and South America. Chinese farmers have used ants as keystone predators to control pests in citrus orchards for over 1,700 years.

REVIEW QUESTIONS

1. You could argue that the classical food web of Bear Island included several communities, each with its own food web. What were some of the different communities that Summerhayes and Elton (1923) included in their web? On the other hand, because the Bear Island food web includes significant movement of energy (food) and nutrients between what many ecologists might consider to be separate communities, what does their food web say about the distinctness of what we call communities?

2. What is a keystone species? How does Paine's experiment demonstrate this concept?

3. When Power (1990) excluded predaceous fish from her river sites, the density of herbivorous insect larvae (chironomids) decreased. Use the food web described by Power to explain this response.

4. Some paleontologists have proposed that overhunting caused the extinction of many large North American mammals at the end of the Pleistocene about 11,000 and 10,000 years ago.

The hunters implicated by paleontologists were a newly arrived predatory species, *Homo sapiens*. Offer arguments for and against this hypothesis.

5. All the keystone species work we have discussed in chapter 17 has concerned the influences of animals on the structure of communities. Can other groups of organisms act as keystones? What about parasites and pathogens?

6. According to Paul Keddy's theory of the centrifugal organization of species, dominant species will displace poorer competitors from the best habitat in a community. There is evidence this occurs in the wetlands he has studied, at least among vascular plant species. How would you design a study to test whether this theory also applies to animal species?

7. Decomposition and parasitism are generally excluded from discussions of food webs. How might this practice give a biased view toward the relative importance of different ecological processes in structuring communities?

8. What evidence is necessary to make a firm declaration as to whether grey wolves are keystone species in Yellowstone National Park? If they are found not to be keystone, does this mean that there was no justifiable reason to reintroduce them to Yellowstone?

For more information on the resources available from McGraw-Hill Ryerson, go to **www.mcgrawhill.ca/he/solutions**.

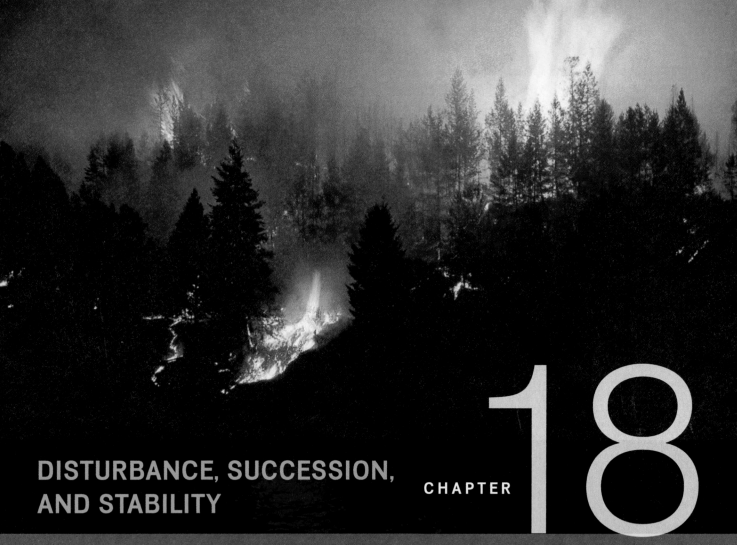

DISTURBANCE, SUCCESSION, AND STABILITY

CHAPTER 18

CHAPTER CONCEPTS

18.1 Intermediate levels of disturbance promote higher diversity.

Concept 18.1 Review

Ecology In Action: Using Disturbances for Conservation

18.2 Community stability may be due to lack of disturbance or community resistance or resilience in the face of disturbance.

Concept 18.2 Review

18.3 Community changes during succession include increases in species diversity and changes in species composition.

Concept 18.3 Review

18.4 Ecosystem changes during succession include increases in biomass, primary production, respiration, and nutrient retention.

Concept 18.4 Review

18.5 Mechanisms that drive ecological succession include facilitation, tolerance, and inhibition.

Concept 18.5 Review

Ecological Tools and Approaches: Using Repeat Photography to Detect Long-Term Change

Summary

Review Questions

468

The first recorded visit to Glacier Bay gave no hint of its eventual contributions to our understanding of biological communities and ecosystems. In 1794, Captain George Vancouver visited the inlet, to what is today called Glacier Bay, Alaska (fig. 18.1). He could not pass beyond the inlet to the bay, however, because his way was blocked by a mountain of ice. Vancouver and Vancouver (1798) described the scene as follows: "The shores of the continent form two large open bays which were terminated by compact solid mountains of ice, rising perpendicularly from the water's edge, and bounded to the north by a continuation of the united lofty frozen mountains that extend eastward from Mount Fairweather."

In 1879, John Muir explored the coast of Alaska, relying heavily on Vancouver's earlier descriptions. Muir (1915)

(a)

(b)

Figure 18.1 Glacier Bay National Park, Alaska, a laboratory for studying ecological succession. *(a)* The lower reaches of the Muir Glacier in August 1941. Note the bare terrain in the foreground of the photo. *(b)* The same scene 63 years later in 2004, at which point the Muir Glacier had retreated 8 km up the valley and out of the view to the left, leaving open water where the ice had been hundreds of metres thick. Notice that the once bare foreground is now covered by thick vegetation.

commented in his journal that Vancouver's descriptions were excellent guides except for the area within Glacier Bay. Where Vancouver had met "mountains of ice," Muir found open water. He and his guides from the Hoona tribe paddled their canoe through Glacier Bay in rain and mist, feeling their way through uncharted territory. They eventually found the glaciers, which Muir estimated had retreated 30 to 40 km up the glacial valley since Vancouver's visit 85 years earlier.

Though the surrounding mountains were filled with mature boreal forest, Muir found no such forests at the upper portions of the bay. He and his party had to build their campfires with the stumps and trunks of long-dead trees exposed by the retreating glaciers. Muir recognized that this fossil wood was a remnant of a forest that had been covered by advancing glaciers centuries earlier. He also saw that plants quickly colonized the areas uncovered by glaciers and that the oldest exposed areas, where Vancouver had long ago met his mountains of ice, already supported forests.

Muir's observations in Glacier Bay were published in 1915 and read the same year by the ecologist William S. Cooper. Cooper saw Glacier Bay as the ideal laboratory for the study of ecological **succession**, the gradual community change in an area following *disturbance* (first introduced in chapter 9). As we discuss below, disturbances can be small or large, may remove a few individuals within a community, or may result in the creation of entirely new habitats. Glacier Bay was ideal for the study of succession because the history of glacial retreat could be accurately traced back to 1794 and perhaps farther. Today, as the world becomes increasingly warmer there is a net retreat of glaciers globally, and thus this process of succession is more than a lesson in ecological history. It is a way to understand the future of natural communities. Though species compositions will vary among locations, we can learn much from understanding the changes found in Glacier Bay.

When glaciers retreat, they do not leave behind soil, seeds, nor living vegetation. Instead, they typically leave only water, rocks, sand, and silt. Such harsh conditions and lack of viable seed permit the growth of few plant species, and thus there tend to be few species able to colonize an area during the first few decades after it is exposed by the retreating glacier. These plants, the first in a successional sequence, form a **pioneer community**. The most common members of the pioneer community around Glacier Bay are horsetail, *Equisetum varietaum*, willow herb, *Epilobium latifolium*, willows, *Salix* sp., cottonwood seedlings, *Populus balsamifera*, mountain avens, *Dryas drummondii*, and Sitka spruce, *Picea sitchensis*.

After another decade or so at Glacier Bay, the pioneer community gradually grades into a community dominated by mats of *Dryas*, a dwarf shrub. These *Dryas* mats also contain scattered alder, *Alnus crispa*, *Salix*, *Populus*, and *Picea*. This community then changes into a shrub-thicket dominated by *Alnus*. Soon after the closure of the *Alnus* thicket, however, *Populus* and *Picea* will grow above it, covering about 50% of the area on sites 50 to 70 years old.

In 75 to 100 years, succession at Glacier Bay leads to a forest community dominated by *Picea*. Mosses carpet the understory of this spruce forest, and here and there grow seedlings of western hemlock, *Tsuga heterophylla*, and mountain hemlock, *Tsuga mertensiana*. Eventually, the population of *Picea* declines and the forests are dominated by *Tsuga*. On landscapes with shallow slopes these hemlock forests eventually give way to muskeg, a landscape of peat bogs and scattered tussock meadows.

Because succession around Glacier Bay occurs on newly exposed geological substrates not significantly modified by organisms, ecologists refer to this process as **primary succession**. Primary succession also occurs on newly formed volcanic surfaces such as lava flows, in outflows of streams where silt deposition can lead to the buildup of new land, and in any situation where new substrate is exposed or created. In contrast, when disturbance removes members from an existing community without destroying the soil or creating new substrate, **secondary succession** follows. For instance, secondary succession occurs after agricultural lands are abandoned, after a forest fire, or after a flood.

Succession may continue indefinitely (e.g., cyclic succession), or may end with a community whose populations remain stable until disrupted by subsequent disturbance. In the latter case, this final successional community is called the **climax community**. The nature of the climax community depends upon environmental circumstances. The communities we discussed in chapter 2—temperate forests, tundra, etc.—were essentially the climax communities for each of the climatic regimes that we considered. Other community types, such as grasslands, can be referred to as **disclimax communities**. Disclimax communities are maintained only through continual disturbances, such as grazing and drought. The climax community around Glacier Bay is determined by the prevailing climate and local topography. On well-drained, steep slopes the climax community is hemlock forest. In poorly drained soil on shallow slopes the climax community is muskeg.

Studies of succession show that communities and ecosystems are not static through time. In many cases, the general direction of change in community structure and ecosystem processes is predictable, at least over the short term. In other cases, the outcome of succession is not predictable, and instead it may end in a number of **alternative states**. Disturbances will not impact all communities equally, and instead some communities are less prone to change than others. These communities exhibit **stability**, the tendency to withstand or recover from disturbance. In this chapter we describe disturbance and the concept of equilibrium, what succession looks like, some of the mechanisms that cause it, and some of aspects of communities associated with increased stability.

the question, "What is a disturbance?" Wayne Sousa (1984), who examined the role of disturbance in structuring natural communities, defined disturbance as "a discrete, punctuated killing, displacement, or damaging of one or more individuals (or colonies) that directly or indirectly creates an opportunity for new individuals (or colonies) to become established." P. S. White and S. Pickett (1985) defined disturbance as "any relatively discrete event in time that disrupts ecosystem, community or population structure and changes resources, substrate availability, or the physical environment." They also caution, however, that we must be mindful of spatial and temporal scale. For example, disturbance to bryophyte (mosses and liverworts) communities growing on boulders along the margin of a stream can occur at spatial scales of fractions of metres and annual temporal scales that are irrelevant to the surrounding forest community. Consequently, a disturbance for one organism may have little or no impact on another, and the nature of disturbance may be quite different in different environments.

There are innumerable potential sources of disturbance to communities. White and Pickett listed 26 major sources of disturbance roughly divided into abiotic forces such as fires, hurricanes, ice storms, and flash floods; biotic factors such as disease and predation; and human-caused disturbances. How might we expect populations to respond to disturbances?

Attempts to understand species interactions such as competition and predation through mathematical modelling have often viewed populations as having more or less constant densities over time. In general, these models (chapters 13 and 14) predict that population densities will not change once **equilibrium** has been reached. In a system at equilibrium, stability is maintained by opposing forces such that if population changes are altered by some event, they will soon return to the equilibrial state. However, as every ecologist knows, the abundances of real populations never remain exactly the same from year to year, or even season to season. Changes in the environment (abiotic conditions, food, etc.) cause changes to growth optima, carrying capacities, and the values of the other parameters of the models we have discussed. When environmental change is sufficiently large we call it a disturbance, and these can have significant impacts on species diversity and ecosystem properties.

As we described above, some areas may move through a seemingly orderly series of community changes following a disturbance, resulting in a climax community. However, what happens to the diversity of the system before equilibrium is obtained? What happens if additional disturbances occur regularly, such that no equilibrium is ever reached? We begin by discussing disturbances and a **nonequilibrial theory** of species diversity.

18.1 Disturbance and Diversity

Intermediate levels of disturbance promote higher diversity. To understand why this may be true, we need to first ask

The Intermediate Disturbance Hypothesis

Joseph Connell (1975, 1978) proposed that disturbance is a prevalent feature of nature that influences the

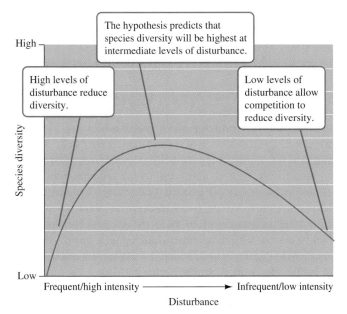

The hypothesis predicts that species diversity will be highest at intermediate levels of disturbance.

High levels of disturbance reduce diversity.

Low levels of disturbance allow competition to reduce diversity.

High

Low

Species diversity

Frequent/high intensity ⟶ Infrequent/low intensity

Disturbance

Figure 18.2 The intermediate disturbance hypothesis (data from Connell 1978).

diversity of communities. This was a direct counter to the prevalent assumption of equilibrial conditions made by most competition-based models of diversity. As you may recall from chapter 13, high levels of diversity are contrary to the predictions of the competitive exclusion principle, and thus substantial research was focused on ways in which organisms could persist even in the face of competition. Connell took a different approach, proposing that high diversity is a consequence of continually changing conditions, not of competitive accommodation at equilibrium. His "Intermediate Disturbance Hypothesis" instead predicts that intermediate levels of disturbance promote higher levels of diversity (fig. 18.2).

Connell suggested that *both* high and low levels of disturbance lead to reduced species diversity. He reasoned that if disturbance is frequent and intense, the community will consist of those few species able to colonize and complete their life cycles between frequent disturbances (colonizers, pioneer species, r-selected species, ruderals, etc.). He also predicted that diversity will be low if disturbances are infrequent and of low intensity. Why? Connell reasoned that in the absence of significant disturbance, the community is eventually limited to the species that are the most effective competitors. Thus at low disturbance, Connell's model predicts one would find predominately the best competitors (also known as climax species, k-selected species, and competitors)

In the intermediate disturbance hypothesis there is thus a shift in species composition from competitors to colonizers as disturbance intensity and/or frequency increases. Assuming unique traits are needed to successfully perform each ecological strategy, low diversity is predicted at both extremes of the disturbance gradient. But why does Connell also predict

that intermediate levels of disturbance promote higher diversity? Connell suggested that at intermediate levels of disturbance there is sufficient time between disturbances for a wide variety of species to colonize but not enough time to allow competitive exclusion. Thus, at intermediate disturbances, species of all competition and colonization strategies may be found.

Importantly, although this model is based on continual disturbance, and thus inherently non-equilibrial, it does predict a fairly constant result—a certain number of species for a given level of disturbance. This model does not suggest disturbance results in random change, but instead suggests that how species respond to disturbances might be predictable based upon the ecological principles we have discussed throughout the text. The concept that the ecological patterns we observe are not necessarily those of systems at rest, is becoming a more common viewpoint among ecologists (chapter 23).

Disturbance and Diversity in the Intertidal Zone

The most classic experimental test of Connell's intermediate disturbance hypothesis was performed by Wayne Sousa (1979a). Sousa studied the effects of disturbance on the diversity of marine algae and invertebrates growing on boulders in the intertidal zone. Disturbance to this community comes mainly from ocean waves generated by winter storms. These waves, which can exceed 2.5 m in height, are large enough to overturn intertidal boulders, killing the algae and barnacles growing on their upper surfaces. Meanwhile, the newly exposed underside of the boulder is available for colonization by algae and marine invertebrates.

Because boulders of different sizes turn over at different frequencies and in response to waves of different heights, Sousa predicted that the level of disturbance experienced by the community living on boulder surfaces depends upon boulder size. Smaller boulders are turned over more frequently and therefore experience a high frequency of disturbance, middle-sized boulders experience an intermediate level of disturbance, and large boulders experience the lowest frequency of disturbance.

Sousa quantified the relationship between boulder size and probability of being moved by waves by measuring the force required to dislodge boulders of different sizes. He measured the exposed surface area of a series of boulders and then measured the force required to dislodge each. To make a measurement he wrapped a chain around a boulder, attached a spring scale to the chain, and pulled in the direction of incoming waves until the boulder moved. He recorded the number of kilograms registered on the scale when the boulder moved and then converted his measurements to force expressed in newtons (newtons [N] = kg × 9.80665). As you might expect, there was a positive relationship between size and the force required to move boulders. What was Sousa assuming as he made these measurements? He assumed that the force required to move a boulder with his

apparatus was proportional to the force required for waves to move it.

Sousa verified this assumption by documenting the relationship between his force measurements and movement by waves. He established six permanent study sites and measured the force required to move the boulders in each. He next mapped the locations of boulders by photographing the study plots and then checked for boulder movements by taking additional photographs monthly for two years. Sousa divided the boulders in the study sites into three classes based on the force required for movement: (1) ≤ 49 N, (2) 50 to 294 N, and (3) > 294 N. These classes translated into frequent movement (42% per month = frequent disturbance), intermediate movement (9% per month = intermediate disturbance), and infrequent movement (1% per month = infrequent disturbance).

The number of species living on boulders varied with frequency of disturbance (fig. 18.3). Most of the frequently disturbed boulders supported a single species, few supported five species, and none supported six or seven species. Most of the boulders experiencing a low frequency of disturbance supported one to three species, few supported six species, and none supported seven. The boulders supporting the greatest diversity of species were those subject to intermediate levels of disturbance. Most of these supported three to five species, many supported six species, and some supported seven species.

Disturbance and Diversity in Temperate Grasslands

What sorts of disturbances might alter diversity in grasslands? Fire, drought, and grazing are all at home on the range, though the activity by a diversity of mammals is among the most common natural disturbances. Historically,

the magnitude of disturbance on the North American prairie ranged from trampling by bison herds and fire to the death of an individual plant. One of the most important and ubiquitous sources of disturbance to grasslands is burrowing by mammals.

April Whicker and James Detling (1988) proposed that prairie dogs (*Cynomys* spp.), which occupied about 40 million hectares of North American grasslands as late as 1919, were an important source of disturbance on the North American prairies. Prairie dogs are herbivorous rodents that weigh approximately 1 kg as adults and live in colonies containing 10 to 55 individuals per hectare. Prairie dogs build extensive burrow systems that are 1 to 3 m deep and about 15 m long, with tunnel diameters of 10 to 13 cm and two entrances. To build a burrow with these dimensions a prairie dog must excavate 200 to 225 kg of soil, which it deposits in mounds 1 to 2 m in diameter around burrow entrances.

Burrowing and grazing by prairie dogs have substantial effects on the structure of plant communities at several spatial scales. Figure 18.4 shows the areas of Wind Cave National Park occupied by prairie dogs. Because of the activities of these rodents, each of these areas supports vegetative communities distinct from the surrounding landscape. Within a colony, prairie dog activities create patchiness on a smaller scale, with areas of forbs and shrubs, grass and forbs, and grass within the surrounding matrix of prairie grassland. Through their careful study of the plant community, Whicker and Detling estimate that across all species, plant diversity is greatest in areas experiencing intermediate levels of disturbance by prairie dogs (fig. 18.5). However, they also realized this does not mean that all types of species respond similarly to disturbance. Instead, shrub diversity was invariant to disturbance, while grass diversity tended to decrease. Why? The answer lies in the natural history of the prairie dogs and the surrounding plants.

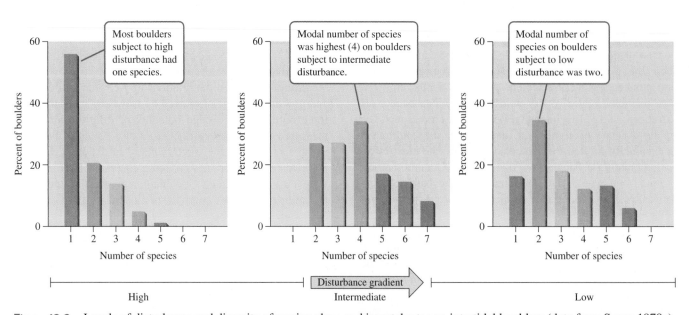

Figure 18.3   Levels of disturbance and diversity of marine algae and invertebrates on intertidal boulders (data from Sousa 1979a).

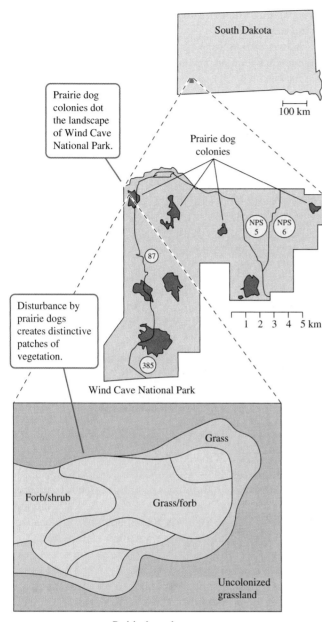

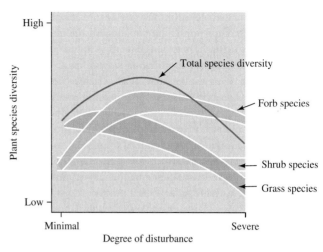

Figure 18.5   Due to differences in life-history and niche requirements, different groups of species may respond differently to different levels of disturbance (from Whicker and Detling 1988).

Figure 18.4   Disturbance by prairie dogs and patchiness of vegetation (data from Coppock et al. 1983, Whicker and Detling 1988).

How does disturbance by prairie dogs foster higher diversity? The mechanisms underlying this effect are essentially the same as those operating in the intertidal boulder field studied by Sousa. By burrowing and piling earth and by grazing and clipping vegetation, prairie dogs remove vegetation from areas around their burrows. These bare patches are then open for colonization by plants. However, some plants (e.g., shrubs) are more resistant to this digging, and other species (e.g., forbs) tend to be the most likely to colonize these open patches. Those species investing most heavily in dispersal are usually the first to arrive. However, these early colonists can be displaced by better competitors that arrive later. The persistence of both good colonizers and

good competitors in a plant community depends upon intermediate levels of disturbance. Too much disturbance and the community is dominated by the good colonizers; too little disturbance and the better competitors dominate. In other words, the details of a species' life-history and niche requirements, combined with a specific set of changes associated with a particular species, determine how diversity changes as a function of disturbance.

Is the Intermediate Disturbance Hypothesis Generally True?

Though the intermediate disturbance hypothesis is a useful model for understanding how disturbances may alter species diversity, not all researchers find empirical support for the model's prediction. Robin Mackey and David Currie, of the University of Ottawa, conducted a meta-analysis on 116 published diversity–disturbance relationships (Mackey and Currie 2001). These examples include animals, plants, terrestrial systems, and aquatic systems. They found that unimodal relationships such as those proposed by Connell were surprisingly rare, occurring in less than 20% of the studies. Instead, most systems showed no significant relationship between diversity and disturbance, and many showed a negative significant relationship. Jeremy Fox, of the University of Calgary, has recently called the theory a "zombie idea," one that never seems to go away (Fox 2013). He argues that in addition to the empirical shortcomings, the model is theoretically flawed and ecologists should abandon it.

What does this mean? First, this is what science looks like. Though we textbook authors do our best to smooth out complexities in an effort to help students understand general concepts, the leading edge of science is full of uncertainty. Opinions are expressed, data is collected, and resolution eventually is reached . . . maybe. What we can say is the relationship between diversity and disturbance

is complex, and cannot be simply described by any single line of any singular form. Ecologists, and students of ecology, should not view this hypothesis as a law. Instead, the intermediate disturbance hypothesis is helpful in the same way that we use the Lotka–Volterra models or physicists use models of Newtonian motion. For these models to be perfectly accurate requires a set of highly unrealistic interactions (e.g., only two species compete with each other; no friction or atmosphere). The value of such models is not to use them to predict outcomes for specific situations but to identify the core processes that may be important. By testing these models under diverse conditions, ecologists (and physicists) are able to eventually understand how natural systems work. Here, we see that the impacts of disturbance on diversity will be dependent upon both the biology of the organisms in a system, and the details of the disturbances they encounter. Once again, understanding basic natural history is important if we wish to understand complex ecological interactions.

As we will discuss next, not all communities are equally prone to change in response to disturbance.

CONCEPT 18.1 REVIEW

1. What is the difference between equilibrium and non-equilibrium models of diversity?
2. According to the intermediate disturbance hypothesis, could area in which human disturbances occur sustain higher levels of species diversity than areas without human disturbance?
3. How does a species' life-history characteristics influence its response to disturbance?

ECOLOGY IN ACTION

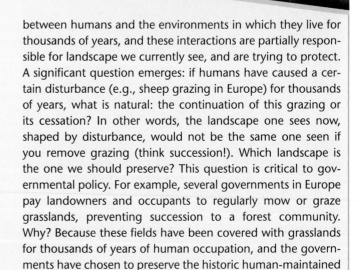

Using Disturbances for Conservation

A variety of ecological topics routinely stimulate controversy in the public and among researchers. We have already discussed several of these, including issues related to fisheries, the Species at Risk Act, reintroduction of top predators, and impacts of hunting on evolution. Here we discuss another, the incorporation of disturbances into conservation programs. The goal of this section is not to suggest all uses of disturbances are appropriate in all conservation programs. Instead, our intention is to show you how the basic information you have learned about succession has direct consequences for the conservation of Canada's wild areas.

Like ecologists, land managers have historically viewed communities as static, discrete entities. Each park was seen as an island, rather than a piece connected to a larger whole, and one that can itself change through time. At the core of this philosophical approach to communities has been the tendency to encourage the preservation of "pristine wilderness," areas free from any disturbances (Gillson and Willis 2004). In this mindset, natural communities were to be protected from disturbances such as grazing and fire (Hobbs and Huenneke 1992). However, as we have seen in this chapter, communities are naturally dynamic, with substantial variation in species composition over space and time. If this is true for most communities, and currently ecological thought believes it to be so, then the idea of trying to "protect" a community from change is at odds with basic ecological understanding.

In a summary of paleoecological work, Gillson and Willis (2004) were able to show that there have been interactions between humans and the environments in which they live for thousands of years, and these interactions are partially responsible for landscape we currently see, and are trying to protect. A significant question emerges: if humans have caused a certain disturbance (e.g., sheep grazing in Europe) for thousands of years, what is natural: the continuation of this grazing or its cessation? In other words, the landscape one sees now, shaped by disturbance, would not be the same one seen if you remove grazing (think succession!). Which landscape is the one we should preserve? This question is critical to governmental policy. For example, several governments in Europe pay landowners and occupants to regularly mow or graze grasslands, preventing succession to a forest community. Why? Because these fields have been covered with grasslands for thousands of years of human occupation, and the governments have chosen to preserve the historic human-maintained landscape, rather than a landscape without human intervention (that hasn't been seen for many centuries).

It is issues like these that are shaking the foundations of many common practices in conservation biology. Should you manage a reserve to maintain the diversity of a single area, or of greater diversity on the landscape? As a reflection of this shifting mindset, fires are now routinely set in many of the National Parks of Canada (fig. 18.6), not to preserve a single community, but instead to protect a *disturbance regime.* This, in turn, will result in the desired diversity of communities. For example, an aggressive anti-fire program over the last several decades has resulted in tree encroachment into alpine

Figure 18.6 A controlled fire being set as part of ecosystem management in Jasper National Park.

meadows, putting these habitats at risk. By reintroducing fire to these systems, park managers hope to restore these unique habitats.

There are few places where controversies regarding using disturbances as a conservation tool rage as strongly as they do in grasslands. As we have discussed, grasslands are a generally unstable habitat, often changing to forest or shrubland in the absence of disturbances. We generally view some combination of fire, drought, and grazing as necessary to maintain grassland habitats for extended periods of time. What are land managers supposed to do if they have been charged with the goal of protecting a grassland? Clearly they cannot alter the frequency of droughts. As we have already seen, fire can be used, under some conditions. Fire is less often a viable tool if the land being managed is near either private land and houses, or near major civic infrastructure (e.g., highways, bridges). The large native herbivores, such as bison, have been fairly

efficiently removed from the grasslands of North America. The question that then faces the land manager is "Do I allow cattle to graze on this conservation land?" What do you think should happen? Is it justified to bring in an alien species (domesticated cattle) in an attempt to preserve a native habitat (grasslands)? If so, who gets to decide how many cattle and when they graze, the conservation organization or the ranchers that own the herd? Should the ranchers be paying for the right to graze, or instead should the conservation organization be paying to have their land grazed? These questions are not trivial, and need to be resolved, as it is clear that the effects of herbivores on plant diversity and community structure can vary as a function of the types of herbivore and site conditions (Olff and Ritchie 1998).

Some ecologists are taking the issue of what is natural even further. Josh Donlan and colleagues have proposed rewilding North America (Donlan et al. 2005). Donlan argues that humans have been, in part, responsible for the loss of a diverse mega-fauna that existed in North America 13,000 years ago. At that time there were species of camels, cheetahs, elephants, and lions throughout the Great Plains. Donlan argues that these species played critical roles in the ecology of these systems (think keystone species and ecosystem engineers, chapter 17). By reintroducing their extant relatives (from Africa and Asia), they propose to reinstate the natural disturbance regime while also providing a new home to species that are likely to go extinct throughout parts of Asia and Africa. Needless to say, this proposal is controversial.

Hopefully, the points we have raised here have encouraged you to rethink some assumptions regarding the preservation of natural areas. If the plants and animals are always changing, can one ever succeed in preserving a single community without controlled disturbances? Clearly, the next generation of ecologists will be pivotal in further integrating current ecological understanding into the preservation of natural areas.

18.2   Community and Ecosystem Stability

Community stability may be due to lack of disturbance or community resistance or resilience in the face of disturbance. The simplest definition of *stability* is the absence of change. In an ecological context, a community or ecosystem may be stable for a variety of reasons. Most obviously, in the absence of a disturbance, local conditions may remain constant over time. For instance, the benthic communities of the deep sea may remain stable over long periods of time because of constant physical conditions.

A second, and more interesting, situation occurs when communities and ecosystems may remain stable even when

exposed to potential disturbance. Consequently, ecologists generally define stability as the persistence of a community or ecosystem in the face of disturbance, rather than simply a lack of change. Stability may result from two very different characteristics of the community. **Resistance** is the ability of a community or ecosystem to maintain structure and/or function in the face of potential disturbance. **Resilience** is the ability of a community to return to its original structure after a disturbance. A resilient community or ecosystem may be completely disrupted by disturbance but quickly return to its former state, and thus over long periods of time be relatively stable (fig. 18.7)

One of the difficulties faced by ecologists studying stability is the need to conduct studies over a long period of time.

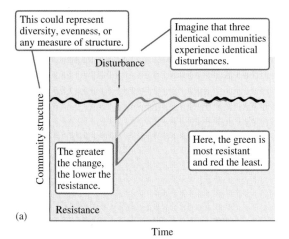

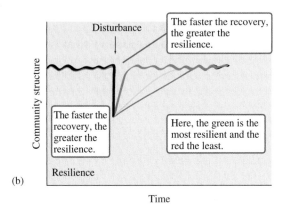

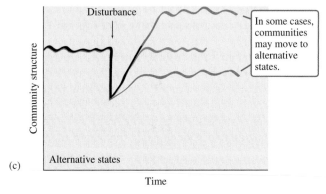

Figure 18.7 Visual representations of stability concepts. In all cases, imagine that three identical communities experience identical disturbances at identical points in time. The green communities are the most stable, the yellow exhibit intermediate stability, and the red are the least stable. (*a*) High resistance and high stability occurs when the communities change very little in response to a disturbance. (*b*) High resilience and high stability occurs when communities recover quickly to a pre-disturbance state. (*c*) In some situations, communities may never recover from a disturbance. Instead, community structure may stabilize at one of many alternative states.

Long-term data is critical, as stability—both resistance and resilience—is something that can only be observed through time. Fortunately, long-term studies are become more common in ecology. We begin with one of the longest, the Park Grass Experiment.

Lessons from the Park Grass Experiment

The Park Grass Experiment is the prototype of all long-term experimental studies in ecology. Started at the Rothamsted Experimental Station in Hertfordshire, England, between 1856 and 1872, its purpose was to study the effects of several fertilizer treatments on the yield and structure of a hay meadow community. Because the Park Grass Experiment has continued without interruption for nearly one and a half centuries, it provides one of the most valuable records of long-term community dynamics. That record provides some unique insights into the nature of community stability.

Jonathan Silvertown (1987) used data from the Park Grass Experiment to respond to the suggestion that existing studies do not conclusively demonstrate that any ecological community is stable. The composition of the plant community at the Park Grass Experiment has been monitored since 1862, and this record reveals at least one level of stability. Over this period, virtually no new species have colonized the meadow. Instead, changes in community composition occurred as a consequence of increases or decreases in species already present in the meadow at the beginning of the experiment. However, Silvertown was able to go much deeper into the data to understand stability.

A key requirement of strong science is the ability to quantify a concept so that it can be objectively measured. Here, Silvertown used variation in community composition as a measure of stability. He represented composition as the proportion of the community consisting of grasses, legumes, or other species. The analysis of composition was restricted to the period from 1910 to 1948 to avoid the early period of the experiment when the meadow community was adjusting to the various fertilizer treatments (i.e., undergoing transient dynamics). Figure 18.8 shows the relative proportions of grasses, legumes, and other plants on plots receiving three different treatments: plot 3, no fertilizer; plot 7, P, K, Na, and Mg; and plot 14, N, P, K, Na, and Mg. The differences in vegetation on the three plots were mostly produced by the different fertilizer treatments and developed early in the Park Grass Experiment.

The proportion of grasses, legumes, and other plants in the study plots varied from year to year, mainly in response to variation in precipitation. Despite this annual variation, figure 18.8 indicates that the proportions of three plant groups remained remarkably similar over the interval of the study. A quantitative analysis of trends in biomass revealed no significant changes in the biomass of the three plant groups in plots 3 and 7 and only a minor, but statistically significant, decrease in the biomass of grasses on plot 14. In other words, the data presented in figure 18.8 show remarkable stability in the proportion of grasses, legumes, and other species over an extended period of time.

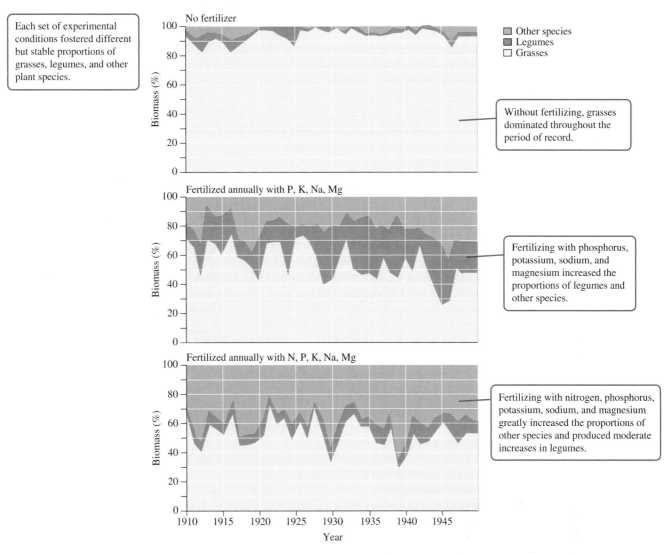

Each set of experimental conditions fostered different but stable proportions of grasses, legumes, and other plant species.

Without fertilizing, grasses dominated throughout the period of record.

Fertilizing with phosphorus, potassium, sodium, and magnesium increased the proportions of legumes and other species.

Fertilizing with nitrogen, phosphorus, potassium, sodium, and magnesium greatly increased the proportions of other species and produced moderate increases in legumes.

Figure 18.8   Proportions of grasses, legumes, and other plant species under three experimental conditions (data from Silvertown 1987).

Does the stability of Silvertown's three major groups of plants in the Park Grass Experiment hold up if we examine community structure at the species level? It turns out that while the proportions of grasses, legumes, and other species remained fairly constant, populations of individual species changed substantially. Mike Dodd and his colleagues (1995) used census data from 1920 to 1979 to examine plant population trends. The result of their analysis showed that some species increased in abundance, some decreased, some showed no trend, while others increased and then decreased (fig. 18.9).

The contrasting results obtained by Silvertown and by Dodd's project suggest that whether a community or ecosystem appears stable may depend upon how we view it. At a very coarse level of resolution, the Park Grass community has remained absolutely stable. It was a meadow community when the Park Grass Experiment began in 1856 and it remains so today. When Silvertown increased the resolution

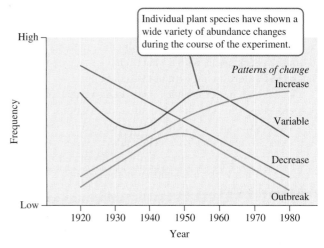

Individual plant species have shown a wide variety of abundance changes during the course of the experiment.

Patterns of change
Increase
Variable
Decrease
Outbreak

Figure 18.9   Patterns of species abundance during 60 years of the Park Grass Experiment (data from Dodd et al. 1995).

to distinguish between grasses, legumes, and other species, the community again appeared stable. However, when Dodd and his colleagues increased the resolution still further and examined trends in the abundances of individual species, the Park Grass community no longer appeared stable.

We now turn to a stream, where frequent disturbance offers another means to understand one potential mechanism that leads to increased stability.

Replicate Disturbances and Desert Stream Stability

Sycamore Creek, a tributary of the Verde River, lies approximately 32 km northeast of Phoenix, Arizona, where it drains approximately 500 km² of mountainous desert terrain. Evaporation nearly equals precipitation within the Sycamore Creek catchment, so flows are generally low and often intermittent. However, the creek is also subject to frequent flash floods.

Numerous studies of disturbance and recovery in Sycamore Creek, Arizona, have produced a highly detailed picture of community, ecosystem, and population responses. For instance, one study shows that resistance in the spatial structure of the Sycamore Creek ecosystem underlies spatial variation in ecosystem resilience. Maury Valett and his colleagues (1994) studied the interactions between surface and subsurface waters in Sycamore Creek to study the influence of these linkages on resilience. They tested the hypothesis that resilience is higher where hydrologic linkages between the surface and subsurface water increase the supply of nitrogen. They proposed a controlling role for nitrogen because it is the nutrient that limits primary production in Sycamore Creek.

Valett and his colleagues studied two stream sections at middle elevations in the 500 km² Sycamore Creek catchment. They measured the flow of water between the surface and subsurface along these reaches with *piezometers*. Piezometers can be used to measure the vertical hydraulic gradient, which indicates the direction of flow between surface water and water flowing through the sediments of a streambed. Positive vertical hydraulic gradients indicate flow from the streambed to the surface in upwelling zones. Negative vertical hydraulic gradients indicate flow from the surface to the streambed in downwelling zones. Zero vertical hydraulic gradients indicate stationary zones; areas with no net exchange between surface waters and water flowing within the sediments.

Valett and his colleagues measured vertical hydraulic gradient along the lengths of both study sections, producing hydrologic maps for both. The upper end of each study reach was an upwelling zone. The middle reaches were stationary zones and the lower reaches were downwelling zones. Figure 18.10 shows the distributions of these zones across one of the study reaches.

The concentration of nitrate in surface water in the two study reaches varies directly with vertical hydraulic gradient (fig. 18.11). Upwelling zones, which are fed by nitrate-rich waters upwelling from the sediments, have the highest concentrations of nitrate. Nitrate concentrations gradually decline with distance downstream through the stationary and downwelling zones.

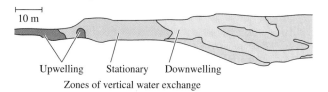

Upwelling   Stationary   Downwelling
Zones of vertical water exchange

Figure 18.10   Patterns of upwelling and downwelling in a reach of Sycamore Creek, Arizona (data from Valett et al. 1994).

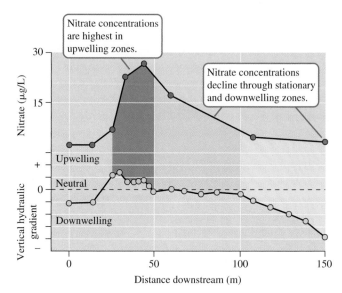

Figure 18.11   Relationship of nitrate to vertical hydraulic gradient in Sycamore Creek, Arizona (data from Valett et al. 1994).

The higher concentrations of nitrate in the upper reaches of each study section are associated with higher algal production. Algal biomass accumulates at a higher rate in upwelling zones compared to downwelling zones. Valett and his colleagues used rate of algal biomass accumulation as a measure of rate of recovery from disturbance (=resilience). Because the rate at which algal biomass accumulates in upwelling zones is so much higher than in downwelling zones, they concluded that the rate of ecosystem recovery is higher in upwelling zones. This pattern supports their hypothesis that algal communities in upwelling zones are more resilient.

The team also found that while flash floods caused rapid changes to the biotic community, the spatial arrangement of upwelling, stationary, and downwelling zones remained stable over time. In other words, this aspect of the spatial structure of the Sycamore Creek ecosystem is highly resistant to flash flooding. The location of upwelling, stationary, and downwelling zones remained stable in the face of numerous intense floods.

The spatial stability of the Sycamore Creek ecosystem in the face of potential disturbance is an example of ecosystem resistance. However, what is the source of this stable spatial structure? This spatial stability can be explained by considering geomorphology, especially the distribution of bedrock.

Subsurface water is forced to the surface in areas where bedrock lies close to the surface. Upwelling zones in Sycamore Creek are located in such areas, and since flooding does not move bedrock, the locations of upwelling zones are stable. Therefore, this aspect of stability is controlled by landscape structure. Next, we discuss how an aspect of the community itself, rather than the surrounding landscape, can influence stability.

Biodiversity and Stability

In chapter 16 we discussed how species diversity was often positively associated with increased ecological function. It may thus come as no surprise that species diversity also can confer increased stability—both through increased resistance and resilience. There are numerous studies testing for such diversity–stability relationships in many types of natural systems, and synthetic analyses have begun to emerge.

Boris Worm, of Dalhousie University, and an international team of researchers (Worm et al. 2006) have compiled experimental and long-term observational data sets to explore the effect of marine biodiversity on aquatic stability. Across 32 experiments in which researchers manipulated diversity (either species or genetic), increased stability (both resistance and resilience) typically resulted. In analyzing long-term data of economically and ecologically important marine species found within 12 coastal systems, areas of high regional (gamma) diversity had a smaller proportion of fisheries that have collapsed relative to areas of lower regional diversity (fig. 18.12). Why might this matter? One potential management implication is that fisheries in areas of lower diversity are at more risk of collapse than those from richer marine systems. Consequently, more care may need to be taken in the establishment of harvest quotas. Similar results are also found on land (Hooper et al. 2005). However, rather than describe more patterns, let us talk about why diversity may confer increased stability.

Let us consider some disturbance, such as a drought in a grassland. If there is a single species present, the overall stability of the system is going to be determined by the performance of that single species. Thus, the system may be highly stable, or highly unstable, depending upon that single species' ability to cope with the disturbance. Let us now imagine another grassland with 50 species. The overall stability of that system will be determined by the combined performances of all of these species. The chance that some species will be able to cope with drought is increased, relative to there just being a single species present. This is the **insurance hypothesis**, in which diversity increases stability due to increased probability of there being some species able to cope with any particular disturbance. Or put another way, diversity buffers a community from the potential consequences of a disturbance, or any environmental change. A key expectation of this idea is that the overall response of a community is not driven by the same species every year; instead, different species should become important under different conditions. In a recent review of studies that was conducted by Forest Isbell of McGill University and colleagues (Isbell et al. 2011), it appears there is support for this idea. Isbell summarized the data from 17 biodiversity experiments conducted in grasslands, similar to those described in chapter 16. Combined, these studies contained 147 plant species. Overall, 84% of these species were found to be important to ecosystem function at some point in time, under some conditions, or in response to some disturbance.

CONCEPT 18.2 REVIEW

1. What causes community resilience?
2. How might taxonomic resolution—that is, how precisely we identify organisms—influence an assessment of community stability?
3. How can one measure the stability of a natural system?

18.3 Community Changes During Succession

Community changes during succession include increases in species diversity and changes in species composition. So far, we have discussed what disturbances are and how characteristics of the landscape and community may enhance stability. However, in many cases stability will be lost, and disturbances significantly impact communities. In this section we focus on what happens next.

Some of the most detailed studies of ecological succession have focused on the studies of forests. Though primary and secondary forest succession require different amounts of time, the changes in species diversity that occur in each appear remarkably similar. Over the course of succession, nearly every aspect of community structure changes. There are shifts

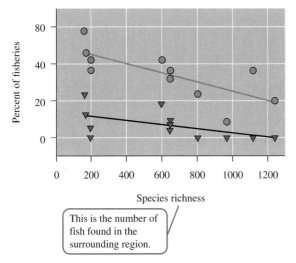

Figure 18.12 Increased regional species diversity is associated with reduced proportions of fisheries that have collapsed (circles) or have gone extinct (triangles).

in dominance, evenness, species diversity and composition, as well as changes to the abiotic environment. Underlying these shifts are the basic ecological interactions we have discussed throughout this book. Dispersal, niche requirements, competition, exploitation, and associated mutualists all influence when and if a species is found in a location undergoing succession. It is important to recognize that succession is the outcome of ecological processes; it is not a process itself. Communities do not act as a whole, moving from one form to another. Instead, individuals survive, thrive, or perish as a function of how well their biology is suited to local conditions. As these conditions change, so too do the species that become dominant. These changes are what we observe and call succession.

In some cases, changes during succession are highly predictable, and they appear to follow assembly rules (chapter 17) leading to a particular climax community. In many other cases, succession does not lead to a single end-point, and instead the outcome may be one of any number of alternative stable states (fig. 18.6c). We begin here by describing the classical form of succession.

Primary Succession at Glacier Bay

We return to Glacier Bay, Alaska, and look with a bit more depth at primary succession following glacial retreat. Succession can take a very long time—centuries or even millennia. This is well beyond the life-span of even a young ecologist, let alone the length of typical research grant! How then to study this process? A typical tool in succession research is the use of a **chronosequence**. A chronosequence is a group of communities or ecosystems that represent a range of ages or times since disturbance. The idea is that if you know the time since disturbance at many locations, then by sampling different locations at the same time you can measure changes through succession. For example, figure 18.13 provides a map showing the approximate locations of the glacial extent since 1794. By measuring community structure at locations in which the glacier retreated 10, 100, and 1,000 years ago, you can swap space for time and infer successional changes. Though chronosequences require making many important assumptions (e.g., climate and gamma diversity have not changed over time), they are a key research tool in long-term ecological studies.

In their study of Glacier Bay, William Reiners and colleagues (1971) worked at sites carefully chosen for similarity in physical features but differing substantially in time since glacial retreat. Their eight study sites were below 100 m elevation, were on glacial till, an unstratified and unsorted material deposited by a glacier, and all had moderate slopes. The study sites ranged in time since glacial retreat from 10 to 1,500 years. By minimizing site differences (e.g., slope and substrate), they give more confidence in the use of the chronosequence approach.

Their youngest site, which was approximately 10 years old, supported a pioneer community of scattered *Epilobium*, *Equisetum*, and *Salix*. Site 2 was about 23 years old and supported a mix of pioneer species and clumps of *Populus* and *Dryas*. Site 3, which was approximately 33 years old, supported a mat of *Dryas* enclosing clumps of *Salix*, *Populus*, and *Alnus*. Site 4 was 44 years old and was dominated by a mat of *Dryas* with few open patches. Site 5, which was approximately 108 years old, was dominated by a thicket of *Alnus* and *Salix* with enough emergent *Populus* and *Picea* to form a partial canopy. Site 6 was a 200-year-old forest of *Picea*. Using geological methods, Reiners and his colleagues dated site 7 at 500 years and site 8 at 1,500 years. Both sites were located on Pleasant Island, which, because it is located outside the mouth of Glacier Bay, had escaped the most recent glaciation. Site 7 was an old forest of *Tsuga* that contained a few *Picea*. Site 8 was a muskeg with scattered Lodgepole pines, *Pinus contorta*.

The total number of plant species in the eight study sites increased with time since glacial retreat. As you can see in figure 18.14, species richness increased rapidly in the early

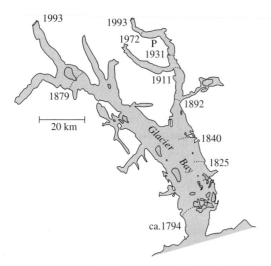

Figure 18.13 A map of Glacier Bay, showing the glacial extent since 1794.

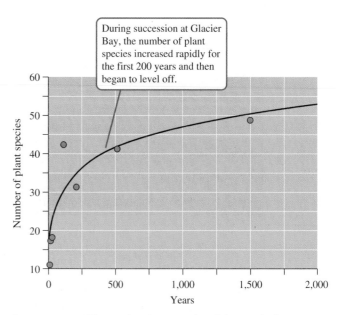

Figure 18.14 Change in plant species richness during primary succession at Glacier Bay, Alaska (data from Reiners et al. 1971).

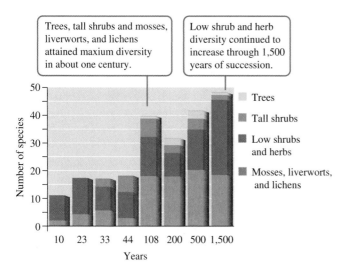

The timing of increasing species richness differs among plant growth forms.

Trees, tall shrubs and mosses, liverworts, and lichens attained maxium diversity in about one century.

Low shrub and herb diversity continued to increase through 1,500 years of succession.

Trees
Tall shrubs
Low shrubs and herbs
Mosses, liverworts, and lichens

Figure 18.15 Succession of plant growth forms at Glacier Bay, Alaska (data from Reiners et al. 1971).

years of succession at Glacier Bay and then more slowly during the later stages. However, not all groups of plants increased in diversity throughout succession. Though the species richness of mosses, liverworts, and lichens reached a plateau after about a century of succession (fig. 18.15), the diversity of low shrubs and herbs continued to increase throughout succession. In contrast, the diversity of tall shrubs and trees increased until the middle stages of succession and then declined in later stages.

The pattern of increased species richness with increased age of the stand that Reiners and his colleagues described for the successional sequence around Glacier Bay is typical of both primary and secondary succession. However, the tempo of succession can vary greatly among systems. The late successional climax community at Glacier Bay was

1,500 years old. In the following example of secondary succession, the climax forest community emerges in approximately one-tenth of that time.

Secondary Succession in Boreal Forest

Boreal forests are a dominant community type in Canada, and though we often think of the boreal as isolated areas of old forest, the reality is often very different. In addition to the ever-increasing pressures of oil and gas exploration, forestry, and peat extraction, the boreal forest is a dynamic community with frequent natural disturbances.

Fires are common throughout the boreal forest, with lightning strikes a frequent source of fire initiation. What exactly does fire do to a forest (fig. 18.16)? The answer depends upon the intensity of the fire, with some fires being minor and affecting only low-lying vegetation, and others being severe and burning both the tops of the trees and through the accumulated litter on the forest floor to the soil. However, if we ignore the extreme ends of the fire intensity distribution, we find a few common consequences of fire. First, fire can kill plants. Death of canopy trees increases light penetration to the soil floors, allowing the recruitment and growth of smaller trees and seedlings that may have escaped the fire, or plants that were able to quickly colonize through seed or clonal growth. Fire effects do not end with their immediate impacts on plant survival. Fire can cause increases in nutrient availability through the breakdown of organic matter and by stimulating microbial activity. In combination, these factors provide a high light environment with high resource availability. Following fire, recolonization by plants is rapid, with new plant growth occurring within days or weeks (unless it is winter!).

But how do plants know to colonize a burned area? Many plants possess life-history traits that facilitate regrowth following fire. These fire-tolerant species are widespread throughout the boreal forest. For example, although aspen stems can burn during a fire, the root systems generally survive. Soon after a fire, you will find thousands of young

1944   1916   1823   1760

Figure 18.16 Changes in boreal forest composition along a chronosequence in Quebec. Dates refer to the year of the last fire.

aspen sprouts emerging from these living root systems. This re-sprouting strategy is found in other species, such as paper birch, but rarely to the same density that is found with aspen. Other species may not be able to re-sprout, but fire may trigger seed dispersal or germination. For example, black spruce (*Picea mariana*) and jack pine (*Pinus banksiana*) produce seeds inside of cones covered with a thick layer of pitch. The pitch burns off during fire, releasing the seed. In other communities, compounds contained within smoke itself can serve as a stimulant promoting seed germination. The life-history trade-offs we discussed in chapter 9 are very relevant to understanding the process of succession. Species that invest in large numbers of seeds, which are able to disperse over great distances, are more likely to encounter the open environments of a post-burn fire. Following fire it is common to see species such as fireweed (*Epilobium angustifolium*), blue-joint grass (*Calamagrostis canadensis*), and many other fast-growing species blanketing the forest floor, until they are shaded out by trees. These species have life-history traits well suited to living in disturbed habitats, but not as well suited for life within a mature forest. Knowing that some, but not all, species of the boreal forests have adaptations to recover following fire, what do you expect secondary succession in the boreal forest to look like?

Yves Bergeron of the Université de Québec has been studying the secondary succession of southern boreal forests for decades. The work of Bergeron and his students has provided us with a much clearer understanding of how fire can alter plant community structure in the boreal forest. In one study (Bergeron 2000), we can see a general pattern in species change over time following fire. Bergeron conducted an extensive survey of forest composition in the southern extent of the boreal forest in Quebec, establishing a series of transects and study plots in the forests surrounding Lake Duparquet. These forests contain a mixture of dominant plant species, including jack pine, black and white spruce, balsam poplar, and paper birch. Bergeron wanted to know whether the distribution of these species on the landscape could be explained by fire. In other words, would you tend to find certain types of boreal species in areas that were recently burned and other species in areas that have not been burned for quite some time? Bergeron sampled forest stands that were established after different forest fires, with the most recent occurring in 1964 and the oldest in 1760. The results were striking. Bergeron found that prior to the fires there was substantial variation in forest composition, and following fire there was a regular pattern to successional changes over time (fig. 18.17). Soon after fire, forests were dominated by hardwood species, such as aspen, birch, willow, and pin cherry. These species were eventually replaced by white spruce and balsam fir, with white cedar becoming common even later. Bergeron found that these dynamics were also influenced by periodic outbreaks of spruce budworms, once again emphasizing the point we made in chapter 17 that all communities will be influenced by multiple ecological factors. Despite this complexity, Bergeron was

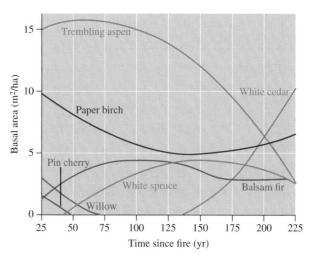

Figure 18.17 Following fire, the composition of the southern boreal forest changes over the course of secondary succession (data from Bergeron 2000).

able to paint a portrait of secondary succession in the southern boreal forests of Canada. His interpretation of this process can help explain the observed heterogeneity in forest types within the boreal, as these areas may be in different stages of the long-term movement toward the local climax community.

As we see next, succession also is found in systems where animals, rather than plants, are among the dominant organisms covering the ground.

Succession in Rocky Intertidal Communities

When we discussed the influence of disturbance on local species diversity earlier in this chapter, we saw how an intertidal boulder stripped of its cover of attached organisms was soon colonized by algae and barnacles (fig. 18.18). Looking back on that pattern of community change we can now see it as an example of ecological succession. Wayne Sousa (1979a, 1979b) showed that the first species to colonize open space on intertidal boulders were a green alga in the genus *Ulva* and the barnacle *Chthamalus fissus*. The next arrivals were several species of perennial red algae: *Gelidium coulteri*, *Gigartina leptorhynchos*, *Rhodoglossum affine*, and *Gigartina canaliculata*. Finally, if there was no additional disturbance for a few years, *G. canaliculata* grew over the other species and dominated 60% to 90% of the space.

Sousa explored succession on intertidal boulders with several experiments. In one of them, he followed succession on small boulders that he had cleaned and stabilized. As in forest succession, the number of species increased with time (fig. 18.19). Notice in the figure that the average number of species increased until about 1 to 1.5 years and then levelled off at about five species.

Primary forest succession around Glacier Bay may require about 1,500 years, and secondary forest succession in the boreal forest takes about 200 years. Meanwhile the successional changes described by Sousa occurred within about

1.5 years. In the next example, ecological succession within a desert stream occurs in less than 2 months.

Succession in Stream Communities

Rapid succession has been well documented in Sycamore Creek, Arizona, which has been studied for nearly two decades by Stuart Fisher and his colleagues (1982). Fisher's research team reported on the successional events following flash floods. Intense floods occurred on Sycamore Creek on August 6, 12, and 16, 1979, with peak flows of 7, 3, and 2 m³ per second. Floods of this intensity mobilize the stones and sand of the stream, scouring some areas and depositing sediments in others. In the process, most stream organisms are destroyed. The three floods of August 1979 eliminated approximately 98% of algal and invertebrate biomass in Sycamore Creek.

In 63 days following these floods, Fisher and his colleagues observed rapid changes in both the diversity and composition of algae and invertebrates. Patterns among primary producers were especially clear. Two days after the floods, the majority of the stream bottom consisted of bare sand with some patches of diatoms. Five days after the flood, diatoms covered about half the streambed. Within 13 to 22 days, diatoms almost completely covered the stream bottom. Other algae, especially blue-green algae and mats consisting of a mixture of the green alga *Cladophora* and blue-green algae, appeared in significant quantities by day 35. By day 63, the bottom of Sycamore Creek consisted of a patchwork of areas dominated by diatoms, blue-green algae, and mats of *Cladophora* and blue-green algae. The diversity of diatoms and other algae, as measured by H' (see chapter 16), levelled off after only 5 days and then began to decline after about 50 days (fig. 18.20).

Figure 18.18   Succession in the intertidal zone involves colonization and competition for limited space among species as different as attached marine algae, sea anemones, mussels, and barnacles.

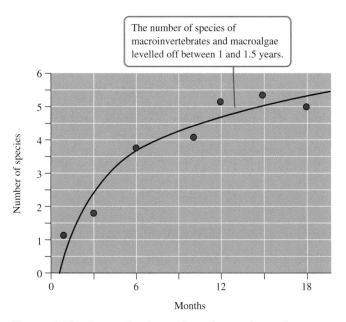

Figure 18.19   Succession in number of macroinvertebrate and macroalgae species on intertidal boulders (data from Sousa 1979a).

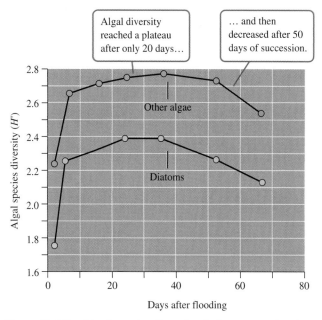

Figure 18.20   Algal species diversity during succession in Sycamore Creek, Arizona (data from Fisher et al. 1982).

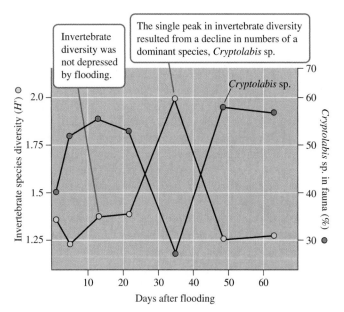

Figure 18.21 Invertebrate species diversity during succession in Sycamore Creek, Arizona (data from Fisher et al. 1982).

Invertebrate diversity was strongly influenced by a single dominant species of crane fly, *Cryptolabis* sp. (fig. 18.21). Large numbers of *Cryptolabis* larvae in Sycamore Creek depressed H' diversity for all collections except for the collection on day 35, when most of the population emerged as adults. Throughout their collections over the 63-day period of the study, the researchers reported that they collected 38 to 43 species of aquatic invertebrates out of a total of 48 species collected during their studies. In other words, most macroinvertebrate species survived the flood.

Where did these invertebrate species find refuge from the devastating floods of August 1979? The invertebrate community of Sycamore Creek is dominated by insects whose adults are terrestrial. During the floods of August, many adult insects were in the aerial stage and the flood passed under them. These aerial adults were the source of most invertebrate recolonization of the flood-devastated Sycamore Creek.

We now move from the flowing waters of the desert stream to the relatively still waters of lakes. Here too we will find predictable patterns of community succession.

Shallow Lake Succession

Freshwater lakes experience succession in two time scales. Over the short time scale of seasons or years there are changes in species composition following some disturbance such as flooding, freezing, or introduction of novel species. Such changes are similar in concept to what we have seen in the previous examples of succession in forests and streams. However, lakes also experience succession on a geological time scale. Most lakes, particularly small lakes, eventually disappear. This too is succession and involves predictable changes in species composition as a result of changing

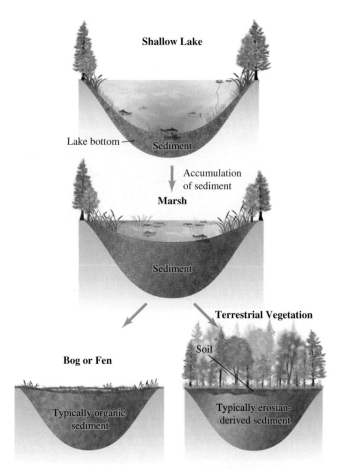

Figure 18.22 Shallow lakes can undergo succession. Terrestrialization is most common with accumulation of inorganic sediments, while transition to wetland habitats is more common with organic sedimentation.

conditions in the lake (fig. 18.22). The mechanisms that drive lake succession vary as a function of local conditions. One form of lake succession is the process of *terrestrialization*, driven by **sedimentation**, the deposition of suspended matter onto the lake bottom. The exact composition of the sediment will vary among locations; it may be organic (e.g., peat), inorganic (e.g., sand), or some mixture of these and other materials.

We begin by imagining a small, shallow lake. Surrounding the lake will likely be a variety of mosses, cattails, and other plants that can grow in water-logged soils. As this is a shallow lake, there are likely to be substantial amounts of aquatic vegetation even far from the lake edge. Now ask yourself a question: what happens to all of the plant litter surrounding and inside the lake when it falls from the plants? Obviously, much of this will fall into the water and settle onto the bottom of the lake. In these cool regions, decomposition is generally slower than litter accumulations, such that the bottom of the lake gradually rises as litter is accumulated across years and decades. Sedimentation can also occur rapidly if the lake becomes eutrophied through inputs of fertilizers, which stimulates algal growth. When algae in lakes die, they too fall

to the bottom, creating layers of detritus. An additional source of sediment may come from upland erosion, which may flow into and fill the bottom of the lake.

Sedimentation can eventually fill the lake bottom, leading to the conversion of the system into an alternative habitat type. The exact habitat will depend upon the type of sediment (organic vs. inorganic), lake depth, and other local conditions. Explaining how different wetland and upland habitat types are formed is well beyond the scope of this course, but we encourage those interested to take some courses in limnology!

In general, changes driven by accumulation of sediment can eventually result in a conversion of the lake into a marsh-like habitat with standing water surrounding substantial amounts of vegetation. Depending upon the specific conditions (e.g., rate of water flow out of the lake, pH, etc.), continued organic sedimentation can convert the marsh into a fen or bog (chapter 3). In other conditions, particularly when sedimentation is from erosion rather than organic sources, the lake can develop into a drier upland forest community. A critical aspect of this form of succession is that it blurs the lines between aquatic and terrestrial systems. High levels of deposition from terrestrial vegetation into a shallow lake can cause succession from one to the other. As we have seen many times throughout the book, terms like aquatic and terrestrial are convenient for scientists to use to describe communities, but they mask the rich complexity of interconnections that actually exist.

It is important to also recognize that not all lakes will undergo this form of long-term succession. Deep lakes are unlikely to have large amounts of vegetation growing throughout the water, and thus relatively little sedimentation occurs. Similarly, lakes with steep, rock-lined boundaries are likely to experience little encroachment by the surrounding terrestrial vegetation, either slowing or preventing succession. Finally, a critical component of lake succession is that sedimentation rates are greater than decomposition rates. If microbial activity is high enough to decompose the litter, or if there is sufficient outflow of water from the lake (carrying sediment), succession is less likely to occur.

As we have just shown, ecological succession involves predictable changes in community structure. As you will see next, succession also leads to predictable changes in ecosystem structure and function.

CONCEPT 18.3 REVIEW

1. What are the primary differences in succession rates in forest, rocky intertidal, and stream communities?
2. How do life-history traits influence whether a species is likely to be found early or late in succession?
3. Why is lake succession likely to occur in shallow lakes with low pH and cool temperatures?

18.4 Ecosystem Changes During Succession

Ecosystem changes during succession include increases in biomass, primary production, respiration, and nutrient retention. In the last section, we saw how plant and animal community structure changes during primary and secondary succession. However, as the species diversity and composition of communities change, they cause changes to a number of ecosystem properties. Further, time itself can influence ecosystem processes through a number of mechanisms, such as the weathering of bedrock. In this section, we review evidence that many ecosystem properties also change during succession. For instance, many properties of soils, such as the nutrient and organic matter content, change during the course of succession.

Ecosystem Changes at Glacier Bay

Again, we return to Glacier Bay in Alaska. Stuart Chapin and his colleagues (1994) documented substantial changes in ecosystem structure during succession at Glacier Bay. They focused on four study areas of approximately 2 km² each. Their first site had been deglaciated for about 5 to 10 years and was in the pioneer stage. Their second site had been deglaciated 35 to 45 years previously and was dominated by a mat of *Dryas. Dryas* was just beginning to invade this site when it was studied by Reiners' group more than 20 years earlier. The third site had been deglaciated about 60 to 70 years before and was in the alder, *Alnus*, stage. This site was studied by Reiners when it was a young thicket of alder and by Cooper when it was in the pioneer stage. The fourth site studied by Chapin and his colleagues had been deglaciated 200 to 225 years earlier and was a forest of spruce, *Picea*.

Chapin and his research team measured changes in several ecosystem characteristics across these study sites, including the quantity of soil. Total soil depth and the depth of all major soil horizons all show significant increases from the pioneer community to the spruce stage (fig. 18.23). Chapin and colleagues also found that the organic content and moisture concentrations of the soil had also increased substantially, while soil bulk density and phosphorus concentration decreased with time since glacial retreat.

Why are these changes in soil properties important? They demonstrate that succession involves more than just changes in the composition and diversity of species. Soils are the foundation upon which terrestrial ecosystems are built, and if it changes, so too will many other aspects of the ecosystem. We can see from this study that the physical and biological properties of ecosystems are inseparable. Organisms acting upon mineral substrates contribute to the building of soils upon which spruce forests eventually grow around Glacier Bay. Soils, in turn, strongly influence the kinds of organisms that grow in a place.

Four Million Years of Ecosystem Change

The detailed knowledge of ecosystem change that has emerged through studies at Glacier Bay is impressive. However, the sequence of ages represented by the chronosequence are limited. In 1794, when Captain George Vancouver encountered a

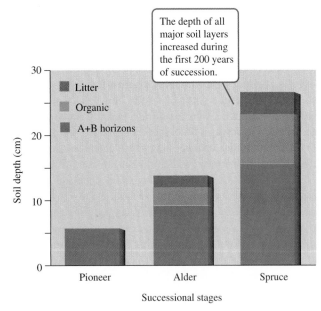

Figure 18.23 Soil building during primary succession at Glacier Bay, Alaska (data from Chapin et al. 1994).

wall of ice at the mouth of Glacier Bay, the island of Kauai in the Hawaiian Island chain supported forest ecosystems growing on soils that had developed on lava flows that were over four million years old. The Hawaiian Islands have formed over a hot spot on the Pacific tectonic plate and have been transported on that plate to the northwest, forming a chain of islands that vary greatly in age. The youngest island in the group is the big island of Hawaii, which is currently growing over the hot spot. The big island is made up of volcanic rocks that vary from fresh lava flows to flows that are approximately 150,000 years old. Meanwhile, the islands to the northwest are sequentially older. As in Glacier Bay, teams of ecologists have probed the chronosequence represented by the Hawaiian Island chain for information on ecosystem development. However, in Hawaii the chronosequence spans not hundreds of years but millions.

Lars Hedin and colleagues (2003) examined nutrient distributions and losses on a chronosequence of forest ecosystems on the islands of Hawaii, Molokai, and Kauai. The youngest ecosystems, which were on Hawaii, had developed on basaltic lava flows that were 300, 2,100, 20,000, and 150,000 years old. The study site on Molokai had developed on rocks that were 1,400,000 years old and the oldest study site, which was on Kauai, was 4,100,000 years old. All sites currently have an average annual temperature of about 16°C and receive approximately 2,500 mm of precipitation annually. They also all support forest communities dominated by the native tree, *Metrosideros polymorpha*.

Over the chronosequence represented by their six study sites, Hedin and colleagues encountered changes in a wide range of soil features. Earlier studies had demonstrated that primary production in the Hawaiian forest ecosystems is limited by nitrogen early in succession and by phosphorus later in succession. Organic matter, which is absent from fresh lava, increased in soils over the first 150,000 years of the chronosequence (fig. 18.24). Increases in soil organic matter also occur

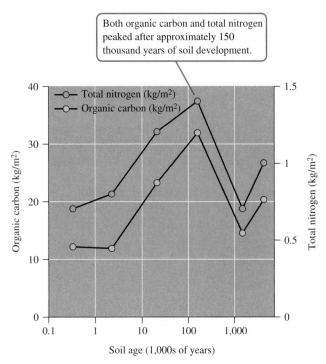

Figure 18.24 Changes in the organic carbon and total nitrogen content of soils developing on Hawaiian lava flows ranging in age from 300 years old to 4.1 million years old (data from Hedin et al. 2003).

over the course of succession at Glacier Bay. However, in the Hawaiian chronosequence, organic matter was lower at the 1.4 million- and 4.1 million-year-old sites. Figure 18.24 also shows that changes in soil nitrogen content followed almost precisely the pattern exhibited by soil organic matter.

The pattern of change in the total phosphorus content of soils was remarkably different (fig. 18.25). The total amount of phosphorus in soils showed no obvious pattern of change with site age. However, the forms of phosphorus changed substantially over the chronosequence. Weatherable mineral phosphorus was largely depleted by 20,000 years. Meanwhile the percentage of soil phosphorus in refractory forms, which are not readily available to plants, increased, varying from 68% to 80% of total phosphorus across ecosystems that had developed on lava flows 20,000 years old or older. On these older soils, primary production is limited by phosphorus availability.

Hedin and colleagues found changes in rates of nutrient loss across the chronosequence. Over the course of four million years of ecosystem development, these tropical forest ecosystems show progressively higher rates of nitrogen loss but decreased rates of phosphorus loss (fig. 18.26). In other words, for approximately 2,000 years these ecosystems are highly retentive of nitrogen but as nitrogen content increases in their soils, they begin to lose nitrogen at a higher rate. Most losses are due to leaching to groundwater. In contrast, as phosphorus becomes progressively less available, and eventually limiting to primary production in these ecosystems, they become more retentive of phosphorus. As we shall see in the next example, intact vegetative cover may play a key role in nutrient retention in forest ecosystems.

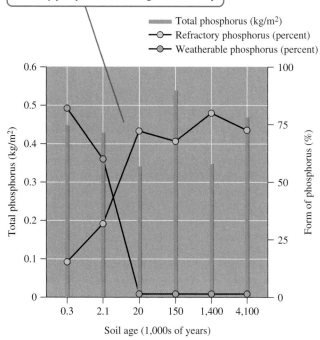

While total phosphorus showed no clear change with soil age, weatherable phosphorus and refractory phosphorus both changed dramatically.

Figure 18.25 Changes in the total phosphorus and percentages of total phosphorus in weatherable and refractory (low availability) forms (data from Hedin et al. 2003).

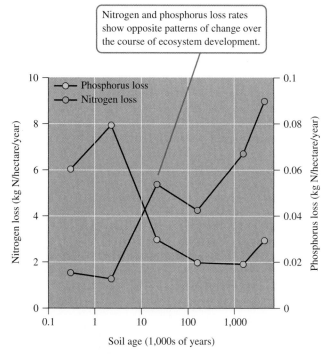

Nitrogen and phosphorus loss rates show opposite patterns of change over the course of ecosystem development.

Figure 18.26 Nitrogen and phosphorus loss rates from soils developing on Hawaiian lava flows ranging in age from 300 years old to 4.1 million years old (data from Hedin et al. 2003).

Recovery of Nutrient Retention Following Disturbance

Bormann and Likens (1981) monitored a control and an experimental stream catchment for three years in the Hubbard Brook Experimental Forest. This forest, located in New Hampshire, provides some of the best evidence of the ecosystem changes that occur during succession in forested communities. They were particularly interested in the effects of clear-cut logging on nutrient dynamics. As we have seen throughout the book, often the best way to study natural processes is generally through experimental manipulation. Here, they cut down the forest surrounding their experimental catchment and suppressed regrowth of vegetation with herbicides for three years (Likens et al. 1978). By suppressing vegetative growth, they delayed succession.

When herbicide applications were stopped, succession proceeded and nutrient losses by the forest ecosystem decreased dramatically. As you can see in figure 18.27, the herbicide suppressed vegetative growth on the experimental catchment for at least three consecutive years. It was during this period that the experimental catchment lost large quantities of nutrients, including calcium, potassium, and nitrate.

When herbicide applications stopped in 1969, Likens' group observed simultaneous increases in primary production and decreases in nutrient loss. However, the researchers point out that uptake by vegetation cannot account completely for reduced nutrient loss and that losses of calcium, potassium, and nitrate all peaked during the time when herbicide was still being applied. They suggest that some of the reduced losses during this period can be attributed to reduced amounts of these nutrients in the ecosystem. In other words, nutrient losses were reducing nutrient pools. However, vegetative uptake is clearly implicated since once succession was allowed to occur, nutrient losses from the experimental catchment declined rapidly. Though losses of nitrate returned to pre-disturbance levels within four years, calcium and potassium losses remained elevated above pre-disturbance levels even after seven years of forest succession.

A Model of Ecosystem Recovery

As a result of their observations on the Hubbard Brook Experimental Forest, Bormann and Likens proposed a model for recovery of ecosystems from disturbance (fig. 18.28). Their biomass accumulation model divides the recovery of a forest ecosystem from disturbance into four phases: (1) a reorganization phase of 10 to 20 years, during which the forest loses biomass and nutrients, despite accumulation of living biomass; (2) an aggradation phase of more than a century, when the ecosystem accumulates biomass, eventually reaching peak biomass; (3) a transition phase, during which biomass declines somewhat from the peak reached during the aggradation phase; and (4) a steady-state phase, when biomass fluctuates around a mean level.

How well does the biomass accumulation model represent the process of forest succession? Does a similar sequence of stages occur during succession in other ecosystems? For

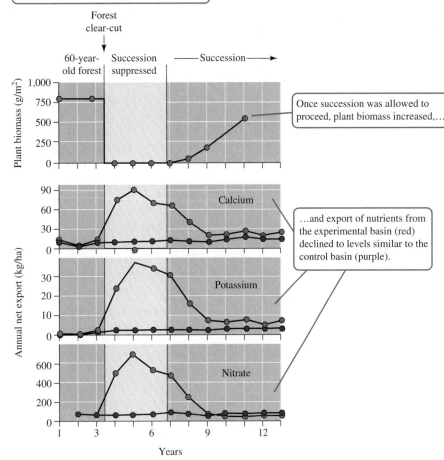

Figure 18.27   Succession following deforestation and nutrient retention (data from Likens et al. 1978).

instance, do ecosystems eventually reach a steady state? The generality of the biomass accumulation model can be tested on ecosystems, such as Sycamore Creek, Arizona, that undergo rapid succession. Such ecosystems give the ecologist the chance to study multiple successional sequences. As we will see in the following example, the patterns of ecosystem change during succession on Sycamore Creek suggest that several ecosystem features eventually reach a steady state.

Succession and Stream Ecosystem Properties

Patterns similar to those proposed by the biomass accumulation model were recorded by Fisher's research group during just 63 days of post-flood succession in Sycamore Creek, Arizona. Algal biomass increased rapidly for the first 13 days following disturbance and then increased more slowly from day 13 to day 63 (fig. 18.29). Sixty-three days after the flood, algal biomass showed clear signs of levelling off. The biomass of invertebrates, the chief animal group in Sycamore Creek, increased rapidly for 22 days following the flood and then, like the algal portion of the ecosystem, began to level off.

Ecosystem metabolic parameters showed even clearer signs of levelling off before the end of the 63-day study (fig. 18.30). Gross primary production (see chapter 19), measured as grams of O_2 produced per square metre per day, increased very rapidly until day 13, increased more slowly between days 13

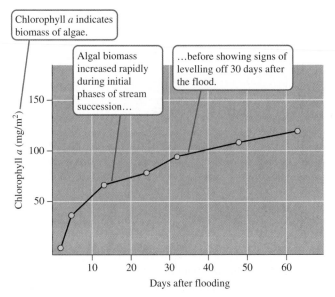

Figure 18.28   The biomass accumulation model of forest succession (data from Bormann and Likens 1981).

Figure 18.29   Changes in biomass during stream succession (data from Fisher et al. 1982).

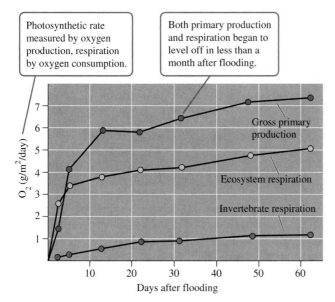

Figure 18.30 Ecosystem processes during succession in Sycamore Creek, Arizona (data from Fisher et al. 1982).

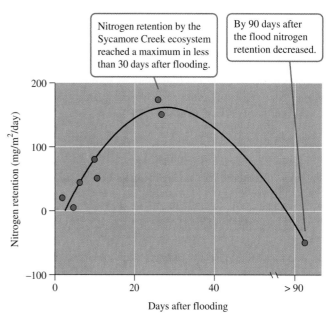

Figure 18.31 Nitrogen retention during stream succession (data from Grimm 1987).

and 48, and then levelled off between days 48 and 63. Total ecosystem respiration, measured as oxygen consumption per square metre per day, increased quickly for only five days after the flood and then began to level off. Respiration by invertebrates, which at its maximum represented about 20% of total ecosystem respiration, levelled off by day 63.

Nancy Grimm (1987) studied nitrogen dynamics in Sycamore Creek following floods that occurred from 1981 to 1983. As in the earlier studies by Fisher and his colleagues (1982), Grimm found that during succession, algal biomass and whole ecosystem metabolism quickly reached a maximum and then levelled off, as did the quantity of nitrogen in the system.

In addition, however, Grimm examined patterns of nitrogen retention during stream succession. She estimated the nitrogen budget in each of her study reaches by comparing the nitrogen inputs at the upstream end to nitrogen outputs at the downstream end. Each 60 to 120 m study reach began where subsurface flows upwelled to the surface and ended downstream, where water disappeared into the sand. Grimm used the ratio of dissolved inorganic nitrogen entering the study reach in the upwelling zone to the amount leaving at the lower end as a measure of nitrogen retention by the stream ecosystem.

Figure 18.31 shows that in the early stages of succession, approximately equal amounts of dissolved inorganic nitrogen entered and left Grimm's study reaches. What do equal levels of input and output indicate regarding nutrient retention? A balance between input and output means that the ecosystem shows no, or zero, retention. The level of retention increased rapidly during succession, levelling off at nearly 200 mg N per square metre per day, about 28 days after a flood. In other words, the study reach was accumulating 200 mg N per square metre per day. Then, between 28 days and 90 days after the flood, the study reach showed progressively lower retention until it eventually exported a little more dissolved inorganic nitrogen than came in with groundwater.

The results of Grimm's study raise several questions. First, what mechanisms underlie retention? Grimm attributes most retention by the Sycamore Creek ecosystem to uptake by algae and invertebrates, since levels of nitrogen retention are consistent with the rates at which nitrogen was accumulated by algal and animal populations. What causes the stream reaches to eventually export nitrogen? Grimm suggested that at 90 days postflood her study sites may have stopped accumulating biomass or may have even begun to lose biomass. A loss of biomass in the later stages of succession is consistent with the predictions of the Bormann and Likens biomass accumulation model.

The major point here is that succession, which produces changes in species composition and species diversity, also changes the structure and function of ecosystems ranging from forests to streams. However, we are left with a major question concerning this important ecological process. What mechanisms drive succession? Ecologists have proposed that the mechanisms underlying succession may fall into one of three categories. Those mechanisms are the subject of the next section.

CONCEPT 18.4 REVIEW

1. Why are the changes in soil properties during the course of succession documented by Stuart Chapin and his colleagues ecologically significant?
2. What would equal levels of nitrogen input and output in the stream reaches (sections) studied by Nancy Grimm indicate?
3. How are the biomass accumulation model of Bormann and Likens (see fig. 18.28) and Grimm's observations of changes in nitrogen retention during succession in Sycamore Creek similar?

18.5 Mechanisms of Succession

Mechanisms that drive ecological succession include facilitation, tolerance, and inhibition. Succession occurs in terrestrial and aquatic environments in response to a diversity of disturbances. What are the underlying mechanisms that cause these changes? Over the last several decades there has been a move away from viewing succession as a process in and of itself, and toward a focus on the interactions of individuals within a community. By focusing on the individual, ecologists have been able to identify several general mechanisms that can cause successional change within a community. We begin, however, with some history.

An early model for successional change was proposed by Frederic Clements in 1916. Clements viewed succession as analogous to the development of an organism (1916, 1936), and that the climax community was a kind of *superorganism* (as a point of reference, *Superman* did not appear until 1938). He argued that each wave of species in a successional sequence facilitated the establishment and growth of the next wave. This process of *serial replacement* would continue until the climax community was established, which, according to Clements, was then able to maintain itself in perpetuity, or at least until another disturbance occurred.

Henry Gleason (1926, 1939) opposed this idea, arguing that species are distributed independently of each other, with overlaps in distribution the result of coincidence, not mutual interdependence. Gleason advocated an individualistic approach to understanding communities and succession, arguing that specific conditions and random events could alter the course of succession. By Gleason's model, the outcome of succession was not nearly as neat and orderly as that proposed by Clements, and instead local interactions and conditions would influence the pattern of community change that was observed. Gleason and Clements had a difficult professional relationship, and there was heated debate among them and their supporters.

Today, most modern ecologists hold a view more similar to that of Gleason than Clements, though interestingly, many members of the general public (and most students in my Ecology and Plant Ecology classes) seem to fall (initially) toward the side of Clements. One of the key observations in contrast to Clements' model is that succession does not always result in the same climax community, even under similar environmental conditions. Instead a system may have a number of alternative stable states, depending upon which specific mechanisms occur during succession. Substantial research has shown that a variety of processes, such as dispersal limitation, influence of herbivores and predators, and simple chance events, can have very dramatic impacts on the direction and speed of successional pathways. Though the climax concept is useful in understanding the general concepts of succession, it should not be taken to imply that succession results in a specific community with deterministic distributions and abundances of species. Instead, although there are repeatable patterns in community structure, communities are groups of individuals, rather than a *superorganism* that follows a predictable developmental pathway.

Frank Egler was among the first to clearly articulate the contrasting ideas related to succession presented by Gleason and Clements (Egler 1954), and by doing so, Egler ushered in a new wave of research in community ecology. Egler presented two alternatives as to how succession might work in a given location. First was **relay floristics**, which was the name Egler gave to Clements' views of how succession operated (fig. 18.32a). In relay floristics, one group of species colonizes an area immediately following disturbance. These pioneer species are then replaced by a second wave of species, and so on until the climax community was reached. A critical point of this model is that each stage facilitates the establishment of the next wave, resulting in very little overlap of species distributions in the different successional stages. As an alternative model Egler presented **initial floristics** (fig. 18.32b). In this model you still find that different species are dominant in different time periods following disturbance, but species occurrences can overlap greatly throughout succession. Most important is the idea that many species, even those we associate with late successional communities, may establish immediately following

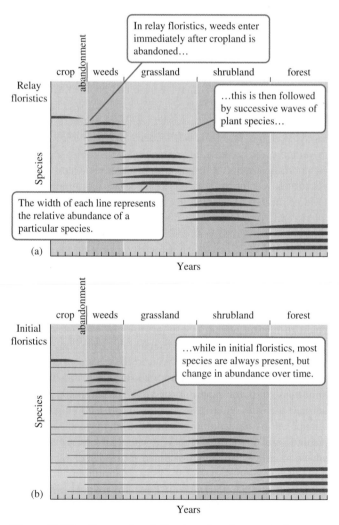

Figure 18.32 Succession following abandonment of cropland according to (*a*) relay floristics, and (*b*) initial floristics as presented by Egler (1954).

a disturbance. This pattern appears to occur in much of the western boreal forest in Canada. For example, white spruce (*Picea glauca*), a species commonly associated with the climax community of the western mixedwood boreal forest, can often establish immediately following fires. The plants can remain as saplings for decades, when they may eventually become dominant species (Peters et al. 2006). Peters and his colleagues also show that in some boreal stands, establishment of spruce can occur decades after fire, supporting the idea of delayed regeneration. The fact that the same species of tree can show different patterns of regeneration in nearby forest stands is strong support for Gleason's individualistic concept, and soundly refutes Clements' notion that species replacement is clean and orderly.

Following Egler, Joseph Connell and Ralph Slatyer (1977) provided what remains the unifying concepts for the mechanisms of succession. They presented three models of succession: (1) facilitation, (2) tolerance, and (3) inhibition (fig. 18.33) This paper has stimulated substantial research, and we explore the models here.

Facilitation

The **facilitation model** proposes that many species may attempt to colonize newly available space but only certain species, with particular characteristics, are able to establish themselves. Species capable of colonizing new sites are called pioneer species. According to the facilitation model, pioneer species modify the environment in such a way that it becomes less suitable for themselves and more suitable for species characteristic of later successional stages. In other words, these early successional species facilitate colonization by later successional species. Early successional species disappear as they make the environment less suitable for themselves and more suitable for other species. Replacement of early successional species by later successional species continues in this way until resident species no longer facilitate colonization by other species. This final stage in a chain of facilitations and replacements is the climax community.

It is critical to understand that there is no "intent" on the part of early species to facilitate their own replacement. Instead, this facilitation is a consequence of their own niche requirements and the impacts of their growth on local conditions. For example, seeds that require high light levels to germinate will do well following a disturbance. However, the growth of those plants will reduce light levels, reducing their own ability to germinate underneath the maternal plants. Their growth would also facilitate the germination of plants that require low light levels for their seeds.

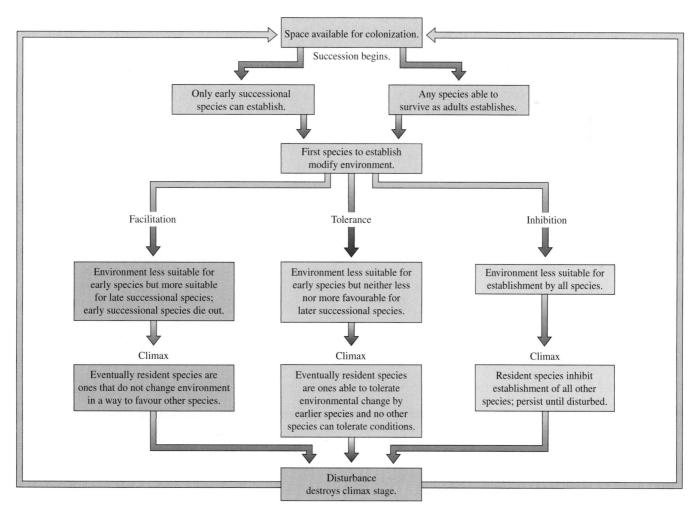

Figure 18.33 Alternative successional mechanisms (data from Connell and Slatyer 1977).

Tolerance

According to the **tolerance model**, the initial stages of colonization are not limited to a few pioneer species. Juveniles of species dominating at climax can be present at even the earliest stages of succession (e.g., initial floristics). In this model, species colonizing early in succession do not facilitate colonization by species characteristic of later successional stages. They do not modify the environment in a way that makes it more suitable for later successional species. Later successional species are simply those tolerant of environmental conditions created earlier in succession. The climax community is established when the list of tolerant species has been exhausted.

Inhibition

Like the tolerance model, the **inhibition model** assumes that any species that can survive in an area as an adult can colonize the area during the early stages of succession. However, the inhibition model proposes that the early occupants of an area modify the environment in a way that makes the area less suitable for both early and late successional species. Simply, early arrivals inhibit colonization by later arrivals. Later successional species can only invade an area if space is opened up by disturbance of early colonists. In this case, succession culminates in a community made up of long-lived, resistant species. The inhibition model assumes that late successional species come to dominate an area simply because they live a long time and resist damage by physical and biological factors.

Which of these models does the weight of evidence from nature support? As you will see in the following examples, most studies of succession support the facilitation model, the inhibition model, or some combination of the two.

Mechanisms of Succession Following Deglaciation

The complex mechanisms underlying succession were well demonstrated by the detailed studies of Chapin's research team (1994). They combined field observations, field experiments, and greenhouse experiments to explore the mechanisms underlying primary succession at Glacier Bay, Alaska. Like Morris and Wood, they found that no single factor or mechanism determines the pattern of primary succession at Glacier Bay, Alaska.

Figure 18.34 summarizes the complex influences of four successional stages on establishment and growth of spruce seedlings. During the pioneer stage, there is some inhibition of spruce germination. Any spruce seedlings that become established, however, have high survivorship but low growth rates. Spruce seedling growth rates and nitrogen supplies are increased somewhat during the *Dryas* stage. However, this facilitation during the *Dryas* stage is offset by poor germination and survivorship, along with increased seed predation and mortality.

Strong facilitation of spruce seedlings first occurs in the alder stage. During this stage, germination and survivorship remain low and seed mortality, root competition, and light competition are significant. However, these inhibitory effects are offset by increased soil organic matter, nitrogen, mycorrhizal activity, and growth rates. The net effect of alder on spruce seedlings is facilitation.

In the spruce stage, the net influence on spruce seedlings is inhibitory. Germination is high during the spruce stage but this is counterbalanced by several inhibitory effects. Growth rates and survivorship are low and nitrogen availability is reduced. In addition, seed predation and mortality, root competition, and light competition are all high.

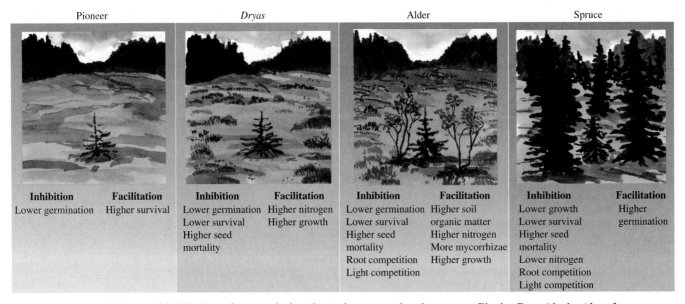

	Pioneer		*Dryas*		Alder		Spruce

Inhibition	**Facilitation**	**Inhibition**	**Facilitation**	**Inhibition**	**Facilitation**	**Inhibition**	**Facilitation**
Lower germination	Higher survival	Lower germination	Higher nitrogen	Lower germination	Higher soil	Lower growth	Higher
		Lower survival	Higher growth	Lower survival	organic matter	Lower survival	germination
		Higher seed		Higher seed	Higher nitrogen	Higher seed	
		mortality		mortality	More mycorrhizae	mortality	
				Root competition	Higher growth	Lower nitrogen	
				Light competition		Root competition	
						Light competition	

Figure 18.34   Inhibition and facilitation of spruce during the major successional stages at Glacier Bay, Alaska (data from Chapin et al. 1994).

These results remind us that nature is far more complex and subtle than models such as that proposed by Connell and Slatyer. However, even in other systems, we still find facilitation, inhibition, and tolerance to be useful categories for understanding the mechanisms of succession.

Successional Mechanisms in the Rocky Intertidal Zone

What mechanisms drive succession by algae and barnacles in the intertidal boulder fields studied by Sousa? The alternative mechanisms proposed by Sousa were those of Connell and Slatyer: facilitation, tolerance, and inhibition. Sousa used a series of experiments to test for the occurrence of these alternative mechanisms. He conducted his first experiments on 25 cm^2 plots on concrete blocks placed in the intertidal zone. In this experiment, Sousa explored the influence of *Ulva* on recruitment by later successional red algae by keeping *Ulva* out of four experimental plots and leaving four other control plots undisturbed. This experiment showed that *Ulva* strongly inhibits recruitment by red algae (fig. 18.35).

In a second set of experiments, Sousa studied the effects of the middle successional species *Gigartina leptorhynchos* and *Gelidium* on establishment of the late successional *Gigartina canaliculata*. He selectively removed middle successional species from a set of four experimental plots while simultaneously monitoring another set of four control plots. These experiments were conducted in 100 cm^2 areas on natural substrate, dominated by either *G. leptorhynchos* or *Gelidium*. When Sousa removed these middle successional species, the experimental plots were quickly reinvaded by *Ulva* and eventually by significantly higher densities of *G. canaliculata*, the late successional species. The effects of these successional algae support the inhibition model for succession.

The inhibition model of succession proposes that early successional species are more vulnerable to a variety of physical and biological factors causing mortality. If algal succession in the intertidal boulder fields studied by Sousa follows the inhibition model, then early successional species should be more vulnerable to various sources of mortality.

Sousa addressed the question of relative vulnerability of algal species with several experiments. In one, he studied the relative vulnerability of intertidal algae to physical stress, especially exposure to air, intense sunlight, and drying wind. He studied the vulnerabilities of the five dominant algal species in his study area by tagging 30 individuals of each species and monitoring their survivorship for two months during a period when low tide occurred during the afternoon, when air temperatures are highest. The results of this study show that the early successional species, *Ulva*, had lower survivorship than the middle or late successional species (fig. 18.36).

Sousa also designed several different field and laboratory experiments to explore differential vulnerability to herbivores. The results of all these experiments indicated that the early successional species *Ulva* is more vulnerable to herbivores

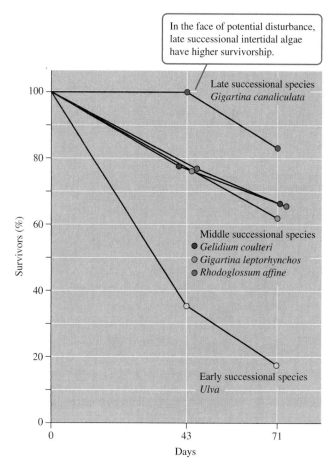

Figure 18.36   Survivorship of early, middle, and late successional species (data from Sousa 1979b).

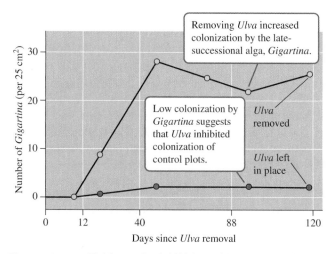

Figure 18.35   Evidence for inhibition of later successional species (data from Sousa 1979a).

than later successional species. These results and those of the several other manipulations performed by Sousa support the inhibition model of succession.

Some studies of intertidal succession, however, have demonstrated facilitation. Teresa Turner (1983) pointed out that the bulk of intertidal studies had supported the inhibition model and that the few studies documenting facilitation had shown that facilitation was not obligate. However, she went on to report a case of obligate facilitation during intertidal succession.

Turner described the successional sequence at her Oregon study site as follows. High waves during winter storms create open space in the lower intertidal zone. In May, these open areas are colonized by *Ulva*, the same early colonist of open areas in Sousa's study area, over 1,000 km south of Turner's study site. *Ulva* is eventually replaced by several middle successional species, especially the red algae *Rhodomela larix*, *Cryptosiphonia woodii*, and *Odonthalia floccosa*. Through this middle stage, the pattern of succession appears much as that in the intertidal boulder field studied by Sousa. However, in the lower intertidal area studied by Turner, the dominant late successional species was not an alga but a flowering plant, the surfgrass *Phyllospadix scouleri*.

Turner proposed that recruitment of *Phyllospadix* by seeds depends upon the presence of macroscopic algae. The seeds of *Phyllospadix* are large and bear two parallel, barbed projections. These projections hook and hold the seeds to attached algae. From this attached position, the seed germinates, first producing leaves and then roots by which the plant will anchor itself to the underlying rock. Once established, *Phyllospadix* spreads and consolidates space by vegetative growth.

Turner tested whether recruitment by *Phyllospadix* is facilitated by attached algae by clearing eight 0.25 m² plots of all attached algae. She then compared the number of new *Phyllospadix* seeds in these plots with the number in eight nearby control plots. The control plots remained undisturbed with their algal populations intact except that all *Phyllospadix* seeds were removed at the start of the study. Turner's control areas were dominated by the red alga *Rhodomela larix*, a species prominent in the middle successional stages in her study area and to which *Phyllospadix* seeds attach.

Turner set up and manipulated her study plots in September and then checked them the following March, after the period of seed dispersal. Over the fall and winter a brown alga, *Phaeostrophion irregulare*, colonized the removal plots but the blade-like form of this species apparently does not allow attachment by *Phyllospadix* seeds. When Turner checked the removal and control plots, she found a total of 48 seeds, 46 on the control plots (all attached to *Rhodomela*) and 2 on the removal plots (fig. 18.37). Both seeds on the removal plots were attached to two isolated branches of *Rhodomela* that had sprouted from remnant holdfasts.

During three years, Turner systematically searched an area of about 200 m² for *Phyllospadix* seeds and found a total

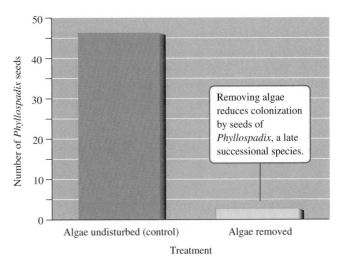

Figure 18.37 Evidence for facilitation of colonization by an intertidal plant, *Phyllospadix scouleri* (data from Turner 1983).

of 298. All were attached to algae. These data support the hypothesis that middle successional algae facilitate recruitment and establishment of *Phyllospadix* and that this facilitation is obligate. As a consequence of Turner's study and others, we can say that facilitation and inhibition occur during intertidal succession. Other research, which we review in the next example, has shown that facilitation and inhibition also occur during forest succession.

Successional Mechanisms in Forests

We now turn from succession in the marine intertidal zone, a place where succession occurs in a matter of a few years, to succession in boreal forests. Forest succession takes hundreds of years to complete and so cannot be observed directly within the period of a typical research project. Therefore, most research on the mechanisms driving succession in forests has focused on the earliest stages.

Mechanisms of Succession in a Boreal Forest

We have already described how succession in boreal forests often results in a transition from hardwood species such as aspen toward dominance by softwood species, such as spruce and fir. Why? We can also think of this issue from an evolutionary perspective. There is certainly no fitness benefit gained by aspen when it is replaced by spruce (rather than its own offspring), so why do aspen plants it let it happen? The answer may seem familiar. Specific life-history traits possessed by aspen allow it to perform some ecological processes extremely well (such as recovery following fire), but at the same time, it is unable to perform other ecological processes. Aspen, as it turns out, has seedlings that are shade-intolerant, while spruce has shade-tolerant seedlings (chapter 5). Aspen trees also produce very small seeds (for a tree) able to travel long distances. Following fire, sunlight

at the forest floor is very high. Any existing aspen trees will re-sprout, and high dispersal ability of aspen seeds also means there is a good probability of seeds in the area that will quickly germinate. These seedlings and sprouts grow rapidly, soon casting deep shade onto the forest floor. During this period of rapid aspen (and other pioneer species) growth, there has been increased opportunity for the more poorly dispersed seeds to enter the community. Seeds of spruce and other species are able to germinate and seedlings are able to establish themselves in this shade. Seeds of aspen and other species can not. As a result, beneath the canopy of aspen, you will find young spruce and fir trees, not aspen. In other words, aspen recovery following fire actually results in inhibition of further aspen recruitment. In contrast, the conditions following fire, including felled logs and other dead plants, can facilitate the establishment of the spruce seedlings.

At this point in the growth of the forest, there are two possible events. First, the aspen trees can grow to maturity, and then like all organisms, individual trees will eventually die. What happens in the forest? The small spruce trees have been growing beneath the aspen, and will quickly grow to fill the gap in the canopy made by the death of the aspen. Over time, this can lead to dominance by the softwood tree species. But as we have said before, succession is not inevitable, and communities do not develop or progress. This is very similar to our understanding of evolution. Evolution does not move toward a particular goal (does not optimize traits), but it does result in change. In the boreal system, one clear reminder that succession is not inevitable is the reality that fire can burn the aspen stand well before spruce has become dominant.

If the forest burns again, the floor is once again an excellent place for re-sprouting and regrowth by the aspen. If spruce seeds are still available, seedlings will once again establish. Depending upon the frequency of fires, regions of the boreal forest may never obtain significant softwood dominance (if fires are frequent), or if fires are rare, the hardwoods will be missing. Because of variation in fire frequency, and because of interspecific differences in life histories, the boreal forest is a mosaic of different communities, interspersed throughout the landscape. We will discuss more about the role of landscapes in ecology in chapter 21.

As complicated as the dynamics of boreal forest succession may seem, we have yet to discuss one critical issue. What role do the plants themselves have in influencing whether there is a fire? At first, this may seem a ridiculous idea—lightning strikes are the dominant form of fire initiation, and these are driven by weather patterns. As important as plants are, they do not control the weather. However, Meg Krawchuk, a graduate student at the University of Alberta, along with her colleagues in Alberta and the Canadian Forest Service in Ontario, has shown that both climate and forest composition can influence the probability of fire initiation in the boreal mixedwoods (Krawchuk et al. 2006; fig. 18.38). The research team analyzed an 11-year database of fire histories for 91,000 km^2

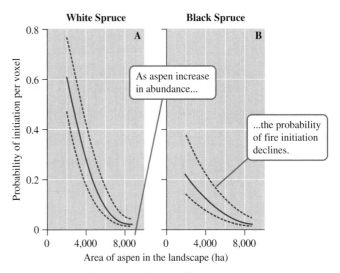

Figure 18.38 The probability of fire initiation changes as a function of forest composition in the boreal mixedwood forest (data from Krawchuk et al. 2006). The dashed lines represent confidence intervals around the mean regression line.

of mixedwood forest in central-eastern Alberta. The study area was divided into smaller units of approximately 10,000 hectares and one year in spatial and temporal dimensions, called *voxels*. For each voxel, the research team had detailed information on forest composition, meteorological records, and whether any fires occurred. Because of the comprehensive nature of their database, they were then able to construct statistical models that determined the relative contribution of both climate and forest composition on the probability of fire initiation. Their results were quite striking. As expected, fires were more likely to occur in areas that were hotter and drier than those that were cooler and wetter. However, even after accounting for this climate effect, there was a substantial impact of forest composition. Aspen inhibit fire initiation (fig. 18.38), with the probability of fire initiation decreasing as forests move from white or black spruce dominance toward that of aspen. In other words, aspen are inhibiting fires, while spruce are facilitating them.

The result may appear a bit surprising, particularly given that aspen can only successfully recruit following a disturbance! It may not be quite as hard to understand if we instead focus on the spruce. As we discussed previously, their seeds will establish soon after a fire, and in many cases cones can not even open unless a fire is present (lodgepole and jackpine also exhibit this interesting fire-dependence). It may make sense that spruce contains a variety of flammable resins and have a growth structure (fuels near the forest floor) that promotes fire, as fire itself is necessary for spruce to most efficiently complete its life cycle! The end result, however, is that spruce facilitates its own replacement, albeit temporary, by aspen. It is because of patterns like this that most ecologists do not believe in the concept of a single climax community, and instead see communities as dynamic.

In fact, in many communities ecologists do not necessarily view there being even a single climax community, but instead, depending upon local conditions and chance events, there may be alternative stable states. Under this model, a single piece of land can persist as alternative types of communities, depending upon some set of factors. This issue will be more fully explored in our discussion of landscape ecology, chapter 21.

In this and the previous two sections we have discussed community and ecosystem changes and the mechanisms producing those changes. In the next section, we consider a companion topic: community and ecosystem stability.

CONCEPT 18.5 REVIEW

1. What is the role of disturbance in the Connell and Slatyer succession model?
2. Suppose *Gigartina* had colonized the plots where Sousa had removed *Ulva* and where he had left *Ulva* in place at the same rates. This result would be consistent with which successional model?
3. How does spruce inhibit its own replacement by aspen?

ECOLOGICAL TOOLS AND APPROACHES

Using Repeat Photography to Detect Long-Term Change

While some graduate students look over their shoulders, Raymond Turner and Julio Betancourt of the U.S. Geological Survey carefully examine a photograph of a desert landscape taken about 100 years earlier. Their goal is to take another photograph of the same scene to document long-term change in the plant community. To do so they must return to the same location and take a photograph from exactly the same spot.

The larger landmarks such as hills and ridges will help them find the general location, but they need finer-scale reference points to locate the exact spot. Turner finally indicates a small boulder about 30 cm in diameter in the foreground, saying, "This should get us close and those small junipers will help orient the cameras." Betancourt agrees. The students are incredulous that someone should think that they can find a small boulder and two small trees after a century. However, long practice at repeat photography has taught Turner what can be found after a century in the arid lands of the American Southwest.

A field trip later takes the group to the general area of the site. After a careful search, Betancourt finds the remains of the two junipers. They have died sometime during the last half century. Next, Turner finds the small boulder. They use a few more landmarks to orient the camera and then position it within about 1 m of the spot from which the century-old photo was taken.

Using techniques such as these, Ray Turner and his colleagues have produced a very useful photographic record of vegetation changes from throughout the southwestern United States and northwestern Mexico. For instance, a series of repeat photographs beginning in 1907 document substantial vegetation change in MacDougal Crater in northern Sonora, Mexico (Turner 1990). The crater is about 137 m deep and was formed by a volcanic eruption about 200,000 years ago. MacDougal Crater is protected by its steep walls from livestock and other human impacts. This protection removes the possibility that observed changes in vegetation might be the result of human influences.

Figure 18.39 shows a series of photographs taken of MacDougal Crater from 1907 to 1984. While most changes depicted by these photographs are subtle, there is one obvious change in the lower left corner, the location of a population of saguaro cactus, *Carnegiea gigantea*. The saguaro, which appear as small stick figures in the photo, increase in number between the 1907 photograph and the 1959 photograph. Though difficult to see with the naked eye, the saguaros are clearly visible with a magnifying glass. Get a magnifying glass and compare the numbers of *Carnegiea* in the 1907 and 1959 photographs.

Close-up photos reveal even more detail. Figure 18.40 shows photographs taken in 1959, 1984, and 1998. The growing conditions were so poor in 1959 that the live saguaro in the photograph formed permanent constrictions on its stems that are still visible in the 1984 photograph. This saguaro died between 1984 and 1998. The dead shrubs in the 1984 photograph are the remains of creosote bushes, *Larrea tridentata*,

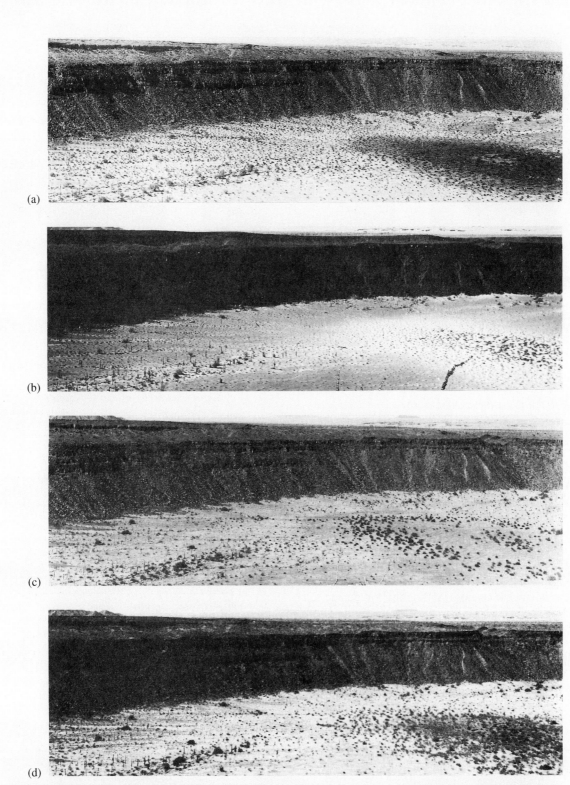

Figure 18.39 Detecting change in plant populations using repeat photography: (*a*) MacDougal Crater, Sonora, Mexico, in 1907, (*b*) in 1959, (*c*) in 1972, and (*d*) in 1984.

(a)   (b)   (c)

Figure 18.40 Details of plant population biology from repeat photography: (a) saguaro cactus in MacDougal Crater, Sonora, Mexico, in 1959, (b) same scene in 1984, and (c) in 1998. By 1998, the two cactus in the foreground of the 1959 photo had died and fallen.

that apparently died in response to the same drought that formed the constrictions on the saguaro stems.

Using repeat photographs, Turner was able to quantify changes in the plant community of MacDougal Crater. One of the changes he documented was a decrease in the population of *Larrea* and an increase in the population of saguaros (fig. 18.41). From 1907 to 1986 the number of *Larrea* in Turner's study area decreased from 103 to 48. Over the same interval, the number of saguaros increased from 38 to 159 in 1972 and then declined to 140 by 1986.

Some of the most important questions asked by ecologists concern changes in the distribution and abundance of organisms. Repeat photography is an easily overlooked tool that is helping to document changes in plant distribution and abundance during the past century.

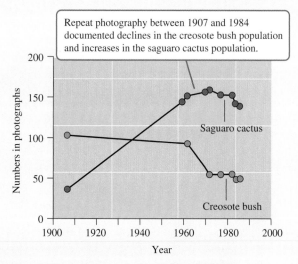

Figure 18.41 Changes in populations of creosote bushes and saguaro cactus determined by repeat photography (data from Turner 1990).

SUMMARY

Natural communities experience a diversity of disturbances, which can have immediate and prolonged impacts of community structure and ecological function. *Succession* is the gradual change in plant and animal communities in an area following disturbance or the creation of new substrate.

Primary succession occurs on newly exposed geological substrates not significantly modified by organisms. *Secondary succession* occurs in areas where disturbance destroys a community without destroying the soil. Succession may end with a climax community whose populations remain stable until

disrupted by disturbance. In other cases, communities may never recover, and instead persist in an alternative state.

18.1 Intermediate levels of disturbance promote higher diversity.

Joseph Connell (1975, 1978) proposed that high diversity is a consequence of continually changing conditions, not of competitive accommodation at equilibrium. He predicted that intermediate levels of disturbance would foster higher levels of diversity. At intermediate levels of disturbance, a wide array of species can colonize open habitats, but there is not enough time for the most effective competitors to exclude the other species. Wayne Sousa (1979a), who studied the effects of disturbance on the diversity of sessile marine algae and invertebrates growing on intertidal boulders, found support for the intermediate disturbance hypothesis. Diversity in prairie vegetation also appears to be higher in areas receiving intermediate levels of disturbance. Across many systems there is no widespread support for a general relationship between disturbance and diversity. Instead, observed patterns are due to interactions among life-history traits of the resident species, and the details of the disturbance they encounter.

18.2 Community stability may be due to lack of disturbance, or community resistance or resilience in the face of disturbance.

Ecologists generally define stability as the persistence of a community or ecosystem in the face of disturbance. Resistance is the ability of a community or ecosystem to maintain structure and/or function in the face of potential disturbance. The ability to bounce back after disturbance is called resilience. A resilient community or ecosystem may be completely disrupted by disturbance but quickly return to its former state. Studies of the Park Grass Experiment suggest that our perception of stability is affected by the scale of measurement. Studies in Sycamore Creek indicate that resilience is sometimes influenced by resource availability and that resistance may result from landscape-level phenomena. Some areas likely form alternative stable states depending upon the disturbance regime.

18.3 Community changes during succession include increases in species diversity and changes in species composition.

Primary forest succession around Glacier Bay may require about 1,500 years, while secondary forest succession on the Piedmont Plateau takes about 150 years. Meanwhile, succession in the boreal forest requires 100 to 200 years and succession within a desert stream occurs in less than two months. Over even longer time periods, some lakes will undergo succession, becoming fens, bogs, or forest. Despite the great differences in the time required, all these successional sequences show increased species diversity over time.

18.4 Ecosystem changes during succession include increases in biomass, primary production, respiration, and nutrient retention.

Succession at Glacier Bay produces changes in several ecosystem properties, including increased soil depth, organic content, and moisture. Over the same successional sequence, several soil properties show decreases, including soil bulk density and phosphorus concentration. During ecosystem development on lava flows in Hawaii, organic matter and nitrogen content of soils increased over the first 150,000 years and then declined by 1.4 years and 4.1 million years. Weatherable mineral phosphorus in soils was largely depleted on lava flows 20,000 years old. The percentage of soil phosphorus in refractory form made up the majority of phosphorus on lava flows 20,000 years old or older. Nitrogen losses from these ecosystems increased over time, while phosphorus losses decreased. Succession at the Hubbard Brook Experimental Forest increased nutrient retention by the forest ecosystem. Several ecosystem properties change predictably during succession in Sycamore Creek, Arizona, including biomass, primary production, respiration, and nitrogen retention.

18.5 Mechanisms that drive ecological succession include facilitation, tolerance, and inhibition.

Most studies of succession support the facilitation model, the inhibition model, or some combination of the two. Both facilitation and inhibition occur during intertidal succession. Facilitation and inhibition also occur during secondary and primary forest succession.

Succession is a very long process, and thus studies through time are critical. Ecologists use a diversity of techniques, including chronosequences, long-term longitudinal studies, and repeat photography.

REVIEW QUESTIONS

1. According to the intermediate disturbance hypothesis, both low and high levels of disturbance can reduce species diversity. Explain possible mechanisms producing this relationship. Include trade-offs between competitive and dispersal abilities in your discussion.

2. The dams that have been built on many rivers often stabilize river flow by increasing flows below the dam during droughts and decreasing the amount of flooding during periods of high rainfall. Explain how these stabilized flows can be considered as a disturbance. Using the intermediate disturbance hypothesis, predict how stabilized flows would affect the diversity of river organisms below reservoirs.

3. The successional studies in Sycamore Creek produced patterns of variation in diversity that differed significantly from those observed during primary succession at Glacier Bay or algal and barnacle succession in the intertidal zone. What may have been responsible for these different results? How might have differences in the longevity of species contributed to the different patterns observed by researchers? (Hint: Think about what we might observe in the other communities if they were studied for a longer period of time.)

4. The rapid succession shown by the Sycamore Creek ecosystem is impressive. How might natural selection influence the life cycles of the organisms living in Sycamore Creek? Imagine a creek that floods about twice per century. How quickly would you expect the community and ecosystem to recover following one of these rare floods? Explain your answer in terms of natural selection by flooding on the life cycles of organisms.

5. In the studies of mechanisms underlying succession, ecologists have found a great deal of evidence for both facilitation and inhibition. However, they have found little evidence for the tolerance model. Explain this lack of support for the tolerance model.

6. Ecological succession has been compared to the development of an organism and the climax community to a kind of superorganism. Which of the following graphs showing hypothetical distributions of species along an environmental gradient supports the superorganismic view of communities? How does the other graph support the individualistic view of species held by Gleason? (A, B, C, and D represent the distributions of species along an environmental gradient.)

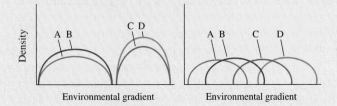

7. Species have come and gone in response to changing global climates during the history of the earth. Some of the mass extinctions of the past have resulted in the deaths of over 90% of existing species. What do these biological changes suggest about the long-term stability of the species composition of climax communities?

8. Succession seems to lead to predictable changes in community and ecosystem structure. Predict the characteristics of a frequently disturbed community/ecosystem versus a largely undisturbed community/ecosystem. What do your predictions suggest about a future biosphere increasingly disturbed by a growing human population? How does the intermediate disturbance hypothesis (see chapter 17) figure into your answer?

9. Describe the successional pathway of the boreal forest. Is there a climax community that is stable?

10. In lake succession, shallow lakes can be converted into bogs or fens, or into a drier terrestrial habitat such as a forest. What factors do you think are likely to influence the direction of succession for a given body of water?

PRODUCTION AND ENERGY FLOW

CHAPTER 19

CHAPTER CONCEPTS

19.1 Terrestrial primary production is generally limited by temperature and moisture.
Concept 19.1 Review
Ecology In Action: Interactions Across Community Boundaries

19.2 Aquatic primary production is generally limited by nutrient availability.
Concept 19.2 Review

19.3 Energy losses limit the number of trophic levels in ecosystems.
Concept 19.3 Review

19.4 A variety of species can influence rates of primary production in aquatic and terrestrial ecosystems.
Concept 19.4 Review
Ecological Tools and Approaches: Using Stable Isotope Analysis to Trace Energy Flow Through Ecosystems
Summary
Review Questions

501

The interactions between organisms and their environments are fuelled by complex fluxes and transformations of energy. The magnitude, speed, and efficiencies of these transformation are influenced by the traits of the organisms, as well as the supply of water, light, and a diversity of mineral nutrients. We can imagine a simple situation, with sunlight shining down on the canopy of a forest. Immediately, some of that light is reflected, some is converted to heat energy, and some is absorbed by chlorophyll. Included in these solar inputs will be infrared radiation. This too will be absorbed by the molecules in organisms, soil, and water, increasing their kinetic state and raising the temperature of the forest. Forest temperature affects the rate of biochemical reactions and transpiration by forest vegetation.

Forest plants use photosynthetically active solar radiation (chapter 7) to synthesize sugars. Some of this fixed energy supports a plant's own respiration; some supports growth and reproduction. Not all of the energy will likely be used immediately, and instead some of the fixed energy will be stored as nonstructural carbohydrates (e.g, starch) in roots, seeds, or fruits. Plants do not live alone, so it is likely that some fraction of the energy fixed by forest vegetation is consumed by herbivores. The remainder will end up as soil organic matter, consumed by detritivores. Energy fixed by forest vegetation powers bird flight through the forest canopy and fuels the muscle contractions of earthworms as they burrow through the forest soil. The forest vegetation is sunlight transformed, as are all the associated bacteria, fungi, and animals and all their activities (fig. 19.1).

We can view any biological community as a system that absorbs, transforms, and stores energy. In this view, physical, chemical, and biological structures and processes are inseparable; changes in one will impact the other. When we look at a forest (or coral reef, or grassland, etc.) in this way we view it as an *ecosystem*. An ecosystem is a biological community as well as all of the abiotic factors influencing that community. The term ecosystem and its definition were first proposed in

Figure 19.1 In most ecosystems, sunlight provides the ultimate source of energy to power all biological activity, including the movement of these deer and the growth of the plants upon which they feed.

1935 by the British ecologist Arthur Tansley. Tansley wrote: "Though the organisms may claim our primary interest . . . we cannot separate them from their special environment, with which they form one physical system. It is the [eco]systems so formed which, from the point of view of the ecologist, are the basic units of nature on the face of the earth." Though evolutionary biologists may disagree with aspects of this statement, the point Tansley is making is clear—the living and nonliving components of nature are intertwined. To study how a given location works, rather than learn details about a particular species, study the ecosystem.

Ecosystem ecologists study the flow of energy, water, and nutrients through and within ecosystems and, as suggested by Tansley, pay as much attention to physical and chemical processes as they do to biological ones. Some fundamental areas of interest for ecosystem ecologists are biomass production, energy flow, carbon storage, and nutrient cycling; all topics of great societal concern. In chapter 20 we discuss nutrient cycling. Here in chapter 19 we focus on energy capture and its flow through an ecosystem. We saw in chapter 7 how the photosynthetic machinery of plants uses solar energy to synthesize sugars. In chapter 7 we considered photosynthesis from the perspective of the individual plant. Here we step back from the biochemical and physiological details of photosynthesis and back even from the individual organism to look at photosynthesis at the level of the whole ecosystem.

Primary production is the fixation of energy by autotrophs in an ecosystem. In most systems this will be the plants, algae, and cyanobacteria, though other chemo-autotrophs are dominant in some ecosystems (chapter 3). The **rate of primary production (= primary productivity)** is the amount of energy fixed over some interval of time. Primary production can be further subdivided into gross and net primary production. **Gross primary production** is the total amount of energy fixed by all the autotrophs in the ecosystem, independent of any costs associated with either energy fixation or basal metabolism of the organisms. **Net primary production (NPP)** is the amount of energy left over after autotrophs have met their own energetic needs. NPP is gross primary production minus respiration by primary producers and it is the amount of energy available to the consumers in an ecosystem. In most systems, NPP is the difference between photosynthesis and respiration. Ecologists have measured primary production in a variety of ways but mainly as the rate of carbon uptake by primary producers or by the amount of biomass or oxygen produced.

Energy fixed through primary production eventually moves from the primary producers to other parts of the ecosystem. In chapter 7, we examined the biology of herbivores, detritivores, and carnivores. In chapters 14 and 15 we discussed the ecology of exploitation, and in chapter 17 we used food webs as a means of representing the trophic structure of communities. Ecosystem ecologists are also concerned with trophic networks, as the outcome of feeding is the movement of energy through an ecosystem. Ecosystem ecologists have simplified the trophic structure of ecosystems by typically arranging species into trophic levels based on the predominant

source of their nutrition (i.e., where they get their energy). A **trophic level** is a position in a food web and is determined by the number of transfers of energy from primary producers to that level. Primary producers occupy the first trophic level in ecosystems since they convert inorganic forms of energy, principally light, into biomass. Herbivores are often called primary consumers and occupy the second trophic level. Carnivores are secondary consumers and occupy the third trophic level. Carnivores that feed on other carnivores occupy a fourth trophic level. Since each trophic level may contain several species, in some cases hundreds, an ecosystem perspective simplifies trophic structure in comparison to trophic networks and food webs (fig. 19.2). Consuming members of all trophic levels are parasites and detritivores, which themselves are often prey for other consumers.

It is important to remember that such energetic descriptions of ecosystems are gross simplifications of what is actually found in natural systems. As we saw in chapter 17, food webs are complex, not simple cartoons in a textbook. Nonetheless, the trophic level approach is a useful means for organizing our understanding of energy flow within an ecosystem. Because of its importance and because rates of primary production vary substantially from one ecosystem to another, ecosystem ecologists study the factors controlling rates of primary production in ecosystems. In this chapter, we discuss the major patterns of variation in primary production in terrestrial and aquatic ecosystems and key experiments designed to determine the mechanisms producing those patterns. We then discuss how energy flows through different trophic levels, and how these processes can be altered through the activity of organisms within the ecosystem. We begin by describing patterns of primary production.

19.1   Patterns of Terrestrial Primary Production

Terrestrial primary production is generally limited by temperature and moisture. As we surveyed the major terrestrial biomes in chapter 2, you probably got a sense of the geographic variation in rates of primary production. Globally, the variables most highly correlated with variation in terrestrial primary production are *temperature* and *moisture*. Highest rates of terrestrial primary production occur under warm, moist conditions.

The importance of temperature and moisture to net primary productivity (NPP) can be seen in a map of primary productivity across Canada (fig. 19.3). This map was developed by Jing Chen and colleagues from the Canada Centre of Remote Sensing based at the University of Toronto (Liu et al. 2002). Describing patterns across a large geographic extent, such as the whole of Canada, cannot be done with traditional field samples. In chapter 1, we presented the idea that larger-scale sampling, often involving remote sensing done by satellites, has opened up an area of research unimaginable just a few decades ago. We discuss the importance of remote sensing to address questions in large-scale ecology in chapter 22, and we presented other examples in chapter 1. Here it is enough to recognize that the data collected by Chen and colleagues was acquired through image collection and analysis, rather than purely field sampling.

Across Canada, Chen and colleagues found NPP was 1.22 gigatonnes of carbon (Gt C) per year. However, this production was highly spatially variable. Seventy-eight percent of Canada's NPP occurs in the boreal forest, even though these forests only occupy 40% of the land base. Productivity is low in the northern regions of Canada, as well as along the Rocky Mountain and Pacific Coast mountain ranges in Alberta and British Columbia. This should not be surprising, as mountain peaks and high

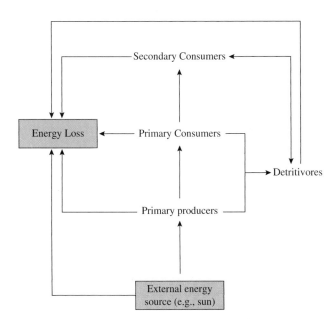

Figure 19.2   From an energetic perspective, food webs can be organized by understanding from where each trophic level obtains its energy. Presented here is a system containing three trophic levels.

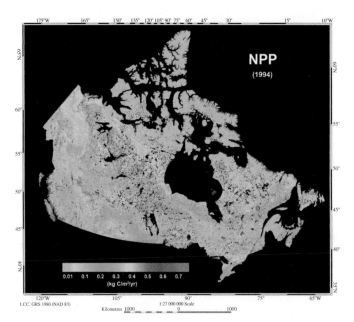

Figure 19.3   Estimated terrestrial net primary productivity across Canada.

latitudes are quite cold, which limits plant growth. However, there is another large area of low productivity found primarily in southern Alberta and Saskatchewan. This region is commonly referred to as Palliser's Triangle, named after John Palliser, who in early surveys of the region deemed this region unsuitable for agriculture. The farmers of western Canada would beg to differ. This region is the northern extent of the Great Plains, and with warm summers it has become a major region of wheat and canola production. In Palliser's Triangle, it is soil moisture, not temperature, that predominantly limits NPP.

Many scientists have conducted similar surveys of NPP for other countries and regions of the world. More often than not, temperature and moisture are regularly found to be strongly correlated with variation in NPP. Such patterns are so common that ecologists have developed a metric allowing them to more accurately understand the abiotic controls on NPP.

Actual Evapotranspiration and Terrestrial Primary Production

Michael Rosenzweig (1968) estimated the influence of moisture and temperature on rates of primary production by plotting the relationship between annual net primary productivity and annual actual evapotranspiration for many different terrestrial ecosystems. **Actual evapotranspiration (AET)** is the total amount of water that evaporates and transpires off a landscape during a given time period, measured in millimetres of water. Here, we are referring to AET over an entire

year. AET is affected by both temperature and precipitation. Ecosystems with the highest AET are those that are warm and receive large amounts of precipitation. Conversely, ecosystems tend to have low levels of AET either because they receive little precipitation, are very cold, or both. Both hot deserts and cold tundra exhibit low levels of AET.

Figure 19.4 shows Rosenzweig's plot of the positive relationship between net primary productivity and AET for different ecosystems. Tropical forests show the highest levels of both net primary productivity and AET. At the other end of the spectrum, hot, dry deserts and cold, dry tundra show the lowest levels of AET and NPP. Intermediate levels occur in temperate forests, temperate grasslands, woodlands, and high-elevation forests.

Rosenzweig's analysis is useful in explaining variation in primary productivity across the whole spectrum of terrestrial ecosystems, and figure 19.4 suggests that AET can explain a large amount of the variation in NPP across diverse terrestrial ecosystems. What controls variation in primary productivity within similar ecosystems, such as two different grasslands? O. E. Sala and his colleagues (1988) explored the factors controlling primary productivity in the central grassland region of the United States. Their study was based on data collected by the U.S. Department of Agriculture Soil Conservation Service at 9,498 sites. To make this large data set more manageable, the researchers grouped the sites into 100 representative study areas.

The study areas extended from Mississippi and Arkansas in the east to New Mexico and Montana in the west and from North Dakota to southern Texas. Primary productivity was highest in the eastern grassland study areas and lowest in the western study areas. This east–west variation corresponds to the westward changes from tall-grass prairie to short-grass prairie that we reviewed in chapter 2. Sala and his colleagues found that this east–west variation in primary productivity among grassland ecosystems correlated significantly with the amount of rainfall (fig. 19.5).

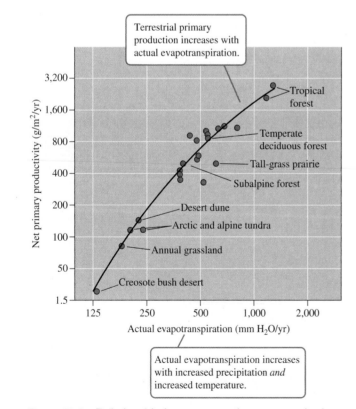

Figure 19.4 Relationship between actual evapotranspiration and net above-ground primary productivity in a series of terrestrial ecosystems (data from Rosenzweig 1968).

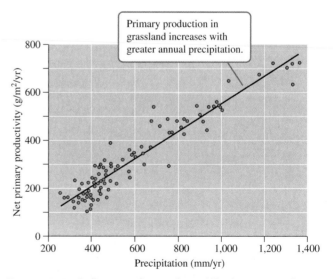

Figure 19.5 Influence of annual precipitation on net above-ground primary productivity in grasslands of central North America (data from Sala et al. 1988).

Compare the plot by Sala and his colleagues (fig. 19.5) with the one constructed by Rosenzweig (fig. 19.4). Both graphs have primary productivity plotted on the vertical axis as a dependent variable. However, while the Rosenzweig plot includes ecosystems where the growing season varies widely in temperature, ranging from tundra to tropical rain forest, the plot by Sala and his colleagues includes grasslands only. In addition, different variables are plotted on the horizontal axes of the two graphs. While Rosenzweig plotted actual evapotranspiration, which depends upon temperature and precipitation, Sala and his colleagues plotted precipitation only. Sala and his colleagues found that including temperature in their analysis did not improve their ability to predict net primary production. One potential cause for the lack of temperature effect in grasslands is that warm temperatures occur during the growing season at all of the study areas included by Sala and his colleagues, otherwise they would not be grasslands! An interesting question to think about is whether this can help us understand what might happen to productivity in grasslands in the face of atmospheric warming.

These researchers found strong correlations between AET or precipitation and rates of terrestrial primary productivity. However, their models are unable to completely explain the variation in primary productivity among the study ecosystems. For instance, in figure 19.4, ecosystems with annual AET levels of 500 to 600 mm of water showed annual rates of primary production ranging from 300 to 1,000 g per square metre! In figure 19.4, grassland ecosystems receiving 400 mm of annual precipitation had annual rates of primary production ranging from about 100 to 250 g per square metre. Some of this variation will be driven by differences in soil fertility.

Soil Fertility and Terrestrial Primary Productivity

Farmers have long known that adding fertilizers to soil can increase agricultural production. However, it was not until the nineteenth century that scientists began to quantify the influence of specific nutrients, such as nitrogen (N) or phosphorus (P), on rates of primary productivity. Justus Liebig (1840) pointed out that nutrient supplies often limit plant growth. He also suggested that nutrient limitation to plant growth could be traced to a single limiting nutrient. This hypothetical control of primary productivity by a single nutrient was later called Liebig's Law of the Minimum. We now know that Liebig's perspective, though remaining influential, is also too simplistic. Usually several factors, including a number of nutrients, simultaneously affect levels of terrestrial primary production in natural systems. However, Liebig's work led the way to a concept that remains true today: variation in soil fertility can affect rates of terrestrial primary production.

Liebig's work, and most practical experience prior to Liebig, concerned the productivity of agricultural ecosystems. Do nutrients influence rates of primary production in other ecosystems, such as the tundra or deserts, where human manipulation has been less prominent? Ecologists have demonstrated the significant influence of nutrients on terrestrial primary production through numerous experiments involving the addition of nutrients to natural ecosystems.

Ecologists have increased primary productivity through experimentation by adding nutrients to a wide variety of terrestrial ecosystems, including arctic tundra, alpine tundra, grasslands, deserts, and forests. For example, Gaius Shaver and Stuart Chapin (1986) studied the potential for nutrient limitation in arctic tundra. They added commercial fertilizer containing nitrogen, phosphorus, and potassium to several tundra ecosystems in Alaska. They made a single application of fertilizer to half of their experimental plots and two applications to the remaining experimental plots.

Shaver and Chapin measured NPP at their control and experimental sites two to four years after the first nutrient additions. Nutrient additions increased net primary production (by 23%–300%) at all of the study sites. The response to fertilization was substantial and clear at most study sites. Four years after the initial application of fertilizer, NPP on Kuparuk Ridge was twice as high on the fertilized plots compared to the unfertilized control plots (fig. 19.6).

You may recall from chapter 14 that a large number of Canadian researchers conducted a large-scale experiment manipulating resources, prey, and predators in an attempt to understand the linkages between plants, hares, and lynx in the Yukon. As part of this study, Roy Turkington, of the University of British Columbia, along with researchers from the University of Alberta, Nova Scotia Agricultural College, University of Toronto, and University of Sussex, analyzed the response of the boreal vegetation to long-term nutrient additions (Turkington et al. 1998). The research team added fertilizer to two large (1 km²) plots, and monitored plant growth in these, and two control plots, for six years. Fertilizer was added each year, always including nitrogen, and in some years P and K were also added. The response they found varied more than what we saw on Kuparuk Ridge.

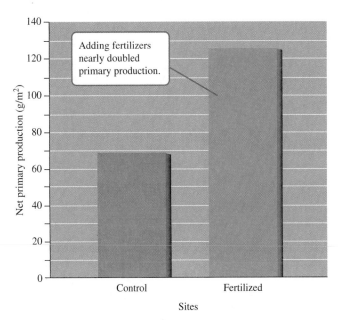

Figure 19.6   Effect of addition of nitrogen, phosphorus, and potassium on net above-ground primary production in arctic tundra (data from Shaver and Chapin 1986).

One of the great strengths of the Turkington study is that they did not simply measure total production in the plots, but instead measured each of the major plant groups separately. By doing this, they found a rather interesting story (fig. 19.7). Overall, the biomass of the system increased, indicating soil fertility did in fact limit primary production. However, the exact effects of adding nutrients varied among the different plant types. The fast growing herbaceous species responded very quickly, while effects on tree growth only became apparent later in the study. Additionally, several plant species showed a reduction in growth due to fertilization. How is this possible if the boreal forest is nutrient limited? The answer is straightforward: not all plant species are equally limited by mineral nutrients. Instead, species differ in the shape of their performance curves related to nitrogen, light, or any other resource that occupies a niche-axis (chapter 9). Some species will have traits that allow them to grow and reproduce under low-resource conditions, while others require higher resource levels. Under low nutrient conditions, stress-tolerant species (chapter 9) will do just fine. However, by adding nutrients, the stress has been removed, and now the faster growing and more competitively dominant species are able to take over. In other words, even though an ecosystem may be nutrient limited, this does not mean that all species increase in growth if nutrients are added. This is a critical point to understand about ecosystem ecology. The factors that limit NPP, or other ecosystem processes, do not necessarily limit the growth of all species within the ecosystem.

Experiments such as these have shown that despite the major influence of temperature and moisture on rates of primary production in terrestrial ecosystems, variation in nutrient availability can also have measurable influence. As we shall see in the next section, a variety of nutrients are often the main factors limiting primary production in aquatic ecosystems.

Species	Variable	Magnitude
Cryptogams		
Lichens	percent cover	−26%
Moss	percent cover	−25%
Herbaceous species		
Achillea millefolium	percent cover	+22%
	biomass	+33%
Anemone parviflora	percent cover	−124%
Epilobium angustifolium	percent cover	+176%
	biomass	+96%
Festuca altaica	percent cover	+173%
Lupinus arcticus	percent cover	−119%
	biomass	no change
Mertensia paniculata	percent cover	+192%
	biomass	+224%
Solidago multiradiata	percent cover	+66%
All species	percent cover	+18%
Dwarf shrubs		
Arctostaphylos uva-ursi	percent cover	−41%
Linnaea borealis	percent cover	−54%
Shrubs		
Betula glandulosa	percent cover	+37%
	biomass	no change
Salix glauca	growth rate	+146%
	biomass	no change
Trees		
Picea glauca	twig growth	+15%–50%
	cone crop	no change
	seed fall	no change

Figure 19.7 Addition of mineral nutrients to the boreal forest can have different effects on different plant species (data from Turkington et al. 1998).

ECOLOGY IN ACTION

Interactions Across Community Boundaries

In chapter 18, we observed there is growing acceptance that communities are not static entities, but instead are constantly in a state of flux due to natural and human-induced disturbances. More progressive conservation programs generally try to incorporate some aspect of disturbance into the management plan. Here we will explore a related topic. The factors that influence the growth and ecosystem dynamics of a particular community (e.g., forest, lake, etc.) include not only those factors internal to the community that we have discussed (biodiversity, consumers), but also can include processes in the surrounding communities. There is an increasing realization that to preserve a particular community will require an understanding of nutrient inputs from the surrounding area, as changes in primary production can have cascading effects on competitive interactions, herbivory, and community structure.

Many communities receive **allochthonous inputs** of nutrients and biomass. Allochthonous inputs are derived/created within a community external to the one in which they are eventually deposited. For example, the nutrients and energy contained in leaves that fall from trees into a stream are an allochthonous input into the stream ecosystem. Thomas Reimchen and his colleagues and students at the University of Victoria have studied the role that bears feeding upon salmon have on the primary production of coastal forests (fig. 19.8). Coastal forests tend to be nitrogen-limited, and thus they are likely very sensitive to any additions of nitrogen into the system. Large numbers of salmon spawn in the rivers throughout coastal British Columbia, and

(a)

(b)

Figure 19.8   (*a*) Feeding by bear on salmon results in large allochthonous inputs of nutrients into (*b*) the forest surrounding salmon spawning grounds.

enormous quantities of these fish are eaten by bears, wolves, and other animals. Let's look at this interaction from an ecosystem perspective. You have fish that leave the streams at a very small size and move into the ocean. There, they live for many years, growing to large size. The resources they use for this growth come from the marine environment. They then move back into freshwater, where they either are consumed by terrestrial animals or die in the streams. In either case, many of the nutrients they carried with them from the ocean are released onto land (as bear feces and urine or as decomposing fish carcasses), on the stream edges (for fish that die in the stream), or they are swept with the currents into the ocean. In other words, the exploitative interaction between bear and salmon causes an allochthonous input of nutrients into coastal forests. Reimchen and his group have been working to determine whether such nutrient inputs alter primary production of the forests.

As you will see in the Ecological Tools and Approaches section of this chapter, ecologists are able to use stable isotope analyses to determine the source of different nutrients in different trophic levels. We will not go into the details here; it is sufficient to understand that animal tissue that comes from marine habitats contains a higher percentage of ^{15}N than similar tissue from terrestrial habitats. As a result, if plants near the water's edge consume the nitrogen that comes from the ocean, rather than the nitrogen that is found on land, they should have more ^{15}N in their leaves than plants that do not have access to this marine-derived nitrogen source (MDN).

Reimchen and his colleagues (Mathewson et al. 2003) were able to test whether this was true by comparing ^{15}N levels of several riparian plant species collected in different positions along a stream, in each of two watersheds. Specifically, they recognized that some waterfalls are impenetrable barriers to salmon, such that plants below the waterfall would have access to MDN, while those above would not. When they measured the plant tissues, they found their

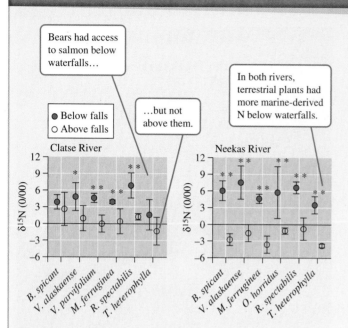

Figure 19.9 ^{15}N concentrations were higher for most plants species when they had access to marine-derived nitrogen (data from Mathewson et al. 2003).

hunch was correct; most species tested were enriched in ^{15}N below the waterfall but not above it (fig. 19.9). More importantly, for most samples more than 30% of the nitrogen in the plant tissues came from the ocean! To put it mildly, this is

strong evidence that the bear-salmon interaction has strong impacts on nutrient inputs on land. But does it actually alter the composition and production of these forests? Again, Mathewson and colleagues (2003) have data suggesting yes. Plants generally associated with low-N soils were much more abundant above the waterfalls, while plants associated with high-N soils were much more abundant below the falls. This is initial evidence to suggest that not only do salmon alter nitrogen levels, they can alter the outcome of interactions among plant species!

The idea that fish can influence plant competition and forest community composition has significant implications for any conservation program of the coastal forests. It suggests that if you want to preserve the forest, you also need to protect the fish that feed the forest. Without the large number of salmon that die each year and serve as fertilizer for the riparian forest, there will most certainly be a shift in plant species composition, and a loss of the ecosystem we are trying to preserve. Realization of this concept serves as the foundation of ecosystem-based management, where the goal is to protect an entire set of interactions, rather than specific communities. A recent success story is the Great Bear Rainforest, a newly protected, five-million acre expanse of coastal rainforest along the coast of British Columbia and Alaska. An understanding of the basic ecological principles occurring in nature serves as the foundation for such an ambitious conservation program.

CONCEPT 19.1 REVIEW

1. Why was precipitation alone, without temperature, sufficient to account for most of the variation in grassland net primary production across central North America?
2. How are the desert dune ecosystem and the arctic and alpine tundra ecosystems indicated in figure 19.4 the same?
3. Why do different species respond differently to nutrient addition, even if the net primary production is nutrient limited?

19.2 Patterns of Aquatic Primary Production

Aquatic primary production is generally limited by nutrient availability. Limnologists and oceanographers have measured rates of primary production and nutrient concentrations in many lakes, streams, coastal and oceanic study sites. These studies have produced one of the best documented patterns in the biosphere: the positive relationship between

nutrient availability and rate of primary production in aquatic ecosystems.

Patterns and Models

A quantitative relationship between phosphorus, an essential plant nutrient, and phytoplankton biomass was first described for a series of lakes in Japan (Hogetsu and Ichimura 1954, Ichimura 1956, Sakamoto 1966). The ecologists studying this relationship found a strong correspondence between total phosphorus and phytoplankton biomass.

Soon after the ecologists from Japan studied this relationship, there emerged two Canadian researchers who further explored nutrient controls on aquatic productivity. Peter Dillon, now an Industrial Research Chairholder at Trent University, and Frank Rigler, formerly of University of Toronto. Rigler was an exceptionally influential person in the field of aquatic ecology, and today the Society of Canadian Limnologists has named its highest award, the Frank H. Rigler Award, in his honour. Since his work with Rigler, Dillon has continued to study nutrient issues in lakes, influencing governmental policy through ecological studies. In their work, Dillon and Rigler (1974) described a similar positive relationship between phosphorus and phytoplankton biomass for lake ecosystems throughout the Northern Hemisphere (fig. 19.10)

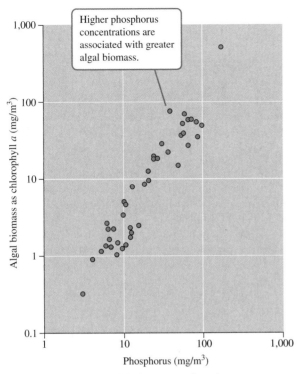

Figure 19.10   Relationship between phosphorus concentration and algal biomass in north temperate lakes (data from Dillon and Rigler 1974).

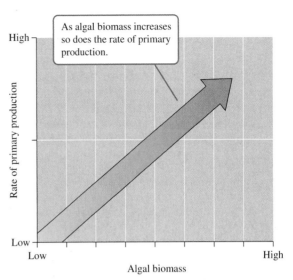

Figure 19.11   Relationship between algal biomass and rate of primary production in temperate zone lakes (data from Smith 1979).

as was found in Japan. Remarkably, the slopes of the lines describing the relationship between phosphorus and phytoplankton biomass for the Japanese and Canadian lakes were nearly identical.

The data from Japan and North America strongly support the hypothesis that nutrients, particularly phosphorus, control phytoplankton biomass in lake ecosystems. However, what is the relationship between phytoplankton biomass and the rate of primary production? This relationship was explored by Val Smith (1979) for 49 lakes of the north temperate zone. The data from these lakes showed a strong positive correlation between chlorophyll concentrations and photosynthetic rates (fig. 19.11). Smith also examined the relationship between total phosphorus concentration and photosynthetic rate directly.

Some of the most influential experiments in ecology are those in which Canadian ecologists moved beyond correlation, and began whole-lake experimental manipulations.

Whole-Lake Experiments on Primary Production

In chapter 1, we introduced some experiments on primary production conducted at the Experimental Lakes Area by David Schindler and his colleagues. Here we provide more information about the groundbreaking work by the team of ELA researchers. The Experimental Lakes Area was founded in northwestern Ontario, Canada, in 1968, as a place in which aquatic ecologists could manipulate whole-lake ecosystems (Mills and Schindler 1987, Findlay and Kasian 1987). For instance, ecologists

manipulated nutrient availability in a lake called Lake 226 using a vinyl curtain to divide Lake 226 into two 8-hectare basins, each containing about 500,000 m³ of water. Each half of Lake 226 was fertilized from 1973 to 1980. The researchers added a mixture of carbon in the form of sucrose and nitrate to one basin and carbon, nitrate, and phosphate to the other basin. They stopped fertilizing the lakes after 1980 and then studied the recovery of the Lake 226 ecosystem from 1981 to 1983.

Both sides of Lake 226 responded significantly to nutrient additions; however, the side that received phosphorus showed a much more dramatic increase on phytoplankton growth (fig. 1.6). Prior to the manipulation, Lake 226 supported about the same biomass of phytoplankton as two reference lakes (fig. 19.12). However, when experimenters began adding the nutrient mix that included phosphorus to Lake 226, phytoplankton biomass quickly surpassed that in the reference lakes (and in the other half of Lake 226 that did not receive phosphorus). Phytoplankton biomass remained elevated in Lake 226 until the experimenters stopped adding fertilizer at the end of 1980. Then, from 1981 to 1983 the phytoplankton biomass in Lake 226 declined significantly.

Correlations between phosphorus concentrations and primary productivity, as well as whole-lake experimental manipulation, support the generalization that nutrient availability controls primary productivity in freshwater ecosystems. Now, let's examine the evidence for this relationship in marine ecosystems.

Global Patterns of Marine Primary Production

The geographic distribution of net primary production in the sea indicates a positive influence of nutrient availability on rates of primary production. The highest rates of primary production by marine phytoplankton are generally concentrated

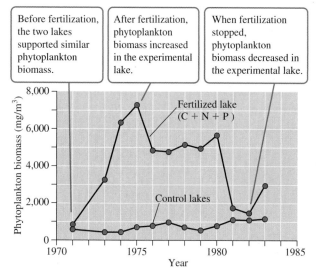

Before fertilization, the two lakes supported similar phytoplankton biomass.

After fertilization, phytoplankton biomass increased in the experimental lake.

When fertilization stopped, phytoplankton biomass decreased in the experimental lake.

Figure 19.12 A whole-lake experiment shows the effect of nutrient additions on average phytoplankton biomass (data from Findlay and Kasian 1987).

in areas with higher levels of nutrient availability along the margins of continents over continental shelves and in areas of upwelling (fig. 19.13). Along continental margins, nutrients are renewed by runoff from the land and by biological or physical disturbance of bottom sediments. As we saw in chapter 3, the upwelling that brings nutrient-laden water from the depths to the surface is concentrated along the west coasts of continents and around the continent of Antarctica, areas that appear dark red on figure 19.13a, indicating high to very high rates of primary production. Meanwhile, the central portions of the major oceans show low levels of nutrient availability and low rates of primary production. The main source of nutrient renewal in the surface waters of the open ocean is vertical mixing. Vertical mixing is generally blocked in open tropical oceans by a permanent thermocline. Consequently, the surface waters of open tropical oceans contain very low concentrations of nutrients and show some of the lowest rates of marine primary production.

Figure 19.13b highlights that NPP patterns are not static, but instead change over time. Between the periods of 1979–86 and 1997–2002, global marine NPP decreased 6%, attributed to changing temperatures and decreased atmospheric deposition of iron, an essential element for phytoplankton. However, these changes in NPP were not uniform. Oceans near coastlines, particularly near large urban centres, showed great increases in NPP. Decreases tended to be in the open oceans, particularly in northern latitudes.

What is the experimental evidence for nutrient limitation of marine primary production? There have been no experiments done in the marine environment that are equivalent to the whole-lake manipulations at the Experimental Lakes Area, in large part because ocean waters are interconnected. However, there have been a number of nutrient addition studies. For example, researchers were able to alter the nutrient inputs and concentrations in Himmerfjärden,

Sweden, a brackish water coastal inlet of the Baltic Sea with a surface area of 195 km^2 (see fig. 19.14; Granéli et al. 1990). (For comparison, the lake sub-basins manipulated in the whole-lake experiments were < 0.1 km^2.) The researchers combined this large-scale manipulation with small-scale culture flask experiments, providing critical data for understanding nutrient controls of production in a marine system. The results of this manipulative experiment indicate that nitrogen limitation of primary production can shift to phosphorus limitation by altering nitrogen:phosphorus ratios. Increasing additions of phosphorus to Himmerfjärden reinforced nitrogen limitation, while decreasing phosphorus additions and increasing nitrogen additions led to increased phosphorus limitation. There is also substantial evidence that marine productivity can, at certain times and in some locations, be influenced by dissolved iron concentrations (Moore et al. 2004).

Additional evidence for nutrient controls of marine primary production is found in the observation of increasing numbers and sizes of **dead zones** throughout the world's ocean. Dead zones are hypoxic areas (<2mg/L oxygen), typically a consequence of pollution, eutrophication, and high rates of decomposition, that are essentially devoid of marine life. Diaz and Rosenberg (2008) compiled the global distribution of oceanic dead zones, finding evidence for over 400 locations (Fig. 19.15). Paleoecological evidence suggests these areas are not typically recurring over long time scales; and instead the number of such zones reported has been doubling each decade for the last 50 years (Diaz and Rosenberg 2008). Dead zones are aggregated along coastlines, and predominantly in areas with high levels of human influence. Major causes appear to be nutrient runoff associated with fertilization of agricultural fields within the surrounding watershed, as well as general nutrient-rich pollution being dumped into oceans. One of the largest dead zones is in the Gulf of Mexico, near the outflow of the Mississippi river. The size of the dead zone varies as a function of rainfall and other climatic conditions, and can exceed 15,000 km^2 in some years (Rabalais et al. 2002). Though a number of local factors influence whether a dead zone forms and whether it persists, the general sequence of events is one we have discussed many times before. High rates of limiting nutrients enter the marine system. In response, certain groups of organisms (typically algae and cyanobacteria) grow rapidly, forming an algal bloom. As these organisms die, microbial activity associated with decomposition increases. The heterotrophic organisms have substantial food, and thus consume the available oxygen. An outcome of this process is an area with oxygen levels too low to support other marine life. It is a common, though unfortunate, example of how marine primary production can be limited by nutrients.

Ecologists have been able to identify major drivers governing primary production both on land and in aquatic systems. However, ecologists also recognize that such general causes do not always apply to specific locations. Dillon and Rigler suggested that limnologists pay attention to the

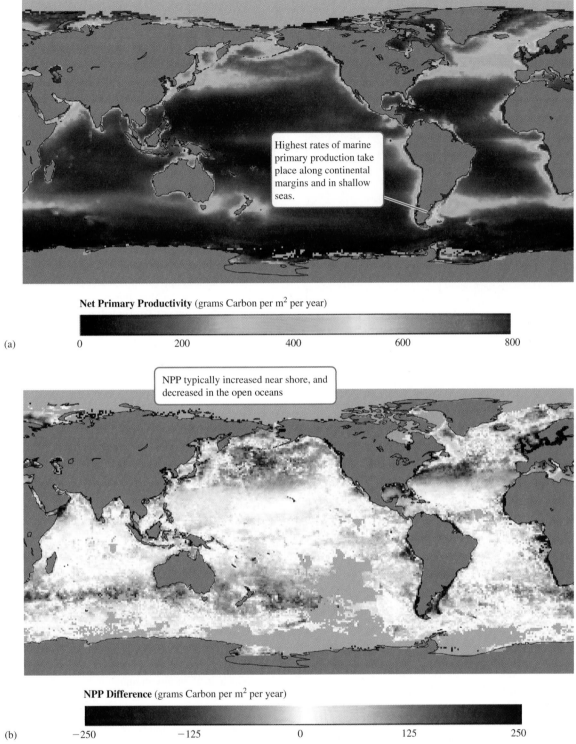

Figure 19.13   (*a*) Geographic variation in marine primary productivity (NASA Earth Observatory). (*b*) Change in ocean NPP between 1979–86 and 1997–2002 (data from NASA Earth Observatory).

scatter of points around lines showing a relationship between nutrient concentrations and phytoplankton biomass (F.A.O. 1972). We call that scatter of points residual variation (see appendix A). Residual variation is that proportion of variation not explained by the independent variable, in this case, by nutrient concentration. Dillon and Rigler suggested that

environmental factors besides nutrient availability significantly influence phytoplankton biomass. One of those factors is the intensity of predation on the zooplankton that feed on phytoplankton. As we shall see in the next section, consumers can influence rates of primary production in both terrestrial and aquatic ecosystems.

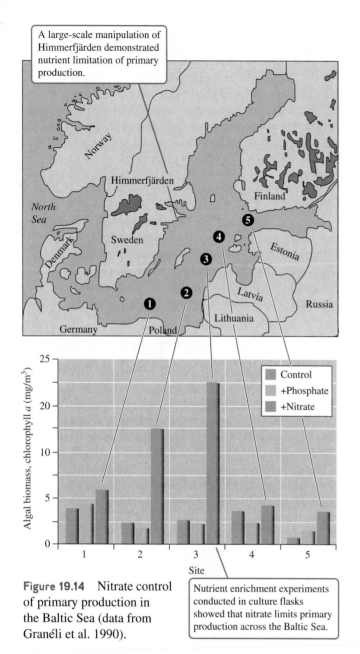

A large-scale manipulation of Himmerfjärden demonstrated nutrient limitation of primary production.

Nutrient enrichment experiments conducted in culture flasks showed that nitrate limits primary production across the Baltic Sea.

Figure 19.14 Nitrate control of primary production in the Baltic Sea (data from Granéli et al. 1990).

19.3 | Trophic Levels

Energy losses limit the number of trophic levels in ecosystems. An understanding of thermodynamics tells us that with each transfer or conversion of energy, some energy is lost. What are the consequences for these losses of energy in ecosystems? To answer this question, we first need to quantify the flow of energy through ecosystems. One of the very first ecologists to do this was Raymond Lindeman.

A Trophic-Dynamic View of Ecosystems

Raymond Lindeman (1942) published a revolutionary paper with the title, *The Trophic-Dynamic Aspect of Ecology*. In this paper, Lindeman articulated a view of ecosystems centred on energy fixation, storage, and flows that remains influential to this day. Like Tansley before him, Lindeman pointed out the difficulty and artificiality of separating organisms from their environment and promoted an ecosystem view of nature. Lindeman concluded that the ecosystem concept is fundamental to the study of **trophic dynamics**, which he defined as the transfer of energy from one part of an ecosystem to another. Viewing organisms as simply stored energy will not come easy for everyone, excepting of course science fiction fans who are accustomed to the idea of sentient energy. For the rest of us, we have spent substantial time focusing on the details of species interactions, based upon a deep understanding of natural history; putting that aside requires an alternative way of viewing organisms. Such an approach is critical to understanding energy flow in natural systems.

Lindeman suggested grouping organisms within an ecosystem into trophic levels: primary producers, primary consumers, secondary consumers, tertiary consumers, and so forth. In this scheme, each trophic level feeds on the one immediately below it, and is food for the level immediately above it. Energy enters the ecosystem as primary producers (typically) engage in photosynthesis and convert solar energy into biomass. As energy is transferred from one trophic level to another, energy is lost due to limited consumption and assimilation, respiration by consumers, and heat production. As a result of these losses, the quantity of energy in an ecosystem stored in any given trophic level decreases with each successive trophic level.

This loss of energy in unavoidable, and comes from basic physical properties described by the laws of thermodynamics (fig. 19.16). The first law is simple, and explains that energy can only be transformed, not created. For example, plants can convert sunlight into plant biomass, deer convert plant biomass (stored sunlight) into deer biomass (still stored sunlight), and wolves convert deer biomass into wolf biomass (yet again, stored sunlight). The only way for such a system to gain new energy is for it to come from the sun, and then be converted by the plants. But even there, energy is not being created. Instead, nuclear and chemical reactions occur in and on the sun, converting other forms of stored energy into solar radiation. Back on Earth, we find that the deer's growth can be limited by plant biomass, and the wolf's growth can be limited by the deer. In theory, one might expect the deer to be able to

CONCEPT 19.2 REVIEW

1. Suppose that when you add nitrogen to one half of a lake, you observe no change in phytoplankton biomass but when you add phosphorus to the other half of the lake, phytoplankton biomass more than doubles. What is the most likely explanation of your results?

2. Suppose you fertilize a region of an ocean with nitrogen only, another region with phosphorus only, and a third region with nitrogen plus phosphorus and observe no change in phytoplankton biomass. What is the most likely explanation of your results?

3. How does the global distribution of oceanic dead zones influence our understanding of what controls NPP in marine systems?

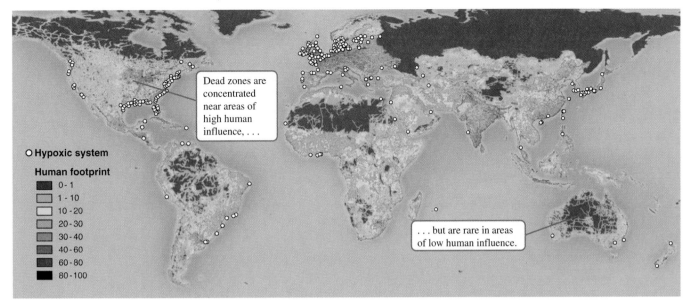

Figure 19.15   Over 400 eutrophication-associated dead zones have been identified around the world (from Diaz and Rosenberg 2008). Here, the extent of human influence on the land is reflected as the Human Footprint, reported as a percentage.

Two Laws of Thermodynamics Relevant to Ecology

1. The total amount of energy in the universe is constant. Thus, energy can only be transformed, and not created.

2. Heat energy will move from a warmer body to a cooler one. This is equivalent to the idea that entropy will tend to increase over time in a closed system.

Figure 19.16   There are several laws of thermodynamics critical to understanding physical processes. Two of those laws important for understanding the movement of energy among trophic levels are presented here.

eat 100% of the plants, and thus the amount of stored energy in the herbivore trophic level could be close to the amount fixed by the plants. This is where both the second law of thermodynamics and some basic ecology come in (fig. 19.16).

Entropy, the focus of the second law, is a complicated concept, generally better suited for physics class than ecology. However, the bit relevant here is that energy, in the form of heat, will move from warm areas (e.g., a deer) to cool areas (e.g., night sky). Where did that heat energy come from? It was the product of metabolism within the deer, and its movement into the atmosphere means that some of the plant energy the deer consumed is lost to the sky in the form of heat. It cannot become more deer, nor wolf, nor anything. All organisms warmer than ambient temperature suffer from this energy loss explained by the second law of thermodynamics. Actually, so too do inanimate objects, which is why my coffee is cooling as I write this. Though many organisms have a number of ways to minimize this loss of heat energy (chapter 5), some loss will still occur.

An additional reason why consumers do not contain 100% of the energy found in producers comes from our understanding of exploitation in chapter 14. Most of a plant a deer may encounter is inedible, and thus the energy stored within is inaccessible. Thick trunks and most woody structures, roots, and a variety of other plant parts simply are not edible by most organisms. Further, deer will never find all the plants in an ecosystem, and thus much of even the potentially edible plant biomass will never be consumed. Combined, these ecological realities limit the potential size of the consumer trophic level, even were energy transfer to be completely efficient. The same thing happens as we move from consumers to predators; deer to wolf. In chapter 14, we talked about how refugia allow some prey to avoid predation. In an ecosystem context, this means that much of the consumer biomass is unavailable for conversion into predator biomass.

Because higher trophic levels cannot create new energy, lose heat energy, and cannot find and consume all potential food, there is an inevitable pyramid-shaped distribution of energy among trophic levels in *every* natural ecosystem. Lindeman called these **trophic pyramids** Eltonian pyramids, since Charles Elton (1927) was the first to propose that the distribution of energy among trophic levels is shaped like a pyramid. Both terms are regularly used by ecologists.

Figure 19.17 shows the distribution of annual primary production among trophic levels in Cedar Bog Lake and in Lake Mendota, Wisconsin. As predicted by Elton, the distribution of energy across trophic levels in both lakes is shaped like a pyramid. Note, too, that both lakes have fairly few trophic levels; Lake Mendota includes four trophic levels, while Cedar Bog Lake includes just three. We will come back to the topic of limits to the number of trophic levels found within an ecosystem shortly.

Following Lindeman's pioneering work, many other ecologists studied energy flow within ecosystems. One of

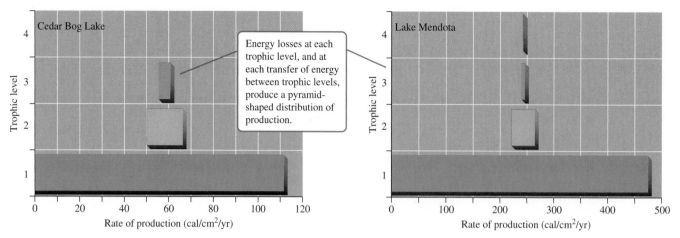

Figure 19.17   Annual production by trophic level in two lakes (data from Lindeman 1942).

the most comprehensive of these later studies focused on the Hubbard Brook Experimental Forest we first discussed in chapter 18.

Energy Flow in a Temperate Deciduous Forest

James Gosz and his colleagues (1978) studied energy flow in the Hubbard Brook Experimental Forest, which is managed for research by the U.S. Forest Service. They concentrated their efforts on a stream catchment called watershed 6, which was left undisturbed so it could serve as a control for experimental studies on other stream catchments. The energy flow in the Hubbard Brook Experimental Forest was quantified as kilocalories (kcal) per square metre per year. The results of the analysis are shown in figure 19.18.

First, you will notice that figure 19.18 does not look anything like the trophic pyramids presented in figure 19.17! The pyramids are useful when one is trying to provide a rough snapshot of the energy distributions within an ecosystem. The energy budget that Gosz and colleagues provide is a much more detailed examination of where all of the energy that enters the ecosystem goes. Both approaches are useful, though for answering slightly different questions.

Let's examine the distribution of organic matter among the major components of the Hubbard Brook ecosystem. The largest single pool of energy in the forest, 122,442 kcal/m^2, occurred as dead organic matter. Most of the dead organic matter, 88,120 kcal/m^2, was organic matter in the upper 36 cm of soil. The remainder, 34,322 kcal/m^2, occurred as plant litter on the forest floor. Total living-plant biomass amounted to 71,420 kcal/m^2, of which 59,696 kcal/m^2 was stored in above-ground biomass and 11,724 kcal/m^2 as below-ground biomass.

The total standing stock of energy occurring as dead organic matter and living-plant biomass was 193,862 kcal/m^2. This estimate by Gosz and his colleagues dwarfs the energy stored in all other portions of the ecosystem. For instance, the

energetic content of a caterpillar population during a severe population outbreak amounted to only 160 kcal/m^2 (compared to the greater than 190,000 kcal/m^2 of plant biomass)! However, even this amount far exceeds the total energetic content of all vertebrate biomass. The researchers estimated that the total energetic content of the most numerous vertebrates, including chipmunks, mice, shrews, salamanders, and birds, amounted to less than 1 kcal/m^2. In other words, in this fairly typical ecosystem, animals make up an amazingly small fraction of the biomass, and in terms of energetic abundance, vertebrates are essentially absent. This is again a critical point to understand about ecosystems and energy flow: the study of energy in ecosystems is often the same as the study of the plants and the microbes that feed upon organic matter. Now that we have inventoried the major standing stocks of energy, let's look at energy flow through the Hubbard Brook Forest.

The main source of energy for the ecosystem is solar radiation. The total input of solar energy to the study area during the growing season was estimated to be 480,000 kcal/m^2 (expressed as 100% in figure 19.18). Of this total energy input, 15% was reflected, 41% was converted to heat, and 42% was absorbed during evapotranspiration. About 2.2% of the solar input was fixed by plants as gross primary production. Plant respiration accounted for 1.2%, leaving about 1% as net primary production. In other words, only about 1% of the solar input to the Hubbard Brook ecosystem was available to the herbivores and detritivores that made up the second trophic level.

About 1,199 kcal/m^2 of NPP in the Hubbard Brook Forest went into plant growth. Herbivores consumed only about 41 kcal/m^2, approximately 1% of NPP. Most of the energy available to consumers, approximately 3,037 kcal/m^2, occurred as surface litter fall. About 150 kcal/m^2 of the litter fall was stored as organic matter on the forest floor. The remainder was used by consumers. An additional source of detritus, amounting to 437 kcal/m^2, occurred below ground as root exudate and litter. Most of the energy consumed by grazers and detritivores, approximately 3,353 kcal/m^2, was lost as consumer respiration.

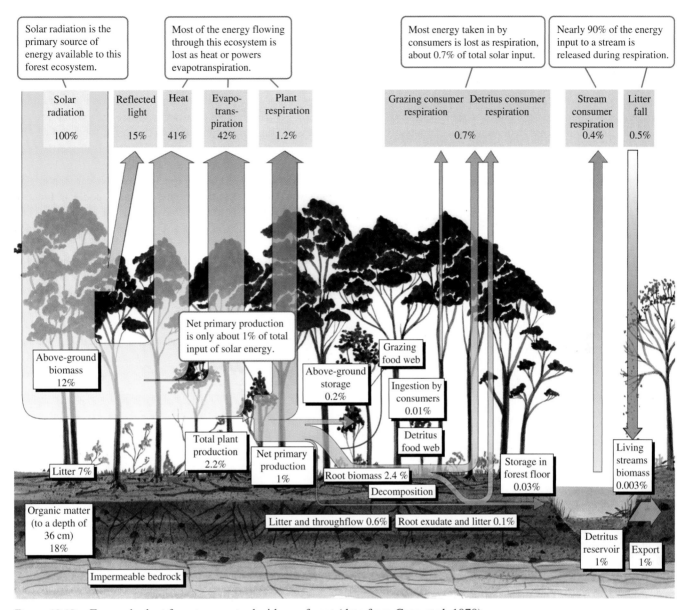

Solar radiation is the primary source of energy available to this forest ecosystem.

Most of the energy flowing through this ecosystem is lost as heat or powers evapotranspiration.

Most energy taken in by consumers is lost as respiration, about 0.7% of total solar input.

Nearly 90% of the energy input to a stream is released during respiration.

| Solar radiation | Reflected light | Heat | Evapo-trans-piration | Plant respiration | | Grazing consumer respiration | Detritus consumer respiration | | Stream consumer respiration | Litter fall |
| 100% | 15% | 41% | 42% | 1.2% | | 0.7% | | | 0.4% | 0.5% |

Net primary production is only about 1% of total input of solar energy.

Above-ground biomass 12%

Grazing food web

Above-ground storage 0.2%

Ingestion by consumers 0.01%

Detritus food web

Total plant production 2.2%

Net primary production 1%

Root biomass 2.4 %

Decomposition

Storage in forest floor 0.03%

Living streams biomass 0.003%

Litter 7%

Organic matter (to a depth of 36 cm) 18%

Litter and throughflow 0.6% Root exudate and litter 0.1%

Detritus reservoir 1%

Export 1%

Impermeable bedrock

Figure 19.18 Energy budget for a temperate deciduous forest (data from Gosz et al. 1978).

Limits to the Number of Trophic Levels

One consistent feature of ecosystems across the planet is that all tend to have relatively few trophic levels, with three to five being typical. Some ecosystems will have more (seven to eight) but these tend to be rare. Why don't we tend to find systems with 10, 15, or even 25 trophic levels? Clear answers to this question still elude ecologists, though there are several hypotheses that have been put forward. Many hypotheses focus on energy loss, and that is where we begin.

The energy budget constructed by Gosz and his colleagues gives us a basis for understanding how energy loss can limit the number of trophic levels in natural ecosystems. Net primary production in the Hubbard Brook Forest ecosystem was less than 1% of the input of solar energy. In other words, over 99% of the solar energy available to the Hubbard Brook was unavailable for use by a second trophic level. Of the NPP available to consumers, approximately 96% is lost as

consumer respiration. This leaves very little for a third trophic level. Such losses with each transfer of energy in a food chain will limit the number of trophic levels that can be supported in an ecosystem. As these losses between trophic levels accumulate, eventually there will be insufficient energy remaining to support a viable population of an even higher trophic level.

Although energy limitations may be an important factor restricting the number of trophic levels in an ecosystem, it is not the only hypothesis that has been put forward. Let us consider what a 5th or 6th or 10th trophic level actually represents. These would be organisms that primarily feed upon high level predators, not simply additional types of predators that feed upon primary consumers. These would be animals that hunt great white sharks, eagles, and cheetah. You may see some problems here. First, the prey for these hypothetical predators are going to be in extremely low abundance (the trophic pyramid is still there!). At some point, natural selection

operating through optimal foraging (chapter 5) would likely favour choosing more abundant prey at lower trophic levels. Why spend all that time hunting a rare, hard-to-catch prey if more abundant and less dangerous prey exist? A third issue may be an evolutionary constraint. Though we might imagine body designs that would catch these top predators, that does not mean that any putative ancestor possessed the raw genetic material that would allow for evolution of those traits.

Energy limitation can play a big role in determining the trophic structure of ecosystems. As we see next, a number of biotic processes can also be important.

CONCEPT 19.3 REVIEW

1. If we assume that the Hubbard Brook Forest ecosystem studied by James Gosz and colleagues is subject to a trophic cascade (top-down control), can we explain why herbivores consume such a small amount of plant net primary production?
2. What are the relative amounts of net primary production consumed by herbivores versus plant litter-feeders (detritivores) living on the forest floor?
3. How do the laws of thermodynamics influence the number of trophic levels found in an ecosystem?

19.4 Biotic Influences

A variety of species can influence rates of primary production in aquatic and terrestrial ecosystems. In the first section of chapter 19, we emphasized the effects of physical and chemical factors on rates of primary production. More recently, ecologists have discovered that primary production is also affected by a diversity of species interactions as well. For example, in chapter 16 we discussed how the genotypic and species diversity within a community enhanced primary production. Here, we focus on the impacts of herbivory and predation.

Ecologists refer to the influences of physical and chemical factors on ecosystems, such as temperature and nutrients, as **bottom-up controls**. The influences of consumers on ecosystems are known as **top-down controls**. In the previous two sections, we discussed bottom-up controls on rates of primary production. Here we discuss top-down control.

Piscivores, Planktivores, and Lake Primary Production

Stephen Carpenter, James Kitchell, and James Hodgson (1985) proposed that while nutrient inputs determine the potential rate of primary production in a lake, piscivorous and planktivorous fish can cause significant deviations from

potential primary production. In support of their hypothesis, Carpenter and his colleagues (1991) cited a negative correlation between zooplankton size, an indication of grazing intensity, and primary production.

Carpenter and Kitchell (1988) proposed that the influences of consumers on lake primary production can extend to other levels throughout food webs. Since they visualized the effects of consumers coming from the top of food webs to the base, they called these effects on ecosystem properties trophic cascades. The trophic cascade hypothesis (fig. 19.19) is very similar to the keystone species hypothesis (chapter 17). However, notice that the trophic cascade model is focused on the effects of consumers on ecosystem processes, such as primary production, and not on their effects on species diversity.

Carpenter and Kitchell (1993) interpreted the trophic cascade in their study of lakes as follows: Piscivores, such as largemouth bass, feed on planktivorous fish and invertebrates. Because of their influence on planktivorous fish, largemouth bass indirectly affect populations of zooplankton. By reducing populations of planktivorous fish, largemouth bass reduce

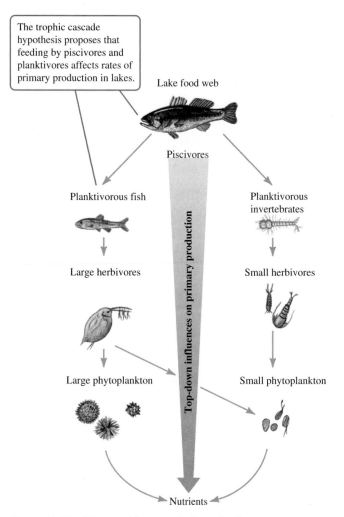

The trophic cascade hypothesis proposes that feeding by piscivores and planktivores affects rates of primary production in lakes.

Figure 19.19   The trophic cascade hypothesis.

feeding pressure on zooplankton and zooplankton populations. Large-bodied zooplankton, the preferred prey of size-selective planktivorous fish (see chapter 7), soon dominate the zooplankton community. A dense population of large zooplankton reduces phytoplankton biomass and the rate of primary production. This interpretation of the trophic cascade is consistent with the negative correlation between zooplankton body size and primary production reported by Carpenter and his research team.

Carpenter and Kitchell tested their trophic cascade model by manipulating the fish communities in two lakes and using a third lake as a control. Figure 19.20 shows the overall design of their experiment. Two of the lakes contained substantial populations of largemouth bass. A third lake had no bass, due to occasional winterkill, but contained an abundance of planktivorous minnows. The researchers removed 90% of the largemouth bass from one experimental lake and put them into the other. They simultaneously removed 90% of the planktivorous minnows from the second lake and introduced them to the first. They left a reference lake unmanipulated as a control.

The responses of the study lakes to the experimental manipulations support the trophic cascade hypothesis (fig. 19.20). Reducing the planktivorous fish population led to reduced rates of primary production. In the absence of planktivorous minnows, the predaceous invertebrate *Chaoborus* became more numerous. *Chaoborus* fed heavily upon the smaller herbivorous zooplankton, and the herbivorous zooplankton assemblage shifted in dominance from small to large species. In the presence of abundant, large herbivorous zooplankton, phytoplankton biomass and rate of primary production declined.

Adding planktivorous minnows produced a complex ecological response. Increasing the planktivorous fish population led to increased rates of primary production. However, though the researchers increased the population of planktivorous fish in this experimental lake, they did so in an unintended way. Despite the best efforts of the researchers, a few bass remained. So, by introducing a large number of minnows they basically fed the remaining bass. An increased food supply combined with reduced population density induced a strong numerical response by the bass population (see chapter 11). The manipulation increased the reproductive rate of the remaining largemouth bass 50-fold, producing an abundance of young largemouth bass that feed voraciously on zooplankton.

The lake ecosystem responded to the increased biomass of planktivorous fish (young largemouth bass) as predicted at the

Experimental manipulations

Reduced piscivore (bass) biomass
Increased planktivore biomass

Increased piscivore (bass) biomass
Decreased planktivore biomass

Decreased herbivores
Increased phytoplankton

Responses

Increased herbivores
Decreased phytoplankton

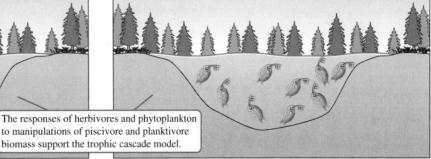

The responses of herbivores and phytoplankton to manipulations of piscivore and planktivore biomass support the trophic cascade model.

Figure 19.20 Experimental manipulations of ponds and responses.

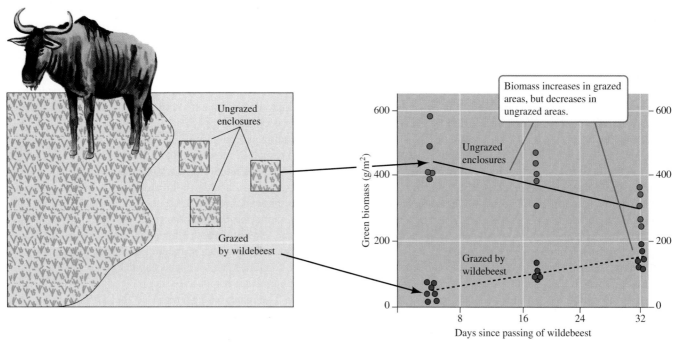

Figure 19.21   Growth response by grasses grazed by wildebeest (data from McNaughton 1976).

outset of the experiment. The biomass of zooplankton decreased sharply, the average size of herbivorous zooplankton decreased, and phytoplankton biomass and primary production increased.

The results of these whole-lake experiments show that the trophic activities of a few species can have large effects on ecosystem processes. However, the majority of trophic cascades described by ecologists have been in aquatic ecosystems with algae as primary producers. This pattern prompted Donald Strong (1992) to ask, "Are trophic cascades all wet?" Strong suggested that trophic cascades most likely occur in ecosystems of lower species diversity and reduced spatial and temporal complexity. These are characteristics of many aquatic ecosystems. Despite these restrictions, consumers have significant effects on rates of primary production in some terrestrial ecosystems; one of those is the Serengeti grassland ecosystem.

Grazing by Large Mammals and Primary Productivity on the Serengeti

The Serengeti-Mara, a 25,000 km^2 grassland ecosystem that straddles the border between Tanzania and Kenya, is one of the last ecosystems on earth where great numbers of large mammals still roam freely. Sam McNaughton (1985) reported estimated densities of the major grazers in the Serengeti that included 1.4 million wildebeest, *Connochaetes taurinus albujubatus;* 600,000 Thomson's gazelle, *Gazella thomsonii;* 200,000 zebra, *Equus quagga;* 52,000 buffalo, *Syncerus caffer;* 60,000 topi, *Damaliscus korrigum;* and large numbers of 20 additional grazing mammals. McNaughton estimated that these grazers consume an average of 66% of the annual above-ground primary productivity on the Serengeti. In light of this estimate, the potential for consumer influences on primary productivity seems very high.

Over two decades of research on the Serengeti ecosystem in Tanzania led McNaughton to appreciate the complex interrelations of abiotic and biotic factors there. For instance, both soil fertility and rainfall stimulate plant production and the distributions of grazing mammals. However, grazing mammals also affect water balance, soil fertility, and plant production.

As you might predict, the rate of primary production on the Serengeti is positively correlated with the quantity of rainfall. However, McNaughton (1976) also found that grazing can increase above-ground primary production. Similar to the methods used by Jefferies in chapter 15, McNaughton fenced in some areas in the western Serengeti to explore the influence of herbivores on production. The migrating wildebeest that flooded into the study site grazed intensively for four days, consuming approximately 85% of plant biomass. During the month after the wildebeest left the study area, biomass within the enclosures decreased, while the biomass of vegetation outside the enclosures increased (fig. 19.21). Similar to the geese in arctic wetlands, these mammals caused compensatory growth of many grass species. Compensatory growth was likely caused by reduced self-shading and improved water balance due to reduced leaf area and reduced respiration. Compensatory growth was highest at intermediate grazing intensities (fig. 19.22). Apparently, light grazing is insufficient to produce compensatory growth and very heavy grazing reduces the capacity of the plant to recover.

What McNaughton and his colleagues described is essentially a trophic cascade in a terrestrial environment where the feeding activities of consumers have a major influence on ecosystem properties. The Serengeti is now an exceptional terrestrial ecosystem but it was not always so. As we saw in chapter 2, the extensive grasslands of North America and Eurasia were

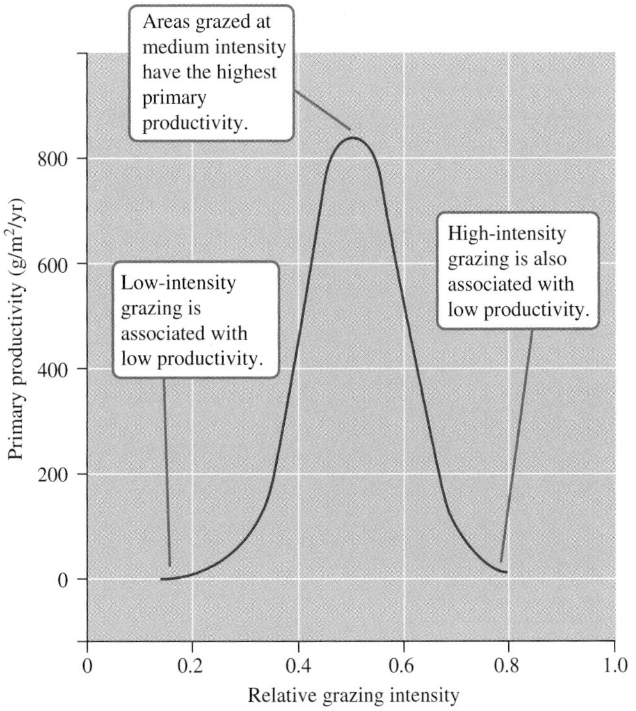

Figure 19.22 Grazing intensity and primary productivity of Serengeti grassland (data from McNaughton 1985).

also once populated by vast herds of mammalian grazers. Historians estimate that the population of North American bison in the middle of the nineteenth century numbered up to 60 million. Such a dense concentration of grazers must have had significant influences upon the grassland ecosystems of which they were part. It appears that terrestrial consumers, as well as the aquatic ones studied by Carpenter and Kitchell, can have important influences on primary production.

In the Ecological Tools section we review how ecologists can use stable isotope analyses to determine the trophic position of a species within an ecosystem.

CONCEPT 19.4 REVIEW

1. Since increased phytoplankton biomass decreases water clarity in lakes, how should fishing pressure on the bass population in a lake ecosystem, such as that pictured in figure 19.17, impact water clarity?
2. Why is it more difficult to obtain evidence for trophic cascades in terrestrial ecosystems, as opposed to lakes?

ECOLOGICAL TOOLS AND APPROACHES

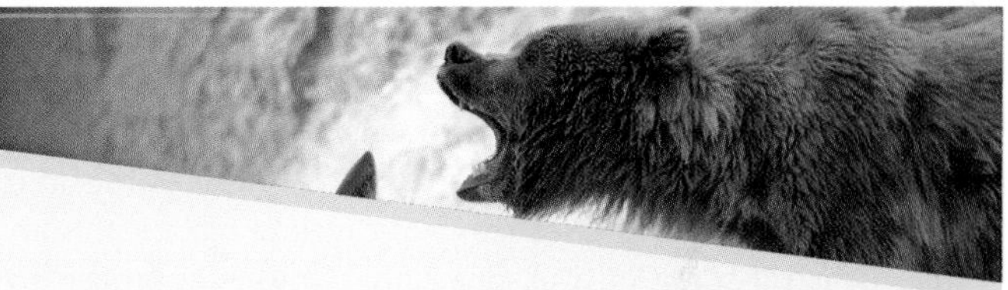

Using Stable Isotope Analysis to Trace Energy Flow Through Ecosystems

How do ecologists study the flow of energy through ecosystems? First, they identify the organisms that make up the biological part of the ecosystem. Next, they determine who eats who. They may identify consumers down to species or assign them broader taxonomic categories (e.g., insectivorous birds). Next, they assign organisms to trophic levels and determine (1) the biomass of each trophic level, (2) the rate of energy or food intake by each trophic level, (3) the rate of energy assimilation, (4) the rate of respiration, and (5) rates of loss of energy to predators, parasites, etc. Finally, ecologists combine their information on individual trophic levels to construct a trophic pyramid such as that constructed by Lindeman (see fig.19.17) or an energy flow diagram such as that by Gosz and his colleagues (see fig. 19.18).

One of the fundamental steps in constructing a trophic pyramid or energy flow diagram is assigning organisms to trophic levels. While this task may sound easy it is not. Most assignments are based on studies of feeding habits. If food items are easily identified and feeding habits are well studied and do not change significantly over time or from place to place, you may accurately identify feeding relations and assign organisms to trophic levels. However, if feeding habits are variable or if food items are difficult to identify, it may be difficult to assign organisms accurately to a particular trophic level. One of the most useful tools for making such assignments is stable isotope analysis (see chapter 6 and the Ecology in Action in this chapter).

Seasonal Shifts in the Diet of the Arctic Fox

In this book, we have presented food webs as static descriptions of the natural communities. However, life is not a cartoon, and the composition of an individual's diet varies greatly over the course of its lifetime, years, seasons, or even days. Further, individuals within a population of a single species may consume different prey, resulting in a diverse diet at the species level. The reasons for this are obvious: different food items become available at different times of year due to phenological patterns in plant growth, animal migration, and activity and different animals may specialize on and/or prefer different types of food. Stable isotopes can serve as a useful tool for deciphering the actual complexity of food webs.

James Roth has been studying the feeding behaviour of the animals near Churchill, Manitoba, for nearly a decade. Arctic foxes, *Alopex lagopus*, are a common carnivore of the area with a broad diet. The foxes are known to eat lemmings, bird eggs, and birds. However, some of these food items are

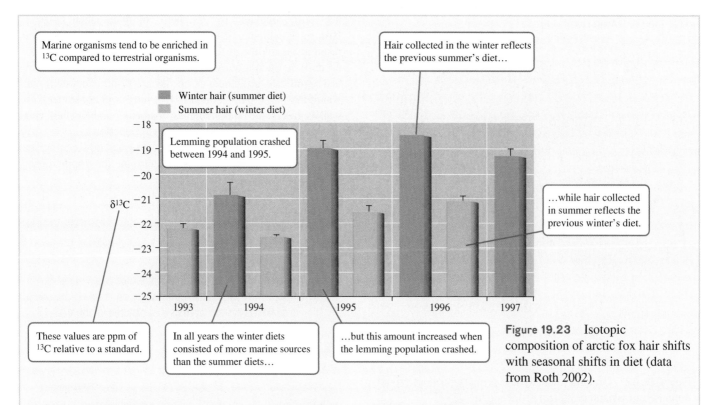

Marine organisms tend to be enriched in ^{13}C compared to terrestrial organisms.

Hair collected in the winter reflects the previous summer's diet…

Winter hair (summer diet)
Summer hair (winter diet)

Lemming population crashed between 1994 and 1995.

…while hair collected in summer reflects the previous winter's diet.

$\delta^{13}C$

These values are ppm of ^{13}C relative to a standard.

In all years the winter diets consisted of more marine sources than the summer diets…

…but this amount increased when the lemming population crashed.

Figure 19.23   Isotopic composition of arctic fox hair shifts with seasonal shifts in diet (data from Roth 2002).

available primarily during the summer, while the foxes are year-round residents of the north. Additionally, lemmings have notoriously large population booms and busts (no, they do not march themselves off to death to "save the species"); consequently they will not always be available in high numbers as a food item. It has been hypothesized that in the winter the foxes can walk along the sea ice and scavenge seal meat from polar bear kill sites. Roth used a stable isotope approach to study seasonal shifts in the diets of the foxes (Roth 2002).

To measure seasonal shifts in diet, Roth needed samples from the foxes that would reflect short-term, rather than long-term, diet composition. In other words, he needed some animal tissue that grows rapidly. The Arctic foxes moult twice each year, and thus Roth was able to make the reasonable assumption that the dark brown hair produced at the start of spring would have the isotopic composition of their winter food, and the white hair produced at the start of winter would reflect their summer diet. Roth then took samples of fox hair over three years, as well as samples of the eggs of Canada geese, caribou, lemmings, and other possible food sources. Roth measured $^{13}C/^{12}C$ ratios for all samples.

There was a substantial shift in $^{13}C/^{12}C$ ratios across seasons (fig. 19.23), with substantially more ^{13}C in the winter diet than summer diet. This shift is consistent with a shift towards more marine-based food items in winter, as these animals tend to be enriched in ^{13}C relative to terrestrial animals. In a mark-recapture study, Roth found that the lemming population went from approximately 13 animals per hectare in 1994 to less than 4 animals per hectare in 1995, 1996, and 1997. Using a variety of analytical methods, Roth was able to estimate that when lemmings were abundant, marine food sources represented only about 17% of the foxes' diet. Immediately after the lemming population crash, marine food, such

as leftovers scavenged from polar bear kills, represented over 40% of the foxes' diet.

This study is a great example of how stable isotopes allow ecologists to study complex phenomena, such as the relative contribution of different food items to the diet of animals. The results also have important implications for the future of the arctic fox. Due to rapid global warming in the North, sea ice is forming later and breaking up earlier than it has over the last several decades. The impacts of this will most immediately be felt by polar bear populations, as their hunting grounds become less available. If this change results in decreasing number of polar bears, and polar bear kill sites, it could mean a great reduction in a winter food source for the arctic fox.

Using Stable Isotopes to Identify Sources of Energy in a Salt Marsh

The main energy source in a salt marsh in eastern North America is primary production by the salt marsh grass *Spartina*, most of which is consumed as detritus. The detritus of *Spartina* is carried into tidal creeks at high tide, where it is consumed by a variety of organisms, including crabs, oysters, and mussels. However, *Spartina* is not the only potential source of food for these organisms. The waters of the salt marsh also contain organic matter from upland plants and carry phytoplankton. How much might these other food sources contribute to energy flow through the salt marsh ecosystem?

Bruce Peterson, Robert Howarth, and Robert Garritt (1985) used stable isotopes to determine the relative contributions of *Spartina*, phytoplankton, and upland plants to the nutrition of the ribbed mussel, *Geukensia demissa*, a dominant filterfeeding species in New England salt marshes. The researchers pointed out that determining the trophic structure of salt marshes is

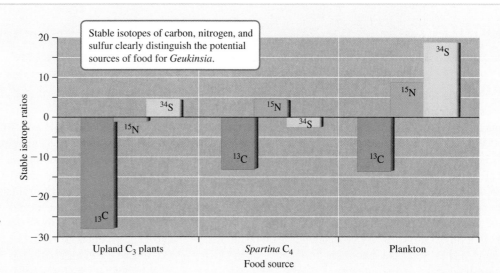

Figure 19.24 Isotopic content of potential food sources for the ribbed mussel, *Geukensia demissa*, in a New England salt marsh (data from Peterson et al. 1985).

difficult because detritus from different sources is difficult to identify visually, because there are several potential sources of detritus, and because organisms may frequently change their feeding habits. It is difficult to accurately quantify the relative contributions of alternative energy sources to a species like *Geukensia* using traditional methods. Those methods will also probably miss transient dietary switches entirely.

As a solution for these problems, Peterson and his colleagues used the ratios of stable isotopes of carbon, nitrogen, and sulfur to assess the relative contributions of alternative food sources to the nutrition of the mussel. They used the stable isotopes of these three elements because their ratios are different in phytoplankton, upland C_3 plants (see chapter 7), and *Spartina*, a C_4 grass (fig. 19.24). Upland plants, with a $\delta^{13}C = -28.6‰$, are the most depleted of ^{13}C, while *Spartina*, with a $\delta^{13}C = -13.1‰$,

is the least depleted. Stable isotopes of sulfur and nitrogen are also distributed differently among these potential energy sources. For instance, *Spartina*, with a $\delta^{34}S = -2.4‰$, has the lowest relative concentration of ^{34}S, while plankton, with a $\delta^{34}S = +18.8‰$, has the highest concentration of ^{34}S.

Because of these differences in isotopic concentrations, the researchers were able to identify the relative contributions of potential food sources to the diet of the mussel (fig. 19.25). Their analyses showed that *Geukensia* gets most of its energy from plankton and *Spartina* but that the relative contributions of these two food sources depends upon location. In the interior of the marsh, the mussel feeds mainly on *Spartina*, while near the mouth of the marsh it depends mainly on plankton. This is an example of how analyses of stable isotopes can provide us with a window to the otherwise hidden biology of species.

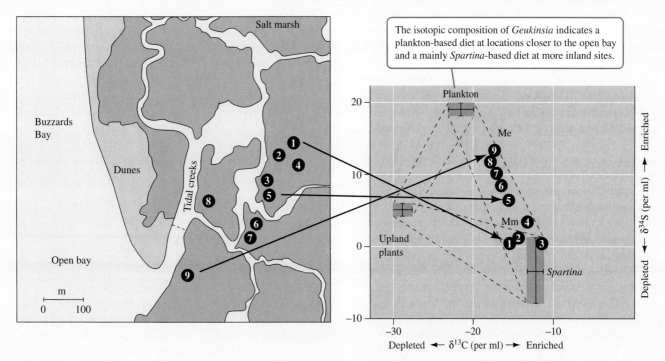

Figure 19.25 Variation in isotopic composition of ribbed mussels, *Geukensia demissa*, by distance inland in a New England salt marsh (data from Peterson et al. 1985).

SUMMARY

We can view a forest, a stream, or an ocean as a system that absorbs, transforms, and stores energy. In this view, physical, chemical, and biological structures and processes are inseparable. When we look at natural systems in this way we view them as ecosystems. An *ecosystem* is a biological community plus all of the abiotic factors influencing that community.

Primary production, the fixation of energy by autotrophs, is one of the most important ecosystem processes. The rate of primary production is the amount of energy fixed over some interval of time. Gross primary production is the total amount of energy fixed by all the autotrophs in the ecosystem. Net primary production is the amount of energy left over after autotrophs have met their own energetic needs.

19.1 Terrestrial primary production is generally limited by temperature and moisture.

The variables most highly correlated with variation in terrestrial primary production are temperature and moisture. Highest rates of terrestrial primary production occur under warm, moist conditions. Temperature and moisture conditions can be combined in a single measure called annual actual evapotranspiration, or AET, which is the total amount of water that evaporates and transpires off a landscape during the course of a year. Annual AET is positively correlated with net primary production in terrestrial ecosystems. However, significant variation in terrestrial primary production results from differences in soil fertility.

19.2 Aquatic primary production is generally limited by nutrient availability.

One of the best documented patterns in the biosphere is the positive relationship between nutrient availability and rate of primary production in aquatic ecosystems. Phosphorus concentration usually limits rates of primary production in freshwater ecosystems, while nitrogen concentration usually limits rates of marine primary production. In many areas of high human impact, there are large marine dead zones, areas essentially devoid of life.

19.3 Energy losses limit the number of trophic levels in ecosystems.

Ecosystem ecologists have simplified the trophic structure of ecosystems by arranging species into trophic levels based upon the predominant source of their nutrition. A trophic level is determined by the number of transfers of energy from primary producers to that level. As energy is transferred from one trophic level to another, energy is lost due to limited assimilation, respiration by consumers, and heat production. As a result of these losses, the quantity of energy in an ecosystem decreases with each successive trophic level, forming a pyramid-shaped distribution of energy among trophic levels. As losses between trophic levels accumulate, eventually there is insufficient energy to support a viable population at a higher trophic level. Along with energy limitation, optimal foraging, evolutionary constraints, and decreasing stability may also limit the number of trophic levels in an ecosystem.

19.4 A variety of species can influence rates of primary production in aquatic and terrestrial ecosystems.

Trophic cascades can occur in terrestrial and aquatic ecosystems. Piscivorous fish can indirectly reduce rates of primary production in lakes by reducing the density of plankton-feeding fish, leading to increased densities of herbivorous zooplankton, and decreased densities of phytoplankton. Intense grazing in the Serengeti can lead to compensatory growth by plants. These effects may also cascade up the food chain, increasing herbivore biomass.

Stable isotope analysis can be used to trace the flow of energy through ecosystems. The ratios of different stable isotopes of important elements such as nitrogen and carbon are generally different in different parts of ecosystems. As a consequence, ecologists can use isotopic ratios to study the trophic structure and energy flow through ecosystems.

REVIEW QUESTIONS

1. Population, community, and ecosystem ecologists study structure and process. However, they focus on different natural characteristics. Contrast the important structures and processes in a forest from the perspectives of population, community, and ecosystem ecologists.

2. M. Huston (1994) pointed out that the well-documented pattern of increasing annual primary production from the poles to the equator is strongly influenced by the longer growing season at low latitudes. The following data are from table 14.10 in Huston. The data cited by Huston are from Whittaker and Likens (1975).

Forest Type	Annual NPP (t/ha/yr)	Length of Growing Season (months)	Monthly NPP (t/hae/mo)
Boreal forest	8	3	2.7
Temperate forest	13	6	?
Tropical forest	20	12	?

Complete the missing data to compare the *monthly* production of boreal, temperate, and tropical forests. How does this short-term perspective of primary production in high-, middle-, and low-latitude forests compare to an annual perspective? How does the short-term perspective change our perception of tropical versus high-latitude forests?

3. Many migratory birds spend approximately half the year in temperate forests during the warm breeding season and the other half of the year in tropical forest. Given the analyses you made in question 2, which forest appears to be more productive from the perspective of these migratory birds?

4. Turkington and colleagues (1998) found that although forests increased in primary productivity in response to fertilization, there was substantial variation among species. What do these differences in response say about using the responses of individual species to predict responses at the ecosystem level? What about the reverse—can we predict the responses of individual species or growth forms from ecosystem-level responses?

5. Compare the pictures of trophic structure that emerged from our discussions of food webs in chapter 18 with those in chapter 19. What are the strengths of each perspective? What are their limitations?

6. Over the last several decades, NPP near coastal areas has typically increased, while it decreased in open areas. Why might this pattern have emerged?

7. Suppose you are studying a community of small mammals that lives on the boundary between a riverside forest and a semidesert grassland. One of your concerns is to discover the relative contributions of the grassland and the forest to the nutrition of small mammals living between the two ecosystems. Design a research program to find out.

8. Most of the energy that flows through a forest ecosystem flows through detritus-based food chains, and the detritus consists mainly of dead plant tissues (e.g., leaves and wood). In contrast, most of the energy flowing through a pelagic marine or freshwater ecosystem flows through grazing food chains with phytoplankton constituting the major primary producers. Ecologists have determined that on average, a calorie or joule of energy takes only several days to pass through the pelagic ecosystem but a quarter of a century to pass through the forest ecosystem. Explain.

9. In chapter 18, we examined the influences of keystone species on the structure of communities. In chapter 19, we reviewed trophic cascades. Discuss the similarities and differences between these two concepts. Compare the measurements and methods of ecologists studying keystone species versus those studying trophic cascades.

10. Are top-down or bottom-up processes more important in controlling primary production? Design an experiment to test your hypothesis.

For more information on the resources available from McGraw-Hill Ryerson, go to **www.mcgrawhill.ca/he/solutions**.

NUTRIENT AND ELEMENTAL CYCLING

CHAPTER 20

CHAPTER CONCEPTS

20.1 All common elements have global cycles that include biotic and abiotic pools.

Concept 20.1 Review

20.2 Decomposition rate is influenced by temperature, moisture, and chemical composition of litter and the environment.

Ecology in Action: How Decomposition Can Change the World

Concept 20.2 Review

20.3 Plants and animals can modify the distribution and cycling of nutrients in ecosystems.

Concept 20.3 Review

20.4 Human activities and natural disturbance can dramatically impact nutrient cycling.

Concept 20.4 Review

Ecological Tools and Approaches: Altering Aquatic and Terrestrial Ecosystems

Summary

Review Questions

t is fair to say that the eyes of many students glaze over when we begin to lecture about nutrient cycling. Many students want to "run with the wolves," not follow an atom of nitrogen through an ecosystem. However, many students are also concerned about issues such as global warming and nitrogen deposition. The science of these issues lies in understanding the content of this chapter. For example, when people talk about acid rain, what they really mean is that through their actions humans have moved large pools of nitrogen or sulfur from one location and then transformed the element and moved it into another location. When people talk about global warming, what they really mean is that humans have again moved large pools of an element (carbon) from one location, transformed it, and moved it into another location. The balance of pools of elements has very significant consequences for the quality of human life on this planet. It is through the study of ecosystem ecology that ecologists are able to understand the consequences of these disruptions to nutrient cycles, hopefully providing the science needed to make evidence-based political and social solutions. This may not be as exciting as chasing a wolf in the forest, but it does have the potential to impact the lives of billions of people.

The exchange of nutrients between organisms and their environment is an essential feature of an ecosystem. A diatom living in the surface waters of a lake absorbs a phosphate molecule from the surrounding water. It incorporates the phosphate into its DNA during cell division. A few hours later, one of the diatom's daughter cells is eaten by a cladoceran, an algae-feeding member of the zooplankton. The cladoceran incorporates the phosphate into a molecule of ATP. The cladoceran lives two days more and then is eaten by a planktivorous minnow. Within the minnow, the phosphate is combined with a lipid to form a phospholipid molecule in the cell membrane of one of the minnow's neural cells. A few weeks later, the minnow is eaten by a northern pike and the phosphate is incorporated into the pike's skeleton. During the following winter, the pike is caught by an intrepid person dropping a hook through the ice. The fish is filleted on site, with the fillets packed for home. The offal and skeleton are dropped back down the fishing hole, settling to the bottom of the lake. These tissues are attacked by bacteria and fungi that gradually decompose the remains of the pike. During decomposition, the phosphate in the skeleton is dissolved in the surrounding water. The following spring the very same phosphate molecule is taken up by another diatom, completing its cycle through the lake ecosystem (fig. 20.1).

One of the principles we learned in chapter 19 was that energy makes a one-way trip through ecosystems. Energy eventually leaves ecosystems due to inefficient transformation of energy and lost heat energy, with significant implications for population sizes and trophic structure. In contrast, elements such as phosphorus (P), carbon (C), nitrogen (N), potassium (K), and iron (Fe) may move among biotic and abiotic components of ecosystems many times before they leave an ecosystem. Every element found in ecosystems will have a cycle that involves movement from location to location, and transformation into different forms (e.g., oxidized, reduced, a salt, elemental).

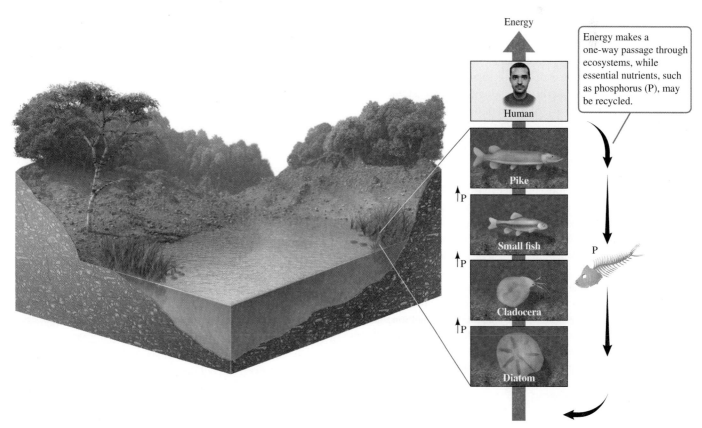

Figure 20.1   Phosphorus cycle in a lake ecosystem.

Elements that are required for the development, maintenance, and reproduction of organisms are called **nutrients**, and ecologists refer to the use, transformation, movement, and reuse of nutrients within and among ecosystems as **nutrient cycling**. Because of the physiological importance of nutrients, their relative scarcity, and their influence on rates of primary production, nutrient cycling is one of the most significant ecosystem processes studied by ecologists. Only a subset of elements in an ecosystem are required by living organisms and therefore labelled as *essential*. For example, though uranium may be found in an organism, it is not an *essential* nutrient. Essential nutrients can be further subdivided as **macronutrients** and **micronutrients**. Macronutrients are those essential elements required in large concentrations within an organism, while micronutrients are those required in only small concentrations. Carbon, hydrogen, oxygen, and phosphorus are macronutrients for all life on earth. However, the designation of other elements as macro or micro will depend upon the organism in question. For example, silica can be considered a macronutrient for diatoms, but not for many other taxonomic groups. Because essential nutrients are typically actively taken up by organisms, they generally have a significant biotic component to their nutrient cycle.

All nutrients will cycle at several different scales of organization. For example, nitrogen taken up by a root in the soil will be translocated within a plant, perhaps into a growing leaf. As we discussed in chapter 5, that nitrogen is likely to be translocated to a new position within the plant prior to the leaf falling from the plant. In other words, there is a nutrient cycle that occurs within an individual organism. That nitrogen will eventually leave that plant, where it may be used by other organisms or sit unused—with this process repeating through time. Thus, within an ecosystem is a second scale of nutrient cycling. A third scale exists when we realize that sometimes that nitrogen will leave the ecosystem through leaching, fire, or some other process. The nitrogen does not disappear, instead it enters a new ecosystem (or resides in the atmosphere) where additional cycles may occur. Such nested scales of nutrient cycling occur for all nutrients used by living organisms, not just nitrogen.

20.1 Nutrient Cycles

All common elements have global cycles that include biotic and abiotic pools. As described above, ecological actions and chemical processes result in the movement of elements from one pool to another. Elements may reside in one pool for millennia, or minutes—depending upon a large number of biotic and abiotic processes.

There are too many different elements in ecosystems for us to describe the cycles of each. Instead, we have chosen three nutrient cycles that play especially prominent roles in natural systems: the *phosphorus cycle*, the *nitrogen cycle*, and the *carbon cycle*. Nutrients not described here, such as sulfur, can also be important for both natural systems and the quality of human life.

The Phosphorus Cycle

Phosphorus is essential to the energetics, genetics, and structure of living systems, forming part of ATP, RNA, DNA, and phospholipid molecules. While of great biological importance, phosphorus is not very abundant in the biosphere. Increases in phosphorus in aquatic systems can cause large algal blooms (chapter 19), with cascading effects on fish and other aquatic species. Although phosphorus typically does not limit terrestrial plant growth, there are exceptions. In very old soils, such as those found in parts of the Canadian Shield and under wet tropical forests (chapter 2), phosphorus levels can be extremely low, limiting plant growth. Similar phosphorus limitations can occur in areas subjected to long-term agricultural production.

The global phosphorus cycle does not include a substantial atmospheric pool of phosphorus (fig. 20.2). Instead, the largest quantities of phosphorus occur in mineral deposits and marine sediments. Sedimentary rocks that are especially rich in phosphorus are often mined for fertilizer and applied to agricultural soils. Soil may contain substantial quantities of phosphorus; however, much of this phosphorus occurs in chemical forms not directly available to plants.

Phosphorus is slowly released to terrestrial and aquatic ecosystems through the weathering of rocks. As phosphorus is released from mineral deposits, it is absorbed by plants and recycled within ecosystems. However, much phosphorus is washed into rivers and eventually finds its way to the oceans, where it will remain in dissolved form until eventually finding its way to the ocean sediments. Further, bedrock contains only a certain amount of phosphorus, and the longer it is weathered, the less remains to enter into biological systems. In areas of the world that have experienced very long-term weathering, such as the Canadian Shield and tropical wet forests, one typically finds very low amounts of plant-available soil phosphorus. In contrast, low P in agriculture systems is common not due to weathering of bedrock, but instead due to continual removal of phosphorus-containing plant biomass. Due to the limited amounts of P available, many agricultural practices are based upon *phosphorus mining*, an inherently non-sustainable system where P outputs are greater than natural P inputs.

Ocean sediments will eventually be transformed into phosphate-bearing sedimentary rocks that through geological uplift can form new land. William Schlesinger (1991) points out that the phosphorus released by the weathering of sedimentary rocks has made at least one passage through the global phosphorus cycle.

The Nitrogen Cycle

Nitrogen is important to the structure and functioning of organisms, forming part of key biomolecules such as amino acids, nucleic acids, and the porphyrin rings of chlorophyll and hemoglobin. In addition, as we saw in chapter 19, nitrogen supplies may limit rates of primary production in marine and terrestrial environments. Much of modern agriculture attempts to overcome nitrogen limitation through elaborate fertilization programs. Nitrogen is also released into the atmosphere through the burning of coal (along with sulfur), contributing to acidification of many lakes in Canada and the United States. Later in this chapter we will discuss human impacts on the nitrogen cycle; here we focus on an overview of the general cycle itself.

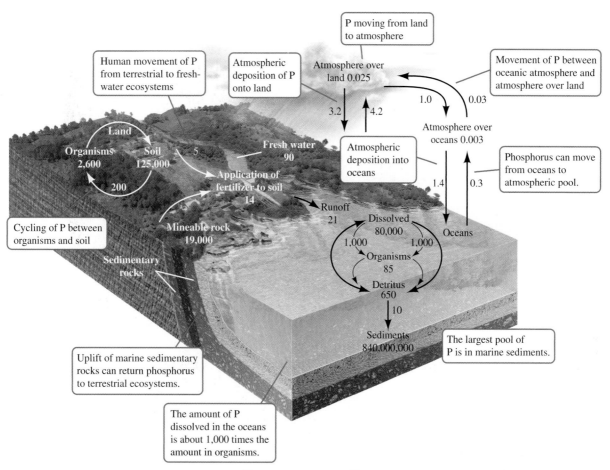

Figure 20.2   The phosphorus cycle. Numbers are 10^{12} g P or fluxes as 10^{12} g P per year (data from Schlesinger 1991, after Richey 1983, Meybeck 1982, Graham and Duce 1979).

Two critical aspects of the nitrogen cycle are **mineralization** and **immobilization**. Mineralization is the conversion of organic forms of nitrogen (e.g., proteins) into mineral forms (e.g., ammonia and nitrate). Immobilization is the reverse process, the conversion of mineral forms of nitrogen into organic forms. Because mineral nitrogen is often limiting plant growth, the balance between these processes can greatly alter productivity. Microbes play a central role in nitrogen cycling.

The nitrogen cycle includes a major atmospheric pool in the form of molecular nitrogen, N_2 (fig. 20.3). However, only a few organisms, all prokaryotes, can use this atmospheric supply of molecular nitrogen directly. These organisms, called nitrogen fixers, include (1) some cyanobacteria, or blue-green algae, of freshwater, marine, and soil environments, (2) free-living soil bacteria such as *Azotobacter* and *Azospirillum*, (3) *Rhizobia* bacteria associated with the roots of leguminous plants, and (4) *Frankia* bacteria, associated with the roots of alders and several other species of woody plants (fig. 20.4). Because of the strong triple bonds between the two nitrogen atoms in the N_2 molecule, nitrogen fixation is an energy-demanding process. During nitrogen fixation, N_2 is reduced to ammonia, NH_3. Nitrogen fixation takes place under aerobic conditions in terrestrial and aquatic environments, where nitrogen-fixing bacteria oxidize sugars to obtain the required energy. Nitrogen fixation also occurs as a physical process

associated with the high pressures and energy generated by lightning; or through similar conditions through industrial production of nitrogen fertilizers. Pre-industrialization, the vast majority of the nitrogen cycling within ecosystems ultimately entered these cycles through nitrogen fixation by organisms or lightning. As we discuss later, humans now use large quantities of fossil fuels to generate the energy needed to break these triple bonds, creating mineral forms of nitrogen, and thus increase plant growth. In other words, humans are swapping the stored energy in fuels for the potential growth of plants through increased nitrogen.

Once nitrogen is fixed by nitrogen-fixing organisms (or lightening or burning of fossil fuels), it becomes available to other organisms within an ecosystem. Upon the death of an organism, the nitrogen in its tissues can be released by fungi and bacteria involved in the decomposition process. These fungi and bacteria release nitrogen as ammonium, $NH4^+$, a process called **ammonification**. Ammonium may be converted to nitrate, NO_3^-, by other bacteria in a process called **nitrification**. Ammonium and nitrate can be used directly by some bacteria, fungi, or plants. The nitrogen in dead organic matter can also be used directly by some mycorrhizal fungi, which can be passed on to plants. The nitrogen in bacterial, fungal, and plant biomass may pass on to populations of animal consumers or back to the pool of dead organic matter, where it will be recycled again.

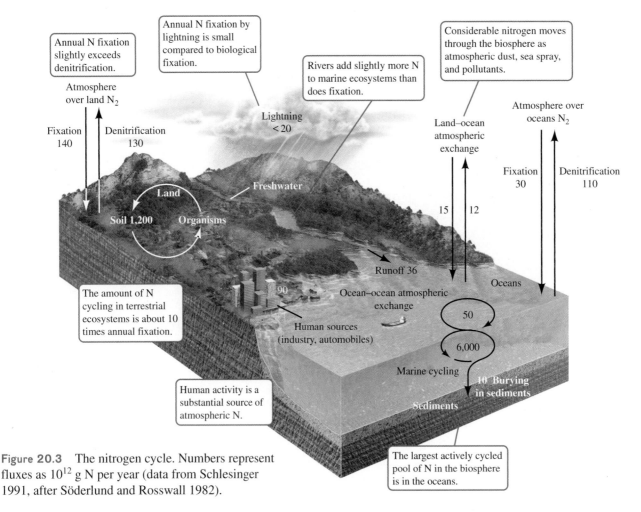

Figure 20.3   The nitrogen cycle. Numbers represent fluxes as 10^{12} g N per year (data from Schlesinger 1991, after Söderlund and Rosswall 1982).

Nitrogen may exit the organic matter pool of an ecosystem through denitrification. **Denitrification** is an energy-yielding process that occurs under anaerobic conditions and converts nitrate to molecular nitrogen, N_2. The molecular nitrogen produced by denitrifying bacteria moves into the atmosphere and can only re-enter the organic matter pool through nitrogen fixation. The mean residence time of fixed nitrogen in the biosphere is about 625 years. In contrast, the mean residence time of phosphorus in the biosphere is in the order of thousands of years.

The Carbon Cycle

Carbon is an essential part of all organic molecules. As constituents of the atmosphere, carbon compounds such as carbon dioxide, CO_2, and methane, CH_4, substantially influence global climate. This connection between atmospheric carbon and climate has drawn all nations of the planet into discussions of the ecology of carbon cycling, and is discussed more fully in chapter 23.

Carbon moves between organisms and the atmosphere as a consequence of two reciprocal biological processes: photosynthesis and respiration (fig. 20.5). Photosynthesis removes CO_2 from the atmosphere, while respiration by primary producers and consumers, including decomposers, returns carbon to the atmosphere in the form of CO_2. In aquatic ecosystems, CO_2 must first dissolve in water before being used by aquatic primary producers. Once dissolved in water, CO_2 enters a chemical equilibrium with bicarbonate, HCO_3^-, and carbonate, CO_3^-. Carbonate may precipitate out of solution as calcium carbonate and may be buried in ocean sediments.

While some carbon cycles rapidly between organisms and the atmosphere, some remains sequestered in relatively unavailable forms for long periods of time. Carbon in soils, peat, fossil fuels, and carbonate rock would generally take a long time to return to the atmosphere. However, fossil fuels have become a major source of atmospheric CO_2 as humans have tapped

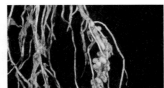
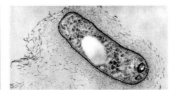

Figure 20.4   Some of the bacteria that can fix atmospheric nitrogen, converting it into a form usable by plants. Shown are (left to right) cyanobacteria, *Rhizobia* nodules, *Rhizobia*, and *Frankia*.

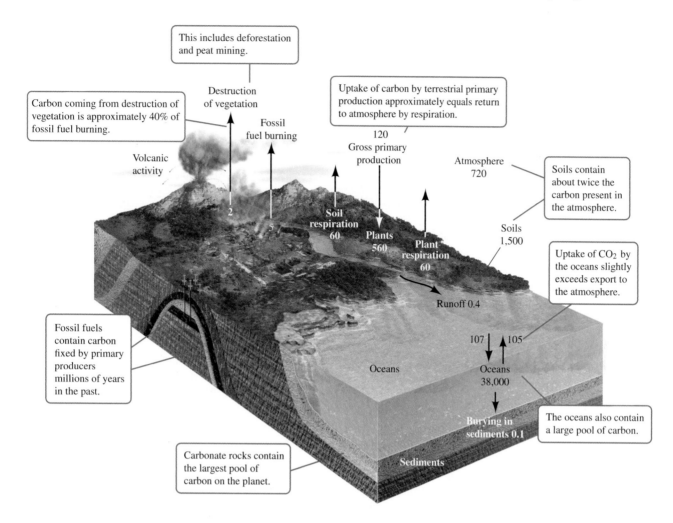

Figure 20.5 The carbon cycle. Numbers are storage as 10^{15} g or fluxes as 10^{15} g per year (data from Schlesinger 1991).

into fossil fuel supplies to provide energy. We will discuss the effects of humans on the carbon cycle later in the chapter.

Ecosystem ecologists study the factors controlling the movement, storage, and conservation of nutrients within ecosystems. You can see broad outlines of these processes in figures 20.1, 20.2, and 20.3. However, much remains to be learned, especially concerning the factors controlling rates of nutrient exchange within and between ecosystems. Nutrient exchange is substantially affected by the process of decomposition, which we will discuss below.

CONCEPT 20.1 REVIEW

1. A critical aspect of nutrient cycles is the movement of elements from one pool into another. What are the largest pools for phosphorus, nitrogen, and carbon?
2. Which fluxes move the most phosphorus, nitrogen, and carbon among pools?
3. The answers to 1 & 2 will be different for phosphorus, nitrogen, and carbon. Why?

20.2 Rates of Decomposition

Decomposition rate is influenced by temperature, moisture, and chemical composition of litter and the environment. The rate at which nutrients, such as nitrogen and phosphorus, are made available to the primary producers of terrestrial ecosystems is determined largely by the rate at which nutrient supplies are converted from organic to inorganic forms (mineralization). Mineralization takes place principally during **decomposition**, which is the breakdown of organic matter accompanied by the release of carbon dioxide.

Decomposition occurs partially through weathering, but predominantly involves biotic interactions. Arthropods, fungi, and bacteria are common detritivores, using dead organic matter as their main energy source. As with all biological processes, decomposition rates are influenced by temperature, moisture, as well as the chemical composition of the dead material. Key chemical characteristics influencing decomposition rates include nitrogen concentration, phosphorus concentration, the carbon:nitrogen ratio, and lignin content. Ecologists have studied how several of these variables affect rates of leaf decomposition in Mediterranean ecosystems.

Decomposition in Two Mediterranean Woodland Ecosystems

Antonio Gallardo and José Merino (1993) studied how chemical and physical factors affect rates of decomposition of leaf litter in two Mediterranean woodland ecosystems in southwestern Spain (fig. 20.6). The mean annual temperature at the two sites differs by only 0.5° C and both sites experience Mediterranean climates with wet winters and dry summers. However, they differ significantly in annual rainfall. While Doñana Biological Reserve receives about 500 mm of rain annually, Monte La Sauceda receives about 1,600 mm; a difference driven by an elevational difference among sites. These two sites were ideally suited to study the effects of moisture on rates of decomposition.

Gallardo and Merino also explored the effects of litter chemistry on decomposition by using leaves from nine tree and shrub species that differed in concentrations of tannins, lignin, nitrogen, and phosphorus. You may remember from chapter 2 that many of the native plants from areas with a Mediterranean climate produce tough or sclerophyllous leaves. Gallardo and Merino also explored the influence of leaf toughness on decomposition rate.

The core research methodology in studies of decomposition is refreshingly straightforward. If you wanted to see how long dead material takes to disappear what would you do? Here, approximately 2 g of air-dried leaves from each of the study species was put into several nylon mesh litter bags and placed at the Doñana Biological Reserve and at Monte La Sauceda. The litter bags had a mesh size of 1 mm—small enough to reduce the loss of small leaves, yet large enough to permit aerobic microbial activity and entry of small soil invertebrates. Every two months for two years Gallardo and Merino retrieved litter bags from each study site.

In the laboratory, the researchers measured the mass of leaf tissue remaining in replicate litter bags for each species. Figure 20.6 shows that the amount of leaf mass lost by ash leaves, *Fraxinus angustifolia*, was much higher at Monte La Sauceda. In fact, all species showed higher decomposition rates at Monte La Sauceda, supporting the idea that precipitation accelerates decomposition.

Differences in decomposition rates among species were similar at the two sites. For instance, the leaves of ash, *Fraxinus*, showed the greatest mass loss at both study sites, while the oak, *Quercus lusitanica*, showed the lowest mass loss at both study sites. Differences in mass loss by the nine species reflected differences in the physical and chemical characteristics of their leaves. In general, decomposition was fastest in species with high nitrogen and low leaf toughness (fig 20.7).

As we will see in the next example, the lignin—one aspect of leaf toughness—and nitrogen content also influence decomposition rates in temperate forest ecosystems.

Decomposition in Forest Ecosystems

Jerry Melillo, John Aber, and John Muratore (1982) used litter bags to study leaf decomposition in a temperate forest in New Hampshire. Their study species were beech, *Fagus grandifolia*; sugar maple, *Acer saccharum*; paper birch, *Betula papyrifera*; red maple, *Acer rubrum*; white ash, *Fraxinus americana*; and pin cherry, *Prunus pennsylvanica*. They also compared their results with decomposition of leaves from white pine, chestnut oak, white oak, red maple, and flowering dogwood in a temperate forest in North Carolina.

In both the New Hampshire and North Carolina forests, the researchers found a negative correlation between the leaf mass remaining after one year of decomposition and the ratio of lignin to nitrogen concentrations in leaves, % lignin:% N.

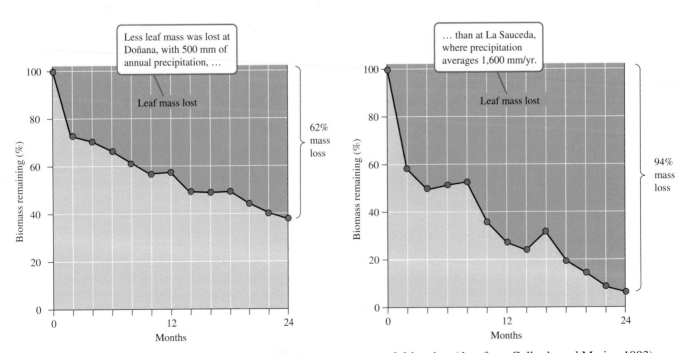

Figure 20.6   Decomposition of *Fraxinus angustifolia* leaves at wetter and drier sites (data from Gallardo and Merino 1993).

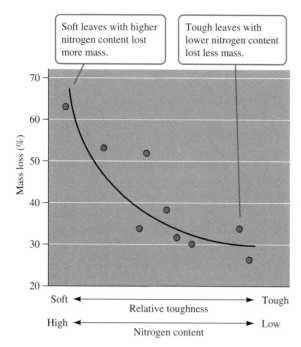

Figure 20.7 Influence of leaf toughness and nitrogen content on decomposition (data from Gallardo and Merino 1993).

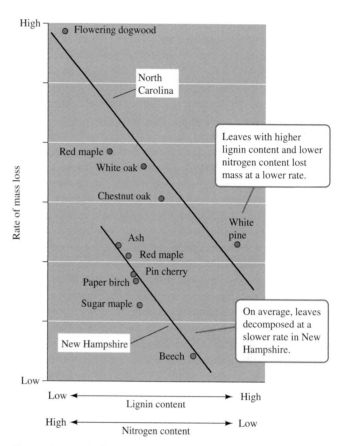

Figure 20.8 Influence of lignin and nitrogen content of leaves on decomposition (data from Melillo et al. 1982).

In other words, leaves with higher lignin:nitrogen ratios lost less mass during the year-long study. As you can see in figure 20.8, the amount of leaf mass remaining was lower at the North Carolina site than at the New Hampshire site. What factors were responsible for these higher rates of decomposition at the North Carolina site? Melillo and his colleagues suggested that higher nitrogen availability in the soils at the North Carolina site may contribute to the higher rates of decomposition observed there. However, higher temperatures at the North Carolina site may also contribute to higher decomposition rates.

Studies in both temperate and Mediterranean regions suggest that rates of decomposition are positively correlated with temperature and moisture. Can we combine these two factors into one? In chapter 19, we reviewed how ecologists studying the effect of climate on terrestrial primary production combined temperature and precipitation into a single measure called actual evapotranspiration, or AET. Vernon Meentemeyer (1978) analyzed the relationship between AET and decomposition and found a significant positive relationship.

If decomposition rates increase with increased evapotranspiration, how would you expect rates of decomposition in tropical and temperate ecosystems to compare? As you probably predicted, rates of decomposition are generally higher in tropical ecosystems. The average annual mass loss in tropical forests shown in figure 20.9 is 120%, or three times the average rate measured in temperate forests. These higher rates probably reflect the effects of higher AET in tropical forests and indicate complete decomposition in less than a year.

Soil nutrient content has also been shown to have a strong positive effect on rates of nutrient cycling in tropical forests. Three forest ecologists, Masaaki Takyu, Shin-Ichiro Aiba, and Kanehiro Kitayama, took advantage of natural variation in nutrient content on different geologic formations and different topographic situations to explore the factors influencing

tropical rain forest functioning in Borneo (Takyu et al. 2003). Takyu, Aiba, and Kitayama established research sites on ridges, which tend to have soils with lower nutrient content, and lower slopes, where nutrient content is higher, on three different rock types. The younger Quaternary sedimentary rock in their study area was approximately 30,000 to 40,000 years old and soils developing on these rocks tended to have higher nutrient content compared to soils on the other rock types in

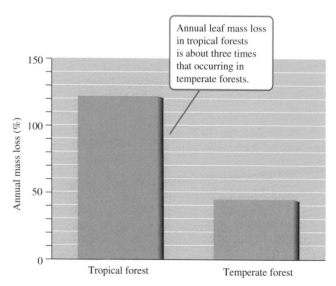

Figure 20.9 Decomposition in tropical and temperate forests (data from Anderson and Swift 1983).

the study, especially on lower slopes (fig. 20.10). Two older rock types were both approximately 40 million years old. One, a Tertiary sedimentary rock, supported soils that were considerably more fertile than the other, a Tertiary ultrabasic rock.

Takyu, Aiba, and Kitayama's study clearly demonstrated the influence of soil fertility on rates of decomposition and nutrient cycling. Because all study sites were at approximately the same elevation and all were on south-facing aspects, the research team was able to isolate the influences of geologic conditions, especially soil characteristics. Takyu, Aiba, and Kitayama found higher rates of above-ground net primary production, higher rates of litter fall, and higher rates of decomposition on sites with higher concentrations of soluble phosphorus in topsoil, particularly on soils formed on the lower slopes of Quaternary and Tertiary rock formations. These results show that while climate may have a primary influence on decomposition rates, within climatic regions nutrient availability has an ecologically significant effect on decomposition and nutrient cycling rates.

In summary, decomposition in terrestrial ecosystems is influenced by moisture, temperature, soil fertility, and the chemical composition of litter, especially the concentrations of nitrogen and lignin. With the obvious exception of moisture, these factors also influence decomposition rates in aquatic ecosystems, which we examine next.

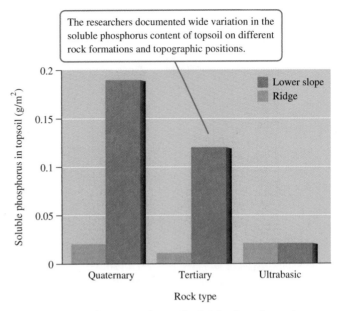

Figure 20.10 Concentrations of soluble phosphorus in topsoils formed on three rock types and at two topographic positions in Borneo (data from Takyu et al. 2003).

ECOLOGY IN ACTION

How Decomposition Can Change the World

In chapters 19 and 20 we have provided a foundation for understanding the most basic ecosystem functions: primary production and nutrient cycling. We have discussed how these ecological services can be altered by human activities, by the abiotic environment, and by interactions within the ecosystems themselves. The question I am sure that many of you are asking is, so what? Although nutrient cycling is widely recognized by ecologists as one of the most critical aspects of ecosystem ecology, and that alteration of the rates of decomposition can have cascading effects altering a variety of other ecological interactions and patterns of diversity, this message is not often clearly transmitted to undergraduate students and the general population. Instead, decomposition is often viewed as among the dullest of subjects: studying things we can't see eating things that are dead. Why would anyone want to devote their life to the study of the rate at which dead leaves and roots turn into CO_2 and other molecules? The answer, quite simply, is that changes in decomposition will more directly and indirectly alter processes humans care about (such as climate change and biomass production) than nearly any other ecological process you will find in this book. Certainly, studying bear and elk in a national park is a great life, and understanding the ecology of these organisms is a worthwhile endeavour. However, a 10% increase or

decrease in predation rates or population sizes of these charismatic creatures may alter their population sizes, but it is not going to have any impact on global processes. A 10% change in decomposition will.

Here we discuss one such example: the potential impact of altered rates of decomposition in the arctic and sub-arctic regions of the world. As we saw in chapters 2 and 3, northern regions are home to large expanses of peatlands and deep organic soils. Additionally, these regions represent a large portion of the land mass on the planet. These areas are quite cold for much of the year, and in many areas deep layers of permafrost keep the layers of the ground frozen year round (fig. 20.11). What actually is frozen in the north? Is it simply clay, sand, and other layers of mineral soil? No. Although soil particles are frozen, much of the permafrost is organic matter—dead plants, animals, bacteria, and fungi. Put another way, the north is home to an enormous pool of frozen carbon, which could potentially be liberated into the atmosphere with a bit of liquid water and some warming. Let's try to put this into a larger perspective.

Between 20% to 60% of the carbon stored in the soil in the world is found in the northern regions, including the boreal forest and arctic tundra. This volume of C is roughly 10–100 times the amount of C released each year through

Figure 20.11 Permafrost is found in much of Northern Canada.

Figure 20.12 Open-top chambers, such as the one pictured here in a polar desert on Ellesmere Island, are commonly used to study the effects of warming on ecological processes.

deforestation and the burning of fossil fuels (Hobbie et al. 2000). Because of the magnitude of carbon stored in these soils, even a small change in decomposition rates has the potential to greatly alter the amount of carbon entering the atmosphere. As we discuss later in this chapter, increases in the amount of CO_2 in the atmosphere can further enhance global temperatures. So, if decomposition rates in the arctic increase due to increased temperatures, this could increase atmospheric warming, which in turn would further enhance decomposition rates. In other words, the effects of temperature on decomposition rates are of global importance. But as you might imagine, the story is not quite this simple.

What are the impacts of temperature on decomposition in the north? The answer to this question is complicated, and involves many ecological puzzles not yet solved. Although we often view the arctic as a homogeneous expanse of land, the reality is quite different. There are numerous community types in the north, including salt marshes, dry grasslands, peatlands, and forested areas. The plants of different community types differ in tissue composition and, importantly, in the effects of increased temperature on decomposition rates (Shaver et al. 2006). In general, it is thought that the wetter areas will show

the greatest increase in decomposition in response to increased temperatures (Shaver et al. 2006; Aerts 2006). In contrast, it is thought that in the drier regions of the north it is soil moisture, rather than soil temperature, that limits decomposition rates. However, there is much variation among studies in the actual change in decomposition that has occurred, and some of this variation appears due to different types of experimental treatments being imposed (Aerts 2006; fig. 20.12). Some data even suggests that increased decomposition associated with warming may result in increased N mineralization, essentially fertilizing parts of the arctic. This in turn may stimulate plant growth, resulting in increased, rather than decreased, storage of C in the soil! It is too early to say for certain what the direct effect of altered temperature will be on decomposition rates, though there is grave concern among many researchers.

A second complication is that even if increased temperature has a minimal effect on the rate of decomposition of the unfrozen parts of soil, it could greatly impact global carbon cycles if it causes a partial thawing of the permafrost. There already exists substantial evidence that this is occurring throughout much of the high Arctic (Serreze et al. 2000). As a consequence of this thawing, more organic matter is being decomposed, even though the rate of decomposition is constant. Again, the impact on global carbon cycles will depend upon whether the increase in nitrogen that also occurs is enough to stimulate plant growth.

The effects of temperature on decomposition are not limited to direct impacts due to increased temperatures. Instead, decomposition rates can also be altered through changes in litter composition and changes in the soil fauna (fig. 20.13). In particular, *Sphagnum* mosses have very low decomposition rates, and may even reduce decomposition of the surrounding

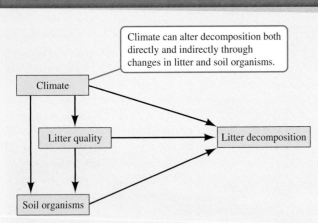

Figure 20.13   Climate, litter chemistry, and soil organisms will all interact to affect rates of decomposition (data from Aerts 2006).

vegetation (Aerts 2006). Although long-term studies are few in number, those that have occurred suggest that moss abundances decrease under warming (Aerts 2006), supporting the idea that warming can enhance decomposition through a shift in plant composition and litter quality. As we discussed in chapter 2, the functional ecology and description of soil fauna communities is very poorly understood, and this lack of information is even more pronounced in northern systems.

As you can see here, the functional consequences of warming on soil communities are unknown, and major discoveries wait for the next generation of ecologists. That is, of course, if they are willing to take on the challenge of working (with organisms they can't see that eat dead things) on questions whose answers could change the world.

Decomposition in Aquatic and Wetland Ecosystems

Jack Webster and Fred Benfield (1986) reviewed what was known about the decomposition of plant tissues in freshwater ecosystems. Among the most important variables that emerged from their analysis were leaf species, temperature, and nutrient concentrations in the aquatic ecosystem.

Webster and Benfield summarized the rates of leaf breakdown for 596 types of woody and nonwoody plants decaying in aquatic ecosystems and found that the average daily breakdown rate varied more than tenfold. As in terrestrial ecosystems, the chemical composition of litter significantly influences rates of decomposition in aquatic ecosystems.

The nutrient content of stream water can also influence rates of decomposition. Keller Suberkropp and Eric Chauvet (1995) studied how water chemistry affects rates of leaf decomposition, using the leaves of yellow poplar, *Liriodendron tulipifera*. They placed the leaves in several streams in the temperate zone that differed in water chemistry and were able to estimate the daily rate of mass loss.

Suberkropp and Chauvet found that leaves decayed faster in streams with higher concentrations of nitrates (fig. 20.14). This result is consistent with the suggestion by Melillo's research team that higher rates of decomposition at one of their study sites was due to higher availability of soil nitrogen. Similar results were found in streams draining a tropical forest. Amy Rosemond and colleagues (2002) found leaf decomposition rate increased markedly as phosphorus concentration increased to about 20 μg per litre, after which decomposition rate levelled off.

As in terrestrial ecosystems, litter chemistry and nutrient availability in the environment affect decomposition rates in aquatic ecosystems. These impacts of litter composition on water chemistry are found in all aquatic systems, including lakes and oceans, as well as wetland systems such as bogs and fens. The patterns discussed in this section emphasize the role played by the physical and chemical environment in the process of decomposition. As we shall see in the next section, animals and plants can also significantly affect the nutrient dynamics of ecosystems.

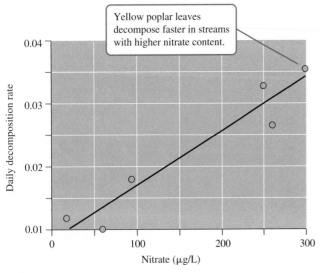

Figure 20.14   Stream nitrate and decomposition of *Liriodendron* leaves (data from Suberkropp and Chauvet 1995).

CONCEPT 20.2 REVIEW

1. During the past 30 years, thousands of papers have been published on decomposition within ecosystems. Why have ecologists spent so much time studying decomposition?
2. Why does litter chemistry alter decomposition rates?

20.3 | Organisms and Nutrients

Plants and animals can modify the distribution and cycling of nutrients in ecosystems. In chapters 17 and 18, we discussed how interactions among organisms can cause changes to community structure, and in chapter 19 we discussed how these interactions influenced energy flow in ecosystems. These ecological interactions also impact nutrient cycling. One of the great realizations in ecosystem ecology over the last several decades has been that although the same ecological processes occur in terrestrial and aquatic habitats (e.g., decomposition, herbivory, predation), there are consistent difference in the patterns of nutrient cycling between these ecosystems. Jonathan Shurin, formerly of the University of British Columbia, has summarized many of the critical differences in nutrient cycling between aquatic and terrestrial habitats (fig. 20.15; Shurin et al. 2006).

As we saw in chapter 19, there is strong evidence for top-down control of productivity in some aquatic systems, while terrestrial systems are primarily controlled by bottom-up processes. However, Shurin describes a number of other differences in the trophic structure and distribution of nutrients among terrestrial and aquatic systems (fig. 20.15). For example, aquatic systems tend to have a greater proportion of autotrophs being consumed by herbivores than by detritivores when compared to terrestrial systems. A consequence of this is that these systems tend to have a lower proportion of carbon and nutrients stored in detritus and detritivores than in terrestrial systems. Shurin and colleagues (2006) suggest that driving these differences are fundamental differences in

life-history, morphology, and chemistry between phytoplankton and terrestrial plants. In general, phytoplankton appear less well-defended than terrestrial plants (chapter 15), resulting in higher consumption rates of phytoplankton by zooplankton than of terrestrial plants by herbivores. Additionally, growth rates of phytoplankton are generally much higher than terrestrial plants, facilitating rapid nutrient cycling.

Overall, species interactions, life-histories, and environmental chemistry can all interact to influence nutrient cycling within an ecosystem. This should serve as a reminder that although we have divided this book into different sections, this does not mean that ideas presented in the first few chapters are not relevant to our discussion here (this is why professors often have cumulative final exams!). We now move away from general differences that occur among ecosystems and present a few specific examples of how organisms can influence the distribution and dynamics of nutrients within ecosystems.

Nutrient Cycling in Streams

Before we consider how stream animals influence the dynamics of nutrient turnover in streams, we have to consider some special features of this ecosystem. As we saw in chapter 3, the most distinctive feature of stream and river ecosystems is water flow. Jack Webster (1975) was the first to point out that because nutrients in streams are subject to downstream transport, there is little nutrient cycling in one place. Water currents move nutrients downstream. Webster suggested that rather than a stationary cycle, stream nutrient dynamics are

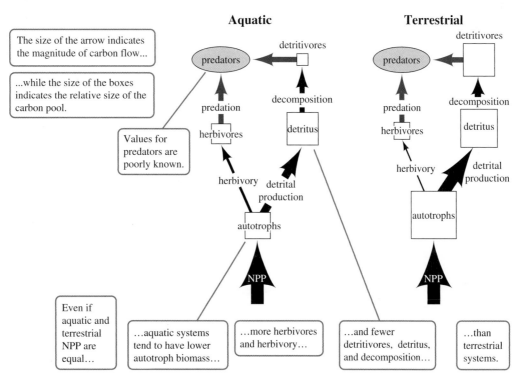

Figure 20.15   General differences in food webs and carbon flow among terrestrial and aquatic ecosystems (adapted from Shurin et al. 2006).

better represented by a spiral. He coined the term **nutrient spiraling** to describe stream nutrient dynamics (fig. 20.16).

As an atom of a nutrient completes a cycle within a stream, it may pass through several ecosystem components such as an algal cell, an invertebrate, a fish, or a detrital fragment. Each of these ecosystem components may be displaced downstream by current, and therefore contribute to nutrient spiraling. The length of stream required for an atom of a nutrient to complete a cycle is called the **spiraling length**. Spiraling length is related to the rate of nutrient cycling and average velocity of nutrient movement downstream. Denis Newbold and his colleagues (1983) represented spiraling length, S, as:

$$S = VT$$

where V is the average velocity at which a nutrient atom moves downstream and T is the average time for a nutrient atom to complete a cycle. If velocity, V, is low and the time to complete a nutrient cycle, T, is short, nutrient spiraling length is short. Where spiraling lengths are short, a particular nutrient atom may be used many times before it is washed out of a stream system.

The tendency of an ecosystem to retain nutrients is called **nutrient retentiveness**. In stream ecosystems, retentiveness is inversely related to spiraling length. Short spiraling lengths are equated with high retentiveness and long spiraling lengths with low retentiveness. Any factors that influence spiraling length affect nutrient retention by stream ecosystems.

Stream Invertebrates and Spiraling Length

Nancy Grimm (1988) showed that aquatic macroinvertebrates significantly increase the rate of nitrogen cycling in Sycamore Creek, Arizona. Streams in the arid American Southwest support high levels of macroinvertebrate biomass. Grimm estimated invertebrate population densities as high as 110,000 individuals per square metre and dry biomass as high as 9.62 g per square metre. More than 80% of macroinvertebrate biomass in Sycamore Creek was made up of species that feed on small organic particles, a feeding group that stream ecologists call *collector-gatherers*. The collector-gatherers of Sycamore Creek are dominated by two families of mayflies, Baetidae and Tricorythidae, and one family of Diptera, Chironomidae.

Grimm quantified the influence of macroinvertebrates on the nitrogen dynamics in the creek, where primary production is limited by nitrogen availability. She developed nitrogen budgets for stream invertebrates, mainly insect larvae and snails, by quantifying their rates of nitrogen ingestion, egestion (defecation), excretion, and accumulation during growth. By combining these rates with her estimates of macroinvertebrate biomass, Grimm was able to estimate the contribution of macroinvertebrates to the nutrient dynamics of the Sycamore Creek ecosystem.

Her measurements indicated that macroinvertebrates could play an important role in nutrient spiraling. To determine whether they play such a role, what information do we need? We need to know how much of the available nitrogen they ingest. If invertebrates ingest a large proportion of the nitrogen pool, then their influences on nitrogen spiraling may be substantial. Grimm measured the nutrient retention of Sycamore Creek as the daily difference between nitrogen inputs and outputs in her study area. These measurements showed an average rate of retention of nitrogen as 250 mg per square metre per day. Grimm set this rate of retention as 100% and

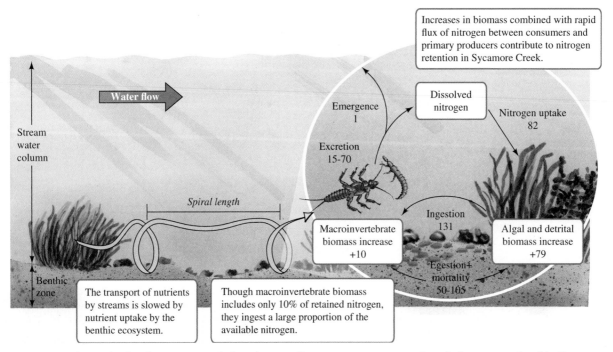

Figure 20.16 Nutrient spiraling in streams. Relative nitrogen fluxes are percentages of total nitrogen retained in Sycamore Creek, Arizona (data from Grimm 1988).

then expressed her estimates of flux rates as a percentage of this total (fig. 20.16). Nitrogen ingestion rates by macroinvertebrates averaged about 131%. How can ingestion rates be greater than 100%? What this means is that the collector-gatherers in the study stream re-ingest nitrogen in their feces. This is a well-known habit of detritivores, many of which gain more nutritional value from their food by processing it more than once.

Grimm suggests that rapid recycling of nitrogen by macroinvertebrates may increase primary production in Sycamore Creek. Stream macroinvertebrates excreted and recycled 15% to 70% of the nitrogen pool as ammonia. By their high rates of feeding on the particulate nitrogen pool and their high rates of excretion of ammonia, the macroinvertebrates of the creek reduce the T in the equation for spiral length, $S = VT$. This effect coupled with the 10% of nitrogen tied up in macroinvertebrate biomass, which reduces V, reduces the nitrogen spiral length and increases the nutrient retentiveness of Sycamore Creek.

The Effect of Vertebrate Species on Nutrient Cycling in Aquatic Ecosystems

As we saw in chapter 7, organisms allocate nutrients in different ways. In general, adult animals of a given species maintain a relatively constant nutrient content of their body. Most herbivores and detritivores must overcome large differences between the low nutrient content of their food and their own elemental requirements. Remember that when an element is in high demand, it will be sequestered from food to build tissues, whereas other elements will be egested or excreted. Therefore, differences in the ratio of nitrogen:phosphorus (N:P) for different species could influence the ratio of N:P recycled into the environment.

Michael Vanni, Alexander Flecker, James Hood, and Jenifer Headworth (2002) sought to find out how animal species identity and N:P ratio affect nutrient cycling in the Rio Las Marías, a tropical stream in Venezuela. They measured the N:P ratio of 26 fish species and 2 amphibian species. The species in the study had diets of mainly algae and detritus. Excretion of nitrogen and phosphorus was quantified by confining individuals of each species in a plastic bag containing filtered stream water for about 1 hour and then analyzing the nutrient content of the water.

Vanni and his colleagues found a negative correlation between the excretion ratios of N:P and the N:P of each species (fig. 20.17). The N:P ratios of fish and amphibians varied from about 4 to 23. This variation in N:P ratio was mainly caused by differences in allocation of phosphorus for each species. For example, armored catfish species (Loricariidae) had the highest phosphorus content and lowest N:P. These fish species require large amounts of phosphorus relative to other fish and amphibians to make their bonelike armor. As a result, armored catfish had a low N:P ratio and excreted relatively less phosphorus than fish and tadpole species with higher N:P ratios and lower phosphorus demands.

How important is the transport of nutrients by animals across ecosystem boundaries? The life cycle of anadromous

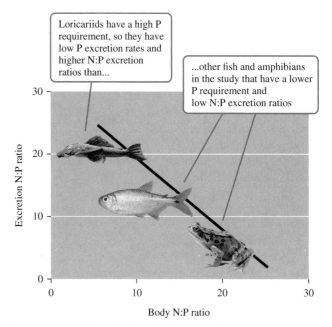

Figure 20.17 The relationship between the nutrient composition of vertebrate consumers and excretion ratios of nitrogen:phosphorus in a tropical stream (data from Vanni et al. 2002).

Pacific salmon, (*Oncorhynchus* spp.) is a dramatic example of how animals can affect nutrient cycling across ecosystem boundaries. *Oncorhynchus* spp. spend most of their lives at sea before they return to spawn and die in the streams and lakes where they were born. Annual spawning of *Oncorhynchus* spp. provides an important seasonal food resource for mammals and birds, and the marine-derived nutrients from salmon carcasses are utilized by multiple trophic levels in both freshwater and terrestrial ecosystems (fig. 20.18; Naiman et al. 2002).

As we shall see in the next section, consumers can also substantially affect nutrient cycling in terrestrial ecosystems.

Figure 20.18 Salmon transport nutrients from marine to freshwater and terrestrial ecosystems during and after spawning.

Animals and Nutrient Cycling in Terrestrial Ecosystems

As we saw in chapter 16, burrowing animals, such as ground squirrels and pocket gophers, affect local plant diversity. These burrowers also alter the distribution and abundance of nitrogen within their ecosystems.

Pocket gophers can significantly affect their ecosystems because their mounds may cover as much as 25% to 30% of the ground surface. This deposition represents a massive reorganization of soils and a substantial energy investment, since the cost of burrowing is 360 to 3,400 times that of above-ground movements. Estimates of the amount of soil deposited in mounds by gophers range from 10,000 to 85,000 kg per hectare per year.

Nancy Huntly and Richard Inouye (1988) found that pocket gophers altered the nitrogen cycle at the Cedar Creek Natural History Area in Minnesota by bringing nitrogen-poor subsoil to the surface (fig. 20.19). The result was greater horizontal heterogeneity in nitrogen availability and greater heterogeneity in light penetration. These effects on the nitrogen cycle in prairie ecosystems help explain some of the positive influences that pocket gophers have on plant diversity.

April Whicker and James Detling (1988) found that the feeding activities of prairie dogs also influence the distribution of nutrients within prairie ecosystems. This should not be surprising since these researchers estimate that prairie dogs consume or waste 60% to 80% of the net annual production from the grass-dominated areas around their colonies. One result of this heavy grazing is that above-ground biomass is reduced by 33% to 67% and the young grass tissue that remains is higher in nitrogen content (fig. 20.20). This higher nitrogen content may influence the behaviour of bison, which spend a disproportionate amount of their time grazing near prairie dog colonies.

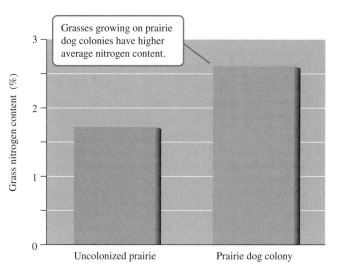

Figure 20.20   Early season nitrogen content of grasses growing on uncolonized prairie and on a young prairie dog colony (data from Whicker and Detling 1988).

Bison and other large herbivorous mammals, such as moose and African buffalo, may also influence the cycling of nutrients within terrestrial ecosystems. Sam McNaughton and his colleagues (1988) report a positive relationship between grazing intensity and the rate of turnover of plant biomass in the Serengeti Plain of eastern Africa. Figure 20.21 suggests that increased grazing increases the rate of nutrient cycling. Without grazing, nutrient cycling occurs more slowly through decomposition and through the feeding of small herbivores.

Steve Côte and colleagues at the Université Laval (Côte et al. 2004) suggest that deer may have similar effects in the forests of North America. Deer populations have increased rapidly for several decades throughout much of North America, reaching densities as high as 10/km^2 throughout the

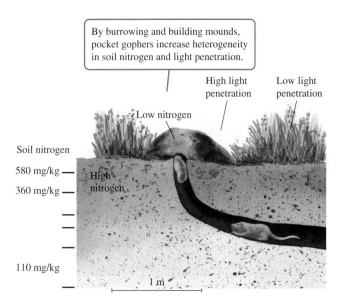

Figure 20.19   Pocket gophers and ecosystem structure (data from Huntly and Inouye 1988).

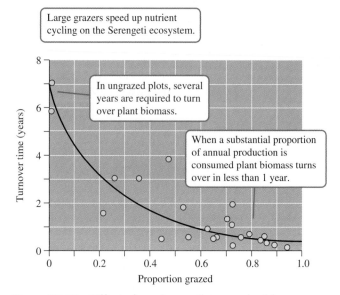

Figure 20.21   Effect of grazing on time required for turnover of plant biomass on the Serengeti ecosystem (data from McNaughton et al. 1988).

temperate forests (chapter 2). The causes of this population boom are numerous, ranging from reforestation on abandoned farmland, increased forage availability, and reduced predation by hunters and natural predators (Côte et al. 2004). Many forests are now experiencing an intensity of grazing that was not common in the evolutionary history of the species of these communities. As a result, many of the seedlings of the common canopy tree species, such as oak and maple, are poorly defended against high levels of predation. In areas of high deer density, prolonged predation appears to be shifting the community towards species that are less palatable, such as conifers and ferns (Côte et al. 2004). This makes perfect sense given our understanding of natural selection, life histories, and the intermediate disturbance hypothesis. What is less obvious, but potentially of greater long-term effect, is what may be happening in the soil.

Although deer impacts on nutrient cycling are not as well studied as are the pocket gopher and Serengeti examples we have already discussed, there is accumulating evidence that deer can alter ecosystem processes. Côte and colleagues (2004) have found evidence that deer browsing can reduce the frequency of ectomycorrhizal infections among dominant trees, which could have negative implications for nutrient uptake. Additionally, intense grazing causes dominance of plant species that have substantial morphological and chemical defences. These species produce litter of lower quality than the former dominant plants, and thus rates of decomposition are reduced. As a result, previously dominant plants seem hurt both through reduced nitrogen availability due to reduced decomposition, as well as decreased foraging ability due to reduced mycorrhizae.

In the next section, we discuss how human activities and other disturbances alter nutrient cycling within ecosystems.

CONCEPT 20.3 REVIEW

1. The Great Plains of North America have experienced many changes over the last 200 years. How have the extermination of wild bison and the introduction of crested wheatgrass likely influenced nutrient cycling?
2. How can differences in the intensity of herbivory cause differences in nutrient cycling between terrestrial and aquatic ecosystems?
3. How does spiraling length influence the nutrient retentiveness of a stream?

20.4 Human Impacts on Elemental Cycles

Human activities and natural disturbance can dramatically impact nutrient cycling. Throughout the text we have emphasized how disturbances, both natural and anthropogenic, influence ecological and evolutionary processes. This remains true as we focus here on nutrients, rather than communities and populations.

Industrial Activity and Nitrogen Deposition

How has human activity altered the nitrogen cycle? To address this question, we need to review the sources and amounts of nitrogen fixed in the absence of human manipulation. Vitousek (1994) summarized the natural background levels of nitrogen fixation as follows. The nitrogen fixed in terrestrial environments by free-living nitrogen-fixing bacteria and nitrogen-fixing plants totals approximately 100 terragrams (Tg) of nitrogen (N) per year (1 Tg = 10^{12} g). Nitrogen fixation in marine environments adds an additional 5 to 20 Tg N per year; fixation by lightning adds about 10 Tg N per year. These estimates of nonhuman sources of fixed nitrogen total approximately 130 Tg N per year.

Human additions to the nitrogen cycle now are as great or even exceed these "natural" sources of nitrogen fixation. One of the traditional ways that humans have manipulated the nitrogen cycle is by planting agricultural land with nitrogen-fixing crops. At some point, agriculturists learned that rotating legumes such as alfalfa and soybeans with crops such as wheat and canola could increase crop yields. We now know that those increased yields are due mainly to nitrogen additions to the soil by the bacteria that are associated with legumes. Vitousek estimated that the plant–microbe mutualism that results in nitrogen-fixing crops, fixes about 30 Tg N per year. As you know, farmers also apply nitrogen fertilizers produced through industrial processes. The nitrogen fixed by the fertilizer industry amounts to more than 80 Tg N per year. Finally, Vitousek estimated that the internal combustion engines in cars, trucks, and other conveyances emit about 25 Tg N per year as oxides of nitrogen. Smil (1990) estimated the total emission of nitrogen from all combustion of fossil fuels, including coal-fired electrical generation as well as internal combustion engines, at 35 Tg N per year. The main point here is that on a global scale, nitrogen fixation resulting from human activity fixes as much if not more nitrogen (135–145 Tg N versus 130 Tg N) than all nonhuman sources of fixed nitrogen combined (fig. 20.22).

The massive human contribution to the global nitrogen cycle is a recent phenomenon. For instance, the industrial production of fertilizers dates from the early twentieth century, and Vitousek estimated that 50% of all the commercial fertilizer produced prior to 1993 was applied to land between 1982 and 1993. Figure 20.23 shows that human contributions to the global nitrogen cycle have increased exponentially.

What are some of the consequences of these human-induced alterations to the global nitrogen cycle? Nitrogen addition can cause local reductions in plant and fungal diversity. Nitrogen enrichment appears to also alter the mutualistic relationship between plants and mycorrhizal fungi. Consequently, nitrogen enrichment over large regions threatens the health and survival of entire ecosystems as we know them. The health of forests near industrial areas has been in rapid decline. By creating environmental conditions favourable to some species and unfavourable to others, large-scale nitrogen enrichment threatens biological diversity.

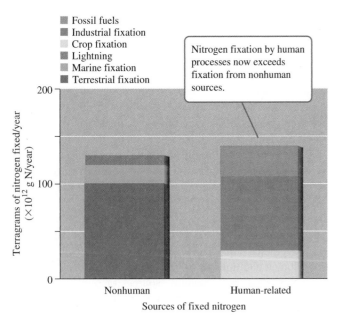

Figure 20.22 Human and nonhuman sources of fixed nitrogen (data from Vitousek 1994).

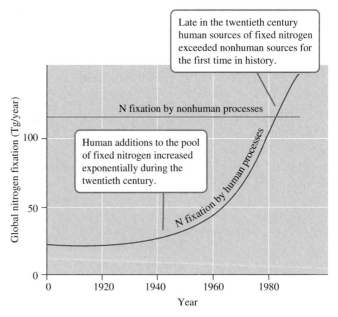

Figure 20.23 Increase in nitrogen fixation by human processes during the twentieth century (data from Vitousek 1994).

The impacts of large-scale nitrogen deposition have been studied by Scott Wilson and his graduate student, Martin Köchy, of the University of Regina (Köchy and Wilson 2001). The researchers were working in Elk Island National Park in Alberta, testing the effects of plant litter on nutrient dynamics. To do this, they measured the nitrogen that was mineralized beneath plant litter, and then in areas away from litter. They hypothesized that decomposition of the litter would result in higher levels of nitrogen. However, when they took their samples to the lab and analyzed them, they found the opposite pattern: areas away from litter had more nitrogen available than areas under litter. How was this possible? Köchy and Wilson hypothesized that the nitrogen they were measuring in the exposed plots was coming from the atmosphere. Because the magnitude of nitrogen deposition was so high, clearly greater than the nitrogen mineralized in litter, they decided to investigate its potential ecological effects.

It comes as little surprise to most people that highly urbanized areas will suffer substantial nitrogen deposition. Köchy and Wilson were interested in whether there was evidence of ecological shifts due to nitrogen deposition in less densely populated areas. Additionally, nitrogen deposition is often associated with forest encroachment on grasslands. In other words, when more nitrogen is available, trees tend to competitively exclude many grasses. Köchy and Wilson realized that an ideal location for this study was in the northern region of the North American Great Plains. This area is sparsely populated, and much of the area exists as a mosaic of grasslands and forests. They decided to measure nitrogen dynamics and forest encroachment in six national parks in Manitoba, Saskatchewan, and Alberta (fig. 20.24). In each location, they measured nitrogen deposition, the amount of nitrogen available to plants in the soil, and the extent of forest invasion into land previously occupied by grasslands.

Measures of nitrogen were relatively straightforward. Within each site they collected nitrogen that was absorbed by ion-exchange resin bags. These bags are filled with small beads of a resin that absorbed nitrogen, and the amounts absorbed can be determined in the lab. Bags were placed above the soil surface to measure deposition, and below the soil surface to measure nitrogen availability to plants. Measures of forest expansion required a completely different set of methods. The researchers obtained aerial photographs of the parks ranging from 1930 to 1995. They selected a 3.5 km^2 area in each of the earliest photographs that contained both forest and grassland. They then measured any changes in forest and grassland cover through the subsequent photographs.

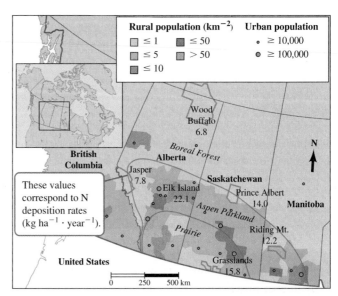

Figure 20.24 Population densities surrounding six national parks in western Canada (data from Köchy and Wilson 2001).

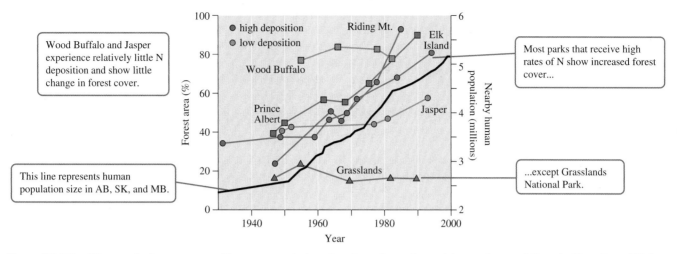

Figure 20.25 Changes in forest area and human population size throughout the prairie provinces of Canada (data from Köchy and Wilson 2001).

The results were striking. Nitrogen deposition varied among parks, and was highest in parks surrounded by high human population densities (Elk Island, Prince Albert) and lowest in areas of low population densities (Jasper, Wood Buffalo). High rates of nitrogen deposition were also positively associated with high levels of nitrogen availability in the soils. Through their studies of photographs, they found that in the last 50 to 60 years there has been an increase in forest cover in Elk Island, Prince Albert, and Riding Mountain national parks, but not Jasper, Wood Buffalo, or Grasslands (fig. 20.25). Statistical analyses indicated these changes are positively correlated to both precipitation and nitrogen deposition rates, suggesting that both water and extra nitrogen lead to increased forest cover in the North American Great Plains. Additionally, in those parks with increased forest cover, the timing of change appears synchronized with the timing of human population growth in the prairies (fig. 20.25).

These results are just one of many examples suggesting that atmospheric nitrogen is causing shifts in the composition of natural communities. These changes have occurred over only the last several decades, and likely will continue into the foreseeable future. As we show next, industrial activities have also greatly impacted the carbon cycle.

Human Influence on Carbon Cycles

Globally, human activity has greatly increased the amount of carbon that occurs as atmospheric CO_2, leading to increased global temperatures. Industrial activity has increased steadily since about the year 1800. Over the same period, atmospheric CO_2 has increased steadily. The evidence discussed here shows that most of this atmospheric increase is due to the burning of fossil fuels. Soulé pointed out that changes in atmospheric composition are likely to affect global climate and will certainly affect the biota of all terrestrial ecosystems. The effect of human activity on atmospheric CO_2 and other gases is one of the most thoroughly studied aspects of global ecology.

The concentration of CO_2 in the atmosphere has been dynamic over much of earth's history. Scientists have very carefully reconstructed atmospheric composition by studying air bubbles trapped in ice. As ice built up on glaciers in places such as Greenland and Antarctica, air spaces within the ice preserved a record of the ancient atmosphere. A record of atmospheric composition during the last 160,000 years was extracted and analyzed by a joint team of scientists from France and the former Soviet Union (Lorius et al. 1985, Barnola et al. 1987). This international team studied a 2,083 m core of ice drilled by Soviet scientists and engineers near the Antarctic station of Vostok. Vostok, located in eastern Antarctica at a latitude of over 78° S, has a mean annual temperature of −55° C, ideal conditions for preserving samples of the atmosphere in ice. The Vostok research station sits on the high Antarctic plateau, where the ice is about 3,700 m thick. The amazing physical feat of extracting such a long ice core in such difficult physical circumstances is equalled by the dramatic climatic record contained within the Vostok ice core.

To extract air trapped within ice, scientists place sections of an ice core into a chamber and create a vacuum, removing traces of the current atmosphere in the process. The ice, still under vacuum, is then crushed and the air it contains is released into the chamber. Sampling devices then measure the CO_2 concentration of the air released from the ice. The Barnola team made 66 measurements along the length of the Vostok ice core. At each location they were also able to estimate the air temperature at the time the ice was formed. The scientists made measurements of CO_2 every 25 m along the length of the ice core from about 850 m depth to the bottom of the core. These lower sections of the core correspond to ages from 50,000 to 160,000 years. Because there were many fractures in the core above 850 m depth, the upper portion of the core was generally sampled at intervals greater than 25 m.

Figure 20.26 shows the variation in CO_2 concentration revealed by the Vostok ice core. The core indicated two very large fluctuations in atmospheric CO_2 concentration. Overall,

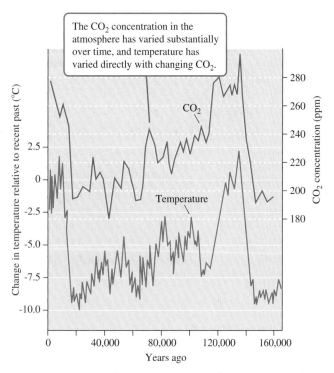

Figure 20.26   A 160,000-year record of atmospheric CO_2 concentrations and temperature change (data from Barnola et al. 1987).

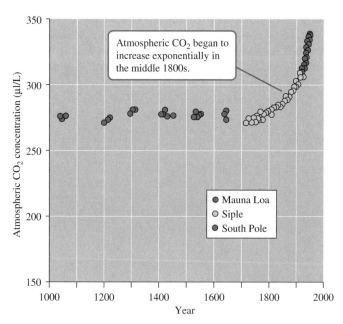

Figure 20.27   A 1,000-year atmospheric CO_2 record (data from Post et al. 1990).

it shows that CO_2 concentrations have oscillated between low concentrations of approximately 190 to 200 parts per million (ppm) and high concentrations of 260 to 280 ppm. About 160,000 years ago, the atmospheric concentration of CO_2 was less than 200 ppm. This early period in the Vostok ice core corresponds to an ice age. Then, about 140,000 years ago, the atmospheric concentration of CO_2 began to rise abruptly. This rise in CO_2 corresponds to a warmer interglacial period. High levels of CO_2 persisted until about 120,000 years ago. The concentration of CO_2 then declined and remained at relatively low concentrations until about 13,000 years ago, when atmospheric CO_2 again increased abruptly.

Notice that the fluctuations in CO_2 within the Vostok ice core correspond to variation in temperature (fig. 20.26). The periods of low CO_2 correspond to the low temperatures experienced during ice ages, while the periods of high CO_2 correspond to warmer, interglacial periods.

The most recent measurements in the Vostok ice core are about 2,000 years old. How has atmospheric CO_2 varied during the most recent 2,000 years? W. Post and colleagues (1990) assembled atmospheric CO_2 records from a number of sources to estimate atmospheric concentrations during the last 1,000 years (fig. 20.27). The first 1,000 years of the record come from the South Pole ice core, which was analyzed by Ulrich Siegenthaler and colleagues (1988) of the University of Bern, Switzerland. This record shows that the concentration of CO_2 remained relatively constant for approximately 800 years. Another study at the University of Bern provided a CO_2 record for the most recent 200 years (Friedli et al. 1986). This part of the CO_2 record comes from the Siple ice core,

from Siple Station at about 75° S latitude. While the Siple ice core does not allow us to look as far back in time as the Vostok record, it provides a very detailed estimate of recent concentrations of atmospheric CO_2. H. Friedli and colleagues dated the beginning of the Siple record at about A.D. 1744. At that time, about two and a half centuries ago, the atmospheric concentration of CO_2 was about 277 ppm. This estimated concentration is almost identical to those made by the Siegenthaler team for the same time period using the South Pole ice core. Therefore, both the South Pole and Siple ice cores indicate that the CO_2 concentration in the middle 1700s was approximately the same as at the end of the Vostok record, about 2,000 years earlier.

The Siple record showed that CO_2 increased exponentially from 1744 to 1953. The Friedli team estimated the 1953 concentration of CO_2 at 315 ppm. However, the trace in CO_2 concentrations shown in figure 20.27 extends beyond 1953 and above 315 ppm. Where do these later measurements come from? These later CO_2 concentrations are direct measurements made on Mauna Loa, Hawaii, by Charles Keeling and his associates over a period of about 40 years (Keeling and Whorf 1994).

Keeling's measurements complement the ice core data from the Vostok, South Pole, and Siple stations in two ways. First, they extend the record into the present. Second, they help validate the measurements of CO_2 made from the ice cores. How do Keeling's measurements lend credence to the ice core data? Look carefully at the plot of CO_2 concentrations shown in figure 20.27. Notice that two of the measurements made from the Siple ice core overlap the period when Keeling and his team made measurements at Mauna Loa. Notice also that the two estimates made independently by Keeling at Mauna Loa and by Friedli and his colleagues from the Siple ice core are almost identical.

The data in figure 20.28 indicate that during the nineteenth and twentieth centuries the concentration of atmospheric CO_2 increased dramatically. This period of increase coincides with the Industrial Revolution. However, what evidence is there that human activity caused this observed increase? Vitousek provided evidence by pointing out that the annual increase in atmospheric carbon in the form of CO_2 is about 3,500 Tg (1 Tg $= 10^{12}$ g), while the annual burning of fossil fuels releases about 5,600 Tg carbon as CO_2. So, fossil fuel burning alone produces more than enough CO_2 to account for recent increases in atmospheric concentrations.

If we look carefully at the pattern of CO_2 increase between 1860 and 1960 we find additional evidence for a human influence. Figure 20.28 shows three interruptions in the otherwise steady increase in the burning of fossil fuels. Those periods correspond to three major disruptions of global economic activity: World War I, the Great Depression, and World War II. At the end of each of these major global upheavals, the increase in atmospheric CO_2 resumed. These patterns provide circumstantial evidence that humans are responsible for the modern increase in atmospheric CO_2. However, there is also direct evidence.

Additional evidence that human industrial activity is at the heart of recent increases in atmospheric CO_2 comes from analyses of atmospheric concentrations of various carbon isotopes (see chapter 19). One of the most useful carbon isotopes for determining the contribution of fossil fuels to atmospheric CO_2 is radioactive ^{14}C. Because ^{14}C has a half-life of 5,730 years, fossil fuels, which have been buried for millions of years, contain very little of this carbon isotope. Consequently, burning fossil fuel adds CO_2 to an atmosphere that has little ^{14}C. If fossil fuel additions are a major source of increased atmospheric CO_2, then the relative concentration of ^{14}C in the atmosphere should be declining.

A recent decline in atmospheric ^{14}C was first described by Hans Suess (1955), a scientist with the U.S. Geological Survey. Suess made his discovery by analyzing the ^{14}C content of wood. He analyzed the ^{14}C content of wood laid down by single trees at various times during their growth. He found that annual growth rings laid down in the late 1800s had significantly higher concentrations of ^{14}C than those laid down in the 1950s. Suess proposed that the ^{14}C content in wood was being progressively reduced because burning of fossil fuels was reducing the atmospheric concentration of ^{14}C. Because of his pioneering work, reduced atmospheric ^{14}C as a consequence of fossil fuel burning is called the **Suess effect**.

Robert Bacastow and Charles Keeling (1974) compiled ^{14}C data from several studies of ^{14}C in trees and plotted the date when the wood was formed against the relative ^{14}C content of the wood. As figure 20.29 shows, the concentration of ^{14}C was fairly stable from A.D. 1700 until about 1850. After 1850, ^{14}C concentrations in wood declined significantly. The curved line in figure 20.29 shows the predictions of ^{14}C concentrations based upon global patterns of fossil fuel burning and estimated rates of exchange of carbon between the ocean, the earth's biota, and the atmosphere.

What can we conclude from this evidence? Several things are clear. First, the concentration of CO_2 in the atmosphere has varied widely during the last 160,000 years and closely parallels variation in global temperatures. High levels of atmospheric CO_2 have corresponded to higher global temperatures. Second, the atmospheric concentration of CO_2 has increased substantially in the past two centuries. This modern increase has exceeded all levels reached during the past 160,000 years. Third, there is little doubt that the present levels of CO_2 in the atmosphere are strongly influenced by the burning of fossil fuels.

Deforestation and Nutrient Loss

As Gene Likens and Herbert Bormann watched, work crews felled the trees covering an entire stream basin in the Hubbard

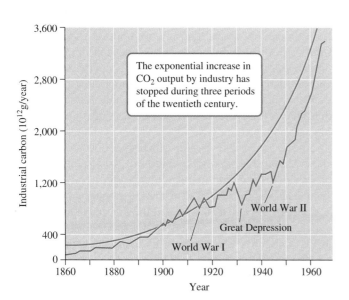

Figure 20.28 Deviations from recent exponential increases in fossil fuel burning (data from Bacastow and Keeling 1974).

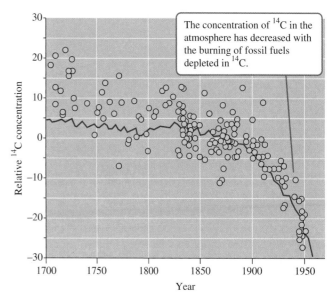

Figure 20.29 The Suess effect (data from Bacastow and Keeling 1974).

Brook Experimental Forest of New Hampshire. The felling of these trees was a key part of an experiment that Likens and Bormann had designed to study how forests affect the loss of nutrients, such as nitrogen, from forested lands (Bormann and Likens 1994; Likens and Bormann 1995). They had studied two small stream valleys for three years before cutting the trees in one of the valleys. The undisturbed stream valley would act as a control against which to compare the response of the deforested stream valley (fig. 20.30).

Before they deforested the experimental basin, Likens and Bormann inventoried the distribution of nutrients. Those measurements indicated that over 90% of the nutrients in the ecosystem were tied up in soil organic matter. Most of the rest, 9.5%, was in vegetation. They estimated the rates at which some organisms fix atmospheric nitrogen and the rates at which weathering releases nutrients from the granite bedrock of the stream basins. They also measured the input of nutrients to the forest ecosystem from precipitation and nutrient outputs with stream water. The annual nutrient outputs in streamflow amounted to less than 1% of the amount contained within the forest ecosystems. After this preliminary work, Likens and Bormann cut the trees on their experimental stream basin. They then used herbicides to suppress regrowth of vegetation in their experimental basin and continued to apply herbicides for three years.

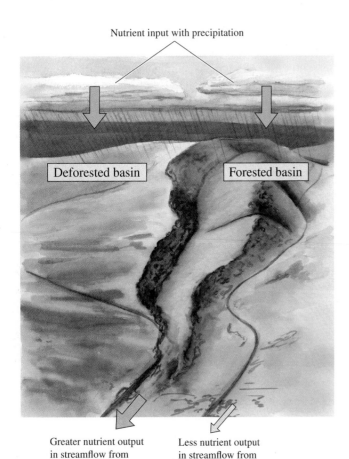

Nutrient input with precipitation

Deforested basin

Forested basin

Greater nutrient output in streamflow from deforested stream basin.

Less nutrient output in streamflow from forested stream basin.

Figure 20.30   This whole-stream-basin manipulation demonstrated the influence of forest trees on nutrient budgets of northeastern hardwood forests.

The increased rates of nutrient loss following forest cutting were dramatic. The connection between forest cutting and increased nutrient output is shown clearly by plotting nutrient concentrations in the streams draining experimental and control stream basins. Figure 20.31 shows the highly significant increases in nitrate losses following deforestation, which were 40 to 50 times higher than those in the deforested basin.

The development of vegetation following a disturbance affects many ecosystem processes, including nutrient cycling (see chapter 18). Monica Turner and her colleagues (2009) demonstrated biological influences on nutrient retention from forest ecosystems following the stand-replacing fires of 1988 in Yellowstone National Park, Wyoming. These forests are dominated by Lodgepole pine (*Pinus contorta*) with a diverse understory plant community that quickly regenerated following the fire (Turner et al. 2003). The studies of the Yellowstone fires suggest that the young, rapidly growing *P. contorta* forest and understory vegetation was a nitrogen sink in the ecosystem. Turner's work also indicates that not all ecosystems lose nutrients following a disturbance and that many factors affect nutrient retention over time.

What do these results suggest about the role of vegetation in preventing losses of nitrogen from forest ecosystems? Over the short term, at least, uptake by vegetation in ecosystems with high rates of plant growth should be able to rapidly reduce nitrogen loss following disturbance.

Now let's consider how disturbance affects nutrient losses from stream ecosystems, where nutrient loss appears to be highly episodic and associated with disturbance during flooding.

Flooding and Nutrient Export by Streams

How do the nutrient dynamics of stream ecosystems respond to variations in stream flow? Judy Meyer and Gene Likens (1979) examined the long-term dynamics of phosphorus in Bear Brook, a stream ecosystem in the Hubbard Brook Experimental Forest. They found that during periods of average flow, the ratio of annual phosphorus inputs to exports varied from 0.56 to 1.6 and that the balance depended upon stream discharge. Meyer and Likens found that exports were highly episodic and associated with periods of high flow.

How did Meyer and Likens determine the phosphorus dynamics of Bear Brook ecosystem? They measured the geological and meteorological inputs and the geological exports of phosphorus in the stream, which they divided into three size fractions: (1) dissolved phosphorus, <0.45 μm, (2) phosphorus associated with fine particles, 0.45 μm to 1 mm, and (3) phosphorus associated with coarse particles, >1 mm.

Meyer and Likens inventoried the movement and storage of phosphorus in the Bear Brook ecosystem. They measured the inputs of dissolved phosphorus at 12 seeps (areas of groundwater input) along the length of the stream. They also measured meteorological inputs, which included precipitation and forest litter falling or blowing into the stream. The only significant export of phosphorus in the ecosystem was transport with streamflow. The researchers measured the amount of particulate

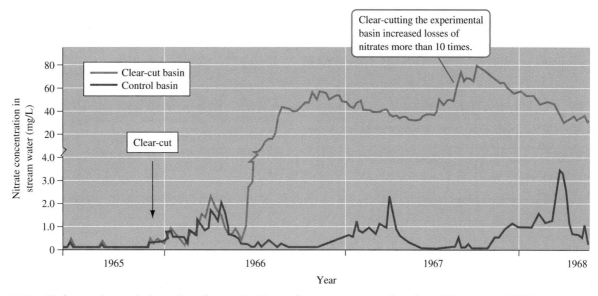

Figure 20.31 Deforestation and nitrate loss from a deciduous forest ecosystem (data from Likens et al. 1970).

matter transported by the Bear Brook ecosystem by collecting the organic matter deposited behind the weir (a small dam used to measure streamflow) on the stream and by collecting organic matter captured by nets set at seven sites. They estimated the amount of organic matter stored by removing all the organic matter in 42 randomly located 1 m^2 areas of stream bottom.

During 1974 to 1975, Meyer and Likens estimated an almost exact balance between inputs and exports of phosphorus, with approximately 1,250 mg of phosphorus per square metre of input and approximately 1,300 mg of phosphorus per square metre of output. Despite a balance between input and output, their data indicated significant transformation of phosphorus-size fractions. Phosphorus inputs to Bear Brook were almost evenly divided between dissolved (28%), fine particulate (37%), and coarse particulate (35%) fractions. However, 62% of exports were fine particulates. Clearly physical and biological processes converted dissolved and coarse particulate forms of phosphorus into fine particulate forms.

Meyer and Likens used their estimates to reconstruct the long-term phosphorus dynamics of Bear Brook. During 1974 to 1975, the ratio of phosphorus export to input was almost exactly one (1.04). However, the Meyer and Likens model of phosphorus dynamics indicated considerable year-to-year variation in this ratio during the period from 1963 to 1975, which included the wettest and driest years in the 20-year precipitation record for the area. The predicted ratio of output to input over this interval was highly correlated with annual streamflow. The ratio ranged from 0.56 in the driest year to 1.6 in the wettest year (fig. 20.32). In other words, during the driest year only 56% of phosphorus inputs were exported, while during the wettest year exports amounted to 160% of inputs. In wet years the stream ecosystem's standing stocks of phosphorus were reduced by high levels of export.

The patterns of inputs and exports of phosphorus from Bear Brook were highly pulsed during Meyer and Likens' study (fig. 20.33). They estimated that from 1974 to 1975, 48% of total annual input of phosphorus to Bear Brook entered during

10 days and that 67% of exports left the ecosystem during 10 days. The annual peak in phosphorus input was associated with autumn leaf fall, and an annual pulse of export was associated with spring snowmelt. Most phosphorus export, however, was irregular because it was driven by flooding caused by intense storms that might occur during any month of the year. If we consider floods as a source of disturbance, the behaviour of stream ecosystems is consistent with the generalization that disturbance increases the loss of nutrients from ecosystems.

Aquatic ecologists study the nutrient dynamics of aquatic ecosystems like Bear Brook because, as we saw in chapter 19, nutrient availability is a key regulator of aquatic primary production. As we shall see in the Ecological Tools and Approaches section, nutrient enrichment of ecosystems by human activity is a worldwide problem.

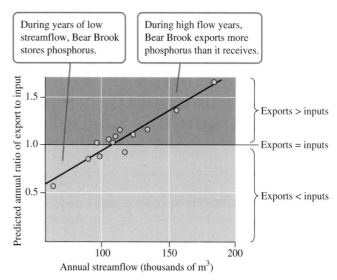

Figure 20.32 Annual streamflow and ratio of phosphorus export to input in Bear Brook, New Hampshire (data from Meyer and Likens 1979).

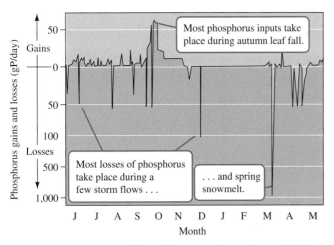

Figure 20.33   Daily gains and losses of phosphorus (P) by the Bear Brook ecosystem from 1974 to 1975 (data from Meyer and Likens 1979).

CONCEPT 20.4 REVIEW

1. How do human industrial activities impact nitrogen and carbon cycles?
2. What were the similarities and differences between the experiments by Vitousek and his colleagues and that of Likens and Bormann?
3. Flood control on streams and rivers has often been cited as a potential threat to populations of aquatic animals and riparian trees that require flooding for reproduction. How might flow regulation also alter stream ecosystem nutrient dynamics?

ECOLOGICAL TOOLS AND APPROACHES

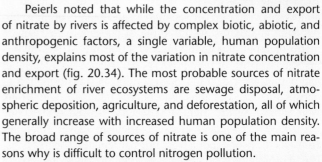

Altering Aquatic and Terrestrial Ecosystems

Human activity increasingly affects ecosystem nutrient cycles. Agriculture and forestry can remove nutrients from ecosystems. However, increasingly, human activity enriches ecosystems with nutrients, especially with nitrogen and phosphorus. Nitrogen enrichment comes from a variety of sources: combustion of fossil fuels, agricultural fertilizers, land clearing, forest burning, industry, and animal waste.

Nitrogen from anthropogenic sources enters the atmosphere as emissions or particulates, producing air pollution. Nitrogen fertilization occurs when biologically available forms of nitrogen fall from the atmosphere as either **wet** (precipitation) or **dry** (dry fall) **deposition**. In the temperate coastal forests of southern Chile, far from urban and industrial centres, inputs from nitrogen deposition amount to about 0.1 to 1.0 kg per hectare per year. In contrast, in the Netherlands, with its high population density and intense agriculture, the deposition of nitrogen to forest ecosystems adds up to about 60 kg of nitrogen per hectare per year.

Humans are also a major source of nutrient inputs to aquatic ecosystems. Nutrient enrichment of aquatic ecosystems can result in water quality problems and eutrophication, a process generally resulting in increased primary production, anoxic conditions, and reduced biodiversity. Benjamin Peierls and his colleagues (1991) examined the relationship of human population density within river basins and nitrate concentration and export by 42 major rivers. These rivers, which deliver approximately 37% of the total freshwater flow to the oceans, support human population densities ranging from 1 to 1,000 individuals per square kilometre.

Peierls noted that while the concentration and export of nitrate by rivers is affected by complex biotic, abiotic, and anthropogenic factors, a single variable, human population density, explains most of the variation in nitrate concentration and export (fig. 20.34). The most probable sources of nitrate enrichment of river ecosystems are sewage disposal, atmospheric deposition, agriculture, and deforestation, all of which generally increase with increased human population density. The broad range of sources of nitrate is one of the main reasons why is difficult to control nitrogen pollution.

Cities are home to an increasing proportion of the human population. Worldwide, more people live in or near urban areas than in the more rural countryside. This concentration of people in cities is also associated with the concentration and transformation of energy, materials, and waste in a small area, which can have disproportionate impacts on nutrient cycling. Prompted by a need for better understanding of urban areas, ecological studies of nutrient pools and fluxes within whole watersheds, like those of Hubbard Brook Experimental Forest, are being applied to these human-dominated ecosystems.

One of the first questions asked by ecologists is whether urban ecosystems within a watershed are a source or a sink for nutrients. Peter Groffman and his colleagues (2004) compared the nitrogen budgets of forested, agricultural, and urbanized watersheds as part of the Baltimore Ecosystem Study with surprising results. They constructed a budget by calculating inputs and outputs of nitrogen for each watershed type. Nitrate concentrations were measured as a major component of nitrogen outputs in streams draining each watershed.

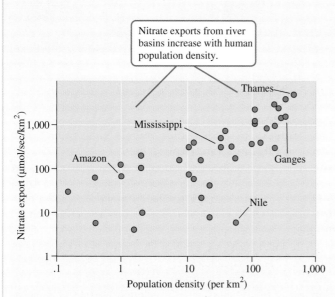

Figure 20.34 Human population density and nitrate export from river basins (data from Peierls et al. 1991).

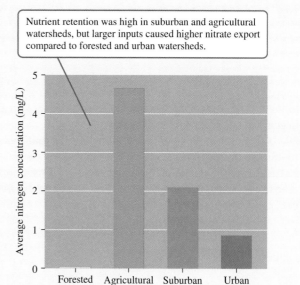

Figure 20.35 Nitrate export in streams draining watersheds with different land use in Baltimore County, Maryland (data from Pickett et al. 2008).

As expected, mean nitrate concentrations were very low in the forested watershed (fig. 20.35). However, nitrate levels in dense urban areas were lower than those in either the suburban or agricultural watersheds.

What caused higher nitrate concentrations in streams draining the agricultural and suburban watersheds? First, Groffman and his colleagues compared nitrogen inputs into the different watersheds. All of these watersheds receive similar amounts of atmospheric nitrogen deposition. The first major difference in inputs was in the application of fertilizers. Estimates of nitrogen inputs from fertilizers were highest for agricultural areas, but application rates of fertilizer to residential lawns in suburban areas were also substantial. They also found that centralized urban sanitary systems can leak nitrogen, but are controllable. In contrast, residential septic systems in suburban areas are designed to discharge nitrate and can contribute to nitrate concentrations in streams.

The difference in nitrogen outputs from these watersheds could not be explained by inputs alone. Another surprising result of Groffman's study was that the suburban watershed retained an estimated 75% of nitrogen inputs, approaching retention values of forested watersheds (95%). So even though the suburban areas had higher nitrogen inputs, only a quarter of this nitrogen was exported downstream. Groffman and his colleagues attribute this high capacity for nitrogen retention in suburban areas to actively growing lawns, woodlots, and riparian areas that serve as nitrogen sinks. These permeable areas within the watershed have the potential to decrease nitrogen export to surface water through biological uptake and denitrification of nitrate. High nitrogen retention has also been observed for

the large metropolitan area of Phoenix, Arizona (Baker et al. 2001). These results call into question a common assumption that human alteration of the environment limits ecological processes in urbanized areas.

If urban areas can retain a large proportion of nitrogen inputs, why do we observe high nitrate export to rivers dominated by human activity worldwide? Studies of nitrogen budgets in cities are very limited and, to date, incomplete. For instance, the nitrogen budget for Baltimore did not include the large flux of food into and sewage out of the study watersheds. Wastewater is piped out for treatment on much larger streams or bays where wastewater effluent can be safely discharged. Most cities around the globe are facing the challenge of minimizing nitrogen pollution without proper infrastructure and planning. In a review of urban ecological studies, Emily Bernhardt and her colleagues (2008) suggest that cities need to integrate nitrogen reduction strategies into their management plans to minimize impacts on water quality. However, while scientists can make recommendations based on their research, they do not make or implement policy. Cities are dynamic, complex, socio-ecological systems that require close cooperation of scientists, managers, and citizens to minimize nutrient pollution.

In summary, we know there is a direct connection between human activity and nutrient enrichment of ecosystems and that nutrient enrichment has a number of negative consequences. Application of an ecosystem approach to studies of nitrogen pools and fluxes within urban watersheds has advanced our understanding of nutrient cycling in urban systems, but much work remains at this frontier of ecology.

SUMMARY

The elements organisms require for development, maintenance, and reproduction are called *nutrients*. Ecologists refer to the use, transformation, movement, and reuse of nutrients in ecosystems as *nutrient cycling*.

20.1 All common elements have global cycles that include biotic and abiotic pools.

Nutrient cycling is one of the most ecologically significant processes studied by ecosystem ecologists. The **carbon**, **nitrogen**, and **phosphorus cycles** have played especially prominent roles in studies of nutrient cycling. Chemical transformations move C, N, and P among different biotic and abiotic pools. Human actions and natural processes influence the rate of chemical flux and the size of each pool.

20.2 Decomposition rate is influenced by temperature, moisture, and chemical composition of litter and the environment.

The rate of decomposition affects the rate at which nutrients such as nitrogen and phosphorus are made available to primary producers. Rates of decomposition in terrestrial ecosystems are higher under warm, moist conditions. The rate of decomposition in terrestrial ecosystems increases with nitrogen content and decreases with the lignin content of litter. The chemical composition of litter and the availability of nutrients in the surrounding environment also influence rates of decomposition in aquatic ecosystems.

20.3 Plants and animals can modify the distribution and cycling of nutrients in ecosystems.

Aquatic and terrestrial systems have significant differences in their nutrient cycles. The dynamics of nutrients in streams are best represented by a spiral rather than a cycle. The length of stream required for an atom of a nutrient to complete a cycle is called the spiraling length. Stream macroinvertebrates can substantially reduce spiraling length of nutrients in stream ecosystems. Animals can also alter the distribution and rate of nutrient cycling in terrestrial ecosystems.

20.4 Human activities and natural disturbance can dramatically impact nutrient cycling.

Analyses of air trapped in ice show that the concentration of CO_2 in the atmosphere has varied widely during the last 160,000 years and closely parallels variation in global temperatures. High levels of atmospheric CO_2 have corresponded to higher global temperatures. The buildup of atmospheric CO_2 during the past two centuries has reached levels of atmospheric CO_2 not equalled in the past 160,000 years. The present level of CO_2 in the atmosphere is strongly influenced by burning of fossil fuels. Increases in atmospheric CO_2 concentration are associated with increased global temperatures and a variety of environmental impacts. Human land use and pollution can also alter cycling of other elements in ecosystems. Vegetation exerts substantial control on nutrient retention by terrestrial ecosystems. Vegetative controls on nutrient loss from forest ecosystems appear to be most important in environments that are warm and moist during the growing season. Vegetative controls appear to be less important in cold and/or dry environments. Nutrient loss by stream ecosystems is highly pulsed and associated with disturbance by flooding.

Nutrient enrichment by humans is altering aquatic and terrestrial ecosystems. Nitrate concentration and export by the earth's major rivers correlate directly with human population density. A study of an urban watershed showed that cities can have higher nutrient retention than previously expected. Ecosystem-scale studies can be used as a tool to improve management of urban areas and to address challenging water quality problems.

REVIEW QUESTIONS

1. Of all the naturally occurring elements in the biosphere, why have the cycles of carbon, nitrogen, and phosphorus been so intensively studied by ecologists? (Hint: Think about the kinds of organic molecules of which these elements are constituents. Also think back to our discussions, in chapter 19, of the influences of nitrogen and phosphorus on rates of primary production.)

2. Parmenter and Lamarra (1991) studied decomposition of fish and waterfowl carrion in a freshwater marsh. During the course of their studies they found that the soft tissues of both fish and waterfowl decomposed faster than the most rapidly decomposing plant tissues. Explain the rapid decomposition of these animal carcasses.

3. Review figure 19.4, in which Rosenzweig (1968) plotted the relationship between actual evapotranspiration and net primary production. How do you think that decomposition rates change across the same ecosystems? Using what you learned in chapter 20, design an experiment to test your hypothesis.

4. Melillo, Aber, and Muratore (1982) suggested that soil fertility may influence the rate of decomposition in terrestrial ecosystems. Design an experiment to test this hypothesis. If you test for the effects of soil fertility, how will you control for the influences of temperature, moisture, and litter chemistry?

5. Many rivers around the world have been straightened and deepened to improve conditions for navigation. Side effects of these changes include increased average water velocity and decreased

movement of water into shallow riverside environments such as eddies and marginal wetlands. What are the probable influences of these changes on nutrient spiraling length? Use the model of Newbold et al. (1983) in your discussion.

6. Likens and Bormann (1995) found that vegetation substantially influences the rate of nutrient loss from small stream catchments in the northern hardwood forest ecosystem. How do vegetative biomass and rates of primary production in these forests affect their capacity to regulate nutrient loss? How much do you think vegetation affects nutrient movements in desert ecosystems?

7. McNaughton, Ruess, and Seagle (1988) proposed that grazing by large mammals increases the rate of nitrogen cycling on the savannas of East Africa. Explain how passing through a large mammal could increase the rate of breakdown of plant biomass. In chapter 19, we also saw how grazing mammals may increase the rate of primary production on the savanna. How might the disappearance of the large mammals of East Africa affect ecosystem processes on the savanna?

8. If rates of decomposition are higher in ecosystems with higher nutrient availability, how should nutrient enrichment affect rates of decomposition? Because of its effects on fungal diversity, could nutrient enrichment of ecosystems affect rates of decomposition differently over the short term versus the long term?

9. Atmospheric warming may cause increases or decreases to decomposition in the arctic. A shift in either direction has the potential to greatly alter the atmospheric concentration of CO_2, which can further alter global temperatures. However, the science is not conclusive on what direction of effect will occur. What do you believe is the role of the scientist in public debate on this issue? More generally, should a scientist speak out on environmental issues? If so, when?

For more information on the resources available from McGraw-Hill Ryerson, go to www.mcgrawhill.ca/he/solutions.

LARGE-SCALE ECOLOGY

Many ecological processes occur at spatial scales much larger than individual ecosystems, and many patterns emerge only if we step back and look at natural systems from a great distance. We also gain a unique perspective on ecological understanding when we are able to see changes through time, recognizing that natural systems are dynamic. In this final section, we explore the mechanisms and consequences of interactions at scales much greater than individuals, populations, communities, or even ecosystems. Here we explore the ecology of landscapes (chapter 21), geographic regions (chapter 22), and changes through time (chapter 23).

Chapter 21 Landscape Ecology
Chapter 22 Macroecology
Chapter 23 Global Ecology

LANDSCAPE ECOLOGY

CHAPTER 21

CHAPTER CONCEPTS

21.1 Landscapes are created and change in response to geological processes, climate, activities of organisms, and fire.

Concept 21.1 Review

21.2 Landscape structure includes the size, shape, composition, number, and position of patches, or landscape elements, in a landscape.

Concept 21.2 Review

21.3 Landscape structure influences processes such as the flow of energy, materials, and species distributions across a landscape.

Ecology in Action: Linear Disturbances Across the Landscape

Concept 21.3 Review

Ecological Tools and Approaches: Linking Population, Behavioural, and Landscape Ecology

Summary

Review Questions

n every region on earth and at every stage in history, human survival has required a basic understanding of landscapes. In contemporary ecology, a **landscape** is a heterogeneous area consisting of distinctive patches—that landscape ecologists refer to as **landscape elements**—organized into a mosaic-like pattern. The elements of a mountain landscape may include forests, meadows, bogs, and streams, while those in an urban landscape include parks, industrial districts, and residential areas.

While our distant ancestors did not articulate a formal definition of landscape, their lives reflected their understanding of landscape structure and process. Hunters and gatherers were familiar with variation across the landscapes in which they lived. They learned where to find plants useful as food or medicines, where game animals hid, fed, watered, and how their food sources moved with the seasons. Later, pastoralists learned how to locate forage for livestock, how the most productive pastures changed with the seasons and between years of drought and years with ample rain, and where in the landscape predators and other dangers were likely to be encountered (fig. 21.1). Settled agriculturalists learned which areas were most suitable for planting row crops, which were areas were best for cereal grains or vineyards, and how to work and shape the land to guide the movement of water and avoid soil losses (fig. 21.2). The establishment of cities required managing the movements of food, waste, and water between the urban centre and the surrounding agricultural and wild lands.

With mounting environmental pressures from human populations, the need for understanding the ecology of entire landscapes has grown, resulting in the formation of the subdiscipline of landscape ecology. Jianguo Wu and Richard Hobbs (2007) point out that the precise meaning of the term landscape ecology is still debated among landscape ecologists. However, drawing from its many definitions, Wu and Hobbs identify a thematic thread uniting the discipline and on

that basis define *landscape ecology* as the study of the relationship between spatial pattern and ecological processes over a range of scales. Though most landscape ecologists work at fairly large spatial scales (km, not cm), the concepts of landscape ecology can been applied to spatial patterns and ecological processes ranging from those relevant to ground beetles moving across a few metres of grassland (Wiens et al. 1997) to very large regional scales measured in thousands of square kilometres.

Three facets of landscape ecology distinguish it from the other subdisciplines of ecology presented in this text. The first is that landscape ecology is generally highly interdisciplinary. Gunther Tress, Bärbel Tress, and Gary Fry (2005) point out that **interdisciplinary research** involves researchers from multiple disciplines working closely to produce an understanding that integrates across disciplines. Interdisciplinary research can include several scientific disciplines or extend beyond the boundaries of the natural sciences into the social sciences and humanities. The second characteristic distinguishing landscape ecology from other subdisciplines is that it has included humans, and human influences on landscapes, since its beginnings. As a consequence, landscape ecology is often intertwined with conservation biology—though not all studies in landscape ecology necessarily have a conservation focus. Third, and perhaps most central to the discipline, landscape ecology focuses on understanding the extent, origin, and ecological consequences of spatial heterogeneity across multiple spatial scales.

The full scope of landscape ecology cannot be covered in a single chapter. However, we will sample the discipline by reviewing some studies concerning core areas of landscape ecology. In earlier chapters, we discussed structure, process, and change within the context of populations, communities, and ecosystems. In chapter 21, we revisit structure, process, and change within the context of landscapes. We begin by asking, "where does a landscape come from?"

Figure 21.1   Managing large bands of grazing animals requires detailed knowledge of local landscapes, especially the locations of good forage, water, and shelter.

Figure 21.2   Successful agriculturalists must have a basic understanding of landscape structure and process. These terraced rice fields in China are the result of human engineering of the landscape to retain water and prevent erosion.

21.1 Origins of Landscapes

Landscapes are created and change in response to geological processes, climate, activities of organisms, and fire. What creates the landscapes we see? Many forces combine in numerous ways to produce the diversity of landscape elements found in natural systems. In chapter 18, we saw how fire initiated succession in the boreal forest and other communities. We also discussed how Parks Canada was using fire and other disturbances to manage the biodiversity of the National Parks. In chapter 17, we discussed how the activity of ecosystem engineers could alter the landscape. For example, beaver dams increase riparian areas, and have impacts on patterns of tree diversity. In this section, we discuss more explicitly how geological process, climate, organisms, and fire contribute to the creation of landscapes.

Geological Processes, Climate, and the Landscape

Geological processes such as volcanism, sedimentation, and erosion interact with local climatic conditions to form many landscape elements. For instance, the alluvial deposits along a river valley provide growing conditions different from those on thin, well-drained soils on nearby hills. A volcanic cinder cone in the middle of a sandy plain offers different environmental conditions than the surrounding plain. Distinctive ecosystems may develop on each of these geological surfaces, creating patchiness in the landscape. In the following example, we shall see how glaciers have contributed to the vegetative patchiness found in much of Canada and other countries of mid-to-high latitudes.

Glaciations and Vegetation Mosaics in Northern North America

Around 20,000 years ago, most of what is now Canada and the northern United States was covered by glaciers. The landscape that we see now is largely a result of the behaviour of ice

and snow, creating a mosaic of soil conditions, landforms, and the substrate that forms today's ecosystems. Twenty-thousand years is hardly a blink of the eye in terms of geological time; however, the impact of glaciers in moving rocks and scouring the land more than compensates for their ephemeral nature. We begin with a brief overview of the rise and fall of glaciers. Evelyn Pielou, who we first encountered in chapter 16, has provided a most readable account of the role glaciations have played in developing the landscape around us (Pielou 1991).

Earth's climate is subject to not only the immediate consequences of human activities, but also a variety of naturally occurring cycles. Over the last many millions of years, we have had periods of **glacial ages**, within which occur **glaciations**. Glacial ages can last millions of years, within which are approximately 100,000-year cycles that include very cold periods lasting between 60,000 and 90,000 years (glaciations), and warmer periods lasting 10,000–40,000 years (**interglacials**). We are currently living within an interglacial period of a glacial age. The last glaciation was the Wisconsin, and it reached its peak 20,000 years ago (fig. 21.3*b*). During the current interglacial period, only remnants of glaciers remain (fig. 21.3*a*), and in their place is our current landscape, which was formed as plants and other species migrated out from areas not covered in ice.

The effects of glaciers on the physical structure of landscapes are dramatic, and can been seen throughout Canada (fig. 21.4). Glaciers have an unrivalled ability to move soil and rock over great distances, literally reshaping the landscape. As a glacier moves forward, it carries with it large volumes of rock, scouring the landscape. More erosion occurs when rocks are ripped out of the earth and water enters cracks in the surrounding material and freezes, further widening the cracks and weakening the rock's structure. When alpine glaciers flow down valleys in mountains, they cause a U-shaped cross-section in the valley, in contrast to the familiar V-shape of valleys created by streams. Throughout a valley created

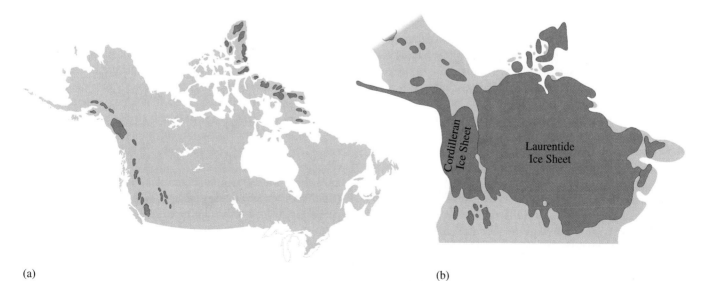

(a)   (b)

Figure 21.3 Distribution of glaciers in North America (*a*) in the late twentieth century, and (*b*) 18,000 years ago (data from Pielou 1991).

(a)

(b)

(c)

(d)

Figure 21.4 Impacts of glaciers on landscapes can be seen as (*a*) a U-shaped valley in Labrador, (*b*) a drumlin field in Manitoba, (*c*) eskers in Québec, and (*d*) a till plain in the Northwest Territories.

by glaciers will be **talus**, great rock piles pushed aside and left behind by glaciers. Continental glaciers also leave a variety of signatures in the landscape. When the glaciers retreat, they leave behind large masses of **till**, unsorted material that includes clay, rocks, and boulders. When the till is piled up by either being pushed to the side or left behind with glacial retreat, they form **moraines**. Marking the furthest extent of glaciers are terminal moraines, formed by the materials that were pushed forward during the glacial advance. When a glacier passes over a moraine left by a prior glacier, it can be reshaped into **drumlins**, a hill (or series of hills) drained by streams. When much debris flows out of streams fed by glaciers, long narrow ridges called **eskers** can be formed. When a block of ice becomes detached from the glacier, melting in place, a depression is formed called a **kettle**. As depressions generally fill with water, kettle lakes dot landscapes carved by glaciers.

These physical structures are common throughout Canada and a close look while biking across the Canadian Shield will reveal the impacts of glaciers on the shape of a landscape.

The story of the landscape does not end with glacial melting; instead, for the plants and animals, it just begins.

Glacial retreat reveals a bare rocky substrate. No soil, no seedbank, no plants. Very quickly, however, seeds and spores arrive and new plants grow initiating primary succession (chapter 18). We have seen evidence for these plant migrations throughout the text, such as the work of Margaret Davis (chapter 1). But where exactly do these migrating plants come from? Some of these seeds come from **glacial refugia**, areas that through a variety of interactions between geology and climate were never glaciated, while others come from populations that were south of the terminal extent of the glaciers (fig. 21.5). A special type of refugia is the **nunatak**, mountain peaks that were surrounded, but not covered, by continental glaciers. Of course, not all mountains served as refugia, and instead many are (and were) home to a number of alpine glaciers that also carve a landscape into the rock.

What the colonizing plants encountered following the melt was a very heterogeneous landscape. In some areas there was nothing but large rocks, a substrate nearly impossible

Figure 21.5 The cypress hills in Alberta and Saskatchewan were the northern-most location that remained south of the glacial advance in North America. As a result, this area is home to unique vegetation and likely played a critical role in seed production and dispersal following the melt.

to get roots into. Others areas had fine glacial till, facilitating root growth. These geological differences persist to this day, and a great variety of ecosystems can be found within a short distance along moraines, eskers, and kettles. The spatial arrangements of these different ecosystems are caused by interactions between species-specific traits of the colonizing plants and the changes to the landscape caused by the power of glaciers.

The effects of glaciers are most visibly obvious through their direct influence on the shape of the land on which they rested. However, their true impact can be global in scale. Global sea levels rise and fall with glaciers. As we saw in chapter 3, large volumes of water are stored in glaciers. When glaciers melt, much of that water ends up in the ocean, contributing to a rise in sea levels. The effects of rising sea levels are obvious, and highlight the ephemeral (on a geological time scale) nature of mangrove islands and coral atolls (chapter 3). However, we can also imagine back to when much of the water currently found in the oceans was stored as ice across much of North America. During these periods of lower sea levels, many now isolated islands were connected by land bridges. These connections served as corridors for the movement of numerous species, allowing the colonization of new habitats.

Organisms and Landscape Structure

Organisms of all sorts, including people, influence the structure of landscapes. Many studies of landscape change have focused on the conversion of forest to agricultural landscapes. In North America, an often-cited example of this sort of landscape change is that of Cadiz Township, Green County, Wisconsin (Curtis 1956). In 1831, approximately 93.5% of Cadiz Township was forested. By 1882, the percentage of forested land had decreased to 27% and by 1902 forest cover

had fallen to less than 9%. Between 1902 and 1950, the total area of forest decreased again to 3.4%. Similar changes in landscape structure have been observed throughout the midwestern region of the United States. However, in some other forested regions of North America and Europe, the pattern of recent landscape change has been different.

In eastern North America, many abandoned farms have reverted to forest and in these landscapes forest cover has increased. Recent increases in forest cover have also been observed in some parts of northern Europe. One such area is the Veluwe region in the central Netherlands. Maureen Hulshoff (1995) reviewed the landscape changes that have occurred in the Veluwe region during the past 1,200 years. The Veluwe landscape was originally dominated by a mixed deciduous forest. Then, from AD 800 to 1100, people gradually occupied the area and cut the forest. Consequently, forests were gradually converted to heathlands, which are landscapes dominated by low shrubs and used for livestock foraging. Later, small areas of cropland were interspersed with the extensive heathlands. During the tenth and eleventh centuries, some areas were devegetated completely and converted to areas of drifting sand. The problem of drifting sand continued to increase until the end of the nineteenth century, when the Dutch government began planting pine plantations on the Veluwe landscape, a practice that continued into the twentieth century.

Figure 21.6 shows the changes in the composition of the Veluwe landscape from 1845 to 1982. The greatest change over this period was a shift in dominance from heathlands to forests. In 1845, heathlands made up 66% of the landscape, while forests constituted 17%. By 1982, coverage by heathlands had fallen to 12% of the landscape and forest coverage had risen to 64%. The figure also shows modest but ecologically significant changes in the other landscape elements. The

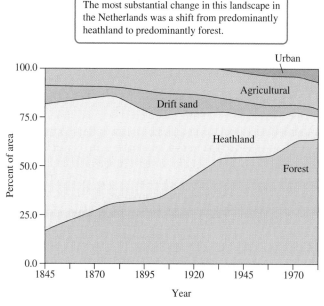

Figure 21.6 Change in a Dutch landscape (data from Hulshoff 1995).

area of drift sand reached a peak in 1898 and then dropped and held steady at 3% to 4% from 1957 to 1982. Urban areas established a significant presence beginning in 1957. Finally, coverage by agricultural areas has varied from 9% to 16% over the study interval, the least variation shown by any of the landscape elements.

As total coverage by forest and heathlands changed within the Veluwe landscape, the number and average area of forest and heath patches also changed. These changes indicate increasing fragmentation of heathlands and decreasing fragmentation of forests. For instance, between 1845 and 1982, the number of forest patches declined, while the average area of forest patches increased. During this period, the number of heath patches increased until 1957. Between 1957 and 1982, the number of heath patches decreased as some patches were eliminated. The average area of heath patches decreased rapidly between 1845 and 1931 and then remained approximately stable from 1931 to 1982.

During the period that Cadiz Township in Wisconsin was losing forest cover, this landscape element was increasing in the Veluwe district of the Netherlands. These two examples show how human activity has changed landscape structure. However, what forces drive human influences on landscapes? In both Cadiz Township and the Veluwe landscape, the driving forces were economic. A developing agricultural economy converted Cadiz Township from forest to farmland. The Veluwe landscape was converted from heathland to forest as the local sheep-raising economy collapsed in response to the introduction of synthetic fertilizers and inexpensive wool from Australia.

As we enter the twenty-first century, economically motivated human activity continues to change the structure of landscapes all over the globe. We examine current trends in land cover at the global scale in chapter 23. Before we do that, however, let's examine the effects of some other species on landscape structure.

In chapters 17 and 18, we discussed keystone species and ecosystem engineers. As you may remember, beaver activity can change the course of streams, create ponds, and alter forest structure. Using the terms from this chapter, we now explore in more depth how beavers create and modify landscape structure.

The influences of beavers on landscape structure once shaped the face of entire continents. At one time, beavers modified nearly all the temperate stream valleys in the Northern Hemisphere. The range of beavers in North America extended from arctic tundra to the Chihuahuan and Sonoran Deserts of northern Mexico, a range of approximately 15 million km^2. Before European colonization, the North American beaver population numbered 60 to 400 million individuals. However, fur trappers eliminated beavers from much of their historical range and nearly drove them to extinction. With protection, North American beaver populations are recovering and large areas once again show the influence of beavers on landscape structure.

Carol Johnston and Robert Naiman and their colleagues have carefully documented the substantial effects of beavers

on landscape structure (e.g., Naiman et al. 1994). Much of their work has focused on the effects of beavers on the 298 km^2 Kabetogama Peninsula in Voyageurs National Park, Minnesota. Following their near extermination, beavers reinvaded the Kabetogama Peninsula beginning about 1925. From 1927 to 1988, the number of beaver ponds on the peninsula increased from 64 to 834, a change in pond density from 0.2 to 3.0 per square kilometre. Over this 63-year period, the area of new ecosystems created by beavers, including beaver ponds, wet meadows, and moist meadows, increased from 200 ha, about 1% of the peninsula, to 2,661 ha, about 13% of the peninsula. Foraging by beavers altered another 12% to 15% of upland areas.

Beaver activity has changed the Kabetogama Peninsula from a landscape dominated by boreal forest to a complex mosaic of ecosystems. Figure 21.7 shows how beavers have changed a 45 km^2 catchment on the peninsula. Between 1940 and 1986, beavers increased landscape complexity within this catchment. Similar changes have occurred over nearly the entire peninsula.

Naiman and his colleagues quantified the effects of beaver over 214 km^2, or 72%, of the Kabetogama Peninsula. Within this area, there are about 2,763 ha of low-lying area that can be impounded by beavers. In 1927, the majority of the landscape, 2,563 ha, was dominated by forest. In 1927, moist meadow, wet meadow, and pond ecosystems covered only 200 ha. By 1988, moist meadows, wet meadows, and beaver ponds covered over 2,600 ha and boreal forest was limited to 102 ha. Between 1927 and 1988, beavers transformed most of the landscape.

The changes in landscape structure induced by beavers substantially alter landscape processes such as nutrient

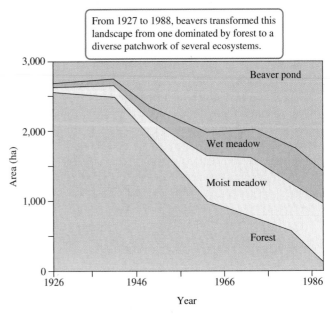

Figure 21.7   Beaver-caused landscape changes on the Kabetogama Peninsula, Minnesota (data from Naiman et al. 1994).

retention. Beaver activity between 1927 and 1988 increased the quantity of most major ions and nutrients in the areas affected by impoundments. The total quantity of nitrogen increased by 72%, while the amounts of phosphorus and potassium increased by 43% and 20%, respectively. The quantities of calcium, magnesium, iron, and sulfate stored in the landscape increased by even greater amounts.

Naiman and his colleagues offer three possible explanations for increased ion and nutrient storage in this landscape: (1) beaver ponds and their associated meadows may trap materials eroding from the surrounding landscape, (2) the rising waters of the beaver ponds may have captured nutrients formerly held in forest vegetation, and (3) the habitats created by beavers may have altered biogeochemical processes in a way that promotes nutrient retention. Whatever the precise mechanisms, beaver activity has substantially altered landscape structure and processes on the Kabetogama Peninsula.

Fire and the Structure of a Mediterranean Landscape

Fire contributes to the structure of landscapes ranging from tropical savanna to boreal forest. However, fire plays a particularly prominent role in regions with a Mediterranean climate. As we saw in chapter 2, terrestrial ecosystems in regions with Mediterranean climates, which support Mediterranean woodlands and shrublands, are subject to frequent burning. Hot, dry summers combined with vegetation rich in essential oils create ideal conditions for fires, which can be easily ignited by lightning or humans. In regions with a Mediterranean climate, fire is responsible for a great deal of landscape structure and change.

Richard Minnich (1983) used satellite photos to reconstruct the fire history of southern California and northern Baja California, Mexico, from 1971 to 1980, and found that the landscapes of both areas consist of a patchwork of new and old burns. Though these regions experience similar Mediterranean climates and support similar natural vegetation, their fire histories diverged significantly in the early twentieth century. For centuries, lightning-caused fires burned, sometimes for months, until they burned out naturally. In addition, Spanish and Anglo-American residents would set fire to the land routinely to improve grazing for cattle and sheep. Then, early in the twentieth century, various government agencies in southern California began to suppress fires to protect property within an increasingly urbanized landscape.

Minnich proposed that the different fire histories of southern California and northern Baja California might produce landscapes of different structure. He suggested that fire suppression allowed more biomass to accumulate and set the stage for large, uncontrollable fires. His specific hypothesis was that the average area burned by wildfires would be greater in southern California.

Minnich tested his hypothesis using satellite images taken from 1972 to 1980 (fig. 21.8). He found that between 1972 and 1980 the total area burned in the two regions was fairly similar (fig. 21.9). However, the size of burns differed significantly between the two regions. The frequency of small burns below 1,000 ha was higher in northern Baja California, while large burns above 3,000 ha were more frequent in southern California. Consequently, median burn size in southern California, 3,500 ha, was over twice that observed in Baja California, 1,600 ha (fig. 21.9).

These results are consistent with Minnich's hypothesis, but do they show conclusively that differences in fire management in southern California and Baja California have produced a difference in burn area? Other factors may contribute to the observed differences in the fire mosaic, including climatic differences, differences in age structure of vegetation, and topographic differences. The exploration of fire's influence on the structure of Mediterranean landscapes continues.

Geological processes, fire, organisms, and climate lead to the development of the landscapes we see around the world. Knowing this, the next step for the ecologist is to understand how landscapes are organized, and determine whether such organization has biological consequences.

Figure 21.8 Areas of Mediterranean shrubland in southern California periodically burn over large areas, destroying human habitations in the process.

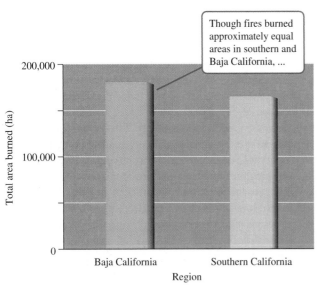

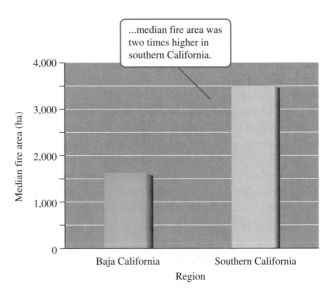

Figure 21.9 Characteristics of fires in the Mediterranean landscapes of southern and Baja California from 1972 to 1980 (data from Minnich 1983).

CONCEPT 21.1 REVIEW

1. What similarities are shared between beavers and glaciers in constructing the shape of a landscape?
2. Do the patterns described by Minnich (fig. 21.9) conclusively show that the differences in burn area in the two regions are the result of different fire management practices?
3. What are some common means by which humans modify landscape structure?

21.2 Landscape Structure

Landscape structure includes the size, shape, composition, number, and position of patches, or landscape elements, in a landscape. Much of ecology focuses on studies of structure and process; landscape ecology is no exception. We are all familiar with the structure, or anatomy, of organisms. In chapters 10 to 12 we discussed the structure of populations, and in chapters 16 to 20 we considered the structure of communities and ecosystems. What constitutes landscape structure? **Landscape structure** consists mainly of the size, shape, composition, number, and position of patches (landscape elements), within a landscape. As you look across a landscape you can usually recognize its constituent ecosystems as distinctive patches, which might consist of forests, fields, ponds, marshes, or urban areas. Landscape ecologists define a **patch** as a relatively homogeneous area that differs from its surroundings; for example, an area of forest surrounded by agricultural fields, or an agricultural field surrounded by forest. The patches within a landscape form the mosaic that we call landscape structure. The background in this mosaic is called the **matrix**, which is the element within the landscape that is the most spatially continuous.

Most questions in landscape ecology require that ecologists first quantify landscape structure. The following examples show how this has been done on some landscapes and how some aspects of landscape structure are not obvious without quantification.

The Structure of Six Landscapes in Ohio

In 1981, G. Bowen and R. Burgess published a quantitative analysis of several Ohio landscapes. These landscapes consisted of forest patches surrounded by other types of ecosystems. Six of the 10 km by 10 km areas analyzed are shown in figure 21.10. If you look carefully at this figure you see that the landscapes, which are named after nearby towns, differ considerably in total forest cover, the number of forest patches, the average area of patches, and the shapes of patches. Some of the landscapes are well forested, and others are not. Some contain only small patches of forest, while others include some large patches. In some landscapes, the forest patches are long and narrow, while in others they are much wider. These general differences are clear enough, but we would find it difficult to give more precise descriptions unless we quantified our impressions.

First, let's consider total forest cover, as this varies substantially among the six landscapes. The Concord landscape, with 2.7% forest cover, is the least forested. At the other extreme, forest patches cover 43.6% of the Washington landscape. Differences between these extremes are clear, but what about some of the less obvious differences. Compare the Monroe and Somerset landscapes (fig. 21.10) and try to estimate which is more forested and by how much. Somerset may appear to have greater forest cover, but how much more? You may be surprised to discover that Somerset, with 22.7% forest cover, has twice the forest cover of the Monroe landscape, which includes just 11.8% forest cover (fig. 21.11).

ECOLOGICAL TOOLS AND APPROACHES

Linking Population, Behavioural, and Landscape Ecology

How much change to the landscape is too much to sustain natural populations of animals? What areas of the landscape are used by species of concern and thus are a high conservation priority? What areas on the landscape are rarely used, and thus industrial development may have a less negative impact if located there? These are critical questions in ecology and conservation biology. In the last several years, there has been a growing appreciation that animal behaviour and landscapes are intimately tied. To begin to provide answers to the questions above, ecologists must work across disciplines, and truly understand the systems in which they work. The rapid increase in available computing power has facilitated research, allowing the construction of detailed models predicting which ecological parameters are, or are not, likely to influence animal populations on the landscape. In this section, we will explore how ecologists are working at blending population, landscape, and behavioural ecology, with important consequences for management and conservation of natural resources.

Using Thresholds to Estimate Risk

There is significant societal pressure to develop natural areas. Development can take a variety of forms, including oil and gas exploration, construction of residential areas, forestry, agriculture, water extraction, dams, and road construction. As we have seen in this chapter, every activity that occurs changes the structure of the landscape. In some cases, these changes have no meaningful consequence for the long-term sustainability of natural populations. In other cases, these changes may cause the collapse of a population. Assuming politicians value land-use planning that protects both economic interests and ecological sustainability, it is critical that ecologists provide tools that help identify risk. The key question becomes: how much habitat loss and change in landscape structure is too much?

The answer to this depends upon whether the effects of habitat loss and changes to landscape structure have proportional or disproportional effects on populations (fig. 21.24). Lenore Fahrig, whom we have highlighted before, has written a review exploring the impacts of fragmentation and habitat loss on populations (Fahrig 2003). She has found that the majority of theoretical studies suggest that the relationship between habitat amount and population sizes will be nonlinear. If this is true, it means that at some amount of habitat, well above zero, a population will go extinct (fig. 21.24). Fahrig suggests that habitat fragmentation can alter the exact location of this threshold, though empirical data is sparse. Regardless of the data available right now, thresholds are

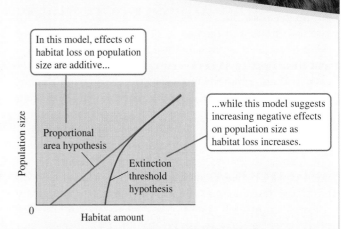

Figure 21.24   Two possible relationships between habitat abundance and population sizes (Fahrig 2003).

one tool that may allow a researcher to predict at what point development may switch a landscape from one that can support sustainable populations (or the organisms of interest) to one that cannot.

These ideas form the basis of **conservation thresholds**, points at which habitat loss and fragmentation cause populations to tip from sustainable to extinct. Ecologists are charged with finding those tipping points before they are reached. If these thresholds can be identified, then they can be incorporated into a regional land-use plan, ensuring adequate areas are left undeveloped, while also allowing for development in areas that are redundant in terms of population sustainability. This approach recognizes that different citizens value different things (development, wilderness, sustainability), and the threshold approach holds promise by setting the point at which balanced land uses are no longer viable. We turn to New Brunswick for an example.

Marc-André Villard and a former graduate student, Jean-Sébastien Guénette, of the Université de Moncton, explored whether thresholds could be a useful concept for conservation planning of forest bird species (Guénette and Villard 2005). The researchers conducted their study in a 1,891 km² managed forest in northwestern New Brunswick. About 27% of the landscape consists of hills covered with forests dominated by sugar maples and American beech. In the valleys and on hilltops there also exists coniferous (20%) and mixed-wood forests (13%). The remaining area consists of forest plantations (spruce), roads, and water. The dominant human land use in this area is logging. The deciduous stands are logged by removing subsets of a stand (approximately 20% to 40% volume in a process called single-tree selection) every 20 to 50 years. The coniferous forests are clear-cut, with tree-planting crews hired to (generally) plant monocultures

of seedlings in their place. Guénette and Villard wanted to understand how forest birds (songbirds and woodpeckers) responded to this diverse landscape and these disturbance regimes.

To measure bird communities, they laid out 5 to 10 sampling stations in each of 43 sites. The sites were located using a stratified, systematic design (chapter 16), ensuring that they sampled all ecosystem types on the landscape. In each of three summers, they went to the sampling stations and recorded the presence of birds. They did this by arriving very early in the day and identifying any bird they saw during a 15-minute interval. During five of the intervals, they played a recording of a Black-capped Chickadee mobbing call. Many bird species respond to these calls, which makes them easier to detect. In addition to the detailed data on birds, the researchers also sampled the plant community composition at each station. They measured a total of 23 plant variables such as canopy height, groundcover, and sapling densities.

The more complicated aspects of the study came at the time of statistical analyses. Quite simply, Guénette and Villard had an enormous data set. They had measures of all bird species across the landscape, along with information on land-use practices, and 23 measures of the vegetation. The first step was to use a statistical procedure called *ordination* (see appendix A) to collapse the vegetation data into few dimensions. A strength of ordination techniques is that they allow an ecologist to take a complicated and multi-dimensional data set (such as that Guénette and Villard had compiled) and collapse many variables into just a few dimensions. Ordinations work by creating new variables that represent trends in groups of variables. In the resulting ordination diagram (fig. 21.25), each data point represents a single sampling station. In the Guénette and Villard study, data points that are close together represent areas that were similar in the vegetation measures taken. Knowing that, you can see that the plant communities differ among harvest treatment types (fig. 21.25). Additionally, when they looked at what variables were correlated with each axis, they

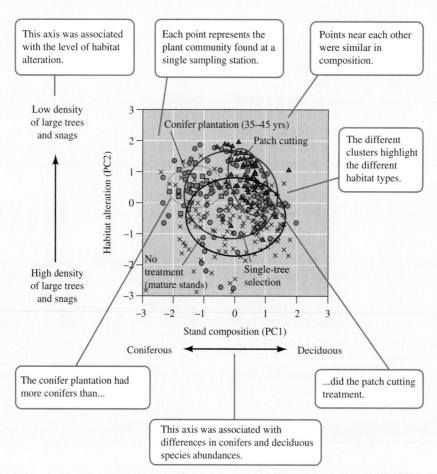

Figure 21.25   Results of an ordination describing variation in the local vegetation among 390 sampling stations (data from Guénette and Villard 2005).

found that the x-axis was driven primarily by species composition, and the y-axis by variables related to harvest. The critical tests of the study are then to determine how bird distributions were correlated with this y-axis, the measure of habitat alteration.

Of the 42 bird species that were regularly found at the stations, 25 were significantly associated with the degree of habitat alteration (y-axis in figure 21.25). Of these, eight species were sensitive, decreasing in abundance with increasing alteration even after controlling for differences in plant species composition. Another seven species had a positive relationship with habitat alteration, even after accounting for differences in plant species composition. Why would a species respond positively to logging? Birds, like all taxonomic groups, consist of species with diverse life-history strategies (chapter 9). The environment of high resources and rapid growth following logging is clearly suitable for a suite of colonizing bird species. Returning to the sensitive species, was there evidence of a threshold?

As you might expect, the answer depends to some extent on which species is being looked at (fig. 21.26). The ovenbird, golden-crowned kinglet, and winter wren show clear nonlinearity in the relationship between occurrence and habitat alteration, while the Blackburnian warbler does not. The models suggested that you would only find all the sensitive species when canopy closure was about 70%, or there were at least 80 large trees/ha. Going below either of these thresholds increased the probability of losing at least one species. Which species would be lost depends on species-specific traits and which forest type is being studied. Knowing that thresholds exist, at least for these species, provides land managers with the information they need to develop a management plan that allows for the long-term sustainability of populations.

As effective as conservation thresholds may be to predict a population's collapse, they are not the only such method available to ecologists and conservation biologists. Next we explore an alternative approach, resource selection functions.

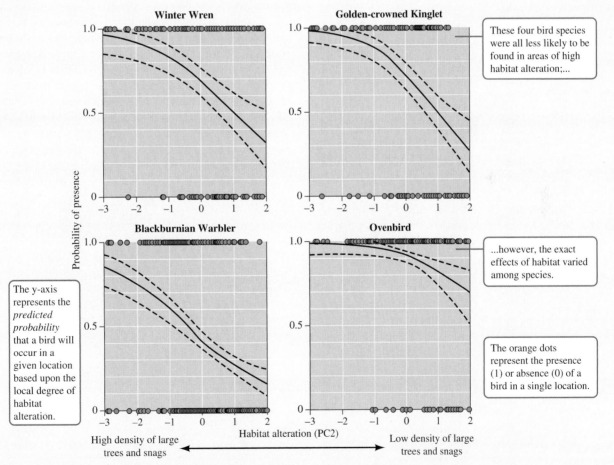

Figure 21.26 The results of the ordination presented in figure 21.25 are used here to help predict the occurrence of four bird species. Solid lines indicate predicted probabilities of occurrence while the dotted lines represent variation in that prediction (data from Guénette and Villard 2005).

Using Resource Selection Functions to Link Movement to the Landscape

As we have seen, thresholds can be a valuable tool in helping ecologists and land managers understand the point at which development is likely to cause collapse of natural populations. There exists a complementary approach that is also proving to be critical to the development of scientifically sound management strategies. This approach, resource selection functions (RSF), also blends measures of the local environment, landscape, and animal behaviour in models that allow researchers to describe (and predict) where animals will be found on the landscape. As we have discussed previously in the chapter, this information is critical to the development of corridors that actually serve as corridors. Only by knowing what habitat animals will actually use can you hope to be successful in having functional links between isolated fragments.

Mark Boyce, of the University of Alberta, has been a leading advocate for greater use of RSFs in ecology. Boyce argues that the basis of RSFs is very straightforward: if you want to know the distribution and abundance of species on a landscape, then it makes sense to know the distribution of resources on the landscape (Boyce and McDonald 1999). The mathematics behind RSF are beyond the scope of this textbook, but the output from the models they produce is very understandable. If a model determines that some factor, such as elk density, is associated with the probably of some other factor, such as the presences of wolves, then the model will generate a probability function. In this case, the RSF would represent the probability of finding a wolf as a function of elk density. To develop this model requires locating large numbers of individuals of the species of concern through one of the methods previously discussed in chapter 10 (e.g., radiotelemetry, trapping, etc.). At the same time, the researchers would measure all aspects of their locations. Additional data would be collected about locations that the animals were not found in. The factors measured could include abiotic conditions, abundance of predators and prey, vegetation and habitat complexity, and any other factor thought to influence the ecology of that particular species.

A statistical model would then be constructed that relates the location of animals to these landscape and environmental measures. Those factors found to be of minimal explanatory power are usually discarded, resulting in a model that identifies what are likely the most important factors influencing the distribution of the animals on this particular landscape. Perhaps in this case that would include elk density, snow depth, and slope. What is particularly attractive about RSF is that these functions can all be combined on a map of the landscape, showing exactly where animals are most likely to occur (fig. 21.27).

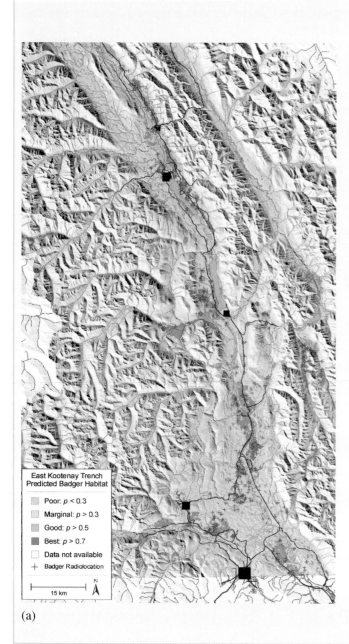

East Kootenay Trench
Predicted Badger Habitat

- Poor: $p < 0.3$
- Marginal: $p > 0.3$
- Good: $p > 0.5$
- Best: $p > 0.7$
- Data not available
- + Badger Radiolocation

15 km
N

(a)

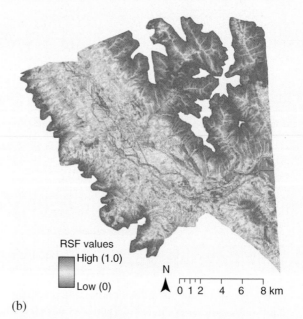

RSF values
High (1.0)
Low (0)

N
0 1 2   4   6   8 km

(b)

Figure 21.27   RSFs predict the preferred and avoided habitat for (*a*) badgers in the east Kootenays of British Columbia (Apps et al. 2002), and (*b*) grizzly bears around Canmore, Alberta (Chetkiewicz et al. 2006).

The maps that are developed are then very helpful guides for land managers, allowing them to visually understand which habitats on the landscape are preferred by the species of concern. This approach is rapidly spreading throughout western Canada, including the large national parks of Jasper and Banff.

RSFs, like thresholds, show that ecologists are developing the research tools that are critical to understanding the factors that drive species distributions and abundances. At the core of the models is the realization that there will not be a single factor that is most important, but instead a suite of processes and conditions will influence the distribution of the species of concern.

SUMMARY

A landscape is a heterogeneous area composed of several ecosystems. The ecosystems making up a landscape generally form a mosaic of visually distinctive patches. These patches are called *landscape elements. Landscape ecology* is the study of landscape structure and processes.

21.1 Landscapes are created and change in response to geological processes, climate, activities of organisms, and fire.

Geological features produced by processes such as volcanism, sedimentation, and erosion interact with climate to provide a primary source of landscape structure. Repeated glaciations in North America have created much of the landscape that is currently found in Canada. We are currently living in an interglacial period, with the last glaciation reaching a peak approximately 20,000 years ago. Glacial movement causes scouring and translocation of substantial amounts of soil, creating a topologically diverse landscape. The resulting variation in soil textures influences the distribution of plant species and ecosystems. While geological processes and climate set the basic template for landscape structure, the activities of organisms, from plants to elephants, can be an additional source of landscape structure and change. Economically motivated human activity changes the structure of landscapes all over the globe. Beavers can quickly change landscape structure and processes over large regions. Fire contributes to the structure of landscapes ranging from tropical savanna to boreal forest. However, fire plays a particularly prominent role in regions with a Mediterranean climate.

21.2 Landscape structure includes the size, shape, composition, number, and position of patches, or landscape elements, in a landscape.

Most questions in landscape ecology require that ecologists quantify landscape structure. Until recently, however, geometry, which means earth measurement, could offer only rough approximations of complex landscape structure. Today, an area of mathematics called fractal geometry can be used to quantify the structure of complex natural shapes. One of the findings of fractal geometry is that the length of the perimeter of complex shapes depends upon the size of the device used to measure the perimeter. One implication of this result is that organisms of different sizes may use the environment in very different ways.

21.3 Landscape structure influences processes such as the flow of energy, materials, and species distributions across a landscape.

Landscape ecologists have proposed that landscape structure, especially the size, number, and isolation of habitat patches, can interact with other ecological processes such as competition, predation, and behaviour to influence populations and communities. Studies of the movements of small mammals in a prairie landscape show that a smaller proportion of individuals moves in more fragmented landscape but that the individuals that do move will move farther. Not all studies of landscape structure suggest biologically meaningful effects on natural populations. Fragmentation of the boreal forest appears to have only minor effects on the species composition of boreal bird communities. However, some species responded quite strongly, indicating that landscape structure can interact with species-specific traits. Habitat loss and local processes such as habitat quality appear to have stronger impacts on most species than landscape structure. However, some species, particularly large mobile species, appear to be strongly affected by changes in landscape structure. Habitat corridors may reduce the negative effects of fragmentation and patch isolation for some species; however, there is little empirical data indicating current practices in corridor design result in the desired conservation goals. Not all ecosystems on a landscape are equally permeable to animal movement, and thus the contrast between a patch and the surrounding matrix ecosystem can serve as another factor altering animal movement. The source of water for lakes in a Wisconsin lake district is determined by their positions in the landscape, which in turn determine their hydrologic and chemical responses to drought.

Society requires scientific knowledge about the ecological impacts of landscape development. Providing answers requires a coordinated approach among landscape, population, and behavioural ecologists. Ecologists are currently using threshold models to understand the potential impacts of habitat loss on the distribution of forest bird species. These models require the use of ordination, a statistical procedure that reduces the dimensionality of ecological data sets. Resource selection functions can be used to predict habitats of high and low value for focal species. These approaches are critical to the development of successful corridors, conservation programs, and finding actual balances between development and species protection.

REVIEW QUESTIONS

1. How does landscape ecology differ from ecosystem and community ecology? What questions might an ecosystem ecologist ask about a forest? What questions might a community ecologist ask about the same forest? Now, what kinds of questions would a landscape ecologist ask about a forested landscape?

2. How should the *area* of forest patches in an agricultural landscape affect the proportion of bird species in a community that are associated with forest edge habitats? How should patch area affect the presence of birds associated with forest interiors?

3. In the figure below, the green areas represent forest fragments surrounded by agriculture. Landscapes 1 and 2 contain the same total forest area. Will landscape 1 or 2 contain more forest interior species? Explain.

4. How might the shapes of forest patches in a landscape affect the proportion of birds in the community associated with forest edge habitat? How might patch shape affect the presence of birds associated with forest interior?

5. In this chapter, we have presented evidence that landscape structure can influence population growth. In section III, we presented the idea that some populations exist as metapopulations. Describe the similarities and the differences between landscape ecology and metapopulations. Do aspects of the landscape necessarily influence metapopulation dynamics?

6. Consider the above options for preserving patches of riverside forest. Again, the two landscapes contain the same total area of forest but the patches in the two landscapes differ in shape. Which of the two would be most dominated by forest edge species?

7. How do the positions of patches in a landscape affect the movement of individuals among habitat patches and among portions of a metapopulation? Again, consider the hypothetical landscapes shown in question 6. Which of the two landscapes would promote the highest rate of movement of individuals between forest patches? Can you think of any circumstances in which it might be desirable to reduce the movement of individuals across a landscape? (Hint: Think of the potential threat of pathogens that are spread mainly by direct contact between individuals within a population.)

8. Use fractal geometry and the niche concept to explain why the canopy of a forest should accommodate more species of predaceous insects than insectivorous birds. Assume that the numbers of bird and predaceous insect species are limited by competition.

9. Several of the studies we have discussed in this chapter find few effects of landscape structure on some natural populations. Other species, however, respond very strongly to changes in landscape structure. What aspects of an organism's life-history are likely to determine whether or not a species responds? What types of shifts in landscape structure are most likely to cause biological effects?

10. How do the activities of animals affect landscape heterogeneity? You might use either beaver or human activity as your model. What parallels can you think of between the influence of animal activity on landscape heterogeneity and the intermediate disturbance hypothesis? Which is concerned with the effect of disturbance on species diversity?

MACROECOLOGY

CHAPTER **22**

CHAPTER CONCEPTS

22.1 Information about a species' current distribution and niche requirements can be combined with spatial information to predict invasion and range expansion.

Concept 22.1 Review

22.2 On islands and habitat patches on continents, species richness increases with area and decreases with isolation.

Concept 22.2 Review

22.3 Species richness on islands can be modelled as a dynamic balance between immigration and extinction of species.

Concept 22.3 Review

22.4 Species richness generally increases from middle and high latitudes to the equator.

Concept 22.4 Review

22.5 Long-term historical and regional processes significantly influence the structure of biotas and ecosystems.

Ecology In Action: Biodiversity Hotspots

Concept 22.5 Review

Ecological Tools and Approaches: Global Positioning Systems, Remote Sensing, and Geographic Information Systems

Summary

Review Questions

On June 5, 1799, Alexander von Humboldt and Aimé Bonpland sailed out of the port of Coruña in northwest Spain. Their small Spanish ship managed to slip past a British naval blockade and sail on, first to the Canary Islands and then to South America. Humboldt was a Prussian engineer and scientist and Bonpland was a French botanist. Humboldt came equipped with the finest scientific instruments of the time and was prepared to systematically survey the lands that he and Bonpland would visit. He wrote a letter to a friend a few hours before his ship left port outlining his purpose for the expedition: "I shall try to find out how the forces of nature interreact upon one another and *how the geographic environment influences plant and animal life* [emphasis added]."

Humboldt and Bonpland carried passports issued by the court of King Carlos IV of Spain, giving them permission to conduct scientific studies throughout the Spanish Empire, which then stretched from California to Texas in North America and south to the tip of South America. They had complete access to a vast area of the earth's surface that was essentially unexplored scientifically, and they put that access to productive use. Because their discoveries were so numerous and their explorations so thorough, Simón Bolívar, the liberator of most of Spanish America, referred to Humboldt as "the discoverer of the New World."

Humboldt's expedition was one of the most ambitious scientific explorations of the age. During the course of their expedition, Humboldt and Bonpland travelled nearly 10,000 km through South and North America. They travelled on foot, by canoe, or on horseback, visiting latitudes ranging between 12° S and 52° N. They also climbed to nearly 5,900 m on the slopes of Chimborazo; the highest recorded ascent by anyone in history up to that time (fig. 22.1).

The physical feats of their expedition, however, never took precedence over their scientific purpose. For instance, on their climb of Chimborazo, they faced the uncertain dangers of high altitude. Yet, as blood oozed from their lips and gums, Humboldt and Bonpland recorded the altitudinal distributions of plants and animals. Later, Humboldt organized their observations of climate and plant distributions into ingenious visual representations of plant geography. What he did not accomplish, he inspired others to. One of those inspired to follow in Humboldt's footsteps was Charles Darwin. Darwin said that his reading of Humboldt's expedition to South America set the course of his whole life.

In the early decades of ecology, many ecologists continued in this tradition, studying broadscale patterns. For example, Robert H. MacArthur (1972) defined a subdiscipline of *geographic ecology* as the "search for patterns of plant and animal life that can be put on a map." As ecology matured in the 1970s and 1980s, there was increased emphasis placed on mechanism, and these decades saw the emergence of experimental ecology and decreased emphasis on broad pattern description. In 1989, James Brown and Brian Maurer published an influential paper in which they argued that, "Without a complementary emphasis on large-scale phenomena, there is little basis for determining which results simply reflect the idiosyncrasies of individual species and particular sites and which reflect the operation of more universal processes" (Brown and Mauer 1989). In other words, Brown and Mauer argued that without *macroecology*, there is no context in which to place what we learn from *microecological* studies. This paper led to the widespread adoption of the term *macroecology* in reference to large-scale studies of species abundances and distribution, though it is itself conceptually linked to MacArthur's term of *geographic ecology*. Although terminology is in debate, the underlying importance of studying ecological patterns over large spatial scales is not.

The development of macroecology continues as new generations of scientists equipped with a diversity of tools, both ancient and modern, search for the elusive patterns that can be put on maps. The breadth of macroecology is as vast as its subject. Consequently, we concentrate our discussions in chapter 22 on just a few aspects of the field: the distribution of species, island biogeography, latitudinal patterns of species diversity, and the influences of large-scale regional and historical processes on biological diversity.

22.1 Ecological Niche Modelling

Information about a species' current distribution and niche requirements can be combined with spatial information to predict invasion and range expansion. Ecologists have done a good job at explaining why many of the natural patterns we see likely have arisen. In other words, scientists are very good at describing the mechanisms that generate the natural history we can observe *now*. However, society needs us to predict the patterns we will see in the *future*. The field of population ecology has addressed this issue through its reliance on population growth models (chapter 12). However, these models rarely integrate information about both the species of interest and its niche requirements. Yes, it is helpful to describe why a novel disease or invasive species moved across a landscape, but it would be more helpful to be able to alert officials about the most at-risk locations for the spread of a disease (Mak et al. 2010) or an invasive species (Peterson and Vieglais

Figure 22.1 On the slopes of Chimborazo, a 6,310 m high volcanic peak in the Andes Mountains of Ecuador, Alexander von Humboldt and Aimé Bonpland meticulously recorded the altitudinal distributions of plants.

2001). It would also be helpful to be able to predict how climate change may alter species distributions before the changes occur (Peterson et al. 2004). Ecologists have begun to make great strides in this form of predictive ecology, and it only is possible through a mash-up of diverse data sets coupled with geographic information. This new approach goes by many names, including ecological niche modelling, species distribution modelling, and habitat modelling. Regardless of what it is called, the goal is to combine a species' niche requirements with the spatial distribution of environmental conditions on a landscape or across a region to identify specific locations about where a species could occur.

In chapter 9, we first presented the concept of the niche, defining it as the combination of environmental factors that influence the growth, survival, and reproduction of a species. One of the critical aspects of this niche definition is that the niche is an abstract representation of the conditions a species needs, it was not an actual physical location on a map. However, to make specific predictions about how a species' range may change over time, we need to convert the abstract concept of the niche to specific locations across a landscape. How do you actually do this? In theory, it is pretty straightforward, and requires three basic steps: (1) identify the niche of the species of concern, (2) determine the distribution of environmental conditions throughout the geographic area of concern, and (3) combine this information to produce a map of potential distributions of the species of concern. In reality, this is a very difficult task requiring detailed field work coupled with complex statistical analyses. To demonstrate the complexity and potential benefits of this approach, we present two examples.

Predicting the Spread of an Invasive Crab Species Throughout North America

In chapter 14, we mentioned that a relaxation of exploitative relationships may lead to novel species rapidly increasing their range, and invading throughout a landscape. Here, we show how ecological niche modelling can be used to identify the locations into which a species may invade, with the hope of preventative actions being taken to reduce or eliminate the environmental risk.

Hugh MacIsaac is a professor at the University of Windsor, the Chair of the Department of Fisheries and Oceans' Invasive Species Research group, and one of the world's leading researchers studying invasive species. MacIsaac and colleagues recently published a study investigating the invasion risk of the Chinese mitten crab (*Eriocheir sinensis*) to habitats throughout North America (Herborg et al. 2007). The mitten crab (fig. 22.2) is native to Asia, occurring throughout China, North Korea, and Hong Kong. The crab has spread throughout the planet by hitchhiking in ballast water of trade-ships, and intentional introduction as seafood (Herborg et al. 2007). The crab is now widespread throughout Europe, and has a very spotty distribution within North America. MacIsaac and colleagues recognized that a spotty distribution now does not mean there will be a spotty distribution in the future, and they wanted a way to predict the relative risk of invasion in the

major ports throughout North America. To make such predictions realistic, the research team needed to understand the biology of the organism. Because this species is not yet widespread in North America, they needed to gather information from Europe and Asia.

Determining the niche of an organism is very difficult, and there a number of methods that have been used over the years. The standard approach used in ecological niche modelling is to obtain (1) a list of locations where the study organism has been found (compiling new field data, museum records, etc.), (2) spatially explicit environmental information for the region in which the organism is found, and (3) similar environmental information for areas where the organism has not been found. Later in the chapter we will discuss how such spatially explicit data is collected (remote sensing). For now it is enough to know that just as molecular tools have revolutionized the field of evolutionary ecology, easy access to satellites has revolutionized large-scale ecological studies. MacIsaac and colleagues had data on the distribution of *Eriocheir sinensis* in the crab's native range in Asia. They then chose 12 environmental parameters they thought may represent different niche axes (and for which they had spatially explicit data). These included parameters such as local topography, minimum and maximum temperatures, and precipitation. They then used a variety of statistical procedures (which are beyond the scope of this text) to relate these data sets, allowing them to generate an equation that described the multivariate environmental conditions under which the mitten crab had a high probability of occurring. This equation was a mathematical approximation of the species' niche, generated from data in locations where the crab currently exists. The research team then applied the niche equation to the environmental conditions found throughout North America. The resulting map indicates strength of the match between niche requirements as determined from its Asian distribution, and local environmental conditions in North America (fig. 22.3*a*).

Figure 22.3*a* looks quite troubling, as much of the United States (and pieces of Canada) have suitable environmental conditions for the growth and spread of this invasive species. However, MacIsaac and colleagues recognized that there is

Figure 22.2 Chinese Mitten Crab, *Eriocher sinensis*.

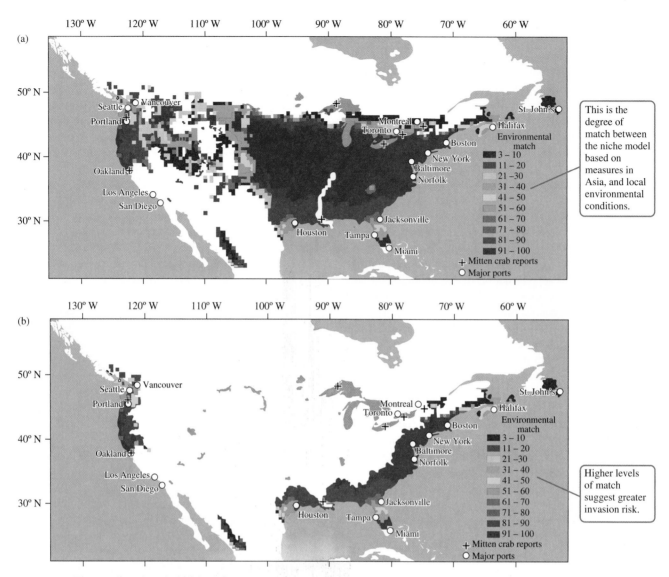

Figure 22.3 The predicted probabilities of Chinese mitten crabs occurring in different locations throughout North America. (*a*) This map assumes the crab can successfully maintain a population independent of distance from salt water. (*b*) A more biologically realistic model limits crab populations to <355 km away from a salt water source. Note that in both figures a "+" indicates mitten crabs were found, though this does not imply a population had successfully established (Data from Herborg et al. 2007).

more to this story that is critical for assessing invasion risk. First, there are issues related to the basic biology of this species. *Eriocheir sinensis* has a *catadromous* life cycle with planktonic larvae maturing in brackish-saline water, while the adult lives primarily in freshwater (essentially the opposite of the *anadromous* life cycle of salmon). As a result, when the researchers looked at existing distributions of this crab throughout Europe, they found that all reported occurrences were less than 1,261 km from the sea, and 90% of occurrences were less than 355 km from the sea (Herborg 2007). This is critical information, and suggests locations in North America more than 355 km from the sea are unlikely to be invaded. When this niche axis (distance to ocean) is also applied to the data, we find a greatly reduced (though still troublesome!) potential range in North America (fig. 22.3*b*).

A second issue that could influence invasion risk is the frequency with which this species is actually introduced at different locations. The dominant vectors for invasion are ships that pick up ballast water in Europe and Asia, and dump that water (and planktonic larvae) in foreign ports. MacIsaac and colleagues were able to estimate the frequency with which that happened in the major shipping ports in the United States. Using that information, coupled with the maps they generated describing environmental match (fig. 22.3*b*), they were able to identify specific ports as being most vulnerable due to a combination of environmental match and large ballast volumes. Such predictive ecology can help governmental officials focus their search efforts for this species in those locations, rather than spending limited dollars searching in areas unlikely to be invaded. This approach has the potential to greatly

reduce the likelihood that this species will gain a foothold in North America.

Similar studies have now been conducted for many species. There are readily available environmental data sets for much of the world, and geo-referenced occurrence data is found in most research museums and collections. Though the statistics involved are complicated, there are user-friendly interfaces that greatly facilitate ecological niche modelling. Heck, you can even predict where black rhinos could live if they were introduced to Canada! There are, however, some problems. First, though this is called niche modelling, this process focuses only on where a species is found in its native range, not where it could live. In other words, this is ecological *realized* niche modelling, and does not use the *fundamental* niche. This may be a critical flaw if the factors that restrict a species are biological (competitors, predators, pathogens) rather than environmental. A second issue is even more basic. How do you know the species you are modelling?

Using Ecological Niche Modelling to Predict the Distribution of a Crypto-Zoological Species

One use of ecological niche modelling is to identify the niche conditions for a rare or at-risk species, and then use that information to help identify potential locations on the landscape where that species may be found. Such efforts would provide scientists with more accurate information on the health of populations of at-risk species, leading to the development of more accurate conservation plans. For example, a team of researchers using niche modelling were able to find extant populations of a rare plant species, previously believed to be extinct, in a region of Brazil (de Siqueira et al. 2009). Ecological niche modelling, however, can go even further—and has been used to predict the distribution of sasquatch (Lozier et al. 2009).

Sasquatch, or Bigfoot, is one of many *crypto-zoological* species: species for whom existence has not yet been confirmed. What can an ecologist do to help determine where to find the Loch Ness Monster, chupacabra, unicorns, or sasquatch? Although there are no confirmed museum records of this large ape-like creature, there are a number of geo-referenced sightings throughout western North America. In total, Lozier and colleagues were able to find 551 records of sightings or auditory detections, and another 95 records of footprints. They were also able to obtain spatially explicit environmental information for nine variables they felt could be important niche axes (e.g., temperature and precipitation information). By combining these data sets, they were able to model the combinations of environmental conditions that typically were found in locations where sasquatch was reported to occur, and then put this information onto a map (fig. 22.4*a*). This resulting predicted distribution suggests sasquatch may have a range that includes Mexico, most of California, the Pacific Northwest, Vancouver Island, and the lower mainland of British Columbia. When Lozier and colleagues incorporated potential future environmental conditions associated with climate change (chapter 23), they found a striking potential for range expansion of this species (fig. 22.4*b*). Sasquatch should move eastward under predicted future climatic conditions, giving great opportunity for future sightings.

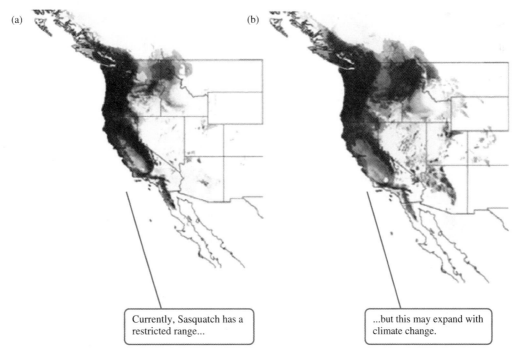

Figure 22.4 Darker values indicate a higher probability of occurrence of sasquatch under (*a*) current and (*b*) future climate conditions. The data come from an ecological niche model based upon putative sightings, recordings, and footprint records. (Lozier et al. 2009).

What is the point of modelling a species that has never been confirmed to exist? In a second analysis, they found the predicted range of sasquatch in the northwest was virtually identical to that of black bears. Interestingly, a bear standing on its hind legs approximates the size of a large ape-like creature. Lozier and colleagues suggest that perhaps the real lesson is that if the core data used in niche modelling is not accurate (e.g., putative sightings), even pretty maps will be meaningless. In other words, we find once again that basic natural history is critical to ecology. Predications are only as good as the raw data, and to acquire good data requires scientists to get away from the computer; relying less on public reports and more on scientifically validated collections.

But there is another potential benefit, one less tongue-in-cheek. When done well, ecological niche modelling can highlight areas in which rare species are likely to occur, and where they could move to under future environmental conditions. If the core data is accurate, this form of predictive ecology can be of great value to land managers and conservation biologists.

In the next section, we move away from describing the geographic distribution of a single species, and focus on broader patterns of diversity. We start with one of the oldest ecological patterns ever described—the relationship between area and species diversity.

CONCEPT 22.1 REVIEW

1. What types of information are needed to conduct ecological niche modelling?
2. Why does the ability to accurately identify a species, or know that identifications by others are accurate, influence the validity an ecological niche model?

22.2 Area, Isolation, and Species Richness

On islands and habitat patches on continents, species richness increases with area and decreases with isolation.

Island Area and Species Richness

David Currie, of the University of Ottawa, and his graduate student, Attila Kalmar, examined the relationship between island area and bird species (Kalmar and Currie 2006). They compiled data on 346 marine islands scattered throughout the globe. Islands included in the database varied in size from 0.1 km^2 to 800,000 km^2, and were found in all major climatic regions on the planet. They then searched through field guides, checklists, and journals to compile lists of the breeding bird species found on each of the islands. Across all islands, there was a clear relationship between island area and

the number of bird species found (fig. 22.5a). The large dataset also showed that some islands have substantially lower diversity for their size than would be expected. Kalmar and Currie suggested that island area results in an upper bound to diversity, while other factors such as extreme temperatures and precipitation can suppress diversity on the island. The relationship between island area and number of species is not just a property of bird assemblages. Sven Nilsson, Jan Bengtsson, and Stefan Ås (1988) explored patterns of species richness among woody plants, carabid beetles, and land snails on 17 islands in Lake Mälaren, Sweden. The islands ranged in area from 0.6 to 75 ha and were all forested. The researchers were careful to choose islands that showed few or no signs of human disturbance. One of the results of their study was

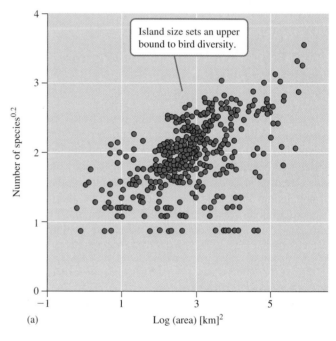

(a)

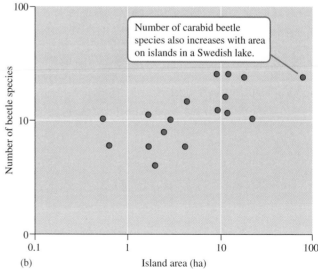

(b)

Figure 22.5 Relationship between island area and number of species (data from Kalmar and Currie 2006; Nilsson et al. 1988).

that island area was the best single predictor of species richness in all three groups of organisms. Figure 22.5*b* shows the relationship found between island area and number of carabid beetles.

When most of us think of islands, the picture that generally comes to mind is a small bit of land in the middle of an ocean. However, many habitats on continents are so isolated that they can be considered as islands.

Habitat Patches on Continents: Mountain Islands

The many isolated mountain ranges that extend across the Great Basin and southwestern regions of North America are now continental islands. During the late Pleistocene, 11,000 to 15,000 years ago, forest and woodland habitats extended unbroken from the Rocky Mountains to the Sierra Nevada in California. Then, as the Pleistocene ended and the climate warmed, forest and alpine habitats contracted to the tops of the high mountains scattered across the American Southwest. As montane habitats retreated to higher elevations, woodland, shrubland, grassland, or desert scrub vegetation invaded the lower elevations. As a consequence of these changes, once-continuous forest and alpine vegetation was converted to a series of island-like habitat patches associated with mountains and therefore called *montane*.

As montane vegetation contracted to mountaintops, montane animals followed. Mark Lomolino, James H. Brown, and Russell Davis (1989) studied the diversity of montane mammals on isolated mountains in the American Southwest. Similar to the studies of islands, the team found that montane mammal richness was positively correlated with habitat area. As figure 22.6 shows, the area of the 27 montane islands ranged from less than 7 km^2 to over 10,000 km^2, while the number of montane mammals on them ranged from 1 to 16.

Lakes as Islands

Lakes can also be considered as habitat islands—aquatic environments isolated from other aquatic environments by land. However, lakes differ widely in their degree of isolation. Seepage lakes, which receive no surface drainage, are

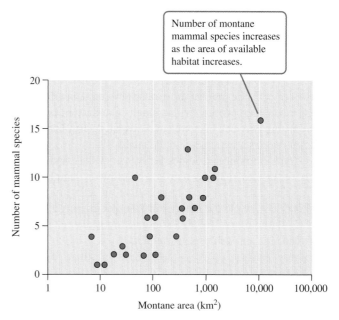

Figure 22.6   Area of montane habitat and number of montane mammal species on isolated mountain ranges in the American Southwest (data from Lomolino et al. 1989).

completely isolated, while drainage lakes, which have stream inlets and/or outlets, are less isolated (see chapter 21).

Bill Tonn, now of the University of Alberta, and John Magnuson of the University of Wisconsin (1982) studied patterns of species composition and richness among fish inhabiting lakes in northern Wisconsin. They focused their research on 18 lakes in the Northern Highlands Lake District of Wisconsin and Michigan. The study was conducted in Vilas County, Wisconsin, which includes over 1,300 lakes (fig. 22.7). With so many lakes at their disposal, Tonn and Magnuson could match lakes carefully for a variety of characteristics. All 18 study lakes had similar bottom substrates and similar maximum depths. However, the lakes spanned a considerable range of surface area (2.4–89.8 ha).

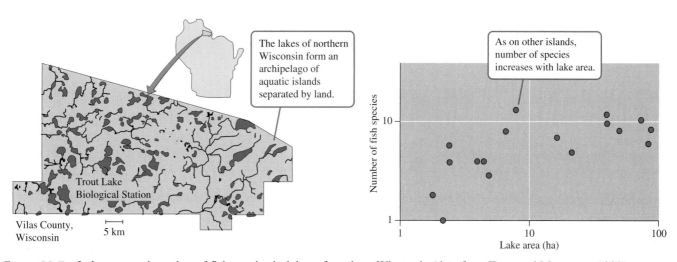

Figure 22.7   Lake area and number of fish species in lakes of northern Wisconsin (data from Tonn and Magnuson 1982).

Tonn and Magnuson collected a total of 23 species, 22 in summer and 18 in winter. If we combine their winter and summer collections on each lake and plot total species richness against area, there is a significant positive relationship (fig. 22.7). Once again, we see that the number of species increases with the area of an insular environment. However, these researchers worked with a single lake district. Is there a relationship between lake area and diversity when lakes from several regions are included in the analysis?

Clyde Barbour and James H. Brown (1974) studied patterns of species richness across a worldwide sample of 70 lakes. The lakes in their sample ranged in area from 0.8 to 436,000 km^2, while the number of fish species ranged from 5 to 245. Barbour and Brown also found a positive relationship between area and fish species richness.

Island Isolation and Species Richness

There is often a negative relationship between the isolation of an island and the number of species it supports. However, because organisms differ substantially in dispersal rates, an island that is very isolated for one group of organisms may be completely accessible to another group.

Marine Islands

We now return to the study of Kalmar and Currie (2006), who explored patterns of diversity among marine islands distributed across the planet. Because the researchers knew the location of each island (fig. 22.8a), they were able to measure the linear distance between the island and the nearest continental shore. The relationship between isolation and bird species

richness is clear: the more isolated the island, the fewer bird species that will be found (fig. 22.8b).

Comparative studies of diversity patterns on islands remind us that different organisms have markedly different dispersal abilities. Mark Williamson (1981) summarized the data for the relationship between island area and species richness for various groups of organisms inhabiting the Azore and Channel Islands. The Azore Islands lie approximately 1,600 km west of the Iberian Peninsula, while the Channel Islands are very near the coast of France. While vastly different in distance from mainland areas, both island groups experience moist temperate climates and have biotas that are of European origin. Consequently, a comparison of their biotas should reveal the potential influence of isolation on diversity.

Figure 22.9 shows Williamson's summary of species area relationships for ferns and fernlike plants (pteridophytes) and land- and water-breeding birds. Both groups of organisms show a positive relationship between island area and diversity on both the Channel and Azore Islands. However, while birds show a clear influence of isolation on diversity, pteridophytes do not. Notice that bird species richness is lower on Azore Islands compared to Channel Islands of similar size. Meanwhile, pteridophyte diversity is similar on islands of comparable size in the two island groups.

These differences in pattern show that the 1,600 km of ocean between the Azore Islands and the European mainland reduces the diversity of birds but not pteridophytes. These differences in the effect of isolation reflect differences in the dispersal rates of these organisms. While land birds must fly across water barriers, pteridophytes produce large quantities of light spores that are easily dispersed by wind. One species

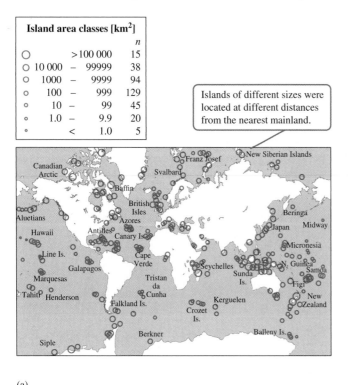

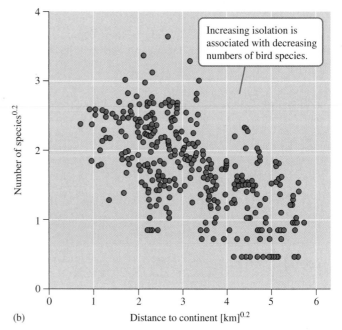

(a)   (b)

Figure 22.8   (*a*) The location and size of islands studied by Kalmar and Currie (2006). (*b*) Relationship between island isolation and the number of bird species found on the island.

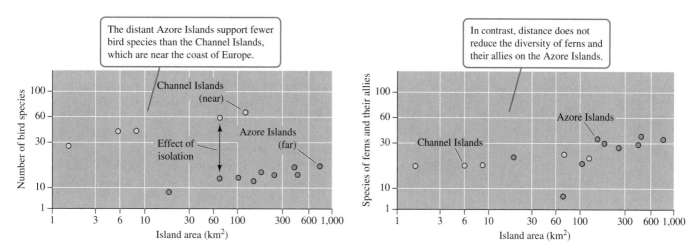

Figure 22.9 Influence of isolation on diversity of birds and ferns and their allies on the Channel and Azore Islands (data from Williamson 1981).

of pteridophyte, bracken fern, has naturally established populations throughout the globe, including New Guinea, Britain, Hawaii, and New Mexico. When we consider the potential effects of isolation on diversity, we must also consider the dispersal capabilities of the study organisms.

Isolation of a Thermophilic Cyanobacteria

Studies of geographic isolation generally focus on plants, mammals, birds, and other relatively large taxa. Part of this bias comes from the general bias toward the study of larger organisms that we have discussed throughout the book. Another aspect comes from a long-standing assumption that free-living microbes are widely distributed, and thus unlikely to show effects of isolation on patterns of population and community structure. There is substantial support for this idea, with numerous examples of widespread distributions of bacteria on land and in the water. However, as Thane Papke, from Dalhousie University, and his colleagues show, some microbes show effects of geographic isolation.

In locations throughout the world, springs can be heated by a variety of sources (geothermal heat, magma, etc.), causing

what are commonly referred to as hot springs. We may be most familiar with the hot springs found in the Rocky Mountains, a prime destination for visitors of Banff, Jasper, and other parks. Or we may think of Old Faithful Geyser in Yellowstone National Park in the United States. Environmental conditions in hot springs can be extreme, with some hot springs having water temperatures near boiling point (or even above in the case of a geyser). Even the cooler hot springs will be elevated in temperature compared to the surrounding (non-hot) springs. It may come as no surprise that hot springs are home to a number of thermophilic bacteria. These microbes have very narrow niche requirements, and many species are unable to live outside of hot springs. As a result, these bacteria living in hot springs scattered across the world are similar to birds or mammals that can only live on mountaintops or other isolated habitats. Therefore, if isolation from other habitats can cause shifts in community structure, there should be variation in the composition of the microbial populations found in hot springs across the planet.

Prior work has indicated that one genus of cyanobacteria, *Synechococcus* (fig. 22.10), is particularly diverse, and this group was the focus for Papke and his colleagues (Papke

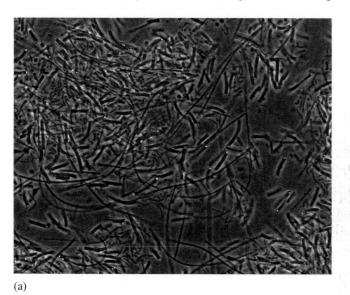

(a)

(b)

Figure 22.10 Cyanobacteria of (*a*) the genus *Synechococcus* form and (*b*) mats that line hot springs in locations around the world.

CONCEPT 22.2 REVIEW

1. In chapter 21, we discussed how species number decreases with increasing habitat loss. Drawing from the information in this section, provide an explanation for that pattern.
2. In figure 22.5*a*, island size appears to set a maximal, rather than minimal, boundary for bird diversity. Why?
3. Why can mountaintops also be considered *islands* in this biogeographic context?

et al. 2003). As we discussed in chapter 4, the definition of species is complicated, and the biological species concept simply does not apply to the microbial world. Instead, researchers measure diversity by determining the number of genetically distinct clones they find within some sample. Papke and colleagues were able to isolate clones from numerous hot springs in North America, Japan, New Zealand, and Italy. Because they sampled multiple hot springs in different regions within each of these widely separated geographic locations, they were able to explore variation in species composition of this group of cyanobacteria. If geographic isolation is not important, one would expect to find most clones of *Synechococcus* even in widely separated locations.

Across their samples there was clear evidence for geographical isolation. This isolation occurred at the largest scale, such as North America vs. Japan, as well as finer scales, such as variation among hot springs within North America. Importantly, the variation among locations could not be explained by variations in the chemical properties of the hot springs. Instead, hot springs with similar chemical properties contained different species assemblages if they were isolated from each other. These results show that geographical isolation can impact even the smallest of organisms, such as these cyanobacteria. The study of geographic ecology of microbes remains in its infancy, with substantial surprises yet to be uncovered.

In the next section, we take a dynamic, rather than static, view of island diversity. This will serve as the foundation for one of the most influential theories in ecology, the equilibrium model of island biogeography.

22.3 The Equilibrium Model of Island Biogeography

Species richness on islands can be modelled as a dynamic balance between immigration and extinction of species. The examples we just reviewed show clear relationships between species richness and island area and isolation. When confronted with such a pattern, scientists look for explanatory mechanisms. What mechanisms might increase species richness on large islands and reduce richness on small and isolated islands? MacArthur and Wilson (1963, 1967) proposed a model that explained patterns of species diversity on islands as the result of a balance between rates of immigration and extinction (fig. 22.11). This model is called the **equilibrium model of island biogeography**.

Figure 22.11 shows that the model presents rates of immigration and extinction as a function of numbers of species on islands. How might rates of immigration and extinction be influenced by the numbers of species on an island? To answer this question, we need to understand what MacArthur and Wilson meant by rates of immigration and extinction. They defined the *rate of immigration* as the rate of arrival of *new* species on an island. *Rate of extinction* was the rate at which species went extinct on the island. MacArthur and Wilson reasoned that rates of immigration would be highest on a new island with no organisms, since every species that arrived at the island would be new. Then as species began to accumulate on an island, the rate of immigration would decline since fewer and fewer arrivals would be *new* species. They called the point at which the immigration line touches the horizontal axis *P* because it is the point representing the entire pool of species that might immigrate to the island.

How might numbers of species on an island affect the rate of extinction? MacArthur and Wilson predicted that the rate of extinction would rise with increasing numbers of species on an island for three reasons: (1) the presence of more species creates a larger pool of potential extinctions, (2) as the number of species on an island increases, the population size of each might diminish, increasing risk of extinction, and (3) as the number of species on an island increases, the potential for competitive interactions between species will increase.

Since the immigration line falls and the extinction line rises as number of species increases, the two lines must cross as shown in figure 22.11. What is the significance of the point where the two lines cross? The point where the two lines cross predicts the number of species that will occur on an island. Thus, the equilibrium model represents the diversity of species on islands as the result of a dynamic balance between immigration and extinction.

MacArthur and Wilson used the equilibrium model to predict how island size and isolation should affect rates of immigration and extinction. They proposed that the rate of immigration is mainly determined by an island's distance from a source of immigrants; for example, the distance of an oceanic island from a mainland. They proposed that rates of extinction on islands would be determined mainly by island size. These predictions are represented in figure 22.12. Notice that the figure predicts that large, near islands will support the greatest number of species, while small, far islands will support the lowest number of species. The model predicts that small, near islands and large, far islands will support intermediate numbers of species.

The equilibrium model of island biogeography is a special type of ecological model, called a *neutral model*. In ecology,

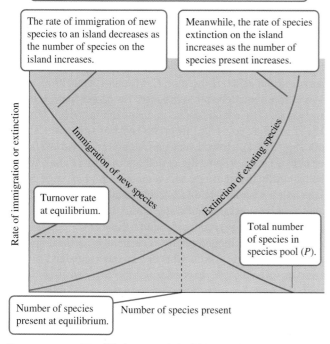

According to the equilibrium model of island biogeography, the number of species on an island is determined by a balance between species immigration and extinction.

The rate of immigration of new species to an island decreases as the number of species on the island increases.

Meanwhile, the rate of species extinction on the island increases as the number of species present increases.

Rate of immigration or extinction

Immigration of new species

Extinction of existing species

Turnover rate at equilibrium.

Total number of species in species pool (P).

Number of species present at equilibrium.

Number of species present

Figure 22.11   Equilibrium model of island biogeography (data from MacArthur and Wilson 1963).

neutral models are ones that predict the outcome of ecological interactions independent of any differences among species. For example, the predictions of MacArthur and Wilson about the abundance of organisms on islands assumes that all species have the same probability of immigration and extinction. This is, of course, a biologically unjustifiable assumption. However, the critical issue here is whether making such a seemingly absurd assumption has any consequence for the accuracy of their patterns. Can one predict, to some rough approximation, the diversity of species on islands assuming all species are functionally the same?

The predictions of the equilibrium model of island biogeography are consistent with the patterns of island diversity reviewed in the previous section. Large islands hold more species than small islands, and islands near sources of immigrants hold more species than islands far from sources of immigrants. We should expect the equilibrium model to be consistent with known variation in species richness across islands since MacArthur and Wilson designed their model to explain the known patterns. Did the equilibrium model make any new predictions? The main new predictions were (1) that island diversity is the outcome of a highly dynamic balance between immigration and extinction, and (2) that the rates of immigration and extinction are determined mainly by the isolation and area of islands. In other words, the equilibrium model predicts that the species composition on islands is not static but changes over time. Ecologists call this change in species composition **species turnover**.

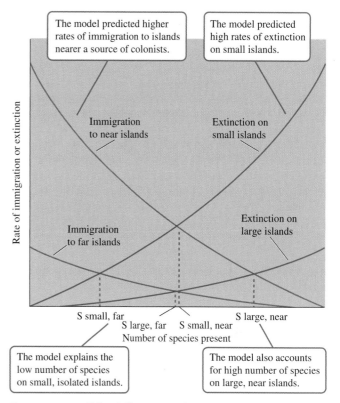

The equilibrium model of island biogeography explained variation in number of species on islands by the influences of isolation and area on rates of immigration and extinction.

The model predicted higher rates of immigration to islands nearer a source of colonists.

The model predicted high rates of extinction on small islands.

Rate of immigration or extinction

Immigration to near islands

Extinction on small islands

Immigration to far islands

Extinction on large islands

S small, far

S large, far   S small, near

S large, near

Number of species present

The model explains the low number of species on small, isolated islands.

The model also accounts for high number of species on large, near islands.

Figure 22.12   Island distance and area and rates of immigration and extinction (data from MacArthur and Wilson 1963).

Species Turnover on Islands

In the equilibrium model of island biogeography, the equilibrium number of species predicted to be found on an island is determined by the value of species richness (x-axis) where immigration and extinction rates intersect (fig. 22.12). However, another critical prediction of this theory is that distance from mainland and island size will influence the rate of species turnover on the island. In other words, on some islands species will be predicted to persist for long periods, while the same species are predicted to persist only briefly on other islands. Using this model, how can we predict which islands will have higher, or lower, turnover rates? The answer lies in taking a close look at the y-axis, the one that describes immigration and extinction rates. Just as the value of the x-axis at equilibrium indicates the equilibrium species richness, the value of the y-axis at equilibrium indicates the equilibrium turnover rate. You can see in figure 22.13 that turnover rates are predicted to be highest on small, near islands, and lowest on large, far islands. These conditions are different for where we predict the highest, and lowest, number of species. It may seem paradoxical to talk about species turnover at equilibrium. However, it is important to remember that this model

of biogeography predicts solely the number of species and rate of change, not the identity of the species on the island. Based upon this model, do you think that species composition is likely to be at equilibrium on any island? As you will see below, species turnover on islands is much more than a theoretical concept.

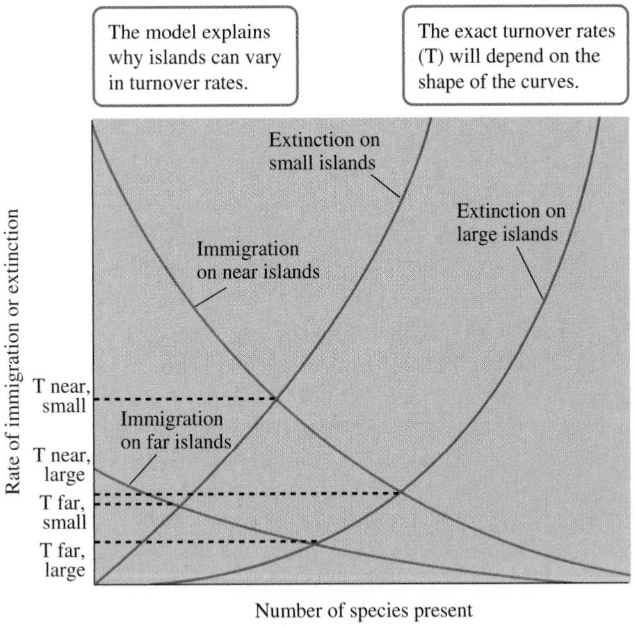

Turnover of bird species was demonstrated on the California Channel Islands by Jared Diamond (1969). Diamond surveyed the birds of the nine California Channel Islands in 1968, approximately 50 years after an earlier survey by A. B. Howell. The islands range in area from less than 3 to 249 km² and lie 12 to 61 km from the coast of southern California (fig. 22.14). Howell had thoroughly censused all of the islands except for San Miguel and Santa Rosa Islands, where he had difficulty getting permission to do bird surveys. In his later study, Diamond had full access to all the islands and was able to survey all land and water birds.

The results of Diamond's study support the equilibrium model of island biogeography. The number of bird species inhabiting the California Channel Islands remained almost constant over the 50 years between the two censuses. However, this stability in numbers of species was the result of an

Figure 22.13 Island distance and size influence species turnover rates (from MacArthur and Wilson 1963).

The model explains why islands can vary in turnover rates.

The exact turnover rates (T) will depend on the shape of the curves.

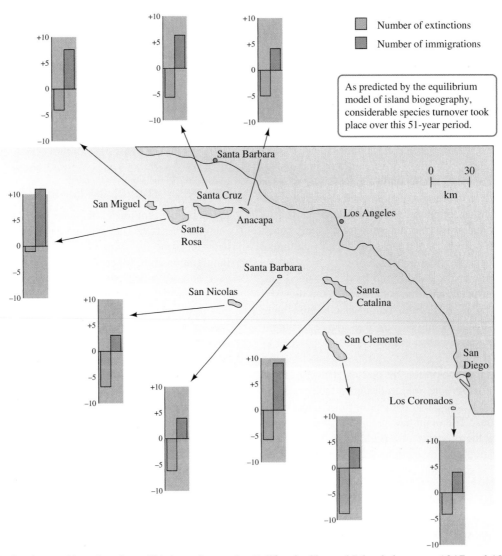

Figure 22.14 Extinction and immigration of bird species on the California Channel Islands between 1917 and 1968 (data from Diamond 1969).

approximately equal number of immigrations and extinctions on each of the islands (fig. 22.14). Diamond's study is an excellent example of how theory can guide field ecology. He discovered the dynamics underlying the diversity of birds on the California Channel Islands because he went out to test the MacArthur-Wilson equilibrium model of island biogeography. Additional insights into this model have been provided by experiments.

Experimental Island Biogeography

As Diamond conducted his surveys of the California Channel Islands, Daniel Simberloff and Edward O. Wilson were engaged in experimental studies of mangrove islands in the Florida Keys (Wilson and Simberloff 1969, Simberloff and Wilson 1969). The Florida Keys support very large stands of mangroves, which are dominated by the red mangrove, *Rhizophora mangle*. Many of these stands occur as small islands that lie hundreds of metres from the nearest large patch of mangroves (fig. 22.15). Simberloff and Wilson chose eight of these small mangrove islands for their experimental study. Their study islands were roughly circular and varied from 11 to 18 m in diameter and 5 to 10 m in height. The distance of islands from large areas of mangroves that could act as a source of colonists varied from 2 to 1,188 m.

The main fauna inhabiting the small mangrove islands of the Florida Keys are arthropods, chiefly insects. Simberloff and Wilson estimated that of the approximately 4,000 species of insects in the Florida Keys, about 500 species inhabit mangroves. Of these 500 species, about 75 commonly live on small mangrove islands. In addition to insects, the mangroves supported 15 species of spiders and other arthropods. The number of insect species on the experimental islands averaged 20 to 40 and the number of spider species ranged from 2 to 10.

Simberloff and Wilson chose two of the islands to act as controls and designated the six others as experimental islands. They carefully surveyed all the islands prior to defaunating the experimental islands. The islands were defaunated by enclosing them with a tent and then fumigating with methyl bromide. Fumigating was done at night to avoid heat damage to the mangrove trees. Simberloff and Wilson examined the trees immediately after fumigating and found that, with the possible exception of some wood-boring insect larvae, all arthropods had been killed. They followed recolonization by periodically censusing the arthropods on each island for approximately one year.

The number of species recorded on the two control islands was virtually identical at the beginning and end of the experiment. Though the number did not change significantly over the period of study, Simberloff and Wilson reported that species composition changed considerably. In other words, there had been species turnover on the control islands, a result consistent with the equilibrium model of island biogeography.

The equilibrium model was also supported by the recolonization studies of the experimental islands. Following defaunation, the number of arthropod species increased on all of the islands. All the islands, except the farthest island, eventually supported about the same number of species as they did prior to defaunation (fig. 22.16). Again, however, the composition of arthropods on the islands was substantially different, indicating species turnover. Species turnover is also indicated by the colonization histories of individual islands, which include many examples of species appearing and then disappearing from the community.

The process of colonization of species onto islands can be studied either by removing organisms from existing islands, as Simberloff and Wilson did when they defaunated their mangrove islands, or by creating new islands. Many new islands formed in a large lake in southern Sweden when the level of the lake was dropped at the end of the nineteenth century. Fortunately, some biologists recognized the rare opportunity offered by the new islands and studied their colonization by plants. These studies have continued for a century.

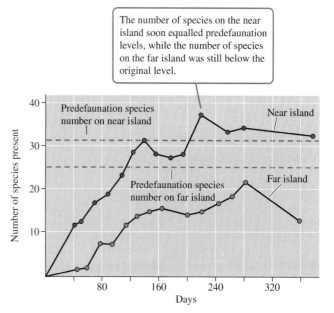

Figure 22.16   Colonization curves for two mangrove islands that were near and far from sources of potential colonists (data from Simberloff and Wilson 1969).

Figure 22.15   Some mangrove islands in the Florida Keys, which number in the thousands, are convenient places to test the equilibrium model of island biogeography.

Colonization of New Islands by Plants

The site of this long-term study is Lake Hjälmaren, which covers about 478 km² in Sweden (fig. 22.17). The level of Lake Hjälmaren was lowered 1.3 m between 1882 and 1886 and exposed many new islands. The first plant surveys of the new islands were conducted in 1886, and the islands were surveyed again in 1892, from 1903 to 1904, from 1927 to 1928, and from 1984 to 1985. Håkan Rydin and Sven-Olov Borgegård

(1988) summarized the earlier surveys of these new islands and conducted their own surveys in 1985. The result was a unique long-term record of the colonization of 40 islands.

The study islands vary in area from 65 m² to over 25,000 m² and support a limited diversity of plants. Rydin and Borgegård estimated that approximately 700 species of plants occur around Lake Hjälmaren. Of these 700 plant species, the number recorded on individual islands during the first century of their existence varied from 0 to 127. As expected, this variation in species richness correlated positively with island area over the entire history of the islands and accounted for 44% to 85% of the variation in species richness among islands. Measures of island isolation accounted for 4% to 10% of the variation in plant species richness among islands through the 1903–04 census. Island isolation did not account for significant variation in species richness among islands in subsequent censuses.

Rydin and Borgegård used the censuses of 30 islands to estimate rates of plant immigration and extinction (fig. 22.17). The historical record documents many immigrations and extinctions. There has been a slight excess of immigrations over extinctions on small- and medium-sized islands during the entire 100 years of record. What do these higher rates of immigration indicate? They show that small and medium islands continue to accumulate species. In contrast, large islands attained approximately equal rates of immigration and extinction sometime between 1928 and 1985. Over this period, approximately 30 plants became extinct on each large island and another 30 new species arrived. In other words, it appears that the number of species may have reached equilibrium on large islands.

The observed patterns of colonization were consistent with the predictions of the equilibrium model of island biogeography. Plant species richness on the islands of Lake Hjälmaren, like arthropod richness on the mangrove islands studied by Simberloff and Wilson, appears to be maintained by a dynamic interplay between immigration and local extinction. Many studies support the basic predictions of the equilibrium model of island biogeography. However, many questions remain.

For instance, why do larger islands support more species? Is the greater species richness on large islands due to a direct effect of area or do large islands support higher species richness because they include a greater diversity of habitats? Rydin and Borgegård found that measures of habitat diversity on the study islands accounted for only 1% to 2% of the variation in plant species richness. However, they point out that while some large islands with few habitats support low numbers of plant species, some small islands, with diverse habitats, support higher species richness than would be expected on the basis of area alone. The researchers point out that it is very difficult to separate the effects of habitat diversity from the effects of area. As we shall see in the next example, there is at least one experiment that came close to demonstrating that species richness on islands can be directly affected by area.

Manipulating Island Area

Daniel Simberloff (1976) tested the effect of island area on species richness experimentally. He surveyed the arthropods inhabiting nine mangrove islands that ranged in area from 262

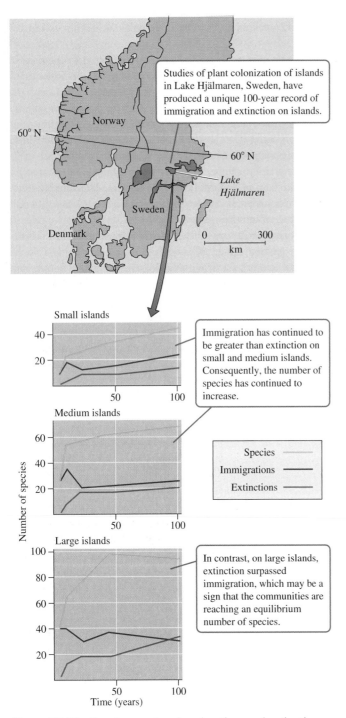

Figure 22.17 Species number, immigration, and extinction on 30 islands in Lake Hjälmaren, Sweden (data from Rydin and Borgegård 1988).

to 1,263 m². The distance of these islands from large areas of mangrove forest ranged from 2 to 432 m. The islands were up to five times the size of the mangrove islands fumigated by Simberloff and Wilson in their earlier study of recolonization and so contained a larger number of arthropod species.

Simberloff kept one island as a control, while reducing the area of the eight other islands by 32% to 76%. Island area was reduced during low tide by removing whole sections of the islands. Workers cut mangroves off below the high tide level and loaded the cut trees and branches on a barge. They then moved the cut material away from the island, where they sank it into deeper water (green mangrove wood sinks). Simberloff reduced the area of four experimental islands twice and the area of the other four experimental islands once only.

The results of Simberloff's experiment show a positive relationship between area and species richness. In all cases where island area was reduced, species richness decreased (fig. 22.18). Meanwhile, species richness on the control island, which was not changed in area, increased slightly. Additional insights are offered by the contrasting histories of islands whose areas were reduced once and those whose areas were reduced twice. For instance, the area of Mud 2 island was reduced from 942 to 327 m² and the richness of its arthropod fauna fell from 79 to 62 species. The area of Mud 2 was not reduced further, and its arthropod richness remained almost constant. Meanwhile, the islands whose area was reduced twice lost species with each reduction in area. Simberloff's results showed that area itself, without increased habitat heterogeneity, has a positive influence on species richness.

Island Biogeography Update

The equilibrium theory of island biogeography has had a major influence on the disciplines of biogeography and ecology. However, much has been discovered in the 40 years since

MacArthur and Wilson proposed their theory. For instance, James Brown and Astrid Kodric-Brown (1977) showed how higher rates of immigration to near islands can reduce extinction rates. As a consequence, we now know that, contrary to the original MacArthur-Wilson model, island distance from sources of colonists also influences rates of extinction. Similarly, Mark Lomolino (1990) extended the original model when he proposed the *target hypothesis*, demonstrating that island area can alter rates of immigration to islands. Brown and Lomolino (2000) pointed out that we have also discovered that species richness is not in equilibrium on many islands. In addition, we now know that species richness on islands is affected by differences among species groups in their speciation, colonization, and extinction rates. And perhaps most significantly, area and isolation are only two of several environmental factors that affect species richness on islands. Brown and Lomolino suggest that we may be on the eve of another revolution in theories that will replace the MacArthur-Wilson model. If so, it will be the result of research largely inspired by their theory as well as by our fascination for the islands themselves.

Experiments on islands such as those of Simberloff and Wilson demonstrate the value of an experimental approach to answering ecological questions. However, there are important ecological patterns that occur over such large scales that experiments are virtually impossible. The ecologists who study these large-scale patterns must rely on other approaches. In the next section, we discuss one of these important large-scale patterns, latitudinal variation in species richness.

CONCEPT 22.3 REVIEW

1. Why are virtually all estimates of immigration and extinction rates on islands underestimates of the true rates?
2. What result would have been grounds for Diamond to reject the equilibrium model of island biogeography based on his studies of the California Channel Islands?
3. In the course of studies by Simberloff and Wilson (1969) and Simberloff (1976), several mangrove islands were defaunated and several were partially destroyed to reduce island area. Do such experiments raise ethical issues?

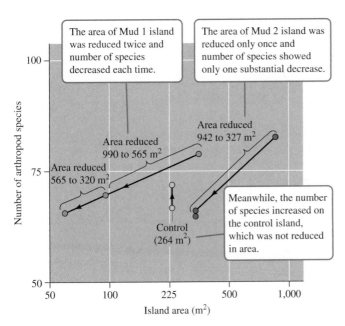

Figure 22.18   Effect of reducing mangrove island area on number of arthropod species (data from Simberloff 1976).

22.4 Latitudinal Gradients in Species Richness

Species richness generally increases from middle and high latitudes to the equator. Most groups of organisms are more species-rich in the tropics than they are at higher latitudes. This well-known increase in species richness toward the equator was apparent to scientists by the middle of the eighteenth century as taxonomists, led by Carolus Linnaeus, described tropical species sent back to Europe by explorers. Explorers

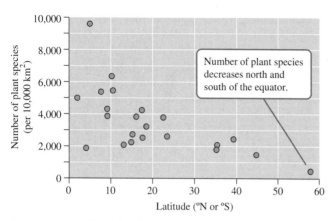

Figure 22.19 Variation in number of vascular plant species with latitude in the Western Hemisphere (data from Reid and Miller 1989).

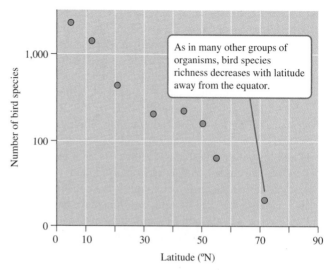

Figure 22.20 Latitudinal variation in number of bird species from Central to North America (data from Dobzhansky 1950).

and naturalists, such as Humboldt, Darwin, and Wallace, described overwhelming biological diversity in the tropics.

Figures 22.19 and 22.20 show examples of how plant species richness (Reid and Miller 1989) and bird species richness (Dobzhansky 1950) decrease as you move away from the equator and toward the poles. However, this pattern is not always found, as shown in figure 22.21, leading some ecologists to question whether it was in fact a general phenomenon. In a recent meta-analysis, Helmut Hillebrand took on the daunting task of summarizing all of the published studies testing for latitudinal gradients in diversity (Hillebrand 2004). In total, he found 232 studies that described 581 gradients for different taxa. These studies included terrestrial, marine, and freshwater habitats, spanned between 10° and 90° latitude, sampled areas between 1 m^2 and 1,000,000 km^2, and included taxa that ranged in body size across 12 orders of magnitude.

Across all of these studies, there was evidence for a clear and widespread pattern of increased diversity with decreasing latitudes (Hillebrand 2004). Even among the approximately 1/3 of studies that reported a lack of statistical support for a latitudinal gradient, the overall trend was toward greater diversity at low latitudes. Hillebrand was also able to show that on average those non-significant studies had lower sample size and sampled a more narrow range of latitudes than studies that demonstrated a latitudinal gradient in diversity. This finding is an important reminder that a study's design and sample size can influence the direction and strength of the results (appendix A). Though most studies demonstrated at least a trend toward increased diversity in the tropics, a small number of studies (<5%) did demonstrate lower diversity in the low latitudes. These are clearly exceptions belonging to a small number of taxa.

Underneath the general pattern of a latitudinal gradient of biodiversity, Hillebrand (2004) uncovered a number of ecological factors that influenced the strength of this relationship. The latitudinal gradient was quite strong for both marine and terrestrial taxa, and though significant, less strong for freshwater organisms (fig. 22.22a). The strength of the latitudinal gradient was greatest for higher trophic levels (fig. 22.22b) and for larger organisms (fig. 22.22c). The data set included

both large and small autotrophs (e.g., algae and trees) and large and small carnivores (e.g., chaetognaths and cats), and so the findings of stronger latitudinal gradients for both larger organisms and predators likely reflects two separate mechanisms.

Overall, the pattern of increased numbers of species in the tropics is pervasive and dramatic. There are some variations due to biotic realm, size, and feeding biology, but in general this is a robust pattern. As this pattern is so well documented, and has been for nearly a century, it would stand to reason that ecologists know the underlying mechanisms. Unfortunately, proposed explanations are nearly as diverse as the taxa being studied, and there is no broad agreement among ecologists.

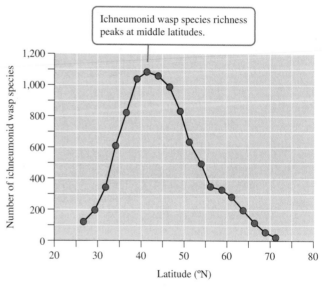

Figure 22.21 An exception to the general decline in species number with latitude: latitudinal variation in ichneumonid wasp species richness (data from Janzen 1981).

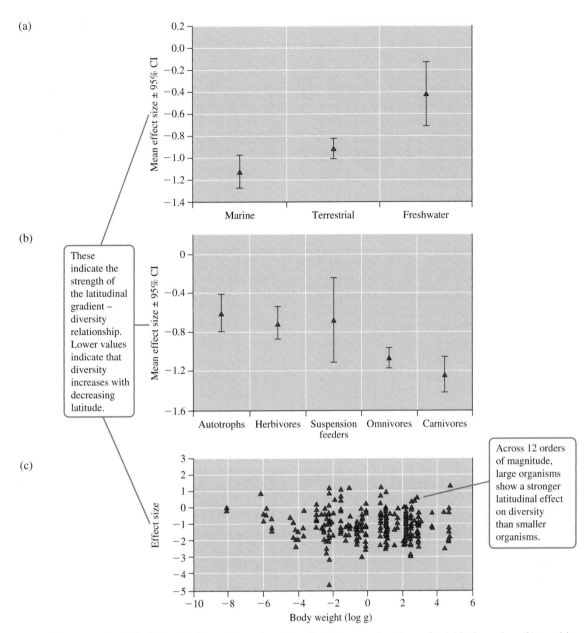

(a)

(b)

These indicate the strength of the latitudinal gradient – diversity relationship. Lower values indicate that diversity increases with decreasing latitude.

(c)

Across 12 orders of magnitude, large organisms show a stronger latitudinal effect on diversity than smaller organisms.

Figure 22.22 The strength of the latitudinal gradient of species diversity as a function of (*a*) biotic realm, (*b*) trophic position, and (*c*) organism body size. In all cases, negative values indicate increased diversity at lower latitudes, and more negative values indicate a stronger relationship (from Hillebrand 2004).

One recent review suggests that 30 different mechanisms for the gradient have been proposed (Willig et al. 2003). But there is good news: a series of recent reviews by international teams of researchers have begun to provide clarity to one of ecology's most pervasive patterns (Mittelbach et al. 2007; Currie et al. 2004; Schemske et al. 2009). Here we describe just a few of the proposed mechanisms—ones that appear not to have been clearly refuted by data. That said, there is no promise these will still be the ones we talk about in the next edition of this text! Though there is no expectation that there is a single cause, the generality of the pattern does suggest the cause(s) should also be general, and not taxa specific.

Time and Area Effects

The latitudinal gradient is extremely old, found in fossils at least 250 million years old (Willig et al. 2003). Alfred Russel Wallace, the man who independently developed a theory of evolution by natural selection, was the first to propose a mechanism for the latitudinal diversity gradient (Wallace 1878). He suggested that there are more species in the tropics because the tropics are older and they are disturbed less frequently than other regions of the earth. More specifically, tropical regions have been less affected by glacial cycles (chapter 21), potentially allowing for more time for speciation to occur.

A related issue is that there is a greater area covered by tropical regions than other biomes, both currently and through much of geological history. As we have discussed previously in this chapter, species diversity tends to increase as area increases. It may not be immediately apparent that the tropics, which mainly occupy the area between the tropics of Cancer and Capricorn, include a greater area of both land and water than do higher latitudes. The reason for this is that the typical world map is based upon the *Mercator projection*, a projection that increases the apparent area at high latitudes. However, if you look at a world globe you will immediately see that the tropical areas of the earth constitute a vast area.

Rosenzweig (1992) quantified the amount of land surface area in various latitudinal zones using a computer map of the earth. He divided the globe into tropical ($\pm 26°$ of latitude), subtropical (26° to 36°), temperate (36° to 46°), boreal (46° to 56°), and tundra (>56°). He then measured the area of land within these latitudinal zones and found that the area of land within the tropics far exceeds that of other areas (fig. 22.23).

Not only is there more land (and water) at tropical latitudes, but in addition, temperatures are more uniform across this tropical belt. This pattern was put in the context of geographic ecology by Terborgh (1973), who plotted mean annual temperatures against latitude. As figure 22.24 shows, there is little difference in mean annual temperatures between about 0° and 25° latitude. Because this temperature pattern occurs both north and south of the equator, mean annual temperature changes little over about 50° of latitude within the tropics. However, above 25° latitude, mean annual temperature declines linearly with latitude. What is the biological significance of this latitudinal pattern of temperature variation? One implication is that tropical organisms can disperse over large areas and not meet with significant changes in temperature.

How do patterns of temperature variation affect rates of speciation and extinction? Rosenzweig proposed that the larger area of tropical regions should reduce extinction rates in two ways. First, large, physically similar areas will allow tropical species to be distributed over a larger area. Within these larger areas, there should be more refuges in which to survive environmental disturbances. Because of their larger range, tropical species should also have greater total population sizes. Larger populations are less likely to become extinct.

Mittelbach et al. (2007) review a number of recent studies that provide some support for the time and area hypotheses. For example, they found that many clades of temperate species are actually nested within larger clades of tropical species. This suggests the origin of much of the temperate diversity we see is rooted in older tropical species. In another case, they find that tree diversity could not be explained by current biome area, but it was well explained when they included biome area over geological time.

Rate of Diversification

A second potential cause of the diversity gradient could be increased species diversification rates in the tropics, relative to low latitudes. What could cause increased speciation rates? One mechanism could be the interactions among species.

Throughout much of this text, we have discussed the evolutionary implications of ecological interactions. These have included character displacement, host-race formation, changes in host–parasite dynamics, and a number of other responses. Over time, and under a number of conditions (chapter 4), these evolutionary responses could lead to speciation. As a result, a number of ecologists have suggested that biotic interactions (e.g., competition, predation, herbivory, parasitism) are stronger in the tropics than at higher

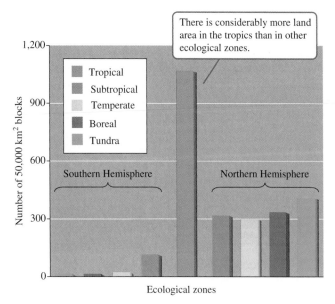

Figure 22.23   Land area in five latitudinal biomes (data from Rosenzweig 1992).

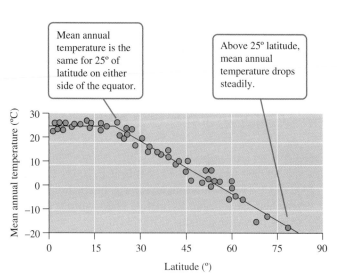

Figure 22.24   Mean annual temperature by latitude (data from Rosenzweig 1992, after Terborgh 1973).

latitudes, leading to increased speciation and increased diversity (reviewed by Schemske et al. 2009).

Data comparing the intensity of ecological interactions along latitudinal gradients are relatively sparse, though they have been compiled by Schemske et al. 2009. They were able to find over 50 studies looking at predation, herbivory, parasitism, some mutualisms, and a variety of other interactions. Across all of these studies, not a single one reported greater intensities of interactions in high latitudes, some reported no latitudinal gradient in species interactions, and most reported greater intensities of interactions at low latitudes. Schemske et al. (2009) strongly emphasize the need for more data on this question, but to date, it appears that there is a latitudinal gradient in species interactions. If interactions lead to specialization and diversification, this could contribute to the generation of the latitudinal gradient in species diversity.

Mittelbach et al. (2007) present a number of other mechanisms that could increase diversification rates in the tropics, some of which may increase speciation rates (as that above), and others may reduce extinction rates. Many of these mechanisms will be tied to the age and area of the topics, highlighting that no single mechanism is likely at play. For example, climatic variation at low latitudes may slow down speciation and increase extinction rates, larger areas increase the chance for parapatric and sympatric speciation (chapter 4), and increased productivity in the tropics may increase population sizes, altering extinction probabilities.

In summary, many factors may contribute to higher tropical species richness, including ecological, geological, and evolutionary hypotheses. Despite being aware of this pattern for over a century, ecologists have yet to agree on the relative importance of these and a number of other potential mechanisms. Although we have no final answer to the causes of this pattern, we now turn to another example of geographic ecology: the relationship between local and regional diversity.

CONCEPT 22.4 REVIEW

1. Why is there no one factor that seems to explain latitudinal gradients in species diversity?
2. Why do ecologists use evolutionary biology when discussing the mechanisms of this ecological pattern?

22.5 Historical and Regional Influences

Long-term historical and regional processes significantly influence the structure of biotas and ecosystems. Macroecological patterns in diversity can be caused by local factors, such as area and ecological interactions. However, as we saw in the previous section, unique historical and geographic factors can also influence regional patterns in species richness. Here we will further explore how regional processes can influence local diversity.

Patterns of Local and Regional Diversity

What determines the number of species that are found in a given location? In this chapter, we have discussed how this could, influenced by area and isolation. In prior chapters we have also described how competition, herbivory, and a variety of local processes can alter community structure. One factor we have not yet considered is the relatively straightforward idea that the number of species found in a community must be no greater than the regional species pool. Only species that are present somewhere in the region could possibly be found in any particular community, and thus the size of the species pool serves as an upper bound of local diversity. Therefore, as regional diversity increases, local diversity increases too. Or does it? We have seen before that the presence of competitive dominant species may actually exclude other species from entering a community. Similarly, abiotic stress or herbivory could be so extreme in a given community that only a few, specially adapted species may persist, regardless of how many species are in the region. Similar statements could be made about all the ecological processes we discussed in section IV of the book. In short, even if there were an unlimited number of species in the regional pool, local processes might limit the number of species found in any particular community. These contrasting predictions can be summarized in a graph describing the hypothetical relationships between local and regional species richness (fig. 22.25). In both models, a line with a slope of 1 represents the theoretical maximum. In model I, there is a linear relationship between local and regional diversity. Such a relationship indicates that local diversity is a constant fraction of regional diversity. In model II, there is species saturation at high levels of regional diversity. This model predicts that there is only a set amount of niche space within a community, and thus species exclusion occurs through local processes. What does the data suggest?

Ronald Karlson, Howard Cornell, and Terence Hughes have provided one of the most comprehensive tests of this question (Karlson et al. 2004). They sampled the diversity

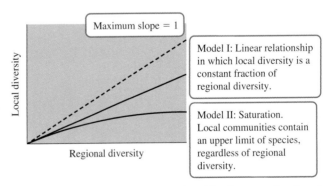

Figure 22.25 Hypothetical relationships between local and regional diversity.

Figure 22.26 A rich diversity of life lives in and among coral reefs.

of corals around 15 islands that were spread across five Indo-Pacific regions (fig. 22.26). In total, these locations represented a 10,000 km gradient, and represented a truly ambitious research project. In each location, they measured coral diversity in three habitat types: (1) reef flats that were 5 to 10 m inshore of breaking waves; (2) reef crests that were seaward of breaking waves and at a depth of 1 to 2 m; and

(3) reef slopes, which were also seaward of breaking waves but at a depth of 6 to 7 m. Through extensive dives below the water's surface, they sampled a total of 41,710 coral colonies. There were clear differences in diversity among the five regions and three habitats they sampled (fig. 22.27). Reef flats consistently had the lowest diversity, and reef slopes the highest in nearly all regions. When they compared local and regional diversity, they found a clear linear relationship for all three habitats (fig. 22.28), supporting model I. Karlson and his colleagues are not the only ones to find support for a regional effect on local diversity. A group of researchers from the United States and Canada found similar results for a number of groups of zooplankton in lakes throughout North America (Shurin et al. 2000).

Why does regional richness increase local dispersal? One likely mechanism is **dispersal limitation**. This idea suggests that many species in a region are capable of living in more communities; however, they simply have not successfully dispersed into those areas. As we see next, there can be a variety of other influences of the region on local patterns of diversity.

Exceptional Patterns of Diversity

There are major differences in species richness that cannot be explained by differences in area. For instance, consider the regions with Mediterranean climates that we discussed in chapter 2, which support Mediterranean woodlands and shrublands. Such regions include the Cape region of South Africa (90,000 km^2), southwestern Australia (320,000 km^2), and the California Floristic Province (324,000 km^2). These regions have similar climates but differ significantly in area. Which of these areas should contain the greatest number of species? The positive relationship between area and species richness that we have seen repeatedly earlier in this chapter leads us to predict that southwestern Australia and the California Floristic Province, with more than three times the area of the Cape region of South Africa, will contain the

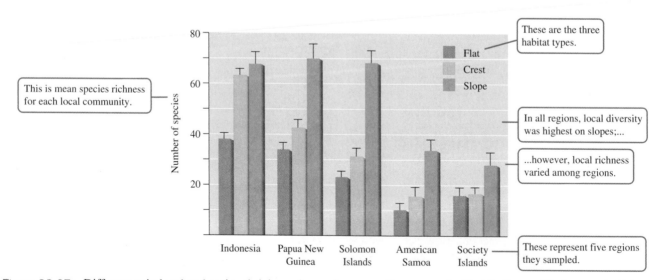

Figure 22.27 Differences in local and regional richness in coral communities across the Pacific Ocean (Karlson et al. 2004).

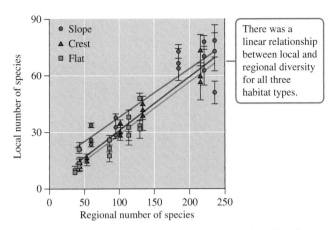

Figure 22.28 Relationship between local and regional diversity of coral communities in the Pacific Ocean (Karlson et al. 2004).

greatest biological diversity. Southwestern Australia and the California Floristic Province have the same area and approximately the same number of species. However, as figure 22.29 shows, the Cape region, the smallest area, contains more than twice the number of plant species as the other two regions.

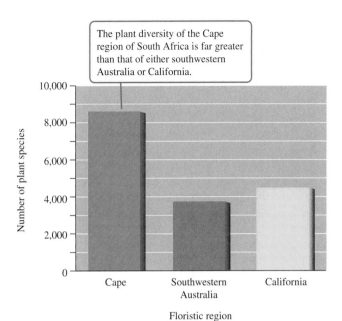

Figure 22.29 Number of plant species living in three regions with Mediterranean climates (data from Bond and Goldblatt 1984).

ECOLOGY IN ACTION

Biodiversity Hotspots

Species are not distributed evenly across the globe; instead, biodiversity is concentrated into specific areas of the planet known as *biodiversity hotspots*. The realization that biodiversity is clustered into these hotspots across the planet is important for a variety of reasons. First, it is an intriguing ecological pattern that is certainly worthy of explanation. Second, the concentration of biodiversity across the planet suggests that loss of certain habitats and areas to development will result in a greater ecological cost than similar development in other areas. In other words, by identifying biodiversity hotspots, ecologists may provide ecological triage, identifying those areas that are most urgently in need of treatment and repair.

As we discussed in chapter 10, there are different types of rarity for species, with different consequences for conservation. Of particular concern are the species that have a very narrow range, and are endemic to a very small area. Even small amounts of development can threaten these species, if it were to occur in their relatively restricted habitat.

One concern about the hotspot approach to identifying areas of critical conservation need has been that high levels of species richness do not necessarily equate to high levels of rare and endemic species. Instead, it is possible that areas are particularly diverse due to large numbers of cosmopolitan species, ones not likely in need of protection. Jeremy Kerr,

of York University, has analyzed this issue for several taxa. He has found that patterns of richness were generally correlated with patterns of endemism, supporting the hotspot approach (Kerr 1997). However, he also found that the location of biodiversity hotspots varied among taxa, and protection of area for one group of species could not be assumed to provide an umbrella that would reach over and cover other taxa. Instead, each taxonomic group is likely going to have its own locations in most critical need of protection.

Norman Myers and colleagues have produced one of the more comprehensive studies identifying terrestrial biodiversity hotspots (Myers et al. 2000). They focused specifically on endemic plants, mammals, birds, reptiles, and amphibians. They state that because plants are "essential to virtually all forms of animal life," an area could only qualify as a hotspot if it contained a minimum of 0.5% of the world's plant species as endemics (this equates to 1,500 of the 300,000 known species). Only if a location met these criteria would information regarding endemic vertebrates be added for comparison. The research team did not include invertebrates in this analysis primarily because a large proportion of invertebrate diversity remains undescribed by science, and thus accurate information is lacking. An area only made the final cut for inclusion as a hotspot if it was under significant threat of development,

with at least 70% or more of the vegetation lost. This criteria was added to allow this list to identify areas in need of urgent protection, rather than simply a map of diversity patterns.

In total, Myers et al. (2000) identified 25 hotspots around the globe (fig. 22.30). These areas represent only 1.4% of the planet's land base, yet contain 44% of the known plant species. In total, 88% of the primary vegetation in these areas has already been lost to development. It should come as no surprise that a majority of these sites are in tropical areas, where diversity is high and pressure to develop the land is strong. Figure 22.31 shows that these hotspots vary in terms of biodiversity and habitat threat. For example, the top five hotspots contain 20% of all plant and 16% of all vertebrate species and yet only occupy 0.4% of the earth's surface. Clearly, not all areas on the planet are ecologically equivalent, nor of equal conservation priority.

Diversity hotspots can be identified in marine systems as well. By definition, these cannot be exactly the same place as

Figure 22.30   Identified terrestrial biodiversity hotspots around the planet (data from Myers et al. 2000).

the terrestrial hotspots. However, if these areas were in close proximity to one another, such as marine areas immediately offshore a terrestrial hotspot, it may facilitate conservation efforts. There have been numerous efforts to identify marine

Hotspot	Original extent of primary vegetation (km²)	Remaining primary vegetation (km²) (% of original extent)	Area protected (km²) (% of hotspot)	Plant species	Endemic plants (% of global plants, 300,000)	Vertebrate species	Endemic vertebrates (% of global vertebrates, 27,298)
Tropical Andes	1,258,000	314,500 (25.0)	79,687 (25.3)	45,000	20,000 (6.7%)	3,389	1,567 (5.7%)
Mesoamerica	1,155,000	231,000 (20.0)	138,437 (59.9)	24,000	5,000 (1.7%)	2,859	1,159 (4.2%)
Caribbean	263,500	29,840 (11.3)	29,840 (100.0)	12,000	7,000 (2.3%)	1,518	779 (2.9%)
Brazil's Atlantic Forest	1,227,600	91,930 (7.5)	33,084 (35.9)	20,000	8,000 (2.7%)	1,361	567 (2.1%)
Choco/Darien/Western Ecuador	260,600	63,000 (24.2)	16,471 (26.1)	9,000	2,250 (0.8%)	1,625	418 (1.5%)
Brazil's Cerrado	1,783,200	356,630 (20.0)	22,000 (6.2)	10,000	4,400 (1.5%)	1,268	117 (0.4%)
Central Chile	300,000	90,000 (30.0)	9,167 (10.2)	3,429	1,605 (0.5%)	335	61 (0.2%)
California Floristic Province	324,000	80,000 (24.7)	31,443 (39.3)	4,426	2,125 (0.7%)	584	71 (0.3%)
Madagascar*	594,150	59,038 (9.9)	11,548 (19.6)	12,000	9,704 (3.2%)	987	771 (2.8%)
Eastern Arc and Coastal Forests of Tanzania/Kenya	30,000	2,000 (6.7)	2,000 (100.0)	4,000	1,500 (0.5%)	1,019	121 (0.4%)
Western African Forests	1,265,000	126,500 (10.0)	20,324 (16.1)	9,000	2,250 (0.8%)	1,320	270 (1.0%)
Cape Floristic Province	74,000	18,000 (24.3)	14,060 (78.1)	8,200	5,682 (1.9%)	562	53 (0.2%)
Succulent Karoo	112,000	30,000 (26.8)	2,352 (7.8)	4,849	1,940 (0.6%)	472	45 (0.2%)
Mediterranean Basin	2,362,000	110,000 (4.7)	42,123 (38.3)	25,000	13,000 (4.3%)	770	235 (0.9%)
Caucasus	500,000	50,000 (10.0)	14,050 (28.1)	6,300	1,600 (0.5%)	632	59 (0.2%)
Sundaland	1,600,000	125,000 (7.8)	90,000 (72.0)	25,000	15,000 (5.0%)	1,800	701 (2.6%)
Wallacea	347,000	52,020 (15.0)	20,415 (39.2)	10,000	1,500 (0.5%)	1,142	529 (1.9%)
Philippines	300,800	9,023 (3.0)	3,910 (43.3)	7,620	5,832 (1.9%)	1,093	518 (1.9%)
Indo-Burma	2,060,000	100,000 (4.9)	100,000 (100.0)	13,500	7,000 (2.3%)	2,185	528 (1.9%)
South-Central China	800,000	64,000 (8.0)	16,562 (25.9)	12,000	3,500 (1.2%)	1,141	178 (0.7%)
Western Ghats/Sri Lanka	182,500	12,450 (6.8)	12,450 (100.0)	4,780	2,180 (0.7%)	1,073	355 (1.3%)
SW Australia	309,850	33,336 (10.8)	33,336 (100.0)	5,469	4,331 (1.4%)	456	100 (0.4%)
New Caledonia	18,600	5,200 (28.0)	526.7 (10.1)	3,332	2,551 (0.9%)	190	84 (0.3%)
New Zealand	270,500	59,400 (22.0)	52,068 (87.7)	2,300	1,865 (0.6%)	217	136 (0.5%)
Polynesia/Micronesia	46,000	10,024 (21.8)	4,913 (49.0)	6,557	3,334 (1.1%)	342	223 (0.8%)
Totals	17,444,300	2,122,891 (12.2)	800,767 (37.7)	†	133,149 (44%)	†	9,645 (35%)

Figure 22.31   Details of the diversity and development found in the top 25 terrestrial hotspots (data from Myers et al. 2000).

* Madagascar includes the nearby islands of Mauritius, Reunion, Seychelles, and Comores.
† These totals cannot be summed owing to overlapping between hotspots.

biodiversity hotspots recently. A group of researchers from Canada, the United States, and Australia investigated the location of marine hotspots, focusing primarily on tropical reefs (Roberts et al. 2002). They found that the 10 richest hotspots contain only 16% of the world's reefs but 44% to 54% of the endemic reef species. In another example from marine systems, Boris Worm, Heike Lotze, and Ransom Myers of Dalhousie University have identified the majority of biodiversity hotspots for large ocean predators such as tunas, sharks, and billfish, which occur at intermediate, rather than tropical latitudes (Worm et al. 2003). These locations are generally at the intersection of the ranges of temperate and tropical prey species, and are generally concentrated around variation in ocean bottom topography (e.g., reefs, shelf breaks, etc.).

Biodiversity is not spread evenly around the globe, and efforts such as these provide critical information for conservation programs. Though Canada is not home to the extreme concentrations of biodiversity found in countries at lower latitudes, there are pockets within Canada that are relatively high in biodiversity. For example, the Carolinean Canada forests of southwestern Ontario have over 2,000 species of plants. This is a large number considering the entire country most likely has less than 5,000 species!.

Understanding the distribution of diversity is a critical outcome of ecological research, and an essential part of any conservation program. It is up to the next generation of ecologists to find ways to protect these areas.

The failure of area to explain a significant regional diversity pattern is not unique to this example. For instance, Roger Latham and Robert Ricklefs (1993) reported a striking contrast in diversity of temperate zone trees that cannot be explained by an area effect. As we saw in chapter 2, the temperate forest biome covers approximately equal areas in Europe (1.2 million km^2), eastern Asia (1.2 million km^2), and eastern North America (1.8 million km^2). The species area relationship would lead us to predict that these three regions would support approximately equal levels of biological diversity. However, eastern Asia contains nearly three times more tree species than eastern North America and nearly six times more species of trees than Europe.

Historical and Regional Explanations

How can we explain these exceptional patterns of biological diversity? What mechanisms produced these patterns, which are contrary to generalizations discussed in chapter 22 and earlier chapters? In each case, it appears that geography and history offer convincing explanations.

The Cape Floristic Region of South Africa

Pauline Bond and Peter Goldblatt (1984) attributed the unusual species richness of the Cape floristic region to several historic and geographic factors. Selection for a distinctively Mediterranean flora in southern Africa began during the late Tertiary period, about 26 million years ago. At that time, the climate became progressively cooler and drier, conditions that selected for succulence, fire resistance, and smaller, sclerophyllous leaves. The initial sites for evolution of the Cape flora were likely in south-central Africa, not in the Cape region itself. At that time, Africa lay farther south and the Cape region had a cool, moist climate and supported an evergreen forest.

As Africa drifted northward, the climate of southern Africa became more arid and the ancestors of today's Cape flora gradually migrated toward the Cape region. By the time Africa neared its present latitudinal position during the late Pliocene, about three million years ago, southern Africa was very arid and the Cape region had a Mediterranean climate. Bond and Goldblatt suggest that plant speciation within this region was promoted by the highly dissected landscape, the existence of a wide variety of soil types, and repeated expansion, contraction, and isolation of plant populations during the climatic fluctuations of the Pleistocene. They suggest that extinction rates were reduced by the existence of substantial refuge areas, even during times of peak aridity.

The Diversity of Temperate Trees

How did eastern Asia, eastern North America, and Europe, three temperate regions of approximately equal area and climate, end up with such different numbers of tree species? Latham and Ricklefs offer persuasive geographic and historical reasons. They propose that we need to consider what trees in the three regions faced during the last glacial period and how those conditions may have affected extinction rates.

Refer to chapter 2 and study the distributions of temperate forest in eastern Asia, eastern North America, and Europe. Now examine the distributions of mountains in eastern Asia, eastern North America, and Europe shown in chapter 2. Notice that while there are no mountain barriers to north–south movements of organisms in eastern Asia and eastern North America, the mountains in Europe form barriers that are oriented east to west. Now imagine what happened to a tree species as glaciers began to advance during the last ice age and the climate of Europe became progressively colder. Temperate trees would have had their southward retreat largely cut off by mountain ranges running east to west.

This hypothesis proposes that the lower species richness of European trees has been at least partly a consequence of higher extinction rates during glacial periods. How would you test this hypothesis? Latham and Ricklefs searched the fossil

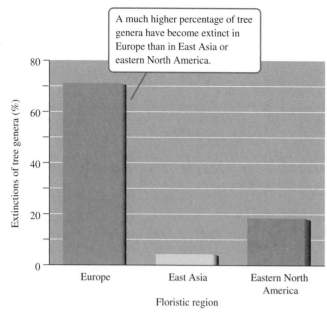

Figure 22.32 Extinctions of tree genera in Europe, East Asia, and eastern North America since the middle Tertiary period (data from Latham and Ricklefs 1993).

record for extinctions in the three regions. They estimated the number of genera that have become extinct in the three regions during the last 30 to 40 million years. Their analysis showed that most of the plant genera that once lived in Europe have become extinct. A larger proportion of genera has become extinct in Europe than in either eastern Asia or eastern North America (fig. 22.32).

Now consider eastern North America. The only mountain range, the Appalachians, runs north to south. Consequently, in eastern North America, temperate trees had an avenue of retreat in the face of advancing glaciers and cooling climate. The movement of temperate tree populations in the face of climate change has been well documented by paleontologists such as Margaret Davis. There are also no mountain barriers

in eastern Asia, where temperate trees can migrate even farther south than in eastern North America.

Higher rates of extinction during glacial periods can explain the lower diversity of trees in Europe. However, why does eastern North America include fewer tree species than eastern Asia? Latham and Ricklefs conclude that the fossil record and present-day distributions of temperate trees indicate that most temperate tree taxa originated in eastern Asia. These Asian taxa subsequently dispersed to Europe and North America. In addition, after the dispersal routes between eastern Asia and eastern North America were closed off, speciation continued in Asia, producing several endemic Asian genera. In other words, there are fewer tree species in eastern North America because most taxa originated in eastern Asia and never dispersed to North America.

Throughout this chapter we have shown how geographic factors can influence local species diversity. Many aspects of geographic variation in species richness can be explained by historical and regional processes, and do not necessarily rely on the processes described in section V. The ecologist interested in understanding patterns of diversity at large spatial scales must consider processes occurring over similarly large scales and over long periods of time. As we shall see in chapter 23, a large-scale, long-term perspective is also essential for understanding global ecology.

CONCEPT 22.5 REVIEW

1. Why should history have such a strong influence on regional diversity patterns?
2. How does the combined evidence from studies of the flora of Mediterranean regions and the diversity of trees in temperate forest regions increase confidence that historical differences can outweigh the potential influence of area on diversity?

ECOLOGICAL TOOLS AND APPROACHES

Global Positioning Systems, Remote Sensing, and Geographic Information Systems

Modern tools have revolutionized the field of macroecology. One of the reasons there is renewed interest among ecologists in studying the classic patterns of ecology is that the availability of inexpensive and highly accurate spatial data allows for improved analyses and understanding. Today, ecologists generally geo-reference their study location, and often record their data on geographic information systems (GIS). GIS are computer-based systems that store, interpret, integrate, analyze, and display geographic information. In addition, the ecologists of today have access to more information of greater

accuracy because of continued improvements in remote sensing and global positioning systems. Once again, we find that development of new and better methodologies is critical to advancement in ecology.

Global Positioning Systems

Where are you? This is one of the most basic questions the geographer can ask. Scientists, engineers, navigators, and explorers have spent centuries devising methods to measure elevation, latitude, and longitude. Recent technological advances have improved the accuracy of these measurements.

Alexander von Humboldt would appreciate these recent technological advances. As he explored South and North America, he carefully determined the latitude, longitude, and elevation of important geographic features. For instance, Humboldt was particularly interested in verifying the existence and location of a waterway called the Casiquiare Canal. The Casiquiare reportedly connected the Orinoco River with the Rio Negro, which flows into the Amazon. A connection between two major river systems would make the Casiquiare unique, but its existence was widely doubted.

Humboldt halted his expedition at the junction of the Casiquiare and the Rio Negro so that he could record the latitude and longitude. Biting insects tormented the explorers as they waited for nightfall. Luckily, that night the clouds parted and Humboldt could see the stars well enough to take sightings and determine their position. At other times, he was not so lucky. He once waited for nearly a month for the weather to clear sufficiently to make his sightings on the stars. Today, equipped with a global positioning system, Humboldt could have determined the latitude and longitude of the junction of the Casiquiare and the Rio Negro any time he wished, regardless of weather.

A **global positioning system (GPS)** determines locations on the earth's surface, including latitude, longitude, and altitude, using satellites as reference points. These satellites, which orbit the earth at a height of about 21,000 km, continuously transmit their position and the time. The satellites keep track of time with an extremely accurate atomic clock that loses or gains 1 second in about 30,000 years. A global positioning system receives the signals broadcast by these satellites. Because the system also includes an extremely accurate clock, the time required for the satellite signal to reach the receiver can be used as a measure of the distance between the two. With measurements of the distance to four satellites, a global positioning system can determine the latitude, longitude, and altitude of any point on earth with great accuracy (fig. 22.33). GPS units are now widely available, inexpensive, and embedded in many electronic devices. These items are so easy to use that even my mother, with her car-mounted unit, can navigate through new cities with minimal stress. It is difficult to overstate the importance that access to accurate spatial data has for the ability to address many ecological questions. I suppose we all owe the U.S. military a "thank you," as they led the development of this technology (including paying those research bills), and in the last decade allowed civilians to have improved accuracy in their positioning records.

While navigation satellites and global positioning systems can accurately locate places on the ground, other satellites provide a wealth of other information about those localities. These remote sensing satellites transmit pictures of the earth that are extremely valuable to ecologists.

Remote Sensing

Remote sensing refers to gathering information about an object without direct contact with it, mainly by gathering and

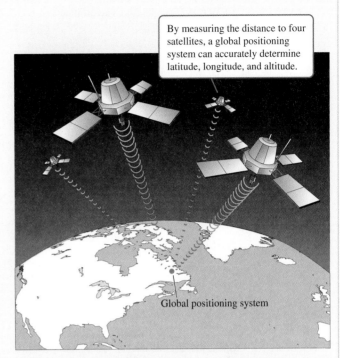

By measuring the distance to four satellites, a global positioning system can accurately determine latitude, longitude, and altitude.

Global positioning system

Figure 22.33   Global positioning systems determine latitude, longitude, and altitude by measuring the distance from several satellites.

processing electromagnetic radiation emitted or reflected by the object. Using this definition, the original remote sensor was the eye. However, we generally associate remote sensing with technology that extends the senses, technology ranging from binoculars and cameras to satellite-mounted sensors.

Remote-sensing satellites are generally fitted with electro-optical sensors that scan several bands of the electromagnetic spectrum. These sensors convert electromagnetic radiation into electrical signals that are in turn converted to digital values by a computer. These digital values can be used to construct an image. The earliest of the *Landsat* satellites monitored four bands of electromagnetic radiation, two bands of visible light (0.5 to 0.6 μm and 0.6 to 0.7 μm), and two bands in the near infrared (0.7 to 0.8 μm and 0.8 to 1.1 μm). From this beginning, satellite imaging systems have become progressively more sophisticated both in terms of the number of wavelengths scanned and the spatial resolution.

Satellite-based remote sensing has produced detailed images of essentially every square metre of the earth's surface. You may have already seen many of these through readily available services such as Google Earth. Ecologists use a diversity of satellite-based imaging processes to monitor a variety of ecological processes, including "greenness" and primary productivity. For example, the Department of Fisheries and Oceans uses remote sensing to monitor changes in ocean productivity, often measured as chlorophyll-a concentrations (fig. 22.34). When images are taken at different points in time, it is possible to measure changes. The most obvious changes

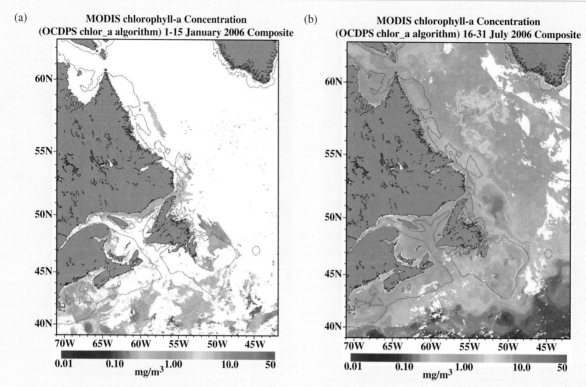

Figure 22.34 Measures of ocean chlorophyll-a concentrations from part of Atlantic Canada in (*a*) January 2006, and (*b*) July 2006.

would be seasonal shifts in productivity (fig. 22.34), but could also include other factors.

Incorporating satellite imaging with a variety of methods of analysis also allows scientists to categorize large geographic regions by the dominant vegetation. For example, using the Advanced Very High Resolution Radiometer satellite network, a team of researchers at the Canada Centre for Remote Sensing were able to develop a land cover map for all of Canada (fig. 22.35). It is important to recognize that there exists a great diversity of satellites capable of conducting remote-sensing operations for ecological research. Some satellites, like those used to produce figure 22.35, are very good at imaging vast geographic regions (such as all of Canada!), but have relatively coarse resolution, such as 1 km^2. In contrast, other satellite systems can image the earth from space at a resolution of less than 1 m^2. Such detailed information is likely critical to assess change or characterize habitats within a local area (e.g., a single province), but would produce too great a volume of data to characterize larger areas (such as all of Canada).

Remote sensing allows ecologists to gather large volumes of data across a very large spatial scale—even more data than could be collected with an army of eager undergraduate assistants! However, these large quantities of data create another problem. Ecologists need a system for storing, sorting, analyzing, and displaying these large quantities of geographic information. This is the problem addressed by geographic information systems.

Geographic Information Systems

In the days of Humboldt, geographers often had too little data. Today, with new tools for gathering great quantities of information, geographers and geographic ecologists can be overwhelmed by data. **Geographic information systems (GIS)**, computer-based systems for storing, sorting, analyzing, and displaying geographic data, are designed to handle large quantities of data. Sometimes GIS are confused with computerized map-making. While these systems can produce maps, they do much more. Much of population ecology is concerned with understanding the factors controlling the distribution and abundance of organisms. However, the geographic context of populations has often been lost. Geographic information systems preserve this geographic information. Because they preserve geographic context, the systems provide ecologists with a valuable tool for exploring large-scale population responses to climate change. GIS serves as a critical tool for many studies we have already discussed, including the ability to rapidly quantify landscape elements and conduct ecological niche modelling.

As we shall see in chapter 23, rapid global change challenges the field of ecology to continue to address large-scale environmental questions. As ecologists address these compelling questions, GIS, global positioning systems, and remote sensing will be increasingly valued parts of their tool kit.

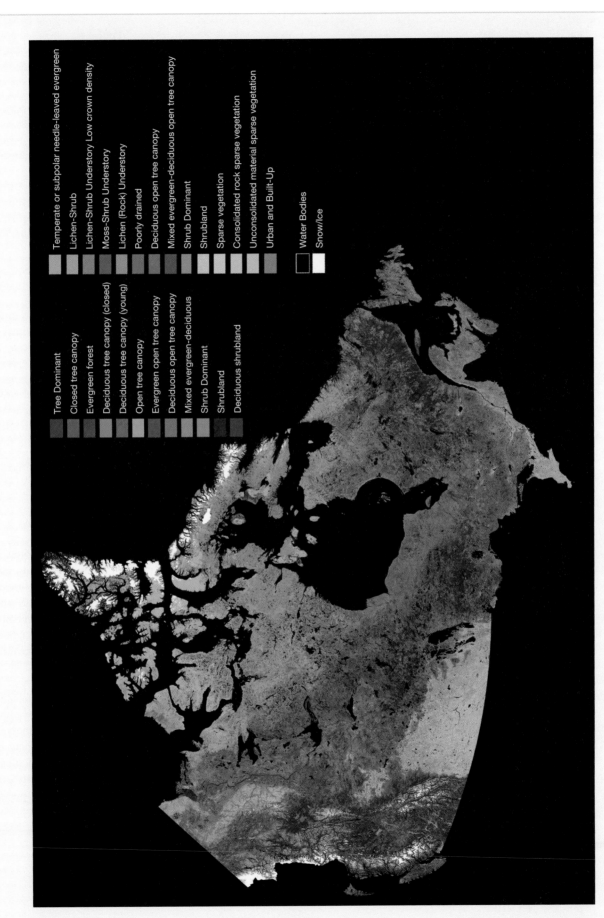

Figure 22.35 Land cover map for all of Canada, based upon satellite imaging.

Macroecology focuses on large-scale patterns of the distribution and diversity of organisms and ecological processes. Research areas include island biogeography, latitudinal patterns of species diversity, and the influences of regional and historical process on diversity and function.

22.1 Information about a species' current distribution and niche requirements can be combined with spatial information to predict invasion and range expansion.

Ecological niche modelling is a new approach designed to predict the potential distribution of a species across a broad geographic range. To create such models, an ecologist combines geo-referenced information about where a species is found with spatially explicit information about the environmental conditions that exist, resulting in statistical description of a species' niche. This information can then be applied to new locations, predicting where one could find rare species, predict range shifts associated with climate change, and predict where an invasive species may spread. However, data quality is critical to accurate predictions, and pretty maps alone do not represent strong science.

22.2 On islands and habitat patches on continents, species richness increases with area and decreases with isolation.

Larger oceanic islands support more species of most groups of organisms than small islands. Isolated oceanic islands generally contain fewer species than islands near mainland areas. In addition to true islands, many habitats on continents (e.g., mountain tops, lakes) are so isolated that they can be considered as islands. However, because organisms differ substantially in dispersal rates, an island that is very isolated for one group of organisms may be completely accessible to another group.

22.3 Species richness on islands can be modelled as a dynamic balance between immigration and extinction of species.

The equilibrium model of island biogeography proposes that the difference between rates of immigration and extinction determines the species richness on islands. The equilibrium model of island biogeography assumes that rates of species immigration to islands are mainly determined by distance from sources of immigrants. The model assumes that rates of extinction on islands are determined mainly by island size. Species turnover is also predicated to vary as a function of isolation and island area. The predictions of the equilibrium model of island biogeography are supported by observations of species turnover on the islands and by colonization studies of mangrove islands in Florida and new islands in Lake Hjälmaren, Sweden.

22.4 Species richness generally increases from middle and high latitudes to the equator.

Most groups of organisms are more species-rich in the tropics. Many factors may contribute to higher tropical species richness, and these can be roughly categorized as (1) time and area effects, and (2) changes in the rate of diversification. Fully understanding the causes of this diversity gradient requires integration information about phylogenetic patterns, geography, and local ecological interactions.

22.5 Long-term historical and regional processes significantly influence the structure of biotas and ecosystems.

Much geographic variation in species richness can be explained by historical and regional processes. Regional diversity can influence the diversity of local communities through a variety of mechanisms. Some exceptional situations that seem to have resulted from unique historical and regional processes include the exceptional species richness of the Cape floristic region of South Africa, and the high species richness of temperate trees in East Asia. Dispersal among communities can result in meta-communities. These connections may buffer some effects of environmental change.

Global positioning systems, remote sensing, and geographic information systems are important tools for effective geographic ecology. A global positioning system determines locations on the earth's surface, including latitude, longitude, and altitude, using satellites as reference points. Remote-sensing satellites are generally fitted with electro-optical sensors that scan several bands of the electromagnetic spectrum. These sensors convert electromagnetic radiation into electrical signals that are in turn converted to digital values by a computer. These digital values can be used to construct an image. Geographic information systems are computer-based systems that store, analyze, and display geographic information. Global positioning systems, remote sensing, and geographic information systems are increasingly valuable parts of the ecologist's tool kit. Ecologists are using these new tools to study large-scale, dynamic ecological phenomena such as interannual variation in primary production, land cover categorization, and potential responses to climate change.

REVIEW QUESTIONS

1. The following data (Preston 1962a) give the area and number of bird species on islands in the West Indies:

Island	Area	Log$_{10}$ Area	# Species	Log # Species
Cuba	43,000	4.633	124	2.093
Isle of Pines	11,000	4.041	89	1.949
Hispaniola	47,000	4.672	106	2.021
Jamaica	4,470	3.650	99	1.996
Puerto Rico	3,435	3.536	79	1.898
Bahamas	5,450	3.736	74	1.869
Virgin Islands	465	2.667	35	1.544
Guadalupe	600	2.778	37	1.568
Dominica	304	2.483	36	1.556
St. Lucia	233	2.367	35	1.544
St. Vincent	150	2.176	35	1.544
Grenada	120	2.079	29	1.462

The numbers are expressed in two ways: as simple measurements and counts, and as the logarithms of area and numbers of species. Use these data to plot your own species–area relationship. Plot area on the horizontal axis and number of species on the vertical axis. First plot the simple measurements of area and species number on one graph, and then plot the logarithms of area and species number on another graph. Which gives you the tightest relationship between area and species richness?

2. We discussed how Diamond (1969) documented immigrations and extinctions on the California Channel Islands by comparing his censuses of the birds of the islands with the birds recorded over 50 years earlier. Disregarding the numbers for San Miguel and Santa Rosa Islands, which were not well censused in 1917, Diamond showed that an average of approximately six bird species became extinct on California Channel Islands between 1917 and 1968. During the same period, an average of approximately five new bird species immigrated to the islands. Diamond suggested that his estimates of immigration and extinction were likely underestimates of the actual rates. Explain why his comparative study produced underestimates of rates of immigration and extinction.

3. Suppose you are about to study the bird communities on the islands shown on the right, which are identical in area but lie at different distances from the mainland. According to the equilibrium model of island biogeography, which of the islands should experience higher rates of immigration? What does the equilibrium model of island biogeography predict concerning relative rates of extinction on the two islands?

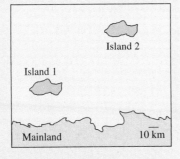

4. Now, suppose you are going to study the bird communities on the islands shown on the right, which lie equal distances from the mainland but differ in area. According to the equilibrium model of island bio-

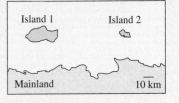

geography, what should be the relative rates of immigration to the two islands? On which islands should rates of extinction be lowest? Explain.

5. Review the major hypotheses proposed to explain the higher species richness of tropical regions compared to temperate and high-latitude regions. How are each of these hypotheses related to relative rates of speciation and extinction in tropical regions and temperate and high-latitude regions?

6. Explain how speciation and extinction rates might be affected by the area of continents. What evidence is there to support your explanation? What does the influence of area on rates of extinction and speciation have to do with higher species richness in tropical regions compared to temperate and high-latitude regions?

7. Ricklefs (1987) pointed out that many large-scale contrasts in species richness and composition cannot be explained by local processes such as competition and predation. Ricklefs proposed that differences in history and geography can leave a unique stamp on regional biotas. The mammals of Australia, including kangaroos, koalas, and duck-billed platypuses, must be one of the best-known examples of a unique biota. How have history and geography, as opposed to local processes, combined to produce this unique assemblage of mammals?

8. Most examples of regional and latitudinal variation in species richness cited in chapter 22 have been terrestrial. Consider regional variation in marine biotas. Like birds on land, fish are one of the best-studied groups of marine organisms. Moyle and Cech (1982) cite the following patterns of fish species richness:

Atlantic and Gulf Coasts of North America		Pacific Coast of North America	
Area	*Species*	*Area*	*Species*
Texas	400	Gulf of California	800
South Carolina	350	California	550
Cape Cod	250	Canada	325
Gulf of Maine	225		
Labrador	61		
Greenland	34		

As you can see, fish species richness decreases northward on both coasts. However, the Pacific coast generally supports a larger number of species. This contrast may be another situation requiring historical- and geographic-level explanations. Explore and explain this contrast in species richness using information from the fields of marine biology, oceanography,

and ichthyology. Moyle and Cech (1982) and Briggs (1974) are good starting points.

9. The diversity of a local community is often linearly related to regional diversity. However, local diversity usually is lower than regional diversity. Why does local diversity not equal regional diversity? If the relationship between local and regional diversity does not saturate, does this mean that local processes such as competition are not important in structuring local communities?

10. How would you construct a map of the biodiversity hotspots for Canada? What information would you need for this to be accurate? How would you choose which taxa to include in constructing the map? Why does North America have very few biodiversity hotspots on global maps?

For more information on the resources available from McGraw-Hill Ryerson, go to **www.mcgrawhill.ca/he/solutions**.

GLOBAL ECOLOGY

CHAPTER 23

CHAPTER CONCEPTS

23.1 Over a geologic time scale, the Earth and its biological diversity exhibit a near-constant state of flux.

Concept 23.1 Review

23.2 Human activities have generated substantial threats to biological diversity.

Ecology In Action: Being an Ecologist

Concept 23.2 Review

23.3 Ecological information can be integrated with economic data to help meet conservation goals in a political landscape.

Concept 23.3 Review

Ecological Tools and Approaches: Cooperative Research Networks & Distributed Ecology

Summary

Review Questions

What does the world look like? This is a simple question for which there is no single answer. As individuals, we live for a short period time in a small location. Even with constant news feeds to our phones and homes, we may still not be aware of what happens over long time spans or over large geographic expanses. For example, though we now take satellite imagery as simply another way of viewing our world, it was as recently as 1957 that the former Soviet Union successfully launched Sputnik, the first successful artificial satellite, into an earth orbit. The social and scientific impacts of this small beeping ball bouncing through space were substantial. Soon after Sputnik, the United States launched the *Apollo 8* mission to the moon. It was that voyage that produced images of the Earth rising above the moon's horizon (fig. 23.1). That image, of Earth as a shining blue ball against the blackness of space, instantaneously changed the perspective that most people held of the planet. Today, most people in Canada, and throughout much of the world, "know" what the Earth looks like as a whole, not solely the boundaries of their village, city, or country.

But what happens if we move back in time, and ask what the astronauts would have seen if they had taken this picture 10,000, 1,000,000, or 100,000,000 years ago? What if instead of simply visualizing land and water, the cameras on the spacecraft were able to photograph the distribution and forms of biological diversity on the planet? What would we then consider to be the "normal" pattern of biodiversity throughout the planet? Would we be able to accept that over deep time, there is no "normal" pattern of life nor even land and water?

Going back through time, we would find land masses to be different shapes and in different locations than those with which we are now familiar. In Canada, many regions that are

Figure 23.1   Oasis in space: earthrise over the moon's horizon.

currently cold and dry were at some point warm and wet—rich in species and high in productivity. Through repeated imagery over hundreds of millions of years, we would see that both the generation and extinction of substantial biological diversity is a common occurrence on the planet. The world, both in its structure and its diversity, has been in a constant state of change. The earth is not a static blue ball on a black background, but instead a dynamic system whose changes are slow, at least relative to our own limited life spans.

Though slow changes to Earth's geography, atmosphere, and biological diversity are more typical than stasis, human activities are now causing a period of unusually rapid change. Forests have been cut, burned, and turned over, providing us with building materials, parking lots, and pastures. Vast expanses of grasslands have been replaced with crops and cities. Aquatic systems have been drained, contaminated, and depleted of fish. Unlike times past, these changes are happening at a speed we can see and understand—even if we do not yet know the consequences of these changes or whether undesired effects can be mitigated or reversed.

It was not too long ago that this is where ecology textbooks would stop, with an acknowledgement that change was happening and that people were driving much of the most significant alterations to the environment. But the field of ecology is maturing, and its connections to other disciplines have become stronger. It is now recognized that ecological function and ecological services are not simply ideas for students to be tested upon, but instead, that these concepts have economic and societal value. Estuaries are both beautiful and critical for the efficient filtering of water. Removing the estuary thus causes more than a loss of biological diversity; it imposes economic and societal costs through the loss of the filtering services. Economic valuations of natural services have become widespread and are beginning to force developers and planners to look at the whole of construction, not just the cost of buildings, roads, and power lines. Ecologists are also recognizing that conservation itself imposes a cost on society. Throughout much of the world land is privately owned, and restricting the use of that land by its owners reduces personal liberty. Ecologists and economists are now working together to develop models that can maximize conservation goals while minimizing economic and societal costs. In this way, ecology is more than just a subject taught in school, it is a body of knowledge central to development and sustainability.

As we move to address questions relevant to longer periods of time, or to questions that explicitly include human impacts, the line among research disciplines becomes blurrier. In this final chapter, we will discuss the work of diverse groups of researchers, including geologists, biologists, physicists, chemists, sociologists, and economists. We begin by understanding that in deep time, this planet has undergone substantial change.

23.1 Patterns of Biological Diversity Change Through Time

Over a geologic time scale, the Earth and its biological diversity exhibit a near-constant state of flux. Ecological communities, and the species that live within them, are ephemeral . . . if we look through the lens of geological time. As has hopefully been evident throughout this book, abiotic conditions impose significant pressures on the organisms that live within a given location. These pressures can impact the fitness of an individual, the persistence of a population, and the structure and function of communities and ecosystems. Thus, it may come as no surprise that in the past, as continents moved, oceans disappeared, and climatic patterns changed, so too has the biological diversity of planet.

Plate Tectonics

One of the most obvious features we use to describe a single location is whether it is predominantly terrestrial, aquatic, or a wetland. Though we recognize that disturbances, such as floods, beaver activity, and volcanoes, can submerge a forest or create land where there was once water, it is easy to view such changes as exceptions to the rule of geologic constancy. However, over deep geologic time, the movement of tectonic plates has created the landscapes we see now, and destroyed many others that we never will.

Much as the atmosphere consists of many different layers, so too does the physical structure of the earth. A coarse description would list the solid inner and liquid outer cores, surrounded by a mantle, and then the outer layer called the crust (fig. 23.2). However, much as soil scientists define

many horizons and sub-horizons in the soil (chapter 2), geologists use substantially more detail in their description of the earth's layers. Here, we are primarily concerned with the surface lithosphere that sits upon the slowly flowing asthenosphere. The lithosphere consists of the hard crust, along with the uppermost (solid) layer of the mantle. The asthenosphere is weaker and more fluid. Quite simply, the solid lithosphere sits and moves upon the more fluid asthenosphere. Where the lithosphere breaks, we observe faults. Currently, the lithosphere is arranged into 15 major tectonic plates, though this number and their sizes have changed over time (fig. 23.3).

Today, the idea that plates move over time, crashing into each other, separating, subsiding, and generally causing mayhem to the physical structure of the earth's surface is commonly understood; it is taught early and often in schools around the world. However, when the theory of continental drift (later subsumed by the theory of plate tectonics) was first proposed in the early 1900s, the idea was revolutionary. The idea that the physical structure of the planet was dynamic rather than fixed challenged geological and religious

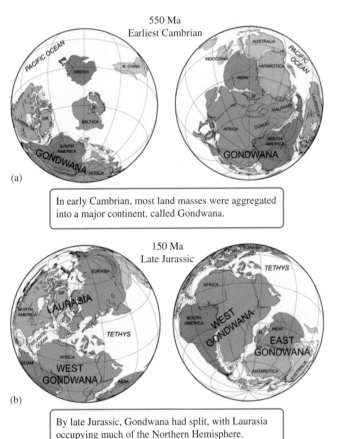

550 Ma
Earliest Cambrian

(a)

In early Cambrian, most land masses were aggregated into a major continent, called Gondwana.

150 Ma
Late Jurassic

(b)

By late Jurassic, Gondwana had split, with Laurasia occupying much of the Northern Hemisphere.

Figure 23.3 Reconstructions of tectonic plate locations approximately (*a*) 550 million years ago, and (*b*) 150 million years ago. (Ma = mega annum, referring to 1 million years). For reference, current continents are colour coded.

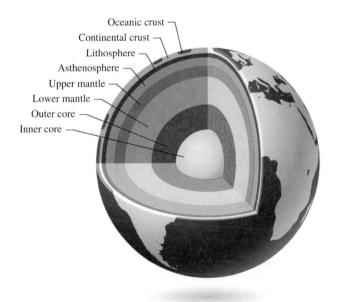

Oceanic crust
Continental crust
Lithosphere
Asthenosphere
Upper mantle
Lower mantle
Outer core
Inner core

Figure 23.2 The Earth is made up of several layers.

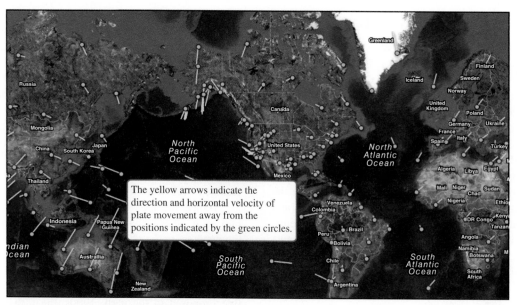

The yellow arrows indicate the direction and horizontal velocity of plate movement away from the positions indicated by the green circles.

Figure 23.4 Using measurements from the global positioning system, researchers at NASA are able to visualize the movement of the Earth's plates.

doctrine, resulting in substantial debate. However, through decades of data collection, scientists have been able to support this revolutionary concept with solid evidence; among the most compelling of which is the ability to use satellite imagery to show plate movement over time (fig. 23.4). Rather than repeat a course in earth sciences in this ecology text, the question to ask here is: Why should ecologists care? As we discuss next, processes occurring over long time scales, such as tectonic plate movement and atmospheric cycles, influence the past and current diversity and distribution of species on the planet.

Extinction Events

Extinction is the expected fate of new taxa; some estimates suggest that only 1% of the species ever to occupy the earth are currently extant (Novacek 2001). However, given that ecologists cannot agree on how many species are currently extant (chapter 2), let alone how many were extant 100 million years ago, you should be a bit skeptical of this claim of 1%. Regardless of the true estimate, the concept it promotes emphasizes the importance of time in structuring natural systems, as the diversity we find on the planet now is just a small sliver of the total species pool over the history of the planet. As exciting as it might be to be able to swim alongside trilobites within Canada's oceans, the best we can hope for is to encounter them as fossils encased in stone.

Though extinction is expected, the rate of extinction has varied greatly over time (fig. 23.5). There is broad agreement that there have been five mass extinction events over the last 550 million years (Raup and Sepkoski 1982), each characterized by the loss of over 75% of the species estimated prior to the event (Barnosky et al. 2011). Some of these events may be

familiar, such as the recent Cretaceous event (approximately 65 million years ago), the Permian event (approximately 250 million years ago), and the more distant Ordovician event (approximately 443 million years ago) (Barnosky et al. 2011). The causes of these events are diverse, and include periods of massive global warming or cooling, asteroid impacts, sea level changes, extensive volcanic activity, and changes in atmospheric composition. As you might expect, plate tectonic activity and solar periodicity can trigger or exaggerate some of these other more proximate causes of extinction. These causes are not exclusionary of each other, and multiple factors can lead to each mass extinction event.

Extinction events obviously have major impacts on biodiversity patterns through the loss of numerous genera and species. However, they can also impact biodiversity through periods of rapid speciation following the event (Erwin 2001). Why should extinction lead to high speciation? Though taxa die out during these events, this does not mean that all of the resources and habitats upon which they depended also disappeared. Instead, adaptive radiation was often able to act on the few taxa remaining, as much of the niche space was no longer occupied by other species. Further, in many cases, extinction events are frequently associated with changes in the climate of the planet and chemistry of the oceans and atmosphere. Such changes would impose new opportunities and challenges for the species that remained, leading to further selection and speciation. One of the most well-known examples is the rapid diversification of birds and mammals following the extinction event approximately 65 million years ago.

The first tetrapods (four-footed animals) to colonize land appeared during the mid-Devonian period, over 350 million years ago (if not earlier). Today, there are over 30,000 species of tetrapods living on Earth. The rise in diversity of tetrapods is linked to evolutionary innovation following a series

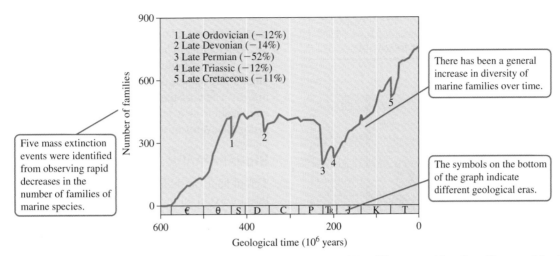

Figure 23.5 Estimated number of families of marine organisms over the last 600 million years (data from Raup and Sepkoski 1982). Estimates of the fraction of genera and species lost are substantially higher.

of extinction events. One way of viewing the evolutionary innovation that can occur over time is to imagine the number of habitable ecological modes that are both possible and that are found in existing taxa. An ecological mode is analogous to an ecologist's description of an organism's niche, though the mode represents a potential way of existing (e.g., tree-nesting insectivore). This is in contrast with a formal statistical description of an organism's performance on multiple niche axes (chapter 9). Recently, a group of British and Canadian scientists have been able to show a tight linkage between the number of tetrapod families and the number of occupied modes over the last 350 Ma (fig. 23.6) (Sahney et al. 2010). Particularly noticeable is the rapid rise in occupied modes

following the extinction of the dinosaurs during the Cretaceous event. In other words, it appears that when dinosaurs were no longer the dominant tetrapods, birds and mammals underwent substantial diversification both in terms of ecological modes and number of families. Sahney et al. (2010) suggest only 36% of the potential ecological modes have so far been occupied by tetrapods, in contrast to 78% occupancy by marine animals. If true, this suggests there is substantial room for future innovation among tetrapods.

Room for future innovation may prove to be very important, as there is evidence suggesting we are currently in the midst of the sixth mass extinction event (Barnosky et al. 2011). It may not be surprising that anthropogenic changes

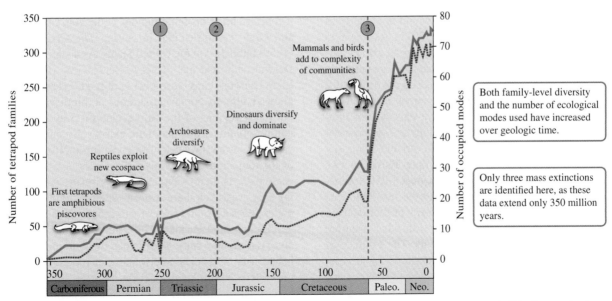

Figure 23.6 The estimated number of tetrapod families (red) and ecological modes used by tetrapods (blue) over the last 350 million years.

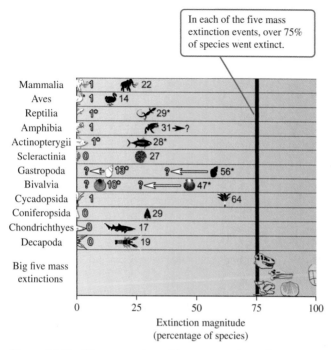

Figure 23.7 The proportion of known species to have gone extinct (white) or are threatened (black) in the last 500 years. Some taxonomic groups have not been fully assessed (asterisks), and thus these estimates may be inaccurate (data from Barnosky et al. 2011).

associated with land use, spread of invasive species, and changes to global climate have been identified as key drivers of the changing patterns. We have already discussed several of these issues, and we will talk broadly about land use later in this chapter. Here, we present some of the evidence suggesting that the concern about the current magnitude and rate of biodiversity loss is warranted.

Using the definition of 75% species loss (as opposed to genera or families) as an indicator of a mass extinction event, the loss of species in the last 500 years would not qualify as a major extinction event (Barnosky et al. 2011). As shown in figure 23.7, few species are known to have gone extinct during that time period; however, a high percentage are currently threatened. Importantly, the threatened taxa do not belong to a single clade, but are instead widespread among many groups of organisms. Further, mass extinction events do not typically take 500 years; instead their durations are on the order of 2,000,000 years, though the number is variable (Barnosky et al. 2011). To account for the issue of time, Barnosky asks the question: How long would it take to reach 75% extinction if the extinction rates observed over the last 500 years continue? The answer ranges from hundreds of thousands to millions of years; timelines consistent with what occurred during the last five mass extinction events. The estimate of time to reach 75% extinction drops to less than 2,500 years if you assume species currently critically endangered become extinct within 100 years; it drops to less than 600 years if you make the same assumption about currently threatened species. However, these numbers are based upon projections of the

future, and one of the things we have all learned from years of reading science fiction is that the future can be changed.

Later in this chapter, we will discuss some examples of novel ways ecological information is being applied to lessen human impacts on the world around us. But first we need to discuss a few of the impediments to species movement and colonization as a means of emphasizing the importance of historical events in structuring modern communities.

Biogeographical Barriers

Throughout the book we have discussed dispersal both in the context of an individual species' life-history, and also its impacts on community assembly. The physical arrangement of land and sea can facilitate, or inhibit, dispersal of species from one location to another. In the equilibrium model of island biogeography, this was implicit to the idea that islands far from mainland should have lower immigration rates than islands near the mainland. Similarly, glaciations wipe out species from large areas, though as mentioned in chapter 21, some areas remain as refugia—uncovered by the massive ice sheets. Following the most recent glaciation event in North America, these refugia served as a critical source of seeds and immigrants of many species. Though the last glaciation event was a long time ago, from the perspective of a person it is easy to forget that many species are still in a process of migration, slowly moving and occupying previously glaciated areas. Thus the barrier of ice, once removed, is still causing a reshuffling of species composition throughout Canada and elsewhere. However, in deeper geological time, we can look at the effect of the position of continents on species distribution, rather than the presence or absence of ice. Let us address this by considering the trees we see outside, as well as those seen by our colleagues in Norway, Russia, China, and other forested countries of the Northern Temperate zone.

Asa Gray is a name few students know, but in the late 1800s and early 1900s he was a formidable presence as a leading botanist and natural historian in North America. He was a good friend of his more famous colleague, Charles Darwin, and Gray was influential in getting *The Origin of Species* (1859) published in the United States. As a sign of his respect, Darwin dedicated one of his books to Gray (Darwin 1877). Like Darwin, Gray travelled and read extensively, which allowed him to compare patterns of biodiversity throughout many regions of the world. One of Gray's most important observations was that there exists substantial geographic variation in the diversity of trees within the forested regions of the temperate zone (Gray 1878). This is a bit puzzling to ecologists, as there is typically less climatic variability moving east–west then there is north–south, and thus they would not expect such high levels of variation in species diversity.

Latham and Ricklefs (1993) decided to explore Gray's observation more fully. They began by combing through published lists of species, and found that for every tree species in western North America, there are two in Europe, four in eastern North America, and twelve in eastern Asia. Why? It is not due to unequal area in these regions, since on that basis eastern North America should have the most tree species.

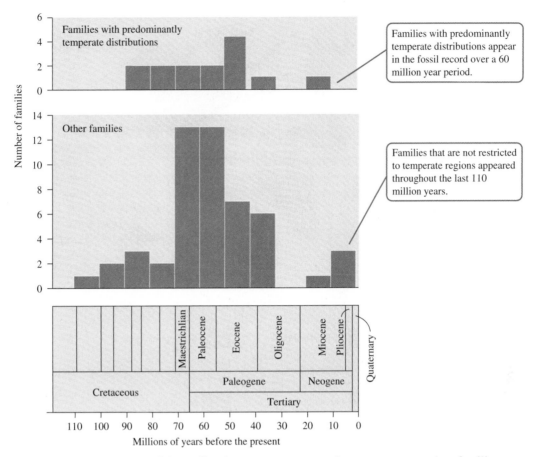

Figure 23.8 The frequency distribution of the earliest known occurrences of extant temperate plant families.

Curiously, much of the observed variation in species diversity occurs at high taxonomic levels, such as that of family, and not simply diversity within a genus. Highlighting the diversity of Asian forests, Latham and Ricklefs found that 95% of all temperate tree families have at least one representative species in eastern Asia, and only 3% of temperate tree species do not occur in eastern Asia. Latham and Ricklefs (1993) suggest this, along with other patterns in the taxonomic composition of these forests, points to differences among continents in their abilities to have been colonized by different forest taxa.

To begin to put deep history into this story, Latham and Ricklefs (1993) turned to the work of paleontologists and geologists. There they found that the fossil record suggests that most families of temperate zone trees first appeared 30 to 90 million years ago, during the late Cretaceous/early Tertiary periods (fig. 23.8). Interestingly, of the four forest zones they studied, during this period a continuous zone of forest vegetation spanned from high latitudes down to the tropics only in the region occupied by what is now southeastern Asia (fig. 23.9). Latham and Ricklefs suggest that these circumstances facilitated colonization by tropical tree species, and facilitated evolution of new taxa. As a consequence, they suggest most of the temperate diversity that now occurs globally originated in eastern Asia. The ability of the trees to colonize other regions of the world was limited by several factors, including (1) geographic barriers, such as

oceans, that separated Asia from other continents, and (2) atmospheric cooling that required species to have evolved freezing-tolerance to successfully migrate through the northern route.

Though researchers are able to go into modern forests and directly measure herbivory, competition, and the role of heterogeneity in determine local biodiversity patterns, the work of Latham and Ricklefs highlights the importance of understanding that some patterns can only be explained with the help of paleontologists. This study is a reminder that patterns generated over millions of years may not be easily explained by processes occurring within the lifetime of an individual. Next, we continue to emphasize how ecological patterns can be driven by processes over long time scales. However, rather than continuing to look at the fossils below us, we discuss climate cycles found in the atmosphere around us.

Atmospheric Cycles: The Southern and North Atlantic Oscillations

Geological changes have had, and continue to have, substantial impacts on the current composition of natural communities. However, at shorter time scales we find additional examples of earth-system processes that influence biological diversity. Two of the most relevant to those of us in Canada are the **Southern** and **North Atlantic Oscillations**.

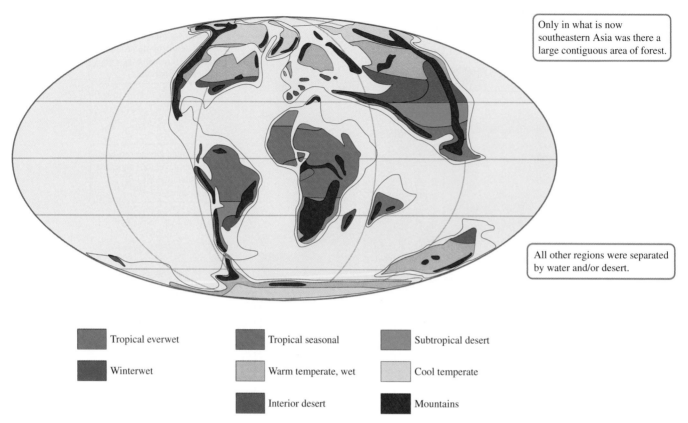

Only in what is now southeastern Asia was there a large contiguous area of forest.

All other regions were separated by water and/or desert.

Tropical everwet

Winterwet

Interior desert

Tropical seasonal

Warm temperate, wet

Mountains

Subtropical desert

Cool temperate

Figure 23.9   Distribution of major biomes and landforms during the late Cretaceous. Areas in brown indicate areas with substantial highland regions.

In 1904, a British mathematician named Gilbert Walker was appointed Director General of Observatories in India. Walker arrived in India shortly after a disastrous famine from 1899 to 1900 caused by crop failures during a drought. This tragic event led him to search for a way to predict the rainfall associated with the Asian monsoons. Walker (1924) eventually found a correspondence between barometric pressure across the Pacific Ocean and the amount of rain falling during the monsoons. He found that reduced barometric pressure in the eastern Pacific was accompanied by increased barometric pressure in the western Pacific. In a similar fashion, when the barometric pressure fell in the western Pacific, it rose in the eastern Pacific. Walker called this oscillation in barometric pressure the Southern Oscillation.

Today, meteorologists monitor the state of the Southern Oscillation with the Southern Oscillation Index. The value of the index is determined by the difference in barometric pressure between Tahiti and Darwin, Australia (fig. 23.10). Walker noticed that low values of the Southern Oscillation Index were associated with drought in Australia, Indonesia, India, and parts of Africa. Walker also suggested that winter temperatures in Canada were connected to the Southern Oscillation.

The connection between Walker's Southern Oscillation and patterns of ocean temperature during El Niños was eventually described by Jacob Bjerknes (1966, 1969).

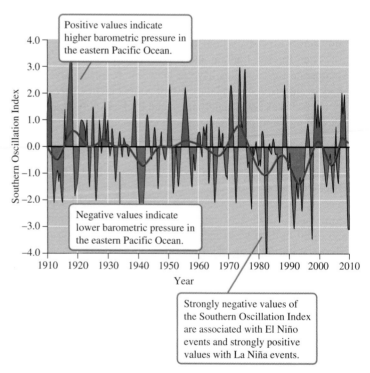

Positive values indicate higher barometric pressure in the eastern Pacific Ocean.

Negative values indicate lower barometric pressure in the eastern Pacific Ocean.

Strongly negative values of the Southern Oscillation Index are associated with El Niño events and strongly positive values with La Niña events.

Figure 23.10   The Southern Oscillation Index shows the difference in barometric pressures between Tahiti and Darwin, Australia.

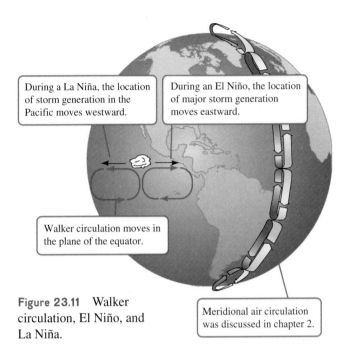

Figure 23.11 Walker circulation, El Niño, and La Niña.

> During a La Niña, the location of storm generation in the Pacific moves westward.

> During an El Niño, the location of major storm generation moves eastward.

> Walker circulation moves in the plane of the equator.

> Meridional air circulation was discussed in chapter 2.

forms rain clouds. Bjerknes called this atmospheric system **Walker circulation** after Sir Gilbert Walker. The El Niño Southern Oscillation affects the climate of North America, South America, Australia, southern Asia, Africa, and parts of southern Europe (fig. 23.12).

During the mature phase of an **El Niño**, the sea surface in the eastern tropical Pacific Ocean is much warmer than average and the barometric pressure over the eastern Pacific is lower than average. The combination of warm sea surface temperatures and low barometric pressure promotes the formation of storms over the eastern Pacific Ocean. These storms bring increased precipitation to much of North and South America. During an El Niño, the sea surface in the western Pacific is cooler than average and the barometric pressure is higher than average. These conditions produce drought over much of the western Pacific region.

Periods of lower sea surface temperature and higher-than-average barometric pressure in the eastern tropical Pacific have been named **La Niñas**. During a La Niña period, a pool of warm seawater moves far into the western Pacific. This warm water, combined with lower barometric pressures in the western Pacific Ocean, generates many storms. Consequently, La Niña brings higher-than-average precipitation to the western Pacific. However, La Niñas also bring drought to much of North and South America. While often associated with the tropics, the influence of the El Niño Southern Oscillation extends well into temperate regions. During El Niños, much of the northern United States, Canada, and Alaska are much warmer than average. During La Niñas, these regions are colder than average. As you might expect, this global climate system affects ecological systems around the globe.

Bjerknes proposed that the gradient in sea surface temperature across the central Pacific Ocean produces a large-scale atmospheric circulation system that moves in the plane of the equator, as shown in figure 23.11. Air over the warmer western Pacific rises, flows eastward in the upper atmosphere, and then sinks over the eastern Pacific. This air mass then flows westward along with the southeast trade winds, gradually warming and gathering moisture. This westward-flowing air eventually joins the rising air in the western Pacific. As this warm and moist air rises, it

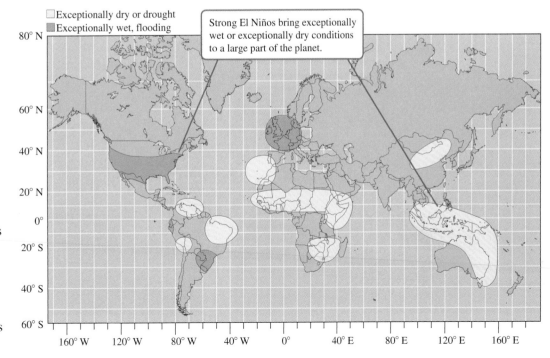

Figure 23.12 Effects of the exceptionally strong El Niño of 1982 to 1983 on patterns of global precipitation (data from Diaz and Kiladis 1992).

> ☐ Exceptionally dry or drought
> ■ Exceptionally wet, flooding

> Strong El Niños bring exceptionally wet or exceptionally dry conditions to a large part of the planet.

El Niño and Marine Populations

Some of the most dramatic ecological responses to El Niño occur in marine populations along the west coast of South America. Long before the recent discovery of the global extent of its effects, El Niño was known to produce declines in coastal populations of anchovies and sardines and the seabirds that feed upon them. How does El Niño induce these population declines? They are produced by changes in the pattern of sea surface temperatures and coastal circulation. Figure 23.13*b* shows sea surface temperatures off the west coast of South America during average conditions. Notice that under average conditions, coastal waters are relatively cool along most of the west coast of South America and that a tongue of cool water extends westward toward the open Pacific Ocean. This cool water is brought to the surface by upwelling. Upwelling along the coast is driven by the southeast trade winds, while the offshore upwelling is driven by the east winds of the Walker circulation.

With the onset of an El Niño, the easterly winds slacken and the pool of warm water in the western Pacific moves eastward. Eventually this pool of warm water reaches the west coast of South America and then moves north and south along the coast (fig. 23.13*a*). During the mature phase of an El Niño, the warm surface water along the west coast of South America shuts off upwelling. Consequently, the supply of nutrients that upwelling usually delivers to surface waters is also shut off. A lower nutrient supply reduces primary production by phytoplankton. This decline in primary production reduces the supply of food available to consumers in the coastal food web and is followed by declines in populations of fish and their predators.

Remote sensing of phytoplankton pigments in surface waters around the Galápagos Islands shows that the 1982–83 El Niño reduced average primary production and dramatically changed the location of production hot spots. Changes in the rate and distribution of primary production induced reproductive failure, migration, and widespread death among seabird populations in the Galápagos Islands and along the west coast of South America during the 1982–83 El Niño. Many seabirds abandoned their nests with the onset of this El Niño and migrated either north or south along the coast of South America. Virtually no birds reproduced and most of the migrating birds starved. Population declines were dramatic. The adult populations of three seabird species on the coast of Peru declined from 6.01 million to 330,000 between March 1982 and May 1983, a population decline of approximately 95%.

The 1982–83 El Niño also had a major impact on fur seal and sea lion populations, mainly through reductions in food supply. The main food fish for the South American fur seal, *Arctocephalus australis*, is the anchoveta, *Engraulis ringens. Engraulis* normally lives at depths of 0 to 40 m. However, during the 1982–83 El Niño, it moved away from fur seal colonies to cooler water at depths of up to 100 m. In response, fur seals dived deeper and shifted their diets to other fish. Both on the mainland and on the Galápagos, female fur seals increased their foraging time. Since females are away from their young while foraging, the pups in both populations did not get enough food and all died. On the Galápagos, nearly 100% of mature male fur seals died, while the mortality of adult females and nonterritorial males was approximately 30%. A large fur seal colony at Punta San Juan, Peru, declined from 6,300 to 4,200 individuals.

Though the Southern Oscillation is typically better known among the general public, the North Atlantic Oscillation typically has a stronger influence on the biological diversity of northern systems, including much of Canada.

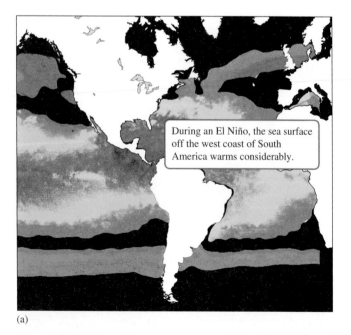

(a)

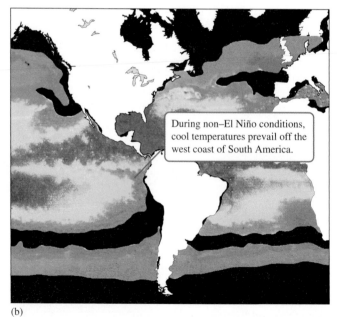

(b)

Figure 23.13   Sea surface temperature during (*a*) El Niño and (*b*) non–El Niño conditions.

The North Atlantic Oscillation (NAO) is a fluctuation in atmospheric pressure between Iceland and the Azores off the coast of Portugal (fig. 23.14). Like El Niño, the NAO has been identified for over 200 years (Saabye 1776), though only recently has its importance in driving large-scale ecological patterns been realized (Otterson et al. 2001). A major effect of changes in the NAO is a shift in the direction and speed of wind over the Atlantic Ocean between 40° and 60° latitude, particularly during winter months. When the NAO is in the positive phase, there are high atmospheric pressures below 55° and lower pressures toward the Arctic (Stenseth et al. 2003). This has the effect of moving the storms that travel across the Atlantic Ocean toward the north (the area of lower pressure), resulting in increased storm activity in southern Europe, higher temperatures over much of Europe and North America, reduced precipitation across much of the Canadian Arctic, and cool temperatures in eastern Canada. When the NAO is in the negative phase, these patterns are reversed, with the storm activity focused on southern Europe, cooler temperatures, and more precipitation in the Canadian Arctic. There is substantial variation in the strength of NAO among years (fig. 23.15), though the last few decades have been dominated primarily by strongly positive years. As a sign of the importance of the NAO on ecological communities, approximately 33% of the interannual variation in winter temperatures in the Northern Hemisphere is attributed to variation in the NAO (Hurrell 1996).

Eric Post and Nils Stenseth have explored the impacts of variation in the NAO on populations of a variety of organisms (Post and Stenseth 1999). As we saw in chapter 9, plant phenology is responsive to changes in temperature and is already shifting in response to global warming. Therefore it is reasonable to expect that other large-scale phenomena, such as the NAO, may also be important in determining the timing of flowering across large geographic regions. Ungulates were chosen for study because they are herbivores, and may be affected by any changes in the plant communities. Snow depth and the timing of snow can also impact large foragers, with potential impacts on population growth. Additionally, these large mammals are of great concern to indigenous communities, conservation biologists, and the general public, and thus an understanding of whether large-scale climatic variation influences their populations is critically needed.

To test whether there was a link between the NAO, plant phenology, and ungulate populations, the researchers gathered information from numerous data sets. The NAO index was available online through the National Center for Atmospheric Research in the United States. Long-term records on plant phenology were available in the literature for 43 species of flowering plants located in 37 sites across Norway. Several of the species included serve as important food sources for native ungulates. For all species, they

(a) **Positive North Atlantic Oscillation Phase**

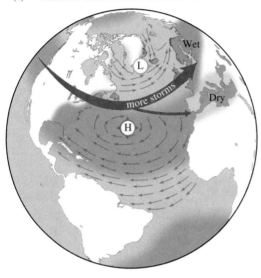

(b) **Negative North Atlantic Oscillation Phase**

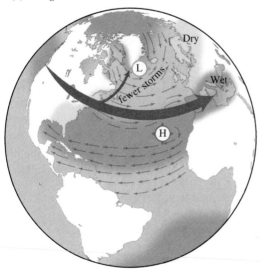

Figure 23.14 Large-scale impacts of the (*a*) positive, and (*b*) negative phases of the North Atlantic Oscillation. Areas that will be wetter than usual are indicated in blue, with drier areas in yellow.

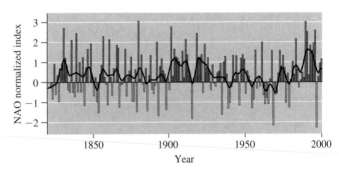

Figure 23.15 Variation in the NAO over time (Otterson et al. 2001). Zero represents the standardized average NAO index, with values in red corresponding to the positive phase and values in blue the negative phase.

had data on the date of first flowering in each year, and for many species they also had data for the date of first fruit set. The researchers also compiled previously published data on 16 populations of 7 ungulate species, including reindeer, moose, red deer, Soay sheep, feral goats, muskoxen, and caribou. The exact measures varied among populations and species, but often included such things as body size, fecundity, and survival of juveniles. In contrast to the data on plant phenology, the data on ungulate populations came from sites located across the north, including Europe, North America, and Scandinavia.

In general, plants flowered earlier in Norway following a positive NAO winter, which corresponds to a warmer, wetter year. The correlations between flowering and NAO varied among species and locations, and were strongest for non-woody species, species from the more southerly latitudes within Norway, and species that typically bloom early, rather than late. For example the date of first flowering of *Anemone nemorosa* spanned a 30-day range around 57° and only a 10 to 20 day range around 63°. Of all the measures of ungulate populations, 72% also showed signification covariation with the NAO. There was evidence that the NAO influenced growth and fecundity in all the species studied, explaining between 40% to 70% of the variation in body size and fecundity. The exact effects of positive NAO years varied among species and locations. In general, mainland populations had greater fecundity and smaller body size during positive NAO years, while maritime populations had increased body size and reduced fecundity during positive NAO winters. In total, this study provides clear evidence that the North Atlantic Oscillation can impact a diversity of populations across a broad geographic area.

Closely related to the NAO is the **Northern Hemisphere Annular Mode** (NAM), formerly referred to as the Arctic Oscillation. The NAM is generally of a direction opposite to the NAO such that when one is in positive phase, the other is generally in negative phase. Because of this synchrony it is not clear whether the resulting ecological effects are driven primarily by variation in NAO or the NAM. Regardless of which large-scale climatic system is driving the changes that are observed, it is very clear that these systems have impacts on ecological systems similar in scale to that of El Niño.

CONCEPT 23.1 REVIEW

1. Why do plate tectonics influence the diversity of life the ecologists find in different locations?

2. How common are mass extinction events, and what are some of their ecological consequences?

3. Why is it important for ecologists to understand phases of atmospheric cycles when studying long-term ecological processes?

23.2 Human Activity Transforms the World

Human activities have generated substantial threats to biological diversity. In the previous section, we emphasized that the planet has always undergone periods of dramatic shifts, with pronounced consequences for the species that inhabit the land and sea. Even now, changes are occurring, though the most obvious ones are not driven not by geologic processes, nor are they a function of atmospheric cycles. Rather, the changes are due to the work of a truly effective ecosystem engineer, *Homo sapiens*. In chapter 20, we discussed the effects of industrialization on nutrient and carbon cycling. Here we focus more generally on our seemingly inexhaustible consumption of the natural products produced through ecological processes.

Humans have changed the face of the earth. Human activities, mainly agriculture and urbanization, have significantly altered one-third to one-half of the ice-free land surface of the earth. Marshes have been drained and filled to build urban areas or airports. Tropical forests have been cut and converted to pasture. The courses of rivers have been changed. The Aral Sea in central Asia has been so starved for water that it is nearly dry. We will begin by taking a broad overview of some global patterns of land use. However, it is important to recognize that although the actions taken by individuals and governments in different countries can be summed to describe the global condition, not every country faces the same challenges. In a classic paper, Soulé (1991) suggests that the economic status of countries will strongly influence whether challenges to biodiversity are likely to be strong or weak (Fig. 23.16).

Human Appropriation of Net Primary Production

One of the best ways to understand the influence of humans on the planet is to ask a question right at the base of life: How much of the planet's net primary productivity (NPP) is used by humans? Though simple to ask, this question is hard to answer. One of the most thorough analyses comes from Helmut Haberl and colleagues in Europe (Haberl et al. 2007). In a suite of analyses based upon global terrestrial data in 2000, the team of researchers estimates that humans appropriate nearly 24% of global NPP on land (HANPP = Human appropriation of net primary productivity). As can be seen in figure 23.17, the spatial distribution of HANPP is highly variable, with usage highest through much of Canada, the United States, Europe, and Southeast Asia. You will also note that HANPP is negative in some regions; these tend to be desert or other very low productivity systems where human activities such as irrigation cause increased NPP.

Digging deeper into the data, Haberl and colleagues were able to isolate different human activities, identifying their individual contributions to HANPP. Direct harvest was the largest cause, accounting for over half of the measured HANPP. Perhaps not surprisingly, in areas occupied by cropland HANPP exceeded 80%. In contrast, HANPP in forests was only 7%,

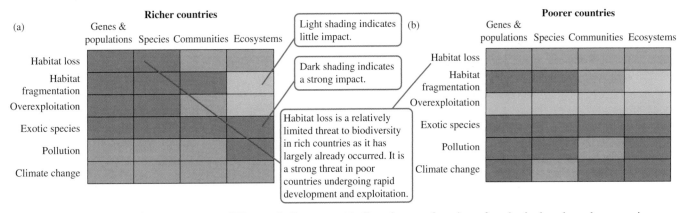

Figure 23.16 Human influences present different challenges to biodiversity as a function of ecological scale and economic status of a country (Soulé 1991).

and was 19% in areas regularly grazed by animals. Though croplands and grazing areas account for only 12% of the non-ice covered regions of the plant, human activities in those regions account for over 75% of HANPP! Changes in land use, such as the construction of cities and industrial activities, is also responsible for a sizable fraction of the HANPP. More specifically, human land use has reduced global NPP by over 9%. However, as mentioned above, some human activities, such as irrigation, increase NPP (Haberl et al. 2007).

Though humans are restricted to land as our primary habitat, we are increasingly exploiting the oceans for food. A global team of researchers, led by then-Ph.D. student Wilf Swartz from the University of British Columbia, has compiled the most complete understanding of the growth of fisheries (Swartz et al. 2010). One of the key differences in exploitation among terrestrial and aquatic systems is what humans tend to harvest. On land, it is predominantly plants; in water, it is predominately animals. Further, those harvested animals may

themselves be herbivorous, feeding upon algae, or carnivorous, feeding upon other fish at a diversity of trophic positions. To allow comparison, a means of standardizing for this variation in trophic position is necessary. Swartz and his colleagues calculated the primary production required (PPR) to produce a given level of harvest by a fishery. For two catches of equal biomass, PPR will be higher for the harvested species that feeds at a higher trophic level, as more primary production is needed to produce equal amounts of carnivores than herbivores (chapter 19). Similar to Haberl's measures of HANPP, Swartz and his colleagues present their PPR results to be used as a measure of the intensity of exploitation by humans.

Swartz and his colleagues were able to calculate PPR throughout the world's oceans, historically (in 1950) and more recently (in 2005). The change is striking (fig. 23.18). There has been a substantial increase the in areas heavily exploited since 1950. Interestingly, much of this growth has

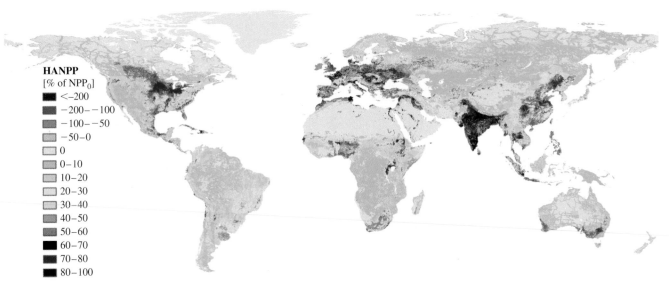

Figure 23.17 A map showing the percentage of NPP that is used by people. Negative values can occur through irrigation and other agricultural activities.

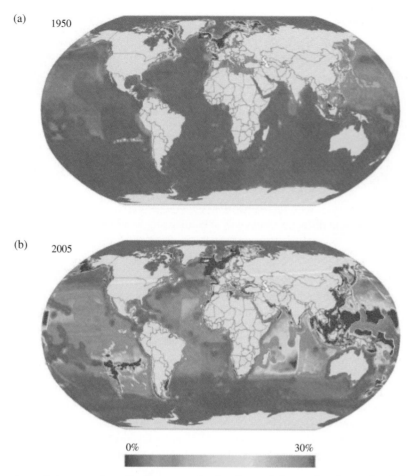

(a) 1950

(b) 2005

0%   30%

Figure 23.18   Maps showing what proportion of primary production is needed to maintain marine fisheries in (*a*) 1950 and (*b*) 2005.

been in southern latitudes, as much of the northern latitudes were already heavily exploited in 1950. Swartz and colleagues also highlight that though this expansion in exploitation resulted in nearly a fivefold increase in yields, increases in agricultural lands result in substantially greater agricultural yield increases. Specifically, they contrast a doubling of agricultural production between 1961 and 1995 although the agricultural land base increased only 10% (Tilman 1999) with a 2.4-fold increase in fishery yields during this same time period, though that was associated with almost a fourfold increase in area. Despite its relative efficiency, agricultural expansion has changed the landscape of the world.

The Agricultural Footprint

The most dominant human land uses are cropland and pastures, which together cover nearly 40% of the land surface of the planet (fig. 23.19). Associated with conversion of native grasslands and forests to croplands and rangelands has been a 700% increase in fertilizer use, and a 70% increase in irrigated croplands in the last 40 years. These two activities associated with modern agricultural practices place enormous pressures on freshwater resources and global nitrogen cycles. It is estimated that 85% of the freshwater used by humans goes to agriculture, and this represents 10% of the global reserves.

In addition to more nitrogen being deposited from the atmosphere, fertilizers routinely leach into streams and groundwater, decreasing the quality of the water and changing aquatic ecosystems that surround agricultural fields.

In the last 300 years, between 7 to 11 million km^2 of forest have been cleared for timber and for conversion into agricultural land. Grasslands have not fared any better, with little native prairie remaining in many areas of the world, including North America (fig. 23.19). The rates of changes in land use vary across the planet. Foley and colleagues suggest that as societies develop economically, so too does their impact on the surrounding land (fig. 23.20). Much of the land base in North America and Europe has already been altered, and thus most people do not recognize the extensive changes that these lands have already undergone. The large expanses of land that remain relatively intact, such as the boreal forest and arctic tundra, are regions that historically were economically unviable for development. However, continued changes to the world timber markets; new technologies for processing oil sands; discovery of extensive gas fields, diamonds, and other valuable minerals; and thinning ice and snow packs are placing significant pressures for development in formerly remote areas. In other parts of the world, such as the Amazon Basin and much of Africa, the rapid phase of development is just beginning. These changes present an interesting moral

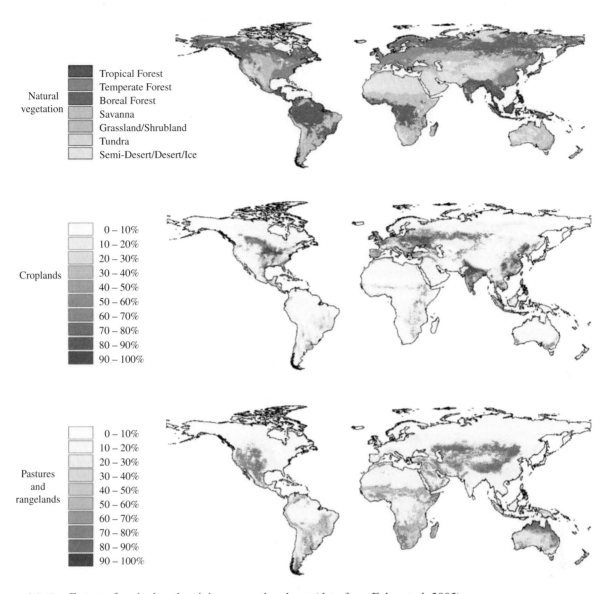

Figure 23.19 Extent of agricultural activity across the planet (data from Foley et al. 2005).

question: do North American and European societies have the right to suggest developing nations not develop their land, when these northern societies did exactly the same thing just a few centuries ago? Alternatively, do developed countries have a moral obligation to protect the world's biodiversity, as they may be the only countries that can afford to do so? Needless to say, there are no easy answers, even though the questions are of great importance.

In addition to direct impacts on vegetation cover (and thus habitat for animals and microbes), land-use changes have significant impact on global climate. For example, changes in the reflectance of land cover alter albedo (chapter 5), and thus temperatures. Burning large expanses of land to clear forest for agricultural or pastureland releases large reserves of CO_2 into the atmosphere. Although historically there has been expansion of cropland and rangeland throughout the planet, of greatest current concern is the rate of deforestation of the

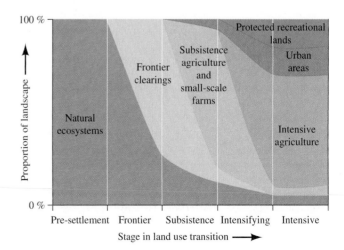

Figure 23.20 Changes in land use as societies develop (Foley et al. 2005).

tropical forests. These activities are of global concern due both to the speed at which they occur, and because the tropical forests are home to many of the most significant biodiversity hotspots (chapter 22).

Tropical Deforestation

Back when I was in university in the 1990s, there was great public concern about the rate of deforestation in the tropics. Today, as I write for university students, that concern is no less strong, nor is deforestation any less a threat to biological diversity in the tropics. As we saw in chapter 22, many of the biodiversity hotspots on the planet are in the tropics, and tropical forests support half or more of earth's species. In the face of worldwide concern, we need accurate estimates of the state of tropical forests.

The most basic questions to ask are how much tropical forest is there, and how much tropical forest has been cut? David Skole and Compton Tucker (1993) provide us with answers to some of these questions. These researchers reported that tropical forest occurs in 73 countries and once covered 11,610,350 km^2. However, three-fourths of the world's tropical forests occur in just 10 countries. The largest single tract of tropical forest, nearly one-third of the total, occurs in Brazil. Brazil is also the country with the highest rate of deforestation.

While there has been general agreement that rates of deforestation in Brazil are high, estimates of those rates vary widely. Skole and Tucker set out to provide an accurate estimate of deforestation rates in the Amazon Basin. They based their estimate on photographs taken by Landsat satellites in 1978 and 1988. The images they used, Landsat Thematic Mapper photos, provide high-resolution information. As you can see in figure 23.21, Thematic Mapper photos clearly show areas of deforestation, regrowth on deforested plots, and areas of isolated forest. Skole and Tucker entered these high-resolution images into a geographic information system (see chapter 22), which they used to create computerized maps of deforestation within the Amazon Basin.

Let's look at the maps in figure 23.22 and see what they tell us. First, notice that large areas, coloured light brown in the map, were not forested. These areas, concentrated in the southeastern Amazon Basin, have a semiarid climate and support scrubby vegetation. Some areas, shown in light violet, were covered by clouds and could not be analyzed. Skole and Tucker used the 1978 image to estimate the amount of deforestation that had occurred prior to 1978. They then compared the 1978 and 1988 photos to determine the amount of deforestation during that decade. They divided the Amazon Basin into 16 km by 16 km squares for their analysis. One of those areas is enlarged in an inset on figure 23.22. These insets show the amount of deforestation

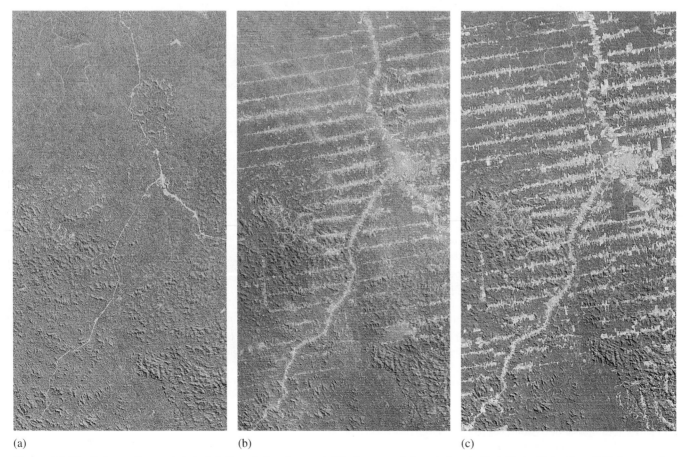

(a)   (b)   (c)

Figure 23.21   Information on tropical deforestation from satellite images: deforestation in Rondônia State, Brazil (light areas), in (*a*) 1975, (*b*) 1986, and (*c*) 1992.

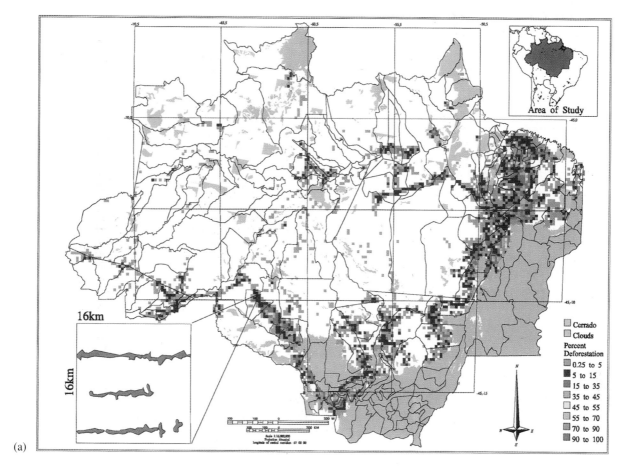

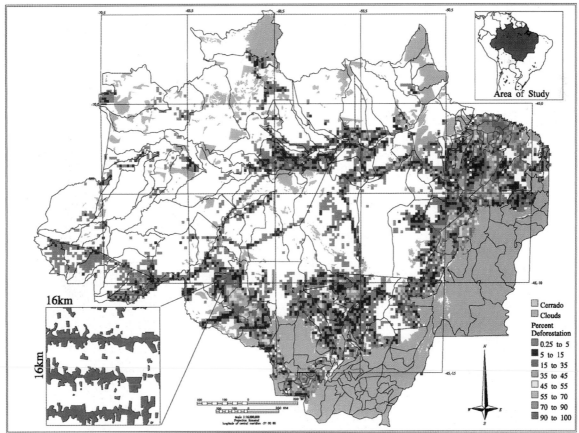

Figure 23.22 Deforestation in Amazonia between (*a*) 1978 and (*b*) 1988 (data from Skole and Tucker 1993).

in 1978 and in 1988. Notice that the deforested area in the inset increased significantly between 1978 and 1988.

Skole and Tucker used their analyses of 16 km by 16 km areas to estimate the percentage of the land surface that had been deforested across the entire Amazon Basin. On their maps, white indicates completely forested areas, while various colours indicate increasing degrees of deforestation. At one end of their spectrum, grey indicates 0.25% to 5% deforested; at the other end, red indicates 90% to 100% deforested. Notice that the colour of the area covered by the inset is purple on the 1978 map and green on the 1988 map. Change in colour on the map of the entire basin from 1978 to 1988 reflects the increase in deforested area during that period.

How much of the Brazilian Amazon has been deforested? Skole and Tucker estimated that by 1978, 78,000 km^2 had been deforested. They also estimated that the annual rate of deforestation between 1978 and 1988 was about 15,000 km^2 per year. While this estimate indicates considerable deforestation, it is considerably lower than earlier estimates that ranged from 21,000 to 80,000 km^2 per year. Skole and Tucker estimated that the total area deforested by 1988 was 230,000 km^2. This estimate, which was slightly lower than the official estimate by the Brazilian government, is probably the most accurate estimate of deforestation within the Amazon Basin made to date.

Although these rates of deforestation are high, we need to remember they represent only the bare minimum of impact on biological systems. In chapter 21, we discussed issues of edge effects and fragmentation. Deforestation causes changes to the distribution and characteristics of landscape elements, with a number of additional consequences for the resident species.

Skole and Tucker provided a detailed picture of land cover changes in the Amazon Basin. However, what is the global rate of tropical deforestation? No one can answer this question precisely, but the best estimates indicate that 52% to 64% of tropical deforestation occurs outside Brazil. Therefore, a conservative estimate of the global rate of deforestation from 1978 to 1988 would be approximately 30,000 km^2 per year.

Figure 23.23 Deforestation in the forests of British Columbia.

How much land cover change is occurring outside the tropics? Though most people have focused on tropical deforestation, massive deforestation has occurred in temperate and boreal regions. As we saw in chapter 2, the temperate forest regions of Europe, eastern China, Japan, and North America support some of the densest human populations on earth. Large areas of Europe were deforested by the Middle Ages (Williams 1990), and much of the forest of eastern North America was cut by the middle 1800s. The majority of old-growth temperate forests in northwestern North America have been cut (fig. 23.23), and the remaining old-growth forests are threatened by deforestation. In addition, vast areas of boreal forest are being cut in Russia and Canada. As you can see, deforestation is not limited to tropical regions.

Kates, Turner, and Clark (1990) estimated that human activity has transformed approximately half the ice-free land cover of the earth. In the process, many of the major terrestrial biomes of the earth (see chapter 2) have been highly fragmented. Others, such as tropical dry forest, have been nearly eliminated by conversion to agriculture. Because of the negative effect of reduced area on diversity (see chapter 22), these massive land conversions present a major threat to global diversity. However, land cover changes also have the potential to contribute, directly and indirectly, to other issues of concern, including the spread of invasive species.

ECOLOGY IN ACTION

Being an Ecologist

I am a tenured professor, at a large research-intensive university. I have devoted my professional life to the discovery of knowledge, its critical evaluation and interpretation, and its dissemination to others through my published works (including

this book!), public talks, and through teaching. I do this not because I live a life full of despair and dread about the state of the environment, but instead, because I am hopeful. I believe my training in science, and the training of many thousands

more in Canada each year, will lead toward solutions to many current problems. Even more, I believe that scientific literacy is critical to the development of effective governmental regulations, policies, and a willingness to enforce them. An even more basic reason why I work so hard on the science of ecology is that I simply love my job. Though the endless pursuit of grant dollars, the repeated questions of "will this be on the test? and soul-draining administrative duties are occupational hazards, they pale in comparison to my job's benefits. I know that when my group discovers something, we are the first—ever—to have learned this new nugget of information. There is true satisfaction in my work when I see students who had struggled with a difficult concept finally get it, and be able to converse with a depth of understanding unlike that which they had achieved before. It is a pleasure to be able to speak in front of non-scientific audiences about my research, and help bring to them the excitement of discovery that drives much of what I do. However, I am only one type of ecologist, the classic academic who combines research and teaching in my daily activities. I do, in fact, own a tweed jacket with patches on the elbows. This job is great for me, but it is not great for everyone.

A question I hear every year from students is, "What do ecologists do?" The short answer is, "everything." Similar to nearly all science degrees, engaged students with ecological training will have developed the capacity for analytical thought and the writing abilities that are valued by many businesses and industries. However, to offer a more specific answer, I return to the University of Alberta. We are a large school. In my department alone, Biological Sciences, we have among the most academic ecologists of any school in Canada, we have well over 125 graduate students in ecology, and approximately 750 undergraduate students take our introductory ecology course each year. Though most of the ecological researchers on campus are in my department, I also have many colleagues in the Departments of Renewable Resources, Earth and Atmospheric Sciences, and Agriculture. To get a sense of the diversity of career paths that have been taken by our students, I polled the ecology group on campus. In return, I received a dizzying array of occupations filled by recent UA graduates. I recognize that specific jobs will differ among schools and locations; however, the general breadth of jobs that emerge from training at a single school should help show the breadth of options for those that take up the noble endeavour of training in ecology. Some of the jobs below can be stepped into right after convocation; others require more specialized training in graduate or professional schools.

Government

All levels of government, from municipal to federal, hire substantial numbers of individuals with training in ecology. Why? There is abundant legislation on nearly all uses of land, sea, and air and government needs help updating the legislation, turning legislation into regulation, and monitoring activities. Additionally, governments own/run parks, and these need to be staffed and managed to achieve both recreational and conservation goals.

Governments employ many individuals to harvest and extract natural resources. Positions range from that of providing information to individual producers (e.g., range agrologist), to setting harvest quotas for fisheries and wild game, to those involved with developing policy, to those focused on monitoring environmental impacts. One specialized job is that of a wildlife forensic DNA specialist. In this position, individuals use techniques in molecular ecology to explore crimes involving wildlife (e.g., poaching, smuggling, etc.). Think *CSI* meets *The Nature of Things*. Other jobs include:

Parks Scientist/Manager/Technician

Parks are bound by many regulations regarding the protection of wildlife and preservation of ecosystem integrity. Meeting these demands requires a diverse group of employees, from taxa-focused specialists through to ecosystem ecologists. Parks employees are also involved in mitigating human–wildlife conflict through trail and road design and through public awareness campaigns. Many are also hired to assist with weed/invasive species control, implement fire/grazing as a conservation tool, collect entrance fees, assist/manage interpretive programs, and assist with essentially any other task performed in a park.

Conservation Coordinator/Biodiversity Management

Many governments have specialized individuals who work directly with the public, offering guidance to individuals in terms of enhancing local conservation efforts. Duties may also include management of invasive species and/or recovery of species-at-risk.

Nongovernmental Organizations (NGOs)

There are many groups dedicated to specific issues related to the environment. These may be groups focused on the preservation and recovery of a single species, or groups that focus on broader issues such as climate change. NGOs may be political lobbying organizations, they may be focused on education, or they may be primarily action oriented (e.g., wildlife recovery). Such organizations are a very common home to students of ecology, who often start as internships or volunteers (someone needs to staff those fundraising campaigns!). A few examples of environmentally oriented NGOs in Alberta include the Alberta Biodiversity Monitoring Institute and the Alberta Conservation Association. Nationally and internationally, these include the Nature Conservancy, Sierra Club, and many other organizations.

Outreach and Science Interpretation

Though most of us imagine that training in science leads to traditional careers as scientists, for many individuals their true passion lies in outreach and interpretation. The combination of skills that allow you to both understand scientific information and also have a sense of design, rhetoric, or strong writing is rare but critical to many careers. Examples include science writer and illustrator, editor/publisher, film maker and visual artist, tour guide/eco-adventure leader, and biological interpreter in parks and museums.

Education

A unique form of science interpretation is a career as a teacher in K–12 or post-secondary classrooms. In many parts of Canada, individuals who possess depth in scientific literacy combined with strong math skills are highly desired. Personal experience in research, such as conducting an undergraduate project or assisting in a research lab, adds further depth of understanding that can be invaluable when helping the next generation of students develop to their full potential. Teaching science at the post-secondary level nearly always requires a Ph.D., or at least a M.Sc. Requirements for K–12 teaching vary among provinces.

Industry and Private Business

Companies associated with resource extraction and the harvest of natural products, housing and commercial development, and any number of other industries regularly hire ecology students to fill a diversity of positions. Many other students will find employment as consultants, either working for a firm or freelance, with the clients including government, industry, and NGOs. Combined, these industry-related positions are critical to conducting rare species surveys, making environmental impact assessments, developing plans to mitigate environmental risk, and implementing restoration and reclamation efforts.

Many science graduates develop their own businesses, and thus create their own jobs. These may be related to their ecological training (e.g., integrated pest management), their personal interests (e.g., beekeeper and honey maker), or may capture the benefits of sharp analytical thought (e.g., financial analyst).

Law, Medicine, Dentistry, Pharmacy, Architecture

In my lab alone, over the last 14 years undergraduates have moved on to each of these professional schools immediately following graduation. The idea that you must study biomedical health or be pre-med to pursue a medical degree is false. The idea that only undergraduate degrees in the humanities lead to law is wrong. What professional schools are looking for are students who are highly capable, have applied themselves to difficult tasks, who write and speak well, and who demonstrate personal integrity and maturity. Though non-traditional paths to professional schools may require more work in terms of scheduling your classes to meet both degree and pre-req course requirements, it is often worth challenging untested assumptions about your future.

Researcher

Researchers find employment in industry, government, and academia. However, in all three cases, your level of responsibility is related (in part) to which degree you hold. In most organizations, only Ph.D.s will be given the flexibility to design and lead projects, while those with M.Sc. and B.Sc. degrees will (often) perform more of the technical work. Academia is a unique path, as it integrates teaching and research. The relative amount of time an individual spends teaching versus research varies highly among universities; though not surprisingly, at research-intensive universities, the majority of time and effort of a professor will typically be devoted toward research (and graduate teaching). An additional path for a researcher can be found in museums, both through curation of collections and interpretation of information. These may or may not be affiliated with universities, run by a non-profit organization, or managed by government. The larger museums often serve not only as a location for science interpretation, but through the work of researchers, also as places of discovery.

Invasive Species

Throughout the text we have shown examples of how the introduction of a new species to a community can have dramatic consequences for community structure and nutrient cycling. Species introductions are happening across the planet at an ever-increasing pace, and as Soulé suggests, these pose one of the most critical threats to ecological integrity and biodiversity of native communities. We begin with a definition of *biotic invaders* (fig. 23.24). According to Richard Mack and colleagues (Mack et al. 2000), these are defined as "species that establish a new range in which they proliferate, spread, and persist to the detriment of the environment." This is a generally accepted definition; in fact, Mack's paper has been cited by other researchers over 500 times since it was published. This definition is critical because it differentiates invaders from alien or exotic species. The latter words describe species that historically were not found in a given location, but through some form of dispersal (human mediated or not), are now found in a novel area. For instance, in Canada there are about 4,200 species of vascular plants, and it is estimated that nearly one-third of these are exotic species. However, most exotic species are not invasive, and instead represent a relatively small fraction of the biomass and drive only a small portion of the ecosystem function. What we are concerned about here are the few species able to establish, spread, and dominate an area: the biotic invaders.

For example, smallmouth and rock bass are two invaders of Canadian lakes. A collaboration between the Ontario Ministry of Natural Resources and researchers at McGill University has demonstrated how these fish cause significant changes to the trophic structure of lakes they invade (Vander Zanden et al. 1999). These species are generally intentionally introduced to lakes well beyond their native range in an effort to increase fishing opportunities. By using stable isotopes to understand feeding relationships (chapter 19), the research team found the introduced species caused a decline in the abundance of native prey-fish, and caused the native lake trout to feed more on zooplankton. Such shifts in trophic structure are likely to have cascading effects on phytoplankton and nutrient cycles.

As in the example of sport-fish, humans often play an important role in transporting species from one location to another. This is likely not too surprising—humans are able to travel across the planet much more efficiently than the historical dispersal vectors of plant and animals. For some species, such as these fish, Pacific oysters, a variety of horticultural plants, and a diversity of bird species, introductions are intentional. These are often when a person, or governmental organization, has decided to improve the use of land through new economic activities (e.g., fishing, oyster farms) or through aesthetic desires for non-native flora and fauna. Many other introductions are unintentional, such as the zebra mussel and lamprey in the Great Lakes, a variety of insect pests, and numerous agricultural weeds. These species are often introduced when ships dump ballast water near new lands, as contaminants in food shipments, and through other forms of unintentional release. Regardless of the cause of introduction, species are quickly being introduced to novel locations across the world.

We have shown many of the ecological consequences of invasion throughout this book. David Pimentel and colleagues have conducted an assessment of some of the economic costs of invasive species within the United States, estimating the damages and loss due to these species is nearly $120 billion ($US) per year (Pimentel et al. 2005). Although the data available for Canada are not as clear, Hugh MacIsaac and colleagues from the University

(a)

(b)

(c)

(d)

Figure 23.24   Invasive species in Canada include (*a*) zebra mussels, *Dreissena polymorpha*, (*b*) sea lamprey, *Petromyzon marinus*, (*c*) Dutch elm disease, *Ophiostoma ulmi*, and (*d*) purple loosestrife, *Lythrum salicaria*.

of Windsor (chapter 22) suggest costs associated with just 16 non-indigenous species can exceed $13 billion ($CAD) annually (Colautti et al. 2006). Why are these numbers so large? To begin with, there are a lot of alien species. Pimentel and colleagues report that there are an estimated 750,000 species in the United States, with 50,000 of these being alien-invasive species. The economic costs associated with these species include attempted control programs as well as losses due to reduced agricultural production. For example, there are an estimated 25,000 alien species of plants alone in the United States. Of these alien plant species, many are major weeds in crops and Pimentel estimates they cost $24 billion ($US) per year in reduced agricultural yield, and an additional $3 billion ($US) per year in herbicides and other control programs. Rats are estimated to cause $19 billion ($US) per year in damages due to feeding upon stored grains, fires associated with gnawing on wires, and disease transmission. The nearly 30 million feral cats in the United States (compared to the 63 million pet cats) feed upon native birds and other animals. Pimentel estimates a loss of $17 billion ($US) per year from these cats due to lost opportunities (and expenses) associated with bird watching, hunting, and other activities. Another $14 billion and $21 billion ($US) per year are associated with introduced insect and microbial pests of crops, with another $14 billion ($US) per year for introduced livestock diseases.

The impacts of invasive species on the functioning and biological integrity of natural areas is clear. The economic costs of these species is simply enormous. Due to continued movement by people, continued desires to improve native lands, and continued development, we are unlikely to see any reduction in these costs in the near future. It will be up to the current and next generations of ecologists to figure out how the negative effects of these species introductions can be reduced, and maybe even how some of these species can be eliminated.

CONCEPT 23.2 REVIEW

1. Why do patterns of human appropriation of ocean and terrestrial productivity differ spatially?
2. How does the harvest efficiency of croplands and fisheries differ? Why?
3. Why is reducing land cover through deforestation or agriculture a threat to biodiversity?

23.3 Ecologically Informed Decision Making

Ecological information can be integrated with economic data to help meet conservation goals in a political landscape. There was a time when ecological research was focused nearly exclusively on wild areas; where researchers avoided field sites and study locations obviously impacted by humans. There were, of course, exceptions, such as Schindler's classic work on lake eutrophication due to phosphorus pollution (chapter 19).

However, when thumbing through copies of *Ecology* or *The American Naturalist* from even as late as the 1970s, it would be hard to have realized the extent of human impacts on the earth described earlier in this chapter. Times have changed. Ecologists of today benefit from two things not available to the early ecologists. First, we benefit from the hard work of our predecessors that has resulted in a broad set of theories regarding how the natural world functions. It is much easier to improve ideas and theories than it is to create them *de novo*. Second, for the last several decades, issues of great environmental concern have been in the front pages of newspapers and lead stories on news broadcasts throughout the world. Society has said there are problems, and they need to be fixed. In this section, we present several examples of how ecologists have moved out of the wild, and are addressing issues on the human-dominated landscape within which we all live. As this landscape is one full of politics, it is not surprising that the economics of ecological decisions plays a central role.

Costs of Conservation

Globally, there is recognition that the protection of biological diversity is important, as evidenced by national laws (e.g., species-at-risk legislation) and international agreements (e.g., Convention of Biological Diversity). However, recovery programs for species that are threatened or endangered are not cheap, and it is typically difficult to convince the public to sign a blank cheque for such efforts. What are needed are robust cost estimates, and these can emerge when ecologists, economists, and political scientists work together.

Donal McCarthy has recently led a large international team in developing cost estimates for reducing the extinction risk for 211 of the over 1,100 globally threatened bird species (McCarthy et al. 2012). In their economic model, they set the conservation goal of preventing species extinction as equivalent to downlisting a species one step in the IUCN listing categories (chapter 10). Birds were chosen in part because of the high quality of data available, allowing for more confidence in the resulting analyses. As you might imagine, measuring the costs of conservation—and the extinction risk—for a single species is difficult; doing so for over 200 species is impossible for a single person. Thus, the authors enlisted help of experts. For each species, they contacted experts familiar with its ecology and recovery costs, and asked them to estimate both the current amount spent on conservation for that species, as well as the total costs expected to successfully downlist the species within ten years. They then combined this information with data related to the habitat needs of each species, the GDP of the nation(s) that contains the breeding range, and other factors. So, what is the bill?

Based upon 2012 dollar values, the estimated recovery costs ranged from $0.04 to $8.96 million per species (median = $0.848 million). After validating these estimates based upon true costs of successful recovery of 25 species, they extrapolated their results to project the cost of recovering all 1,115 bird species. In total, they estimate a price tag of $1.23 billion for each of the next ten years. Interestingly, the price decreases as the degree of risk increases; they suggest this is due to the most endangered species having the smallest distributions (and thus land purchase costs are reduced). Recognizing that the ranges for some species

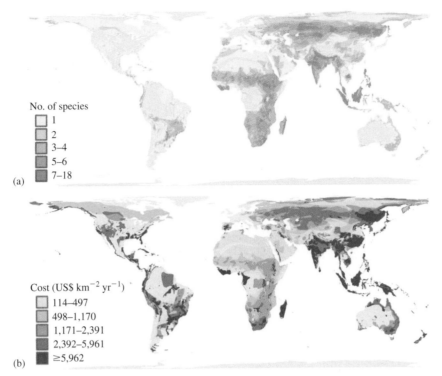

(a)

No. of species
- 1
- 2
- 3–4
- 5–6
- 7–18

(b)

Cost (US$ km^{-2} yr^{-1})
- 114–497
- 498–1,170
- 1,171–2,391
- 2,392–5,961
- ≥5,962

Figure 23.25   Maps showing (*a*) the distribution of bird species red-listed, and (*b*) the estimated conservation costs of those 1,097 globally threatened species.

overlap, such that land purchases may benefit multiple species, a more realistic estimate is a total cost of $0.88 billion per year. Whether this is viewed as a very large cost or not is likely highly dependent upon your country of origin.

Not surprisingly, the distribution of red-listed bird species is not uniform across the world, and instead most are concentrated near the equator (fig. 23.25*a*). Consequently, most of the costs associated with species recovery will be in countries considered low or lower middle income (McCarthy et al. 2012; fig. 23.25*b*). As these countries are poorly suited to pay for such conservation activities, large-scale political solutions will be needed. Making matters even more complicated is the recognition that birds are only one of many taxonomic groups that contain red-listed species. When they extrapolate their costs to other species, they conservatively estimate global costs of $3.41 billion per year to downlist all listed species within ten years. If the goal is moved away from simply delisting species to a broader goal of protecting areas of global biodiversity significance to reduce future listings (e.g., high diversity, endemic species, etc.), the costs rise to over $76 billion annually (McCarthy et al. 2012). For all countries, this is a large number.

Integrating Ecosystem Services into Decision Making

Clearly, conservation actions have real costs, and for many governments these cannot be incurred without assistance. However, equally important to knowing the costs of action are science-driven estimates of the costs of inaction. Throughout the book, we have discussed a diversity of ecological services (chapter 16), such as nutrient cycling, water filtration, and biomass production. These services have economic value, and as ecosystems deteriorate, their value also declines. Thus,

conservation costs can result in economic gains and be seen as an investment in natural capital. However, the framework for how you might incorporate the value of natural capital into economic decisions has generally been lacking. Gretchen Daily and colleagues have recently presented a framework in which ecology and economics can be more formally integrated into decision-making processes (Daily et al. 2009; fig. 23.26).

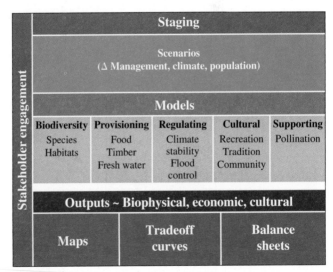

Figure 23.26   A decision-making process that allows investment in natural capital to be included at the planning stage of projects. In this model, diverse group of stakeholders meet to discuss the issues and alternative plausible outcomes. Scientific and economic information is then incorporated into models. This information is then integrated to give the stakeholders the needed information to make a complete decision.

This decision-making framework has been integrated into a more formal tool called InVEST (Integrated Valuation of Ecosystem Services and Trade-offs) (http://www.naturalcapitalproject.org/). A key feature is that a number of costs and benefits of a given scenario (e.g., population growth, development) are explicitly discussed. This requires participants to understand trade-offs, rather than to focus solely on a single output (e.g., economic return on investment). The InVEST model is currently being applied to the future planning of the marine environment of the west coast of Vancouver Island (Guerry et al. 2012).

The west coast of Vancouver Island is a base for commercial activities (fisheries, logging, etc.), a tourist destination, a source of renewable energy, and is the object of deep beliefs among First Nations peoples and others regarding the natural landscape (Guerry et al. 2012). Consequently, any changes to the system, whether to increase conservation or to increase development, impact many stakeholders. Guerry and her team modified the InVEST model to address the specific issues relevant to this system; the outputs of the model are spatially explicit and relevant to stakeholders. For example, in a focal study of Lemmens Inlet, the research team was able to map the impacts of no policy change (=baseline), increased conservation, and industrial expansion on the quality of a number of factors (fig. 23.27). For more general discussions, these

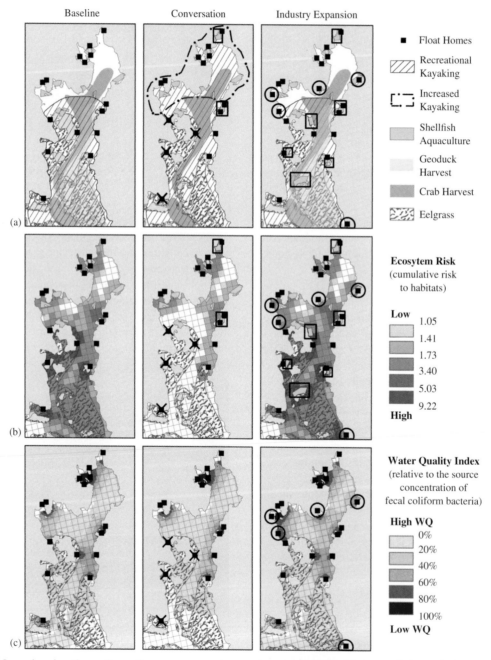

Figure 23.27   Maps showing three alternative management scenarios proposed for Lemmens Inlet, BC. In the baseline scenario, no changes are proposed. The remaining two scenarios focus on increased (conservation) or decreased (industry expansion) restrictions on float homes and aquaculture. (*a*) The location of different activities, (*b*) the cumulate risks to nearshore habitats, and (*c*) impacts on water quality.

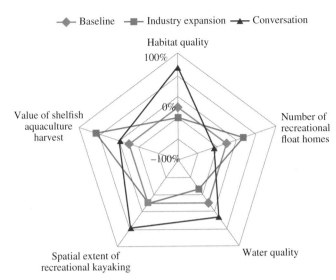

Figure 23.28 By focusing on five major outcomes, this modelling approach allows for visualization of potential costs and benefits of the different scenarios.

results can be visualized in a way that highlights trade-offs (fig. 23.28). It is hoped that these more synthetic planning exercises will help governments better understand not simply the costs of conservation, but also the value of protecting existing natural capital.

Using Ecological Understanding to Reduce Costs

As critical as it will be to show costs and benefits to conservation, it is also critical to have the dollars spent on conservation goals used as efficiently as possible. Or to use economic terms, there is a need to maximize the return on investment (ROI) on conservation efforts. In an ambitious study, John Withey and colleagues used an ROI approach to identify areas of priority for land conservation—over the entire 48 lower states in the U.S. mainland (Withey et al. 2013). Again, this was done through collaborations among ecological and social scientists, and recognized existing political boundaries.

Within the United States, as in Canada, many land-use decisions are made at the county, rather than state (or provincial) level. Consequently, that was the unit of measure used by Withey and his colleagues. For nearly all of the 3,109 counties in the lower 48 states, the researchers collected several critical pieces of data.

Biodiversity

Though ideally this would be a measure of all species found within each county, such data do not exist. The authors chose to focus exclusively on the number of vertebrate species, as these are both a manageable (low) number, and of relatively high data quality.

Risk and Gain

For each species, they calculated the percentage of its range that was currently under protection from development; those with high values would likely receive little value from increased land protection. For each county, they also estimated the threat of development both through the percent of area that exists as anthropogenic land cover (e.g., roads, cities, etc.), as well as the rate of change from natural to anthropogenic cover.

Costs

Using a number of economic assumptions and models, the authors estimated the cost of acquiring land for protection in each county. This estimate took into consideration the current land use and cover-type (e.g., forest, grassland, cropland) as well as land values.

By combining these data into a ROI model, Withey et al. (2013) were able to show areas in which conservation efforts would be most, or least, effective (fig. 23.29). As is clear, the conservation gain per dollar spent is highly variable, though typically highest in the central United States. Not surprisingly, general ROI is lowest on the coasts, where land prices tend to be very high. However, federal regulation requires protection of all species, not only those that live in the central United States. Withey and his colleagues were able to use their model to address a related question: if you wanted to protect a minimum percent of the range of all species, where would land be purchased most cost effectively? The answer is highly dependent upon the protected target (fig. 23.30).

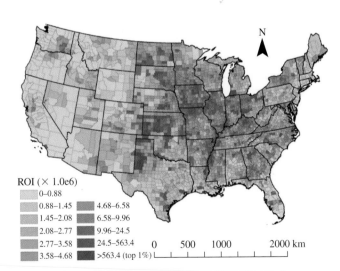

Figure 23.29 ROI for conservation efforts focused on vertebrate animals in the United States. The units for ROI are species saved with purchase of 1,000 ha of land per dollar spent.

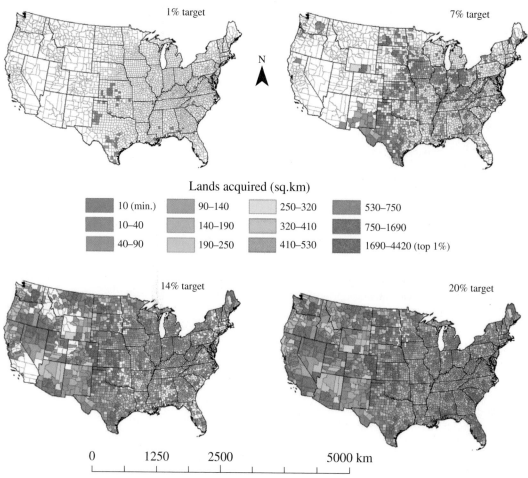

Figure 23.30 The amount of land needed to be purchased to ensure different levels of habitat protection for all vertebrate species.

At the lowest target, 1%, very little additional land will be needed, and it is generally in low-cost counties. However, as the protection target increases, it becomes clear that very large tracts of land will need to be purchased in the more expensive regions of the county. Tools such as those presented here are opening a new era for applying ecological knowledge to conservation. As we see next, this is not the only change happening in how ecologists conduct and use their research.

CONCEPT 23.3 REVIEW

1. In figure 23.29, Withey and colleagues presented a map describing what counties in the United States would show the greater return on conservation investment. What types of data are necessary are needed to generate such tools of conservation?

2. Why is it important to incorporate aspects of the natural environment into decision-making tools related to development?

3. In this section, nearly all papers were published by large research teams, as opposed to the work of a lonely genius. What aspects of the application of ecological knowledge require such collaborations?

ECOLOGICAL TOOLS AND APPROACHES

Cooperative Research Networks & Distributed Ecology

How do you know if the ecological changes you observe are due to local processes, or are instead part of a widespread phenomenon? For an individual researcher, it is not practical to set up experiments and studies throughout a single province, across a country, or around the world. Instead, the limited resources of time and money restrict most studies to a relatively small spatial scale over a very narrow window of time. As should be clear from this chapter, such approaches are not likely to allow scientists to observe—let alone understand— change. To overcome such limitations, researchers often form networks, casual or formal, working together to address specific issues in ecology. As global questions become more pressing, and as scientists increasingly recognize the limitations of the traditional silo approach to ecological enquiry, the culture of how many ecologists conduct research is changing.

To effectively address the complex problems, scientists must appreciate a variety of scientific disciplines and be capable of working effectively within multidisciplinary teams. Such teams can conduct studies at spatial and temporal scales impossible for an individual researcher. As these networks develop, there have emerged two main approaches: (1) broad monitoring, and (2) coordinated distributed experiments (sensu Fraser et al. 2013).

Broad Monitoring

A key to understanding whether patterns are regional or global in extent is to have a standardized monitoring program spread over a large geographical area. Some networks may be very focused in which data they collect, while others are quite broad. For example, FLUXNET is a network of towers established in a diversity of habitat types that measure micrometeorology such as CO_2 concentrations. The goals of these measures include providing a comprehensive understanding of the relationship between climate and ecosystem productivity; and to understand long-term changes in microenvironment, including greenhouse gases. Towers are established in over 200 locations in 45 countries, including 22 sites in Canada. Hank Margolis of the Université Laval oversees the FLUXNET-Canada network, and has recently summarized some of the findings that are beginning to emerge (Margolis et al. 2006), including (1) the forests of Canada are becoming a reduced carbon sink due to increased disturbances such as insect outbreaks and fire, (2) changes in precipitation and evapotranspiration associated with climate change will have strong effects on the carbon balance of forests and peatlands throughout Canada, and (3) recent studies indicate that root production and soil respiration play a very significant role in total ecosystem carbon fluxes, and thus more study is needed below ground.

The United States has long been a leader in large-scale ecological modelling. For the last several decades, the U.S. Long-Term Ecological Research (LTER) network has fostered large-scale ecological research. One of the central purposes of this research network is to foster cooperative, interdisciplinary research over large geographic areas. These sites include tropical forests, arctic tundra, temperate forests, grasslands, coastal ecosystems, deserts, and two cities. They extend from sea level to elevations over 4,000 m and from the Arctic to the Antarctic. The first International Long-Term Ecological Research (ILTER) workshop was held in 1993 (Nottrott et al. 1994). Scientists from around the world met to establish active interactions and collaboration between the LTER network and long-term ecological research programs from around the globe. Today, ILTER coordinates the efforts of 38 independent networks found in over 30 countries (including Canada) on five continents (fig. 23.31).

More recently, the United States has created NEON, the National Ecological Observatory Network. The goal of NEON is to understand continental-scale ecology, an unprecedented and ambitious project. To move toward this goal, NEON has divided the United States into 20 eco-climatic domains based upon the types of eco-climatic variables discussed throughout this book. Within each domain they have established one core site. In some domains they also have a paired aquatic site and additional sites focused on human impacts. In total, there are currently 106 sites within NEON. The intent is to have coordinated and detailed measures of the biotic and abiotic components of the United States for decades; what questions and solutions will emerge are not known, but they are likely to be significant.

Compared to the United States, Canada remains slow to recognize the need for ongoing federal support for long-term international research networks. Consequently, networks in Canada are typically focused on marshalling efforts of many individuals toward common goals, rather than designating formal locations across Canada as priorities for in-depth research. Nonetheless, such networks can be extremely productive. For example, ArcticNet (http://www.arcticnet.ulaval.ca/) involves over 140 researchers throughout Canada and other Northern countries with a primary focus on climate change impacts. The centre of the network is headed at Université Laval, led by Martin Fortier. Critical to ArcticNet's mission is the involvement of local communities and cultures, along with social scientists, to help individuals understand and mitigate change. A second Canadian example is EMAN, the Environmental Monitoring and Assessment Network. EMAN is a loose network of organizations that form a partnership to study ecosystem changes. Members of the network record observations of

Figure 23.31   The International Long-Term Ecological Research Network includes member networks located in over 30 countries.

plant phenology, frog abundance, ice break, and the spread of invasive earthworms, among other activities. These organizations are scattered throughout Canada and include governmental organizations, individual researchers, schools, and members of the general public. Because of the varied quality and limited central coordination, EMAN has not provided the same level of ecological understanding that has emerged from the LTER. However, networks such as ArcticNet and EMAN can serve as a starting point from which Canada can build.

Distributed Ecology

From observations will come hypotheses and models of ecological function. However, a critical aspect of scientific understanding is challenging hypotheses with data, and few tools are more powerful than the artfully designed experiment. However, individual ecological experiments suffer from the same limitation found within individual observations: an inability to know whether the measured response is general or idiosyncratic. A common approach for seeking synthesis is to combine the results of independent experiments in a meta-analysis. We present the results of many such efforts throughout the book. However, meta-analyses have substantial flaws and limitations of scale, potential bias, and sometimes a misunderstanding of the underlying natural history being studied (Whittiker 2010; Hillebrand et al 2010). However, more often than not, they are the best means available to try and draw a synthetic answer to a specific hypothesis.

In a recent paper, Lauch Fraser from Thomson Rivers University, along with a number of colleagues, have drawn attention to an alternative approach: coordinated distributed experiments (Fraser et al. 2013). The name is drawn from computing science, where complex problems can be solved by distributing the work among many individual computers. In this model, the costs to the individual (e.g., computer) are small, relative to the value of the solution to the computing problem. Fraser and colleagues suggest such a model may be well suited to ecological research, where there is a need for replication over a large geographic scale, though individual budgets are typically tight. Two of the most successful examples of distributed ecological experiments involve substantial involvement by Canadian researchers: ITEX (International Tundra Experiment) and NutNet (Nutrient Network), focused on ecosystem responses to warming in the tundra (Henry and Molau 1997) and fertilization effects on biodiversity (Adler et al. 2011). Fraser suggests that what made these such strong efforts, and what is required in general for distributed ecological experiments to be successful are a few key criteria. These include a clear hypothesis, standardized and inexpensive design, broad geographic replication, and clear rules for data sharing among team members. Many of these requirements swim against the current of academic independence. However, like the oceans, scientific tides change, and a growing number of ecologists are recognizing the scientific value of collaboration.

SUMMARY

Chapter 23 focuses on global-scale processes and phenomena, including the movement of tectonic plates, large-scale weather systems, and global change induced by humans. We also discuss novel approaches to conservation, integration, and ecological and economic information.

23.1 Over a geologic time scales, the Earth and its biological diversity exhibit a near-constant state of flux.

The surface of the earth consists of numerous tectonic plates whose movement has changed the distribution of land and water of the planet. Through geographic isolation, this geologic movement has influenced the distribution of species, including temperate tree species.

Over deep time, there have been substantial changes in the number of types of species found on the planet. Some estimates suggest only 1% of all species that have ever existed are currently extant. There have been at least five mass extinction events over the last 500 million years, in which at least 75% of species present at the start of the event were extinct by the end of the event. The causes are varied, and include climate change, tectonic activity, and chemical changes in the atmosphere. Current evidence suggests human activity is moving us into the sixth such extinction event. Though only a small number of species have currently gone extinct in the last 500 years, the extinction rate is high, and many species are at risk.

In addition to changes on the earth's surface, the earth's atmosphere is very dynamic. The El Niño Southern Oscillation is a large-scale weather system that involves variation in sea surface temperature and barometric pressure across the Pacific and Indian Oceans. During the mature phase of an El Niño, the sea surface in the eastern tropical Pacific Ocean is much warmer than average and the barometric pressure over the eastern Pacific is lower than average. El Niño brings increased precipitation to much of North America and parts of South America and drought to the western Pacific. Periods of lower sea surface temperature and higher-than-average barometric pressures in the eastern tropical Pacific have been named La Niñas. La Niña brings drought to much of North America and South America and higher-than-average precipitation to the western Pacific. The North Atlantic Oscillation and the Northern Hemisphere Annular Mode influence the weather across more northern latitudes. The NAO is a fluctuation in pressure between Iceland and Portugal. In the positive phase there are cooler temperatures in eastern Canada, less precipitation in the Canadian Arctic, and wetter, warmer weather in northern Europe. These patterns reverse when the NAO is in the negative phase. The NAM (Arctic Oscillation) is a mirror image of the NAO, also impacting global weather. The variation in weather caused by these oscillations has dramatic effects on marine and terrestrial populations around the world.

23.2 Human activities have generated substantial threats to biological diversity.

Human activities, mainly agriculture and urbanization, have significantly altered one-third to one-half of the ice-free land surface of the earth. A striking example of these pressures is the appropriation of 24% of the terrestrial NPP by people. In marine lands, substantial amounts of primary productivity are used to support the world's fisheries. Human activity has converted substantial extents of land into agricultural systems, with associated applications of fertilizer and water use for irrigation. These activities have placed significant pressures on aquatic systems. A widely cited example of land cover change is tropical deforestation. From 1978 to 1988, the rate of deforestation in the Amazon Basin of Brazil averaged about 15,000 km^2 per year. By 1988, the total area deforested within the Amazon Basin was 230,000 km^2. By adding in edge effects and the effects of isolation, the area of Amazonian forest affected by deforestation increases from 230,000 km^2 to 588,000 km^2. The global rate of tropical deforestation from 1978 to 1988 was about 30,000 km^2 per year. Massive deforestation has also occurred outside of the tropics. Because of the negative effect of reduced habitat area on diversity, these massive land conversions present a major threat to global biological diversity. An associated cost of human activities is the global spread of invasive species. Combined, these species are posing substantial harm to natural systems and result in massive economic costs to people.

23.3 Ecological information can be integrated with economic data to help meet conservation goals in a political landscape.

Ecology is no longer a new science, nor are many of its results of purely theoretical value. Increasingly, the science of ecology is being used to address the issue of conservation biology. This requires collaboration among scientists, economists, government, and other stakeholders. The costs of conservation are very high; however, the protection of natural capital is also of economic value. New frameworks have been developed that allow for more holistic conversations at the time of development planning, which incorporate economic and ecological costs and benefits. Ecologists are increasingly using the tools of economics to increase the ROI of conservation, allowing managers to prioritize land purchases. This represents a new phase to conservation, one where ecological issues are not viewed independently from societal values.

Cooperative research networks aid global ecology. The present possibility of rapid climate change poses a substantial challenge to the scientific community. Studying ecology at a global scale requires that scientists develop new tools and approaches. New devices, often employing the most recent technological developments, are becoming more and more common in the tool kit of ecologists. However, some

of the most important developments required for global-scale research may involve changes in the culture of science. The complexity and large scale of global change requires that scientists work in multidisciplinary, national, and international teams. International networks of scientists now work on global-scale ecological problems in a research environment that emphasizes information sharing and a team approach to research.

REVIEW QUESTIONS

1. Ecologists are now challenged to study global ecology. The role played by humans in changing the global environment makes it imperative that we understand the workings of the earth as a global system. However, this study requires approaches that are significantly different from those that can be applied to traditional areas of ecological study. Historically, much of ecology focused on small areas and short-term studies. What are some of the main differences between global ecology and, for instance, the study of interspecific competition (see chapter 13) or forest succession (see chapter 18)? How will these differences affect the design of studies at the global scale?

2. Geologists, atmospheric scientists, and oceanographers have been conducting global-scale studies for some time. What role will information from these disciplines play in the study of global ecology? Why will global ecological studies generally be pursued by interdisciplinary teams? How can ecologists play a useful role in global studies?

3. What changes in sea surface temperatures and atmospheric pressures over the Pacific Ocean accompany El Niño? What physical changes accompany La Niña? How do El Niño and La Niña affect precipitation in North America, South America, and Australia?

4. Large-scale climatic processes, such as the North Atlantic Oscillation, are not amenable to experimental research. How would you design a study to determine whether the NAO impacts natural populations of plant and animals in different regions of Canada?

5. Our perception of the "normal" distributions of continents is strongly coloured by our living at only one small point in geological time. Why is it important that anyone interested in understanding the distribution of species also understand the past movement of tectonic plates?

6. There have been at least five mass extinction events, and we may be in a sixth. However, though current trends support this view, this sixth event has not yet happened. What evidence do you need, as a scientist, to determine whether you do, or do not, support the argument that humans are creating a sixth mass extinction event?

7. Deforestation poses significant risk to a number of biodiversity hotspots in the tropics. In Canada, deforestation of the boreal forest is also very high; however, there are few specific areas of concentrated biodiversity in these high-latitude forests. Does this mean that rates of deforestation are not of ecological concern in the boreal? How do you balance the need for economic development with a desire to preserve large areas of undisturbed forest?

8. Invasive species have been discussed throughout the text, in many different contexts. They are widely viewed as one of the greatest threats to biodiversity. Their spread is greatly facilitated by the increased pressures humans are putting on the planet. Why?

9. Humans have appropriated a large proportion of the terrestrial and marine NPP for our own use. Even then, fisheries more often collapse than remain stable. As the earth's population is projected to continue growing in the future, these pressures will likely increase. How can we determine at what point human appropriation of NPP is too high to allow for the delivery of critical ecological services?

10. The conservation costs of even a small group of taxa (birds) is extremely high. When we include other major taxonomic groups, it is likely enormous. How can ecologists use a ROI approach to optimize the protection of multiple types of species?

11. Why is it important that ecological information be included in development plans at the start of a project, rather than simply consulting with ecologists when a project has already been completed?

Building a Statistical Toolbox

In chapter 1 we presented an overview of the scientific method, highlighting its importance to ecologists. A central component of the scientific method is the continual testing of theory and ideas with data. Throughout this text we have provided a broad overview of the types of data needed to answer questions at a variety of temporal and spatial scales. However, due to the complexity of nature, ecological data are often "messy," and in their raw form hard to interpret. Because of the importance objective data have in the scientific method, many statistical approaches have been developed to help discern patterns from seemingly incomprehensible pages of data. In this appendix, we provide a brief overview of the methods ecologists use to relate their collected data to their previously formed hypotheses and ideas. As a group, these critical ecological tools are referred to as statistical methods.

The idea of statistics will cause some students to panic, others to give up, and others to just want to go to sleep. Some advice to those dreading what comes next in this section: **Don't Panic!** The key to understanding statistics is to realize that they sound intimidating to *everyone* at first. However, with practice and experience you will learn the needed vocabulary, and you will see both the utility and surprising simplicity of these approaches. As an aside, the basic statistics described here are used in nearly all scientific disciplines, not just ecology.

Describing a Group

Imagine you are an ecologist in the Yukon, conducting a study on the size of male caribou in a population. After learning the procedures for handling large mammals in the wild, you and your field crew fly across the tundra in a helicopter catching animals and weighing them. Aside from a very tired body, you bring back to your tent at base camp a rumpled notebook full of the weights of all the animals you have caught. Your professor is in camp with you and has asked you to give her an overview of the data collected. What do you do?

One of the most common and important steps in the processing of data is the production of summary statistics. In an ideal world, every caribou in a population could be measured easily and cheaply. However in the real world, helicopter time is expensive, animals are evasive, and your classes start in September, thus you have a limited summer field season. As a result, you are going to only sample a small proportion of the individuals that actually exist within the population, and you will only be able to *estimate* population measures. A *statistic* is a number that is used by scientists to estimate a measurable characteristic (e.g., weight) of an entire population.

Looking at your notebook, you see you have measured 11 caribou. The average weight of these 11 animals is referred to as the **sample mean**, and this is one of the most common and useful of summary statistics. Because of its importance, it is worth describing how it is calculated. Consider the following sample of the weights of the 11 caribou measured:

Caribou Number	1	2	3	4	5	6	7	8	9	10	11
Weight (kg)	145	131	154	169	167	175	117	146	166	134	158

What is the average weight of caribou in this population? Since we did not catch all the males, we cannot know the *true* population mean, however, our sample of 11 males does allow us to calculate a *sample* mean.

To calculate the sample mean, divide the sum of measurements by the number of animals measured:

$$\overline{X} = \frac{\Sigma X}{n}$$

Where,

Sample mean $= \overline{X}$

n = sample size = 11

Sum of measurements $= \Sigma X$

$\Sigma X = 145 + 131 + 154 + 169 + 167 + 175 + 117 + 146 + 166 + 134 + 158 = 1,662$

$\overline{X} = 1662/11$

$\overline{X} = 151.1$ kg

So, your hard day's work is boiled down to a single number: 151.1 kg. This is the sample mean, your estimate of the true weight of the male caribou in the population at the time of this study. To be even more precise, we calculated the *arithmetic mean* in this example. Ecologists use other types of means, such as the *geometric mean* and the *harmonic mean*. However, a discussion of the uses of these other statistics is beyond the scope of this text.

While the sample mean is very useful, it is not the most appropriate statistic for some situations. One of the assumptions underlying the use of the sample mean is that the observations are drawn from a population with a normal, or bell-shaped, distribution (fig. A.1). This assumption was reasonable for the caribou example, but there will be many cases in which the distribution of values within a population deviates substantially from a **normal distribution**. In those situations, it is generally better to use another estimator of the population average. One such

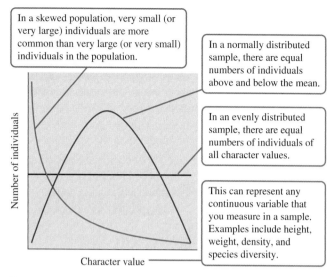

Figure A.1   Normal, skewed, and even distributions of values of a given character (e.g., weight) among individuals within a population.

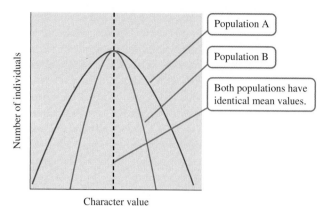

Figure A.2   Populations A and B have identical mean values for this character; however, the variation around the mean appears much greater in population A than in population B.

statistic is the **sample median**. The sample median is simply the middle value when samples are ranked numerically. In our caribou example, there were 11 samples, with the middle caribou being the 6th largest (= sixth smallest), which was 154 kg. Notice that this value is very similar to the sample mean of 151.1 kg. This will be common in populations with normal distributions.

However, when the distribution of samples within a population is skewed, such that there are few very large or very small values, the sample median may give a better estimate of the typical individual within the population. Imagine you are once again back at base camp in the Yukon. Your professor wakes you up at 4 a.m., ready for a long day at work (it is light nearly 24 hours a day during the summer). Today you will be measuring the number of leaves found on individuals of *Dryas octopetala* (common name = avens). The area you will be sampling has been grazed heavily by caribou, and though not a preferred food source for these animals, many avens have been damaged by the animal's hooves. Back at camp you are again asked to provide a summary of the day's data.

Avens Number	1	2	3	4	5	6	7	8	9	10	11	12	13	14
Number of leaves	1	6	2	4	12	15	1	3	9	1	18	2	1	3

In this example there is an even number of samples, and thus the median value will be the average of the 7th and 8th largest (and smallest) individuals:

$$\text{Sample median} = \frac{3+3}{2} = 3 \text{ leaves per plant}$$

$$\text{The sample mean} = \frac{\Sigma X}{11} = \frac{78}{14} = 5.6 \text{ leaves per plant}$$

The estimate of the population mean is nearly twice that of the population median. In this case it is clear that the sample

median, which represents the middle value of observations, more closely estimates the number of leaves you are likely to encounter on an individual plant on this day.

Being able to describe the typical individual in a population of samples using means and medians is a critical first step, but there is much more information left behind in your data books. A second important question we can ask is, how much *variation* exists among individuals (fig. A.2)? This is important for several reasons. For example, two or more samples may have the same mean but quite different amounts of variation among the samples. That variation itself may have either an ecological cause, or may influence some ecological process, and thus being able to describe variation is a critical tool for all ecologists.

Imagine now that it is the next field season and your hard work last summer resulted in a strong letter of recommendation from your supervisor. As a result, you were able to secure another field job, and you are now working on the east coast of Newfoundland, studying the diversity of invertebrate species in the rocky intertidal zones. Your basic research methods involve laying down a 50 × 50 cm quadrat (= 0.25 m²) and counting the different number of species of algae, barnacles, snails, and other macroscopic organisms you can find. You are able to finish 10 samples before lunch, and as you are eating your peanut butter and jelly sandwich (which tastes a bit salty), your professor requests a summary of the data.

Sample Number	1	2	3	4	5	6	7	8	9	10
Number of species per 0.25 m²	15	6	18	17	8	9	12	15	10	12

You quickly estimate the mean and median as 12.2 and 12 species per 0.25 m² plot. How do you quantify the variation around those numbers? The simplest index of variation is the **range**, which is the difference between the largest and smallest observations:

$$\text{Range} = 18 - 6 = 12$$

The range does not represent variation in samples very well since very different sets of observations can have the same range. A better representation of the variation in a sample is one that uses all the observations relative to the sample mean, and not just the largest and smallest samples.

The underlying distribution of the population of samples influences nearly all choices about which statistics to use. For non-normally distributed data, one common method to represent variation is to divide the samples into four equal parts, called quartiles, and use the range of measurements between the upper bound of the lowest quartile and the lower bound of the highest quartile. This representation of variation in a sample is called the **interquartile range**. For illustration, imagine you have been asked to study the recovery of mayfly nymphs following a flash flood of Tesuque Creek, New Mexico, a high mountain stream in the southern Rocky Mountains. You took samples from two forks, one disturbed and one undisturbed by the flood. Median densities are 4.5 *Baetis bicaudatus* nymphs per 0.1 m² benthic sample from the disturbed fork and 40 nymphs per 0.1 m² benthic sample in the undisturbed fork. Interquartile ranges can be seen from the data (sorted from lowest density to highest):

Sample Number	1	2	3	4	5	6	7	8	9	10	11	12
Number of nymphs, disturbed fork	2	2	**2**	3	3	4	5	6	6	**8**	10	126
Number of nymphs, undisturbed fork	12	30	**32**	35	37	38	42	48	52	**58**	71	79
Quartiles	1st			2nd			3rd			4th		

Notice that the interquartile range for the undisturbed fork is from 32 to 58; for the disturbed fork, the interquartile range is 2 to 8. In both cases, 50% of the quadrat counts in each sample fall within the respective range.

For populations that follow a normal distribution, there exist a variety of preferred methods for estimating the variation around the mean. One commonly used index is the sample **variance**. It is calculated by squaring the differences between the sample mean and each of the individual observations, adding them up to produce the "sum of squares." This value is then divided by the sample size minus one:

$$\text{Sum of squares} = \Sigma(X - \overline{X})^2$$

Using our measures of intertidal diversity, the sums of squares equals:

$$\Sigma(X - \overline{X})^2 = (15 - 12.2)^2 + (6 - 12.2)^2 + (18 - 12.2)^2 +$$
$$(17 - 12.2)^2 + (8 - 12.2)^2 + (9 - 12.2)^2 +$$
$$(12 - 12.2)^2 + (15 - 12.2)^2 +$$
$$(10 - 12.2)^2 + (12 - 12.2)^2 = 143.6$$

To calculate the sample variance, divide the sum of squares by the sample size minus 1. The sample size in this case is 10 measurements.

$$\text{Sample variance} = S^2 = \frac{\Sigma(X - \overline{X})^2}{n - 1} = \frac{143.6}{10 - 1} = 15.96 \text{ (Species per quadrat)}^2$$

Notice that the unit of the sample variance is the *square* of species number per quadrat, not species number itself. Because the sample variance is expressed in squares of the original units, we generally take the square root of the variance to calculate a measure of variation called the sample **standard deviation**.

$$\text{Standard deviation} = S = \sqrt{S^2} = \sqrt{15.96} = 3.99 \text{ species per quadrat}$$

While it took a little effort to calculate it, the standard deviation of 3.99 species per quadrat provides us with a standardized index of the variation in species number found in our intertidal study. This value, in addition to the mean of 12.2 species per quadrat, helps us understand patterns in complex ecological data sets. As you move forward in your scientific training, you will frequently use both mean and standard deviation, so you might as well take the time to truly understand them now!

As you may recall, our measures of sample mean and standard deviation are only *estimates* of the true values in the system. The only way we could ever know the true values themselves is to measure every nook and cranny of the intertidal zone, a feat that would both be extraordinarily difficult and unnecessary. It is instead much more cost effective to sample only enough to have a reliable estimate of the true values. How do you know how close a given sample mean is to the true population means?

The answer to this question depends upon two factors: the variation within the population and the number of measurements in our sample of the population. Common sense suggests that we are more likely to estimate the true mean of a population that has low variability than one that has high variability. Similarly, more observations in our sample will bring us closer to the true value than few observations. Here we will build a way of representing the precision of a given estimate of a population means. Our first step will be to calculate a statistic called the **standard error** of the mean, $s_{\overline{X}}$:

$$s_{\overline{X}} = \sqrt{\frac{s^2}{n}} + \frac{s}{\sqrt{n}}$$

where s^2 is the sample variance, s is the sample standard deviation, and n is the number of observations (sample size).

Applying this formula to our intertidal example, we find:

$$s_{\overline{X}} = \frac{s}{\sqrt{n}} = \frac{3.99}{\sqrt{15}} = 1.26 \text{ species per quadrat}$$

Now let us imagine we have sampled a second intertidal region, which surprisingly has given us the same sample mean (12.2) and the same standard deviation (3.99). However, because we were feeling refreshed after lunch, we were able to take 15, rather than 10 observations. The standard error calculated for this sample is:

$$s_{\overline{X}} = \frac{s}{\sqrt{n}} = \frac{3.99}{\sqrt{15}} = 1.03 \text{ species per quadrat}$$

Notice that because there were more quadrats in the second sample, the size of the standard error is reduced. In other words, due to increased sample size, our second sample mean is a more accurate estimate of the true population mean. We can further refine our estimate of the true population mean through the calculation of confidence intervals.

A **confidence interval** is a range of values within which the true population mean occurs with a particular probability. That probability is called the **level of confidence**, and is calculated as one minus the significance level, α, which is generally 0.05 (see the next section for a discussion of what "significance" represents):

$$\text{Level of confidence} = 1 - \alpha = 1 - 0.05 = 0.95$$

Using this level confidence produces the 95% confidence interval:

$$\text{Confidence interval (CI) for } \mu = \overline{X} \pm s_{\overline{x}}t$$

where the true population mean, $\overline{X}$, is the sample mean, $s_{\overline{x}}$ is the standard error, and t is a value from the Student's t table.

The Student's t table is available in most statistics textbooks, and is available on the Connect website. The table summarizes the values of a statistical distribution known as the Student's t distribution, and these values are used in a variety of statistical tests. The exact value of t used for calculating a confidence interval is determined by the degrees of freedom of our sample (calculated as $n - 1$) and the significance level we want, which in this cases is $\alpha = 0.05$.

Continuing the example of samples of diversity from two intertidal communities with identical means and standard deviations, but differing in sample size, we find that 2.26 and 2.14 are the t values for sample sizes of 10 and 15 respectively (at $\alpha = 0.05$). Using that information, we calculate:

Community 1: $\text{CI} = 12.2 \pm 1.26 \times 2.26 = 12.2 \pm 2.85$ species per quadrat

Community 2: $\text{CI} = 12.2 \pm 1.03 \times 2.14 = 12.2 \pm 2.20$ species per quadrat

With this confidence interval, we can say that there is a 95% probability that the true mean number of species per quadrat in community 1 is between 9.35 ($12.2 - 2.85$) and 15.05 ($12.2 + 2.85$). For community 2, the true mean number of species per quadrat is between 10 and 14.4. Put another way, the true population mean will fall within our confidence intervals 19 times out of 20. Although the mean and standard deviation are the same for the two communities, we have narrower confidence intervals for the community that we sampled more heavily.

Statistical Testing

Even though describing populations is important to many ecologists, this is only a very narrow component to the scientific method. Scientists use this information to formulate questions about the natural world and convert their questions into testable hypotheses. To evaluate the validity of a hypothesis,

it is important to know whether an observed result is different from that predicted by the hypothesis. As you will see below, the most commonly used statistical methods do not allow scientists to prove anything to be true, but instead are designed to test whether a hypothesis is false. A critical aspect of ecology is the construction of *falsifiable hypotheses*. Imagine the following two statements:

1. Blue flowers are pollinated by bumblebees.

2. Blue flowers are *not* pollinated by bumblebees.

The first assertion is very hard to test and essentially unfalsifiable. Why? Imagine you see a blue flower pollinated by a bumblebee. That would support #1 and reject #2. But now imagine you do NOT see a blue flower pollinated by a bumblebee. That supports #2, but you cannot reject #1, as the bees may have been sleeping, you may have been lazy, or you just had back luck in your sampling. In other words, #1 is a poor statistical hypothesis, as there is no data you can collect that would falsify it. In contrast, #2 is a good statistical hypothesis, as it can be falsified.

Because of the importance of falsifiable hypotheses, ecologists typically make a distinction between their working hypothesis and a statistical null hypothesis, with the latter being the one that is tested. For example, an ecologist may hypothesize that male elk are generally heavier than female elk. To test this, the ecologist will reword this as a *null hypothesis*, such as "there is no difference in mean weight between male and female elk." Data could be collected, at which point the ecologist needs to test whether the data support or reject the null hypothesis.

To determine this, we need to differentiate between the variation we find in our data that would be expected due to chance from the variation between our data and predictions that are unlikely to be caused by chance alone. When we find differences that are very unlikely to occur by chance, we refer to them as *significant* differences. The critical point here is in identifying when an observed measure, such as mean weight of elk, differs significantly from some theoretical explanation, such as the mean values for males and females will be the same. That judgment is based upon the probability of being incorrect, and there are two ways we can be incorrect.

In one scenario, we could find a significant difference between our data and our predictions, when in fact no actual difference exists. Or to put it a more formal way, we could reject our null hypothesis (that males and female elk are the same weight) when in fact our null hypothesis is true. This type of error is a *type I error*, and should occur at the frequency of α, which ecologists generally set as $P = 0.05$. Type I error rates are also called false positives, and if $\alpha = 0.05$, they will occur 5% of the time. A second type of error is a *type II error*, or a false negative. In type II errors, the data fail to reject the null hypothesis when in fact it is false. The frequency of type II errors is determined by β, which is often set to $\beta = 0.20$. In other words, in a typical study, there is a 5% probability of being wrong due to a false positive, and a 20% probability of being wrong due to false negatives—not

a particularly appealing reality! Why don't ecologists simply lower these values? α and β are related mathematically, such that decreasing one causes an increase in the other. As a result, we must balance these two unavoidable risks, and have historically felt reducing false positive rates was more important than reducing false negative rates, though there has recently been disagreement with this historical decision. If ecologists cannot simply reduce both of these errors by decree, what can we do? As you might imagine, the risks of errors will be associated to the variation in the data we are collecting. The larger the variance in our populations, the larger the risk of type I and II errors. Therefore, increasing sample size can reduce error rates. A second factor, though outside of our control, is **effect size**, the relative magnitude of difference between our two groups (i.e., are male elk 2% or 200% bigger than females). The larger the effect size, the lower the risk of statistical errors. In other words, for the same amount of sampling effort, ecologists are more likely to detect big effects than small effects, even if both actually occur.

Type I and type II errors are hazards of all statistical tests, and are not limited to ecology. As a result, all researchers place great importance in the quality of experimental designs and the ability to replicate studies, as results repeated by others give more confidence than results found only once.

The Null Hypothesis Is:		
True		*False*
The Data Find the Null Hypothesis to Be:		
True	**Data = Reality**	*Type II Error*
False	*Type I Error*	**Data = Reality**

between two variables, and we present a few in figure A.3. The most basic scatterplot is one in which there is no relationship between X and Y (fig. A.3*a*). In contrast, figure A.3*b* shows a negative relationship between the variables, in which larger values of X are associated with smaller values of Y. Figure A.3*c* shows a positive relationship, where larger values of X are associated with larger values of Y.

Scatterplots provide a visual overview of the relationships among variables in a study; however, it is equally important to perform statistical tests on the data to determine whether these relationships are likely to have arisen by chance. Two main analyses can be used for this, **correlation** and **regression**. A simple test for correlation asks whether two continuous variables are related. A regression analysis requires a plausible causal link between the two variables. For example, if we measure soil N and P, we might ask whether these variables are correlated. There is no reason to think that high soil N will cause high (or low) soil P. Instead, it is likely that some other factor generates high soil fertility for all soil nutrients. Because there is no plausible causal relationship, we test for a correlation. For parametric data, a test for correlation is generally done using the *product-moment method*, which results in the index *r*. *r* can range from -1 to $+1$, with low negative values representing a strong negative correlation and high positive values representing a strong positive correlation. Correlations in nonparametric data can be tested using the *Spearman-Rank correlation*, which results in the index r_S. The main difference between the parametric and nonparametric tests is that the former uses the actual data in its calculations, while the latter tests for correlations among ranks (smallest value = 1, second smallest = 2, etc.).

Common Statistical Tests

As we discussed before, some populations of samples will be normally distributed, while others will be non-normally distributed. Different statistical tests make different assumptions about the underlying distribution of the data. In general, these can be divided into *parametric* and *nonparametric* procedures, with the former based upon normal distributions, and the latter allowing for other distributions. In the remainder of this chapter we will discuss examples where a statistical test is needed, and provide solutions based upon parametric and nonparametric procedures. In general, we will not be providing the mathematical formulae for the procedures described, and instead we suggest that you to investigate statistics courses and books for more detailed information.

Relationships Among Variables

Ecologists are often interested in the relationship between two variables, which we might call X and Y. For example, an ecologist might be interested in seeing if there is a numerical response between predator and prey (chapter 14). One way of visualizing such relationships is with an X−Y scatterplot, with prey density on the *x*-axis and predator density on the *y*-axis. There are an infinite number of possible relationships

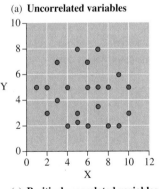

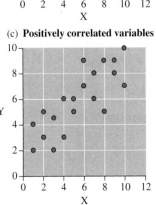

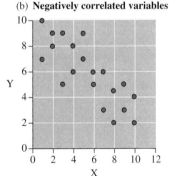

Figure A.3 A scatterplot is a useful tool for exploring relationships between any two variables X and Y.

Regression analysis is more formal in its treatment of the two variables, and is only conducted on normally-distributed data. In this analysis, there is a plausible causal link between the two factors, such that you believe the level of factor X (**independent variable**) influences the level of factor Y (**dependent variable**). For example, in a study of predator–prey interactions, you may believe that predators will move toward areas of high prey density, and thus there would be a positive relationship between these variables. In regression analysis we construct X-Y plots as before; however, we now also determine the equation for a line, called the **regression line**. The regression line is the line that best fits the relationship between X and Y. When this line is linear, the regression equation takes the form:

$$Y = bX + a$$

where a is the Y-intercept and b is the slope of the line, also called the **regression coefficient**.

Figure A.4 shows different possible outcomes of a regression analysis between predator and prey densities in three different communities. You can see from the figures that the slope varies among communities, suggesting different factors influence the relationship between prey and predator in these communities.

One statistic that can be derived from both correlation and regression analyses is the *coefficient of determination*, or R^2. This value can be calculated by squaring the r value from a correlation. There are additional methods for calculating this value in regression analysis, but the principle is the same. R^2 is a very commonly used value in ecology, and it tells us how much of the variation in Y is explained by variation in X (fig. A.4). High values represent "tighter fits" of the data to the regression line. As you can see in figure A.4, in addition to variations in slopes, the communities differ in R^2, suggesting a weaker relationship between predator–prey densities in some communities than others.

Significance values (*P-values*) can be determined for both correlations and regression, again with the risks of type I and II errors. It is important to recognize that just because you believe there to be a causal relationship between two variables

does not mean that there actually is a causal relationship between the variables, even if the statistical test is significant. The only clear way to demonstrate causality is with manipulative experiments, which is why experiments are given such prominence in science.

Differences Among Groups—Continuous Data

Correlations and regressions are very useful tools for describing relationships between two variables. However, many ecological problems involve a single variable, but multiple groups. For example, suppose you are concerned about the impacts of acid rain on the diversity of plant species in the boreal forest. You have conducted an experiment in northern Québec in which you added low pH water to ten 2 × 2 m plots, and neutral pH water to an additional ten plots over the course of several growing seasons. At the end of the experiment you measure the number of vascular plant species found in each plot:

Measurement	*1*	*2*	*3*	*4*	*5*	*6*	*7*	*8*	*9*	*10*
Low pH— Species Number	6	4	4	5	7	4	6	6	4	7
Neutral pH— Species Number	12	8	10	8	13	10	16	9	6	5

You can use are a variety of parametric and nonparametric methods to determine whether the mean number of plants is significantly reduced through the addition of low pH water. The first would simply be to graph the mean values and calculate confidence intervals for each group, as we have done in figure A.5. As you can see in the figure, the average number of plant species is lower when acidified water is added to the forest. Recall from before that the true population means for each of the study populations has a 95% chance of falling somewhere within the 95% confidence intervals. Now notice that the 95% confidence intervals do not overlap. This indicates there is less than a 5% chance that the two samples were drawn from a single larger statistical population with a common mean species density. In other words, we have a basis for saying there is a statistically significant effect of adding low

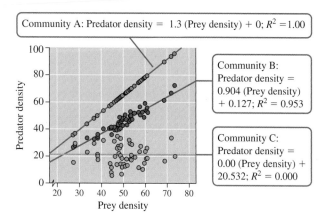

Figure A.4 Regression analysis indicates the strength and slope of the relationship between prey and predator densities in three hypothetical communities.

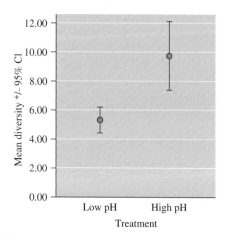

Figure A.5 Mean species diversity and 95% confidence limits for hypothetical plots treated with low and high pH water.

pH water on species diversity. There are, however, more direct ways of testing for such a difference.

As we saw in the analyses of correlation between two variables, parametric and nonparametric approaches differ in whether they use the raw data or the ranked data. We find the same difference in the analysis of groups. In our example of species diversity, we have two groups and we want to know whether the mean diversity differs between groups. The parametric procedure would be the *t*-test, and a nonparametric approach would use the *Mann-Whitney Test*. Because the *t*-test is so widely used, we present the formula here:

$$t = \frac{|\overline{X}_a - \overline{X}_n|}{s_{\overline{X}a} - \overline{X}n}$$

In this equation:

$\overline{X}_a$ = mean of sample from acidified water treatment = 5.3

$\overline{X}_n$ = mean of sample from neutral water control = 9.7

$s_{\overline{X}a} - \overline{X}n$ = the standard error of the difference between means, which is calculated as:

$$s_{\overline{X}a} - \overline{X}n = \sqrt{\frac{S_p^2}{n_a} + \frac{S_p^2}{n_n}}$$

where:

n_a = number of acidified water addition plots = 10

n_n = number of neutral water addition plots = 10

S_p^2 = pooled estimate of the variance, calculated as:

$$S_p^2 = \frac{SS_a + SS_n}{DF_a + DF_n}$$

In this equation:

SS_a = sum of squares for the samples from the acidified water addition treatment = 14.1

SS_n = sum of squares for the samples from the neutral water addition treatment = 98.1

DF_a = degrees of freedom for the acidified water addition treatment = 9

DF_n = degrees of freedom for the neutral water addition treatment = 9

Using this information, we calculate $S_p^2 = 6.23$ (species per plot)^2.

We can now calculate the standard deviation of the difference between means:

$$s_{\overline{X}a} - \overline{X}n = \sqrt{\frac{S_p^2}{n_a} + \frac{S_p^2}{n_n}} = \sqrt{\frac{6.23}{10} + \frac{6.23}{10}} = 1.12 \text{ species per plot}$$

Now we have all the values we need to calculate *t*:

$$t = \frac{|\overline{X}_a - \overline{X}_n|}{s_{\overline{X}a} - \overline{X}n} = \frac{|5.3 - 9.7|}{1.12} = 3.93$$

At this point we need to compare the calculated *t* with the appropriate critical value. To do this, we need to know both the desired level of significance ($P<0.05$ in this case), and the pooled degrees of freedom:

$$DF_{pooled} = DF_a + DF_n = 9 + 9 = 18$$

The Student's *t* for $P<0.05$ and DF = 18 is 2.10. Since our calculated value of *t*, 3.93, is greater than this critical value, the probability that the population means are the same *is less than* 0.05. Therefore we reject the null hypothesis that applying acidified and neutral water have equal effects on species diversity, and instead accept the alternative hypothesis that acidification of water reduces diversity in this forest.

The *t*-test and Mann-Whitney tests are very useful tools for comparing differences between two groups. However, there are many ecological questions that require comparison among more than two groups, and different statistical tools are needed. For example, an ecologist may wish to know whether bluegill sunfish densities differ depending upon the species identity of the dominant predator found within the pond. To test this, one approach would be to create many artificial ponds (cattle watering tanks are often used), stocking each with a constant number of sunfish. To each pond you have added one predator species, such as large-mouth bass, northern pike, or grass pickerel. After adding the predators, you measure any changes in sunfish density. With enough replicate ponds, you can test the null hypothesis that "predator species identity has no impact on sunfish density." For parametric data, the standard statistical approach for comparing among multiple groups is *ANOVA*, or the *analysis of variance*. The most commonly used test for comparisons of more than two groups with nonparametric data is the *Kruskal-Wallis* test. As with the other nonparametric tests we have discussed, this test is based upon a rank-sum approach.

A detailed explanation of how an ANOVA is calculated is beyond the scope of this text, and thus we provide only an overview here. The most basic ANOVA is a *one-way* ANOVA, in which there is a single *factor*, such as predator species identity. In this example, we want to know whether bluegill sunfish densities are differentially affected by three predators (bass, pike, and pickerel). You choose an experimental approach, using cattle watering tanks as experimental lakes. In each tank you place a known density of bluegills and one of the three species of predators, and after several weeks you measure bluegill densities. In this study, we have a single factor (predator species identity) with three levels (bass, pike, and pickerel). It is important to note that this experiment does not have a **control**, such as tanks without any predators. Why? The answer is due to the specific research question that is being asked: "does predator species identity impact sunfish densities." This is different from the question of whether predators alter sunfish densities. In our example, we are not interested in the density of sunfish in the absence of predators, only if sunfish obtain different densities with different predators. The details of the research question being tested will determine the appropriate experimental treatments and controls for each research project.

In the ANOVA we derive a statistic and compare it to a critical value to determine whether the differences we

observe among groups are likely to have occurred by chance. If not, then we reject our null hypothesis and accept the alternative hypothesis that predator identity significantly impacts bluegill densities. A critical underlying assumption of the ANOVA is that all samples taken come from a single statistical population. This assumption is the null hypothesis, and the goal of the statistical test is to determine the likelihood that it is true. Like all populations, there will exist variation in the individual values of data around the mean. In ANOVA, significant effects of the factors are found if the amount of variation that can be attributed to the factor (between groups) is high relative to the amount of variation within a single level of a factor (within groups). In other words, if most of the overall variation in the data set is due to difference among groups, you likely will find a significant difference among groups. The test statistic used in ANOVA is the *F*-ratio, as it is a ratio of between-group variation to within-group variation.

ANOVAs are very flexible statistical tools, and can be expanded to allow for more than a single factor in the experimental model. For example, suppose you believe that predator identity only will impact bluegill densities if the predators are at low abundance. At high abundance, you think all predators will be very efficient at reducing prey numbers. To test this, you again use experimental ponds in which you vary species identity (Factor A, 3 levels), but you also include a second factor of predator density by stocking predators at either high or low densities (Factor B, 2 levels). In a *factorial design*, you have treatment combinations such that every level of every factor is found in combination with each other. In this example, you would have a total of six treatment combinations: (1) predator A, low density, (2) predator A, high density, (3) predator B, low density, (4) predator B, high density, (5) predator C, low density, and (6) predator C, high density.

ANOVA partitions the total variation in the data set into groups including predator identity (between groups), predator density (between groups), and the overall with-in group variation. In two-way ANOVAs (and other multi-way ANOVAs), an additional term may explain some of the variation in the data, and that is the interaction between the two factors (predator identity × predator density). Interaction terms are critical to many ecological studies, as many processes are likely to be important not by themselves, but in combination with other factors. For example, in this case you have predicted that predator species identity will only impact sunfish density if predator density is low, and this can be seen in figure A.6. In more general terms, this means that the effect of one factor is dependent upon the level of another factor. Such situations are common in ecology, and you encountered many throughout the text. It is the ability to extend beyond two levels and include more than one factor that make ANOVAs a statistical workhorse in ecology.

Differences Among Groups—Categorical Data

So far we have only discussed ecological questions that generate continuous response variables, such as number of species or elk weight. However, many types of ecological data are categorical, such as flower colour or gender. If you were

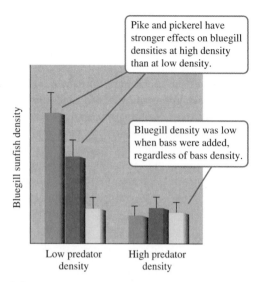

Figure A.6 Hypothetical interaction between predator species identity and predator density on bluegill sunfish densities.

interested in whether some factor influenced flower colour, *t*-tests would clearly be inappropriate: what is the average of blue and red? (No, it is not purple!) Fortunately there exists a set of statistical approaches that allow an ecologist to test whether the distributions of character states in a population differ from what would be expected by chance.

The simplest method to test hypotheses concerning the relationship between observed and hypothesized frequencies is the **chi-square (χ^2)** "goodness of fit" test. This test is used to judge how well an observed distribution of frequencies matches one expected from a particular hypothesis. Let's explore this test using the frequency of flower colours in a hypothetical population of *Claytonia virginica*, Spring Beauty. These plants are common in the forest understory throughout much of central and eastern North America, and different plants produce flowers that vary in colour from pure white to very dark pink. You explore a population in southern Ontario and are able to find 90 plants in flower, with individual plants displaying either white, light pink, or dark pink flowers. Let's consider this hypothetical data set and test the hypothesis that the three phenotypes are present in equal frequencies in the population.

Flower Colour	*Observed Frequency (O)*	*Expected Frequency (E)*
White	45	30
Light Pink	30	30
Dark Pink	15	30

Because our null hypothesis is that the phenotypes are present in equal proportions, and we have three possible phenotypes, our expected frequency for each phenotype is simply 1/3 the total number of samples (90) in our study population. The values of 45, 30, and 15 represent the number of individuals we encountered of each phenotype in this hypothetical population. The question then becomes: Is 45, 30, 15 significantly different from 30, 30, 30?

The value of χ^2 is calculated as:

$$\chi^2 = \Sigma \frac{(O - E)^2}{E}$$

where O is the observed frequency of a particular group and E is the expected frequency.

For this example:

$$\chi^2 = \Sigma \frac{(O - E)^2}{E} = \frac{(45 - 30)^2}{30} + \frac{(30 - 30)^2}{30} + \frac{(15 - 30)^2}{30} = 15$$

The next step is to determine whether this value of χ^2 is greater than that expected by chance, given this number of degrees of freedom. To do this, we again consult a list of critical χ^2 values, in this case for 2 degrees of freedom and $P<0.05$. Our observed value of 15 is greater than the critical value of 5.991, and thus we can conclude that there is a significant difference in the frequencies of the three flower colour phenotypes in this population.

The χ^2 "goodness of fit" test is a powerful tool for identifying differences in frequencies among groups within a single population. However, how would you test whether some treatment (e.g., fertilization) had a significant impact on the frequency of flower colours? These questions are analogous to those we address using ANOVA and *t*-tests for continuous data, but the "goodness of fit" test is insufficient. Fortunately, there exist several statistical approaches, such as the χ^2 "test for independence" and Fisher's exact test that are well suited for this purpose. We direct you to the Online Learning Centre for more information on the "test for independence." You will also find more approaches to analyzing categorical data in advanced courses and statistical textbooks.

More Complex Problems

Believe it or not, the statistics we have just described are only a basic introduction to what is a very diverse and complex set of analytical tools. Like all tools, proficiency increases with use. Also like all tools, they are generally used for a reason. In ecology, we simply are unable to answer even the most basic questions without a means to synthesize extremely complex data sets. In other words, statistical methods are just as important to ecology as are sampling natural populations, coming up with good questions, or any other part of the scientific method.

As the complexity of the scientific question increases, so too does the statistical methodology. Imagine the following ecological research questions. Many questions are centred on how whole communities, rather than individual species, respond to environmental changes. These questions are *multivariate*, rather than *univariate* in nature, which means that each species of the community represents a different dimension in the analysis. In more practical terms, this means you need a statistical method that allows for more than one *response variable*, not just more than one factor. Fortunately a variety of methods have been developed including MANOVA (multivariate analysis of variance), ordinations, and other classification methods. These latter approaches help reduce the complexity of data sets, allowing the ecologist to see underlying patterns. Although we will not discuss the details of these approaches here, results from such analyses were presented throughout the text.

Two factors that also greatly increase the complexity of ecological studies are variations in ecological patterns and processes in space and time. In other words, precipitation might strongly influence plant growth in some years but not in others. Similarly, elk may compete for forage in some locations but not in others. Understanding the contributions of spatial and temporal patterns can be critical to a holistic understanding of a natural system. Fortunately, there are advanced statistical methods to address these questions as well.

GLOSSARY

A

A horizon a biologically active soil layer consisting of a mixture of mineral materials, such as clay, silt, and sand, as well as organic material, derived from the overlying O horizon; generally characterized by leaching.

absolute density See *density*.

abundance the total number of individuals, or biomass, of a species present in a specified area.

abyssal zone a zone of the ocean depths between 4,000 and 6,000 m.

acclimation physiological adjustment to change in an environmental factor, such as temperature or salinity.

actual evapotranspiration (AET) the amount of water lost from an ecosystem to the atmosphere due to a combination of evaporation and transpiration by plants.

adaptation an evolutionary process that changes anatomy, physiology, or behaviour, resulting in an increased ability of a population to live in a particular environment. The term is also applied to the anatomical, physiological, or behavioural characteristics produced by this process.

adhesion-adapted seeds with hooks, spines, or barbs that disperse by attaching to passing animals.

age distribution the distribution of individuals among age groups in a population; also called age structure.

albedo the proportion of incident radiation reflected by a surface.

allele one of the alternative forms of the same gene.

allochthonous inputs organic matter derived or created in a community external to the one in which they are eventually deposited.

allopatric speciation speciation that occurs when isolating mechanisms evolve among geographically separated populations.

allopolyploidy a process of speciation initiated by hybridization of two different species.

alluvial groundwater water that is derived from a surface stream in contrast to groundwater that is derived from underground streams and high water tables.

alternative states an ecological theory that suggests that a given location can persist as different community types depending upon disturbance regimes, nutrient inputs, and other external factors.

amensalism an ecological interaction in which one organism is harmed while other participants are neither harmed nor helped. A "–0" interaction.

ammonification the conversion of organic forms of nitrogen to ammonium, generally mediated by bacteria.

anadromous fish that hatch and spawn in fresh water, but live most of their lives in salt water.

aposematic colouration bright and conspicuous colouration displayed by many toxic or distasteful potential prey species.

arbuscular mycorrhizal fungi (AMF) mycorrhizae in which the mycorrhizal fungus produces arbuscules (sites of exchange between plant and fungus), hyphae (fungal filaments), and vesicles (fungal energy storage organs within root conex cells).

arbuscule a bush-shaped organ on an endomycorrhizal fungus that acts as a site of material exchange between the fungus and its host plant.

archaea prokaryotes distinguished from bacteria on the basis of structural, physiological, and other biological features.

aril a fleshy covering of some seeds that attracts birds and other vertebrates, which act as dispersers of such seeds.

assortative mating mating among phenotypically similar (positive assortative mating), or dissimilar (negative assortative mating), individuals.

atoll a circle of low islands and coral reefs that ring a lagoon, generally formed on a submerged mountain called a seamount.

autotroph an organism that can synthesize organic molecules using inorganic molecules and energy from either sunlight (photosynthetic autotrophs) or from inorganic molecules, such as hydrogen sulphide (chemosynthetic autotrophs).

B

B horizon a subsoil in which materials leached from above, generally from the A horizon, accumulate. May be rich in clay, organic matter, iron, and other materials.

barrier reef a long, ridgelike reef that parallels the mainland and is separated from it by a deep lagoon.

Batesian mimicry evolution of a nonnoxious species to resemble a poisonous or inedible species.

bathypelagic zone a zone within the deep ocean that extends from about 1,000 to 4,000 m.

behavioural ecology study of the relationships between organisms and environment that are mediated by behaviour.

benthic refers to the bottom of bodies of waters such as seas, lakes, or streams.

bioaccumulation the process by which toxic substances increase in concentration within a living organism due to intake rates greater than excretion and metabolism.

biocontrol the deliberate introduction of some agent (herbivore, pathogen, etc.) that will exploit an invasive species, reducing its population size.

biological species concept a group of actually or potentially inter-breeding populations, which are reproductively isolated from other such groups.

biomagnification increase in toxin levels with increased trophic position within a food web, due to predators eating contaminated prey.

biome large-scale classification of terrestrial habitats, distinguished primarily by their predominant plants and are associated with particular climates. They consist of distinctive plant formations such as the tropical rain forest biome and the desert biome.

biosphere the portions of earth that support life; also refers to the total global ecosystem.

bog peat-forming wetlands with precipitation being the source of water entering the system.

boreal forest northern forests that occupy the area south of arctic tundra. Though dominated by coniferous trees, they also contain aspen and birch. Also called taiga.

bottom-up control control of a community or ecosystem by physical or chemical factors, such as temperature or nutrient availability.

brood parasite a species (generally birds) that lays its eggs in the nests of others, relying on the unrelated individuals to provide parental care

bundle sheath a structure, which surrounds the leaf veins of C_4 plants, made up of cells where four-carbon acids produced during carbon fixation are broken down to three-carbon acids and CO_2.

buttress roots large roots on all sides of a tree that occur above the soil surface, providing structural support rather than nutrient capture.

C

C horizon a soil layer composed of largely unaltered parent material, little affected by biological activity.

C_3 photosynthesis the photosynthetic pathway used by most plants and all algae, in which the product of the initial reaction is phosphoglyceric acid, or PGA, a three-carbon acid.

C_4 photosynthesis photosynthesis in which CO_2 is fixed in mesophyll cells by combining it with phosphoenol pyruvate, or PEP, to produce a four-carbon acid. Plants using C_4 photosynthesis are generally more drought tolerant than plants employing C_3 photosynthesis.

CAM (crassulacean acid metabolism) photosynthesis a photosynthetic pathway largely limited to succulent plants in arid and semiarid environments, in which carbon fixation takes place at night, when lower temperatures reduce the rate of water loss during CO_2 uptake. The resulting four-carbon acids are stored until daylight, when they are broken down into pyruvate and CO_2.

carnivore an organism that consumes flesh; approximately synonymous with predator.

carrying capacity (K) the maximum population of a species that a particular ecosystem can sustain.

caste a group of individuals that are physically distinctive and engage in specialized behaviour within a social unit, such as a colony.

cavitation rapid formation of air bubbles within the xylem of plants.

character displacement changes in the physical characteristics of a species' population as a consequence of natural selection for reduced interspecific competition.

chemosynthetic autotrophs that use inorganic molecules as a source of carbon and energy.

chi-square (χ^2) a statistic used to measure how much a sample distribution differs from a theoretical distribution.

chronosequence a series of communities or ecosystems representing a range of ages or times since disturbance.

climate diagram a standardized form of representing average patterns of variation in temperature and precipitation that identifies several ecologically important climatic factors such as relatively moist periods and periods of drought.

climax community a community that occurs late in succession and whose populations remain stable until disrupted by disturbance.

cline See *ecocline*.

clumped distribution individuals in a population have a much higher probability of being found in some areas than in others; individuals are aggregated rather than dispersed.

coefficient of relationship the probability that the alleles at a given locus will be identical by descent among two individuals in the population.

coevolution a reciprocal evolutionary interaction between two or more species.

cohort a group of individuals of the same age.

cohort life table a life table based on individuals born (or beginning life in some other way) at the same time.

colonization cycle   when stream populations are maintained through a dynamic interplay between downstream drift and upstream dispersal.

combined response   the combined effect of functional and numerical responses by consumers on prey populations; determined by multiplying the number of prey eaten per predator times the number of predators per unit area, giving the number of prey eaten per unit area. Combined response is generally expressed as a percentage of the total number of prey.

commensalism   an ecological interaction in which one organism receives a benefit while other participants are neither harmed nor helped. A "+,0" interaction.

community   an association of interacting species living in a particular area; also often defined as all of the organisms living in a particular area.

community assembly rules   the processes that limit or promote coexistence.

community ecology   the scientific study of interactions among species within a community.

community structure   attributes of a community, such as the number of species or the distribution of individuals among species within the community.

competition coefficient   expresses the magnitude of the negative effect of individuals of one species on individuals of a second species.

competitive exclusion principle   two species with identical niches cannot coexist indefinitely.

competitive hierarchies   a nested ranking of species by competitive ability.

conduction   the movement of heat between objects in direct physical contact.

confidence interval   a range of values within which the true population mean occurs with a particular probability called the level of confidence.

conservation threshold   a level of habitat loss and/or fragmentation below which a population is sustainable, and above which the population is likely to go extinct.

constitutive defences   chemical or morphological defences that are produced continuously, regardless of whether the organism has been previously attacked. Contrast with induced defences.

consumptive effects of predation   the direct effects of predators on prey populations through the capture and consumption of living prey.

control   in an experiment, the individuals/plots/units to which the experimental treatment of interest is not applied.

convection   the process of heat flow or transfer to a moving fluid, such as wind or flowing water.

cooperative breeding   a social system in which adults help in the care for young that are not necessarily their own.

Coriolis effect   a phenomenon caused by the rotation of the earth, which produces a deflection of winds and water currents to the right of their direction of travel in the Northern Hemisphere and to the left of their direction of travel in the Southern Hemisphere.

correlation   a statistical test to determine whether two variables are related.

corridors   regions of a landscape that provide connections among habitat fragments, potentially resulting in enhanced flow or movement of individuals or genes.

D

dead zones   hypoxic areas (< 2mg/L oxygen) in aquatic systems, typically a consequence of pollution, eutrophication, and high rates of decomposition, that are essentially devoid of marine life.

decomposition   the breakdown of organic matter accompanied by the release of carbon dioxide and other inorganic compounds; a key process in nutrient cycling.

denitrification   the conversion of nitrate to gaseous nitrogen, generally mediated by bacteria.

density   the number of individuals in a population per unit area.

density-dependent factor   biotic factors in the environment, such as disease and competition, whose effects on populations may be related to, or depend upon, local population density.

density-independent factor   abiotic factors in the environment, such as floods and extreme temperature, whose effects on populations may be independent of population density.

dependent variable   the variable traditionally plotted on the vertical or "Y" axis of a scatter plot.

desert   an arid biome occupying approximately 20% of the land surface of the earth in which water loss due to evaporation and transpiration by plants exceeds precipitation during most of the year.

detritivore   organisms that feed on nonliving organic matter.

diffusion   transport of material due to the random movement of particles; net movement is from areas of high concentration to areas of low concentration.

directional selection   a form of natural selection that favours an extreme phenotype over other phenotypes.

disclimax community   a community whose species composition is maintained through time by frequent disturbances such as drought or grazing.

disease   an atypical conditions in living organisms that causes some sort of physiological impairment.

dispersal limitation   the absence of a species from a community due to a lack of propagules entering the community.

disruptive selection   a form of natural selection that favours two or more extreme phenotypes over the average phenotype in a population.

distribution   the natural geographic range of an organism or the spatial arrangement of individuals in a local population.

disturbance   White and Pickett (1985) define disturbance as any relatively discrete event that disrupts an ecosystem, community, or population structure and changes resources, substrate availability, or the physical environment.

DNA sequencing   methods for determining the sequence of nucleic acids in DNA molecules.

dominance   a species that is substantially more common than the other species in the community.

drift   the active or passive downstream movement of stream organisms.

drumlin   a smooth hill, or series of hills, formed as a glacier cuts through a moraine.

dry deposition   fallout of particulate material from the air by means other than with precipitation in rain or snow.

E

ecocline   a gradual change in genotype and/or phenotype of a species over a large geographic area.

ecological density   the number of individuals of a species per unit area of suitable habitat.

ecological function   any of a number of biological, chemical, or physical processes that occur within an ecological system; typically with relevance to human needs or uses. Examples include biomass production, nutrient cycling, and provisioning of suitable habitat for wildlife.

ecological network   the interactions that occur among co-occurring species in a community.

ecological services   the processes and resources provided by ecological systems that are of value to humans.

ecological stoichiometry   the study of the balance of multiple chemical elements in ecological interactions, for example, in trophic interactions.

ecology   study of the relationships between organisms and the environment.

ecosystem ecology   the subdiscipline of ecology that focuses on the flow of energy and nutrients among the biotic and abiotic components of an ecosystem.

ecosystem engineers   species whose activity creates, or fundamentally alters, habitats.

ecotone   a spatial transition from one type of ecosystem to another; for instance, the transition from a woodland to a grassland.

ecotype   a genetically identifiable subclass of a species that has evolved in response to local environmental conditions.

ectomycorrhizae (ECM)   an association between a fungus and plant roots in which the fungus forms a mantle around roots and a netlike structure around root cells.

ectotherm   an organism that relies mainly on external sources of energy for regulating body temperature.

effect size   statistical measurement of the magnitude of a treatment effect.

El Niño   a large-scale coupled oceanic-atmospheric system that has major effects on climate worldwide. During an El Niño, the sea surface temperature in the eastern Pacific Ocean is higher than average and barometric pressure is lower.

elaiosome   a structure on the surface of some seeds generally containing oils attractive to ants, which act as dispersers of such seeds.

emigration   the movement of an organism out of a population.

endemic   naturally occurring in only a single geographic region.

endotherm   an organism that relies mainly on internal sources of energy for regulating body temperature.

epilimnion   the warm, well-lighted surface layer of lakes.

epipelagic zone   the warm, well-lighted surface layer of the oceans.

epiphyte   a plant, such as an orchid, that grows on the surface of another plant but that is not parasitic.

equilibrium   a state of balance in a system in which opposing factors cancel each other.

equilibrium model of island biogeography   a model developed by MacArthur and Wilson that predicts species diversity and rates of turnover on islands as a function of island sizes and location.

esker   a long and narrow ridge of glacial debris deposited by meltwater.

estivation   a dormant state that some animals enter during the summer; involves a reduction of metabolic rate.

estuary   the lowermost part of a river, which is under the influence of the tides and is a mixture of seawater and freshwater.

euphotic zone   the upper parts of aquatic environments that receive enough light to support photosynthesis.

eusociality   highly specialized sociality generally including (1) individuals of more than one generation living together, (2) cooperative care of young, and (3) division of individuals into sterile, or nonreproductive, and reproductive castes.

eutrophic   a term applied to lakes, and sometimes to other ecosystems, with high nutrient content and high biological production.

eutrophication   nutrient enrichment of a water body through natural processes or pollution, generally causing rapid algal growth and reduced dissolved oxygen levels.

evaporation   the process by which a liquid changes from liquid phase to a gas, as in the change from liquid water to water vapour.

evolution   a change in gene frequencies within a population over time.

evolutionary stable strategy   a behavioural strategy that is resistant to invasion, and most likely to be maintained by natural selection.

exploitation   an interaction between species that enhances the fitness of the exploiting individual—the predator, the herbivore, etc.—while reducing the fitness of the exploited individual—the prey or host.

exploitative competition   use of a shared and limiting resource by two or more individuals.

exponential population growth   a J-shaped pattern of population increase where the change in numbers with time is the product of the per capita rate of increase, r, and population size, N.

F

facilitation model   a situation in which pioneer species modify the environment in such a way that it becomes less suitable for themselves and more suitable for species characteristic of later successional stages.

facultative mutualism   a mutualistic relationship between two species that is not required for the survival of the two species.

fecundity   the number of offspring produced by an organism.

fecundity schedule   a table of birthrates for females of different ages in a population.

female   sex that produces larger, more energetically costly gametes (eggs or ova).

fen   peat-forming wetlands that obtain water both through precipitation and groundwater.

fetch   the longest distance over which wind can blow across a body of water; directly related to the maximum size of waves that can be generated by wind.

fitness   the number of offspring contributed by an individual relative to the number of offspring produced by other members of the population. Ultimately defined as the relative genetic contribution of individuals to future generations.

flood pulse concept   a theory of river ecology identifying periodic flooding as an essential organizer of river ecosystem structure and functioning.

food web   a summary of the feeding relationships within an ecological community.

founder effect   a decrease in genetic diversity associated with the formation of a new, small population.

frequency-dependent selection   the fitness of a genotype depends upon its relative abundance within a population.

fringing reef   a coral reef that forms near the shore of an island or continent.

functional response   an increase in animal feeding rate, which eventually levels off, that occurs in response to an increase in food availability.

fundamental niche   the physical conditions under which a species might live, in the absence of interactions with other species.

G

generalist   a predator or herbivore that regularly includes a variety of prey species as part of its diet.

generation time, T   the average age within a population at which a female gives birth to her offspring. Note that this number is larger than the age of first reproduction if the female has multiple reproductive events.

geographic information system (GIS)   a computer-based system that stores, analyzes, and displays geographic information, generally in the form of maps.

geometric population growth   generations do not overlap and successive generations differ in size by a constant ratio.

geometric rate of increase (λ)   the ratio of the population size at two points in time: $\lambda = N_{t+1}/N_t$ where N_{t+1} is the size of the population at some future time and N_t is the size of the population at some earlier time.

glacial age   periods of variably cool and warm global temperatures that can last for millions of years. Within a glacial age will be a number of glaciations and interglacial periods.

glacial refugia   areas that occur within the extent of a glacial landscape that remained uncovered by glaciers.

glaciation   cold periods generally lasting between 60,000–90,000 years within a glacial age. During glaciations, glaciers increase in size across the planet.

global ecology   the subdiscipline of ecology that focuses on the study of the biosphere.

global positioning system (GPS)   a device that determines locations on the earth's surface, including latitude, longitude, and altitude, using radio signals from satellites as references.

gonadosomatic index (GSI)   an index of reproductive effort calculated as ovary weight divided by body weight and adjusted for the number of batches of offspring produced per year.

granivore   an animal that feeds chiefly on seeds.

gross primary production   the total amount of energy fixed by all the autotrophs in an ecosystem.

group selection   selection on traits benefiting a group, even if these traits are detrimental to the individual that possesses the trait.

guild   a group of organisms that make their living in a similar way; for example, the seed-eating animals in a desert, the fruit-eating birds in a tropical rain forest, or the filter-feeding invertebrates in a stream.

gyre   a large-scale, circular oceanic current that moves to the right (clockwise) in the Northern Hemisphere and to the left (counter-clockwise) in the Southern Hemisphere.

H

habitat fragmentation   the division of a previously intact habitat into several isolated patches, typically due to human development and resource extraction.

hadal zone   the deepest parts of the oceans, below about 6,000 m.

haplodiploidy   sex inheritance in which males are haploid and females are diploid.

Hardy-Weinberg principle   a principle that in a population mating at random in the absence of evolutionary forces, allele frequencies will remain constant.

herbivore   organisms that eats plants.

herd immunity   resistance of a population to the spread of a disease due to high rates of immunity among individuals within the population.

heritability   the proportion of total phenotypic variation in a trait attributable to genetic variation; determines the potential for evolutionary change in a trait.

hermaphrodite   an individual capable of producing both sperm or pollen and eggs or ova.

heterotroph   an organism that uses organic molecules both as a source of carbon and as a source of energy.

hibernation   a dormant state, involving reduced metabolic rate, that occurs in some animals during the winter.

homeotherm   an organism that uses metabolic energy to maintain a relatively constant body temperature; such organisms are often called warm-blooded.

horizontal transmission   the transfer of diseases among different individuals of the same generation.

host race   genetically distinct subpopulations or species that are spatially differentiated as a function of their host species.

humus   partially decomposed organic matter, generally found in soil.

hydrologic cycle   the sun-driven cycle of water through the biosphere through evaporation, transpiration, condensation, precipitation, and runoff.

hyperosmotic   organisms with body fluids with a lower concentration of water and higher solute concentration than the external environment.

hyphae   long, thin filaments that form the basic structural unit of fungi.

hypolimnion   the deepest layer of a lake below the epilimnion and thermocline.

hypoosmotic   organisms with body fluids with a higher concentration of water and lower solute concentration than the external environment.

hyporheic zone   a zone below the benthic zone of a stream; a zone of transition between surface, streamwater flow, and groundwater.

I

I_{sat}   the irradiance required to saturate the photosynthetic capacity of a photosynthetic organism.

immigration   the movement of an organism into a population.

immobilization   the conversion of inorganic ions, such as nitrate, into organic compounds, such as proteins.

inbreeding   mating between close relatives. Inbreeding tends to increase levels of homozygosity in populations and often results in offspring with lower survival and reproductive rates.

inclusive fitness   overall fitness determined by the survival and reproduction of an individual, plus the survival and reproduction of genetic relatives of the individual.

independent variable   the variable traditionally plotted on the horizontal or "X" axis of a scatter plot.

induced defences   chemical or morphological defences that are produced or enhanced in response to an attack by a predator or herbivore.

inhibition model   a model of succession that proposes that early occupants of an area modify the environment in a way that makes the area less suitable for both early and late successional species.

initial floristics   a model of succession in which most species are able to colonize a habitat soon after a disturbance. Species become more or less abundant over time due to shifts in limiting resources and environmental conditions.

insurance hypothesis   the theory that increased diversity increases community stability due to an increased probability of there being some species present in the community able to cope with any particular disturbance.

interdisciplinary research   investigations that involve researchers from multiple disciplines working closely to produce an understanding that integrates across disciplines; may include several scientific disciplines or extend beyond the boundaries of the natural sciences into the social sciences and humanities.

interference competition   form of competition involving direct antagonistic interactions between individuals.

interglacial periods   relatively short warm periods (10,000–40,000 years) that occur between glaciations in a glacial age. During interglacials, glaciers retreat across the planet. Even without human-induced climate change, the planet is currently in an interglacial period.

interquartile range   a range of measurements that includes the middle 50% of the measurements or observations in a sample, bounded by the lowest value of the highest 25% of measurements and the highest value of the lowest 25% of measurements.

intersexual selection   sexual selection occurring when members of one sex choose mates from among the members of the opposite sex on the basis of some anatomical or behavioural trait, generally leading to the elaboration of that trait.

interspecific competition   competition between individuals of different species.

intertidal zone   See *littoral zone.*

intrasexual selection   sexual selection in which individuals of one sex compete among themselves for mates.

intraspecific competition   competition between individuals of the same species.

intrinsic rate of increase   the maximum per capita rate of population increase; may be approached under ideal environmental conditions for a species.

introduced (exotic or non-native) species   a species currently found outside its historical range. Determination of the date used to define a historical range is arbitrary.

invasive species   a species that is able to rapidly increase its population size and species range, often to the detriment of the surrounding species. Both native and introduced species have the potential to be invasive species

irradiance   the level of light intensity, often measured as photon flux density.

isoclines of zero population growth   lines, in the graphical representation of the Lotka–Volterra competition model, where population growth of the species in competition is zero.

isolating mechanisms   some process that prevents the production of a viable offspring between two individuals. Isolating mechanisms are critical to species integrity, and can occur pre- or postzygote formation.

isosmotic   organisms with body fluids containing the same concentration of water and solutes as the external environment.

iteroparity   reproduction that involves production of an organism's offspring in two or more events, generally spaced out over the life time of the organism.

K

kettle   a small depression on the landscape formed by a block of glacial ice melting in place.

keystone species   species that, despite low biomass, exert strong effects on the structure of the communities they inhabit.

kin selection   selection in which individuals increase their inclusive fitness by helping increase the survival and reproduction of relatives (kin) that are not offspring.

L

La Niña   the opposite of an El Niño, where the sea surface temperature in the eastern Pacific Ocean is lower than average and barometric pressure is higher.

landscape   an area of land containing a patchwork of ecosystems.

landscape ecology   the study of landscape structure and processes.

landscape elements   the ecosystems in a landscape, which generally form a mosaic of visually distinctive patches.

landscape structure   the size, shape, composition, number, and position of ecosystems within a landscape.

large-scale phenomena   phenomena of a geographic scale rather than a local scale.

lateritic soil   soils containing high concentrations of iron and aluminum and low concentrations of many essential plant nutrients. These soils are commonly caused by extensive weathering of the parent materials.

law of toleration   the abundance and distribution of an animal can be determined by the deviation between the local conditions and the optimum set of conditions for a species.

level of confidence   one minus the significance level, α, which is generally 0.05; for example, level of confidence = $1 - 0.05 = 0.95$.

LHF horizon   the L, F, and H layers, known collectively as the LFH horizon, consist of leaves, twigs, and other organic materials. LFH horizons are found primarily in upland habitats, such as forests.

life history   the adaptations of an organism that influence aspects of its biology, such as the number of offspring it produces, its survival, and its size and age at reproductive maturity.

life table   age-specific survival and death, or mortality, rates in a population.

light compensation point (LCP)   that amount of light necessary for a plant's respiration rate to equal its photosynthetic rate.

limnetic zone   the open lake beyond the littoral zone.

littoral zone   the shallowest waters along a lake or ocean shore; where rooted aquatic plants may grow in lakes.

logistic equation $dN/dt = r_{max} N(K - N/K)$. This equation can be rearranged and presented as $dN/dt = r_{max} N(1 - N/K)$.

logistic population growth   a pattern of growth that produces a sigmoidal, or S-shaped, population growth curve; population size levels off at carrying capacity (K).

M

macroclimate   the prevailing climate for a region.

macroecology   a subdiscipline of ecology that focuses on the study of ecological patterns and processes that occur over a large geographic extent.

macronutrient   essential elements required in large concentrations within an organisms.

male   sex that produces smaller less costly gametes (sperm or pollen).

mangrove forest   a forest of subtropical and tropical marine shores dominated by salt-tolerant woody plants, such as *Rhizophora* and *Avicennia*.

marginal value theorem   developed by Eric Charnov, this is a theory based on optimality that describes the "optimal" time for a forager to move from one food patch to another.

masting   the synchronous production of large quantities of fruits by plants, such as oaks and some grass species.

mating system   the social structure of a population in relation to sexual interactions and offspring rearing. Examples include monogamy and polygynandry.

matric force   a force resulting from water's tendency to adhere to the walls of containers such as cell walls or the soil particles lining a soil pore.

matrix   the landscape element within a landscape mosaic that is the most continuous spatially, for example, the forest that surrounds small isolated patches of meadow.

maximum sustainable yield (MSY)   the maximum harvest of a species that can occur without reducing population growth rates.

Mediterranean woodland and shrubland   a biome associated with mild, moist winter conditions and usually with dry summers. Vegetation is characterized by small, tough (sclerophyllous) leaves and adaptations to fire. This biome is found around the Mediterranean Sea and in western North America, Chile, southern Australia, and southern Africa. Also known as chaparral, garrigue, maquis, and fynbos.

mesocosm   an experimental system that is intermediate between field and laboratory conditions.

mesopelagic zone   a middle depth zone of the oceans, extending from about 200 to 1,000 m.

meta-analysis   a statistical technique that combines the results of several studies on a single topic to test specific hypotheses.

metabolic heat   energy released within an organism during the process of cellular respiration.

metabolic water   water released during oxidation of organic molecules.

metalimnion   a depth zone between the epilimnion and hypolimnion characterized by rapid decreases in temperature and increases in water density with depth. Often used synonymously with the term *thermocline*.

metapopulation   a group of subpopulations living in separate locations with active exchange of individuals among subpopulations.

microclimate   a small-scale variation in climate caused by a distinctive substrate, location, or aspect.

microcosm   small models of natural systems that allow experimental manipulation

micronutrient   essential elements required in only small concentrations.

microsatellite DNA   sequence of randomly repetitive DNA, 10 to 100 base pairs long.

mineralization   the breakdown of organic matter from organic to inorganic form during decomposition.

mixotroph   species that are able to gain energy both from photosynthesis and from consuming organic or inorganic compounds.

monogamy   a mating system in which one male and one female have an exclusive relationship, at least for some duration of time.

moraine   large piles of glacial till, typically formed along the edges of a glacier.

Müllerian mimicry   comimicry among several species of noxious organisms.

mutualism   interactions between individuals of different species that benefit both partners.

mycorrhizae   a mutualistic association between fungi and the roots of plants.

N

natural selection   differential reproduction and survival of individuals in a population due to environmental influences on the population; proposed by Charles Darwin as the primary mechanism driving evolution.

neap tide   tides occurring during the 1st and 3rd quarter phases of the moon, when tidal fluctuations are the smallest.

nectar robbers   animals that visit flowers and remove nectar without providing pollination services

neritic zone   a coastal zone of the oceans, extending to the margin of a continental shelf, where the ocean is about 200 m deep.

net primary production (NPP)   the amount of energy left over after autotrophs have met their own energetic needs (gross primary production minus respiration by primary producers); the amount of energy available to the consumers in an ecosystem.

net reproductive rate (R_0)   the average number of offspring produced by an individual in a population.

neutralism   an ecological interaction in which all participants are neither harmed nor helped. A "0, 0" interaction.

niche   the set of biotic and abiotic conditions in which an organism is able to survive and reproduce. See also *fundamental niche* and *realized niche*.

nitrification   the conversion of ammonia to nitrate, generally mediated by bacteria.

nitrogen use efficiency (NUE)   the magnitude of plant growth per unit nitrogen.

nonconsumptive effects of predation   changes to prey that result as a consequence of predators being present, including shifts in morphological traits, stress-physiology, and altered behaviour.

nonequilibrial theory   theories of ecological systems that do not assume equilibrial conditions.

nonsymbiotic relationship   An ecological relationship in which the participants live most of their lives distant from each other. For example, the birds that pollinate a flower.

nontarget effects   negative effects of a biocontrol agent on species other than the intended invasive target.

normal distribution   a bell-shaped distribution, proportioned so that predictable proportions of observations or measurements fall within one, two, or three standard deviations of the mean.

North Atlantic Oscillation (NAO)   an interannual fluctuation in atmospheric pressure between Iceland and the Azores off the coast of Portugal. Changes in the NAO are associated with altered climate and can have impacts on numerous plant and animal species.

Northern Hemisphere Annular Mode (NAM)   an interannual fluctuation in atmospheric pressure in the northern polar regions; generally synchronized with the North Atlantic Oscillation.

numerical response   change in the density of a predator population in response to increased prey density.

nunatak   a unique form of glacial refugia in which a mountain peak was surrounded, but not covered by, continental glaciers.

nutrient   chemical substance required for the development, maintenance, and reproduction of organisms.

nutrient cycling   the use, transformation, movement, and reuse of nutrients in ecosystems.

nutrient retentiveness   the tendency of an ecosystem to retain nutrients.

nutrient spiraling   a representation of nutrient dynamics in streams which, because of downstream displacement of organisms and materials, are better represented by a spiral than a cycle.

O

O (organic) horizon   the most superficial soil layer containing substantial amounts of organic matter, including whole leaves, twigs, other plant parts, and highly fragmented organic matter.

obligate mutualism   a mutualistic relationship in which species are so dependent upon the relationship that they cannot live in its absence.

oceanic zone   the open ocean beyond the continental shelf with water depths generally greater than 200 m.

oligotrophic   refers to lakes of low nutrient content, abundant oxygen, and low primary production.

omnivore a heterotrophic organism that eats a wide range of food items, usually including both animal and plant matter.

optimal foraging theory attempts to model how organisms feed as an optimizing process, a process that maximizes or minimizes some quantity, such as energy intake or predation risk.

optimization a process that maximizes or minimizes some quantity.

optimum sustainable yield (OSY) the rate of harvest of a species which maximizes the difference between revenue and costs.

osmosis diffusion of water down its concentration gradient.

overcompensation increased plant growth following herbivory, compared to growth of plants that did not experience herbivory.

P

P_{max} maximum rate of photosynthesis for a particular species of plant growing under ideal physical conditions.

parallel evolution the independent evolution of similar traits in geographically separated species.

parapatric speciation speciation that occurs when a population expands into a new habitat-type within the pre-existing range of the parent species.

parthenogenesis the production of offspring by a female without fertilization of the egg.

patch a relatively homogeneous area in a landscape that differs from its surroundings, for example, an area of forest surrounded by agricultural fields.

peat partially decomposed organic matter that builds up in certain poorly drained wetland habitats.

pelagic a term referring to marine life zones or organisms above the bottom; for instance, tuna are pelagic fish that live in the epipelagic zone of the oceans.

per capita rate the rate of some ecological process (e.g., births) divided by the number of individuals in a population.

per capita rate of increase usually symbolized as r, equals per capita birthrate minus per capita death rate: $r = b - d$.

permafrost a permanently frozen layer of soil that remains frozen even during the summer months.

phenology the study of the relationship between climate and the timing of ecological events, such as the date of arrival of migratory birds on their wintering grounds, the timing of spring plankton blooms, or the onset and ending of leaf fall in a deciduous forest.

phenotypic plasticity the ability to produce different phenotypes from a single genotype as a function of local conditions.

photic zone the upper layers of an ocean or lake in which there is enough light to support photosynthesis.

photon flux density the number of photons of light striking a square metre surface each second.

photorespiration an energetically wasteful process in plants that occurs when O_2 binds to RUBISCO, leading to the release of CO_2 from the plant.

photosynthesis process in which the photosynthetic pigments of plants, algae, or bacteria absorb light and transfer their energy to electrons; the energy carried by these electrons is used to synthesize ATP and NADPH, which in turn serve as donors of electrons and energy for the synthesis of sugars.

photosynthetic describes organisms capable of photosynthesis.

photosynthetically active radiation (PAR) wavelengths of light between 400 and 700 nm that photosynthetic organisms use as a source of energy.

phreatic zone the region below the hyporheic zone of a stream; contains groundwater.

physiological ecology the scientific study of how physiological limitations and adaptation influence the ability of organisms to cope with biotic and abiotic stress

phytophagous plant-eating.

phytoplankton microscopic photosynthetic organisms that drift with the currents in the open sea or in lakes.

pioneer community the first community, in a successional sequence of communities, to be established following a disturbance.

pistil female organ of a flower.

plant growth form a combination of a plant's structure and its growth dynamics; includes trees, vines, annual plants, sclerophyllous vegetation, grasses, and forbs.

poikilotherm an organism whose body temperature varies directly with environmental temperatures; commonly called cold-blooded.

pollen vector biotic or abiotic agents, such as wind and bees, that move pollen from an anther to a stigma.

polyandry a mating system in which one female mates with multiple males while each male mates with just one female.

polygynandry a mating system in which groups of multiple males and multiple females mate with each other.

polygyny a mating system in which one male mates with multiple females while each female mates with just one male.

population a group of potentially interbreeding individuals of a single species inhabiting a specific area.

population ecology the scientific study of the structure and dynamics of populations

population structure patterns of mortality, age distributions, sex ratios, and dispersal within a population.

predator a heterotrophic organism that kills and eats other organisms for food; usually an animal that hunts and kills other animals for food.

predator satiation a defensive tactic in which prey reduce their individual probability of being eaten by occurring at very high densities; predators can only capture and eat so many prey and so become satiated when prey are at very high densities.

primary production the fixation of energy by autotrophs in an ecosystem.

primary productivity a measure of plant growth rate, per unit area, per unit time. This is in contrast to standing biomass.

primary succession succession on newly exposed geological substrates, not significantly modified by organisms; for instance, on newly formed volcanic lava or on substrate exposed during the retreat of a glacier.

prokaryotes organisms with cells that have no membrane-bound nucleus or organelles; includes the bacteria and the archaea.

promiscuity a mating system where individuals may have multiple sexual partners.

psychrophilic a term applied to organisms that live and thrive at temperatures below 20° C.

R

radiation the transfer of heat through electromagnetic radiation, mainly infrared light.

random distribution individuals within a population have an equal chance of living anywhere within an area.

range the difference between the largest and smallest values in a set of measurements or observations.

range of tolerance the entire set of conditions, such as air temperature or soil moisture, under which an organism is potentially able to survive. Levels outside of this range will be lethal.

rank-abundance curve portrays the number of species in a community and their relative abundance; constructed by plotting the relative abundance of species against their rank in abundance.

rate of primary production the amount of energy fixed by the autotrophs in an ecosystem over some interval of time.

realized niche the actual niche of a species whose distribution is restricted by biotic interactions such as competition, predation, disease, and parasitism.

reciprocal altruism a mutually beneficial behaviour in which one individual helps another in expectation of a reciprocal behaviour.

regression a statistical procedure to determine whether a dependent variable is related to an independent variable.

regression coefficient the slope of a regression line.

regression line the line that best fits the relationship between two variables, X and Y.

regular distribution individuals in a population are uniformly spaced.

relative humidity a measure of the water content of air relative to its content at saturation; relative humidity = water vapour density/saturation water vapour density × 100.

relay floristics a model of succession in which species colonize a habitat in sequential waves. The first wave of colonizers is replaced by the second wave, and so on, until a climax community is established.

remote sensing gathering information about an object without direct contact with it, mainly by gathering and processing electromagnetic radiation emitted or reflected by the object; such measurements are typically made from remote sensing satellites.

reproductive effort the allocation of energy, time, and other resources to the production and care of offspring, generally involving reduced allocation to other needs such as maintenance and growth.

resilience the capacity to recover structure and function after disturbance; a highly resilient community or ecosystem may be completely disrupted by disturbance but quickly returns to its former state.

resistance the capacity of a community or ecosystem to maintain structure and/or function in the face of potential disturbance.

resource limitation limitation of population growth by resource availability.

restriction enzymes the enzymes produced by bacteria to cut up foreign DNA, used in DNA studies to cut DNA molecules at particular places called restriction sites.

restriction fragments the DNA fragments resulting from the cutting of a DNA molecule by a restriction enzyme.

restriction sites the particular locations where a restriction enzyme cuts a DNA molecule.

rhodopsin light-absorbing pigments found in the eyes of animals and in bacteria and archaea.

riparian vegetation vegetation growth along rivers or streams.

riparian zone the transition between the aquatic environment of a river or stream and the upland terrestrial environment, generally subject to periodic flooding and elevated groundwater table.

river continuum concept a model that predicts change in physical structure, dominant organisms, and ecosystem processes along the length of temperate rivers.

root exudates organic compounds, such as amino acids, enzymes, and carbohydrates, that are secreted by plant roots into the surrounding soil.

ruderals plants or animals that live in highly disturbed habitats and that may depend on disturbance to persist in the face of potential competition from other species.

S

salinity the salt content of water.

salt marsh a marine shore ecosystem dominated by herbaceous vegetation, found mainly along sandy shores from temperate to high latitudes.

sample mean the average of a sample of measurements or observations; an estimate of the true population mean.

sample median the middle value in a series of measurements or observations, chosen so that there are equal numbers of measurements in the series that are larger than the median and smaller than the median.

saturation water vapour pressure the pressure exerted by the water vapour in air that is saturated with water vapour.

scatterhoarded seeds gathered by mammals and stored in scattered caches or hoards.

secondary succession   succession where disturbance has destroyed a community without destroying the soil; for instance, forest succession following a forest fire or logging.

sedimentation   the deposition of suspended matter onto a surface, such as a lake bottom.

selection coefficient (s)   the relative selection costs or benefits (decreased or increased fitness) associated with a particular biological trait.

self-incompatibility   incapacity of a plant to fertilize itself; such plants must receive pollen from another plant to develop seeds.

self-thinning   reduction in population density as a stand of plant increases in biomass, due to intraspecific competition.

self-thinning rule   a rule resulting from the observation that plotting the average weight of individual plants in a stand against density often produces a line with an average slope of approximately $-\frac{3}{2}$.

semelparity   reproduction that involves production of all of an organism's offspring in one event, generally over a short period of time.

sex ratio   the relative frequency of each sex type in a population.

sex types   the distribution of male and female fertility among individuals of a species. For example, males, females, and hermaphrodites would be three possible sex types.

sexual selection   results from differences in reproductive rates among individuals as a result of differences in mating success due to intrasexual selection, intersexual selection, or a mixture of the two forms of sexual selection.

sigmoidal population growth curve   an S-shaped pattern of population growth, with population size levelling off at the carrying capacity of the environment.

single nucleotide polymorphisms (SNPs)   single base pair changes in DNA sequences that are used to quantify genetic diversity.

size-selective predation   prey selection by predators based on prey size.

small-scale phenomena   takes place on a local scale.

sociality   group living generally involving some degree of cooperation between individuals.

soil   the upper layer of the earth's land surface, consisting of organic matter and minerals.

solifluction   the slow movement of tundra soils down slopes as a result of annual freezing and thawing of surface soil and the actions of water and gravity.

Southern Oscillation   an oscillation in atmospheric pressure that extends across the Pacific Ocean.

spate   sudden flooding in a stream.

specialist   a predator or herbivore that regularly feeds upon a single, or very few, prey species.

species composition   the species that occur in a given community.

species diversity   a measure of diversity that increases with species evenness and species richness.

species evenness   the relative abundance of species in a community or collection.

species richness   the number of species in a community or collection.

species turnover   changes in species composition on islands resulting from some species becoming extinct and others immigrating.

spiraling length   the length of stream required for an atom of a nutrient to complete a cycle from release into the water column to re-entry into the benthic ecosystem.

spring tide   tides occurring during new and full moons, when tidal fluctuations are greatest.

stability   a community's ability to withstand or recover from disturbance.

stabilizing selection   a form of natural selection that acts against extreme phenotypes; can act to impede changes in populations.

stable age distribution   a population in which the proportion of individuals in each age class is constant.

stable isotope analysis   analysis of the relative concentrations of stable isotopes, such as ^{13}C and ^{12}C, in materials; used in ecology to study the flow of energy and materials through ecosystems.

stamen   male organ of a flower.

standard deviation   the square root of the variance.

standard error   an estimate of variation among means of samples drawn from a population.

standing biomass   the amount of plant biomass found at a given location at a single point in time. This is in contrast to primary productivity.

static life table   a life table constructed by recording the age at death of a large number of individuals; involves a snapshot of survival within a population during a short interval of time.

stream order   a numerical classification of streams in terms of where they occur in a stream drainage network. Headwater streams are first-order streams, joining of two first-order streams forms a second-order stream, joining of two second-order streams forms a third-order stream, and so forth.

stress   any strong negative environmental condition that induces physiological responses in an organism or alters the structure of functioning of an ecosystem.

succession   the gradual change in plant and animal communities in an area following disturbance or the creation of new substrate.

Suess effect   reduced concentration of ^{14}C in the atmosphere as a consequence of fossil fuel burning.

survivorship curve   a graphical summary of patterns of survival in a population.

symbionts   an organism in a symbiotic relationship (a close and typically interdependent, relationship between two or more species). The outcome of the relationship may or may not be mutually beneficial.

symbiotic relationship   an ecological relationship in which the participants live most of their lives in close proximity to each other. For example, the fungi and plants that form mycorrhizae or the fungi and algae that form lichens.

sympatric speciation   speciation that occurs when isolation mechanisms evolve among populations with overlapping geographic ranges.

T

taiga   northern forests that occupy the area south of arctic tundra. Though dominated by coniferous trees, they also contain aspen and birch. Also called boreal forest.

talus   rock piles pushed aside and left behind by glaciers.

temperate forest   deciduous or coniferous forests generally found between 40° and 50° of latitude, where annual precipitation averages anywhere from about 650 mm to over 3,000 mm; this biome receives more winter precipitation than temperate grasslands.

temperate grassland   grasslands growing in middle latitudes that receive between 300 and 1,000 mm of annual precipitation, with maximum precipitation usually falling during the summer months.

thermal neutral zone   the range of environmental temperatures over which the metabolic rate of a homeothermic animal does not change.

thermocline   a depth zone in a lake or ocean through which temperature changes rapidly with depth, generally about 1°C per metre of depth.

thermophilic   a term applied to organisms that tolerate or require high-temperature environments.

till   unsorted materials, such as clay, rocks, and boulders, left behind by glaciers.

tolerance model   a model of succession in which initial stages of colonization are not limited to a few pioneer species; juveniles of species dominating at climax can be present from the earliest stages of succession, and species colonizing early in succession do not facilitate colonization by species characteristic of later successional stages. Later successional species are simply those tolerant of environmental conditions early in succession.

top-down control   the control or influence of consumers on ecosystem processes.

torpor   a state of low metabolic rate and lowered body temperature.

trophic (feeding) biology   the study of the feeding biology of organisms.

trophic dynamics   the transfer of energy from one part of an ecosystem to another.

trophic level   trophic position in an ecosystem; for instance primary producer, primary consumer, secondary consumer, tertiary consumer, and so forth.

trophic pyramid   a graphical representation of the amount of energy contained in different trophic levels within an ecosystem. Traditionally they have primary producers at the bottom and top consumers at the top. Due to losses of energy between levels, the resulting graph is pyramid shaped.

tropical dry forest   a broadleaf deciduous forest growing in tropical regions having pronounced wet and dry seasons; trees drop their leaves during the dry season.

tropical rain forest   a broadleaf evergreen forest growing in tropical regions where conditions are warm and wet year-round.

tropical savanna   a tropical grassland dotted with scattered trees; characterized by pronounced wet and dry seasons and periodic fires.

tundra   a northern biome dominated by mosses, lichens, and dwarf willows, receiving low to moderate precipitation and having a very short growing season.

type I survivorship curve   a pattern of survivorship with high rates of survival among young and middle-aged individuals, followed by high rates of mortality among the aged.

type II survivorship curve   a pattern of survivorship with constant rates of survival throughout life.

type III survivorship curve   a pattern of survivorship with a period of extremely high rates of mortality among the young, followed by a relatively high rate of survival.

U

upwelling   movement of deeper ocean water to the surface; occurs most commonly along the west coasts of continents and around Antarctica.

V

vapour pressure deficit (VPD)   the difference between the actual water vapour pressure and the saturation water vapour pressure at a particular temperature.

variance   a measure of variation in a population or a sample from a population.

vertical transmission   the transfer of a disease from parent to offspring.

vesicle   storage organ in vesicular-arbuscular mycorrhizal fungi.

W

Walker circulation   a large-scale atmospheric circulation system that moves in the plane of the equator.

water potential   the capacity of water to do work, which is determined by its free energy content; water flows from positions of higher to lower free energy. Increasing solute concentration decreases water potential.

water vapour pressure   the atmospheric pressure exerted by the water vapour in air; increases as the water vapour in air increases.

weed   a species that a person does not want in a certain location at a certain point in time.

wet deposition   washing of materials from the atmosphere onto the earth surface with rain or snow.

Z

zonation of species   pattern of separation of species into distinctive vertical habitats or zones.

zooplankton   animals that drift in the surface waters of the oceans or lakes; most zooplankton are microscopic.

Adams, P. A. and J. E. Heath. 1964. Temperature regulation in the sphinx moth, *Celerio lineata. Nature* 201:20–22.

Addicott, J. F. 1986. Variation in the costs and benefits of mutualism: the interaction between yuccas and yucca moths. *Oecologia* 70:486–94.

Addicott, J. F. 1996. Cheaters in yucca/moth mutualism. *Nature* 380(6570): 114–15.

Adler, P. B., E. W. Seabloom, E. T. Borer, H. Hillebarnd, Y. Hautier, A. Hector, W. S. Harpole, L. R. O'Halloran, J. B. Grace, T. M. Anderson, J.D. Bakker, L. A. Biederman, C. S. Brown, Y. M. Buckley, L. B. Calabrese, C.-J. Chu, E. E. Cleland, S. L. Collins, K. L. Cottingham, M. J. Crawley, E. I. Damschen, K. F. Davies, N. M. DeCrappeo, P. A. Fay, J. Firn, P. Frater, E. I. Gasarch, D. S. Gruner, N. Hagenah, J. H. R. Lambers, H. Humphries, V. L. Jin, A. D. Kay, K. P. Kirkman, J. A. Klein, J. M. H. Knops, K. J. La Pierre, J. G. Lambrinos, W. Li, A. S. MacDougall, R. L. McCulley, B. A. Melbourne, C. E. Mitchell, J. L. Moore, J. W. Morgan, B. Mortensen, J. L. Orrock, S. M. Prober, D. A. Pyke, A. C. Risch, M. Schuetz, M. D. Smith, C. J. Stevens, L. L. Sullivan, G. Wang, P. D. Wragg, J. P. Wright, L. H. Yang. 2011. Productivity is a poor predictor of plan species richness. *Science* 333(6050):1750–3.

Aerts, R. 2006. The freezer defrosting: global warming and litter decomposition rates in cold biomes. *Journal of Ecology* 94:713–24.

Agrawal, A. A. and P. M. Kotanen. 2003. Herbivores and the success of exotic plants: a phylogenetically controlled experiment. *Ecology Letters* 6(8):712–15.

Alberta Environment and Sustainable Resource Development. 2013. Total Tailings Ponds Surface Area. http://environment.alberta.ca/apps/osip. Accessed September 26, 2013.

Allen, E. B. and M. F. Allen. 1986. Water relations of xeric grasses in the field: interactions of mycorrhizae and competition. *New Phytologist* 104:559–71.

Anderson, K. G. 2006. How well does paternity confidence match actual paternity? *Current Anthropology* 47:513–20.

Anderson, J. M. and M. J. Swift. 1983. Decomposition in tropical forests. In S. L. Sutton, T. C. Whitmore, and A. C. Chadwick. eds. *Tropical Rain Forest: Ecology and Management.* Oxford: Blackwell Scientific Publications.

Anderson, M. J., T. O. Crist, J. M. Chase, M. Vellend, B. D. Inouye, A. L. Freestone, N. J. Sanders, H. V.

Cornell, L. S. Comita, K. F. Davies, S. P. Harrison, N. J. B. Kraft, J. C. Stegen, and N. G. Swenson. 2011. Navigating the multiple meanings of β diversity: a roadmap for the practicing ecologist. *Ecology Letters,* 14:19–28.

Anderson, R. M. and R. M. May. 1979. Population biology of infectious-diseases *Nature* 280(5721): 361–67.

Angilletta, M. J., Jr. 2001. Thermal and physiological constraints on energy assimilation in a widespread lizard (*Sceloporus undulatus*). *Ecology* 82:3044–56.

Apps, C. D., N. J. Newhouse, and T. A. Kinley. 2002. Habitat associations of American badgers in southeastern British Columbia. *Canadian Journal of Zoology-Revue Canadienne De Zoologie* 80(7):1228–39.

Arcese, P. 1987. Age, intrusion pressure and defence against floaters by territorial male song sparrows. *Animal Behaviour* 35:773–84.

Arnemo, J. M., P. Ahlqvist, R. Andersen, F. Berntsen, G. Ericsson, J. Odden, S. Brunberg, P. Segerstrom, and J. E. Swenson. 2006. Risk of capture-related mortality in large free-ranging mammals: experiences from Scandinavia. *Wildlife Biology* 12:109–13.

Arnqvist, G. and L. Rowe. 2002. Antagonistic coevolution between the sexes in a group of insects. *Nature* 415(6873):787–89.

Ashman, T. L. and D. J. Schoen. 1994. How long should flowers live? *Nature* 371(6500):788–91.

Ashman, T. L. and D. J. Schoen. 1997. The cost of floral longevity in *Clarkia tembloriensis:* An experimental investigation. *Evolutionary Ecology* 11(3):289–300.

Bacastow, R. and C. D. Keeling. 1974. Atmospheric carbon dioxide and radiocarbon in the natural carbon cycle: II. Changes from AD 1700 to 2070 as deduced from a geochemical model. In G. M. Woodwell and E. V. Pecan. eds. *Carbon and the Biosphere.* BHNL/CONF 720510. Springfield, Va.: National Technical Information Service.

Bailey, N. T. J. 1951. On estimating the size of mobile populations from recapture data. *Biometrika* 38: 293–306.

Bailey, N. T. J. 1952. Improvements in the interpretation of recapture data. *Journal of Animal Ecology* 21: 120–27.

Baillie, J. E. M., C. Hilton-Taylor, and S. N. Stuart (Ed.). 2004. *2004 IUCN Red List of Threatened Species. A Global Species Assessment.* Gland, Switzerland and Cambridge, UK: IUCN.

Baker, C. S., J. M. Straley, and A. Perry. 1992. Population characteristics of individually identified humpback whales in southeastern Alaska: summer and fall 1986. *Fishery Bulletin* 90:429–37.

Baker, L. A., D. Hope, Y. Xu, J. Edmonds, and L. Lauver. 2001. Nitrogen balance for the Central Arizona–Phoenix (CAP) ecosystem. *Ecosystems* 4(6):582–602.

Baker, M. C., L. R. Mewaldt, and R. M. Stewart. 1981. Demography of white-crowned sparrows (*Zonotrichia leucophrys nuttalli*). *Ecology* 62: 636–44.

Baldwin, J. and P. W. Hochachka. 1970. Functional significance of isoenzymes in thermal acclimation: acetylcholinesterase from trout brain. *Biochemical Journal* 116:883–87.

Balvanera P., A. B. Pfisterer, N. Buchmann, J. S. He, T. Nakashizuka, D. Raffaelli, and B. Schmid. 2006. Quantifying the evidence for biodiversity effects on ecosystem functioning and services. *Ecology Letters* 9:1146–56.

Barbour, C. D. and J. H. Brown. 1974. Fish species diversity in lakes. *American Naturalist* 108:473–89.

Barnes, R. S. K. and R. N. Hughes. 1988. *An Introduction to Marine Ecology.* Oxford: Blackwell Scientific Publications.

Barnola, J. M., D. Raynaud, Y. S. Korotkevich, and C. Lorius. 1987. Vostok ice core provides 160,000-year record of atmospheric CO_2, *Nature* 329:408–14.

Barnosky, A. D., N. Matzke, S. Tomiya, G. Wogan, B. Swartz, T. Quental, C. Marshall, J. L. McGuire, E. L. Lindsey, K. C. Maguire, B. Mersey, and E. A. Ferrer. 2011. Has the Earth's sixth mass extinction already arrived? *Nature* 471:51–7.

Barrie, L. A. and 24 others. 1997. *Canadian Arctic Contaminant Assessment Report.* Ottawa, Canada: Department of Indian and Northern Affairs.

Baur, B. and A. Baur. 1993. Climatic warming due to thermal radiation from an urban area as possible cause for the local extinction of a land snail. *Journal of Applied Ecology* 30: 333–40.

Béjà, O., E. N. Spudich, J. L. Spudich, M. Leclerc, and E. F. Delong. 2001. Proteorhodopsin phototrophy in the ocean. *Nature* 411:786–89.

Béjà, O., L. Aravind, E. V. Koonin, M. T. Suzuki, A. Hadd, L. P. Nguyen, S. B. Jovanovich, C. M. Gates, R. A. Feldman, J. L. Spudich, E. N. Spudich, and E. F. Delong. 2000. Bacterial rhodopsin: evidence for a new type of phototrophy in the sea. *Science* 289:1902–06.

Béjà, O., M. T. Suzuki, J. F. Heidelberg, W. C. Nelson, C. M. Preston, T. Hamada, J. A. Eisen, C. M. Fraser, and E. F. Delong. 2002. Unsuspected diversity among marine aerobic anoxygenic phototrophs. *Nature* 415:630–33.

Bell, G., M. J. Lechowicz, and M. J. Waterway. 2000. Environmental heterogeneity and species diversity of forest sedges. *Journal of Ecology* 88(1):67–87.

Bennett, K. D. 1983. Postglacial population expansion of forest trees in Norfolk, UK. *Nature* 303:164–67.

Bennet, A. F. and R. E. Lenski. 2007. An experimental test of evolutionary trade-offs during temperature adaptation. *Proceedings of the National Academy of Sciences of the United States.* 104 supplement 1:8649–54.

Ben-Shahar, Y., A. Robichon, M. B. Sokolowski, and G. E. Robinson. (2002). Influence of gene action across different time scales on behavior. *Science* 296(5568):741–44.

Bergeron, Y. 2000. Species and stand dynamics in the mixed woods of Quebec's southern boreal forest. *Ecology* 81(6):1500–16.

Bernhardt, E. S., L. E. Band, C. J. Walsh, and P. E. Berke. 2008. Understanding, managing, and minimizing urban impacts on surface water nitrogen loading. *Annals of the New York Academy of Sciences* 1134:61–96.

Bernhardt, T. 2010. The Canadian Biodiversity website. http://canadianbiodiversity.mcgill.ca/english/index.htm.

Berry, J. and O. Björkman. 1980. Photosynthetic response and adaptation to temperature in higher plants. *Annual Review of Plant Physiology* 31:491–543.

Berteaux, D., D. Reale, A. G. McAdam, and S. Boutin. 2004. Keeping pace with fast climate change: Can arctic life count on evolution? *Integrative and Comparative Biology* 44(2):140–51.

Bertschy, K. A. and M. G. Fox. 1999. The influence of age-specific survivorship on pumpkinseed sunfish life histories. *Ecology* 80:2299–313.

Beschta, R. L. and W. J. Ripple. 2009. Large predators and trophic cascades in terrestrial ecosystems of the western United States. *Biological Conservation* 142:2401–14.

Bird, D. F. and J. Kalff. 1986. Bacterial grazing by planktonic lake algae. *Science* 4737:493–5.

Bird R. D. 1930. Biotic communities of the Aspen parkland of central Canada. *Ecology* 11:356–442

Bjerknes, J. 1966. A possible response of the atmospheric Hadley circulation to equatorial anomalies of ocean temperature. *Tellus* 18:820–9.

Bjerknes, J. 1969. Atmospheric teleconnections from the equatorial Pacific. *Monthly Weather Review* 97:163–72.

Blais, J. M., D. W. Schindler, D. C. G. Muir, L. E. Kimpe, D. B. Donald, and B. Rosenberg. 1998. Accumulation of persistent organochlorine compounds in mountains of western Canada. *Nature* 395:685–88.

Bloch, N. and D. J. Irschick. 2005. Toe-clipping dramatically reduces clinging performance in a pad-bearing lizard (*Anolis carolinensis*). *Journal of Herpetology* 39:288–93.

Bloom, A. J., F. S. Chapin III, and H. A. Mooney. 1985. Resource limitation in plants—an economic analogy. *Annual Review of Ecology and Systematics* 16:363–92.

Boag, D. A. and J. O. Murie. 1981. Population ecology of Columbian ground-squirrels in southwestern Alberta. *Canadian Journal of Zoology* 59:2230–40.

Boag, P. T. and P. R. Grant. 1978. Heritability of external morphology in Darwin's finches. *Nature* 274:793–94.

Boag, P. T. and P. R. Grant. 1984a. The classical case of character release: Darwin's finches (*Geospiza*) on Isla Daphne Major, Galápagos. *Biological Journal of the Linnean Society* 22:243–87.

Boag, P. T. and P. R. Grant. 1984b. Darwin's finches on Isla Daphne Major, Galápagos: breeding and feeding ecology in a climatically variable environment. *Ecological Monographs* 54:463–89.

Bolduc, E., C. M. Buddle, N. J. Bostanian, and C. Vincent. 2005. Ground-dwelling spider fauna (Araneae) of two vineyards in southern Quebec. *Environmental Entomology* 34(3):635–45.

Bollinger, G. 1909. *Zur Gastropodenfauna von Basel und Umgebung.* Ph.D. dissertation. University of Basel, Switzerland.

Bond, P. and P. Goldblatt. 1984. Plants of the Cape Flora. *Journal of South African Botany. Supplementary Volume No. 13.*

Bonner, J. T. 1965. *Size and Cycle: An Essay on the Structure of Biology.* Princeton, N.J.: Princeton University Press.

Boonstra, R., D. Hik, G. R. Singleton, A. Tinnikov. 1998. The Impact of Predator-Induced Stress on the Snowshoe Hare Cycle. *Ecological Monographs* 68(3):371–94.

Booth, R. E. and J. P. Grime. 2003. Effects of genetic impoverishment on plant community diversity. *Journal of Ecology* 91(5):721–30.

Bormann, F. H. and G. E. Likens. 1981. *Pattern and Process in a Forested Ecosystem.* New York: Springer-Verlag.

Bormann, F. H. and G. E. Likens. 1994. *Pattern and Process in a Forested Ecosystem.* New York: Springer-Verlag.

Bowen, G. W. and R. L. Burgess. 1981. A quantitative analysis of forest island pattern in selected Ohio landscapes. ORNL/TM 7759. Oak Ridge National Laboratory, Oak Ridge, Tenn.

Boyce, M. S. and L. L. McDonald. (1999). Relating populations to habitats using resource selection functions. *Trends in Ecology & Evolution* 14(7):268–72.

Braune, B. M., P. M. Outridge, A. T. Fisk, D. C. G. Muir, P. A. Helm, K. Hobbs, P. F. Hoekstra, Z. A. Kuzyk, M. Kwan, R. J. Letcher, W. L. Lockhart, R. J. Norstrom, G. A. Stern, and I. Stirling. 2005. Persistent organic pollutants and mercury in marine biota of the Canadian Arctic: An overview of spatial and temporal trends. *Science of the Total Environment* 351:4–56.

Briggs, J. C. 1974. *Marine Zoogeography.* New York: McGraw-Hill.

Brisson, J. and J. F. Reynolds. 1994. The effects of neighbors on root distribution in a creosote bush (*Larrea tridentata*) population. *Ecology* 75:1693–702.

Brock, T. D. 1978. *Thermophilic Microorganisms and Life at High Temperatures.* New York: Springer-Verlag.

Broders, H. G., S. P. Mahoney, W. A. Montevecchi, and W. S. Davidson. 1999. Population genetic structure and the effect of founder events on the genetic variability of moose, *Alces alces,* in Canada. *Molecular Ecology* 8:1309–15.

Brown, G. P. and P. J. Weatherhead. 1999. Demography and sexual size dimorphism in northern water snakes, *Nerodia sipedon. Canadian Journal of Zoology* 77:1358–66.

Brown, J. H. 1984. On the relationship between abundance and distribution of species. *American Naturalist* 130:255–79.

Brown, J. H. and A. Kodric-Brown. 1977. Turnover rates in insular biogeography: effects of immigration on extinction. *Ecology* 58:445–9.

Brown, J. H. and B. A. Mauer. 1989. Macroecology: The division of food and space among species on continents. *Science* 243:1145–50.

Brown, J. H. and J. C. Munger. 1985. Experimental manipulation of a desert rodent community: food addition and species removal. *Ecology* 66:1545–63.

Brown, J. H. and M. V. Lomolino. 2000. Concluding remarks: historical perspective and the future of island biogeography theory. *Global Ecology and Biogeography* 9:87–92.

Brown, J. H., D. W. Mehlman, and G. C. Stevens. 1995. Spatial variation in abundance. *Ecology* 76:2028–43.

Brown J. S., J. W. Laundre, and M. Gurung. 1999. The ecology of fear: Optimal foraging, game theory, and trophic interactions. *Journal of Mammalogy* 80(2):385–99.

Brown, W. L. and E. O. Wilson. 1956. Character displacement. *Systematic Zoology* 5:49–64.

Bshary, R. 2003. The cleaner wrasse, *Labroides dimidiatus,* is a key organism for reef fish diversity at Ras Mohammed National Park, Egypt. *Journal of Animal Ecology* 72:169–72.

Caddy, J. F. 1999. Fisheries management in the twenty-first century: will new paradigms apply? *Reviews in Fish Biology and Fisheries* 9(1):1–43.

Cahill, J. F., J. P. Castelli, and B. B. Casper. 2001. The herbivory uncertainty principle: visiting plants can alter herbivory. *Ecology* 82:307–12.

Calow, P. and G. E. Petts. 1992. *The Rivers Handbook.* London: Blackwell Scientific Publications.

Callan, R. N. Pl. Nibbelink, T. P. Rooney, J. E. Wiedenhoeft, and A. P. Wydeven. 2013. Recolonizing wolves trigger a trophic cascade in Wisconsin (USA). *Journal of Ecology.* 101:837–45.

Canada. Environment Canada. Canadian Wildlife Service. Minister's Round Table under the *Species At Risk Act.* 2006. *Conserving Wildlife Species and Recovering Species at Risk in Canada.*

Canada. Natural Resources Canada. 2010. www.nrcan.gc.ca/forests.

Canada. Species At Risk Act Public Registry. 2007. www.sararegistry.gc.ca/approach/act/default_e.cfm

Cardillo, M., A. Purvis, W. Sechrest, J. L. Gittleman, J. Bielby, and G. M. Mace. 2004. Human population density and extinction risk in the world's carnivores. *Plos Biology* 2(7):909–14.

Cardinale, B. J., M. A. Palmer, and S. L. Collins. 2002. Species diversity enhances ecosystem functioning through interspecific facilitation. *Nature.* 415:426–9.

Cargill, S. M. and R. L. Jefferies. 1984. The effects of grazing by lesser snow geese on the vegetation of a sub-arctic salt-marsh. *Journal of Applied Ecology* 21(2):669–86.

Carignan, V. and M.-A. Villard. 2002. Selecting indicator species to monitor ecological integrity: a review. *Environmental Monitoring and Assessment* 78:45–6.

Carpenter, F. L., M. A. Hixon, C. A. Beuchat, R. W. Russell, and D. C. Patton. 1993. Biphasic mass gain in migrant hummingbirds: body composition changes, torpor, and ecological significance. *Ecology* 74:1173–82.

Carpenter, S. R. and J. F. Kitchell. 1988. Consumer control of lake productivity. *BioScience* 38:764–9.

Carpenter, S. R. and J. F. Kitchell. 1993. *The Trophic Cascade in Lakes.* Cambridge. England: Cambridge University Press.

Carpenter, S. R., J. F. Kitchell, and J. R. Hodgson. 1985. Cascading trophic interactions and lake productivity. *BioScience* 35:634–39.

Carpenter, S. R., T. M. Frost, J. F. Kitchell, T. K. Kratz, D. W. Schindler, J. Shearer, W. G. Sprules, M. J. Vanni, and A. P. Zimmerman. 1991. Patterns of primary production and herbivory in 25 North American lake ecosystems. In J. Cole. G. Lovett. and S. F. Findlay. eds. *Comparative Analyses of Ecosystems: Patterns, Mechanisms, and Theories.* New York: Springer-Verlag.

Carroll, S. P. and C. Boyd. 1992. Host race radiation in the soapberry bug: natural history with the history. *Evolution* 46:1052–69.

Carruthers, R. I., T. S. Larkin, H. Firstencel, and Z. Feng. 1992.

Influence of thermal ecology on the mycosis of a rangeland grasshopper. *Ecology* 73:190–204.

Caughley, G. 1977. *Analysis of Vertebrate Populations.* New York: John Wiley & Sons.

Caughley, G., J. Short, G. C. Grigg, and H. Nix. 1987. Kangaroos and climate: an analysis of distribution. *Journal of Animal Ecology* 56:751–61.

Cavieres, L., M. T. K. Arroyo, A. Penaloza, M. A. Molina-Montenegro, C. Torres. 2002. Nurse effect of Bolax *gummifera* cushion plants in the alpine vegetation of the Chilean Patagonian Andes. *Journal of Vegetation Science.* 13(4):547–54.

Census of Marine Life. 2010. www.coml.org/highlights-2010.

Central Intelligence Agency. 2007. *The World Factbook.* https://www.cia.gov/library/publications/the-world-factbook/index.html.

Chapin, F. S., III, L. R. Walker, C. L. Fastie, and L. C. Sharman. 1994. Mechanisms of primary succession following deglaciation at Glacier Bay, Alaska. *Ecological Monographs* 64:149–75.

Chapman, V. J. 1977. *Wet Coastal Ecosystems.* Amsterdam: Elsevier Scientific Publishing.

Charnov, E. L. 1973. *Optimal Foraging: Some Theoretical Explorations.* Ph.D. Dissertation. University of Washington. Seattle.

Charnov, E. L. 1976. Optimal foraging: the marginal value theorem. *Theoretical Population Biology* 9:129–36.

Charnov, E. L. 2002. Reproductive effort, offspring size and benefit-cost ratios in the classification of life histories. *Evolutionary Ecology Research* 4:1–10.

Charnov, E. L., J. Maynard Smith, and J. J. Bull. 1976. Why be a hermaphrodite? *Nature* 263:125–26.

Charnov, E. L. R. Warne, and M. Moses. 2001. Lifetime reproductive effort. *American Naturalist* 170: E129–E142.

Chetkiewicz, C. L. B., C. C. S. Clair, and M. S. Boyce. 2006. Corridors for conservation: Integrating pattern and process. *Annual Review of Ecology Evolution and Systematics* 37:317–42.

Chiariello, N. R., C. B. Field, and H.A. Mooney. 1987. Midday wilting in a tropical pioneer tree. *Functional Ecology* 1:3–11.

Christian, C. E. 2001. Consequences of a biological invasion reveal the importance of mutualism for plant communities. *Nature* 413:635–39.

CIA World Factbook. 2010. Field Listing: Roadways. https://www.cia.gov/library/publications/the-world-factbook/fields/2085.html?countryName=&countryCode=&regionCode=%C2%A8.

Clausen, J., D. D. Keck, and W. M. Hiesey. 1940. *Experimental Studies on the Nature of Species. I. The Effect of Varied Environments on Western North American Plants.* Washington D. C.: Carnegie Institution of Washington, Publication no. 520.

Clements, F. E. 1916. *Plant Succession: An Analysis of the Development of Vegetation*. Washington, D.C.: Carnegie Institution of Washington. Publication 242.

Clements, F. E. 1936. Nature and structure of the climax. *Journal of Ecology* 24:252–84.

Clevenger, A. P. and N. Waltho. 2005. Performance indices to identify attributes of highway crossing structures facilitating movement of large mammals. *Biological Conservation* 121(3):453–64.

Cody, M. L. and J. M. Diamond. 1975. *Ecology and Evolution of Communities*. Harvard University Press. Cambridge, MA.

Coffey, H. M. P. and L. Farrig. 2012. Relative effects of vehicle pollution, moisture and colonization sources on urban lichens. *Journal of Applied Ecology* 49:1467–74.

Colautti, R. I., S. A. Bailey, C. D. A. van Overdijk, K. Amundsen, and H. J. MacIsaac. 2006. Characterised and projected costs of nonindigenous species in Canada. *Biological Invasions* 8(1):45–59.

Coltman, D. W., P. O'Donoghue, J. T. Jorgenson, J. T. Hogg, C. Strobeck, and M. Festa-Bianchet. 2003. Undesirable evolutionary consequences of trophy hunting. *Nature* 426:655–58.

Connell, J. H. 1961a. The effects of competition. predation by *Thais lapillus* and other factors on natural populations of the barnacle, *Balanus balanoides*. *Ecological Monographs* 31:61–104.

Connell, J. H. 1961b. The influence of interspecific competition and other factors on the distribution of the barnacle *Chthamalus stellatus*. *Ecology* 42:710–23.

Connell, J. H. 1975. Some mechanisms producing structure in natural communities: a model and evidence from field experiments. In M. L. Cody and J. Diamond. eds. *Ecology and Evolution of Communities*. Cambridge. Mass.: Harvard University Press.

Connell, J. H. 1978. Diversity in tropical rain forests and coral reefs. *Science* 199:1302–10.

Connell, J. H. 1980. Diversity and the coevolution of competitors, or the ghost of competition past. *Oikos* 35:131–38.

Connell, J. H. 1983. On the prevalence and relative importance of interspecific competition: evidence from field experiments. *American Naturalist* 122:661–96.

Connell, J. H. and R. O. Slatyer. 1977. Mechanisms of succession in natural communities and their role in community stability and organization. *The American Naturalist* 111:1119–44.

Conti, M. E. and G. Cecchetti. 2001. Biological monitoring: lichens as bioindicators of air pollution assessment–a review. *Environmental Pollution* 114:471–92.

Cooper, P. D. 1982. Water balance and osmoregulation in a free-ranging tenebrionid beetle, *Onymacris unguicularis*, of the Namib Desert. *Journal of Insect Physiology* 28: 737–42.

Coppock, D. L., J. K. Delling, J. E. Ellis, and M. I. Dyer. 1983. Plant herbivore interactions in a North American mixed-grass prairie: effects of black-tailed prairie dogs on intraseasonal aboveground plant biomass and nutrient dynamics and plant species diversity. *Oecologia* 56:1–9.

COSEWIC. 2006. *Canadian Species at Risk*. Committee on the Status of Endangered Wildlife in Canada.

Côte, S. D., T. P. Rooney, J. P. Tremblay, C. Dussault, and D. M. Waller. 2004. Ecological impacts of deer overabundance. *Annual Review of Ecology Evolution and Systematics* 35:113–47.

Coupland, R. T. and R. E. Johnson. 1965. Rooting characteristics of native grassland species in Saskatchewan. *Journal of Ecology* 53:475–507.

Crutsinger, G. M., M. D. Collins, J. A. Fordyce, Z. Gompert, C. C. Nice, and N. J. Sanders. 2006. Plant genotypic diversity predicts community structure and governs an ecosystem process. *Science*. 313(5789): 966–8.

Culp, J. M. and G. J. Scrimgeour. 1993. Size dependent diel foraging periodicity of a mayfly grazer in streams with and without fish. *Oikos* 68:242–50.

Currie, D.J., G. G. Mittelbach, H. V. Cornell, R. Field, J. F. Guegan, B. A. Hawkins, D. M. Kaufman, J. T. Kerr, T. Oberdorff, E. O'Brien, and J. R. G. Turner. 2004. Predictions and tests of climate-based hypotheses of broad-scale variation in taxonomic richness. *Ecology Letters* 7(12): 1121–34.

Curtis, J. T. 1956. The modification of mid-latitude grasslands and forests by man. In W. L. Thomas. Jr. ed. *Man's Role in Changing the Face of the Earth*. Chicago: University of Chicago Press.

Daily, G. C., S. jPolasky, J. Goldstein, P. M. Kareiva, H. A. Monney, L. Pejchar, T. H. Ricketts, J. Salzman, and R. Shallenberger. 2009. *Frontiers in Ecology and the Environment* 7(1):21–8.

Damuth, J. 1981. Population density and body size in mammals. *Nature* 290:699–700.

Darimont, C. T., S. M. Carlson, M. T. Kinnison, P. C. Paquet, T. E. Reimchen, and C. C. Wilmers. 2009. Human predators outpace other agents of trait change in the wild. *PNAS* 106:952–4.

Darwin, C. 1839. *Journal of Researches into the Geology and Natural History of the Various Countries Visited During the Voyage of H.M.S. 'Beagle' Under the Command of Captain FitzRoy, R.N., From 1832–1836.* London: Henry Colborn.

Darwin, C. 1842a. *The Structure and Distribution of Coral Reefs*. London: Smith. Elder and Company. Reprinted by the University of California Press. Berkeley. 1962.

Darwin, C. 1842b. *Journal of Researches into the Geology and Natural History of the Various Countries Visited During the Voyage of H.M.S. 'Beagle' Under the Command of Captain FitzRoy, R.N., From 1832–1836.* London: Henry Colborn.

Darwin, C. 1859. *The Origin of Species by Means of Natural Selection, or the Preservation of Favored Races in the Struggle for Life*. New York: Modern Library.

Darwin, C. 1871. *The Descent of Man, and Selection in Relation to Sex*. London: John Murray.

Darwin, C. 1877. *The Different Forms of Flowers on Plants of the Same Species*. London: John Murray.

Davis, M. B. 1981. Quaternary history and the stability of forest communities. In D. C. West, H. H. Shugart, and D. B. Botkin. eds. *Forest Succession: Concepts and Application*. New York: Springer-Verlag.

Davis, M. B. 1983. Quaternary history of deciduous forests of eastern North America and Europe. *Annals of the Missouri Botanical Garden* 70:550–63.

Davis, M. B. 1989. Retrospective studies. In G. E. Likens. ed. *Long-Term Studies in Ecology*. New York: Springer-Verlag.

Dawson, T. E., S. Mambelli, A. H. Plamboeck, P. H. Templer, and K. P. Tu. 2002. Stable isotopes in plant ecology. *Annual Review of Ecology and Systematics* 33:507–99.

Deevey, E. S. 1947. Life tables for natural populations of animals. *Quarterly Review of Biology* 22:283–314.

de Leon, L. F., E. Bermingham, J. Podos, and A. P. Hendry. 2010. Divergence with gene flow as facilitated by ecological differences: within-island variation in Darwin's finches. *Philosophical transactions of the Royal Society B-Biological Sciences* 365:1041–1052.

Demeester, L. 1993. Genotype, fish-mediated chemicals, and phototactic behavior in daphnia-magna. *Ecology* 74(5):1467–74.

Dempson, J. B., M. F. O'Connell, and N. M. Cochrane. 2001. Potential impact of climate warming on recreational fishing opportunities for Atlantic salmon, *Salmo salar L.*, in Newfoundland, Canada. *Fisheries Management and Ecology* 8:69–82.

Denno, R. F. and G. K. Roderick. 1992. Density-related dispersal in planthoppers: effects of interspecific crowding. *Ecology* 73:1323–34.

Derocher, A. E., I. Stirling, and W. Calvert. 1997. Male-biased harvesting of polar bears in western Hudson bay. *Journal of Wildlife Management* 61:1075–82.

Derocher, A. E., H. Wolkers, T. Colborn, M. Schlabach, T. S. Larsen, and O. Wiig. 2003. Contaminants in Svalbard polar bear samples archived since 1967 and possible population level effects. *Science of the Total Environment* 301(1–3):163–74.

de Siqueira, M. F., G. Durigan, P. de Marco Jr, and A. T. Peterson. 2009. Something from nothing: Using landscape similarity and ecological niche modeling to find rare plant species. *Journal for Nature Conservation* 17:25–32.

Dewailly, E. A., J. P. Nantel, J. P. Weber, and F. Meyer. 1989. High levels of PCBs in breast milk of Inuit women from Arctic Quebec. *Bulletin of Environmental Contamination and Toxicology* 43:641–46.

Diamond, J. M. 1969. Avifaunal equilibria and species turnover rates on the Channel Islands of California. *Proceedings of the National Academy of Sciences* 64:57–63.

Diamond, J. M. 1984. "Normal" extinctions of isolated populations. In N.H. Nitecki. *Extinctions*. Chicago, Chicago University Press.

Diaz, H. F. and G. N. Kiladis. 1992. Atmospheric teleconnections associated with the extreme phases of the Southern Oscillation. In H. F. Diaz and V. Markgraf. eds. *El Niño Historical and Paleoclimatic Aspects of the Southern Oscillation*. Cambridge. England: Cambridge University Press.

Diaz, R. J. and R. Rosenberg. 2008. Spreading dead zones and consequences for Marine Ecosystems. *Science* 321(5891):926–9.

Diffendorfer, J. E., M. S. Gaines, and R. D. Holt. 1995. Habitat fragmentation and movements of three small mammals (*Sigmodon, Microtus,* and *Peromyscus*). *Ecology* 76:827–39.

Dillon, P. J. and F. H. Rigler. 1974. The phosphorus–chlorophyll relationship in lakes. *Limnology and Oceanography* 19:767–73.

Dirzo, R. and A. Miranda. 1990. Contemporary neotropical defaunation and forest structure, function, and diversity—a sequel to John Terborgh. *Conservation Biology* 4:444–7.

Dobzhansky, T. 1950. Evolution in the tropics. *American Scientist* 38:209–21.

Dodd, M., J. Silvertown, K. McConway, J. Potts, and M. Crawley. 1995. Community stability: a 60-year record of trends and outbreaks in the occurrence of species in the Park Grass Experiment. *Journal of Ecology* 83:277–85.

DOE. 2000. The Human Genome Project Information. www.ornl.gov/TechResources/Human_Genome/home.html

Donkor, N. T. and J. M. Fryxell. 1999. Impact of beaver foraging on structure of lowland boreal forests of Algonquin Provincial Park, Ontario. *Forest Ecology and Management,* 118:83–92.

Donlan, J., H. W. Greene, J. Berger, C. E. Bock, J. H. Bock, D. A. Burney, J. A. Estes, D. Foreman, P. S. Martin, G. W. Roemer, F. A. Smith, and M. E. Soulé. 2005. Re-wilding North America. *Nature* 436(7053): 913–14.

Douglas, M. R. and P. C. Brunner. 2002. Biodiversity of central alpine *Coregonus* (Salmoniformes); impact of one-hundred years of management. *Ecological Applications* 12:154–72.

Downing, J. A., Y. T. Prairie, J. J. Cole, C. M. Duarte, L. J. Tranvik, R. G. Striegl, W. H. McDowell, P. Kortelainen, N. F. Caraco, J. M. Melack, and J. J. Middelburg. 2006. The global abundance and size distribution of lakes, ponds, and impoundments. *Limnology and Oceanography* 51:2388–97.

Drew, M. C. 1975. Comparison of effects of a localized supply of phosphate, nitrate, ammonium and potassium on growth of seminal root system, and shoot, in barley. *New Phytologist* 75(3):479–90.

Dubois, F. D. and L. A. Giraldeau. 2005. Fighting for resources: The economics of defense and appropriation. *Ecology* 86(1):3–11.

Dulvy, N. K., R. E. Forrest. 2010. Life histories, population dynamics, and extinction risks in Chondrichthyans. In J. C. Carrier, J. A. Musick, and M. R. Heithaus, eds. *Sharks and Their Relatives II: Biodiversity, Adaptive Physiology, and Conservation.* Boca Raton, FL, CRC Press.

Dyer, S. J., J. P. O'Neill, S. M. Wasel, and S. Boutin. 2002. Quantifying barrier effects of roads and seismic lines on movements of female woodland caribou in northeastern Alberta. *Canadian Journal of Zoology-Revue Canadienne De Zoologie* 80(5):839–45.

Ecological Stratification Working Group. 1996. *A National Ecological Framework for Canada.* Agriculture and Agri-Food Canada, Research Branch, Centre for Land and Biological Resources Research and Environment Canada, State of Environment Directorate, Ottawa/Hull.

Edney, E. B. 1953. The temperature of woodlice in the sun. *Journal of Experimental Biology* 30:331–49.

Egler, F. E. 1954. Vegetation science concepts I. Initial floristic composition. A factor in old-field vegetation development. *Vegetatio* 4:412–17.

Ehleringer, J. R. 1980. Leaf morphology and reflectance in relation to water and temperature stress. In N. C. Turner and P. J. Kramer. eds. *Adaptations of Plants to Water and High Temperature Stress.* New York: Wiley-Interscience.

Ehleringer, J. R., J. Roden, and T. E. Dawson. 2000. Assessing ecosystem-level water relations through stable isotope ratio analyses. In O. E. Sala. R. B. Jackson, H. A. Mooney. and R. W. Howarth. eds. *Methods in Ecosystem Science.* New York: Springer.

Ehleringer, J. R., S. L. Phillips, W. S. F. Schuster, and D. R. Sandquist. 1991. Differential utilization of summer rains by desert plants. *Oecologia* 88:430–34.

Eliason, E. J., T. D. Clark, M. J. Hague, L. M. Hanson, Zoe S. Gallagher, K. M. Jeffries, M. K. Gale, D. A. Patterson, S. G. Hinch, and A. P. Farrell. 2011. Differences in thermal tolerance among sockeye salmon populations. *Science.* 332:109–12.

Elton, C. 1924. Periodic fluctuations in the numbers of animals: their causes and effects. *British Journal of Experimental Biology* 2:119–63.

Elton, C. 1927. *Animal Ecology.* London: Sidgewick & Jackson.

Endler, J. A. 1980. Natural selection on color patterns in *Poecilia reticulata.* *Evolution* 34:76–91.

Endler, J. A. 1995. Multiple-trait coevolution and environmental gradients in guppies. *Trends in Ecology & Evolution* 10:22–9.

Erickson, G. M., P. J. Currie, B. D. Inouye, and A. A. Winn. 2006. Tyrannosaur Life Tables: An Example of Nonavian Dinosaur Population Biology. *Science* 313:213.

Erwin, D. H. 2001. Lessons from the past: Biotic recoveries from mass extinctions. *Proceedings of the National Academy of Sciences of the United States of America* 98:5399–403.

Evans, M. S., D. Muir, W. L. Lockhart, G. Stern, M. Ryan, and P. Roach. 2005. Persistent organic pollutants and metals in the freshwater biota of the Canadian Subarctic and Arctic: An overview. *Science of the Total Environment* 351:94–147.

F. A. O. 1972. *Atlas of the Living Resources of the Sea.* 3d ed. Rome: F. A. O.

Fahrig, L. 1997. Relative effects of habitat loss and fragmentation on population extinction. *Journal of Wildlife Management* 61(3):603–10.

Fahrig, L. 2003. Effects of habitat fragmentation on biodiversity. *Annual Review of Ecology Evolution and Systematics* 34:487–515.

Fahrig, L. 2005. When is a landscape perspective important? In J. A. Wiens and M. R. Moss, eds. *Issues and Perspective in Landscape Ecology.* Cambridge, Cambridge University Press.

Findlay, D. L. and S. E. M. Kasian. 1987. Phytoplankton community responses to nutrient addition in Lake 226, Experimental Lakes Area, northwestern Ontario. *Canadian Journal of Fisheries and Aquatic Sciences* 44(Suppl. 1):35–46.

Fisher, R. A. 1930. *The genetical theory of natural selection.* Oxford, Clarendon Press.

Fisher, S. G., L. J. Gray, N. B. Grimm, and D. E. Busch. 1982. Temporal succession in a desert stream ecosystem following flash flooding. *Ecological Monographs* 52:93–110.

Foley, J. A., R. DeFries, G. P. Asner, C. Barford, G. Bonan, S. R. Carpenter, F. S. Chapin, M. T. Coe, G. C. Daily, H. K. Gibbs, J. H. Helkowski, T. Holloway, E. A. Howard, C. J. Kucharik, C. Monfreda, J. A. Patz, I. C. Prentice, N. Ramankutty, and P. K. Snyder. 2005. Global consequences of land use. *Science* 309(5734):570–4.

Forbes, S. A. 1887. The lake as a microcosm. *Bulletin of the Peoria Scientific Association.* Reprinted in the Bulletin of the Illinois State Natural History Survey 15 (1925):537–50.

Forel, F. A. 1892. *Le Léman: Monograhie limnologique.* Tome I, Géographie, Hydrographie, Géologie, Climatologie, Hydrologie. Lausanne, F. Rouge. Reprinted Genève, Slatkine Reprints, 1969.

Forman, R. T. T. and L. E. Alexander. 1998. Roads and their major ecological effects. *Annual Review of Ecology and Systematics* 29:207–31.

Fortin, M. J., R. J. Olson, S. Ferson, L. Iverson, C. Hunsaker, G. Edwards, D. Levine, K. Butera, and V. Klemas. 2000. Issues related to the detection of boundaries. *Landscape Ecology,* 15:453–66.

Fortin, M. J., T. H. Keitt, B. A. Maurer, M. L. Taper, D. M. Kaufmann, and T. M. Blackburn. 2005. Species' geographic ranges and distributional limits: pattern analysis and statistical issues. *Oikos,* 108:7–17.

Fox, J. W. 2013. The intermediate disturbance hypothesis should be abandoned. *Trends in Ecology & Evolution* 28(2):86–92.

Frank, P. W., C. D. Boll, and R. W. Kelly. 1957. Vital statistics of laboratory cultures of *Daphnia pulex* De Geer as related to density. *Physiological Zoology* 30:287–305.

Frankham, R. and K. Ralls. 1998. Inbreeding leads to extinction. *Nature* 392:441–42.

Fraser, L. H., H. A. L. Henry, C. N. Carlyle, S. R. White, C. Beierkuhnlein, J. F. Cahill, B. B. Casper, E. Cleland, S. L. Collins, J. S. Dukes, A. K. Knapp, E. Lind, R. Long, Y. Luo, P. B. Reich, M. D. Smith, M. Sternberg, and R. Turkington. 2013. Coordinated distributed experiments: an emerging tool for testing global hypotheses in ecology and environmental science. *Frontiers in Ecology and the Environment* 11(3):147–55.

Friedli, H., H. Lotscher, H. Oeschger, U. Siegenthaler, and B. Stauffer. 1986. Ice core record of the $^{13}C/^{12}C$ ratio of atmospheric CO_2 in the past two centuries. *Nature* 324:237–8.

Friedmann, H. 1955. The honey-guides. *Bulletin of the United States National Museum* 208:1–292.

Fu, C. H., R. Mohn, and L. P. Fanning. 2001. Why the Atlantic cod (*Gadus morhua* stock off eastern Nova Scotia has not recovered. *Canadian Journal of Fisheries and Aquatic Sciences* 58(8):1613–23.

Funk, D. J., P. Nosil, and W. J. Etges. 2006. Ecological divergence exhibits consistently positive associations with reproductive isolation across disparate taxa. *Proceedings of the National Academy of Sciences of the United States of America* 103(9):3209–13.

Gallardo, A. and J. Merino. 1993. Leaf decomposition in two Mediterranean ecosystems of southwest Spain: influence of substrate quality. *Ecology* 74:152–61.

Gamberg, M., B. Braune, E. Davey, B. Elkin, P. F. Hoekstra, D. Kennedy, C. Macdonald, D. Muir, A. Nirwal, M. Wayland, and B. Zeeb. 2005. Spatial and temporal trends of contaminants in terrestrial biota from the Canadian Arctic. *Science of the Total Environment* 351:148–64.

Garant, D., I. A. Fleming, S. Einum and L. Bernatchez. 2003. Alternative male life-history tactics as potential vehicles for speeding introgression of farm salmon traits into wild populations. *Ecology Letters* 6(6):541–9.

Gaston, K. J. 1996. The multiple forms of the interspecific abundance-distribution relationship. *Oikos* 76:211–20.

Gaston, K. J., T. M. Blackburn, J. J. D. Greenwood, R. D. Gregory, R. M. Quinn, and J.H. Lawton. 2000. Abundance-occupancy relationships. *Journal of Applied Ecology* 37:39–59.

Gaudet, C. L. and P. A. Keddy. 1988. A comparative approach to predicted competitive ability from plant traits. *Nature* 334:242–43.

Gause, G. F. 1934. *The Struggle for Existence.* Baltimore: Williams & Wilkins. Reprinted by Hafner Publishing Company. New York. 1969.

Gauslaa, Y. 1984. Heat resistance and energy budget in different Scandinavian plants. *Holarctic Ecology* 7:1–78.

Gauthier-Clerc, M., J. P. Gendner, C. A. Ribic, W. R. Fraser, E. J. Woehler, S. Descamps, C. Gilly, C. Le Bohec, and Y. Le Maho. 2004. Long-term effects of flipper bands on penguins. *Proceedings of the Royal Society of London Series B-Biological Sciences* 271:S423–26.

Gedney, N., P. M. Cox, R. A. Betts, O. Boucher, C. Huntingford, and P. A. Stott. 2006. Detection of a direct carbon dioxide effect in continental river runoff records. *Nature* 439(7078):835–38.

Gallardo, A. and J. Merino. 1993. Leaf decomposition in two Mediterranean ecosystems of southwest Spain: influence of substrate quality. *Ecology* 74:152–61.

Gersani, M., J. S. Brown, E. E. O'Brien, G. M. Maina, and Z. Abramsky. 2001. Tragedy of the commons as a result of root competition. *Journal of Ecology* 89(4):660–69.

Getzin, S., C. Dean, F. L. He, J. A. Trofymow, K. Wiegand, and T. Wiegand. 2006. Spatial patterns and competition of tree species in a Douglas-fir chronosequence on Vancouver Island. *Ecography* 29(5):671–82.

Gibbs, H. L. and P. R. Grant. 1987. Ecological consequences of an exceptionally strong El Niño event on Darwin's finches. *Ecology* 68:1735–46.

Gibbs, R. J. 1970. Mechanisms controlling world water chemistry. *Science* 170:1088–90.

Gillson, L. and K. J. Willis. 2004. "As Earth's testimonies tell: wilderness conservation in a changing world." *Ecology Letters* 7(10):990–8.

Gleason, H. A. 1926. The individualistic concept of the plant association. *Torrey Botanical Club Bulletin* 53:7–26.

Gleason, H. A. 1939. The individualistic concept of the plant association. *American Midland Naturalist* 21:92–110.

Gobeil, J. F. and M. A. Villard. 2002. Permeability of three boreal forest landscape types to bird movements as determined from experimental translocations. *Oikos* 98(3):447–58.

Gorrell, J. C., A. G. McAdam, D. W. Coltman, M. M. Humphries, and S. Boutin. 2010. Adopting kin enhances inclusive fitness in asocial red squirrels. *Nature Communications* 1:22, doi:10.1038/ncomms1022.

Gosz, J. R., R. T. Holmes, G. E. Likens, and F. H. Bormann. 1978. The flow of energy in a forest ecosystem. *Scientific American* 238(3):92–102.

Graham, W. F. and R. A. Duce. 1979. Atmospheric pathways of the phosphorus cycle. *Geochimica et Cosmochimica Acta* 43:1195–208.

Granéli, E., K. Wallström, U. Larsson, W. Granéli, and R. Elmgren. 1990. Nutrient limitation of primary production in the Baltic Sea area. *Ambio* 19:142–51.

Grant, B. R. and P. R. Grant. 1989. *Evolutionary Dynamics of a Natural Population.* Chicago: University of Chicago Press.

Grant, P. R. 1986. *Ecology and Evolution of Darwin's Finches.* Princeton. N.J.: Princeton University Press.

Grassle, J. F. 1973. Variety in coral reef communities. In O. A. Jones and R. Endean. eds. *Biology and Geology of Coral Reefs.* Vol. 2. New York: Academic Press.

Grassle, J. F. 1991. Deep-sea benthic biodiversity. *BioScience* 41(7): 464–69.

Gray, A. 1878. "Forest Geography and Archaeology": a lecture delivered before the Harvard University Natural History Society, April 18, 1878, *American Journal of Science and Arts* 16:85–94, 183–196.

Griffith, S. C., I. P, F. Owens, K. A. Thuman. 2002. Extra pair paternity in birds: a review of interspecific variation and adaptive function. *Molecular Ecology* 11:2195-212.

Grime, J. P. 1973. Competition and diversity in herbaceous vegetation. *Nature* 244:311.

Grime, J. P. 1977. Evidence for the existence of three primary strategies in plants and its relevance to ecological and evolutionary theory. *American Naturalist* 111:1169–94.

Grime, J. P. 1979. *Plant Strategies and Vegetation Processes.* New York: John Wiley & Sons.

Grimm, N. B. 1987. Nitrogen dynamics during succession in a desert stream. *Ecology* 68:1157–70.

Grimm, N. B. 1988. Role of macroinvertebrates in nitrogen dynamics of a desert stream. *Ecology* 69:1884–93.

Grinnell, J. 1917. The niche-relationships of the California Thrasher. *Auk* 34:427–33.

Grinnell, J. 1924. Geography and evolution. *Ecology* 5:225–29.

Groffman, P. M., N. L. Law, K. T. Belt, L. E. Band, and G. T. Fisher. 2004. Nitrogen fluxes and retention in urban watershed ecosystems. *Ecosystems.* 7:393–403.

Gross, M. R. 1985. Disruptive selection for alternative life histories in salmon. *Nature* 313:47–8.

Gross, M. R. 1991. Salmon breeding behavior and life history evolution in changing environments. *Ecology* 72:1180–6.

Gross, J. E., L. A. Shipley, N. T. Hobbs, D. E. Spalinger, and B. A. Wunder. 1993. Functional response of herbivores in food-concentrated patches: tests of a mechanistic model. *Ecology* 74:778–91.

Grutter, A. S. 1999. Cleaner fish really do clean. *Nature* 398:672–3.

Guénette, J. S. and M. A. Villard. 2005. Thresholds in forest bird response to habitat alteration as quantitative targets for conservation. *Conservation Biology* 19(4):1168–80.

Guerry, A. D., M. H. Ruckelshaus, K. K. Arkema, J. R. Bernhardt, G. Guannel, C.-K Kim, M. Marsik, M. Papenfus, J. E. Toft, G. Verutes, S. A. Wood, M. Beck, F. Chan, K. M. A. Chan, G. Gelfenbaum, B. D. Gold, B. S. Halpern, W. B. Labiosa, S. E. Lester, P. S. Levin, M. McField, M. L. Pinsky, M. Plummer, S. Polasky, P. Ruggiero, D. A. Sutherland, H. Tallis, A. Day,

and J. Spencer. 2012. Modeling benefits from nature: using ecosystem services to inform coastal and marine spatial planning. *International Journal of Biodiversity Science, Ecosystem Services & Management* 8(1-2):107–21.

Gumel, A. B., S. G. Ruan, T. Day, J. Watmough, F. Brauer, P. van den Driessche, D. Gabrielson, C. Bowman, M. E. Alexander, S. Ardal, J. H. Wu, and B. M. Sahai. 2004. Modelling strategies for controlling SARS outbreaks. *Proceedings of the Royal Society of London Series B-Biological Sciences* 271(1554): 2223–32.

Gunderson, D. R. 1997. Trade-off between reproductive effort and adult survival in oviparous and viviparous fishes. *Canadian Journal of Fisheries and Aquatic Sciences* 54:990–98.

Gurevitch, J., L. L. Morrow, A. Wallace, and J. S. Walsh. 1992. A meta-analysis of competition in field experiments. *American Naturalist* 140:539–72.

Haberl, H., K. H. Erb, F. Krausmann, V. Gaube, A. Bondau, C. Pluzar, S. Gingrich, W. Lucht, and M. Fischer-Kowalski. 2007. Quantifying and mapping the human appropriation of net primary production in earth's terrestrial ecosystems. *Proceedings of the National Academy of Sciences Journal* 104(31):12942–7.

Hadley, N. F. and T. D. Schultz. 1987. Water loss in three species of tiger beetles (*Cicindela*): correlations with epicuticular hydrocarbons. *Journal of Insect Physiology* 33:677–82.

Hamilton, W. D. 1964. The genetical evolution of social behaviour, I and II. *Journal of Theoretical Biology* 7:1–52.

Handford, P., G. Bell, and T. Reimchen. 1977. A gillnet fishery considered as an experiment in artificial selection. *Journal of Fisheries Research Board of Canada* 34:954–61.

Hanski, I. 1982. Dynamics of regional distribution: the core and satellite hypothesis. *Oikos* 38:210–21.

Hanski, I., M. Kuussaari, and M. Nieminen. 1994. Metapopulation structure and migration in the butterfly *Melitaea cinxia. Ecology* 75:747–62.

Hardie, K. 1985. The effect of removal of extraradical hyphae on water uptake by vesicular-arbuscular mycorrhizal plants. *New Phytologist* 101:677–84.

Hardin, G. 1960. The competitive exclusion principle. *Science* 131:1292–97.

Harper, J. L., P. H. Lovell, and K. G. Moore. 1970. The shapes and sizes of seeds. *Annual Review of Ecology and Systematics* 1:327–56.

Haukioja, E., K. Kapiainen, P. Niemelä, and J. Tuomi. 1983. Plant availability hypothesis and other explanations of herbivore cycles: complementary or exclusive alternatives? *Oikos* 40:419–32.

Hawkes, C. V. and J. J. Sullivan. 2001. The impact of herbivory on plants in different resource conditions: A meta-analysis. *Ecology* 82(7):2045–58.

Heath, J. E. and P. J. Wilkin. 1970. Temperature responses of the desert cicada, *Diceroprocta apache* (Homoptera, Cicadidae). *Physiological Zoology* 43:145–54.

Hebert, P. D. N., A. Cywinska, S. L. Ball, and J. R. DeWaard. 2003. Biological identifications through DNA barcodes. *Proceedings of the Royal Society of London Series B-Biological Sciences* 270(1512):313–21.

Hedin, L. O., P. M. Vitousek, and P. A. Matson. 2003. Nutrient losses over four million years of tropical forest development. *Ecology* 84:2231–55.

Hegazy, A. K. 1990. Population ecology and implications for conservation of *Cleome droserifolia:* a threatened xerophyte. *Journal of Arid Environments* 19:269–82.

Heinrich, B. 1979. *Bumblebee Economics.* Cambridge, Mass.: Harvard University Press.

Heinrich, B. 1984. Strategies of thermoregulation and foraging in two vespid wasps, *Dolichovespula maculata* and *Vespula vulgaris. Journal of Comparative Physiology* B154:175–80.

Heinrich, B. 1993. *The Hot-Blooded Insects.* Cambridge, Mass.: Harvard University Press.

Heisenberg, W. 1927. Über den anschaulichen Inhalt der quantentheoretischen Kinematik und Mechanik, *Zeitschrift für Physik,* 43:172–98. English translation: J. A. Wheeler and H. Zurek. 1983. *Quantum Theory and Measurement.* Princeton Univ. Press, 62–84.

Hendry, A. P., S. K. Huber, L. F. de Leon, A. Herrel, and J. Podos. 2010. Disruptive selection in a bimodal population of Darwin's finches. *Philosophical Transactions of the Royal Society B-Biological Sciences* 276:753–59.

Hengeveld, R. 1988. Mechanisms of biological invasions. *Journal of Biogeography* 15:819–28.

Henry, G. H. R. and U. Molau. 1997. Tundra plants and climate change: the International Tundra Experiment (ITEX). *Global Change Biology* 3(S1):1–9.

Herborg, L. M., C. L. Jerde, D. M. Lodge, G. M. Ruiz, and H. J. MacIsaac. 2007. Predicting invasion risk using measures of introduction effort and environmental niche models. *Ecological Applications* 17:663–74.

Heske, E. J., J. H. Brown, and S. Mistry. 1994. Long-term experimental study of a Chihuahuan Desert rodent community: 13 years of competition. *Ecology* 75:438–45.

Hik, D. S. and R. L. Jefferies. 1990. Increases in the net aboveground primary production of a salt-marsh forage grass—a test of the predictions of the herbivore-optimization model. *Journal of Ecology* 78(1):180–95.

Hillebrand, H. 2004. On the generality of the latitudinal diversity gradient. *American Naturalist* 163:192–211.

Hillebrand, H. and B. J. Cardinale. 2010. A critique for meta-analyses and the productivity–diversity relationship. *Ecology* 91(9):2545–9.

Hillis, D. M., B. K. Mable, A. Larson, S. K. Davis, and E. A. Zimmer. 1996. Nucleic acids IV: sequencing and cloning. In D. M. Hillis, C. Moritz, and B. K. Mable. eds. *Molecular Systematics.* Sunderland, Mass.: Sinauer Associates, Inc.

Hobbie, S. E., J. P. Schimel, S. E. Trumbore, and J. R. Randerson. 2000. Controls over carbon storage and turnover in high-latitude soils. *Global Change Biology* 6: 196–210.

Hobbs, R. J. and L. F. Huenneke. 1992. Disturbance, diversity, and invasion—implications for conservations. *Conservation Biology* 6(3):324–37.

Hobson, K. A. 1999. Tracing origins and migration of wildlife using stable isotopes: A review. *Oecologia* 120:314–26.

Hodkinson, I. D. and S. J. Coulson. 2004. Are high Arctic terrestrial food chains really that simple? The Bear Island food web revisited. *Oikos* 106:427–31.

Hogetsu, K. and S. Ichimura. 1954. Studies on the biological production of Lake Suwa. 6. The ecological studies in the production of phytoplankton. *Japanese Journal of Botany* 14:280–303.

Hölldobler, B. and E. O. Wilson. 1990. *The Ants.* Cambridge, Mass.: The Belknap Press of Harvard University Press.

Holling, C. S. 1959. The components of predation as revealed by a study of small mammal predation of the European pine sawfly. *The Canadian Entomologist* 91:293–320.

Hooper, D. U., F. S. Chapin, III, J. J. Ewel, A. Hector, P. Inchausti, S. Lavorel, J. H. Lawton, D. Lodge, M. Loreau, S. Naeem, B. Schmid, H. Setälä, A. J. Symstad, J. Vandermeer, and D. A. Wardle. 2005. Effects of biodiversity on ecosystem functioning: a consensus of current knowledge. *Ecological Monographs* 75:3–35.

Houde, A. E. 1997. *Sex. Color, and Mate Choice in Guppies.* Princeton, N.J.: Princeton University Press.

Houghton, J. 2001. The science of global warming. *Interdisciplinary Science Reviews* 26(4):247–57.

Howe, W. H. and F. L. Knopf. 1991. On the imminent decline of the Rio Grande cottonwoods in central New Mexico. *Southwestern Naturalist* 36:218–24.

Huang, H. T. and P. Yang. 1987. The ancient cultured citrus ant. *BioScience* 37:665–7.

Hudson, P. J., A. P. Dobson, and D. Newborn. 1992. Do parasites make prey vulnerable to predation? *Journal of Animal Ecology* 61:681–92.

Huffaker, C. B. 1958. Experimental studies on predation: dispersion factors and predator-prey oscillations. *Hilgardia* 27:343–83.

Hulshoff, R. M. 1995. Landscape indices describing a Dutch landscape. *Landscape Ecology* 10:101–11.

Huntly, N. and R. Inouye. 1988. Pocket gophers in ecosystems: patterns and mechanisms. *BioScience* 38: 786–93.

Hurrell, J. W. 1996. Influence of variations in extratropical wintertime teleconnections on Northern Hemisphere temperature. *Geophysical Research Letters* 23(6):665–8.

Huston, M. 1994. *Biological Diversity.* New York: Cambridge University Press.

Hutchings, J. A. 1996. Spatial and temporal variation in the density of northern cod and a review of hypotheses for the stock's collapse. *Canadian Journal of Fisheries and Aquatic Sciences* 53(5):943–62.

Hutchinson, G. E. 1957. Concluding remarks. *Cold Spring Symposia on Quantitative Biology* 22:415–27.

Hutchinson, G. E. 1961. The paradox of the plankton. *American Naturalist* 95:137–45.

Hutchinson, G. E. 1978. *An Introduction to Population Ecology.* New Haven, Conn.: Yale University Press.

Ichimura, S. 1956. On the standing crop and productive structure of phytoplankton community in some lakes of central Japan. *Japanese Botany Magazine Tokyo* 69:7–16.

Innes, D. J. and P. D. N. Hebert. 1988. The origin and genetic-basis of obligate parthenogenesis in *daphnia-pulex. Evolution* 42(5):1024–35.

Innes, D. J. and R. L. Dunbrack. 1993. Sex allocation variation in *Daphnia-pulex. Journal of Evolutionary Biology* 6(4):559–75.

Iriarte, J. A., W. L. Franklin, W. E. Johnson, and K. H. Redford. 1990. Biogeographic variation of food habits and body size of the American puma. *Oecologia* 85:185–90.

Isack, H. A. and H.-V. Reyer. 1989. Honeyguides and honey gatherers: interspecific communication in a symbiotic relationship. *Science* 243:1343–46.

Isbell, F. V. Calcagno, A. Hector, J. Conolly, W. S. Harpole, P. B. Reich, M. Scherer-Lorenzen, B. Schmid, D. Tilman, J. van Ruijven, A. Weigelt, B. J. Wilsey, E. S. Zavaleta, and M. Loreau. 2011. High plant diversity is needed to maintain ecosystem services. *Nature* 477:199–202.

Jakobsson, A. and O. Eriksson. 2000. A comparative study of seed number, seed size, seedling size and recruitment in grassland plants. *Oikos* 88:494–502.

Janzen, D. H. 1966. Coevolution of mutualism between ants and acacias in Central America. *Evolution* 20:249–75.

Janzen, D. H. 1967a. Fire, vegetation structure, and the ant x acacia interaction in Central America. *Ecology* 48:26–35.

Janzen, D. H. 1967b. Interaction of the bull's-horn acacia (*Acacia cornigera* L.) with an ant inhabitant (*Pseudomyrmex ferruginea* F. Smith) in eastern Mexico. *The University of Kansas Science Bulletin* 47:315–558.

Janzen, D. H. 1978. Seeding patterns of tropical trees. In P. B. Tomlinson and M. H. Zimmermann. eds. *Tropical Trees as Living Systems.* Cambridge, England: Cambridge University Press.

Janzen, D. H. 1981a. Guanacaste tree seed-swallowing by Costa Rican range horses. *Ecology* 62:587–92.

Janzen, D. H. 1981b. Enterolobium cyclocarpum seed passage rate and survival in horses, Costa Rican Pleistocene seed dispersal agents. *Ecology* 62:593–601.

Janzen, D. H. 1985. Natural history of mutualisms. In D. H. Boucher. ed. *The Biology of Mutualism: Ecology and Evolution.* London: Croom Helm.

Jarvis, J. U. M. 1981. Eusociality in a mammal: cooperative breeding in naked mole-rat colonies. *Science* 212:571–73.

Jenny, H. 1980. *The Soil Resource.* New York: Springer Verlag.

Johnson, N. C. 1993. Can fertilization of soil select less mutualistic mycorrhizae. *Ecological Applications* 3:749–57.

Jones, C. G., J. H. Lawton, and M. Shachak. 1994. Organisms as Ecosystem Engineers. *Oikos* 69:373–86.

Jonsen, I. D. and P. D. Taylor. 2000. Fine-scale movement behaviors of calopterygid damselflies are influenced by landscape structure: an experimental manipulation. *Oikos* 88(3):553–62.

Kairiukstis, L. A. 1967. In J. L. Tselniker (ed.) Svetovoi rezhim fotosintez i produktiwnost lesa. (Light regime, photosynthesis and forest productivity) Nauka, Moscow.

Kallio, P. and L. Kärenlampi. 1975. Photosynthesis in mosses and lichens. In J. P. Cooper. ed. *Photosynthesis and Productivity in Different Environments.* Cambridge, England: Cambridge University Press.

Kalmar, A. and D. J. Currie. 2006. A global model of island biogeography. *Global Ecology and Biogeography* 15(1):72–81.

Karlson, R. H., H. V. Cornell, and T. P. Hughes. 2004. Coral communities are regionally enriched along an oceanic biodiversity gradient. *Nature* 429(6994):867–70.

Kaser, S. A. and J. Hastings. 1981. Thermal physiology of the cicada, *Tibicen duryi. American Zoologist* 21:1016.

Kates, R. W., B. L. Turner II, and W. C. Clark. 1990. The great transformation. In B. L. Turner II, W. C. Clark, R. W. Kates, J. F. Richards, J. T. Mathews, and W. B. Meyer, eds. *The Earth as Transformed by Human Action.* Cambridge, England: Cambridge University Press.

Katona, S. K. 1989. Getting to know you. *Oceanus* 32:37–44.

Keddy, P. A. and B. Shipley. 1989. Competitive Hierarchies in Herbaceous Plant-Communities. *Oikos* 54:234–41.

Keeler, K. H. 1981. A model of selection for facultative nonsymbiotic mutualism. *American Naturalist* 118:488–98.

Keeler, K. H. 1985. Benefit models of mutualism. In D. H. Boucher. ed. *The Biology of Mutualism: Ecology and Evolution.* London: Croom Helm.

Keeling, C. D. and T. P. Whorf. 1994. Atmospheric CO_2 records from sites in the SIO air sampling network. In T. A. Boden, D. P. Kaiser, R. J. Sepanski, and F. W. Stoss. eds. *Trends '93: A Compendium of Data on Global Change.* ORNL/CDIAC-65, Oak Ridge, Tenn.: Carbon Dioxide Information Analysis Center, Oak Ridge National Laboratory.

Keith, L. B. 1963. *Wildlife's Ten-year Cycle.* Madison, Wis.: University of Wisconsin Press.

Keith, L. B. 1983. Role of food in hare population cycles. *Oikos* 40:385–95.

Keith, L. B., J. R. Cary, O. J. Rongstad, and M. C. Brittingham. 1984. Demography and ecology of a declining snowshoe hare population. *Wildlife Monographs* 90:1–43.

Kembel, S. K. and J. F. Cahill, Jr. 2005. Plant phenotypic plasticity belowground: a phylogenetic perspective on root foraging tradeoffs. *American Naturalist* 166:216–30.

Kerr, J. T. 1997. Species richness, endemism, and the choice of areas for conservation. *Conservation Biology* 11(5):1094–100.

Kevan, P. G. 1975. Sun-tracking solar furnaces in high arctic flowers: significance for pollination and insects. *Science* 189:723–26.

Kidron, G. J., E. Barzilay, and E. Sachs. 2000. Microclimate control upon sand microbiotic crusts, Western Negev Desert, Israel. *Geomorphology* 36: 1–18.

Killingbeck, K. T. and W. G. Whitford. 1996. High foliar nitrogen in desert shrubs: an important ecosystem trait or defective desert doctrine? *Ecology* 77:1728–37.

Klemmedson, J. O. 1975. Nitrogen and carbon regimes in an ecosystem of young dense ponderosa pine in Arizona. *Forest Science* 21:163–68.

Klironomos, J. N. 2003. Variation in plant response to native and exotic arbuscular mycorrhizal fungi. *Ecology* 84(9):2292–2301.

Klironomos, J. N. and M. M. Hart. 2001. Food-web dynamics—Animal nitrogen swap for plant carbon. *Nature* 410(6829):651–52.

Kloppers, E. L., C. C. St. Clair, and T. E. Hurd. 2005. Predator-resembling aversive conditioning for managing habituated wildlife. *Ecology and Society* 10(1):31. www.ecologyandsociety.org/vol10/iss1/art31/.

Knutson, R. M. 1974. Heat production and temperature regulation in eastern skunk cabbage. *Science* 186:746–47.

Knutson, R. M. 1979. Plants in heat. *Natural History* 88:42–47.

Köchy, M. and S. D. Wilson. 2001. Nitrogen deposition and forest expansion in the northern Great Plains. *Journal of Ecology* 89(5):807–17.

Kodric-Brown, A. 1993. Female choice of multiple male criteria in guppies: interacting effects of dominance, coloration and courtship. *Behavioral Ecology and Sociobiology* 32:415–20.

Koh, L. P., R. R. Dunn, N. S. Sodhi, R. K. Colwell, H. C. Proctor, and V. S. Smith. 2004. Species coextinctions and the biodiversity crisis. *Science* 305(5690):1632–34.

Kolber, Z. S., C. L. Van Dover, R. A. Niederman, and P. G. Falkowski. 2000. Bacterial photosynthesis in surface waters of the open ocean. *Nature* 407:177–79.

Kontiainen, P., J. E. Brommer, P. Karell, and H. Pietiäinen. 2008. Heritability, plasticity and canalization of Ural owl egg size in a cyclic environment. *Journal of Evolutionary Biology* 21:88–96.

Korpimäki, E. 1988. Factors promoting polygyny in European birds of prey—a hypothesis. *Oecologia* 77:278–85.

Korpimäki, E. and K. Norrdahl. 1991. Numerical and functional responses of kestrels, short-eared owls, and long-eared owls to vole densities. *Ecology* 72:814–26.

Kotanen, P. M. and R. L. Jefferies. 1997. Long-term destruction of sub-arctic wetland vegetation by lesser snow geese. *Ecoscience* 4(2):179–82.

Krawchuk, M. A., S. G. Cumming, M. D. Flannigan, and R. W. Wein. 2006. Biotic and abiotic regulation of lightning fire initiation in the mixedwood boreal forest. *Ecology* 87(2):458–68.

Krebs, C. J. 2006. Ecology after 100 years: Progress and pseudo-progress. *New Zealand Journal of Ecology* 30(1):3–11.

Krebs, C. J., R. Boonstra, S. Boutin, and A. R. E. Sinclair. 2001. What drives the 10-year cycle of snowshoe hares? *BioScience* 51:25–36.

Krebs, C. J., S. Boutin, R. Boonstra, A. R. E. Sinclair, J. N. M. Smith, M. R. T. Dale, K. Martin, and R. Turkington. 1995. Impact of food and predation on the snowshoe hare cycle. *Science* 269:1112–15.

Krebs, C.J., S. Boutin, and R. Boonstra (eds.). 2001. *Ecosystem Dynamics of the Boreal Forest: The Kluane Project.* Oxford, Oxford University Press.

Kubien, D. S., S. von Cammerer, R. T. Furbank, and R. F. Sage. 2003. C-4 photosynthesis at low temperature. A study using transgenic plants with reduced amounts of Rubisco. *Plant Physiology* 132(3):1577–85.

Lack, D. 1968. *Ecological Adaptations for Breeding in Birds.* Methuen Ltd, London.

Lacy, R. C. 1997. Importance of genetic variation to the viability of mammalian populations. *Journal of Mammalogy* 78:320–35.

Laird, R. A. and B. S. Schamp. 2006. Competitive intransitivity promotes species coexistence. *American Naturalist* 168:182–93.

Lamb, E. G., A. U. Mallik, and R. W. Mackereth. 2003. The early impact of adjacent clearcutting and forest fire on riparian zone vegetation in northwestern Ontario. *Forest Ecology and Management* 177(1–3):529–38.

Lamberti, G. A. and V. H. Resh. 1983. Stream periphyton and insect herbivores: an experimental study of grazing by a caddisfly population. *Ecology* 64:1124–35.

Landhausser, S. M. and V. J. Lieffers. 2001. Photosynthesis and carbon allocation of six boreal tree species grown in understory and open conditions. *Tree Physiology* 21(4):243–50.

Larcher, W. 1995. *Physiological Plant Ecology.* 3d ed. Berlin: Springer.

Latham, R. E. and R. E. Ricklefs. 1993. Continental comparisons of temperate-zone tree species diversity. In R. E. Ricklefs and D. Schluter. eds. *Species Diversity in Ecological Communities.* Chicago: University of Chicago Press.

Lechowicz, M. J. and G. Bell. 1991. The ecology and genetics of fitness in forest plants: Microspatial heterogeneity of the edaphic environment. *Journal of Ecology* 79(3):687–96.

Ledig, F. T., V. Jacob-Cervantes, P. D. Hodgskiss, and T. Eguiluz-Piedra. 1997. Recent evolution and divergence among populations of a rare Mexican endemic, Chihuahua spruce, following Holocene climatic warming. *Evolution* 51:1815–27.

Lemon, W. C. 1993. Heritability of selectively advantageous foraging behavior in a small passerine. *Evolutionary Ecology* 7(4):421–28.

Levang-Brilz, N. and M. E. Biondini. 2002. Growth rate, root development and nutrient uptake of 55 plant species from the Great Plains Grasslands, USA. *Plant Ecology* 165:117–44.

Leverich, W. J. and D.A. Levin. 1979. Age-specific survivorship and reproduction in *Phlox drummondii*. *American Naturalist* 113:881–903.

Levins, R. 1968. *Evolution in Changing Environments*. Princeton, New Jersey: Princeton University Press.

Lie, E., H. J. S. Larsen, S. Larsen, G. M. Johnsen, A. E. Derocher, N. J. Lunn, R. J. Norstrom, O. Wiig, and J. U. Skaare. 2004. Does high organochlorine (OC) exposure impair the resistance to infection in polar bears (*Ursus maritimus*)? Part I: Effect of OCs on the humoral immunity. *Journal of Toxicology and Environmental Health-Part a-Current Issues* 67(7):555–82.

Lie, E., H. J. S. Larsen, S. Larsen, G. M. Johnsen, A. E. Derocher, N. J. Lunn, R. J. Norstrom, O. Wiig, and J. U. Skaare. 2005. Does high organochlorine (OC) exposure impair the resistance to infection in polar bears (*Ursus maritimus*)? Part II: Possible effect of OCs on mitogen- and antigen-induced lymphocyte proliferation. *Journal of Toxicology and Environmental Health-Part a-Current Issues* 68(6):457–84.

Liebig, J. 1840. *Chemistry in its Application to Agriculture and Physiology*. London: Taylor and Walton.

Ligon, J. D. 1999. *The Evolution of Avian Mating Systems*. Oxford: Oxford University Press.

Likens, G. E. and F. H. Bormann. 1995. *Biogeochemistry of a Forested Ecosystem*. 2d ed. New York: Springer-Verlag.

Likens, G. E., F. H. Bormann, N. M. Johnson, D. W. Fisher, and R. S. Pierce. 1970. Effects of forest cutting and herbicide treatment on nutrient budgets in the Hubbard Brook watershed-ecosystem. *Ecological Monographs* 40:23–47.

Likens, G. E., F. H. Bormann, R. S. Pierce, and W. A. Reiners. 1978. Recovery of a deforested ecosystem. *Science* 199:492–6.

Lindeman, R. L. 1942. The trophic-dynamic aspect of ecology. *Ecology* 23:399–418.

Liu, J., J. M. Chen, J. Cihlar, and W. Chen W. 2002. Net primary productivity mapped for Canada at 1-km resolution. *Global Ecology and Biogeography* 11:115–29.

Lomolino, M. V. 1990. The target hypothesis—the influence of island area on immigration rates of non-volant mammals. *Oikos* 57:297–300.

Lomolino, M. V., J. H. Brown, and R. Davis. 1989. Island biogeography of montane forest mammals in the American Southwest. *Ecology* 70:180–94.

Long, S. P. and C. F. Mason. 1983. *Saltmarsh Ecology*. Glasgow: Blackie.

Lorius, C., J. Jouzel, C. Ritz, L. Merlivat, N. I. Barkov, Y. S. Korotkevich, and V. M. Kotlyakov. 1985. A 150,000-year climatic record from Antarctic ice. *Nature* 316:591–6.

Lotka, A. J. 1925. *Elements of Physical Biology*. Baltimore, Md.: Williams and Wilkins.

Lotka, A. J. 1932b. Contribution to the mathematical theory of capture. I. Conditions for capture. *Proceedings of the National Academy of Science* 18:172–200.

Lotka, A. J. 1932a. The growth of mixed populations: two species competing for a common food supply. *Journal of the Washington Academy of Sciences* 22:461–69.

Louda, S. M., R. W. Pemberton, M. T. Johnson, and P. A. Follett. 2003. Nontarget effects—The Achilles' Heel of biological control? Retrospective analyses to reduce risk associated with biocontrol introductions. *Annual Review of Entomology* 48:365–96.

Lozier, J. D., P. Aniello, and M. J. Hickerson. 2009. Predicting the distribution of Sasquatch in western North America: anything goes with ecological niche modeling. *Journal of Biogeography* 36:1623–7.

MacArthur, R. H. 1958. Population ecology of some warblers of northeastern coniferous forests. *Ecology* 39:599–619.

MacArthur, R. H. 1972. *Geographical Ecology*. New York: Harper & Row.

MacArthur, R. H. and E. O. Wilson. 1963. An equilibrium theory of insular zoogeography, *Evolution* 17:373–87.

MacArthur, R. H. and E. O. Wilson. 1967. *The Theory of Island Biogeography*. Princeton, N.J.: Princeton University Press.

MacArthur, R. H. and E. R. Pianka. 1966. On optimal use of a patchy environment. *American Naturalist* 100:603–9.

MacArthur, R. H. and J. W. MacArthur. 1961. On bird species diversity. *Ecology* 42:594–98.

MacDonald, J. S., E. A. MacIsaac, and H. E. Herunter. 2003. The effect of variable-retention riparian buffer zones on water temperatures in small headwater streams in sub-boreal forest ecosystems of British Columbia. *Canadian Journal of Forest Research* 33:1371–82.

Mack, R. N., D. Simberloff, W. M. Lonsdale, H. Evans, M. Clout, and F. A. Bazzaz. 2000. Biotic invasions: Causes, epidemiology, global consequences, and control. *Ecological Applications* 10(3):689–710.

Mackay, R. L. and D. J. Currie. 2001. The diversity-disturbance relationship: is it generally strong and peaked? *Ecology* 82:3479–92.

MacLachlan, A. 1983. Sandy beach ecology—a review. In A. MacLachlan and T. Erasmus. eds. *Sandy Beaches as Ecosystems*. The Hague: Dr. W. Junk Publishers.

MacLulich, D. A. 1937. Fluctuation in the numbers of the varying hare (*Lepus americanus*). *University of Toronto Studies in Biology Series No. 43*.

Mak, S., M. Morshed, and B. Henry. 2010. Ecological Niche Modelling of Lyme Disease in British Columbia, Canada. *Journal of Medical Entomology* 47:99–105.

Mallet, J. 2008. Hybridization, ecological races and the nature of species: empirical evidence for the ease of speciation. *Phil Trans R Soc B*. 363:2971–86.

Mandelbrot, B. 1982. *The Fractal Geometry of Nature*. New York: W. H. Freeman.

Mao, J. S., M. S. Boyce, D. W. Smith, F. J. Singer, D. J. Vales, J. M. Vore, and E. H. Merrill. 2005. Habitat selection by elk before and after wolf reintroduction in Yellowstone National Park. *Journal of Wildlife Management* 69:1691–1707.

Marchand, P. J. 1996. *Life in the cold*. Hanover, NH, University Press of New England.

Margolis, H. A., L. B. Flanagan, and B. D. Amiro. 2006. The Fluxnet-Canada Research Network: Influence of climate and disturbance on carbon cycling in forests and peatlands. *Agricultural and Forest Meteorology* 140(1-4):1–5.

Margulis, L. and R. Fester. 1991. *Symbiosis as a Source of Evolutionary Innovation: Speciation and Morphogenesis*. Cambridge. Mass.: MIT Press.

Maron, J. L. and E. Crone. 2006. Herbivory: effects on plant abundance, distribution and population growth. *Proceedings of the Royal Society B-Biological Sciences* 273(1601):2575–84.

Marshall, D. L. 1990. Non-random mating in a wild radish, *Raphanus sativus*. *Plant Species Biology* 5: 143–56.

Marshall, D. L. and M. W. Folsom. 1991. Mate choice in plants: an anatomical to population perspective. *Annual Review of Ecology and Systematics* 22:37–63.

Marshall, D. L. and M. W. Folsom. 1992. Mechanisms of nonrandom mating in wild radish. In R. Wyatt. ed. *Ecology and Evolution of Plant Reproduction: New Approaches*. New York: Chapman and Hall.

Marshall, D. L. and O. S. Fuller. 1994. Does nonrandom mating among wild radish plants occur in the field as well as in the greenhouse? *American Journal of Botany* 81:439–45.

Marshall, D. L., M. W. Folsom, C. Hatfield, and T. Bennett. 1996. Does interference competition among pollen grains occur in wild radish? *Evolution* 50:1842–48.

Mathewson, D. D., M. D. Hocking, and T. E. Reimchen. 2003. Nitrogen uptake in riparian plant communities across a sharp ecological boundary of salmon density. *BMC Ecology* 3:4.

Matter, S. F. M. Ezzeddine, E. Duirmit, J. Mashburn, R. Hamilton, T. Lucas, and J. Roland. 2009. Interactions between habitat quality and connectivity affect immigration but not abundance or population growth of the butterfly, *Parnassius smintheus*. *Oikos* 118:1461–70.

May, R. M. 1975. Patterns of species abundance and diversity. In M. L. Cody and J. M. Diamond. eds. *Ecology and Evolution of Communities*. Cambridge, Mass.: Harvard University Press.

Maynard Smith, J. 1982. *Evolution and the Theory of Games*. Cambridge, Cambridge University Press.

Mayr, E. 1942. *Systematics and the Origin of Species*. New York: Columbia University Press.

Mazerolle, M. J. and M. A. Villard. 1999. Patch characteristics and landscape context as predictors of species presence and abundance: A review. *Ecoscience* 6(1):117–24.

McCarthy, D. P., P. F. Donald, J. P. W. Scharlemann, G. M. Buchanan, A. Balmford, J. M. H. Green, L. A. Bennun, N. D. Burgess, L. D. C. Fishpool, S. T. Garnett, D. L. Leonard, R. F. Malony, P. Morling, H. M. Schaefer, A. Symes, D. A. Wiedenfeld, and S. H. M. Butchart. 2012. Financial costs of meeting global biodiversity conservation targets: Current spending and unmet needs. *Science* 338(6109):946–9.

McCormick, S. D. 2001. Endocrine control of osmoregulation in teleost fish. *American Zoologist* 41:781–94.

McCullough, D. A. 1999. A review and synthesis of effects of alterations to the water temperature regime on freshwater life stages of salmonids, with special reference to chinook salmon. Environmental Protection Agency. *EPA 910-R-99-010*.

McKinnon, J. S., S. Mori, B. K. Blackman, L. David, D. M. Kingsley, L. Jamieson, J. Chou, and D. Schluter. 2004. Evidence for ecology's role in speciation. *Nature* 429(6989):294–98.

McLean, M. A., D. Parkinson. 2000. Field evidence of the effects of the epigeic earthworm *Dendrobaena octaedra* on the microfungal community in pine forest floor. *Soil Biology & Biochemistry* 32(3): 351–60.

McNaughton, S. J. 1976. Serengeti migratory wildebeest: facilitation of energy flow by grazing. *Science* 191:92–4.

McNaughton, S. J. 1985. Ecology of a grazing ecosystem: the Serengeti. *Ecological Monographs* 55:259–94.

McNaughton, S. J., R. W. Ruess, and S. W. Seagle. 1988. Large mammals and process dynamics in African ecosystems. *BioScience* 38:794–800.

Meentemeyer, V. 1978. An approach to the biometeorology of decomposer organisms. *International Journal of Biometeorology* 22:94–102.

Melillo, J. M., J. D. Aber, and J. F. Muratore. 1982. Nitrogen and lignin control of hardwood leaf litter decomposition dynamics. *Ecology* 63:621–6.

Messier, F. 1994. Ungulate population models with predation: a case study with the North American moose. *Ecology* 75:478–88.

Meybeck, M. 1982. Carbon, nitrogen, and phosphorus transport by world rivers. *American Journal of Science* 282: 401–50.

Meyer, J. L. and G. E. Likens. 1979. Transport and transformation of phosphorus in a forest stream ecosystem. *Ecology* 60:1255–69.

Meyer, J. R., S. P. Ellner, N. G. Hairston, L. E. Jones, and T. Yoshida. 2006. Prey evolution on the time scale of predator-prey dynamics revealed by allele-specific quantitative PCR. *Proceedings of the National Academy of Sciences of the United States of America* 103(28):10690–95.

Miller, R. B. 1923. First report on a forestry survey of Illinois. *Illinois Natural History Bulletin* 14:291–377.

Mills, E. L., J. H. Leach, J. T. Carlton, and C. L. Secor. 1994. Exotic species and the integrity of the Great Lakes. *BioScience* 44:666–76.

Mills, K. H. and D. W. Schindler. 1987. Preface. *Canadian Journal of Fisheries and Aquatic Sciences* 44(Suppl. 1):3–5.

Milne, B. T. 1993. Pattern analysis for landscape evaluation and characterization. In M. E. Jensen and P. S. Bourgeron. eds. *Ecosystem Management: Principles and Applications*. Gen. Tech. Report PNW-GTR-318. Portland, Ore.: U.S. Department of Agriculture Forest Service, Pacific Northwest Research Station.

Minnich, R. A. 1983. Fire mosaics in southern California and northern Baja California. *Science* 219:1287–94.

Mittelbach, G. G., D. W. Schemske, H. V. Cornell, A. P. Allen, J. M. Brown, M. B. Bush, S. P. Harrison, A. H. Hurlbert, N. Knowlton, H. A. Lessios, C. M. McCain, A. R. McCune, L. A. McDade, M. A. McPeek, T. J. Near, T. D. Price, R. E. Ricklefs, K. Roy, D. F. Sax, F. Dov, D. Schluter, J. M. Sobel, and M. Turelli. 2007. Evolution and the latitudinal diversity gradient: speciation, extinction and biogeography. *Ecology Letters* 10(4):315–31.

Molles, M. C., Jr. 1978. Fish species diversity on model and natural reef patches: experimental insular biogeography. *Ecological Monographs* 48:289–305.

Mooers, A. O., L. R. Prugh, M. Festa-Bianchet, and J. A. Hutchings. 2007. Biases in legal listings under Canadian endangered species legislation. *Conservation Biology* 21:572–75.

Moore, D. R. J., P. A. Keddy, C. L. Gaudet, and I. C. Wisheu. 1989. Conservation of Wetlands—Do Infertile Wetlands Deserve a Higher Priority. *Biological Conservation* 47:203–17.

Moore, J. 1983. Responses of an avian predator and its isopod prey to an acanthocephalan parasite. *Ecology* 64:1000–15.

Moore, J. 1984a. Altered behavioral responses in intermediate hosts—an acanthocephalan parasite strategy. *American Naturalist* 123:572–77.

Moore, J. 1984b. Parasites that change the behavior of their host. *Scientific American* 250:108–15.

Moore, J. A. H. and T. J. Roper. 2003. Temperature and humidity in badger *Meles meles* setts. *Mammal Review* 33:308–13.

Moore, J. K., S. C. Doney, and K. Kindsay. 2004. Upper ocean ecosystem dynamics and iron cycling in a global three-dimensional model. *Annual Review of Ecology and Systematics* 33:235–63.

Mooring, M. S. and W. M. Samuel. 1999. Premature loss of winter hair in free-ranging moose (*Alces alces*) infested with winter ticks (*Dermacentor albipictus*) is correlated with grooming rate. *Canadian Journal of Zoology-Revue Canadienne De Zoologie* 77(1):148–56.

Moran, P. A. P. 1949. The statistical analysis of the sunspot and lynx cycles. *Journal of Animal Ecology* 18:115–16.

Morita, R. Y. 1975. Psychrophilic bacteria. *Bacteriological Reviews* 39:144–67.

Moritz, R. E., C. M. Bitz, and E. J. Steig. 2002. Dynamics of recent climate change in the Arctic. *Science* 297:1497–502.

Mortensen, P. B. and L. Buhl-Mortensen. 2005. Deep-water corals and their habitats in The Gully, a submarine canyon off Atlantic Canada. In A. Freiwald and J. Murray Roberts, eds. *Cold-water corals and ecosystems*. Berlin: Springer 247–77.

Mosser, J. L., A. G. Mosser, and T. D. Brock. 1974. Population ecology of *Sulfolobus acidocaldarius*. I. Temperature strains. *Archives for Microbiology* 97:169–79.

Moyle, P. B. and J. J. Cech Jr. 1982. *Fishes and Introduction to Ichthyology*. Englewood Cliffs. N.J.: Prentice Hall.

Muir, J. 1915. *Travels in Alaska*. Boston: Houghton Mifflin.

Müller, K. 1954. Investigations on the organic life in north Swedish streams. *Reports of the Institute of Freshwater Research of Drottningholm* 35:133–48.

Müller, K. 1974. Stream drift as a chronobiological phenomenon in running water ecosystems. *Annual Review of Ecology and Systematics* 5:309–23.

Mullon, C., P. Freon, and P. Cury. 2005. The dynamics of collapse in world fisheries. *Fish and Fisheries* 6(2):111–20.

Munger, J. C. and J. H. Brown. 1981. Competition in desert rodents: an experiment with semipermeable exclosures. *Science* 211:510–12.

Munz, P., I. Hudea, J. Imad, and R. J. Smith. 2009. When zombies attack!: Mathematical modelling of an outbreak of zombie infection. In J. M. Tchuenche and C. Chiyaka. *Infectious Disease Modelling Research Progress*. Nova Science Publishers, Inc.

Murie, A. 1944. The wolves of Mount McKinley. *Fauna of the National Parks of the U.S.. Fauna Series No.5*. Washington, D.C.: U.S. Department of the Interior, National Park Service.

Murie, A. 1961. *A naturalist in Alaska*. New York: Devin-Adair Company.

Murie, J. O. 1985. A comparison of life history traits in two populations of Columbian ground squirrels in Alberta, Canada. *Acta Zool. Fennica* 173:43–5.

Murphy, P. G. and A. E. Lugo. 1986. Ecology of tropical dry forest. *Annual Review of Ecology and Systematics* 17:67–88.

Murphy-Klassen, H. M., T. J. Underwood, S. G. Sealy, and A. A. Czyrnyj. 2005. Long-term trends in spring arrival dates of migrant birds at Delta Marsh, Manitoba, in relation to climate change. *Auk* 122(4):1130–48.

Muscatine, L. and C. F. D'Elia. 1978. The uptake. retention, and release of ammonium by reef corals. *Limnology and Oceanography* 23:725–34.

Myers, N., R. A. Mittermeier, C. G. Mittermeier, G. A. B. da Fonseca, and J. Kent. 2000. Biodiversity hotspots for conservation priorities. *Nature* 403(6772):853–8.

Naiman, R. J., G. Pinay, C. A. Johnston, and J. Pastor. 1994. Beaver influences on the long-term biogeochemical characteristics of boreal forest drainage networks. *Ecology* 75:905–21.

Naiman, R. J., R. E. Bilby, D. E. Schindler, and J. M. Helfield. 2002. Pacific salmon, nutrients, and the dynamics of freshwater and riparian ecosystems. *Ecosystems* 5:399–417.

NASA Earth Observatory. 2003. Ocean plant life slows down and absorbs less carbon. http://earthobservatory.nasa.gov/Newsroom/view.php?id=23717.

Neptune Canada. 2010. http://neptunecanada.ca

Newbold, J. D., J. W. Elwood, R. V. O'Neill, and A. L. Sheldon. 1983. Phosphorus dynamics in a woodland stream ecosystem: a study of nutrient spiraling. *Ecology* 64:1249–65.

Newman, E. I. 1973. Competition and diversity in herbaceous vegetation. *Nature* 244:310–11.

Nilsson, S. G., J. Bengtsson, and S. Ås. 1988. Habitat diversity or area *per se?* Species richness of woody plants, carabid beetles and land snails on islands. *Journal of Animal Ecology* 57:685–704.

Norris, R. D., P P. Marra, T. K. Kyser, and L. M. Ratcliffe. 2005. Tracking habitat use of a long-distance migratory bird, the American redstart *Setaphaga ruticilla*, using stable-carbon isotopes in cellular blood. *Journal of Avian Biology* 36164–70.

Nottrott, R. W., J. F. Franklin, and J. R. Vande Castle. 1994. *International Networking in Long-Term Ecological Research*. Seattle: U.S. LTER Network Office, University of Washington.

Novacek, M. G. 2001. *The Biodiversity Crisis: Losing What Counts* New York: New Press.

Ødegaard, F. 2000. How many species of arthropods? Erwin's estimate revised. *Biological Journal of the Linnean Society* 71(4):583–97.

O'Donoghue, M., S. Boutin, C. J. Krebs, and E. J. Hofer. 1997. Numerical responses of coyotes and lynx to the snowshoe bare cycle. *Oikos* 80:150–62.

O'Donoghue, M., S. Boutin, C. J. Krebs, G. Zuleta, D. L. Murray, and E. J. Hofer. 1998. Functional responses of coyotes and lynx to the snowshoe hare cycle. *Ecology* 79:1193–208.

O'Dowd, D. J. and A. M. Gill. 1984. Predator satiation and site alteration following fire: mass reproduction of alpine ash (*Eucalyptus delegatensis*) in southeastern Australia. *Ecology* 65:1052–66.

Olff, H. and M. E. Ritchie. 1998. Effects of herbivores on grassland plant diversity. *Trends in Ecology & Evolution* 13(7):261–5.

Olsen, E. M., M. Heino, G. R. Lilly, M. J. Morgan, J. Brattey, B. Ernande, and U. Dieckmann. 2004. Maturation trends indicative of rapid evolution preceded the collapse of northern cod. *Nature* 428:932–35.

Olsen, G. H., M. Mauritzen, A. E. Derocher, E. G. Sormo, J. U. Skaare, O. Wiig, and B. M. Jenssen. 2003. Space-use strategy is an important determinant of PCB concentrations in female polar bears in the Barents sea. *Environmental Science & Technology* 37(21):4919–24.

Ottersen, G., B. Planque, A. Belgrano, E. Post, P. C. Reid, and N. C. Stenseth. 2001. Ecological effects of the North Atlantic Oscillation. *Oecologia* 128(1):1–14.

Packer, C. and A. E. Pusey. 1982. Cooperation and competition within coalitions of male lions: kin selection or game-theory? *Nature* 296:740–42.

Packer, C. and A. E. Pusey. 1983. Cooperation and competition in lions: reply. *Nature* 302:356.

Packer, C. and A. E. Pusey. 1997. Divided we fall: cooperation among lions. *Scientific American* 276(5):52–59.

Packer, C., D. A. Gilbert, A. E. Pusey, and S. J. O'Brien. 1991. A molecular genetic analysis of kinship and cooperation in African lions. *Nature* 351:562–65.

Packer, L. 1991. The evolution of social-behavior and nest architecture in sweat bees of the subgenus evylaeus (Hymenoptera, halictidae)—a phylogenetic approach. *Behavioral Ecology and Sociobiology* 29(3):153–60.

Paine, R. T. 1966. Food web complexity and species diversity. *American Naturalist* 100:65–75.

Paine, R. T. 1969. A note on trophic complexity and community stability. *American Naturalist* 103:91–93.

Paine, R. T. 1976. Size-limited predation: an observational and experimental approach with the *Mytilus-Pisaster* interaction. *Ecology* 57:858–73.

Palumbi, S. R. 2001. Humans as the world's greatest evolutionary force. *Science* 293:1786–90.

Papke, R. T., N. B. Ramsing, M. M. Bateson, and D. M. Ward. 2003. Geographical isolation in hot spring cyanobacteria. *Environmental Microbiology* 5(8):650–9.

Pappers, S. M., G. van der Velde, N. J. Ouborg, and J. M. van Groenendael. 2002. Genetically based polymorphisms in morphology and life history associated with putative host races of the water lily leaf beetle *Galerucella nymphaeae*. *Evolution* 56:1610–21.

Park, T. 1948. Experimental studies of interspecific competition. I. Competition between populations of flour beetles *Tribolium confusum* Duval and *Tribolium castaneum* Herbst. *Ecological Monographs* 18:267–307.

Park, T. 1954. Experimental studies of interspecific competition. II. Temperature, humidity and competition in two species of *Tribolium*. *Physiological Zoology* 27:177–238.

Park, T., D. B. Mertz, W. Grodzinski, and T. Prus. 1965. Cannibalistic predation in populations of flour beetles. *Physiological Zoology* 38:289–321.

Parmenter, R. R. and V.A. Lamarra. 1991. Nutrient cycling in a freshwater marsh: the decomposition of fish and waterfowl carrion. *Limnology and Oceanography* 36:976–87.

Parmenter, R. R., C. A. Parmenter, and C. D. Cheney. 1989. Factors influencing microhabitat partitioning among coexisting species of arid-land darkling beetles (Tenebrionidae): behavioural responses to vegetation architecture. *The Southwestern Naturalist* 34:319–29.

Parmesan, C. and G. Yohe. 2003. A globally coherent fingerprint of climate change impacts across natural systems. *Nature* 421(6918):37–42.

Partel, M. and S. D. Wilson. 2002. Root dynamics and spatial pattern in prairie and forest. *Ecology* 83(5):1199–203.

Pauly, D., V. Christensen, J. Dalsgaard, R. Froese, and F. Torres. 1998. Fishing down marine food webs. *Science* 279(5352):860–63.

Pearcy, R. W. 1977. Acclimation of photosynthetic and respiratory carbon dioxide exchange to growth temperature in *Atriplex lentiformis* (Torr.) Wats. *Plant Physiology* 59:795–99.

Pearcy, R. W. and A. T. Harrison. 1974. Comparative photosynthetic and respiratory gas exchange characteristics of *Atriplex lentiformis* (Torr.) Wats. in coastal and desert habitats. *Ecology* 55:1104–11.

Peckarsky, B. L. 1980. Behavioural interactions between stoneflies and mayflies: behavioural observations. *Ecology* 61:932–43.

Peckarsky, B. L. 1982. Aquatic insect predator-prey relations. *BioScience* 32:261–66.

Peckarsky, B. L., P. A. Abrams, D. I. Bolnick, L. M. Dill, J. H. Grabowski, B. Luttbeg, J. L. Orrock, S. D. Peacor, E. L. Preisser, O. J. Schmitz, and G. C. Trussell. 2008. Revisiting the classics: Considering nonconsumptive effects in textbook examples of predator-prey interactions. *Ecology* 89(9):2416–25.

Peierls, B. L., N. F. Caraco, M. L. Pace, and J. J. Cole. 1991. Human influence on river nitrogen. *Nature* 350:386–7.

Peters, R. H. and K. Wassenberg. 1983. The effect of body size on animal abundance. *Oecologia* 60:89–96.

Peters, V. S., S. E. Macdonald, and M. R. T. Dale. 2006. Patterns of initial versus delayed regeneration of white spruce in boreal mixedwood succession. *Canadian Journal of Forest Research-Revue Canadienne de Recherche Forestière* 36(6):1597–609.

Peterson, A. T. and D. A. Vieglais. 2001. Predicting species invasions using ecological niche modelling: New approaches from bioinformatics attack a pressing problem. *Bioscience* 51:363–71.

Peterson, B. J., R. W. Howarth, and R. H. Garritt. 1985. Multiple stable isotopes used to trace the flow of organic matter in estuarine food webs. *Science* 227:1361–3.

Pianka, E. R. 1970. On r and K selection. *American Naturalist* 102:592–97.

Pianka, E. R. 1972. r and K selection or b and d selection. *American Naturalist* 106:581–88.

Pickett, S. T. A., M. L. Cadenasso, J. M. Grove, P. M. Groffman, L. E. Band, C. G. Boone, W. R. Burgch Jr., C. S. B. Grimmond, J. Hom, J. C. Jenkins, N. L. Law, C. H. Nilon, R. V. Pouyat, K. Szlavec, P. S. Warren, and M. A. Wilson. 2008. Beyond urban legends: an emerging framework of urban ecology, a illustrated by the Baltimore Ecosystem Study. *BioScience* 58:139–50.

Pielou, E. C. 1966. Measurement of diversity in different types of biological collections. *Journal of Theoretical Biology* 13:131–44.

Pielou, E. C. 1977. *Mathematical Ecology*. New York, Wiley.

Pielou, E. C. 1991. *After the ice age: the return of life to glaciated North America*. University of Chicago Press. 5–38.

Pimentel, D., R. Zuniga, and D. Morrison. 2005. Update on the environmental and economic costs associated with alien-invasive species in the United States. *Ecological Economics* 52(3):273–88.

Pimlott, D. H. 1953. *Newfoundland Moose*. Transactions of the North American Wildlife Conference, 18:563–81.

Platt, T. 1975. Spectral Analysis in Ecology. *Annual Review of Ecology and Systematics* 6:189–210.

Platt, T. and Jassby, A.D. 1976. Relationship between photosynthesis and light for natural assemblages of coastal marine phytoplankton. *Journal of Phycology* 12:421–30.

Podos, J. 2010. Acoustic discrimination of sympatric morphs in Darwin's finches: a behavioural mechanism for assortative mating? *Philosophical transactions of the Royal Society B-Biological Sciences* 365:1031–39.

Polischuk, S. C., R. J. Norstrom, and M. A. Ramsay. 2002. Body burdens and tissue concentrations of organochlorines in polar bears (*Ursus maritimus*) vary during seasonal fasts. *Environmental Pollution* 118(1):29–39.

Post, E. and N. C. Stenseth. 1999. Climatic variability, plant phenology, and northern ungulates. *Ecology* 80(4):1322–39.

Post, W. M., T.-H. Peng, W. R. Emanuel, A. W. King, V. H. Dale, and D. L. DeAngelis. 1990. The global carbon cycle. *American Scientist* 78:310–26.

Poulin, R. and W. L. Vickery. 1995. Cleaning symbiosis as an evolutionary game—to cheat or not to cheat. *Journal of Theoretical Biology* 175(1):63–70.

Power, M. E. 1990. Effects of fish on river food webs. *Science* 250:811–14.

Power, M. E., D. Tilman, J. A. Estes, B. A. Menge, W. J. Bond, L. S. Mills, G. Daily, J. C. Castilla, J. Lubchenko, and R. T. Paine. 1996. Challenges in the quest for keystones. *BioScience* 46:609–20.

Preisser, E. L., D. I. Bolnick, and M. F. Benard. 2005. Scared to death? The effects of intimidation and consumption in predator-prey interactions. *Ecology* 86(2):501–9.

Preston, F. W. 1948. The commonness, and rarity, of species. *Ecology* 29:254–83.

Preston, F. W. 1962a. The canonical distribution of commonness and rarity: part I. *Ecology* 43:185–215.

Preston, F. W. 1962b. The canonical distribution of commonness and rarity: part II. *Ecology* 43:410–32.

Province of British Columbia. 2010. B.C. Wild (Capture) Salmon Production. www.env.gov.bc.ca/omfd/fishstats/graphs-tables/wild-salmon.html.

Purvis, A., J. L. Gittleman, G. Cowlishaw, and G. M. Mace. 2000. Predicting extinction risk in declining species. *Proceedings of the Royal Society of London Series B-Biological Sciences* 267(1456):1947–52.

Raup, D. M., J. J. Sepkoski. 1982. Mass extinctions in the marine fossil record. *Science, New Series* 215(4539):1501–3.

Reabalais, N. N., R. E. Turner, and W. J. Wiseman. 2002. Gulf of Mexy hypoxia, aka "The dead zone." *Annual Review of Ecology and Systematics*. 33:235–63.

Rabinowitz, D. 1981. Seven forms of rarity. In H. Synge. ed. *The Biological Aspects of Rare Plant Conservation*. New York: John Wiley & Sons.

Ralph, C. J. 1985. Habitat association patterns of forest and steppe birds of northern Patagonia, Argentina. *The Condor* 87:471–83.

Rawson, T. 2001. *Changing Tracks—Predators and Politics in Mt. McKinley National Park*, Fairbanks: Univ. of Alaska Press.

Reader, R. J., S. D. Wilson, J. W. Belcher, I. Wisheu, P. A. Keddy, D. Tilman, E. C. Morris, J. B. Grace, J. B. McGraw, H. Olff, R. Turkington, Y. Klein, B. Leung, B. Shipley, R. Van Hulst, E. Johansson, C. Nilsson, J. Gurevitch, K. Grigulis, and B. E. Beisner. 1994. Plant competition in relation to neighbor biomass: An intercontinental study with *Poa pratensis*. *Ecology* 75(6):1753–60.

Réale, D., A. G. McAdam, S. Boutin, and D. Berteaux. 2003. Genetic and plastic responses of a northern mammal to climate change. *Proceedings of the Royal Society of London Series B-Biological Sciences* 270(1515):591–96.

Recher, H. R., G. Gowing, T. Armstrong. (1985). Causes and Frequency of Deaths among Birds Mist-Netted for Banding Studies at Two Localities. *Australian Wildlife Research* 12(2):321–6.

Redford, K. H. 1992. The empty forest. *BioScience* 42:412–22.

Reich, P. B., D. Tilman, F. Isbell, K. Mueller, S. E. Hobbie, D. F. B. Flynn, and N. Eisenhauer. 2012. Impacts of biodiversity loss escalate through time as redundance fades. *Science* 336(6081):589–92.

Reid, W. V. and K. R. Miller. 1989. *Keeping Options Alive: The Scientific Basis for Conserving Biodiversity*. Washington, D.C.: World Resources Institute.

Reiners, W. A., I. A. Worley, and D. B. Lawrence. 1971. Plant diversity in a chronosequence at Glacier Bay, Alaska. *Ecology* 52:55–69.

Reynolds, H. L. and C. D'Antonio. 1996. The ecological significance of plasticity in root weight ratio in response to nitrogen: Opinion. *Plant and Soil* 185:75–97.

Reynolds, J. D. 2003. Life histories and extinction risk. In T. M. Blackburn and K. J. Gaston. *Macroecology*. Oxford, Blackwell Publishing.

Richey, J. E. 1983. The phosphorus cycle. In B. Bolin and R. B. Cook. eds. *The Major Biogeochemical Cycles and Their Interaction*. New York: John Wiley & Sons.

Ricklefs, R. E. 1987. Community diversity: relative roles of local and regional processes. *Science* 235:167–71.

Ripple, W. J. and R. L. Beschta. 2006. Linking wolves to willows via risk-sensitive foraging by ungulates in the northern Yellowstone ecosystem. *Forest Ecology and Management* 230:96–106.

Risch, S. J. and C. R. Carroll. 1982. Effect of a keystone predaceous ant, *Solenopsis geminata,* on arthropods in a tropical agroecosystem. *Ecology* 63:1979–83.

Roark, E. B., T. P. Guilderson, R. B. Dunbar, S. J. Fallon, and A. D. Mucciarone. 2009. Extreme longevity in proteinaceous deep-sea corals. *PNAS* 106:5204–08.

Roberts, C. M., C. J. McClean, J. E. N. Veron, J. P. Hawkins, G. R. Allen, D. E. McAllister, C. G. Mittermeier, F. W. Schueler, M. Spalding, F. Wells, C. Vynne, and T. B. Werner. 2002. Marine biodiversity hotspots and conservation priorities for tropical reefs. *Science* 295(5558):1280–4.

Robertson, G. P., M. A. Huston, F. C. Evans, and J. M. Tiedje. 1988. Spatial variability in a successional plant community: patterns of nitrogen availability. *Ecology* 69:1517–24.

Roland, J., N. Keyghobadi, and S. Fownes. 2000. Alpine Parnassius butterfly dispersal: effects of landscape and population size. *Ecology* 81:1642–53.

Rood, S. B., G. M. Samuelson, J. H. Braatne, C. R. Gourley, F. M. R. Hughes, and J. M. Mahoney. 2005b. Managing river flows to restore floodplain forests. *Frontiers in Ecology and the Environment* 3(4):193–201.

Rood, S. B., G. M. Samuelson, J. K. Weber, and K. A. Wywrot. 2005a. Twentieth-century decline in streamflows from the hydrographic apex of North America. *Journal of Hydrology* 306(1-4):215–33.

Rood, S. B., J. H. Braatne, and F. M. R. Hughes. 2003. Ecophysiology of riparian cottonwoods: stream flow dependency, water relations and restoration. *Tree Physiology* 23(16):1113–24.

Rooney, R. C. and S. E. Bayley. 2011. Setting appropriate reclamation targets and evaluating success: aquatic vegetation in natural and post-oilsands mining wetlands in Alberta, Canada. *Ecological Engineering* 37:569–79.

Root, T. 1988. *Atlas of Wintering North American Birds.* Chicago: University of Chicago Press.

Root, T. L., J. T. Price, K. R. Hall, S. H. Schneider, C. Rosenzweig, and J. A. Pounds. 2003. Fingerprints of global warming on wild animals and plants. *Nature* 421(6918):57–60.

Rosell, F., O. Bozser, P. Collen, and H. Parker. 2005. Ecological impact of beavers *Castor fiber* and *Castor canadensis* and their ability to modify ecosystems. *Mammal Review* 35:248–76.

Rosemond, A. D., C. M. Pringle, A. Ramirez, M. J. Paul, and J. L. Meyer. 2002. Landscape variation in phosphorus concentration and effects on detritus-based tropical streams. *Limnology and Oceanography* 47:278–89.

Rosenzweig, M. L. 1968. Net primary productivity of terrestrial environments: predictions from climatological data. *American Naturalist* 102:67–84.

Rosenzweig, M. L. 1992. Species diversity gradients: we know more and less than we thought. *Journal of Mammalogy* 73:715–30.

Roth J.D. 2002 Temporal variability in arctic fox diet as reflected in stable-carbon isotopes; the importance of sea ice. *Oecologia* 133:70–7.

Rowe, L., G. Arnqvist, A. Sih, and J. Krupa. 1994. Sexual conflict and the evolutionary ecology of mating patterns—water striders as a model system. *Trends in Ecology & Evolution* 9(8):289–93.

Rydin, H. and S-O. Borgegård. 1988. Plant species richness on islands over a century of primary succession: Lake Hjälmaren. *Ecology* 69:916–27.

Ryther, J. H. 1969. Photosynthesis and fish production in the sea. *Science* 166:72–76.

Saabye, H. E. 1776. Fragments of a diary kept in Greenland during the years 1770–1779. In H. Ostermann (ed.). 1942. *Reports from Greenland.* Copenhagen: GED Gad Commission.

Saccheri, I., M. Kuussaari, M. Kankare, P. Vikman, W. Fortelius, and I. Hanski. 1998. Inbreeding and extinction in a butterfly metapopulation. *Nature* 392:491–94.

Sage, R. F. 1999. Why C4 photosynthesis? In R. F. Sage and R. K. Monson, *C4 Plant Biology.* San Diego: Academic Press.

Sage, R. F. 2004. The evolution of C-4 photosynthesis. *New Phytologist* 161(2):341–70.

Sage, R. F. and D. S. Kubien. 2003. *Quo vadis* C₄? An ecophysiological perspective on global change and the future of C₄ plants. *Photosynthesis Research* 77:209–25.

Sahney, S. M. J. Benton, P. A. Ferry. 2010. Links between global taxonomic diversity, ecological diversity and the expansion of vertebrates on land. *Biology Letters* 6:544–7.

Sakai, A. and C. J. Weiser. 1973. Freezing resistance of trees in North America with reference to tree regions. *Ecology* 54(1):118–26.

Sakamoto, M. 1966. Primary production by phytoplankton community in some Japanese lakes and its dependence on lake depth. *Archive für Hydrobiologie* 62:1–28.

Sala, O. E., W. J. Parton, L. A. Joyce, and W. K. Laurenroth. 1988. Primary production of the central grassland regions of the United States. *Ecology* 69:40–5.

Samuel, B. 2004. *White as a Ghost: Winter Ticks and Moose.* Edmonton, Federation of Alberta Naturalists.

Scheu S., D. Parkinson. 1994. Effects of Invasion of an Aspen Forest (Canada) by *Dendrobaena-Octaedra* (Lumbricidae) on Plant-Growth. *Ecology* 75(8):2348–61.

Schemske, D.W., G. G. Mittelbach, H. V. Cornell, J. M. Sobel, and K. Roy. 2009. Is there a latitudinal gradient in the importance of biotic interactions? *Annual Review of Ecology Evolution and Systematics* 40:245–69.

Schenk, H. J. 2006. Root competition: beyond resource depletion. *Journal of Ecology* 94(4):725–39.

Schenk, H. J. and R. B. Jackson. 2002. The global biogeography of roots. *Ecological Monographs* 72:311–28.

Schimel, D. S. 1995. Terrestrial ecosystems and the carbon cycle. *Global Change Biology* 1:77–91.

Schindler, D. W. 1974. Eutrophication and recovery in experimental lakes: Implications for lake management. *Science,* 184:897–99.

Schindler, D. W. 1977. Evolution of phosphorus limitation in lakes. *Science,* 195:260–62.

Schindler, D. W. 1987. Detecting ecosystem responses to anthropogenic stress. *Canadian Journal of Fisheries and Aquatic Sciences* 44:6–25.

Schindler, D. W. 1990. Experimental perturbations of whole lakes as tests of hypotheses concerning ecosystem structure and function. *Oikos* 57:25–41.

Schindler, D. W., K. G. Beaty, E. J. Fee, D. R. Cruikshank, E. R. Debruyn, D. L. Findlay, G. A. Linsey, J. A. Shearer, M. P. Stainton, and M. A. Turner. 1990. Effects of Climatic Warming on Lakes of the Central Boreal Forest. *Science,* 250:967–70.

Schindler, D. W., K. H. Mills, D. F. Malley, D. L. Findlay, J. A. Shearer, I. J. Davies, M. A. Turner, G. A. Linsey, and D. R. Cruikshank. 1985. Long-Term Ecosystem Stress—The Effects of Years of Experimental Acidification on a Small Lake. *Science,* 228:1395–1401.

Schlesinger, W. H. 1991. *Biogeochemistry: An Analysis of Global Change.* New York: Academic Press.

Schluter, D. 1994. Experimental evidence that competition promotes divergence in adaptive radiation. *Science* 266:798–800.

Schluter, D. and J. D. McPhail. 1992. Ecological character displacement and speciation in sticklebacks. *The American Naturalist* 140:85–108.

Schmidt-Nielsen, K. 1964. *Desert Animals: Physiological Problems of Heat and Water.* Oxford: Clarendon Press.

Schmidt-Nielsen, K. 1969. The neglected interface. The biology of water as a liquid-gas system. *Quarterly Review of Biophysics* 2:283–304.

Schmidt-Nielsen, K. 1983. *Animal Physiology: Adaptation and Environment.* 3d ed. Cambridge, England: Cambridge University Press.

Schmiegelow, F. K. A., C. S. Machtans, and S. J. Hannon. 1997. Are boreal birds resilient to forest fragmentation? An experimental study of short-term community responses. *Ecology* 78(6):1914–32.

Schmitt, J., A. C. McCormac, and H. Smith. 1995. A test of the adaptive plasticity hypothesis using transgenic and mutant plants disabled in phytochrome-mediated elongation responses to neighbors. *American Naturalist* 146(6):937–53.

Schoener, T. W. 1983. Field experiments on interspecific competition. *American Naturalist* 122:240–85.

Scholander, P. F., R. Hock, V. Walters, F. Johnson, and L. Irving. 1950. Heat regulation in some arctic and tropical mammals and birds. *Biological Bulletin* 99:237–58.

Schultz, T. D., M. C. Quinlan, and N. F. Hadley. 1992. Preferred body temperature, metabolic physiology, and water balance of adult *Cicindela longilabris*: a comparison of populations from boreal habitats and climatic refugia. *Physiological Zoology* 65:226–42.

Schumacher, H. 1976. *Korallenriff.* Munich: BLV Verlagsgellschaft mbH.

Serreze, M. C., J. E. Walsh, F. S. Chapin, T. Osterkamp, M. Dyurgerov, V. Romanovsky, W. C. Oechel, J. Morison, T. Zhang, and R. G. Barry. 2000. Observational evidence of recent change in the northern high-latitude environment. *Climatic Change* 46:159–207.

Shaver, G. R. and F. S. Chapin III. 1986. Effect of fertilizer on production and biomass of tussock tundra, Alaska, U.S.A. *Arctic and Alpine Research* 18:261–8.

Shaver, G. R., A. E. Giblin, K. J. Nadelhoffer, K. K. Thieler, M. R. Downs, J. A. Laundre, and E. B. Rastetter. 2006. Carbon turnover in Alaskan tundra soils: effects of organic matter quality, temperature, moisture and fertilizer. *Journal of Ecology* 94:740–53.

Shelford, V. E. 1911. Physiological animal geography. *Journal of Morphology.* 22:551–618.

Sherman, P. W. 1977. Nepotism and evolution of alarm calls. *Science* 197(4310):1246–53.

Sherman, P.W., J. U. M. Jarvis, and S. H. Braude. 1992. Naked mole rats. *Scientific American* 257(8):72–78.

Shine, R. and E. L. Charnov. 1992. Patterns of survival, growth, and maturation in snakes and lizards. *American Naturalist* 139:1257–69.

Shipley B. 1993. A Null Model for Competitive Hierarchies In Competition Matrices. *Ecology* 74:1693–99.

Shurin, J. B., D. S. Gruner, and H. Hillebrand. 2006. All wet or dried up? Real differences between aquatic and terrestrial food webs. *Proceedings of the Royal Society B-Biological Sciences* 273:1–9.

Shurin, J. B., J. E. Havel, M. A. Leibold, and B. Pinel-Alloul. 2000. Local and regional zooplankton species richness: A scale-independent test for saturation. *Ecology* 81(11):3062–73.

Siegenthaler, U., H. Friedli, H. Loetscher, E. Moor, A. Neftel, H. Oeschger, and B. Stauffer. 1988. Stable-isotope ratios and concentrations of CO₂ in air from polar ice cores. *Annals of Glaciology* 10:151–6.

Silvertown, J. 1987. Ecological stability: a test case. *American Naturalist* 130:807–10.

Simard, S. W., D. A. Perry, M. D. Jones, D. D. Myrold, D. M. Durall, and R. Molina. 1997. Net transfer of carbon between ectomycorrhizal tree species in the field. *Nature* 388(6642):579–82.

Simberloff, D. S. 1976. Experimental zoogeography of islands: effects of island size. *Ecology* 57:629–48.

Simberloff, D. S. 1998. Flagships, umbrellas, and keystones: Is single-species management passe in the landscape era? *Biological Conservation* 83:247–57.

Simberloff, D. S. and E. O. Wilson. 1969. Experimental zoogeography of islands: the colonization of empty islands. *Ecology* 50:278–96.

Sinclair, A. R. E. 1977. *The African Buffalo.* Chicago: University of Chicago Press.

Sinclair, A.R.E. 2003. Mammal population regulation, keystone processes and ecosystem dynamics. *Philosophical Transactions of the Royal Society of London Series B-Biological Sciences* 358:1729–40.

Singer, M. C. and P. Wedlake. 1981. Capture does affect probability of recapture in a butterfly species. *Ecological Entomology* 6:215–16.

Skole, D. and C. Tucker. 1993. Tropical deforestation and habitat fragmentation in the Amazon: satellite data from 1978 to 1988. *Science* 260:1905–10.

Smil, V. 1990. Nitrogen and phosphorus. In B. L. Turner II. W. C. Clark, R. W. Kates. J. F. Richards. J. T. Mathews. and W. B. Meyer. eds. *The Earth as Transformed by Human Action.* Cambridge, England: Cambridge University Press.

Smith, C. L. and J. C. Tyler. 1972. Space resource sharing in a coral reef fish community. Natural History Museum of Los Angeles County. *Science Bulletin* 14:125–70.

Smith J. M. 1964. Group selection and kin selection. *Nature* 201:1145–7 doi:10.1038/2011145a0 Letter.

Smith, J. N. M. and P. Arcese. 1994. Brown-headed cowbirds and an island population of song sparrows—a 16-year study. *Condor* 96(4):916–34.

Smith, V. H. 1979. Nutrient dependence of primary productivity in lakes. *Limnology and Oceanography* 24:1051–64.

Smol, J. P., A. P. Wolfe, H. J. B. Birks, M. S. V. Douglas, V. J. Jones, A. Korhola, R. Pienitz, K. Ruhland, S. Sorvari, D. Antoniades, S. J. Brooks, M. A. Fallu, M. Hughes, B. E. Keatley, T. E. Laing, N. Michelutti, L. Nazarova, M. Nyman, A. M. Paterson, B. Perren, R. Quinlan, M. Rautio, E. Saulnier-Talbot, S. Siitonen, N. Solovieva, and J. Weckstrom. 2005. Climate-driven regime shifts in the biological communities of arctic lakes. *Proceedings of the National Academy of Sciences* 102:4397–402.

Snelgrove, P. V. R. 1999. Getting to the bottom of marine biodiversity: Sedimentary habitats. *Bioscience* 49:129–38.

Snelgrove, P. V. R. 2000. Linking biodiversity above and below the marine sediment-water interface. *Bioscience* 50:1076–88.

Söderlund, R. and T. Rosswall. 1982. The nitrogen cycles. In O. Hutzinger. ed. *The Handbook of Environmental Chemistry*, vol. I, part B. *The Natural Environment and the Biogeochemical Cycles*. New York: Springer-Verlag.

Soulé, M. E. 1991. Conservation—Tactics for a Constant Crisis. *Science* 253(5021):744–50.

Sousa, W. P. 1979a. Disturbance in marine intertidal boulder fields: the nonequilibrium maintenance of species diversity. *Ecology* 60:1225–39.

Sousa, W. P. 1979b. Experimental investigations of disturbance and ecological succession in a rocky intertidal algal community. *Ecological Monographs* 49:227–54.

Sousa, W. P. 1984. The role of disturbance in natural communities. *Annual Review of Ecology and Systematics* 15:353–91.

Spector, W. S. 1956. *Handbook of Biological Data*. Philadelphia: W. B. Saunders.

Stastny, M., U. Schaffner, and E. Elle. 2005. Do vigour of introduced populations and escape from specialist herbivores contribute to invasiveness? *Journal of Ecology* 93(1):27–37.

Stenseth, N. C., G. Ottersen, J. W. Hurrell, A. Mysterud, M. Lima, K. S. Chan, N. G. Yoccoz, and B. Adlandsvik. 2003. Studying climate effects on ecology through the use of climate indices: the North Atlantic Oscillation, El Niño, Southern Oscillation and beyond. *Proceedings of the Royal Society of London Series B-Biological Sciences* 270(1529):2087–96.

Stevens E. D., J. W. Kanwisher, and F. G. Carey. 2000. Muscle temperature in free-swimming giant Atlantic bluefin tuna (*Thunnus thynnus L.*). *Journal of Thermal Biology* 25:419–23.

Stevens, O. A. 1932. The number and weight of seeds produced by weeds. *American Journal of Botany* 19:784–94.

Stireman, J. O., J. D. Nason, and S. B. Heard. 2005. Host-associated genetic differentiation in phytophagous insects: General phenomenon or isolated exceptions? Evidence from a goldenrod-insect community. *Evolution* 59(12):2573–87.

Stireman, J. O., J. D. Nason, S. B. Heard, and J. M. Seehawer. 2006.

Cascading host-associated genetic differentiation in parasitoids of phytophagous insects. *Proceedings of the Royal Society B-Biological Sciences* 273(1586):523–30.

Storey, K. B. and J. M. Storey. 1992. Natural freeze tolerance in ectothermic vertebrates. *Annual Review of Physiology* 54:619–37.

Strahler, A. N. 1952. Dynamic Basis of Geomorphology. *Geological Society of America Bulletin* 63(9):923–38.

Strong, D. R. 1992. Are trophic cascades all wet? Differentiation and donor-control in speciose ecosystems. *Ecology* 73:747–54.

Suberkropp, K. and E. Chauvet. 1995. Regulation of leaf breakdown by fungi in streams: influences of water chemistry. *Ecology* 76:1433–45.

Suess, H. E. 1955. Radiocarbon concentration in modern wood. *Science* 122:415–7.

Sugihara, G. 1980. Minimal community structure: an explanation of species abundance patterns. *American Naturalist* 116:770–87.

Summerhayes, V. S. and C. S. Elton. 1923. Contribution to the ecology of Spitsbergen and Bear Island. *Journal of Ecology* 11:214–86.

Swartz, W. E. Sala, S. Tracey,k R. Watson, D. Pauly. 2010. The spatial expansion and ecological footprint of fisheries (1950 to present). *PloS ONE* 5(12):e15143.

Swift, J. 1726. *Travels into Several Remote Nations of the World, in Four Parts. By Lemuel Gulliver, First a Surgeon, and then a Captain of Several Ships.* London: Benjamin Motte.

Swift, M., O. Heal, and J. Anderson. 1979. *Decomposition in Terrestrial Ecosystems*. Oxford, UK: Blackwell Scientific Publications.

Takyu, M., S.-I. Aiba, and K. Kitayama. 2003. Changes in biomass, productivity and decomposition along topographical gradients under different geological conditions in tropical lower montane forests on Mount Kinabalu, Borneo. *Oecologia* 134:397–404.

Tansley, A. G. 1917. On competition between *Galium saxatile* L. (*G. hercynicum* Weig.) and *Galium sylvestre* Poll. (*G. asperum* Schreb.) on different types of soil. *Journal of Ecology* 5:173–79.

Tansley, A. G. 1935. The use and abuse of vegetational concepts and terms. *Ecology* 16:284–307.

Tennyson, A. 1849. *In Memoriam A. H. H.*, http://en.wikisource.org/wiki/In_Memoriam_A._H._H.#LVI.

Terborgh, J. 1973. On the notion of favorableness in plant ecology. *American Naturalist* 107:481–501.

Terborgh, J. 1988. The big things that run the world: a sequel to E. O. Wilson. *Conservation Biology* 2:402–3.

Thompson, J. N. 1994. *The Coevolutionary Process*. Chicago, University of Chicago Press.

Thomson, D. A. and C. E. Lehner. 1976. Resilience of a rocky intertidal fish community in a physically unstable environment. *Journal of Experimental Marine Biology and Ecology* 22:1–29.

Thoreau, H. D. 1854. *Walden*. G. S. Haight ed. Reprinted 1942. New York: W. J. Black.

Tilman, D. 1977. Resource competition between planktonic algae: an experimental and theoretical approach. *Ecology* 58:338–48.

Tilman, D. 1982. *Resource Competition and Community Structure*. Princeton University Press. Princeton.

Tilman, D. 1987. The importance of the mechanisms of interspecific competition. *The American Naturalist* 129(5):767–74.

Tilman, D. 1999. Global environmental impacts of agricultural expansion: The need for sustainable and efficient practices. *Proceedings of the National Academy of Sciences Journal* 96(11):5995–6000.

Todd, A. W. and L. B. Keith. 1983. Coyote demography during a snowshoe hare decline in Alberta. *Journal of Wildlife Management* 47:394–404.

Tonn, W. M. and J. J. Magnuson. 1982. Patterns in the species composition and richness of fish assemblages in northern Wisconsin lakes. *Ecology* 63:1149–66.

Toolson, E. C. 1987. Water profligacy as an adaptation to hot deserts: water loss rates and evaporative cooling in the Sonoran Desert cicada, *Diceroprocta apache* (Homoptera, Cicadidae). *Physiological Zoology* 60:379–85.

Toolson, E. C. and N. F. Hadley. 1987. Energy-dependent facilitation of transcuticular water flux contributes to evaporative cooling in the Sonoran Desert cicada. *Diceroprocta apache* (Homoptera, Cicadidae). *Journal of Experimental Biology* 131:439–44.

Tourney, J. W. and R. Kienholz. 1931. Trenched plots under forest canopies. *Yale University School of Forestry Bulletin* 30:1–31.

Tracy, R. L. and G. E. Walsberg. 2000. Prevalence of cutaneous evaporation in Merriam's kangaroo rat and its adaptive variation at the subspecific level. *Journal of Experimental Biology* 203:773–81.

Tracy, R. L. and G. E. Walsberg. 2001. Intraspecific variation in water loss in a desert rodent, *Dipodomys merriami*. *Ecology* 82:1130–37.

Tracy, R. L. and G. E. Walsberg. 2002. Kangaroo rats revisited: re-evaluating a classic case of desert survival. *Oecologia* 133:449–57.

Tress, G., B. Tress, and G. Fry. 2005. Clarifying integrative research concepts in landscape ecology. *Landscape Ecology* 20:479–93.

Turkington R., E. John, C. J. Krebs, M. R. T. Dale, V. O. Nams, R. Boonstra, S. Boutin, K. Martin, A. R. E. Sinclair, and J. N. M. Smith. 1998. The effects of NPK fertilization for nine years on boreal forest vegetation in northwestern Canada. *Journal of Vegetation Science* 9:333–46.

Turner, M. G., E. A. H. Smithwick, D. B. Tinker, and W. H. Romme. 2009. Variation in foliar nitrogen and aboveground net primary production in young postfire lodgepole pine. *Canadian Journal of Forest Research* 39:1024–35.

Turner, M. G., W. H. Romme, and D. B. Tinker. 2003. Surprises and lessons

from the 1988 Yellowstone fires. *Frontiers in Ecology and the Environment* 1:351–8.

Turner, R. M. 1990. Long-term vegetation change at a fully protected Sonoran Desert site. *Ecology* 71:464–77.

Turner, T. 1983. Facilitation as a successional mechanism in a rocky intertidal community. *The American Naturalist* 121:729–38.

Turner, T. F. and J. C. Trexler. 1998. Ecological and historical associations of gene flow in darters (Teleostei: Percidae). *Evolution* 52:1781–801.

U.S. Bureau of the Census, International Data Base. 2011. www.census.gov/pub/ipc/www/idbnew.html.

Underwood, T. J. and S. G. Sealy. 2006. Influence of shape on egg discrimination in American robins and gray catbirds. *Ethology* 112(2):164–73.

United Nations Population Information Network. www.un.org/popin/.

Urton, E. J. M. and K. A. Hobson. 2005. Intrapopulation variation in gray wolf isotope (delta N-15 and delta C-13) profiles: implications for the ecology of individuals. *Oecologia* 145(2):317–26.

USDA Agricultural Research Service. 2011. http://ars.usda.gov/Research/docs.htm?docid=11059&page=6.

USFWS. 2010. Species profile: Whooping crane (*Grus americana*). http://ecos.fws.gov/speciesProfile/profile/speciesProfile.action?spcode=B003.

USGS. 2000. Monitoring Grizzly Bear Populations Using DNA. www.mesc.nbs.gov/glacier/beardna.htm.

Usher, M. B., P. Davis, J. Harris, and B. Longstaff. 1979. A profusion of species? Approaches towards understanding the dynamics of the population of microarthropods in decomposer communities. In R. M. Anderson, B. D. Turner, and L. R. Taylor. *Population Dynamics*. Blackwell Scientific Publications, Oxford. 359–84.

Valett, H. M., S. G. Fisher, N. B. Grimm, and P. Camill. 1994. Vertical hydrologic exchange and ecological stability of a desert stream ecosystem. *Ecology* 75:548–60.

Vancouver, G. and J. D. Vancouver. 1798. *A Voyage of Discovery to the North Pacific Ocean*. London: G. G. and J. Robinson.

Vander Zanden, M. J., J. M. Casselman, and J. B. Rasmussen. 1999. Stable isotope evidence for the food web consequences of species invasions in lakes. *Nature* 401(6752):464–7.

Vanni, M. J., A. S. Flecker, J. M. Hood, and J. L. Headworth. 2002. Stoichiometry of nutrient recycling by vertebrates in a tropical stream: linking species identity and ecosystem p4rocesses. *Eology Letters* 5:285–93.

Vannote, R. L., G. W. Minshall, K. W. Cummins, J. R. Sedell, and C. E. Cushing. 1980. The river continuum. *Canadian Journal of Fisheries and Aquatic Sciences* 37:130–37.

Van Ruijven, J. and F. Berendse. 2005. Diversity-productivity relationships: Initial effects, long-term patterns, and underlying mechanisms. *Proceedings of the National Academy of Sciences of the United States of America* 102(3):695–700.

Van Valen, L. 1973. A new evolutionary law. *Evolutionary Theory* 1:1–30.

Verhulst, P. F. and A. Quetelet. 1838. Notice sur la loi que la population suit dans son accroisissement. *Correspance in Mathematics and Physics* 10:113–21.

Verreault, J., D. C. G. Muir, R. J. Norstrom, I. Stirling, A. T. Fisk, G. W. Gabrielsen, A. E. Derocher, T. J. Evans, R. Dietz, C. Sonne, G. M. Sandala, W. Gebbink, F. F. Riget, E. W. Born, M. K. Taylor, J. Nagy, and R. J. Letcher. 2005. Chlorinated hydrocarbon contaminants and metabolites in polar bears (Ursus maritimus) from Alaska, Canada, East Greenland, and Svalbard: 1996–2002. *Science of the Total Environment* 351:369–90.

Victoria Experimental Network Under the Sea. 2010. Project VENUS. www.venus.uvic.ca.

Vitousek, P. M. 1994. Beyond global warming: ecology and global change. *Ecology* 75:1861–76.

Volterra, V. 1926. Variations and fluctuations of the number of individuals in animal species living together. Reprinted 1931. In R. Chapman. *Animal Ecology.* New York: McGraw-Hill.

Wade, M. J. 1977. Experimental-study of group selection. *Evolution* 31(1): 134–53.

Wagner, R. G., K. M. Little, B. Richardson, and K. McNabb. 2006. The role of vegetation management for enhancing productivity of the world's forests. *Forestry* 79:57–79.

Walker, G. T. 1924. Correlation in seasonal variations of weather. no. 9: a further study of world weather. *Memoirs of the Indian Meteorology Society* 24:275–332.

Wall, D. H., A. H. Fitter, and E. A. Paul. 2005. Developing new perspectives from advances in soil biodiversity research. In R. D. Bardgett, M. B. Usher, and D. W. Hopkins. *Biological diversity and function in soils.* Cambridge, Cambridge University Press.

Wallace, A. E. 1878. *Tropical Nature and Other Essays.* New York: Macmillan.

Walter, H. 1985. *Vegetation of the Earth.* 3rd ed. New York: Springer-Verlag.

Wan, C. S. M. and R. F. Sage. 2001. Climate and the distribution of C-4 grasses along the Atlantic and Pacific coasts of North America. *Canadian Journal of Botany-Revue Canadienne De Botanique* 79(4):474–86.

Ward, J. V. 1985. Thermal characteristics of running waters. *Hydrobiologia* 125:31–46.

Warwick, S. I. , A. Légère, M.-J. Simard, T. James. 2008. Do escaped transgenes persist in nature? The case of an herbicide resistance transgene in a weedy *Brassica rapa* population. *Molecular Ecology* 17(5):1387–95.

Watwood, M. E. and C. N. Dahm. 1992. Effects of aquifer environmental factors on biodegradation of organic contaminants. In *Proceedings of the International Topical Meeting on Nuclear and Hazardous Waste Management Spectrum '92.* La Grange Park. Ill.: American Nuclear Society.

Webster, J. R. 1975. Analysis of potassium and calcium dynamics in stream ecosystems on three southern Appalachian watersheds of contrasting vegetation. Ph.D. thesis, University of Georgia. Athens.

Webster, J. R. and E. F. Benfield. 1986. Vascular plant breakdown in freshwater ecosystems. *Annual Review of Ecology and Systematics* 17:567–94.

Webster, K. E., T. K. Kratz, C. J. Bowser, J. J. Magnuson, and W. J. Rose. 1996. The influence of landscape position on lake chemical responses to drought in northern Wisconsin. *Limnology and Oceanography* 41:977–84.

Weiher E. and P. A. Keddy. 1999. *Ecological Assembly Rules: Perspectives, Advances, Retreats.* Cambridge. England: Cambridge University Press.

Weiser, C. J. 1970. Cold resistance and injury in woody plants. *Science* 169(3952):1269–78.

Werner, E. E. and G. G. Mittelbach. 1981. Optimal foraging: field tests of diet choice and habitat switching. *American Zoologist* 21:813–29.

Westoby, M. 1984. The self-thinning rule. *Advances in Ecological Research* 14:167–255.

Westoby, M., M. Leishman, and J. Lord. 1996. Comparative ecology of seed size and dispersal. *Philosophical Transactions of the Royal Society of London Series B* 351:1309–18.

Wetzel, R.G. 1975. *Limnology.* Philadelphia: W. B. Saunders.

Whicker, A. D. and J. K. Detling. 1988. Ecological consequences of prairie dog disturbances. *BioScience* 38:778–85.

White, C. S. and J. T. Markwiese. 1994. Assessment of the potential for *in sutu* bioremediation of cyanide and nitrate contamination at a heap leach mine in central New Mexico. *Journal of Soil Contamination* 3:271–83.

White, J. 1985. The thinning rule and its application to mixtures of plant populations. In J. White. ed. *Studies in Plant Demography.* New York: Academic Press.

White, J. and J. L. Harper. 1970. Correlated changes in plant size and number in plant populations. *Journal of Ecology* 58:467–85.

White, P. S. and S. T. A. Pickett. 1985. Natural disturbance and patch dynamics: an introduction. In S. T. A. Pickett and P. S. White. eds. *The Ecology of Natural Disturbance and Patch Dynamics.* New York: Academic Press.

Whittaker, R. H. 1956. Vegetation of the Great Smoky Mountains. *Ecological Monographs* 26:1–80.

Whittaker, R. H. 1965. Dominance and diversity in land plant communities. *Science* 147:250–60.

Whittaker, R. H. 1972. Evolution and measurement of species diversity. *Taxon* 21(2/3):213–51.

Whittaker, R. A. 2010. Meta-analysis and mega-mistakes: calling time on meta-analysis of the species richness–productivity relationship. *Ecology* 91(9):2522–33.

Whittaker, R. H. and G. E. Likens. 1973. The primary production of the biosphere. *Human Ecology* 1: 299–369.

Whittaker, R. H. and G. E. Likens. 1975. The biosphere and man. In *Primary Productivity of the Biosphere.* New York: Springer-Verlag.

Whittaker, R. H. and W. A. Niering. 1965. Vegetation of the Santa Catalina Mountains. Arizona: a gradient analysis of the south slope. *Ecology* 46:429–52.

Whittaker, W. H. 1975. *Communities and Ecosystems.* New York: Macmillan Publishing Co.

Wiebe, H. H., R. W. Brown, T. W. Daniel, and E. Campbell. 1970. Water potential measurement in trees. *BioScience* 20:225–26.

Wiens, J. A., R. L. Schooley, and R. D. Weeks. 1997. Patchy landscapes and animal movements: do beetles percolate? *Oikos* 78:257–64.

Williams, G. C. 1966. *Adaptation and Natural Selection.* Princeton, N.J., Princeton University Press.

Williams, G. C. and R. M. Nesse. 1991. The dawn of Darwinian medicine. *Quarterly Review of Biology* 66(1): 1–22.

Williams, K. S., K. G. Smith, and F. M. Stephen. 1993. Emergence of 13-yr periodical cicadas (Cicadidae, *Magicicada*): phenology, mortality, and predator satiation. *Ecology* 74:1143–52.

Williams, M. 1990. Forests. In B. L. Turner II, W. C. Clark. R. W. Kates. J. F. Richards. J. T. Mathews. and W. B. Meyer. eds. *The Earth as Transformed by Human Action.* Cambridge, England: Cambridge University Press.

Williamson, M. 1981. *Island Populations.* Oxford: Oxford University Press.

Willig, M. R., D. M. Kaufman, and R. D. Stevens. 2003. Latitudinal gradients of biodiversity: Pattern, process, scale, and synthesis. *AREES* 34:273–309.

Willis, C. K. R., J. E. Lane, E. T. Liknes, D. L. Swanson, and R. M. Brigham. 2005. Thermal energetics of female big brown bats (*Eptesicus fuscus*). *Canadian Journal of Zoology-Revue Canadienne De Zoologie* 83(6): 871–79.

Wilmers, C. C. and W. M. Getz. 2005. Gray wolves as climate change buffers in Yellowstone. *Plos Biology* 3:571–6.

Wilmers, C. C., R. L. Crabtree, D. W. Smith, K. M. Murphy, and W. M. Getz. 2003. Trophic facilitation by introduced top predators: grey wolf subsidies to scavengers in Yellowstone National Park. *Journal of Animal Ecology* 72:909–16.

Wilson, D. R. and J. F. Hare. 2004. Ground squirrel uses ultrasonic alarms. *Nature* 430(6999):523.

Wilson, E. O. 1980. Caste and division of labor in leafcutter ants (Hymenoptera: Formicidae: *Atta*), I: The overall pattern in *A. sexdens. Behavioral Ecology and Sociobiology* 7:143–56.

Wilson, E. O. and D. S. Simberloff. 1969. Experimental zoogeography of islands: defaunation and monitoring techniques. *Ecology* 50:267–78.

Wilson, R. P. and C. R. McMahon. 2006. Measuring devices on wild animals: what constitutes acceptable practice? *Frontiers in Ecology and the Environment* 4(3):147–54.

Wilson, R. P., W. S. Grant, and D. C. Duffy. 1986. Recording devices on free-ranging marine animals: does measurement affect foraging performance. *Ecology* 67: 1091–93.

Winemiller, K. O. 1990. Spatial and temporal variation in tropical fish trophic networks. *Ecological Monographs* 60:331–67.

Winemiller, K. O. 1992. Life history strategies and the effectiveness of sexual selection. *Oikos* 63:318–27.

Winemiller, K. O. 1995. Fish ecology. pp. 49–65 In Vol. 2 *Encyclopedia of Environmental Biology.* New York: Academic Press. Inc.

Winemiller, K. O. and K. A. Rose. 1992. Patterns of life-history diversification in North American fishes: implications for population regulation. *Canadian Journal of Fisheries and Aquatic Sciences* 49:2196–218.

Winston, M. L. 1992. Biology and management of Africanized bees. *Annual Review of Entomology* 37:173–93.

Wirsing, A. J., M. R. Heithaus, and L. M. Dill. 2007. Fear factor: do Dugongs (*Dugong dugon*) trade food for safety from tiger sharks (*Galeocerdo cuvier*)? *Oecologia* 153:1031–40.

Wisheu, I. C. and P. A. Keddy. 1992. Competition and Centrifugal Organization of Plant-Communities— Theory and Tests. *Journal of Vegetation Science* 3:147–56.

Withey, J. C., J. J. Lawler, S. Polasky, A. J. Plantinga, E. J. Nelson, P. Kareiva, C. B. Wilsey, C. A. Schloss, T. M. Nogeire, A. Ruesch, J. Ramos Jr., and W. Reid. 2013. Maximising return on conservation investment in the conerminuous USA. *Ecology Letters* 15:1249–56.

Worm, B., H. K. Lotze, and R. A. Myers. 2003. Predator diversity hotspots in the blue ocean. *Proceedings of the National Academy of Sciences of the United States of America* 100(17):9884–88.

Wu, J. and R. Hobbs. 2007. Landscape ecology: the state of the science. Topic 15, pp. 271–287. In J. Wu and R. Hobbs, eds. *Key Topics in Landscape Ecology.* Cambridge, UK: Cambridge University Press.

WWF. 2006. *Living Planet Report 2006.* Gland, Switzerland: WWF—World Wildlife Fund for Nature.

Wynne-Edwards, V. C. 1962. *Animal Dispersion in Relation to Social Behavior.* London, Oliver & Boyd.

Yoda, K., T. Kira, H. Ogawa, and K. Hozumi. 1963. Intraspecific competition among higher plants. XI. Self-thinning in overcrowded pure stands under cultivated and natural conditions. *Journal of Biology Osaka City University* 14:107–29.

Zhu, Y., H. Chen, J. Fan, Y. Wang, Y. Li, J. Chen, J. Fan, S. Yang, L. Hu, H. Leung, T. W. Mew, P. S. Teng, Z. Wang, and C. C. Mundt. 2000. Genetic diversity and disease control in rice. *Nature.* 406: 718–22.

CREDITS

Section Openers:
Section I: Stephen J. Krasemann/Photographers Choice/Getty Images; Section II: Thomas Kitchin & Victoria Hurst/Getty Images; Section III: © Rebecca Case; Section IV: Rich Palmer, University of Alberta and Bamfield Marine Sciences Centre; Section V: Baldcoconut/Dreamstime.com/GetStock.com; Section VI: Patrick Thompson.

Chapter 1:
Chapter 1: © Kyle Knopff; Figure 1.1a: AVHRR, NDVI, Seawifs, MODIS, NCEP, DMSP, and Sky2000 star catalog; AVHRR and Seawifs texture: Reto Sockli, Visualization: Marit Jentoft-Nilsen, VAL, NASA GSFC; Figure 1.1b: Jacques Descloitres, MODIS Rapid Response Team, NASA/GSFC; 1.1c–g: Maria Didkowsky, MSc Environmental Biology and Ecology; Figure 1.3 Tom Vezo/Minden Pictures; Figure 1.5: David Schindler, 1974, *Science* 184:897-899; Figure 1.6: David Schindler, from Schindler, D. 1974. *Science* 184: 897-899; Figure 1.8: SeaWiFS data courtesy of GeoEYe and NASA, Image provided by the Remote Sensing Unit at BIO, created in collaboration with NASA GSFC www.mar.dfo-mpo.gc.ca/science/ocean/ias/seawifs/seawifs_1.html; Figure 1.9: Alexander Lowry/Photo Researchers; Figure 1.10: Marie-Josée Fortin.

Chapter 2:
Chapter 2: Dean van't Schip/All Canada Photos/Getty Images; Figure 2.1a: © Preston J. Garrison/Visuals Unlimited; Figure 2.1b: © Dorling Kindersley/Getty Images; Figure 2.7: Scott Chang; Figure 2.8: David Walter; Figure 2.10: Alasdair Veitch; Figure 2.12: Peter Kershaw; Figure 2.13: © Stefan Wackerhagen/Getty Images; Figure 2.15: © Victor Lieffers, Dept. of Renewable Resources, University of Alberta; Figure 2.16: © Carr Clifton/Minden Pictures; Figure 2.18: © Michio Hoshino/Minden Pictures; Figure 19a: Rinusbaak/Dreamstime.com/GetStock.com; Figure 2.19b: Darcy C. Henderson; Figure 2.21: James F. Cahill; Figure 2.22: © Carr Clifton/Minden Pictures; Figure 2.24: © Wardene Weisser/Bruce Coleman; Figure 2.25a: © Frans Lanting/Minden Pictures; Figure 2.25b: Miles Derksen; Figure 2.27a: © Eric Toolson; Figure 2.27b: blickwinkel/Laule/GetStock.com; Figure 2.28: Angelo Cavalli/Alamy/GetStock.com; Figure 2.30a, b: Jeffrey Klemens; Figure 2.32: Frans Lanting/Minden Pictures; Figure 2.34a: Stefan A. Schnitzer; Figure 2.34b: © Niall Corbet @ www.flickr/photos/niallcorbet/Getty Images; Figure 2.35: David Hik; Figure 2.38a: © Oldrich Karasek/Peter Arnold; Figure 2.38b: © Francois Gohier/Photo Researchers; Figure 2.39: "Canada (Ecozones and Ecoregions) 1:7.5M" © Agriculture and Agri-Food Canada; and is published by the Government of Canada and that the reproduction has not been produced in affiliation with, or with the endorsement of the Government of Canada 2010; Figure 2.40: A National Ecological Framework for Canada, Alberta Ecoregion Map www1.agric.gov.ab.ca/$department/deptdocs.nsf/All/sag6299?OpenDocument#figure4 Used with permission of Geographic Information Systems Unit, Alberta Agriculture and Rural Development Land Use; Figure 2.41: Sheri Hendsbee.

Chapter 3:
Chapter 3: © Norbert Rosing/National Geographic/Getty Images; Figure 3.1: © Photodisc/Getty; Figure 3.3: © DAJ/Getty RF; Figure 3.4: © Peter David/Getty Images; Figure 3.7a: © Kelvin Aitken/Peter Arnold, Inc.; Figure 3.7b: ©Fred McDonnaughey/Photo Researchers; Figure 3.8: © NOAA; Figure 3.10: Bob Semple; Figure 3.11: © Mike Severns/Tom Stack & Associates; Figure 3.13 a–c: Deep Sea Discoveries off Canada's East Coast, Fisheries and Oceans Canada. Reproduced with permission of the Minister of Public Works and Government Services Canada, 2010; Figure 3.14: © Charles V. Angelo/Photo Researchers; Figure 3.15: Sally Leys; Figure 3.17: © Jim Zipp/Photo Researchers; Figure 3.19 a, b: ©Doug Sherman/Geofile; Figure 3.20: Dennis Ho-Jay Wong; Figure 3.21: © Norbert Rosing/National Geographic/Getty Images; Figure 3.22a: © p. Robles Gil/Bruce Coleman; Figure 3.22b: © Gary Meszaros/Visuals Unlimited/Getty Images; Figure 3.24: ©Digital Vision/Getty RF; Figure 3.28: © Lee Foote; Figure 3.29: ©Digital Vision/Getty RF; Figure 3.33 a, b: ©Creatas/PunchStock RF; Figure 3.37: NASA Geospatial Interoperability Office, Jet Propulsion Laboratory, California Institute of Technology, US Geological Survey, Imaging by Pete Giencke; Figure 3.43a: Jacana/Photo Researchers; Figure 3.43b: © David M. Dennis/MAXX Images Figure 3.44: Adapted from Figure 3.1 from Mitsch, W.J. and Gosselink, J. G, Wetlands, Third Edition. © John Wiley and Sons; Figure 3.45a: © Tui De Roy/Minden Pictures/Getty Images; Figure 3.45b: © Peter Essick/Aurora Photos; Figure 3.46: Aaron Ellison; Figure 3.47a: Kathleen Ruhland; Figure 3.47b: Kathleen Ruhland and Daniel Selbie; Figure 3.48: (top) John Smol; Figure 3.48: (bottom) Bronwyn Keatly.

Chapter 4:
Chapter 4: © Art Wolfe/Iconica/Getty Images; Figure 4.1: ©Corbis RF; Figure 4.2: © FPG/Getty Images; Figure 4.3: © A. Scott Earle; Figure 4.5: © Corbis RF; Figure 4.6: © Tom McHugh/Photo Researchers, Inc.; Figure 4.9a: Bob Semple; Figure 4.9b: Jocelyn Poissant; Figure 4.10a, b: Reprinted by permission from Macmillan Publishers Ltd: NATURE, Evidence of maturation at smaller sizes during years with fishing than in the years following the moratorium. Figures 4.10 a) and b) Nature, Olsen et al. (2004), p. 428:932, copyright (2004). Used with permission via Rightslink; Figure 4.11 a, b: Reprinted by permission from Macmillan Publishers Ltd: NATURE, Mean-weight and horn-length breeding values have decreased over the last 30 of trophy hunting; Figures 4.11 a) & b) *Nature*, Coltman et al. (2003) *Nature* p. 428:655, copyright (2003). Used with permission via Rightslink; Figure 4.18: from table 4 (modified). Broders et al. 1999. Population genetic structure and the effect of founder events on the genetic variability of moose, *Alces alces*, in Canada. Molecular Ecology (1999). Used with permission via Rightslink, 1309–1315; Figure 4.19: © Ken Pilsbury/Natural Visions; Figure 4.22: Figure 1b-c, from Funk et al. (2006) PNAS 103:page 3210. Copyright 2006 National Academy of Sciences, USA; Figure 4.23: © Ernie Cooper; Figure 4.24: Reprinted by permission from Macmillan Publishers Ltd: NATURE, Evidence for ecology's role in speciation, J. McKinnon et al. Nature p. 429:294, May 20, 2004 Publisher: Nature Publishing Group. Used with permission via Rightslink; Figure 4.25: Consortium for the Barcode of Life, Smithsonian Institution; Figure 4.26: from Mallet 2008 (Table 2). *Phil Trans Royal Soc B* 363:2971–2986.

Chapter 5:
Chapter 5: age fotostock/SuperStock; Figure 5.1: © Steve McCutcheon/Visuals Unlimited; Figure 5.2: © Walt Anderson/Visuals; Figure 5.4a: © Corbis RF; Figure 5.4b: © Medioimages/PunchStock RF; Figure 5.4c: © Courtesy Saewan Koh; Figure 5.9: Faye Smith; Figure 5.26: NOAA/Department of Commerce; Figure 5.31 (clockwise from top left): A.E. Derocher, University of Alberta; David Hik; Gustaf Samelius; Outdoorsman/Dreamstime.com/GetStock.com; Brian Dust; Figure 5.33: J.M. Storey.

Chapter 6:
Chapter 6: Paul Nicklen/National Geographic/Getty Images; Figure 6.2a: from Brown, Ross. D. Environment Canada, Atmospheric Science and Technology Directorate, Climate Research Division, Climate Processes Section, Toronto; Figure 6.2b: Original map data provided by The Atlas of Canada http://atlas.gc.ca/ © 2006. Produced under licence from Her Majesty the Queen in Right of Canada, with permission of Natural Resources Canada; Figure 6.13: Rooting depth varies across a broad geographical gradient. Data from Schenk and Jackson, 2002. The global biogeography of roots. *Ecological Monographs* 72:311–328. Ecological monographs by Ecological Society of America. Reproduced with permission of Ecological Society of America, etc. in the format Book via Copyright Clearance Center; Figure 6.17: Data from Tracy and Walsberg 2001; Figure 6.18a: Nstanev/Dreamstime.com; Figure 6.18b: © John D. Cunningham/Visuals Unlimited; Figure 6.20a–c: Stewart Rood; Figure 6.21a: © Doug Sokell/Visuals Unlimited; Figure 6.21b: © Leonard Lee Rue III/Photo Researchers; Figure 6.26a: © From Toolson and Hadley: Energy-Dependent facilitation of transcuticular water flux contributes to evaporative cooling in the Sonoran Desert cicada, *Diceroprocta apache* (homoptera: Cidiadiae). *The Journal of Experimental Biology*, 1987, vol. 131; Figure 6.26b: © From Toolson and Hadley: Energy-Dependent facilitation of transcuticular water flux contributes to evaporative cooling in the Sonoran Desert cicada, Diceroprocta apache (homoptera: Cidiadiae). *The Journal of Experimental Biology*, 1987, vol. 131; Figure 6.31a: Blickwinkel/Hartl/Getstock.com; Figure 6.31b: Mark Conlin/Getstock.com; Figure 6.31c: Kike Calvo/vwpics/Getstock.com; Figure 6.31d: Steven Kazlowski/Getstock.com.

Chapter 7:
Chapter 7: © Don Johnstoll All Canada Photos/Getty Images; Figure 7.1: © D. Holden Bailey/Tom Stack & Associates; Figure 7.9: Swift, M., O. Heal, and J. Anderson. 1979. *Decomposition in Terrestrial Ecosystems*. Oxford. U.K: Blackwell Scientific Publishing; Figure 7.10: Brent Moores/Getty Images; Figure 7.12 fish: Bob Semple; Figure 7.12 wolverine: Visceralimage/Dreamstime.com/GetStock.com; Figure 7.12 mountain lion: Brand X Pictures/PunchStock; Figure 7.12 Malachite Kingfisher: Digital Vision/PunchStock; Figure 7.12 praying mantis: IT Stock/PunchStock; Figure 7.12 crab: Bonfire007/Dreamstime.com/Getstock.com; Figure 7.13a: With kind permission from Springer Science+Business Media: *Oecologia*, May 9, 2005, Volume 145, Issue 2, p.316–325, Figures 2 and 3, "Intrapopulation variation in gray wolf isotope profiles: Implications of the ecology of individuals." Erin J.M Urton, Jan 1, 2005, ISSN 0029-8549. Via Rightslink; Figure 7.13b: With kind permission from Springer Science+Business Media: *Oecologia*, May 9, 2005, Volume 145, Issue 2, p.316–325, Figures 2 and 3, "Intrapopulation variation in gray wolf isotope profiles: Implications of the ecology of individuals." Erin J.M Urton, Jan 1, 2005, ISSN 0029-8549. Via Rightslink; Figure 7.17: Blickwinkel/NaturimBild/GetStock.com; Figure 7.26 a, b: adapted from Figures 1 and 4 from Drew. 1975. *New Phytologist* 75:479–490; Figure 7.27: Reprinted from *Plant Biology*, Vol. 1, Sage, R.F. and Monson, R.K., "The Biogeography of C4," pages 316–317. 1999, with permission from Elsevier; Figure 7.28: Adapted from Wan and Sage (2001) *Canadian Journal of Botany*, Figure 3b, p. 79:474–486.

Chapter 8:
Chapter 8: Eastcott Momatiuk/Stone/Getty Images; Figure 8.1: © Gregory G. Dimijian/Photo Researchers; Figure 8.2 clockwise from upper left: Courtesy of David Hik; Steven J. Kazlowski/GHG/Aurora Photos; Gustaf Samelius; Krista Bush; Figure 8.4: Ryan W. Taylor; Figure 8.5 a, b: Todd Underwood, Spencer Sealy, Influence of Shape on Egg Discrimination in American Robins and Gray Catbirds,

John Wiley and Sons, *Ethology* 2006. P112-164-173. Copyright Clearance Centre; Figure 8.6: Table from Todd Underwood, Spencer Sealy, *Influence of Shape on Egg Discrimination in American Robins and Gray Catbirds*, John Wiley and Sons, Ethology 2006. P112-164-173. Copyright Clearance Centre; Figure 8.7: © pjmalsbury/iStockPhoto; Figure 8.8 a–c: Kloppers et al. 2005; Figure 8.9: Data from Kloppers et al. 2005; Figure 8.12: Mark W. Moffett/Minden Pictures; Figure 8.9: Wilson, 1980; Figure 8.16: Anderson 2006. figure 1 from KG Anderson. 2006. How well does paternity confidence match actual paternity? *Current Anthropology* 47:513–520; Figure 8.17: © Dr. Paul A. Zahl/Photo Researchers Inc.; Figure 8.23: Chris MacQuarrie; Figure 8.24: © Richard Parker/Photo Researchers.

Chapter 9:

Chapter 9: © John White Photos/Getty Images; Figure 9.1: Tim Ennis/Getstock.com; Figure 9.2: © Gary Meszaros/Visuals Unlimited/Getty Images; Figure 9.3: Turner and Trexler 1998; Figure 9.4: Turner and Trexler 1998; Figure 9.5: Turner and Trexler 1998; Figure 9.6: Frans Lanting/Minden Pictures; Figure 9.7: Stevens 1932; Figure 9.8: Westoby, Leishman, and Loard 1996; Figure 9.9: Jakobsson and Eriksson 2000; Figure 9.10 a, b: Shine and Charnov 1992 and Gunderson 1997; Figure 9.11: Gunderson 1997; Figure 9.12: M.R. Gross. 1991. Salmon breeding behavior and life history evolution in changing environments. *Ecology* 72:1180–1186. Ecology by Ecological Society of America. Reproduced with permission of Ecological Society of America, in the format Book via Copyright Clearance Center; Figure 9.13: Breck P. Kent/Animals, Animals; Figure 9.14: Bertschy and Fox 1999; Figure 9.16: Bertschy and Fox 1999; Figure 9.17: Bertschy and Fox 1999; Figure 9.18 gorilla: Elliothurwitt/Dreamstime.com/GetStock.com; Figure 9.18 snow leopard: Mrolands/Dreamstime.com/Getstock.com; Figure 9.18 peregrine falcon: Klikk/Dreamstime.com/Getstock.com; Figure 9.18 great white shark: Tom Campbell/Robert Harding; Figure 9.18 Swift fox: Colette6/Dreastime.com/Getstock.com; Figure 9.18 woodpecker: Image by R. Ehrnsberger, J. Dabert, and H. Proctor; Figure 9.19: David Innes; Figure 9.21a: © David Schleser/Photo Researchers; Figure 9.21b: Corbis Digital Stock; Figure 9.26: data from Charnov 2002, Charnov et al. 2007; Figure 9.28: Grant 1986; Figure 9.29: Boag and Grant 1984b; Figure 9.30: Grant 1986; Figure 9.31: Grant 1986; Figure 9.32: Courtesy, Mark McCorry, University College Dublin; Figure 9.34: Root et al. 2003. Fingerprints of global warming on wild animals and plants. *Nature* 421(6918): 57–60; Figure 9.35: Murphy-Klassen et al. figure 4 *Auk,* 122: 1120–1148 (2005); Figure 9.36: Colleen Cassady St. Clair; Figure 9.37: Adapted from Gjerdrum et al. (2003) PNAS 100:9377-9382. Copyright 2003 National Academy of Sciences, U.S.A; Figure 9.38: Reale et al. 2003. Genetic and plastic responses of a northern mammal to climate change. *Proceeding of the Royal Society of London Series B-Biological Sciences* 270(1515):591–96.

Chapter 10:

Chapter 10: Kevin van der Leek Photography/Flickr/Getty Images; Figure 10.1a: Mark K. Peck; Figure 10.1b: Gustaf Samelius; Figure 10.5a: A.J. Southward; Figure 10.5b: © Diane Nelson; Figure 10.14a: Natural History Museum Rotterdam; Figure 10.14b: Courtesy Daniel W. Schneider and John Lyons; Figure 10.15: Boyan Tracz; Figure 10.17a: © Natalie Fobes, www.fobesphoto.com; Figure 10.20: J.A. Trofymow, Canadian Forest Service; Figure 10.21: Getzin Stephan, Dean Charmaine, He Fangliang, "Spatial patterns and competition of tree species in a douglas-fir chronosequence on Vancouver Island," *Ecography* (2006). John Wiley and Sons. Copyright Clearance Center; Figure 10.24a: Photo by Gordon Court; Figure 10.24b: Andrew Fyson; Figure 10.24c: Ed Snucins; Figure 10.24d: Joyce Gould; Figure 10.28: Damuth 1981; Figure 10.29: Peters and Wassenberg 1983; Figure 10.32: © Joseph Van Os/The Image Bank/Getty Images; Figure 10.33a: © Heather Proctor; Figure 10.33b: Roger Benoit; Figure 10.33c: Jeffery Newton; Figure 10.33d: JC Cahill; Figure 10.33e: Anthony Bertrand; Figure 10.33f: Greg Becic; Figure 10.33g: Rolf Vinebrook; Figure 10.33h: Gordon G. McNickle; Figure 10.34: © Michio Hoshino/Minden Pictures; Figure 10.35 a, b: © Tom Fernald, College of the Atlantic, Bar Harbor, Maine.

Chapter 11:

Chapter 11: James C. Cahill; Figure 11.1: The Murie Archives at The Murie Center, Moose, WY; Figure 11.2: Leonard Lee Rue III/Photo Researchers; Figure 11.3: Murie 1944; Figure 11.6: Deevey 1947, Baker, Mewaldt, and Stewart 1981, Brown and Weatherhead 1999; Figure 11.7: Hegazy 1990; Figure 11.8b: From Erickson, G.M., Currie, P.J., Inouye, B.D., Winn, A.A. 2006. Tyrannosaur life tables: An example of nonavian dinosaur population biology. *Science,* 313 p. 213–217. Reprinted with permission from AAAS; Figure 11.9: David Beaune; Figure 11.11: Howe and Knopf 1991; Figure 11.13 a, b: Douglas Dix; Figure 11.14: Ian Stirling; Figure 11.15: Derocher et al. 1997. Figure 2 A.E Derocher, I Stirling, and W Calvert. 1997. Male-biased harvesting of polar bears in western Hudson bay. *Journal of Wildlife Management* 61:1075–1082.The Wildlife Society, Allen Press Publishing Services.

Chapter 12:

Chapter 12: Getty Image/DAL; Figure 12.1a: © M.I Walker/Science Source/Photo Researchers; Figure 12.1b: © James Bell/Science Source/Photo Researchers; Figure 12.3 a, b: © Peter R. Grant, Princeton University; Figure 12.4: Gibbs and Grant 1987; Figure 12.5: Gibbs and Grant 1987; Figure 12.7: © Peter R. Grant, Princeton University; Figure 12.9: Leverich and Levin 1979; Figure 12.12: Bonner, J. T. 1965. *Size and Cycle: An Essay on the Structure of Biology.* Princeton, N.J.: Princeton University Press; Figure 12.16: Bennett 1983; Figure 12.17: Brian Johns; Figure 12.18: USGS 2005, USFWS Whooping Crane Coordinator; Figure 12.19: Data from Bennett 1983; Figure 12.21: Gause 1934; Figure 12.22: Gause 1934; Figure 12.23: Connell 1961a 1961b; Figure 12.24: Sinclair 1977; Figure 12.28: Frank, Boll, and Kelly 1957; Figure 12.32: United Nations Population Information Network; Figure 12.34: Data from the U.S. Bureau of the Census, International Data Base 2005; Figure 12.35 a, b: United Nations Population Information Network and the U.S. Bureau of the Census, International Data Base 2006.

Chapter 13:

Chapter 13: Chris Cheadle/All Canada Photos/Getty Images; Figure 13.1: Shannon White; Figure 13.3: © Jodi Jacobson/Peter Arnold; Figure 13.4: © George Haling/Photo Researchers, Inc.; Figure 13.6: Data from Westoby 1984; Figure 13.7: Data from White and Harper 1970; Figure 13.8: Data from Denno and Roderick 1992; Figure 13.9: Reprinted from *Animal Behaviour,* 35, Arcese, P., "Age, intrusion pressure and defense," p.776 © 1987 with permission from Elsevier; Figure 13.11: Figure 2b, Reader et al. (1994) *Ecology,* 75: 1753–1760. Reproduced with permission from the Ecological Society of America; Figure 13.14: Data from Gause 1934; Figure 13.16: Data from Park 1954; Figure 13.17: Data from Park 1954. Experimental studies of interspecific competition. II. Temperature, humidity and competition in two species of Tribolium. *Physiological Zoology* 27:177–238. Used with permission of Rightslink; Figure 13.18: © Heather Angel; Figure 13.22: © Dr. James H. Brown; Figure 13.23 a, b: © Dr. James H. Brown; Figure 13.26: Photo by Brett Purdy; Figure 13.27: Figure 3 reprinted from Schluter & McPhail (1992), "Ecological Character Displacement and Speciation. . ." *American Naturalist,* 140. Reprinted with permission of University of Chicago Press via Rightslink; Figure 13.28: from Dolph Schluter, "Experimental Evidence that Competition Promotes Divergence in Adaptive Radiation," Science, 266:798-801 (fig. 1). Copyright 1994 AAAS. Reprinted with permission from AAAS; *Science,* 266:798–801 (fig.1). Copyright 1994 AAAS; Figure 13.29: Reprinted by permission from Macmillan Publishers Ltd: *Nature,* Gaudet, Connie L., and Paul A Keddy, "A comparative approach to predicting competitive ability from plant traits," copyright 1988.Volume 334, Issue 6179, pp. 242–243 (1988).

Chapter 14:

Chapter 14: Robert Postma/First Light/Getty Images; Figure 14.1: © Mark Newman/Photo Researcher, Inc.; Figure 14.2 a & b: David Hik; Figure 14.3: "The effects of grazing by lesser snow geese on the vegetation of a sub-arctic salt marsh" Cargill and Jefferies. (1984). *Journal of Applied Ecology,* 21 Figure 2b and 3b, 669–686. Reproduced with permission of Blackwell Publishing; Figure 14.4: Bob Jefferies; Figure 14.17 a & b: Courtesy, Dr. Gary A. Lamberti; Figure 14.8 a & b: Ken Puliafico; Figure 14.9: Reproduced with permission from the Ecological Society of America; Figure 14.10: Joe McDonald/Visuals Unlimited/Getty Images; Figure 14.11: Data from MacLulich 1937; Figure 14.12: Data from Krebs et al. 1995, 2001; Figure 14.13: Fig 1 from Rudy Boonstra, David Hik, Grant R. Singleton, Alexander Tinnikov (1998) THE IMPACT OF PREDATOR-INDUCED STRESS ON THE SNOWSHOE HARE CYCLE. *Ecological Monographs:* Vol. 68, No. 3, pp. 371–394; Ecological monographs by Ecological Society of America. Reproduced with permission of Ecological Society of America, in the format Book via Copyright Clearance Center; Figure 14.14a: David Peart/arabianEye/Getty Images; Figure 14.14b: Alastair Pollock Photography/Getty Images; Figure 14.18: Gause (1934) The Struggle for Existence; Figure 14.19a: Seraphzheng/Dreamstime.com GetStock.com; Figure 14.19b: Evelyng23/Dreamstime.com/GetStock.com; Figure 14.20: Gause (1934) The Struggle for Existence; Figure 14.23: Data from O'Dowd and Gill 1984. Predator satiation and site alteration following fire: mass reproduction of alpine ash (*Eucalyptus delegatensis*) in southeastern Australia. *Ecology* 65:1052–66; Ecology by Ecological Society of America. Reproduced with permission of ECOLOGICAL SOCIETY OF AMERICA, in the format Book via Copyright Clearance Center; Figure 14.25: Data from Williams, Smith, and Stephen 1993; Figure 14.27: © Gregory G. Dimijian/Photo Researchers; Figure 14.27: Data from Paine 1976; Figure 14.28: Data from Paine 1976; Figure 14.30: Photo by T. Yoshida and R.O Wayne; Figure 14.31: Meyer et al. (2006). "Prey evolution on the time scale of predator-prey dynamics revealed by the allele-specific quantitative PCR." *Proceedings of the National Academy of Sciences,* 103: 10690–10695. Page 10692, Figure 3, Copyright 2006, National Academy of Sciences, U.S.A; Figure 14.32 a–c: Courtesy of Graham Cox, Stephen Heard, and Chris Kolaczan.

Chapter 15:

Chapter 15: Photograph by Francois Teste; Figure 15.1: © Anthony Mercieca/Photo Researchers; Figure 15.3 a–d: Bill Samuel; Figure 15.4: Bill Samuel; Figure 15.5: Data from Park 1948. Experimental studies of interspecific competition. I. Competition between populations of flour beetles *Trinbolium confusum* Duval and *Tribolium castaneum* Herbst. *Ecological Monographs* 18:267–307. Ecological monographs by ECOLOGICAL SOCIETY OF AMERICA. Reproduced with permission of ECOLOGICAL SOCIETY OF AMERICA, ETC. in the format Book via Copyright Clearance Center; Figure 15.6: © Robert & Linda Mitchell; Figure 15.7: Data from Janzen 1966; Figure 15.8: Data from Janzen 1966; Figure 15.9: Data from Janzen 1966; Figure 15.10a: Aquanaut4/Dreamstime.com; Figure 15.10b: Mychadre77/Dreamstime.com; Figure 15.10c: Data from Muscatimne and D'Elia; Figure 15.11: Reprinted by permission from Macmillan Publishers Ltd: NATURE, "Population biology of infectious diseases: Part I: A compartmental model of the population growth of a disease-causing organism", Roy M. Anderson* & Robert M. May, *Nature* 280, 361 - 367 (02 August 1979). Used with permission via Rightslink; Figure 15.12a: Photo12/Getstock.com; Figure 15.12b: Data from http://en.wikipedia.org/wiki/List_of_zombie_films March 12, 2010; Figure 15.13: Gumel et al. (2004). "Modelling strategies from controlling SARS outbreaks," *Proceedings of the Royal Society of London.* B. 271: 2223–2232. Figure 1 (appearing on page 2224) and Figure 5 (appearing on page 2230) reprinted with permission; Figure 15.14: Fig 3 from P. Munz, I. Hudea, J. Imad, R.J. Smith. 2009. When zombies attack!: Mathematical modeling of an outbreak of zombie infection (infectious disease modeling research progress 2009, in J.M. Tchuenche and C. Chiyaka, eds.); Figure 15.16: Gumel et al. (2004). "Modelling strategies from controlling SARS outbreaks," *Proceedings of the Royal Society of London.* B. 271: 2223–2232. Figure 1 (appearing on page 2224) and Figure 5 (appearing on page 2230) reprinted with permission; Figure 15.17: Table 1 from Paul E. M. Fine, Herd Immunity: History, Theory, Practice, *Epidemiologic Reviews* Vol. 15

Figure 1: "The present extent of perennial ice in North America." Reprinted with permission; Figure 21.4a: Alasdair Veitch; Figure 21.4b: Reproduced with the permission of Natural Resources Canada 2011, courtesy of the Geological Survey of Canada photo number 2004-067. Photographer: Lynda Dredge; Figure 21.4c: Reproduced with the permission of Natural Resources Canada 2011, courtesy of the Geological Survey of Canada photo number 2004-093. Photographer: Jean Veillette; Figure 21.4d: Reproduced with the permission of Natural Resources Canada 2011, courtesy of the Geological Survey of Canada photo number 2004-259. Photographer: Lynda Dredge; Figure 21.5: Darwin Wiggett/First Light/Getty Images; Figure 21.6: Data from Hulshoff 1995; Figure 21.7: Data from Naiman et al. 1994; Figure 21.8: © Steve Starr/Stock Boston; Figure 21.9: Data from Minnich 1983; Figure 21.10: Data from Bowen and Burgess 1981; Figure 21.11: Data from Bowen and Burgess 1981; Figure 21.12: Data from Bowen and Burgess 1981; Figure 21.13: Data from Milne 1993; Figure 21.14: Figures 1.1 and 1.2, p.4 Chapter 1, When is a landscape perspective important? By Lenore Fahrig. Reprinted with the permission of Cambridge University Press; Figure 21.15: Data from Diffendorfer, Gaines, and Holt 1995; Figure 21.16: Data from Diffendorfer, Gaines, and Holt 1995; Figure 21.17: Schmiegelow et al. (1997). *Ecology.* 78:1914–1932. Reprinted with permission; Figure 21.18: Figures 1, 2, and 3 from Schmiegelow et al. (1997). *Ecology.* 78:1914–1932. Reprinted with permission; Figure 21.19: Fahrig 1997. Relative effects of habitat loss and fragmentation on population extinction. *Journal of Wildlife Management* 61(3):603–10. Used with permission via Rightslink; Figure 21.20: © Richard O. Bierregaard, Jr./University of North Carolina, Biology Department; Figure 21.21: Johnson and Taylor. (2000). "Fine-scale movement behaviours of calopterygid damselflies are influenced by landscape structure: An experimental manipulation." *Oikos.* Reprinted by permission of Blackwell Publishing OIKOS issue 3, vol. 88: 553–562. Copenhagen 2000 part b & c of figure 3; Figure 21.22: Data from Webster et al. 1996; Figure 21.23: Tony Clevenger/WTI-Montana State University; Figure 21.24: Figure 8 from Fahrig. (2003). *Annual review of Ecology, Evolution, and Systematics.* 34:487–515. Reprinted with permission from *The Annual Review of Ecology, Evolution, and Systematics,* Volume 34. © 2003 by Annual Reviews: www.annualreviews.org; Figure 21.25: Guenette and Villard. (2005). "Thresholds in Forest Bird Response to Habitat Alteration as Quantitative Targets for Conservation." *Conservation Biology.* Reprinted with permission of Blackwell Publishing; Figure 21.26: Guenette and Villard. (2005). "Thresholds in Forest Bird Response to Habitat Alteration

as Quantitative Targets for Conservation." *Conservation Biology.* Reprinted with permission of Blackwell Publishing; Figure 21.27a: Figure 3 from Apps et al. (2002). *Canadian Journal of Zoology.* 80:1228–1239. Reprinted with permission; Figure 21.27b: Figure 1b from Chetkiewicz et al. (2006). *Annual Review of Ecology, Evolution, and Systematics.* 37:317–342. Reprinted with permission from *The Annual Review of Ecology, Evolution, and Systematics.* Volume 37. © 2006 by Annual Reviews: www.annualreviews.org.

Chapter 22:

Chapter 22: Getty Images/DAL; Figure 22.1: © Norman Owen Tomalin/Bruce Coleman; Figure 22.2: © Mike Lane/Getstock; Figure 22.3: figure 1 of LM Herborg, CL Jerde, DM Lodge, GM Ruiz, and HJ MacIsaac. 2007. Predicting invasion risk using measures of introduction effort and environmental niche models. *Ecological Applications* 17:663–674; Figure 22.4: figure 2 of JD Lozier, P Aniello, and MJ Hickerson. Predicting the distribution of Sasquatch in western North America: anything goes with ecological niche modeling. *Journal of Biogeography* 36:1623–1627; Figure 22.5a: Kalmar and Currie. (2006). "A global model of island biogeography." *Global Ecology & Biogeography.* Reprinted with permission of Blackwell Publishing; Figure 22.5b: Nilsson, Bengtsson, and As 1988; Figure 22.6: Data from Lomolino, Brown, and Davis 1989; Figure 22.7: Data from Tonn and Magnuson 1982; Figure 22.8: Kalmar A, Currie DJ. 2006. A global model of island biogeography. *Global Ecology & Biogeography* 15: 72–81 Figure 4; Figure 22.9: Data from Williamson 1981; Figure 22.10 a, b: Dave Ward; Figure 22.11: Data from MacArthur and Wilson 1963; Figure 22.12: Data from MacArthur and Wilson 1963; Figure 22.13: MacArthur and Wilson. An equilibrium theory of insular zoogeography. *Evolution* 17:373–87. © 1963. Reprinted with permission of Blackwell Publishing Ltd; Figure 22.14: Data from Diamond 1969; Figure 22.15: © H.W. Kitchen/Photo Researchers; Figure 22.16: Data from Simberloff and Wilson 1969; Figure 22.17: Data from Rydin and Borgegard 1988; Figure 22.18: Data from Simberloff 1976; Figure 22.19: Data from Reid and Miller; Figure 22.20: Data from Dobzhansky 1950; Figure 22.21: Data from Janzen 1981; Figure 22.22: H. Hillebrand. 2004. On the generality of the latitudinal diversity gradient, *American Naturalist* 163:192–211; Figure 22.23: Data from Rosenzweig 1992; Figure 22.24: Data from Rosenzweig, after Terborgh 1973; Figure 22.26: Robert Semple; Figure 22.27: Coral communities are regionally enriched along an oceanic biodiversity gradient. Author(s): Cornell, Howard V. DOI: 10.1038/NATURE02685

Date: Jan 24, 2004 Volume: 429 Issue: 6994 Page: 867:870. With permission from Rightslink via Copyright Clearance Center; Figure 22.28: Coral communities are regionally enriched along an oceanic biodiversity gradient Author(s): Cornell, Howard V. DOI: 10.1038/NATURE02685 Date: Jan 24, 2004 Volume: 429 Issue: 6994 Page: 867:870. With permission from Rightslink via Copyright Clearance Center; Figure 22.29: Data from Bond and Coldblatt 1984; Figure 22.30: Data from Myers et al. 2000; Figure 22.31: "Biodiversity hotspots for conservation priorities" Da Fonseca, Gustavo A. B., Feb 24, 2000 ISSN: 0028-0836 Volume: 403 Issue: 6772, 853, Nature Publishing; Figure 22.32: Data from Latham and Ricklefs 1993; Figure 22.34: MODIS data courtesy of NASA, image created by the Remote Sensing Unit at BIO, in collaboration with NASA GSFC; Figure 22.35: Land Cover of Canada, http://atlas.nrcan.gc.ca/site/english/maps/environment/land/landcover. Reproduced with the permission of Natural Resources Canada 2011, courtesy of the Atlas of Canada.

Chapter 23:

Chapter 23: AGE Fotostock/Dal; Figure 23.1: © NASA; Figure 23.2: U.S. Geographical Survey; Figure 23.3: The University of Texas, Institute for Geophysics; Figure 23.4: Imagery © 2013 NASA, Terrametrics; Figure 23.5: Fig 2 from David M. Raup and J. John Sepkoski Jr, "Mass Extinctions in the Marine Fossil Record," *Science* 19 March 1982: Vol. 215 no. 4539 pp. 1501-1503. Reprinted with permission from AAAS; Figure 23.7: Reprinted by permission from Macmillan Publishers Ltd: NATURE, Has the Earth's sixth mass extinction already arrived?. Figure 2, *Nature*, Barnosky et al. (2011), 471, pp. 51–57, copyright (2011). Used with permission via Rightslink; Figure 23.8 and Figure 23.9: 1) Ricklefs and Latham (1994). *Species Diversity in Ecological Communities.* Chicago, IL: University of Chicago Press, Figure 26.10. Reprinted with permission; Figure 23.12: Data from Diaz and Kiladis (1992); Figure 23.14: www.ldeo.columbia.edu/res/pi/NAO/; Figure 23.15: Otterson et al. (2001). "Ecological effects of the North Atlantic Oscillation." *Oecologica.* 128:1–14. With kind permission from Springer Science and Business Media; Figure 23.16: Figure 2 from Soule, *Science* 253:744–750 (1991). Reprinted with permission from AAAS; Figure 23.17: 1) Adapted from Haberl (2007) PNAS, Figure 1 from Haberl (only lower panel), PNAS, "Quantifying and mapping the human appropriation of net primary production in earth's terrestrial ecosystems," Vol. 104:12942–12947. Copyright 2007 National Academy of Sciences, U.S.A; Figure 23.18: 1) Wilf Swartz, Enric Sala,

Sean Tracey, Reg Watson, Daniel Pauly. "The Spatial Expansion and Ecological Footprint of Fisheries (1950 to Present)." PLoS ONE, 2010; 5 (12): e15143 DOI: 10.1371/journal.pone.0015143. Reprinted with permission; Figure 23.19: Figures 1 and 2 from Foley et al., *Science* 309:570–574 (2005). Reprinted with permission from AAAS; Figure 23.20: Figures 1 and 2 from Foley et al., *Science* 309:570–574 (2005). Reprinted with permission from AAAS; Figure 23.21: USGA/EROS; Figure 23.22: Data from Skole and Tucker 1993; Figure 23.23: Anina Hundsdorfer; Unnumbered Figure: skynesher/iStockPhoto; Figure 23.24a: Randy Westbrooks, U.S. Geological Survey, Bugwood.org; Figure 23.24b: U.S. Fish and Wildlife Service Archive, U.S. Fish and Wildlife Service, Bugwood.org; Figure 23.24c: R. Scott Cameron, Advanced Forest Protection, Inc., Bugwood.org; Figure 23.24d: Randy Westbrooks, U.S. Geological Survey, Bugwood.org; Figure 23.25: 1) From McCarthy et al., 2012. "Financial Costs of Meeting Global Biodiversity Conservation Targets: Current Spending and Unmet Needs." *Science*, 338, p. 946. Reprinted with permission from AAAS; Figure 23.26 1) From Daily et al., "Ecosystem services in decision making: time to deliver," Frontiers in Ecology and the Environment 7:21-28, 2009. Frontiers in Ecology and the Environment by ECOLOGICAL SOCIETY OF AMERICA. Reproduced with permission of ECOLOGICAL SOCIETY OF AMERICA, ETC. in the format Book via Copyright Clearance Center; Figure 23.27: 1): "Modeling benefits from nature: using ecosystem services to inform coastal and marine spatial planning," Anne D. Guerry, Mary H. Ruckelshaus, Katie K. Arkema et al., Figure 4, *International Journal of Biodiversity Science*, Ecosystem Services & Management, June 1, 2012, reprinted by permission of the publisher (Taylor & Francis Ltd, http://www.tandf.co.uk/journals); Figure 23.28: 1) "Modeling benefits from nature: using ecosystem services to inform coastal and marine spatial planning," Anne D. Guerry, Mary H. Ruckelshaus, Katie K. Arkema et al., Figure 5, *International Journal of Biodiversity Science*, Ecosystem Services & Management, June 1, 2012, reprinted by permission of the publisher (Taylor & Francis Ltd, http://www.tandf.co.uk/journals); Figure 23.29: 1) From Withey et al. (2012). "Maximising return on conservation investment in the conterminous USA." *Ecology Letters*, Vol. 15, Issue 11, Figure 2. Reprinted with permission of Blackwell Publishing; Figure 23.30: 1) From Withey et al. (2012). "Maximising return on conservation investment in the conterminous USA." *Ecology Letters*, Vol. 15, Issue 11, Figure 3. Reprinted with permission of Blackwell Publishing.

INDEX

A

A horizon, 21, 21*f*
Aber, John, 530
Abiotic stressors, 232, 312, 313, 315, 332, 595
Aboriginal Traditional Knowledge Subcommittee, 280
Abrams, Peter, 374
Absolute density, 264
Abundance, estimating, 22, 286–290, 291
　animal activity, 288
　challenges of, 286–288, 291
　Lincoln-Peterson index, 288
　marking/tagging and recapture, 288, 291
　whale population size, 288–290
　winter conditions, in, 287
Abundance, patterns of, 424–425, 424*f*, 444
Abyssal zone, 56
Acacia ants (*Pseudomyrmex* spp.), 396–397, 396*f*, 397*f*
Acacias, swollen thorn, 396–397, 396*f*, 397*f*, 417
Acanthocephalan (*Plagiorhynchus cylindraceus*), 393–394, 393*f*
Acapulco, Mexico, 39, 40*f*
Acclimation, 126–127, 126*f*, 140, 189
Acetylcholine, 124
Acetylcholinesterase, 124
Acid rain, 525
Acidification, lake, 7
Actual evapotranspiration (AET), 504–505, 522
Adams, Phillip, 135
Adaptational biochemistry, 124
Adaptations, Darwin and, 91
Adaptive behaviour, 204–205
　adaptationist approach, 205, 206
Addicott, John, 405–406
Adelaide, Australia, 33*f*
Adelina tribolii, 395, 396*f*
Adhesion-adapted seeds, 235, 236
Adler, P.B., 634
Admiralty Island, Alaska, 560–561, 561*f*
Adoption, red squirrels, by, 206, 207, 208
Advanced Very High Resolution Radiometer satellite network, 602
Aerts, Rien, 533, 534*f*
African buffalo (*Syncerus caffer*), 297, 324, 324*f*
African lions, 209–212, 209*f*, 229
　female lion prides, 209, 229
　kin selection, 209
　male relations, reproduction and, 209, 211–212, 212*f*, 229
Africanized honeybees, 268–269, 268*f*, 269*f*, 290
Age, sediment core, 85
Age distribution, 296, 301–303, 308, 330, 330*f*
　cohort life table vs., 296
　tree populations, stable and declining, 301–302
　variable climates and shifts in, 302–303, 303*f*
Agrawal, Anurag, 368, 369
Agricultural footprint, 620–622, 621*f*, 635
　changes in land use, 620–621, 621*f*, 635
Agriculture and Agri-Food Canada, 113
Aiba, Shin-Ichiro, 531–532
Air, water content of, 148–150
Alaska, 330
Albedos, 118, 119*f*, 621

Alberta Biodiversity Monitoring Institute, 626
Alberta Conservation Association, 626
Alberta Forest Service, 563
Alexander, Lauren, 570
Alfalfa (*Medicago sativa*), 190, 340*f*
Algae
　niches, heterogeneity and diversity of, 429–430, 444, 483–484, 483*f*
　phosphorus and, 508–509, 509*f*
Algae (*Chlorella vulgaris*), 386, 386*f*
Algae (*Ulva*), 482, 493, 493*f*, 494
Algae, filamentous (*Cladophora*), 456, 456*f*
Algonquin Provincial Park, Ontario, 458
Alleles, 91, 103, 105, 108
　frequency changes, 104*f*
Allen, Edie, 407, 408*f*
Allen, Michael, 407, 408*f*
Allenspark, Colorado, 45*f*
Allequash, 569, 569*f*
Allocation, principle of energy, 115, 121–122, 144, 191, 194, 207, 211, 222, 232, 250, 306, 370, 386, 386*f*, 395, 452, 453, 466
Allochthonous inputs, 506, 507, 507*f*
Allopatric speciation, 108, 108*f*, 109, 114, 266
　competition and, 354, 355, 356, 356*f*
Allopolyploidy, 252
Alluvial groundwater, 160
Alpha diversity, 423, 433, 444
Alpine fish, 94–95
Alternative hypothesis, AP-7
Alternative states, 470
Altitude, 117–118, 118*f*
Altruism, 205, 229, 404
　adoption, 206, 207, 208
　brood parasites, 207, 207*f*, 229
　Brown-headed Cowbird (*Molothrus ater*), 207–208, 207*f*, 229
　group selection, 206
　kin selection, 206–207, 229
　manipulation, 206, 207
　multi-level selection, 206
　natural selection and, 206–208
　reciprocal, 206, 208
Amazon, 601
Amazon Basin, 620, 622, 623*f*, 624, 635
Amazonian Peru, 463–464, 464*f*
Amensalism, 336, 337*f*
American crow (*Corvus brachyrhynchos*), 277, 278*f*
American redstart (*Setophaga ruticilla*), 5, 5*f*, 6, 6*f*
American robin (*Turdus migratorius*), 207, 298, 298*f*
Ammonification, 527
Ammonium, 398–399, 398*f*
Ammonium to nitrite, oxidation of, 187, 187*f*
Anadromous fish, 123, 168, 169*f*
Analysis of variance (ANOVA), AP-7–AP-8, AP-8*f*, AP-9
　control, AP-7
　factorial design, AP-8
　multi-way ANOVA, AP-8
　one-way ANOVA, AP-7
Anchoveta (*Engraulis ringens*), 616
Andadromous life cycle, 580
Anderson, J.M., 531*f*
Anderson, Kermyt, 217
Anderson, M.J., 423
Anderson, Roy, 400, 400*f*
Anemone nemorosa, 618
Angilletta, Michael, 125, 125*f*, 131–132

Animal Care Committees, 300
Animal display, 378–379
Animal-dispersed seeds, 235, 236
Animals
　aquatic, endothermic, 134–135, 134*f*, 144
　burrowing, impact of, 537–538
　carbon: nitrogen ratio and, 180, 184, 199
　ectothermic, temperature regulation by, 131–132, 132*f*, 144
　endangered, 10
　endothermic, temperature regulation by, 132–136, 133*f*
　energy and nutrient intake by, 188
　essential nutrients for, 180
　food density and animal functional response, 190–191
　gomphotheres, 15, 15*f*
　herbivorous, 15
　heterotrophic, 176*f*
　internal water regulation by, 153–165
　movement of and landscape structure, 561–562, 562*f*, 567–568, 568*f*, 575
　nitrogen isotopic signatures, 185, 185*f*
　size of and population density, 282–283, 282*f*, 283*f*, 291
　temperature and performance of, 123, 124–125
　transition zones, 9
　variation in life histories within vertebrate animals, 248, 248*f*
　water acquisition by, 153, 154, 154*f*
　water conservation by, 156–159
Annapolis Valley, Nova Scotia, 568
ANOVA. *See* Analysis of variance (ANOVA)
Antarctic, 263, 329
Anthropod diversity, 464, 465*f*
Anthropogenic alteration, 71*f*
Antibiotic resistance, 98
Ant-plant protection mutualism, 412, 413–414, 418, 465, 466
　Keeler's conditions for, 413–414
Ants, 212–214, 424
　leafcutters, 212–213, 212*f*, 214
　seed dispersal by, 462, 463*f*, 466
　seed-harvesting species, 212
Aphids, 165*f*, 340, 382
Apollo 8, 608
Aposematic colouration, 378, 379, 389
Apple maggot (*Rhagoletis pomonella*), 388
Apps, C.D., 574*f*
Aquatic environment
　water and salt balance in, 165–171
　water movement in, 150–151
Aquatic environment, natural history of, 54–84
　biology of, 87
　intertidal zones, 64–67
　ocean-land transitions, 67–71
　oceans, 54–59
　peatlands, 81–84
　reconstructing lake communities, 84–87, 88
　running waters, 71–76
　shallow marine waters, 59–64
　still waters, 76–81
Aquatic invertebrates, 282–283, 283*f*, 291
Aquatic primary production, 508–512, 545
　global patterns of marine primary production, 509–512, 511*f*, 512*f*
　patterns and models of, 508–509
　whole-lake experiments on, 509, 510, 510*f*, 517–518

Aquatic temperatures, 119–121
　dissolved oxygen levels, 121
　latent heat of fusion, 120
　latent heat of vaporization, 120
　oxygen-limiting conditions, 121
　riparian vegetation, 121
　specific heat, 120
　thermal stability and, 120
　variation in, 120*f*
Aral Sea, 618
Arbuscular mycorrhizal fungi (AMF), 407, 410, 418
Arcese, Peter, 207, 340–341, 341*f*
Archaea, 175, 176, 176*f*
Arctic and alpine plants, thermoregulation of, 117*f*, 129–130
　cushion plants, 129–130, 130*f*, 131*f*
Arctic cod, 238
Arctic fox (*Alopex lagopus*), 519–520, 520*f*
Arctic habitat, pollution and, 305, 306, 308
Arctic Ocean, 263
Arctic Oscillation, 618
Arctic terns (*Sterna paradisaea*), 263, 263*f*
ArcticNet, 633, 634
Area, species richness and, 582–584, 604
　manipulation of, 590–591, 591*f*
Argentine ant (*Linepithema humile*), 462, 462*f*, 463*f*
Aridity, 148
Aril, 235
Aripo River, 218, 219*f*
Arithmetic mean, AP-1
Arizona Madrone (*Arbutus arizonica*), 279, 279*f*
Armored catfish (Loricariidae), 537
Arnemo, Jon M., 300
Arnqvist, Goran, 222–223
Artemesia frigida, 156
Ås, Stefan, 582
Asexual reproduction, 216, 232, 243
Ash leaves (*Fraxinus angustifolia*), 530, 531*f*
Ash Meadows killifish (*Empetrichthys merriami*), 286
Ash Meadows milkvetch (*Astragalus phoenix*), 286
Ash Meadows stickleaf (*Mentzelia leucophylla*), 286
Ashman, Tia-Lynn, 405
Aspects, 118, 118*f*
Aspen Parkland, 423, 423*f*, 449, 450*f*, 451
Assortative mating, 109
Asterionella formosa, 430, 430*f*
Asthenosphere, 609
Atlantic cod (*Gadus morhua*), harvest of, 98–99, 98*f*
　age of maturity, 99, 99*f*
　collapse of fisheries, 327–328
Atlantic Ocean, 617
Atlantic salmon (*Salmo salar*), 113
Atlantic sturgeon (*Acipenser oxyrinchos*), 169*f*
Atmospheric circulation, 16–18, 18*f*
Atmospheric CO_2, 151, 542*f*, 621
　human influences on, 541–543, 548
Atmospheric cycles: Southern and North Atlantic Oscillations, 613–618, 614*f*, 615*f*, 635
Atolls, coral, 61, 87
ATP synthesis, 176, 177
At-risk species, predicting distribution of, 581–582
Aurora trout (*Salvelinus fontinalis timagamiensis*), 280*f*

Australian alpine ash (*Eucalyptus delgatensis*, 382, 382f
Australian tree (genus *Eucalyptus*), 381–382
Autotrophs, 175, 179, 180, 502, 522, 535
  chemosynthetic, 175, 185–187, 199–200
  photosynthetic, 175
Avens (*Dryas octopetala*), AP-2
Aversive conditioning, 210–211
Avoidance conditioning, 211f
Azore Islands, 585f, 617
Azospirillum, 527
Azotobacter, 527

B

B horizon, 21f, 22
Bacastow, Robert B., 543, 543f
Bacillus pyocyaneus, 346
Bacteria
  carbon: nitrogen ratio, 199
  chemosynthetic, 175, 200
  photosynthetic, 175
  trophic diversity of, 175–176, 198–199, 200
  use of to solve environmental problems, 198–199
Bailey, N., 288
Baillie, Jonathan E.M., 284
Baja California, Mexico, 557–558, 558f
Baker, J.L., 298f
Baker, Lawrence A., 547
Baker, Scott, 289–290
Bald-faced hornets, 378
Baldwin, John, 124, 125f
Ballooning, 380
Balsam fir, 354
Baltimore Ecosystem Study, 546, 547f
Balvanaera, Patricia, 434, 435f
Banff National Park, 210, 211, 567, 569, 570, 570f
Bank voles (*Clethrionomys glareolus*), 100
Barbour, Clyde, 584
Barcode of Life Initiative, 112
Barley plant root growth vs. nutrient distributions, 195, 195f
Barnacles (*Balanus glandula*), 455f
Barnacles (*Balanus balanoides*), 266, 266f, 267f, 324, 324f
  mortality of, 266–267, 267f
  niches and, 350
Barnacles (*Chthamalus fissus*), 482
Barnacles (*Chthamalus stellatus*), 266–267, 266f, 267f, 295
  dispersal of, 268f
  mortality of, 266–267, 267f
  niches and, 350
Barnacles, gooseneck (*Pollicipes polymerus*), 454, 455, 455f
Barnes, R.S.K., 40f
Barnola, J.M., 541, 542f
Barnosky, A.D., 611, 612
Barrie, L.A., 305
Barrier reefs, 61, 87
Barro Colorado Island, Panama, 463
Barzilay, E., 118
Batesian mimicry, 378, 379f, 389
Bathypelagic zone, 56
Baur, Anette, 142
Baur, Bruno, 142
Bay of Fundy, 65, 65f
Bay-breasted warbler (*D. castanea*), 4
Bayley, Suzanne, 438f
Beagle, H.M.S., 90, 102
Beans (Fabaceae), 235
Bear Brook, 544–545, 545f, 546f
Bear Island, Norway, 447–448, 448f, 466
Beaver, North American (*Castor canadensis*), impact of, 458–461, 458f, 466, 556–557
Bedstraw
  Galium pumilum, 349, 349f
  Galium saxatile, 349, 349f, 350
  Galium sylvestre, 349, 349f, 350
Beech trees (*Fagus grandifolia*), 8, 8f, 530
Bees (Halictidae), 205

Beetles
  Chrysolina quadrigemina, 381
  genus *Lepidochora*, 154–155
  Tribolium castaneum, 348, 348f, 395, 396f
  Tribolium confusum, 348, 348f, 395, 396f
Behaviour modification by parasites, 393–394
Behavioural ecology, 3, 183, 202–230
  diversity of behaviour, 204f
  evolution and behaviour, 203–208
  mating, 216–226
  sociality, 208–216
Behavioural isolation, 107f, 108
Behavioural traits, 48
Béjà, Oded, 175, 176
Belem, Kisangani, 41, 41f
Belen, New Mexico, 302, 302f
Bell, Graham, 195, 431, 432f, 433
Beltian bodies, 396
Benfield, Fred, 534
Bengtsson, Jan, 582
Bennett, Albert, 121, 122f
Bennett, K., 321, 321f
Ben-Shahar, Yehuda, 204
Benthic, 56, 58, 63, 67, 76f, 79, 80f
  algae, 454, 456–457, 456f, 457f
  ecosystem, 536
  zone, 72, 73f
Berendse, F., 435
Bergeron, Yves, 482, 482f
Bernhardt, T., 22
Bernhardt, Emily, 547
Berry, J., 126f
Berteaux, D., 257
Bertschy, Kirk, 239–240, 240f, 241f
Beschta, R., 460, 461
Beta diversity, 423, 444
Betancourt, Julio, 496
Betula payrifera, 411, 411f
BIDE dynamics, 311–315, 323, 332
  BIDE per capita rates vs. total number, 312
  density dependence and independence, 312–313, 312f, 315
  environment and birth and death among Galápagos finches, 313–315
  equations for, 311–312, 319
  rainfall, cactus finches, and cactus reproduction, 313–315
Big bluestem grass (*Andropogon gerardii*), 408–409, 409f, 410
Big Muskellunge, 569, 569f
Big Sulphur Creek, California, 365
Bioaccumulation, 305, 306
BioCON, 433–434, 434f, 436
Biocontrol agents, 369
BioDIV, 433–434, 434f, 436
Biodiversity
  aquatic systems, 62–63, 63f
  cost reduction for, 631
  deforestation, impact of, 624, 635
  ecological services, 433–434, 434f
  fertilizer, impact of on, 634
  hotspots, 597–599, 598f, 622
  loss of, 433, 546, 612
  marine species, 58, 59
  oceanic organisms, 57, 59
  stability and, 479, 479f
  tropical rain forest, 58
Biodiversity Institute of Ontario, 112
Biodiversity patterns, 609–618, 635
  atmospheric cycles, 613–618, 614f, 615f, 635
  biogeographical barriers, 612–613, 613f, 614f
  extinction events, 610–612, 611f, 612f, 635
  plate tectonics, 609–610, 609f, 610f, 635
Biogeoclimatic Ecosystem Classification, 46
Biological desert, 58
Biological species concept, 107

Biology
  bogs, 83–84, 83f
  boreal forest, 28
  buttress roots, 42, 42f
  coral reefs, 61
  deserts, 36, 36f
  epiphytes, 42, 42f
  fens, 83–84, 83f
  intertidal zones, 66–67
  kelp, 61–62
  lakes, 79f
  mangrove forests, 71
  Mediterranean woodland and shrubland, 34, 34f
  ocean, 57–58, 58f
  rivers, 74–75, 76f
  salt marshes, 71
  streams, 74–75, 76f
  temperate forest, 30, 30f
  temperate grassland, 32, 32f
  tropical dry forest, 39–40
  tropical rain forest, 42–43
  tropical savanna, 38
  tundra, 26
Biomagnification, 305, 306
Biomass accumulation model, 487–488, 488f
  phases of, 487, 488, 489
Biomass production, 502, 532, 629
  species diversity and, 422, 433–434, 434f, 444
Biomes, 16, 18, 503
  boreal forest, 26–28, 27f, 28f, 50, 57
  Canadian, winter ecology and, 46–49
  chaparral, 32
  climate-biome relationships, 24, 24f
  deserts, 34–37, 35f, 36f, 50, 148
  foundation of terrestrial: soil, 19–22
  fynbos, 33
  garrigue, 32
  mallee, 33
  matoral, 32
  Mediterranean woodland and shrubland, 24f, 32–34, 33f, 34f, 50
  mountains, 50
  mountainsides, on, 43–46
  natural history and geography of, 23–46
  oceans, 54–59, 54f
  temperate forest, 24f, 28–30, 29f, 30f, 50, 57
  temperate grassland, 24f, 30–32, 31f, 32f, 50
  tropical dry forest, 39–40, 39f, 40f, 50
  tropical rain forest, 40–43, 41f, 50, 58, 148
  tropical savanna, 24f, 37–38, 38f, 50
  tundra, 24f, 25–26, 25f, 26f, 49–50, 57
  water availability, 148
Biondini, Mario, 195
Bioremediation, 198–199
Biotic factors, 312, 313, 315, 332
  large mammal grazing and primary productivity, 518–519, 519f, 522
  piscivores, planktivores, and lake primary production, 516–518, 522
Biotic invaders, 627, 627f
Bird, David, 187
Bird, Ralph, 449, 450f, 451, 466
Bird Banding Laboratory (BBL), 300
Birds
  classification of altricial, 248–250, 249f, 250f, 259
  extinction and immigration of, 588–589, 588f
  island area and number of, 582–584, 582f
  island isolation and number of, 584–585, 584f, 585f
  latitude and species richness, 592, 592f
  life-history patterns among, 244–246, 248
  migration, 255–256, 256f
  red-listed species, 628–629, 629f
Birth, defined, 311
Birth rates, 316, 330
  disease and, 400f

Bjerknes, Jacob, 614–615
Björkman, O., 126f
Black spruce (*Picea mariana*), 482
Blackburnian warbler (*D. fusca*), 4
Black-capped chickadee (*Poecile atricapilla*), 48–49, 48f
Black-throated green warbler (*D. virens*), 4
Blais, Jules M., 305
Bloch, N., 300
Bloom, Arnold, 194
Blue fin tuna, 134f, 135f, 144
Bluegill sunfish (*Lepomis macrochirus*), 383
  foraging by, 193–194, 194f
Bluehead wrasse males, 203, 203f
Blue-joint grass (*Calamagrostis canadensis*), 482
Boag, David A., 294, 305
Boag, Peter, 95, 102, 313
Body temperature regulation, 128–137, 144, 264
  ectothermic animals, 131–132
  endothermic animals, 132–136
  extreme temperature, 122f, 137–142, 138f
  heat gain vs. loss, balancing, 128–129
  plants, 129–131, 136–137
Bogs, 21, 28, 81–84, 82f, 485, 499
  geography, 81
  physical conditions, 82–83
  structure, 81–82, 82f
Bolax gummifera, 130
Bolduc, Elise, 442, 442f
Bolívar, Simón, 578
Bollinger, G., 142, 143
Bombay, India, 39, 40f
Bond, Pauline, 597f, 599
Bonner, John Tyler, 318f
Bonpland, Aimé, 578
Boonstra, Rudy, 373, 374
Booth, Rosemary, 439, 439f
Boreal cordillera ecozone, 46
Boreal forest, 24f, 26–28, 27f, 50, 57, 81, 105, 131, 139, 175, 266, 354, 371, 373, 423, 424, 469, 532, 620
  biology, 28
  boreal birds, 563–564, 564f, 565f, 575
  climate, 27–28, 27f
  fertilizers and primary productivity, 506, 506f
  fire, 481–482, 481f, 482f, 557, 575
  geography, 27, 27f
  human influences, 28, 28f
  light response curve plants, 189, 189f
  photosynthetically active radiation (PAR) and, 176, 177f
  regeneration of using seedlings, 189
  secondary succession in, 481–482, 481f, 482f, 499
  soils, 28
  succession mechanisms in, 354, 491, 494–496, 499
  vegetation, 27
  water availability, 148
Boreal plain ecozone, 46
Boreal shield ecozone, 46
Borgegård, Sven-Olov, 590
Bormann, F. Herbert, 487, 488f, 489, 543–544
Bottom-up controls, 516, 535
Boulder, Colorado, 45f
Boulders and burrows, microclimate and, 119
Boutin, Stan, 206, 373, 570
Bow Valley, Banff, 210
Bowen, G., 558, 559f, 560f
Box turtle, 157f
Boyce, Mark, 567, 574
Boyd, Christin, 101–102
Braude, Stanton, 214, 215f
Braune, B.M., 306
Breeding Bird Survey, 278
Brigham, Mark, 141
Brillouin diversity index, 426
Brisson, Jacques, 276–277
Broad monitoring, 633–634

Brock, Thomas, 127
Broderick, Matthew, 226
Broders, Hugh, 105, 106, 111
Brommer, Jon, 97
Brood parasite, 207, 207f, 229, 414
Brown, Gregory P., 298f, 318f
Brown, James H., 278, 278f, 279, 284, 351, 351f, 352, 353f, 578, 583, 584, 591
Brown, Joel, 374
Brown, William L., 354
Brown algae (*Phaeostrophion irregulare*), 494
Brown bats (*Eptesicus fuscus*), 141, 142f
Brown-headed Cowbird (*Molothrus ater*), 207–208, 207f, 229
Brunner, Patrick, 94–95, 113
Bryophyte, 470
Bshary, Redouan, 461–462
Buffalo (*Syncerus caffer*), 518
Buhl-Mortensen, P., 59
Bull, James, 216
Bumblebees, thermoregulation of, 135–136
Bundle sheath, 178
Burgess, R., 558, 559f, 560f
Burrowing owl (*Athene cunicularia*), 280f
Butterfly (*Melitaea cinxia*) extinction, genetic diversity and, 105–106, 106f, 111
Buttress roots, 42, 42f
Buttress zone, 61

C

C horizon, 21f, 22
C₃ plants, 177, 177f, 178, 179, 196, 253
   climate, impact of on, 197
   distribution of, 197
   photosynthesis, 177, 177f, 196, 199
C₄ plants, 178, 178f, 179, 199, 253
   distribution of, 196, 196f
   increased temperature, impact of, 197, 197f
   photosynthesis, 178, 178f, 196, 199
   predicting distribution of, 196–197
Cactus (*Opuntia helleri*), 314–315, 315f
Cactus finch (*Geospiza conirostris*), 302–303, 303f
Caddisflies, 435, 435f, 436f
Caddisfly (*Helicopsyche borealis*), 365–366, 365f, 366f, 367f
Caddy, J.F., 327
Cadiz Township, Green County, 555, 556
Cahill, James, 195, 300
Calcium, 180, 487
California, 557, 557f, 558f
California Floristic Province, 596, 604
California roach (*Hesperoleucas symmetricus*), 456, 456f
Callan, R., 460
Calvin cycle reactions, 177, 179
CAM plants, 179, 179f, 199
Camas quamash, 404f
Cambridge Botanical Garden, 349
Camels, water budgets of, 161–162, 161f, 162f, 172
Camouflage, 378
Canada
   biodiversity of, 22
   historical and projected populations of, 331, 331f
   population density of, 330
Canada Centre for Remote Sensing, 602
Canada Goose, 256f
Canada Sensor of Remote Sensing, 503
Canadian Centre for DNA Barcoding, 112
Canadian Forest Service, Ontario, 495
Canadian Healthy Oceans Network (CHONe), 62
Canadian Shield, 526, 554
Canadian Wildlife Service, 256, 278, 280, 563–564
Canary Islands, 578
Canmore, Alberta, 574f
Caño Volcán, Venezuela, 449, 449f
Canola
   Brassica napus, 113
   Brassica rapa, 113

Canopy, 61
Cape floristic region, South Africa, 596, 597f, 599, 604
Cape May warbler (*Dendroica tigrina*), 4
Capital Reef National Park, Utah, 74f
Carabid beetles, island area and number of, 582f, 583
Carbon, 7, 23, 180, 181, 411, 502, 526
Carbon cycle, 528–529, 529f, 533, 548, 618
   human influences on, 529, 541–543, 548
   photosynthesis, 528
   respiration, 528
Carbon dioxide, atmospheric, 151, 528
Carbon fixation, 177, 178, 179
Carbon gain, nutrient gain vs., 407–410
Carbon: nitrogen (C:N) ratios, 180, 180f, 181, 182–183, 183f, 184, 199, 367
   cyanide breakdown and, 199, 199f
   sucrose, impact of addition of, 199
Cardillo, Marcel, 242
Cardinale, Bradley, 435, 436, 436f
Carex, 431–433, 432f
Carey, Francis, 134
Cargill, S.M., 363, 364f
Carignan, Vincent, 437
Carnivores, 180, 184–185, 199, 502, 503, 619
   carbon: nitrogen ratio, 184
   extinction risk, 242
   nitrogen isotopic signatures, 185, 185f
   size and shape of, 184, 184f
   size-selective predation, 185
Carnivourous plants, 188
Carpenter, F.L., 141
Carpenter, Stephen, 516–517, 519
Carroll, Lewis, 387
Carroll, Ronald, 464, 465f
Carroll, Scott, 101–102
Carruthers, R.I., 132
Carrying capacity (K), 323, 323f, 324, 325, 333, 338, 343, 346, 363, 454
Casiquiare Canal, 601
Castes, 213
Catadromous life cycle, 580
Catch rate, 328
Categorical data, AP-8–AP-9
   chi-square (X²) /goodness of fit test, AP-8–AP-9
   Fisher's exact test, AP-9
   test for independence, AP-9
Caughley, G., 264, 269f
Cavers, Paul, 354
Cavieres, Lohengrin, 130, 131f
Cavitation, 160
Cecchetti, G., 437
Cedar Bog Lake, 513, 514f
Cedar Creek, Minnesota, 434f
Cedar Creek Natural History Area, 408, 409, 537
Census of Marine Life, 63
Center for Limnology, 568
Central Intelligence Agency (CIA), 304
Centrifugal organization of species, 452–453, 453f, 466
Chaffinch, 269f
Change, 7–10
Channel Islands, California, 585f, 588–589, 588f
Chaparral, 32
Chapin, Stuart, 485, 492, 505, 505f
Character displacement, 354–356, 356f, 359, 428, 594
Charnov, Eric, 192, 193, 216, 237–238, 248–250, 249f, 250f, 258, 259
Chauvet, Eric, 534
Chemical composition, nutrient requirements and, 180
Chemical conditions
   bogs, 83
   coral reefs, 61
   fens, 83
   intertidal zones, 66
   kelp, 61
   lakes, 78
   mangrove forests, 69–71
   oceans, 57

rivers, 74, 75f
   salt marshes, 69–71
   streams, 74
Chemoautotrophs, 186, 187f
Chemostats, 386
Chemosynthesis, 58, 58f, 186
Chemosynthetic autotrophs, 175, 185–187, 199
   chemosynthetic bacteria, 175, 186, 200
Chen, Jing, 503
Cheney, C.D., 119
Chestnut trees, 8
Chetkiewicz, Cheryl-Lesley, 567, 574f
Chiariello, Nona, 159, 159f
Chihuahua spruce (*Picea chihuahuana*), 103–104, 106, 114
Chihuahuan Desert, 276, 350, 351f, 352, 556
Chilean alpine plants, 130, 131f
Chimborazo, Andes Mountains, 578, 578f
China, 331
Chinese mitten crab (*Eriocheir sinensis*), 579–580, 579f, 580f
Chinook salmon, 124
Chironomids (*Pseudochironomous*), 456f, 457, 457f
Chi-square (X²) test, AP-8–AP-9
Chitons, herbivorous, 454
Chlorophyll, 8f, 176, 365f, 367, 509, 526
Christian, Caroline, 462
Christmas Bird Counts, 277, 278f
Chronosequence, 480, 485, 486
Churchill, Manitoba, 25f, 68, 363
CIA World Factbook, 570
Cicada (*Diceroprocta apache*), 147, 147f, 163–164, 164f, 165f
Cicada (*Tibicen duryi*), 163–165
Cicadas' approach to desert living, 162–165, 163f, 172
Citrus ant (*Oecophylla smaragdina*), 465
Clark, William C., 624
Clausen, Jens, 92, 93, 93f, 113
Cleaner wrasse (*Labroides dimidiatus*), 461–462, 462f, 466
Clear winged grasshopper (*Cannula pellucida*), 132, 132f
Clements, Frederic, 490
Clevenger, Anthony, 570
Climate
   age distribution shifts in variable climates, 302–303, 303f
   atmospheric carbon and, 528
   boreal forest, 27–28
   diagrams, 18–19, 19f, 20f, 49, 128
   geological processes and landscape and, 553–555, 575
   kangaroo distributions and, 264–265, 265f, 290
   Mediterranean woodland and shrubland, 32, 33, 33f
   mountains, 44, 45f
   temperate forest, 29–30, 29f
   temperate grassland, 31–32, 31f
   tropical rain forest, 41f
   tropical savanna, 37, 38f
   tundra, 25–26, 25f
Climate change, 7, 22, 197, 532, 579, 581, 602
   bird migration, 255–256
   changes in land use and, 621–622
   climate fingerprint, 254–255, 258, 259
   competition and, 347–348, 349
   dispersal range changes, 269–270, 290
   lakes, 86, 86f
   life history information re, 254–258, 255f
   reproduction and, 256–258, 259
Climate-lake linkage, 86–87
Climatic stability, 63
Climatic variation, 16–19
   temperature, precipitation, and atmospheric circulation, 16–18
Climax community, 470, 480, 481, 482, 490, 491, 492, 495, 496, 498
Cline, 107

Clumped distribution, 274–275, 275f, 276, 277, 278, 279, 280, 328, 329, 330, 380
Coalitions. *See* African lions, male coalitions, reproduction and
Coarse particulate organic matter (CPOM), 75, 76f
Coastal forests, 506, 507
Cocha Cashu Biological Station, Manu National Park, Peru, 464
Cod (*Gadus morhua*), 327–328
Codling moth (*Carpocapsa* spp.), 182
Cody, Martin, 447
Coefficient of determination, AP-6
Coefficient of relationship, 206
Co-evolution, 223, 387
   Red Queen hypothesis, 387, 389
   stable cycling, 387, 389
Co-evolutionary response, 366
Coexistence, 466
   competitive equivalence, 348, 359
   mechanisms of and competitive exclusion principle, 347–349
   non-equilibrium conditions, 349, 359
   prediction of by modelling, 345–346
   spatial heterogeneity in the strength of competition, 347, 359
   variation in competitive ability within species, 347–348, 349, 359
Coffey, Heather, 437–438
Coho salmon (*Oncorhynchus kisutch*), 238–239, 239f, 258
Cohort, 295
Cohort life table, 295
Colautti, Robert I., 627–628
Cold-blooded, 129
Coleridge, Samuel, 52
Collard dove (*Streptopelia decaocto*), 322, 322f
Collector-gatherers, 536–537
Collembola
   Entomobryidae, 23f
   Neelidae, 23f
Colonization cycle, 271, 271f
Colonization of new islands by plants, 590, 590f, 604
Colonization of species, 589, 589f, 591, 604
Colouration, as warning, 367
Coltman, David, 99
Columbian ground squirrel (*Spermophilus columbianus*), 294
Columbus, Christopher, 59
Combined response, prey density and, 381, 381f
Commensalism, 336, 337f, 392
Committee on the Status of Endangered Wildlife in Canada (COSEWIC), 280, 281
Common Nighthawk, 255
Commonness and rarity, 284–286, 285f, 291
   geographic range of a species, 284, 291
   habitat tolerance, 284, 291
   local population size, 284, 291
Communities and ecosystems, 420–549
Community assembly rules, 447, 451, 466, 469
   centrifugal organization of species, 452–453, 453f, 466
   competitive asymmetries, 451–453, 466
   competitive equivalence, 451
   competitive hierarchies, 451–452
Community boundaries
   allochthonous inputs, 506, 507f
   interactions across, 506–508
Community changes during succession, 479–485, 499
Community ecology, 3, 4
Community phylogenetics, 90
Community structure and function, 421–445, 558, 627
   community defined, 422, 444
   community structure defined, 422–423

diversity, functional consequences of 433–436, 444
ecological function, 422
environmental complexity and species diversity, 428–433, 444
genetic diversity and ecological processes, 438–440, 444
species abundances and diversity, 423–428, 444
species richness, 423, 429, 444
Compartmental models of population growth, 400–403, 401*f*, 417
Compensatory growth, 518, 519*f*
Competition, 67, 177, 251, 267, 312, 334–360, 362, 370, 428, 430
climate, changes in and, 347–348, 349
community and, 447, 451
diversity and, 451–453, 466
exploitative, 338, 338*f*, 339, 341, 347, 359
focal plant study, 342
forest management, role of in, 354–355
forms of, 337–338, 358–359
individuals, among, 275
interference, 337, 338, 338*f*, 340–341, 359
interspecific, 337, 338, 341, 343–346, 349–350, 359, 400
intraspecific, 337, 338, 339–340, 340*f*, 358, 400
intraspecific interference, 341
latitude and, 594
mathematical and laboratory models, 343–349, 359
mortality of trees and, 276
natural systems, evidence of in, 338–343
niches and, 349–356, 359
plant competition vs. productivity, 342, 342*f*
plant roots, 337–338, 338*f*, 341–342
plant traits and competitive ability, 357–358, 357*f*
population equivalents, 344
root distributions, underground, 276–277
spatial aggregation and, 276
Competition coefficients, 344
Competitive ability, 386
Competitive equivalence, 348, 359, 451
Competitive exclusion, 344, 345, 346, 350, 354, 365, 368, 386, 428, 429, 430, 435, 451, 454
principle of, 347, 359, 375, 471
mechanisms of coexistence and, 347–349
Competitive hierarchies, 451–452, 452*f*, 466
Competitive species, plant, 246–247, 246*f*, 259
Competitive transitivity, 451, 452
Complementarity, 435, 436, 440, 444
Concentration gradient, 150, 171
Conduction, 128, 129, 131, 131*f*, 135, 137*f*
Confidence interval, AP-4, AP-6*f*
Connell, Joseph, 266, 267, 267*f*, 324, 324*f*, 341, 350, 351*f*, 354, 470–471, 471*f*, 491, 491*f*, 493, 499
Conservation, costs of, 628–629, 629*f*, 635
Conservation, using disturbances for, 474–475
Conservation biology, 459
Conservation genetics, 90, 111
Conservation thresholds, 571
Consortium for the Barcode of Life, Smithsonian Institution, 112*f*
Constitutive defences, 370
Construction, 397–399, 398*f*
Consumptive effects of predators, 370, 372, 373, 374, 375, 389
Conti, M.E., 437
Continuous data, AP-6–AP-8
analysis of variance (ANOVA), AP-7–AP-8
desired level of significance, AP-7
Kruskal-Wallis test, AP-7

Mann-Whitney test, AP-7
pooled degrees of freedom, AP-7
t-test, AP-7
Control by parasites, 393–394
Convection, 128, 129, 130*f*, 131, 131*f*, 135
Convention of Biological Diversity, 628
Cooper, Paul, 155
Cooper, William S., 469, 485
Cooperation, 205, 208, 209, 211, 212, 227, 229, 404
Cooperative breeders, 208–212, 215
African lions, 209–212
Cooperative research networks and distributed ecology, 633–634, 635–636
broad monitoring, 633–634
distributed ecology, 634
Coordinated distributed experiments, 634
Copepod, 311*f*
Coppock, David Layne, 473
Coral (phylum Cnidaria), 64
Coral (*Pocillopora damicornis*), 398–399, 398*f*
Coral (*Tubastrea aurea*), 398–399, 398*f*
Coral atolls, 61, 555
Coral bleaching, 64
Coral reefs, 59–64, 60*f*, 87, 175
biology, 61–62
chemical conditions, 61
cleaner wrasse (*Labroides dimidiatus*), impact of, 461–462, 462*f*
Deep-sea corals, 61*f*
diversity, 595–596, 597*f*
ecosystem engineers of, 458
human influences, 62
local and regional richness, 596, 596*f*
mutualism and, 397–399, 398*f*, 417
structure, 61
Core habitat, 452, 453*f*, 466
Coriolis effect, 18, 18*f*, 49
Cornell, Howard, 595
Corn-squash agroecosystem, 464
Correlation analysis, AP-5
product-moment method, AP-5
Spearman-Rank correlation, AP-5
Coruña, Spain, 578
Cost reduction using ecology, 631–632, 635
biodiversity, 631
land acquisition costs, 631–632, 631*f*, 632*f*, 635
return on investment (ROI), 631, 635
risk and gain, 631
Côte, Steve, 538–539
Cotton rats (*Sigmodon hispidus*), 561, 562
Cottonwood seedlings (*Populus balsamifera*), 469
Cottonwoods (*Populus* spp.), 159–161, 160*f*
alluvial groundwater, 160
cavitation, 160
Coulson, Stephen J., 448
Countercurrent heat exchangers, 134, 134*f*
blue fin tuna lateral swimming muscles, 134*f*, 135*f*
dolphin flippers, in, 134*f*
Coupland, R., 156
Coyotes (*Canis latrans*), 372
Crane fly (*Cryptolabis* sp.), 484, 484*f*
Crassulacean acid metabolism (CAM) photosynthesis, 179, 179*f*, 199
Creosote bush (*Larrea tridentata*), 276–277, 422, 422*f*, 424, 497*f*, 498
Critical value, AP-7
Crone, Elizabeth, 369
Crossing structures, 570, 570*f*
Crust, 609, 609*f*
Crustaceans, shrimp-like (*Euphausia superba*), 447
Crustsinger, Greg, 439, 440*f*
Cryoprotectants, 141
Crypto-zoological species, 581
Crystal Lake, 568, 569*f*
Crystallaria, 233
Current, 270–271
Currie, David, 473, 582, 582*f*, 584, 584*f*, 593
Currie, Phil, 299

Curtis, J.T., 555
Cushion plant forms, 129–130
Cyanide
breakdown of by bacteria, 198, 200
leaching process, 198–199
Cyanobacterium, 437, 527, 528*f*
Synechococcus, 585, 586*f*
Cyclical parthenogenesis, 243, 244
Cyclotella meneghiniana, 430, 430*f*

D

Dahm, Cliff, 198
Daily, Gretchen, 629
Daisies (Asteraceae), 235
Dall sheep (*Ovis dalli*), 294, 294*f*, 296, 296*f*, 297, 298, 371, 463
Dalsgaard, Johanne, 327
Dams, 160
flows, and Cottonwoods (*Populus* spp.) and, 159–161, 160*f*
impact of, 458, 461
riparian forests, impact on, 160
Damselfish, 337, 337*f*, 338
Damselflies
Calopteryx aequabilis, 568, 568*f*
Calopteryx maculata, 568, 568*f*
Damuth, John, 282, 282*f*
Dandelion (*Taraxacum officinale*), 268*f*
D'Antonio, Carla, 195
Daphne Major, 252, 313, 314*f*
Daphnia, genetic control of anti-predator movement patterns, 204
Darimont, Chris, 463
Darters, 233, 233*f*
egg size and gene flow, 233–234, 234*f*, 258
female size and number of eggs, 233, 234*f*, 258
number of eggs and gene flow, 233–234, 234*f*, 258
Darwin, Australia, 39, 40*f*, 614, 614*f*
Darwin, Charles, 61, 90–92, 90*f*, 91*f*, 95, 98–100, 113, 578, 592, 612
competition, 341
energy limitation, 121
finches, disruptive selection in, 102–103
secondary sexual characteristics, 217
sexual selection, 217–218
Davis, Margaret, 7–8, 10, 12, 269, 554, 600
Davis, Russell, 583
Dawson, Canada, 27*f*
Dawson, Todd, E., 170
Day, Troy, 402
DDT, 285
de León, Luis, 102
de Siqueira, Marinez Ferreira, 581
Dead zones, 510, 513*f*
Death, 138–139, 144–145, 400, 400*f*
dynamics of, 311–315
Decomposition, 19, 21, 22, 26, 34, 449, 466, 510, 529, 565
actual evapotranspiration (AET) and, 531, 531*f*
aquatic and wetland ecosystems and, 534, 548
forest ecosystems, in, 530–532, 532*f*
impact of on humans, 532–534
leaf, 529, 530–532, 530*f*
Mediterranean woodland ecosystems, in, 530, 530*f*, 531*f*
rates of, 87, 529–534, 548
Deep-sea anglerfish, 54, 55*f*
Deep-sea corals, 61*f*
Deer mice (*Peromyscus maniculatus*), 284, 561, 562
Deevey, Edward S., 297*f*, 298*f*
Deforestation
edge effects and, 565–566, 566*f*
global, 624, 635
nutrient loss and, 543–544, 544*f*, 548
tropical, 622–624, 622*f*, 623*f*, 635
Deglaciation, succession anad, 492–493
D'Elia, C., 398–399
Delong, Edward, 175, 176
Delta Marsh, 207, 255, 256

Delta Waterfowl and Wetland Research Station, 255
DeMeester, L., 204
Dempson, Brian, 124
Denali National Park, Alaska, 294, 296
Denitrification, 528, 547
Denno, Robert, 340, 340*f*
Density
absolute, 264
ecological, 264
Density-dependent factors, 311, 312, 312*f*, 313, 322, 323, 323*f*, 327, 332
Density-dependent populations, 273*f*
Density-independent factors, 311, 312, 312*f*, 313, 332
Density-independent populations, 273*f*
Dependent variable, AP-6
Depositional horizon, 21*f*
Deroche, Andrew, 307
Desert shrubs
Atriplex lentiformis, 126
Cleome droserifolia, 298, 298*f*
Desert tortoise, 157*f*
Deserts, 16, 21, 24*f*, 34–37, 35*f*, 50, 129, 264
biology, 36, 36*f*
climate, 34–35, 35*f*
dissimilar organisms with similar life approaches, 161–162, 161*f*, 162*f*, 172
geography, 34, 35*f*, 39*f*
human influences, 36–37
plant thermoregulation, 130–131, 131*f*
shrubs, below ground distribution of, 276–277
soils, 36
stream communities, succession in, 483–484, 483*f*, 484*f*
stream stability, replicate disturbance and, 478–479, 499
terrestrial animals, water acquisition by, 154–155, 155*f*
thermal microclimates in, 118, 119*f*
two arthropods with opposite approaches to, 162–165, 163*f*
vegetation, 36
water availability, 148
water conservation, 156–159
Desired level of significance, AP-7
Detling, James, 472, 473*f*, 538, 538*f*
Detritivores, 23*f*, 180–181, 199, 448*f*, 502, 503*f*, 514, 535, 537
feeding problems faced by, 181
size and shape of, 181, 182*f*
Diamond, Jared, 241, 447, 588–589, 588*f*
Diapausing eggs, 243, 244
Diatoms, 85, 85*f*, 311*f*, 430, 447, 483, 525
Diaz, R.J., 510, 513*f*
Didinium nasutum, 379, 379*f*
Diet composition, 192–193
seasonal shifts in Arctic fox's, 519–520, 520*f*
Diffendorfer, James, 561–562, 562*f*, 563
Diffusion, 150
Dill, Larry, 374
Dillon, Peter, 508, 509*f*, 510–511
Diploid eggs, 243
Diplura (*Japygidae*), 23*f*
Dipodomys merriami, 352
Dipodomys ordi, 352
Dipodomys spectabilis, 352
Diqiu, 52
Directional selection, 96*f*, 97, 100, 114
Dirzo, R., 464
Disclimax communities, 470
Disease, 267, 277, 312, 347
Disease, ecology of, 399–403, 417
compartmental models, 400–403, 401*f*, 417
horizontal transmission, 399, 400
SARS, 402–403, 402*f*, 403*f*, 418
vaccination, herd immunity and, 403, 403*f*, 418
vertical transmission, 399, 400
zombie attacks, preparing for, 401–402, 401*f*, 402*f*

Dispersal, 267–272, 268f, 277, 290, 311, 380, 612
  ballooning, 380
  changing food supply, in response to, 270
  emigration, 267
  expanding populations, of, 268–269
  expansion rates of animal populations, 268–269, 269f
  immigration, 267
  migration vs., 267
  range changes due to climate change, 269–270, 290
  rivers and streams, in, 270–272, 290
  seed, 381–382, 382f
  temporal, 354
Dispersal limitation, 595
Disruptive selection, 96f, 97, 109, 114
  Coho salmon (*Oncorhynchus kisutch*), 239
  Darwin's finches, in, 102–103
Distributed ecology
  coordinated distributed experiments, 634
  criteria for successful, 634
  International Tundra Experiment (ITEX), 634
  NutNet (Nutrient Network), 634
Distribution
  biomes, 16, 18, 23, 24
  changes in, 7–10, 290
  competition and, 341
  coral reefs, 60f
  deserts, 35, 35f
  human population, 329, 329f
  intertidal species, 64, 64f, 66, 66f
  kelp, 60f
  lakes, 77f
  mangrove forests, 68f
  Mediterranean woodland and shrubland, 32
  rain forests, 40f
  salt marshes, 68f
  temperate grassland, 31f
  tropical dry forests, 40f
  tropical savanna, 38f
  wetlands, 82f
Distribution and abundance of populations and species, 261–292
  commonness and rarity, 284–286, 291
  dispersal. See Dispersal
  distribution limits. See Distribution limits
  distribution patterns. See Distribution patterns
  metapopulations, 272–274
  organism size and population density, 282–284
Distribution limits, 264–267, 274
  barnacles along intertidal exposure gradient, 266–267, 266f, 267f
  kangaroo distributions and climate, 264–265, 265f, 290
  physical environment and, 265–266, 290
  tiger beetle, 265–266, 265f, 266f, 290
Distribution patterns, 274–280, 290
  clumped, 274–275, 275f, 276, 277, 278, 279, 280
  individuals, of, large scale, 277–280
  individuals, of, small scale, 274–277
  random, 274–275, 275f
  regular, 274–275, 275f
Disturbance
  conservation and, 474–475
  diversity and, 470–474, 475, 499
  intensity of, 246, 246f
  intermediate disturbance hypothesis, 470–471, 471f, 499
  intertidal zones, diversity in, 471–472, 472f, 482, 499
  nutrient retention, recovery of following, 487–488, 499
  regime of, 474

replicate and desert stream stability, 478–479, 499
  temperate grasslands, diversity and in, 472–473, 499
Disturbance, succession, and stability, 468–500
  community and ecosystem stability, 475–479, 499
  community changes during succession, 479–485, 499
  disturbance and diversity, 470–474, 499
  ecosystem changes during succession, 485–489, 499
  mechanisms of succession, 490–496, 499
Diurnal tides, 65
Diversity
  alpha, 423, 433, 444
  beta, 423, 444
  competition and, 451–453, 466
  dispersal limitation, 595
  disturbance and, 470–474, 475, 499
  diversity-function relationships, causes of, 434–436, 444
  ecological processes and genetic, 438–440, 444
  environmental complexity and species diversity, 428–433, 444
  exceptional patterns of, 596–599
  fragmentation and, 565
  functional consequences of, 433–436, 444
  gamma, 423, 433
  genotypic, 423
  heterogeneity and, 429–433, 451
  integrative index of, 425–427
  latitude and rates of, 594–595
  local and regional, 595–596, 604
  scales of, 423, 423f
  species diversity, 423, 425, 426f, 432, 433–434, 479, 612
  species evenness, 425–426, 426f, 429, 431, 444
  species richness, 423, 425, 431, 432, 444
  temperate trees, of, 599–600, 604
DNA, 111–112, 114
  barcode, 112, 114
Dobzhansky, Theodosius, 592, 592f
Dodd, Mike, 477–478, 477f
Dolphin flippers, thermoregulation in, 134f
Domain Archaea, 127
Dominant alleles, 91
Dominant species, 424, 425, 457, 458f, 461
Doñana Biological Reserve, 530, 530f
Donkor, Noble, 458–459
Donlan, Josh, 475
Donor: recipient interactions in social relations, 205
Dos Santos, João, 415
Douglas, Marlis, 94–95, 113
Douglas-fir (*Pseudotsuga menziesii*), 276, 279, 279f
Douglas-fir forest, tree distribution in, 275–276, 275f, 276f, 290
Downing, J.A., 77f
Drainage lakes, 568, 583
Dredging, salt marsh, 71, 71f
Drew, M.C., 195
Drift, 271
Droughts, lake response to, 568–569
Drumlins, 554
Dry (dry fall) deposition, 546
Dryas, 469, 480, 485, 492
Dryas integrifolia, 117, 117f, 129
Dubois, Luc-Alain, 228
Duce, Robert A., 527f
Duckweed (*Lemna*), 283f
Dugong dugon, 374, 375f
Dulvy, Nicholas K., 243
Dunbrack, R.L., 244
Dutch Elm disease (*Ophiostoma ulmi*), 313, 627f

Dwarf shrub (*Dryas*), 469
Dyer, Simon, 570
Dzamiin Uuded, Mongolia, 19, 20, 35–36, 35f

E

E.S. George Reserve, 430
Earth, layers of, 609, 609f
Earthworm (*Dendrobaena octaedra*), 23
East Pacific Rise, 58f
Eastern fence lizard (*Sceloporus undulatus*), 125, 125f, 131–132, 132f
Eastern skunk cabbage (*Symplocarpus foetidus*), 136, 137f
Ecodistricts, 46
Ecoline, 107
Ecological boundaries, 9
Ecological density, 264
Ecological divergence, reproductive isolation and, 109–110, 109f, 114
Ecological function, 422, 433, 435f, 438, 444
Ecological genomics, 90
Ecological health, 437
Ecological intactness, 437
Ecological integrity, 437
Ecological isolation, 107–108, 107f
Ecological mode, 611, 611f
Ecological networks, 447, 466
  food webs, 447–451, 448f
  host-parasitoid networks, 447
  mutualistic networks, 447
  trophic networks, 447
Ecological niche modelling, 578–582, 604
  crypto-zoological species, predicting distribution using, 581–582, 581f
  invasive crab species, predicting North American spread using, 579–581, 580f
Ecological research
  sampling, 4–11
  unintended consequences of, 300–301
Ecological services, 433–434, 436
Ecological stoichiometry, 180
Ecological succession, 469
Ecological tools and approaches
  abundance, estimating, 286–290, 291
  altering aquatic and terrestrial ecosystems, 546–547, 548
  behaviour, using game theory to understand, 226–228
  biological effects of climate change, using life histories as indicators of, 254–258
  bioremediation, 198–199
  Canadian biomes and winter ecology, 46–49
  climatic warming and local extinction of land snail, 142–144, 143f, 145
  cooperative research networks and distributed ecology, 633–634, 635–636
  energy flow through ecosystems, traced by stable isotope analysis, 519–521, 522
  evolution and exploitation, 385–388, 389
  geographic information systems (GIS), 602, 604
  global positioning systems, remote sensing, and geographic information systems, 600–603, 604
  human population and, 328–332, 333
  human-mediated change, using population structure to assess impact of, 305–308
  humans as keystone species, 463–465, 466
  lake communities, reconstructing, 84–87, 88
  long-term change, using repeat photography to detect, 496–498, 499
  mechanisms by which plants compete, identifying, 357–358, 357f, 359

mutualism and humans, 414–417, 418
  plant water uptake, using stable isotopes to study, 169–171
  remote sensing, 601–602, 602f, 604
  sampling communities, 440–443, 444
Ecologists, career paths of, 624–626
Ecology
  community, 3, 4, 263, 336, 423, 426, 438, 439, 440, 441, 444, 452, 490
  ecosystem, 3, 420, 447, 502, 503, 506, 522, 529, 532, 535, 548, 561, 625
  fear, of, 211, 460
  forest birds, of, 4–6
  goal of, 22
  levels in, 3f
  overview of, 2–4
  physiological, 3–4, 152, 153, 189, 197, 257, 261, 263, 395, 452
  population and behavioural and landscape ecology, linking, 571–575
  population genetics and, 111–113
  population. See Population ecology
  scientific discipline, 2
  scientific method, 10–11, 11f
  scope of, 10–11
  temporal scale of, 3–4
  threatened species, 280–282
  traditional vs. landscape ecologists' view of, 561, 562f
Economics, ecology and, 628–632, 635
  conservation costs, 628–629, 629f, 635
  cost reduction, 631–632, 635
  decision-making framework using, 629, 629f, 630f, 631f, 635
  ecosystem services, integration of into decisions, 629–631
  InVEST (Integrated Valuation of Ecosystem Services and Trade-offs), 630, 630f
Ecoregions, 46, 47
Ecosystems, 2, 21
  aquatic and terrestrial, altering, 546–547, 548
  aquatic and wetland, decompensation in, 534–548
  beavers, impact of, 458–461, 466
  bottom-up controls, 516, 535
  community stability and, 475–479, 476f, 499
  controlled fire introduction, impact of, 474–475, 475f
  controls of, 6–7
  decompensation, terrestrial, 530–532, 548
  ecology of, 3
  engineers, 458–461, 466, 475, 556
  functional consequences of diversity, 433
  Glacier Bay, Alaska, changes to at, 485–487, 499
  grassland, 518–519, 519f, 522
  integration of services into decision making, 629–631
  number of trophic levels in, limits to, 513, 515–516, 522
  nutrient cycling in terrestrial 537–539, 548
  phosphorus cycle in lake, 525f
  recovery, model of, 487–488, 488f, 499
  tundra warming, response to, 634
  Serengeti-Mara, 518–519, 519f, 522
  stable isotope analysis, 519–521, 522
  stream ecosystem properties, succession and, 488–489, 488f, 489f, 499
  succession, changes during, 485–489, 499
  top-down controls, 516, 535
  terrestrial vs. aquatic, 535f, 548
  trophic cascades, 516
  trophic levels in, 512–516, 522
  trophic pyramids, 513, 514, 515, 522
  whole-lake, 509, 517–518

Ecotones, 9
Ecotypes, 93, 107
Ecozones, Canadian, 46–48, 47f
Ectomycorrhizae (ECM), 407, 410, 412, 418, 539
Ectotherms, 129, 136, 138, 140, 144, 181
  thermoregulation by, 131–132, 144, 181
Edge effects, 565–566, 566f, 624, 635
Edney, E.B., 119
Eel River, California, 455–457, 456f, 457f
Effect size, AP-5
Egg number, gene flow and, 233–234, 234f, 258
Egg size
  gene flow and, 233–234, 234f, 258
  stabilizing selection and, 97–100
Egler, Frank, 490, 491
Ehleringer, James, 131, 170, 171f
El Garrapatero, Santa Cruz Island, Galápagos, 102, 103, 103f
El Niño, 314, 315, 315f, 614–615, 615f, 617, 618, 635
  global precipitation, 615, 615f, 635
  marine populations, 616–618, 616f, 635
Elaiosomes, 235, 462
Elemental cycles, human impacts on, 539–546, 548
Eliason, Erika, 124
Elk (Cervus elaphus), 210, 210f, 567
Elk Island National Park, Alberta, 395, 395f, 540, 541
Elle, Elizabeth, 368
Ellesmere Island, 533f
Elton, Charles, 250, 371, 447, 447–448, 448f, 466, 513
Eltonian pyramids, 513
Emigration, 267, 290, 295, 380, 400
  dynamics of, 311–315, 312f
Emily Murphy Park, Edmonton, 336, 336f
Encelia californica, 131
Encelia farinosa, 131
Endangered Species Act, 281
Endemic, 58, 597
Endeostigmata (Nanorchestidae), 23f
Endeostigmata (Terpnacaridae), 23f
Endler, John, 218–219, 219f, 220, 220f, 221f
Endothermic animal thermoregulation, 132–136
  aquatic animals, 134–135, 134f, 144
  environmental temperature and metabolic rates, 132–134, 133f
  insect flight muscles, 135–136, 136f
Endothermic plant thermoregulation, 136–137
Endotherms, 129, 138, 139, 140, 149
Enemy release hypothesis, 368
Energy, production and, 501–523
Energy and nutrient capture, 191–196
Energy and nutrient limitation, 188–191
  food density and animal functional response, 190–191
  photon flux and photosynthetic response curves, 188–190
Energy and nutrient relations, 174–201
Energy balance equation, 305–306
Energy budget, 141, 142, 145, 191, 232, 264, 514, 515, 515f
  pie diagrams and, 139, 139f, 145
Energy flow, 502, 535
  diagram of, 515f, 519
  temperate deciduous, in, 514, 515f
  stable isotope analysis and, 519–521, 522
Energy intake, predator's rate of, 193
Energy limitation, 121
Energy sources
  chemical composition and nutrient requirements, 180
  chemosynthetic autotrophs, 185–187
  heterotrophs, 180–185
  inorganic molecules, 175, 199
  mixotrophy and omnivory, 187–188
  organic molecules, 175, 199

photosynthesis, 176–179
solar radiation, 175, 199
Entropy, 513
Environment Canada, 5, 48, 280
Environmental complexity, species diversity and, 428–433, 444
  forest sedges, environmental heterogeneity influences on, 431–433, 432f
  niches, heterogeneity, and diversity of algae and plants, 429–430
  species composition, 432
  structural complexity, the niche, and bird species diversity, 428–429
  terrestrial plants, environmental heterogeneity effects on, 430, 431f
Environmental impact of population, 332
Environmental Monitoring and Assessment Network, 633–634
Environmental resistance to population growth, 325
Environmental temperature, metabolic rate and, 132–134, 133f
Enzyme activity, temperature and, 123, 124–125, 125f, 129, 144
Ephemerellidae mayflies, 384, 385f
Epilimnion, 77
Epipelagic zone, 56, 57, 87
Epiphytes, 42, 42f, 84, 87, 392
Equilibrium life-history strategy, 247–248, 247f
  r vs. K and Grime's classification systems vs., 248
Equilibrium model of island biogeography, 585, 586–591, 587f, 604, 612
  colonization of new islands by plants, 590, 590f, 591
  experimental island biogeography, 589, 604
  island area, manipulation of, 590–591, 591f
  species turnover, island, 587–589, 588f, 604
Equilibrium species richness, 587
Equilibrium turnover rate, 587–588
Equivalent land capability, 438
Erickson, Gregory M., 299
Erigone atra, 442f
Erigone blaesa, 442f
Eriksson, Ove, 236, 236f
Erosion, 553
Erwin, Douglas H., 610
Escherichia coli, 121, 122f
Eskers, 554, 555
Estivation, 141, 145
Estuary, 67, 69, 70, 70f, 71, 87, 168
Etheostoma, 233
Ethology, 203
Eukaryotic organisms, 189, 392–393
Euphotic zone, 78, 176
Eurasian badger (Meles meles), 119
Eurasian collared doves, 269f
European kestrel (Falco tinnunculus), 270, 270f
European rabbit, 269f
European starling (Sturnus vulgaris), 393
Eusocial species, 212–214
Eusociality, 208, 212, 229
  characteristics of, 208, 229
  evolution of, 214–215, 215f
Eutrophic lakes, 78, 79, 80f
Eutrophication, 6–7, 9, 11, 78, 510, 513f, 546, 628
Evans, G.O., 306
Evaporation, 16, 128, 129, 130, 133
Evaporative cooling, 163–165, 164f, 165f
Even distribution, AP-2, AP-2f
Evenness, species, 425–426, 426f
Evil quartet, 241
Evolution, 96–106
  co-evolution, 387
  Darwin, Charles and, 90
  eusociality, of, 214–215, 215f
  evolutionary dynamics, 387–388
  exploitation and, 385–388, 389

genetic drift, 103–105
Hardy-Weinberg principle, 96
human-induced, 98–100, 98f, 99f, 100f
natural history and, 13–114
natural selection, process of, 96–103
natural selection, theory of, 90, 91, 102, 113, 593
parallel, 109, 114
plants, response in, 358
predation and, 385–387, 389
speciation and, 89–114, 106–114
Evolution and behaviour, 203–208
  adaptive behaviour, 204–205
  altruism and natural selection, 206–208
  genetic effect on behaviour, 203–205
  inclusive fitness and types of behaviour, 205–208, 229
  interspecific variation in behaviour, 205
  intraspecific variation in behaviour, 205
Evolutionary constraint, 516, 522
Evolutionary significant units, 95
Evolutionary stable strategies (ESS), 226–227, 228, 229, 239
Evolutionary trade-offs, 121–122, 144
  allocation, principle of, 121–122, 144, 370
Exclusion, competitive, 344, 345, 346, 354, 368, 375
Expanding populations, dispersal and, 268–269
Experimental Lakes Area (ELA), 6–7, 7f, 84, 509, 510, 568
Exploitation, 362, 365, 377, 389, 399, 404, 405, 406, 407, 459f, 502, 513
  disease and, 392, 399
  evolution and, 385–388, 389
  forms of, 362
  intraspecific, 395
  parasites and, 392
Exploitative competition, 338, 338f, 339, 341, 359
Exploitative relationships, invasive species and, 368–369, 579
Exponential population growth, 320–322, 323, 343, 376
  anatomy of the equation for, 320f
  conditions for, 321–322
  importance of, 322, 332
  slowing of, 322
  tree populations, in, 321
Extinct organisms, 90
Extinction, 114, 117, 142–144, 284, 291, 586–587, 587f, 588f, 589, 590, 590f, 591, 595, 604, 610–612, 611f, 612f, 635
  Arianta arbustorum, 142–144, 143f, 144f, 145
  commonness, rarity and, 284–285, 285f, 286, 291
  Cretaceous event, 610, 611, 611f, 613, 613f, 614f
  Devonian event, 610, 611f
  fragmentation and, 565, 566f
  Glanville fritillary butterfly (Melitaea cinxia), genetic diversity and, 105–106, 106f
  heterozygosity and, 106
  island distance and, 591
  life histories and risk of, 241–243, 242f
  Lotka-Volterra model of interspecific competition, 344
  mass extinction defined, 612
  metapopulations and, 273f
  Ordovician event, 610, 611f
  Permian event, 610, 611f
  protection of threatened species, 280–282
  rates of, 586, 610, 611f
  risk of, 241
  speciation and, 610
  species coextinctions, 243
  species loss, causes of, 241
  Triassic event, 611f

Extreme temperatures, surviving, 122f, 137–142, 144–145
  acclimation, 140
  death, 138–139, 144–145
  fur, fat, and feathers, 139–140, 145
  inactivity, tolerance, and avoidance, 140–141
  metabolic rate, reducing, 141–142
  migration, 139
  resistance, 139
  winter conditions, 138f, 140, 145

F
Facilitation, 130, 435, 436, 444, 491, 491f, 492f, 493, 494, 495, 499
Factorial design, AP-8
Facultative mutualism, 392, 414
  ant-plant protection mutualisms, 412, 413–414, 418
Fahrig, Lenore, 437–438, 561, 564, 566f, 571
Falsifiable hypotheses, AP-4
Faya Largeau, Chad, 35, 35f
Fear, ecology of, 373–375, 389, 460
Fecundity, 233, 318, 319
  fish, 247–248
  schedule of, 316, 332
Federal Biodiversity Partnership, 280
Feeding relationships, 447–451, 447f, 453, 627
  cross community boundaries, 449–451, 450f
Fens, 21, 28, 81–84, 82f, 485, 499
  geography, 81
  physical conditions, 82–83
  structure, 81–82, 82f
Fernandina, 90f
Ferrel cells, 17, 18f
Fertilizer
  hay meadow community, effect on 476–478, 477f, 499
  mycorrhhizae and, 408–409, 409f, 418
  primary productivity and, 505–506, 505f, 522
Festa-Bianchet, Marco, 281
Fester, René, 392
Fetch, 253
Field studies, 338, 359
Fight or flight responses, 374f
Finch (Geospiza fortis), 251, 251f, 252
  seed depletion by and average seed hardness, 252, 252f
Finch (Geospiza fuliginosa), 251, 251f
Finch (Geospiza magnirostris), 251, 251f
Findlay, David L., 509, 510f
Fine, Paul E.M., 403f
Fine particulate organic matter (FPOM), 75, 76f
Fire
  boreal forest, impact of in, 481–482, 481f, 482f, 495, 495f, 553
  Mediterranean landscape structure and, 557–558, 557f, 558f, 575
  reintroduction of, 474–475, 475f, 553, 621
Fire ant (Solenopsis geminata), 464, 465f
Fireweed (Epilobium angustifolium), 482
Fish
  cleaner fish as keystone species, 461–462, 466
  keystone species in river food webs, as, 455–457, 466
  life-history patterns among, 247–248, 259
  piscivorous, 516–518, 522
  planktivorous, 516–518, 522
  plant competition, impact on by, 506–508, 508f
  predatory, 455–457, 456f
  reproductive allocation, adult survival and, 237–241
Fish and Wildlife Services of the United States, 278
Fish crow (Corvus ossifragus), 277, 278f
Fisher, R.A., 303

Fisher, Stuart, 483, 488, 489
Fisheries, 326–328, 474
    Atlantic cod (*Gadus morhua*), collapse
        of, 327–328
    growth of, 619–620, 635
    maximum sustainable yield (MSY),
        327, 327f
Fisheries and Oceans Canada, 124
Fisheries Research Board of Canada, 6
Fisher's exact test, AP-9
Fishing, selection and, 99
Fishkill, 78
Fitness, 338f, 341, 369, 389
    competition and, 337, 338, 338f, 341,
        349, 354, 356, 357, 358
    Darwin and, 91, 96, 99, 100, 203–204
    disease and, 399
    herbivory and predation and, 389
    inclusive, 205–206, 229
    Levin and, 121–122
    mutualism and, 412–413
    natural selection and, 228
Flagship species, 459
Flash floods
    dispersal in, 271
    impact of, 478, 483
Flea beetle (*Longitarsus jacobaeae*),
    368, 369f
Flecker, Alexander, 537
Floaters, 359
Flood pulse concept, 74
Floods
    impact of, 160–161, 302
    nutrient export, stream, 544–546, 548
Florida Keys, 589, 604
Fluking, 288, 289f
FLUXNET, 633
Focal plant study, 342
Foley, Jonathan A., 620, 621f
Folsom, Michael W., 222, 224
Food cycles, 447
Food density and animal functional
    response, 190–191
Food supply, dispersal in response to
    changes in, 270, 270f, 290
Food supply, population size and,
    371–372
Food webs, 447–451, 448f, 452, 464,
    466, 535f
    feeding relationships, cross community,
        449–451, 450f
    great complexity of, 449, 449f, 466
    humans, impact of on, 463, 466
    river, fish as keystone species in,
        455–457, 456f, 457f, 466
    species diversity and structure of, 454
    stable isotope analysis, use of,
        519–520
    trophic cascades, 516
    trophic levels, 503, 503f
Foraging, 180, 369, 370, 375
    bluegill sunfish (*Lepomis
        macrochirus*), by, 193–194
    honey bees, genetic control in, 204
    monocots vs. dicots, by, 195–196
    optimal foraging theory, 191–196, 404,
        516, 522
    plants, by, 194–196
    prey predictions, 193–194
    root: shoot ratios, 195, 200
Forbes, Stephen A., 77
Forel, F.A., 76–81
Forests
    birds, ecology of, 4–6
    beavers' impact on, 458–461, 466
    boreal. *See* Boreal forest
    management of, 354–355
    ecosystem, recovery of, 487–488, 488f
    sedges of, environmental heterogeneity
        influence on diversity of,
        431–433, 432f
    succession in, 479–482, 499
    sustainability, mycorrhizae and,
        410–412, 411f
    temperate deciduous, energy flow in,
        514, 515f

Forman, Richard, 570
Forrest, Robyn E., 243
Fortier, Martin, 633
Fortin, Marie-Josée, 9, 9f, 10
Fossil fuel burning, 527, 528, 529, 529f,
    533, 539, 540f, 541, 543, 543f, 548
Founder effect, 104–105, 105f
Fownes, Sherri, 273
Fox, Jeremy, 473
Fox, Michael, 239–240, 240f, 241f
Fractal geometry, 560–561, 575
Fragmentation, habitat and population,
    272, 561–562
    boreal bird communities, effects of,
        563–564, 564f, 565f, 575
    conservation thresholds, 571
    deforestation, impact of on, 624
    edge effects and, 565–566, 566f
    habitat loss and, 564–565, 566f, 571,
        571f, 575
    population dynamics and, 566–567
Frank, P.W., 326f
Frank H. Rigler Award, 508
Frankham, Richard, 106
Frankia, 527, 528f
Fraser, Lauchlan, 452, 634
Frederick Sound, Alaska, 289, 290
Freeze tolerance, 140–141
Frenchman Bay, Maine, 289f
Frequency-dependent selection, 304,
    308, 387
Freshwater
    bony fish osmoregulation, 167,
        168f, 172
    ecosystem, 52
    invertebrate osmoregulation, 167,
        168f, 172
    phyla in, 58, 59f
    supply of, 52–53
Freshwater Institute, 6
Friedli, H., 542
Friedmann, H., 415
Fringing reefs, 61, 87
Fry, fish, 456–457, 456f
Fry, Gary, 552
Fryxell, John, 458–459
Fu, During, 328
Fuller, Ollar, 225, 225f
Functional consequences of diversity,
    433–436, 434f
    biodiversity, impact of, 433–434, 434f
    complementarity, 435, 436, 444
    diversity-function relationships, causes
        of, 434–436, 440
    facilitation, 435, 436, 444
    sampling effect, 435–436, 444
Functional groups, 444, 449
Functional response, 200, 381, 381f
    food density and, 190–191
    hare density and, 372
    low vs. medium and high prey
        densities, 190, 190f
    type 1, 190, 190f, 200, 372
    type 2, 190, 190f, 372
    type 3, 190, 190f
Fundamental niche, 250, 251, 251f, 259,
    349, 453f
Fungi, heterotrophic, 176f
Fungivores, 23f
Funk, Dan, 109, 109f, 110
Fur, fat, and feathers, 139–140, 145
Fynbos, 33, 462, 462f, 466

G

Gaines, Michael, 561–562
Galápagos finches, 102
    caterpillars vs. *Geospiza fortis*
        fledglings, 313, 314f
    environment and birth and death
        among, 313–315, 313f
    Geospiza conirostris, 313
    Geospiza fortis, 313, 314f, 315
    Geospiza scandens, 313
    rainfall vs. *Geospiza conirostris* eggs
        laid, 313, 315f

Galápagos finches, feeding niches of,
    251–252, 251f, 252f, 259
    beak morphology of, 251–252
    body size vs. seed size eaten,
        251–252, 251f
    hardness of seeds vs. beak depth,
        252, 252f
Galápagos Islands, 90, 91, 95, 98–100,
    102, 185, 302, 308, 313, 313f,
    315, 616
Gallardo, Antonio, 530, 530f
Gamberg, M., 306
Game theory, 226–228, 229
    defence of resources model, animal, 228
    evolutionary stable strategies (ESS),
        226–227, 228, 229
    Hawk-Dove game, 227, 229
    modern ecology, in, 228
Gamma diversity, 423, 433
Garant, D., 113
Garden pea (*Pisum sativum*), 92
Garden spider (*Argiope* sp.), 268f
Garrigue, 32
Garritt, Robert, 520
Gaston, Kevin, 284
Gaudet, Connie, 357–358, 357f, 452
Gault Nature Reserve, Quebec, 431f
Gause, G.F., 323, 323f, 346, 346f, 347,
    349, 378f, 379–380, 379f
Gauslaa, Yngvar, 130
Gauthier-Clerc, M., 300
Gedney, Nicola, 151
Gelidium coulteri, 482, 493, 493f
Gene flow, metapopulations and, 273f
Gene frequency, 97f, 114
Gene sequencing, 105, 111, 112f, 114
Generalists, 388
Generation time, 316, 318
    equation for, 318
    Nerodia spideon, for, 318f
Genetic control of life history, 243–244
Genetic diversity, 97, 102, 103, 108,
    111, 114
    butterfly extinction and, 105–106, 106f
Genetic diversity and ecological
    processes, 438–440, 444
    functional consequences of, 438–440
Genetic drift, 97f, 103–105, 106, 108, 109,
    110, 114
    Chihuahya spruce (*Picea
        chihuahuana*), 103–104
    founder effect in Newfoundland moose
        (*Alces alces*), 104–105, 105f
    process of, 103–105
Genetic stocks, 113
Genetic variation, 93, 93f, 96, 103,
    106, 243
    heritability and, 95
    measurement of, 111
Genetics, impact on behaviour,
    203–204, 229
Genotype, 91, 103, 399, 439
Genotypic variation, 95
Genovesa, Galápagos Islands, 302,
    313–315
Geographic ecology, 578
Geographic information systems (GIS),
    600, 602, 604
Geographic mosaic, 387
Geographic range and population density,
    284–285, 291
Geographic speciation. *See* Allopatric
    speciation
Geography
    bogs, 81
    boreal forest, 27, 27f
    coral reefs, 59, 60f
    deserts, 34, 35f, 39f
    fens, 81
    intertidal zones, 64
    kelp, 59, 60f
    lakes, 77
    mangrove forests, 68, 68f
    Mediterranean woodland and
        shrubland, 32–33, 33f
    mountains, 43–44, 44f

oceans, 54–55, 55f
rivers, 72, 72f
salt marshes, 68, 68f
streams, 72
temperate forests, 29, 29f
temperate grassland, 30–31, 31f
tropical dry forests, 39, 40f
tropical rain forests, 40–41, 41f
tropical savanna, 37, 38f
tundra, 25, 25f
Geological processes, climate and
    landscape and, 553–555, 575
    glaciations and vegetation mosaics,
        northern North America,
        553–555, 575
    organisms and landscape structure,
        555–557, 556f, 575
Geometric mean, AP-1
Geometric population growth, 319–320,
    319f, 332
Geometric rate of increase, 316, 317, 317f,
    319, 372
    equation for, 317, 320, 320f
Geos, 52
Geospiza fortis, 95
Gersani, Mordechi, 228
Getz, W.M., 460
Getzin, Stephan, 276, 276f
Ghost moose, 394–395, 417
Giant sequoia (*Sequoia gigantea*),
    283, 295
Gibbs, H. Lisle, 314f
Gigartina canaliculata, 482, 493, 493f
Gigartina leptorhynchos, 482, 493, 493f
Gigaspora gigantea, 408
Gigaspora margarita, 408
Gill, A., 382, 382f
Gillson, L., 474
Giraldeau, Frédérique, 228
Glacial ages, 553
Glacial refugia, 554
Glaciations, vegetation mosaics in
    northern North America and,
    553–555, 575
    drumlins, 554
    eskers, 554
    glacial refugia, 554, 612
    glacier distribution, 553, 553f
    glaciers, impact of, 553, 554f, 575
    interglacial periods, 553, 575
    kettles, 554
    moraines, 554
    talus, 554
    till, 554
Glacier Bay, Alaska, 469, 492
    ecosystem changes at, 485–487, 499
    primary succession at, 480–481, 480f,
        481f, 482, 499
Glacier National Park, 111, 469f
Glanville fritillary butterfly (*Melitaea
    cinxia*), 105–106, 106f, 114, 272
Glass sponges (*Aphrocallistes vastus*), 63f
Gleason, Henry, 490, 491
Global biodiversity, 422
Global climatic cycles, 160
Global ecology, 3, 600, 607–636
    biological diversity patterns over time,
        609–618, 635
    decision making and, 628–632, 635
    human activity transforms the world,
        618–628, 635
Global population growth, human,
    331–332, 331f, 333
Global positioning systems (GPS)
    telemetry, 300, 301, 600–601, 601f,
        610, 610f
Global Species Assessment, 284
Global warming, 26, 117, 124, 142, 145,
    160, 254, 308, 525, 617
    atmospheric CO_2 and, 533,
        541–543, 548
    impact of, 533f
Global Water Policy Project, 52
Glomus etunicatum, 410
Glomus intradix, 408
Gobeil, Jean-François, 568

Gobi Desert, Mongolia, 118
Goldblatt, Peter, 597f, 599
Goldenrod (*Solidago altissima*), 439
Gold-mining ores, leaching of and cyanide breakdown, 198–199
Gomphotheres, 15, 15f
Gonadosomatic index (GSI), 238, 240, 241f
Gondwana, 609f
Goodness of fit test, AP-8–AP-9
Google Earth, 601
Gorrell, Jamie, 206, 207
Goshawks (*Accipiter gentilis*), 372
Gosz, James, 514, 515, 519
Graham, William F., 527f
Granéli, Edna, 510, 512f
Granivores, 352, 352f, 353f
Grant, Peter, 95, 102, 251, 251f, 252f, 302, 303f, 313
Grant, Rosemary, 302, 303f, 313
Grass (*Agropyron smithii*), 407, 408f
Grass (*Typha*), 452, 452f, 453, 453f
Grasses (Poaceae), 235
Grasshoppers, thermoregulation by, 132, 132f
Grassle, J.F., 58, 63
Gray, Asa, 612
Gray catbirds, 207
Gray wolves, keystone species, as, 460–461, 460f
Grazing, nutrient cycling and, 538–539
Grazing, primary production and, 516, 538f
   large mammal, 519f, 522
Great Barrier Reef, 61, 392
Great Bear Rainforest, B.C., 232, 232f, 508
Great horned owls (*Bubo virginianus*), 372
Great Lakes of North America, 77f, 627
Great Pacific Garbage Patch, 59
Great Smoky Mountains, Tennessee, 74f, 279–280, 279f
Greater honeyguide (*Indicator indicator*), 414–415, 414f, 418
   guiding behaviour of, 415–417, 416f
Greece, 330
Green sturgeon (*Acipenser medirostri*), 281
Greenhouse effect, 26
Grey kangaroo, eastern (*Macropus giganteus*), 264–265, 265f
Grey kangaroo, western (*Macropus fuliginosus*), 264–265, 265f
Grey wolf (*Canis lupus*), 294
Griffith, Simon, C., 217
Grime, Phil, 246–247, 259, 342, 342f, 439, 439f
   classification of plant life-history strategies, 246, 246f, 259
   Grime's triangle, 247
Grimm, Nancy, 489, 489f, 536–537
Grinnell, Joseph, 250
Groffman, Peter, 546–547
Gross, John, 190
Gross, Mart, 238, 239, 239f
Gross primary production, 502, 522
Ground finch (*Geospiza fortis*), 102, 103f
Ground-hugging growth form, 129, 130f
Groundwater flow through lakes, 568
Group living, 203
Group selection, 206
Groups, describing using statistics, AP-1–AP-4
Groups, differences among, AP-6–AP-8
Grutter, Alexander, 461
Guanacaste National Park, 15
Guanacaste tree (*Enterolobium cyclocarpum*), 15–16, 15f
Guénette, Sébastien, 571–572, 572f, 573f
Guerry, Anne, 630
Guilds, 423–424, 444, 449
Gumel, Abba B., 402
Gunderson, Donald, R., 237, 258

Guppy (*Poecilia reticulata*), 218, 218f, 229
   mate choice and sexual selection in, 218–222, 219f, 220f
   mate choice by female guppies, 220–222
Gurevitch, Jessica, 341
Gyres, 57

H

Haberl, Helmut, 618, 619
Habitat corridors, organism movement and, 567–568, 574, 575
   matrix, role of in influencing animal movement, 567–568, 575
Habitat loss, 241, 619f
   conservation thresholds, 571, 575
   fragmentation and, 561, 564–565, 566f, 571, 571f, 575
Habitat modelling, 579
Habitat patches, 552, 553, 556, 558, 559, 560, 560f, 561, 562, 563, 563f, 564, 565, 566, 567, 570, 575
   continents, on: mountain islands, 583
Habitat tolerance, 284–285, 291
Hadal zone, 56
Hadley, Neil F., 147f, 156–157, 157f, 163, 164–165, 164f
Hadley, Neil, F., 265
Hadley cells, 17, 18f
Hair samples, isotope analysis of, 185
Hall, Roland, 84
Halorates plumosus, 442f
Hamilton, William D., 205–206, 214, 227
Hammocks, 82
Han, Ji, 464, 465
Handford, P., 98
Handling time, 190, 193, 194
Hannon, Susan, 563
Hanski, Ilka, 106, 284
Haplodiploidy, 214, 216f
Haploid eggs, 243
Hardie, Kay, 407
Hardin, Garrett, 347
Hardy, George, H., 96
Hardy-Weinberg principle, 96, 102, 103, 108
Hare, James, 207
Harelip sucker (*Lagochila lacera*), 285–286
Harem mating system, 304
Harmonic mean, AP-1
Harper, Jayson K., 340f
Harper, J.L., 235
Harrison, A.T., 126f
Harsh environments, 183
Hart, M., 412
Hastings, Jon, 163
Haukioja, Erkki, 372
Hawaiian lava flows, 486, 486f, 487f
Hawkes, Christine, 363
Headworth, Jennifer, 537
Heard, S., 388
Heat exchange
   conduction, 128, 128f, 129, 131, 131f, 135, 137f
   convection, 128, 128f, 129, 131, 131f, 135
   evaporation, 128, 128f, 129, 130, 133, 164f
   metabolic heat, 128
   radiation, 128, 128f, 129, 130f, 131, 132, 137f, 143, 145, 176
Heat gain vs. loss, balancing, 128–129
Heath, James, 135, 163
Hebert, Paul, 112, 243–244
Hedin, Lars O., 486, 486f
Hegazy, A.K., 298, 298f
Heidegger, Martin, 444
Heinrich, Bernd, 135–136, 136f, 378
Heisenberg, Werner, 301
Heisenberg Uncertainty Principle, 301
Heithaus, Michael R., 374
Hemlock (*Tsuga canadensis*), 279, 279f
Hemlock trees, northward expansion of, 269, 269f

Hendry, Andrew, 102, 103f
Hengeveld, R., 269f
Henry, G.H.R., 634
Herbicides, nutrient production and, 487, 499
Herbivore-host interactions, 367
Herbivores, 180, 181–184, 195, 199, 362, 363, 502, 503, 514, 535, 537, 619
   carbon: nitrogen ratio, 182–183, 184
   feeding problems faced by, 181, 182–183
   plant communities, effect of on, 464
   plant population growth, impact of on, 369
   size and shape of, 182, 183f
   symbionts, 183
Herbivory, 447, 449, 595
   constitutive defences, 370
   herbivorous stream insect, algal food and, 365–366, 365f, 366f, 389
   induced defences, 370
   latitude and, 594, 595
   primary production and, 516–518, 522
   snow goose grazing and a sub-arctic salt marsh, 363–365, 363f, 364f, 389, 457
Herbivory and predation, 183, 362f
   exploitation, 362
   plant defence, 362–370, 370f, 372, 389
   predator avoidance, 378–385, 389
   predator-prey dynamics, mathematical model of, 375–378, 389
   prey populations, impacts of predators on, 370–375, 389
Herborg, Leif-Matthias, 579, 580f
Herd immunity, 403, 403f, 418
Heritability of traits, 97, 100
   genetic variation and, 95
Hermaphrodites, 216, 229
   conditions favouring, 216
Herrel, Anthony, 102
Heske, Edward, 352, 353f
Heterogeneity, 429–433, 444, 452
Heterotrophs, 175, 180–185, 199
Heterozygous genotypes, 91, 105, 106
Hibernation, 141, 145
Hierarchies, competitive, 451–452
Hiesey, William, 92, 93, 93f, 113
Hik, David, 364
Hillebrand, Helmut, 592, 593f, 634
Hillis, D.M., 111
Himmerfjärden, Sweden, 510, 512f
Hobbie, J.E., 533
Hobbs, Richard, 474, 552
Hobson, Keith, 5, 185
Hochachka, Peter, W., 124, 125f
Hodgson, James, 516
Hodkinson, Ian D., 448
Hogetsu, Taizo, 508
Holdfasts, 61
Hölldobler, Bert, 212, 213
Holling, C.S., 190, 270, 381
Hollows, 82
Holt, Robert, 561–562
Home range, 562
Homeotherms, 128, 129, 133
Homoptera, 340, 382, 465
Homozygous genotypes, 91, 105
Honey badger (*Mellivora capensis*), 415
Honey gathering, 414, 418
Honeybees, genetic control of foraging in, 204, 205
Honeybees (*Apis melifera scutellata*), 268
Hood, James, 537
Hooper, David, 479
Horizontal transmission, 399, 400
Horned lark, 255
Horse, 269f
Horsetail (*Equisetum variertaum*), 469
Hosie Islands, Barkley Sound, B.C., 63f
Host races, 388
Host-herbivore interactions, 389
Host-parasitoid networks, 447
Host-pathogen interactions, 376
Hot springs, 585
Houde, Anne, 220

Houghton, John, 254
Howarth, Robert, 520
Howell, A.B., 588
Huang, H., 464, 465
Hubbard Brook Experimental Forest, New Hampshire, 487, 488f, 499, 514, 543–544, 546
   energy flow in temperate deciduous forests, 514, 515f
   net primary production (NPP), 515
Huber, Sarah, 102
Hudson Bay Company, 371f
Huennecke, L.F., 474
Huffaker, C., 380, 380f
Hugh, Terence, 595
Hughes, R.N., 40f
Hulshoff, Maureen, 555, 555f
Human appropriation of net primary production (NAPP), 618–620, 619f
Human Footprint, 513f
Human influences
   agricultural footprint, 620–622, 621f, 635
   biodiversity, threat to from, 618–628, 619f, 635
   bogs, 84
   boreal forest, in, 28, 28f
   carbon cycle, on, 541–543, 548
   coral reefs, 62
   dead zones, 510, 513f
   deforestation and nutrient loss, 543–544, 544f, 548
   deserts, 36–37
   elemental cycles, 539–546, 548
   fens, 84
   flooding and nutrient export by streams, 544–546, 548
   human appropriation of net primary production (HANPP), 618–620
   indicators of, 436–438
   industrial activity and nitrogen deposition, 539–541
   intertidal zones, 67
   invasive species, 627–628, 635
   kelp, 62
   lakes, 79–81, 81f
   mangrove forests, 71
   Mediterranean woodland and shrubland, 34
   nitrogen cycle, on, 526, 527
   ocean, 58–59
   rivers, 76
   salt marshes, 71, 71f
   streams, 76
   temperate forests, 30
   temperate grassland, 32
   tropical deforestation, 622–624, 622f, 623f, 635
   tropical dry forests, 40
   tropical rain forests, 43, 44–46
   tropical savanna, 38
   tundra, 26
Human population, 328–332, 333
   distribution and abundance, 329–330, 329f
   growth of, 331–332, 331f, 333
   structure and dynamics of, 330–331
   variation in density of, 329–330, 329f
Human-induced evolution, 98–100, 98f, 100f
Human-mediated change, 305–308
   pollution and industrialization, 305, 308
Humans as keystone species, 463–465, 466
   ants and agriculture, 464–465, 466
   empty forest, 463–464, 464f, 466
Human-wildlife conflict, 209–211
   aversive conditioning, 210–211
   elk (*Cervus elaphus*), 210–211, 210f, 211f, 567
   grizzly/black bears, 210
   habituated animals, 209
   hyperabundant animals, 209
   pirating gulls (*Larus* species), 210
Humboldt, Alexander von, 592, 601, 602

Humboldt Current, 60*f*
Hummingbirds, 141
    torpor, 141–142, 141*f*
Humpback whales, 288–290, 289*f*
    Megaptera novaeangliae, 288, 289*f*
Humphries, Murray, 206
Humus, 21
Hungary, 330, 331*f*
    historical and projected populations of,
        331, 331*f*
    per capita rate of increase, 331
Hunters, animal communities in tropical
    rain forests and, 463–464, 464*f*, 466
Huntly, Nancy, 537, 538*f*
Hurrell, James W., 617
Hutchings, Jeffrey, 281, 328
Hutchinson, G. Evelyn, 250, 259, 299,
    429–430
Hutchinsonian niche, 250
Hybrid inviability, 107*f*, 108
Hybrid sterility, 107*f*, 108
Hybridization, 112–113, 113*f*, 114
Hydrocarbons, 157
Hydrogen, 526
Hydrologic cycle, 52–54, 53*f*, 87,
    148–149, 151, 568
Hydrologically mounded lakes, 568
Hyperosmotic aquatic organism, 151,
    151*f*, 166, 166*f*, 171
Hyperthermophilic microbes, 127
Hypervolume, 250, 251
Hyphae, 407
Hypolimnion, 77, 78*f*
Hypoosmotic aquatic organism, 151, 151*f*,
    166, 167, 171
Hyporheic zone, 72, 73*f*, 76
Hypothalamic-pituitary-
    adrenal feedback system, 374*f*

I

Iceland, 617
Ice/snow dominated, 24*f*
Ichimura, T., 508
Ichneumonid wasp, 592*f*
Immigration, 267, 290, 295, 379, 380,
    400, 586–587, 587*f*, 588*f*, 589, 590,
    590*f*, 591, 604
    dynamics of, 311–315, 312*f*
    rate of, defined, 586
Immobilization, 527
Inactivity, tolerance, and avoidance, 140–141
Inbreeding, 106
Inclusive fitness, 205–208, 229
    coefficient of relationship, 206
    cooperative behaviours, 209
    Hamilton's theory of, 205–206, 207
    kin selection, 205
    sociality, challenge of to, 208
Independent variable, AP-6
Indiana Dunes National Lakeshore, 235
Indicator species, 459
Indicators of human impact on
    communities, 436–438
    lichens and vehicular pollution,
        437–438
    wetlands and oil sands, 438
Individuals, 115–260
Induced defences, 370
Industrial activity and nitrogen
    disposition, 539–541
Industrial Revolution, 543
Infestation, 394–395
Infrared light, 176
Infrared radiation, 176
Inheritance, 91
    particulate, 91
Inhibition, 492, 492*f*, 493, 493*f*, 494,
    495, 499
Initial floristics, 490, 490*f*, 492
Innes, David, 243–244
Inorganic molecules, 175, 199
Inouye, Richard, 537, 538*f*
Insects
    endothermic, thermoregulation in,
        135–136, 136*f*
    generalists, 388

herbivorous, 397, 397*f*, 417, 424, 434
host races, 388
life-history patterns among, 244–246
predatory, 456–457, 456*f*, 457*f*
soft-scale, mutualism and, 465
specialists, 388
Insurance hypothesis, 479
Integrative index of diversity
    Brillouin's index, 426
    Margalef's index, 426
    Pielou's index, 426–427
    Shannon-Wiener index, 426,
        427*f*, 429
    Simpson's index, 426
Interactions, 334–419
Interdisciplinary research, 552
Interference competition, 226, 337, 338,
    338*f*, 359
    song sparrows, among, 340–341
Interglacials, 553, 575
Intermediate disturbance hypothesis, 447,
    459, 470–471, 471*f*, 499
    diversity and, 470–471, 472*f*, 499
    support for, 473–474
International Barcode of Life Project,
    112, 112*f*
International Long-Term Ecological
    Research (ILTER), 633, 634*f*
International Tundra Experiment
    (ITEX), 634
International Union for the Conservation
    of Nature (IUCN), 241, 281,
    284, 628
Interquartile range, AP-3
Intersexual selection, 218
Interspecific competition, 337, 338, 341,
    354, 359
    barnacle niches, 350, 351*f*
    logistic population growth and,
        343–344
    Lotka-Volterra model of, 343–346,
        359, 375–378
    mathematical/laboratory models of,
        343–346
    niches and, 349–350
    seed germination in soil, 349–350, 350*f*
Interspecific variation in behaviour, 205
Intertidal communities, succession in
    rocky, 482–483, 483*f*
Intertidal zones, 56, 59, 64–67, 65*f*, 87
    barnacles along, 266–267, 266*f*, 267*f*,
        350, 351*f*
    biology, 66–67, 168
    chemical conditions, 66
    disturbance and diversity, 471–472,
        472*f*, 499
    geography, 64
    human influences, 67
    physical conditions, 64–66
    structure, 64, 65*f*
    succession mechanisms in rocky, 493–
        494, 499
    vulnerability of species, succession
        and, 493–494, 493*f*
Intrasexual selection, 217–218
Intraspecific competition, 337, 338, 340*f*,
    347, 358, 376
    logistic population growth and, 343,
        346
    planthoppers, among, 339–340
    plants, in, 339, 340*f*
    self-thinning, 339, 339*f*, 340*f*, 359
Intraspecific interference competition, 341
Intraspecific variation in behaviour, 205
Intrinsic rate of increase, 324
Introduced species, 368
    competition with, 241
Introgression, gene, 113, 114
Intrusion pressure, 341
    territory owner age and, 341, 341*f*
Invasive species, 627–628, 627*f*, 635
    biocontrol, 369
    economic costs of, 627–628
    exploitative relationships and,
        368–369
    nontarget effects, 369

InVEST (Integrated Valuation of
    Ecosystem Services and
    Trade-offs), 630
Iriarte, Augustin, 185, 186*f*
Irradiance, 188, 188*f*, 200
Irschick, D.J., 300
Isabela Island, 90*f*
Isack, H.A., 414, 415, 416*f*, 417
Isbell, Forest, 479
Island area, species richness and,
    582–584, 604
    habitat patches on continents, 583
    lakes as islands, 583–584, 583*f*
    manipulation of, 590–591
Island biogeography, experimental,
    589, 604
Island isolation, species richness and,
    584–586, 590, 604
    marine islands, 584–585, 584*f*, 585*f*
    thermophilic cyanobacteria, isolation
        of, 585, 586*f*
Isoclines of zero population growth,
    344–346, 345*f*, 376–377, 377*f*
    orientation of using Lotka-Volterra
        model, 345*f*
Isolating mechanisms, 107–108, 107*f*
Isolation, species richness and, 582,
    584–586, 590, 590*f*, 604
Isosmotic aquatic organism, 151, 151*f*
Isozymes, 111
    electrophoresis of, 224
Iteroparity, 245

J

Jack pine (*Pinus banksiana*), 482
Jackson, R.B., 156
Jakobsson, Anna, 236, 236*f*
Janzen, Daniel, 15, 16, 50, 381, 396–397,
    397*f*, 592*f*
Jarvis, Jennifer, 214, 215, 215*f*
Jassby, Alan, 8
Jeffries, Robert L., 363, 364, 364*f*, 365
Johnson, Nancy, 408
Johnson, R., 156
Johnston, Carol, 556
Jones, Clive G., 458
Jonsen, Ian, 567–568

K

K selection, 245*f*, 259
Ka honua, 52
Kabetogama Peninsula, Voyageurs
    National Park, Minnesota,
    556–557, 556*f*
Kairiukstis, L.A., 177*f*
Kalff, Jacob, 187
Kallio, P., 126*f*
Kalmar, Attila, 582, 582*f*, 584, 584*f*
Kananaskis region, Rocky Mountains, 273
Kangaroo distributions and climate,
    264–265, 265*f*, 290
Kangaroo rats Merriam's (genus
    Dipodomys), 155, 352, 352*f*, 353*f*
Kärenlampi, L., 126*f*
Karlson, Ronald, 595, 596*f*, 597*f*
Karrell, Patrik, 97
Kaser, Stacy, 163
Kasian, S.E.M., 509, 510*f*
Kates, Robert W., 624
Katona, Steven, 288
Keck, David, 92, 93, 93*f*, 113
Keddy, Paul, 357–358, 357*f*, 447, 452,
    453, 453*f*, 466
Keeler, Kathleen, 412, 413–414
Keeling, Charles D., 542, 543, 543*f*
Keith, Lloyd, 371, 372
Kelp, 59–64, 59*f*
    chemical conditions, 61
    forests, 87
    geography, 59, 60*f*
    human influences, 62
    structure, 61
Kembel, Steve W., 195
Kemmerer, Wyoming, 118

Kentucky bluegrass (*Poa pratensis*), 342
Kerr, Jeremy, 597
Kettles, 554, 555
Kevan, Peter, 117
Keyghobadi, Nusha, 273
Keystone species, 454–461, 455*f*, 466,
    475, 516, 556
    beavers, impact as, 458–461, 466
    definition refined, 457–458, 458*f*,
        459–461
    fish as in river food webs, 455–457,
        457*f*, 466
    food web structure and species
        diversity, 454, 466
    starfish, removal of, 454–455, 455*f*
    terrestrial communities, in, 457
    wolves, impact of, 460–461, 460*f*
Kidron, G.J., 118
Kienholz, R., 337
Killer whales, studies of, 290
Killifish (*Rivulus hartii*), 218, 219, 219*f*,
    220*f*, 221*f*
Killingbeck, K.T., 181*f*
Kin selection, 205, 206–207, 229
    Belding's ground squirrels' alarm
        calls, 207
    coefficient of relationship, 206
    cooperative behaviours, 209
    eusociality and, 214
    fitness gains vs. costs, 206
    haplodiploidy, 214, 216*f*
    Richardson's ground squirrels' alarm
        calls, 207
    Sciuridae family's alarm calls, 207
    squirrel adoption, 206, 207, 208
Kinetic state, 56
King penguins (*Aptenodytes patagonicus*),
    flipper bands and, 300–301, 301*f*
Kinsella, Alberta, 33*f*
Kipling, Rudyard, 205
Kisangani, Zaire, 41*f*
Kitayama, Kanehiro, 531–532
Kitchell, James, 516–517, 519
Klamath River, 381
Klemmedson, J.O., 183*f*
Klironomos, John, 410, 410*f*, 412
Kloppers, Elsabé, 210
Kluane, Yukon, 373, 562
Kluane Lake, Yukon, 257
Kluane National Park, Yukon, 27*f*
Kluane Red Squirrel Project, 206
Knut Schmidt-Nielsen, 155
Knutson, Roger, 136–137, 137*f*
Köchy, Martin, 540, 540*f*, 541*f*
Kodric-Brown, Astrid, 220–222, 221*f*, 591
Koffler Scientific Reserve, Jokers Hill, 368
Koh, Lian Pin, 243
Kolber, Zbigniew S., 176
Kontiainen, Pekka, 97, 100, 101*f*
Kootenays, B.C., 574*f*
Korpimäki, Erkki, 270, 270*f*, 371
Kotanen, Peter, 364, 368, 369
Krawchuk, Meg, 495
Krebs, Charles J., 372–373, 373*f*, 562–563
Krill, 58
Kruskal-Wallis test, AP-7
Kuala Lumpur, Malaysia, 19, 20, 20*f*,
    41, 41*f*
Kubien, David S., 197
Kuparuk Ridge, 505
Kuusaari, Mikko, 106

L

La Niñas, 615, 615*f*, 635
La Pérouse Bay, Manitoba, 67–68, 363, 364
La terre, 52
Laboratory models of competition,
    343–349, 359
    paramecia, experiments with, 346–347
Laccaria bicolor, 412
Lack, David, 217
Lacy, Robert, 439
Lagoon, 61
Laird, R.A., 451
Lake algae (*Dinobryon*), 187, 187*f*

Lake Duparquet, 482
Lake Hjälmaren, Sweden, 590, 590f, 604
Lake Lucerne, Switzerland, 94f
Lake Mälaren, Sweden, 582
Lake Mendota, Wisconsin, 513, 514f
Lake Seminole, Florida, 277
Lakes, 76–81, 77f, 87
    chemical conditions, 78
    chemistry of and landscape position,
        568–569, 569f, 575
    community reconstruction, 84–87, 88
    deep, succession and, 485
    districts, 77
    drainage, 568, 583
    eutrophication, 510, 513f, 628
    geography, 77
    groundwater flow through, 568
    human influences, 79–81, 81f
    hydrologically mounded, 568
    islands, as, 583–584, 583f
    physical conditions, 77–78
    primary production in, 516–518, 522
    seepage, 583
    shallow, succession and, 484–485, 484f
    structure, 77, 78f
    whole-lake experiments on primary
        production, 509, 510, 510f
Lamb, E., 427, 428f
Lamberti, Gary, 365, 365f, 366, 366f
Lanceleaf stonecrop (Sedum
        lanceolatum), 273
Land snail, climatic warming and
        extinction of, 142–144, 145
    Arianta arbustorum, 142–144, 143f,
        144f, 145
    Cepea nemoralis, 142, 143–144, 144f
Landhausser, Simon, 189–190, 189f
Landsat satellites, 601, 622
Landsat Thematic Mapper, 622
Landscape, origins of, 553–558, 575
    fire and Mediterranean landscape
        structure, 557–558, 557f,
        558f, 575
    geological processes, climate, and
        landscape, 553–555, 575
    organisms and landscape structure,
        555–557, 555f, 556f
Landscape ecology, 3, 9, 228, 495, 496,
        551–576
    landscape defined, 552, 575
Landscape elements, 552, 558, 575
Landscape processes, 552, 552f,
        561–569, 575
    habitat corridors and organism
        movement, 567–568, 575
    habitat fragmentation, 561, 575
    landscape position and lake chemistry,
        568–569, 569f, 575
    traditional vs. landscape ecologists'
        view of, 561, 562f
Landscape structure, 552, 552f,
        558–561, 575
    animal movement and, 567–568,
        568f, 575
    beavers' impact on, 556–557, 556f
    crossing structures, 570, 570f
    fractal geometry, 560–561, 575
    linear disturbances across landscape,
        569–570
    matrix, 558
    movement of animals and, 561–562,
        562f, 575
    Ohio landscapes, 558–560, 559f, 560f
    organisms, relative importance of on,
        562–567
    quantifying of, 558–561, 559f, 575
Larcher, W., 177f
Large-scale distribution, 277–280
    North American bird populations,
        277–279
    plant abundance along moisture
        gradients, 279–280, 290
Large-scale ecology, 550–636
Las Cruces, New Mexico, 276
Latent heat of fusion, 120
Latent heat of vaporization, 120

Lateritic soils, 42
Latham, Roger, 599–600, 600f, 612–613
Latitude, 16–17, 17f, 18f
Latitudinal gradients in species richness,
        591–595, 592f, 593f, 604
    rate of diversification, 594–595
    time and area effects, 593–594,
        594f, 604
Law of toleration, 122, 122f
Lawrence Lake, Michigan, 194
Leaf decomposition, 529, 530–532, 534
Leafcutter ants (atta sexdens), 212–213,
        212f, 214
    castes and behaviours of, numbers of,
        213, 213f
    division of labour among, 215f
    haplodiploidy, 214, 216f
    naked mole rat (Heterocephalus
        glaber) vs., 214–215, 215f
Leafhoppers, 340, 359, 382
Leaves, nitrogen content in dead vs. live,
        181, 181f
Lechowicz, Martin, 195, 431, 433
Ledig, Robert, Gerhard, 104
Lehner, C.E., 428f
Leishman, Michelle, 235, 258
Lemmens Inlet, B.C., 630, 630f, 631f
Lemon, William C., 204
Lenski, Richard, 121, 122f
Lethbridge, Alberta, 31f, 32
Levang-Brilz, Nichole, 195
Level of confidence, AP-4
    equation for, AP-4
Leverich, Wesley J., 297f, 319, 320
Levin, Donald A., 297f, 319, 320
Levins, Richard, 121
LFH horizons, 21, 21f
Lichens, vehicular pollution and, 437–438
Lie, Elisabeth, 307
Liebig, Justus, 505
Liebig's Law of the Minimum, 194, 505
Lieffers, Victor, 189–190, 189f
Life histories and extinction risk, 241–243
    slow vs. fast life histories, 241
Life histories and the niche, 231–260, 264,
        265, 268, 274, 276, 278
    fundamental and realized niches,
        250–253, 259
    life history classification. See Life
        history classification
    trade-offs, 232–244, 258
Life history classification, 244–250, 259
    Charnov: variation in vertebrate
        animals, 248, 248f, 249, 259
    lifetime reproductive effort and relative
        offspring size, 248–250
    opportunistic, equilibrium, and
        periodic life histories,
        247–248, 247f
    plant life histories, 246–247, 342, 453
    r and K selection, 244–246, 259
Life history, genetic control of, 243–244
Life in water, 51–88, 52f
    hydrologic cycle, 52–54, 53f
    intertidal zones, 64–67
    ocean-land transitions, 67–71
    oceans, 54–59
    peatlands, 81–84
    rivers/streams, 71–76
    shallow marine waters, 59–64
    still waters, 76–81
Life on land, 14–50
    biome, natural history and geography
        of, 23–46
    climatic variation, large-scale, 16–19
    soil, foundation of, 19–22
Life tables, 295, 308, 316, 317, 318, 319
Life-form groups, 444
Light
    bogs, 82–83
    changes in, 176–177
    coral reefs, 61
    fens, 82–83
    intertidal zones, 64
    kelp, 61
    lakes, 77–78

mangrove forests, 69
    ocean, 56, 56f
    properties of, 176
    reactions, 177
    rivers, 73
    salt marshes, 69
    streams, 73, 74f
Light compensation point (LCP),
        188–189, 188f, 189–190, 200
Ligia oceanica, 119
Lignin, 529, 530–532, 532f, 548
Ligon, David, 208
Likens, Gene Elden, 487, 488f, 489,
        543–545, 545f, 546f
Limnetic zone, 77, 78f
Limpets, herbivorous, 454
Lincoln-Peterson index, 288, 290
Lindeman, Raymond, 512, 513, 519
Linnaean classification system, 107
Linnaeus, Carolus, 107, 591
Liolaemus lizards, 140
Liriodendron leaves, 534f
Lithosphere, 609
Litter, chemical composition of, 530, 533,
        534, 534f
Litter buildup, 23
Little Qualicum River, B.C., 123f
Littoral zone, 56, 77, 78f
Liu, Jiangui, 503
Lizards
    Charnov's classification of, 248–250,
        249f, 250f, 259
    thermoregulation by, 125f,
        131–132, 132f
Local diversity, patterns of, 595–596, 604
Lodgepole pine (Pinus contorta), 354,
        480, 544
Logging activity, stream temperature
        and, 124
Logistic (sigmoidal) population growth,
        322, 323–326, 323f, 324f, 327,
        332–333, 339, 346, 376, 400
    carrying capacity (K), 323, 323f, 324,
        325, 333, 338, 343, 346, 363
    interspecific competition, 343
    intraspecific competition and, 343
    intrinsic rate of increase, 324
    population density vs. per capita rate of
        increase, 326, 326f, 333
    population growth rate as a function of
        population size, 325, 325f, 327,
        333, 346
    realized/actual per capita rate of
        increase, 324, 325, 331
    sigmoidal (S-shaped) population
        growth curve, 323, 323f, 363
Logistic equation, 324, 325, 333, 343
    integrated form of, 325, 325f
Lomolino, Mark, 583, 583f, 591
Long-eared owls (Asio otus), 270, 270f
Longreach, Australia, 37, 38f
Long-tailed weasels (Mustela
        frenata), 372
Long-Term Ecological Research (LTER)
        network, 633
Lord, Janice, 235, 258
Lorenz, Konrad, 203
Lorius, Claude, 541
Lotka, Alfred, 343, 344, 375, 377, 380
Lotka-Volterra interspecific competition
        model, 343–346, 347, 349, 359, 474
    isoclines of zero population growth,
        344–346, 345f
    oscillation of predator and prey
        populations, 377–378, 377f, 379,
        379f, 380, 380f
    predator-prey model, 375–378, 376f,
        377f, 378f, 380
    refuges and predator-prey
        relations, 380
    resource-ratio model vs., 346
Lotze, Heike, 599
Louda, Svata M., 369
Lower intertidal zone, 64, 65f
Lozier, J.D., 581–582, 581f
Lugo, Ariel, 40

Lymington Hampshire, England, 252–253
Lymphocyte proliferation, 307
Lynx (Lynx canadensis, 371, 371f,
        372, 505
Lythrum salicaria, 357

M

MacArthur, John, 429, 429f
MacArthur, Robert, 4–5, 6, 10, 11, 12, 15,
        193, 244, 245, 428–429, 429f, 578,
        586–587, 587f, 588f, 589, 591
MacDonald, Steve, 124
MacDougal Crater, Mexico, 496–498, 497f
Machtans, Craig, 563–564
MacIsaac, Hugh, 579, 627
Mack, Richard N., 368–369, 627f
Mackerel (Scomber scombrus), 298
Mackey, Robin, 473
MacLachlan, P., 67
MacLulich, D., 371
Macroclimate, 117, 144
Macroecology, 3, 577–606
    area, isolation, and species richness,
        582–586, 604
    biodiversity hotspots, 597–599, 598f
    ecological niche modelling,
        578–582, 604
    equilibrium model of island
        biogeography, 586–591,
        587f, 604
    historical and regional influences
        and explanations, 595–600,
        595f, 604
    latitudinal gradients in species
        richness, 591–595, 592f,
        593f, 604
    tools of, 600–603, 604
Macrofauna, 63f, 182f
Macronutrients, 526
Macropodidea, 264
Magellan, Ferdinand, 59
Magnitogorsk, Russia, 31f, 32
Magnuson, John, 583–584, 583f
Mak, S., 578
Mako sharks, 233
Malau, U., 634
Males, 216
Mallard, 256f
Mallee, 33
Mallet, James, 113
Malthus, Thomas, 90
Mammals
    Charnov's life-history classification of,
        248–250, 249f, 250f, 259
    population density vs. size of, 283,
        283f, 291
Mandarte Island, B.C., 340
Mandelbrot, Benoit, 560
Mangrove forests, 67–71, 68f, 81, 82f, 87
    biology, 71
    chemical conditions, 69–71
    geography, 68, 68f
    human influences, 71
    physical conditions, 69
    structure, 68–69, 70f
Mangrove islands, 555, 590–591, 591f
Manipulation, 206, 207, 229, 362
Manipulative experiments, AP-6
Mantle, 609f
Mao, J.S., 460
Maple trees, northward expansion of,
        269, 269f
Map-making, 602
Marchand, P.J., 140
Margalef' diversity index, 426
Marginal value theorem, 192, 192f
Margolis, Hank, 633
Margulis, Lynn, 392
Marine biodiversity hotspots,
        598–599, 616
Marine bony fish, osmoregulation by,
        166–167, 167f, 172
Marine environment, 58, 59f
    phyla in, 59f
    waste, dumping of in, 58

Marine invertebrates, water and salt
balance in, 166–167, 167*f*, 172
Marine island, isolation and, 584–585,
584*f*, 585*f*
Marine population, El Niños, impact of
on, 616–618, 616*f*, 635
Marine primary production, 8, 8*f*,
509–512, 511*f*, 512*f*
Marine zooplankton (*Calanus
finmarchicus*), 284
Marine-derived nitrogen (MDN),
507–508, 508*f*
Mark and recapture techniques, 273, 288,
289*f*, 290, 291, 300–301, 317
Markwiese, James, 198–199, 199*f*
Maron, John, 369
Marshall, Diane L., 222, 224, 225*f*
Masting, 381
Mathematical models, competition and,
343–349, 359
Mathewson, D., 507–508, 508*f*
Mating systems and mate choice,
216–226, 229
colouration and mate choice, 220, 229
guppy (*Poecilia reticulata*), sexual
selection and in, 218–222,
218*f*, 229
male behaviour and mating
success, 220
male competitive interactions and
mating success, 220, 229
mating systems, 216–217
monogamy, 216
nonrandom mating, wild radish
(*Raphanus sativus*), 223–226,
223*f*, 224*f*, 225*f*, 229
polyandry, 217
polygynandry, 217
polygyny, 217
reproductive strategies, evolution
of, 216
reproductive success by male
attractiveness and dominance,
221, 221*f*
sex types, 216
sexual conflict among water striders,
222–223, 222*f*, 229
sexual selection, 216, 217–222, 229
Matoral, 32
Matric forces, 152
Matrix, 558
animal movement and, 567–568, 575
Maui, Hawaiian Islands, 286
Maumee River, Ohio, 286
Mauna Loa, Hawaii, 542
Maurer, Brian, 578
Maximum potential population growth
rate, 344, 381
Maximum sustainable yield (MSY),
327, 327*f*
May, Robert, 400, 400*f*, 425
Mayr, Ernst, 107
Mazerolle, Marc, 566
McAdam, Andrew, 206
McCarthy, Donal P., 628
McCormick, Stephen, D., 168
McCullough, D., 124
McDonald, Lyman, 574
McKinnon, Jeffrey, S., 109, 110
McLean, M.A., 23
McMahon, C.R., 301
McNaughton, Sam, 518, 519*f*, 538, 538*f*
McPhail, John, 354, 355–356
Mean square distances, 562
Mechanical isolation, 107*f*, 108
Mediterranean Sea, 212
Mediterranean woodland and shrubland,
24*f*, 32–34, 50
biology, 34, 34*f*
climate, 32, 33, 33*f*, 557, 575
ecosystem decomposition, 530,
530*f*, 531*f*
fire, impact of, 557–558, 557*f*,
558*f*, 575
geography, 32–33, 33*f*
human influences, 34

soils, 33
vegetation, 34
Meentemeyer, Vernon, 531
Megafauna, 59, 182*f*
Mehlman, David, 278, 278*f*
Meiofauna, 63*f*
Meiosis, 243, 244
Melillo, Jerry, 530, 531, 531*f*, 534
Mendel, Johann (Gregor), 91–92, 113
Mendelian genetics, 91
Mercator projection, 594
Mercury, 305
Merriam's kangaroo rats (*Dipodomys
merriami*), 155, 155*f*, 157
Mesocosm studies, 338, 349, 359
Mesofauna, 181, 182*f*
Mesopelagic zone, 56
Mesostigmata (*Ologamasidae*), 23*f*
Mesostigmata (*Zerconidae*), 23*f*
Mesquite trees (*Prosopis juliflora*), 163,
165, 165*f*
Messier, François, 190–191
Meta-analysis, 195, 254, 255, 375, 389,
473, 592, 634
Metabolic heat, 128, 129, 132, 133,
134, 136
Metabolic rate, temperature and, 132–134,
133*f*, 144
Metabolic rate, reducing, 141–142, 145
Metabolic water, 155
Metabolizable energy intake (MEI),
125, 125*f*
Metalimnion, 77, 78*f*
Metapopulations, 267, 272–274, 284, 290,
400, 567
Alpine butterfly, of, 273–274, 290
characteristics of, 273*f*
Methane, 528
Mexican pinyon pine (*Pinus cembroides*),
279, 279*f*
Meybeck, M., 527*f*
Meyer, Judy, 544–545, 545*f*, 546*f*
Meyer, Justin, 386, 387
Microbial activity, temperature and,
127–128, 127*f*
Microbivores, 23*f*
Microclimate, 117–121, 144
altitude and aspect, 117–118
aquatic temperatures, 119–121
boulders and burrows, 119
snow, effect of, 118, 119*f*, 120*f*
stones, effect of on, 119
vegetation and ground colour,
118–119, 119*f*, 120*f*
Microcosms, 386
Microecology, 578
Microfauna, 181, 182*f*
Microflora, 182*f*
Micronutrients, 526
Microsatellite DNA, 94, 105, 111, 114,
207, 386
Middle intertidal zone, 64, 65*f*
Migration, 139, 267
Migratory Bird Treaty, 322
Migratory patterns
Miller, K.R., 592, 592*f*
Miller, R.B., 301
Mills, K.H., 509
Milne, Bruce, 560
Mineralization, 527, 529, 533
Minimal community structure, 424
Mink (*Mustela vison*), 372
Minnich, Richard, 557–558, 558*f*
Mires, 81
Mississippi Delta, 277
Mississippi Valley, 269
Mist nets, 286–287, 300
Mistry, Shahroukh, 352, 353*f*
Mite (*Typhlodromus occidentalis*), 380,
380*f*
Mitosis, 243, 244
Mitranda, A., 464
Mittelbach, Gary G., 193–194, 593,
594, 595
Mixed function oxidases (MFOs), 183, 187

Mixotrophy, 187–188
Moisture
decomposition rate and, 529, 531, 533
primary production and, 503, 522
and, 529
Moisture gradient, plant abundance along,
279–280, 279*f*
Molecular ecology, 111
Mongolia, 330
Monogamy, 216
genetic, 217
social, 217
Montane habitat and species richness, 583,
583*f*
Monte La Sauceda, 530, 530*f*
Mooers, Arnie, 281
Moore, A.H., 119
Moore, D.R.J., 453*f*
Moore, Janice, 393–394
Mooring, Michael S., 395
Moors, 81
Moose (*Alces alces*), 394, 394*f*, 395*f*
feeding on plants, 190, 191*f*
Moraines, 554, 555
Moran, P., 371
Moray eel, 175
Morgan Lake, 568, 569, 569*f*
Morita, Richard, 127, 127*f*
Moritz, Craig, 86
Morphological traits, 48
Morris, William F., 492
Mortality, 295, 297, 299, 303, 308
Mortensen, P.B., 59
Moses, Melanie, 248
Mosquito larvae, freshwater (genus
Aedes), osmoregulation by, 168*f*
Mosquito larvae, saltwater (genus *Aedes*),
osmoregulation by, 166–167
Mosquito larvae, saltwater (genus *Aedes*),
osmoregulation by, 167, 167*f*
Moss (*Pleurozium schreberi*), 126
Moss (*Sphagnum*), 533–534
Mosser, Jerry, 127
Mortality rates vs. reproductive age,
237–238, 237*f*
Mount Desert Island, Maine, 429
Mount Kilimanjaro, Africa, 45
Mount McKinley National Park, Alaska,
294, 295
Mountain avens (*Dryas drummondii*), 469
Mountain islands, habitat patches
and, 583
Mountain sheep (*Ovis canadensis*),
harvest of, 98, 98*f*, 99–100, 100*f*
Mountains, 43–46, 43*f*, 50
biology, 44
climate, 44, 45*f*
geography, 43–44, 44*f*, 599
human influences, 44
soils, 44
Muir, John, 469
Muir Glacier, 469*f*
Mukkaw Bay, Washington, 454
Müller, Karl, 271
Müllerian mimicry, 379, 379*f*, 389
Mullon, Christian, 326
Multi-level selection, 206
Multiple regression analysis, 357
Multivariate analysis of variance
(MANOVA), AP-9
Munger, J.C., 351
Munz, Philip, 401–402, 401*f*, 402*f*
Muratore, John, 530
Murie, Adolph, 294–295, 294*f*, 296,
299, 371
Murie, Jan O., 294, 295, 305
Murie, Olaus, 294, 294*f*
Murphy, Peter, 40
Murphy-Klassen, H.M., 255, 256*f*
Muscatine, L., 398–399
Muskegs, 81
Muskox (*Ovibos moschatus*), 263,
263*f*, 264
Mussel (*Mytilus californianus*), 384, 384*f*,
454, 455
Mustards (Brassicaceae), 235

Mutualism, 336, 337*f*, 362, 417, 447,
539, 563
cheaters, 406, 418
community structure and, 461, 466
complex interactions, 393–399, 417
construction: ant-plant mutualisms,
412, 413–414, 418
cost-benefit analyses, 405, 405*f*, 410,
412–414, 418
evolution and, 412–414, 418
facultative, 392, 404, 413, 414,
417, 418
fitness and, 412–413
humans and, 414–417, 418
Keeler's cost-benefit analysis of,
412–414
latitude and, 595
Lotka-Volterra equations and, 412
mycorrhizae, 392–399
non-obligate pollination, 405
obligate, 392, 396, 404, 405, 406,
413, 417
protection: ants and bullshorn acacia,
396–397, 396*f*, 397*f*, 404,
413, 417
zooxanthellae and corals, 397–399,
398*f*, 417
Mutualism, parasitism, and disease,
391–419.
disease, ecology of, 399–403, 417
Mutualist-exploiter continuum,
404–412, 418
mycorrhizae, 404, 407–412, 418
pollination, 404–407, 404*f*
Mutualistic keystones, 461–463
cleaner fish as keystone species,
461–462, 466
seed dispersal ants as, 462–463,
463*f*, 466
Mutualistic networks, 447
Mutualist-parasite continuum, 392
Mycorrhizae, 392, 404, 407–412, 418,
424, 434, 435*f*, 447, 539
arbuscular mycorrhizal fungi (AMF),
407, 418
ectomycorrhizae (ECM), 407, 410,
412, 418
fertilizers and, 408–409, 409*f*, 418
forest sustainability and, 410–412, 411*f*
nutrient availability and mutualistic
balance sheet, 408–410, 418
nutrient gain vs. carbon gain, 407–410
water balance in plants and, 407–408,
408*f*
Myers, Norman, 597–598, 598*f*
Myers, Ransom, 599

N

NADPH synthesis, 177
Naiman, Robert J., 458, 537, 556–557,
556*f*
Naked mole rat (*Heterocephalus glaber*), ,
213–215
division of labour, 215*f*
leafcutter ants (*atta sexdens*) vs.,
214–215, 215*f*
Namib Desert, Africa, 35*f*, 155
National Audubon Society, 278*f*
National Center for Atmospheric
Research, 617
National Ecological Framework for
Canada, 46
National Ecological Observatory Network
(NEON), 633
National Institute for Research,
Amazonia, 565
National Wildlife Research Centre, 278
Natural history, 2, 4, 10
soils, of, 19–23, 23*f*
winter, of, 46–49
Natural history and evolution, 13–114
Natural Resources Canada, 354
Natural Resources Red List, 241
Natural selection, 2, 90, 106, 108, 109,
113, 114, 200, 203–208, 264, 320

age of reproductive maturity vs. mortality rates, 238
altruism, 205, 206–208, 229, 404
climate change and, 258, 259
colour pattern in guppies, 218
cooperation, 203, 205, 208, 227, 229, 404
directional selection, 96f, 97, 100, 114
disruptive selection, 96f, 97, 114
evolutionary stable strategies (ESS), 226–227, 228
finches, Darwin's, 102–103
gene frequency, shift in, 97f, 114
heritability and, 399
heritability of traits, 95, 203
individuals' fitness, 203, 228, 229
organism's feeding: optimal foraging theory, 191, 194
parallel evolution, 109–110
phenotypic variation, 92–95, 113
plants, in, 366
predation and evolutionary change, 218, 385–387
process of, 96–103
selfishness, 205, 227
sex ratios, 303
soapberry bug (Jadera haematoloma), rapid adaptation, 97–100, 101f, 114
spitefulness, 205
stabilizing selection, 96–100, 96f, 114
theory of, summarized, 91
ural owls (Strix uralensis) egg size among, 97–100
Natural systems, competition in, 338–343, 359
competition as a common ecological interaction, 341–343, 359
interference competition, 340–341
intraspecific competition, plant, 339–340
intraspecific competition, planthopper, 340, 340f
Nature Conservancy, 626
n-dimensional hypervolume, 250, 259
Neap tides, 65, 253, 267f
Nectar robbers, 406
Negative assortative mating, 109
Negatively correlated variables, AP-5, AP-5f
Negev Desert, 118
Neptune Canada, 63
Neritic zone, 56
Nesse, Randolph, 399
Net primary production (NPP), 502, 510, 510f, 522
actual evapotranspiration (AET) and, 504, 504f
fertilizer, impact of on, 505
humans, impact of on, 619, 619f, 635
precipitation, impact of on, 504, 504f, 505
temperature and moisture, impact of on, 503–504, 503f, 506
Net reproductive rate (Ro), 316, 316f, 317
equation for, 317
Nerodia spideon, for, 318f
Netherlands, 330
Neutral model, 587
Neutralism, 336, 337f
Nevins Lake, Michigan, 568
New Hampshire, 337
New Jersey, 330
Newbold, Denis, 536
Newfoundland and Labrador Department of Forest Researcher and Agrifoods, 105
Newfoundland moose (Alces alces), 104–105, 106, 111
Newman, Edward, 342, 342f
Niche, life histories and. See Life histories and the niche
Niche modelling, 602
Niches, fundamental and realized, 250–253, 259, 264, 368

barnacles, niche overlap and competition between, 350, 351f
character displacement, 354–356, 359, 428
complementarity, 435, 436, 440
Galàpagos finches, feeding niches of, 251–252, 251f, 252f, 259
heterogeneity, diversity of algae and plants and, 429–430, 431, 432
n-dimensional hypervolume, 250, 251, 259
niche, defined, 232, 250, 264, 579
plants, competition among and, 349–350, 350f
salt marsh grass, habitat niche of, 252–253
small rodents, competition and, 350–353, 352f, 353f
structural complexity, bird species diversity and, 428–429
Nicholson River, Queensland, Australia, 71f
Nieminen, Marko, 106
Niering, William, 279, 279f
Nilsson, Sven, 582, 582f
Nine-banded armadillo, 269f
Nitrates, 430, 431f, 487
deforestation and, 545f
export of from rivers and human population density, 546, 547f
marine primary production, 510, 512f, 522
stream level and decomposition rates, 534, 534f
vertical hydraulic gradient and levels of, 478, 478f
Nitrifying bacteria (Nitrosomonas spp.), 187f
Nitrogen, 7, 23, 180, 338f, 398, 478, 526, 546
cycling of, 187
dry deposition, 546
leaf content: dead vs. live, 181, 181f
nitrifying bacteria, 187, 187f
primary productivity and, 505, 505f, 526, 527
retention of during stream succession, 489, 489f
wet deposition, 546
Nitrogen cycle, 526–528, 528f, 537–538, 538f, 548
ammonification, 527
denitrification, 528
human impacts on, 526, 527
immobilization, 527
industrial activity and nitrogen deposition, 539–541
microbes, role of, 527
mineralization, 527, 529, 533
nitrification, 527
nitrogen fixers, 527, 528
Nitrogen deposition, 539–541, 540f
Nitrogen fixation, 414, 527, 528, 539, 540f
Nitrogen isotopic signatures, 185, 185f
Nitrogen use efficiency (NUE), 181
Nitrogen: phosphorus (N:P) ratio, nutrient composition and, 537, 537f
Niwot Ridge, Colorado, 45f
Non-consumptive effects of predators, 370, 373–375, 377, 389, 460, 570
Non-equilibrium conditions, 349, 359
Nonparametric procedures, AP-5, AP-6, AP-7
Nonrandom mating, 102, 103
Nonsymbiotic relationships, 392
Nontarget effects, 369
Non-verterbrae species, 22
Normal distribution, AP-1, AP-2f, AP-6
Norrdahl, Kai, 270, 270f, 371
Norris, Ryan, 5, 6, 7
North American bird populations, 277–279
North American elk, 269, 269f
North American Great Plains, 540
North Atlantic Humpback Catalog, 288
North Atlantic Oscillation (NAO), 613, 616–618, 617f, 635
Northern Hemisphere, 49, 284, 321, 441, 508, 556, 594f, 617

boreal forest, 27
climatic diagrams, 19
northern aspect, 118
oceanic gyres, 57
solar energy, 16–17, 17f
temperate forest, 29
tropical dry forest, 40f
winds: Coriolis effect, 18, 18f
Northern Hemisphere Annular Mode (NAM), 618, 635
Northern Highlands Lake District of Wisconsin and Michigan, 583
Northern water snake (Nerodia sipedon), 298, 298f, 317–319
Nottrott, R.W., 633
Novacek, Michael J., AP-4, AP-5, AP-7, AP-8
Null hypothesis, AP-4, AP-5, AP-7, AP-8
Numbers, protection in, 381, 383f, 389
Numerical responses, prey availability and, 270, 270f, 371, 372, 381, 381f
Nunatak, 554
Nunavut, 119f, 263, 281, 330
NutNet (Nutrient Network), 634
Nutrient
leaching of, 23
loss, deforestation and, 543–544
macronutrients, 526
micronutrients, 526
retentiveness, 536
spiraling, 536, 536f, 548
Nutrient cycling, 422, 444, 451, 460, 502, 526–529, 532, 535, 545f, 546, 548, 568, 618, 627, 629
animals in terrestrial ecosystems, 537–539, 548
aquatic vs. terrestrial ecosystems, in, 535, 535f, 548
carbon cycle, 528–529, 529f, 548
decomposition, rates of, 87, 529–534, 548
deer impact on, 539
grazing and, 538–539
human influences on, 539–546, 540f, 548
nitrogen cycle, 526–528, 528f, 548
organisms and nutrients, 535–539, 548
phosphorus cycle, 526, 527f, 548
streams, in, 535–537, 548
vertebrate effect on nutrient cycling in aquatic ecosystems, 537
Nutrient gain, carbon gain vs., 407–410
nutrient availability and mutualistic balance sheet, 408–410, 418
water balance in plants and, 407–408
Nutrient retention, recovery of post-disturbance, 487–488, 499
ecosystem recovery model, 487–488, 488f

O

O horizons, 21, 37
Oak leaves (Quercus lusitanica), 530
Obligate mutualisms, 392, 405, 406
Obligate parthogenesis, 243, 244, 244f
Oceanic zone, 56
Ocean-land transitions, 67–71
Oceanography of lakes, 76
Oceans, 54–59, 54f, 87, 168
biology of, 57–58, 58f
chemical conditions, 57
geography, 54–55, 55f
human influences on, 58–59
oceanic circulation, 55f
physical conditions, 56–57
structure, 56, 56f
vertical structuring, 57f
Ocotilla plant, 158, 158f
Ødegaard, Frode, 388
O'Donoghue, M., 372
O'Dowd, D., 382, 382f
Offspring, size and number of, 233–237, 244, 258
fish egg size and number, 233–237
Oil development, 7
Oil sands, reclamation of, 438
Old Faithful Geyser, 585
Old Man River, 160f, 161

Olff, H., 475
Oligotrophic lakes, 78, 79, 80f
Olsen, E.M., 98, 99
Olsen, G.H., 307
Omnivores, 187
Omnivory, 187–188
Onychomys leucogaster, 352, 353f
Onychomys torridus, 352
Onymacris unguicularis, 154–155
Opportunistic life-history strategy, 247–248, 247f
r vs. K and Grime's classification systems vs., 248
Optimal foraging theory, 191–196, 200, 203, 385, 516, 522
Bluegill sunfish (Lepomis macrochirus), foraging by, 193–194, 194f
diet composition, 192–193
feeding on one prey, 193
feeding on two or more prey, 193
grasslands, by, 195–196
handling time, 190, 193, 194
marginal value theorem, 192, 192f
movement among patches, 192
optimization, 193
plants, by, 194–196
prey encounter rate, 192–193
root: shoot ratios, 195, 200
searching costs, 193
Optimization, 193
Ordinations, 437, 438, 572, 572f, 573f, AP-9
Organ Pipe National Monument, 422
Organic molecules, 175, 199
Organism size and population density, 282–284, 290
animals, of, 282–283, 282f, 283f, 291
plants, of, 283–284, 283f, 291
Organisms
aquatic, 16
biology of, 8
changes to, 8
importance of landscape structure on, 555, 556f, 562–567, 575
temperature and performance of, 122–128
Organisms and nutrients, 535–539, 548
Oribatida
Brachychthoniidae, 23f
Cosmochthoniidae, 23f
Hermanniidae, 23f
Lohmannidae, 23f
Phenopelopidae, 23f
Phthiracaroidea, 23f
Suctobelboideae, 23f
Orinoco River, 601
Osa Peninsula, Costa Rica, 271
Osmosis, 150
Osmotic pressure, 150–151, 152, 172, 314
Osoyoos, B.C., 35f
Otterson, G., 617
Overcompensation, 363, 364
Over-exploitation, 241
Overpopulation theories, 371
Oxygen, 526
aquatic temperatures, 121
bogs, 83
coral reefs, 61
dissolved vs. gaseous, levels of, 121
fens, 83
intertidal zones, 66
kelp, 61
lakes, 78
mangrove forests, 70–71
oceans, 57
rivers, 74
salt marshes, 70–71
streams, 74

P

Pacific salmon (Oncorhynchus spp.), 537, 538f
Pacific Trash Vortex, 59
Packer, Craig, 209, 212, 212f
Packer, Laurence, 205

Paine, Robert, 383–384, 384*f*, 454–455, 455*f*, 457, 466
Paleoecological Environmental Assessment and Research Laboratory (PEARL), 84, 85*f*
Paleolimnology, 84
Palliser, John, 504
Palliser's Triangle, 504
Palm (*Protchardia munroi*), 286
Palumbi, Stephen, R., 98–100
Paper birch (*Betula papyrifera*), 530
Papke, Thane, 585
Pappers, S.M., 95
Paradox of the plankton, 429
Parallel evolution, 109–110, 114
Paramecium aurelia, 346, 346*f*, 347*f*
Paramecium caudatum, 346, 346*f*, 347*f*, 379, 379*f*
Parametric procedures, AP-5, AP-6, AP-7
Parapatric speciation, 108, 108*f*, 114, 595
Parasite-host system, 380, 393, 594
Parasites, 23*f*, 392, 448*f*, 466
Parasitic interactions, 362
Parasitism, 392–399, 447
control: behaviour modification by parasites, 393–394, 417
infestation: ghost moose and winter ticks, 394–395, 417
interactions: predation and competition and, 395–396, 396*f*, 417
latitude and, 594, 595
Park, Thomas, 347, 348*f*, 349, 395, 396*f*
Park Grass Experiment, 476–478, 477*f*, 499
Parkinson, Dennis, 23
Parks Canada, 280, 553, 570
Parmenter, C.A., 119
Parmenter, Robert, R., 118
Parmesan, Camille, 254
Partel, M., 195–196
Parturition date, climate change and, 257–258, 258*f*
Patch reefs, 61
Patches. *See* Habitat patches
Paternity tests, human, 216–217, 217*f*, 316
Pathogens, 399, 400, 401, 448*f*, 466
Patterns of species' abundances, 424–425
distribution of commonness and rarity, 424
dominance, 424, 425
minimal community structure, 424
Preston's curves: lognormal distributions, 425, 444
relative abundance, 424–425, 424*f*, 444
Pauly, Daniel, 327
PCB levels in polar bears, impact of, 306–307
Pearcy, Robert, W., 126*f*
Peatlands, 81–84, 533
Peckarsky, Barbara L., 374, 384
Peers, G., 210
Peierls, Benjamin, 546, 547*f*
Pelagic, 56
PEP carboxylase, 178
Per capita rate of increase, 312, 316, 318, 331, 332, 344, 374
population density, impact of, 312, 312*f*, 332
Percidae, 233
Percina, 233
Peregrine falcon, 281
Peregrine falcon (*Falco peregrinus*), 284–285, 285*f*
Performance of organisms, temperature and, 122–128, 144
animals, 123, 124–125
enzyme function, 123, 124–125, 125*f*
law of toleration, 122, 122*f*
microbial conditions and temperature, 127–128
range of tolerance, 123
reproduction and, 124
Periodic life-history strategies, 247–248, 247*f*
r vs. K and Grime's classification systems vs., 248

Periodical cicadas (*Magicicada* spp.), 382–383, 383*f*
Peripheral habitat, 452, 466
Periphyton, 85
Permafrost, 26, 532–533, 533*f*
Peroganathus flavus, 352
Peroganathus penicillatus, 352
Peromyscus maniculatus, 352
Perry, Anjanette, 289
Persistent organic pollutants (POPs), 305–307
Peters, Robert, 282, 283*f*
Peters, Vern, 490
Peterson, A.T., 578, 579
Peterson, Bruce, 520–521, 521*f*
Petroleum extraction, 67
Petroleum leaks, benzene breakdown by bacteria, 198, 198*f*, 200
Phenology, climate change and, 254–256, 257, 259
Phenotype, 91, 92, 95, 97, 107, 257
Phenotypic plasticity, 93, 97, 189, 257, 258, 259
Phenotypic variation, 92–95, 96, 113, 463
alpine fish, 94–95
heritability, genetic variation and, 95
plants, 92–94
Philadelphia, Pennsylvania, 29*f*
Phlox drummondii, 297, 297*f*, 316–317, 316*f*, 319–320, 319*f*, 322
Phosphate, 430, 430*f*
Phosphoenolspyruvate (PEP), 178, 179
Phosphoglyceric acid (PGA), 177
Phosphorus, 6–7, 9, 78, 180, 407, 486, 487*f*, 505, 505*f*, 508, 509*f*, 522, 526, 534, 537, 544–545, 545*f*, 546, 546*f*, 628
Phosphorus cycle, 526, 527*f*, 548
Phosphorus mining, 526
Photic zone, 57
Photography, using to detect long-term change, 496–498, 497*f*, 498*f*, 499
Photoidentification, 288, 289, 289*f*, 290
Photon flux density (PFD), 176, 188, 189*f*, 199, 200
photosynthetic response curves and, 188–190, 200
Photons, 176
Photorespiration, 178, 197, 199
Photosynthesis, 26, 138, 144, 175, 176–179, 185, 367, 502
acclimation, 126–127, 126*f*
alternative pathways, 176–179, 199
atmospheric CO_2 and, 528
C_3 photosynthesis, 177, 177*f*, 199
C_4 photosynthesis, 178, 178*f*, 199
Calvin cycle reactions, 177, 179
carbon fixation, 177, 178, 179
chlorophyll concentration and, 509
coral reefs, 61
crassulacean acid metabolism (CAM) photosynthesis, 179, 179*f*, 199
equation for, 126
extreme temperatures and, 126–127, 126*f*
intertidal zones, 64
irradiance, 188
irradiance (I_{sat}), 188*f*
kelp, 61
lakes, 61
light reactions, 177–179, 177*f*
mangrove forests, 71
measuring PAR, 176–177
ocean, 57, 58
optimal temperatures for, 126, 126*f*
peatland, 82, 83
phosphorus and, 509
photon flux density (PFD) and photosynthetic response curves, 188–190
P_{max}, 188, 188*f*
rate of, 126
salt marshes, 71
shut down of, 178
solar-powered biosphere, 176

streams, 73
water conservation pathways for, 159, 160
Photosynthetic autotrophs, 175
photosynthetic bacteria, 175
photosynthetic protists, 175
Photosynthetic response curves, 188, 188*f*, 200
differences in, 189–190
Photosynthetically active radiation (PAR), 176–177, 177*f*, 199
measurement of, 176–177
photon flux density (PFD), 176, 188, 189*f*,199, 200
Phreatic zone, 72, 73*f*, 76
Phyla, 58, 59*f*, 63
Phylogenetic species concept, 107
Physical conditions
bogs, 82–83
coral reefs, 61
fens, 82–83
intertidal zones, 64–66
kelp, 61
lakes, 77–78
mangrove forests, 69
ocean, 56–57
rivers, 73–74, 75*f*
salt marshes, 69
streams, 73–74, 74*f*
Physiological ecology, 3–4, 152, 153, 189, 197, 257, 261, 263, 395, 452
Physiological traits, 48
Phytochrome system, 358
Phytometer, 357, 359
Phytophagous species, 388, 389
Phytoplankton, 8, 57, 76*f*, 85, 256, 455*f*, 511, 520, 535
iron and, 510
paradox of the, 429–430
phosphorus and, 508, 509
Pianka, Eric R., 193, 245, 248
Picea chihuahuana, 103–104
Pickett, S., 470
Pie diagrams, 139, 139*f*, 145
Pielou, Evelyn, 441, 553, 553*f*
Pielou index of diversity, 426–427
Piezometers, 478
Pike cichlid (*Crenicichla alta*), 218, 219, 219*f*, 220*f*, 221*f*
Pill bug (*Armadillidium vulgare*), 393–394
Pimentel, David, 627
Pimlott, D.H., 105
Pin cherry (*Prunus pennsylvanica*), 530
Pine beetles, 7
Pine tissues, C: N ratio, 183*f*
Pine trees (*Pinus edulis*), 163
Pioneer community, 469
Pirating gulls (*Larus* species), 210
Pistils, 223
Pitcher plant (*Sarracenia purpurea*), 83*f*
Pitfall traps, 300
PKG, 204
Planktivorous fish, 516–518, 522
Plant growth forms, 236
Plant litter, 118
Plant-animal interactions, 184, 364
Plant-fungal interactions, 408–410, 409*f*
Planthopper (*Prokelisia marginata*), 340, 340*f*
Planthoppers, intraspecific competition among, 339–340
Plant-pollinator interaction, 392, 392*f*
Plants, 21*f*, 228, 246*f*
abiotic stress, 246, 247
abundance of along moisture gradients, 279–280, 290
adaptive hypothesis, 357–358
bear-salmon interaction, impact of on, 506–508, 508*f*
biology, 7
boreal forest, 28
C_3, 177, 177*f*, 178, 179, 521
C_4, 178, 178*f*, 179, 521
cacti, Galápagos finches and, 313–315
CAM, 179, 179*f*

carbon: nitrogen ratio, 180, 180*f*, 182–183, 183*f*, 184
carnivorous, 188
colonization of new islands by, 590, 590*f*, 604
competition, 246–247, 259, 452
competition mechanisms, 357–358, 357*f*
competitive hierarchies in, 452
defence strategies of, 181
defences against herbivory, 366–370, 372, 389
dispersal mechanism and seed mass, 235, 235*f*, 258
distribution, 7, 452
disturbance, intensity of, 246
diversity, impact of, 439–440, 439*f*, 440*f*, 444
diversity of, production and, 434, 435*f*
energy intake by, limits on, 188–190
essential nutrients for, 180
evolutionary response, 358
evolutionary stable strategies (ESS), 228
focal plant study, 342
Grime's classification of plant life-history strategies, 246, 246*f*, 259
herbaceous, 26
herbivory and defence of, 362–370, 370*f*
heterogeneity and survival of, 431–432, 432*f*, 451
heterotrophic, 176
intraspecific competition, 339, 340*f*
land, internal water regulation by, 154
latitude and species richness, 592, 592*f*
life histories of, 246–247, 342, 453
light response curve for, 189, 189*f*
mating, behavioural ecology of, 223–226
matric forces, 152
monocots vs. dicots, foraging of, 195–196
net reproductive rate (Ro) of, 316*f*
niches, heterogeneity and diversity of, 429–430
niches and competition among, 349–350, 453, 453*f*
nitrogen use efficiency (NUE) of, 181
optimal foraging, 194–196
photosynthetic, 176*f*
phytochrome system, 358
planthoppers, impact of on, 340, 340*f*
prairie dog grazing and burrowing, effect of, 472
red to far-red (R:FR) wavelength ratio, 358
root and shoot biomass in varied nutrient conditions, 195
root exudates, 22
root growth vs. nutrient levels, 195, 195*f*, 228
ruderals, 246, 246*f*, 247, 259
seed mass and number, 235, 235*f*, 258
seed number and size, 234–237, 235*f*
seed size and recruitment, 236, 236*f*
self-thinning, 283, 291, 339, 339*f*, 340*f*, 359
shade avoidance, 358
size of and population density, 283–284, 283*f*, 291
size vs. competitive ability, 357–358
soil nitrogen levels, impact of on, 506–508, 508*f*
stomatal closure, 159, 160, 162, 178
succession and, 480–482, 480*f*, 481*f*, 482*f*
summer vs. winter rainfall, use of, 170–171, 171*f*, 172
sun vs. shade, 189–190
survival pattern, 297, 297*f*
survivorship vs. seed production by *P. drummondii*, 316*f*
toxins in, 184, 369–370
transgenic, 358
transition zones, 9

transpiration, 151
tundra, in, 26
variation in, 92–94
vegetation history, 8, 8f
water conservation, 156–159
water movement between soils and, 151–153, 153f, 172
water potential in, 152
water regulation, 153–165
water sources used by, 170–171, 171f, 172
Plants, thermogenic, temperature regulation by, 136–137, 144, 145
eastern skunk cabbage (*Symplocarpus foetidus*), 136, 137f
Plants, thermoregulation of, 129–131
arctic and alpine plants, 117f, 129–130
desert plants, 130–131
Plate tectonics, 609–610, 609f, 610, 610f, 635
Platt, Trevor, 8, 10
P_{max}, 188, 188f, 189
Pocket gophers, ecosystems and, 537–538, 538f
Pocket mouse (*Perognathus* sp.), 352f
Podos, Jeffrey, 102, 103
Poikilothermic ectotherms, 136
Poikilotherms, 128, 129, 283f, 291
Point Barrow, Alaska, 25f
Polar bear (*Ursus Maritimus*), 306–307, 306f, 308f
Polar cells, 17, 18f
Polar easterlies, 18
Polischuk, S.C., 307
Pollen, lake sediment, in, 7, 8f, 269, 290, 321, 321f
Pollen vector, 404, 418
Pollination, 404–407, 447, 510, 565
cheaters, 406, 418
cost-benefit analyses, mutualisms and, 405, 405f, 418
nectar robbers, 406
pollen vector, 404, 418
Polluted areas, bacteria and remediation of, 187
Pollution, urban, 437–438, 628
Polymerase chain reaction (PCR), 111
Pond turtle, 157f
Ponds, 76–81
Pooled degrees of freedom, AP-7
Population
characteristics of, 264
defined, 263, 290
density, 264, 282–284, 291, 333, 339, 339f
density and competition, 343
density and planthopper performance, 340, 340f
size of and population density, 284–285, 291
Population, behavioural and landscape ecology, link between, 571–575
resource selection functions (RSF), use of, 574–575
thresholds, use of, 571–573, 575
Population change, rates of, 316–319, 316f, 332
estimating rates when generations overlap, 317–319
geometric rate of increase, 317, 317f
net reproductive rate (Ro), 316f, 317
Phlox drummondii, for, 316–317, 316f, 332
short-lived plants, estimating, 316–317, 316f
Population dynamics and growth, 310–333
BIDE dynamics, 311–315, 311f, 332
fisheries, 326–328
fragmentation, 566–567
logistic population growth, 322, 323–326, 332–333
variation within, 92–95
Population ecology, 3, 261–333, 578
Population equivalents, 344
Population growth, geometric and exponential, 319–322, 332, 447

exponential, 320–322, 320f, 323, 343
geometric, 319–320, 319f, 320, 320f
J-shaped curve, 319
Population growth, logistic, 322, 323–326, 332–333, 400
sigmoidal growth curve, 323, 323f
Population growth models, 244, 578
compartmental models, 400–401, 400f, 417
Population structure, 293–309, 558
age distribution, 301–303, 308, 330, 330f
human population and, 330–331
pollutants and, 305–308
sex ratios, 303–305, 308
survival patterns, 295–299, 308
Port Hardy, B.C., 29f
Positive assortative mating, 109
Positively correlated variables, AP-5, AP-5f
Post, Eric, 617
Post, W., 542
Post, W.M., 542f
Postel, Sandra, 52
Postzygotic isolating mechanism, 107, 107f, 109, 114
Potassium, 487
Poulin, R., 228
Power, Mary, 455–457, 457f, 458f, 461
Prairie dogs (*Cynomys* spp.), 472, 538, 538f
Prairie voles (*Microtus ochrogaster*), 561, 562
Prawn (*Leander squilla*), 298
Precipitation, 16–18, 19, 49
biomes and, 24f
boreal forest, 27f, 28
deserts, 35, 35f
heating the earth and, 49
Mediterranean woodland and shrubland, 33f
mountains, 44, 45f
temperate forests, 29, 29f, 30, 31–32
temperate grassland, 31f
tropical dry forests, 39, 40f
tropical rain forests, 41f
tropical savanna, 37, 38f
tundra, 25f, 26
Predation, 67, 218–219, 267, 270, 277, 290, 312, 347, 449
Atlantic cod (*Gadus morhua*,)
by seals, 328
carnivourous plants, 188
defence against, 180
guppies (*Poecilia reticulata*)
colouration and, 218, 219f, 220f
latitude and, 594, 595
male ornamentation, 218–220
parasitism and competition and, 395–396, 396f, 417
predator-prey interactions, 362, 389
primary production, 516
seed, 381
selective pressure, cause of, 385–387
size-selective, 185, 383–385, 384f, 389
water striders (Heteroptera) mating struggles and, 222–223
Predator avoidance, 378–385, 389
animal display, 378–379
exploited organisms and refuge variety, 380–385
refuges and prey persistence, 379–380, 379f
Predator satiation, 381–383, 389
Australian tree, 381–382
periodical cicadas (*Magicicada* spp.), 382–383, 383f
size as a refuge, 383–385, 384f
Predator-prey dynamics, 98, 370–378, 381, 389, 392, 395, 400, 505
mathematical model of, 375–378, 389
Predators, 23f, 350, 362
species diversity, impact on, 454, 455f
intertidal communities, effect on, 464
keystone species, as, 454–461, 466
Predators, impacts of on prey populations, 370–375, 389

experimental test of food and, 372–373
non-consumptive effects of predators, 373–375, 389, 460
snowshoe hares (*Lepus americanus*) and their predators, abundance cycles of, 370–372, 371f
Predictive ecology, 578–582
Preisser, Evan, 375
Preston, Frank, 424–425
Preston's curves, 425, 425f, 444
Prey
abundance, 192–193
predictions, 193–194
Prezygotic isolating mechanism, 107, 107f, 109, 114
Prides. *See* African lions, female lion prides
Primary production, 502, 516, 522, 532, 537, 546
aquatic, patterns of, 508–512, 522, 545
grazing by large mammals and, 518–519, 519f, 522
gross, 502, 522
lake, 516–518, 522
marine, global patterns of, 509–512, 511f, 512f, 522
net, 502, 522
piscivores and planktivores and, 516–518, 522
terrestrial, patterns of, 503–508, 522, 531
whole-lake experiments on, 509, 510, 510f, 517–518, 522
Primary production required (PPR), 619–620, 620f
Primary productivity, 8, 8f, 23, 363, 488, 489f, 499, 502, 522, 601
Primary succession, 470, 479, 485, 498, 554
Glacier Bay, at, 480–481, 480f, 499
Primates, extinction risk, 242
Prince Albert National Park, 185f
Prince Edward Island, 330
Proctor, Heather, 243
Production and energy flow, 501–523
aquatic primary production, 508–512
biotic influences, 516–519, 522
primary production, 502, 516, 522
terrestrial primary production, 503–508, 522
trophic levels, 512–516, 522
Productivity, plant competition vs., 342, 342f
Product-moment method, AP-5
Project Venus, 63
Prokaryotes, 175, 176f, 527
Promiscuity, 217
polyandry, 217
polygynandry, 217
polygyny, 217
Prostigmata
Labidostomatidae, 23f
Stigmaeidae, 23f
Trombiculidae, 23f
Protection, 396–397, 396f, 397f
Protein variability, 111
Protists
heterotrophic, 175, 176f
photosynthetic, 175, 176f
Protozoa (*Paramecium caudatum*), 323, 323f
Pseudotsuga menziesii, 411, 411f
Psychrophilic marine bacteria, 127, 127f
Puget Sound, B.C., 290
Puget Sound rockfish, 238
Puma/mountain lion (*Felis concolour*), 383
size of vs. prey size, 185, 186f
Pumpkinseed sunfish (*Lepomis gibbosus*), 239–241, 239f, 258–259
adult to juvenile survival probabilities, 240f
adult to juvenile survival ratio and reproductive effort, 241f
adult to juvenile survival ratios and reproductive maturity age, 241f

Punta San Juan, Peru, 616
Purple loosestrife (*Lythrum salicaaria*), 627f
Purugh, Laura, 281
Purvis, Andy, 241–242
Pusey, Anne E., 209, 212
Putative sightings, 582

Q

Quagga mussel (*Dreissena rostriformis*), 81
Quarantine, 402–403, 402f, 403f, 418
response time, 402–403
Quartiles, AP-3
Quetelet, Adolphe, 324
Quinlan, Michael, 265

R

r selection, 245f, 259
r vs. K selection, 244–246, 249, 259
Grime's classification system vs., 247
Winemiller's and Rose's classification systems vs., 248
Rabalais, Nancy, 510
Rabinowitz, Deborah, 284
Radiation, 128, 129, 130f, 131, 131f, 132, 137f, 143, 145, 176
Radioactive ^{14}C, 543, 543f
Rainbow trout (*Oncorhynchus mykiss*), 124
Rainfall, plant uptake by, 170–171, 171f, 172
Ralls, Katherine, 106
Ramets, 431
Random distribution, 274–275, 275f
Random sampling, 442–443, 442f
Range, AP-2–AP-3
Range agrologist, 625
Range of tolerance, 123, 251
Rank-abundance curves, 427–428, 427f, 428f
Rarity, 311, 597
extensive geographic range, broad habitat tolerance, and small local population, 284–285
extensive geographic range, large local population, and narrow habitat tolerance, 285–286
extreme: restricted geographic range, narrow habitat tolerance, and small local population, 286
seven forms of, 284–286, 285f
Ras Mohammed National Park, Egypt, 461
Raup, David, 611, 611f
Rawson, Timothy, 294
Reader, Richard, 342, 342f
Réale, D., 257, 258f
Realized niche, 251, 251f, 259, 349, 350, 453f
Realized/actual per capita rate of increase, 324, 325, 333
population density and, 326, 326f
population size and, 325, 325f, 327
Recher, Harold F., 300
Reciprocal altruism, 206, 208
Red algae
Cryptosiphonia woodii, 494
Odonthalia floccosa, 494
Rhodomela larix, 494
Red clover (*Trifolium pratence*, 407
Red deer (*Cervus elaphus*), 297
Red foxes (*Vulpes vulpes*), 372
Red kangaroo (*Macropus rufus*), 264–265, 265f
Red mangrove (*Rhizophora mangle*), 589, 589f
Red maple (*Acer rubrum*), 279f, 280, 530
Red Queen hypothesis, 387, 389
Red Sea, 60f, 462, 462f
Red squirrel (*Tamiasciurus hudsonicus*), 257, 258f
Red to far-red (R: FR) wavelength ratio, 358
Red-eyed vireos (*Vireo olivaceus*), 278, 278f
Redford, Kent, 463–464, 464f

Red-osier dogwood (*Cornus stolonifera*), 140
Redpath Museum, 22
Red-shouldered hawk, 281
Redwood, coastal (*Sequoia sempervirens*), 283*f*
Reef crest, 61
Reef-building corals, 61, 62*f*
Reeves, Keanu, 567
Refractory phosphorus, 486, 487*f*, 499
Refuges, exploited organisms and, 380–385, 389
  predator satiation, 381–383, 389
  protection in numbers, 381, 383*f*, 389
  size and, 383–385, 384*f*
  spatial refuge, 380–381, 389
Refuges and prey persistence, 379–380, 379*f*, 380*f*
Refugia, 378, 389, 513
Regional diversity, patterns of, 595–596, 604
Regression analysis, AP-5, AP-6
  dependent variable, AP-6
  independent variable, AP-6
  regression coefficient, AP-6
  regression line, AP-6
Regular distribution, 274–275, 275*f*
Reich, Peter, 433, 434, 436
Reid, W.V., 592, 592*f*
Reimchen, Thomas, 506, 507
Reiners, William, 480, 480*f*, 481, 481*f*, 485
Reins, France, 29*f*
Reithrodontomys megalotis, 352
Relative humidity, 149
Relay floristics, 490, 490*f*
Remote operated vehicle, 63*f*
Remote sensing, 579, 601–602, 602*f*, 604
Reproduction
  age distribution, 301, 308
  climate change and, 256–258, 302–303, 303*f*, 308
  respiration and, 306
  sexual vs. asexual, 243, 259
  temperature, and performance and, 124
Reproductive allocation, adult survival and, 237–241, 258
  mortality vs. age of reproductive maturity, 237, 237*f*
  variation among species, 237–238, 258
  variation within species, 238–241, 258
Reproductive effort, 237, 239, 240, 241*f*, 249, 258
  mortality and, 238
Reproductive isolation
  behavioural isolation, 107*f*, 108
  defined, 107–108
  ecological divergence, 109–110, 109*f*, 114
  ecological isolation, 107–108, 107*f*
  isolating mechanisms, 107, 107*f*
  mechanical isolation, 107*f*, 108
  temporal isolation, 107*f*, 108
Reproductive maturity, fish, 247–248
Research on Avian Protection Project (RAPP), 211
Reservoirs, hydrologic cycle, 53, 53*f*
  turnover times, 53
Resh, Vincent, 365, 365*f*, 366, 366*f*
Residual variation, 511
Resilience, 475, 476*f*, 478, 499
Resistance, 366, 475, 476*f*, 478, 499
  natural selection, 98
  thermoregulation, 139–142
Resource limitation, 337, 338, 339, 340, 342, 346, 359
Resource selection functions (RSF), use of, 574–575, 574*f*
Resource-ratio model, Lotka-Volterra model of interspecific competition vs., 346
Respiration, 502
  atmospheric CO_2 and, 528
Response variables, AP-9
Restriction enzymes, 111
Restriction fragments, 111

Restriction sites, 111
Return on investment (ROI), conservation efforts and, 631, 631*f*, 635
Reyer, H.U., 414, 415, 416*f*, 417
Reynolds, Heather, 195
Reynolds, James, 276–277
Reynolds, John, 241
Rhizobia, 527, 528*f*
Rhodoglossum affine, 482
Rhodopsin, 175–176
Ribbed mussel (*Geukensia demissa*), 520–521, 521*f*
Ribulose biophosphate (RuBP), 177, 178
Richardson's ground squirrel, 207
Richie, Jerry C., 527*f*
Ricklefs, Robert, 599–600, 600*f*, 612–613
Rigler, Frank, 508, 509*f*, 510–511
Rio Claro, Costa Rica, 271–272, 271*f*
Rio Grande cottonwoods (*Populus deltoides* ssp. *Wislizenii*), 302, 302*f*
Rio Las Marías, Venezuela, 537
Rio Negro, 601
Riparian vegetation, 121
Riparian zone, 72, 73*f*
Ripple, William J., 460, 461
Risch, Stephen, 464, 465*f*
Risk, using thresholds to estimate, 571–573, 575
Ritchie, M.E., 475
River continuum concept, 75, 76*f*
River discharge, 74
River food webs, 455–457, 457*f*, 466
Rivers, 71–76, 71*f*, 87
  biology, 74–75, 76*f*
  chemical conditions, 74, 75*f*
  dispersal in, 270–272, 290
  geography, 72, 72*f*
  human influences, 76
  physical conditions, 73–74, 75*f*
  structure, 72–73
Roads, effect on landscape structure, 570
Roark, E.B., 59
Robertson, G., 430, 431*f*
Rocky Mountain Parnassian butterfly (*Parnassius smintheus*), 273–274, 273*f*, , 274*f* 290
Rocky Mountains, 99, 160, 272, 583
Roderick, George, 340, 340*f*
Roland, Jens, 273, 273*f*, 274
Rondônia State, Brazil, 622*f*
Rood, Stewart B., 159–161
Rooney, Rebecca, 438*f*
Root, Terry, 254, 255*f*, 277, 278, 279
Root competition, 337–338, 338*f*, 341–342
Root development, plant, 156, 156*f*
Root exudates, 22
Root growth, nutrient levels and, 195, 195*f*, 200
Root systems of creosote bushes
  actual, 277*f*
  excavated, 277*f*
  hypothetical circular, 277*f*
Rooting depth, 156, 156*f*
Roper, T.J., 119
ROPOS, 63*f*
Rose, Kenneth, 247–248, 247*f*, 259
Rosell, F., 458
Rosemond, Amy, 534
Rosenberg, R., 510, 513*f*
Rosenzweig, Michael, 504, 504*f*, 505, 594, 594*f*
Rosswall, T., 528*f*
Roth, James, 519–520
Rothamsted Experimental Station, Hertfordshire, England, 476
Rotifers, 188
  Brachionus calyciflorus, 386, 386*f*
  Floscularia conifera, 297, 297*f*
Rowe, Locke, 222–223
Royal Society of Canada, 381
RUBISCO
  RuBP carboxylase (RUBISCO), 177, 178
  RuBP oxygenase (RUBISCO), 178
Ruderals, 246*f*, 247, 259, 354

Rufous hummingbirds, 141
Running waters, 71–76
Rwanda, historical and projected populations of, 331, 331*f*
Rydin, Håkan, 590
Ryther, J.H., 58

S

Saabye, Hans Egede, 617
Sable Gully, 59, 61*f*
Saccheri, Ilik, 106, 111
Sachs, E., 118
Safe sites, 190
Sage, Rowan, 197
Sage, Tammy L., 179
Saguaro cactus, 161–162, 161*f*, 162*f*, 172
Saguaro cactus, (*Carnegiea gigantea*), 496, 497*f*, 498, 498*f*
Sahney, S., 611
Sakai, A., 140
Sakamoto, M., 508
Sala, O.E., 504–505, 504*f*
Salinity
  bogs, 83
  changing levels of, adapting to, 168
  coral reefs, 61
  fens, 83
  intertidal zones, 66, 168
  kelp, 61
  lakes, 78, 87, 148
  mangrove forests, 69–70
  oceans, 57
  rivers, 74, 75*f*, 148
  salt marshes, 69–70, 168
  streams, 74
Salmon
  bears, interactions with, 506–508, 507*f*
  life history plasticity of, 238–239
  recruitment, impact of stream temperature on, 122*f*, 123–124
  spawning of, 506–507
Salmonidae, 123
Salt marsh grass (*Spartina alterniflora*), 340
Salt marsh grass (*Spartina anglica*), 252, 259
Salt marshes, 67–71, 67*f*, 68*f*, 81, 82*f*, 87, 533
  biology, 71, 168
  Carex subspathacea, 363, 364
  chemical conditions, 69–71
  energy sources in, using stable isotope analysis to study, 520–521
  geography, 68, 68*f*
  habitat niche of, 252–253, 259
  human influences, 71, 71*f*
  physical conditions, 69
  Puccinellia phryganodes, 363, 364
  Spartina, 520–521
  structure, 68–69, 69*f*
Salt pans, 68, 71*f*
Sample mean, AP-1
  equation for, AP-1
Sample median, AP-2
  equation for, AP-2
Sample standard deviation, AP-3
  equation for, AP-3
Sample variance, AP-3
Sampling communities, 440–443
  locations, 442–443
  pilot studies, 443, 444
  random sampling, 442–443, 442*f*
  stratified random sampling, 443
  stratified sampling, 442–443, 442*f*
  systematic sampling, 442–443, 442*f*
  timing, 441–442, 442*f*, 444
  where, when, who, and how much, 441, 444
Sampling effect, 435–436
Samuel, Bill, 394–395, 395*f*
San Diego, California, 33*f*
San Fernando, Venezuela, 37, 38*f*
Santa Catalina Mountains, Arizona, 279, 280
Sapindaceae plant family, 101, 101*f*

Sapling bank, 30
Sargasso Sea, 454
SARS, quarantine during, 402–403, 402*f*, 403*f*, 418
Sartre, Jean-Paul, 444
Sasquatch (Big Foot), 581, 581*f*
Satellite imaging systems, 601–602
  land cover map for Canada, 602, 603*f*
Saturation water vapour density, 149, 149*f*
Saturation water vapour pressure, 149, 149*f*
Scattered alder (*Alnus crispa*), 469
Scatterhoarded seeds, 235, 236
Scatterplots, AP-5
Schamp, B.S., 451
Schemske, D.W., 593, 595
Schenk, H. Jochen, 156, 228
Scheu, S., 23
Schimel, David, 22
Schindler, David, 6, 6*f*, 9, 11, 52, 78, 84, 373, 509, 628
Schlesinger, William, 526, 527*f*, 528*f*, 529*f*
Schluter, Dolph, 110, 354, 355–356
Schmidt-Nielsen, K., 128
Schmiegelow, Fiona, 563–564, 564*f*
Schmitt, Johanna, 204, 358
Schoen, Daniel, 405
Schoener, Thomas, 341
Scholander, P.F., 132, 133*f*, 136*f*
Scholander, P.F., 132, 133*f*, 136*f*
Schultz, Thomas, 156, 156–157, 157*f*, 265–266, 265*f*, 266*f*
Schumacher, Joel, 40*f*
Scientific method, 10–11, 11*f*, AP-1
Sciuridae family rodents, 207
Scorpian posture, 384–385, 385*f*
Scorpions' approach to desert living, 162–165, 163*f*, 165, 172
Scots pine (*Pinus sylvestris*), 321, 321*f*
Scutellospora calospora, 408
Sea lamprey, 81*f*
  Petromyzon marinus, 169*f*, 627*f*
Sea star (*Pisaster ochraceus*), 384, 384*f*
Sea urchin (*Diadema*), 62*f*
Seafloor, 186
Seals, 447
Sealy, Spencer, 207, 255
Sea-surface temperature (SST), 256–257, 257*f*
  puffin chick hatch dates and, 257, 257*f*
Secondary sexual characteristics, 217
Secondary succession, 470, 479, 485, 498
Sediment core, 84–85, 85*f*, 86, 449
  age, 85
  diatoms, 85, 85*f*
Sedimentation, 484–485, 484*f*, 553
Seed dispersal mutualists as keystone species, 462–463, 463*f*, 466
Seed predation, 381
Seed size and number, 234–237, 235*f*, 258
Seepage lakes, 583
Selection coefficients, 413
Self-incompatibility, 223, 224
Selfishness, 205, 227
Self-thinning, 283, 291, 339, 339*f*, 340*f*, 354, 359
Semelparity, 245
Semidiurnal tides, 64
Senecio jacobaea, 368, 369*f*
Sepkoski, Jack, 611, 611*f*
Serengeti, 209, 324*f*
Serengeti Plain, 538, 538*f*
Serengeti-Mara, 518, 522
Serial replacement, 490
Serreze, Mark C., 533
Sessile organisms, 424
Setts, 119
Sex and mating systems, 203
Sex determination, environmental, 304
Sex ratios, 303–305, 307, 308
Sex types, 216, 229, 303
  females, 216, 229
  hermaphrodites, 216, 229
  males, 216, 229

Sexual conflict, 222–223
　co-evolution of male and female water strider armaments, 223, 229
Sexual selection, 203, 216, 217–222, 229
　intersexual selection, 218
　intrasexual selection, 217–218
Sexually transmitted disease, 222
Shade avoidance plants, 358, 499
Shallow lakes, succession in, 484–485, 484f, 499
Shallow marine waters, 59–64. *See also* Kelp; Coral reefs
Shannon-Wiener diversity index, 426, 427f, 429, 439
Shark Bay, Australia, 374
Sharks, osmoregulation by, 166–167, 166f
　trimethylamine oxide (TMAO), 166, 172
Shaver, Gaius, 505, 505f, 533
Shelford, Victor, 122
Sherman, Paul, 207, 214, 215f
Shine, Richard, 237–238, 258
Shipley, Bill, 452
Short tandem repeats (STR), 105
Short-eared owls (*Asio flammeus*), 270, 270f
Shurin, Jonathan, 535, 595
Siegenthaler, Ulrich, 542
Sierra Club, 626
Sierra Madre Occidental, Mexico, 104
Sierra Nevada, 583
Sigmoidal (S-shaped) population growth curve, 323, 323f, 338
Significance values (P-values), AP-6
Significant differences, AP-4
Silicate, 430, 430f
Silvertown, Jonathan, 476–478, 477f
Simard, Suzanne, 410–411, 411f
Simberloff, Daniel, 459–460, 589, 589f, 590–591, 591f
Simple sequence repeats (SSR), 105
Simpson diversity index, 426
Sinclair, Tony, 324, 324f, 459
Singapore, 330
Singer, Michael C., 300
Single nucleotide polymorphisms (SNPs), 111
Siple Station, 542
Site tenacious, 100
Sitka spruce (*Picea sitchensis*), 469, 470
Six spotted mite (*Eotetranychus sexnaculatus*), 380, 380f
Size-selective predation, 185, 383–385, 384f, 389
Skewed distribution, AP-2, AP-2f
Skole, David, 565, 622, 623f, 624
Slayter, Ralph, 491, 491f, 493
Small rodents, competition and niches of, 350–353, 351f, 352f, 353f
Small scale distribution, 274–277
　below ground desert shrub distributions, 276–277
　distributions of Vancouver Island tree species, 275–276
　Douglas-fir forest, 275–276, 275f, 276f, 290
Smil, Vaclav, 539
Smith, James, 207
Smith, John Maynard, 206, 216, 226, 227
Smith, Val, 509
Smol, John, 84, 86
Smyth County, Virginia, 286
Snail (*Neritina Latissima*), 271–272, 271f
Snares, 300
Snelgrove, Paul, 62
Snow
　albedo, effect on, 118, 119f
　coverage, northern latitudes, 148f
　insulative properties of, 140, 145
Snow goose grazing, sub-Arctic salt marsh and, 363–365, 363f, 364f, 457
Snowshoe hares (*Lepus americanus*) and their predators, abundance cycles of, 370–372, 371f
　ecology of fear, 374, 389
　food supply, role of, 371–372

historical fluctuations in hare and lynx, 371, 371f
　Krebs' experiment, 372–373, 373f
　predators, role of, 372, 389
Soapberry bug (*Jadera haematoloma*), rapid adaptation to new host plants, 100–102, 101f, 114
Sociality, 208–216, 229
　cooperative breeders, 208–212
　cooperative feeding, 208, 229
　degree of, 208
　eusocial species, 212–214
　eusociality, 208, 229
　evolution of eusociality, 214–215, 215f
Society of Canadian Limnologists, 508
Sockeye salmon (*Oncorhynchus nerka*), 169f
Socorro, New Mexico, 286
Socorro isopod (*Thermosphaeroma thermophilum*), 286
Söderlund, R., 528f
Soil, 180–181, 449
　A horizon, 21, 21f, 49
　B horizon, 21f, 22, 49
　boreal forest, 28
　C horizon, 21f, 22, 49
　description of, 19–22
　deserts, 36
　ecosystem changes during succession, 485–486, 487f
　fauna, 533–534
　fertility of and terrestrial primary production, 505–506, 505f, 522
　humus, 21–22
　lateritic soils, 42
　LFH horizons, 21, 49
　matric forces, 152
　Mediterranean woodland and shrubland, 33
　mountains, 44
　natural history, 19–23, 23f
　nitrogen level, impact of on plants, 506–508, 508f
　nutrient cycling and decompensation, 531, 532f
　O horizon, 21, 37, 49
　permafrost, 26
　profile of, exposed, 21f
　root exudates, 22
　solifluction, 26, 26f
　species in, diversity of, 23, 23f, 188
　structure of, 19–22
　temperate forest, 30
　temperate grassland, 32
　terrestrial biomes, 19–22
　tropical dry forest, 39
　tropical rain forest, 41–42
　tropical savanna, 38
　tundra, 26
　water movement between plants and, 151–153
　water potential in, 153
Solar radiation, 175, 199, 502, 514, 515f
Solar-driven air circumstances, 18f
Solidago altissima, 388, 388f
Solidago gigantea, 388, 388f
Solifluction, 26, 26f
Song sparrows (*Melospiza melodia*), 340–341, 341f, 359
Sonoran Desert, 147, 158, 163, 279, 422f, 556
Soulé, Michael E., 618, 619f, 627
Soulé, Peter T., 541
Sousa, Wayne, 470, 471–472, 472f, 473, 482–483, 483f, 493, 493f, 494, 499
South American fur seal (*Arctocephalus australis*), 616
Southern Hemisphere, 38f, 49, 594f
　boreal forest, 27
　climatic diagrams, 19
　Mediterranean woodland and shrubland, 33
　oceanic gyres, 57
　solar energy, 16–17, 17f
　southern aspect, 118
　temperate forest, 29

temperate grassland, 31
　tropical dry forest, 40f
　tropical savanna, 38f
　winds: Coriolis effect, 18, 18f
Southern Oscillation, 613–618, 635
Southern Oscillation Index, 614–615, 614f, 616
Sparkling Lake, 568, 569f
Spartina alterniflora, 252
Spartina anglica, 252–253, 252f
　fetch of the estuary and distribution of, 253
　tidal fluctuations and distribution of, 253, 253f
Spartina maritima, 252
Spates, 271
Spatial change, 7–10
Spatial extent, 274
Spatial heterogeneity in the strength of competition, 347, 359
Spatial refuges, 380–381, 389
Spawning streams, 123–124, 123f
Spearman-Rank correlation, AP-5
Specialists, 388
Speciation, 106–114, 234, 387–388, 593, 594–595
　allopatric, 108, 108f, 109, 114
　causes of, 108–109
　fuzzy species boundaries, 112–113, 114
　molecular revolution and, 111–113, 114
　parapatric, 108, 108f, 109, 114
　reproductive isolation and, 114
　species, defined, 107, 585
　species identification, 85, 112
　sympatric, 108, 108f
　temperature variation, 594
Species abundances and diversity, 423–428, 444
　diversity defined, 423
　integrative index of species diversity, 425–427
　patterns of species' abundances, 424–425
　rank-abundance curves, 427–428, 427f, 428f
Species at Risk Act (SARA), 241, 280, 281, 311, 474
Species composition, 432
Species distribution modelling, 579
Species diversity, 423, 433–434, 434f, 439, 444, 594
Species evenness, 425–426, 426f, 429, 431, 444, 447
Species interactions and community structure, 446–467
　community assembly rules, 447
　competitive asymmetries, 451–453, 466
　ecological networks, 447–451, 466
　feeding relationships, 447, 447f
　food webs, 447–451
　keystone species, 454–461, 466
　mutualistic keystones, 461–463, 466
Species introduction, 627–628, 635
Species richness, 423, 425, 429, 431, 432, 438, 443, 444, 447, 459, 459f, 462f, 480–481, 480f, 564, 565f, 590–591, 604
　latitudinal gradients in, 591–595, 592f, 593f, 604
Species selection, 435–436
Species Specialist Subcommittees, 280
Species turnover, island, 587–589, 588f, 604
Specific heat, 120
Spector, W.S., 180f
Sphinx moths (*Manduca sexta*), 135–136, 136f
Spiders, ground-dwelling, 442, 442f
Spiraling length, 536, 548
　stream invertebrates and, 536–537, 548
Spitefulness, 205
Splash zone, 64
Spring Beauty (*Claytonia virginica*), AP-8
Spring tides, 65, 253, 267f

Springtail (*Folsomia candida*), 412
Spruce trees (*Picea* spp.), 7–8, 8f, 485
Sputnik, 608
Square, AP-3
St. Clair, Colleen, 210–211, 567
St. John's wort (*Hypericum perforatum*), 381
St. Mary River, 161
Stability, community and ecosystem, 470
　biodiversity and, 479, 479f
　desert stream stability, replicate disturbances and, 478–479, 499
　Park Grass Experiment, 476–478, 477f, 499
　resilience, 475, 476f, 478, 499
　resistance, 475, 476f, 478, 499
　stability, defined, 475
Stabilizing selection, 96–97, 96f, 114, 129
　ural owl (*Strix uralensis*) egg size among, 97–100, 101f
Stable age distribution, 317
Stable cycling, 387, 389
Stable isotope analysis, 5, 6, 172, 507
　energy flow through ecosystems, 519–521, 522
　water uptake by plants, 160, 169–171, 171f
Stamens, 223
Standard error, AP-3–AP-4
　equation for, AP-3
Standing biomass, 363, 364f
Starfish (*Heliaster kubinijii*), 454
Starfish (*Pisaster*), 454–455, 455f
Stastny, Michael, 368
Static life table, 295–296
Statistical methods, AP-1
Statistical testing, 9–10, AP-4–AP-5
　common tests, AP-5–AP-9
　differences among groups: categorical data, AP-8–AP-9
　differences among groups: continuous data, AP-6–AP-8
　effect size, AP-5
　falsifiable hypotheses, AP-4
　more complex problems, AP-9
　nonparametric procedures, AP-5
　null hypothesis, AP-4, AP-5
　parametric procedures, AP-6
　relationships among variables, AP-5–AP-6
　significant differences, AP-4
　type I error, AP-4, AP-6
　type II error, AP-4, AP-6
Statistical toolbox, building a, AP-1–AP-9
Statistics defined, AP-1
Stearns, Stephen, 232
Steelhead trout (*Oncorhynchus mykiss*), 169f, 456
Stems, 61
Stenseth, Nils, 617
Stevens, E.D., 134
Stevens, George, 278, 278f
Stevens, O.A., 235, 235f
Sticklebacks (*Gasterosteus aculeatus*), 355, 356f
Sticky cinquefoil (*Potentilla glandulosa*), 92, 92f, 93f
Still waters, 76–81
Stipes, 61
Stireman, J.O. III, 388
Stones, microclimate and, 119
Storage tanks, leaky, 198
　benzene breakdown by bacteria, 198, 198f, 200
Storey, Janet, 140
Storey, Kenneth, 140
Straley, Janice, 289
Stratified random sampling, 443
Stratified sampling, 442–443, 442f, 572
Stream order, 72, 73f
Streams, 71–76, 87
　biology, 74–75, 76f, 160
　chemical conditions, 74
　dam construction and temperature of, 124, 160
　dispersal in, 270–272, 290

Streams—*Cont.*
ecosystem properties and succession, 488–489, 488f, 489f, 499
flooding and nutrient export by, 544–546, 548
geography, 72
human influences, 76, 160
invertebrates and spiraling length, 536–537, 548
logging activity and temperature of, 124
nutrient content of, decomposition and, 534
nutrient cycling in, 535–537, 548
nutrient retentiveness, 536
nutrient spiraling, 536, 536f, 548
physical conditions, 73–74, 74f
salmon recruitment and temperature of, 123–124
spiraling length, 536, 548
stream flow, changes in, 160, 535, 544–545, 545f
structure, 72–73, 73f
succession in stream communities, 483–484, 483f, 484f, 499
vertebrates and nutrient cycling in, 537
Stress, impact of, 374, 374f, 389
Stress tolerant species, 246, 247, 505
plant, 246, 246f
stress, defined, 246
Strong, Donald, 518
Structure
bogs, 81–82, 82f
coral reefs, 61
fens, 81–82, 82f
intertidal zones, 64, 65f
kelp, 61
mangrove forests, 68–69, 70f
oceans, 56, 56f
rivers, 72–73
salt marshes, 68–69, 69f
streams, 72–73, 73f
Student's *t* distribution, AP-4
Student's *t* table, AP-4
Suberkropp, Keller, 534
Subniveanl traps, 288
Subpopulations, 272, 290, 400
Subtidal zone, 64, 65f
Succession, 469–470, 474
chronosequence, 480
community changes during, 479–485, 499
cyclic, 470
deep lakes, 484
ecological, 469, 479
ecosystem changes during, 485–489, 499
facilitation model, 491, 491f, 492f, 493, 494, 495, 499
forests, mechanisms in, 494–496, 499
inhibition model, 492, 492f, 493, 493f, 494, 495, 499
initial floristics, 490, 490f, 492
mechanisms, 490–496, 499
nutrient retention and, 487, 488f, 499
post-deglaciation, mechanisms of, 492–493
primary, 470, 479, 480–481, 480f, 481f, 485, 498, 499
relay floristics, 490, 490f
rocky intertidal communities, in, 482–483, 483f
rocky intertidal zones, mechanisms of in, 493–494, 499
secondary, 470, 479, 481–482, 481f, 482f, 485, 498, 499
shallow lakes, in, 484–485, 484f, 499
stream communities, 483–484, 483f, 484f, 499
stream ecosystem properties and, 488–489, 488f, 489f, 499
tolerance model, 492, 493, 499
Suess, Hans, 543
Suess effect, 543, 543f
Sugar maple (*Acer saccharum*), 530
Sugihara, George, 424, 425
Sulfolobus, 127

Sullivan, Jon, 363
Sulphur oxidation, temperature and rate of, 127, 127f
Sulphur oxidizing bacteria, 186–187, 186f
Sum of squares, AP-3, AP-7
equation for, AP-3
Summary statistics, AP-1
arithmetic mean, AP-1
sample mean, AP-1
Summerhayes, Victor, 447
Sunlight
boreal forest, 28
deserts, 36
ecosystems, 502, 502f
latitudinal variation and, 49
tundra, 26
Sunspot cycles hypothesis, 371
Superorganism, 490
Supratidal fringe, 64, 65f, 87
Surfgrass (*Phyllospadix scouleri*), 494, 494f
Survival, patterns of, 295–299, 308, 330, 374
age distribution, 296
cohort life table, 295
comparisons among familiar vertebrates, 299f
constant rates of survival, 298, 299, 299f
environmental variation and, 431–432
estimating, 295–296
high survival, young individuals, 296–297, 299, 299f, 308
low survival, young individuals, 298, 299, 299f, 308
static life table, 295–296
Survivorship, fish, 247–248
Survivorship curve, 295, 297, 297f, 298, 308, 317
types of, 298–299, 299f
Swartz, Wilf, 619–620
Sweep nets, 287
Swift, Jonathan, 395
Swift, M.J., 182f, 531f
Swift fox (*Vulpes velox*), 281
Swingle, Walter, 465
Sycamore Creek, Arizona, 478–479, 478f, 483–484, 483f, 484f, 488–489, 489f, 536–537, 536f
Symbionts, 183
Symbioses, cleaning, 228, 392
Symbiotic relationships, 392
Sympatric speciation, 108f, 109, 114, 388, 389, 595
competition and, 354, 355, 356, 356f
Synthetic communities, 433
Systematic sampling, 442–443, 442f

T
Table mountain pine (*Pinus pungens*), 279f, 280
Tahiti, 614, 614f
Tahoua, Niger, 37, 38f
Taiga, 26
Taiyuan, China, 31f, 32
Takyu, Masaaki, 531–532, 532f
Talus, 554
Tansley, Arthur, 349–350, 350f, 502, 512
Taranto, Italy, 33f
Target hypothesis, 591
Taylor, Philip, 567–568, 568f
Taylor's Checkspot (*Euphydryas editha taylori*), 280f
Tegeticula altiplanella, 405, 406f, 418
Temperate deciduous forest, 514
energy flow in, 515f
Temperate forest, 24f, 28–30, 50, 57, 74, 84, 176, 470
biology, 30, 30f
climate, 29–30
diversity of, 599–600, 604, 612–613, 613f, 614f
geography, 29
human influences, 30
soils, 30
vegetation, 30

Temperate grasslands, 24f, 30–32, 31f, 50
biology, 32, 32f
climate, 31–32
disturbance and diversity in, 472–473, 475, 499
geography, 30–31
human influences, 32
soils, 32
vegetation, 32
Temperature, 16–18, 19
biomes and, 24f
bog, 83
coral reef, 61
decomposition rate and, 529, 531, 533
extinction rates and, 594
fen, 83
fluctuations, 119–121, 458
intertidal zones, 64
kelp, 61
lake, 78, 79f
large mammal response to changes in, 617–618
latitudinal variations in, 594, 594f
mangrove forests, 69
ocean, 56–57
plant response to changes in, 617–618
primary production and, 503, 522
river, 73
salt marsh, 69
speciation rates and, 594
stream, 73, 458
tundra, 25–26, 25f
Temperature regulation. *See* Body temperature, regulation of
Temperature relations, 115–145
body temperature, regulating, 128–137
evolutionary trade-offs, 121–122
extreme temperatures and photosynthesis, 126–127, 144
extreme temperatures, surviving, 137–142
microclimates, 117–121
performance of organisms, temperature and, 122–128
Temporal change, 7–10
Temporal isolation, 107f, 108
Tennesseelium formicum, 442f
Tennyson, Lord Alfred, 373
Terborgh, John, 463, 594, 594f
Terminal moraines, 554
Terrestrial biodiversity hotspots, 597–598, 598f
Terrestrial biomes, 14, 624
Terrestrial communities, beavers' impact on, 458
Terrestrial ecosystems, 530–532, 548
altering, 546–547, 548
aquatic ecosystems vs., 535f, 548
nutrient cycling in by animals, 537–539, 548
Terrestrial environment, phyla in, 58, 59f
Terrestrial invertebrates, 283, 283f, 291
Terrestrial plants
environmental heterogeneity, 430, 431f
niches of, 430, 444
phytoplankton vs., 535, 535f
Terrestrial primary production, patterns of, 503–506, 522
actual evapotranspiration (AET) and, 504–505, 504f, 522
moisture, 503, 522
soil fertility and, 505–506, 505f, 522
temperature, 503, 522
Terrestrialization, 484, 484f
Test for independence, AP-9
Tetrapods, 610–611, 611f
Thermal neutral zone, 133, 133f
arctic vs. tropical mammals, 133f
Thermal stability, aquatic environments, of, 120–121
Thermal stratification, 56, 57, 79f, 87
Thermocline, 56, 57, 77
Thermodynamics, ecology and, 512–513, 513f
Thermophilic cyanobacteria, isolation of, 585, 586f

Thermophilic microbes, 127, 127f
Thermoregulation. *See* Body temperature, regulation of
Thompson, John, 387
Thomson, D.A., 428f
Thomson's gazelle (*Gazella thomsonii*), 518
Thoreau, Henry David, 77
Threatened species, use of ecology to protect, 280–282
Three-spined sticklebacks (*Gasterosteus aculeatus*), 110, 100f, 456, 456f
Thresholds, use of to estimate risk, 571–573, 574, 575
conservation thresholds, 571, 575
Thuja plicata, 411, 411f
Thunder Bay, Ontario, 427, 428f
Tibetan Plateau, 284
Tick (*dermacentor albipictus*), 394, 394f, 395f
Tidal creeks, 68
Tidal dissipation, 433
Tidal fluctuation, 64–65, 68–69, 87
Tiger beetles
Cicindela obsoleta, 156–157, 157f, 161
Cicindela oregona, 156–157, 157f
cold climate (*Cicindela longilabris*), 265–266, 265f, 266f, 290
Tiger sharks, 374
Tiksi, Russia, 25f
Till, 554, 555
Tilman, David, 342, 346, 430, 433
Time-energy budget, 191
Tit-for-tat, 208, 229
Tobacco plant, genetic control of anti-competitor growth in, 204
Todd, Arlen, 372
Toe-clipping, 300
Tolerance, 366, 492, 493, 499
Tonn, Bill, 583–584, 583f
Toolson, Eric, 147, 163–165, 164f
Top-down controls, 516, 535
Topi (*Damaliscus korrigum*), 518
Torpor, 141–142, 141f, 142f, 145
Total atmospheric pressure, 149
saturation water vapour pressure, 149, 149f
Tourney, J., 337
Tracy, Richard, 157–158
Trade-offs, 115, 232–244, 243, 258, 264
adult survival and reproductive allocation, 237–241, 243, 258
competitive ability and stress tolerance, 453, 453f
fecundity, survivorship and reproductive maturity age in fish, 247–248, 258
genetic control of life history, 243–244
life-history strategies, 241, 243, 247, 249, 482
offspring, size and number of, 233–237, 258
reproduction vs. respiration, 306
seed size and number in plants, 234–237, 235f, 258
speciation, impact on, 234
Trans-Canada Highway, 567, 569, 570f
Transpiration, 151, 154
atmospheric CO_2 and, 151
Trees
age, trunk diameter and, 301
exponential growth by, 321
extinction of, 599–600, 600f
populations of, 301–302
temperate trees, diversity of, 599–600, 604
Tress, Bärbel, 552
Tress, Gunther, 552
Trexler, Joel, 233–234, 258
Triangle Island, B.C., 256, 256f, 257f
Trimethylamine oxide (TMAO), 166, 172
Trochosa ruricola, 442f
Trophic (feeding) biology, 175
Trophic cascade hypothesis, 516–518, 516f, 517f
Trophic dependency, 241